Frederick Forsyth

THREE COMPLETE NOVELS

Also by Frederick Forsyth

THE SHEPHERD

THE DEVIL'S ALTERNATIVE

Frederick Forsyth

THREE COMPLETE NOVELS

The Day of the Jackal

The Odessa File

The Dogs of War

AVENEL BOOKS · NEW YORK

This edition is published by Avenel Books, distributed by Crown
Publishers, Inc., by arrangement with The Viking Press.
a b c d e f g h
AVENEL 1981 EDITION

Manufactured in the United States of America

Library of Congress Cataloging in Publication Data

Forsyth, Frederick, 1938-
    Three complete novels.

    Originally published: Forsyth's three. New York: Viking Press,
1980
    Contents: The day of the jackal — The Odessa file — The dogs
of war.
    I. Title.
PR6056.0699A6 1981   823'.914   81–2081
ISBN 0–517–34346–0   AACR2

Acknowledgment is made to St. Martin's Press, Inc., and Macmillan & Co., Ltd, for permission to reprint a quotation from *Collected
Poems* by Thomas Hardy.

CONTENTS

PREFACE

When I sat down in the cold, bleak opening days of the year 1970 to type out my first attempt at a novel, it was neither the desire for literary achievement nor the determination to pass on some message for humanity that inspired me.

My motive was much simpler to explain. It just happened I was a reporter and erstwhile foreign correspondent without a job; a freelance journalist with no commission in hand; a thirty-two-year-old wanderer with neither apartment, car, savings, nor prospects. With few places to go but up, it occurred to me I needed to make a few dollars—but quickly. Which shows how little I knew about authorship and publishing. Nothing about the financial side of authorship is quick.

Years later, people said of that book, hammered out on a battered old portable typewriter in thirty-five days, that it was innovative; that the use of real men in public office, their real names given in the text and blended in with fictional characters, had not been done before; that the wealth of technical and procedural detail, drawn from the corridors of power on the one hand and the back alleys of the underworld on the other, was unprecedented; that the blend of real events, checkable in newspaper archives, with fictional allegations, which were neither provable nor disprovable, was something new. The true irony is that at the time I neither knew nor suspected any of this. I simply wrote the story of the blond foreign assassin who tried to drop French President Charles de Gaulle in his tracks the way it seemed to me it might damn nearly have happened.

I was not then, and indeed never have been, a great devotee of thrillers; most of my reading diet is nonfiction. But as a traveler I had of course grabbed a number of paperback thrillers off the airport bookstand and found many of them illogical, inaccurate, predictable, or plain downright incredible. I thought, rightly or wrongly, that if these had been accepted for publication by some editor somewhere, the tale I had carried in my head since those tense, cliff-hanging days back in Paris seven years earlier might even sell a few thousand copies. No more.

The only thing I consciously did that was intended to be different concerned the character of the hero, or anti-hero: the assassin himself. Usually the major character in a novel is lengthily described, a three-dimensional figure. I thought, since this assassin is to be a shadow, an insubstantial, fleeting, will-o'-the-wisp wraith to the French security authorities in the book, and even to his employers, the OAS, let us keep him just the same for the reader—a flitting shadow of whom we never learn more than that he was there and almost succeeded.

It was out of this decision that the title sprang. If he was to have no face, no passport, no documents on file, he must have no name. Yet he needed some kind of name—so, a code name. Cobra? Wolf, bear, lion, tiger, panther, leopard, wolverine, hawk? All predators prepared to kill. All hunters. But too common, used before. I needed something more secretive; something that comes by night, soft-footed, stealthy, wary; something that is seldom seen, gone before sunrise, back to some secret, silent place in the shadows. Two days before January 1, 1970, the name came to me. Just after nine in the morning of the first day of the new decade I rolled the first sheet through the typewriter and, two-fingered as always, pecked out the words *The Day of the Jackal.*

Ten years later, people still tell me they think *Jackal* was the best I ever did. Personally, I don't know. Books to an author are a bit like kids; it's hellishly hard to make a choice. What I wrote in 1970 was instinctive, self-taught; the story, with its twists and turns, with the convolutions of the two manhunts (of the Jackal for his presidential target and of the police for the Jackal), was written the way it was because it seemed to me that was the only way to describe it. With hindsight, I suppose, of the three novels in this volume, *Jackal* may be described as the "cunning" one. For that was what the events were like: a pitting against each other of two forces, each cunning, devious, undercover, ruthless, and utterly lethal.

By the early spring of 1971, even before the novel was published, it had become plain it was going to be a bigger seller than either I or the publisher had expected. The foreign contracts and the royalty advances were coming in, bigger each time. That was when it was said to me: "Great, now do another one like it." It was rather like a guy who has never swum before falling by chance off the top board, executing by an incredible fluke a perfect Olympic-quality triple-somersault dive, and then being told as he drags himself spluttering out of the pool: "Lovely, sonny, now do it again."

I found myself in a quandary. What to write? To start with, I tried to analyze, belatedly, the format and theme of *Jackal.* I came up with this: two manhunts; a stationary target, unable to move by force of circumstance; a hunter seeking to destroy the target; the protectors of the target seeking to identify and liquidate the hunter before he can reach home base. I searched around for a theme and came up with the (then) continuing secret hunt for the cream of the missing Nazi mass-murderers. Occasionally, I knew, the tip of this iceberg surfaced, as in the case of Adolf Eichmann, snatched by an Israeli commando and brought back to stand trial and hang in Jerusalem. But under the surface? There must be more, plenty more. I began to ferret. By November 1971 I was ready to sit down again and write *The Odessa File.*

I remembered the tail end of the Second World War. I had seen the pictures that came out of Germany, watched the documentaries filmed in death camps. I knew Germany intimately and spoke the lingo well enough to pass for a German. But I had never really dived deep into the history of that time. During those long researches during 1971 as I went through the archives of the Nazi elite, burrowing into the personal life of Eduard Roschmann, a new dimension of repugnance was added to my feelings. At first I thought my revenge-seeking hunter should be Jewish; then I revised that notion—too conventional. Better a young German, himself Aryan, apprised twenty years after the events, filled with disgust, seeking to bring to justice one single one of his compatriots. Acutally, quite a lot of what I went through during the research period went into Peter Miller's experiences—the closed doors, the sudden cessation of helpfulness, the official obscurantism, the missing files.

So, a few explanatory words about the second novel in this volume. Every word in the diary of Salomon Tauber was told to me personally by Jewish survivors of Riga. Every incident described in that diary really happened. The tale of the old woman made to dance till she dropped was told me by an eyewitness. I talked long into the night by the firelight with the ex-Kapo who helped his wife into the gassing van and feels to this day he is not worthy to go to Israel. Everything described about Eduard Roschmann at Riga actually happened.

After the book was published, many readers felt the allegations went beyond believable fact. Some, with good intentions, protested there could not really be an Odessa. Sorry; there *was* an Odessa and for three decades after the war its members did what I alleged. Ensured the most expensive defense for accused comrades; sprang some from jail; tipped off others, who fled in time; provided false identity documents; funded small business enterprises for former colleagues; underwrote industries; provided jobs and havens for the fallen-on-hard-times; abstracted files; blocked inquiries; stultified judicial progress; subsidized magazines and newspapers; held reunions; contributed to political campaigns; infiltrated commerce, industry, public service, the police, judiciary, central and local government.

Nor were other parts of the book imaginary. There *was* a rocket program mounted by Nasser for eventual use against Israel; its key scientists *were* ex-Hitlerites; the 7,000-strong German colony at Maadi *was* impregnated with Nazis; Israeli intelligence *did* sabotage the program; there *was* a civil war in Yemen, during which Nasser tested warheads with chemical rather than explosive contents; and the rockets *did* fail to fly because they lacked guidance systems.

Finally, Roschmann himself. He, too, existed. His career was just as I described it, taken from his own curriculum vitae in his own hand and from the supporting SS documents, all of which I read. He fled for the second time to South America in the late 1950s or early 1960s. About three years ago he was denounced in Argentina, where he had been living for years, by a neighbor who had seen the film *The Odessa File* in a nearby movie house.

Arrested by the Argentinian police, he was held while West Germany slapped in a request for extradition. The local magistrate granted him bail. He skipped bail and escaped to the sanctuary of Paraguay. There, a few weeks later, he died of a heart attack—brought on, I hope, by the exertions of his flight. He was sixty-eight. Fingerprints were flown from Vienna and tallied with those of the corpse. The clincher was the two missing toes; just as I described it, he had got frostbite in two toes while wandering through the Austrian snow. pursued by the British police, in the winter of 1947, and the toes were later amputated at Rimini, Italy. The corpse had the same two toes missing, old scars in their place.

If I had to describe *Jackal* as the cunning novel, *Odessa* would probably rate as the humane one.

By the first days of January 1972, after handing in the manuscript of *Odessa*, I found myself with one book outstanding to complete the three-novel contract I had signed back in 1970. I decided to make a break with the manhunt theme and try for a new subject. Not unnaturally, my thoughts went back to the third area of the world I knew pretty well from my reporting days: the west of Africa.

This is a harsh land—in climate, in flora, in fauna, but most of all in its predators. The gentlest of these have four legs, the cruelest have two. It would be fashionable to suppose that of these last the totality were white in pigmentation. Not true; the worst of the miseries I have seen inflicted upon the suffering masses were imposed by fellow Africans. By and large, the role of the white in Africa today is that of paymaster, provider, and mentor. No external inspirators are needed.

So I wrote of mercenaries—the nice ones with guns for hire, the nasty ones with checkbooks at the ready. And of a monster, a tyrant, a mad despot, who was thought by some readers to be a lampoon until recent reports described the true faces of Idi Amin and Jean-Bédel Bokassa—and they told only the half of it.

Not a nice book, *The Dogs of War*. Not a fashionable tome. An odor of cordite, corruption, and vultures here. But take your pick. The only other odor is of sanctimoniousness, hypocrisy, and convenient concern.

So, *Dogs of War*, the third book, is the tough one, the raw tale, the story that does not seek to avoid stepping on toes or pulling punches. And if in the end the only man who cares a damn for the ones Frantz Fanon called "the wretched of the earth" turns out to be a hired gunman, maybe that is just my own acid joke. Or maybe that is the way it was when I was there.

Anyway, I hope you enjoy them all.

The Day of the Jackal

PART 1
Anatomy of a Plot

ONE

It is cold at 6:40 in the morning of a March day in Paris, and seems even colder when a man is about to be executed by firing squad. At that hour on March 11, 1963, in the main courtyard of the Fort d'Ivry a French Air Force colonel stood before a stake driven into the chilly gravel as his hands were bound behind the post, and stared with slowly diminishing disbelief at the squad of soldiers facing him twenty metres away.

A foot scuffed the grit, a tiny release from tension, as the blindfold was wrapped around the eyes of Lieutenant-Colonel Jean-Marie Bastien-Thiry, age thirty-five, blotting out the light for the last time. The mumbling of the priest was a helpless counterpoint to the crackling of twenty rifle bolts as the soldiers charged and cocked their carbines.

Beyond the walls a Berliet truck blared for a passage as some smaller vehicle crossed its path towards the centre of the city; the sound died away, masking the "Take your aim" order from the officer in charge of the squad. The crash of rifle fire, when it came, caused no ripple on the surface of the waking city, other than to send a flutter of pigeons skywards for a few moments. The single "whack" seconds later of the coup-de-grace was lost in the rising din of traffic from beyond the walls.

The death of the officer, leader of a gang of Secret Army Organisation killers who had sought to shoot the President of France, was to have been an end—an end to further attempts on the President's life. By a quirk of fate it marked a beginning, and to explain why, it is first necessary to explain why a riddled body came to hang from its ropes in the courtyard of the military prison outside Paris on that March morning. . . .

The sun had dropped at last behind the palace wall, and long shadows rippled across the courtyard bringing a welcome relief. Even at 7 in the evening of the hottest day of the year the temperature was still twenty-five degrees centigrade. Across the sweltering city the Parisians piled querulous wives and yelling children into cars and trains to leave for the weekend in the country. It was August 22, 1962, the day a few men waiting beyond the city boundaries had decided that the President, General Charles de Gaulle, should die.

While the city's population prepared to flee the heat for the relative cool of the rivers and beaches, the cabinet meeting behind the ornate façade of the Elysée Palace continued. Across the tan gravel of the front courtyard, now cooling in welcome shadow, sixteen black Citroen DS sedans were drawn up nose to tail, forming a circle round three quarters of the area.

The drivers, lurking in the deepest shade close to the west wall where the shadows had arrived first, exchanged the inconsequential banter of those who spend most of their working days waiting on their masters' whims.

There was more desultory grumbling at the unusual length of the Cabinet's deliberations, until a moment before 7:30 a chained and bemedalled usher appeared behind the plate glass doors at the top of the six steps of the palace and gestured towards the guards. Among the drivers, half-smoked Gauloises were dropped and ground into the gravel. The security men and guards stiffened in their boxes beside the front gate and the massive iron grilles were swung open.

The chauffeurs were at the wheels of their limousines when the first group of ministers appeared behind the plate glass. The usher opened the doors and the members of the Cabinet straggled down the steps exchanging a few last-minute wishes for a restful weekend. In order of precedence the sedans eased up to the base of the steps, the usher opened the rear door with a bow, the Ministers climbed into their respective cars and were driven away past the salutes of the Garde Républicaine and out into Faubourg Saint Honoré.

Within ten minutes they were gone. Two long black DS 19 Citroens remained in the yard, and each slowly cruised to the base of the steps. The first, flying the pennant of the President of the French Republic, was driven by François Marroux, a police driver from the training and headquarters camp of the Gendarmerie Nationale at Satory. His silent temperament had kept him apart from the joking of the ministerial drivers in the courtyard; his ice-cold nerves and ability to drive fast and safely kept him de Gaulle's personal driver. Apart from Marroux, the car was empty. Behind it the second DS 19 was also driven by a gendarme from Satory.

At 7:45 another group appeared behind the glass doors, and again the men on the gravel stiffened to attention. Dressed in his habitual double-breasted charcoal grey suit and dark tie, Charles de Gaulle appeared behind the glass. With old-world courtesy he first ushered Madame Yvonne de Gaulle through the doors, then took her arm to guide her down the steps to the waiting Citroen. They parted at the car, and the President's wife climbed into the rear seat of the front vehicle on the left-hand side. The General got in behind her from the right.

Their son-in-law, Colonel Alain de Boissieu, then chief-of-staff of the Armoured and Cavalry units of the French Army, checked that both rear doors were safely shut, then took his place in the front beside Marroux.

In the second car two others from the group of functionaries who had accompanied the presidential couple down the steps took their seats. Henri d'Jouder, the hulking bodyguard of the day, a Kabyle from Algeria, took the front seat beside the driver, eased the heavy revolver under his left armpit, and slumped back. From then on his eyes would flicker incessantly, not over the car in front, but over the pavements and street corners as they flashed past. After a last word to one of the duty security men to be left behind, the second man got into the back alone. He was Commissaire Jean Ducret, chief of the Presidential Security Corps.

From beside the west wall two white-helmeted motorcyclists gunned their engines into life and rode slowly out of the shadows towards the gate. Before the entrance they stopped ten feet apart and glanced back. Marroux pulled the first Citroen away from the steps, swung towards the gate, and drew up behind the motorcycle outriders. The second car followed. It was 7:50 p.m.

Again the iron grille swung open, and the small cortege swept past the ramrod guards into the Faubourg Saint Honoré and from there into the Avenue de Marigny. From under the chestnut trees a young man in a white crash helmet astride a scooter watched the cortege pass, then slid away from the kerb and followed. Traffic was normal for an August weekend, and no advance warning of the President's departure had been given. Only the whine of the motorcycle sirens told traffic cops on duty of the approach of the convoy, and they had to wave and whistle frantically to get the traffic stopped in time.

The convoy picked up speed in the tree-darkened avenue and erupted into the sunlit Place Clemenceau, heading straight across towards the Pont Alexandre III. Riding in the slipstream of the official cars, the scooterist had little difficulty in following. After the bridge Marroux followed the motor-cyclists into the Avenue General Gallieni and thence into the broad Boulevard des Invalides. The scooterist at this point had his answer—the route de Gaulle's convoy would take out of Paris. At the junction of the Boulevard des Invalides and the rue de Varennes he eased back the screaming throttle and swerved towards a corner cafe. Inside, taking a small metal token from his pocket, he strode to the back of the cafe where the telephone was situated and placed a local call.

Lieutenant-Colonel Jean-Marie Bastien-Thiry waited in the suburb of Meudon. He was marrried, with three children, and he worked in the Air Ministry. Behind the conventional façade of his professional and family life, he nurtured a deep bitterness towards Charles de Gaulle, who, he believed, had betrayed France and the men who in 1958 had called him back to power by yielding Algeria to the Algerian nationalists.

He personally had lost nothing through the loss of Algeria, and it was not personal consideration that motivated him. In his own eyes he was a patriot, a man convinced that he would be serving his beloved country by slaying the man he thought had betrayed her. Many thousands shared his views at that time, but few in comparison were fanatical members of the Secret Army Organisation, which had sworn to kill de Gaulle and bring down his government. Bastien-Thiry was such a man.

He was sipping a beer when the call came through. The barman passed him the phone, then went to adjust the television set at the other end of the bar. Bastien-Thiry listened for a few seconds, muttered, "Very good, thank you," into the mouthpiece, and set it down. His beer was already paid for. He strolled out of the bar onto the pavement, took a rolled newspaper from under his arm, and carefully unfolded it twice.

Across the street a young woman let drop the lace curtain of her first floor flat, and, turning to the twelve men who lounged about the room, she said, "It's route number two." The five youngsters, amateurs at the business of killing, stopped twisting their hands and jumped up.

The other seven were older and less nervous. Senior among them in the assassination attempt and second-in-command to Bastien-Thiry was Lieute-nant Alain Bougrenet de la Tocnaye, an extreme right-winger from a family of landed gentry. He was thirty-five, married, with two children.

The most dangerous man in the room was Georges Watin, aged thirty-nine, a bulky-shouldered, square-jowled OAS fanatic, originally an agri-

cultural engineer from Algeria, who in two years had emerged again as one
of the OAS's most dangerous trigger-men. From an old leg-wound he was
known as "the Limp."

When the girl announced the news, the twelve men trooped downstairs via
the back of the building to a side street where six vehicles, all stolen or hired,
had been parked. The time was 7:55.

Bastien-Thiry had personally spent days preparing the site of the assassination, measuring angles of fire, speed and distance of the moving vehicles, and the degree of firepower necessary to stop them. The place he had
chosen was a long straight road called the Avenue de la Libération, leading
up to the main cross-roads of Petit-Clamart. The plan was for the first group
containing the marksmen with their rifles to open fire on the President's car
some two hundred yards before the cross-roads. They would shelter behind
an Estafette van parked by the roadside, beginning their fire at a very
shallow angle to the oncoming vehicles.

By Bastien-Thiry's calculations, 150 bullets should pass through the leading car by the time it came abreast of the van. With the presidential car
brought to a stop, the second OAS group would sweep out of a side road to
blast the security police vehicle at close range. Both groups would spend a
few seconds finishing off the presidential party, then spring for the three
getaway vehicles in another side street.

Bastien-Thiry himself, the thirteenth of the party, would be the lookout
man. By 8:05 the groups were in position. A hundred yards on the Paris side
of the ambush, Bastien-Thiry stood idly by a bus stop with his newspaper.
Waving the newspaper would give the signal to Serge Bernier, leader of the
first commando, who would be standing by the Estafette. He would pass the
order to the gunmen spreadeagled in the grass at his feet. Bougrenet de la
Tocnaye would drive the car to intercept the security police, with Watin the
Limp beside him clutching a submachine gun.

As the safety catches flicked off beside the road at Petit-Clamart, General
de Gaulle's convoy cleared the heavier traffic of central Paris and reached
the more open avenues of the suburbs. Here the speed increased to nearly
sixty miles per hour.

As the road opened out, François Marroux flicked a glance at his watch,
sensed the testy impatience of the old General behind him, and pushed the
speed up even higher. The two motorcycle outriders dropped back to take
up station at the rear of the convoy. De Gaulle never liked such ostentation
sitting out in front and dispensed with them whenever he could. In this
manner the convoy entered the Avenue de la Division Leclerc at Petit-
Clamart. It was 8:17 p.m.

A mile up the road Bastien-Thiry was experiencing the effects of his big
mistake. He would not learn of it until told by the police as he sat months
later in Death Row. Investigating the timetable of his assassination, he had
consulted a calendar to discover that dusk fell on August 22 at 8:35,
seemingly plenty late enough even if de Gaulle was late on his usual schedule, as indeed he was. But the calendar the Air Force colonel had consulted
was wrong. On August 22, 1962, dusk fell at 8:10. Those twenty-five minutes
were to change the history of France. At 8:18 Bastien-Thiry discerned the
convoy hurtling down the Avenue de la Libération towards him at seventy
miles per hour. Frantically he waved his newspaper.

Across the road and a hundred yards down, Bernier peered angrily through the gloom at the dim figure by the bus stop. "Has the colonel waved his paper yet?" he asked of no one in particular. The words were hardly out of his mouth when he saw the shark-nose of the President's car flash past the bus stop and into vision. "Fire," he screamed to the man at his feet. They opened up as the convoy came abreast of them, firing with a ninety-degree lay-off at a moving target passing them at seventy miles per hour.

That the car took twelve bullets at all was a tribute to the killers' marksmanship. Most of those hit the Citroen from behind. Two tires shredded under the fire, and although they were self-sealing tubes the sudden loss of pressure caused the speeding car to lurch and go into a front-wheel skid. That was when François Marroux saved de Gaulle's life.

While the ace marksman, ex-legionnaire Varga, cut up the tires, the remainder emptied their magazines at the disappearing rear window. Several slugs passed through the bodywork, and one shattered the rear window, passing within a few inches of the presidential nose. In the front seat Colonel de Boissieu turned and roared, "Get down," at his parents-in-law. Madame de Gaulle lowered her head towards her husband's lap. The General gave vent to a frosty "What, again?" and turned to look out of the back window.

Marroux held the shuddering steering wheel and gently turned into the skid, easing down the accelerator as he did so. After a momentary loss of power the Citroen surged forward again towards the intersection with the Avenue du Bois, the side-road where the second commando of OAS men waited. Behind Marroux the security car clung to his tail, untouched by any bullets at all.

For Bougrenet de la Tocnaye, waiting with engine running in the Avenue du Bois, the speed of the approaching cars gave him a clear choice: to intercept and commit suicide as the hurtling metal cut him to pieces, or let the clutch in a half-second too late. He chose the latter. As he swung his car out of the side road and into line with the presidential convoy, it was not de Gaulle's car he came alongside, but that of the marksman bodyguard d'Jouder and Commissaire Ducret.

Leaning from the right-hand side window, outside the car from the waist up, Watin emptied his submachine gun at the back of the DS in front, in which he could see de Gaulle's haughty profile through the smashed glass. "Why don't those idiots fire back?" de Gaulle asked querulously. D'Jouder was trying to get a shot at the OAS killers across ten feet of air between the two cars, but the police driver blocked his view. Ducret shouted to the driver to stick with the President, and a second later the OAS were left behind. The two motorcycle outriders, one having nearly been unseated by de la Tocnaye's sudden rush out of the side road, recovered and closed up. The whole convoy swept into the roundabout and road-junction, crossed it, and continued towards Villacoublay.

At the ambush site the OAS men had no time for recriminations. They were to come later. Leaving the three cars used in the operation, they leapt aboard the getaway vehicles and disappeared into the descending gloom.

From his car-borne transmitter Commissaire Ducret called Villacoublay and told them briefly what had happened. When the convoy arrived ten minutes later, General de Gaulle insisted on driving straight to the apron where the helicopter was waiting. As the car stopped, a surge of officers and officials surrounded it, pulling open the doors to assist a shaken Madame de Gaulle to her feet. From the other side the General emerged from the debris and shook glass splinters from his lapel. Ignoring the panicky solicitude of the surrounding officers, he walked round the car to take his wife's arm.

"Come, my dear, we are going home," he told her, and finally gave the Air Force staff his verdict on the OAS: "They can't shoot straight." With that he guided his wife into the helicopter and took his seat beside her. He was joined by d'Jouder, and they took off for a weekend in the country.

On the tarmac François Marroux sat ashen-faced behind the wheel. Both tires along the right-hand side of the car had finally given out, and the DS was riding on its rims. Ducret muttered a quiet word of congratulations to him, then went on with the business of clearing up.

While journalists the world over speculated on the assassination attempt and for lack of anything better filled their columns with personal conjectures, the French police, headed by the Sûreté Nationale and backed up by the Secret Service and the Gendarmerie, launched the biggest police operation in French history. Soon it was to become the biggest manhunt the country had yet known, only later to be surpassed by the manhunt for another assassin whose story remains unknown but who is still listed in the files by his code-name, the Jackal.

They got their first break on September 3, and, as is so often the case with police work, it was a routine check that brought results. Outside the town of Valence, south of Lyons on the main road from Paris to Marseilles, a police roadblock stopped a private car containing four men. They had stopped hundreds that day to examine identity papers, but in this case one of the men in the car had no papers on him. He claimed he had lost them. He and the other three were taken to Valence for routine questioning.

At Valence it was established that the other three in the car had nothing to do with the fourth, apart from having offered him a lift. They were released. The fourth man's fingerprints were taken and sent to Paris, just to see if he was who he said he was. The answer came back twelve hours later: the fingerprints were those of a twenty-two-year-old deserter from the Foreign Legion, who faced charges under military law. But the name he had given was quite accurate—Pierre-Denis Magade.

Magade was taken to the headquarters of the Service Régional of the Police Judiciaire at Lyons. While waiting in an anteroom for interrogation, one of the police guarding him playfully asked, "Well, what about Petit-Clamart?"

Magade shrugged helplessly. "All right," he answered, "what do you want to know?"

As stunned police officers listened to him and stenographers' pens scratched across one notebook after another, Magade "sang" for eight hours. By the end he had named every one of the participants of Petit-Clamart, and nine others who had played smaller roles in the plotting stages or in procuring the equipment. Twenty-two in all. The hunt was on, and this time the police knew whom they were looking for.

In the end only one escaped, and has never been caught to this day. Georges Watin got away and is presumed to be living in Spain along with most of the other OAS chiefs.

The interrogation and preparation of the charges against Bastien-Thiry,

Bougrenet de la Tocnaye, and the other leaders of the plot were finished by December, and the group went on trial in January 1963.

While the trial was on, the OAS gathered its strength for another all-out attack on the Gaullist government, and the French Secret Service fought back tooth and claw. Under the pleasant norms of Parisian life, beneath the veneer of culture and civilisation, one of the bitterest and most sadistic underground wars of modern history was fought out.

The French Secret Service is called the Service de Documentation Extérieure et de Contre-Espionage, known for short as SDECE. Its duties are both those of espionage outside France and counter-espionage within, though each service may overlap the other's territory on occasion. Service One is pure intelligence, subdivided into bureaux known by the initial R for Renseignement (Information). These subdivisions are R 1, Intelligence Analysis; R 2, Eastern Europe; R 3, Western Europe; R 4, Africa; R 5, Middle East; R 6, Far East; R 7, America/Western Hemisphere. Service Two is concerned with counter-espionage. Three and Four comprise the Communist Section in one office, Six is Finance, and Seven, Administration.

Service Five has a one-word title—Action. This office was the core of the anti-OAS war. From the headquarters in a complex of nondescript buildings off the Boulevard Mortier, close to the Porte des Lilas, a dingy suburb of northeast Paris, the hundred toughs of the Action Service went out to war. These men, mainly Corsicans, were trained to a peak of physical fitness, then taken to Satory camp, where a special section shut off from the rest taught them everything known about destruction. They became experts in fighting with small arms and in unarmed combat—Karate and Judo. They underwent courses in radio communication, demolition and sabotage, interrogation with and without the use of torture, kidnapping, arson, and assassination.

Some spoke only French, others were fluent in several languages and at home in any capital in the world. They had the authority to kill in the course of duty and often used it.

As the activities of the OAS became more violent and brutal, the Director of the SDECE, General Eugène Guibaud, finally took the muzzle off these men and let them loose on the OAS. Some of them enlisted in the OAS and infiltrated its highest councils. From here they were content to provide information on which others could act, and many OAS emissaries on missions into France or other areas where they were vulnerable to the police were picked up on information provided by Action Service men inside the terrorist organization. On other occasions wanted men could not be inveigled into France and were ruthlessly killed outside the country. Many relatives of OAS men who simply disappeared believed ever after that the men had been liquidated by the Action Service.

Not that the OAS needed lessons in violence. They hated the Action Service men (known as the Barbouzes, or Bearded Ones, because of their undercover role) more than any policeman. In the last days of the struggle for power between the OAS and the Gaullist authorities inside Algiers, the OAS captured seven Barbouzes alive. The bodies were later found hanging from balconies and lamp-posts minus ears and noses. In this manner the undercover war went on, and the complete story of who died under torture at whose hands in which cellar will never be told.

The remainder of the Barbouzes stayed outside the OAS at the beck and call of the SDECE. Some of them had been professional thugs from the underworld before being enlisted, kept up their old contacts, and on more than one occasion enlisted the aid of their former underworld friends to do a particularly dirty job for the government. It was these activities that gave rise to talk in France of a "parallel" (unofficial) police, supposedly at the orders of one of President de Gaulle's right-hand men, M. Jacques Foccart. In truth no "parallel" police existed; the activities attributed to them were carried out by the Action Service strong-arms or temporarily enlisted gang-bosses from the "milieu."

Corsicans, who dominated both the Paris and Marseilles underworld and the Action Service, know a thing or two about vendettas, and after the slaying of the seven Barbouzes of Mission C in Algiers, a vendetta was declared against the OAS. In the same manner as the Corsican underworld helped the Allies during the landings in the South of France in 1944 (for their own ends; they later cornered most of the vice trade along the Côte d'Azur as a reward), so in the early sixties the Corsicans fought for France again in a vendetta with the OAS. Many of the OAS men who were *pieds-noirs* (Algerian-born Frenchmen) had the same characteristics as the Corsicans, and at times the war was almost fratricidal.

As the trial of Bastien-Thiry and his fellows wore on, the OAS campaign also got under way. Its guiding light, the behind-the-scenes instigator of the Petit-Clamart plot, was Colonel Antoine Argoud. A product of one of France's top universities, the Ecole Polytechnique, Argoud had a good brain and dynamic energy. As a lieutenant under de Gaulle in the Free French, he had fought for the liberation of France from the Nazis. Later he commanded a regiment of cavalry in Algiers. A short, wiry man, he was a brilliant but ruthless soldier, and by 1962 he had become operations chief for the OAS in exile.

Experienced in psychological warfare, he understood that the fight against Gaullist France had to be conducted on all levels, by terror, diplomacy, and public relations. As part of the campaign he arranged for the head of the National Resistance Council, the political wing of the OAS, former French Foreign Minister Georges Bidault, to give a series of interviews to newspapers and television across Western Europe to explain the OAS's opposition to General de Gaulle in "respectable" terms.

Argoud was now putting to use the fine intellect that had once made him the youngest colonel in the French Army and now made him the most dangerous man in the OAS. He set up for Bidault a series of interviews with major networks and newspaper correspondents, during which the old politician was able to put a cloak of sober rectitude over the less acceptable activities of the OAS thugs.

The success of Bidault's Argoud-inspired propaganda operation alarmed the French government as much as the terror tactics and the wave of plastic bombs exploding in cinemas and cafes all over France. Then on February 14 another plot to assassinate General de Gaulle was uncovered. The following day he was due to give a lecture at the Ecole Militaire on the Champ de Mars. The plot was that on entering the hall he was to be shot in the back by an assassin perched among the eaves of the adjacent block.

Those who later faced trial for the plot were Jean Bicnon, a captain of artillery named Robert Poinard, and an English-language teacher at the Military Academy, Madame Paule Rousselet de Liffiac. The trigger-man was to have been Georges Watin, but once again the Limp got away. A rifle with sniperscope was found at Poinard's flat, and the three were arrested. It was stated at their later trial that, seeking a way to spirit Watin and his gun into the Academy, they had consulted Warrant Officer Marius Tho, who had gone straight to the police. General de Gaulle duly attended the military ceremony at the appointed time on the 15th but made the concession of arriving in an armour-plated car, to his great distaste.

As a plot, it was amateurish beyond belief, but it annoyed de Gaulle. Summoning Interior Minister Frey the next day, he hammered the table and told the Minister responsible for national security, "This assassination business has gone far enough."

It was decided to make an example of some of the top OAS conspirators to deter the others. Frey had no doubts about the outcome of the Bastien-Thiry trial still going on in the Supreme Military Court, for Bastien-Thiry was at pains to explain from the dock why he thought Charles de Gaulle should die. But something more in the way of a deterrent was needed.

On February 22 a copy of a memorandum which the director of Service Two of SDECE had sent to the Interior Minister landed on the desk of the head of the Action Service. Here is an extract:

"We have succeeded in ascertaining the whereabouts of one of the main ringleaders of the subversive movement, namely ex-Colonel of the French Army Antoine Argoud. He has fled to Germany and intends, according to information from our Intelligence Service there, to remain for several days. . . .

"This being so, it should be possible to get at Argoud and perhaps seize him. As the request made by our official counter-espionage service to the competent German security organisations has been refused, and these organisations now expect our agents to be on the heels of Argoud and other OAS leaders, the operation must, insofar as it is directed against the person of Argoud, be carried out with maximum speed and discretion."

The job was handed over to the Action Service.

In the midafternoon of February 25 Argoud arrived back in Munich from Rome where he had been meeting other OAS leaders. Instead of going straight to Unertlstrasse he took a taxi to the Eden-Wolff Hotel, where he had booked a room, apparently for a meeting. He never attended it. In the hall he was accosted by two men who spoke to him in faultless German. He presumed they were German police and reached into his breast pocket for his passport.

He felt both arms grabbed in a vice-like grip, his feet left the ground, and he was whisked outside to a waiting laundry van. He lashed out and was answered with a torrent of French oaths. A horny hand chopped across his nose, another slammed him in the stomach, a finger felt for the nerve spot below the ear, and he went out like a light.

Twenty-four hours later a telephone rang in the Brigade Criminelle of the Police Judiciaire at 36, Quai des Orfèvres in Paris. A hoarse voice told the answering desk sergeant that he was speaking for the OAS and that Antoine Argoud, "nicely tied up," was in a van parked behind the building. A few minutes later the door of the van was jerked open and Argoud stumbled out into a circle of dumbfounded police officers.

His eyes, bandaged for twenty-four hours, would not focus. He had to be helped to stand. His face was covered with dried blood from a nose-bleed, and his mouth ached from the the gag which the police pulled out of it. When someone asked him, "Are you Colonel Antoine Argoud?" he mumbled, "Yes." Somehow the Action Service had spirited him across the frontier during the previous night, and the anonymous phone call to the police about the parcel waiting them in their own parking lot was just their private sense of humour at work. Argoud was held until June 1968, and then released.

But one thing the Action Service men had not counted on: in removing Argoud, despite the enormous demoralisation this caused in the OAS, they had paved the way for his shadowy deputy, the little known but equally astute Lieutenant Colonel Marc Rodin, to assume command of operations aimed at assassinating de Gaulle. In many ways it was a bad bargain.

On March 4 the Supreme Military Court delivered its verdict on Jean-Marie Bastien-Thiry. He and two others were sentenced to death, as were a futher three still at large including Watin the Limp. On March 8 General de Gaulle listened for three hours in silence to appeal for clemency by the lawyers of the condemned men. He commuted two of the death sentences to life imprisonment, but Bastien-Thiry's condemnation stood.

That night his lawyer told the Air Force colonel of the decision.

"It is fixed for the eleventh," he told his client, and when the latter continued to smile disbelievingly, blurted out, "You are going to be shot."

Bastien-Thiry kept smiling and shook his head.

"You don't understand," he told the lawyer, "no squad of Frenchmen will raise their rifles against me."

He was wrong. The execution was reported on the 8 a.m. news of Radio Europe Number One in French. It was heard in most parts of Western Europe by those who cared to tune in. In a small hotel room in Austria the broadcast was to set off a train of thoughts and actions that brought General de Gaulle nearer to death than at any time in his career. The room was that of Colonel Marc Rodin, new operations chief of the OAS.

TWO

Marc Rodin flicked off the switch of his transistor radio and rose from the table, leaving the breakfast tray almost untouched. He walked over to the window, lit another in the endless chain of cigarettes and gazed out at the snow-encrusted landscape, which the late-arriving spring had not yet started to dismantle.

"Bastards." He murmured the word quietly and with great venom, following up with another sotto voce string of nouns and epithets that expressed his feelings towards the French President, his government, and the Action Service.

Rodin was unlike his predecessor in almost every way. Tall and spare, with a cadaverous face hollowed by the hatred within, he usually masked his emotions with an un-Latin frigidity. For him there had been no Ecole Polytechnique to open doors to promotion. The son of a cobbler, he had escaped to England by fishing boat in the halcyon days of his late teens when the Germans overran France, and had enlisted as a private soldier under the banner of the Cross of Lorraine.

Promotion through sergeant to Warrant Officer had come the hard way, in bloody battles across the face of North Africa under Koenig and later through the hedgerows of Normandy with Leclerc. A field commission during the fight for Paris had got him the officer's chevrons his education and breeding could never have obtained, and in post-war France the choice had been between staying in the Army or reverting to civilian life.

But revert to what? He had no trade but that of cobbler which his father had taught him, and he found the working class of his native country dominated by Communists, who had also taken over the Resistance and the Free French of the Interior. So he stayed in the Army, later to experience the bitterness of an officer from the ranks who saw a new young generation of educated boys graduating from the officer schools, earning in theoretical lessons carried out in classrooms the same chevrons he had sweated blood for. As he watched them pass him in rank and privilege, the bitterness started to set in.

There was only one thing left to do, and that was join one of the colonial regiments, the tough crack soldiers who did the fighting while the conscript army paraded round drill squares. He managed a transfer to the colonial paratroops.

Within a year he had been a company commander in Indochina, living among other men who spoke and thought as he did. For a young man from a cobbler's bench, promotion could still be obtained through combat, and more combat. By the end of the Indochina campaign he was a major, and after an unhappy and frustrating year in France he was sent to Algeria.

The French withdrawal from Indochina and the year he spent in France had turned his latent bitterness into a consuming loathing of politicians and Communists, whom he regarded as one and the same thing. Not until France was ruled by a soldier could she ever be pried loose from the grip of the traitors and lickspittles who permeated her public life. Only in the Army were both breeds extinct.

Like most combat officers who had seen their men die and occasionally buried the hideously mutilated bodies of those unlucky enough to be taken alive, Rodin worshipped soldiers as the true salt of the earth, the men who sacrificed themselves in blood so that the bourgeoisie could live at home in comfort. To learn from the civilians of his native land after his eight years of combat in the forests of Indochina that most of them cared not a fig for the soldiery, to read the denunciations of the military by the Left-wing intellectuals for mere trifles like the torturing of prisoners to obtain vital information, had set off inside Marc Rodin a reaction which, combined with the native bitterness stemming from his own lack of opportunity, had turned into zealotry.

He remained convinced that given enough backing by the civil authorities on the spot and the Government and people back home, the Army could have beaten the Viet-Minh. The cession of Indochina had been a massive betrayal of the thousands of fine young men who had died there—seemingly for nothing. For Rodin there would be, could be, no more betrayals. Algeria would prove it. He left the shore of Marseilles in the spring of 1956 as near a happy man as he would ever be, convinced that the distant hills of Algeria would see the consummation of what he regarded as his life's work, the apotheosis of the French Army in the eyes of the world.

Within two years of bitter and ferocious fighting little happened to shake his convictions. True, the rebels were not as easy to put down as he had thought at first. However many fellagha he and his men shot, however many villages were razed to the ground, however many FLN terrorists died under torture, the rebellion spread until it enveloped the land and consumed the cities.

What was needed, of course, was more help from the Métropole. Here at least there could be no question of a war in a far-flung corner of the Empire. Algeria was France, a part of France, inhabited by three million Frenchmen. One would fight for Algeria as for Normandy, Brittany, or the Alpes-Maritimes. When he got his lieutenant-colonelcy Marc Rodin moved out of the *bled* and into the cities, first Bone then Constantine.

In the *bled* he had been fighting the soldiers of the FLN, irregular soldiers but still fighting men. His hatred of them was as nothing to what consumed him as he entered the sneaking, vicious war of the cities, a war fought with plastic bombs planted by cleaners in French-patronised cafes, supermarkets, and play-parks. The measures he took to cleanse Constantine of the filth who planted these bombs among French civilians earned him in the Casbah the title of Butcher.

All that was lacking for the final obliteration of the FLN and its army, the ALN, was more help from Paris. Like most fanatics, Rodin could blind himself to facts with sheer belief. The escalating costs of the war, the tottering economy of France under the burden of a war becoming increasingly unwinnable, the demoralisation of the conscripts, were a bagatelle.

In June 1958 General de Gaulle returned to power as Prime Minister of France. Efficiently disposing of the corrupt and tottering Fourth Republic, he founded the Fifth. When he spoke the words whose utterance in the mouths of the Generals had brought him back to the Matignon and then in January 1959 to the Elysée, "Algérie Française," Rodin went to his room and cried. When de Gaulle visited Algeria, his presence was for Rodin like that of Zeus coming down from Olympus. The new policy, he was sure, was on the way. The Communists would be swept from their offices, Jean-Paul Sartre must surely be shot for treason, the trade unions would be brought into submission, and the final wholehearted backing of France for her kith and kin in Algeria and for her Army protecting the frontiers of French civilisation would be forthcoming.

Rodin was as sure of this as the rising of the sun in the east. When de Gaulle started his measures to restore France his own way, Rodin thought there must be some mistake. One had to give the old man time. When the first rumours of preliminary talks with Ben Bella and the FLN filtered through, Rodin could not believe it. Although he sympathised with the revolt of the settlers led by Big Joe Ortiz in 1960, he still felt the lack of progress in smashing the fellagha once and for all was simply a tactical move by de Gaulle. Le Vieux, he felt sure, must know what he was doing. Had he not said it, the golden worlds "Algérie Française"?

When the proof came finally and beyond any doubt that Charles de Gaulle's concept of a resuscitated France did not include a French Algeria, Rodin's world disintegrated like a china vase hit by a train. Of faith and hope, belief and confidence, there was nothing left. Just hate. Hate for the system, for the politicians, for the intellectuals, for the Algerians, for the trade unions, for the journalists, for the foreigners; but most of all, hate for That Man. Apart from a few wet-eared ninnies who refused to come, Rodin led his entire battalion into the military putsch of April 1961.

It failed. In one simple, depressingly clever move de Gaulle foiled the putsch before it could get off the ground. None of the officers had taken more than a passing notice when thousands of simple transistor radios were issued to the troops in the weeks before the final announcement that talks were being started with the FLN. The radios were regarded as a harmless comfort for the troops, and many officers and senior NCOs approved the idea. The pop music that came over the air from France was a pleasant distraction for the boys from the heat, the flies, the boredom.

The voice of de Gaulle was not so harmless. When the loyalty of the Army was finally put to the test, tens of thousands of conscripts spread out in barracks across Algeria turned on their radois for the news. After the news they heard the same voice that Rodin himself had listened to in June 1940. Almost the same message. You are faced with a choice of loyalties. I am France, the instrument of her destiny. Follow me. Obey me.

Some battalion commanders woke up with only a handful of officers and most of their sergeants left.

The mutiny was broken like the illusions—by radio. Rodin had been luckier than some. One hundred and twenty of his officers, NCOs, and rankers remained with him. This was because he commanded a unit with a higher proportion of old sweats from Indochina and the Algerian *bled* than most. Together with the other putschistes they formed the Secret Army Organisation, pledged to overthrow the Judas of the Elysée Palace.

Between the triumphant FLN and the loyal Army of France, there was little time left for an orgy of destruction. In the last seven weeks, as the French settlers sold their life's work for a song and fled the war-torn coast, the Secret Army exacted one last hideous revenge on what they had to leave behind. When it was over there remained only exile for the leaders whose names were known to the Gaullist authorities.

Rodin became deputy to Argoud as operations chief of the OAS in exile in the winter of 1961. Argoud's was the flair, the talent, the inspiration behind the offensive the OAS launched on Metropolitan France from then on; Rodin's was the organisation, the cunning, the shrewd common sense.

Had he merely been a tough fanatic, he would have been dangerous but not exceptional. There were many others of that calibre toting guns for the OAS in the early sixties. But he was more. The old cobbler had sired a boy with a good thinking brain, never developed by formal education or army service. Rodin had developed it on his own, in his own way.

When faced with his own concept of France and the honour of the Army, Rodin was as bigoted as the rest; but when faced with a purely practical problem, he could bring to bear a pragmatic and logical concentration that was more effective than all the volatile enthusiasm and senseless violence in the world.

This was what he brought on the morning of March 11 to the problem of killing Charles de Gaulle. He was not fool enough to think the job would be easy; on the contrary, the failures of Petit-Clamart and the Ecole Militaire would make it much harder. Killers alone were not hard to find; the problem was to find a man or a plan that had one single factor built in that would be sufficiently unusual to penetrate the wall of security now built up in concentric rings round the person of the President.

Methodically he listed in his mind the problems. For two hours, chain-smoking before the window until the room became cloudy with a blue haze, he set them up, then devised a plan to demolish or circumvent them. Each plan seemed feasible under most of the critical examination to which he submitted them; each then disintegrated under the final test. Out of this train of thought one problem emerged as virtually insurmountable—the question of security.

Things had changed since Petit-Clamart. The penetration of the Action Service into the ranks and cadres of the OAS had increased to an alarming degree. The recent abduction of his own superior, Argoud, indicated the lengths to which the Action Service was prepared to go to get at and interrogate the leaders of the OAS. Even a blazing row with the German Government was not avoided.

With Argoud already fourteen days under interrogation, the whole OAS leadership had had to go on the run. Bidault had suddenly lost his taste for publicity and self-exposure; others of the CNR had fled panicking to Spain, America, Belgium. There had been a rush for false papers, tickets to far places.

Watching this, the lower ranks had suffered a staggering setback to morale. Men inside France previously prepared to help, to shelter wanted men, to carry packages of arms, to pass messages, even to provide information, were hanging up the phone with a muttered excuse.

Following the failure of Petit-Clamart and the interrogation of the prisoners, three whole networks inside France had had to be closed down. With inside information the French police had raided house after house, uncovered cache after cache of weapons and stores; two other plots to kill de Gaulle had been swamped with police as the conspirators sat down to their second meeting.

While the CNR made speeches in committee and burbled about the restoration of democracy in France, Rodin grimly faced the facts of life as exposed in the bulging briefcase by his bed. Short of funds losing national and international support, membership and credibility, the OAS was crumbling before the onslaught of the French Secret Service and police.

Arriving at the end of his own argument, Rodin muttered, "A man who is not known . . ." He ran through the list of men who he knew would not flinch from assassinating a president. Every one had a file thick as the Bible in French HQ. Why else would he, Marc Rodin, be hiding in a hotel in an obscure Austrian mountain village?

The answer came to him just before noon. He dismissed it for a while, but was drawn back to it with insistent curiosity. If such a man could be found . . . if only such a man existed. Slowly, laboriously, he built another plan around such a man, then subjected it to all the obstacles and objections. The plan passed them all, even the question of security.

Just before the lunch-hour struck Marc Rodin shrugged into his greatcoat and went downstairs. At the front door he caught the first blast of the wind along the icy street. It made him flinch, but cleared the dull headache caused by the cigarettes in the overheated bedroom. Turning left he crunched away towards the post office in the Adlerstrasse and sent a series of brief telegrams, informing his colleagues, scattered under aliases across southern Germany, Austria, Italy, and Spain, that he would not be available for a few weeks because he was going on a mission.

It occurred to him, as he trudged back to the humble rooming house, that some might think he too was chickening out, disappearing from the threat of kidnap or assassination by the Action Service. He shrugged to himself. Let them think what they wished, the time for lengthy explanations was over.

He lunched at the boarding house Stammkarte, the meal of the day being pot roast and noodles. Although years in the jungle and the wilderness of Algeria had left him little discrimination about food, he had difficulty cramming it down. By midafternoon he was gone, bags packed, bill paid, departed on a lonely mission to find a man, or more precisely a type of man he was not sure existed.

As he boarded his train, a BOAC Comet 4B drifted down the flight path towards runway Zero-Four at London Airport. It was inbound from Beirut. Among the passengers filing through the arrivals lounge was a tall, blond Englishman. His face was healthily tanned by the Middle East sun. He felt relaxed and fit after two months of enjoying the undeniable pleasures of the Lebanon and the, for him, even greater pleasure of supervising the transfer of a handsome sum of money from a bank in Beirut to another in Switzerland.

Far behind him in the sandy soil of Egypt, long since buried by the baffled and furious Egyptian police, each with a neat bullet hole through the spine, were the bodies of two German missile engineers. Their departure from life had set back the development of Nasser's Al Goumhouria rocket by several years, and a Zionist millionaire in New York felt his money had been well spent. After passing easily through customs, the Englishman took a hired car to his flat in Mayfair.

It was ninety days before Rodin's search was over, and what he had to show for it was three slim dossiers, each encased in a manila file which he kept with him permanently in his brief-case. It was in the middle of June that he arrived back in Austria and checked into a small boarding house, the Pension Kleist in the Brucknerallee in Vienna.

From the city's main post office he sent off two crisp telegrams, one to Bolzano in northern Italy, the other to Rome. Each summoned his two principal lieutenants to an urgent meeting in his room in Vienna. Within twenty-four hours the men had arrived. René Montclair came by hired car from Bolzano, André Casson flew in from Rome. Each travelled under false name and papers, for both in Italy and Austria the resident officers of the SDECE had both men top-listed on their files and by this time were spending a lot of money buying agents and informers at border checkpoints and airports.

André Casson was the first to arrive at the Pension Kleist, seven minutes before the appointed time of eleven o'clock. He ordered his taxi to drop him at the corner of the Brucknerallee and spent several minutes adjusting his tie in the reflection of a florist's window before walking quickly into the hotel foyer. Rodin had as usual registered under a false name, one of twenty known only to his immediate colleagues. Each of the two he had summoned had received a cable the previous day signed by the name of Schulze, Rodin's code-name for that particular twenty-day period.

"*Herr Schulze, bitte?*" Casson enquired of the young man at the reception desk. The clerk consulted his registration book.

"Room sixty-four. Are you expected, sir?"

"Yes, indeed," replied Casson and headed straight up the stairs. He turned the landing to the first floor and walked along the passage looking for Room 64. He found it halfway along on the right. As he raised his hand to knock, it was gripped from behind. He turned and stared up into a heavy blue-jowled face. The eyes beneath a thick single band of black hair that passed for eyebrows gazed down at him without curiosity. The man had fallen in behind him as he passed an alcove twelve feet back and despite the thinness of the cord carpet Casson had not heard a sound.

"*Vous désirez?*" said the giant as if he could not have cared less. But the grip on Casson's right wrist did not slacken.

For a moment Casson's stomach turned over as he imagined the speedy removal of Argoud from the Eden-Wolff Hotel four months earlier. Then he recognised the man behind him as a Polish Foreign Legionnaire from Rodin's former company in Indochina and Vietnam. He recalled that Rodin occasionally used Viktor Kowalski for special assignments.

"I have an appointment with Colonel Rodin, Viktor," he replied softly. Kowalski's brows knotted even closer together at the mention of his own and his master's name. "I am André Casson," he added. Kowalski seemed unimpressed. Reaching round Casson he rapped with his left hand on the door of Room 64.

A voice from inside replied, "*Oui.*"

Kowalski approached his mouth to the wooden panel of the door.

"There's a visitor here," he growled, and the door opened a fraction. Rodin gazed out, then swung the door wide.

"My dear André. So sorry about this." He nodded to Kowalski. "All right, corporal, I am expecting this man."

Casson found his wrist freed at last, and stepped into the bedroom. Rodin had another word with Kowalski on the threshold, then closed the door again. The Pole went back to stand in the shadows of the alcove.

Rodin shook hands and led Casson over to the two armchairs in front of the gas fire. Although it was mid-June, the weather outside was a fine chill drizzle, and both men were used to the warmer sun of North Africa. The gas fire was full on. Casson stripped off his raincoat and settled before the fire.

"You don't usually take precautions like this, Marc," he observed.

"It's not so much for me," replied Rodin. "If anything should happen I can take care of myself. But I might need a few minutes to get rid of the papers." He gestured to the writing desk by the window where a thick manila folder lay beside his briefcase. "That's really why I brought Viktor. Whatever happened he would give me sixty seconds to destroy the papers."

"They must be important."

"Maybe, maybe." There was nevertheless a note of satisfaction in Rodin's voice. "But we'll wait for René. I told him to come at eleven-fifteen so the two of you would not arrive within a few seconds of each other and upset Viktor. He gets nervous when there is too much company around whom he does not know."

Rodin permitted himself one of his rare smiles at the thought of what would ensue if Viktor became nervous with the heavy Colt under his left armpit. There was a knock at the door. Rodin crossed the room and put his mouth to the wood. "*Oui?*"

This time it was René Montclair's voice, nervous and strained.

"Marc, for the love of God . . . "

Rodin swung open the door. Montclair stood there dwarfed by the giant Pole behind him. Viktor's left arm encircled him, pinning both the accountant's arms to his side.

"*Ça va*, Viktor," murmured Rodin to the bodyguard, and Montclair was released. He entered the room thankfully and grimaced at Casson, who was grinning from the chair by the fire. Again the door closed, and Rodin made his excuses to Montclair.

Montclair came forward and the two shook hands. He had taken off his overcoat to reveal a rumpled dark-grey suit of poor cut which he wore badly. Like most ex-army men accustomed to a uniform, both he and Rodin had never worn suits well.

As host, Rodin saw the other two seated, in the bedroom's two easy chairs. He kept for himself the upright chair behind the plain table that served him for a desk. From the bedside cabinet he took a bottle of French brandy and held it up enquiringly. Both his guests nodded. Rodin poured a generous measure into each of three glasses and handed two to Montclair and Casson. They drank first, the two travellers letting the hot liquor get to work on the chill inside them.

René Montclair, leaning back against the bedhead, was short and stocky, like Rodin a career officer from the Army. But unlike Rodin he had not had a combat command. Most of his life he had been in the administrative branches, and for the previous ten years in the pay-accounts branch of the Foreign Legion. By the spring of 1963 he was treasurer of the OAS.

André Casson was the only civilian. Small and precise, he dressed still like the bank manager he had been in Algeria. He was the coordinator of the OAS-CNR underground in Metropolitan France.

Both men were, like Rodin, hardliners even among the OAS, albeit for different reasons. Montclair had had a son, a nineteen-year-old boy who had been doing his National Service in Algeria three years previously while his father was running the pay-accounts department of the Foreign Legion base outside Marseilles. Major Montclair never saw the body of his son; it had been buried in the *bled* by the Legion patrol that took the village where the young private had been held a prisoner by the guerrillas. But he heard the details of what had been done to the young man afterwards. Nothing remains secret for long in the Legion. People talk.

André Casson was more involved. Born in Algeria, he had devoted his entire life to his work, his flat, and his family. The bank for which he worked had its headquarters in Paris, so even with the fall of Algeria he would not have been out of work. But when the settlers rose in revolt in 1960 he had been with them, one of the leaders in his native Constantine. Even after that he had kept his job, but realised as account after account closed and the businessmen sold out to move back to France that the heyday of French presence in Algeria was over. Shortly after the Army mutiny, incensed by the new Gaullist policy, and the misery of the small-time farmers and traders of the region, fleeing ruined to a country many of them had hardly seen across the water, he had helped an OAS unit to rob his own bank of 30,000,000 old francs. His complicity had been noticed and reported by a junior cashier, and his career with the bank was over. He sent his wife and two children to live with his in-laws at Perpignan, and joined the OAS. His value to them was his personal knowledge of several thousand OAS sympathisers now living inside France.

Marc Rodin took his seat behind his desk and surveyed the other two. They gazed back with curiosity but no questions.

Carefully and methodically Rodin began his briefing, concentrating on the growing list of failures and defeats the OAS had sustained at the hands of the French Secret Service over the past few months. His guests stared gloomily into their glasses.

"We simply must face facts. In the past four months we have taken three severe blows. I don't need to go into the details, you know them all as well as I do.

"Despite Antoine Argoud's loyalty to the cause, there can be no doubt that with modern methods of interrogation, probably including drugs, used on him, the whole organisation stands in jeopardy from the security standpoint. We have to start again, almost from scratch. But even starting from scratch would not be so bad if it were a year ago. Then we could call on thousands of volunteers full of enthusiasm and patriotism. Now that is not so easy. I do not blame our sympathisers too much. They have a right to expect results, not words."

"All right, all right. What are you getting at?" said Montclair. Both listeners knew Rodin was right. Montclair realised better than any that the funds gained in robbing banks across Algeria were expended on the costs of running the organisation, and that the donations from Right-wing industrialists were beginning to dry up. More recently his approaches had been met with ill-concealed disdain. Casson knew his lines of communications with the underground in France were becoming more tenuous by the week, his safe-houses were being raided, and since the capture of Argoud many had withdrawn their support. The execution of Bastien-Thiry could only accelerate this process. The résumé given by Rodin was the truth, but no more pleasant to hear for all that.

Rodin continued as though there had been no interruption.

"We have now reached a position where the prime aim of our cause to liberate France, the elimination of Grand Zohra, without which all further plans must inevitably abort, has become virtually impossible by the traditional means. I hesitate, gentlemen, to commit more patriotic young men to plans which stand little chance of remaining unrevealed to the French Gestapo for more than a few days. In short, there are too many squealers, too many backsliders, too many recusants.

"Taking advantage of this, the Secret Police have now so completely infiltrated the movement that the deliberations of even our highest councils are being leaked to them. They seem to know, within days of the decision being taken, what we intend, what are our plans, and who are our personnel. It is unpleasant to have to face this situation, but I am convinced that if we do not face it we shall continue to live in a fool's paradise.

"In my estimation there is only one method remaining to accomplish our first objective, the killing of Zohra, in a manner that will by-pass the whole network of spies and agents, leave the Secret Police stripped of its advantages, and face them with a situation not only of which they are unaware but which they could hardly frustrate even if they knew about it."

Montclair and Casson looked up quickly. There was dead silence in the bedroom, broken only by the occasional clatter of rain against the window-pane.

"If we accept that my appreciation of the situation is, unfortunately, accurate," continued Rodin, "then we must also accept that all of those we now know as being both prepared and capable of doing the job of eliminating Grand Zohra are equally known to the Secret Police. None of them can move inside France as other than a hunted animal, not only pursued by the conventional police forces but betrayed from behind by the Barbouzes and the stool-pigeons. I believe, gentlemen, that the only alternative left to us is to engage the services of an outsider."

Montclair and Casson gazed at him first in amazement, then dawning comprehension.

"What kind of outsider?" asked Casson at length.

"It would be necessary for this man, whoever he is, to be a foreigner," said Rodin. "He would not be a member of the OAS or the CNR. He would not be known to any policeman in France, nor would he exist on any file. The weakness of all dictatorships is that they are vast bureaucracies. What is not on file does not exist. The assassin would be an unknown and therefore non-existent quantity. He would travel under a foreign passport, do the job, and disappear back to his own country while the people of France rose to sweep away the remnants of de Gaulle's treasonable rabble. For the man to get out would not in any case be vastly important, since we would in any case liberate him after taking power. The important thing is that he be able to get in, unspotted and unsuspected. That is something which at the moment not one of us can do."

Both his listeners were silent, each gazing into his private thoughts as Rodin's plan took shape in their minds also.

Montclair let out a low whistle.

"A professional assassin, a mercenary."

"Precisely," replied Rodin. "It would be quite unreasonable to suppose that an outsider is going to do such a job for the love of us or for patriotism or for the hell of it. In order to get the level of skill and of nerve necessary for this kind of operation, we must engage a true professional. And such a man would only work for money, a lot of money," he added, glancing quickly at Montclair.

"But how do we know we can find such a man?" asked Casson.

Rodin held up his hand.

"First things first, gentlemen. Evidently there is a mass of detail to be worked out. What I wish to know first of all is if you agree in principle to the idea."

Montclair and Casson looked at each other. Both turned to Rodin and nodded slowly.

"*Bien.*" Rodin leaned back as far as the upright chair would allow him. "That then is the first point disposed of—agreement in principle. The second concerns security and is fundamental to the whole idea. In my view there are increasingly few who can be regarded as absolutely beyond suspicion as the possible source of a leak of information. That is not to say I regard any of our colleagues either in the OAS or the CNR as traitors to the cause, not as such. But it is an old axiom that the more people know a secret, the less sure that secret becomes. The whole essence of this idea is absolute secrecy. Consequently, the fewer who are aware of it the better.

"Even within the OAS there are infiltrators who have achieved responsible positions and who yet report our plans to the Secret Police. These men's time will come one day, but for the moment they are dangerous. Among the politicians of the CNR there are those either too squeamish or too gutless to realise the full extent of the project they are supposed to have become committed to. I would not wish to put the life of any man in danger by gratuitously and unnecessarily informing such men of his existence.

"I have summoned you, René, and you, André, here because I am utterly convinced of your loyalty to the cause and your ability to retain a secret. Moreover, for the plan I have in mind, the active cooperation of you, René, as treasurer and paymaster is necessary to meet the hire that any professional assassin will undoubtedly demand. Your cooperation, André, will be necessary to assure such a man of the assistance inside France of a small handful of men loyal beyond doubt in case he should have to call on them.

"But I see no reason why details of the idea should go further than we three. I am therefore proposing to you that we form a committee of ourselves to take the entire responsibility for this idea, its planning, execution, and subsidisation."

There was another silence. At length Montclair said, "You mean we cut out the entire council of the OAS, the whole of the CNR? They won't like that."

"Firstly, they won't know about it," replied Rodin calmly. "If we were to put the idea to them all, it would require a plenary meeting. This alone would attract attention and the Barbouzes would be active to find out what the plenary meeting was called for. There may even be a leak on one of the two councils. If we visited each member in turn, it would take weeks even to get preliminary approval in principle. Then they would all want to know the details as each planning stage was reached and passed. You know what these bloody politicians and committeemen are like. They want to know everything just for the sake of knowing it. They do nothing, but each one can put the whole operation in jeopardy with a word spoken in drunkenness or carelessness.

"Secondly, if the agreement of the entire council of the OAS and the CNR could be obtained to the idea, we would be no further forward, and nearly thirty people would know about it. If, on the other hand, we go ahead, take the responsibility, and it fails, we shall be no further back than we are now. There will be recriminations no doubt, but nothing more. If the plan succeeds we shall be in power and no one will start arguing at that time. The exact means of achieving the destruction of the dictator will have become an academic point. In brief, then, do you two agree to join me as sole planners, organisers, and operators of the idea I have expounded to you?"

Again Montclair and Casson looked at each other, turned to Rodin, and nodded. It was the first time they had met with him since the snatching of Argoud three months earlier. When Argoud had taken the chair, Rodin had kept quietly in the background. Now he had emerged as a leader in his own right. The chief of the underground and the purse were impressed.

Rodin look at them both, exhaled slowly, and smiled.

"Good," he said, "now let us get down to details. The idea of using a professional mercenary assassin first occurred to me on the day I heard over the radio that poor Bastien-Thiry had been murdered. Since that time I have been searching for the man we want. Obviously such men are hard to find; they do not advertise themselves. I have been searching since the middle of March, and the outcome can be summed up in these."

He held up the three manila folders that had been lying on his desk. Montclair and Casson exchanged glances again, eyebrows raised, and remained silent. Rodin resumed.

"I think it would be best if you studied the dossiers, then we can discuss our first choice. Personally, I have listed all three in terms of preference in case the first-listed either cannot or will not take the job. There is only one copy of each dossier, so you will have to exchange them."

He reached into the manila folder and took out three slimmer files. He handed one to Montclair and one to Casson. The third he kept in his own hand, but did not bother to read it. He knew the contents of all three files intimately.

There was little enough to read. Rodin's reference to a "brief" dossier was depressingly accurate. Casson finished his file first, looked up at Rodin and grimaced.

"That's all?"

"Such men do not make details about themselves easily available," replied Rodin. "Try this one." He handed down to Casson the file he held in his hand.

A few moments later Montclair also finished and passed his file back to Rodin, who gave him the dossier Casson had just finished. Both men were again lost in reading. This time it was Montclair who finished first. He looked up at Rodin and shrugged.

"Well . . . not much to go on, but surely we have fifty men like that. Gunslingers are two a penny—"

He was interrupted by Casson.

"Wait a minute, wait till you see this one," He flicked over the last page and ran his eyes down the three remaining paragraphs. When he had finished he closed the file and looked up at Rodin. The OAS chief gave away nothing of his own preferences. He took the file Casson had finished and passed it to Montclair. To Casson he passed the third of the folders. Both men finished their reading together four minutes later.

Rodin collected the folders and replaced them on the writing desk. He took the straight-backed chair, reversed it, and drew it towards the fire, sitting astride it with his arms on the back. From this perch he surveyed the other two.

"Well, I told you it was a small market. There may be more men about who do this kind of work, but without access to the files of a good Secret Service, they are damned hard to find. And probably the best ones aren't even on any files at all. You've seen all three. For the moment let us refer to them as the German, the South African, and the Englishman. André?"

Casson shrugged, "For me there is no debate. On his record, if it is true, the Englishman is out ahead by a mile."

"René?"

"I agree. The German is a bit old for this kind of thing now. Apart from a few jobs done for the surviving Nazis against the Israeli agents who pursue them, he doesn't seem to have done much in the political field. Besides, his motivations against Jews are probably personal, therefore not completely professional. The South African may be all right chopping up nigger politicians like Lumumba, but that's a far cry from putting a bullet through the President of France. Besides, the Englishman speaks fluent French."

Rodin nodded slowly. "I didn't think there would be much doubt. Even before I had finished compiling those dossiers, the choice seemed to stand out a mile."

"Are you sure about this Anglo-Saxon?" Casson asked. "Has he really done those jobs?"

"I was surprised myself," said Rodin. "So I spent extra time on this one. As regards absolute proof, there is none. If there were, it would be a bad sign. It would mean he would be listed everywhere as an undesirable immigrant. As it is, there is nothing against him but rumour. Formally, his sheet is white as snow. Even if the British have him listed, they can put no more than a question mark against him. That does not merit filing him with Interpol. The chances that the British would tip off the SDECE about such a man, even if a formal enquiry were made, are slim. You know how they hate each other. They even kept silent about George Bidault being in London last January. No, for this kind of job the Englishman has all the advantages but one—"

"What's that?" asked Montclair quickly.

"Simple. He will not be cheap. A man like him can ask a lot of money. How are the finances, René?"

Montclair shrugged. "Not too good. Expenditure has gone down a bit. Since the Argoud affair all the heroes of the CNR have gone to ground in cheap hotels. They seem to have lost their taste for the three-star palaces and the television interviews. On the other hand, income is down to a trickle. As you said there must be some action, or we shall be finished for lack of funds. One cannot run this kind of thing on love and kisses."

Rodin nodded grimly. "I thought so. We have to raise some money from somewhere. On the other hand, there would be no point in getting into that kind of action until we know how much we shall need—"

"Which presumes," cut in Casson smoothly, "that the next step is to contact the Englishman and ask him if he will do the job and for how much."

"Yes, well, are we all agreed on that?" Rodin glanced at both men in turn. Both nodded. Rodin glanced at his watch. "It is now just after one o'clock. I have an agent in London whom I must telephone now and ask him to contact this man to ask him to come. If he is prepared to fly to Vienna tonight on the evening plane, we could meet him here after dinner. Either way, we will know when my agent phones back. I have taken the liberty of booking you both into adjoining rooms down the corridor. I think it would be safer to be together protected by Viktor than separated but without defenses. Just in case, you understand."

"You were pretty certain, weren't you?" asked Casson, piqued at being predicted in this manner.

Rodin shrugged. "It has been a long process getting this information. The less time wasted from now on the better. If we are going to go ahead, let us now move fast."

He rose and the other two got up with him. Rodin called Viktor and told him to go down to the hall to collect the keys for rooms 65 and 66, and to bring them back up. While waiting he told Montclair and Casson, "I have to telephone from the main post office. I shall take Viktor with me. While I am gone, would you both stay together in one room with the door locked. My signal will be three knocks, a pause, then two more."

The sign was the familiar three-plus-two that made up the rhythm of the words *Algérie Française* that Parisian motorists had hooted on their car horns in previous years to express their disapproval of Gaullist policy.

"By the way," continued Rodin, "does either of you have a gun?"

Both men shook their heads. Rodin went to the escritoire and took out a chunky MAB 9 mm. that he kept for his private use. He checked the magazine, snapped it back, and charged the breech. He held it out towards Montclair. "You know this *flingue*?" Montclair nodded. "Well enough," he said, and took it.

Viktor returned and escorted the pair of them to Montclair's room. When he returned, Rodin was buttoning his overcoat.

"Come, corporal, we have work to do."

The BEA Vanguard from London to Vienna that evening glided into Schwechat Airport as the dusk deepened into night. Near the tail of the plane the blond Englishman lay back in his seat near the window and gazed out at the lead-in lights as they flashed past the sinking aircraft. It always gave him a feeling of pleasure to see them coming closer and closer until it appeared certain the plane must touch down in the grass of the undershoot area. At the very last minute the dimly lit blur of grass, the numbered panels by the vergeside, and the lights themselves vanished, to be replaced by black-slickened concrete, and wheels touched down at last. The precision of the business of landing appealed to him. He liked precision.

By his side the young Frenchman from the French Tourist Office in Piccadilly glanced at him nervously. Since the telephone call during the lunch-hour he had been in a state of nerves. Nearly a year ago on leave in Paris he had offered to put himself at the disposal of the OAS but since then had been told simply to stay at his desk in London. A letter or telephone call, addressed to him in his rightful name, but beginning "Dear Pierre . . . " should be obeyed immediately and precisely. Since then, nothing, until today, June 15.

The operator had told him there was a person-to-person call for him from Vienna, and had then added "In Austria" to distinguish it from the town Vienne in France. Wonderingly he had taken the call, to hear a voice call him "my dear Pierre." It had taken him several seconds to remember his own code-name.

Pleading a bout of migraine after his lunch-hour, he had gone to the flat

off South Audley Street and given the message to the Englishman who
answered the door. The latter had evinced no surprise that he should be
asked to fly to Vienna in three hours. He had quietly packed an overnight
case, and the pair of them had taken a taxi to Heathrow Airport. The
Englishman had calmly produced a roll of notes enough to buy two return
tickets for cash after the Frenchman had admitted he had not thought of
paying cash and had only brought his passport and a checkbook.

Since then they had hardly exchanged a word. The Englishman had not
asked where they were going in Vienna, or whom they were to meet, or why,
which was just as well because the Frenchman did not know. His instructions
had merely been to telephone back from London airport and confirm his
arrival on the BEA flight, at which he was told to report to General Information on arrival at Schwechat. All of which made him nervous, and the
controlled calm of the Englishman beside him, far from helping, made
things worse.

At the information desk in the main hall he gave his name to the pretty
Austrian girl, who searched in a rack of pigeon-holes behind her, then
passed him a small buff message form. It said simply "Ring 61.44.03, ask for
Schulze." He turned and headed towards the bank of public phones along
the back of the main hall. The Englishman tapped him on the shoulder and
pointed at the booth marked *Wechsel*.

"You'll need some coins," he said in fluent French. "Not even the Austrians are that generous."

The Frenchman blushed and strode towards the money-change counter,
while the Englishman sat himself comfortably in the corner of one of the
upholstered settees against the wall and lit another king-size English filter.
In a minute his guide was back with several Austrian bank-notes and a
handful of coins. The Frenchman went to the telephones, found an empty
booth, and dialed. At the other end Herr Schulze gave him clipped and
precise instructions. It took only a few seconds, then the phone went dead.

The young Frenchman came back to the settee, and the blond man looked
up at him.

"*On y va?*" he asked.

"*On y va.*" As he turned to leave, the Frenchman screwed up the message
form with the telephone number and dropped it on the floor. The Englishman picked it up, opened it out, and held it to the flame of his lighter. It
blazed for an instant and disappeared in black crumbs beneath the elegant
suede boot. They walked in silence out of the building and hailed a taxi.

The centre of the city was ablaze with lights and choked with cars, so it was
not until forty minutes later that the taxi arrived at the Pension Kleist.

"This is where we part. I was told to bring you here, but to take the taxi
somewhere else. You go straight up to Room Sixty-four. You are expected."

The Englishman nodded and got out of the car. The driver turned
enquiringly to the Frenchman. "Drive on," he said, and the taxi disappeared
down the street. The Englishman glanced up at the old Gothic writing on the
street name-plate, then the square roman capitals above the door of the
Pension Kleist. Finally he threw away his cigarette, half smoked, and entered.

The clerk on duty had his back turned, but the door creaked. Without
giving any sign of approaching the desk, the Englishman walked towards the

stairs. The clerk was about to ask what he wanted when the visitor glanced in his direction, nodded casually as to any other menial, and said firmly, *"Guten Abend."*

"Guten Abend, mein Herr," replied the clerk automatically, and by the time he had finished the blond man was gone, taking the stairs two at a time without seeming to hurry. At the top he paused and glanced down the only corridor available. At the far end was Room 68. He counted back down the corridor to what must be 64, although the figures were out of sight.

Between himself and the door of 64 were twenty feet of corridor, the walls being studded on the right by two other doors before 64, and on the left a small alcove partially curtained with red velours hanging from a cheap brass rod.

He studied the alcove carefully. From beneath the curtain, which cleared the floor by four inches, the toe of a single black shoe emerged slightly. He turned and walked back to the foyer. This time the clerk was ready. At least he managed to get his mouth open.

"Get me Room Sixty-four please," said the Englishman. The clerk looked him in the face for a second, then obeyed. After a few seconds he turned back from the small switchboard, picked up the desk phone, and passed it over.

"If that gorilla is not out of the alcove in fifteen seconds I am going back home," said the blond man, and put the phone down. Then he walked back up the stairs.

At the top he watched the door of 64 open and Colonel Rodin appeared. He stared down the corridor for a moment at the Englishman, then called softly, "Viktor." From the alcove the giant Pole emerged and stood looking from one to the other. Rodin said, "It's all right. He is expected." Kowalski glowered. The Englishman started to walk.

Rodin ushered him inside the bedroom. It had been arranged like an office for a recruiting board. The escritoire served for the chairman's desk and was littered with papers. Behind it was the single upright chair in the room. But two other uprights brought in from adjacent rooms flanked the central chair, and these were occupied by Montclair and Casson, who eyed the visitor curiously. There was no chair in front of the desk. The Englishman cast an eye around, selected one of the two easy chairs and spun it around to face the desk. By the time Rodin had given fresh instructions to Viktor and closed the door, the Englishman was comfortably seated and staring back at Casson and Montclair. Rodin took his seat behind the desk.

For a few seconds he stared at the man from London. What he saw did not displease him, and he was an expert in men. The visitor stood above six feet tall, apparently in his early thirties, and with a lean athletic build. He looked fit, the suntanned face had regular but not remarkable features, and the hands lay quietly along the arms of the chair. To Rodin's eye he looked like a man who retained control of himself. But the eyes bothered him. He had seen the soft, moist eyes of weaklings, the dull, shuttered eyes of psychopaths, and the watchful eyes of soldiers. The eyes of the Englishman were open and stared back with frank candor. Except for the irises, which were of flecked grey so that they seemed smoky like the hoar mist on a winter's morning. It took Rodin a few seconds to realise that they had no expression at all. Whatever thoughts did go on behind the smokescreen, nothing came through, and Rodin felt a worm of unease. Like all men created by systems and procedures, he did not like the unpredictable and therefore the uncontrollable.

"We know who you are," he began abruptly. "I had better introduce myself. I am Colonel Marc Rodin—"

"I know," said the Englishman, "you are chief of operations of the OAS. You are Major René Montclair, treasurer, and you are Monsieur André Casson, head of the underground in the Métropole." He stared at each of the men in turn as he spoke, and reached for a cigarette.

"You seem to know a lot already," interjected Casson as the three watched the visitor light up. The Englishman leaned back and blew out the first stream of smoke.

"Gentlemen, let us be frank. I know what you are, and you know what I am. We both have unusual occupations. You are hunted while I am free to move where I will without suveillance. I operate for money, you for idealism. But when it comes to practical details, we are all professionals at our jobs. Therefore we do not need to fence. You have been making enquiries about me. It is impossible to make such enquiries without the news of them soon getting back to the man being asked about. Naturally I wished to know who was so interested in me. It could have been someone seeking revenge or wishing to employ me. It was important to me to know. As soon as I discovered the identity of the organisation interested in me, two days among the French newspaper files in the British Museum were enough to tell me about you and your organisation. So the visit of your little errand boy this afternoon was hardly a surprise. *Bon.* I know who you are, and whom you represent. What I would like to know is what you want."

There was silence for several minutes. Casson and Montclair glanced for guidance at Rodin. The paratroop colonel and the assassin stared at each other. Rodin knew enough about violent men to understand the man facing him was what he wanted. From then on Montclair and Casson were part of the furniture.

"Since you have read the files available, I will not bore you with the motivations behind our organisation, which you have accurately summed up as idealism. We believe France is now ruled by a dictator who has polluted our country and prostituted its honour. We believe his regime can only fall and France be restored to Frenchmen if he first dies. Out of six attempts by our supporters to eliminate him, three were exposed in the early planning stages, one was betrayed the day before the attempt, and two took place but misfired.

"We are considering, but at this stage only considering, engaging the services of a professional to do the job. However we do not wish to waste our money. The first thing we would like to know is if it is possible."

Rodin had played his cards shrewdly. The last sentence, to which he already knew the answer, brought a flicker of expression to the grey eyes.

"There is no man in the world who is proof against an assassin's bullet," said the Englishman. "De Gaulle's exposure rate is very high. Of course, it's possible to kill him. The point is that the chances of escape would not be too high. A fanatic prepared to die himself in the attempt is always the most certain method of eliminating a dictator who exposes himself to the public. I notice," he added with a touch of malice, "that despite your idealism you have not yet been able to produce such a man. Both Pont-de-Seine and Petit-Clamart failed because no one was prepared to risk his own life to make absolutely certain."

"There are patriotic Frenchmen prepared even now—" began Casson hotly, but Rodin silenced him with a gesture. The Englishman did not even glance at him.

"And as regards a professional?" prompted Rodin.

"A professional does not act out of fervour and is therefore more calm and less likely to make elementary errors. Not being idealistic, he is not likely to have second thoughts at the last minute about who else might get hurt in the explosion, or whatever method, and being a professional he has calculated the risks to the last contingency. So his chances of success on schedule are surer than anyone else, but he will not even enter into operation until he has devised a plan that will enable him not only to complete the mission, but to escape unharmed."

"Do you estimate that such a plan could be worked out to permit a professional to kill Grand Zohra and escape?"

The Englishman smoked quietly for a few minutes and stared out of the window. "In principle, yes," he replied at length. "In principle, it is always possible with enough time and planning. But in this case it would be extremely difficult. More so than with most other targets."

"Why more than others?" asked Montclair.

"Because de Gaulle is forewarned—not about the specific attempt but about the general intention. All big men have bodyguards and security men, but over a period of years without any serious attempt on the life of the big man, the checks become formal, the routines mechanical, and the degree of watchfulness is lowered. The single bullet that finishes the target is wholly unexpected and therefore provokes panic. Under cover of this the assassin escapes. In this case there will be no lowering of the level of watchfulness, no mechanical routines, and if the bullet were to get to the target, there would be many who would not panic but would go for the assassin. It could be done, but it would be one of the hardest jobs in the world at this moment. You see, gentlemen, your own efforts have not only failed but have queered the pitch for everyone else."

"In the event that we decide to employ a professional assassin to do this job—" began Rodin.

"You have to employ a professional," cut in the Englishman quietly.

"And why, pray? There are many men still who would be prepared to do the job out of purely patriotic motives."

"Yes, there are still Watin and Curutchet," replied the blond man. "And doubtless there are more Degueldres and Bastien-Thirys around somewhere. But you three men did not call me here for a chat in general terms about the theory of political assassination, nor because you have a sudden shortage of trigger-fingers. You called me here because you have belatedly come to the conclusion that your organisation is so infiltrated by the French Secret Service agents that little you decide remains secret for long, and also because the faces of every one of you is imprinted on the memory of every cop in France. Therefore you need an outsider. And you are right. If the job is to be done, an outsider has to do it. The only questions that remain are who, and for how much. Now, gentlemen, I think you have had long enough to examine the merchandise, don't you?"

Rodin looked sideways at Montclair and raised an eyebrow. Montclair nodded. Casson followed suit. The Englishman gazed out of the window without a shred of interest.

"Will you assassinate de Gaulle?" asked Rodin at last. The voice was quiet, but the question filled the room. The Englishman's glance came back to him, and the eyes were blank again.

"Yes, but it will cost a lot of money."

"How much?" asked Montclair.

"You must understand this is a once-in-a-lifetime job. The man who does it will never work again. The chances of remaining not only uncaught but undiscovered are very small. One must take enough for this one job both to be able to live well for the rest of his days and to acquire protection against the revenge of the Gaullists—"

"When we have France," said Casson, "there will be no shortage—"

"Cash," said the Englishman. "Half in advance and half on completion."

"How much?" asked Rodin.

"Half a million."

Rodin glanced at Montclair, who grimaced. "That's a lot of money, half a million new francs—"

"Dollars," said the Englishman.

"Half a million dollars?" shouted Montclair, rising from his seat. "You are crazy?"

"No," said the Englishman calmly, "but I am the best, and therefore the most expensive."

"We could certainly get cheaper estimates," sneered Casson.

"Yes," said the blond man without emotion, "you would get men cheaper, and you would find they took your fifty-per-cent deposit and vanished or made excuses later as to why it could not be done. When you employ the best you pay. Half a million dollars is the price. Considering you expect to get France itself, you value your country very cheap."

Rodin, who had remained quiet through this exchange, took the point. "*Touché.* The point is, monsieur, we do not have half a million dollars cash."

"I am aware of that," replied the Englishman. "If you want the job done you will have to make that sum from somewhere. I do not need the job, you understand. After my last assignment I have enough to live well for some years. But the idea of having enough to retire is appealing. Therefore I am prepared to take some exceptionally high risks for that price. Your friends here want a prize even greater—France herself. Yet the idea of risks appals them. I am sorry. If you cannot acquire the sum involved, then you must go back to arranging your own plots and seeing them destroyed by the authorities one by one."

He half-rose from his chair, stubbing out his cigarette in the process. Rodin rose with him.

"Be seated, monsieur. We shall get the money." Both sat down.

"Good," said the Englishman, "but there are also conditions."

"Yes?"

"The reason you need an outsider in the first place is because of constant security leaks to the French authorities. How many people in your organisation know of this idea of hiring any outsider at all, let alone me?"

"Just the three of us in this room. I worked out the idea the day after Bastien-Thiry was executed. Since then I have undertaken all the enquiries personally. There is no one else in the know."

"Then it must remain that way," said the Englishman. "All records of all meetings, files, and dossiers must be destroyed. There must be nothing available outside your three heads. In view of what happened in February to Argoud, I shall feel myself free to call off if any of you three are captured. Therefore you should remain somewhere safe and under heavy guard until the job is done. Agreed?"

"*D'accord.* What else?"

"The planning will be mine, as with the operation. I shall divulge the details to no one, not even to you. In short, I shall disappear. You will hear nothing from me again. You have my telephone number in London and my address, but I shall be leaving both as soon as I am ready to move.

"In any event you will only contact me at that place in an emergency. For the rest there will be no contact at all. I shall leave you the name of my bank in Switzerland. When they tell me the first two hundred and fifty thousand dollars has been deposited, or when I am fully ready, whichever is the later, I shall move. I will not be hurried beyond my own judgement, nor will I be subject to interference. Agreed?"

"*D'accord.* But our undercover men in France are in a position to offer you considerable assistance in the way of information. Some of them are highly placed."

The Englishman considered this for a moment. "All right, when you are ready send me by mail a single telephone number, preferably in Paris so that I can ring the number direct from anywhere in France. I will not give anyone my own whereabouts, but simply ring that number for latest information about the security situation surrounding the President. But the man on the end of that telephone should not know what I am doing in France. Simply tell him that I am on a mission for you and need his assistance. The less he knows, the better. Let him be simply a clearing house for information. Even his sources should be confined uniquely to those in a position to give valuable inside information, not rubbish that I can read in the newspapers. Agreed?"

"Very well. You wish to operate entirely alone, without friends or refuge. Be it on your own head. How about false papers? We have two excellent forgers at our disposal."

"I will acquire my own, thank you."

Casson broke in. "I have a complete organisation inside France similar to the Resistance during the German occupation. I can put this entire structure at your disposal for assistance purposes."

"No, thank you. I prefer to bank on my own complete anonymity. It is the best weapon I have."

"But supposing something should go wrong, you might have to go on the run—"

"Nothing will go wrong, unless it comes from your side. I will operate without contacting or being known to your organisation, M. Casson, for exactly the same reason I am here in the first place: because the organisation is crawling with agents and stool-pigeons."

Casson looked fit to explode. Montclair stared glumly at the window trying to envisage raising half a million dollars in a hurry. Rodin stared thoughtfully back at the Englishman across the table.

"Calm, André. Monsieur wishes to work alone. So be it. That is his way. We do not pay half a million dollars for a man who needs the same amount of molly-coddling our own shooters need."

"What I would like to know," muttered Montclair, "is how we can raise so much money so quickly."

"Use your organisation to rob a few banks," suggested the Englishman lightly.

"In any case, that is our problem," said Rodin. "Before our visitor returns to London, are there any further points?"

"What is to prevent you from taking the first quarter of a million and disappearing?" asked Casson.

"I told you, messieurs, I wanted to retire. I do not wish to have half an army of ex-paras gunning for me. I would have to spend more protecting myself than the money I have made. It would soon be gone."

"And what," persisted Casson, "is to prevent us waiting until the job is done and then refusing to pay you the balance of the half million?"

"The same reason," replied the Englishman smoothly. "In that event I should go to work on my own account. And the target would be you three gentlemen. However, I don't think that will occur, do you?"

Rodin interrupted. "Well, if that is all, I don't think we need detain our guest any longer. Oh . . . there is one last point. Your name. If you wish to remain anonymous you should have a code name. Do you have any ideas?"

The Englishman thought for a moment. "Since we have been speaking of hunting, what about the Jackal? Will that do?"

Rodin nodded. "Yes, that will do fine. In fact I think I like it."

He escorted the Englishman to the door and opened it. Viktor left his alcove and approached. For the first time Rodin smiled and held out his hand to the assassin. "We will be in touch in the agreed manner as soon as we can. In the meantime could you begin planning in general terms so as not to waste too much time? Good. Then *bonsoir, Monsieur Chacal.*"

The Pole watched the visitor depart as quietly as he had come. The Englishman spent the night at the airport hotel and caught the first plane back to London in the morning.

Inside the Pension Kleist Rodin faced a barrage of belated questions and complaints from Casson and Montclair, who had both been shaken by the three hours between nine and midnight.

"Half a million dollars," Montclair kept repeating. "How on earth do we raise half a million dollars?"

"We may have to take up Chacal's suggestion and rob a few banks," answered Rodin.

"I don't like that man," said Casson. "He works alone, without allies. Such men are dangerous. One cannot control them."

Rodin closed the discussion. "Look, you two, we devised a plan, we agreed on a proposal, and we sought a man prepared to and capable of killing the President of France for money. I know a bit about men like that. If anyone can do it, he can. Now we have made our play. Let us get on with our side and let him get on with his."

THREE

During the second half of June and the whole of July in 1963 France was rocked by an outbreak of violent crime against banks, jewellers' shops, and post offices that was unprecedented at the time and has never been repeated since. The details of this crime wave are now a matter of record.

From one end of the country to the other, banks were held up with pistols, sawn-off shotguns, and submachine guns on an almost daily basis. Smash and grab raids at jewellers' shops became so common throughout that period that local police forces had hardly finished taking depositions from the shaken and often bleeding jewellers and their assistants than they were called away to another similar case within their own district.

Two bank clerks were shot in different towns as they tried to resist the robbers, and before the end of July the crisis had grown so great that the men of the Corps Républicain de Sécurité, the anti-riot squads known to every Frenchman simply as the CRS, were called in and for the first time armed with submachine guns. It became habitual for those entering a bank to have to pass one or two of the blue-uniformed CRS guards in the foyer, each toting a loaded submachine carbine.

In response to pressure from the bankers and jewellers, who complained bitterly to Government about this crime wave, police checks on banks at night were increased in frequency, but to no avail, since the robbers were not professional cracksmen able to open a bank vault skilfully during the hours of darkness, but simply thugs in masks, armed and ready to shoot if provoked in the slightest way.

The danger hours were in daylight, when any bank or jeweller shop throughout the country could be surprised in the middle of business by the appearance of two or three armed and masked men, and the peremptory cry "*Haut les mains.*"

Three robbers were wounded towards the end of July in different hold-ups, and taken prisoner. Each turned out to be either a petty crook known to be using the existence of the OAS as an excuse for general anarchy or a deserter from one of the former colonial regiments who soon admitted he was an OAS man. But despite the most diligent interrogations at police headquarters, none of the three could be persuaded to say why this rash of robberies had suddenly struck the country, other than that they had been contacted by their *patron* (gang boss) and given a target in the form of a bank or jewel-shop. Eventually the police came to believe that the prisoners did not know what the purpose of the robberies was; they had each been promised a cut of the total, and being small fry had done what they were told.

It did not take the French authorities long to realise that the OAS was behind the outbreak and that for some reason the OAS needed money in a hurry. But it was not until the first fortnight of August, and then in a quite different manner, that the authorities discovered why.

Within the last two weeks of June the wave of crime against banks and other places where money or gems could be quickly and unceremoniously acquired had become sufficiently serious to be handed over to the Commissaire Maurice Bouvier, the much-revered chief of the Brigade Criminelle of the Police Judiciaire. In his surprisingly small, work-strewn office at the headquarters of the PJ at 36, Quai des Orfèvres along the banks of the Seine a chart was prepared showing the cash or, in the case of jewellery, approximate re-sale value of the stolen money and gems. By the latter half of July the total was well over two million new francs, or 400,000 dollars. Even with a reasonable sum deducted for the expenses of mounting the various robberies, and more for paying the hoodlums and deserters who carried them out, that still left, in the Commissaire's estimation, a sizeable sum of money that could not be accounted for.

In the last week of June a report landed on the desk of General Guibaud, the head of the SDECE, from the chief of his permanent office in Rome. It was to the effect that the three top men of the OAS, Marc Rodin, René Montclair, and André Casson, had taken up residence together on the top floor of a hotel just off the Via Condotti. The report added that despite the obvious cost of residing in such an exclusive quarter, the three had taken the entire top floor for themselves, and the floor below for their bodyguards. They were being guarded night and day by no less than eight extremely tough ex-members of the Foreign Legion and were not venturing out at all. At first it was thought they had met for a conference, but as the days passed SDECE came to the view that they were simply taking exceptionally heavy precautions to ensure that they were not the victims of another kidnapping as had been inflicted on Antoine Argoud. General Guibaud permitted himself a grim smile at the sight of the top men of the terrorist organisation themselves now cowering in a hotel in Rome, and filed the report in a routine manner. Despite the bitter row still festering between the French Foreign Ministry at the Quai d'Orsay and the German Foreign Ministry in Bonn over the infringement of German territorial integrity at the Eden-Wolff Hotel the previous February, Guibaud had every reason to be pleased with his Action Service men who had carried out the coup. The sight of the OAS chiefs running scared was reward enough in itself. The General smothered a small shadow of misgiving as he surveyed the file of Marc Rodin and nevertheless asked himself why a man like Rodin should scare that easily. As a man with considerable experience in his own job and an awareness of the realities of politics and diplomacy, he knew he would be most unlikely ever to obtain permission to organise another snatch-job. It was only much later that the real significance of the precautions the three OAS men were taking for their own safety became clear to him.

In London the Jackal spent the last fortnight of June and the first two weeks of July in carefully controlled and planned activity. From the day of his return he set himself among other things to acquire and read almost every word written about or by Charles de Gaulle. By the simple expedient of going to the local lending library and looking up the most recent books on de Gaulle he compiled a comprehensive bibliography about his subject.

After that he wrote off to various well-known bookshops, using a false name and a forwarding address in Praed Street, Paddington, and acquired the necessary books by post. These he scoured until the small hours each morning in his flat, building up in his mind a most detailed picture of the incumbent of the Elysée Palace from his boyhood until the time of reading. Much of the information he gleaned was of no practical use, but here and there a quirk or character trait would emerge that he noted in a small exercise book. Most instructive concerning the character of the French President was the third volume of the General's memoirs, *The Edge of the Sword (Le Fil de l'Epée)*, in which Charles de Gaulle was at his most illuminating about his own personal attitude to life, his country, and his destiny as he saw it.

The Jackal was neither a slow nor a stupid man. He read voraciously and planned meticulously, and possessed the faculty to store in his mind an enormous amount of factual information on the off-chance that he might later have a use for it.

But although his reading of the works of Charles de Gaulle, and the books about him by the men who knew him best, provided a full picture of the proud and disdainful President of France, it still did not solve the main question that had been baffling him since he accepted the assignment in Rodin's bedroom in Vienna on June 15. By the end of the first week in July he still had not worked out the answer to this question—when, where, and how should the "hit" take place? As a last resort he went down to the reading room of the British Museum and, after signing his application for permission to do research with his habitual false name, started to work his way through the back copies of France's leading daily newspaper, *Le Figaro*.

Just when the answer came to him is not exactly known, but it is fair to presume it was within three days from July 7. Within those three days, starting with the germ of an idea triggered by a columnist writing in 1962, cross-checking back through the files covering every year of de Gaulle's presidency since 1945, the assassin managed to answer his own question. He decided within that time precisely on what day, come illness or bad weather, totally regardless of any considerations of personal danger, Charles de Gaulle would stand up publicly and show himself. From that point on, the Jackal's preparations moved out of the research stage and into that of practical planning.

It took long hours of thought, lying on his back in his flat staring up at the cream painted ceiling and chain-smoking his habitual king-size filter cigarettes, before the last detail had clicked into place.

At least a dozen ideas were considered and rejected before he finally hit on the plan he decided to adopt, the "how" that had to be added to the "when" and "where" that he had already decided.

The Jackal was perfectly aware that in 1963 General de Gaulle was not only the President of France; he was also the most closely and skilfully guarded figure in the western world. To assassinate him, as was later proved, was considerably more difficult than to kill President John F. Kennedy of the United States. Although the English killer did not know it, French security experts who had through American courtesy been given an opportunity to study the precautions taken to guard the life of President Kennedy had returned somewhat disdainful of those precautions as exercised by the American Secret Service. The French experts' rejection of the American methods was later justified when in November 1963 John Kennedy was killed in Dallas by a half-crazed amateur while Charles de Gaulle lived on, to retire in peace and eventually to die in his own house.

What the Jackal did know was that the security men he was up against were at least among the best in the world, that the whole security apparatus around de Gaulle was in a state of permanent forewarning of the likelihood of some attempt being made on their charge's life, and that the organisation for which he worked was riddled with security leaks. On the credit side he could reasonably bank on his own anonymity and on the choleric refusal of his victim to cooperate with his own security forces.

On the chosen day, the pride, the stubbornness, and the absolute contempt for personal danger of the French President would force him to come out into the open for a few seconds no matter what the risks involved.

The SAS airliner from Kastrup, Copenhagen, made one last swing into line in front of the terminal building at London, trundled forward a few feet, and halted. The engines whined on for a few seconds, then they also died away. Within a few minutes the steps were wheeled up, and the passengers started to file out and down, nodding a last goodbye to the smiling stewardess at the top. On the observation terrace the blond man slipped his dark glasses upwards onto his forehead and applied his eyes to a pair of binoculars. The file of passengers coming down the steps was the sixth that morning to be subjected to this kind of scrutiny, but as the terrace was crowded in the warm sunshine with people waiting for arriving passengers and trying to spot them as soon as they emerged from their aircraft, the watcher's behaviour aroused no interest.

As the eighth passenger emerged into the light and straightened up, the man on the terrace tensed slightly and followed the new arrival down the steps. The passenger from Denmark was a priest or pastor, in a clerical grey suit with a dog-collar. He appeared to be in his late forties from the iron-grey hair cut at medium length that was brushed back from the forehead, but the face was more youthful. He was a tall man with wide shoulders, and he looked physically fit. He had approximately the same build as the man who watched him from the terrace above.

As the passengers filed into the arrivals lounge for passport and customs clearance, the Jackal dropped the binoculars into the leather brief-case by his side, closed it, and walked quietly back through the glass doors and down into the main hall. Fifteen minutes later the Danish pastor emerged from the customs hall holding a grip and a suitcase. There appeared to be nobody to meet him, and his first call was made to the Barclays Bank counter to change money.

From what he told the Danish police when they interrogated him six weeks later, he did not notice the blond young Englishman standing beside him at the counter, apparently waiting his turn in the queue but quietly examining the features of the Dane from behind dark glasses. At least he had no memory of such a man. But when he came out of the main hall to board the BEA coach to the Cromwell Road terminal, the Englishman was a few paces behind him holding his brief-case, and they must have travelled into London on the same coach.

At the terminal the Dane had to wait a few minutes while his suitcase was unloaded from the luggage trailer behind the coach, then wend his way past the checking-in counters to the exit signs marked with an arrow and the international word "Taxis." While he did so, the Jackal strode round the back of the coach and across the floor of the coach-park to where he had left his car in the staff car-park. He hefted the brief-case into the passenger seat of the open sports model, climbed in, and started up, bringing the car to a halt close to the left-hand wall of the terminal from where he could glance to the right down the long line of waiting taxis under the pillared arcade. The Dane climbed into the third taxi, which cruised off into the Cromwell road, heading towards Knightsbridge. The sports car followed.

The taxi dropped the oblivious priest at a small but comfortable hotel in Half Moon Street, while the sports car shot past the entrance and within a few minutes had found a spare parking metre on the far side of Curzon Street. The Jackal locked the brief-case in the trunk, bought a midday edition of the *Evening Standard* at the newsagent in Shepherd Market, and was back in the foyer of the hotel within five minutes. He had to wait another twenty-five before the Dane came downstairs and handed back his room key to the receptionist. After she hung it up, the key swayed for a few seconds from the hook, and the man in one of the foyer arm chairs apparently waiting for a friend, who lowered his newspaper as the Dane passed into the restaurant, noted that the number of the key was 47. A few minutes later, as the receptionist bobbed back into the rear office to check a theatre booking for one of the guests, the man in the dark glasses slipped quietly and unnoticed up the stairs.

A two-inch-wide strip of flexible mica was not enough to open the door of Room 47, which was rather stiff, but the mica strip stiffened by a whippy little artist's palette knife did the trick, and the spring lock slipped back with a click. As he had only gone downstairs for lunch, the pastor had left his passport on the bedside table. The Jackal was back in the corridor within thirty seconds, leaving the folder of traveller's cheques untouched in the hopes that without any evidence of a theft the authorities would try to persuade the Dane that he had simply lost his passport somewhere else. And so it proved. Long before the Dane had finished his coffee, the Englishman had departed unseen, and it was not until much later in the afternoon, after a thorough and mystified search of his room, that the pastor mentioned the disappearance of his passport to the manager. The manager also searched the room, and after pointing out that everything else including the wallet of traveller's cheques was intact, brought all his advocacy to bear to persuade his bewildered guest that there was no need to bring the police to his hotel since he had evidently lost his passport somewhere in transit. The Dane, being a kindly man and not too sure of his ground in a foreign country, agreed despite himself that this was what must have happened. So he reported the loss to the Danish Consulate-General the next day, was issued with travel documents with which to return to Copenhagen at the end of his fortnight's stay in London, and thought no more about it. The clerk at the Consulate-General who issued the travel documents filed the loss of a passport in the name of Pastor Per Jensen of Sankt Kjeldskirke in Copenhagen, and thought no more about it either. The date was July 14.

Two days later a similar loss was experienced by an American student from Syracuse, New York. He had arrived at the Oceanic Building of London Airport from New York, and he produced his passport in order to change the first of his traveller's cheques at the American Express counter.

After changing the cheque he placed the money in an inside pocket of his jacket, and the passport inside a zipped pouch which he stuffed back into a small leather hand-grip. A few minutes later, trying to attract the attention of a porter, he put the grip down for a moment and three seconds later it was gone. At first he remonstrated with the porter, who led him to the Pan American enquiries desk, which directed him to the attention of the nearest terminal security police officer. The latter took him to an office where he explained his dilemma.

After a search had ruled out the possibility that the grip might have been taken by someone else accidentally in mistake for his own, a report was filed listing the matter as a deliberate theft.

Apologies were made and regrets were expressed to the tall and athletic young American about the activities of pickpockets and bag-snatchers in public places, and he was told of the many precautions the airport authorities took to try to curb their thefts from incoming foreigners. He had the grace to admit that a friend of his was once robbed in a similar manner in Grand Central Station.

The report was eventually circulated in a routine manner to all the divisions of the London Metropolitan Police, together with a description of the missing grip, its contents, and the papers and passport in the pouch. This was duly filed, but as weeks passed and no trace was found of either the grip or its contents, no more was thought of the incident.

Meanwhile Marty Schulberg went to his consulate in Grosvenor Square, reported the theft of his passport, and was issued with travel documents enabling him to fly back to the United States after his month's vacation touring the highlands of Scotland with his exchange-student girl friend. At the consulate the loss was registered, reported to State Department in Washington, and duly forgotten by both establishments.

It will never be known just how many incoming passengers at London Airport's two overseas arrivals passenger buildings were scanned through binoculars from the observation terraces as they emerged from their aircraft and headed down the steps. Despite the difference in their ages, the two who lost their passports had some things in common. Both were around six feet tall, had broad shoulders and slim figures, blue eyes, and a fairly close facial resemblance to the unobtrusive Englishman who had followed and robbed them. Otherwise, Pastor Jensen was aged forty-eight, with grey hair and gold-rimmed glasses for reading; Marty Schulberg was twenty-five, with chestnut brown hair and heavy-rimmed executive glasses which he wore all the time.

These were the faces the Jackal studied at length on the writing bureau in his flat off South Audley Street. It took him one day and a series of visits to theatrical costumiers, opticians, a man's clothing store in the West End specializing in garments of American type and mainly made in New York to acquire a set of blue-tinted clear-vision contact lenses; two pairs of spectacles, one with gold rims and the other with heavy black frames, and both with clear lenses; a complete outfit consisting of a pair of black leather loafers, T-shirt and underpants, off-white slacks and a sky-blue nylon windbreaker with a zip-up front and collars and cuffs in red and white wool, all made in New York; and a clergyman's white shirt, starched dog-collar, and black bib. From each of the last three the maker's label was carefully removed.

His last visit of the day was to a men's wig and toupee emporium in Chelsea run by two homosexuals. Here he acquired a preparation for tinting the hair a medium grey and another for tinting it chestnut brown, along with precise and coyly delivered instructions on how to apply the tint to achieve the best and most natural-looking effect in the shortest time. He also bought several small hairbrushes for applying the liquids. Otherwise, apart from the complete set of American clothes, he did not make more than one purchase at any one shop.

The following day, July 18, there was a small paragraph at the bottom of an inside page of *Le Figaro*. It announced that in Paris the Deputy Chief of the Brigade Criminelle of the Police Judiciaire, Commissaire Hippolyte Dupuy, had suffered a severe stroke in his office at the Quai des Orfèvres and had died on his way to hospital. A successor had been named. He was Commissaire Claude Lebel, Chief of the Homicide Division, and in view of the pressure of work on all the departments of the Brigade during the summer months, he would take up his new duties forthwith. The Jackal, who read every French newspaper available in London each day, read the paragraph after his eye had been caught by the word "Criminelle" in the headline, but thought nothing of it.

Before starting his daily watch at London Airport, he had decided to operate throughout the whole of the forthcoming assassination under a false identity. It is one of the easiest things in the world to acquire a false British passport. The Jackal followed the procedure used by most mercenaries, smugglers, and others who wish to adopt an alias for passing national boundaries. First he took a car trip through the Home Counties of the Thames Valley looking for small villages. Almost every English village has an attractive little church, and a graveyard nestling in its shadow. In the third cemetery he visited the Jackal found a gravestone to suit his purpose, that of Alexander Duggan who died at the age of two and a half years in 1931. Had he lived, the Duggan child would have been a few months older than the Jackal in July 1963. The elderly vicar was courteous and helpful when the visitor presented himself at the vicarage to announce that he was an amateur genealogist engaged in attempting to trace the family tree of the Duggans. He had been informed that there had been a Duggan family that had settled in the village in years past. He wondered, somewhat diffidently, if the parish records might be able to help him in his search.

The vicar was kindness itself, and on their way over to the church a compliment on the beauty of the little Norman building and a contribution to the donations box for the restoration fund improved the atmosphere yet more. The records showed that both the Duggan parents had died over the past seven years, and, alas, their only son Alexander had been buried in this very churchyard over thirty years before. The Jackal idly turned over the pages in the parish register of births, marriages, and deaths for 1929, and for the month of April the name of Duggan, written in a crabbed and clerkly hand, caught his eye.

Alexander James Quentin Duggan, born April 3, 1929, in the Parish of Saint Mark's, Sambourne Fishley.

He noted the details, thanked the vicar profusely, and left. Back in London he presented himself at the Central Registry of Births, Marriages and Deaths, where a helpful young assistant accepted without query his visiting card showing him to be a partner in a firm of solicitors of Market Drayton, Shropshire, and his explanation that he was engaged in trying to trace the whereabouts of the grandchildren of one of the firm's clients who had recently died and left her estate to her grandchildren. One of these grandchildren was Alexander James Quentin Duggan, born at Sambourne Fishley, in the parish of Saint Mark's on April 3, 1929.

Most civil servants in Britain do their best to be helpful when confronted by a polite enquiry, and in this case the assistant was no exception. A search of the records showed that the child in question had been registered precisely according to the enquirer's information, but had died on November 8, 1931, as the result of a road accident. For a few shillings the Jackal received a copy of both the birth and death certificates. Before returning home he stopped at a branch office of the Ministry of Labour and was issued with a passport application form, at a toyshop where for fifteen shillings he bought a child's printing set, and at a post office for a one-pound postal order.

Back in his flat he filled in the application form in Duggan's name, giving exactly the right age, date of birth, etc., but his own personal description. He wrote in his own height, colour of hair and eyes, and for profession put down simply "businessman." The full names of Duggan's parents, taken from the child's birth certificate, were also filled in. For the reference he filled in the name of Reverend James Elderly, vicar of Saint Mark's, Sambourne Fishley, to whom he had spoken that morning, and whose full name and title of LLD had obligingly been printed on a board outside the church gate. The vicar's signature was forged in a thin hand in thin ink with a thin nib, and from the printing set he made up a stamp reading:

SAINT MARK'S PARISH CHURCH
SAMBOURNE FISHLEY

which was placed firmly next to the vicar's name. The copy of the birth certificate, the application form, and the postal order were sent off to the Passport Office in Petty France. The death certificate he destroyed. The brand new passport arrived at the accommodation address by post four days later as he was reading that morning's edition of *Le Figaro*. He picked it up after lunch. Late that afternoon he locked the flat and drove to London Airport, where he boarded the flight to Copenhagen, paying in cash again to avoid using a cheque book. In the false bottom of his suitcase, in a compartment barely thicker than an ordinary magazine and almost undetectable except to the most thorough search, was two thousand pounds, which he had drawn earlier that day from his private deed box in the vaults of a firm of solicitors in Holborn.

The visit to Copenhagen was brisk and businesslike. Before leaving Kastrup Airport, he booked himself on the next afternoon's Sabena flight to Brussels. In the Danish capital it was far too late to go shopping, so he booked in at the Hotal D'Angleterre on Kongens Nytorv, ate like a king at the Seven Nations, had a mild flirtation with two Danish blondes while strolling through the Tivoli Gardens, and was in bed by one in the morning.

The next day be bought a lightweight clerical grey suit at one of the best known men's outfitters in central Copenhagen, a pair of sober black walking shoes, a pair of socks, a set of underwear and three white shirts with collars attached. In each case he bought only what had the Danish maker's name on a small cloth tab inside. In the case of the three white shirts, which he did not need, the point of the purchase was simply to acquire the tabs for transference to the clerical shirt, dog-collar, and bib that he had bought in London while claiming to be a theological student on the verge of ordination.

His last purchase was a book in Danish on the notable churches and cathedrals of France. He lunched off a large cold collation at a lakeside restaurant in the Tivoli Gardens, and caught the 3:15 plane to Brussels.

FOUR

Why a man of the undoubted talents of Paul Goossens should have gone wrong in middle age was something of a mystery even to his few friends, his rather more numerous customers, and the Belgian police. During his thirty years as a trusted employee of the Fabrique Nationale at Liège he had established a reputation for unfailing precision in a branch of engineering where precision is absolutely indispensable. Of his honesty also there had been no doubt. He had also during those thirty years become the company's foremost expert in the very wide range of weapons that that excellent company produces, from the tiniest lady's automatic to the heaviest of machine guns.

His war record had been remarkable. Although he had continued after the Occupation to work in the arms factory run by the Germans for the Nazi war effort, later examination of his career had established beyond doubt his undercover work for the Resistance, his participation in private in a chain of safe-houses for the escape of downed Allied airmen, and at work his leadership of a sabotage ring that ensured a fair proportion of the weapons turned out by Liège either never fired accurately or blew up at the fiftieth shell, killing the German crews. All this, so modest and unassuming was the man, had been wormed out of him later by his defence lawyers and triumphantly produced in court on his behalf. It had gone a long way to mitigating his sentence, and the jury had also been impressed by his own halting admission that he had never revealed his activities during the war because post-liberation honours and medals would have embarrassed him.

By the time in the early fifties that a large sum of money had been embezzled from a foreign customer in the course of a lucrative arms deal, and suspicion had fallen upon him, he was a departmental chief in the firm, and his own superiors had been loudest in informing the police that their suspicions with regard to the trusted M. Goossens were ridiculous.

Even at the trial his managing director spoke for him. But the presiding judge took the view that to betray a position of trust in such a manner was all the more reprehensible, and he had been given ten years in prison. On appeal it was reduced to five. With good conduct he had been released after three and a half.

His wife had divorced him and taken the children with her. The old life of the suburban dweller in a neat flower-rimmed detached house in one of the prettier outskirts of Liège (there are not many) was over, a thing of the past. So was his career with F.N. He had taken a small flat in Brussels, later a house further out of town, as his fortunes prospered from his private business as the source of illegal arms to half the underworld in Western Europe.

By the early sixties he had the nickname l'Armurier, the Armourer. Any Belgian citizen can buy a lethal weapon—revolver, automatic, or rifle—at any sports or gun shop in the country on production of a national identity card proving Belgian nationality. Goossens never used his own, for at each sale of the weapon and subsequent ammunition the sale is noted in the gunsmith's log-book, along with the name and I.D. card of the purchaser. Goossens used other people's cards, either stolen or forged.

He had established close links with one of the city's top pickpockets, a man who, when not languishing in prison as a guest of the state, could remove any wallet from any pocket at ease. These he bought outright for cash from the thief. He also had at his disposal the services of a master forger who, having come badly unstuck in the late forties over the production of a large amount of French francs in which he had inadvertently left the "u" out of "Banque de France" (he was young then), had finally gone into the false passport business with much greater success. Lastly, when Goossens needed to acquire a firearm for a customer, the client who presented himself at the gunsmith's with a neatly forged I.D. card was never himself but always an out-of-work and out-of-jail petty crook or an actor resting between conquests of the stage.

Of his own "staff" only the pickpocket and the forger knew his real identity. So also did some of his customers, notably the top men in the Belgian underworld, who not only left him alone to his devices but also offered him a certain amount of protection in refusing to reveal when captured where they had got their guns, simply because he was so useful to them.

This did not stop the Belgian police being aware of a portion of his activities, but it did prevent them ever being able to catch him with the goods in his possession or being able to get testimony that would stand up in court and convict him. They were aware of and highly suspicious of the small but superbly equipped forge and workshop in his converted garage, but repeated visits had revealed nothing more than the paraphernalia for the manufacture of wrought-metal medallions and souvenirs of the statues of Brussels. On their last visit he had solemnly presented the Chief Inspector with a figurine of the Manneken-Pis as a token of his esteem for the forces of law and order.

He felt no qualms as he waited on the morning of July 21, 1963, for the arrival of an Englishman who had been guaranteed to him over the phone by one of his best customers, a former mercenary in the services of Katanga from 1960 to 1962 who had since masterminded a protection business among the whorehouses of the Belgian capital.

The visitor turned up at noon, as promised, and M. Goossens showed him into his little office off the hall.

"Would you please remove your glasses?" he asked when his visitor was seated and, as the tall Englishman hesitated, added, "You see I think it is better that we trust each other insofar as we can while our business association lasts. A drink, perhaps?"

The man whose passport would have announced him as Alexander Duggan removed his dark glasses and stared quizzically at the little gunsmith as two beers were poured. M. Goossens seated himself behind his desk, sipped his beer, and asked quietly. "In what way may I be of service to you, monsieur?"

"I believe Louis rang you earlier about my coming?"

"Certainly," M. Goossens nodded. "Otherwise you would not be here."

"Did he tell you what is my business?"

"No. Simply that he knew you in Katanga, that he could vouch for your discretion, that you needed a firearm, and that you would be prepared to pay in cash, sterling."

The Englishman nodded slowly. "Well, since I know what your business is, there is little reason why you should not know mine. Besides which, the weapon I need will have to be a specialist gun with certain unusual attachments. I—er—specialise in the removal of men who have powerful and wealthy enemies. Evidently, such men are usually powerful and wealthy themselves. It is not always easy. They can afford specialist protection. Such a job needs planning and the right weapon. I have such a job on hand at the moment. I shall need a rifle."

M. Goossens again sipped his beer, nodded benignly at his guest.

"Excellent, excellent. A specialist like myself. I think I sense a challenge. What kind of rifle had you in mind?"

"It is not so much the type of rifle that is important. It is more of a question of the limitations that are imposed by the job, and of finding a rifle which will perform satisfactorily under those limitations."

M. Goossens eyes gleamed with pleasure.

"A one-off," he purred delightedly. "A gun that will be tailor-made for one man and one job under one set of circumstances, never to be repeated. You have come to the right man. I sense a challenge, my dear monsieur. I am glad that you came."

The Englishman permitted himself a smile at the Belgian's professorial enthusiasm. "So am I, monsieur."

"Now tell me, what are these limitations?"

"The main limitation is of size, not in length but in the physical bulk of the working parts. The chamber and breech must be no bulkier than that—" He held up his right hand, the tip of his middle finger touching the end of the thumb in the form of a letter o less than two and a half inches in diameter.

"That seems to mean it cannot be a repeater, since a gas chamber would be larger than that, nor can it have a bulky spring mechanism for the same reason," said the Englishman. "It seems to me it must be a bolt-action rifle."

M. Goossens was nodding at the ceiling, his mind taking in the details of what his visitor was saying, making a mental picture of a rifle of great slimness in the working parts.

"Go on, go on," he murmured.

"On the other hand it cannot have a bolt with a handle that sticks out sideways like the Mauser seven-ninety-two or the Lee Enfield three-o-three. The bolt must slide straight back towards the shoulder, gripped between forefinger and thumb for the fitting of the bullet into the breech. Also there must be no trigger guard, and the trigger itself must be detachable so that it can be fitted just before firing."

"Why?" asked the Belgian.

"Because the whole mechanism must pass into a tubular compartment for storage and carrying, and the compartment must not attract attention. For that it must not be larger in diameter than I have just shown, for reasons I shall explain. It is possible to have a detachable trigger?"

"Certainly, almost all is possible. Of course, one could design a single-shot rifle that breaks open at the back for loading like a shotgun. That would dispense with the bolt completely, but it would involve a hinge, which might be no saving. Also it would be necessary to design and manufacture such a rifle from scratch, milling a piece of metal to make the entire breech and chamber. Not an easy task in a small workshop, but possible."

"How long would that take?" asked the Englishman.

The Belgian shrugged and spread his hands. "Several months, I am afraid."

"I do not have that amount of time."

"In that case it will be necessary to take an existing rifle purchasable in a shop and make modifications. Please go on."

"Right. The gun must also be light in weight. It need not be of heavy calibre, the bullet will do the work. It must have a short barrel, probably not longer than twelve inches—"

"Over what range will you have to fire?"

"This is still not certain, but probably not more than a hundred and thirty metres."

"Will you go for a head or chest shot?"

"It will probably have to be head. I may get a shot at the chest, but the head is surer."

"Surer to kill, yes, if you get a good hit," said the Belgian. "But the chest is surer to get a good hit. At least, when one is using a light weapon with a short barrel over a hundred and thirty metres with possible obstructions. I assume," he added, "from your uncertainty on this point of the head or the chest that there may be someone passing in the way?"

"Yes, there may be."

"Will you get the chance of a second shot, bearing in mind that it will take several seconds to extract the spent cartridge and insert a fresh one, close the breech, and take aim again?"

"Almost certainly not. I just might get a second if I use a silencer and the first shot is a complete miss which is not noticed by anyone nearby. But even if I get a first hit through the temple, I need the silencer to effect my own escape. There must be several minutes of clear time before anyone nearby realises even roughly where the bullet has come from."

The Belgian continued nodding, by now staring down at his deskpad.

"In that case, you better have explosive bullets. I shall prepare a handful along with the gun. You know what I mean?"

The Englishman nodded. "Glycerine or mercury?"

"Oh mercury, I think. So much neater and cleaner. Are there any more points covering this gun?"

"I'm afraid so. In the interests of slimness, all the woodwork of the handgrip beneath the barrel should be removed. The entire stock must be removed. For firing it must have a frame-stock like a Sten gun, each of the three sections of which, upper and lower members and shoulder-rest, must unscrew into three separate rods. Lastly, there must be a completely effective silencer and a telescopic sight. Both of these too must be removable for storage and carrying."

The Belgian thought for a long time, sipping his beer until it was drained. The Englishman became impatient.

"Well, can you do it?"

M. Goossens seemed to emerge from his reverie. He smiled apologetically.

"Do forgive me. It is a very complex order. But yes, I can do it. I have never failed yet to produce the required article. Really, what you have described is a hunting expedition in which the equipment must be carried past certain checks in such a manner as to arouse no suspicion. A hunting expedition supposes a hunting rifle, and that is what you shall have. Not as small as a twenty-two calibre, for that is for rabbits and hares. Nor as big as a Remington three hundred, which would never conform to the limitations of size you have demanded.

"I think I have such a gun in mind, and easily available here in Brussels at some sports shops. An expensive gun, a high-precision instrument. Very accurate, beautifully tooled, and yet light and slim. Used a lot for chamois and other small deer, but with explosive bullets just the thing for the bigger game. Tell me, will the—er—gentleman be moving slowly, fast, or not at all?"

"Stationary."

"No problems then. The fittings of a frame-stock of three separate steel rods and the screw-in trigger are mere mechanics. The tapping of the end of the barrel for the silencer and the shortening of the barrel by eight inches I can do myself. One loses accuracy as one loses eight inches of barrel. Pity, pity. Are you a marksman?"

The Englishman nodded.

"Then there will be no problem with a stationary human being at a hundred and thirty metres with a telescopic sight. As for the silencer, I shall make it myself. They are not complex, but difficult to obtain as a manufactured article, particularly long ones for rifles which are not usual in hunting. Now, monsieur, you mentioned earlier some tubular compartments for carrying the gun in its broken-down form. What had you in mind?"

The Englishman rose and crossed to the desk, towering over the little Belgian. He slipped his hand inside his jacket, and for a second there was a flicker of fear in the smaller man's eyes. For the first time he noticed that whatever expression was on the killer's face, it never touched his eyes, which appeared clouded by streaks of grey like wisps of smoke covering all expression that might have touched them. But the Englishman produced only a silver propelling pencil.

He spun round M. Goossens's note pad and sketched rapidly for a few seconds.

"Do you recognize that?" he asked, turning the pad back to the gunsmith.

"Of course," replied the Belgian after giving the precisely drawn sketch a glance.

"Right. Well now, the whole thing is composed of a series of hollow aluminum tubes which screw together. This one"—tapping with the point of the pencil at a place on the diagram—"contains one of the struts of the rifle stock. This here contains the other strut. Both are concealed within the tubes that make up this section. The shoulder-rest of the rifle is this—here—in its entirety. This is therefore the only part which doubles up with two purposes without changing in any way.

"Here"—tapping at another point on the diagram as the Belgian's eyes widened in suprise—"at the thickest point is the largest diameter tube which contains the breech of the rifle with the bolt inside it. This tapers to the barrel without a break. Obviously, with a telescopic sight being used there need be no foresight, so the whole thing slides out of this compartment when the assemblage is unscrewed. The last two sections—here and here—contain the telescopic sight itself and the silencer. Finally the bullets. They should be inserted into this little stump at the bottom. When the whole thing is assembled it must pass for precisely what it looks. When unscrewed into its seven component parts, the bullets, silencer, telescope, rifle, and the three struts that make up the triangular frame stock can be extracted for reassembly as a fully operational rifle. OK?"

For a few seconds longer the little Belgian looked at the diagram. Slowly he rose, then held out his hand.

"Monsieur," he said with reverence, "it is a conception of genius. Undetectable. And yet so simple. It shall be done."

The Englishman was neither gratified nor displeased.

"Good," he said. "Now, the question of time. I shall need the gun in about fourteen days, can that be arranged?"

"Yes. I can acquire the gun within three. A week's work should see the modifications achieved. Buying the telescopic sight presents no problems. You may leave the choice of the sight to me, I know what will be required for the range of a hundred and thirty metres you have in mind. You had better calibrate and zero the settings yourself at your own discretion. Making the silencer, modifying the bullets and constructing the outer casing . . .yes, it can be done within the time allowed if I burn the candle at both ends. However, it would be better if you could arrive back here with a day or two in hand, just in case there are some last minute details to talk over. Could you be back in twelve days?"

"Yes, any time between seven and fourteen days from now. But fourteen days is the deadline. I must be back in London by August the fourth."

"You shall have the completed weapon with all last details arranged to your satisfaction on the morning of the fourth if you can be here yourself on August first for final discussions and collection, monsieur."

"Good. Now for the question of your expenses and fee," said the Englishman. "Have you an idea how much they will be?"

The Belgian thought for a while. "For this kind of job, with all the work it entails, for the facilities available here and my own specialised knowledge, I must ask a fee of one thousand English pounds. I concede that is above the rate for a simple rifle. But this is not a simple rifle. It must be a work of art. I believe I am the only man in Europe capable of doing it justice, of making a perfect job of it. Like yourself, monsieur, I am in my field the best. For the best, one pays. Then on top there would be the purchasing price of the weapon, bullets, telescope, and raw materials . . . say, the equivalent of another two hundred pounds."

"Done," replied the Englishman without argument. He reached into his breast pocket again and extracted a bundle of five-pound notes. They were bound in lots of twenty. He counted out five wads of twenty notes each.

"I would suggest," he went on evenly, "that in order to establish by bona fides I make you a down payment as an advance and to cover costs of five hundred pounds. I shall bring the remaining seven hundred on my return in eleven days. Is that agreeable to you?"

"Monsieur," said the Belgian skilfully pocketing the notes, "it is a pleasure to do business both with a professional and a gentleman."

"There is a little more," went on his visitor as though he had not been interrupted. "You will make no further attempt to contact Louis or ask him or anyone else who I am or what is my true identity. Nor will you seek to enquire for whom I am working, nor against whom. In the event that you should try to do so it is certain I shall hear about the enquiries. In that event you will die. On my return here, if there has been any attempt to contact the police or to lay a trap, you will die. Is that understood?"

M. Goossens was pained. Standing in the hallway he looked up at the Englishman, and an eel of fear wriggled in his bowels. He had faced many of the tough men of the Belgian underworld when they came to him for special or unusual weapons, or simply a run-of-the-mill snub-nosed Colt Special. These were hard men. But there was something distant and implacable about the visitor from across the Channel who intended to kill an important and well-protected figure. Not another gangland boss, but a big man, perhaps a politician. He thought of protesting or expostulating, then decided better.

"Monsieur," he said quietly. "I do not want to know about you, anything about you. The gun you will receive will bear no serial number. You see, it is of more importance to me that nothing you do should ever be traced back to me than that I should seek to know more than I do about you. *Bonjour, monsieur.*"

The Jackal walked away into the bright sunshine and two streets away found a cruising taxi to take him back to the city centre and the Hotel Amigo.

He suspected that in order to acquire guns Goossens would have to have a forger in his employ somewhere, but preferred to find and use one of his own. Again Louis, his contact from the old days in Katanga, helped him. Not that it was difficult. Brussels has a long tradition as the centre of the forged identity-card industry, and many foreigners appreciate the lack of formalities with which assistance in this field can be obtained. In the early sixties Brussels had also become the operations base of the mercenary soldier, for this was before the emergence in the Congo of the French and South African/British units who later came to dominate the business. With Katanga gone, over three hundred out of work "military advisers" from the old Tshombe regime were hanging around the bars of the red-light quarter, many of them in possession of several sets of identity papers.

The Jackal found his man in a bar off the rue Neuve after Louis had arranged the appointment. He introduced himself, and the pair retired to a corner alcove. The Jackal produced his driving licence, which was in his own name, issued by the London County Council two years earlier and with some months still to run.

"This," he told the Belgian, "belonged to a man now dead. As I am banned from driving in Britain, I need a new front page in my own name."

He put the passport in the name of Duggan in front of the forger. The man opposite glanced at the passport first, took in the newness of the passport, the fact that it had been issued three days earlier, and glanced shrewdly at the Englishman.

"*En effet*," he murmured, then flicked open the little red driving licence. After a few minutes he looked up.

"Not difficult, monsieur. The English authorities are gentlemen. They do not seem to expect that official documents might perhaps be forged, therefore they take few precautions. This paper"—he flicked the small sheet gummed onto the first page of the licence, which carried the licence number and the full name of the holder—"could be printed by a child's printing set. The watermark is easy. This presents no problems. Was that all you wanted?"

"No, there are two other papers."

"Ah. If you will permit my saying so, it appeared strange that you should wish to contact me for such a simple task. There must be men in your own London who could do this within a few hours. What are the other papers?"

The Jackal described them to the last detail. The Belgian's eyes narrowed in thought. He took out a packet of Bastos, offered one to the Englishman, who declined, and lit one for himself.

"That is not so easy. The French identity card, not too bad. There are plenty about from which one can work. You understand, one must work from an original to achieve the best results. But the other one. I do not think I have seen such a one. It is a most unusual requirement."

He paused while the Jackal ordered a passing waiter to refill their glasses. When the waiter had gone he resumed.

"And then the photograph. That will not be easy. You say there must be a difference in age, in hair colouring and length. Most of those wishing for a false document intend that their own photograph shall be on the document, but with the personal details falsified. But to devise a new photograph which does not even look like you as you now appear, this complicates things."

He drank off half of his beer, still eyeing the Englishman opposite him. "To achieve this it will be necessary to seek out a man of the approximate age of the bearer of the cards, who also bears a reasonable similarity to yourself, at least as far as the head and face is concerned, and cut his hair to the length you require. Then a photograph of this man would be put onto the cards. From that point on it would be up to you to model your subsequent disguise on this man's true appearance, rather than the reverse. You follow me?"

"Yes," replied the Jackal.

"This will take some time. How long can you stay in Brussels?"

"Not long," said the Jackal. "I must leave fairly soon, but I could be back on August first. From then I could stay another three days. I have to be returning to London on the fourth."

The Belgian thought again for a while, staring at the photograph in the passport in front of him. At last he folded it closed and passed it back to the Englishman after copying onto a piece of paper from his pocket the name Alexander James Quentin Duggan. He pocketed both the piece of paper and the driving licence.

"All right. It can be done. But I have to have a good portrait photograph of yourself as you are now, full-face and profile. This will take time. And money. There are extra expenses involved . . . it may be necessary to undertake an operation into France itself with a colleague adept in picking pockets in order to acquire the second of these cards you mention. Obviously, I shall ask around Brussels first, but it may be necessary to go to these lengths—"

"How much?" cut in the Englishman.

"Twenty thousand Belgian francs."

The Jackal thought for a moment. "About a hundred and fifty pounds sterling. All right. I will pay you a hundred deposit and the remainder on delivery."

The Belgian rose. "Then we had better get the portrait photos taken. I have my own studio."

They took a taxi to a small basement flat more than a mile away. It turned out to be a seedy and run-down photographer's studio, with a sign outside indicating that the premises were run as a commercial establishment specialising in passport photographs developed while the customer waited. Inevitably stuck in the window were what a passer-by must have presumed to be the high-points of the studio owner's past work—two portraits of simpering girls, hideously retouched, a marriage photo of a couple sufficiently unprepossessing to deal a nasty blow to the whole concept of wedlock, and two babies. The Belgian led the way down the steps to the front door, unlocked it, and ushered his guest inside.

The session took two hours, in which the Belgian showed a skill with the camera that could never have been possessed by the author of the portraits in the window. A large trunk in one corner, which he unlocked with his own key, revealed a selection of expensive cameras and flash equipment, besides a host of facial props including hair tints and dyes, toupees, wigs, spectacles in great variety, and a case of theatrical cosmetics.

It was halfway through the session that the Belgian hit on the idea that obviated the necessity to seek out a substitute to pose for the real photograph. Studying the effect of thirty minutes working on the Jackal's face with makeup, he suddenly dived into the chest and produced a wig.

"What do you think of this?" he asked.

The wig was of hair coloured iron-grey and cut *en brosse.*

"Do you think that your own hair, cut to this length and dyed this colour, could look like this?"

The Jackal took the wig and examined it. "We can give it a try and see how it looks in the photo," he suggested.

And it worked. The Belgian came out of the developing room half an hour after taking six photos of his customer with a sheaf of prints in his hand. Together they pored over the desk. Staring up was the face of an old and tired man. The skin was an ashen gray and there were dark rings of fatigue or pain beneath the eyes. The man wore neither beard nor moustache, but the grey hair on his head gave the impression he must have been in his fifties at least, and not a robust fifty at that.

"I think it will work," said the Belgian at last.

"The problem is," replied the Jackal, "that you had to work on me with cosmetics for half an hour to achieve this effect. Then there was the wig. I cannot emulate all that by myself. And here we were under lights, whereas I shall be in the open air when I have to produce these papers I have asked for."

"But this is precisely not the point," reposted the forger. "It is not so much that you will not be a dead image of the photograph, but that the photograph will not be a dead likeness of you. This is the way the mind of a man examining papers works. He looks at the face first, the real face, then asks for the papers. Then he sees the photograph. He already has the image of the man standing beside him in his mind's eye. This affects his judgment. He looks for points of similarity, not the opposite.

"Secondly, this photograph is twenty-five by twenty centimetres. The photograph in the identity card will be three by four. Thirdly, a too precise likeness should be avoided. If the card was issued several years previously, it is impossible that a man should not change a bit. In the photograph here we have you in open-necked striped shirt with collar attached. Try to avoid that shirt for example, or even avoid an open-necked shirt at all. Wear a tie, or a scarf or a turtle-necked sweater.

"Lastly, nothing that I have done to you cannot be easily simulated. The main point of course is the hair. It must be cut *en brosse* before this photo is presented, and dyed grey, perhaps even greyer than in the photograph, but not less so. To increase the impression of age and decrepitude, grow two or three days of beard stubble. Then shave with a cut-throat razor, but badly, nicking yourself in a couple of places. Elderly men tend to do this. As for the complexion, this is vital. To extract pity it must be grey and tired, rather waxy and ill-looking. Can you get hold of some pieces of cordite?"

The Jackal had listened to the exegesis of the forger with admiration, though nothing showed on his face. For the second time in a day he had been able to contact a professional who knew his job thoroughly. He reminded himself to thank Louis appropriately—after the job was done.

"It might be arranged," he said cautiously.

"Two or three small pieces of cordite, chewed and swallowed, produce within half an hour a feeling of nausea, uncomfortable but not disastrous. They also turn the skin a grey pallor and cause facial sweating. We used to use this trick in the Army to simulate illness and avoid fatigue and route marches."

"Thank you for the information. Now for the rest, do you think you can produce the documents in time?"

"From the technical standpoint, there is no doubt of it. The only remaining problem is to acquire an original of the second French document. For that I may have to work fast. But if you come back in the first few days of August, I think I can have them all ready for you. You—er—had mentioned a down payment to cover expenses—"

The Jackal reached into his inside pocket and produced a single bundle of twenty five-pound notes, which he handed the Belgian.

"How do I contact you?" he asked.

"I would suggest by the same way as tonight."

"Too risky. My contact man may be missing, or out of town. Then I would have no way of finding you."

The Belgian thought for a minute. "Then I shall wait from six until seven each evening in the bar where we met tonight on each of the first three days of August. If you do not come, I shall presume the deal is off."

The Englishman had removed the wig and was wiping his face with a towel soaked in removing spirit. In silence he slipped on his tie and jacket. When he was finished he turned to the Belgian.

"There are certain things I wish to make clear," he said quietly. The friendliness was gone from the voice and the eyes stared at the Belgian as bleak as a Channel fog. "When you have finished the job, you will be present at the bar as promised. You will return to me the new licence and the page removed from the one you now have. Also the negatives and all prints of the photographs we have just taken. You will also forget the names of Duggan and of the original owner of that driving licence. The name of the two French documents you are going to produce you may select yourself, providing it is a simple and common French name. After handing them over to me you will forget that name also. You will never speak to anyone of this commission again. In the event that you infringe any of these conditions, you will die. Is that understood?"

The Belgian stared back for a few moments. Over the past three hours he had come to think of the Englishman as a run-of-the-mill customer who simply wished to drive a car in Britain and masquerade for his own purposes as a middle-aged man in France. A smuggler, perhaps, running dope or diamonds from a lonely Breton fishing port into England.

"It is understood, monsieur."

A few seconds later the Englishman was gone into the night. He walked for five blocks before taking a taxi back to the Amigo, and it was midnight when he arrived. He ordered cold chicken and a bottle of Moselle in his room, bathed thoroughly to get rid of the last traces of make-up, then slept.

The following morning he checked out of the hotel and took the Brabant Express to Paris. It was July 22.

The head of the Action Service of the SDECE sat at his desk on that same morning and surveyed the two pieces of paper before him. Each was a copy of a routine report filed by agents of other departments. At the head of each piece of blue flimsy was a list of department chiefs entitled to receive a copy of the report. Opposite his own designation was a small tick. Both reports had come in that morning and in the normal course of events Colonel Rolland would have glanced at each, taken in what they had to say, stored the knowledge somewhere in his fearsome memory, and had them filed under separate headings. But there was one word that cropped up in each of the reports, a word that intrigued him.

The first report that arrived was an interdepartmental memo from R 3 (Western Europe) containing a synopsis of a despatch from their permanent office in Rome. The despatch was a straight-forward report to the effect that Rodin, Montclair, and Casson were still holed up in their top floor suite and were still being guarded by their eight guards. They had not moved out of the building since they established themselves there on June 18. Extra staff had been drafted from R 3 Paris to Rome to assist in keeping the hotel under round-the-clock surveillance. Instructions from Paris remained unchanged: not to make any approach but simply to keep watch. The men in the hotel had established a routine for keeping in touch with the outside world three weeks previously ("see R 3 Rome report of June 30"), and this was being maintained. The courier remained Viktor Kowalski. End of message.

Colonel Rolland flicked open the buff file lying on the right of his desk next to the sawn-off 105 mm. Shell case that served for a copious ashtray and was even by then half-full of Disque Bleue stubs. His eyes strayed down the R 3 Rome report of June 30 till he found the paragraph he wanted.

Each day, it said, one of the guards left the hotel and walked to the head post office of Rome. Here a Poste Restante pigeonhole was reserved in the name of one Poitiers. The OAS had not taken a postal box with a key, apparently for fear it might be burgled. All mail for the top men of the OAS was addressed to Poitiers and was kept by the clerk on duty at the Poste Restante counter. An attempt to bribe the original such clerk to hand over the mail to an agent of R 3 had failed. The man had reported the approach to his superiors and had been replaced by a senior clerk. It was possible that mail for Poitiers was now being screened by the Italian security police, but R 3 had instructions not to approach the Italians to ask for cooperation. The attempt to bribe the clerk had failed, but it was felt the initiative had to be taken. Each day the mail arriving overnight in the post office was handed to the guard, who had been identified as one Viktor Kowalski, formerly a corporal of the Foreign Legion and a member of Rodin's original company in Indochina. Kowalski seemingly had adequate false papers identifying him to the post office as Poitiers, or a letter of authority acceptable to the post office. If Kowalski had letters to post, he waited by the post box inside the main hall of the building until five minutes before collection time, dropped the mail through the slit, then waited until the entire box-full was collected and taken back into the heart of the building for sorting. Attempts to interfere with the process of either collection or despatch of the OAS chiefs' mail would entail a degree of violence, which had already been precluded by Paris. Occasionally Kowalski made a telephone call, long-distance, from the Overseas Calls telephone counter, but here again attempts either to learn the number asked for or to overhear the conversation had failed. End of message.

Colonel Rolland let the cover of the file fall back on the contents and took up the second of the two reports that had come in that morning. It was a police report from the Police Judiciaire of Metz stating that a man had been questioned during a routine raid on a bar and had half-killed two policemen in the ensuing fight. Later at the police station he had been identified by his fingerprints as a deserter from the Foreign Legion by the name of Sandor Kovacs, Hungarian by birth and a refugee from Budapest in 1956. Kovacs, a note from PJ Paris added at the end of the information from Metz, was a notorious OAS thug long wanted for his connection with a series of terror murders of loyalist notables in the Bone and Constantine areas of Algeria during 1961. At that time he had operated as partner of another OAS gunman still at large, former Foreign Legion corporal Viktor Kowalski. End of message.

Rolland pondered the connection between the two men yet again, as he had done for the previous hour. At last he pressed a buzzer in front of him and replied to the "*Oui, mon colonel*" that came out of it.

"Get me the personal file on Viktor Kowalski. At once."

He had the file up from archives in ten minutes, and spent another hour reading it. Several times he ran his eye over one particular paragraph. As other Parisians in less demanding professions hurried past on the pavement below to their lunches, Colonel Rolland convened a small meeting consisting of himself, his personal secretary, a specialist in handwriting from the documentation department three floors down, and two strong-arm men from his private Praetorian Guard.

"Gentlemen," he told them, "with the unwilling but inevitable assistance of one not here present, we are going to compose, write, and despatch a letter."

FIVE

The Jackal's train arrived at the Gare du Nord just before lunch, and he took a taxi to a small but extremely comfortable hotel in the rue de Suresne, leading off from the Place de la Madeleine. While it was not a hotel in the same class as the D'Angleterre of Copenhagen or the Amigo of Brussels, he had reasons for wishing to seek a more modest and less known place to stay while in Paris. For one thing his stay would be longer, and for another there was far more likelihood of running into somebody in Paris in late July who might have known him fleetingly in London under his real name than in either Copenhagen or Brussels. Out on the street he was confident that the wraparound dark glasses he habitually wore, and which in the bright sunshine of the boulevards were completely natural, would protect his identity. The possible danger lay in being seen in a hotel corridor or foyer. The last thing he wished at this stage was to be halted by a cheery "Well, fancy seeing you here," and then the mention of his name within the hearing of a desk clerk who knew him as Mr. Duggan.

Not that his stay in Paris had anything about it to excite attention. He lived quietly, taking his breakfast of croissants and coffee in his room. From the delicatessen across the road from his hotel he bought a jar of English marmalade to replace the black currant jam provided on the breakfast tray, and asked the hotel staff to include the jar of marmalade on his tray each morning in place of the jam.

He was quietly courteous to the staff, spoke only a few words of French with the Englishman's habitually atrocious pronunciation of the French language, and smiled politely when addressed. He replied to the management's solicitous enquiries by assuring them that he was extremely comfortable and thank you.

"*M. Duggan,*" the hotel proprietress told her desk clerk one day, "*est extrêmement gentil. Un vrai* gentleman." There was no dissent.

His days were spent out of the hotel in the pursuits of the tourists. On his first day he bought a street map of Paris, and from a small notebook marked off on the map the places of interest he most wanted to see. These he visited and studied with remarkable devotion, even bearing in mind the architectural beauty of some of them or the historical association of the others.

He spent three days roaming round the Arc de Triomphe or sitting on the terrace of the Café de l'Elysée scanning the monument and the rooftops of the great buildings that surround the Place de l'Etoile. Anyone who had followed him in those days (and no one did) would have been surprised that even the architecture of the brilliant M. Haussmann should have attracted so devoted an admirer. Certainly no watcher could have divined that the quiet and elegant English tourist stirring his coffee and gazing at the buildings for so many hours was mentally working out angles of fire, distances from the upper stories to the Eternal Flame flickering beneath the Arc, and the chances of a man fleeing down a rear fire escape unnoticed into the milling crowds.

After three days he left the Etoile and visited the ossuary of the martyrs of the French Resistance at Montvalérien. Here he arrived with a bouquet of flowers, and a guide, touched by the gesture of the Englishman to the guide's one-time fellow Resistants, gave him an exhaustive tour of the shrine and a running commentary. He was hardly to perceive that the visitor's eyes kept straying away from the entrance to the ossuary towards the high walls of the prison which cut off all direct vision into the courtyard from the roofs of the surrounding buildings. After two hours he left with a polite "thank-you" and a generous but not extravagant *pourboire*.

He also visited the Place des Invalides, dominated on its southern side by the Hôtel des Invalides, home of Napoleon's tomb and shrine to the glories of the French Army. The western side of the enormous square, formed by the rue Fabert, interested him most, and he sat for a morning at the corner cafe where the rue Fabert adjoins the tiny triangular Place de Santiago du Chili. From the sixth or seventh floor of the building above his head, 146, rue de Grenelle, where that street joins the rue Fabert at an angle of ninety degrees, he estimated that a gunman would be able to dominate the front gardens of the Invalides, the entrance to the inner courtyard, most of the Place des Invalides, and two or three streets. A good place for a last stand, but not for an assassination. For one thing, the distance from the upper windows to the gravelled path leading from the Invalides Palace to where cars would be drawn up at the base of the steps between the two tanks was over two hundred metres. For another, the view downwards from the windows of number 146 would be partly obscured by the topmost branches of the dense lime trees growing in the Place de Santiago and from which the pigeons dropped their off-white tributes onto the shoulders of the uncomplaining statue of Vauban. Regretfully, he paid for his Vittel Menthe and left.

A day was spent in the precincts of Notre Dame cathedral. Here amid the rabbit warren of the Ile de la Cité were back stairways, alleys, and passageways, but the distance from the entrance to the cathedral to the parked cars at the foot of the steps was only a few metres, and the rooftops of the Place du Parvis were too far away, while those of the tiny abutting Square Charlemagne were too close and easy for security forces to infest with watchers.

His last visit was to the square at the southern end of the rue de Rennes. He arrived on July 28. Once called the Place de Rennes, the square had been renamed when the Gaullists took power in the City Hall, and was now called Place du 18 Juin 1940. The Jackal's eyes strayed to the shining new name plate on the wall of the building and remained there. Something of what he had read the previous month returned to him. June 18, 1940, the day when the lonely but lofty exile in London had taken the microphone to tell the French that if they had lost a battle, they had not lost the war.

There was something about this square, with the crouching bulk of the Gare Montparnasse on its southern side, full of memories for the Parisians of the war generation, that caused the assassin to stop. Slowly he surveyed the expense of tarmac, crisscrossed now by a maelstrom of traffic pounding down the Boulevard de Montparnasse and joined by other streams from the rue d'Odessa and the rue de Rennes. He looked round at the tall, narrow-fronted buildings on each side of the rue de Rennes that also overlooked the square. Slowly he wended his way round the square to the southern side and peered through the railings into the courtyard of the station. It was a-buzz with cars and taxis bringing or taking away tens of thousands of commuter passengers a day, one of the great mainline stations of Paris. By that winter it would become a silent hulk, brooding on the events, human and historical, that had taken place in its steely, smoky shadow. The station was destined for demolition in 1964, when a new station was to be built five hundred yards along the railway line.

The Jackal turned with his back to the railings and looked down the traffic artery of the rue de Rennes. He was facing the Place du 18 Juin 1940, convinced that this was the place the President of France would come one last time, on the appointed day. The other places he had examined during the past week were possibles; this one, he felt sure, was the certainty. Within a short time there would be no more Gare Montparnasse, the columns that had looked down on so much would be smelted for suburban fences and the forecourt that had seen Berlin humiliated and Paris preserved would be just another executives' cafeteria. But before that happened, he, the man with the kepi and two gold stars, would come once again. But in the meantime the distance from the top floor of the corner house on the western side of the rue de Rennes and the centre of the forecourt was about 130 metres.

The Jackal took in the landscape facing him with a practised eye. Both corner houses on the rue de Rennes where it debouched into the square were obvious choices. The first three houses up the rue de Rennes were possibles, presenting a narrow firing angle into the forecourt. Beyond them the angle became too narrow. Similarly, the first three houses that fronted the Boulevard de Montparnasse running straight through the square east to west were possibles. Beyond them the angles became too narrow again, and the distance too great. There were no other buildings that dominated the forecourt that were not too far away, other than the station building itself. But this would be out of bounds, its upper office windows overlooking the forecourt crawling with security men. The Jackal decided to study the three corner houses on the western side of the rue de Rennes first, and sauntered over to a cafe on the corner at the eastern side, the Café Duchesse Anne.

Here he sat on the terrace a few feet from the roaring traffic, ordered a coffee, and stared at the houses across the street. He stayed for three hours. Later he lunched at the Hansi Brasserie Alsacienne on the far side, and studied the eastern façades. For the afternoon he sauntered up and down, looking at closer quarters into the front doors of the blocks of apartments he had picked out as possibles.

He moved on eventually to the houses that fronted the Boulevard de Montparnasse itself, but here the buildings were offices, newer and more briskly busy.

The next day he was back again, sauntering past the façades, crossing the road to sit on a pavement bench under the trees and toying with a newspaper while he studied the upper floors. Five or six floors of stone façade, topped by a parapet, then the steeply sloping black-tiled roofs containing the attics, pierced by mansard windows, once the quarters of the servants, now the homes of the poorer pensionnaires. The roofs, and possibly the mansards themselves, would certainly be watched on the day. There might even be watchers on the roofs, crouching among the chimney stacks, their field glasses on the opposite windows and roofs. But the topmost floor below the attics would be high enough, providing one could sit well back into the darkness of the room not to be visible from across the street. The open window, in the sweltering heat of a Paris summer, would be natural enough.

But the further back one sat inside the room, the narrower would be the angle of fire sideways down into the forecourt of the station. For this reason the Jackal ruled out the third house into the rue de Rennes on each side of the street. The angle would be too narrow. That left him four houses to choose from. As the time of day he expected to fire would be the midafternoon, with the sun moving towards the west, but still high enough in the sky to shine over the top of the station roof into the windows of the houses on the east side of the street, he eventually chose those two on the west side. To prove it, he waited until four o'clock on July 29 and noticed that on the west side the topmost windows were receiving only a slanting ray from the sun, while it still fiercely lit the houses on the east.

The next day he noticed the concierge. It was his third day sitting either at a cafe terrace or on a pavement bench, and he had chosen a bench a few feet from the doorways of the two blocks of flats that still interested him. Within a few feet, behind him and separated by the pavement down which pedestrians scurried endlessly, the concierge sat in her doorway and knitted. Once, from a nearby cafe, a waiter strolled over for a chat. He called the concierge Madame Berthe. It was a pleasant scene. The day was warm, the sun bright, reaching several feet into the dark doorway while it was still in the southeast and south, high in the sky over the station roof across the square.

She was a comfortable grandmotherly soul, and from the way she chirped "Bonjour, monsieur" to the people who occasionally entered or left her block, and from the cheerful "Bonjour, Madame Berthe" that she received each time in return, the watcher on the bench twenty feet away judged that she was well-liked. A good-natured body, and with compassion for the unfortunate of this world. For shortly after two in the afternoon a cat presented itself and within a few minutes, after diving into the dark recesses of her loge at the rear of the ground floor, Madame Berthe was back with a saucer of milk for the creature she referred to as her little Minet.

Shortly before four she bundled up her knitting, put it into one of the capacious pockets of her pinafore, and shuffled on slippered feet down the road to the bakery. The Jackal rose quietly from his bench and entered the apartment block. He chose the stairs rather than the lift and ran silently upwards.

The stairs ran round the lift shaft, and at each curve on the rear of the building, the stairs halted to make room for a small half-landing. On each second floor this landing gave access through a door in the rear wall of the block to a steel fire escape. At the sixth and top floor, apart from the attics, he opened the rear door and looked down. The fire escape led to an inner courtyard, around which were the rear entrances to the other blocks that made up the corner of the square behind him. On the far side of the courtyard the hollow square of buildings was penetrated by a narrow co-vered alleyway leading towards the north.

The Jackal closed the door quietly, replaced the safety bar, and mounted the last half-flight to the sixth floor. From here, at the end of the passage, a humbler staircase led to the upper attics. There were two doors in the passage giving access to flats overlooking the inner courtyard and two others for flats on the front of the building. His sense of direction told him either of these front flats contained windows looking down into the rue de Rennes, or half-sideways onto the square and beyond it for the forecourt of the station. These were the windows he had been observing for so long from the street below.

One of the name plates next to the bell pushes of the two front flats he now confronted bore the inscription "Mlle Béranger." The other bore the name "M. et Mme Charrier." He listened for a moment but there was no sound from either of the flats. He examined the locks; both were embedded in the woodwork, which was thick and strong. The tongues of the locks on the far side were probably of the thick bar of steel type so favoured by the security-conscious French, and of the double-locking variety. He would need keys, he realised, of which Mme Berthe would certainly have one for each flat somewhere in her little loge.

A few minutes later he was running lightly down the stairs the way he had come. He had been in the block less than five minutes. The concierge was back. He caught a glimpse of her through the frosted glass pane in the door of her cubbyhole, then he had turned and was striding out of the arched entrance.

He turned left up the rue de Rennes, passed two other blocks of apart-ments, then the façade of a post office. At the corner of the block was a narrow street, the rue Littre. He turned into it, still following the wall of the post office. Where the building ended there was a narrow covered alleyway. The Jackal stopped to light a cigarette and while the flame flickered glanced sideways down the alley. It gave access to a rear entrance into the post office for the telephone exchange switchboard night staff. At the end of the tunnel was a sunlit courtyard. On the far side he could make out in the shadows the last rungs of the fire escape of the building he had just left. He had found his escape route.

At the end of the rue Littre he turned left again into the rue de Vaugirard and walked back to where it joined the Boulevard de Montparnasse. He had reached the corner and was looking up and down the main street for a free taxi, when a police motorcyclist swept into the road junction, jerked his machine onto its stand, and in the center of the junction began to halt the traffic. By shrill blasts on his whistle he stopped all the traffic coming out of the rue de Vaugirard, as well as that heading down the Boulevard from the direction of the station. The cars coming up the Boulevard from Duroc were imperiously waved into the right hand side of the road. He had barely got them all stopped when the distant wail of police sirens was heard from the direction of Duroc. Standing on the corner looking down the length of the Boulevard de Montparnasse, the Jackal saw five-hundred yards away a motorcade sweep into the Duroc junction from the Boulevard des Invalides and start to head towards him.

In the lead were two black-leather-clad motorcyclists, white helmets gleaming in the sun, sirens blaring. Behind them appeared the shark-like snouts of two DS 19 Citroens in the line astern. The policeman in front of the Jackal stood bolt upright facing away from him, left arm gesturing rigidly down towards the Avenue du Maine on the southern side of the junction, right arm bent across the chest, palm downwards, indicating priority passage for the approaching motorcade.

Heeling over to the right, the two motorcyclists swept into the Avenue du Maine, followed by the two limousines. In the back of the first one, sitting upright behind the driver and the A.D.C., staring rigidly in front of himself, was a tall figure in a charcoal-grey suit. The Jackal had a fleeting glimpse of the uptilted head and the unmistakable nose before the convoy was gone. The next time I see your face, he silently told the departing image, it will be in closer focus through a telescopic sight. Then he found a taxi and was taken back to his hotel.

Farther down the road, near the exit from the Duroc Métro station from which she had just emerged, another figure had watched the passing of the President with more than usual interest. She had been about to cross the road when a policeman had waved her back. Seconds later the motorcade swept out of the Boulevard des Invalides across the expanse of cobbles and into the Boulevard de Montparnasse. She too had seen the distinctive profile in the back of the first Citroen, and his eyes had glowed with a passionate fervour. Even when the cars had gone, she stared after them, until she saw the policeman looking her up and down. Hastily she had resumed her crossing of the road.

Jacqueline Dumas was then twenty-six years old and of considerable beauty, which she knew how to show off to its best advantage for she worked as a beautician in an expensive salon behind the Champs Elysées. On the evening of July 30 she was hurrying home to her little flat off the Place de Breteuil to get ready for her evening's date. Within a few hours she knew she would be naked in the arms of the lover she hated, and she wanted to look her best.

A few years earlier the thing that mattered most in her life was her next date. Hers was a good family, a tight-knit group with her father working as a respectable clerk in a banking house, mother being a typical middle-class French housewife and Maman, she finishing her beautician's course, and Jean-Claude doing his National Service. The family lived in the outer suburb of Le Vésinet, not in the best part, but a nice house all the same.

The telegram from the Ministry of the Armed Forces had come one day at breakfast towards the end of 1959. It said that the Minister was required with infinite regret to inform Monsieur and Madame Armand Dumas of the death in Algeria of their son Jean-Claude, private soldier in the First Colonial Paratroops. His personal effects would be returned to the bereaved family as soon as possible.

For some time Jacqueline's private world disintegrated. Nothing seemed to make sense, not the quiet security of the family at Le Vésinet or the chatter of the other girls at the salon on the charms of Yves Montand or the latest dance craze imported from America, le Rock. The only thing that seemed to pound through her mind was that little Jean-Claude, her darling baby brother, so vulnerable and gentle, hating war and violence, waiting only to be alone with his books, scarcely more than a boy whom she loved to spoil, had been shot dead in a battle in some God-forsaken *wadi* in Algeria. She began to hate. It was the Arabs, the loathsome, dirty, cowardly "melons" who had done it.

Then François came. Quite suddenly one winter morning he turned up at the house on a Sunday when the parents were away visiting relatives. It was December, there was snow in the avenue and crusted onto the garden path. Other people were pale and pinched, and François looked tanned and fit. He asked if he could speak to Mademoiselle Jacqueline. She said, "*C'est moi-même*" and what did he want? He replied he commanded the platoon in which one Jean-Claude Dumas, private soldier, had been killed, and he bore a letter. She asked him in.

The letter had been written some weeks before Jean-Claude died, and he had kept it in his pocket during the patrol in the *djebel* looking for a band of fellagha who had wiped out a settler family. They had not found the guerrillas, but had run into a battalion of the ALN, the trained troops of the Algerian national movement, the FLN. There had been a bitter skirmish in the half light of dawn and Jean-Claude had taken a bullet through the lungs. He gave the letter to the platoon commander before he died.

Jacqueline read the letter and cried a little. It said nothing of the last weeks, just chatter about the barracks at Constantine, the assault courses, and the discipline. The rest she learned from François: the pull-back through the scrub for four miles while the outflanking ALN closed in, the repeated calls on the radio for air support, and at eight o'clock the arrival of the fighter-bombers with their screaming engines and thundering rockets. And how her brother, who had volunteered for one of the toughest regiments to prove he was a man, had died like one, coughing blood over the knees of a corporal in the lee of a rock.

François had been very gentle with her. As a man he was hard as the earth of the colonial province in whose four years of war he had been forged as a professional soldier. But he was very gentle with the sister of one of his platoon. She liked him for that and accepted his offer to dine in Paris. Besides, she feared her parents would return and surprise them. She did not want them to hear how Jean-Claude had died, for both had managed to numb themselves to the loss in the intervening two months and somehow carry on as usual. Over dinner she swore the lieutenant to silence and he agreed.

But for her the curiosity became insatiable, to know about the Algerian war, what really happened, what it really stood for, what the politicians were really playing at. General de Gaulle had come to the presidency from the premiership the previous January, swept into the Elysée on a tide of patriotic fervour as the man who would finish the war and still keep Algeria French. It was from François that she first heard the man her father adored referred to as a traitor to France.

They spent François's leave together, she meeting him every evening after work in the salon to which she had gone in January 1960 from the training school. He told her of the betrayal of the French Army, of the Paris government's secret negotiations with the imprisoned Ahmed Ben Bella, leader of the FLN, and of the pending handover of Algeria to the melons. He had returned to his war in the second half of January, and she had snatched a brief time alone with him when he managed to get a week's leave in August in Marseilles. She had waited for him, building him in her private thoughts into the symbol of all that was good and clean and virile in French young manhood. She had waited throughout the autumn and winter of 1960, with his picture on her bedside table throughout the day and evening, pushed down her nightdress and clasped to her belly while she slept.

In his last leave of the spring of 1961 he had come again to Paris, and when they walked down the boulevards, he in uniform, she in her prettiest dress, she thought he was the strongest, broadest, handsomest man in the city. One of the other girls at work had seen them, and the next day the salon was a-buzz with news of Jacqui's beautiful "para." She was not there; she had taken her annual holiday to be with him all the time.

François was excited. There was something in the wind. The news of the talks with the FLN was public knowledge. The Army, the real Army, would not stand for it much longer, he promised. That Algeria should remain French was, for both of them, the combat-hardened twenty-seven-year-old officer and the adoring twenty-three-year-old mother-to-be, an article of faith.

François never knew about the baby. He returned to Algeria in March 1961 and on April 21 several units of the French Army mutinied against the Metropolitan government. The First Colonial Paras were in the mutiny almost to a man. Only a handful of conscripts scuttled out of barracks and made rendezvous at the Prefet's office. The professionals let them go. Fighting broke out between the mutineers and the loyal regiments within a week. Early in May François was shot in a skirmish with a loyalist Army unit.

Jacqueline, who had expected no letter from April onwards, suspected nothing until she was told the news in July. She quietly took a flat in a cheap suburb of Paris and tried to gas herself. She failed because the room had too many gas leaks, but lost the baby. Her parents took her away with them for their August annual holidays, and she seemed to have recovered by the time they returned. In December she became an active underground worker for the OAS.

Her motives were simple: François, and after him Jean-Claude. They should be avenged, no matter by what means, no matter what the cost to herself or anyone else. Apart from this passion, she was without an ambition in the world. Her only complaint was that she could not do more than run errands, carry messages, occasionally a slab of plastic explosive stuffed into a loaf in her shopping bag. She was convinced she could do more. Did not the "flics" on the corners, carrying out snap searches of passers-by after one of the regular bombings of cafés and cinemas, inevitably let her pass after one flutter of her long dark eyelashes, one pout of her lips?

After the Petit-Clamart affair one of the would-be killers had spent three nights at her flat off the Place de Breteuil while on the run. It had been her big moment, but then he had moved on. A month later he had been caught, but had said nothing of his stay with her. Perhaps he had forgotten. But to be on the safe side, her cell leader instructed her to do no more work for the OAS for a few months, until the heat wore off. It was January 1963 when she began carrying messages again.

And so it went on, until in July a man came to see her. He was accompanied by her cell leader, who showed him great deference. He had no name. Would she be prepared to undertake a special job for the Organisation? Of course. Perhaps dangerous, certainly distasteful? No matter.

Three days later she was shown a man emerging from a block of flats. They were sitting in a parked car. She was told who he was, and what was his position. And what she had to do.

By mid-July they had met, apparently by chance, when she sat next to the man in a restaurant and smiled shyly at him while asking for the loan of the salt cellar on his table. He had spoken, she had been reserved, modest. The reaction had been the right one. Her demureness interested him. Without seeming to, the conversation blossomed, the man leading, she docilely following. Within a fortnight they were having an affair.

She knew enough about men to be able to judge the basic types of appetites. Her new lover was accustomed to easy conquests, experienced women. She played shy, attentive, but chaste, reserved on the outside with just a hint now and again that her superb body was one day not to be completely wasted. The bait worked. For the man the ultimate conquest became a matter of top priority.

In late July her cell leader told her their cohabitation should begin soon. The snag was the man's wife and two children, who lived with him. On July 29 they left for the family's country house in the Loire Valley, while the husband was required to stay on in Paris for his work. Within a few minutes of his family's departure he was on the phone to the salon to insist that Jacqueline and he should dine alone at his flat the following night.

Once inside her flat, Jacqueline Dumas glanced at her watch. She had three hours to get ready, and although she intended to be meticulous in her preparations, two hours would suffice. She stripped and showered, drying herself in front of the full-length mirror on the back of the wardrobe door, watching the towel run over her skin with unfeeling detachment, raising her arms high to lift the full, rose-nippled breasts with none of the feeling of anticipatory delight she used to feel when she knew they would soon be caressed in François's palms.

She thought dully of the coming night, and her belly tightened with revulsion. She would, she vowed, she would go through with it, no matter with kind of loving he wanted. From a compartment in the back of the bureau she took her photo of François, looking out of the frame with the same old ironic half-smile he had always smiled when he saw her flying the length of the station platform to meet him. The picture's soft brown hair, the cool buff uniform with the hard-muscled pectorals beneath, against which she loved once long ago to rest her face, and the steel paratrooper's wings, so cool on a burning cheek. They were all still there—in celluloid. She lay on the bed and held François above her looking down as he did when they made love, asking superfluously, "*Alors, petite, tu veux? . . .*" She always whispered, "*Oui, tu sais bien . . .*" And then it happened.

When she closed her eyes she could feel him inside her, hard and hot and throbbing strength, and hear the softly growled endearments in her ear, the final stifled command "*Viens, viens . . .*" which she never disobeyed.

She opened her eyes and stared at the ceiling, holding the warmed glass of the portrait to her breasts. "François," she breathed, "help me, please help me tonight."

On the last day of the month the Jackal was busy. He spent the morning at the Flea Market, wandering from stall to stall with a cheap holdall by his side. He bought a greasy black beret, a pair of well-scuffed shoes, some not-too-clean trousers, and, after much searching, a long once-military greatcoat. He would have preferred one of lighter material, but military greatcoats are seldom tailored for midsummer and in the French Army are made of Duffel. But it was long enough, even on him, stretching to well below the knee, which was the important thing.

As he was on his way out, his eye was caught by a stall full of medals, mostly stained with age. He bought a collection, together with a booklet describing French military medals with faded colour pictures of the ribbons and captions telling the reader for which compaigns or for what kind of acts of gallantry the various medals were awarded.

After lunching lightly at Queenie's on the rue Royale he slipped round the corner to his hotel, paid his bill, and packed. His new purchases went into the bottom of one of his two expensive suitcases. From the collection of medals and with the help of the guide-book he made up a bar of decorations starting with the Médaille Militaire for courage in the face of the enemy, and adding the Médaille de la Libération and five campaign medals awarded to those who fought in the Free French Forces during the Second World War. He awarded himself decorations for Bir Hakeim, Libya, Tunisia, D-Day, and the Second Armoured Division of General Philippe Leclerc.

The rest of the medals, and the book, he dumped separately into two waste paper baskets attached to lamp posts up the Boulevard Malesherbes. The hotel desk clerk informed him there was the excellent Etoile du Nord express for Brussels leaving the Gare du Nord at five-fifteen. This he caught, and dined well, arriving in Brussels in the last hours of July.

<u>SIX</u>

The letter for Viktor Kowalski arrived in Rome the following morning. The giant corporal was crossing the foyer of the hotel on his return from picking up the daily mail from the post office when one of the bell-hops called after him, "*Signor, per favore . . .* "

He turned, as surly as ever. The wop was one he did not recognise, but there was nothing unusual in that. He never noticed them as he bulled his way across the floor of the foyer towards the lift. The dark-eyed young man held a letter in his hand as he came to Kowalski's side.

"*E una lettera, signor. Per un Signor Kowalski . . . non cognosco questo signor. . . . E forse un francese . . .* "

Kowalski did not understand a word of the babble of Italian, but he got the sense and he recognised his own name, badly pronounced though it was. He snatched the letter from the man's hand and stared at the scrawled name and address. He was registered under another name, and not being a reading man had failed to notice that five days earlier a Paris newspaper had had a scoop announcing that three of the top men of the OAS were now holed up on the top floor of the hotel.

So far as he was concerned, no one was supposed to know where he was. And yet the letter intrigued him. He did not often receive letters, and as with most simple people the arrival of one was an important event. He had cottoned from the Italian, now standing with spaniel eyes by his side staring up as if he, Kowalski, was the fount of human knowledge who would solve the dilemma, that none of the desk staff had heard of a guest of that name and did not know what to do with the letter.

Kowalski looked down. "*Bon. Je vais demander,*" he said loftily. The Italian's brow did not uncrease.

"*Demander, demander,*" repeated Kowalski, pointing upwards through the ceiling.

The Italian saw the light. "*Ah, sì. Domandare. Prego, Signor. Tante grazie . . .*"

Kowalski strode away leaving the Italian gesticulating his gratitude. Taking the lift to the eighth floor, he emerged to find himself confronted by the desk-duty man in the corridor, automatic drawn and cocked. For a second the two stared at each other. Then the other slipped on the safety catch and pocketed the gun. He could see only Kowalski, no one else in the lift. It was purely routine, happening every time the lights above the lift doors indicated that the ascending lift was coming beyond the seventh floor.

Apart from the desk-duty man, there was another facing the fire escape door at the end of the corridor and another at the head of the stairs. Both the stairs and the fire escape were booby-trapped, although the management did not know this, and the booby-traps could be rendered harmless only when the current to the detonators was cut off from a switch under the desk in the corridor.

The fourth man on the day shift was on the roof above the ninth floor where the chiefs lived, but in case of attack there were three others now asleep in their rooms down the corridor who had been on night shift, but who would awake and be operational in a few seconds if anything happened. On the eighth floor the lift doors had been welded closed from the outside, but even if the light above the lift on the eighth floor indicated the lift was heading right for the top it was a sign for a general alarm. It had only happened once and then by accident, when a bell-hop delivering a tray of drinks had pressed the button for "Nine." He had been quickly discouraged from this practice.

The desk man telephoned upstairs to announce the arrival of the mail, then signalled to Kowalski to go up. The ex-corporal had already stuffed the letter addressed to himself into his inside pocket while the mail for his chiefs was in a steel case chained to his left wrist. Both the lock for the chain and for the flat case were spring-loaded, and only Rodin had the keys. A few minutes later the OAS colonel had unlocked both, and Kowalski returned to his room to sleep before relieving the desk man in the late afternoon.

In his room back on the eighth floor he finally read his letter, starting with the signature. He was surprised that it should be from Kovacs, whom he had not seen for a year and who hardly knew how to write, as Kowalski had some difficulty in reading. But by dint of application he deciphered the letter. It was not long.

Kovacs began by saying that he had seen a newspaper story on the day of writing, which a friend had read aloud to him, saying that Rodin, Montclair, and Casson were hiding at that hotel in Rome. He had supposed his old friend Kowalski would be with them, hence was writing on the offchance of reaching him.

Several paragraphs followed to the effect that things were getting tough in

France these days, with the *flics* everywhere asking for papers, and orders still coming through for smash-and-grab raids on jewellers. He had personally been in four, said Kovacs, and it was no joke, particularly when one had to hand over the proceeds. He had done better in Budapest in the good old days, even though these had only lasted for a fortnight.

The last paragraph recounted that Kovacs had met Michel some weeks before, and Michel had said that he had been talking to JoJo, who had said little Sylvie was sick with Luke-something; anyway it was to do with her blood having gone wrong, but that he Kovacs hoped she would soon be all right and Viktor should not worry.

But Viktor did worry. It worried him badly to think that little Sylvie was ill. There was not a great deal that had ever penetrated into the heart of Viktor Kowalski in his thirty-six violent years. He had been twelve years old when the Germans invaded Poland and one year older when his parents were taken away in a dark van. Old enough to know what his sister was doing in the big hotel behind the cathedral that had been taken over by the Germans and was visited by so many of their officers, which so upset his parents that they protested to the military governor's office. Old enough to join the partisans. He had killed his first German at fifteen. He was seventeen when the Russians came, but his parents had always hated and feared them, and told him terrible tales about what they did to Poles, so he left the partisans, who were later executed on orders of the commissar, and went westwards like a hunted animal towards Czechoslovakia. Later it was Austria and a Displaced Persons camp for the tall raw-boned gangling youth who spoke only Polish and was weak from hunger. They thought he was another of the harmless flotsam of post-war Europe. On American food his strength returned. He broke out one spring night in 1946 and hitched south towards Italy, and thence into France in company with another Pole he had met in DP camp who spoke French. In Marseilles he broke into a shop one night, killed the proprietor, who disturbed him, and was on the run again. His companion left him, advising Viktor there was only one place to go—the Foreign Legion. He signed on the next morning and was in Sidi-Bel-Abbes before the police investigation in war-torn Marseilles was really off the ground. The Mediterranean city was still a big import-base for American foodstuffs, and murders committed for these foodstuffs were not uncommon. The case was dropped in a few days when no immediate suspect came to light. By the time he learned this, however, Kowalski was a legionnaire.

He was nineteen and at first the old sweats called him "*petit bonhomme.*" Then he showed them how he could kill, and they called him Kowalski.

Six years in Indochina finished off what might have been left in him of a normally adjusted individual, and after that Kowalski was sent to Algeria. In between he had a posting to a weapons training course for six months outside Marseilles. There he met Julie, a tiny but vicious scrubber in a dockside bar, who had been having trouble with her mec. Kowalski knocked the man six metres across the bar and out cold for ten hours with one blow. The man enunciated oddly for years afterwards, so badly was the lower mandible shattered.

Julie liked the enormous legionnaire, and for several months he became her "protector" by night, escorting her home after work to the sleazy attic in the Vieux Port. There was a lot of lust, particularly on her side, but no love between them, and even less when she discovered she was pregnant. The child, she told him, was his, and he may have believed it because he wanted to. She also told him she did not want the baby, and knew an old woman who would get rid of it for her. Kowalski clouted her and told her if she did that he would kill her. Three months later he had to return to Algeria. In the meantime he had become friendly with another Polish ex-legionnaire, Josef Grzybowski, known as JoJo the Pole, who had been invalided out of Indochina and had settled with a jolly widow running a snack-stall on wheels up and down the platforms at the main station. Since their marriage in 1953 they had run it together, JoJo limping along behind his wife taking the money and giving out the change while his wife dispensed the snacks. On the evenings when he was not working, JoJo liked to frequent the bars haunted by the legionnaires from the nearby barracks to talk over old times. Most of them were youngsters, recruits since his own days at Tourane, Indochina, but one evening he ran into Kowalski.

It was to JoJo that Kowalski had turned for advice about the baby. JoJo agreed with him. They had both been Catholics once.

"She wants to have the kid done in," said Viktor.

"*Salope*," said JoJo.

"Cow," agreed Viktor. They drank some more, staring moodily into the mirror at the back of the bar.

"Not fair to the kid," said Viktor.

"Not right," agreed JoJo.

"Never had a kid before," said Viktor after some thought.

"Nor me, even being married and all," replied JoJo.

Somewhere in the small hours of the morning, very drunk, they agreed on their plan and drank to it with the solemnity of the truly intoxicated. The next morning JoJo remembered his pledge, but could not think how to break the news to Madame. It took him three days. He skated warily round the subject once or twice, then blurted it out while he and the missis were in bed. To his amazement, Madame was delighted. And it was arranged.

In due course Viktor returned to Algeria, then to rejoin Major Rodin, who now commanded the battalion, and to a new war. In Marseilles JoJo and his wife, by a mixture of threats and cajolement, supervised the pregnant Julie. By the time Viktor left Marseilles she was already four months gone and it was too late for an abortion, as JoJo menacingly pointed out to the pimp with the broken jaw who soon came hanging around. This individual had become wary of crossing legionnaires, even old veterans with gammy legs, so he obscenely foreswore his former source of income and looked elsewhere.

Julie was brought to bed in late 1955 and produced a girl, blue-eyed and golden-haired. Adoption papers were duly filed by JoJo and his wife, with the concurrence of Julie. The adoption went through. Julie went back to her old life, and the JoJos had themselves a daughter, whom they named Sylvie. They informed Viktor by letter, and in his barracks bed he was strangely pleased. But he did not tell anyone. He had never actually owned anything within his memory that, if revealed, had not been taken away from him.

Nevertheless, three years later, before a long combat mission in the Algerian hills, the chaplain had proposed to him that he might like to make a will. The idea had never even occurred to him before. He had never had anything to leave behind for one thing, since he spent all his accumulated pay in the bars and whorehouses of the cities when given his rare periods of leave, and what he had belonged to the Legion. But the chaplain assured him that in the modern Legion a will was perfectly in order, so with considerable assistance he made one, leaving all his worldly goods and chattels to the daughter of one Jòsef Grzybowski, former legionnaire, presently of Marseilles. Eventually a copy of this document, along with the rest of his dossier, was filed with the archives of the Ministry of the Armed Forces in Paris. When Kowalski's name became know to French security forces in connection with the Bone and Constantine terrorism in 1961, this dossier was unearthed along with many others and came to the attention of Colonel Rolland's Action Service at the Porte des Lilas. A visit was paid to the Grzybowskis, and the story came out. Kowalski never learned this.

He saw his daughter twice in his life, once in 1957 after taking a bullet in the thigh and being sent on convalescent leave to Marseilles, and again in 1960 when he came to the city when on escort duty for Lieutenant Colonel Rodin, who had to attend a court martial as a witness. The first time the little girl was two, the next time four and a half. Kowalski arrived laden with presents for the JoJos and toys for Sylvie. They got on very well together, the small child and her bear-like Uncle Viktor. But he never mentioned her to anyone else, not even Rodin.

And now she was sick with Luke-something, and Kowalski worried a lot throughout the rest of the morning. After lunch he was upstairs to have the steel etui for the mail chained to his wrist. Rodin was expecting an important letter from France containing further details of the total sum of money amassed by the series of robberies, and he wanted Kowalski to pay a second visit to the post office for the afternoon mail arrivals.

"What," the corporal suddenly blurted out, "is Luke-something?"

Rodin, attaching the chain to his wrist, looked up in surprise.

"I've never heard of him," he replied.

"It's a malady of the blood," explained Kowalski.

From the other side of the room where he was reading a glossy magazine Casson laughed.

"Leukaemia, you mean," he said.

"Well, what is it, monsieur?"

"It's cancer," replied·Casson, "cancer of the blood."

Kowalski looked at Rodin in front of him. He did not trust civilians.

"They can cure it, the *toubibs, mon colonel?*"

"No, Kowalski, it's fatal. There's no cure. Why?"

"Nothing," mumbled Kowalski, "just something I read."

Then he left. If Rodin was surprised that his bodyguard who had never been known to read anything more complex than standing orders of the day had come across that word in a book, he did not show it and the matter was soon swept from his mind. For the afternoon's mail brought the letter he was waiting for, to say that the combined OAS bank accounts in Switzerland now contained over $250,000.

Rodin was satisfied as he sat down to write and despatch the instructions to the bankers transferring that sum to the account of his hired assassin. For the balance he had no qualms. With President de Gaulle dead, there would be no delay before the industrialists and bankers of the extreme Right-wing, who had financed the OAS in its earlier and more successful days, produced the other $250,000. The same men who had replied to his approaches for a further advance of cash only a few weeks earlier with mealy-mouthed excuses that the "lack of progress and initiative shown over recent months by the forces of patriotism" had decreased their chances of ever seeing a return on previous investments, would be clamouring for the honour of backing the soldiers who shortly afterwards would become the new rulers of a re-born France.

He finished the instructions to the bankers as darkness fell, but when he saw the orders Rodin had written instructing the Swiss bankers to pay over the money to the Jackal, Casson objected. He argued that one vitally important thing they had all three promised their Englishman was that he would have a contact in Paris capable of supplying him constantly with the latest accurate information about the movements of the French President, along with any changes in the security routines surrounding him that might occur. These could, indeed probably would, be of vital importance to the assassin. To inform him of the transfer of the money at this stage, Casson reasoned, would be to encourage him to go into action prematurely. Whenever the man intended to strike was obviously his own choice, but a few extra days would make no difference. What might very well make a difference between success and another, certainly the last, failure would be the question of information provided to the killer.

He, Casson, had received word that very morning in the mail that his chief representative in Paris had succeeded in placing an agent very close to one of the men in de Gaulle's immediate entourage. A few days more would be necessary before this agent was in a position to acquire consistently reliable information as to the General's whereabouts and above all his travelling intentions and his public appearances, neither of which were being publicly announced in advance any more. Would Rodin therefore please stay his hand for a few more days until Casson was in a position to supply the assassin with a telephone number in Paris from which he could receive the information that would be vital to his mission?

Rodin reflected long over Casson's argument, and eventually agreed that he was right. Neither man could be aware of the Jackal's intentions, and in fact the transmission of the instructions to the bankers, followed later by the letter to London containing the Paris telephone number, would not have caused the assassin to alter any detail of his schedule. Neither terrorist in Rome could know that the killer had already chosen his day and was proceeding with his planning and contingency precautions with clockwork precision.

Sitting up on the roof in the hot Roman night, his bulky form merging into the shadow of the air conditioner ventilation stack, the Colt .45 resting easily in a practised hand, Kowalski worried about a little girl in a bed in Marseilles with Luke-something in her blood. Shortly before dawn he had an idea. He remembered that the last time he had seen JoJo in 1960, the ex-legionnaire had talked of getting a telephone in his flat.

On the morning that Kowalski received his letter, the Jackal left the Amigo hotel in Brussels and took a taxi to a corner of the street where M. Goossens lived. He had rung the armourer over breakfast in the name of Duggan, which was how Goossens knew him, and the appointment was for 11 a.m. He arrived at the corner of the street at 10:30 and spent half an hour surveying

the street from behind a newspaper on a kerbside bench in the little public
gardens at the end of the street.

It seemed quiet enough. He presented himself at the door at 11 sharp, and
Goossens let him in and led him to the little office off the hallway. After the
Jackal had passed, M. Goossens carefully locked the front door and put it on
the chain. Inside the office the Englishman turned to the armourer.

"Any problems?" he asked. The Belgian looked embarrassed.

"Well, yes, I am afraid so."

The assassin surveyed him coldly, with no expression on his face, the eyes
half closed and sullen.

"You told me that if I came back on August 1 I could have the gun by
August 4 to take home with me," he said.

"That's perfectly true, and I assure you the problem is not with the gun,"
said the Belgian. "Indeed the gun is ready, and franky I regard it as one of
my masterpieces, a beautiful specimen. The trouble has been with the other
product, which evidently had to be made from scratch. Let me show you."

On top of the desk lay a flat case about two feet long by eighteen inches
broad four inches deep. M. Goossens opened the case and the Jackal looked
down on it as the upper half fell back to the table.

It was like a flat tray, divided into carefully shaped compartments, each
exactly the shape of the component of the rifle that it contained.

"It was not the original case, you understand," expained M. Goossens.
"That would have been much too long. I made the case myself. It all fits."

It fitted very compactly. Along the top of the open tray was the barrel and
breech, the whole no longer than eighteen inches. The Jackal lifted it out
and examined it. It was very light, and looked rather like a submachine gun
barrel. The breech contained a narrow bolt which was closed shut. It ended
at the back with a knurled grip no larger than the breech into which the rest
of the bolt was fitted.

The Englishman took the knurled end of the bolt between forefinger and
thumb of the right hand, gave it a sharp turn anti-clockwise. The bolt
unlocked itself and rolled over in its groove. As he pulled the bolt slid back to
reveal the gleaming tray into which the bullet would lie, and the dark hole at
the rear end of the barrel. He rammed the bolt back home and twisted it
clockwise. Smoothly it locked into place.

Just below the rear end of the bolt an extra disc of steel had been expertly
welded onto the mechanism. It was half an inch thick but less than an inch
round, and in the top part of the disc was a cutout crescent to allow free
passage backwards of the bolt. In the centre of the rear face of the disc was a
single hole half an inch across; the inside of this hole had been threaded as if
to take a screw.

"That's for the frame of the stock," said the Belgian quietly.

Jackal noticed that where the wooden stock of the original rifle had been
removed no trace remained except the slight flanges running along the
underside of the breech where the woodwork had once fitted. The two holes
made by the retaining screws that had secured the wooden stock to the rifle
had been expertly plugged and blued. He turned the rifle over and examined the underside. There was a narrow slit beneath the breech. Through
it he could see the underside of the bolt that contained the firing pin which
fired the bullet. Through both slits protruded the stump of the trigger. It

had been sawn off flush with the surface of the steel breech.

Welded to the stump of the old trigger was a tiny knob of metal, also with a threaded hole in it. Silently M. Goossens handed him a small sliver of steel, an inch long, curved and with one end threaded. He fitted the threaded end into the hole and twiddled it quickly with forefinger and thumb. When it was tight the new trigger protruded below the breech.

By his side the Belgian reached back into the tray and held up a single narrow steel rod, one end of it threaded.

"The first part of the stock assembly," he said.

The assassin fitted the end of the steel rod into a hole at the rear of the breech and wound it till it was firm. In profile the steel rod seemed to emerge from the back of the gun and cant downwards at thirty degrees. Two inches from the threaded end, up near the mechanism of the rifle, the steel rod had been lightly flattened, and in the centre of the flattened portion a hole had been drilled at an angle to the line of the rod. This hole now faced directly backwards. Goossens held up a second and shorter steel rod.

"The upper strut," he said.

This too was fitted into place. The two rods stuck out backwards, the upper one at a much shallower angle to the line of the barrel so that the two rods separated from each other like two sides of a narrow triangle with no base. Goossens produced the base. It was curved, about five or six inches long, and heavily padded with black leather. At each end of the shoulder guard, or butt of the rifle, was a small hole.

"There's nothing to screw here," said the armourer, "just press it onto the ends of the rods."

The Englishman fitted the end of each steel rod into the appropriate hole and smacked the butt home. The rifle now, when seen in profile, looked more normal, with a trigger and a complete stock sketched in outline by the upper and lower strut and the base plate. The Jackal lifted the butt-plate into his shoulder, left hand gripping the underside of the barrel, right forefinger round the trigger, left eye closed, and right eye squinting down the barrel. He aimed at the far wall and squeezed the trigger. There was a soft click from inside the breech.

He turned to the Belgian, who held what looked like a ten-inch long black tube in each hand.

"Silencer," said the Englishman. He took the proffered tube and studied the end of the rifle barrel. It had been finely "tapped" or threaded. He slipped the wider end of the silencer over the barrel and wound it quickly round and round until it would go no more. The silencer protruded off the end of the barrel like a long sausage. He held his hand out from his side and M. Goossens slipped the telescopic sight into it.

Along the top of the barrel were a series of pairs of grooves gouged into the metal. Into these the sprung clips on the underside of the telescope fitted, ensuring the telescopic sight and the barrel were exactly parallel. On the right hand side and on the top of the telescope were tiny grub screws for adjusting the crossed hairs inside the sight. Again the Englishman held up the rifle and squinted as he took aim. To a casual glance he might have been an elegant, check-suited English gentleman in a Piccadilly gunshop trying out a new sporting gun. But what had been ten minutes before a handful of odd-looking components was no sporting gun any more; it was a high-velocity, long-range, fully silenced assassin's rifle. The Jackal put it down. He turned to the Belgian and nodded, satisfied.

"Good," he said, "very good. I congratulate you. A beautiful piece of work."

M. Goossens beamed.

"There still remains the question of zeroing the sights and firing some practise shots. Do you have any shells?"

The Belgian reached into the drawer of the desk and pulled out a box of a hundred bullets. The seals of the packet had been broken, and six shells were missing.

"These are for practice," said the armourer. "I have taken six others out for converting them to explosive tips."

The Jackal poured a handful of the shells into his hand and looked at them. They seemed terribly small for the job one of them would have to do, but he noticed they were the extra long type of that calibre, the extra explosive charge giving the bullet a very high velocity and consequently increased accuracy and killing power. The tips too were pointed, where most hunting bullets are snub-nosed, and where hunting bullets have a dull leaden head, these were tipped with cupronickel. They were competition rifle bullets of the same calibre as the hunting gun he held.

"Where are the real shells?" asked the assassin.

M. Goossens went to the desk again and produced a screw of tissue paper.

"Normally, of course, I keep these in a very safe place," he explained, "but since I knew you were coming, I got them out."

He undid the screw of paper and poured the contents out onto the white blotter. At first glance the bullets looked the same as those the Englishman was pouring from his cupped hand back into the cardboard box. When he had finished he took one of the bullets off the blotter and examined it closely.

From a small area round the extreme tip of the bullet the cupronickel had been finely sanded away to expose the lead inside. The sharp tip of the bullet had been slightly blunted, and into the nose a tiny hole had been drilled down the length of the nose-cap for a quarter of an inch. Into this aperture a droplet of mercury was poured, then the hole was tamped with a drop of liquid lead. After the lead had hardened, it too was filed and papered until the original pointed shape of the bullet tip had been exactly re-created.

The Jackal knew about these bullets, although he had never had occasion to use one. Far too complex to be used en masse except if factory-produced, banned by the Geneva Convention, more vicious than the simple dum-dum, the explosive bullet would go off like a small grenade when it hit the human body. On firing, the droplet of mercury would be slammed back in its cavity by the forward rush of the bullet, as when a car passenger is pressed into his seat by a violent acceleration. As soon as the bullet struck flesh, gristle, or bone, it would experience a sudden deceleration.

The effect on the mercury would be to hurl the droplet forwards towards the plugged front of the bullet. Here its onward rush would rip away the tip of the slug, splaying the lead outwards like the fingers of an open hand or the petals of a blossoming flower. In this shape the leaded projectile would tear through nerve and tissue, ripping, cutting, slicing, leaving fragments of itself over an area the size of a tea-saucer. Hitting the head, such a bullet would not emerge, but would demolish everything inside the cranium, forcing the bone-shell to fragment.

The assassin put the bullet carefully back on the tissue paper. Beside him the mild little man who had designed it was looking up at him quizzically.

"They look all right to me. You are evidently a craftsman, M. Goossens. What then is the problem?"

"It is the other, monsieur. The tubes. These have been more difficult to fabricate than I had imagined. First I used aluminum as you suggested. But please understand I acquired and perfected the gun first. That is why I only got around to doing the other things a few days ago. I had hoped it would be relatively simple, with my skill and the machinery I have in my workshop.

"But in order to keep the tubes as narrow as possible, I bought very thin metal. It was too thin. When threaded on my machine for later assembly piece by piece, it was like tissue paper. It bent when the slightest pressure was put upon it. In order to keep the inside measurements big enough to accommodate the breech of the rifle at its widest part, and yet get thicker-metalled tubes, I had to produce something that simply would not look natural. So I decided on stainless steel.

"It was the only thing. It looks just like aluminum, but slightly heavier. Being stronger, it can be thinner. It can take the thread and still be tough enough not to bend. Of course, it is a harder metal to work, and it takes time. I began yesterday . . . "

"All right. What you say is logical. The point is, I need it, and I need it perfect. When?"

The Belgian shrugged. "It is difficult to say. I have all the basic components, unless other problems crop up. Which I doubt. I am certain the last technical problems are licked. Five days, six days, A week perhaps . . . "

The Englishman showed no signs of his annoyance. The face remained impassive, studying the Belgian as he completed his explanations. When he finished, the other was still thinking.

"All right," he said at last. "It will mean an alteration of my travelling plans. But perhaps not as serious as I thought the last time I was here. That depends to a certain degree on the results of a telephone call I shall have to make. In any event, it will be necessary for me to acclimatise myself to the gun, and that may as well be done in Belgium as anywhere else. But I shall need the gun and the undoctored shells, plus one of the doctored ones. Also, I shall need some peace and quiet in which to practise. Where would one pick in this country to test a new rifle in conditions of complete secrecy? Over a hundred and thirty to a hundred and fifty metres in the open air?"

M. Goossens thought for a moment. "In the forest of the Ardennes," he said at length. "There are great reaches of forest there where a man may be alone for several hours. You could be there and back in a day. Today is Thursday, the weekend starts tomorrow and the woods might be too full of people picnicking. I would suggest Monday, the fifth. By Tuesday or Wednesday, I hope to have the rest of the job finished."

The Englishman nodded, satisfied.

"All right. I think I had better take the gun and the ammunition now. I shall contact you again on Tuesday or Wednesday next week."

The Belgian was about to protest when the customer forestalled him.

"I believe I still owe you some seven hundred pounds. Here"—he dropped another few bundles of notes onto the blotter—"is a further five hundred. The outstanding two hundred pounds you will receive when I get the rest of the equipment."

"*Merci, monsieur,*" said the armourer, scooping the five bundles of twenty five-pound notes into his pocket. Piece by piece he disassembled the rifle, placing each component carefully into its green baize-lined compartment in the carrying case. The single explosive bullet the assassin had asked for was wrapped in a separate piece of tissue paper and slotted into the case beside the cleaning rags and brushes. When the case was closed, he proffered it and the box of shells to the Englishman, who pocketed the shells and kept the neat attaché case in his hand.

M. Goossens showed him politely out.

The Jackal arrived back at his hotel in time for a late lunch. First he placed the case containing the gun carefully in the bottom of the wardrobe, locked it, and pocketed the key.

In the afternoon he strolled unhurriedly into the main post office and asked for a call number in Zurich, Switzerland. It took half an hour for the call to be put through and another five minutes until Herr Meier came on the line. The Englishman introduced himself by quoting a number and then giving his name.

Herr Meier excused himself and came back two minutes later. His tone had lost the cautious reserve it had previously had. Customers whose accounts in dollars and Swiss francs grew steadily merited courteous treatment. The man in Brussels asked one question, and again the Swiss banker excused himself, this time to be back on the line in less than thirty seconds. He had evidently had the customer's file and statement brought out of the safe and was studying it.

"No, *mein Herr,*" the voice crackled into the Brussels phone booth. "We have here your letter of instructions requiring us to inform you by letter express airmail the moment any fresh in-payments are made, but there have been none over the period you mention."

"I only wondered, Herr Meier, because I have been away from London for two weeks and it might have come in my absence."

"No, there has been nothing. The moment anything is paid in, we shall inform you without delay."

In a flurry of Herr Meier's good wishes, the Jackal put the phone down, settled the amount charged, and left.

He met the forger in the bar off the rue Neuve that evening, arriving shortly after 6. The man was there already, and the Englishman spotted a corner seat still free, ordered the forger to join him with a jerk of his head. A few seconds after he had sat down and lit a cigarette, the Belgian joined him.

"Finished?" asked the Englishman.

"Yes, all finished. And very good work, even if I do say so myself."

The Englishman held out his hand.

"Show me," he ordered. The Belgian lit one of his Bastos and shook his head.

"Please understand, monsieur, this is a very public place. Also one needs a good light to examine them, particularly the French cards. They are at the studio."

Jackal studied him coldly for a moment, then nodded.

"All right. We'll go and have a look at them in private."

They left the bar a few minutes later and took a taxi to the corner of the street where the basement studio was situated. It was still a warm, sunny evening, and though the street was narrow and no sun percolated, the Englishman wore the wraparound dark glasses to avoid recognition. One old man passed them coming the other way, but he was bent with arthritis and shuffled with his head to the ground.

The forger led the way down the steps and unlocked the door from a key on his ring. Inside the studio it was almost as dark as if it were night outside. A few shafts of dullish daylight filtered between the ghastly photographs stuck to the inside of the window beside the door, so that the Englishman could make out the shapes of the chair and table in the outer office. The forger led the way through the two velvet curtains into the studio and switched on the centre light.

From inside his pocket he drew a flat brown envelope, tipped it open, and spread the contents on the small round mahogany table that stood to one side, a prop for the taking of portrait photographs. The table he then lifted over to the centre of the room and placed it under the centre light. The twin arc lamps above the tiny stage at the far back of the studio remained unlit.

"Please, monsieur." He smiled broadly and gestured towards the three cards lying on the table. The Englishman picked the first up and held it under the light. It was his driving licence, the first page covered by a stuck-on tab of paper. This informed the reader that Mr. Alexander James Quentin Duggan of London W.1. is hereby licensed to drive motor vehicles of Groups 1a, 1b, 2, 3, 11, 12, and 13 only from 10 DEC 1960 until 9 DEC 1963 inclusive. Above this was the licence number (an imaginary one of course) and the words "London County Council" and "Road Traffic Act 1960." Then, "DRIVING LICENCE" and "Fee of 15/—received." So far as Jackal could tell, it was a perfect forgery, certainly good enough for his purposes.

The second card was simply a French *carte d'identité* in the name of André Martin, aged fifty-three, born at Colmar and resident in Paris. His own photograph, aged by twenty years, with iron-grey hair cut *en brosse,* muzzy and embarrassed, stared out of a tiny corner of the card. The card itself was stained and dogeared, a working man's card.

The third specimen drew his closest attention. The photograph on it was slightly different from the one on the I.D. card, for the date of issue of each card was different by several months, since the renewal dates would probably not have coincided precisely, had they been real. The card bore another portrait of himself that had been taken nearly two weeks earlier, but the shirt seemed to be darker and there was a hint of stubble round the chin of the photo on the card he now held. This effect had been achieved by skilful retouching, giving the impression of two different photographs of the same man, taken at different times and in different clothes. In both cases the draughtsmanship of the forger was excellent. Jackal looked up and pocketed the cards.

"Very nice," he said. "Just what I wanted. I congratulate you. There is fifty pounds outstanding, I believe."

"That is true, monsieur. *Merci.*" The forger waited· expectantly for the money. The Englishman drew a single wad of ten five-pound notes from his pocket but held them extended between forefinger and thumb. He said, "I believe there is something more, no?"

The Belgian tried unsuccessfully to look as if he did not comprehend.
"Monsieur?"

"The genuine front page of the driving licence. The one I said I wanted
back."

There could be no doubt now that the forger was acting. He raised his
eyebrows in extravagant surprise, as if the thought had just occurred to him,
and turned away. He walked several paces one way, head bowed as if deep in
thought, hands held behind his back. Then he turned and walked back.

"I thought we might be able to have a little chat about that piece of paper,
monsieur."

"Yes?" The Jackal's tone gave nothing away. It was flat, without expression, apart from a slight interrogative. The face said nothing either, and the
eyes seemed half shrouded as if they stared only into their own private
world.

"The fact is, monsieur, that the original front page of the driving licence,
with, I imagine, your real name on it, is not here. Oh, please, please"—he
made an elaborate gesture as if to reassure one seized by anxiety, which the
Englishman gave no sense of being—"it is in a very safe place. In a private
deed box in a bank, which can be opened by no one but me. You see,
monsieur, a man in my precarious line of business has to take precautions,
take out, if you like some form of insurance."

"What do you want?"

"Now, my dear sir, I had hoped that you might be prepared to do business
on the basis of an exchange of ownership of that piece of paper, business
based on a sum somewhat above the last figure of a hundred and fifty
pounds which we mentioned in this room."

The Englishman sighed softly, as if slightly puzzled by the ability of man to
complicate unnecessarily his own existence on this earth. He gave no other
sign that the proposal of the Belgian interested him.

"You are interested?" asked the forger, coyly. He was playing his part as if
he had rehearsed it at length; the oblique approach, the supposedly subtle
hints. It reminded the other of a bad B-picture.

"I have met blackmailers before," said the Englishman, not an accusation,
just a flat statement in a flat voice. The Belgian was shocked.

"Ah, monsieur, I beg you. Blackmail? Me? What I propose is not blackmail, since that is a process that repeats itself. I propose simply a trade. The
whole package for a certain sum of money. After all, I have in my deed box
the original of your licence, the developed plates, and all the negatives of the
photographs I took of you, and, I am afraid"—he made a regretful grimace
to show he was afraid—"one other picture taken of you very quickly while
you were standing under the arc lights without your makeup. I am sure these
documents, in the hands of the British and French authorities, could cause
you some inconvenience. You are evidently a man accustomed to paying in
order to avoid the inconveniences of life—"

"How much?"

"One thousand pounds, monsieur."

The Englishman considered the proposition, nodding quietly as if it was
of mild academic interest only.

"It would be worth that amount to me to recover those documents," he
conceded.

The Belgian grinned triumphantly. "I am most glad to hear it, monsieur."

"But the answer is no," went on the Englishman as if he were still thinking hard. The Belgian's eyes narrowed.

"But why? I do not understand. You say it is worth a thousand pounds to you to have them back. It is a straight deal. We are both used to dealing in desirable property and being paid for it."

"There are two reasons," said the other mildly. "Firstly, I have no evidence whatever that the original negatives of the photographs have not been copied, so that the first demand would not be succeeded by others. Nor have I any evidence that you have not given the documents to a friend, who, when asked to produce them will suddenly decide that he no longer has them, unless he too is sweetened to the tune of another thousand pounds."

The Belgian looked relieved. "If that is all that worries you, your fears are groundless. It would be in my interest not to entrust the documents to any partner, for fear that he might not produce them. I do not imagine you would part with a thousand pounds without receiving the documents. So there is no reason for me to part with them. I repeat, they are in a bank deposit box.

"From the point of view of repeated requests for money, that would not make sense. A photostat copy of the driving licence would not impress the British authorities, and even if you were caught with a false driving licence, it would only cause you some inconvenience, but not enough to justify several payments of money to me. As for the French cards, if the French authorities were informed that a certain Englishman were masquerading as a non-existent Frenchman called André Martin, they might indeed arrest you if you passed in France under that name. But if I were to make repeated requests for money, it would become worth your while to throw the cards away and get another forger to make you a new set. Then you would no longer need to fear exposure while in France as André Martin, since Martin would have ceased to exist."

"Then why cannot I do that now?" asked the Englishman, "since another complete set would cost me probably no more than an extra hundred and fifty pounds?"

The Belgian gestured with hands apart, palms upwards.

"I am banking on the fact that convenience and the time element to you are worth money. I think you need those André Martin papers and my silence in not too long a time. To get another set made would involve a lot more time, and they would not be as good. Those you have are perfect. So you want the papers, and my silence, and both now. The papers you have. My silence costs a thousand pounds."

"Very well, since you put it like that. But what makes you think I have a thousand pounds right here in Belgium?"

The forger smiled tolerantly, as one who knows all the answers but has no rooted objections to exposing them to satisfy the whims of a close friend.

"Monsieur, you are an English gentlemen. It is clear to all. Yet you wish to pass for a middle-aged French working man. Your French is fluent and almost without accent. That is why I put the birthplace of André Martin as Colmar. You know, Alsatians speak French with a trace of accent like your own. You pass through France disguised as André Martin. Perfect, a stroke of genius. Who would ever think of searching an old man like Martin? So whatever you are carrying on you must be valuable. Drugs perhaps? Very fashionable in certain smart English circles these days. And Marseilles is one of the main supply centres. Or diamonds? I do not know. But the business you are in is profitable. English milords do not waste their time with picking pockets on racecourses. Please, monsieur, we stop playing games, *hein?* You telephone your friends in London and ask them to cable a thousand pounds to you at the bank here. Then tomorrow night we exchange packages and—hop—you are on your way, not so?"

The Englishman nodded several times, as if in rueful contemplation of a past life full of errors. Suddenly he raised his head and smiled engagingly at the Belgian. It was the first time the forger had seen him smile, and he felt enormously relieved that this quiet Englishman had taken the matter so calmly without the usual twisting around to seek an outlet. But in the long run no problems. The man had come around. He felt the tension drain out of him.

"Very well," said the Englishman, "you win. I can have a thousand pounds here by noon tomorrow. But there is one condition."

"Condition?" At once the Belgian was wary again.

"We do not meet here."

The forger was baffled. "There is nothing wrong with this place. It is quiet, private—"

"There is everything wrong with this place from my point of view. You have just told me that you took a clandestine picture of me here. I do not wish our little ceremony of handing over our respective packages to be interrupted by the quiet click of a camera from some concealed point where one of your friends has thoughtfully hidden himself . . . "

The Belgian's relief was visible. He laughed aloud.

"You need have no fears of that, *cher ami.* This place is mine, very discreet, and nobody comes in here unless they are invited in by me. One has to be discreet, you understand, for I make a sideline from here in taking pictures for the tourists, you know, very popular but not quite the kind of work one does in a studio on the Grand' Place."

He held up his left hand, the forefinger and thumb forming the letter O, and ran the extended forefinger of the right hand through the circular aperture several times to indicate the sex act in progress.

The Englishman's eyes twinkled. He grinned wide, then started to laugh. The Belgian laughed too at the joke. The Englishman clapped his hands against the Belgian's upper arms, and the finger tightened on the biceps muscles, holding the forger steady, his hands still going through their erotic gestures. The Belgian was still laughing when he got the impression that his private parts had been hit by an express train.

The head jerked forward, the hands discontinued their mime and dropped downwards to the crushed testicles from which the man who held him had withdrawn his right knee, and the laugh turned to a screech, a gurgle, a retch. Half unconscious, he slithered to his knees, then tried to roll forwards and sideways to lie on the floor and nurse himself.

The Jackal let him slip quite gently to his knees. Then he stepped round and over the fallen figure, straddling the exposed back of the Belgian. His right hand slipped round and past the Belgian's neck and with it he gripped his own left biceps. The left hand was placed against the back of the forger's head. He gave one short, vicious twist to the neck, backwards, upwards, and sideways.

The crack as the cervical column snapped was probably not very loud, but in the quiet of the studio it sounded like a small pistol going off. The forger's body gave one last contraction, them slumped as limp as a rag doll. The Jackal held on for a moment longer before letting the body fall face down on the floor. The dead face twisted sideways, hands buried beneath the hips still clutching the privates, tongue protruding slightly between the clenched teeth, half bitten through, eyes open and staring at the faded pattern of the linoleum.

The Englishman walked quickly across to the curtains to make sure they were closed completely, then went back to the body. He turned it over and patted the pockets, finding the keys eventually in the left-hand side of the trousers. In the far corner of the studio stood the large trunk of props and make-up trays. The fourth key he tried opened the lid, and he spent ten minutes removing the contents and piling them in untidy heaps on the floor.

When the trunk was quite empty, the killer lifted the body of the forger by the armpits and hefted it over to the trunk. It went in quite easily, the limp limbs buckling to conform with the contours of the interior of the trunk. Within a few hours rigor mortis would set in, jamming the corpse into its adopted position at the bottom of the case. The Jackal then started replacing the articles that had come out. Wigs, women's underwear, toupees, and anything else that was small and soft were stuffed into the crevices between the limbs. On top went the several trays of make-up brushes and tubes of grease. Finally the jumble of remaining pots of cream, two negligees, some assorted sweaters and jeans, a dressing-gown, and several pairs of black fishnet stockings was placed on top of the body, completely covering it and filling the trunk to the brim. It took a bit of pressure to make the lid close, but then the hasp went home and the padlock was shut.

Throughout the operation the Englishman had handled the pots and jars by wrapping his hand in a piece of cloth from inside the case. Using his own handkerchief he now wiped off the lock and all outer surfaces of the trunk, pocketed the bundle of five-pound notes that still lay on the table, wiped that too, and replaced it against the wall where it had stood when he came in. Finally he put out the light, took a seat on one of the occasional chairs against the wall, and settled down to wait until darkness fell. After a few minutes he took out his box of cigarettes, emptied the remaining ten into one of the side pockets of his jacket, and smoked one of them, using the empty box as the ash-tray and carefully preserving the used stub by putting it into the box when it was finished.

He had few illusions that the disappearance of the forger could remain undetected forever but thought there was a likelihood that a man like that would probably have to go underground or travel out of town at periodic intervals. If any of his friends remarked on his sudden failure to appear at his normal haunts, they would probably put the fact down to that. After a while a search would start, first of all among the people connected with the forging or pornographic photo business. Some of these might know about the studio and visit it, but most would be deterred by the locked door. Anyone who did penetrate into the studio would have to ransack the place, force the lock on the trunk, and empty it before finding the body.

A member of the underworld, doing this, would probably not report the matter to the police, he reasoned, thinking the forger had fallen foul of a gangland boss. No maniac customer interested in pornography alone would have bothered to hide the body so meticulously after a killing in passion. But eventually the police would have to know. At that point a photograph of the forger would doubtless be published, and the barman would probably remember his departure on the evening of August 1 in company with a tall blond man in a check suit and dark glasses. But it was an extremely long shot that anyone would for months to come examine the dead man's deed box, even if he had registered it in his own name.

He had exchanged no words with the barman, and the order for drinks he had given to the waiter in the same bar had been two weeks earlier. The waiter would have to have a phenomenal memory to recall the slight trace of foreign accent in the order for two beers. The police would launch a perfunctory search for a tall blond man, but even if the enquiry got as far as Alexander Duggan, the Belgian police would still have to go a long way to find the Jackal. On balance, he felt he had at least a month, which was what he needed. The killing of the forger was as mechanical as stamping on a cockroach. The Jackal relaxed, finished a second cigarette, and looked outside. It was 9:30, and a deep dusk had descended over the narrow street. He left the studio quietly, locking the outer door behind him. No one passed him as he went quietly down the street. Half a mile away he dropped the unidentifiable keys down a large drain set into the pavement and heard them splash into the water several feet down in the sewer beneath the street. He returned to his hotel in time for a late supper.

The next day, Friday, he spent shopping in one of the working-class suburbs of Brussels. From a shop specialising in camping equipment he bought a pair of hiking boots, long woollen socks, denim trousers, check, woollen shirt, and a haversack. Among his other purchases were several sheets of thin foam rubber, a string shopping bag, a ball of twine, a hunting knife, two thin paint brushes, a tin of pink paint and another of brown. He thought of buying a large Honeydew melon from an open fruit stall, but decided not to, as it would probably go rotten over the weekend.

Back at the hotel he used his new driving licence, now matching his passport in the name of Alexander Duggan, to order a self-drive hire car for the following morning, and prevailed on the head reception clerk to book him a single room with shower/bath for the weekend at one of the resorts along the sea coast. Despite the lack of accommodation available in August, the clerk managed to find him a room in a small hotel overlooking the picturesque fishing harbour of Zeebrugge, and wished him a pleasant weekend by the sea.

SEVEN

While the Jackal was doing his shopping in Brussels, Viktor Kowalski was wrestling with the intricacies of international telephone enquiries from Rome's main post office.

Not speaking Italian, he had sought the aid of the counter clerks, and eventually one of them had agreed that he spoke a little French. Laboriously Kowalski explained to him that he wished to telephone a man in Marseilles,

France, but that he did not know the man's telephone number. Yes, he knew the name and address. The name was Grzybowski. That baffled the Italian, who asked Kowalski to write it down. This Kowalski did, but the Italian, unable to believe that any name could start "Grzyb . . . " spelt it out to the operator at the international exchange as "Grib . . . " thinking that Kowalski's written "z" had to be an "i." No name Josef Gribowski existed in the Marseilles telephone directory, the operator informed the Italian at the other end of the phone. The clerk turned to Kowalski and explained that there was no such person.

Purely by chance, because he was a conscientious man anxious to please a foreigner, the clerk spelt the name out to underline that he had got it right.

"*Il n'existe pas, monsieur. Voyons: jay, air, eee*—"

"*Non, jay, air, zed* . . . " cut in Kowalski.

The clerk looked perplexed.

"*Excusez moi, monsieur. Jay, air, zed? Jay, air, zed, ee-grec, bay?*"

"*Oui*," insisted Kowalski, "G-R-Z-Y-B-O-W-S-K-I."

The Italian shrugged and presented himself to the switchboard operator once again.

"Get me international enquiries, please."

Within ten minutes Kowalski had JoJo's telephone number, and half an hour later he was through. At the end of the line the ex-legionnaire's voice was distorted by crackling, and he seemed hesitant to confirm the bad news in Kovac's letter. Yes, he was glad Kowalski had rung, he had been trying to trace him for three months.

Unfortunately, yes, it was true about the illness of little Sylvie. She had been getting weaker and thinner, and when finally a doctor had diagnosed the illness, it had already been time to put her to bed. She was in the next bedroom at the flat from which JoJo was speaking. No it was not the same flat, they had taken a newer and larger one. What? The address? JoJo gave it slowly, while Kowalski, tongue between pursed lips, slowly wrote it down.

"How long do the quacks give her?" he roared down the line. He got his meaning over to JoJo at the fourth time of trying. There was a long pause.

"*Allo? Allo?*" he shouted when there was no reply. JoJo's voice came back.

"It could be a week, maybe two or three," said JoJo.

Disbelievingly, Kowalski stared at the mouthpiece in his hand. Without a word he replaced it on the cradle and blundered out of the booth. After paying the cost of the call he collected the mail, snapped the steel case on his wrist tight shut, and walked back to the hotel. For the first time in many years his thoughts were in a turmoil, and there was no one to whom he could turn for orders how to solve the problem by violence.

In his flat in Marseilles, the same one he had always lived in, JoJo also put down the receiver when he realized Kowalski had hung up. He turned to find the two men from the Action Service still where they had been, each with his Colt .45 Police Special in his hand. One was trained on JoJo, the other on his wife, who sat ashen-faced in the corner of the sofa. "Bastards," said JoJo with venom. "Shits."

"Is he coming?" asked one of the men.

"He didn't say. He just hung up on me," said the Pole.

The black, flat eyes of the Corsican stared back at him.

"He must come. Those are the orders."

"Well, you heard me. I said what you wanted. He must have been shocked. He just hung up. I couldn't prevent him doing that."

"He had better come, for your sake, JoJo," repeated the Corsican.

"He will come," said JoJo resignedly. "If he can, he will come. For the girl's sake."

"Good. Then your part is done."

"Then get out of here," shouted JoJo, "Leave us alone."

The Corsican rose, the gun still in his hand. The other man remained, seated, looking at the woman.

"We'll be going," said the Corsican, "but you two will come with us. We can't have you talking about the place or ringing Rome now, can we, JoJo?"

"Where are you taking us?"

"A little holiday. A nice pleasant hotel in the mountains. Plenty of sun and fresh air. Good for you, JoJo."

"For how long?" asked the Pole dully.

"For as long as it takes."

The Pole stared out of the window at the tangle of alleys and fish stalls that crouch behind the picture postcard frontage of the Old Port.

"It is the height of the tourist season. The trains are full these days. In August we make more than all the winter. It will ruin us for several years."

The Corsican laughed as if the idea amused him.

"You must consider it rather a gain than a loss, JoJo. After all, it is for France, your adopted country."

The Pole spun round. "I don't give a shit about politics. I don't care who is in power, what party wants to make a fuck-up of everything. But I know people like you. I have been meeting them all my life. You would serve Hitler, your type. Or Mussolini, or the OAS if it suited you. Or anybody. Regimes may change, but bastards like you never change . . . " He was shouting, limping towards the man with the gun whose snout had not quivered a millimetre in the hand that held it.

"JoJo," screamed the woman from the sofa. "I beg you—leave him alone!"

The Pole stopped and stared at his wife as if he had forgotten she was there. He looked round the room at the figures in it one by one. They all looked back at him, his wife imploring, the two Secret Service toughs without noticeable expression. They were used to reproaches which had no effect on the inevitable. The leader of the pair nodded towards the bedroom.

"Get packed. You first, then the wife."

"What about Sylvie? She will be home from school at four. There will be no one to meet her," said the woman.

The Corsican still stared at her husband.

"She will be picked up by us on the way past the school. Arrangements have been made. The headmistress has been told her granny is dying and the whole family has been summoned to her death bed. It's all very discreet. Now move."

JoJo shrugged, gave a last glance at his wife, and went into the bedroom to pack, followed by the Corsican. His wife continued to twist her handkerchief between her hands. After a while she looked up at the other agent on the end of the sofa. He was younger than the Corsican, a Gascon.

"What—what will they do to him?

"Kowalski?"

"Viktor."

"Some gentlemen want to talk to him. That is all."

An hour later the family was in the back seat of a big Citroen, the two agents in the front, speeding towards a very private hotel high in the Vercors.

The Jackal spent the weekend at the seaside. He bought a pair of swimming trunks and spent the Saturday sunning himself on the beach at Zeebrugge, bathed several times in the North Sea, and wandered around the little harbour town and along the mole where British soldiers and sailors had once fought and died in a welter of blood and bullets. Some of the walrus-moustached old men who sat along the mole and threw for sea bass might have remembered forty-six years before, had he asked them, but he did not. The English present that day were a few families scattered along the beach enjoying the sunshine and watching their children play in the surf.

On Sunday morning he packed his bags and drove leisurely through the Flemish countryside, strolling through the narrow streets of Ghent and Bruges. He lunched off the unmatchable steaks broiled over a timber fire served by the Siphon restaurant at Damm, and in the midafternoon turned the car back towards Brussels. Before turning in for the night, he asked for an early call with breakfast in bed and a packed lunch, explaining that he wished to drive into the Ardennes the following day and visit the grave of his elder brother who had died in the Battle of the Bulge between Bastogne and Malmédy. The desk clerk was most solicitous, promising that he would be called without fail for his pilgrimage.

In Rome Viktor Kowalski spent a much less relaxed weekend. He turned up regularly on time for his periods of guard duty, either as the desk man on the landing on the eighth floor, or on the roof by night. He slept little in his periods off duty, mostly lying on his bed off the main passage on the eighth floor, smoking and drinking the rough red wine that was imported by the gallon flagon for the eight ex-legionnaires who made up the guard. The crude Italian rosso could not compare for bite with the Algerian pinard that sloshes inside every legionnaire's pannikin, he thought, but it was better than nothing.

It habitually took Kowalski a long time to make up his mind on anything independently, but by Monday morning he had come to his decision.

He would not be gone long, perhaps just a day, or maybe two days if the planes did not connect properly. In any event, it was something that had to be done. He would explain to the *"patron"* afterwards. He was sure the *"patron"* would understand, even though he would be damned angry. It occurred to him to tell the colonel of the problem and ask for forty-eight hours' leave, but he felt sure that the colonel, although a good commanding officer who also stuck by his men when they got into trouble, would forbid him to go. He would not understand about Sylvie, and Kowalski knew he could never explain. He could never explain anything in words. He sighed heavily as he got up for the Monday morning shift. He was deeply troubled by the thought that for the first time in his life as a legionnaire, he was going to go A.W.O.L.

The Jackal rose at the same time and made his meticulous preparations. He showered and shaved first, then ate the excellent breakfast placed on the tray by his bedside. Taking the case containing the rifle from the locked wardrobe, he carefully wrapped each component in several layers of foam rubber, securing the bundles with twine. These he stuffed into the bottom of his rucksack. On top went the paint tins and brushes, the denim trousers and check shirt, the socks and the boots. The string shopping bag went into one of the outer pockets of the rucksack, the box of bullets into the other.

He dressed himself in one of his habitual striped shirts, a dove-grey lightweight suit as opposed to his usual check worsted ten-ounce, and a pair of light black leather loafers from Gucci. A black silk knitted tie completed the ensemble. He went down to his car, parked in the hotel lot, and locked his rucksack in the trunk. Returning to the foyer, he took delivery of his packed lunch, nodded a reply to the desk clerk's wishes for a *bon voyage,* and by 9 was speeding out of Brussels along the old E 40 highway towards Namur. The flat countryside was already basking in a warm sunshine that gave a hint of a scorching day to come. His road-map told him it was ninety-four miles to Bastogne, and he added a few more to find a quiet place in the hills and forests to the south of the little town. He estimated he would do the hundred miles by noon easily and gunned the Simca Aronde into another long, flat straight across the Walloon plain.

Before the sun had reached its zenith, he was through Namur and Marche, following the signposts that indicated Bastogne was approaching. Passing through the little town that had been torn to pieces by the guns of Hasso von Manteuffel's King Tiger tanks in the winter of 1944, he took the road southwards into the hills. The forests grew thicker, the winding road more frequently darkened by great elms and beeches and less often sliced by a single beam of sunshine between the trees.

Five miles beyond the town the Jackal found a narrow track running off into the forest. He turned the car down it and after another mile found a second trail leading away into the forest. He turned the car a few yards up this and hid it behind a clump of undergrowth. For a while he waited in the cool shade of the forest, smoking a cigarette and listening to the ticking of the engine block as it cooled, the whisper of wind through the upper branches, and the distant cooing of a pigeon.

Slowly he climbed out, unlocked the trunk, and laid the rucksack on the hood. Piece by piece he changed his clothes, folding the impeccable dove-grey suit along the back seat of the Aronde and slipping on the denim slacks. It was warm enough to do without a jacket, and he changed the collared and tied shirt for the lumberjack check shirt. Finally, the expensive shoes gave way to the hiking boots and woollen socks into which he tucked the bottoms of the denims.

One by one he unwrapped the component parts of the rifle, fitting it together piece by piece. The silencer he slipped into one trouser pocket, the telescopic sight into the other. He tipped twenty shells from the box into one breast pocket of his shirt, the single explosive shell, still in its tissue-paper wrapper into the other.

When the rest of the rifle was assembled, he laid it on the hood of the car and went round to the trunk again and took from it the purchase he had made the previous evening from a market stall in Brussels before returning to the hotel, and which had lain in the trunk all night. It was the Honeydew melon. He locked the trunk, tipped the melon into the empty rucksack along with the paint, brushes and hunting knife, locked the car, and set off into the wood. It was just after noon.

Within ten minutes he had found a long, narrow clearing, a glade where from one end one could get a clear vision for 150 yards. Placing the gun beside a tree, he paced out 150 paces, then sought a tree from which the place where he had left the gun was visible. He tipped the contents of the rucksack out onto the ground, prised the lids off both tins of paint, and set to work on the melon. The upper and lower parts of the fruit were painted quickly brown over the dark green skin. The centre section was colored pink. While both colours were still wet, he used his forefinger to draw crudely a pair of eyes, a nose, moustache, and mouth.

Jabbing the knife into the top of the fruit to avoid smearing the paint by finger contact, the Jackal gingerly placed the melon inside the string shopping bag. The big mesh and fine string of the bag in no way concealed either the outline of the melon or the design sketched upon it.

Lastly he jabbed the knife hard into the trunk of the tree about seven feet from the ground, and hung the handles of the shopping bag over the hilt. Against the green bark of the tree the pink and brown melon hung suspended like a grotesque autonomous human head. He stood back and surveyed his handiwork. At 150 yards it would serve its purpose.

He closed the two tins of paint and hurled them far into the forest where they crashed through the undergrowth and disappeared. The brushes he jabbed into the ground gristles foremost and stamped on them until they too were lost to view. Taking the rucksack he went back to the rifle.

The silencer went on easily, swivelling round the end of the barrel until it was tight. The telescopic sight fitted snugly along the top of the barrel. He slipped back the bolt and inserted the first cartridge into the breech. Squinting down the sight, he scoured the far end of the clearing for his hanging target. When he found it, he was surprised to find how large and clear it looked. To all appearances, had it been the head of a living man, it would have been no more than thirty yards away. He could make out the crisscross lines of the string of the shopping bag where it restrained the melon, his own finger smears denoting the main features of the face.

He altered his stance slightly, leaned against a tree to steady his aim, and squinted again. The two crossed wires inside the telescopic sight did not appear to be quite centred, so he reached out with the right hand and twiddled the two adjusting screws until the cross in the sight appeared to be perfectly central. Satisfied, he took careful aim at the centre of the melon and fired.

The recoil was less than he had expected, and the restrained "phut" of the silencer hardly loud enough to have carried across a quiet street. Carrying the gun under his arm, he walked back the length of the clearing and examined the melon. Near the upper right hand edge the bullet had scored its path across the skin of the fruit, snapping part of the string of the shopping bag, and had buried itself in the tree. He walked back again and fired a second time, leaving the setting of the telescopic sight exactly where it had been before.

The result was the same, with half an inch of difference. He tried four shots without moving the screws of the telescopic sight until he was convinced his aim was true, but the sight was firing high and slightly to the right. He adjusted the screws.

This next shot was low and to the left. To make quite sure he again walked the length of the clearing and examined the hole made by the bullet. It had penetrated the lower left corner of the mouth on the dummy head. He tried three more shots with the sights still adjusted to this new position, and the bullets all went in the same area. Finally he moved the sights back by a whisker.

The ninth shot went clean through the forehead, where he had aimed. A third time he walked up to the target, and this time he took a piece of chalk from his pockets and chalked the existing area touched by the bullets—the small cluster to the top and right, the second cluster round the left hand side of the mouth, and the neat hole through the centre of the forehead.

From then on he plugged in succession each eye, the bridge of the nose, the upper lip and the chin. Swinging the target into a profile position he used the last six shots through the temple, ear-hole, neck, cheek, jaw and cranium, only one of them being slightly off-target.

Satisfied with the gun, he noted the positioning of the grub-screws that adjusted the telescopic sight and, taking a tube of balsa wood cement from his pocket, squirted the viscous liquid over the heads of both grub screws and the surface of the bakelite adjacent to them. Half an hour and two cigarettes later the cement was hard, and the sights were set for his eyesight with that particular weapon at 130 metres at spot-on accuracy.

From his other breast pocket he took the explosive bullet, unwrapped it and slid it into the breech of the rifle. He took particularly careful aim at the centre of the melon and fired.

As the last plume of blue smoke curled away from the end of the silencer, the Jackal laid the rifle against the tree and walked down the clearing towards the hanging shopping bag. It sagged, limp and almost empty, against the scarred trunk of the tree. The melon that had absorbed twenty led slugs without coming to pieces had disintegrated. Parts of it had been forced through the mesh of the bag and lay scattered on the grass. Pips and juice dribbled down the bark. The remaining fragments of the fruit's flesh lay broken in the lower end of the shopping bag, which hung like a weary scrotum from the hunting knife.

He took the bag and tossed it into some nearby bushes. The target it had once contained was unrecognisable as anything but pulp. The knife he jerked out of the wood and put back in its sheath. He left the tree, retrieved his rifle, and strolled back to the car.

There each component was carefully wrapped in its swaddling of foam rubber sheeting and replaced in the rucksack, along with his boots, socks, shirt, and slacks. He dressed again in his city clothes, locked the rucksack in the boot, and quietly ate his lunch sandwiches.

When he had finished, he left the drive and drove back to the main road, turning left for Bastogne, Marche, Namur, and Brussels. He was back in the hotel shortly after six, and after taking his rucksack up to his room, descended to settle the charge for the hire car with the desk clerk. Before bathing for dinner, he spent an hour carefully cleaning every part of the rifle and oiling the moving parts, stacked it away in its carrying case, and locked it in the wardrobe. Later that night the rucksack, twine, and several strips of foam rubber were dumped into a corporation refuse basket, and twenty-one used cartridge cases went spinning into the municipal canal.

On the same Monday morning, August 5, Viktor Kowalski was again at the main post office in Rome seeking the help of someone who spoke French. This time he wanted the clerk to telephone the Alitalia flight enquiries office and ask the times of planes during that week from Rome to Marseilles and back. He learned that he had missed the Monday flight, for it was leaving Fiumicino in an hour and he would not have time to catch it. The next direct flight was on Wednesday. No, there were no other airlines running a direct flight to Marseilles from Rome. There were indirect flights; would the Signor be interested in that idea? No? The Wednesday flight? Certainly, it left at 11:15 a.m., arriving at Marignane Airport, Marseilles, shortly after noon. The return flight would be the next day. One booking? Single or return? Certainly, and the name? Kowalski gave the name on the papers he carried in his pocket. With passports abolished within the Common Market, the national identity card would be good enough.

He was asked to be at the Alitalia desk at Fiumicino one hour before take-off on Wednesday. When the clerk put the phone down, Kowalski took the waiting letters, locked them into his etui, and left to walk back to the hotel.

The following morning the Jackal had his last meeting with M. Goossens. He rang him over breakfast, and the armourer announced that he was pleased to say the work was finished. If Monsieur Duggan would like to call at 11 a.m.? And please to bring the necessary items for a final fitting.

He arrived again with half an hour in hand, the small attaché case inside an ordinary empty fibre suitcase that he had bought at a secondhand shop earlier in the morning. For thirty minutes he surveyed the street in which the armourer lived before finally walking quietly to the front door. When M. Goossens let him in, he went on into the office without hesitating. Goossens joined him after locking the front door, and closed the office door behind him.

"No more problems?" asked the Englishman.

"No, this time I think we have it." From behind his desk the Belgian produced several rolls of hessian sacking and laid them on the desk. As he undid them, he laid side by side a series of thin steel tubes, so polished they looked like aluminum. When the last one was laid on the desk he held out his hand for the attaché case containing the component parts of the rifle. The Jackal gave it to him.

One by one, the armourer started to slide the parts of the rifle into the tubes. Each one fitted perfectly.

"How was the target practice?" he enquired as he worked.

"Very satisfactory."

Goossens noticed as he handled the telescopic sight that the adjusting screws had been fixed into place with a blob of balsa wood cement.

"I am sorry the calibrating screws should have been so small," he said. "It is better to work off precise markings, but again it was the size of the original screw heads that got in the way. So I had to use these little grub screws. Otherwise the sight would have never fitted into its tube." He slipped the telescope into the steel tube designed for it, and like the other components it fitted exactly. When the last of the five components of the rifle had disappeared from view, he held up the tiny needle of steel that was the trigger, and the five remaining explosive bullets.

"These, you see, I have had to accommodate elsewhere," he explained. He took the black leather padded butt of the rifle and showed his customer how the leather had been slit with a razor. He pushed the trigger into the stuffing inside and closed the slit with a strip of black insulating tape. It looked quite natural. From the desk drawer he took a lump of circular black rubber about one and a half inches in diameter and two inches long.

From the centre of one circular face a steel stud protruded upwards, threaded like a screw.

"This fits onto the end of the last of the tubes," he explained.

Round the steel stud were five holes drilled downwards into the rubber. Into each one he carefully fitted a bullet, until only the brass percussion caps showed to view.

"When the rubber is fitted, the bullets become quite invisible, and the rubber gives a touch of verisimilitude," he explained. The Englishman remained silent. "What do you think?" asked the Belgian with a touch of anxiety.

Without a word the Englishman took the tubes and examined them one by one. He rattled them, but no sound came from inside, for the interiors were lined with two layers of baize to absorb both shock and noise. The longest of the tubes was twenty inches; it accommodated the barrel and breech of the gun. The others were about a foot each, and contained the two struts, upper and lower, of the stock, the silencer, and the telescope. The butt, with the trigger inside its padding, was separate, as was the rubber knob containing the bullets. As a hunting rifle, let alone an assassin's rifle, it had vanished.

"Perfect," said the Jackal, nodding quietly. "Absolutely what I wanted." The Belgian was pleased. Although an expert in his trade, he enjoyed praise as much as the next man, and he was aware that in his field the customer in front of him was also in the top bracket.

The Jackal took the steel tubes, with the parts of the gun inside them, and wrapped each one carefully in the sacking, placing each piece into the fibre suitcase. When the five tubes, butt, and rubber knob were wrapped and packed, he closed the fibre suitcase and handed the attaché case with its fitted compartments back to the armourer.

"I shall not be needing that any more. The gun will stay where it is until I have occasion to use it." He took the remaining two hundred pounds he owed the Belgian from his inner pocket and put it on the table.

"I think our dealings are complete, M. Goossens." The Belgian pocketed the money.

"Yes, monsieur, unless you have anything else in which I may be of service."

"Only one," replied the Englishman. "You will please remember my little homily to you a fortnight ago on the wisdom of silence."

"I have not forgotten, monsieur," replied the Belgian quietly.

He was frightened again. Would this soft-spoken killer try to silence him now, to ensure his silence? Surely not. The enquiries into such a killing would expose to the police the visits of the tall Englishman to this house long before he ever had a chance to use the gun he now carried in a suitcase. The Englishman seemed to be reading his thoughts. He smiled briefly.

"You do not need to worry. I do not intend to harm you. Besides, I imagine a man of your intelligence has taken certain precautions against being killed by one of his customers. A telephone call expected within an hour perhaps? A friend who will arrive to find the body if the call does not come through? A letter deposited with a lawyer, to be opened in the event of your death? For me, killing you would create more problems than it would solve."

M. Goossens was startled. He had indeed a letter permanently deposited with a lawyer, to be opened in the event of his death. It instructed the police to search under a certain stone in the back garden. Beneath the stone was a box containing a list of those expected to call at the house each day. It was replaced each day. For this day, the note described the only customer expected to call, a tall Englishman of well-to-do appearance who called himself Duggan. It was just a form of insurance.

The Englishman watched him calmly.

"I thought so," he said. "You are safe enough. But I shall kill you, without fail, if you ever mention my visits here or my purchase from you to anyone, anyone at all. So far as you are concerned the moment I leave this house I have ceased to exist."

"That is perfectly clear, monsieur. It is the normal working arrangement with all my customers. I may say, I expect similar discretion from them. That is why the serial number of the gun you carry has been scorched from the barrel with acid. I too must protect myself."

The Englishman smiled again. "Then we understand each other. Good day, Monsieur Goossens."

A minute later the door closed behind him, and the Belgian who knew so much about guns and gunmen but so little about the Jackal breathed a sigh of relief and withdrew to his office to count the money.

The Jackal did not wish to be seen by the staff of his hotel carrying a cheap fibre suitcase so although he was late for lunch he took a taxi straight to the mainline station and deposited the case in the left-luggage office, tucking the ticket into the inner compartment of his slim lizard-skin wallet.

He lunched at the Cygne well and expensively to celebrate the end of the planning and preparation stage in France and Belgium, and walked back to the Amigo to pack and pay his bill. When he left, it was exactly as he had come, in a finely cut check suit, wraparound dark glasses, and with two Vuitton suitcases following him in the hands of the porter down to the waiting taxi. He was also 1600 pounds poorer, but his rifle reposed safely inside an unobtrusive suitcase in the luggage office of the station and three finely forged cards were tucked into an inside pocket of his suit.

The plane left Brussels for London shortly after 4, and although there was a perfunctory search of one of his bags at London Airport, there was nothing to be found, and by 7 he was showering in his own flat before dining out in the West End.

EIGHT

Unfortunately for Kowalski, there were no telephone calls to make at the post office on Wedsnesday morning; had there been he would have missed his plane. And the mail was waiting in the pigeonhole for M. Poitiers. He collected the five envelopes, locked them into his steel carrier on the end of the chain, and set off hurriedly for the hotel. By half past nine he had been relieved of both by Colonel Rodin, and was free to go back to his room for sleep. His next turn of duty was on the roof, starting at 7 that evening.

He paused in his room only to collect his Colt .45 (Rodin would never allow him to carry it on the street) and tucked it into his shoulder holster. If he had worn a well-fitting jacket the bulge of the gun and holster would have been evident at a hundred yards, but his suits were as ill-fitting as a thoroughly bad tailor could make them, and despite his bulk they hung on him like sacks. He took the roll of sticking plaster and the beret that he had bought the day before and stuffed them into his jacket, pocketed the roll of lire notes and French francs that represented his past six months' savings, and closed the door behind him.

At the desk of the landing the duty guard looked up.

"Now they want a telephone call made," said Kowalski, jerking his thumb upwards in the direction of the ninth floor above. The guard said nothing, just watched him as the lift arrived and he stepped inside. Seconds later he was in the street, pulling on the big dark glasses.

At the cafe across the street the man with a copy of *Oggi* lowered the magazine a fraction and studied Kowalski through impenetrable sunglasses as the Pole looked up and down for a taxi. When none came, he started to walk towards the corner of the block. The man with the magazine left the cafe terrace and walked to the kerb. A small Fiat cruised out of a line of parked cars further down the street and stopped opposite him. He climbed in and the Fiat crawled after Kowalski at a walking pace.

On the corner Kowalski found a cruising taxi and hailed it. "Fiumicino," he told the driver.

At the airport the SDECE man followed him quietly as he presented himself at the Alitalia desk, paid for his ticket in cash, assured the girl on the desk that he had no suitcases or hand luggage, and was told passengers for the 11:15 Marseilles flight would be called in an hour and five minutes.

With time to kill, the ex-legionnaire lounged into the cafeteria, bought a coffee at the counter and took it over to the plate glass windows from where he could watch the planes coming and going. He loved airports although he could not understand how airplanes worked. Most of his life the sound of aero engines had meant German Messerschmitts, Russian Stormoviks, or American Flying Forts. Later they meant air support with B-26s or Skyraiders in Vietnam, Mystères or Fougas in the Algerian *djebel*. Now at a civilian airport he liked to watch them cruising in to land like big silver birds, engines muted, hanging in the sky as if on threads just before the touch-down. Although socially a shy man, he liked watching the interminable bustle of an airport. Perhaps, he mused, if his life had been different, he would have worked in an airport. But he was what he was, and there was no going back now.

His thoughts turned to Sylvie, and his beetle brows darkened with concentration. It wasn't right, he told himself soberly, it wasn't right that she should die and all those bastards sitting up in Paris should live. Colonel Rodin had told him about them, and the way they had let France down, and betrayed the army, and destroyed the Legion, and abandoned the people in Indochina and Algeria to the terrorists. Colonel Rodin was never wrong.

His flight was called, and he filed through the glass doors and out into the burning white concrete of the apron for the hundred yard walk to the plane.

From the observation terrace the two agents of Colonel Rolland watched him climb the steps into the plane. He now wore the black beret and the piece of sticking plaster on one cheek. One of the agents turned to the other and raised a weary eyebrow. As the Turbo-prop took off for Marseilles, the two men left the rail. On the way through the main hall they stopped at a public kiosk while one of them dialled a Rome local number. He identified himself to the person at the end with a Christian name and said slowly, "He's gone. Alitalia four-five-one. Landing Marignane twelve-ten. *Ciao.*"

Ten minutes later the message was in Paris, and ten minutes after that it was being listened to in Marseilles.

The Alitalia Viscount swung out over the bay of impossibly blue water and turned onto final approach for Marignane Airport. The pretty Roman air hostess finished her smiling walk down the gangway checking that all seat belts were fastened and sat down in her own corner seat at the back to fasten her own belt. She noticed the passenger in the seat ahead of her was staring fixedly out of the window at the glaring off-white desolation of the Rhône Delta as if he had never seen it before.

He was the big lumbering man who spoke no Italian, and whose French was heavily accented from some motherland in eastern Europe. He wore a black beret over his cropped black hair, a dark and rumpled suit, and a pair of dark glasses which he never took off. An enormous piece of sticking plaster obscured one half of his face; he must have cut himself badly, she thought.

They touched down precisely on time, quite close to the terminal building, and the passengers walked across to the customs hall. As they filed through the glass doors, a small balding man standing beside one of the passport police kicked him lightly in the ankle.

"Big fellow, black beret, sticking plaster." Then he strolled quietly away and gave the other the same message. The passengers divided themselves into two lines to pass through the guichets. Behind their grilles the two policemen sat facing each other, ten feet apart, with the passengers filing between them. Each passenger presented his passport and disembarkation card. The officers were of the Security Police, the DST, responsible for all internal state security inside France, and for checking incoming aliens and returning Frenchmen.

When Kowalski presented himself, the blue-jacketed figure behind the grille barely gave him a glance. He banged his stamp down on the yellow disembarkation card, gave the proffered identity card a short glance, nodded, and waved the big man on. Relieved, Kowalski walked on towards the customs benches. Several of the customs officers had just listened quietly to the small balding man before he disappeared into a glass-fronted office behind them. The senior customs officer called to Kowalski.

"Monsieur, your baggage."

He gestured to where the rest of the passengers were waiting by the mechanical conveyor belt for their suitcases to appear from the wire-frame barrow parked in the sunshine outside.

Kowalski lumbered over to the customs officer. "I have no baggage," he said.

The customs officer raised his eyebrows. "No baggage? Well, have you anything to declare?"

"No, nothing," said Kowalski.

The customs man smiled amiably, a smile almost as broad as his sing-song Marseilles accent.

"Very well, go ahead, monsieur." He gestured towards the exit into the taxi rank. Kowalski nodded and went out into the sunshine. Not being accustomed to spending freely, he looked up and down until he caught sight of the airport bus, and climbed into it.

As he disappeared from sight, several of the other customs men gathered round the senior staffer.

"Wonder what they want him for," said one.

"He looked a surly character."

"He won't be when those bastards have finished with him," said a third jerking his head towards the offices at the back.

"Come on, back to work," chipped in the older one. "We've done our bit for France today."

"For *le Grand Charlie,* you mean," replied the first as they split up, and muttered under his breath, "God rot him."

It was the lunch-hour when the bus stopped finally at the Air France offices in the heart of the city, and it was even hotter than in Rome. August in Marseilles has several qualities, but the inspiration to great exertions is not one of them. The heat lay on the city like an illness, crawling into every fibre, sapping strength, energy, the will to do anything but lie in a cool room with the jalousies closed and the fan full on.

Even the Cannebière, usually the bustling bursting jugular vein of Marseilles, after dark a river of light and animation, was dead. The few people and cars on it seemed to be moving through waist-deep treacle. It took half an hour to find a taxi; most of the drivers had found a shady spot in a park to have their siesta.

The address JoJo had given Kowalski was on the main road out of town heading towards Cassis. At the Avenue de la Libération, he told the driver to drop him, so that he could walk the rest. The driver's *"si vous voulez"* indicated plainer than text what he thought of foreigners who considered covering distances of over a few yards in this heat when they had a car at their disposal.

Kowalski watched the taxi turn back into town until it was out of sight. He found the side street named on the piece of paper by asking a waiter at a terrace cafe on the sidewalk. The block of flats looked fairly new, and Kowalski thought the JoJos must have made a good thing of their station food trolley. Perhaps they had got the fixed kiosk that Madame JoJo had had her eyes on for so many years. That at any rate would account for the increase in their prosperity. And it would be nicer for Sylvie to grow up in this neighborhood than round the docks. At the thought of his daughter, and the idiotic thing he had just imagined for her, Kowalski stopped at the foot of the steps to the apartment block. What had JoJo said on the phone. A week? Perhaps two? It was not possible.

He took the steps at a run and paused in front of the double row of letter boxes along one side of the hall. Grzybowski, read one, Apartment 23. He decided to take the stairs since it was only on the second floor.

Apartment 23 had a door like the others. It had a bell-push with a little white card in a slot beside it, with the word "Grzybowski" typed on it. The door stood at the end of the corridor, flanked by the doors of apartments 22 and 24. He pressed the bell. The door in front of him opened and the lunging pickaxe handle swung out of the gap and down towards his forehead.

The blow split the skin but bounced off the bone with a dull "thunk." On each side of the Pole the doors of apartments 22 and 24 opened inwards and men surged out. It all happened in less than half a second. In the same time Kowalski went berserk. Although slow-thinking in most ways, the Pole knew one technique perfectly, that of fighting.

In the narrow confines of the corridor his size and strength were useless to him. Because of his height the pickaxe handle had not reached the full momentum of its downward swing before hitting his head. Through the blood spurting over his eyes he discerned there were two men in the door in front of him and two others on each side. He needed room to move, so he charged forward into Apartment 23.

The man directly in front of him staggered back under the impact; those behind closed in, hands reaching for his collar and jacket. Inside the room he drew the Colt from under his armpit, turned once and fired back into the doorway. As he did so another stave slammed down on his wrist, jerking the aim downwards.

The bullet ripped the kneecap off one of his assailants, who went down with a thin screech. Then the gun was out of his hand, the fingers rendered nerveless from another blow on the wrist. A second later he was overwhelmed as the five men hurled themselves at him. The fight lasted three minutes. A doctor later estimated he must have taken a score of blows to the head from the leather-wrapped coshes before he finally passed out. A part of one of his ears was slashed off by a glancing blow, the nose was broken, and the face was a deep-red mask.

Most of his fighting was by reflex action. Twice he almost reached his gun, until a flying foot sent it spinning to the other end of the sitting room. When he did finally go down onto his face, there were only three attackers left standing to put the boot in.

When they had done and the enormous body on the floor was insensible, only a trickle of blood from the slashed scalp indicating that it was still alive, the three survivors stood back swearing viciously, chests heaving. Of the others, the man shot in the leg was curled against the wall by the door, white-faced, glistening red hands clutching his wrecked knee, a long monotonous stream of obscenities coming through pain-grey lips. Another was on his knees, rocking slowly back and forward, hand thrust deep into the torn groin. The last lay face down on the carpet not far from the Pole, a dull bruise discolouring his left temple where one of Kowalski's haymakers had caught him at full force.

The leader of the group rolled Kowalski over onto his back and flicked up one of the closed eyelids. He crossed to the telephone near the window, dialled a local number, and waited.

He was still breathing hard. When the phone was answered he told the person at the other end, "We got him. . . . Fought? Of course he bloody fought. . . . He got off one bullet, Guerini's lost a kneecap. Capetti took one in the balls and Vissart is out cold. . . . What? Yes, the Pole's alive, those were the orders, weren't they? Otherwise he wouldn't have done all this damage. . . .Well, he's hurt, all right. Dunno, he's unconscious. . . . Look, we don't want a salad basket, we want a couple of ambulances. And make it quick."

He slammed the receiver down and muttered "*Cons*" to the world in general. Round the room the fragments of shattered furniture lay about like firewood, which was all they would be good for. They had all thought the Pole would go down in the passage outside. None of the furniture had been stacked in a neighbouring room, and it had got in the way. He himself had stopped an armchair thrown by Kowalski with one hand full in the chest, and it hurt. Goddamn Pole, he thought, the jerks at the head office hadn't said what he was like.

Fifteen minutes later two Citroen ambulances slid into the road outside the block, and the doctor came up. He spent five minutes examining Kowalski. Finally he drew back the unconscious man's sleeve and gave him an injection. As the two stretcher bearers staggered away towards the lift with the Pole, the doctor turned to the wounded Corsican who had been regarding him balefully from his pool of blood beside the wall.

He prised the man's hands away from his knee, took a look, and whistled.

"Right. Morphine and the hospital. I'm going to give you a knockout shot. There's nothing I can do here. Anyway, *mon petit,* your career in this line is over."

Guerini answered him with a stream of obscenities as the needle went in.

Vissart was sitting up with his hands to his head, a dazed expression on his face. Capetti was upright by now, leaning against the wall retching dry. Two of his colleagues gripped him under the armpits and led him hobbling from the flat into the corridor. The leader helped Vissart to his feet as the stretcher bearers from the second ambulance carried the inert form of Guerini away.

Out in the corridor the leader of the six took a last look back into the desolated room. The doctor stood beside him.

"Quite a mess, *hein?*" said the doctor.

"The local office can clean it up," said the leader. "It's their goddamn apartment."

With that he closed the door. The doors of apartments 22 and 24 were also open, but the interiors were untouched. He pulled the doors closed.

"No neighbours?" asked the doctor.

"No neighbours," said the Corsican, "we took the whole floor."

Preceded by the doctor, he helped the still dazed Vissart down the stairs to the waiting cars.

Twelve hours later, after a fast drive the length of France, Kowalski was lying in a cot in a cell beneath a fortress barracks outside Paris. The room had the inevitable white-washed walls, stained and musty, of all prison cells, with here and there a scratched obscenity or prayer. It was hot and close, with an odour of carbolic acid, sweat, and urine. The Pole lay face up on a narrow iron cot whose legs were embedded in the concrete floor. Apart from the biscuit mattress and a rolled-up blanket under his head, the cot contained no other linen. Two heavy leather straps secured his ankles, two more his thighs and wrists. A single strap pinned his chest down. He was still unconscious, but breathing deeply and irregularly.

The face had been bathed clean of blood, the ear and scalp sutured. A stick of plaster spanned the broken nose, and through the open mouth out of which the breath rasped could be seen the stumps of two broken front teeth. The rest of the face was badly bruised.

Beneath the thick mat of black hair covering the chest, shoulders, and belly other livid bruises could just be discerned, the results of fists, boots, and coshes. The right wrist was heavily bandaged and taped.

The man in the white coat finished his examination, straightened up, and replaced his stethoscope in his bag. He turned and nodded at the man behind him, who tapped at the door. It swung open and the pair of them went outside. The door swung to, and the gaoler slid home the two enormous steel bars.

"What did you hit him with, an express train?" asked the doctor as they walked down the passage.

"It took six men to do that," replied Colonel Rolland.

"Well, they did a pretty good job. They damn nearly killed him. If he weren't built like a bull they would have done."

"It was the only way," replied the Colonel. "He ruined three of my men."

"It must have been quite a fight."

"It was. Now, what's the damage?"

"In layman's terms: possible fracture of the right wrist—I haven't been able to do an X-ray, remember—plus lacerated left ear, scalp, and broken nose. Multiple cuts and bruising, slight internal haemorrhaging, which could get worse and kill him or could clear up on its own. He enjoys what one might call a rude good health—or he did. What worries me is the head. There's concussion all right, whether mild or severe is not easy to say. No signs of a skull fracture, though that was not the fault of your men. He's just got a skull like solid ivory. But the concussion could get worse if he's not left alone."

"I need to put certain questions to him," observed the Colonel, studying the tip of his glowing cigarette. The doctor's prison clinic lay one way, the stairs leading to the ground floor the other. Both men stopped. The doctor glanced at the head of the Action Service with distaste.

"This is a prison," he said quietly. "All right, it's for offenders against the security of the state. But I am still the prison doctor. Elsewhere in this prison what I say, concerning prisoners' health, goes. That corridor"—he jerked his head backwards in the direction from which they had come—"is your preserve. It has been most lucidly explained to me that what happens down there is none of my business, and I have no say in it. But I will say this: if you start 'questioning' that man before he's recovered, with your methods, he'll either die or become a raving lunatic."

Colonel Rolland listened to the doctor's bitter prediction without moving a muscle.

"How long?" he asked. The doctor shrugged.

"Impossible to say. He may regain consciousness tomorrow, or not for days. Even if he does, he will not be fit for questioning—medically fit, that is—for at least two weeks. At the very least. That is, if the concussion is only mild."

"There are certain drugs," murmured the Colonel.

"Yes, there are. And I have no intention of prescribing them. You may be able to get them, you probably can. But not from me. In any case, nothing he could tell you now would make the slightest sense. It would probably be gibberish. His mind is undoubtedly scrambled. It may clear, it may not. But if it does, it must happen in its own time. Mind-bending drugs now would simply produce an idiot, no use to you or anyone else. It will probably be a week before he flickers an eyelid. You'll just have to wait."

With that he turned on his heel and walked back to his clinic.

But the doctor was wrong. Kowalski opened his eyes three days later, on August 10, and the same day had his first and only session with the interrogators.

The Jackal spent the three days after his return from Brussels putting the final touches to his preparations for his forthcoming mission into France.

With his new driving licence in the name of Alexander James Quentin Duggan in his pocket, he went down to Fanum House, headquarters of the Automobile Association, and acquired an International Driving Licence in the same name.

He bought a matching series of leather suitcases from a second hand shop specialising in travel goods. Into one he packed the clothes that would, if necessary, disguise him as Pastor Per Jensen of Copenhagen. Before the packing he transferred the Danish maker's labels from the three ordinary shirts he had bought in Copenhagen to the clerical shirt, dog-collar, and black bib that he had bought in London. These clothes joined the shoes, socks, underwear, and charcoal grey light suit that might one day make up the persona of Pastor Jensen. Into the same suitcase went the clothes of American student Marty Schulberg, loafers, socks, jeans, sweat-shirts, and windbreaker.

Slitting the lining of the suitcase, he inserted between the two layers of leather that comprised the stiffened sides of the case the passport of the two foreigners he might one day wish to become. The last additions to this case-ful of clothes were the Danish book on French Cathedrals, the two sets of spectacles, one for the Dane, the other for the American, the two different sets of tinted contact lenses, carefully wrapped in tissue paper, and the preparations for hair tinting.

Into the second case went the shoes, socks, shirt, and trousers of French make and design that he had bought in the Paris Flea Market, along with the ankle-length greatcoat and black beret. Into the lining of this case he inserted the false papers of the middle-aged Frenchman André Martin. This case remained partly empty, for it would soon also have to hold a series of narrow steel tubes containing a complete sniper's rifle and ammunition.

The third, slightly smaller suitcase was packed with the effects of Alexander Duggan: shoes, socks, underwear, shirts, ties, handkerchiefs, and three elegant suits. Into the lining of this case went several thin wads of ten-pound notes to the value of a thousand pounds, which he had drawn from his private bank account on his return from Brussels.

Each of these cases was carefully locked and the keys transferred to his private key-ring. The dove-grey suit was cleaned and pressed, then left hanging in the wall cupboard of his flat. Inside the breast pocket were his passport, driving licence, international licence, and a folder containing a hundred pounds in cash.

Into the last piece of his luggage, a neat hand case, went shaving tackle, pyjamas, sponge-bag and towel, and the final pieces of his purchases—a light harness of finely sewn webbing, a two-pound bag of plaster of Paris, several rolls of large-weave lint bandages, half a dozen rolls of sticky plaster, three packs of cotton wool, and a pair of stout shears with blunt but powerful blades. The grip would travel as hand-luggage, for it was his experience that in passing customs at whatever airport an attaché case was not usually the piece of luggage selected by the customs officer for an arbitrary request to open up.

With his purchases and packing completed, he had reached the end of his planning. The disguises of Pastor Jensen and Marty Schulberg, he hoped, were merely precautionary tactics which would probably never be used unless things went wrong and the identity of Alexander Duggan had to be abandoned. The identity of André Martin was vital to his plan, and it was possible that the two others would never be required. In that event the entire suitcase could be abandoned in a left-luggage office when the job was over. Even then, he reasoned, he might need either of them for his escape. André Martin and the gun could also be abandoned when the job was over, as he would have no further use for them. Entering France with three suitcases and an attaché case, he estimated he would leave with one suitcase and the hand luggage, certainly not more.

With this task finished, he settled down to wait for the two pieces of paper that would set him on his way. One was the telephone number in Paris which could be used to feed him information concerning the exact state of readiness of the security forces surrounding the French President. The other was the written notification from Herr Meier in Zurich that 250,000 dollars had been deposited in his numbered bank account.

While he was waiting for them, he passed the time by practising walking round his flat with a pronounced limp. Within two days he was satisfied that he had a sufficiently realistic limp to prevent any observer from being able to detect that he had not sustained a broken ankle or leg.

The first letter he awaited arrived on the morning of August 9. It was an envelope postmarked in Rome and bore the message: "Your friend can be contacted at Molitor 5901. Introduce yourself with the words '*Ici Chacal.*' Reply will be '*Ici Valmy.*' Good luck."

It was not until the morning of the 11th that the letter from Zurich arrived. He grinned openly as he read the confirmation that, come what may, provided he remained alive, he was a wealthy man for the rest of his life. If his forthcoming operation was successful, he would be even richer. He had no doubts that he would succeed. Nothing had been left to chance.

He spent the rest of that morning on the telephone booking air passages, and fixed his departure for the following morning, August 12.

The cellar was silent except for the sound of breathing, heavy but controlled, from the five men behind the table, a rasping rattle from the man strapped to the heavy oaken chair in front of it. One could not tell how big the cellar was, nor what was the colour of the walls. There was only one pool of light in the whole place, and it encircled the oak chair and the prisoner. It was a standard table lamp such as is often used for reading, but its bulb was of great power and brightness, adding to the overpowering warmth of the cellar. The lamp was clipped to the left-hand edge of the table, and the adjustable shade was turned so that it shone straight at the chair six feet away.

Part of the circle of light swept across the stained wood of the table, illuminating here and there the tips of a set of fingers, a hand and wrist, a clipped cigarette sending a thin stream of blue smoke upwards.

So bright was the light that by contrast the rest of the cellar was in darkness. The torsos and shoulders of the five men behind the table in a row were invisible to the prisoner. The only way he could have seen his questioners would have been to leave his chair and move to the side, so that the indirect glow from the light picked out their silhouettes.

This he could not do. Padded straps pinned his ankles firmly against the legs of the chair. From each of these legs, front and back, an L-shaped steel bracket was bolted into the floor. The chair had arms, and the wrists of the prisoner were secured to these also by padded straps. Another strap ran round his waist and a third round his massive hairy chest. The padding of each was drenched with sweat.

Apart from the quiescent hands, the top of the table was almost bare. Its only other decoration was a slit bordered in brass and marked along one side with figures. Out of the slit protruded a narrow brass arm with a bakelite knob on the top, which could be moved backwards and forwards up and down the slit. Beside this was a simple on/off switch. The right hand of the man on the end of the table rested negligently close to the controls. Little black hairs crawled along the back of the hand.

Two wires fell beneath the table, one from the switch, the other from the current control, towards a small electrical transformer lying on the floor near the end man's feet. From here a stouter, rubber-clad black cable led to a large socket in the wall behind the group.

In the far corner of the cellar, behind the questioners, a single man sat at a wooden table, face to the wall. A tiny glow of green came from the "on" light of the tape recorder in front of him, although the spools were still.

Apart from the breathing, the silence of the cellar was almost tangible. All the men were in shirt sleeves, rolled up high and damp with sweat. The odour was crushing, a stench of sweat, metal, stale smoke, and human vomit. Even the latter, pungent enough, was overpowered by one even stronger, the unmistakeable reek of fear and pain.

The man in the centre spoke at last. The voice was civilised, gentle coaxing.

"*Ecoute, mon p'tit* Viktor. You are going to tell us. Not now perhaps. But eventually. You are a brave man. We know that. We salute you. But even you cannot hold out much longer. So why not tell us? You think Colonel Rodin would forbid you if he were here. He would order you to tell us. He knows about these things. He would tell us himself to spare you more discomfort. You yourself know, they always talk in the end. *N'est-ce pas,* Viktor? You have seen them talk, *hein?* No one can go on and on and on. So why not now, *hein?* Then back to bed. And sleep, and sleep and sleep. No one will disturb you. . . ."

The man in the chair raised a battered face, glistening with sweat, into the light. The eyes were closed, whether by the great blue bruises caused by the feet of the Corsicans in Marseilles or by the light, one could not tell. The face looked at the table and the blackness in front of it for a while, the mouth opened and tried to speak. A small gobbet of puke emerged and dribbled down the matted chest to the pool of vomit in his lap. The head sagged back until the chin touched the chest again. As it did so the shaggy hair shook from side to side in answer. The voice from behind the table began again.

"Viktor, *écoute-moi.* You're a hard man. We all know that. We all recognise that. You have beaten the record already. But even you can't go on. But we can, Viktor, we can. If we have to, we can keep you alive and conscious for days, weeks. No merciful oblivion like in the old days. One is technical nowadays. There are drugs, *tu sais.* Third degree is finished now, probably gone for good. So why not talk. We understand, you see. We know about the pain. But the little crabs, they do not understand. They just don't understand, Viktor. They just go on and on. . . . You want to tell us, What are they doing in that hotel in Rome? What are they waiting for?"

Lolling against the chest, the great head shook slowly from side to side. It was as if the closed eyes were examining first one and then the other of the little copper crabs that gripped the nipples, or the single larger one whose serrated teeth clipped each side of the head of the penis.

The hands of the man who had spoken lay in front of him in a pool of light, slim, white, full of peace. He waited a few moments longer. One of the white hands separated itself from the other, the thumb tucked into the palm, the four fingers spread wide, and laid itself on the table.

At the far end of the hand of the man by the electric switch moved the brass handle up the scale from figure two to figure four, then took the on/off switch between finger and thumb.

The hand further along the wooden top withdrew the splayed fingers, lifted the forefinger once into the air, then pointed the fingertip downwards in the worldwide signal for "Go." The electric switch went on.

The little metal crabs fixed to the man in the chair and linked by wires to the on/off switch appeared to come alive with a slight buzzing. In silence the huge form in the chair rose as if by levitation, propelled by an unseen hand in the small of the back. The legs and wrists bulged outwards against the straps until it seemed that even with the padding the leather must cut clean through the flesh and bone. The eyes, medically unable to see clearly through the puffed flesh around them, defied medicine and started outwards, bulging into vision and staring at the ceiling above. The mouth was open as if in surprise and it was half a second before the demonic scream came out of the lungs. When it did come, it went on and on and on. . . .

Viktor Kowalski broke at 4:10 in the afternoon, and the tape recorder went on.

As he started to talk, or rather ramble incoherently between whimpers and squeaks, the calm voice from the man in the centre cut across the maunderings with incisive clarity.

"Why are they there, Viktor . . .in that hotel . . .Rodin, Montclair, and Casson . . .what are they afraid of . . .where have they been, Viktor . . .whom have they seen . . .why do they see nobody, Viktor . . .tell us, Viktor . . .why Rome . . .before Rome . . .why Vienna, Viktor . . .where in Vienna . . .which hotel . . .why were they there, Viktor . . ."

Kowalski was finally silent after fifty minutes, his last ramblings as he went into relapse being recorded on tape until they stopped. The voice behind the table continued, more gently, for another few minutes until it became clear there were going to be no more answers. Then the man in the centre gave an order to his subordinates, and the session was over.

The tape recording was taken off the spool and rushed by a fast car from the cellar beneath the fortress into the outskirts of Paris and the offices of the Action Service.

The brilliant afternoon that had warmed the friendly pavements of Paris throughout the day faded to golden dusk, and at nine the street lights came on. Along the banks of the Seine the couples strolled as always on summer nights, hand in hand, slowly as if drinking in the wine of dusk and love and youth that will never, however hard they try, be quite the same again. The open-fronted cafes along the water's edge were alive with chatter and clink of glasses, greetings and mock protests, raillerie and compliments, apologies and passes. The magic of the river Seine on an August evening. Even the tourists were almost forgiven for being there and bringing their dollars with them.

In a small office near the Porte des Lilas the insouciance did not penetrate. Three men sat round a tape recorder that turned slowly on a desk. Through the late afternoon and evening they worked. One man controlled the switches, continuously flicking the spools into playback or re-wind and then playback again on the instruction of the second. This man had a pair of earphones over his head, brow furrowed in concentration as he tried to decipher meaningful words out of the jumble of sounds coming through the phones. A cigarette clipped between his lips, rising blue smoke making his eyes water, he signed with his fingers to the operator when he wanted to hear a passage again. Sometimes he listened to a ten-second passage half a dozen times before nodding to the operator to hold on. Then he would dictate the last passage of speech.

The third man, a young blond, sat behind a typewriter and waited for dictation. The questions that had been asked in the cellar beneath the fortress were easy to understand, coming clear and precise through the earphones. The answers were more disjointed. The typist wrote the transcript like an interview, the questions always on a fresh line and beginning with the letter Q. The answers were on the next line, beginning with the letter R. These were disjointed, involving the use of plenty of spacing dots where the sense broke up completely.

It was nearly twelve midnight before they had finished. Despite the open window, the air was blue with smoke and smelt like a powder magazine.

The three men rose stiff and weary. Each stretched in his own fashion to untwine the bunched and aching muscles. One of the three reached for the telephone, asked for an outside line, and dialled a number. The man with the earphones took them off and re-wound the tape back onto the original spool. The typist took the last sheets out of his machine, extracted the carbons from between them and began to arrange the separate piles of paper into sets of the confession in order of pages. The top set would go to Colonel Rolland, the second to files, and the third to mimeograph for extra copies to be made for department heads, to be distributed if Rolland deemed fit.

The call reached Colonel Rolland at the restaurant where he had been dining with friends. As usual the elegant-looking bachelor civil servant had been his witty and gallant self, and his compliments to the ladies present had been much appreciated, by them if not by their husbands. When the waiter called him to the phone, he apologised and left. The phone was on the counter. The Colonel said simply "Rolland" and waited while his operative at the other end identified himself.

Rolland then did the same by introducing into the first sentence of his conversation the correct pre-arranged word. A listener would have learned that he had received information that his car, which had been under repair, was mended, and could be collected at the Colonel's convenience. Colonel Rolland thanked his informant, and returned to the table. Within five minutes he was excusing himself with urbanity, explaining that he faced a hard day in the morning and ought to get his ration of sleep. Ten minutes later he was alone in his car, speeding through the still crowded city streets towards the quieter faubourg of Porte des Lilas. He reached his office soon after one in the morning, took off his immaculate dark jacket, ordered coffee from the night staff, and rang for his assistant.

The top copy of Kowalski's confession came with the coffee. The first time, he read the twenty-six pages of the dossier quickly, trying to grasp the gist of what the demented legionnaire had been saying. Something in the middle caught his eye, causing him to frown, but he read on to the end without a pause.

His second reading was slower, more cautious, giving greater concentration to each paragraph. The third time, he took a black felt-nib pen from the tray in front of the blotter and read even more slowly, drawing the thick black line of ink through the words and passages relating to Sylvie, Luke-something, Indochina, Algeria, JoJo, Kovacs, Corsican bastards, the Legion. All these he understood, and they did not interest him.

Much of the wandering concerned Sylvie, some of it a woman called Julie, which meant nothing to Rolland. When all this was deleted, the confession would not have covered more than six pages. Out of the remaining passages he tried to make some sense. There was Rome. The three leaders were in Rome. Well, he knew that anyway. But why? This question had been asked eight times. By and large the answer had been the same each time. They did not wish to be kidnapped as Argoud had been in February. Natural enough, thought Rolland. Had he then been wasting his time with the whole Kowalski operation? There was one word the legionnaire had mentioned twice, or rather mumbled twice, in answering these eight identical questions. The word was "secret." As an adjective? There was nothing secret about their presence in Rome. Or as a noun. What secret?

Rolland went through to the end for the tenth time, then back again to the beginning. The three OAS men were in Rome. They were there because they did not wish to be kidnapped. They did not wish to be kidnapped because they possessed a secret.

Rolland smiled ironically. He had known better than General Guibaud that Rodin would not run for cover because he was frightened.

So they knew a secret, did they? What secret? It all seemed to have stemmed from something in Vienna. Three times the word Vienna cropped up, but at first Rolland had thought it must be the town called Vienne that lies twenty miles south of Lyon. But perhaps it was the Austrian capital, not the French provincial town.

They had a meeting in Vienna. Then they went to Rome and took refuge against the possibility of being kidnapped and interrogated until they revealed a secret. The secret must stem from Vienna.

The hours passed, and so did innumerable cups of coffee. The pile of stubs in the shell-case ashtray grew. Before the thin line of paler grey started to tip the grisly industrial suburbs that lie east of the Boulevard Mortier,

Colonel Rolland knew he was on to something.

There were pieces missing. Were they really missing, gone for all time since the message by phone at three in the morning had told him Kowalski would never be questioned again because he was dead? Or were they hidden somewhere in the jumbled text that had come out of the deranged brain as the final reserves of strength failed?

With his right hand Rolland began to jot down pieces of the puzzle that had no seeming place to be there. Kleist, a man called Kleist. Kowalski, being a Pole, had pronounced the word correctly, and Rolland, knowing some German still from his wartime days, wrote it down correctly although it had been spelt wrongly by the French transcriber. Or was it a person? A place perhaps? He rang the switchboard and asked them to seek out the Viennese telephone directory and search for a person or place called Kleist. The answer was back in ten minutes. There were two columns of Kleists in Vienna, all private individuals, and two places of that name: the Ewald Kleist primary school for boys, and the Pension Kleist in the Brucknerallee. Rolland noted both, but underlined the Pension Kleist. Then he read on.

There were several references to a foreigner over whom Kowalski seemed to have mixed feelings. Sometimes he used the word "*bon*," meaning good, to refer to this man; at other times he called him a "*fâcheur*," an annoying or irritating type. Shortly after 5 a.m. Colonel Rolland sent for the tape and tape recorder, and spent the next hour listening to it. When he finally switched off the machine he swore quietly and violently to himself. Taking a fine pen he made several alterations to the transcribed text.

Kowalski had referred to the foreigner not as "*bon*" but as "*blond*." And the word coming from the torn lips that had been written down as "*fâcheur*" had in reality been "*faucheur*," meaning a killer.

From then on the task of piecing together Kowalski's hazy meaning was easy. The word for jackal, which had been crossed out wherever it occurred because Rolland had thought it was Kowalski's way of insulting the men who had hunted him down and were torturing him, took on a new meaning. It became the code name of the killer with the blond hair, who was a foreigner, and whom the three OAS chiefs had met at the Pension Kleist in Vienna days before they had gone into heavily protected hiding in Rome.

Rolland could work out for himself the reason now for the wave of bank and jewel robberies that had rocked France over the preceding eight weeks. The blond, whoever he was, wanted money to do a job for the OAS. There was only one job in the world that could command that kind of money. The blond had not been called in to settle a gang fight.

At seven in the morning Rolland called his communications room and ordered the night duty operator to send off a "blitz" imperative to the SDECE office in Vienna, overriding interdepartmental protocol under which Vienna was within the district of R 3 Western Europe. Then he called in every copy of the Kowalski confession and locked them all in his safe. Finally he sat down to write a report, which had only one listed recipient and was headed "for your eyes only."

He wrote carefully in longhand, describing briefly the operation which he had personally mounted of his own initiative to capture Kowalski; relating the return of the ex-legionnaire to Marseilles, lured by the ruse of a false belief that someone close to him was ill in hospital, the capture by Action

Service agents, a brief mention for the record that the man had been interrogated by agents of the Service and had made a garbled confession. He felt bound to include a bald statement that in resisting arrest the ex-legionnaire had crippled two agents but had also done himself sufficient damage in an attempt at suicide that by the time he was overcome the only possible recourse was to hospitalize him. It was here, from his sick bed, that he had made his confession.

The rest of the report, which was the bulk, concerned the confession itself and Rolland's interpretation of it. When he had finished this he paused for a moment, scanning the roof-tops now gilded by the morning sun streaming in from the east. Rolland had a reputation, as he was well aware, for never overstating his case or exaggerating an issue. He composed his final paragraph with care.

"Enquiries with the intention of establishing corroborative evidence for the existence of this plot are still under way at the hour of writing. However, in the event that these enquiries should indicate the above is the truth, the plot described above constitutes in my view the most dangerous single conception that the terrorists could possibly have devised to endanger the life of the President of France. If the plot exists as described, and if the foreign-born assassin known only by the code-name of the Jackal has been engaged for this attempt on the life of the President, and is even now preparing his plans to execute the deed, it is my duty to inform you that in my opinion we face a national emergency."

Most unusually for him, Colonel Rolland typed the final copy of the report himself, sealed it in an envelope with his personal seal, addressed it, and stamped it with the highest security classification in the Secret Service. Finally he burned the sheets of foolscap on which he had written in longhand and washed the ashes down the plug of the small hand basin in a cabinet in the corner of his office.

When he had finished he washed his hands and face. As he dried them he glanced in the mirror above the wash-stand. The face that stared back at him was, he ruefully admitted, losing its handsomeness. The lean face that had been so dashing in youth and so attractive to women in maturity was beginning to look tired and strained in middle age. Too many experiences, too much knowledge of the depths of bestiality to which man could sink when he fought for his survival against his fellow man, and too much scheming and double-crossing, sending men out to die or to kill, to scream in cellars or to make other men scream in cellars, had aged the head of the Action Service far beyond his fifty-four years. There were two lines down the side of the nose and on down beyond the corners of the mouth that, if they got much longer, would no more be distinguished but simply peasant-like. Two dark smudges seemed to have settled permanently under the eyes, and the elegant grey of the sideburns was becoming white without turning silver.

"At the end of this year," he told himself, "I really am going to get out of this racket." The face looked back at him haggard. Disbelief or simply resignation? Perhaps the face knew better than the mind did. After a certain number of years there was no getting out any more. One was what one was for the rest of one's days. From the Resistance to the security police, then the SDECE, and finally the Action Service. How many men, and how much blood in all those years? he asked the face in the mirror. And all for France. And what the hell does France care? And the face looked back out of the mirror, and said nothing. For they both knew the answer.

Colonel Rolland summoned a motorcycle despatch rider to report to him personally in his office. He also ordered fried eggs, rolls and butter, and more coffee, but this time a large cup of milky coffee, with aspirins for his headache. He handed over the package with his seal and gave the despatch rider his orders. Finishing his eggs and rolls, he took his coffee and drank it on the sill of the open window, the corner that faced towards Paris. He could make out across the miles of roofs the spires of Notre Dame and, in the already hot morning haze that hung over the Seine, the Eiffel Tower further on. It was already well after nine o'clock on the morning of August 11, and the city was busily at work, probably cursing the motorcyclist in the black leather jerkin and the wailing siren who slewed his machine through the traffic towards the eighth arrondissement.

Depending on whether the menace described in the despatch on that motorcyclist's hip could be averted, thought Rolland, might hang whether or not at the end of the year he had a job to retire from.

NINE

The Minister of the Interior sat at his desk later that morning and stared sombrely out of the window into the sunlit circular courtyard beneath. At the far end of the courtyard were the beautifully wrought iron gates, decorated on each half with the coat of arms of the Republic of France, and beyond them the Place Beauvau where streams of traffic from the Faubourg Saint Honoré and the Avenue de Marigny hooted and swirled around the policeman directing them from the centre of the square.

From the other two roads that led into the square, the Avenue de Miromesnil and the rue des Saussaies, other streams of traffic would emerge on a whistled command from the policeman to cross the square and disappear on their way. He seemed to be playing the five streams of lethal Parisian traffic as a bullfighter plays a bull, calmly, with aplomb, dignity, and mastery. M. Roger Frey envied him the ordered simplicity of his task, the assured confidence he brought to it.

At the gates of the ministry two other gendarmes watched their colleague's virtuosity in the centre of the square. They carried submachine guns slung across their backs, and looked out on the world through the wrought-iron grille of the double gates, protected from the furor of the world beyond, assured of their monthly salaries, their continuing careers, their places in the warm August sunshine. The Minister envied them too, for the uncomplicated simplicity of their lives and ambitions.

He heard a page rustle behind him and spun his swivel chair back to face the desk. The man across the desk closed the file and laid it reverently on the desk before the Minister. The two men eyed each other, the silence broken only by the ticking of the ormolu clock on the mantelpiece opposite the door and the subdued roar of traffic from the Place Beauvau.

"Well, what do you think?"

Commissaire Jean Ducret, head of President de Gaulle's personal security corps, was one of the foremost experts in France on all questions of security, and particularly as that subject relates to the protection of a single life against assassination. That was why he held his job, and that was why six known plots to kill the President of France had either failed in execution or been dismantled in preparation up till that date.

"Rolland is right," he said at length. His voice was flat, unemotional, final. He might have been giving his judgement on the probable forthcoming result of a football match. "If what he says is true, the plot is of an exceptional danger. The entire filing system of all the security agencies of France, the whole network of agents and infiltrators presently maintained inside the OAS, all are reduced to impotence in the face of a foreigner, an outsider, working completely alone, without contacts or friends. And a professional into the bargain. As Rolland puts it, it is"—he flicked over the last page of the Action Service chief's report and read aloud—" 'the most dangerous single conception' that one can imagine."

Roger Frey ran his fingers through the iron-grey short-cut hair and spun away towards the window again. He was not a man easily ruffled, but he was ruffled on the morning of August 11. Throughout his many years as a devoted follower of the cause of Charles de Gaulle he had built up the reputation of a tough man behind the intelligence and urbanity that had brought him to the Minister's chair. The brilliant blue eyes that could be warmly attractive or chillingly cold, the virility of the compact chest and shoulders, and the handsome, ruthless face that had brought admiring glances from not a few women who enjoy the companionship of men of power, were no façade in Roger Frey.

In the old days, when the Gaullists had had to fight for survival against American enmity, British indifference, Giraudist ambition, and Communist ferocity, he had learned his in-fighting the hard way. Somehow they had won through, and twice in eighteen years the man they followed had returned from exile and repudiation to take the position of supreme power in France. And for the past two years the battle had been on again, this time against the very men who had twice restored the General to power—the Army. Until a few minutes before, the Minister had thought the last struggle was waning, their enemies once again sliding into impotence and helpless wrath.

Now he knew it was not over yet. A lean and fanatical colonel in Rome had devised a plan that could still bring the whole edifice tumbling down by organising the death of a single man. Some countries have institutions of sufficient stability to survive the death of a president or the abdication of a king, as Britain had shown twenty-eight years earlier and America would show before the year was out. But Roger Frey was well enough aware of the state of the institutions of France in 1963 to have no illusions that the death of his President could only be the prologue to putsch and civil war.

"Well," he said finally, still looking out into the glaring courtyard, "he must be told."

The policeman did not answer. It was one of the advantages of being a technician that you did your job and left the top decisions to those who were paid to take them. He did not intend to volunteer to be the one who did the telling. The Minister turned back to face him.

"*Bien. Merci, Commissaire.* Then I shall seek an interview this afternoon and inform the President." The voice was crisp and decisive. A thing had to be done. "I need hardly ask you to maintain complete silence on this matter until I have had time to explain the position to the President and he has decided how he wishes this affair to be handled."

Commissaire Ducret rose and left, to return across the square and a hundred yards down the road to the gates of the Elysée Palace. Left to himself, the Minister of the Interior spun the buff file round to face him and again read it slowly through. He had no doubt Rolland's assessment was right, and Ducret's concurrence left him no room for manoeuvre. The danger was there, it was serious, it could not be avoided, and the President had to know.

Reluctantly he threw down a switch on the intercom in front of him and told the plastic grille that immediately buzzed at him, "Get me a call to the Secretary General of the Elysée."

Within a minute the red telephone beside the intercom rang. He lifted it and listened for a second.

"*Monsieur Foccart, s'il vous plaît.*" Another pause, then the deceptively soft voice of one of the most powerful men in France came on the line. Roger Frey explained briefly what he wanted and why.

"As soon as possible, Jacques. . . . Yes, I know you have to check. I'll wait. Please call me back as soon as you can."

The call back came within an hour. The appointment was fixed for four that afternoon, as soon as the President had finished his siesta. For a second it crossed the Minister's mind to protest that what he had on the blotter in front of him was more important than any siesta, but he stifled the protest. Like everybody in the entourage of the President, he was aware of the inadvisability of crossing the soft-voiced civil servant who had the ear of the President at all times and a private filing system of intimate information about which more was feared than was known.

At twenty to four that afternoon the Jackal emerged from Cunningham's in Curzon Street after one of the most delicious and expensive lunches that the London sea-food specialists could provide. It was, after all, he mused as he swung into South Audley Street, probably his last lunch in London for some time to come, and he had reason to celebrate.

At the same moment a black DS 19 sedan swung out of the gates of the Interior Ministry of France into the Place Beauvau. The policeman in the centre of the square, forewarned by a shout from his colleagues on the iron gates, held up the traffic from all the surrounding streets, then snapped into a salute.

A hundred metres down the road the Citroen turned towards the grey stone portico in front of the Elysée Palace. Here too the gendarmes on duty, forewarned, had held up the traffic to give the sedan enough turning room to get through the surprisingly narrow archway. The two Gardes Républicaines, standing in front of their sentry boxes on each side of the portico, smacked their white-gloved hands across the magazines of the rifles, in salute, and the Minister entered the forecourt of the palace.

A chain hanging in a low loop across the inner arch of the gate halted the car while the duty inspector of the day, one of Ducret's men, briefly glanced inside the car. He nodded towards the Minister, who nodded back. At a gesture from the inspector the chain was let fall to the ground and the Citroen crunched over it. Across a hundred feet of tan-coloured gravel lay the façade of the palace. Robert, the driver, pulled the car to the right and drove round the courtyard anti-clockwise, to deposit his master at the foot of the six granite steps that lead to the entrance.

The door was opened by one of the two silver-chained, black frock-coated ushers. The Minister stepped down and ran up the steps to be greeted at the plate glass door by the chief usher. They greeted each other formally, and he followed the usher inside. They had to wait for a moment in the vestibule beneath the vast chandelier suspended on its long gilded chain from the vaulted ceiling far above while the usher telephoned briefly from the marble table to the left of the door. As he put the phone down, he turned to the Minister, smiled briefly, and proceeded at his usual majestic, unhurried pace up the carpeted granite stairs to the left.

At the first floor they went down the short, wide landing that overlooked the hallway below, and stopped when the usher knocked softly on the door to the left of the landing. There was a muffled reply of "*Entrez*" from within, the usher smoothly opened the door and stood back to let the Minister pass into the Salon des Ordonnances. As the Minister entered, the door closed behind him without a sound and the usher made his stately way back down the stairs to the vestibule.

From the great south windows on the far side of the Salon the sun streamed through, bathing the carpet in warmth. One of the floor-to-ceiling windows was open, and from the palace gardens came the sound of a wood pigeon cooing among the trees. The traffic of the Champs Elysées five hundred yards beyond the windows and completely shielded from view by the spreading limes and beeches, magnificent in the foliage of full summer, was simply another murmur, not even as loud as the pigeon. As usual when he was in the south-facing rooms of the Elysée Palace, M. Frey, a townman born and bred, could imagine he was in some chateau buried in the heart of the country. The President, as he knew, adored the countryside.

The ADC of the day was Colonel Tesseire. He rose from behind his desk. "*Monsieur le Ministre. . .*"

"Colonel. . ." M. Frey gestured with his head towards the closed double doors with the gilt handles on the left side of the salon. "I am expected?"

"Of course, *Monsieur le Ministre*." Tesseire crossed the room, knocked briefly on the doors, opened one half of them and stood in the entrance.

"The Minister of the Interior, *Monsieur le Président*."

There was a muffled assent from inside. Tesseire stepped back, smiled at the Minister, and Roger Frey went past him into Charles de Gaulle's private study.

There was almost nothing about that room, he had always thought, that did not seem to reflect to the man who occupied it. To the right were the three tall and elegant windows, like those of the Salon des Ordonnances, that gave access to the garden. In the study also one of them was open, and the murmuring of the pigeon, muted as one passed through the door between the two rooms, was heard again coming from the gardens.

Somewhere under those limes and beeches lurked quiet men toting automatics with which they could pick the ace out of the ace of spades at twenty paces. But woe betide the one of them who let himself be seen from the windows of the first floor. The man was enraged by security measures if they obtruded on his privacy. This was one of the heaviest crosses Ducret had to bear, and no one envied him the task of protecting a man for whom all forms of personal protection were an indignity he did not appreciate.

To the left, against the wall containing the glass-fronted bookshelves, was a Louis XV table on which reposed a Louis XIV clock. The floor was covered by a Savonnerie carpet made in the royal carpet factory at Chaillot in 1615. This factory, the President had once explained to him, had been a soap factory before its conversion to carpet making, and hence the name that had always applied to the carpets it produced.

There was nothing in the room that was not simple, nothing that was not dignified, nothing that was not tasteful, and above all nothing that did not exemplify the grandeur of France. And that, so far as Roger Frey was concerned, included the man behind the desk who now rose to greet him with his usual elaborate courtesy.

The minister recalled that Harold King, doyen of British journalists in Paris and the only contemporary Anglo-Saxon who was a personal friend of Charles de Gaulle, had once remarked to him that in all of his personal mannerisms the President was not from the twentieth but from the eighteenth century. Every time he had met his master since then Roger Frey had vainly tried to imagine a tall figure in silks and brocades making those same courteous gestures and greetings. He could see the connection, but the image escaped him. Nor could he forget the few occasions when the stately old man, really roused by something that had displeased him, had used barrack-room language of such forceful crudity as to leave his entourage or Cabinet members stunned and speechless. Security and presidential displeasure went hand in hand, and when Frey thought of the document he carried in his briefcase and the request he was going to have to make, he almost quaked.

"*Mon cher* Frey."

The tall charcoal-grey-suited figure had come round the edge of the great desk behind which he normally sat, hand outstretched in greeting.

"*Monsieur le Président, mes respects.*" He took the proffered hand. At least *le Vieux* seemed to be in a good mood. He found himself ushered to one of the two upright chairs covered in First Empire Beauvais tapestry in front of the desk. Charles de Gaulle, his duty as a host done, returned to his side and sat down, back to the wall. He leaned back, placing the finger tips of both hands on the polished wood in front of him.

"I am told, my dear Frey, that you wished to see me on a matter of urgency. Well, what have you to say to me?"

Roger Frey breathed in deeply once and began. He explained briefly and succinctly what had brought him, aware that de Gaulle did not appreciate long-winded oratory except his own, and then only for public speaking. In private he appreciated brevity, as several of his more verbose subordinates had discovered to their embarrassment.

While he talked, the man across the desk from him stiffened perceptibly. Leaning back further and further, seeming to grow all the while, he gazed down the commanding promontory of his nose at the Minister as if an unpleasant substance had been introduced into his study by a hitherto trusted servant. Roger Frey, however, was aware that at five yards' range his face could be no more than a blur to the President, who concealed his shortsightedness on all public occasions by never wearing glasses except to read speeches.

The Interior Minister finished his monologue, which had lasted barely more than one minute, by mentioning the comments of Rolland and Ducret, and finishing, "I have the Rolland report in my case."

Without a word the presidential hand stretched out across the desk. M. Frey slid the report out of the briefcase and handed it over.

From the top pocket of his jacket Charles de Gaulle took his reading glasses, put them on, spread the folder on his desk, and started to read. The pigeon had stopped cooing as if appreciating that this was not the moment. Roger Frey stared out at the trees, then at the brass reading lamp on the desk next to the blotter. It was a beautifully turned Flambeau de Vermeil from the Restoration, fitted with an electric light, and in the five years of the presidency it had spent thousands of hours illuminating the documents of state that passed during the night across the blotter over which it stood.

General de Gaulle was a quick reader. He finished the Rolland report in three minutes, folded it carefully on the blotter, crossed his hands over it, and asked, "Well, my dear Frey, what do you want of me?"

For the second time Roger Frey took a deep breath and launched into a succinct recitation of the steps he wished to take. Twice he used the phrase, "in my judgement, *Monsieur le Président,* it will be necessary if we are to avert this menace . . ." In the thirty-third second of his discourse he used the phrase "the interest of France."

It was as far as he got. The President cut across him, the sonorous voice rolling the word France into that of a deity in a way no other French voice of his time could equal.

"The interest of France, my dear Frey, is that the President of France is not seen to be cowering before the menace of a miserable hireling, and"—he paused while the contempt for his unknown assailant hung heavy in the room—"of a foreigner."

Roger Frey realised that he had lost. The General did not lose his temper as the Interior Minister feared he might. He began to speak clearly and precisely, as one who has no intention that his wishes should be in any way unclear to his listener. As he spoke, some of the phrases drifted through the window and were heard by Colonel Tesseire.

"*La France ne saurait accepter . . . la dignité et la grandeur assujetties aux misérables menaces d'un . . . d'un* CHACAL . . ."

Two minutes later Roger Frey left the President's presence. He nodded soberly at Colonel Tesseire, walked out through the door of the Salon des Ordonnances and down the stairs to the vestibule.

"There," thought the chief usher as he escorted the Minister down the stone steps to the waiting Citroen and watched him drive away, "goes a man with one hell of a problem, if ever I saw one. Wonder what the Old Man had to say to him." But since he was the chief usher, his face retained the immobile calm of the façade of the palace he had served for twenty years.

"No, it cannot be done that way. The President was absolutely final on that point."

Roger Frey turned from the window of his office and surveyed the man to whom he had addressed the remark. Within minutes of returning from the Elysée he had summoned his chief of personal staff. Alexandre Sanguinetti was a Corsican, another ferocious Gaullist fanatic. As the man to whom the Interior Minister had delegated over the past two years much of the detailed work of master-minding the French state security forces, Sanguinetti had established a renown and a reputation that varied according to the beholder's personal political affiliations or concept of civil rights.

By the extreme Left he was hated and feared for his unhesitating mobilisation of the CRS anti-riot squads and the no-nonsense tactics these 45,000 para-military bruisers used when confronted with a street demonstration from either the Left or the Right.

The Communists called him a Fascist, though some of his methods of keeping public order were reminiscent of the means used in the workers' paradises beyond the Iron Curtain. The extreme Right loathed him equally, quoting the same arguments of the suppression of democracy and civil rights, but more probably because the ruthless efficiency of his public-order measures had gone a long way towards preventing the complete breakdown of order that would have helped precipitate a Right-wing coup ostensibly aimed at restoring that very order.

And the public at large disliked him, because the Draconian decrees that stemmed from his office affected them all with barriers in the streets, examinations of identity cards at most major road junctions, roadblocks on all main roads, and the much-publicized photographs of young demonstrators being bludgeoned to the ground by the truncheons of the CRS. The press had already dubbed him "Monsieur Anti-OAS" and, apart from the relatively small Gaullist press, reviled him roundly. If the odium of being the most criticised man in France affected him at all, he managed to hide it. The deity of his private religion was ensconced in an office in the Elysée Palace, and within that religion Alexandre Sanguinetti was the head of the Curia. He glowered at the blotter in front of him, on which lay the buff folder containing the Rolland report.

"It's impossible. Impossible. He is impossible. We have to protect his life, but he won't let us. I could have this man, this Jackal. But you say we are allowed to take no counter-measures. What do we do? Just wait for him to strike? Just sit around and wait?"

The Minister sighed. He had expected no less from his *chef de cabinet*, but it still made his task no easier. He seated himself behind his desk again.

"Alexandre, listen. Firstly, the position is that we are not yet absolutely certain that the Rolland report is true. It is his own analysis of the ramblings of this—Kowalski, who has since died. Perhaps Rolland is wrong. Enquiries in Vienna are still being conducted. I have been in touch with Guibaud, and he expects to have the answer by this evening. But one must agree that at this stage, to launch a nationwide hunt for a foreigner only known to us by a code-name is hardly a realistic proposition. To that extent, I must agree with the President.

"Beyond that, these are his instructions—no, his absolutely formal orders. I repeat them so that there will be no mistake in any of our minds. There is to be no publicity, no nation-wide search, no indication to anyone outside a small circle around us that anything is amiss. The President feels that if the secret were out the press would have a field day, the foreign nations would jeer, and any extra security precautions taken by us would be interpreted both here and abroad as the spectacle of the President of France hiding from a single man, and a foreigner at that.

"This he will not, I repeat, will not tolerate. In fact"—the Minister emphasised his point with pointed forefinger—"he made quite plain to me that if in our handling of the affair the details, or even the general impression became public knowledge, heads would roll. Believe me, *cher ami,* I have never seen him so adamant."

"But the public programme," expostulated the Corsican, "it must inevitably be changed. There must be no more public appearances until the man is caught. He must surely—"

"He will cancel nothing. There will be no changes, not by an hour or a minute. The whole thing has got to be done in complete secrecy."

For the first time since the dismantling of the Ecole Militaire assassination plot in February, with the arrest of the plotters, Alexandre Sanguinetti felt he was back where he started. In the past two months, even though battling against the wave of bank robberies and smash-and-grab raids, he had permitted himself to hope that the worst was over. With the OAS apparatus crumbling under the twin assaults of the Action Service from within and the hordes of police and CRS from without, he had interpreted the crime wave as the death throes of the Secret Army, the last handful of thugs on the rampage trying to acquire enough money to live well in exile.

Now the last page of Rolland's report made plain that the scores of double agents Rolland had been able to infiltrate into even the highest ranks of the OAS had been outflanked by the anonymity of the assassin. Only three men holed up in a hotel in Rome knew his identity. He could see for himself that the archives of dossiers on everyone who had ever been remotely connected with the OAS had been rendered useless by one simple fact: the Jackal was a foreigner.

"If we are not allowed to act, what can we do?"

"I did not say we were not allowed to act," corrected Frey. "I said we were not allowed to act publicly. The whole thing must be done secretly. That leaves us only one alternative. The identity of the assassin must be revealed by a secret enquiry, he must be traced wherever he is, in France or abroad, and then destroyed without hesitation."

". . . and destroyed without hesitation. That, gentlemen, is the only course left open to us."

The Interior Minister surveyed the meeting seated round the table of the ministry conference room to let the impact of his words sink in. There were fourteen men in the room including himself.

The Minister stood at the head of the table. To his immediate right sat his *chef de cabinet,* and to his left the Prefect of Police, the political head of France's police forces.

From Sanguinetti's right hand down the length of the oblong table sat General Guibaud, head of the SDECE, Colonel Rolland, chief of the Action Service and the author of the report lying before each man. Beyond Rolland were Commissaire Ducret of the Corps de Sécurité Présidentielle, and Colonel Saint-Clair de Villauban, an Air Force colonel of the Elysée staff, a fanatical Gaullist but renowned in the entourage of the President as being equally fanatical concerning his own ambition.

To the left of M. Maurice Papon, the Prefect of Police, were M. Maurice Grimaud, the Director-General of France's national crime force, the Sûreté Nationale, and in a row the five heads of the departments that make up the Sûreté.

Although beloved of novelists as a crime-busting force, the Sûreté Nationale itself is simply the very small and meagrely staffed office that has control over the five crime branches that actually do the work. The task of the Sûreté is administrative, like that of the equally mis-described Interpol, and the Sûreté does not have a detective on its staff.

The man with the national police force of France under his personal orders sat next to Maurice Grimaud. He was Max Fernet, Director of the Police Judiciaire. Apart from its enormous headquarters on the Quai des Orfèvres, vastly bigger than the Sûreté's headquarters at 11, rue des Saussaies, just round the corner from the Interior Ministry, the Police Judiciaire controls seventeen Services Régionaux headquarters, one for each of the seventeen police districts of Metropolitan France. Under these come the borough police forces, 453 in all, being comprised of seventy-four Central Commissariats, 253 Constituency Commissariats and 126 local Postes de Police. The whole network ranges through two thousand towns and villages of France. This is the crime force. In the rural areas and up and down the highways the more general task of maintaining law and order is carried out by the Gendarmerie Nationale and the traffic police, the Gendarmes Mobiles. In many areas, for reasons of efficiency, the gendarmes and the *agents de police* share the same accommodation and facilities. The total number of men under Max Fernet's command in the Police Judiciaire in 1963 was just over twenty thousand.

Running down the table from Fernet's left were the heads of the other four sections of the Sûreté: the Bureau de Sécurité Publique, the Renseignments Généraux, the Direction de la Surveillance du Territoire, and the Corps Républicain de Sécurité.

The first of these, the BSP, was concerned mainly with protection of buildings, communications, highways, and anything else belonging to the state, from sabotage or damage. The second, the RG or central records office, was the memory of the other four; in its Panthéon headquarters archives were 4,500,000 personal dossiers on individuals who had come to the notice of the police forces of France since those forces were founded. They were cross-indexed along five and a half miles of shelves in categories of the names of the persons to whom they applied or the type of crime for which the person had been convicted or merely suspected. Names of witnesses who had appeared in cases, or those who had been acquitted, were also listed. Although the system was not yet computerised, the archivists prided themselves that within a few minutes they could unearth the details of an arson committed in a small village ten years back or the names of witnesses in an obscure trial that had hardly made the newspapers.

Added to these dossiers were the fingerprints of everyone who had ever had his fingerprints taken in France, including many sets that had never been identified. There were also 10,500,000 cards, including the disembarkation card of every tourist at every border crossing point, and the hotel cards filled in by all who stayed at French hotels outside Paris. For reasons of space alone these cards had to be cleared out at fairly short intervals to make way for the vast number of fresh ones that came in each year.

The only cards regularly filled in within the area of France that did not go to the RG were those filled in at the hotels of Paris. These went to the Préfecture de Police in the Boulevard du Palais.

The DST, whose chief sat three places down from Fernet, is the counter-espionage force of France, responsible also for maintaining a constant watch on France's airports, docks, and borders. Before going to the archives, the disembarkation cards of those entering France are examined by the DST officer at the point of entry, to keep tabs on undesirables.

The last man in the row was the chief of the CRS, the 45,000-man force of which Alexandre Sanguinetti had already made such a well publicised and heartily unpopular use over the previous two years.

For reasons of space, the head of the CRS was sitting at the foot of the table, facing down the length of wood at the Minister. There was one last seat remaining, that between the head of the CRS and Colonel Saint-Clair, at the bottom right-hand corner. It was occupied by a large stolid man whose pipe fumes evidently annoyed the fastidious colonel on his left. The Minister had made a point of asking Max Fernet to bring him along to the meeting. He was Commissaire Maurice Bouvier, head of the Brigade Criminelle of the PJ.

"So that is where we stand, gentlemen," resumed the Minister.

"Now you have all read the report by Colonel Rolland which lies in front of each of you. And now you have heard from me the considerable limitations which the President, in the interests of the dignity of France, has felt obliged to impose on our efforts to avert this threat to his person. I will stress again, there must be absolute secrecy in the conduct of the investigation and in any subsequent action to be taken. Needless to say, you are all sworn to total silence and will discuss the matter with no one outside this room until and unless another person has been made privy to the secret.

"I have called you all here because it seems to me that whatever we are to do, the resources of all the departments here represented must sooner or later be called upon, and you, the departmental chiefs, should have no doubt as to the urgency of this affair. It must on all occasions require your immediate and personal attention. There will be no delegation to juniors, except for tasks which do not reveal the reason behind the requirement."

He paused again. Down both sides of the table some heads nodded soberly. Others kept their eyes fixed on the speaker or on the dossier in front of them. At the far end, Commissaire Bouvier gazed at the ceiling, emitting brief bursts of smoke from the corner of his mouth like a Red Indian sending up signals. The Air Force colonel next to him winced at each emission.

"Now," resumed the Minister, "I think I may ask for your ideas on the subject. Colonel Rolland, have you had any success with your enquiries in Vienna?"

The head of the Action Service glanced up from his own report, cast a sideways look at the general who led the SDECE, but received neither encouragement nor a frown.

General Guibaud, remembering that he had spent half the day calming down the head of R 3 Section over Rolland's early morning decision to use the Viennese office for his own enquiries, stared straight ahead of him.

"Yes," said the Colonel. "Enquiries were made this morning and afternoon by operatives in Vienna at the Pension Kleist, a small private hotel in the Brucknerallee. They carried with them photographs of Marc Rodin, René Montclair, and André Casson. There was no time to transmit to them photographs of Viktor Kowalski, which were not on file in Vienna.

"The desk clerk at the hotel stated that he recognised at least two of the men. But he could not place them. Some money changed hands, and he was asked to search the hotel register for the days between June twelfth and eighteenth, the latter being the day the three OAS chiefs took up residence together in Rome.

"Eventually he claimed to have remembered the face of Rodin as a man who booked a room in the name of Schulze on June fifteenth. The clerk said he had a form of business conference in the afternoon, spent the night in that room and left the next day.

"He remembered that Schulze had had a companion, a very big man with a surly manner, which was why he remembered Schulze. He was visited by two men in the morning, and they had a conference. The two visitors could have been Casson and Montclair. He could not be sure, but he thought he had seen at least one of them before.

"The clerk said the men remained in their room all day, apart from one occasion in the late morning when Schulze and the giant, as he called Kowalski, left for half an hour. None of them had any lunch, nor did they come down to eat."

"Were they visited at all by a fifth man?" asked Sanguinetti impatiently. Rolland continued his report as before, in flat tones.

"During the evening another man joined them. The clerk said he remembered because the visitor entered the hotel so quickly, heading straight up the stairs, that the clerk did not get a chance to see him. He thought he must be one of the guests, who had retained his key. But he saw the tail of the man's coat going up the stairs. A few seconds later the man was back in the hall. The clerk was sure it was the same man because of the coat.

"The man used the desk phone and asked to be put through to Schulze's room, number sixty-four. He spoke a few words in French, then replaced the phone and went back up the stairs. He spent some time there, then left without saying another word. Schulze and the other men stayed for the night, then left after breakfast in the morning.

"The only description the clerk could give of the evening visitor was: tall, age uncertain, features apparently regular but he wore wraparound dark glasses, spoke fluent French, and had blond hair left rather long and swept back from the forehead."

"Is there any chance of getting the man to help make up an Identikit picture of the blond?" asked the Prefect of Police, Papon.

Rolland shook his head.

"My—our agents were posing as Viennese plain-clothes police. Fortunately, one of them could pass for a Viennese. But that is a masquerade that could not be sustained indefinitely. The man had to be interviewed at the hotel desk."

"We must get a better description than that," protested the head of the Records Office. "Was any name mentioned?"

"No," said Rolland. "What you have just heard is the outcome of three hours spent interrogating the clerk. Every point was gone over time and time again. There is nothing else he can remember. Short of an Identikit picture, that's the best description he could give."

"Could you not snatch him like Argoud, so that he could make up a picture of this assassin here in Paris?" queried Colonel Saint-Clair.

The Minister interjected,

"There can be no more snatches. The German Foreign Ministry is still enraged over the Argoud snatch. That kind of thing can work once, but not again."

"Surely in a matter of this seriousness the disappearance of a desk clerk can be done more discreetly than the Argoud affair?" suggested the head of the DST.

"It is in any case doubtful," said Max Fernet quietly, "whether an Identikit picture of a man wearing wraparound dark glasses would be very helpful. Very few Identikit pictures made up on the basis of an unremarkable incident lasting twenty seconds two months before ever seem to look like the criminal when he is eventually caught. Most such pictures could be of half a million people, and some are actually misleading."

"So apart from Kowalski, who is dead, and who told everything he knew, which was not much, there are only four men in the world who know the identity of this Jackal," said Commissaire Ducret. "One is the man himself, and the other three are in a hotel in Rome. How about trying to get one of them back here."

Again, the Minister shook his head.

"My instructions on that are formal. Kidnappings are out. The Italian Government would go out of its mind if this kind of thing happened a few yards from the Via Condotti. Besides, there are some doubts as to its feasibility. General?"

General Guibaud lifted his eyes to the assembly.

"The extent and quality of the protective screen Rodin and his two henchmen have built round themselves, according to the reports of my agents who have them under permanent surveillance, rule this out from the practical standpoint also," he said. "There are eight top-class ex-Legion gunmen round them, or seven if Kowalski has not been replaced. All the lifts, stairs, fire escape, and roof are guarded. It would involve a major gun battle, probably with gas grenades and submachine guns, to get one of them alive. Even then, the chances of getting the man out of the country and five hundred kilometres north to France, with the Italians on the rampage, would be very slight indeed. We have men who are some of the world's top experts in this kind of thing, and they say it would be just about impossible short of a commando-style military operation."

Silence descended on the room again.

"Well, gentlemen," said the Minister, "are there any more suggestions?"

"This Jackal must be found. That much is clear," replied Colonel Saint-Clair. Several of the others round the table glanced at each other, and an eyebrow or two was raised.

"That much certainly is clear," murmured the Minister at the head of the table. "What we are trying to devise is a way in which that can be done, within the limits imposed upon us, and on that basis perhaps we can best decide which of the departments here represented would be best suited for the job."

"The protection of the President of the Republic," announced Saint-Clair grandly, "must depend in the last resort, when all others have failed, on the Presidential Security Corps and the President's personal staff. We, I can assure you, Minister, will do our duty."

Some of the hard-core professionals closed their eyes in unfeigned weariness. Commissaire Ducret shot the colonel a glance which, if looks would kill, would have dropped Saint-Clair in his tracks.

"Doesn't he know the Old Man's not listening," growled Guibaud under his breath to Rolland.

Roger Frey raised his eyes to meet those of the Elysée Palace courtier and demonstrated why he was a minister.

"Colonel Saint-Clair is perfectly right, of course," he purred. "We shall all do our duty. And I am sure it has occurred to the Colonel that should a certain department undertake the responsibility for the destruction of this plot, and fail to achieve it, or even employ methods inadvertently capable of bringing publicity contrary to the wishes of the President, certain disapprobation would inevitably descend upon the head of him who had failed."

The menace hung above the long table more tangible than the pall of blue smoke from Bouvier's pipe. Saint-Clair's thin pale face tightened perceptibly, and the worry showed in his eyes.

"We are all aware here of the limited opportunities available to the Presidential Security Corps," said Commissaire Ducret flatly. "We spend our time in the immediate vicinity of the President's person. Evidently this investigation must be far more wide-ranging than my staff could undertake without neglecting its primary duties."

No one contradicted him, for each department chief was aware that what the Presidential Security chief said was true. But neither did anyone else wish the ministerial eye to fall on him. Roger Frey looked round the table, and rested on the smoke-shrouded bulk of Commissaire Bouvier at the far end.

"What do you think, Bouvier? You have not spoken yet."

The detective eased the pipe out of his mouth, managed to let a last squirt of odoriferous smoke waft straight into the face of Saint-Clair, who had turned towards him, and spoke calmly as one stating a few simple facts that had just occurred to him.

"It seems to me, Minister, that the SDECE cannot disclose this man through their agents in the OAS, since not even the OAS know who he is; that the Action Service cannot destroy him since they do not know whom to destroy. The DST cannot pick him up at the border for they do not know whom to intercept, and the RG can give us no documentary information about him because they do not know what documents to search for. The Police cannot arrest him, for they do not know whom to arrest, and the CRS cannot pursue him, since they are unaware whom they are pursuing. The entire structure of the security forces of France are powerless for want of a name. It seems to me therefore that the first task, without which all other proposals become meaningless, is to give this man a name. With a name we get a face, with a face a passport, with a passport an arrest. But to find the name, and do it in secret, is a job for pure detective work."

He was silent again, and inserted the stem of his pipe between his teeth.

What he had said was digested by each of the men round the table. No one could fault it. Sanguinetti, by the Minister's side, nodded slowly.

"And who, Commissaire, is the best detective in France?" asked the Minister quietly. Bouvier considered for a few seconds, before removing his pipe again.

"The best detective in France, messieurs, is my own deputy, Commissaire Claude Lebel."

"Summon him," said the Minister of the Interior.

PART 2
Anatomy of a Manhunt

TEN

An hour later Claude Lebel emerged from the conference room dazed and bewildered. For fifty minutes he had listened as the Minister of the Interior had briefed him on the task that lay ahead.

On entering the room, he had been bidden to sit at the end of the table, sandwiched between the head of the CRS and his own chief, Bouvier. In silence from the other fourteen men he had read the Rolland report, while aware that curious eyes were assessing him from all sides.

When he put the report down, the worry had started inside him. Why call him? Then the Minister started to speak. It was neither a consultation nor a request. It was a directive, followed by a copious briefing. He would set up his own office; he would have unlimited access to all necessary information; the entire resources of the organisations headed by the men seated round the table would be at his disposal. There were to be no limits to the costs incurred.

Several times the need for absolute secrecy, the imperative of the Head of State himself, had been impressed on him. While he listened his heart sank. They were asking, no, demanding the impossible. He had nothing to go on. There was no crime—yet. There were no clues. There were no witnesses, except three whom he could not talk to. Just a name, a code-name, and the whole world to search in.

Claude Lebel was, as he knew, a good cop. He had always been a good cop, slow, precise, methodical, painstaking. Just occasionally he had shown the flash of inspiration that is needed to turn a good cop into a remarkable detective. But he had never lost sight of the fact that in police work ninety-nine percent of the effort is routine, unspectacular enquiry, checking and double-checking, laboriously building up a web of parts until the parts become a whole, the whole becomes a net, and the net finally encloses the criminal with a case that will not just make headlines but stand up in court.

He was known in the PJ as a bit of a plodder, a methodical man who hated publicity and had never given the sort of press conferences on which some of his colleagues had built their reputations. And yet he had gone steadily up the ladder, solving his cases, seeing his criminals convicted. When a vacancy had occurred at the head of the Homicide Division of the Brigade Criminelle three years before, even the others in line for the job had agreed it was fair that Lebel should have the job. He had a good steady record with Homicide and in three years had never failed to procure an arrest, although once the accused was acquitted on a technicality.

As head of Homicide he had come more closely to the notice of Maurice Bouvier, chief of the whole Brigade, and another old-style cop. So when

Deputy Chief Hippolyte Dupuy had died suddenly a few weeks back, it was Bouvier who had asked that Lebel become his new deputy. There were some in the PJ who suspected that Bouvier, bogged down for a lot of the time with administrative details, appreciated a retiring subordinate who could handle the big, headline-making cases quietly, without stealing his superior's thunder. But perhaps they were just being uncharitable.

After the meeting at the ministry, the copies of the Rolland report were gathered up for storage in the Minister's safe. Lebel alone was allowed to keep Bouvier's copy. His only request had been that he be allowed to seek the cooperation, in confidence, of the heads of some of the Criminal Investigation forces of the major countries likely to have the identity of a professional assassin like the Jackal on their files. Without such cooperation, he pointed out, it would be impossible even to start looking.

Sanguinetti had asked if such men could be relied on to keep their mouths shut. Lebel had replied that he knew personally the men he needed to contact, that his enquiries would not be official but would be along the personal-contact basis that exists between most of the Western world's top policemen. After some reflexion, the Minister had granted the request.

And now he stood in the hall waiting for Bouvier and watching the chiefs of department file past him on their way out. Some nodded curtly and passed on; others ventured a sympathetic smile as they said good night. Almost the last to leave, while inside the conference room Bouvier conferred quietly with Max Fernet, was the aristocratic colonel from the Elysée staff. Lebel had briefly caught his name, as the men round the table were introduced, as Saint-Clair de Villauban. He stopped in front of the small and roly-poly Commissaire and eyed him with ill-concealed distaste.

"I hope, Commissaire, that you will be successful in your enquiries, and rapidly so," he said. "We at the Palace will be keeping a very close eye on your progress. In the event that you should fail to find this bandit, I can assure you that there will be . . . repercussions."

He turned on his heel and stalked down the stairs towards the foyer. Lebel said nothing but blinked rapidly several times.

One of the factors in the make-up of Claude Lebel that had led to his successes when enquiring into crime over the previous twenty years, since he had joined the police force of the Fourth Republic as a young detective in Normandy, was his capacity to inspire people with the confidence to talk to him. He had a knack of making simple people, the humble and the lowly who normally fear and dislike policemen, unbutton their thoughts and suspicions to him. The reason he could do this was his seeming air of helplessness, of being, like them, one of the downtrodden and put-upon of this world.

He lacked the imposing bulk of Bouvier, the traditional image of the authority of the law. Nor did he have the smartness with words that exemplified so many of the new breed of young detectives now coming into the force, who could bully and browbeat a witness into tears. He did not feel the lack.

He was aware that most crime in any society is either carried out against, or witnessed by, the little people: the shopkeeper, the sales assistant, the postman, or the bank clerk. These people he could make talk to him, and he knew it.

It was partly because of his size; he was small, and resembled in many ways the cartoonist's image of a hen-pecked husband, which, although no one in the department knew it, was just what he was.

His dress was dowdy, a crumpled suit and a mackintosh. His manner was mild, almost apologetic, and in his request of a witness for information it contrasted so sharply with the attitude the witness had experienced from his first interview with the law that the witness tended to warm towards the detective as a refuge from the roughness of the subordinates.

But there was something more. He had been head of the Homicide Division of the most powerful criminal police force in Europe. He had been ten years a detective with the Brigade Criminelle of the renowned Police Judiciaire of France. Behind the mildness and the seeming simplicity was a combination of shrewd brain and a dogged refusal to be ruffled or intimidatd by anyone when he was carrying out a job. He had been threatened by some of the most vicious gang bosses of France, who had thought from the rapid blinking with which Lebel greeted such approaches that their warnings had been duly taken. Only later, from a prison cell, had they had the leisure to realise they had underestimated the soft brown eyes and the toothbrush moustache.

Twice he had been subjected to intimidation by wealthy and powerful figures, once when an industrialist had wished to see one of his junior employees charged with embezzlement on the basis of a cursory glance at the auditor's evidence, and once when a society blade had wished him to drop investigations into a young actress's death from drugs.

In the first case the enquiry into the affairs of the industrialist had resulted in certain other and far bigger discrepancies being unearthed which had nothing to do with the junior accountant, but which had caused the industrialist to wish he had departed for Switzerland while he had the chance. The second time the society host had ended up with a lengthy period as a guest of the state, during which time he could regret that he had ever bothered to head a vice ring from his Avenue Victor Hugo penthouse.

Claude Lebel's reaction to the remarks of Colonel Saint-Clair was to blink like a rebuked schoolboy and say nothing.

As the last man filed out of the conference room, Maurice Bouvier joined him. Max Fernet wished him luck, shook hands briefly, and headed down the stairs. Bouvier clapped a ham-like hand on Lebel's shoulder.

"*Eh, bien, mon petit* Claude. So that's the way it is, *hein?* All right, it was me who suggested the PJ handle this business. It was the only thing to do. Those others would have talked round in circles forever. Come, we'll talk in the car." He led the way downstairs and the pair of them climbed into the back of the Citroen that waited in the courtyard.

It was past nine o'clock, and a dark purple streak lying over Neuilly was all that remained of the day. Bouvier's car swept down the Avenue de Marigny and over the Place Clemenceau. Lebel glanced out to the right and up the brilliant river of the Champs Elysées, whose grandeur on a summer night never ceased to surprise and excite him, despite the ten years that had passed since he came up from the provinces.

"You'll have to drop whatever you are doing. Everything. Clear the desk completely. I'll assign Favier and Malcoste to take over your outstanding cases. Do you want a new office for this job?"

"No, I prefer to stick to my present one."

"OK, fine, but from now on it becomes headquarters of Operation Find-the-Jackal. Nothing else. Right? Is there anyone you want to help you?"

"Yes. Caron," said Lebel, referring to one of the younger inspectors who had worked with him in Homicide and whom he had brought to his new job as Assistant Chief of the Brigade Criminelle.

"OK, you have Caron. Anyone else?"

"No thank you. But Caron will have to know."

Bouvier thought for a few moments.

"It should be all right. They can't expect miracles. Obviously you must have an assistant. But don't tell him for an hour or two. I'll ring Frey when I get to the office and ask for formal clearance. Nobody else has to know, though. It would be in the press inside two days if it got out."

"Nobody else, just Caron," said Lebel.

"*Bon.* There's one last thing. Before I left the meeting Sanguinetti suggested the whole group who were there tonight be kept informed at regular intervals of progress and development. Frey agreed. Fernet and I tried to head it off, but we lost. There's to be a briefing by you every evening at the Ministry from now on. Ten o'clock sharp."

"Oh God," said Lebel.

"In theory," continued Bouvier with heavy irony, "we shall all be available to offer our best advice and suggestions. Don't worry, Claude, Fernet and I will be there too, in case the wolves start snapping."

"This is until further notice?" asked Lebel.

"I'm afraid so. The hell of it is, there's no time schedule for this operation. You've just got to find this assassin before he gets *le grand* Charles. We don't know whether the man himself has a timetable, or what it could be. It might be for a hit tomorrow morning, maybe not for a month yet. You have to assume you are working full speed until he has been caught, or at least identified and located. From then on I think the Action Service boys can take care of things."

"Bunch of thugs," murmured Lebel.

"Granted," said Bouvier easily, "but they have their uses. We live in hair-raising times, my dear Claude. Added to a vast increase in normal crime, we now have political crime. There are some things that just have to be done. They do them. Anyway, just try and find this jackal, huh."

The car swept into the Quai des Orfèvres and turned through the gates of the PJ. Ten minutes later Claude Lebel was back in his office. He walked to the window, opened it and leant out, gazing across the river towards the Quai des Grands Augustins on the Left Bank in front of him. Although separated by a narrow strip of the Seine where it flowed round the Ile de la Cité, he was close enough to see the diners in the pavement restaurants dotted along the quay and hear the laughter and the clink of bottles on glasses of wine.

Had he been a different kind of man, it might have occurred to him that the powers conferred on him in the last ninety minutes had made him, for a spell at least, the most powerful cop in Europe; that nobody short of the President or the Interior Minister could veto his request for facilities; that he could almost mobilise the army, provided it could be done secretly. It might also have occurred to him that exalted though his powers were, they were dependent upon success; that with success he could crown his career with honours, but that in failure he could be broken, as Saint-Clair de Villauban had indicated.

Because he was what he was, he thought of none of these things. He was puzzling as to how he would explain over the phone to Amélie that he was not coming home until further notice. There was a knock on the door.

Inspectors Malcoste and Favier came in to collect the dossiers of the four cases on which Lebel had been working when he had been called away earlier that evening. He spent half an hour briefing Malcoste on the two cases he was assigning to him, and Favier on the other two.

When they had gone he sighed heavily. There was a knock on the door. It was Lucien Caron.

"I just got a call from Commissaire Bouvier's office," he began. "He told me to report to you."

"Quite right. Until further notice I have been taken off all routine duties and given a rather special job. You've been assigned to be my assistant."

He did not bother to flatter Caron by revealing that he had asked for the young inspector to be his right hand man. The desk phone rang, he picked it up and listened briefly.

"Right," he resumed, "that was Bouvier to say you have been given security clearance to be told what it is all about. For a start you had better read this."

While Caron sat on the chair in front of the desk and read the Rolland file, Lebel cleared all the remaining folders and notes off his desk and stacked them on the untidy shelves behind him. The office hardly looked like the nerve center of the biggest manhunt in France, but police offices never do look like much.

Lebel's office was no more than twelve feet by fourteen, with two windows on the south face looking out over the river towards the lively honeycomb of the Latin Quarter clustering round the Boulevard St. Michel. Through one of the windows the sounds of the night and the warm summer air drifted in. The office contained two desks, one for Lebel, which stood with its back to the window, another for a secretary, which stood along the east wall. The door was opposite the window.

Apart from the two desks and two chairs behind them, there were one other upright chair, an armchair next to the door, six large grey filing cabinets standing along almost the whole of the west wall and whose combined tops supported an array of reference and law books, and one set of bookshelves, situated between the windows and stuffed with almanacs and files.

Of signs of home there was only the framed photograph on Lebel's desk of an ample and determined-looking lady, who was Madame Amélie Lebel, and two children, a plain girl with steel-rimmed glasses and pigtails and a youth with an expression as mild and put-upon as his father.

Caron finished reading and looked up.

"*Merde*," he said.

"As you say, *une énorme merde*," replied Lebel, who seldom permitted himself the use of strong language. Most of the top commissaires of the PJ were known to their immediate staff by nicknames like "*le Patron*" or "*le Vieux*." Claude Lebel, perhaps because he never drank more than a small aperitif, did not smoke or swear, and reminded younger detectives inevitably of one of their former schoolteachers, was known within Homicide and more lately in the corridors of the Brigade chief's administrative floor as "*le Professeur*." Had he not been such a good thieftaker, he would have become something of a figure of fun.

"Nevertheless," continued Lebel, "listen while I fill you in on the details. It will be our last chance."

For thirty minutes he briefed Caron on the events of the afternoon, from Roger Frey's meeting with the President to the meeting in the ministry conference room, to his own brusque summons on the recommendation of Maurice Bouvier, to the final setting up of the office in which they now sat as the headquarters of the manhunt for the Jackal. Caron listened in silence.

"*Mon Dieu,*" he said at last when Lebel had finished, "they *have* fixed you." He thought for a moment, then looked up at his chief with worry and concern. "*Mon commissaire,* you know they have given you this because no one else wants it? You know what they will do to you if you fail to catch this man in time?"

Lebel nodded.

"Yes, Lucien, I know. There's nothing I can do. I've been given the job. So, from now we just have to do it."

"Where on earth do we start?"

"We start by recognising that we have the widest powers ever granted to two cops in France," replied Lebel cheerfully. "So, we use them."

"To start with, get installed behind that desk. Take a pad and note the following. Get my normal secretary transferred or given paid leave until further notice. No one else can be let into the secret. You become my assistant and secretary rolled into one. Get a camp bed in here from emergency stores, linen and pillows, washing and shaving gear. Get a percolator of coffee, some milk and sugar brought from the canteen and installed. We're going to need a lot of coffee.

"Get onto the switchboard and instruct them to leave ten outside lines and one operator permanently at the disposal of this office. If they quibble, refer them to Bouvier personally. As for any other requests from me for facilities, get straight onto the department chief and quote my name. Fortunately, this office now gets top priority from every other ancillary service—by order. Prepare a circular memorandum, copy to every department chief who attended this evening's meeting, ready for my signature, announcing that you are now my sole assistant and empowered to require from them anything that I would ask them for personally if I were not engaged. Got it?"

Caron finished writing and looked up.

"Got it, chief, I can do that tonight. Which is the top priority?"

"The telephone switchboard. I want a good man on that, the best they've got. Get on to Chief of Administration at his home, and again quote Bouvier for authority."

"Right. What do we want from them first?"

"I want, as soon as they can get it, a direct link personally to the Homicide man in seven countries. Fortunately, I know most of them personally from past meetings of Interpol. In some cases I know the Deputy-Chief. If you can't get one, get the other.

"The countries are: United States, that means the Office of Domestic Intelligence in Washington; Britain, Assistant Commissioner (Crime), Scotland Yard; Belgium; Holland; Italy; West Germany; South Africa. Get them at home or in the office.

"When you get each of them one by one, arrange a series of telephone calls from Interpol Communications Room between me and them between seven and ten in the morning at twenty-minute intervals. Better get the Americans in first because of the time difference. Get on to Interpol Communications and book the calls as each Homicide Chief at the other end agrees to be in his own Communications room at the appointed time. The calls should be person-to-person on the UHF frequency, and there is to be no listening in. Impress on each of them that what I have to say is for their ears only and of top priority not only for France but possibly for their own country. Prepare me a list by six in the morning of the schedule of the seven calls that have been booked, in order of sequence."

Caron, looking slightly dazed, glanced up from his several pages of scribbled notes.

"Yes, chief, I've got it. *Bon,* I'd better get to work." He reached out for the telephone.

Claude Lebel passed out of the office and headed for the stairs. As he did so, the clock of Notre Dame farther down the island chimed midnight, and France passed into the morning of August 12.

ELEVEN

Colonel Raoul Saint-Clair de Villauban arrived home just before midnight. He had spent the previous three hours meticulously typing his report on the evening's meeting in the Interior Ministry, which would be on the desk of the Secretary-General of the Elysée first thing in the morning.

He had taken particular pains over the report, tearing up two rough copies before he was satisfied, then carefully typing out the third and final copy by himself. It was irritating to have to engage in the menial task of typing, and he was not used to it, but it had the advantage of keeping the facts from any secretary—a fact that he had not hesitated to point out in the body of the report—and also of enabling him to have the document ready for production first thing in the morning, which he hoped would not go unnoticed. With luck the report would be on the President's desk an hour after being read by the Secretary-General, and this also would do him no harm.

He had used extra care in selecting just the right phraseology to give a slight hint of the writer's disapproval of putting a matter so important as the security of the head of state into the sole hands of a commissaire of police, a man more accustomed by training and experience to uncovering petty criminals of little brains or talent.

It would not have done to go too far, for Lebel might even find his man. But in the event that he did not, it was as well that there was someone sufficiently on his toes to have had doubts about the wisdom of the choice of Lebel at the time.

Moreover, he had certainly not taken to Lebel. A common little man, had been his private judgement. "Possessed no doubt of a competent record," had been his phrasing in the report.

Musing over the first two copies he had written in longhand, he decided that the most advantageous position for him to take would be not to oppose the appointment outright since it had been agreed by the meeting as a whole.

Also if he opposed the selection he would be asked for specific reasons. On the other hand, he determined to keep a close watch on the whole operation, on behalf of the presidential secretariat, and to be the first to point out, with due sobriety, the inefficiencies in the conduct of the investigation as and when they occurred.

His musings on how he could best keep track of what Lebel was up to were interrupted by a telephone call from Sanguinetti to inform him that the Minister had made a last-minute decision to preside over nightly meetings at ten each evening to hear a progress repot from Lebel. The news had delighted Saint-Clair. It solved his problem for him. With a little background homework during the daytime, he would be able to put forceful and pertinent questions to the detective and reveal to the others that at least in the presidential secretariat they were keeping wide awake to the gravity and urgency of the situation.

Privately he did not put the assassin's chances very high, even if there were an assassin in the offing. The presidential security screen was the most efficient in the world, and part of his job in the secretariat was to devise the organisation of the president's public appearances and the routes he would follow. He had few fears that this intensive and highly planned security screen could be penetrated by some foreign gunman.

He let himself in by the front door of his flat and heard his newly installed mistress call from the bedroom.

"Is that you, darling?"

"Yes, *chérie*. Of course it's me. Have you been lonely?"

She came running through from the bedroom, dressed in a filmy black baby-doll nightie, trimmed at throat and hem with lace. The indirect light from the bedroom lamp, shining through the open door of the bedroom, silhouetted the curves of her young woman's body. As usual when he saw his mistress, Raoul Saint-Clair felt a complacent thrill of satisfaction that she was his, and so deeply in love with him.

She threw her bare arms around his neck and gave him a long open-mouthed kiss. He responded as best he could while still clutching his briefcase and the evening paper.

"Come," he said when they separated, "get into bed and I'll join you." He gave her a slap on the bottom to speed her on her way. The girl skipped back into the bedroom, threw herself on the bed, and spread out her limbs, hands crossed behind her neck, breasts upthrust.

Saint-Clair entered the room and glanced at her with satisfaction. She grinned back lasciviously.

During their fortnight together she had learned that only the most blatant suggestiveness and carnality could arouse the courtier. Privately, Jacqueline hated him as much as on the first day they had met, but she learned that what he lacked in virility he made up in loquacity, particularly about his importance in the scheme of things at the Elysée Palace.

"Hurry," she whispered, "I want you."

Saint-Clair smiled with genuine pleasure and took off his shoes, laying them side by side at the foot of the dumb waiter. The jacket followed, its pockets carefully emptied on to the dressing table top. The trousers came next, to be meticulously folded and laid over the protruding arm of the dumb waiter. His long thin legs protruded from beneath the shirt tails like whiskery white knitting needles.

"What kept you so long?" asked Jacqueline. "I've been waiting for ages." Saint-Clair shook his head sombrely.

"Certainly nothing that you should bother your head with, my dear."

"Oh, you're mean." She turned over abruptly onto her side in a mock-sulk, facing away from him, knees bent. His fingers slipped on the tie-knot as he looked across the room at the chestnut hair tumbling over the shoulders and the full hips now uncovered by the shortie night-dress. Another five minutes and he was ready for bed, buttoning the monogrammed silk pyjamas.

He stretched his length on the bed next to her and ran his hand down the dip of the waist and up to the summit of her hip, the fingers slipping down towards the sheet and round the swell of the warm buttock.

"What's the matter, then?"

"Nothing."

"I thought you wanted to make love."

"You just don't give me any explanation. I can't ring you at the office. I've been lying here for hours worrying that something might have happened to you. You've never been this late before without ringing me."

She rolled over onto her back and looked up at him. Propped on his elbow, he slipped his free hand under the nightie and started to knead one of her breasts.

"Look, darling, I've been very busy. There was something of a crisis, something I had to sort out before I could get away. I'd have rung but there were people still working, popping in and out of the office the whole time. Several of them know my wife is away. It would have seemed odd for me to ring home through the switchboard."

She slipped a hand through his pyjama fly to encircle the limp penis, and was rewarded with a light tremor.

"There couldn't have been anything so big you couldn't have let me know you'd be late, darling. I was worrying all night."

"Well, there's no need to worry any more. *Suce-moi,* you know I like that."

She laughed, reached up with her other hand to pull his head down and bit him on the earlobe.

"No, he doesn't deserve it. Not yet anyway." She squeezed the slowly hardening prick in rebuke. The colonel's breathing was noticeably shallower. He started kissing her open-mouthed, his hand kneading first one and then the other nipple so hard that she wriggled.

"*Suce-moi,*" he whispered.

She shifted slightly and undid the pyjama cord. Raoul Saint-Clair watched the mane of brown hair fall forward from her head to shroud his belly, lay back, and sighed with pleasure.

"It seems the OAS are still after the President," he said. "The plot was discovered this afternoon. It's being taken care of. That's what kept me."

There was a soft "plop" as the girl withdrew her head a few inches.

"Don't be silly, darling, they were finished long ago." She went back to her task.

"They're sure as hell not. Now they've hired a foreign assassin to try to kill him. Aeeegh, don't bite."

Half an hour later Colonel Raoul Saint-Clair de Villauban lay asleep, face half-buried in the pillow, snoring gently from his exertions. Beside him his mistress lay staring up through the darkness at the ceiling, dimly lit where the lights from the street outside filtered through a tiny crack where the curtains joined.

What she had learned had left her aghast. Although she had had no previous knowledge of any such plot, she could work out for herself the importance of Kowalski's confession.

She waited in silence until the bedside clock with the luminous dials registered two in the morning. Easing herself out of the bed, she slid the plug of the bedroom telephone extension out of its socket.

Before walking to the door she bent over the colonel, and was grateful he was not the sort of man who liked to sleep in embrace with his bedmate. He was still snoring.

Outside the bedroom she quietly closed the door, crossed the sitting room towards the hall and closed that door after her. From the phone on the hall table she dialed a Molitor number. There was a wait of several minutes until a sleepy voice answered. She spoke rapidly for two minutes, received an acknowledgement, and hung up. A minute later she was back in bed, trying to get to sleep.

Throughout the night crime chiefs of the police forces of five European countries, America, and South Africa were being disturbed or waked with long-distance calls from Paris. Most of them were irritated and sleepy. In Western Europe the time was the same as Paris, the small hours of the morning. In Washington the time was nine in the evening when the call from Paris came through, and the chief of FBI Domestic Intelligence was at a dinner party. It was only at the third attempt that Caron could get him, and then their conversation was marred by the chatter of guests and the clink of glasses from the next room, where the party was in progress. But he got the message and agreed to be in the communications room of the FBI headquarters at ten past one in the morning, Washington time, to take a call from Commissaire Lebel, who would be ringing him from Interpol at ten past seven, Paris time.

The crime chiefs of the Belgian, Italian, German, and Dutch police were all apparently good family men; each was wakened in turn and after listening to Caron for a few minutes agreed to be in his communications room at the time Caron suggested to take a person-to-person call from Lebel on a matter of great urgency.

Van Ruys of South Africa was out of town and would not be able to get back to headquarters by sunrise, so Caron spoke to Anderson, his deputy.

The call reached Mr. Anthony Mallinson, Assistant Commissioner (Crime) for Scotland Yard, in his home at Bexley shortly before four. He growled in protest at the insistent clanging of the bell beside his bed, reached out for the mouthpiece, and muttered, "Mallinson."

"Mister Anthony Mallinson?" asked a voice.

"Speaking." He shrugged to clear the bedclothes from his shoulders, and glanced at his watch.

"My name is Inspector Lucien Caron, of the French Sûreté Nationale. I am ringing on behalf of Commissaire Claude Lebel."

The voice, speaking good but strongly accented English, was coming over clearly. Obviously line traffic at that hour was light. Mallinson frowned. Why couldn't the blighters call at a civilised hour?

"Yes?"

"I believe you know Commissaire Lebel, perhaps, Mister Mallinson?"

Mallinson thought for a moment. Lebel? Oh, yes, little fellow, had been head of Homicide in the PJ. Didn't look much but he got results. Been damn helpful over that murdered English tourist two years back. Could have been nasty in the press if they hadn't caught the killer in double-quick time.

"Yes, I know Commissaire Lebel," he said down the phone. "What's it about?"

Beside him his wife Lily, disturbed by the talking, grumbled in her sleep.

"There is a matter of very considerable urgency, which also requires a great degree of discretion, that has cropped up. I am assisting Commissaire Lebel on the case. It is a most unusual case. The Commissaire would like to place a person-to-person call to you in your communication room at the Yard this morning at nine o'clock. Could you please be present to take the call?"

Mallinson thought for a moment.

"Is this a routine enquiry between cooperating police forces?" he asked. If it were they could use the routine Interpol network. Nine o'clock was a busy time at the Yard.

"No, Mister Mallinson, it is not. It is a question of a personal request by the Commissaire to you for a little discreet assistance. It may be there is nothing that affects Scotland Yard in the matter that has come up. Most probably so. If that is the case, it would be better if there were no formal request placed."

Mallinson thought it over. He was by nature a cautious man and had no wish to be involved in clandestine enquiries from a foreign police force. If a crime had been committed or a criminal had fled to Britain, that was another matter. In that case why the secrecy? Nonetheless, Lebel wanted a bit of help on the Old Boy network and that was what Old Boy networks were for.

"All right, I'll take the call. Nine o'clock."

"Thank you so much, Mister Mallinson."

"Good night." Mallinson replaced the receiver, re-set the alarm clock for six-thirty instead of seven, and went back to sleep.

In a small and fusty bachelor flat, while Paris slept towards the dawn, a middle-aged schoolmaster paced up and down the floor of the cramped bedsitter. The scene around him was chaotic; books, newspapers, magazines and manuscripts lay scattered over the table, chairs and sofa, and even on the coverlet of the narrow bed set into its alcove on the far side of the room. In another alcove a sink overflowed with unwashed crockery.

What obsessed his thoughts in his nocturnal pacings was not the untidy state of his room, for since his removal from his post as headmaster of a lycée at Sidi-bel-Abbès and the loss of the fine house with two manservants that went with it, he had learned to live as he now did. His problem lay elsewhere.

As dawn was breaking over the eastern suburbs, he sat down finally and picked up one of the papers. His eye ran yet again down the second lead story on the foreign news page. It was headlined: "OAS CHIEFS HOLED UP IN ROME HOTEL." After reading it for the last time, he made up his mind, threw on a light mackintosh against the chill of the morning, and left the flat.

He caught a cruising taxi on the nearest boulevard and ordered the driver to take him to the Gare du Nord. Although the taxi dropped him in the forecourt, he walked away from the station as soon as the taxi had left, crossed the road and entered one of the all-night cafes of the area.

He ordered a coffee and a metal disc for the telephone, left the coffee on the counter, and went into the back of the cafe to dial. Directory Enquiries put him on to the International Exchange, and he asked them the number of a hotel in Rome. He got it within sixty seconds, replaced the receiver, and left.

At a cafe a hundred metres down the street he again used the phone, this time to ask Enquiries for the location of the nearest all-night post office from which international calls could be placed. He was told, as he had expected, that there was one round the corner from the mainline station.

At the post office he placed a call to the Rome number he had been given, without naming the hotel represented by the number, and spent an anxious twenty minutes waiting until it came through.

"I wish to speak to Signor Poitiers," he told the Italian voice that answered.

"*Signor Che?*" asked the voice.

"*Il signor francese*. Poitiers. Poitiers. . ."

"*Che?*" repeated the voice.

"*Francese, francese . . .*" said the man in Paris.

"*Ah, si, il signor francese. Un momento, per favore . . .*"

There was a series of clicks, then a tired voice answered in French.

"*Ouay . . .*"

"Listen," said the man in Paris urgently. "I don't have much time. Take a pencil and note what I say. Begins. 'Valmy to Poitiers. The Jackal is blown. Repeat. The Jackal is blown. Kowalski was taken. Sang before dying. Ends.' Got that?"

"*Ouay,*" said the voice. "I'll pass it on."

Valmy replaced the receiver, hurriedly paid his bill, and scurried out of the building. In a minute he was lost in the crowds of commuters streaming out of the main hall of the station. The sun was over the horizon, warming the pavements and the chill night air. Within half an hour the smell of morning and croissants and grinding coffee would vanish beneath the pall of exhaust fumes, body odour, and stale tobacco. Two minutes after Valmy had disappeared, a car drew up outside the post office, and two men from the DST hurried inside. They took a description from the switchboard operator, but it could have described anybody.

In Rome Marc Rodin was awakened at 7:55 when the man who had spent the night on the duty desk on the floor below shook him by the shoulder. He was awake in an instant, half out of bed, and groping for the gun under his pillow. He relaxed and grunted when he saw the face of the ex-legionnaire above him. A glance at the bedside table told him he had overslept anyway. After years in the tropics his habitual waking hour was much earlier, and the August sun of Rome was already high above the roofs. Weeks of inactivity, passing the evening hours playing piquet with Montclair and Casson, drinking too much rough red wine, taking no exercise worth the name, all had combined to make him slack and sleepy.

"A message, *mon colonel*. Someone phoned just now, seemed in a hurry."

The legionnaire proffered a sheet from a note pad on which were scribbled the disjointed phrases of Valmy. Rodin read through the message once, then leapt out of the thinly sheeted bed. He wrapped the cotton sarong he habitually wore, a habit from the East, round his waist, and read the message again.

"All right. Dismiss." The legionnaire left the room and went back downstairs.

Rodin swore silently and intensely for several seconds, crumpling the piece of paper in his hands. Damn, damn, damn, damn Kowalski.

For the first two days after Kowalski's disappearance he had thought the man had simply deserted. There had been several defections of late from the cause, as the conviction set in among the rank and file that the OAS had failed and would fail in its aim of killing Charles de Gaulle and bringing down the present government of France. He had always thought Kowalski would remain loyal to the last. Yet here was evidence that he had for some inexplicable reason returned to France, or perhaps been picked up inside Italy and abducted. Now it seemed he had talked, under pressure, of course.

Rodin genuinely grieved for his dead servitor. Part of the considerable reputation he had built up as a fighting soldier and commanding officer had been based on the enormous concern he showed for his men. These things are appreciated by fighting soldiers more than any military theorist can ever imagine. Now Kowalski was dead and Rodin had few illusions in the manner of his passing.

Still, the important thing was to try to recollect just what Kowalski had had to tell. The meeting in Vienna, the name of the hotel. Of course all of that. The three men who had been at the meeting. This would be no news to the SDECE. But what did he know about the Jackal? He had not been listening at the door, that was certain. He could tell them of a tall blond foreigner who had visited the three of them. That in itself meant nothing. Such a foreigner could have been an arms dealer, or a financial backer. There had been no names mentioned.

But Valmy's message mentioned the Jackal by his code-name. How? How could Kowalski have told them that?

With a start of horror Rodin recalled the scene as they had parted. He had stood in the doorway with the Englishman; Viktor had been a few feet down the corridor, annoyed at the way the Englishman had spotted him in the alcove, a professional outmanoeuvred by another professional, waiting for trouble, almost hoping for it. What had he, Rodin, said? "*Bonsoir, Monsieur Chacal.*" Of course, damn and blast it.

Thinking things over again, Rodin realised that Kowalski could never have got the killer's real name. Only he, Montclair, and Casson knew that. All the same, Valmy was right. With Kowalski's confession in the hands of the SDECE, it was too far blown to be retrievable. They had the meeting, the hotel, probably they had already talked to the desk clerk; they had the face and figure of the man, a code-name. There could be no doubt they would guess what Kowalski had guessed—that the blond was a killer. From then on the net around de Gaulle would tighten; he would abandon all public engagements, all exits from his palace, all chances for an assassin to get him. It was over; the operation was blown. He would have to call off the Jackal, insist on the money back, minus all expense and a retainer for the time and trouble involved.

There was one thing to be settled, and quickly. The Jackal himself must be warned urgently to halt operations. Rodin was still enough of a commanding officer not to send a man out on his orders on a mission for which success had been impossible.

He summoned the bodyguard to whom, since the departure of Kowalski, he had given the duties of going every day to the main post office to collect the mail and, if necessary, make telephone calls, and briefed him at length.

By nine o'clock the bodyguard was in the post office and asked for a telephone number in London. It took twenty minutes before the telephone on the other end began to ring. The switchboard operator gestured the Frenchman to a cabin to take the call. He picked up the receiver as the operator put hers down, and listened to the buzz-buzzz . . . pause . . . bzzz-bzzz of an English telephone ringing.

The Jackal rose early that morning, for he had much to do. The three main suitcases he had checked and re-packed the previous evening. Only the hand-grip remained to be topped up with his sponge bag and shaving tackle. He drank his habitual two cups of coffee, washed, showered, and shaved. After packing the remainder of the overnight toiletries, he closed up the hand luggage and stored all four pieces by the door.

He made himself a quick breakfast of scrambled eggs, orange juice, and more black coffee in the flat's small but compact kitchen, and ate it off the kitchen table. Being a tidy and methodical man, he emptied the last of the milk down the sink, broke the two remaining eggs, and poured them also down the sink. The remainder of the orange juice he drank off, junked the can in the trash basket, and the remainder of the bread, egg shells, and coffee grounds went down the disposal unit. Nothing left would be likely to go rotten during his absence.

Finally he dressed, choosing a thin silk polo-necked sweater, the dove-grey suit containing the private papers in the name of Duggan, and the hundred pounds in cash, dark grey socks, and slim black moccasin shoes. The ensemble was completed by the inevitable dark glasses.

At 9:15 he took his luggage, two pieces in each hand, closed the self-locking flat door behind him, and went downstairs. It was a short walk up Adam Mews to South Audley Street, and he caught a taxi on the corner.

"London Airport, Number Two Building," he told the driver.

As the taxi moved away, the phone in his flat began to ring.

It was ten o'clock when the legionnaire returned to the hotel off the Via Condotti and told Rodin he had tried for thirty minutes to get a reply from the London number he had been given, but had not succeeded.

"What's the matter?" asked Casson, who had heard the explanation given to Rodin and seen the legionnaire dismissed to return to his guard station. The two OAS chiefs were sitting in the drawing room of their suite. Rodin withdrew a piece of paper from his inside pocket and passed it over to Casson.

Casson read and passed it to Montclair. Both men finally looked at their leader for an answer. There was none, Rodin sat staring out of the windows across the baking roofs of Rome, brow furrowed in thought.

"When did it come?" asked Casson eventually.

"This morning," replied Rodin briefly.

"You've got to stop him," protested Montclair. "They'll have half France on the lookout for him."

"They'll have half of France on the lookout for a tall blond foreigner," said Rodin quietly. "In August there are over one million foreigners in France. So far as we know they have no name to go on, no face, no passport. Being a professional, he is probably using a false passport. They still have a long way to go to get him yet. There's a good chance he will be forewarned if he rings Valmy, and then he'll be able to get out again."

"If he rings Valmy, he will of course be ordered to drop the operation," said Montclair. "Valmy will order him."

Rodin shook his head.

"Valmy does not have the authority to do that. His orders are to receive information from the girl and pass it on to the Jackal when he is telephoned. He will do that, but nothing else."

"But the Jackal must realise of his own accord that it is all over," protested Montclair. "He must get out of France as soon as he rings Valmy the first time."

"In theory yes," said Rodin thoughtfully. "If he does he hands back the money. There's a lot at stake, for all of us, including him. It depends how confident he feels of his own planning."

"Do you think he has a chance now—now that this has happened?" asked Casson.

"Frankly, no," said Rodin. "But he is a professional. So am I, in my way. It is a frame of mind. One does not like to stand down an operation one has planned personally."

"Then for God's sake recall him," protested Casson.

"I can't. I would if I could, but I can't. He's gone. He's on his way. He wanted it this way and now he's got it. We don't know where he is or what he is going to do. He's completely on his own. I can't even call up Valmy and order him to instruct the Jackal to drop the whole thing. To do so would risk 'blowing' Valmy. Nobody can stop the Jackal now. It's too late."

TWELVE

Commissaire Claude Lebel arrived back in his office just before 6 in the morning to find Inspector Caron looking tired and strained, in shirtsleeves at his desk.

He had several sheets of foolscap paper in front of him covered with hand-written notes. In the office some things had changed. On top of the filing cabinets an electric coffee percolator bubbled, sending out a delicious aroma of freshly brewed coffee. Next to it stood a pile of paper cups, a tin of unsweetened milk, and a bag of sugar. These had come up from the basement canteen during the night.

In the corner between the two desks a single truckle bed had been set up, covered with a rough blanket. The waste-paper basket had been emptied and stored next to the armchair by the door.

The window was open still, a faint haze of blue smoke from Caron's cigarette drifting out into the cool morning. Beyond the window the first flecks of the coming day mottled the spire of Saint Sulpice.

Lebel crossed to his desk and slumped into the chair. Although it was only twenty-four hours since he had waked from his last sleep, he looked tired, like Caron.

"Nothing," he said. "I've been through the lot over the past ten years. The only foreign political killer who ever tried to operate here was Degueldre, and he's dead. Besides, he was OAS and we had him on file as such. Presumably Rodin has chosen a man who has nothing to do with the OAS, and he's quite right. There were only four contract-hire killers who tried it in France over the past ten years—apart from the home-grown variety—and we got three. The fourth is doing life in Africa somewhere. Besides, they were all gangland killers, not of the calibre to shoot down a President of France.

"I got on to Bargeron of Central Records, and they're doing a complete double-check, but I suspect already that we don't have this man on file. Rodin would in any case insist on that before hiring him."

Caron lit up another Gauloise, blew out the smoke and sighed.

"So we have to start from the foreign end?"

"Precisely. A man of this type must have got his training and experience somewhere. He wouldn't be one of the world's tops unless he could prove it with a string of successful jobs behind him. Not presidents perhaps, but important men, bigger than mere underworld chiefs. That means he must have come to someone's attention somewhere. Surely. What have you arranged?"

Caron picked up one of the sheets of paper, showing a list of names with, in the left-hand column, a series of timings.

"The seven are all fixed," he said. "You start with the head of Domestic Intelligence, FBI, at ten past seven. That's ten past one in the morning, Washington time. I fitted him in first because of the lateness of the hour in America.

"Then Brussels at half past seven, Amsterdam at quarter to eight, and Bonn at eight-ten. The link is arranged with Johannesburg at eight-thirty and with Scotland Yard at nine. Lastly there is Rome at nine-thirty."

"The heads of Homicide in each case?" asked Lebel.

"Or the equivalent. With Scotland Yard it's Mr. Anthony Mallinson, Assistant Commissioner (Crime). It seems they don't have a Homicide section in the Metropolitan Police. Apart from that, yes, except South Africa. I couldn't get Van Ruys at all, so you're talking to Assistant Commissioner Anderson."

Lebel thought for a moment.

"That's fine. I'd prefer Anderson. We worked on a case once. There's the question of language. Three of them speak English. I suppose only the Belgian speaks French. The others almost certainly can speak English if they have to—"

"The German, Dietrich, speaks French," interjected Caron.

"Good, then I'll speak to those two in French personally. For the other five I'll have to have you on the extension as interpreter. We'd better go. Come on."

It was ten to seven when the police car carrying the two detectives drew up outside the innocent green door in the tiny rue Paul Valéry which housed the headquarters of Interpol.

For the next three hours Lebel and Caron sat hunched over the telephone in the basement communications room talking to the world's top crime busters. From the seemingly tangled web of aerials on the roof of the building the high-frequency signals beamed out across three continents, streaming high beyond the stratosphere to bounce off the ionic layer above and home back to earth thousands of miles away to another stick of aluminum jutting from a tiled rooftop.

The wavelengths and scramblers were uninterceptable. Detective spoke to detective while the world drank its morning coffee or final nightcap.

In each telephone conversation Lebel's appeal was much the same.

"No, Commissioner, I cannot yet put this request for your assistance on the level of an official enquiry between our two police forces. . . . Certainly I am acting in an official capacity. . . . It is simply that for the moment we are just not sure if even the intent to commit an offence has been formulated or put into the preparation stage. . . . It's a question of a tip-off, purely routine for the moment. . . . Well, we are looking for a man about whom we know extremely little . . . not even a name, and only a poor description . . . "

In each case he gave the description as best he knew it. The sting came in the tail, as each of his foreign colleagues asked why their help was being sought, and what clues they could possibly go on. It was at that point that the other end of the line became tensely silent.

"Simply this; that whoever this man is or may be, he must have one qualification that marks him out: he would have to be one of the world's top professional contract-hire assassins. . . . No, not a gangland trigger, a political assassin with several successful kills behind him. We would be interested to know if you have anybody like that on your files, even if he has never operated in your own country. Or anybody that even springs to mind."

Inevitably there was a long pause at the other end before the voice resumed. Then it was quieter, more concerned.

Lebel had no illusions that the heads of the Homicide departments of the major police forces of the Western world would fail to understand what he was hinting at but could not say. There was only one target in France that could interest a first-league political killer.

Without exception the reply was the same. Yes, of course. We'll go through all the files for you. I'll try and get back to you before the day is out. Oh, and Claude, good luck.

When he put down the radio-telephone receiver for the last time, Lebel wondered how long it would be before the Foreign Ministers and even Prime Ministers of the seven countries would be aware of what was on. Probably not long. Even a policeman had to report to the politicians something of that size. He was fairly certain the Ministers would keep quiet about it. There was, after all, a strong bond over and above political differences between the men of power the world over. They were all members of the same club, the club of the potentates. They stuck together against common enemies, and what could be more inimical to any of them than the activities of a political assassin? He was aware all the same that if the enquiry did become public knowledge and reached the press, it would be blasted across the world and he would be finished.

The only people who did worry him were the English. If it could only be kept between cops, he would have trusted Mallinson.

But he knew that before the day was out it would have to go higher than Mallinson. It was only seven months since Charles de Gaulle had brusquely rebuffed Britain's bid to the Common Market, and in the wake of the

General's January 23 press conference the London Foreign Office, as even so apolitical a creature as Lebel was aware, had become almost lyrical in its campaign of words planted through the political correspondents against the French President. Would they now use this to get their revenge on the old man?

Lebel stared for a moment at the now silent transmitter panel in front of him. Caron watched him quietly.

"Come on," said the little Commissaire, rising from the stool and heading for the door, "let's get some breakfast and try to get some sleep. There's not much more we can do now."

Assistant-Commissioner Anthony Mallinson put down the telephone with a thoughtful frown and left the communications room without acknowledging the salute of a young policeman who was entering to take up his morning shift. He was still frowning as he went back upstairs to his spacious but soberly appointed office overlooking the Thames.

There was no doubt in his mind of what kind of enquiry Lebel had been making, or of his motives for making it. The French police had got some kind of tip-off that a top-class assassin was on the loose, and that it affected them. As Lebel had predicted to himself, it took very little acumen to work out who could be the only possible target in France in August 1963 for that kind of killer. He considered Lebel's predicament with the knowledge of a long-time policeman.

"Poor bastard," he said aloud as he stared down at the warm and sluggish river flowing past the Embankment beneath his window.

"Sir?" asked his Personal Aide, who had followed him into the office to put the morning mail that needed his attention on the walnut desk.

"Nothing." Mallinson continued to stare out the window as the PA left. However he might feel for Claude Lebel in his task of trying to protect his President without being able to launch an official manhunt, he too had masters. Sooner or later they would have to be told of Lebel's request to him that morning. There was the daily heads-of-department conference at ten, in half an hour's time. Should he mention it there?

On balance he decided not to. It would be enough to write a formal but private memorandum to the Commissioner himself, outlining the nature of Lebel's request. The necessity for discretion would explain later, if necessary, why the matter had not been raised at the morning meeting. In the meantime it would do no harm to put through the enquiry without revealing why it was being made.

He took his seat behind the desk and pressed one of the buttons on the intercom.

"Sir?" his PA's voice came through from the adjoining office.

"Come in here a minute, would you, John?"

The charcoal-grey-suited young detective-inspector came in, notebook in hand.

"John, I want you to get on to Central Records. Speak to Chief Superintendent Markham personally. Tell him the request is from me personally, and that I cannot explain for the moment why I am asking it. Ask him to check every existing record of known living professional assassins in this country—"

"Assassins, sir?" The PA looked as if the Assistant Commissioner had asked for a routine check on all known Martians.

"Yes, assassins. Not, repeat not, run-of-the-mill gangland thugs who either have or are known to be capable of knocking off somebody in a feud in the underworld. Political killers, John, men or a man capable of assassinating a well-guarded politician or statesman for money."

"That sounds more like Special Branch customers, sir."

'Yes, I know. I want to pass the whole thing to Special Branch. But we had better do a routine check first. Oh, and I want an answer one way or the other by midday. OK?"

"Right, sir, I'll get on to it."

Fifteen minutes later Assistant Commissioner Mallinson took his seat at the morning conference.

When he returned to his office he flicked through the mail, pushed it to one side of the desk, and ordered the PA to bring him in a typewriter. Sitting alone, he typed out a brief report for the Commissioner of Metropolitan Police. It mentioned briefly the morning call to his home, the person-to-person call over the Interpol link at nine in the morning, and the nature of Lebel's enquiry. He left the bottom of the memorandum form empty, and locked it away in his desk to get on with the day's work.

Shortly before twelve the PA knocked and entered.

"Superintendent Markham's just been on from CRO," he said. "Apparently there's no one on Criminal Records who can fit that description. Seventeen known contract-hire killers from the underworld, sir; ten in jail and seven on the loose. But they all work for the big gangs, either here or in the main cities. The Super says none would fit for a job against a visiting politician. He suggested Special Branch too, sir."

"Right, John, thank you. That's all I needed."

With the PA dismissed, Mallinson took the half-finished memo from his drawer and re-inserted it into the typewriter. On the bottom he wrote:

"Criminal Records reported upon enquiry that no person fitting the description of type submitted by Commissaire Lebel could be traced in their files. The enquiry was then passed to the Assistant Commissioner, Special Branch."

He signed the memorandum and took the top three copies. The remainder went into the waste-paper basket for classified waste, later to be destroyed.

One of the copies he folded into an envelope and addressed to the Commissioner. The second he filed in the "Secret Correspondence" file and locked it into the wall safe. The third he folded and placed in his inside pocket.

On his desk note-pad he scribbled a message.

> To: Commissaire Claude Lebel, Deputy Director-General, Police Judiciaire, Paris.
>
> From: Assistant-Commissioner Anthony Mallinson, A.C. Crime, Scotland Yard, London.
>
> Message: Following your enquiry this date fullest research criminal records reveals no such personage known to us stop request passing to Special Branch for further checking stop any useful information will be passed to you soonest stop Mallinson.

Time sent: 12.8.63

It was just gone half past twelve. He picked up the phone and, when the operator answered, asked for Assistant Commissioner Dixon, head of Special Branch.

"Hallo, Alec? Tony Mallinson. Can you spare me a minute? . . . I'd love to but I can't. I shall have to keep lunch down to a sandwich. It's going to be one of those days. No, I just want to see you for a few minutes before you go. . . . Fine, good, I'll come right along."

On his way through the office he dropped the envelope addressed to the Commissioner on the PA's desk.

"I'm just going up to see Dixon of the S.B. Get that along to the Commissioner's office, would you, John? Personally. And get this message off to the addressee. Type it out yourself in the proper style."

"Yes, sir." Mallinson stood over the desk while the detective inspector's eyes ran through the message. They widened as they reached the end.

"John . . . "

"Sir?"

"And keep quiet about it, please."

"Yes, sir."

"Very quiet, John."

"Not a word, sir."

Mallinson gave him a brief smile and left the office. The PA read the message for Lebel a second time, thought back to the enquiries he had made with Records that morning for Mallinson, worked it out for himself, and whispered, "Bloody hell."

Mallinson spent twenty minutes with Dixon and effectively ruined the other's forthcoming club lunch. He passed over to the Head of Special Branch the remaining copy of the memorandum to the Commissioner. As he rose to leave he turned at the door, hand on the knob.

"Sorry, Alec, but this really is more up your street. But if you ask me, there's probably nothing and nobody of that calibre in this country, so a good check of records and you should be able to telex Lebel to say we can't help. I must say I don't envy him his job this time."

Assistant Commissioner Dixon, whose job among other things was to keep tabs on all the weird and crazy of Britain who might think of trying to assassinate a visiting politician, not to mention the scores of embittered and cranky foreigners domiciled in the country, felt even more keenly the impossibility of Lebel's position. To have to protect home and visiting politicians from unbalanced fanatics was bad enough, but at least they could usually be relied upon as amateurs to fail in the face of his own corps of case-hardened professionals.

To have one's own head of state the target for a native organisation of tough ex-soldiers was even worse. And yet the French had beaten the OAS. As a professional, Dixon admired them for it. But the hiring of a foreign professional was a different matter. Only one thing could be said in its favour, from Dixon's point of view; it cut the possibles down to so few that he had no doubts there would prove to be no Englishman of the calibre of the man Lebel sought on the books of the Special Branch.

After Mallinson had left, Dixon read the carbon copy of the memorandum. Then he summoned his own PA.

"Please tell Detective Superintendent Thomas I would like to see him here at"—he glanced at his watch, estimated how long a much shortened lunch-hour would take him—"two o'clock sharp."

The Jackal landed at Brussels National just after 12. He left his three main pieces of luggage in an automatic locker in the main terminal building and took with him into town only the hand-grip containing his personal effects, the plaster of Paris, pads of cotton wool, and bandages. At the main station he dismissed the taxi and went to the left-luggage office.

The fibre suitcase containing the gun was still on the shelf where he had seen the clerk deposit it a week earlier. He presented the reclamation slip and was gaiven the case in return.

Not far from the station he found a small and squalid hotel, of the kind that seem to exist in proximity to all main line stations the world over, which ask no questions but get told a lot of lies.

He booked a single room for the night, paid cash in advance in Belgian money that he had changed at the airport, and took his case up to the room himself. With the door safely locked behind him, he ran a basin of cold water, emptied the plaster and bandages onto the bed, and set to work.

It took over two hours for the plaster to dry when he had finished. During this time he sat with his heavy foot and leg resting on a stool, smoking his filter cigarettes and looking out over the grimy array of rooftops that formed the vista from the bedroom window. Occasionally he would test the plaster with his thumb, each time deciding to let it harden a bit more before moving.

The fibre suitcase that had formerly contained the gun lay empty. The remainder of the bandages were re-packed in the hand-grip along with the few ounces of plaster that were left, in case he had to do some running repairs. When he was finally ready, he slid the cheap fibre case under the bed, checked the room for any last tell-tale signs, emptied the ashtray out of the window, and prepared to leave.

He found that with the plaster on, a realistic limp became obligatory. At the bottom of the stairs he was relieved to find the grubby and sleepy-looking desk clerk was in the back room behind the desk, where he had been when the Jackal arrived. Since it was lunchtime, he was eating, but the door with the frosted glass that gave him access to the front counter was open.

With a glance at the front door to make sure no one was coming in, the Jackal clutched his hand-case to his chest, bent onto all fours, and scuttled quickly and silently across the tiled floor. Because of the heat of summer the front door was open and he was able to stand upright on the top of the three steps that led to the street, out of the line of sight of the desk clerk.

He limped painfully down the steps and along the street to the corner where the main road ran past. A taxi spotted him inside half a minute, and he was on his way back to the airport.

He presented himself at the Alitalia counter, passport in hand. The girl smiled at him.

"I believe you have a ticket for Milan reserved two days ago in the name of Duggan," he said.

She checked the bookings for the afternoon flight to Milan. It was due to leave in an hour and a half.

"Yes, indeed," she beamed at him. "Meester Duggan. The ticket was reserved but not paid for. You wish to pay for it?"

The Jackal paid in cash again, was issued with his ticket, and was told he would be called in an hour. With the aid of a solicitous porter who tut-tutted over his plastered foot and pronounced limp, he withdrew his three suitcases from the locker, consigned them to Alitalia, passed through the customs barrier, which, seeing that he was an outgoing traveller, was merely a passport check, and spent the remaining hour enjoying a late lunch in the restaurant attached to the passenger departure lounge.

Everybody concerned with the flight was very kind and considerate towards him because of the leg. He was assisted aboard the coach out to the aircraft and watched with concern as he made his painful way up the steps to the aircraft's door. The lovely Italian hostess gave him an extra wide smile of welcome and saw him comfortably seated in one of the group of seats in the centre of the aircraft that face towards each other. There was more leg room there, she pointed out.

The other passengers took elaborate pains not to knock against the plastered foot as they took their seats, while the Jackal lay back in his seat and smiled bravely.

At 4:15 the airliner was on take-off and was soon speeding southwards, bound for Milan.

Superintendent Bryn Thomas emerged from the Assistant Commissioner's office just before 3, feeling thoroughly miserable. Not only was his summer cold one of the worst and most persistent he had ever been plagued with, but the new assignment with which he had just been saddled had ruined his day.

As Monday mornings went, it had been rotten; first he had learned that one of his men had been given the slip by a Soviet trade delegate whom he was supposed to be tailing, and by mid-morning he had received an inter-departmental complaint from MI-5 politely asking his department to lay off the Soviet delegation, an unmistakable suggestion that in the view of MI-5 the whole matter had better be left to them.

Monday afternoon looked like being worse. There are few things that any policeman, Special Branch or not, likes less than the spectre of the political assassin. But in the case of the request he had just received from his superior, he had not even been given a name to go on.

"No name, but I'm afraid plenty of pack-drill," had been Dixon's bon mot on the subject. "Try and get it out of the way by tomorrow."

"Pack-drill," snorted Thomas when he reached the office. Although the short-list of known suspects would be extremely short, it still presented him and his department with hours of checking of files, records for political trouble-making, convictions, and, unlike the criminal branch, mere suspicions. All would have to be checked. There was only one ray of light in Dixon's briefings: the man would be a professional operator and not one of the numberless bee-in-the-bonnet merchants that made the Special Branch's life a misery before and during any foreign statesman's visit.

He summoned two detective inspectors whom he knew to be presently engaged on low-priority work, told them to drop whatever they were doing, as he had been, and to report to his office. His briefing to them was shorter than Dixon's had been to him. He confined himself to telling them what they were looking for, but not why. The suspicions of the French police that such a man might be out to kill General de Gaulle need have nothing to do with the search through the archives and records of Scotland Yard's Special Branch.

The three of them cleared the desks of outstanding paperwork and settled down.

The Jackal's plane touched down at Linate Airport, Milan, shortly after six. He was helped by the ever-attentive hostess down the steps to the tarmac, and escorted by one of the ground hostesses to the main terminal building. It was at customs that his elaborate preparations in getting the component parts of the gun out of the suitcases and into a less suspicious means of carriage paid dividends. The passport check was a formality but as the suitcases from the hold came rumbling through on the conveyor belt and were deposited along the length of the customs bench, the risks began to mount.

The Jackal secured a porter who assembled the three main suitcases into a line side by side. The Jackal put his hand-grip down beside them. Seeing him limp up to the bench, one of the customs officers sauntered across.

"Signor? This is all your baggage?"

"Er, yes, these three suitcases and this little case."

"You have anything to declare?"

"No, nothing."

'You are on business, signor?"

"No, I've come on holiday, but it turns out it must also include a period of convalescence. I hope to go up to the lakes."

The customs man was not impressed.

"May I see your passport, signor?"

The Jackal handed it over. The Italian examined it closely, then handed it back without a word.

"Please, open this one."

He gestured at one of the three larger suitcases. The Jackal took out his key-ring, selected one of the keys and opened the case. The porter had laid it flat on its side to help him. Fortunately it was the case containing the clothes of the fictitious Danish pastor and the American student. Riffling through the clothes, the customs officer attached no importance to a dark grey suit, underwear, white shirt, loafers, black walking shoes, windbreaker, and socks. Nor did the book in Danish excite him. The cover was a colourplate of Chartres cathedral, and the title, although in Danish, was sufficiently like the equivalent English words not to be remarkable. He did not examine the carefully re-sewn slit in the side lining or find the false identity papers. A really thorough search would have found them, but his was the usual perfunctory run-through that would only have become intensive if he had found something suspicious. The component parts of a complete sniper's rifle were only three feet away from him across the desk, but he suspected nothing. He closed the case and gestured to the Jackal to lock it again. Then he chalked all four cases in quick succession. His job done, the Italian's face broke into a smile.

"*Grazie, signor.* A 'appy holiday."

The porter found a taxi, was well tipped, and soon the Jackal was speeding into Milan, its usually clamorous streets made even noisier by the streams of commuter traffic trying to get home and the constant horn-honking of the drivers. He asked to be taken to the Central Station.

Here another porter was summoned, and he hobbled after the man to the left-luggage office. In the taxi he had slipped the steel shears out of the overnight case into his trouser pocket. At the left-luggage office he deposited the hand-grip and two suitcases, retaining the one containing the long French military overcoat, which also had plenty of spare room.

Dismissing the porter, he hobbled into the men's toilet, to find only one of the wash basins in the long row on the left-hand side of the urinals was in use. He dropped the case and laboriously washed his hands until the other occupant was finished. When the toilet was empty for a second he was across the room and locked into one of the cubicles.

With his foot up on the lavatory seat he chipped silently for ten minutes at the plaster on his foot until it began to drop away, reveaing the cotton wool pads beneath that had given the foot the bulk of a normally fractured ankle encased in plaster.

When the foot was finally clear of the last remnants of plaster, he put back on the silk sock and the slim leather moccasin which had been taped to the inside of his calf while the foot had been in plaster. The remainder of the plaster and cotton wool he gathered up and deposited down the pan. At the first flushing half of it jammed, but it cleared at the second.

He laid the suitcase on top of the toilet and placed the series of circular steel tubes containing the rifle side by side among the folds of the coat until the case was full. When the inside straps were tight the contents of the case were prevented from banging about. Then he closed the case and cast a look outside the door. There were two people at the wash basins and two more standing at the urinals. He left the cubicle, turned sharply towards the door, and was up the steps into the main hall of the station before any had time to notice him, even if they had wished to.

He could not go back to the left-luggage office a fit and healthy man so soon after leaving it as a cripple, so he summoned a porter, explained that he was in a hurry, wished to change money, reclaim his baggage and get a taxi as soon as possible The baggage check he thrust into the porter's hand, along with a thousand-lire note, pointing the man towards the left-luggage office. He himself, he indicated, would be getting his English pounds changed into lire.

The Italian nodded happily and went off to get the luggage. The Jackal changed the last twenty pounds that remained to him into Italian currency and was just finished when the porter returned with the other three pieces of luggage. Two minutes later he was in a taxi speeding dangerously across the Piazza Duca d'Aosta and heading for the Hotel Continentale.

At the reception desk in the splendid front hall he told the clerk, "I believe you have a room for me in the name of Duggan. It was booked by telephone from London two days ago."

Just before 8 the Jackal was enjoying the luxury of a shower and shave in his room. Two of the suitcases were carefully locked into the wardrobe. The third, containing his own clothes, was open on the bed, and the suit for the evening, a navy blue wool-and-mohair summer lightweight, was hanging from the wardrobe door. The dove-grey suit was in the hands of the hotel's valet service for sponging and pressing. Ahead lay cocktails, dinner, and an easy night, for the next day, August 13, would be extremely busy.

THIRTEEN

"Nothing."

The second of the two young detective inspectors in Bryn Thomas's office closed the last of the folders he had been allotted to read and looked across at his superior.

His colleague had also finished, and his conclusion had been the same. Thomas himself had finished five minutes before and had walked over to the window, standing with his back to the room and staring at the traffic flowing past in the dusk. Unlike Assistant Commissioner Mallinson, he did not have a view of the river, just a first-floor vista of the cars churning down Horseferry Road. He felt like death. His throat was raw from cigarettes, which he knew he should not have been smoking with a heavy cold, but could not give up, particularly when under pressure.

His head ached from the fumes, the incessant calls that had been made throughout the afternoon checking on characters turned up in the records and files. Each call-back had been negative. The man was either fully accounted for or simply not of the calibre to undertake a mission like killing the French President.

"Right, that's it, then," he said firmly, spinning round from the window. "We've done all we can, and there just isn't anybody who could possibly fit the guide-lines laid down in the request we have been investigating."

"It could be that there is an Englishman who does this kind of work," suggested one of the inspectors. "But he's not in our files."

"They're all in our files, look you," growled Thomas. It did not amuse him to think that as interesting a creature as a professional assassin existed in his "manor" without being on file somewhere, and his temper was not improved by his cold or his headache.

"After all," said the other inspector, "a political killer is an extremely rare bird. There probably isn't such a thing in this country. It's not quite the English cup of tea, is it?"

Thomas glowered back. He preferred the word "British" to describe the inhabitants of the United Kingdom, and the inspector's inadvertent use of the word "English" he suspected might be a veiled suggestion that the Welsh, Scottish, or Irish could well have produced such a man. But it wasn't.

"All right, pack up the files. Take them back to registry. I'll reply that a thorough search has revealed no such character known to us. That's all we can do."

"Who was the enquiry from, Super?" asked one.

"Never you mind, boy. Someone's got problems by the look of it, but it isn't us."

The two younger men had gathered up all the material and headed for the door. Both had families to get home to, and one was expecting to become a first-time father almost any day. He went straight to the door. The other turned back with a thoughtful frown.

"Super, there's one thing occurred to me while I was checking. If there is such a man, and he's got British nationality, it seems he probably wouldn't operate here anyway. I mean, even a man like that has to have a base somewhere. A refuge, sort of, a place to come back to. Chances are such a man is a respectable citizen in his own country."

"What are you getting at, a sort of Jekyll and Hyde?"

"Well, something like that. I mean, if there is a professional killer about, of the type we've been trying to track, and he's big enough for somebody to pull the kind of weight to get an investigation like this started, with a man of your rank leading it, well the man in question must be big. And if he's that, in his field, he must have a few jobs behind him. Otherwise he wouldn't be anything, would he?"

"Go on," said Thomas, watching him carefully.

"Well, I just thought that a man like that would probably operate only outside his own country. So he wouldn't normally come to the attention of the internal security forces. Perhaps the Service might have got wind of him once. . . ."

Thomas considered the idea, then slowly shook his head.

"Forget it, get on home, boy. I'll write the report. And just forget we ever made the enquiry."

But when the inspector was gone, the idea he had sown remained in Thomas's mind. He could sit down and write the report now. Complete negative. Drawn a blank. There could be no comebacks on the basis of the search of records that had been made. But supposing there was something behind the enquiry from France? Supposing the French had not, as Thomas suspected they had, simply lost their heads over a rumour concerning their precious President? If they really had as little to go on as they claimed, if there was no indication that the man was an Englishman, then they must be checking all over the world in a similar way. Chances were heavily odds-on there was no killer, and if there were, that he came from one of those nations with long histories of political assassinations. But what if the French suspicions were accurate? And if the man turned out to be English, even by birth alone?

Thomas was intensely proud of the record of Scotland Yard, and particularly of the Special Branch. They had never had trouble of this kind. They had never lost a visiting foreign dignitary. He personally had even had to look after that Russian bastard Ivan Serov, head of the KGB, when he came to prepare for Khrushchev's and Bulganin's visit, and there had been scores of Balts and Poles who wanted to get Serov. Not even a shooting, and the place crawling with Serov's own security men, every one packing a gun and quite prepared to use it.

Superintendent Bryn Thomas had two years to go before retirement and the journey back to the little house he and Mag had bought looking out over the green turf to the Bristol Channel. Better be safe, check everything.

In his youth Thomas had been a very fine Rugby player, and there were many who had played against Glamorgan who remembered clearly the inadvisability of making a blind-side break when Bryn Thomas was wing forward. He was too old for it now, of course, but he still took a keen interest in the London Welsh when he could get away from work and go down to the Old Deer Park at Richmond to see them play. He knew all the players well, spending time in the club house chatting with them after a match, and his reputation was enough to ensure that he was always welcome.

One of the players was known to the rest of the members simply to be on the staff of the Foreign Office. Thomas knew he was a bit more than that; the department, under the auspices of the Foreign Secretary but not attached to the Foreign Office, for which Barrie Lloyd worked was the Secret Intelligence Service, sometimes called the SIS, sometimes simply "the Service," and more usually among the public by its incorrect name of MI-6.

The two men met for a drink in a quiet pub down by the river between eight and nine. They talked Rugby for a while, as Thomas bought the drinks. But Lloyd guessed the man from Special Branch had not asked to see him at a riverside pub to talk about a season which would not start for another two months. When they had both got their drinks and given each other a perfunctory "Cheers," Thomas gestured with his head outside onto the terrace that led down to the wharf. It was quieter outside, for most of the young couples from Chelsea and Fulham were drinking up and heading off for dinner.

"Got a bit of a problem, boyo," began Thomas. "Hoped you might be able to help."

"Well. . . if I can," said Lloyd.

Thomas explained about the request from Paris and the blank drawn by Criminal Records and the Special Branch.

"It occurred to me that if there ever was such a man, and a British one at that, he might be the kind who would never get his hands dirty inside this country, see. Might just stick to operations abroad. If he ever had left a trail, maybe he came to the attention of the Service?"

"Service?" asked Lloyd quietly.

"Come on, Barrie. We have to know a lot of things, from time to time." Thomas's voice was hardly above a murmur. From the back they looked like two men in dark suits staring out over the dusky river at the lights of the south bank, talking of the day's dealings in the City. "We had to turn over a lot of files during the Blake investigations. A lot of Foreign Office people got a peek taken at what they were really up to. Yours was one, see. You were in his section at the time he came under suss. So I know what department you work with."

"I see," said Lloyd.

"Now look, I may be Bryn Thomas down at the Park. But I'm also a Superintendent of the S.B., right? You can't be anonymous from everyone now, can you?"

Lloyd stared into his glass.

"Is this an official enquiry for information?"

"No, I can't make it that yet. The French request was an unofficial request from Lebel to Mallinson. He could find nothing in Central Records, so he replied that he couldn't help, but he also had a word with Dixon. Who asked me to have a quick check. All on the quiet, see? Mustn't get out to the press or anything. Chances are there's nothing here in Britain at all that might help Lebel. I just thought I'd cover all the angles, and you were the last."

"This man is supposed to be after de Gaulle?"

"Must be, by the sound of the enquiry. But the French must be playing it very cagey. They obviously don't want any publicity."

"Obviously. But why not contact us direct?"

"The request for suggestions as to a name has been put through on the Old Boy network. From Lebel to Mallinson, direct. Perhaps the French Secret Service doesn't have an Old Boy network with your section."

If Lloyd had noticed the reference to the notoriously bad relations between the SDECE and the SIS, he gave no sign of it.

"What are you thinking?" asked Thomas after a while.

"Funny," said Lloyd staring out over the river. "You remember the Philby case?"

"Of course."

"Still a very sore nerve in our section," resumed Lloyd. "He went over from Beirut in January of sixty-one. Of course, it didn't get out until later, but it caused a hell of a rumpus inside the Service. A lot of people got moved around. Had to be done; he had blown most of the Arab-Section and some others as well. One of the men who had to be moved very fast was our top resident in the Caribbean. He had been with Philby in Beirut six months before, then transferred to Carib.

"The same month, January, the dictator of the Dominican Republic, Trujillo, was assassinated on a lonely road outside Ciudad Trujillo. According to the reports, he was killed by partisans—he had a lot of enemies. Our man came back to London then, and we shared an office for a while until he was re-deployed. He mentioned a rumor that Trujillo's car was stopped, for the ambushers to blow it open and kill the man inside, by a single shot from a marksman with a rifle. It was a hell of a shot—from one hundred and fifty yards at a speeding car. Went through the little triangular window at the driver's side, the one that wasn't of bullet proof glass. The whole car was armoured. Hit the driver through the throat and he crashed. That was when the partisans closed in. The odd thing was, there rumour had it the shooter was an Englishman."

There was a long pause as the two men, the empty beer mugs swinging from their fingers, stared across the now quite darkened waters of the Thames. Both had a mental picture of a harsh, arid landscape in a hot and distant island; of a car careering at seventy miles an hour off a bitumen strip and into the rocky verge; of an old man in fawn twill and gold braid, who had ruled his kingdom with an iron and ruthless hand for thirty years, being dragged from the wreck to be finished off with pistols in the dust by the roadside.

"This—man—in the rumour. Did he have a name?"

"I don't know. I don't remember. It was just talk in the office at the time. We had an awful lot on our plate then, and a Caribbean dictator was the last thing we needed to worry about."

"This colleague, the one who talked to you. Did he write a report?"

"Must have done. Standard practise. But it was just a rumour, understand. Just a rumour. Nothing to go on. We deal in facts, solid information."

"But it must have been filed, somewhere?"

"Suppose so," said Lloyd. "Very low priority, only a bar rumour in that area. Place abounds in rumours."

"But you could just have a look back at the files, like? See if the man on the mountain had a name?"

Lloyd pulled himself off the rail.

"You get on home," he said to the Superintendent. "I'll ring you if there's anything that might help."

They walked back into the rear bar of the pub, deposited the glasses, and made for the street door.

"I'd be grateful," said Thomas as they shook hands. "Probably nothing in it. But just on the offchance."

While Thomas and Lloyd were talking above the waters of the Thames, and the Jackal was scooping the last drops of his zabaglione from the glass in a roof-top restaurant in Milan, Commissaire Claude Lebel attended the first of the progress report meetings in the conference room of the Interior Ministry in Paris.

The attendance was the same as it had been twenty-four hours earlier. The Interior Minister sat at the head of the table, with the department heads down each side. Claude Lebel sat at the other end with a small folder in front of him. The Minister nodded curtly for the meeting to begin.

His *chef de cabinet* spoke first. Over the previous day and night, he said, every customs officer on every border post in France had received instructions to check through the luggage of tall blond male foreigners entering France. Passports particularly were to be checked, and were to be scrutinised by the DST official at the customs post for possible forgeries. (The head of the DST inclined his head in acknowledgement.) Tourists and businessmen entering France might well remark a sudden increase in vigilance at customs, but it was felt unlikely that any victim of such a baggage search would realise it was being applied across the country to tall blond men. If any enquiries were made by a sharp-eyed press man, the explanation would be that they were nothing but routine snap searches. But it was felt no enquiry would ever be made.

He had one other thing to report. A proposal had been made that the possibility be considered of making a snatch of one of the three OAS chiefs in Rome. The Quai d'Orsay had come out strongly against such an idea for diplomatic reasons (they had not been told of the Jackal plot), and they were being backed in this by the President (who was aware of the reason). This must therefore be discounted as a way out of their difficulties.

General Guibaud for the SDECE said a complete check of their records had failed to reveal knowledge of the existence of a professional political killer outside the ranks of the OAS or its sympathisers, and who could not be completely accounted for.

The head of the Renseignements Généraux said a search through France's criminal archives had revealed the same thing, not only among Frenchmen but also among foreigners who had ever tried to operate inside France.

The chief of the DST then made his report. At 7:30 that morning a call had been intercepted from a post office near the Gare du Nord to the number of the Rome hotel where the three OAS chiefs were staying. Since their appearance there eight weeks before, operators on the international switchboard had been instructed to report all calls placed to that number. The one on duty that morning had been slow on the uptake. The call had been placed before he had realised that the number was the one on his list. He had put the call through, and only then rung the DST. However, he had the sense to listen in. The message had been, "Valmy to Poitiers. The Jackal is blown. Repeat. The Jackal is blown. Kowalski was taken. Sang before dying. Ends."

There was silence in the room for several seconds.

"How did they find out?" asked Lebel quietly from the far end of the table. All eyes turned on him, except those of Colonel Rolland, who was staring at the opposite wall deep in thought.

"Damn," he said clearly, still staring at the wall. The eyes swivelled back to the head of the Action Service.

The Colonel snapped out of his reverie.

"Marseilles," he said shortly. "To get Kowalski to come from Rome we used a bait. An old friend called JoJo Grzybowski. The man has a wife and daughter. We kept them all in protective custody until Kowalski was in our hands. Then we allowed them to return home. All I wanted from Kowalski was information about his chiefs. There was no reason to suspect this Jackal plot at the time. There was no reason why they should not know we had got Kowalski—then. Later of course things changed. It must have been the Pole JoJo who tipped off the agent Valmy. Sorry."

"Did the DST pick Valmy up in the post office?" asked Lebel.

"No, we missed him by a couple of minutes, thanks to the stupidity of the operator," said the man from DST.

"A positive chapter of inefficiency," snapped Colonel Saint-Clair suddenly. A number of unfriendly glances were levelled at him.

"We are feeling our way, largely in the dark, against an unknown adversary," replied General Guibaud. "If the colonel would like to volunteer to take over the operation, all the responsibility it implies . . ."

The colonel from the Elysée Palace studiously examined his folders as if they were more important and of greater consequence than the veiled threat from the head of the SDECE. He realised it had not been a wise remark.

"In a way," mused the Minister, "it might be as well they know their hired gun is blown. Surely they must call the operation off now?"

"Precisely," said Saint-Clair, trying to recoup, "the Minister is right. They would be crazy to go ahead now. They'll simply call the man off."

"He isn't exactly blown," said Lebel quietly. They had almost forgotten he was there. "We still don't know the man's name. The forewarning might simply cause him to take extra contingency precautions. False papers, physical disguises . . ."

The optimism to which the Minister's remark had given birth round the table vanished. Roger Frey eyed the little Commissaire with respect.

"I think we had better have Commissaire Lebel's report, gentlemen. After all, he is heading this enquiry. We are here to assist him where we can."

Thus prompted, Lebel outlined the measures he had taken since the previous evening; the growing belief, supported by the check through the French files, that the foreigner could only be on the files of some foreign police force, if at all. The request to make enquiries abroad; request granted. The series of person-to-person phone calls via Interpol to police chiefs of seven major countries.

"The replies came in during the course of today," he concluded. "Here they are: Holland, nothing. Italy, several known contract-hire killers, but all in the employ of the Mafia. Discreet enquiries between the Carabinieri and the Capo of Rome elicited a pledge that no Mafia killer would ever do a political killing except on orders, and the Mafia would not subscribe to killing a foreign statesman." Lebel looked up. "Personally, I am inclined to believe that is probably true.

"Britain. Nothing, but routine enquiries have been passed to another department, the Special Branch, for further checking."

"Slow as always," muttered Saint-Clair under his breath. Lebel caught the remark and looked up again.

"But very thorough, our English friends. Do not underestimate Scotland Yard." He resumed reading.

"America. Two possibilities. One, the right-hand man of a big international arms dealer based in Miami, Florida. This man was formerly a U.S. Marine, later a CIA man in the Caribbean. Fired for killing a Cuban anti-Castroite in a fight just before the Bay of Pigs affair. The Cuban was to have commanded a section of that operation. The American then was taken on by the arms dealer, one of the men the CIA had unofficially used to supply arms to the Bay of Pigs invading force. Believed to have been responsible for two unexplained accidents that happened later to rivals of his employer in the arms business. Arms dealing, it seems, is a very cut-throat business. The man's name is Charles 'Chuck' Arnold. The FBI is now checking for his whereabouts.

"The second man suggested by FBI as a possible. Marco Vitellino, formerly personal bodyguard to a New York gangland boss, Albert Anastasia. This Capo was shot to death in a barber's chair in October fifty-seven, and Vitellino fled America in fear of his own life. Settled in Caracas, Venezuela. Tried to go into the rackets there on his own account, but with little success. He was frozen out by the local underworld. The FBI think that if he was completely broke he might be in the market for a contract killing job for a foreign organisation, if the price were right."

There was complete silence in the room. The fourteen other men listened without a murmur.

"Belgium. One possibility. Psychopathic homicide, formerly on the staff of Tshombe in Katanga. Expelled by United Nations when captured in 1962. Unable to return to Belgium because of pending charges on two counts of murder. A hired gun, but a clever one. Name of Jules Bérenger. Believed also emigrated to Central America. Belgian police are still checking on his possible present whereabouts.

"Germany. One suggestion. Hans-Dieter Kassel, former SS-Major, wanted by two countries for war crimes. Lived after the war in West Germany under an assumed name, and was a contract-killer for ODESSA, the ex-SS members' underground organisation. Suspected of being implicated in the killing of two left-wing Socialists in post-war politics who were urging a government-sponsored intensification of enquiries into war crimes. Later unmasked as Kassel, but skipped to Spain after a tip-off for which a senior police official lost his job. Believed now living in retirement in Madrid."

Lebel looked up again. "Incidentally, this man's age seems to be a bit advanced for this sort of job. He is now fifty-seven."

"Lastly, South Africa. One possible. Professional mercenary. Name: Piet Schuyper. Also one of Tshombe's top gunmen. Nothing officially against him in South Africa, but he's considered undesirable. A crack shot, and a definite penchant for individual killing. Last heard of when expelled from the Congo on the collapse of the Katanga secession early this year. Believed to be still in West Africa somewhere. The South African Special Branch is checking further."

He stopped and looked up. The fourteen men round the table were looking back at him without expression.

"Of course," said Lebel deprecatingly, "it's very vague, I'm afraid. For one thing I only tried the seven most likely countries. The Jackal could be a Swiss, or Austrian, or something else. Then three countries out of seven replied that they had no suggestion to make. They could be wrong. The Jackal could be Italian or Dutch or English. Or he could be South African, Belgian, German, or American, but not among those listed. One doesn't know. One is feeling in the dark, hoping for a break."

"Mere hoping isn't going to get us far," snapped Saint-Clair.

"Perhaps the colonel has a fresh suggestion?" enquired Lebel politely.

"Personally, I feel the man has certainly been warned off," said Saint-Clair icily. "He could never get near the President now that his plan has been exposed. However much Rodin and his henchmen have promised to pay this Jackal, they will ask for their money back and cancel the operation."

"You *feel* the man has been warned off," interposed Lebel softly, "but feeling is not far from hoping. I would prefer to continue enquiries for the present."

"What is the position of these enquiries now, Commissaire?" asked the Minister.

"Already, Minister, the police forces that have made these suggestions are beginning to send by telex the complete dossiers. I expect to have the last by noon tomorrow. Pictures will also come by wire. Some of the police forces are continuing enquiries to try to pin the whereabouts of the suspects down, so that we can take over."

"Do you think they will keep their mouths shut?" asked Sanguinetti.

"There's no reason for them not to," replied Lebel. "Hundreds of highly confidential enquiries are made each year on an unofficial person-to-person basis. Fortunately, all countries, whatever their political outlook, are opposed to crime. So we are not involved in the same rivalries as the more political branches of international relations. Cooperation among police forces is very good."

"Even for political crime?" asked Frey.

"For policemen, Minister, it's all crime. That is why I preferred to contact my foreign colleagues rather than enquire through foreign ministries. Doubtless, the superiors of these colleagues must learn that the enquiry was made, but there would be no good reason for them to make mischief. The political assassin is the world's outlaw."

"But so long as they know the enquiry was made, they can work out the implications and still privately sneer at our President," snapped Saint-Clair.

"I do not see why they should do that. It might be one of them, one day," said Lebel.

"You do not know much about politics if you are not aware how some people would be delighted to know a killer is after the President of France," replied Saint-Clair. "This public knowledge is precisely what the President was so anxious to avoid."

"It is not public knowledge," corrected Lebel. "It is extremely private knowledge, confined to a tiny handful of men who carry in their heads secrets that, if revealed, might well ruin half the politicians of their own countries. Some of these men know most of the inner details of installations that protect Western security. They have to, in order to protect them. If they were not discreet, they would not hold the jobs they do."

"Better a few men should know we are looking for a killer than they should receive invitations to attend the President's funeral," growled Bouvier. "We've been fighting the OAS for two years. The President's instructions were that it must not become press sensation and public talking point."

"Gentlemen, gentlemen," interposed the Minister. "Enough of this. It was I who authorised Commissaire Lebel to make discreet enquires among the heads of foreign police services, after"—he glanced at Saint-Clair—"consulting with the President."

The group's amusement at the colonel's discomfiture was ill-concealed.

"Is there anything else?" asked M. Frey.

Rolland raised a hand briefly.

"We have a permanent bureau in Madrid," he said. "There are a number of refugee OAS in Spain, that's why we keep it there. We could check on the Nazi, Kassel, without bothering the West Germans about it. I understand our relations with the Bonn Foreign Office are still not of the best."

His reference to the Argoud snatch of February and the consequent anger of Bonn brought a few smiles. Frey raised his eyebrows at Lebel.

"Thank you," said the detective, "that would be most helpful, if you could pin the man down. For the rest there is nothing, except to ask that all departments continue to assist me as they have been doing over the past twenty-four hours."

"Then until tomorrow, gentlemen," said the Minister briskly and rose, gathering his papers. The meeting broke up.

Outside on the steps, Lebel gratefully drew in a lungful of the mild night air of Paris. The clocks struck 12 and ushered in Tuesday, August 13.

It was just after 12 when Barrie Lloyd rang Superintendent Thomas at his home in Chiswick. Thomas was just about to put the bedside light out, thinking the SIS man would ring in the morning.

"I found the flimsy of the report we were talking about," said Lloyd. "I was right in a way. It was just a routine report of a rumour running round the island at that time. Marked 'No action to be taken' almost as soon as it was filed. Like I said, we were pretty tied up with other things at that time."

"Was any name mentioned?" asked Thomas quietly, so as not to disturb his wife, who was asleep.

"Yes, a British businessman on the island, who disappeared around that time. He might have had nothing to do with it, but his name was linked in the gossip. Name of Charles Calthrop."

"Thanks, Barrie. I'll follow it in the morning." He put the phone down and went to sleep.

Lloyd, being a meticulous young man, made a brief report of the request and his reply to it, and despatched it to Requirements. In the small hours, the night duty man on Requirements examined it quizzically for a moment, and as it concerned Paris, put it in a pouch for the Foreign Office's France Desk, the entire pouch to be delivered personally according to routine to Head of France when he came in later the same morning.

FOURTEEN

The Jackal rose at his habitual hour of 7:30, drank the tea placed by his bedside, washed, showered, and shaved. Once dressed, he took the wad of a thousand pounds from inside the lining of his suitcase, slipped it into his breast pocket, and went down for breakfast. At nine o'clock he was on the pavement of the Via Manzoni outside the hotel and striding down the road looking for banks. For two hours he went from one to another, changing the English pounds. Two hundred were changed into Italian lire and the remaining eight hundred into French francs.

By midmorning he was finished with his task, and broke for a cup of espresso on a cafe terrace. After that he set out on his second search. After numerous enquiries, he found himself in one of the back streets off the Porta Garibaldi, a working-class area near the Garibaldi station. Here he found what he was looking for, a row of lock-up garages. One of these he hired from the proprietor who ran the garage on the corner of the street. The hire charge for two days was ten thousand lire, well above the odds, but then it was a very short let.

In a local hardware store he bought a set of overalls, a pair of metal clippers, several yards of thin steel wire, a soldering iron, and a foot of solder rod. These he packed into a canvas grip bought at the same store, and deposited the grip in the garage. Pocketing the key, he went off for lunch at a trattoria in the more fashionable centre of the city.

In the early afternoon, after making an appointment by phone from the trattoria, he arrived by taxi at a small and not too prosperous car-hire firm. Here he hired a second-hand 1962 vintage Alfa Romeo sports two-seater. He explained that he wished to tour Italy for the forthcoming fortnight, the length of his holiday in Italy, and return the car at the end of that time.

His passport, British and International driving licenses were in order, and insurance was arranged within the hour from a nearby firm which habitually handled the business of the hire-car firm. The deposit was heavy, the equivalent of over a hundred pounds, but by the midafternoon the car was his, the keys in the ignition, and the proprietor of the firm wishing him a happy holiday.

Previous enquiries with the Automobile Association in London had assured him that as both France and Italy were members of the Common Market, there were no complicated formalities for driving an Italian registered car into France, provided the driving licences, car-registration hire documents, and insurance cover were in order.

From a personal enquiry at the reception desk of the Automobil Club Italiano on the Corso Venezia he was given the name of a highly respectable insurance firm close by, which specialised in offering motor insurance cover for travel in foreign countries. Here he paid cash for extra insurance cover for an expedition into France. This firm, he was assured, enjoyed a mutual relationship with a large French insurance company, and their cover would be accepted without question.

From here he drove the Alfa back to the Continentale, parked it in the hotel car-park, went up to his room, and retrieved the suitcase containing the component parts of the sniper's rifle. Shortly after tea-time he was back in the mews street where he had hired the lock-up garage.

With the door safely shut behind him, the cable from the soldering iron plugged into the overhead light socket, and a high-powered torch lying on the floor beside him to illuminate the underside of the car, he went to work. For two hours he carefully welded the thin steel tubes that contained the rifle parts into the inner flange of the Alfa's chassis. One of the reasons for choosing an Alfa had been because a search through motor magazines in London had taught him that alone among Italian cars the Alfa possessed a stout steel chassis with a deep flange on the inner side.

The tubes themselves were each wrapped in a thin sock of sacking material. The steel wire lashed them tightly inside the flange, and the places where the wire touched the chassis's edge were spot-welded with the soldering iron.

By the time he was finished the overalls were smeared with grease from the garage floor, and his hands ached from the exertions of heaving the wire tighter round the chassis. But the job was done. The tubes were almost undetectable except to a close search made from underneath the car, and would soon be coated with dust and mud.

He packed the overalls, soldering iron, and the remains of the wire into the canvas grip and dumped it under a pile of old rags in the far corner of the garage. The metal clippers went into the glove compartment set in the dashboard.

Dusk was settling again over the city when he finally emerged at the wheel of the Alfa, the suitcase shut into the trunk. He closed and locked the garage door, pocketed the key, and drove back to the hotel.

Twenty-four hours after his arrival in Milan he was again in his room, showering away the exertions of the day, soaking his smarting hands in a bowl of cold water, before dressing for cocktails and dinner.

Stopping at the reception desk before going into the bar for his habitual Campari and soda, he asked for his bill to be made up for settlement after dinner, and for a morning call with a cup of tea at 5:30 the following morning.

After a second splendid dinner he settled the bill with the remainder of his lire and was in bed asleep by shortly after eleven o'clock.

Sir Jasper Quigley stood with his back to the office, hands clasped behind him, and stared down from the windows of the Foreign Office across the immaculate acres of Horse Guards Parade. A column of Household Cavalry in impeccable order trotted across the gravel towards the Annexe and the Mall and on in the direction of Buckingham Palace.

It was a scene to delight and to impress. On many mornings Sir Jasper had stood at his window and gazed down from the ministry at this most English of English spectacles. Often it seemed to him that just to stand at this window and see the Blues ride by, the sun shine, and the tourists crane, and hear across the square the clink of harness and bit, the snort of a mettled horse, and the ooooohs and aaaahs of the crowd was worth all those years in embassies in other and lesser lands. It was rare for him that, watching this sight, he did not feel his shoulders square a little squarer, the stomach draw in a trifle under the striped trousers, and a touch of pride lift the chin to iron out the wrinkles of the neck. Sometimes, hearing the crunch of the hooves on gravel, he would rise from his desk just to stand at the neo-Gothic window and see them pass, before returning to the papers of the business of the state. And sometimes, thinking back on all those who had tried from across the sea to change this scene and supplant the jingle of the spurs with the tramp of boots from Paris or jackboots from Berlin, he felt a little pricking behind the eyes and would hurry back to his papers.

But not this morning. This morning he glowered down like an avenging acid drop, and his lips were pressed so tightly together that, never full or rosy, they had disappeared completely. Sir Jasper Quigley was in a towering rage, and by a small sign here and there it showed. He was, of course, alone.

He was also the Head of France, not in the literal sense of possessing any jurisdiction over the country across the Channel towards friendship with whom so much lip-service had been paid and so little felt during his lifetime, but head of the bureau of the Foreign Office whose business it was to study the affairs, ambitions, activities, and, often, conspiracies of that confounded place and then report upon them to the Permanent Under Secretary and, ultimately, to Her Majesty's Secretary of State for Foreign Affairs.

He possessed, or he would not have got the appointment, all the essential requirements: a long and distinguished record of service in diplomacy elsewhere than in France; a history of soundness in his political judgements, which, although frequently wrong, were inevitably in accord with those of his superiors of the given moment—a fine record and one of which to be justly proud. He had never been publicly wrong or inconveniently right, never supported an unfashionable viewpoint or proffered opinions out of line with those prevailing at the highest levels of the corps.

A marriage to the virtually unmarriageable daughter of the Head of Chancery in Berlin, who had later become an Assistant Deputy Under Secretary of State, had done no harm. It had enabled an unfortunate memorandum in 1937 from Berlin, advising that German rearmament would have no real effect in political terms on the future of Western Europe, to be overlooked.

During the war, back in London, he had been for a while on the Balkan Desk and had forcefully counselled British support for the Yugoslav partisan Mikailovitch and his Chetniks. When the Prime Minister of the time had unaccountably preferred to listen to the advice of an obscure young Captain called Fitzroy MacLean who had parachuted into the place and who advised backing a wretched Communist called Tito, young Quigley had been transferred to France Desk.

Here he had distinguished himself by becoming a leading advocate of British support for General Giraud in Algiers. It was, or would have been, a jolly good policy too, had it not been out-manoeuvred by that other and less senior French general who had been living in London all the while trying to put together a force called the Free French. Why Winston ever bothered with the man was something none of the professionals could ever understand.

Not that any of the French were much use, of course. No one could ever say of Sir Jasper (knighted in '61 for his services to diplomacy) that he lacked the essential qualification for a good Head of France. He had a congenital dislike of France and everything to do with the place. These feelings had become, by the close of President de Gaulle's press conference of January 23, 1963, in which he barred Britain from the Common Market and caused Sir Jasper to have an uncomfortable twenty minutes with the Minister, as nothing compared to his feelings towards the person of the French President.

There was a tap on his door. Sir Jasper swung away from the window. From the blotter in front of him he picked up a piece of blue flimsy paper and held it as though he had been reading it when the knock came.

"Enter."

The younger man entered the office, closed the door behind him, and approached the desk.

Sir Jasper glanced at him over the half-moon glasses.

"Ah, Lloyd. Just looking at this report you filed during the night. Interesting, interesting. An unofficial request lodged by a senior French police detective to a senior British police officer. Passed on to a senior superintendent of the Special Branch, who sees fit to consult, unofficially, of course, a junior member of the Intelligence Service. Mmm?"

"Yes, Sir Jasper."

Lloyd stared across at the spare figure of the diplomat standing by the window studying his report as if he had never seen it before. He had cottoned on at least that Sir Jasper was already well versed in the contents and that the studied indifference was probably a pose.

"And this junior officer sees fit, off his own bat and without reference to higher authority, to assist the Special Branch officer by passing on to him a suggestion. A suggestion, moreover, that without a shred of proof indicates that a British citizen thought to be a businessman may in fact be a cold-blooded killer. Mmmmm?"

"What the hell's the old buzzard getting at?" thought Lloyd.

He soon found out.

"What intrigues me, my dear Lloyd, is that although this request, unofficial of course, is lodged yesterday morning, it is not until twenty-four hours later that the head of the department of the ministry most closely concerned with what happens in France gets to be informed. Rather an odd state of affairs, wouldn't you say?"

Lloyd got the drift. Inter-departmental pique. But he was equally aware that Sir Jasper was a powerful man, versed in the power struggle, which exacted more effort from the members of the hierarchy than did state business.

"With the greatest respect, Sir Jasper, Superintendent Thomas's request to me, as you say an unofficial one, was made at nine last night. The report was filed a midnight."

"True, true. But I notice his request was also complied with before midnight. Now can you tell me why that was?"

"I felt the request for guidance, or possible guidance as to a line of enquiry only, came within the scope of normal inter-departmental cooperation," replied Lloyd.

"Did you now? Did you now?" Sir Jasper had dropped the pose of mild enquiry and some of his pique was coming through. "But not apparently within the scope of inter-departmental cooperation between your service and the France Desk, mmm?"

"You have my report in your hand, Sir Jasper."

"A bit late, sir. A bit late."

Lloyd decided to riposte. He was aware that if he had committed any error in consulting a higher authority before helping Thomas, it was his own chief he should have consulted, not Sir Jasper Quigley. And the head of the SIS was beloved by his staff and disliked by the mandarins of the F.O. for his refusal to allow anyone other than himself to rebuke his subordinates.

"Too late for what, Sir Jasper?"

Sir Jasper glanced up sharply. He was not going to fall into the trap of admitting it was too late to prevent the cooperation with Thomas's request from being fulfilled.

"You realise of course that a British citizen's name is concerned here. A man against whom there is not a shred of evidence, let alone proof. Don't you think it a rather odd procedure to bandy a man's name and, in view of the nature of the request, reputation about in this manner?"

"I hardly think divulging a man's name to a Superintendent of the Special Branch simply as a possible line of enquiry can be described as bandying it about, Sir Jasper."

The diplomat found his lips were pressed hard together as he sought to control his rage. Impertinent pup, but astute too. Needed watching very carefully. He took a grip on himself.

"I see, Lloyd. I see. In view of your evident desire to assist the Special Branch, a most laudable desire of course, do you think it too much to expect you to consult a little before throwing yourself into the breach?"

"Are you asking, Sir Jasper, why you were not consulted?"

Sir Jasper saw red.

"Yes, sir, I am, sir. That is exactly what I am asking."

"Sir Jasper, with the greatest deference to your seniority, I feel I must draw attention to the fact that I am on the staff of the Service. If you disagree with my course of conduct last night, I think it would be more seemly if your complaint went to my own superior officer rather than to me directly."

Seemly? Seemly? Was this young upstart trying to tell a Head of France what was and was not seemly?

"And it shall, sir," snapped Sir Jasper, "and it shall. In the strongest terms."

Without asking for permission Lloyd turned and left the office. He had few doubts that he was in for a roasting from the Old Man, and all he could say in mitigation was that Bryn Thomas's request had seemed urgent, with time possibly a pressing matter. If the Old Man decided that the proper channels should have been gone through, then he, Lloyd, would have to take the rap. But at least he would take it from the O.M. and not from Quigley. Oh, damn Thomas.

However Sir Jasper Quigley was very much in two minds whether to complain or not. Technically he was right, the information about Calthrop, although completely buried in long-discarded files, should have been cleared with higher authority; but not necessarily with himself. As Head of France, he was one of the customers of SIS intelligence reporting, not one of the directors of it. He could complain to that cantankerous genius (not his choice of words) who ran the SIS and probably secure a good ticking off for Lloyd, possibly damage the brat's career. But he might also get a dose of the rough edge of the SIS chief's tongue for summoning an intelligence officer without asking *his* permission, and that thought did not amuse. Besides, the head of SIS was reputed to be extremely close to some of the men at the Very Top. Played cards with them at Blades; shot with them in Yorkshire. And the Glorious Twelfth was only a month away. He was still trying to get invited to some of those parties. Better leave it.

"The damage is done now, anyway," he mused as he gazed out over Horse Guards Parade.

"The damage is done anyway," he remarked to his luncheon guest at his club just after one o'clock. "I suppose they'll go right ahead and cooperate with the French. Hope they won't work too hard, what?"

It was a good joke and he enjoyed it very much. Unfortunately he had not fully estimated his lunch guest, who was also close to some of the men at the Very Top.

Almost simultaneously a personal report from the Commissioner of Metropolitan Police and news of Sir Jasper's little *bon mot* reached the Prime Minister's eyes and ears respectively just before four when he returned to No. 10 Downing Street after questions in the House.

At ten past four the phone in Superintendent Thomas's office rang.

Thomas had spent the morning and most of the afternoon trying to track down a man about whom he knew nothing but the name. As usual when enquiring into a man of whom it was definitely known that he had been abroad, the Passport Office in Petty, France, had been the starting point.

A personal visit there when they opened at 9 in the morning had elicited from them photostat copies of application forms for passports from six separate Charles Calthrops. Unfortunately they all had middle names, and all were different. He had also secured the submitted photographs of each man, on a promise that they would be copied and returned to the Passport Office's archives.

One of the passports had been applied for since January 1961, but that did not necessarily mean anything, although it was significant that no records existed of a previous application by that Charles Calthrop before the one Thomas now possessed. If he had been using another name in the Dominican Republic, how come the rumours that had later linked him with Trujillo's killing had mentioned him as Calthrop? Thomas was inclined to downgrade this late applicant for a passport.

Of the other five, one seemed too old; he would be sixty-five by August of 1963. The remaining four were possibles. It did not matter whether they tallied with Lebel's description of a tall blond, for Thomas's job was one of elimination. If all six could be eliminated from suspicion of being the Jackal, so much the better. He could advise Lebel accordingly with a clear conscience.

Each application form had an address, two in London and two in the provinces. It was not enough simply to ring up, ask for Mr. Charles Calthrop, and then ask if the man had been in the Dominican Republic in 1961. Even if he had been there, he might well deny it now.

Nor were any of the four top-listed suspects marked down as "business-man" in the space for professional status. That too was not conclusive. Lloyd's report of a bar-rumour at the time might call him a businessman, but that could well be wrong.

During the morning the county and borough police, after a telephone request by Thomas, had traced the two provincial Calthrops. One was still at work, expecting to go on holiday with his family on the weekend. He was escorted home in the lunch-break and his passport was examined. It had no entry or exit visas or stamps for the Dominican Republic in 1960 or 1961. It had only been used twice, once for Mallorca and once for the Costa Brava. Moreover, enquiries at his place of work had revealed that this particular Charles Calthrop had never left the accounts department of the soup factory where he worked during January 1961, and he had been on the staff for ten years.

The other outside London was traced to a hotel in Blackpool. Not having his passport on him, he was persuaded to authorise the police of his home town to borrow his house key off the next-door neighbour, go to the top drawer of his desk, and look at the passport. It too bore no Dominican police stamps, and at the man's place of work it was found he was a typewriter mechanic who also had not left his place of work in 1961 except for his summer holidays. His insurance cards and attendance records showed that.

Of the two Charles Calthrops in London one was discovered to be a greengrocer in Catford who was selling vegetables in his shop when the two quiet-spoken men in suits came to talk to him. As he lived above his own shop, he was able to produce his passport within a few minutes. Like the others it gave no indication that the possessor had ever been to the Domini-can Republic. When asked, the greengrocer convinced the detectives that he did not even know where that island was.

The fourth and last Calthrop was proving more difficult. The address given in his application form for a passport four years previously was visited and turned out to be a block of flats in Highgate. The estate agents manag-ing the block searched their records and revealed that he had left that address in December 1960. No forwarding address was known.

But at least Thomas knew his middle name. A search of the telephone directory revealed nothing, but using the authority of Special Branch Tho-mas learned from the General Post Office that one C. H. Calthrop had an unlisted number in West London. The initials tallied with the name of the missing Calthrop—Charles Harold. From there Thomas checked with the registration department of the borough in which the telephone number was located.

Yes, the voice from the Borough Hall told him, a Mr. Charles Harold Calthrop was indeed the tenant of the flat at that address, and was listed on the electoral roll as a voter of that borough.

At this point a visit was made to the flat. It was locked and there was no reply to the repeated rings on the bell. Nobody else in the block seemed to know where Mr. Calthrop was. When the squad car returned to Scotland Yard, Superintendent Thomas tried a new tack. The Inland Revenue was asked to check their records for the tax returns of one Charles Harold Calthrop, private address given. Particular point of interest—who employed him, and who had been employing him over the past three years?

It was at this point that the phone rang. Thomas picked it up, identified himself, and listened for a few seconds. His eyebrows lifted.

"Me?" he asked, "What, personally? . . . Yes, of course, I'll come over. Give me five minutes? . . . Fine, see you."

He left the building and walked across Parliament Square, blowing his nose noisily to clear the blocked sinuses. Far from getting better, his cold seemed to be worse, despite the warm summer day.

From Parliament Square he headed up Whitehall and took the first left into Downing Street. As usual it was dark and gloomy, the sun never penetrating to the inconspicuous cul-de-sac that contains the residence of the Prime Ministers of Britain. There was a small crowd in front of the door of No. 10, kept on the far side of the road by two stolid policemen, perhaps just watching the stream of messengers arriving at the door with buff envelopes to deliver, perhaps hoping to catch a glimpse of an important visage at one of the windows.

Thomas left the roadway and cut to the right across a small courtyard enclosing a little lawn. His walk brought him to the back entrance of No. 10, where he pressed the buzzer beside the door. It opened immediately to reveal a large uniformed police sergeant, who recognised him at once and saluted.

"Afternoon, sir. Mr. Harrowby asked me to show you to his room directly."

James Harrowby, the man who had telephoned Thomas in his office a few minutes before, was the Prime Minister's personal security chief, a handsome man looking younger than his forty-one years. He wore a public-school tie but had a brilliant career as a policeman behind him before he was transferred to Downing Street. Like Thomas, he had the rank of a Superintendent. He rose as Thomas entered.

"Come in, Bryn. Nice to see you." He nodded to the sergeant. "Thank you, Chalmers." The sergeant withdrew and closed the door.

"What's it all about?" asked Thomas. Harrowby looked at him with surprise.

"I was hoping you could tell me. He just rang fifteen minutes ago, mentioned you by name, and said he wanted to see you personally and at once. Have you been up to something?"

Thomas could only think of one thing he had been up to, but he was surprised it had got so high in such a short time. Still, if the P.M. did not wish to take his own security man into his confidence for once, that was his business.

"Not that I know of," he said.

"Harrowby here, Prime Minister. Superintendent Thomas is with me. . . . Yes, sir. Right away." He replaced the receiver.

"Straight in. Almost on the double. You must have been up to something. There are two Ministers waiting. Come on."

Harrowby led the way out of his office and down a corridor towards a green baize door at the far end. A male secretary was coming out, saw the pair of them and stepped back, holding the door open. Harrowby ushered Thomas inside, said clearly, "Superintendent Thomas, Prime Minister," and withdrew, closing the door quietly behind him.

Thomas was aware of being in a very quiet room, high-ceilinged and elegantly furnished, untidy with books and papers, of a smell of pipe tobacco and wood-panelling, a room more like the study of a university don than the office of a Prime Minister.

The figure at the window turned round.

"Good afternoon, Superintendent. Please sit down."

"Good afternoon, sir." He chose an upright chair facing the desk and perched on the edge of it. He had never had occasion to see the Prime Minister that close before, and never in private. He got the impression of a pair of sad, almost beaten eyes, drooping lids, like a bloodhound who has run a long race and taken little joy from it.

There was silence in the room as the Prime Minister walked to his desk and sat behind it. Thomas had heard the rumours round Whitehall, of course, that the P.M.'s health was not all it might be, and of the toll taken by the strain of bringing the government through the rottenness of the Keeler/Ward affair, which had just ended and was still number one talking point throughout the land. Even so, he was surprised at the look of exhaustion and sadness in the man opposite him.

"Superintendent Thomas, it has come to my attention that you are presently conducting an investigation based on a request for assistance telephoned from Paris yesterday morning by a senior detective of the French Police Judiciaire."

"Yes, sir—Prime Minister."

"And that this request stems from a fear among the French security authorities that a man may be on the loose, a professional assassin, hired, presumably by the OAS, to undertake a mission in France at some future time?"

"That was not actually explained to us, Prime Minister. The request was for suggestions as to the identity of any such professional assassin who might be known to us. There was no explanation as to why they wanted such suggestions."

"Nevertheless, what do you deduce from the fact that such a request was made, Superintendent?"

Thomas shrugged slightly.

"The same as yourself, Prime Minister."

"Precisely. One does not need to be a genius to be able to deduce the only possible reason for the French authorities wishing to identify such a— specimen. And what would you deduce to be the eventual target of such a man, if indeed a man of this type has come to the attention of the French police?"

"Well, Prime Minister, I suppose they fear an assassin has been engaged to attempt to kill the President."

"Precisely. Not the first time such an attempt would have been made?"

"No, sir. There have been six attempts already."

The Prime Minister stared at the papers in front of him as if they might give him some clue as to what had happened to the world in the closing months of his premiership.

"Are you aware, Superintendent, that there apparently exist some persons in this country, persons occupying not obscure positions of authority, who would not be displeased if your investigations were not so energetic as they might be?"

Thomas was genuinely surprised.

"No, sir." Where on earth had the P.M. got that tidbit from?

"Would you please give me a résumé of the state of your enquiries up to the present time?"

Thomas began at the beginning, explaining clearly and concisely the trail from Criminal Records to Special Branch, the conversation with Lloyd, the mention of a man called Calthrop, and the investigations that had taken place up to that moment.

When he had finished, the Prime Minister rose and walked to the window, which gave onto the sunlit square of grass in the courtyard. For long minutes he stared down into the courtyard and there was a sag to the set of the shoulders. Thomas wondered what he was thinking.

Perhaps he was thinking of a beach outside Algiers where he had once walked and talked with the haughty Frenchman who now sat in another office three hundred miles away, governing the affairs of his own country. They had both been twenty years younger then, and a lot of things had not happened that were to come later, and a lot of things had not come between them.

Maybe he was thinking of the same Frenchman sitting in the gilded hall of the Elysée Palace eight months earlier destroying in measured and sonorous phrases the hopes of the British Prime Minister of crowning his political career by bringing Britain into the European Community before retiring into the contentment of a man who has fulfilled his dream.

Or possibly he was just thinking of the past agonising months when the revelations of a pimp and a courtesan had almost brought down the Government of Britain. He was an old man, who had been born and brought up in a world that had its standards for good or evil, and had believed in those standards and had followed them. Now the world was a different place, full of a new people with new ideas, and he was of the past. Did he understand that there were new standards now, which he could dimly recognise and did not like?

Probably he knew, looking down onto the sunny grass, what lay ahead. The surgical operation could not long be delayed, and with it retirement from the leadership. Before long the world would be handed over to the new people. Much of the world had already been handed over to them. But would it also be handed over to pimps and tarts, spies and—assassins?

From behind, Thomas saw the shoulders straighten, and the old man in front of him turned round.

"Superintendent Thomas, I wish you to know that General de Gaulle is my friend. If there is the remotest danger to his person, and if that danger would emanate from a citizen of these islands, then that person must be stopped. From now on you will conduct your investigations with unprecedented vigour. Within the hour your superiors will be authorised by me personally to accord you every facility within their powers. You will be subjected to no limits in either expenditure or manpower. You will have the authority to co-opt onto your team whomsoever you wish to assist you, and to have access to the official documentation of any department in the land which may be able to further your enquiries. You will, by my personal order, cooperate without any hint of reserve with the French authorities in this matter. Only when you are absolutely satisfied that, whoever this man may be whom the French are seeking to identify and arrest, he is not a British subject or operating from these shores, may you desist from your enquiries.

At that point you will report back to me in person.

"In the event that this man Calthrop, or any other man bearing a British passport, may reasonably be considered to be the man whom the French are seeking, you will detail this man. Whoever he is, he must be stopped. Do I make myself clear?"

It could not have been clearer. Thomas knew for certain that some piece of information had come to the P.M.'s ears that had sparked off the instructions he had just given. Thomas suspected it had to do with the cryptic remark about certain persons who wished his investigations to make little progress, but he could not be sure.

"Yes, sir," he said.

The P.M. inclined his head to indicate the interview was over. Thomas rose and went to the door.

"Er—Prime Minister?"

"Yes?"

"There is one point, sir. I am not certain whether you would wish me to tell the French yet about the enquiries into the rumour about this man Calthrop in the Dominican Republic two years ago."

"Do you have reasonable grounds to believe as of now that this man's past activities justify fitting him to the description of the man the French wish to identify?"

"No, Prime Minister. We have nothing against any Charles Calthrop in the world except the rumour of two years ago. We do not yet know whether the Calthrop we have spent the afternoon trying to trace is the one who was in the Caribbean in January 1961. If he is not, then we are back to square one."

The Prime Minister thought for a few seconds.

"I would not wish you to waste your French colleagues' time with suggestions based on unsubstantiated rumours two and a half years old. Note the word 'unsubstantiated,' Superintendent. Please continue your enquiries with energy. At the moment you feel there is enough information in your possession concerning this, or any other, Charles Calthrop to add substance to the rumour that he was involved in the affair of General Trujillo, you will inform the French at once and at the same time track the man down, wherever he is."

"Yes, Prime Minister."

"And would you please ask Mr. Harrowby to come to me. I shall issue the authorities you need at once."

Back in Thomas's office, things changed quickly through the rest of the afternoon. Round him he grouped a task force of six of the Special Branch's best detective inspectors. One was recalled from leave; two were taken off their duties watching the house of a man suspected to be passing classified information from the Royal Ordinance Factory to an East European military attaché. Two of the others were the ones who had helped him the day before go through the records of the Special Branch looking for a killer who had no name. The last had been on his day off and was gardening in his greenhouse when the call came through to report to the Branch headquarters immediately.

He briefed them all exhaustively, swore them to silence, and answered a continuous stream of phone calls. It was just after 6 p.m. when the Inland

Revenue found the tax returns of Charles Harold Calthrop. One of the detectives was sent out to bring the whole file back. The rest went to work on the telephone, except one who was sent to Calthrop's address to seek out every neighbour and local tradesman for information as to where the man might be. Photographs taken from the one submitted by Calthrop on his application form for a passport four years previously were printed in the photographic laboratory, and every inspector had one in his pocket.

The tax returns of the wanted man showed that for the past year he had been unemployed, and before that had been abroad for a year. But for most of the financial year 1960/61 he had been in the employ of a firm whose name Thomas recognised as belonging to one of Britain's leading manufacturers and exporters of small arms. Within an hour he had the name of the firm's managing director, and found the man at home at his country house in the stockbroker belt of Surrey. By telephone Thomas made an appointment to see him immediately, and as dusk descended on the Thames his police Jaguar roared over the river in the direction of the village of Virginia Water.

Patrick Monson hardly looked like a dealer in lethal weapons, but then, Thomas reflected, they never do. From Monson Thomas learned the arms firm had employed Calthrop for just under a year. More important, during December 1960 and January 1961 he had been sent by the firm to Ciudad Trujillo to try and sell a consignment of British Army surplus submachine guns to Trujillo's police chief.

Thomas eyed Monson with distaste.

"And never mind what they later get used for, eh boyo," he thought, but did not bother to voice his distaste. Why had Calthrop left the Dominican Republic in such a hurry?

Monson seemed surprised by the question. Well, because Trujillo had been killed, of course. The whole regime fell within hours. What could be expected from the new regime by a man who had come to the island to sell the old regime a load of guns and ammunition? Of course, he'd had to get out.

Thomas pondered. Certainly it made sense. Monson said Calthrop had later claimed he was actually sitting in the office of the dictator's police chief discussing the sale when the news came through that the General had been killed in an ambush outside the town. The Chief of Police had gone white, and left immediately for his private estate where his aircraft and pilot were permanently waiting for him. Within a few hours mobs were rampaging through the streets seeking adherents of the old regime. Calthrop had to bribe a fisherman to sail him out of the island.

Why, Thomas asked eventually, did Calthrop leave the firm? He was dismissed, was the answer. Why? Monson thought carefully for a few moments. Finally he said:

"Superintendent, the arms business is highly competitive. Cut-throat, you might say. To know what another man is offering for sale, and the price he is asking, can be vital for a rival wishing to clinch the same deal with the same buyer. Let us just say that we were not entirely satisfied with Calthrop's loyalty to the company."

In the car back into town Thomas thought over what Monson had told him. Calthrop's explanation at the time as to why he had got out of the

Dominican Republic so fast was logical. It did not corroborate, indeed it tended to negate, the rumour subsequently reported by the Caribbean SIS resident that his name was linked with the killing.

On the other hand, according to Monson, Calthrop was a man who was not above playing a double cross. Could he have arrived as the accredited representative of a small-arms company wishing to make a sale, and at the same time have been in the pay of the revolutionaries?

There was one thing Monson had said that disturbed Thomas: he had mentioned that Calthrop did not know much about rifles when he joined the company. Surely a crackshot would be an expert? But then, of course, he could have learned that while with the company. But if he was a newcomer to rifle shooting, why did the anti-Trujillo partisans want to hire him to stop the General's car on a fast road with a single shot? Or did they not hire him at all? Was Calthrop's own story the literal truth?

Thomas shrugged. It didn't prove anything or disprove anything. Back to square one again, he thought bitterly.

But back at the office there was news that changed his mind. The inspector who had been enquiring at Calthrop's address had reported in. He had found a next-door neighbour who had been out at work all day. The woman said Mr. Calthrop had left some days before and had mentioned he was going touring in Scotland. In the back of the car parked in the street outside the woman had seen what looked like a set of fishing rods.

Fishing rods? Superintendent Thomas felt suddenly chilly, although the office was warm. As the detective finished talking, one of the others came in.

"Super?"

"Yes?"

"Something had just occurred to me."

"Go on."

"Do you speak French?"

"No, do you?"

"Yes, my mother was French. This assassin the PJ are looking for, he's got the code name Jackal, right?"

"So what?"

"Well, Jackal in French is Chacal: C-H-A-C-A-L. See? It could just be a coincidence. He must be as thick as five posts to pick a name, even in French, that's made up of the first three letters of his Christian name and the first three letters of his—"

"Land of my bloody fathers," said Thomas and sneezed violently. Then he reached for the telephone.

FIFTEEN

The third meeting in the Interior Ministry in Paris began shortly after ten o'clock, due to the lateness of the Minister, who had been held up in the traffic on his way back from a diplomatic reception. As soon as he was seated, he gestured for the meeting to start.

The first report was from General Guibaud of the SDECE. It was short and to the point. The ex-Nazi killer, Kassel, had been located by agents of the Madrid office of the Secret Service. He was living quietly in retirement at his rooftop flat in Madrid, had become a partner with another former SS-commando leader in a prosperous business in the city, and so far as could be determined was not involved with the OAS. The Madrid office had in any case had a file on the man by the time the request from Paris for a further check came through, and was of the view that he had never been involved with the OAS at all.

In view of his age, increasingly frequent bouts of rheumatism that were beginning to affect his legs, and a remarkably high alcohol intake, Kassel in the general view could be discounted as a possible Jackal.

As the General finished, eyes turned to Commissaire Lebel. His report was sombre. During the course of the day reports had come into the PJ from the other three countries who had originally suggested possible suspects twenty-four hours earlier.

From America had come news that Chuck Arnold, the gun salesman, was in Colombia trying to clinch a deal for his American employer to sell a consignment of former U.S. Army surplus AR-10 assault rifles to the Chief of Staff. He was in any case under permanent CIA surveillance while in Bogotá, and there was no indication that he was planning anything other than to put through his arms deal, despite official U.S. disapproval.

The file on this man had, however, been telexed to Paris, as had also the file on Vitellino. This showed that although the former Cosa Nostra gunman had not yet been located, he was five feet, four inches tall, immensely broad and squat, with jet black hair and a swarthy complexion. In view of the radical difference in appearance from the Jackal as described by the hotel clerk in Vienna, Lebel felt he too could be discounted.

The South Africans had learned Piet Schuyper was now the head of the private army of a diamond mining corporation in a West African country of the British Commonwealth. His duties were to patrol the borders of the vast mining concessions owned by the company and ensure a continuous disincentive to illicit diamond poachers from across the border. No inconvenient questions were asked of him as to the methods he used to discourage poaching, and his employers were pleased with his efforts. His presence was confirmed by his employers; he was definitely at his post in West Africa.

The Belgian police had checked on their ex-mercenary. A report in the files from one of their Caribbean embassies had been unearthed, which reported the former employee of Katanga had been killed in a bar fight in Guatemala three months previously.

Lebel finished reading the last of the reports from the file in front of him. When he looked up it was to find fourteen pairs of eyes on him, most of them cold and challenging.

"*Alors, rien?*"

The question from Colonel Rolland was that of everyone present. "No, nothing, I'm afraid," agreed Lebel. "None of the suggestions seem to stand up."

"Seem to stand up," echoed Saint-Clair bitterly. "Is that what we have come to with your 'pure detective work'? Nothing seems to stand up?" He glared angrily at the two detectives, Bouvier and Lebel, quickly aware that the mood of the room was with him.

"It would seem, gentlemen," the Minister quietly used the plural form to take in both the police commissaires, "that we are back where we started. Square one, so to speak?"

"Yes, I'm afraid so," replied Lebel. Bouvier took up the cudgels on his behalf.

"My colleague is searching, virtually without clues and without any sort of lead, for one of the most elusive types of men in the world. Such specimens do not advertise their professions or their whereabouts."

"We are aware of that, my dear Commissaire," retorted the Minister, coldly, "the question is—"

He was interrupted by a knock on the door. The Minister frowned; his instructions had been that they were not to be disturbed except in an emergency.

"Come in."

One of the ministry's porters stood in the doorway, diffident and abashed. "*Mes excuses, Monsieur le Ministre.* A telephone call for Commissaire Lebel. From London." Feeling the hostility of the room, the man tried to cover himself. "They say it is urgent . . . "

Lebel rose.

"Would you excuse me, gentlemen?"

He returned in five minutes. The atmosphere was as cold as when he had left it, and evidently the wrangle over what to do next had continued in his absence. As he entered he interrupted a bitter denunciation from Colonel Saint-Clair, who tailed off as Lebel took his seat. The little Commissaire had an envelope in his hand with scribbled writing on the back.

"I think, gentlemen, we have the name of the man we are looking for," he began.

The meeting ended thirty minutes later almost in a mood of levity. When Lebel had finished his relation of the message from London, the men round the table had let out a collective sigh, like a train arriving at its platform after a long journey. Each man knew that at last there was something he could do. Within half an hour they had agreed that without a word of publicity it would be possible to scour France for a man in the name of Charles Calthrop, to find him, and, if deemed necessary, to dispose of him.

The fullest known details of Calthrop, they knew, would not be available until the morning, when they would be telexed from London. But in the meantime Renseignements Généraux could check their miles of shelves for a disembarkation card filled in by this man, for a hotel card registering him at a hotel anywhere in France. The Prefecture of Police could check its own records to see if he was staying at any hotel within the confines of Paris.

The DST could put his name and description into the hands of every border post, port, harbour, and airfield in France, with instructions that such a man was to be held immediately on his touching on French territory.

If he had not yet arrived in France, no matter. Complete silence would be maintained until he arrived, and when he did, they would have him.

"This odious creature, the man they call Calthrop, we have him already in the bag," Colonel Raoul Saint-Clair de Villauban told his mistress that night as they lay in bed.

When Jacqueline finally coaxed a belated orgasm from the colonel to send him to sleep the mantelpiece clock chimed twelve, and it had become August 14.

Superintendent Thomas sat back in his office chair and surveyed the six inspectors whom he had regrouped from their various tasks after putting down the phone following the call to Paris. Outside in the still summer night Big Ben tolled midnight.

His briefing took an hour. One man was allocated to examine Calthrop's youth, where his parents now lived, if indeed he had any; where he had been to school; shooting record, if any, in the cadet corps as a schoolboy; noticeable characteristics, distinguishing marks, etc.

A second was designated to investigate his young manhood, from leaving school, through National Service—record of service and prowess at shooting—employment following discharge from the Army, right up to the time he left the employ of the arms dealers who had dismissed him for suspected double-dealing.

The third and fourth detectives were put on the trail of his activities since leaving his last known employers in October 1961. Where he had been, whom he had seen, what his income had been, from what sources. Since there was no police record and therefore presumably no fingerprints, Thomas needed every known and latest photograph of the man, up to the present time.

The last two inspectors were to seek to establish the whereabouts of Calthrop at that moment. Go over the entire flat for fingerprints, find where he bought the car, check at County Hall, London, for records of issue of a driving licence, and if there were none start checking with the provincial county licencing departments. Trace the car—make, age, colour, registration number. Trace his local garage to see if he was planning a long journey by car, check the cross-Channel ferries, go round all the airline companies for a booking on a plane, no matter what the destination.

All six men took extensive notes. Only when he had finished did they rise and file out of the office. In the corridor the last two eyed each other askance.

"Dry-clean and re-texture," said one. "The complete bloody works."

"The funny thing is," observed the other, "that the old man won't tell us what he's supposed to have done, or be going to do."

"One thing we can be sure of. To get this kind of action, it must have come down right from the top. You'd think the bugger was planning to shoot the King of Siam."

It took a short while to wake up a magistrate and get him to sign a search warrant. By the small hours of the morning, while an exhausted Thomas dozed in the armchair in his office and an even more haggard Claude Lebel sipped black coffee in his office, two Special Branch men went through Calthrop's flat with a fine tooth comb.

Both were experts. They started with the drawers, emptying each one systematically into a bedsheet and sorting the contents diligently. When all the drawers were clean, they started on the woodwork of the drawerless desk for secret panels. After the wooden furniture came two upholstered pieces.

When they had finished with these, the flat looked like a turkey farm on Thanksgiving Day. One man was working over the drawing room, the other the bedroom. After these two came the kitchen and bathroom.

With the furniture, cushions, pillows, and coats and suits in the cupboards dealt with, they started on the floors, ceilings, and walls. By six in the morning the flat was as clean as a whistle. Most of the neighbours were grouped on the landing looking at each other and then the closed door of Calthrop's flat, conversing in whispers that hushed when the two inspectors emerged from the flat.

One was carrying a suitcase stuffed with Calthrop's personal papers, and private belongings. He went down to the street, jumped into the waiting squad car, and drove back to Superintendent Thomas. The other started on the long round of interviews. He began with the neighbours, aware that most would have to head for their places of work within an hour or two. The local tradesmen could come later.

Thomas spent several minutes riffling through the collection of possessions spread all over his office floor. Out of the jumble the detective inspector grabbed a small blue book, walked to the window and started to flick through it by the light of the rising sun.

"Super, have a look at this." His finger jabbed at one of the pages in the passport in front of him. "See . . . Republica Dominicana, Aeroporto Ciudad Trujillo, Decembre 1960, Entrada. . . . He was there all right. This is our man."

Thomas took the passport from him, glanced at it for a moment, then stared out of the window.

"Oh yes, this is our man, boyo. But does it not occur to you that we're holding his passport in our hands?"

"Oh, the sod . . ." breathed the inspector when he saw the point.

"As you say," said Thomas, whose chapel upbringing caused him only very occasionally to use strong language. "If he's not travelling on this passport, then what is he travelling on? Give me the phone, and get me Paris."

By the same hour the Jackal had already been on the road for fifty minutes, and the city of Milan lay far behind him. The hood of the Alfa was down, and the morning sun already bathed the Autostrada 7 from Milan to Genoa. Along the wide straight road he pushed the car well over eighty miles an hour and kept the tachometre needle flickering just below the start of the red band. The cool wind lashed his pale hair into a frenzy around the forehead, but the eyes were protected by the dark glasses.

The road map said it was 210 kilometres to the French frontier at Ventimiglia, about 130 miles, and he was well up on his estimated driving time of two hours. There was a slight hold-up among the truck traffic of Genoa as it headed for the docks just after seven o'clock, but before 7:15 he was away on the A 10 to San Remo and the border.

The daily traffic was already thick when he arrived at 7:50 at the sleepiest of France's frontier points, and the heat was rising.

After a thirty-minute wait in the queue, he was beckoned up to the parking ramp for customs examination. The policeman who took his passport examined it carefully, muttered a brief "*Un moment, monsieur,*" and disappeared inside the customs shed.

He emerged a few minutes later with a man in civilian clothes who held the passport.

"*Bonjour, monsieur.*"

"*Bonjour.*"

"This is your passport?"

"Yes."

There was another searching examination of the passport.

"What is the purpose of your visit to France?"

"Tourism. I have never seen the Côte d'Azur."

"I see. The car is yours."

"No. It's a hired car. I had business in Italy, and it has unexpectedly occasioned a week with nothing to do before returning to Milan. So I hired a car to do a little touring."

"I see. You have the papers for the car?"

The Jackal extended the international driving licence, the contract of hire, and the two insurance certificates. The plain-clothes man examined both.

"You have luggage, monsieur?"

"Yes, three pieces in the trunk, and a hand grip."

"Please bring them all into the customs hall."

He walked away. The policeman helped the Jackal off-load the three suitcases and the hand-grip, and together they carried them to customs.

Before leaving Milan he had taken the old greatcoat, scruffy trousers and shoes of André Martin, the non-existent Frenchman whose papers were sewn into the lining of the third suitcase, and rolled them in a ball at the back of the trunk. The clothes from the other two suitcases had been divided between the three. The medals were in his pocket.

Two customs officers examined each case. While they were doing so, he filled in the standard form for tourists entering France. Nothing in the cases excited any attention. There was a brief moment of anxiety as the customs men picked up the jars containing the hair-tinting dyes. He had taken the precaution of emptying them into after-shave flasks, previously emptied. At that time after-shave lotion was not in vogue in France, it was too new on the market and mainly confined to America. He saw the two customs men exchange glances, but they replaced the flasks in the hand-grip.

Out of the corner of his eye he could see through the windows another man examining the trunk and engine hood of the Alfa. Fortunately, he did not look underneath. He unrolled the greatcoat and trousers in the trunk and looked at them with distaste, but presumed the coat was for covering the hood on winter nights and old clothes were a contingency in case repairs had to be done on the car along the road. He replaced the clothes and closed the trunk.

As the Jackal finished filling in his form, the two customs men inside the shed closed the cases and nodded to the plain-clothes man. He in turn took the entry card, examined it, checked it again with the passport, and handed the passport back.

"*Merci, monsieur. Bon voyage.*"

Ten minutes later the Alfa was booming into the eastern outskirts of Menton. After a relaxed breakfast at a cafe overlooking the old port and yacht basin, the Jackal headed along the Corniche Littorale for Monaco, Nice, and Cannes.

In his London office Superintendent Thomas stirred a cup of thick black coffee and ran a hand over his stubbled chin. Across the room the two inspectors saddled with the task of finding the whereabouts of Calthrop faced their chief. The three were waiting for the arrival of six extra men, all sergeants of the Special Branch released from their routine duties as the result of a string of telephone calls Thomas had been making over the previous hour.

Shortly after nine o'clock, as they reported to their offices and learned of their re-deployment to Thomas's force, the men started to trickle in. When the last had arrived, he briefed them.

"All right, we're looking for a man. There's no need for me to tell you why we want him, it's not important that you should know. What is important is that we get him, and get him fast. Now we know, or think we know, that he's abroad at this moment. We are pretty certain he is travelling under a false passport.

"Here"—he passed out among them a set of photographs, blown-up copies of the portrait photo of Calthrop's passport application form—"is what he looks like. The chances are he will have disguised himself and therefore not necessarily respond to the description. What you are going to have to do is go down to the Passport Office and get a complete list of every application for a passport made recently. Start by covering the last hundred days. If that yields nothing, go back another hundred days. It's going to be a hard grind."

He continued by giving a rough description of the most common way of getting a false passport, which was in fact the method the Jackal had used.

"The important thing is," he concluded, "not to be content with birth certificates. Check the death certificates. So after you've got the list from Passport Office, take the whole operation down to Somerset House, get settled in, divide the list of names among yourselves, and get to work among those death certificates. If you can find one application for a passport submitted by a man who isn't alive any longer, the imposter will probably be our man. Off you go."

The eight men filed out, while Thomas got on to the Passport Office by phone, then the Registry of Births, Marriages and Deaths at Somerset House, to ensure that his team would get the fullest cooperation.

It was two hours later as he was shaving on a borrowed electric razor plugged into his desk lamp that the senior of the two inspectors, who was the leader of the team, phoned back. There were, he said, 841 applications for new passports submitted in the previous hundred days. It was the summer, he explained, holiday time. There were always more in holiday time.

Bryn Thomas hung up and snuffled into his handkerchief.

"Damn summer," he said.

Just after 11 that morning the Jackal rolled into the centre of Cannes. As usual when he wanted something done, he looked for one of the best hotels, and after a few minutes cruising swept into the forecourt of the Majestic. Running a comb through his hair, he strode into the foyer.

Being the middle of the morning most of the guests were out and the hall was not busy. His elegant light suit and confident manner picked him out as an English gentleman and raised no eyebrows when he asked a bell-hop where the telephone booths were. The lady behind the counter that separated the switchboard from the entry to the cloakroom looked up as he approached.

"Please get me Paris, Molitor 5901," he asked.

A few minutes later she gestured him to a booth beside the switchboard and watched him close the sound-proof door behind him.

"*Allo, ici Chacal.*"

"*Allo, ici Valmy.* Thank God you've called. We've been trying to get hold of you for two days."

Anyone looking through the glass panel of the booth's door would have seen the Englishman inside stiffen and frown at the mouthpiece. For most of the ten-minute conversation he remained silent, listening. Occasionally his lips moved as he asked a short, terse question. But nobody was looking; the switchboard operator was busy in a romantic novel. The next thing she saw was the guest towering over her, the dark glasses staring down. From the metre on the switchboard she read off the charge for the call, and was paid.

The Jackal took a pot of coffee on the terrace looking over the Croisette and the glittering sea where brown bathers romped and screamed. Deep in thought, he drew heavily on a cigarette.

The bit about Kowalski he could follow; he remembered the hulking Pole from the hotel in Vienna. What he could not follow was how the bodyguard outside the door had known his code-name, or what he had been hired to do. Perhaps the French police had worked that out for themselves. Perhaps Kowalski had sensed what he was, for he also had been a killer, but oafish and clumsy.

The Jackal took stock. Valmy had advised him to quit and go home, but had admitted he had no direct authority from Rodin to cancel the operation. What had happened confirmed the Jackal's intense suspicions of the security slackness of the OAS. But he knew something that they did not, something that the French police could not know. It was that he was travelling under an assumed name, with a legitimate passport in that name, and three separate sets of false papers including two foreign passports and disguises to match up his sleeve.

Just what did the French police, this man Valmy had mentioned, Commissaire Lebel, have to go on? A rough description: tall, blond, foreign. There must be thousands of such men staying in France in August. They could not arrest every one.

The second advantage he had was that the French police were hunting for a man carrying the passport of Charles Calthrop. Then let them, and good luck. He was Alexander Duggan, and could prove it.

From here on, with Kowalski dead, nobody, not even Rodin and his henchmen, knew who he was or where. He was on his own at last, and that was the way he had always wanted it to be.

Nevertheless, the dangers had increased, there was no doubt of it. With the idea of an assassination once revealed, he would be attacking a fortress of security that was on its guard. The question was could his plan for carrying out the killing beat the security screen. On balance, he was confident that it could.

The question still remained, and it had to be answered. To go back, or to go on? To go back would be to enter into dispute with Rodin and his bunch of thugs over the ownership of the quarter million dollars presently in his account in Zurich. If he refused to hand the bulk of it back, they would not hesitate to track him down, torture him for the signed paper that would release the money from the account, then kill him. To stay ahead of them would cost money, a lot of it, probably the full extent of the money he possessed.

To go on would mean further dangers until the job was over. It would become ever harder to pull back at the last minute as the day approached.

The bill came, he glanced at it and winced. God, the prices these people charged. To live this kind of life a man needed to be rich, to have dollars and dollars and even more dollars. He looked out at the jewelled sea and the lithe brown girls walking along the beach, the hissing Cadillacs and snarling Jaguars that crept along the Croisette, their bronzed young drivers keeping half an eye on the road and the other flicking across the pavements for a likely pick-up. This was what he had wanted for a long time, from the days when he had pressed his nose to the travel agents' windows and gazed at the posters showing another life, another world, far from the drudgery of the commuter train and the forms in triplicate, the paper clips and tepid tea. Over the past three years he had almost made it; a glimpse here, a touch there. He had got used to good clothes, expensive meals, a smart flat, a sports car, elegant women. To go back meant to give it up.

The Jackal paid the bill and left a large tip. He climbed into the Alfa and headed away from the Majestic and into the heart of France.

Commissaire Lebel was sitting at his desk feeling as though he had never slept in his life and probably never would again. In the corner Lucien Caron snored loudly on the camp bed, having been up all night masterminding the search through the records for Charles Calthrop somewhere on the face of France. Lebel had taken over at dawn.

In front of him now was a pile of reports from the various agencies whose task it was to keep check on the presence and whereabouts of foreigners in France. Each one bore the same message. No man of that name had crossed any border point legally since the start of the year, the farthest back the checks had extended. No hotel in the country, either in the provinces or Paris, had taken in a guest of that name, at least not under that name. He was not on any list of undesirable aliens, nor had he ever come to the notice of the French authorities in any way.

As each report came in, Lebel wearily told the informant to go on checking further and further back until any visit Calthrop had ever paid to France could be traced. From that, possibly, could be established whether he had a habitual place of residence, a friend's house, a favourite hotel, where he might even now be masquerading under an assumed name.

Superintendent Thomas's call of that morning had come as yet another blow to hopes of an early capture of the elusive killer. Once again the phrase "back to square one" had been used, but fortunately this time it was only between Caron and himself. The members of the evening council had not yet been informed that the Calthrop lead was probably going to prove abortive. This was something he was going to have to tell them that evening at ten o'clock. If he could not produce an alternative name to Calthrop, he could imagine once again the scorn of Saint-Clair and the silent reproach of the rest.

Two things only could comfort him. One was that at least they now had a description of Calthrop and a photograph of his head and shoulders, full-face to the camera. He had probably changed his appearance considerably if he had taken a false passport, but still, it was better than nothing. The other thing was that no one else on the council could think of anything better to do than what he was doing—checking everything.

Caron had put forward the idea that perhaps the British police had surprised Calthrop while he was away from his flat on an errand in the town; that he had no alternative passport; that he had gone to ground and cried off on the whole operation.

Lebel had sighed.

"That would indeed be lucky," he told his adjutant, "but don't count on it. The British Special Branch reported that all his washing things and shaving gear were missing from the bathroom, and that he had mentioned to a neighbour that he was going away touring and fishing. If Calthrop left his passport behind, it was because he no longer needed it. Don't count on this man making too many errors; I'm beginning to get a feeling about the Jackal."

The man the police of two countries were now searching for had decided to avoid the agonising congestion of the Grande Corniche on its murderous way from Cannes to Marseilles, and to stay away from the southern part of the RN 7 when it turned north out of Marseilles for Paris. Both roads in August he knew to be a refined form of hell on earth.

Safe in his assumed and documented name of Duggan, he decided to drive leisurely up from the coast through the Alpes-Maritimes, where the air was cooler in the altitude, and on through the rolling hills of Burgundy. He was in no particular hurry, for the day he had set for his kill was not yet on him, and he knew he had arrived in France slightly ahead of schedule.

From Cannes he headed due north, taking the RN 85 through the picturesque perfume town of Grasse and on towards Castellane, where the turbulent Verdon river, tamed by the high dam a few miles upstream, flowed more obediently down from Savoy to join the Durance at Cadarache.

From here he pushed on to Barrême and the little spa town of Digne. The blazing heat of the Provençal plain had fallen away behind him, and the air of the hills was sweet and cool even in the heat. When he stopped he could feel the sun blazing down, but when motoring the wind was like a cooling shower and smelled of the pines and woodsmoke from the farms.

After Digne he crossed the Durance and ate lunch in a small but pretty hostelry looking down into the waters. In another hundred miles the Durance would become a grey and slimy snake hissing shallow amid the sun-bleached shingle of its bed at Cavaillon and Plan d'Orgon. But here in the hills it was still a river, the way a river should look, a cool river teeming with fish, shaded along its banks with grass growing all the greener for its presence.

In the afternoon he followed the long northward curving run of the RN 85 through Sisteron, still following the Durance upstream on its left bank until the road forked and the RN 85 headed towards the north. As dusk was falling he entered the little town of Gap. He could have gone on towards Grenoble, but decided that as there was no hurry and more chance of finding rooms in August in a small town, he should look around for a country-style hotel. Just out of town he found the brightly gabled Hôtel du Cerf, formerly a hunting lodge of one of the Dukes of Savoy, and still retaining an air of rustic comfort and good food.

There were several rooms still vacant. He had a leisurely bath, a break with his usual habit of showering, and dressed in his dove-grey suit with a silk shirt and knitted tie, while the room-maid, after receiving several winning smiles, had blushfully agreed to sponge and press the check suit he had worn all day so that he could have it back by morning.

The evening meal was taken in a panelled room overlooking a sweep of the wooded hillside, loud with the chatter of cicadas among the *pinèdes*. The air was warm, and it was only half way through the meal, when a woman diner who wore a sleeveless dress *en décolleté* commented to the mâitre d'hôtel that a chill had entered the air, that the windows were closed.

The Jackal turned round when he was asked if he objected to the window next to which he sat being closed, and glanced at the woman indicated by the mâitre as the person who had asked that they be shut. She was dining alone, a handsome woman in her late thirties with soft white arms and a deep bosom. The Jackal nodded to the mâitre to close the windows and gave a slight inclination of the head to the woman behind him. She answered with a cool smile.

The meal was magnificent. He chose speckled river trout grilled on a wood fire, and tournedos broiled over charcoal with fennel and thyme. The wine was a local Côtes du Rhône, full, rich, and in a bottle with no label. It had evidently come from the barrel in the cellar, the proprietor's personal choice for his vin de la maison. Most of the diners were having it, and with reason.

As he finished his sorbet he heard the low and authoritative voice of the woman behind him telling the mâitre that she would take her coffee in the residents' lounge, and the man bowed and addressed her as "Madame la Baronne." A few minutes later the Jackal had also ordered his coffee in the lounge and headed that way.

The call from Somerset House came for Superintendent Thomas at 10:15. He was sitting by the open window of the office staring down into the now silent street where no restaurants beckoned late diners and drivers into the area. The offices between Millbank and Smith Square were silent hulks, lightless, blind, uncaring. Only in the anonymous block that housed the offices of the Special Branch did the lights burn late as always.

A mile away, in the bustling Strand, the lights were also burning late in the section of Somerset House that housed the death certificates of millions of Britain's deceased citizens. Here Thomas's team of six detective sergeants and two inspectors were hunched over their piles of paper work, rising every few minutes to accompany one of the staff clerks, kept back at work long after the others had gone home, down the rows of gleaming files to check on yet another name.

It was the senior inspector in charge of the team who rang. His voice was tired, but with a touch of optimism, a man hoping that what he had to say would get them all released from the grind of checking hundreds of death certificates that did not exist because the passport holders were not dead.

"Alexander James Quentin Duggan," he announced briefly, after Thomas had answered.

"What about him?" said Thomas.

"Born April third, nineteen-twenty-nine, in Sambourne Fishley, in the parish of Saint Mark's. Applied for a passport in the normal way on the normal form on July fourteenth this year. Passport issued the following day and mailed July seventeenth to the address on the application form. It will probably turn out to be an accommodation address."

"Why?" asked Thomas. He disliked being kept waiting.

"Because Alexander James Quentin Duggan was killed in a road accident in his home village at the age of two and a half, on November eighth, nineteen-thirty-one."

Thomas thought for a moment.

"How many more of the passports issued in the last hundred days remain to be checked?" he asked.

"About three hundred to go," said the voice on the phone.

"Leave the others to continue checking the remainder, just in case there is another phoney among the bunch," instructed Thomas. "Hand over the team leadership to the other fellow. I want you to check out that address to which the passport was sent. Report back to me by phone the moment you have found it. If it's an occupied premises, interview the householder. Bring me back the full details on the phoney Duggan and the file copy of the photograph he submitted with the application form. I want to have a look at this lad Calthrop in his new disguise."

It was just before eleven that the senior inspector phoned back in. The address in question was a small tobacconist and newsagent shop in Paddington, the kind that had a window full of cards advertising the addresses of prostitutes. The owner, living above the shop, had been roused and had agreed he took in mail for customers who had no fixed address. He made a charge for his services. He could not remember a regular customer named Duggan, but it could have been that Duggan only called twice, once to arrange for his mail to be received there, the second time to pick up the one envelope that he was waiting for. The inspector had showed the newsagent a photograph of Calthrop, but the man could not recognise him. He also showed him the photograph of Duggan on the application form, and the man said he thought he remembered the second man, but could not be sure. He felt the man might have worn dark glasses. Many of those who came into his shop to buy the erotic magazines displayed behind the counter wore dark glasses.

"Bring him in," ordered Thomas, "and get back here yourself."

Then he picked up the phone and asked for Paris.

A second time, the call came half way through the evening conference. Commissaire Lebel had explained that beyond a doubt Calthrop was not inside France under his own name, unless he had smuggled himself into the country in a fishing boat or across one of the land borders at an isolated spot. He personally did not think a professional would do that, because at any subsequent spot check by the police he could be caught for not having his papers in order, that is, having no entry stamp on his passport.

Nor had any Charles Calthrop checked into any French hotel in his own name.

These facts were corroborated by the head of the Central Records office, the head of the DST, and the Prefect of Police of Paris, so they were not disputed.

The two alternatives, argued Lebel, were that the man had not made any provision for obtaining a false passport, and had thought he was unsuspected. In that case, the police raid on his flat in London must have caught him short. He explained that he did not believe this, because Superintendent Thomas's men had found gaps in the wardrobe and half-empty clothes drawers, and absence of washing accoutrements and shaving tackle, indicating that the man had left his London flat for a planned absence elsewhere. This was borne out by a neighbour, who reported Calthrop as having said he was going touring by car in Scotland. Neither the British nor the French police had any reason to believe this was true.

The second alternative was that Calthrop had acquired a false passport, and this man was what the British police were presently searching for. In that event, he might either still be not in France but at some other place completing his preparations, or he might already have entered France unsuspected.

It was at this point that several of the conference members exploded.

"You mean he might be here, in France, even in the centre of Paris?" expostulated Alexandre Sanguinetti.

"The point is," explained Lebel, "that he has got his timetable, and only he knows it. We have been investigating for seventy-two hours. We have no way of knowing at which point in the man's timetable we have intervened. The one thing we can be sure of is, that apart from knowing we are aware of the existence of a plot to assassinate the President, the killer cannot know what progress we have made. Therefore we stand a reasonable chance of apprehending an unsuspecting man, as soon as we have him identified under his new name, and located under that name."

But the meeting refused to be mollified. The thought that the killer might even then be within a mile of them, and that in that man's timetable the attempt on the life of the President might be for tomorrow, caused each of them acute anxiety.

"It could be, of course," mused Colonel Rolland, "that having learned from Rodin, through the unknown agent Valmy, that the plan was exposed in principle, Calthrop then left his flat to dispose of the evidence of his preparations. His gun and ammunition for example, could even now be tipped into a lake in Scotland, so that he can present himself to his own police on his return as clean as a whistle. In that event it would be very difficult to bring charges."

The meeting thought over Rolland's suggestion, with increasing signs of agreement.

"Then tell us, Colonel," said the Minister, "if you had been hired for this job, and had learned that the plot was exposed, even if your own identity were still a secret, is that what you would do?"

Certainly, *Monsieur le Ministre*," replied Rolland. "If I were an experienced assassin, I would realise that I must be on some file somewhere, and with the plot exposed it could only be a matter of time before I received a visit from the police and a search of my premises. So I would want to get rid of the evidence, and what better place than an isolated Scottish lake."

The round of smiles that greeted him from the table indicated how much those assembled approved of his speculation.

"However, that does not mean that we should just let him go. I still think we should—take care of this Monsieur Calthrop."

The smiles vanished. There was silence for several seconds.

"I do not follow you, *mon colonel*," said General Guibaud.

"Simply this," explained Rolland. "Our orders were to locate and destroy this man. He may have dismantled his plot for the moment. But he may not have destroyed his equipment, but merely hidden it, in order to pass the scrutiny of the British police. After that, he could simply take up again where he left off, but with a new set of preparations even more difficult to penetrate."

"But surely, when the British police locate him, if he is still in Britain, they will detain him," someone asked.

"Not necessarily. Indeed I doubt it. They will probably have no proof, only suspicions. And our friends the English are notoriously sensitive about what they are pleased to call 'civil liberties.' I suspect they may find him, interview him, and then let him go for lack of evidence."

"Of course the Colonel is right," interjected Saint-Clair. "The British police have stumbled on this man by a fluke. They are incredibly foolish about things like leaving a dangerous man at liberty. Colonel Rolland's section should be authorised to render this man Calthrop harmless once and for all."

The Minister noticed that Commissaire Lebel had remained silent and unsmiling throughout the interchange.

"Well, Commissaire, and what do you think? Do you agree with Colonel Rolland that Calthrop is even now dismantling and hiding, or destroying, his preparations and equipment?"

Lebel glanced up at the two rows of expectant faces on each side of him.

"I hope," he said quietly, "that the Colonel is right. But I fear he may not be."

"Why?" The Minister's question cut like a knife.

"Because," explained Lebel mildly, "his theory, although logical if indeed Calthrop has decided to call off the operation, is based on the theory that he has indeed made that decision. Supposing he has not? Supposing he has either not received Rodin's message or received it but decided to press ahead nevertheless?"

There was a buzz of deprecatory consternation. Only Rolland did not join in. He gazed contemplatively down the table at Lebel. What he was thinking was that Lebel was a far better brain than anyone present seemed prepared to give him credit for. Lebel's ideas, he recognized, could well be as realistic as his own.

It was at this point that the call came through for Lebel. This time he was gone for over twenty minutes. When he came back, he spoke to a completely silent assembly for a further ten minutes.

"What do we do now?" asked the Minister when he had finished. In his quiet way, without seeming to hurry, Lebel issued his orders like a general deploying his troops, and none of the men in the room, all senior to him in rank, disputed a word.

"So there we are," he concluded, "we will all conduct a quiet and discreet nation-wide search for Duggan in his new appearance, while the British police search the records of airline ticket offices, cross-Channel ferries, and so forth. If they locate him first, they pick him up if he is on British soil or inform us if he has left it. If we locate him inside France, we arrest him. If he is located in a third country, we can either wait for him to enter unsuspectingly and pick him up at the border, or . . . take another course of action. At that moment, however, I think my task of finding him will have been achieved. However, until that moment, gentlemen, I would be grateful if you would agree to do this my way."

The effrontery was so bold, the assurance so complete, that nobody could say a thing. They just nodded. Even Saint-Clair de Villauban was silent.

It was not until he was at home shortly after midnight that he found an audience to listen to his torrent of outrage at the thought of this ridiculous little bourgeois policeman having been right, while the top experts of the land had been wrong.

His mistress listened to him with sympathy and understanding, massaging the back of his neck as he lay face down on their bed. It was not until just before dawn, when he was sound asleep, that she could slip away to the hall and make a brief phone call.

Superintendent Thomas looked down at the two separate application forms for passports, and two photographs, spread out on the blotter in the pool of light thrown by the reading lamp.

"Let's run through it again," he ordered the senior inspector seated beside him. "Ready?"

"Sir."

"Calthrop: height, five feet eleven inches. Check?"

"Sir."

"Duggan: height, six feet."

"Thickened heels, sir. You can raise your height up to two and a half inches with special shoes. A lot of short people in show business do it for vanity. Besides, at a passport counter no one looks at your feet."

"All right," agreed Thomas, "thick-heeled shoes. Calthrop: colour of hair, brown. That doesn't mean much, it could vary from pale brown to chestnut brown. He looks to me here as if he had dark brown hair. Duggan also says brown. But he looks like a pale blond."

"That's true, sir. But hair habitually looks darker in photographs. It depends on the light, where it is placed and so forth. And then again, he could have tinted it paler to become Duggan."

"All right. I'll wear that. Calthrop: colour of eyes, brown. Duggan: colour of eyes, grey."

"Contact lenses, sir, it's a simple thing."

"OK. Calthrop's age is thirty-seven, Duggan's is thirty-four last April."

"He had to become thirty-four," explained the inspector, "because the real Duggan, the little boy who died at two and a half, was born in April nineteen-twenty-nine. That couldn't be changed. But nobody would query a man who happened to be thirty-seven but whose passport said he was thirty-four. One would believe the passport."

Thomas looked at the two photographs. Calthrop looked heftier, fuller in the face, a more sturdily built man. But to become Duggan he could have changed his appearance. Indeed, he had probably changed it even for his first meeting with the OAS chiefs, and remained with changed appearance ever since, including the period when he applied for the false passport. Men like this evidently had to be able to live in a second identity for months at a time if they were able to escape identification. It was probably by being this shrewd and painstaking that Calthrop had managed to stay off every police file in the world. If it had not been for that bar rumour in the Caribbean, they would never have got him at all.

But from now on, he had become Duggan, dyed hair, tinted contact lenses, slimmed down figure, raised heels. It was the description of Duggan, with passport number and photograph, that he sent down to the telex room to be transmitted to Paris. Lebel, he estimated, glancing at his watch, should have them all by 2 in the morning.

"After that, it's up to them," suggested the inspector.

"Oh no, boyo, after that there's a lot more work to be done," said Thomas maliciously. "First thing in the morning we start checking the airline ticket offices, the cross-Channel ferries, the continental train ticket offices—the whole lot. We have to find out not only who he is now but where he is now."

At that moment a call came through from Somerset House. The last of the passport applications had been checked, and all were in order.

"OK, thank the clerks and stand down. Eight-thirty sharp in my office, the lot of you," said Thomas.

A sergeant entered with a copy of the statement of the newsagent, who had been taken to his local police station and interviewed there. Thomas glanced at the sworn statement, which said little more than he had told the Special Branch inspector on his own doorstep.

"There's nothing we can hold him on," said Thomas. "Tell them at Paddington nick they can let him go back to his bed and his dirty photos, will you?"

The sergeant said, "Sir," and left.

Thomas settled back in the armchair to try and get some sleep.

While he had been talking it had quietly become August 15.

SIXTEEN

Madame la Baronne de la Chalonnière paused at the door of her room and turned towards the young Englishman who had escorted her there. In the half darkness of the corridor she could not make out the details of his face; it was just a blur in that gloom.

It had been a pleasant evening, and she was still undecided whether she would or would not insist that it end at her doorway. The question had been at the back of her mind for the past hour.

On the one hand, although she had taken lovers before, she was a respectable married woman staying for a single night in a provincial hotel, and not in the habit of permitting herself to be seduced by total strangers. On the other hand, she was at her most vulnerable and was candid enough to admit it to herself.

She had spent the day at the military cadet academy at Barcelonette, high in the Alps, attending the passing-out parade of her son as a newly brevetted second lieutenant in the Chasseurs Alpins, his father's old regiment. Although she had undoubtedly been the most attractive mother at the parade, the sight of her son receiving his officer's bars and commissioned into the French Army had brought home to her with something of a shock. the full realisation that she was a few months short of forty, and the mother of a grown son.

Although she could pass for five years younger, and sometimes felt ten years less than her age, the knowledge that her son was twenty and probably screwing women by now, no more to come home for the school holidays and go shooting in the forests around the family chateau, had caused her to wonder what she was going to do now.

She had accepted the laborious gallantry of the creaking old colonel who was the academy commandant, and the admiring glances of the pink-cheeked class-mates of her own boy, and had felt suddenly very lonely. Her marriage, she had known for years, was finished in all but name, for the Baron was too busy chasing the teenage dollies of Paris between the Bilbo-quet and Castel's to come down to the chateau for the summer, or even to turn up at his son's commissioning.

It had occurred to her, as she drove the family sedan back from the high Alps to stay overnight at a country hotel outside Gap, that she was hand-some, female, and alone. Nothing now seemed to lie in prospect but the attentions of elderly gallants like the colonel at the academy, or frivolous and unsatisfying flirtations with boys, and she was damned if she was going to devote herself to charitable works. Not yet, at any rate.

But Paris was an embarrassment and a humiliation, with Alfred constantly chasing his teenagers and half of society laughing at him and the other half laughing at her.

She had been wondering about the future over coffee in the lounge, and feeling an urge to be told she was a woman and a beautiful one, and not simply Madame la Baronne, when the Englishman had walked across and asked if, as they were alone in the residents' salon, he might take his coffee with her. She had been caught unawares, and too surprised to say no.

She could have kicked herself a few seconds later, but after ten minutes she did not regret accepting his offer. He was, after all, between thirty-three and thirty-five, or so she estimated, and that was the best age for a man. Although he was English, he spoke fluent and rapid French; he was reason-ably good looking and could be amusing. She had enjoyed the deft compli-ments and had even encouraged him to pay them, so that it was close to midnight when she rose, explaining that she had to make an early start the following morning.

He had escorted her up the stairs and at the landing window had pointed outside at the wooded hill slopes bathed in bright moonlight. They had stayed for a few moments looking at the sleeping countryside, until she had glanced at him and seen that his eyes were not on the view beyond the window but on the deep divide between her breasts where the moonlight turned the skin to alabaster white.

He had smiled when detected, and leaned to her ear and murmured,

"Moonlight turns even the most civilised man into a primitive." She had turned and walked on up the stairs, feigning annoyance, but inside her the unabashed admiration of the stranger caused a flutter of pleasure.

"It has been a most pleasant evening, monsieur."

She had her hand on the handle of the door and wondered vaguely whether the man would try to kiss her. In a way she hoped he would. Despite the triteness of the words, she could feel the hunger beginning in her belly. Perhaps it was just the wine, or the fiery Calvados he had ordered with the coffee, or the scene in the moonlight, but she was aware that this was not how she had foreseen the evening ending.

She felt the stranger's arms slip round her back, without a word of warning, and his lips come down onto hers. They were warm and firm. "This must stop," said a voice inside her. A second later she had responded to the kiss, mouth closed. The wine made her head swim, it must have been the effect of the wine. She felt the arms round her tighten preceptibly, and they were hard and strong.

Her thigh was pressed against him below the belly and through the satin of her dress she felt the rigid arrogance of his prick. For a second she withdrew her leg, then pushed it back again. There was no conscious moment of decision-taking; the realisation came without effort that she wanted him, badly, between her thighs, inside her belly, all night.

She felt the door behind her open inwards, broke the embrace, and stepped backwards into her room.

"*Viens, primitif.*"

He stepped into the room and closed the door.

Throughout the night every archive in the Panthéon was checked again, this time for the name Duggan, and with more success. A card was unearthed showing that Alexander James Quentin Duggan entered France on the Brabant Express from Brussels on July 22. An hour later another report from the same frontier post, the customs unit that regularly travels on the express trains from Brussels to Paris and back, doing its task while the train is in motion, was found with Duggan's name among those passengers on the Etoile du Nord Express from Paris to Brussels on July 31.

From the Prefecture of Police came a hotel card filled out in the name of Duggan, and quoting a passport number that matched the one Duggan was carrying, as contained in the information from London, showing that he had stayed in a small hotel near the Place de la Madeleine between July 22 and 30, inclusive.

Inspector Caron was all for raiding the hotel, but Lebel preferred to pay a quiet visit in the small hours of the morning and had a chat with the proprietor. He was satisfied the man he sought was not at the hotel by August 15, and the proprietor was grateful for the Commissaire's discretion in not waking all his guests.

Lebel ordered a plain-clothes detective to check into the hotel as a guest until further notice, and to stay there without moving outside, in case Duggan turned up again. The proprietor was happy to cooperate.

"This July visit," Lebel told Caron when he was back in his office at 4:30, "was a reconnaissance trip. Whatever he has got planned, it's all laid on."

Then he lay back in his chair, gazed at the ceiling, and thought. Why did he stay in a hotel? Why not in the house of one of the OAS sympathisers, like all the other OAS agents on the run? Because he does not trust the OAS sympathisers to keep their mouths shut. He's quite right. So he works alone, trusting nobody, plotting and planning his own operation in his own way, using a false passport, probably behaving normally, politely, without raising any suspicion. The proprietor of the hotel whom he had just interviewed confirmed this. "A real gentleman," he had said. . . . A real gentleman, thought Lebel, and dangerous as a snake. They are always the worst kind, for a policeman, the real gentlemen. Nobody ever suspected them.

He glanced at the two photographs that had come in from London, of Calthrop and Duggan. Calthrop became Duggan, with a change of height, hair and eyes, age, and, probably, manner. He tried to build up a mental picture of the man. What would he be like to meet? Confident, arrogant, assured of his immunity. Dangerous, devious, meticulous, leaving nothing to chance. Armed of course, but with what? An automatic under the left armpit? A throwing knife lashed against the ribs? A rifle? But where would he put it when he went through customs? How would he ever get near to General de Gaulle carrying such a thing, when even women's handbags were suspect within twenty yards of the President, and men with long packages were hustled away without ceremony from anywhere near a public appearance by the President?

Mon Dieu, and that colonel from the Elysée thinks he's just another thug! Lebel was aware he had one advantage: he knew the killer's new name, and the killer did not know that he knew. That was his only ace; apart from that, it all lay with the Jackal, and nobody at the evening conference could or would realise it.

If he ever gets wind of what you know before you catch him, and changes his identity again, Claude my boy, he thought, you are going to be up against it in a big way.

Aloud, he said "Really up against it."

Caron looked up.

"You're right, chief. He hasn't got a chance."

Lebel was short-tempered with him, which was unusual. The lack of sleep must be beginning to tell.

The finger of light from the waning moon beyond the window panes withdrew slowly across the rumpled coverlet and back towards the casement. It picked out the discarded satin dress between the door and the foot of the bed, the discarded brassiere and limp nylons scattered on the carpet. The two figures on the bed were muffled in shadow.

Colette lay on her back and gazed up at the ceiling, the fingers of one hand running idly through the blond hair of the head pillowed on her belly. Her lips parted in a half-smile as she thought back over the night.

He had been good, this English primitive, hard but skilled, knowing how to use fingers and tongue and prick to bring her on five times and himself three. She could still feel the blazing heat going into her when he came, and she knew how badly she had needed a night like this for so long when she responded as she had not for years.

She glanced at the small travelling clock beside the bed. It said a quarter past five. She tightened her grip in the blond hair and pulled.

"Hey."

The Englishman muttered, half asleep. They were both lying naked among the discarded sheets, but the central heating kept the room comfortably warm. The blond head disengaged itself from her hand and slid between her thighs. She could feel the tickle of the hot breath and the tongue flickering in search again.

"No, no more."

She closed her thighs quickly, sat up and grabbed the hair, raising his face until she could look at him. He eased himself up the bed, plunged his face onto one of her full heavy breasts and started to kiss.

"I said no."

He looked up at her.

"That's enough, lover. I have to get up in two hours, and you have to go back to your room. Now, my little English, now."

He got the message and nodded, swinging off the bed to stand on the floor, looking round for his clothes. She slid under the bedclothes, sorted them out from the mess around her knees and pulled them up to the chin. When he was dressed, with jacket and tie slung over one arm, he looked down at her in the half-darkness and she saw the gleam of teeth as he grinned. He sat on the edge of the bed and ran his right hand round to the back of her neck. His face was a few inches from hers.

"It was good?"

"Mmmmmm. It was very good. And you?"

He grinned again. "What do you think?"

She laughed. "What is your name."

He thought for a moment. "Alex," he lied.

"Well, Alex, it was very good. But it is also time you went back to your own room."

He bent down and gave her a kiss on the lips.

"In that case, good night, Colette."

A second later he was gone, and the door closed behind him.

At 7 in the morning as the sun was rising a local gendarme cycled up to the Hôtel du Cerf, dismounted and entered the lobby. The proprietor, who was already up and busy behind the reception desk organising the morning calls and *café complet* for the guests in their rooms, greeted him.

"*Alors*, bright and early?"

"As usual," said the gendarme. "It's a long ride out here on a bicycle, and I always leave you till the last."

"Don't tell me." The proprietor grinned. "We do the best breakfast coffee in the neighborhood. Marie-Louise, bring monsieur a cup of coffee, and no doubt he'll take it laced with a little Trou Normand."

The country constable grinned with pleasure.

"Here are the cards," said the proprietor, handing over the little white cards filled in the previous evening by the newly arrived guests. "There were only three new ones last night."

The constable took the cards and put them in the leather pouch on his belt.

"Hardly worth turning up for," he grinned, but sat on the boyer bench and waited for his coffee and Calvados, exchanging a few words of lustful banter with Marie-Louise when she brought it.

It was not until 8 that he got back to the gendarmerie and commissariat of Gap with his pouchful of hotel registration cards. These were then taken by the station inspector who flicked through them idly and put them in the rack, to be taken later in the day to the regional headquarters at Lyons, and later to the archives of Central Records in Paris. Not that he could see the point of it all.

As the inspector was dropping the cards into the rack in the commissariat, Madame Colette de la Chalonnière settled her bill, climbed behind the wheel of her car and drove off towards the west. One floor above, the Jackal slept on until nine o'clock.

Superintendent Thomas had dozed off when the phone beside him gave a shrill buzz. It was the intercom phone linking his office with the room down the corridor where the six sergeants and two inspectors had been working on a battery of telephones since his briefing had ended.

He glanced at his watch. Ten o'clock. *Damn, not like me to drop off.* Then he remembered how many hours sleep he had had, or rather had not had, since Dixon had summoned him on Monday afternoon. And now it was Thursday morning. The phone buzzed again.

"Hello."

The voice of the senior detective inspector answered.

"Friend Duggan," he began without preliminary. "He left London on a scheduled BEA flight on Monday morning. The booking was taken on Saturday. No doubt about the name. Alexander Duggan. Paid cash at the airport for the ticket."

"Where to? Paris?"

"No, Super. Brussels."

Thomas's head cleared quickly.

"All right, listen. He may have gone but come back. Keep checking airline bookings to see if there have been any other bookings in his name. Particularly if there is a booking for a flight that has not yet left London. Check with advance bookings. If he came back from Brussels, I want to know. But I doubt it. I think we've lost him, although of course he left London several hours before investigations were started, so it's not our fault. OK?"

"Right. What about the search in the U.K. for the real Calthrop? It's tying up a lot of the provincial police, and the Yard's just been on to say that they're complaining."

Thomas thought for a moment.

"Call it off," he said. "I'm pretty certain he's gone."

He picked up the outside phone and asked for the office of Commissaire Lebel at the Police Judiciaire.

Inspector Caron thought he was going to end up in a lunatic asylum before Thursday morning was out. First the British were on the phone at 10:05. He took the call himself, but when Superintendent Thomas insisted on speaking to Lebel, he went over to the corner to rouse the sleeping form on the camp bed. Lebel looked as if he had died a week before. But he took the call. As soon as he had identified himself to Thomas, Caron had to take the receiver back because of the language barrier. He translated what Thomas had to say, and Lebel's replies.

"Tell him," said Lebel when he had digested the information, "that we will handle the Belgians from here. Say that he has my very sincere thanks for his help, and that if the killer can be traced to a location on the continent rather than in Britain, I will inform him immediately so that he can call his men off."

When the receiver was down, both men settled back at their desks.

"Get me the Sûreté in Brussels," said Lebel.

The Jackal rose when the sun was already high over the hills and gave promise of another beautiful summer day. He showered and dressed, taking his check suit, well pressed, from the hands of the maid, Marie-Louise, who blushed again when he thanked her.

Shortly after 10:30 he drove the Alfa down into town and went to the post office to use the long-distance telephone to Paris. When he emerged twenty minutes later, he was tight-lipped and in a hurry. At a hardware store nearby he bought a quart of high-gloss lacquer in midnight blue, a half-pint tin in white, and two brushes, one a fine-tipped camel-hair for lettering, the other a two-inch soft bristle. He also bought a screwdriver. With these in the glove compartment of the car he drove back to the Hôtel du Cerf and asked for his bill.

While it was being prepared, he went upstairs to pack and carried the suitcases down to the car himself. When the three cases were in the trunk and the hand-grip on the passenger seat, he re-entered the foyer and settled the bill. The day clerk who had taken over the reception desk would say later that he seemed hurried and nervous, and paid the bill with a new hundred-franc note.

What he did not say, because he had not seen it, was that while he was in the back room getting change for the note, the blond Englishman turned over the pages of the hotel registry that the clerk had been making up for that day's list of coming clients. Flicking back one page, the Englishman had seen yesterday's inscriptions including one in the name of Mme la Baronne de la Chalonnière, Haute Chalonnière, Corrèze.

A few moments after settling the bill, the roar of the Alfa was heard in the driveway, and the Englishman was gone.

Just before midday more messages came into the office of Claude Lebel. The Sûreté of Brussels rang to say Duggan had only spent five hours in the city on Monday. He had arrived by BEA from London but had left on the afternoon Alitalia flight to Milan. He had paid cash at the desk for his ticket, although it had been booked on the previous Saturday by phone from London.

Lebel at once placed another call with the Milanese police.

As he put the phone down, it rang again. This time it was the DST, to say that a report had been received as normal routine that the previous morning among those entering France from Italy over the Ventimiglia crossing point, and filling in cards as they did so, had been Alexander James Quentin Duggan.

Lebel had exploded.

"Nearly thirty hours, he yelled. "Over a day!" he slammed down the receiver. Caron raised an eyebrow.

"The card," explained Lebel wearily, "has been in transit between Ventimiglia and Paris. They are now sorting out yesterday morning's entry cards from all over France. They say there are over twenty-five thousand of them. For one day, mark you. I suppose I shouldn't have yelled. At least we know one thing—he's here. Definitely. Inside France. If I don't have something for the meeting tonight, they'll skin me. Oh, by the way, ring up Superintendent Thomas and thank him again. Tell him the Jackal is inside France, and we shall handle it from here."

As Caron replaced the receiver after the London call, the Service Régional headquarters of the PJ at Lyons came on the phone. Lebel listened, then glanced up at Caron triumphantly. He covered the mouthpiece with his hand.

"We've got him. He's registered for two days at the Hôtel du Cerf in Gap, starting last night." He uncovered the mouthpiece and spoke down it.

"Now listen, Commissaire, I am not in a position to explain to you why we want this man Duggan. Just take it from me it is important. This is what I want you to do. . . ."

He spoke for ten minutes, and as he finished, the phone on Caron's desk rang. It was the DST again to say Duggan had entered France in a hired white Alfa Romeo sports two-seater, registration MI-61741.

"Shall I put out an all-stations alert for it?" asked Caron.

Lebel thought for a moment.

"No, not yet. If he's out motoring in the countryside somewhere he'll probably be picked up by a country cop who thinks he's just looking for a stolen sports car. He'll kill anybody who tries to intercept him. The gun must be in the car somewhere. The important thing is that he's booked into the hotel for two nights. I want an army round that hotel when he gets back. Nobody must get hurt if it can be avoided. Come on, if we want to get that helicopter, let's go."

While he was speaking the entire police force at Gap was moving steel roadblocks into position on all the exits from the town and the area of the hotel and posting men in the undergrowth round the barriers. Their orders came from Lyons. At Grenoble and Lyons men armed with submachine guns and rifles were clambering into two fleets of Black Marias. At Satory camp outside Paris a helicopter was being readied for Commissaire Lebel's flight to Gap.

Even in the shade of the trees the heat of early afternoon was sweltering. Stripped to the waist to avoid staining more of his clothes than was necessary, the Jackal worked on the car for two hours.

After leaving Gap he had headed due west through Veyne and Aspressur-Buech. It was downhill most of the way, the road winding between the mountains like a carelessly discarded ribbon. He had pushed the car to the limit, hurling it into the tight bends on squealing tires, twice nearly sending another driver coming the other way over the edge into one of the chasms below. After Aspres he picked up the RN 93, which followed the course of the Drôme river eastwards to join the Rhône.

For another eighteen miles the road had hunted back and forth across the river. Shortly after Luc-en-Diois he had thought it time to get the Alfa off the road. There were plenty of side roads leading away into the hills and upland villages. He had taken one at random and after a mile and a half chosen a path to the right leading into the woods.

In the middle of the afternoon he finished painting and stood back. The car was a deep gleaming blue, most of the paint already dry. Although by no means a professional painting job, it would pass muster except if given a close inspection, and particularly in the dusk. The two number plates had been unscrewed and lay face down on the grass. On the back of each had been painted in white an imaginary French number of which the last two letters were 75, the registration code for Paris. The Jackal knew this was the commonest type of car number on the roads of France.

The car's hiring and insurance papers did not now match the blue French Alfa as they had the white Italian one, and if he were stopped for a road check, with improper papers, he was done for. The only question in his mind as he dipped a rag in the petrol tank and wiped the paint stains off his hands was whether to start motoring now and risk the bright sunlight, showing up the amateurishness of the paintwork on the car, or whether to wait until dusk.

He was sure that with his false name discovered, his point of entry into France and a description of his car would soon be known. He was days too early for the assassination, and he needed to find a place to lie low until he was ready. That meant getting to the department of Corrèze 250 miles across country, and the quickest way was by using the car. It was a risk, but he decided it had to be taken. Very well, then, the sooner, the better, before every speed cop in the country was looking for an Alfa Romeo with a blond Englishman at the wheel.

He screwed the new number plates on, threw away what remained of the paint and the two brushes, pulled his polo-necked silk sweater and jacket back on, and gunned the engine into life. As he swept back onto the RN 93, he checked his watch. It was 3:41 in the afternoon.

High overhead he watched a helicopter clattering on its way towards the east. It was seven miles further to the village of Die. He knew well enough not to pronounce it in the English way, but the coincidence of the name occurred to him. He was not superstitious, but his eyes narrowed as he drove into the centre of the town. At the main square near the war memorial a huge black-leather-coated motorcycle policeman was standing in the middle of the road waving him to stop and pull over to the right. His gun was still in its tubes wired to the chassis of the car. He carried no automatic or knife. For a second he hesitated, unsure whether to hit the policeman a glancing blow with the wing of the car and keep driving, later to abandon the car a dozen miles further on and try without a mirror or a washbasin to transform himself into Pastor Jensen, with four pieces of luggage to cope with, or whether to stop.

It was the policeman who made the decision for him. Ignoring him completely as the Alfa began to slow down, the policeman turned round and scanned the road in the other direction. The Jackal slid the car over to the side of the road, watched, and waited.

From the far side of the village he heard the wailing of sirens. Whatever happened, it was too late to get out now. Into the village came a convoy of four Citroen police cars and six Black Marias. As the traffic cop jumped to one side and swept his arm up in salute, the convoy raced past the parked Alfa and headed down the road from which he had come. Through the wired windows of the vans, which gave them the French nickname of salad baskets, he could see the rows of helmeted police, submachine guns across the knees.

Almost as soon as it had come, the convey was gone. The speed cop brought his arm down from the salute, gave the Jackal an indolent gesture that he could now proceed, and stalked off to his motorcycle parked against the war memorial. He was still kicking the starter when the blue Alfa disappeared round the corner heading west.

It was 4:50 p.m. when they hit the Hôtel du Cerf. Claude Lebel, who had landed a mile on the other side of the township and been driven to the driveway of the hotel in a police car, walked up to the front door accompanied by Caron, who carried a loaded and cocked MAT 49 submachine carbine under the mackintosh slung over his right arm. The forefinger was on the trigger. Everyone in the town knew there was something afoot by this time, except the proprietor of the hotel. The hotel had been isolated for five hours, and the only odd thing had been the non-arrival of the trout seller with his day's catch of fresh fish.

Summoned by the desk clerk, the proprietor appeared from his labours over the accounts in the office. Lebel listened to him answer Caron's questions, glancing nervously at the odd-shaped bundle under Caron's arm, and his shoulders sagged.

Five minutes later the hotel was deluged with uniformed police. They interviewed the staff, examined the bedroom, chased through the grounds. Lebel walked alone out into the drive and stared up at the surrounding hills. Caron joined him.

"You think he's really gone, Chief?" Lebel nodded.

"He's gone all right."

"But he was booked for two days. Do you think the proprietor's in this with him?"

"No. He and the staff aren't lying. He changed his mind, some time this morning. And he left. The question now is, where the hell has he gone, and does he suspect yet that we know who he is?"

"But how could he? He couldn't know that. It must be coincidence. It must be."

"My dear Lucien, let us hope so."

"All we've got to go on now, then, is the car number."

"Yes. That was my mistake. We should have put the alert out for the car. Get onto the police R/T to Lyons from one of the sound cars and make it an all-stations alert. Top priority. White Alfa Romeo, Italian, Number MI-61741. Approach with caution, occupant believed armed and dangerous. You know the drill. But one more thing, nobody is to mention it to the press. Include in the message the instruction that the suspected man probably does not know he's suspected, and I'll skin anybody who lets him hear it on the radio or read it in the press. I'm going to tell Commissaire Gaillard of Lyons to take over here. Then let's get back to Paris."

It was nearly six o'clock when the blue Alfa coasted into the town of Valence, where the steel torrent of the RN 7, the main road from Lyons to Marseilles and the highway carrying most of the traffic from Paris to the

Côte d'Azur, thunders along the banks of the Rhône. The Alfa crossed the great road running south and took the bridge over the river towards the RN 533 to Saint Peray on the western bank. Below the bridge, the mighty river smoldered in the afternoon sunlight, ignored the puny steel insects scurrying southwards, and rolled at its own leisurely but certain pace towards the waiting Mediterranean.

After Saint Peray, as dusk settled on the valley behind him, the Jackal gunned the little sports car higher and higher into the mountains of the Massif Central and the province of Auvergne. After Le Puy the going got steeper, the mountains higher, and every town seemed to be a spa where the life-giving streams flowing out from the rocks of the massif had attracted those with aches and eczemas developed in the cities and made fortunes for the cunning Auvergnat peasants who had gone into the business with a will.

After Brioude the valley of the Allier river dropped behind, and the smell in the night air was of heather and drying hay in the upland pastures. He stopped to fill the tank at Issoire, then sped on through the Casino town of Mont Doré and the spa of La Bourdoule. It was nearly midnight when he rounded the headwaters of the Dordogne, where it rises among the Auvergne rocks to flow south and west through half a dozen dams and spend itself into the Atlantic at Bordeaux.

From La Bourdoule he took the RN 89 towards Ussel, the county town of Corrèze.

"You are a fool, *Monsieur le commissaire*, a fool. You had him within your grasp, and let him slip." Saint-Clair had half-risen to his feet to make his point, and glared down the polished mahogany table at the top of Lebel's head. The detective was studying the papers of his dossier, for all the world as if Saint-Clair did not exist.

He had decided that was the only way to treat the arrogant colonel from the Palace, and Saint-Clair for his part was not quite sure whether the bent head indicated an appropriate sense of shame or an insolent indifference. He preferred to believe it was the former. When he had finished and sank back into his seat, Claude Lebel looked up.

"If you will look at the mimeographed report in front of you, my dear colonel, you will observe that we did not have him in our hands," he observed mildly. "The report from Lyons that a man in the name of Duggan had registered the previous evening at a hotel in Gap did not reach the PJ until twelve-fifteen today. We now know that the Jackal left the hotel abruptly at eleven-o-five. Whatever measures had been taken, he still had an hour's start.

"Moreover, I cannot accept your strictures on the efficiency of the police forces of this country in general. I would remind you that the orders of the President are that this affair will be managed in secret. It was therefore not possible to put out an alert to every rural gendarmerie for a man named Duggan, for it would have started a hullabaloo in the press. The card registering Duggan at the Hôtel du Cerf was collected in the normal way at the normal time, and sent with due dispatch to Regional Headquarters at Lyons. Only there was it realised that Duggan was the wanted man. This delay was unavoidable, unless we wish to launch a nation-wide hue-and-cry for the man, and that is outside my brief.

"And lastly, Duggan was registered at the hotel for two days. We do not know what made him change his mind at eleven a.m. today and decide to move elsewhere."

"Probably your police gallivanting about the place," snapped Saint-Clair.

"I have already made it plain, there was no gallivanting before twelve-fifteen, and the man was already seventy minutes gone," said Lebel.

"All right, we have been unlucky, very unlucky," cut in the Minister. "However there is still the question of why no immediate search for the car was instituted. Commissaire?"

"I agree it was a mistake, Minister, in the light of events. I had reason to believe the man was at the hotel and intended to spend the night there. If he had been motoring in the vicinity, and had been intercepted by a motor patrol man for driving a wanted car, he would almost certainly have shot the unsuspecting policeman, and thus forewarned made his escape—"

"Which is precisely what he has done," said Saint-Clair.

"True, but we have no evidence to suggest that he has been forewarned, as he would have been if his car had been stopped by a single patrolman. It may well be he just decided to move on somewhere else. If so, and if he checks into another hotel tonight, he will be reported. Alternately, if his car is seen he will be reported."

"When did the alert for the white Alfa go out?" asked the director of the PJ, Max Fernet.

"I issued the instructions at five-fifteen p.m. from the courtyard of the hotel," replied Lebel. "It should have reached all major road-patrol units by seven, and the police on duty in the main towns should be informed throughout the night as they check in for night-duty. In view of the danger of this man, I have listed the car as stolen, with instructions that its presence be reported immediately to the Regional HQ, but that no approach should be made to the occupant by a lone policeman. If this meeting decides to change these orders, then I must ask that the responsibility for what may ensue be taken by this meeting."

There was a long silence.

"Regrettably, the life of a police officer cannot be allowed to stand in the way of protecting the President of France," murmured Colonel Gallon. There were signs of assent from round the table.

"Perfectly true," assented Lebel. "Providing a single police officer can stop this man. But most town and country policemen, the ordinary men on the beat and the motor patrolman, are not professional gunfighters. The Jackal is. If he is intercepted, shoots down one or two policemen, makes another getaway and disappears, we shall have two things to cope with: one will be a killer fully forewarned and perhaps able to adopt yet a new identity about which we know nothing, the other will be a nation-wide headline story in every newspaper which we will not be able to play down. If the Jackal's real reason for being in France remains a secret for forty-eight hours after the killing story breaks, I will be most surprised. The press will know within days that he is after the President. If anyone here would like to explain that to the General, I will willingly retire from this investigation and hand it over."

No one volunteered. The meeting broke up as usual around midnight. Within thirty minutes it had become Friday, August 16.

SEVENTEEN

The blue Alfa Romeo cruised into the Place de la Gare at Ussel just before one in the morning. There was one cafe remaining open across the square from the station entrance, and a few late-night travellers waiting for a train were sipping coffee. The Jackal dragged a comb through his hair and walked past the stacked-up chairs and tables on the terrace and up to the bar counter. He was cold, for the mountain air was chill as he drove at over sixty miles an hour; and stiff, with aching thighs and arms from hauling the Alfa through innumerable mountain curves; and hungry, for he had not even eaten since dinner twenty-eight hours previously, apart from a buttered roll for breakfast.

He ordered two large buttered slices of a long thin loaf, sliced down the middle and known as a *tartine beurrée*, and four hard-boiled eggs from the stand on the counter. Also a large white coffee.

While the buttered bread was being prepared and the coffee was percolating through the filtre, he glanced round for the telephone booth. There was none, but a telephone stood at the end of the counter.

"Have you got the local telephone directory?" he asked the barman. Without a word, still busy, the barman gestured to a pile of directories on a rack behind the counter.

"Help yourself," he said.

The Baron's name was listed under the words "Chalonnière, M. le Baron de la . . ." and the address was the chateau at La Haute Chalonnière. The Jackal knew this, but the village was not listed on his road map. However the telephone number was given as Egletons, and he found this easily enough. It was another thirty kilometres beyond Ussel on the RN 89. He settled down to eat his eggs and bread.

It was just before two in the morning that he passed a stone by the roadside saying "Egletons, 6 km." and decided to abandon the car in one of the forests that bordered the road. They were dense woods, probably the estate of some local noble, where once boars had been hunted with horse and hound. Perhaps they still were, for parts of Corrèze seem to have stepped straight from the days of Louis XIV.

Within a few hundred metres he had found a drive leading into the forest, separated from the road by a wooden pole slung across the entrance, adorned by a placard saying "Chasse Privée." He removed the pole, drove the car into the wood, and replaced the pole.

From there he drove half a mile into the forest, the headlamps lighting the gnarled shapes of the trees like ghosts reaching down with angry branches at the trespasser. Finally he stopped the car, switched off the headlights, and took the wire cutters and torch from the glove compartment.

He spent an hour underneath the vehicle, his back getting damp from the dew on the forest floor. At last the steel tubes containing the sniper's rifle were free from their hiding place of the previous sixty hours, and he re-packed them in the suitcase with the old clothes and the army greatcoat.

He had a last look round the car to make sure there was nothing left in it that could give anyone who found it a hint of who its driver had been and drove it hard into the centre of a nearby clump of wild rhododendron.

Using the metal shears, he spent the next hour cutting rhododendron branches from nearby bushes and jabbing them into the ground in front of the hole in the shrubbery made by the Alfa, until it was completely hidden from view.

He knotted his tie with one end round the handle of one of the suitcases, the other end round the handle of the second case. Using the tie like a railway porter's strap, his shoulder under the loop so that one case hung down his chest and the other down his back, he was able to grab the remaining two pieces of luggage in his two free hands and start the march back to the road.

It was slow going. Every hundred yards he stopped, put the cases down and went back over his tracks with a branch from a tree, sweeping away the light impressions made in the moss and twigs by the passage of the Alfa. It took another hour to reach the road, duck under the pole, and put half a mile between himself and the entrance to the forest.

His check suit was soiled and grimy, the polo sweater stuck to his back with greasy obstinacy, and he thought his muscles would never stop aching again. Lining the suitcases up in a row, he sat down to wait as the eastern sky grew a fraction paler than the surrounding night. Country buses, he reminded himself, tend to start early.

In fact he was lucky. A farm truck towing a trailer of hay came by at 5:50 heading towards the market town.

"Car broken down?" bawled the driver as he slowed up.

"No. I've got a weekend pass from camp, so I'm hitch-hiking home. Got as far as Ussel last night and decided to push on to Tulle. I've got an uncle there who can fix me a truck to Bordeaux. This was as far as I got." He grinned at the driver, who laughed and shrugged.

"Crazy, walking through the night up here. No one comes this way after dark. Jump on the trailer, I'll take you into Egletons, you can try from there."

They rolled into the little town at 6:45. The Jackal thanked the farmer, gave him the slip round the back of the station, and headed for a cafe.

"Is there a taxi in town?" he asked the barman over coffee.

The barman gave him the number, and he rang to call up the taxi company. There was one car that would be available in half an hour, he was told. While he waited he used the fundamental conveniences of the cold water tap offered by the cafe's lavatory to wash his hands and face, change into a fresh suit, and brush his teeth, which felt furry from cigarettes and coffee.

The taxi arrived at 7:30, an old rattletrap Renault.

"Do you know the village of Haute Chalonnière?" he asked the driver.

"Course."

"How far?"

"Eighteen kilometres." The man jerked his thumb up towards the mountains. "In the hills."

"Take me there," said the Jackal, and hefted his luggage into the roof rack, except for one case that went inside with him.

He insisted on being dropped in front of the Café de la Poste in the village square. There was no use for the taxi driver from the nearby town to know he was going to the chateau. When the taxi had driven away, he brought his luggage into the cafe. Already the square was blazing hot, and two oxen yoked to a hay-cart ruminated their cud reflectively outside while fat black flies promenaded round their gentle patient eyes.

Inside the cafe it was dark and cool. He heard rather than saw the customers shift at their tables to examine the newcomer, and there was a clacking of clogs on tiles as an old peasant woman in a black dress left one group of farm workers and went behind the bar.

"Monsieur?" she croaked.

He put down the luggage and leaned on the bar. The locals, he noticed, were drinking red wine.

"*Un gros rouge, s'il vous plaît, madame.*"

"How far is the chateau, madame?" he asked when the wine was poured. She eyed him keenly from wily black marbles.

"Two kilometres, monsieur."

He sighed wearily. "That fool of a driver tried to tell me there was no chateau here. So he dropped me in the square."

"He was from Egletons?" she asked. The Jackal nodded.

"They are fools at Egletons," she said.

"I have to get to the chateau," he said.

The ring of peasants watching from their tables made no move. No one suggested how he might get there. He pulled out a new hundred-franc note.

"How much is the wine, madame?"

She eyed the note sharply. There was a shifting among the blue cotton blouses and trousers behind him.

"I haven't got change for that," said the old woman.

He sighed.

"If only there were someone with a van, he might have change," he said. Someone got up and approached from behind.

"There is a van in the village, monsieur," growled a voice.

The Jackal turned with mock surprise.

"It belongs to you, *mon ami?*"

"No, monsieur, but I know the man who owns it. He might run you up there."

The Jackal nodded as if considering the merits of the idea.

"In the meantime, what will you take?"

The peasant nodded at the crone, who poured another large glass of rough red wine.

"And your friends? It's a hot day. A thirsty day."

The stubbled face split into a smile. The peasant nodded again to the woman who took two full bottles over to the group round the big table.

"Benoit, go and get the van," ordered the peasant, and one of the men, gulping down his wine in one swallow, went outside.

"What appeals to me about the peasantry of the Auvergne," mused the Jackal as he rattled and bumped the last two kilometres up to the chateau, "is that they are so surly they keep their damn mouths shut—at least to outsiders."

Colette de la Chalonnière sat up in bed, sipped her coffee, and read the letter again. The anger that had possessed her on the first reading had dissipated, to be replaced by a kind of weary disgust.

She wondered what on earth she could do with the rest of her life. She had been welcomed home the previous afternoon after a leisurely drive from Gap by old Ernestine, the maid who had been in service at the chateau since Alfred's father's day, and the gardener, Louison, a former peasant boy who had married Ernestine when she was still an under housemaid.

The pair were now virtually the curators of the chateau of which two thirds of the rooms were shut off and blanketed in dust covers.

She was, she realised, the mistress of an empty castle where there were neither children playing in the park any more nor a master of the household saddling his horse in the courtyard.

She looked back at the cutting from the Paris glossy society magazine that her friend had so thoughtfully mailed to her; at the face of her husband grinning inanely into the flash-bulb, eyes torn between the lens of the camera and the jutting bosom of the girl over whose shoulder he was peering. She was a cabaret dancer, risen from bar hostess, quoted as saying she hoped "one day" to be able to marry the Baron, who was her "very good friend."

Looking at the lined face and scrawny neck of the ageing Baron in the photograph, she wondered vaguely what had happened to the handsome young captain of the Resistance partisans with whom she had fallen in love in 1942 and married a year later when she was expecting her son.

She had been a teenage girl, running messages for the Resistance, when she met him in the mountains. He had been in his mid-thirties, known by the code-name of Pegasus, a lean, hawk-faced, commanding man who had turned her heart. They had been married in a secret ceremony in a cellar chapel by a priest of the Resistance, and she had borne her son in her father's house.

Then after the war had come the restoration of all his lands and properties. His father had died of a heart attack when the Allied armies swept across France, and he had emerged from the heather to become the Baron of Chalonnière, cheered by the peasantry of the countryside as he brought his wife and son back to the chateau. Soon the estates had tired him, the lure of Paris and the lights of the cabarets, the urge to make up for the lost years of his youth in the colonial deserts and of his manhood in the undergrowth, had proved too strong to resist.

Now he was fifty-seven and could have passed for seventy.

The Baroness threw the cutting and its accompanying letter on the floor. She jumped out of bed and stood in front of the full-length mirror on the far wall, pulling open the laces that held the peignoir together down the front. She stood on tip-toe to tighten the muscles of her thighs as a pair of high-heeled shoes would do.

Not bad, she thought. Could be a lot worse. A full figure, the body of a mature woman. The hips were wide, but the waist had mercifully remained in proportion, firmed by hours in the saddle and long walks in the hills. She cupped her breasts one in each hand and measured their weight. Too big, too heavy for real beauty, but still enough to excite a man in bed.

Well, Alfred, two can play at that game, she thought. She shook her head, loosening the shoulder length black hair so that a strand fell forward by her cheek and lay across one of her breasts. She took her hands away and ran them between her thighs, thinking of the man who had been there just over twenty-four hours before. He had been good. She wished now she had stayed on at Gap. Perhaps they could have holidayed together, driving round using a false name, like runaway lovers. What on earth had she come home for?

There was a clatter of an old van drawing up in the courtyard. Idly she drew the peignoir together and walked to the window that gave onto the front of the house. A van from the village was parked there, the rear doors open. Two men were at the back taking something down from the tailboard. Louison was walking across from where he had been weeding one of the ornamental lawns to help carry the load.

One of the men hidden behind the van walked round to the front, stuffing some paper into his trouser pocket, climbed into the driving seat and engaged the grinding clutch. Who was delivering things to the chateau? She had not ordered anything. The van started to pull away and she gave a start of surprise. There were three suitcases and a hand-grip on the gravel, beside them was a man. She recognised the gleam of the blond hair in the sun and smiled wide with pleasure.

"You animal. You beautiful primitive animal. You followed me."

She hurried into the bathroom to dress.

When she came onto the landing, she caught the sound of voices in the hall below. Ernestine was asking what monsieur wanted.

"*Madame la Baronne, elle est là?*"

In a moment Ernestine came hurrying up the stairs as fast as her old legs would carry her. "A gentleman has called, ma'am."

The evening meeting in the ministry that Friday was shorter than usual. The only thing to report was that there was nothing. For the past twenty-four hours the description of the wanted car had been circulated in a routine manner, so as not to arouse undue suspicion, throughout France. It had not been spotted. Similarly, every Regional Headquarters of the Police Judiciaire had ordered its dependent local commissariats in town and country to get all hotel registration cards into HQ by eight in the morning at the latest. At the Regional HQs they were immediately scoured, tens of thousands of them, for the name of Duggan. Nothing had been spotted. Therefore, he had not stayed last night in a hotel, at least, not in the name of Duggan.

"We have to accept one of two premises," explained Lebel to a silent gathering. "Either he still believes he is unsuspected. In other words his departure from the Hôtel du Cerf was an unpremeditated action and a coincidence; in which case there is no reason for him not to use his Alfa Romeo openly and stay openly in hotels under the name of Duggan. In that case he must be stopped sooner or later. In the second case, he has decided to ditch the car somewhere and abandon it, and rely on his own resources. In the latter case, there are a further two possibilities.

"Either he has no further false identities on which to rely; in which case he cannot get far without registering at a hotel or trying to pass a frontier point on his way out of France. Or he has another identity and has passed into it. In the latter case he is still extremely dangerous."

"What makes you think he might have another identity?" asked Colonel Rolland.

"We have to assume," said Lebel, "that this man, having been offered evidently a very large sum by the OAS to carry out this assassination, must be one of the best professional killers in the world. That implies that he has had experience. And yet he has managed to stay clear of any official suspicion, and all official police dossiers. The only way he could do this would be by carrying out his assignments in a false name and with a false appearance. In other words, an expert in disguise as well.

"We know from the comparison of the two photographs that Calthrop was able to extend his height by high-heeled shoes, slim off several kilos in weight, change his eye colour by contact lenses and his hair colour with dye to become Duggan. If he can do that once, we cannot afford the luxury of assuming he cannot do it again."

"But there's no reason to suppose he suspected he would be exposed before he got close to the President," protested Saint-Clair. "Why should he take such elaborate precautions as to have one or more false identities?"

"Because," said Lebel, "he apparently does take elaborate precautions. If he did not, we should have had him by now."

"I note from Calthrop's dossier, as passed on by the British police, that he did his National Service just after the war in their parachute regiment. Perhaps he's using this experience to live rough, hiding out in the hills," suggested Max Fernet.

"Perhaps," agreed Lebel.

"In that case he is more or less finished as a potential danger."

Lebel considered for a moment.

"Of this particular person, I would not like to say that until he is behind bars."

"Or dead," said Rolland.

"If he's got any sense, he'll be trying to get out of France while he's still alive," said Saint-Clair.

On that note the meeting broke up.

"I wish I could count on that," Lebel told Caron back in the office. "But as far as I'm concerned he's alive, well, free, and armed. We keep on looking for him and that car. He had three pieces of luggage, he can't have got far on foot with all that. Find that car and we start from there."

The man they wanted was lying on fresh linen in a chateau in the heart of Corrèze. He was bathed and relaxed, filled with a meal of country pâté and jugged hare, washed down with rough red wine, black coffee, and brandy. He stared up at the gilt curlicues that writhed across the ceiling and planned the course of the days that now separated him from his assignment in Paris. In a week, he thought, he would have to move, and getting away might prove difficult. But it could be done. He would have to think out a reason for going.

The door opened and the Baroness came in. Her hair had been let down around her shoulders and she wore a peignoir held together at the throat but open down the front. As she moved, it swayed briefly open. She was quite naked beneath it, but had kept on the stockings she had worn at dinner and the high-heeled court shoes. The Jackal propped himself up on one elbow as she closed the door and walked over to the bed.

She looked down at him in silence. He reached up and slipped loose the bow of ribbon that held the night-dress closed at the throat. It swung open to reveal the breasts, and as he craned forward his hand slid the lace-edged material off her shoulder. It slid down to the floor without a sound.

She pushed his shoulder so that he rolled back onto the bed, then gripped his wrists and pinned them against the pillow as she climbed over him. He stared back up at her as she knelt above him, her thighs gripping his ribs hard. She smiled down at him, two curling strands of hair falling down to the nipples.

"*Bon, mon primitif,* now let's see you perform."

He eased his head forward as her bottom rose off his chest, and started.

For three days the trail went cold for Lebel, and at each evening meeting the volume of opinion that the Jackal had left France secretly with his tail between his legs increased. By the meeting on the evening of the 19th he was alone in maintaining his view that the killer was still somewhere in France, lying low and biding his time, waiting.

"Waiting for what?" shrilled Saint-Clair that evening. "The only thing he can be waiting for, if he is still here, is an opportunity to make a dash for the border. The moment he breaks cover we have got him. He has every man's arm against him, nowhere to go, no one to take him in, if your supposition that he is completely cut off from the OAS and their sympathisers is correct."

There was murmur of assent from the table, most of whose members were beginning to harden in their opinion that the police had failed, and that Bouvier's original dictum that the location of the killer was a purely detective task had been wrong.

Lebel shook his head doggedly. He was tired, exhausted by lack of sleep, by strain and worry, by having to defend himself and his staff from the constant needling attacks of men who owed their exalted positions to politics rather than experience. He had enough sense to realise that if he was wrong, he was finished. Some of the men round the table would see to that. And if he was right? If the Jackal was still on the trail of the President? If he slipped through the net and closed with his victim? He knew those round the table would desperately seek for a scapegoat. And it would be him. Either way his long career as a policeman was ended. Unless. . . unless he could find the man and stop him. Only then would they have to concede that he had been right. But he had no proof; only an odd faith, that he could certainly never divulge, that the man he was hunting was another professional who would carry out his task no matter what.

Over the eight days since this affair had landed on his lap he had come to a grudging respect for the silent, unpredictable man with the gun who seemed to have everything planned down to the last detail, including the contingency planning. It was as much as his career was worth to admit his feelings amidst the gathering of political appointees around him. Only the massive bulk of Bouvier beside him, hunching his head into his shoulders and glaring at the table, gave him a small comfort. At least he was another detective.

"Waiting for I don't know what," Lebel replied. "But he's waiting for something, or some appointed day. I do not believe, gentlemen, that we have heard the last of the Jackal yet. All the same, I cannot explain why I feel this."

"Feelings!" jeered Saint-Clair. "Some appointed day! Really, Commissaire, you seem to have been reading too many romantic thrillers. This is no romance, my dear sir, this is reality. The man has gone, that's all there is to it." He sat back with a self-assured smile.

"I hope you are right," said Lebel quietly. "In that case, I must tender to you Monsieur le Ministre, my willingness to withdraw from the enquiry and return to the investigation of crime."

The Minister eyed him with indecision.

"Do you think the enquiry is worth pursuing, Commissaire?" he asked. "Do you think a real danger still exists?"

"As to the second question, sir, I do not know. For the former, I believe we should go on looking until we are absolutely certain."

"Very well then. Gentlemen, it is my wish that the Commissaire continue his enquiries and that we continue our evening meetings to hear his reports—for the moment."

On the morning of August 20 Marcango Callet, a gamekeeper, was shooting vermin on the estates of his employer between Egletons and Ussel in the department of Corrèze, when he pursued a wounded wood-pigeon that had tumbled into a clump of wild rhododendron. In the centre of the clump he found the pigeon, fluttering madly on the driving seat of an open sports car that had evidently been abandoned.

At first he thought, as he wrung the bird's neck, that it must have been parked by a pair of lovers who had come into the forest for a picnic, despite the warning notice that he had nailed up on the pole at the entrance to the woods half a mile away. Then he noticed that some of the branches of shrubbery that concealed the car from view were not growing in the ground but had been jabbed into the earth. Further examination showed the cut stumps of the branches on other nearby bushes, the white cuts having been smeared over with earth to darken them.

From the bird droppings on the seats of the car he reckoned it had been there for several days at least. Taking his gun and bird he cycled back through the woods to his cottage, making a mental note to mention the car to the local village constable when he went into the village later that morning to buy some more rabbit snares.

It was nearly noon when the village policeman wound up the hand-cranked telephone in his house and filed a report to the commissariat at Ussel to the effect that a car had been found abandoned in the woods nearby. Was it a white car, he was asked. He consulted his notebook. No, it was a blue car. Was it Italian? No, it was French-registered, make unknown. Right, said the voice from Ussel, a towaway truck will be sent during the afternoon, and he had better be ready waiting to guide the crew to the spot, because there was a lot of work on and everyone was short-staffed, what with a search going on for a white Italian sports car that the bigwigs in Paris wanted to have a look at. The village constable promised to be ready and waiting when the towaway truck arrived.

It was not until after four that afternoon that the little car was towed into the pound at Ussel, and close to five before one of the motor maintenance staff, giving the car a check over for identification, noticed that the paintwork was appallingly badly done.

He took out a screwdriver and scratched at one of the wings. Under the blue, a streak of white appeared. Perplexed, he examined the numberplates, and noticed that they seemed to have been reversed. A few minutes later the front plate was lying in the courtyard face up, exhibiting white lettering MI-61741, and the policeman was hurrying across the yard towards the office.

Claude Lebel got the news just before six. It came from Commissaire Valentin of the Regional Headquarters of the PJ at Clermont Ferrand, capital of the Auvergne. Lebel jerked upright in his chair as Valentin's voice started talking.

"Right, listen, this is important. . . . I can't explain why it's important, I can only say that it is. . . . Yes, I know it's irregular, but that's the way it is. . . . I know you're a full Commissaire, my dear fellow, but if you want confirmation of my authority in this case I'll pass you right on to the Director-General of the PJ.

"I want you to get a team down to Ussel now. The best you can get, and as many men as you can get. Start enquiring from the spot where the car was found. Mark off the map with that spot in the centre and prepare for a square-search. Ask at every farm house, every farmer who regularly drives along that road, every village store and cafe, every hotel and woodcutter's shack.

"You are looking for a tall blond man, English by birth but speaking good French. He was carrying three suitcases and a hand-grip. He carried a lot of money in cash and is well-dressed, but probably looking as if he had slept rough.

"Your men must ask where he was, where he went, what he tried to buy. Oh, and one other thing, the press must be kept out at all costs. . . . What do you mean, they can't? . . . Well, of course the local stringers will ask what goes on. Well, tell them there was a car crash and it's thought one of the occupants might be wandering in a dazed state. . . . Yes, all right, a mission of mercy. Anything, just allay their suspicions. Tell them there's no story the national papers would bother to pay for, not in the holiday season with five hundred road accidents a day. Just play it down. . . . And one last thing, if you locate the man holed up somewhere, don't get near him. Just surround him and keep him there. I'll be down as soon as I can."

Lebel put the phone down and turned to Caron.

"Get on to the Minister. Ask him to bring the evening meeting forward to eight o'clock. I know that's supper time, but it will only be short. Then get on to Satory and get the helicopter again. A night flight, to Ussel, and they'd better tell us where they will be landing so we can get a car laid on to pick me up. You'll have to take over here."

The police vans from Clermont Ferrand, backed up by others contributed by Ussel, set up their headquarters in the village square of the tiny hamlet nearest to where the car had been found, just as the sun was setting. From the radio van, Valentin issued instructions to the scores of squad cars converging on the other villages of the area. He had decided to start with a five mile radius of the spot where the car was found, and work through the night. People were more likely to be home in the hours of darkness. On the other hand, in the twisting valleys and hillsides of the region, there was more chance that in the darkness his men would get lost, or overlook some small woodcutter's shack where the fugitive might be hiding.

There was one other factor that he could not have explained to Paris over the phone, and which he dreaded having to explain to Lebel face to face. Unbeknown to him, some of his men came across this factor before midnight. A group of them were interviewing a farmer in his cottage two miles from the spot where the car was found.

He stood in the doorway in his nightshirt, pointedly refusing to invite the detectives in. From his hand the paraffin lamp cast flickering splashes of light over the group.

"Come on, Gaston, you drive along that road to market pretty often. Did you drive down that road towards Egletons on Friday morning?"

The peasant surveyed them through narrowed eyes.

"Might have done."

"Well, did you or didn't you?"

"Can't remember."

"Did you see a man on the road?"

"I mind my own business."

"That's not what we're asking. Did you see a man?"

"I saw nobody, nothing."

"A blond man, tall, athletic, carrying three suitcases and a handgrip?"

"I saw nothing. *J'ai rien vu, tu comprends.*"

It went on for twenty minutes. At last they went, one of the detectives making a meticulous note in his book. The dogs snarled on the ends of their chains and snapped at the policemen's legs, causing them to skip to one side and step in the compost heap. The peasant watched them until they were back on the road and jolting away in their car. Then he slammed the door, kicked an inquisitive goat out of the way, and clambered back into bed with his wife.

"That was the fellow you gave a lift to, wasn't it?" she asked. "What do they want with him?"

"Dunno," said Gaston, "but no one will ever say Gaston Grosjean helped give away another creature to them." He hawked and spat into the embers of the fire. "*Sales flics.*"

He turned down the wick and blew out the light, swung his legs off the floor and pushed further into the cot against the ample form of his wife. "Good luck to you, friend, wherever you are."

Lebel faced the meeting and put down his papers.

"As soon as this meeting is over, gentlemen, I am flying down to Ussel to supervise the search myself."

There was silence for nearly a minute.

"What do you think, Commissaire, can be deduced from this?"

"Two things, Monsieur le Ministre. We know he must have bought paint to transform the car, and I suspect enquiries will show that if the car was driven through the night from Thursday into Friday morning from Gap to Ussel, that it was already transformed. In that case—and enquiries along these lines are proceeding—it would appear he bought the paint in Gap. If that is so, then he was tipped off. Either somebody rang him or he rang somebody, either here or in London, who told him of the discovery of his pseudonym of Duggan. From that he could work out that we would be onto him before noon, and onto his car. So he got out, and fast."

He thought the elegant ceiling of the conference room was going to crack, so pressing was the silence.

"Are you seriously suggesting," somebody asked from a million miles away, "there is a leak from within this room?"

"I cannot say that, monsieur. There are switchboard operators, telex operators, middle and junior level executives to whom orders have to be passed. It could be that one of them is clandestinely an OAS agent. But one thing seems to emerge ever more clearly. He was tipped off about the unmasking of the over-all plan to assassinate the President of France, and decided to go ahead regardless. And he was tipped off about his unmasking as Alexander Duggan. He has, after all, got one single contact. I suspect it might be the man known as Valmy whose message to Rome was intercepted by the DST."

"Damn," swore the head of the DST, "we should have got the bastard in the post office."

"And what is the second thing we may deduce, Commissaire?" asked the Minister.

"The second thing is that when he learned he was blown as Duggan, he did not seek to quit France. On the contrary, he headed right into the centre of France. In other words, he is still on the trail of the head of state. He has simply challenged the whole lot of us."

The Minister rose and gathered his papers.

"We will not detain you, Monsieur le Commissaire. Find him. Find him, and tonight. Dispose of him if you have to. Those are my orders, in the name of the President."

With that he stalked from the room.

An hour later Lebel's helicopter lifted away from the take-off pad at Satory and headed through the purpling-black sky towards the south.

"Impertinent pig. How dare he? Suggesting that somehow we, the top-most officials of France, were at fault. I shall mention it of course in my next report."

Jacqueline eased the thin straps of her slip from her shoulders and let the transparent material fall to settle in folds round her hips. Tightening her biceps to push the breasts together with a deep cleavage down the middle, she took her lover's head and pulled it towards her bosom.

"Tell me all about it," she cooed.

EIGHTEEN

The morning of August 21 was as bright and clear as the previous fourteen of that summer heat wave had been. From the windows of the Château de la Haute Chalonnière, looking out over a rolling vista of heather-clad hills, it looked calm and peaceful, giving no hint of the tumult of police enquiries that was even then enveloping the town of Egletons eighteen kilometres away.

The Jackal, naked under his dressing gown, stood at the windows of the Baron's study making his routine morning call to Paris. He had left his mistress asleep upstairs after another night of ferocious love-making.

When the connection came through, he began as usual "*Ici Chacal.*"

"*Ici Valmy,*" said the husky voice at the other end. "Things have started to move again. They have found the car . . ."

He listened for another two minutes, interrupting only with a terse question. With a final "*merci,*" he replaced the receiver and fumbled in his pockets for cigarettes and lighter. What he had just heard, he realised, changed his plans whether he liked it or not. He had wanted to stay on at the chateau for another two days, but now he had to leave, and the sooner, the better. There was something else about the phone call that worried him, something that should not have been there.

He had thought nothing of it at the time, but as he drew on his cigarette it niggled at the back of his mind. It came to him without effort as he finished the cigarette and threw the stub through the open window onto the gravel. There had been a soft click on the line soon after he had picked up the receiver. That had not happened during the phone calls over the past three days. There was an extension phone in the bedroom, but surely Colette had been fast asleep when he left her. Surely. . . . He turned and strode briskly up the stairs on silent bare feet and burst into the bedroom.

The phone had been replaced on its cradle. The wardrobe was open and the three suitcases lay about the floor, all open. His own key-ring with the keys that opened the suitcases lay nearby. The Baroness, on her knees amid the debris, looked up with wide staring eyes. Around her lay a series of slim steel tubes, from each of which the hessian caps that closed the open ends had been removed. From one emerged the end of a telescopic sight, from another the snout of the silencer. She held something in her hands, something she had been gazing at in horror when he entered. It was the barrel and breech of the gun.

For several seconds neither spoke. The Jackal recovered first.

"You were listening."

"I—wondered who you were phoning each morning like that."

"I thought you were asleep."

"No. I always wake when you get out of bed. This—thing; it's a gun, a killer's gun."

It was half-question, half-statement, but as if hoping he would explain that it was simply something else, something quite harmless. He looked down at her, and for the first time she noticed that the grey flecks in the eyes had spread and clouded over the whole expression, which had become dead and lifeless like a machine staring down at her.

She rose slowly to her feet, dropping the gun barrel with a clatter among the other components.

"You want to kill him," she whispered. "You are one of them, the OAS. You want to use this to kill de Gaulle."

The lack of any answer from the Jackal gave her the answer. She made a rush for the door. He caught her easily and hurled her back across the room onto the bed, coming after her in three fast paces. As she bounced on the rumpled sheets, her mouth opened to scream. The back-handed blow across the side of the neck into the carotid artery choked off the scream at source, then his left hand was tangled in her hair, dragging her face downwards over the edge of the bed. She caught a last glimpse of the pattern of the carpet when the forehanded chop with the edge of the palm came down to the back of the neck.

He went to the door to listen, but no sound came from below. Ernestine would be preparing the morning rolls and coffee in the kitchen at the back of the house and Louison should be on his way to market shortly. Fortunately, both were rather deaf.

He re-packed the parts of the rifle in their tubes and the tubes in the third suitcase with the Army greatcoat and soiled clothes of André Martin, patting the lining to make sure the papers had not been disturbed. Then he locked the case. The second case, containing the clothes of the Danish pastor Per Jensen, was unlocked but had not been searched.

He spent five minutes washing and shaving in the bathroom that adjoined the bedroom. Then he took his scissors and spent a further ten minutes carefully combing the long blond hair upwards and snipping off the last two inches. Next he brushed into it enough of the hair tint to turn it into a middle-aged man's iron-grey. The effect of the dye was to dampen the hair, enabling him finally to brush it into the style shown in Pastor Jensen's passport, which he had propped on top of the bathroom shelf. Finally he slipped on the blue-tinted contact lenses.

He wiped every trace of the hair tint and washing preparations off the wash basin, collected up the shaving things, and returned to the bedroom. The naked body on the floor he ignored.

He dressed in the undershirt, shorts, socks, and shirt he had bought in Copenhagen, fixed the black bib round his neck, and topped it with the parson's dog-collar. Finally he slipped on the black suit and conventional walking shoes. He tucked the gold-rimmed glasses into his top pocket, re-packed the washing things in the hand-grip, and put the Danish book on French cathedrals in there as well. Into the inside pocket of his suit he transferred the Dane's passport, and a wad of money.

The remainder of his English clothes went back into the suitcase from which they had come, and this too was finally locked.

It was nearly eight o'clock when he finished, and Ernestine would be coming up shortly with the morning coffee. The Baroness had tried to keep their affair from the servants, for both had doted on the Baron when he had been a small boy and later the master of the house.

From the window he watched Louison cycle down the broad path that led towards the gates of the estate, his shopping panier jolting along behind the bicycle. At that moment he heard Ernestine knock at the door. He made no sound. She knocked again.

"*Y a vot' café, madame*," she shrilled through the closed door. Making up his mind, the Jackal called out in French, in a tone half asleep.

"Leave it there. We'll pick it up when we're ready."

Outside the door Ernestine's mouth formed a perfect O. Scandalous.

Whatever were things coming to—and in the Master's bedroom. She hurried downstairs to find Louison, but as he had left had to content herself with a lengthy lecture to the kitchen sink on the depravity of people nowadays, not at all like what the old Baron had been used to. So she did not hear the soft thud as four cases, lowered from the bedroom window on a looped sheet, plumped into the flowerbed on the front of the house.

Nor did she hear the bedroom door locked from the inside, the limp body of her mistress arranged in a natural sleeping position on the bed with the clothes tucked up to the chin, the snap of the bedroom window as it shut behind the grey-haired man crouching outside on the sill, nor the thud as he dropped in a clean fall down to the lawn.

She did hear the roar as Madame's Renault was gunned into life in the converted stable at the side of the chateau, and peering through the scullery window she caught a glimpse as it swung round into the driveway leading to the front courtyard and away down the drive.

"Now what is that young lady up to?" she muttered as she scuttled back upstairs.

In front of the bedroom door the tray of coffee was still luke-warm but untouched. After knocking several times, she tried the door but it would not open. The gentleman's bedroom door was also locked. Nobody would answer her. Ernestine decided there were goings-on, the sort of goings-on that had not happened since the Boche came to stay as guests of the unwilling Baron back in the old days and ask him silly questions about the Young Master.

She decided to consult Louison. He would be at market, and someone in the local cafe would go to fetch him. She did not understand the telephone, but believed that if you picked it up people spoke to you and went and found the person you really wanted to speak to. But it was all nonsense. She picked it up and held it for ten minutes but no one spoke to her. She failed to notice the neat slice through the cord where it joined the skirting board of the library.

Claude Lebel took the helicopter back to Paris shortly after breakfast. As he said later to Caron, Valentin had been doing a first-class job, despite the obstructions of those damned peasants. By breakfast time he had traced the Jackal to a cafe in Egletons where he had had breakfast, and was looking for a taxi driver who had been summoned. Meanwhile he had arranged for roadblocks to be erected in a twenty-kilometer radius around Egletons, and they should be in place by midday.

Because of the calibre of Valentin, he had given him a hint of the importance of finding the Jackal, and Valentin had agreed to put a ring round Egletons, in his own words "tighter than a mouse's asshole."

From Haute Chalonnière the little Renault sped off through the mountains heading south towards Tulle. The Jackal estimated that if the police had been enquiring since the previous evening in ever-widening circles from where the Alfa had been found, they must have reached Egletons by dawn. The cafe barman would talk, the taxi-driver would talk, and they would be at the chateau by the afternoon, unless he had a lucky break.

But even then they would be looking for a blond Englishman, for he had taken good care that no one had seen him as a grey-haired priest. All the same, it was going to be a close-run thing. He whipped the little car through the mountain byways, finally emerging onto the RN 89 eighteen kilometres southwest of Egletons on the road to Tulle, which lay another twenty kilometres ahead. He checked his watch: 9:40.

As he vanished round a bend at the end of the stretch of straight, a small convoy came buzzing down from Egletons. It comprised a police squad car and two closed vans. The convoy stopped in the middle of the straight, and six policemen started to erect a steel roadblock.

"What do you mean, he's out?" roared Valentin to the weeping wife of a taxi-driver in Egletons. "Where did he go?"

"I don't know, monsieur. I don't know. He waits every morning at the station square when the morning train comes in from Ussel. If there are no passengers he comes back here to the garage and gets on with some repair work. If he does not come back it means he has picked up a fare."

Valentin looked around gloomily. It was no use bawling out the woman. It was a one-man taxi business run by a fellow who also did a bit of repair work on cars.

"Did he take anyone anywhere on Friday morning?" he asked, more patiently.

"Yes, monsieur. He had come back from the station because there was no one there, and a call came from the cafe that somebody there wanted a taxi. He had got one of the wheels off, and was worried in case the customer should leave and go in another taxi. So he was cussing all through the twenty minutes it took to put the wheel back on. Then he left. He got the fare, but he never said where he took him." She snuffled. "He doesn't talk to me much," she added by way of explanation.

Valentin patted her on the shoulder.

"All right, madame. Don't upset yourself. We'll wait till he gets back." He turned to one of the sergeants. "Get a man to the main station, another to the square, to the cafe. You know the number of that taxi. The moment he shows up I want to see him—fast."

He left the garage and strode to his car.

"The commissariat," he said. He had transferred the headquarters of the search to Egletons police station, which had not seen activity like it in years.

In a ravine six miles outside Tulle the Jackal dumped the suitcase containing all his English clothes and the passport of Alexander Duggan. It had served him well. The case plummeted over the parapet of the bridge and vanished with a crash into the dense undergrowth at the foot of the gorge.

After circling Tulle and finding the station, he parked the car unobtrusively three streets away and carried his two suitcases and grip the half mile to the railway booking office.

"I would like a single ticket to Paris, second class please," he told the clerk. "How much is that?" He peered over his glasses and through the little grille into the cubbyhole where the clerk worked.

"Ninety-seven new francs, monsieur."

"And what time is the next train please?"

"Twelve-fifty. You've got nearly an hour to wait. There's a restaurant down the platform. Platform 1 for Paris, *je vous en prie*."

The Jackal picked up his luggage and headed for the barrier. The ticket was clipped, he picked up the cases again and walked through. His path was barred by a blue uniform.

"*Vos papiers, s'il vous plaît.*"

The CRS man was young, trying to look sterner than his years would allow. He carried a submachine carbine slung over his shoulder. The Jackal put down his luggage again and proffered his Danish passport. The CRS man flicked through it, not understanding a word.

"*Vous êtes Danois?*"

"*Pardon?*"

"*Vous—Danois.*" He tapped the cover of the passport.

The Jackal beamed and nodded in delight.

"*Dansk—ja, ja.*"

The CRS man handed the passport back and jerked his head towards the platform. Without further interest he stepped forward to bar passage to another traveller coming through the barrier.

It was not until nearly one o'clock that Louison came back, and he had had a glass of wine or two. His distraught wife poured out her tale of woe. Louison took the matter in hand.

"I shall," he announced, "mount to the window and look in."

He had trouble with the ladder to start with. It kept wanting to go its own way. But eventually it was propped against the brickwork beneath the window of the Baroness's bedroom, and Louison made his unsteady way to the top. He came down five minutes later.

"Madame la Baronne is asleep," he announced.

"But she never sleeps this late," protested Ernestine.

"Well, she is doing today," replied Louison, "one must not disturb her."

The Paris train was slightly late. It arrived at Tulle on the dot of one o'clock. Among the passengers who boarded it was a grey-haired Protestant pastor. He took a corner seat in a compartment inhabited only by two middle-aged women, put on a pair of gold-rimmed reading glasses, took a large book on churches and cathedrals from his hand-grip, and started to read. The arrival time in Paris, he learned, was 8:10 that evening.

Charles Bobet stood on the roadside next to his immobilised taxi, looked at his watch, and swore. Half past one, time for lunch, and here he was stuck on a lonely stretch of road between Egletons and the hamlet of Lamazière. With a busted half-shaft. *Merde* and *merde* again. He could leave the car and try to walk to the next village, take a bus into Egletons and return in the evening with a repair truck. That alone would cost him a week's earnings. But then again, the car doors had no locks, and his fortune was tied up in the rattletrap taxi. Better not leave it for those thieving village kids to ransack. Better to be a little patient and wait until a truck came along that could (for a consideration) tow him back to Egletons. He had had no lunch, but there was a bottle of wine in the glove compartment. Well, it was almost empty now.

Crawling around under taxis was thirsty work. He climbed into the back of the car to wait. It was extremely hot on the roadside and no trucks would be moving until the day had cooled a little. The peasants would be taking their siesta. He made himself comfortable and fell asleep.

"What do you mean he's not back yet? Where's the bastard gone?" roared Commissaire Valentin down the telephone. He was sitting in the commissariat at Egletons, ringing the house of the taxi driver and speaking to his own policeman. The babble of the voice on the other end was apologetic. Valentin slammed the phone down. All morning and through the lunch hour radio reports had come in from the squad cars manning the roadblocks. No one remotely resembling a tall blond Englishman had left the twenty-kilometre radius circle round Egletons. Now the sleepy market town was silent in the summer heat, dozing blissfully as if the two hundred policemen from Ussel and Clermont Ferrand had never descended upon it.

It was not until four o'clock that Ernestine got her way.

"You must go up there again and wake Madame," she urged Louison. "It's not natural for anyone to sleep right through the day."

Old Louison, who could think of nothing better than to be able to do just that, and whose mouth tasted like a vulture's crotch, disagreed but knew there was no use in arguing with Ernestine when her mind was made up. He ascended the ladder again, this time more steadily than before, eased up the window and stepped inside. Ernestine watched from below.

After a few minutes the old man's head came out of the window.

"Ernestine," he called hoarsely, "Madame seems to be dead."

He was about to climb back down again when Ernestine screamed at him to open the bedroom door from the inside. Together they peered over the edge of the coverlet at the eyes staring blankly at the pillow a few inches away from the face.

Ernestine took over.

"Louison."

"Yes, my dear."

"Hurry down to the village and fetch Doctor Mathieu. Hurry now."

A few minutes later Louison was pedalling down the drive with all the force his frightened legs could muster. He found Doctor Mathieu, who had tended the ills of the people of Haute Chalonnière for over forty years, asleep under the apricot tree at the bottom of his garden, and the old man agreed to come at once. It was 4:30 when his car clattered into the courtyard of the chateau and fifteen minutes later when he straightened up from the bed and turned round on the two retainers who stood in the doorway.

"Madame is dead. Her neck has been broken," he quavered. "We must fetch the constable."

Gendarme Caillou was a methodical man. He knew how serious was the job of an officer of the law, and how important it was to get the facts straight. With much licking of his pencil he took statements from Ernestine, Louison, and Doctor Mathieu as they sat around the kitchen table.

"There is no doubt," he said, when the doctor had signed his statement, "that murder has been done. The first suspect is evidently the blond Englishman who has been staying here, and who has disappeared in Madame's car. I shall report the matter to headquarters in Egletons."

And he cycled back down the hill.

Claude Lebel rang Commissaire Valentin from Paris at 6:30.

"*Alors,* Valentin?"

"Nothing yet," replied Valentin. "We've had roadblocks up on every road and track leading out of the area since midmorning. He must be inside the circle somewhere, unless he moved far away after ditching the car. That thrice damned taxi driver who drove him out of Egletons on Friday morning has not turned up yet. I've got patrols scouring the roads around here for him—Hold it a minute, another report just coming in."

There was a pause on the line, and Lebel could hear Valentin conferring with someone who was speaking quickly. Then Valentin's voice came back on the line.

"Name of a dog, what's going on round here? There's been a murder."

"Where?" asked Lebel with quickened interest.

"At a chateau in the neighbourhood. The report just came in from the village constable."

"Who's the dead person?"

"The owner of the chateau. A woman. Hold on a moment. . . . The Baroness de la Chalonnière."

Caron watched Lebel go pale.

"Valentin, listen to me. It's him. Has he got away from the chateau yet?"

There was another conference in the police station at Egletons.

"Yes," said Valentin, "he drove away this morning in the Baroness's car. A small Renault. The gardener discovered the body, but not until this afternoon. He though she must have been sleeping. Then he climbed through the window and found her."

"Have you got the number and description of the car?" asked Lebel.

"Yes."

"Then put out a general alert. There's no need for secrecy any more. It's a straight murder hunt now. I'll put out a nation-wide alert for it, but try and pick up the trail near the scene of the crime if you can. Try to get his general direction of flight."

"Right, will do. Now we can really get started."

Lebel hung up.

"Dear God, I'm getting slow in my old age. The name of the Baronne de la Chalonnière was on the guest list at the Hôtel du Cerf the night the Jackal stayed there."

The car was found in a back street in Tulle at 7:30 by a policeman on the beat. It was 7:45 before he was back in the police station at Tulle and 7:55 before Tulle had contacted Valentin. The Commissaire of Auvergne rang Lebel at 8:05.

"About five hundred metres from the railway station," he told Lebel.

"Have you got a railway timetable there?"

"Yes, there should be one here somewhere."

"What was the time of the morning train to Paris from Tulle, and what ime is it due at the Bare d'Austerlitz? Hurry, for God's sake hurry."

There was a murmured conversation at the Egletons end of the line. "Only two a day," said Valentin. "The earlier train left at about one and is due in Paris at . . . here we are, ten past eight . . ."

Lebel left the phone hanging and was half way out of the office yelling at Caron to follow him.

The 8:10 express steamed majestically into the Gare d'Austerlitz precisely on time. It had hardly stopped when the doors down its gleaming length were flung open and the passengers were spilling out onto the platform, some to be greeted by waiting relatives, others to stride towards the series of arches that led from the main hall into the taxi rank. One of these was a tall grey-haired parson in a dog-collar. He was one of the first at the taxi-rank, and humped his three bags into the back of a Mercedes diesel.

The driver slammed the meter over and eased away from the entrance to slide down the incline towards the street. The forecourt had a semi-circular driveway, with one gate for coming and one for going out. The taxi rolled down the slope towards the exit. Both driver and passenger became aware of a wailing sound rising over and above the clamour of passengers trying to attract the attention of taxi drivers before their turn had arrived. As the taxi reached the level of the street and paused before entering the traffic, three squad cars and two Black Marias swept into the entrance and drew to a halt before the main arches leading to the station hall.

"Huh, they're busy tonight, the pricks," said the taxi driver. "Where to, Monsieur l'Abbé?"

The parson gave him the address of a small hotel on the Quai des Grands Augustins.

Claude Lebel was back in his office at nine o'clock, to find a message asking him to ring Commissaire Valentin at the commissariat in Tulle. He was through in five minutes. While Valentin talked, he took notes.

"Have you fingerprinted the car?" asked Lebel

"Of course, and the room at the chateau. Hundreds of them, all matching."

"Get them up here as fast as you can."

"Right, will do. Do you want me to send the CRS man from Tulle railway station up as well?"

"No, thanks, but he can't tell us more than he already has. Thanks for trying, Valentin. You can stand your boys down now. He's in our territory now. We'll have to handle it from here."

"You're sure it is the Danish pastor?" asked Valentin. "It could be coincidence."

"No," said Lebel, "it's him all right. He's junked one of the suitcases, you'll probably find it somewhere between Haute Chalonnière and Tulle. Try the rivers and ravines. But the other three pieces of luggage match too closely. It's him all right."

He hung up.

"A parson this time," he said bitterly to Caron, "a Danish parson. Name unknown, the CRS man couldn't remember the name on the passport. The human element, always the human element. A taxi driver goes to sleep by the roadside, a gardener is too nervous to investigate his employer's oversleeping by six hours, a policeman doesn't remember a name in a passport. One thing I can tell you, Lucien, this is my last case. I'm getting too old. Old and slow. Get my car ready, would you. Time for the evening roasting."

The meeting at the ministry was strained and tense. For forty minutes the group listened to a step-by-step account of the trail from the forest clearing to Egletons, the absence of the vital taxi driver, the murder in the chateau, the tall grey Dane boarding the Paris express at Tulle.

"The long and the short of it," said Saint-Clair icily, when he had finished, "is that the killer is now in Paris, with a new name and a new face. You seem to have failed once again, my dear Commissaire."

"Let us save the recriminations for later," interposed the Minister. "How many Danes are there in Paris tonight?"

"Probably several hundreds, Monsieur le Ministre."

"Can we check them?"

"Only in the morning, when the hotel registration cards come in to the Prefecture," said Lebel.

"I will arrange to have every hotel visited at midnight, two o'clock and four o'clock," proposed the Prefect of Police. "Under the heading of 'Profession' he will have to put 'Pastor' or the hotel clerk will be suspicious."

The room brightened.

"He will probably wrap a scarf round his dog-collar, or take it off, and register as 'Mister Whatever-his-name-is,'" said Lebel. Several people glowered at him.

"At this point, gentlemen, there is only one thing left to do," said the Minister. "I shall ask for another interview with the President and ask him to cancel all public appearances until this man is found and disposed of. In the meantime, every Dane registering in Paris tonight will be checked personally first thing in the morning. I can rely on you for that, Commissaire? *Monsieur le Préfet de Police?*"

Lebel and Papon nodded.

"Then that is all, gentlemen."

"The thing that sticks in my craw," said Lebel to Caron later in their office, "is that they insist on thinking it's just his good luck and our stupidity. Well, he's had good luck, but he's also devilishly clever. And we've had bad luck, and we've made mistakes. I've made them. But there's another element. Twice we've missed him by hours. Once he gets out of Gap with a repainted car in the nick of time. Now he leaves the chateau and kills his mistress into the bargain within hours of the Alfa Romeo being found. And each time it's the morning after I have told that meeting at the ministry that we have him in the bag, and his capture can be expected within twelve hours. Lucien, my dear fellow, I think I'm going to use my limitless powers, and organise a little wire-tapping."

He was leaning against the window ledge, looking out through and across the softly flowing Seine towards the Latin Quarter where the lights were bright and the sound of laughter floated over the floodlit water.

Three hundred yards away another man leaned over his window sill in the summer night and gazed pensively at the bulk of the Police Judiciaire lying to the left of the spot-lit spires of Notre Dame. He was clad in black trousers and walking shoes, with a polo-necked silk sweater covering a white shirt and black bib. He smoked a kingsize English filter cigarette, and the young face belied the shock of iron-grey hair above it.

As the two men looked towards each other unknowingly above the waters of the Seine, the varied chimes of the churches of Paris ushered in August 22.

PART 3
Anatomy of a Kill

NINETEEN

Claude Lebel had a bad night. It was 1:30, and he had barely got to sleep when Caron shook him awake.

"Chief, I'm sorry about this, but I've had an idea. This chap, the Jackal. He's got a Danish passport, right?"

Lebel shook himself awake.

"Go on."

"Well he must have got it from somewhere. Either he had it forged, or he stole it. But as carrying the passport has entailed a change of hair colouring, it looks as if he stole it."

"Reasonable. Go on."

"Well, apart from his reconnaissance trip to Paris in July, he has been based in London. So the chances are he stole it in one of those two cities. Now what would a Dane do when his passport was lost or stolen? He'd go to his Consulate."

Lebel struggled off the cot.

"Sometimes, my dear Lucien, I think you will go far. Get me Superintendent Thomas at his home, then the Danish Consul-General in Paris. In that order."

He spent another hour on the phone and persuaded both men to leave their beds and get back to their offices. Lebel went back to his cot at nearly three o'clock in the morning. At four he was woken by a call from the Préfecture de Police to say that over 980 hotel registration cards filled in by Danes staying in Paris hotels had been brought in by the collections at midnight and 2 a.m., and sorting of them into categories of "probable," "possible," and "others" had already started.

At 6 he was still awake and drinking coffee when the call came from the engineers at the DST, to whom he had given his instructions just after midnight. There had been a catch. He took a car and drove down through the early morning streets to their headquarters with Caron beside him. In a basement communications laboratory they listened to a tape recording.

It started with a loud click, then a series of whirrs as if someone were dialling seven figures. Then there was the long buzz of a telephone ringing, followed by another click as the receiver was lifted.

A husky voice said, "*Allo?*"

A woman's voice said, "*Ici Jacqueline.*"

The man's voice replied, "*Ici Valmy.*"

The woman said quickly, "They know he's a Danish parson. They're checking through the night the hotel registration cards of all Danes in Paris, with card collections at midnight, two, and four o'clock. Then they're going to visit every one."

There was a pause, then a man's voice said, *"Merci."* He hung up, and the woman did the same.

Lebel stared at the slowly turning tape spool.

"You know the number she rang?" Lebel asked the engineer.

"Yes. We can work it out from the length of the delay while the dialling disc spins back to zero. The number was Molitor fifty-nine-o-one."

"You have the address?"

The man passed him a slip of paper. Lebel glanced at it.

"Come on, Lucien. Let's go and pay a call on Monsieur Valmy."

The knock came at seven o'clock. The schoolmaster was brewing himself a cup of breakfast food on the gas-ring. With a frown he turned down the gas and crossed the sitting room to open the door. Four men were facing him. He knew who they were and what they were without being told. The two in uniform looked as if they were going to lunge at him, but the short, mild-looking man gestured for them to remain where they were.

"We tapped the phone," said the little man quietly. "You're Valmy."

The schoolmaster gave no sign of emotion. He stepped back and let them enter the room.

"May I get dressed?" he asked.

"Yes, of course."

It took him only a few minutes, as the two uniformed policemen stood over him, to draw on trousers and shirt, without bothering to remove his pyjamas. The younger man in plain-clothes stood in the doorway. The older man wandered round the flat, inspecting the piles of books and papers.

"It'll take ages to sort through this little lot, Lucien," he said, and the man in the doorway grunted.

"Not our department, thank God."

"Are you ready?" the little man asked the schoolmaster.

"Yes."

"Take him downstairs to the car."

The Commissaire remained when the other four had left, riffling through the papers on which the schoolmaster had apparently been working the night before. But they were all ordinary school examination papers being corrected. Apparently the man worked from his flat; he would have to stay in the flat all day to remain on the end of the telephone in case the Jackal called. It was 7:10 when the telephone rang. Lebel watched it for several seconds. Then his hand reached out and picked it up.

"*Allo?*"

The voice on the other end was flat, toneless.

"*Ici Chacal.*"

Lebel thought furiously.

"*Ici Valmy,*" he said. There was a pause. He did not know what else to say.

"What's new?" asked the voice at the other end.

"Nothing. They've lost the trail in Corrèze."

There was a film of sweat on his forehead. It was vital the man stay where he was for a few hours more. There was a click and the phone went dead. Lebel replaced it and raced downstairs to the car at the kerbside.

"Back to the office," he yelled at the driver.

In the telephone booth in the foyer of a small hotel by the banks of the Seine the Jackal stared out through the glass perplexed. Nothing? There must be more than nothing. This Commissaire Lebel was no fool. They must have traced the taxi driver in Egletons, and from there to Haute Chalonnière. They must have found the body in the chateau, and the missing Renault. They must have found the Renault in Tulle, and questioned the staff at the station. They must have . . .

He strode out of the telephone booth and across the foyer.

"My bill, if you please," he told the clerk. "I shall be down in five minutes."

The call from Superintendent Thomas came in as Lebel entered his office at 7:30.

"Sorry to have been so long," said the British detective. "It took ages to wake the Danish consular staff and get them back to the office. You were quite right. On July fourteenth a Danish parson reported the loss of his passport. He suspected it had been stolen from his room at a West End hotel, but could not prove it. Did not file a complaint, to the relief of the hotel manager. Name of Pastor Per Jensen, of Copenhagen. Description, six feet tall, blue eyes, grey hair."

"That's the one, thank you, Superintendent." Lebel put the phone down. "Get me the Prefecture," he told Caron.

The four Black Marias arrived outside the hotel on the Quai des Grands Augustins at eight-thirty. The police turned Room 37 over until it looked as if a tornado had hit it.

"I'm sorry, *Monsieur le Commissaire*," the proprietor told the rumpled-looking detective who led the raid, "Monsieur Jensen checked out an hour ago."

The Jackal had taken a cruising taxi back towards the Gare d'Austerlitz where he had arrived the previous evening, on the grounds that the search for him would have moved elsewhere. He deposited the suitcase containing the gun and military greatcoat and clothes of the fictitious Frenchman André Martin in the left-luggage office, and retained only the suitcase in which he carried the clothes and papers of American student Marty Schulberg, and the hand-grip with the articles of make-up.

With these, still dressed in the black suit but with a polo sweater covering the dog-collar, he checked into a poky hotel round the corner from the station. The clerk let him fill in his own registration card, being too idle to check the card against the passport on the visitor, as regulations required. As a result the registration card was not even in the name of Per Jensen.

Once up in his room, the Jackal set to work on his face and hair. The grey dye was washed out with the aid of a solvent, and the blond reappeared. This was tinted with the chestnut brown colouring of Marty Schulberg. The blue contact lenses remained in place, but the gold-rimmed glasses were replaced

by the American's heavy-rimmed executive spectacles. The black walking
shoes, socks, shirt, bib and clerical suit were bundled into the suitcase, along
with the passport of Pastor Jensen of Copenhagen. He dressed instead in the
loafers, socks, jeans, T-shirt and windbreaker of the American college boy
from Syracuse, New York.

By midmorning, with the American's passport in one breast pocket and a
wad of French francs in the' other, he was ready to move. The suitcase
containing the last remains of Pastor Jensen went into the wardrobe, and the
key of the wardrobe went down the flush of the bidet. He used the fire
escape to depart, and was no more heard of in that hotel. A few minutes later
he depostied the hand-grip in the left-luggage office at the Gare d'Austerlitz, stuffed the docket for the second case into his back pocket to join the
docket of the first suitcase, and went on his way. He took a taxi back to the
Left Bank, got out at the corner of Boulevard St. Michel and the rue de la
Huchette, and vanished into the crowds of students and young people who
inhabit the rabbit warren of the Latin Quarter of Paris.

Sitting at the back of a smoky dive for a cheap lunch, he started to wonder
where he was going to spend the night. He had few doubts that Lebel would
have exposed Pastor Per Jensen by this time, and he gave Marty Schulberg
no more than twenty-four hours.

"Damn that man Lebel," he thought savagely, but smiled broadly at the
waitress and said, "Thanks, honey."

Lebel was back on to Thomas in London at ten o'clock. His request caused
Thomas to give a low groan, but he replied courteously enough that he
would do everything he could. When the phone went down, Thomas summoned the senior inspector who had been on the investigation the previous
week.

"All right, sit down," he said. "The Frenchies have been back on. It seems
they've missed him again. Now he's in the centre of Paris, and they suspect
he might have another false identity prepared. We can both start as of now
ringing round every consulate in London asking for a list of passports of
visiting foreigners reported lost or stolen since July first. Forget Negroes
and Asiatics. Just stick to Caucasians. In each case I want to know the height
of the man. Everybody above five feet, eight inches is suspect. Get to work."

The daily meeting at the ministry in Paris had been brought forward to
two o'clock in the afternoon.

Lebel's report was delivered in his usual inoffensive monotone, but the
reception was icy.

"Damn the man," exclaimed the Minister half way through, "he has the
luck of the devil."

"No, *Monsieur le Ministre,* it hasn't been luck. At least, not all of it. He has
been kept constantly informed of our progress at every stage. This is why he
left Gap in such a hurry, and why he killed the woman at le Chalonnière and
left just before the net closed. Every night I have reported my progress to
this meeting. Three times we have been within hours of catching him. This
morning it was the arrest of Valmy and my inability to impersonate Valmy

on the telephone that caused him to leave where he was and change into another identity. But the first two occasions he was tipped off in the early morning after I had briefed this meeting."

There was a frigid silence round the table.

"I seem to recall, Commissaire, that this suggestion of yours has been made before," said the Minister coldly. "I hope you can substantiate it."

For answer Lebel lifted a small portable tape recorder onto the table, and pressed the starter button. In the silence of the conference room the conversation tapped from the telephone sounded metallic and harsh. When it finished the whole room stared at the machine on the table. Colonel Saint-Clair had gone ashen grey, and his hands trembled slightly as he shuffled his papers together into his folder.

"Whose voice was that?" asked the Minister finally.

Lebel remained silent. Saint-Clair rose slowly, and the eyes of the room swivelled onto him

"I regret to have to inform you—*Monsieur le Ministre*—that it was the voice of—a friend of mine. She is staying with me at the present time. . . . Excuse me."

He left the room to return to the Palace and write his resignation. Those in the room stared at their hands in silence.

"Very well, Commissaire." The Minister's voice was very quiet. "You may continue."

Lebel resumed his report, relating his request to Thomas in London to trace every missing passport over the previous fifty days.

"I hope," he concluded, "to have a short list by this evening of probably no more than one or two who fit the description we already have of the Jackal. As soon as I know, I shall ask the countries of origin of these tourists in London who lost their passports to provide photographs of those people, for we can be sure the Jackal will by now look more like his new identity than like either Calthrop or Duggan or Jensen. With luck I should have these photographs by noon tomorrow."

"For my part," said the Minister, "I can report on my conversation with President de Gaulle. He has refused point blank to change an item of his itinerary for the future to shield himself from this killer. Frankly, it was to be expected. However, I was able to obtain one concession. The ban on publicity may now be lifted, at least in this respect. The Jackal is now a common murderer. He has slain the Baronne de la Chalonnière in her own home in the course of a burglary of which the objective was her jewellry. He is believed to have fled to Paris and to be hiding here. All right, gentlemen?

"That is what will be released for the afternoon papers, at least the last editions. As soon as you are quite certain as to the new identity, or choice of two or three alternative identities, under which he is now masquerading, Commissaire, you are authorised to release that name or those names to the press. This will enable the morning papers to update the story with a new lead.

"When the photograph of the unfortunate tourist who lost his passport in London comes through tomorrow morning, you can release it to the evening papers, radio, and television for a second up-date to the murder-hunt story.

"Apart from that, the moment we get a name, every policeman and CRS man in Paris will be on the street stopping every soul in sight to examine their papers."

The Prefect of Police, chief of the CRS, and Director of the PJ were taking furious notes. The Minister resumed.

"The DST will check every sympathiser of the OAS known to them, with the assistance of the Central Records Office. Understood?"

The heads of the DST and the RG office nodded vigorously.

"The Police Judiciaire will take every one of its detectives off whatever he is on, and transfer them to the murder hunt."

Max Fernet of the PJ nodded.

"As regards the Palace itself, evidently I shall need a complete list of every movement the President intends to take from now on, even if he himself has not been informed of the extra precautions being taken in his own interest. And, of course, I can rely on the Presidential Security Corps to tighten up the ring round the President as never before. Commissaire Ducret?"

Jean Ducret, head of de Gaulle's personal bodyguard, inclined his head.

"The Brigade Criminelle"—the Minister fixed Commissaire Bouvier with his eye—"obviously has a lot of underworld contacts in its pay. I want every one mobilised to keep an eye out for this man, name and description to be supplied. Right?"

Maurice Bouvier nodded gruffly. Privately, he was disquieted. He had seen a few manhunts in his time, but this was gigantic. The moment Lebel provided a name and a passport number, not to mention a description, there would be nearly 100,000 men from the security forces to the underworld scanning the streets, hotels, bars, and restaurants for one man.

"Is there any other source of information that I have overlooked?" asked the Minister.

Colonel Rolland glanced quickly at General Guibaud, then at Commissaire Bouvier. He coughed.

"There is always the Union Corse."

General Guibaud studied his nails. Bouvier looked daggers. Most of the others looked embarrassed. The Union Corse, brotherhood of the Corsicans, descendants of the Brothers of Ajaccio, sons of the vendetta, was and still is the biggest organised crime syndicate in France. They already ran Marseilles and most of the South Coast. Some experts believed them to be older and more dangerous than the Mafia. Never having emigrated like the Mafia to America in the early years of this century, they had avoided the publicity that had since then made the Mafia a household word.

Twice already Gaullism had allied itself with the Union, and both times found it valuable but embarrassing. For the Union always asked for a kickback, usually in a relaxation of police surveillance of their crime rackets. The Union had helped the Allies to invade the south of France in August 1944, and had owned Marseilles and Toulon ever since. It had helped again in the fight against the Algerian settlers and the OAS after April 1961, and for this had spread its tentacles far north and into Paris.

Maurice Bouvier, as a policeman, hated their guts; but he knew Rolland's Action Service used Corsicans heavily.

"You think they can help?" asked the Minister.

"If this Jackal is as astute as they say," replied Rolland, "then I would reckon that if anyone in Paris can find him the Union can."

"How many of them are there in Paris?" asked the Minister dubiously.

"About eighty thousand. Some in the police, customs officers, CRS, Secret Service, and of course the underworld. And they are organised."

"Use them," said the Minister.

There were no more suggestions.

"Well, that's it then. Commissaire Lebel, all we want from you now is one name, one description, one photograph. After that I give this Jackal six hours of liberty."

"Actually, we have three days," said Lebel who had been staring out of the window. His audience looked startled.

"How do you know that?" asked Max Fernet.

Lebel blinked rapidly several times.

"I must apologise. I have been very silly, not to see it before. For a week now I have been certain that the Jackal had a plan, and that he had picked his day for killing the President. When he quit Gap, why did he not immediately become Pastor Jensen? Why did he not drive to Valence and pick up the express to Paris immediately? Why did he arrive in France and then spend a week killing time?"

"Well, why?" asked someone.

"Because he has picked his day," said Lebel. "He knows when he is going to strike. Commissaire Ducret, has the President got any engagements outside the Palace today, or tomorrow, or Saturday?"

Ducret shook his head.

"And what is Sunday, August twenty-fifth?" asked Lebel.

There was a sigh round the table like wind blowing through corn.

"Of course," breathed the Minister, "Liberation Day. And the crazy thing is, most of us were here with him on that day, the Liberation of Paris, 1944."

"Precisely," said Lebel. "He is a bit of a psychologist, our Jackal. He knows there is one day of the year that General de Gaulle will never spend elsewhere than here. It is, so to speak, his great day. That is what the assassin has been waiting for."

"In that case," said the Minister briskly, "we have got him. With his source of information gone, there is no corner of Paris that he can hide, no single community of Parisians that will take him in, even unwittingly, and give him protection and shelter. We have him. Commissaire Lebel, give us that man's name."

Claude Lebel rose and went to the door. The others were rising and preparing to leave for lunch.

"Oh, there is one thing," the Minister called after Lebel, "how did you know to tap the telephone line of Colonel Saint-Clair's private apartment?"

Lebel turned in the doorway and shrugged.

"I didn't," he said, "so last night I tapped all your telephones. Good day, gentlemen."

At 5 that afternoon, sitting over a beer at a cafe terrace just off the Place de l'Odéon, his face shielded from the sunlight by dark glasses such as everyone else was wearing, the Jackal got his idea. He got it from watching two men stroll by in the street. He paid for his beer, got up, and left. A hundred yards down the street he found what he was looking for, a woman's beauty shop. He went in and made a few purchases.

At 6 that evening papers changed their headlines. The late editions carried a screaming banner across the top: "ASSASSIN DE LA BELLE BARONNE SE REFUGIE A PARIS." There was a photo beneath it of the Baronne de la Chalonnière, taken from a society picture of her five years ago at a party in Paris. It had been found in the archives of a picture agency and the same photo was in every paper. At 6:30, with a copy of *France-Soir* under his arm, Colonel Rolland entered a small cafe off the rue Washington. The dark-jowled barman glanced at him keenly and nodded towards another man in the back of the hall.

The second man came over and accosted Rolland.

"Colonel Rolland?"

The head of the Action Service nodded.

"Please follow me."

He led the way through a door at the back of the cafe and up to a small sitting room on the first floor, probably the owner's private dwelling. He knocked, and a voice inside said, "*Entrez.*"

As the door closed behind him, Rolland took the outstretched hand of the man who had risen from an armchair.

"Colonel Rolland? *Enchanté.* I am the Capo of the Union Corse. I understand you are looking for a certain man. . . . "

It was eight o'clock when Superintendent Thomas came through from London. He sounded tired. It had not been an easy day. Some consulates had cooperated willingly. Others had been extremely difficult.

Apart from women, Negroes, Asiatics, and short men, eight foreign male tourists had lost or had stolen their passports in London during the previous fifty days, he said. Carefully and succinctly he listed them all, with names, passport numbers and descriptions.

"Now let's start to deduct those whom it cannot be," he suggested to Lebel. "Three lost their passports during periods when we know that the Jackal, alias Duggan, was not in London. We've been ckecking airline booking and ticket sales right back to July first as well. It seems on July eighteenth he took the evening flight to Copenhagen. According to BEA, he bought a ticket at their counter in Brussels, paying cash, and flew back to England on the evening of August sixth."

"Yes, that checks," said Lebel. "We have discovered that part of that journey out of London was spent in Paris. From July twenty-second until July thirty-first."

"Well," said Thomas, his voice crackling on the London line, "three of the passports were missing while he was not here. We can count them out, yes?"

"Right," said Lebel.

"Of the remaining five, one is immensely tall, six feet six inches, that's over two metres in your language. Besides which, he's Italian, which means that his height on the fly-leaf of his passport is given in metres and centimetres, which would be immediately understood by a French customs officer, who would notice the difference, unless the Jackal is walking on stilts."

"I agree, the man must be a giant. Count him out. What of the other four?" asked Lebel.

"Well, one is immensely fat, two hundred and forty-two pounds, or well over a hundred kilos. The Jackal would have to be so padded he could hardly walk."

"Count him out," said Lebel. "Who else?"

"Another is too old. He's the right height, but over seventy. The Jackal could hardly look that old unless a real expert in theatrical make-up went to work on his face."

"Count him out too," said Lebel. "What about the last two?"

One's Norwegian, the other American," said Thomas. "Both fit the bill. Tall, wide-shouldered, between twenty and fifty; there are two things that militate against the Norwegian being your man. For one thing he is blond; I don't think the Jackal, after being exposed as Duggan, would go back to his own hair-colouring, would he? He would look too much like Duggan. The other thing is, the Norwegian reported to his consul that he is certain his passport slipped out of his pocket when he fell fully clothed into the Serpentine while boating with a girl-friend. He swears the passport was in his breast pocket when he fell in, and was not there fifteen minutes later when he climbed out. On the other hand, the American made a sworn statement to the police at London Airport to the effect that his hand-grip with the passport inside it was stolen while he was looking the other way in the main hall of the airport building. What do you think?"

"Send me," said Lebel, "all the details of the American. I'll get his photograph from the Passport Office in Washington. And thank you again for all your efforts."

There was a second meeting in the ministry at 10 that evening. It was the briefest so far. Already an hour previously every department of the apparatus of the security of state had received mimeographed copies of the details of Marty Schulberg, wanted for murder. A photograph was expected before morning, in time for the first editions of the evening papers that would be appearing on the streets by 10 in the morning.

The Minister rose.

"Gentlemen, when we first met, we agreed to a suggestion by Commissaire Bouvier that the identification of the assassin known as the Jackal was basically a task for pure detective work. With hind-sight, I would not disagree with that diagnosis. We have been fortunate in having had, for these past ten days, the services of Commissaire Lebel. Despite three changes of identity by the assassin, from Calthrop to Duggan, Duggan to Jensen, and Jensen to Schulberg, and despite a constant leak of information from within this room, he has managed both to identify and, within the limits of this city, to track down our man. We owe him our thanks." He inclined his head towards Lebel, who looked embarrassed.

"However, from now on the task must devolve upon us all. We have a name, a description, a passport number, a nationality. Within hours we shall have a photograph. I am confident that, with the forces at your disposal, within hours after that, we shall have our man. Already every policeman in Paris, every CRS man, every detective, has received his briefing. Before morning, or at latest tomorrow noon, there will be no place to hide for this man.

"And now let me congratulate you again, Commissaire Lebel, and remove from your shoulders the burden and the strain of this enquiry. We shall not be needing your invaluable assistance in the hours to come. Your task is done, and well done. Thank you."

He waited patiently. Lebel blinked rapidly several times and rose from his seat. He bobbed his head at the assembly of powerful men who commanded thousands of underlings and millions of francs. They smiled back at him. He turned and left the room.

For the first time in ten days, Commissaire Claude Lebel went home to bed. As he turned the key in the lock and caught the first shrill rebuke of his wife, the clock chimed midnight and it was August 23.

TWENTY

The Jackal entered the bar an hour before midnight. It was dark and for several seconds he could hardly make out the shape of the room. There was a long bar running down the left hand wall, with an illuminated row of mirrors and bottles behind it. The barman stared at him with unveiled curiosity as the door swung closed.

The shape of the room was long and narrow down the length of the bar, with small tables set on the right-hand wall. At the far end the room broadened into a salon, and here there were larger tables where four or six could sit together. A row of bar stools were against the bar counter. Most of the chairs and stools were occupied by the night's habitual clientele.

The conversation had stopped at the tables nearest the door while the customers examined him, and the hush spread down the room as others further away caught the glances of their companions and turned to study the tall athletic figure by the door. A few whispers were exchanged, and a giggle or two. He spotted a spare bar-stool at the far end and walked between the tables on the right and the bar on the left to reach it. He swung himself onto the bar-stool. Behind him he caught a quick whisper.

"Oh, *regarde-moi ca!* Those muscles, darling, I'm going out of my mind."

The barman slipped down the length of the bar to stand opposite him and get a better look. The carmined lips widened in a coquettish smile.

"*Bonsoir—monsieur.*" There was a chorus of giggles from behind, most of them malicious.

"*Donnez-moi un* Scotch."

The barman waltzed away delighted. A man, a man, a man. Oh there was going to be such a row tonight. He could see the *petites folles* on the far side of the corridor sharpening their claws. Most were waiting for their regular "butches," but some were without a date and had turned up on spec. This new boy, he thought, was going to create an absolute sensation.

The client next to the Jackal turned towards him and gazed with unconcealed curiosity. The hair was a metallic gold, meticulously groomed down onto the forehead in a series of pointed spikes like a young Greek god on an ancient frieze. There the likeness ended. The eyes were mascaraed, the lips a delicate coral, the cheeks dusted with powder. But the make-up could not conceal the tired lines of an aging degenerate, nor the mascara the arid hungry eyes.

"*Tu m'invites?*" The voice was a girlish lisp.

The Jackal slowly shook his head. The drag shrugged and turned back to his companion. They went on with their conversation in whispers and squeaks of mock dismay. The Jackal had taken off his windbreaker and as he reached for his drink, proffered by the barman, the muscles down the shoulders and back rippled under the T-shirt.

The barman was delighted. A "straight"? No, he couldn't be, he wouldn't be here. And not a butch looking for a nance, or why had he snubbed poor little Corrinne when she asked for a drink? He must be . . .how marvellous. A handsome young butch looking for an old-queen to take him home. What fun there was going to be tonight.

The butches started homing in just before midnight, sitting at the back, surveying the crowd, occasionally beckoning the barman for a whispered conversation. The barman would return to the bar and signal to one of the "girls."

"Monsieur Pierre wants to have a word with you, darling. Try and look your best, and for God's sake don't cry like you did last time."

The Jackal made his mark shortly after midnight. Two of the men at the back had been eyeing him for several minutes. They were at different tables and occasionally shot each other venomous glances. Both were in late middle age; one was fat, with tiny eyes buried in obese lids and rolls on the back of his neck that flowed over his collar. He looked gross and piggish. The other was slim, elegant, with a vulture's neck and balding pate across which the few strands of hair were elaborately plastered. He wore a beautifully tailored suit with narrow trousers and a jacket whose sleeves showed a hint of lace at the cuffs. There was a flowing silk foulard artfully knotted at the throat. Something to do with the world of the arts, fashion, or hairstyling, the Jackal thought.

The fat one beckoned to the barman and whispered in his ear. A large note slipped into the barman's tight trousers. He returned across the bar floor.

"The monsieur wonders if you would care to join him for a glass of champagne," whispered the barman, and regarded him archly.

The Jackal put down his whisky.

"Tell the monsieur," he said clearly, so the pansies round the bar could hear, "that he does not attract me."

There were gasps of horror, and several of the flick-knife young men slipped off their bar-stools to come nearer so that they would not miss a word. The barman's eyes opened wide with horror.

"He's offering you champagne, darling. We know him, he's absolutely loaded. You've made a hit."

For reply the Jackal slid off his bar-stool, took his glass of whisky, and sauntered over to the other old queen.

"Would you permit that I sit here?" he asked. "One is embarrassing me."

The arty one almost fainted with pleasure. A few minutes later the fat man, still glowering from the insult, left the bar, while his rival, his bony old hand indolently placed across that of the young American at his table, told his new-found friend what absolutely, absolutely shocking manners some people had.

The Jackal and his escort left the bar after one o'clock. Several minutes before, the man, whose name was Jules Bernard, had asked the Jackal where he was staying. With a show of shamefacedness the Jackal admitted that he had nowhere to stay, and that he was flat broke, a student down on his luck. As for Bernard, he could hardly believe his good fortune. As chance would have it, he told his young friend, he had a beautiful flat, very nicely decorated, and quite quiet. He lived alone, no one ever disturbed him and he never had anything to do with the neighbours in the block, because in the past they had been terribly, terribly rude. He would be delighted if young Martin would stay with him while he was in Paris. With another show, this time of intense gratitude, the Jackal had accepted. Just before they left the bar he had slipped into the lavatory (there was only one) and had emerged a few minutes later with his eyes heavily mascara'ed, powder on his cheeks, and lipstick on his mouth. Bernard looked very put out, but concealed it while they were still in the bar.

Outside on the pavement he protested, "I don't like you in that stuff. It makes you look like all those nasty pansies back in there. You're a very good-looking young boy. You don't need all that stuff."

"Sorry, Jules, I thought it would improve things for you. I'll wipe it all off when we get home."

Slightly mollified, Bernard led the way to his car. He agreed to drive his new friend first to the Gare D'Austerlitz to pick up his bags, before going home. At the first cross-roads a policeman stepped into the road and flagged them down. As the policeman's head came down to the driver's side window, the Jackal flicked the inside light on. The policeman stared for a minute, then his face drew back with an expression of revulsion.

"*Allez*," he commanded without further ado. As the car rolled away he muttered, "*Sales pédés.*"

There was one more stop, just before the station. and the policeman asked for papers. The Jackal giggled seductively.

"Is that all you want?" he asked archly.

"Fuck off," said the policeman and withdrew.

"Don't annoy them like that," protested Bernard *sotto voce*. "You'll get us arrested."

The Jackal withdrew his two suitcases from the left-luggage office without more than a disgusted glance from the clerk in charge, and hefted them into the back of Bernard's car.

There was one more stop on the way to Bernard's flat. This time it was by two CRS men, one a sergeant and the other a private, who flagged them down at the street junction a few hundred metres from where Bernard lived. The private came round to the passenger door and stared into the Jackal's face. Then he recoiled.

"Oh my God. Where are you two going?" he growled.

The Jackal pouted. "Where do you think, sweetie?"

The CRS man screwed up his face in disgust.

"You fucking queers make me sick. Move on."

"You should have asked to see their identity papers," said the sergeant to the private as the tail-lights of Bernard's car disappeared down the street.

"Oh, come on, Sarge," protested the private, "we're looking for a fellow who screwed the arse of a baroness and did her in; not a couple of raving fairies."

Bernard and the Jackal were inside the flat by two o'clock. The Jackal insisted on spending the night on the studio couch in the drawing room and Bernard quelled his objections, although he peeked through the bedroom door as the young American undressed. It was evidently going to be a delicate but exciting chase to seduce the iron-muscled student from New York.

In the night the Jackal checked the refrigerator in the well-appointed and effeminately decorated kitchen, and decided there was enough food for one person for three days, but not for two. In the morning Bernard wanted to go out for fresh milk, but the Jackal detained him, insisting that he preferred tinned milk for his coffee. So they spent the morning indoors talking. The Jackal insisted on seeing the midday television news.

The first item concerned the hunt for the killer of Madame la Baronne de la Chalonnière forty-eight hours earlier. Jules Bernard squealed with horror.

"Oooh, I can't stand violence," he said.

The next second the screen was filled with a face; a good looking young face, with chestnut brown hair and heavy-rimmed glasses, belonging, so the announcer said to the killer, an American student by the name of Marty Schulberg. Would anybody having seen this man, or having any knowledge . . .

Bernard, who was sitting on the sofa, turned round and looked up. The last thing he thought was that the announcer had not been right, for he had said Schulberg's eyes were blue; but the eyes looking down at him from behind the steel fingers that gripped his throat were grey . . .

A few minutes later the door of the hall coat-cupboard closed on the staring distorted features, hair awry and tongue protruding, of Jules Bernard. The Jackal took a magazine out of the rack in the drawing room and settled down to wait for two days.

During those two days Paris was searched as it never had been before. Every hotel from the smartest and most expensive to the sleaziest whorehouse was visited and the guest-list checked; every pension, rooming house, flophouse, and hostel was searched. Bars, restaurants, night-clubs, cabarets, and cafes were haunted by plain-clothesmen, who showed the picture of the wanted man to waiters, barmen, and bouncers. The house or flat of every known OAS sympathiser was raided and turned over. More than seventy young men bearing a passing resemblance to the killer were taken for questioning, later to be released with routine apologies, even these only because they were all foreigners and foreigners have to be more courteously treated than natives.

Hundreds of thousands in the streets, in taxis, and on buses were stopped, and their papers examined. Roadblocks appeared on all the major access points for Paris, and late-night strollers were accosted several times within the space of a mile or two.

In the underworld the Corsicans were at work, silently slipping through the haunts of pimps, prostitutes, hustlers, pickpockets, hoodlums, thieves, and conmen, warning that anyone withholding information would incur the wrath of the Union, with all that that could entail.

A hundred thousand men in the employ of the state, in various capacities from senior detectives to soldiers and gendarmes were on the look-out. The estimated 50,000 of the underworld and its fringe industries vetted the passing faces. Those making a living off the tourist industry by day or night were briefed to keep their eyes open. Students' cafes, bars and talking clubs, social groups and unions were infiltrated with youthful-looking detectives. Agencies specialising in placing foreign-exchange students with French families were visited and warned.

It was on the evening of August 24 that Commissaire Claude Lebel, who had spent the Saturday afternoon pottering about his garden in a cardigan and patched trousers, was summoned by telephone to report to the Minister in his private office. A car came for him at six o'clock.

When he saw the Minister, he was surprised. The dynamic chief of the whole of France's internal security apparatus looked tired and strained. He seemed to have grown older inside forty-eight hours, and there were lines of sleeplessness round the eyes. He gestured Lebel to a chair opposite his desk, and seated himself in the swivel chair in which he liked to be able to spin round from the window with its view of the Place Beauvau back to the desk. This time he did not look out of the window.

"We can't find him," he said briefly. "He's vanished, just disappeared off the face of the earth. The OAS people, we are convinced, just don't know where he is any more than we do. The underworld hasn't had sight nor sound of him. The Union Corse reckons he can't be in town."

He paused and sighed, contemplating the little detective across the desk, who blinked several times but said nothing.

"I don't think we ever really had any idea what kind of a man you have been pursuing these past two weeks. What do you think?"

"He's here, somewhere," said Lebel. "What are the arrangements like for tomorrow?"

The Minister looked as if he was in physical pain.

"The President won't change a thing or permit any of his planned itinerary to be altered. I spoke to him this morning. He was not pleased. So tomorrow remains the same as published. He will rekindle the Eternal Flame under the Arc de Triomphe at ten. High Mass in Notre Dame at eleven. Private meditation at the shrine of the martyred resistants at Montvalérien at twelve-thirty, then back to the Palace for lunch and siesta. One ceremony in the afternoon, presentation of Médailles de la Libération to a group of ten veterans of the Resistance whose services to the Resistance are being rather belatedly recognized.

"That's at four o'clock on the square in front of the Gare de Montparnasse. He chose the place himself. If construction goes ahead according to plan, it may be the last Liberation Day that the old façade of the station remains untouched."

"What about crowd control?" asked Lebel.

"Well, we've all been working on it. Crowds are to be kept back at every ceremony further than ever before. Steel crowd barriers go up several hours before each ceremony, then the area inside the barrier-ring is searched from top to bottom, including the sewers. Every house and apartment is to be searched. Before each ceremony and during it there will be watchers with guns on every nearby roof-top surveying the opposite roofs and windows. Nobody gets through the barriers except officials, and those taking part in the ceremonies.

"We've gone to some extraordinary lengths this time. Even the cornices of Notre Dame, inside and out, will be infiltrated by policemen, right up to the roof and among the spires. All the priests taking part in Mass will be searched for concealed weapons, and the acolytes and choirboys. Even the police and CRS are having special lapel badges issued tomorrow morning at dawn, in case he tries to masquerade as a security man.

"We've spent the past twenty-four hours secretly slipping bullet-proof windows into the Citroen the President will ride in. Incidentally, don't breathe a word of that; not even the President must know. He'd be furious. Marroux will drive him as usual, and he's been told to speed up the pace faster than usual, in case our friend tries for a snap shot at the car. Ducret has drafted in a posse of especially tall officers and officials to try and hedge the General round without him noticing.

"Apart from that, everybody who comes within two hundred metres of him is going to be frisked—no exceptions. It will create havoc with the Diplomatic Corps, and the press is threatening a revolt. All press and diplomatic passes are going to be suddenly changed at dawn tomorrow in case the Jackal tries to slip in as one of them. Obviously, anyone with a package or a lengthy-looking object will be hustled away as soon as spotted. Well, have you any ideas?"

Lebel thought for a moment, twisting his hands between his knees like a schoolboy trying to explain himself to his headmaster. In truth he found some of the workings of the Fifth Republic rather overpowering for a cop who had started on the beat and had spent his life catching criminals by keeping his eyes open a bit wider than anyone else.

"I don't think," he said at length, "that he will risk getting killed himself. He is a mercenary, he kills for money. He wants to get away and spend his money. And he has worked out his plan in advance, during his reconnaissance trip here in the last eight days of July. If he had any doubts, either about the success of the operation or of his chances of getting away, he would have turned back before now.

"So he must have something up his sleeve. He could work out for himself that on one day of the year, Liberation Day, General de Gaulle's pride would forbid him staying at home, no matter what the personal danger. He could probably have worked out that the security precautions, particularly after his presence had been discovered, would be as intensive as you describe, Monsieur le Ministre. And yet he didn't turn back."

Lebel rose and, despite the breach of protocol, paced up and down the room.

"He didn't turn back. And he won't turn back. Why? Because he thinks he can do it, and get away. Therefore, he must have hit on some idea that nobody else has ever thought of. It has to be a bomb triggered by remote control, or a rifle. But a bomb could well be discovered, and that would ruin everything. So it's a gun. That was why he needed to enter France by car. The gun was in the car, probably welded to the chassis or inside the panelling."

"But he can't get a gun near de Gaulle," cried the Minister. "Nobody can get near him, except a few, and they are being searched. How can he get a gun inside the circle of crowd barriers?"

Lebel stopped pacing and faced the Minister. He shrugged.

"I don't know. But he thinks he can, and he's not failed yet, despite having some bad luck and some good. Despite being betrayed and tracked by two of the best police forces in the world, he's here. With a gun, in hiding, perhaps with yet another face and identity card. One thing is certain, Minister. Wherever he is, he must emerge tomorrow. When he does, he must be spotted for what he is. And that comes down to one thing—the old detective's adage of keeping your eyes open.

"There's nothing more I can suggest as regards the security precautions, Minister. They seem perfect, indeed overwhelming. So may I just wander round each of the ceremonies and see if I can spot him? It's the only thing left to do."

The Minister was disappointed. He had hoped for some flash of inspiration, some brilliant revelation from the detective whom Bouvier had described a fortnight earlier as the best in France. And the man had suggested he keep his eyes open. The Minister rose.

"Of course," he said coldly. "Please do just that, Monsieur le Commissaire."

Later that evening the Jackal laid out his preparations in Jules Bernard's bedroom. On the bed were the pair of scuffed black shoes, grey woolen socks, trousers and open-necked shirt, long military greatcoat with a single row of campaign ribbons, and black beret of the French war veteran André Martin. He tossed on top the false papers, forged in Brussels, that gave the wearer of the clothes his new identity.

Beside these he laid out the light webbing harness he had had made in London, and the five steel tubes that looked like aluminum and which contained the stock, breech, barrel, silencer, and telescopic sight of his rifle. Lying beside them was the black rubber stud into which were stuffed five explosive bullets.

He took two of the bullets out of the rubber, and using the pliers from the tool-box under the kitchen sink carefully removed the noses from them. From inside each he slid the small pencil of cordite they contained. These he kept; the cases of the now useless cartridges he threw in the ash-can. He still had three bullets left, and these would suffice.

He had not shaved for two days, and a light golden stubble covered his chin. This he would shave off badly with the cut-throat razor he had bought on his arrival in Paris. Also lying on the bathroom shelf were the flasks of after-shave that in fact contained the grey hair-tint he had once used already for Pastor Jensen, and the solvent spirit. He had already washed out the chestnut brown tint of Marty Schulberg, and sitting in front of the bathroom mirror he cut his own blond hair shorter and shorter, until the tufts stuck up from the top of the head in an untidy brush-cut.

He made one last check to see that all the preparations for the morning were in order, then cooked himself an omelette, settled in front of the television, and watched a variety show until it was time for bed.

Sunday, August 25, 1963, was scorching hot. It was the height of the summer heat wave, as it had been just one year and three days previously when Lieutenant Colonel Jean-Marie Bastien-Thiry and his men had tried to shoot Charles de Gaulle at the roundabout at Petit-Clamart. Although none of the plotters of that evening in 1962 realised it, their action had set off a chain of events that were only to terminate once and for all on the afternoon of the summer Sunday that now blazed down on a city on holiday.

But if Paris was on holiday to celebrate its own liberation from the Germans nineteen years earlier, there were 75,000 among them who sweated in blue-serge blouses and two-piece suits trying to keep the rest in order. Heralded by ecstatic columns of press publicity, the ceremonies to mark the day of liberation were massively attended. Most of those who came, however, hardly had a glimpse of the Head of State as he stalked through solid phalanxes of guards and policemen to officiate at the commemorations.

Apart from being boxed in from public view by a cohort of officers and civil servants who, although delighted to be asked to be in attendance, failed to notice that their one common characteristic was their height and that each in his way served as a human shield for the President, General de Gaulle was also surrounded by all four of his bodyguards.

Fortunately, his short-sightedness, accentuated by his refusal to wear glasses in public, prevented him from noting that behind each elbow and flanking him on each side were the huge bulks of Roger Tessier, Paul Comiti, Raymond Sasia, and Henri d'Jouder.

They were known to the Press as "gorillas," and many thought this was simply a tribute to their looks. In fact, there was a practical reason for their manner of walking. Each man was an expert in combat of all forms, with heavily muscled chest and shoulders. With muscles tensed, the dorsals forced the arms out from the sides so that the hands swung well away from the body. To add to this, each man carried his favourite automatic under his left armpit, accentuating the gorilla-like stance. They walked with hands half-open, ready to sweep the gun out from its shoulder-holster and start firing at the first hint of trouble.

But there was none. The ceremony at the Arc de Triomphe went off exactly as planned, while all along the great amphitheatre of roofs that overlook the Place de l'Etoile hundreds of men with binoculars and rifles crouched behind chimney stacks, watched, and guarded. As the presidential motorcade finally swept down the Champs Elysées towards Notre Dame, they all breathed a sigh of relief and started to come down again.

At the cathedral it was the same. The Cardinal Archbishop of Paris officiated, flanked by prelates and clergy, all of whom had been watched as they robed. In the organ loft two men perched with rifles (not even the Archbishop knew they were there) and watched the gathering below. The worshippers were heavily infiltrated by plain-clothes police, who did not kneel or close their eyes, but who prayed as fervently as the rest the old policeman's prayer: "Please, dear Lord, not while I'm on duty."

Outside, several bystanders, even though they were two hundred metres from the door of the cathedral, were hustled away when they reached inside their jackets. One had been scratching his armpit, the other going for a cigarette case.

And still nothing happened. There was no crack of a rifle from a roof-top, no muffled crump of a bomb. The police even scanned each other, making sure that their colleagues had the indispensable lapel-badge issued that very morning so that the Jackal could not copy it and masquerade as a policeman. One CRS man who lost his badge was arrested on the spot and bustled to a waiting van. His submachine carbine was taken from him, and it was not until the evening that he was released. Even then, it took twenty of his colleagues who personally recognised the man and vouched for him to convince the police that he was who he said he was.

At Montvalérien the atmosphere was electric, although if the President noticed it he gave no sign. In this working-class suburb, the security man had estimated that while actually inside the ossuary the General would be safe. But while his car was wending its way through the narrow streets approaching the prison, slowing down for the corners, the assassin might make his attempt.

In fact, at that moment, the Jackal was elsewhere.

Pierre Valrémy was fed up. He was hot, his blouse was sticking to his back, the strap of his submachine carbine chafed his shoulder through the soaking material, he was thirsty, and it was just lunchtime, which he knew he was going to miss. He was beginning to regret joining the CRS at all.

It had been all very well when he was laid off redundant from his factory job at Rouen and the clerk at the Labour Exchange had pointed to the poster on the wall of a beaming young man in the uniform of the CRS who was telling the world that he had a job with a future and prospects of an interesting life. The uniform in the picture looked as if it had been tailored by Balenciaga himself. So Valrémy had enlisted.

No one had mentioned the life in the barracks that looked like a prison, which was just what it had once been. Nor the drill, nor the night exercises, nor the itchy serge blouse, nor the hours of waiting on street corners in bitter cold or blazing heat for the Great Arrest that never took place. People's papers were always in order, their missions inevitably mundane and harmless, and it was enough to drive anyone to drink.

And now Paris, the first trip out of Rouen he had ever made. He had thought he might see the City of Light. Not a hope, not with Sergeant Barbichet in charge of the squad. Just more of the same. See that crowd barrier, Valrémy. Well, stand by it, watch it, see it don't move, and don't let nobody through it unless they're authorised, see? Yours is a responsible job, my lad.

Responsible indeed! Mind you, they had gone a bit wild over this Paris Liberation Day, bringing in thousands from the provinces to supplement the Paris troops. There had been men from ten different cities in his barracks last night, and the Paris men had a rumour someone was expecting something to happen, else why all the fuss. Rumours, there were always rumours. They never came to anything.

Valrémy turned round and looked back up the rue de Rennes. The crowd barrier he was guarding was one of a chain stretched across the street from one building to the other, about two hundred and fifty metres up the street from the Place du 18 Juin. The facade of the railway station was another two hundred metres beyond the square, fronted by the forecourt in which the ceremony was to take place. In the distance he could see some men inside the forecourt, marking out the places where the old veterans would stand, and the officials, and the band of the Garde Républicaine. Three hours to go, Jesus, would it never end?

Along the line of barriers the first of the public were beginning to assemble. Some of them had fantastic patience, he thought. Fancy waiting in this heat for hours just to see a crowd of heads three hundred metres away and know that de Gaulle was in the middle of that lot, somewhere. Still, they always came when Charlot was about.

There were about a hundred or two hundred scattered along the barriers when he saw the old man. He was hobbling down the street looking like he was never going to make it another half mile. The black beret was stained with sweat and the long greatcoat swished below his knee. There was a row of medals dangling and clinking on his chest. Several of the crowd by the barrier cast him glances full of pity.

These old codgers always kept their medals, Valrémy thought, like it was the only thing they had in life. Well, maybe it *was* the only thing left for some of them. Especially when you had one of your legs shot off. Maybe, thought Valrémy, watching the old man hobbling down the street, he had run around a bit when he was young, when he had two legs to run on. Now he looked like a smashed up old seagull the CRS man had seen once on a visit to the seaside at Kermadec.

Christ, fancy having to spend the rest of your days limping about with one leg, propping yourself up on an aluminum crutch. The old man hobbled up to him.

"*Je peux passer?*" he asked timidly.

"Come on, Dad, let's have a look at your papers."

The old war veteran fumbled inside his shirt, which could have done with a wash. He produced two cards which Valrémy took and looked at. André Martin, French citizen, aged fifty-three, born at Colmar, Alsace; resident in Paris. The other card was for the same man. Written across the top of it were the words: "Mutilé de Guerre."

"Well, you're mutilated all right, pal," thought Valrémy.

He studied the photographs on each card. They were of the same man, but taken at different times. He looked up.

"Take off your beret."

The old man took it off and crumpled it in his hand. Valrémy compared the face in front of him with those in the photograph. It was the same. The man in front of him looked sick. He had cut himself shaving, and small bits of toilet paper were stuck on the cuts where specks of blood still showed. The face was grey-coloured and greasy with a film of sweat. Above the forehead the tufts of grey hair stuck up at all angles, disarranged by the act of sweeping off the beret. Valrémy handed the cards back.

"What do you want to go down there for?"

"I live there," said the old man. "I'm retired on my pension. I have an attic."

Valrémy snatched the cards back. The identity card gave his address as 154, rue de Rennes, Paris 6ème. The CRS man looked at the house above his head. Written over the door was the number 132. Fair enough, 154 must be further down the road. No orders against letting an old man go home.

"All right, pass through. But don't get into no mischief. Charlot's going to be along in a couple of hours."

The old man smiled, putting away his cards and nearly stumbling on his one leg and crutch, so that Valrémy reached out to steady him.

"I know. One of my old pals is getting his medal. I got mine two years ago"—he tapped the Médaille de la Libération on his chest—"but only from the Minister of the Armed Forces."

Valrémy peered at the medal. So that's the Liberation Medal. Hell of a small thing to get a leg shot off for. He remembered his authority and nodded curtly. The old man hobbled away down the street. Valrémy turned to stop another chancer who was trying to slip through the barrier.

"All right, all right, that's enough of that. Stay back behind the barrier."

The last thing he saw of the old soldier was the flash of the greatcoat disappearing into a doorway at the far end of the street next to the square.

Madame Berthe looked up startled as the shadow fell over her. It had been a trying day, what with policemen looking in all the rooms, and she didn't know what the tenants would have said if they had been there. Fortunately all but three were away for the August holidays.

When the police had gone she had been able to settle back in her usual place in the doorway for a bit of quiet knitting. The ceremony due to take place a hundred hards away across the square in the station forecourt in two hours interested her not in the slightest.

"*Excusez-moi, madame*—I was wondering—perhaps a glass of water. It is terribly hot waiting for the ceremony . . ."

She took in the face and form of an old man in a greatcoat such as her long-dead husband had once worn, with medals swinging below the lapel on the left breast. He leaned heavily on a crutch, one single leg protruding from beneath the great coat. His face looked haggard and sweaty. Madame Berthe bundled up her knitting and stuffed it into the pocket of her apron.

"Oh, *mon pauv' monsieur*. Walking around like that—and in this heat. The ceremony is not for two hours yet. You are early. . . . Come in, come in . . ."

She bustled off towards the glass-fronted door of her parlour at the back of the hall to get a glass of water. The war veteran hobbled after her.

Above the running of the water from the kitchen tap she did not hear the door close on the outer lobby; she hardly felt the fingers of the man's left hand slide round her jawbone from behind. And the crash of the bunched knuckles under the mastoid bone on the right side of her head just behind the ear was completely unsuspected. The image of the running tap and the filling glass in front of her exploded into fragments of red and black, and her inert form slid soundlessly to the floor.

The Jackal opened the front of his coat, reached for the waist, and unbuckled the harness that kept his right leg strapped up under his buttocks. As he straightened the leg and flexed the cramped knee, his face tightened with pain. He spent several minutes allowing the blood to flow back into the calf and ankle of the leg before putting any weight on it.

Five minutes later Madame Berthe was trussed up hand and foot with the clothesline from beneath the sink, and her mouth was covered with a large square of sticking plaster. He put her in the scullery and shut the door.

A search of the parlour revealed the keys of the flat in the table drawer. Re-buttoning the coat, he took up the crutch, the same on which he had hobbled through the airports of Brussels and Milan twelve days earlier, and peered outside. The hall was empty. He left the parlour, locked the door after him, and loped up the stairs.

On the sixth floor he chose the flat of Mademoiselle Béranger and knocked. There was no sound. He waited and knocked again. From neither that flat nor the next door one of M. and Mme. Charrier came a sound. Taking the keys he searched for the name Béranger, found it and entered the flat, closing and locking the door after him.

He crossed to the window and looked out. Across the road, on the rooftops of the blocks opposite, men in blue uniforms were moving into position. He was just in time. At arm's length he unclipped the window lock and swung both halves of the frame quietly inwards until they came back against the inside of the living room wall. Then he stepped well back. A square shaft of light fell through the window onto the carpet. By contrast, the rest of the room appeared darker.

If he stayed away from that square of light, the watchers opposite would see nothing.

Stepping to the side of the window, keeping to the shadows of the withdrawn curtains, he found he could look downwards and sideways into the forecourt of the station 130 metres away. Eight feet back from the window and well to one side, he set up the living room table, removing the table-cloth and pot of plastic flowers and replacing them with a pair of cushions from the armchair. These would form his firing rest.

He stripped off his greatcoat and rolled up his sleeves. The crutch came to pieces section by section. The black rubber ferrule on the end was unscrewed and revealed the shining percussion caps of his three remaining shells. The nausea and sweating inspired by eating the cordite out of the other two was only beginning to leave him.

The next section of the crutch was unscrewed, and from it slid the silencer. The second section came away to disgorge the telescopic sight. The thickest part of the crutch, where the two upper supports merged into the main stem, revealed the breech and barrel of the rifle.

From the Y-shaped frame above the join, he slid the two steel rods which, when fitted together, would become the frame of the rifle's stock. Lastly the padded armpit-support of the crutch; this alone concealed nothing except the trigger of the rifle embedded in the padding. Otherwise the armpit-support slid onto the stock of the gun as it was, to become the shoulder guard.

Lovingly and meticulously he assembled the rifle—breech and barrel, upper and lower component of the stock, shoulder-guard, silencer, and trigger. Lastly he slid on the telescopic sight and clipped it fast.

Sitting on a chair behind the table, leaning slightly forward with the gun barrel resting on top of the upper cushion, he squinted through the telescope. The sunlit square beyond the windows and fifty feet down leapt into focus. The head of one of the men still marking out the standing positions for the forthcoming ceremony passed across the line of sight. He tracked the target with a gun. The head appeared large and clear, as large as a melon had looked in the forest glade in the Ardennes.

Satisfied at last, he lined the three cartridges up on the edge of the table like soldiers in a row. With finger and thumb he slid back the rifle's bolt and eased the first shell into the breech. One should be enough, but he had two spare. He pushed the bolt forward again until it closed on the base of the cartridge, gave a half-twist and locked it. Finally he laid the rifle carefully among the cushions, and fumbled for cigarettes and matches.

Drawing hard on his first cigarette, he leant back to wait for another hour and three quarters.

TWENTY-ONE

Commissaire Claude Lebel felt as if he had never had a drink in his life. His mouth was dry and the tongue stuck to the roof of it as though it were welded there. Nor was it just the heat that caused this feeling. For the first time in many years he was really frightened. Something, he was sure, was going to happen during that afternoon, and he still could find no clue as to how or when.

He had been at the Arc de Triomphe that morning, and at Notre Dame and at Montvalérien. Nothing had happened. Over lunch with some of the men from the committee, which had met for the last time at the ministry that day at dawn, he had heard the mood change from tenseness and anger to something almost of euphoria. There was only one more ceremony to go, and the Place du 18 Juin, he was assured, had been scoured and sealed off.

"He's gone," said Rolland as the group who had lunched together at a brasserie not far from the Elysée Palace while General de Gaulle lunched inside it, emerged into the sunlight. "He's gone, fucked off. And a very wise thing too. He'll surface somewhere, sometime, and my boys will get him."

Now Lebel prowled disconsolately round the edge of the crowd held two hundred metres down the Boulevard Montparnasse, so far away from the square that no one could see what was going on. Each policeman and CRS man he spoke to on the barriers had the same message. No one had passed through since the barriers went up at twelve.

The main roads were blocked, the side roads were blocked, the alleys were blocked. The rooftops were watched and guarded, the station itself, honeycombed with offices and attics facing down onto the forecourt, was crawling with security men. They perched atop the great engine sheds, high above the silent platforms from which all trains had been diverted for the afternoon to the Gare Saint-Lazare.

Inside the perimeters every building had been scoured from basement to attic. Most of the flats were empty, their occupants away on holiday at the seaside or the mountains.

In short, the area of the Place du 18 Juin was sealed off, as Valentin would say, "tighter than a mouse's asshole." Lebel smiled at the memory of the language of the Auvergnat policeman. Suddenly the grin was wiped off. Valentin had not been able to stop the Jackal either.

He slipped through the side streets, showing his police pass to take a short cut, and emerged in the rue de Rennes. It was the same story. The road was blocked off two hundred metres from the square, the crowds massed behind the barriers, the street empty except for the patrolling CRS men. He started asking again.

Seen anyone? No, sir. Anyone been past, anyone at all? No sir. Down in the forecourt of the station he heard the band of the Garde Républicaine tuning their instruments. He glanced at his watch. The General would be arriving any time now. Seen anybody pass, anyone at all? No, sir. Not this way. All right, carry on.

Down in the square he heard a shouted order, and from one end of the Boulevard de Montparnasse a motorcade swept into the Place du 18 Juin. He watched it turn into the gates of the station forecourt, police erect and at the salute. All eyes down the street were watching the sleek black cars. The crowd behind the barrier a few yards from him strained to get through. He looked up at the rooftops. Good boys. The watchers on the roof ignored the spectacle below them; their eyes never stopped flickering across the rooftops and windows across the road from where they crouched on the parapets, watching for a slight movement at a window.

He had reached the western side of the rue de Rennes. A young CRS man stood with his feet planted squarely in the gap where the last steel crowd carrier abutted the wall of Number 132. He flashed his card at the man, who stiffened.

"Anybody passed this way?"

"No, sir."

"How long have you been here?"

"Since twelve o'clock, sir, when the street was closed."

"Nobody been through the gap?"

"No sir. Well . . . only the old cripple, and he lives down there."

"What cripple?"

"Oldish fellow, sir. Looked sick as a dog. He had his I.D. card, and Mutilé de Guerre card. Address given as 154, rue de Rennes. Well, I had to let him through, sir. He looked all in, real sick. Not surprised with him in that greatcoat, and in this weather and all. Crazy, really."

"Greatcoat?"

"Yessir. Great long coat. Military, like the old soldiers used to wear. Too hot for this weather though."

"What was wrong with him?"

"Well, he was too hot, wasn't he, sir?"

"You said he was war-wounded. What was wrong with him?"

"One leg, sir. Only one leg. Hobbling along he was, on a crutch."

From down in the square the first clear peals from the trumpets sounded. "*Allons, enfants de la patrie, le jour de gloire est arrivé. . . .*" Several of the crowd took up the familiar chant of the "Marseillaise."

"Crutch?" To himself, Lebel's voice seemed a small thing, very far away. The CRS man looked at him solicitously.

"Yessir. A crutch, like one-legged men always have. An aluminum crutch . . ."

Lebel was taking off down the street yelling at the CRS man to follow him.

They were drawn up in the sunlight in a hollow square. The cars were parked nose to tail along the wall of the station façade. Directly opposite the cars, along the railings that separated the forecourt from the square, were the ten recipients of the medals to be distributed by the Head of State. On the east side of the forecourt were the officials and diplomatic corps, a solid mass of charcoal grey suiting, with here and there the red rosebud of the Legion of Honour.

The western side was occupied by the serried red plumes and burnished casques of the Garde Républicaine, the bandsmen standing a little out in front of the guard of honour itself.

Round one of the cars up against the station façade clustered a group of protocol officials and Palace staff. The band continued to play the "Marseillaise."

The Jackal raised the rifle and squinted down into the forecourt. He picked the war veteran nearest to him, the man who would be the first to get his medal. He was a short, stocky man, standing very erect. His head came clearly into the sight, almost a complete profile. In a few minutes, facing this man, about one foot taller, would be another face, proud, arrogant, topped by a khaki kepi adorned with the two gold stars on the front.

"*Marchons, marchons, qu'un sang impur . . .*" Boom-boom. The last notes of the national anthem died away, replaced by a great silence. The roar of the Commander of the Guard echoed across the station yard. "General Salute. . . Prese-e-ent ARMS." There were three precise crashes as white-gloved hands smacked in unison across rifle butts and magazines, and heels came together. The crowd around the car parted, falling back into halves. From the centre a single tall figure emerged and began to stalk towards the line of war veterans. At fifty metres from them the rest of the crowd stopped, except the Minister of Veterans' Affairs, who would introduce the veterans to their President, and an official carrying a velvet cushion with a row of ten pieces of metal and ten coloured ribbons on it. Apart from these two, Charles de Gaulle marched forward alone.

"This one?"

Lebel stopped, panting, and gestured towards a doorway.

"I think so, sir. Yes, this was it, second from the end. This was where he came in."

The little detective was gone down the hallway, and Valrémy followed him, not displeased to be out of the street, where their odd behavior in the middle of a serious occasion was attracting disapproving frowns from some of the higher brass standing at attention against the railings of the station yard. Well, if he was put on the carpet, he could always say that the funny little man had posed as a Commissaire of Police, and that he had been trying to detain him.

When he got into the hall, the detective was shaking the door of the concierge's parlour.

"Where's the concierge?" he yelled.

"I don't know, sir."

Before he could protest the little man had smashed the frosted glass panel with his elbow, reached inside and opened the door.

"Follow me," he called, and dashed inside.

"You're damned right I'm going to follow you," thought Valrémy. "You're off your chump."

He found the little detective at the door of the scullery. Looking over the man's shoulder he saw the concierge tied up on the floor, still unconscious.

"Shit." Suddenly it occurred to him the little man was not joking. He *was* a police commissaire, and they *were* after a criminal. This was the big moment he had always dreamed of, and he wished he was back in barracks.

"Top floor," shouted the detective, and was gone up the stairs with a speed that surprised Valrémy, who pounded after him, unslinging his carbine as he ran.

The President of France passed before the first man in the line of veterans and stopped slightly to listen to the Minister explain who he was and what was his citation for valour shown on that day nineteen years before. When the Minister had finished, he inclined his head towards the veteran, turned towards the man with the cushion, and took the proffered medal. As the band began a softly played rendering of "La Marjolaine," the tall General pinned the medal onto the rounded chest of the elderly man in front of him. Then he stepped back for the salute.

Six floors up and 130 metres away the Jackal held the rifle very steady and squinted down the telescopic sight. He could see the features quite clearly, the brow shaded by the peak of the kepi, the peering eyes, the prow-like nose. He saw the raised saluting hand come down from the peak of the cap, the crossed wires of the sight were spot on the exposed temple. Softly, gently, he squeezed the trigger. . . .

A split second later he was staring down into the station forecourt as if he could not believe his eyes. Before the bullet had passed out of the end of the barrel, the President of France had snapped his head forward without warning. As the assassin watched in disbelief, he solemnly planted a kiss on each cheek of the man in front of him. As he himself was a foot taller, he had had to bend forward and down to give the traditional kiss of congratulation that is habitual among the French and certain other nations, but which baffles Anglo-Saxons.

It was later established the bullet had passed a fraction of an inch behind the moving head. Whether the President heard the whipcrack of the bullet is not known. He gave no sign of it. The Minister and the official heard nothing; neither did those fifty metres away.

The slug tore into the sun-softened tarmacadam of the forecourt, its disintegration taking place harmlessly inside more than an inch of tar. "La Marjolaine" played on. The President, after planting the second kiss, straightened up and moved sedately on towards the next man.

Behind his gun, the Jackal started to swear, softly, venomously. He had never missed a stationary target at 150 yards in his life before. Then he calmed down; there was still time. He tore open the breech of the rifle, ejecting the spent cartridge to fall harmlessly onto the carpet. Taking the second one off the table he pushed it home and closed the breech.

Claude Lebel arrived panting on the sixth floor. He thought his heart was going to burst from his chest. There were two doors leading towards the front of the building. He looked from one to the other as the CRS man joined him, submachine carbine held on his hip, pointing forward.

As Lebel hesitated in front of the two doors, from behind one of them came a low but distinct "phut." Lebel pointed at the door lock with his forefinger.

"Shoot it off," he ordered, and stepped back. The CRS man braced himself on both feet and fired. Bits of wood and metal, and spent, flattened slugs flew in all directions. The door buckled and swung drunkenly inwards. Valrémy was first into the room, Lebel on his heels.

Valrémy could recognise the grey tufts of hair, but that was all. The man had two legs, the greatcoat was gone, and the forearms that gripped the rifle were on a strong young man. The gunman gave him no time; rising from his seat behind the table, swinging in one smooth motion at a half-crouch, he fired from the hip. The single bullet made no sound; the echoes of Valrémy's gunburst were still ringing in his ears. The slug from the Jackal's rifle tore into his chest, struck the sternum, and exploded. There was a feeling of tearing and ripping and of great sudden stabs of pain; then even they were gone. The light faded as if summer had turned to winter. A piece of carpet came up and smacked him on the cheek, except that it was his cheek that was lying on the carpet. The loss of feeling swept up through the thighs and belly, then the chest and neck. The last thing he remembered was a salty taste in the mouth, like he had had after bathing in the sea at Kermadec, and a one-legged old gull sitting on a post. Then it was all dark.

Above his body Claude Lebel stared into the eyes of the other man. He had no trouble with his heart; it did not seem to be pumping any more.

"Chacal," he said. The other man said simply, "Lebel." He was fumbling with the gun, tearing open the breech. Lebel saw the glint of the cartridge case as it dropped to the floor. The man swept something off the table and stuffed it into the breech. His grey eyes were still staring at Lebel.

"He's trying to fix me rigid," thought Lebel with a sense of unrealism. "He's going to shoot. He's going to kill me."

With an effort he dropped his eyes to the floor. The boy from the CRS had fallen sideways; his carbine had slipped from his fingers and lay at Lebel's feet. Without conscious thought he dropped to his knees, grabbed the MAT 49, swinging it upwards with one hand, the other clawing for the trigger. He heard the Jackal snap home the breech of the rifle as he found the trigger of the carbine. He pulled it.

The roar of the exploding ammunition filled the small room and was heard in the square. Later press enquiries were met with the explanation that it had been a motorcycle with a faulty silencer which some ass had kicked into life a few streets away at the height of the ceremony. Half a magazine full of nine-millimetre bullets hit the Jackal in the chest, picked him up, half-turned him in the air, and slammed his body into an untidy heap in the far corner of the room. As he fell, he brought the standard lamp with him. Down below, the band struck up *"Mon Régiment et Ma Patrie."*

Superintendent Thomas had a phone call at 6 that evening from Paris. He sent for the senior inspector of his staff.

"They got him," he said. "In Paris. No problems, but you'd better get up to his flat and sort things out."

It was eight o'clock when the inspector was having a last sort-through of Calthrop's belongings that he heard someone come into the open doorway. He turned. A man was standing there scowling at him. A big-built, burly man.

"What are you doing here?" asked the inspector.

"I might ask you just the same thing. What the hell do you think you're doing?"

"All right, that's enough," said the inspector. "Let's have your name."

"Calthrop," said the newcomer, "Charles Calthrop. And this is my flat. Now what the hell are you doing to it?"

The inspector wished he carried a gun.

"All right," he said quietly, warily, "I think you'd better come down to the Yard for a little chat."

"Too bloody right," said Calthrop. "You've got a bit of explaining to do."

But in fact it was Calthrop who did the explaining. They held him for twenty-four hours, until three separate confirmations came through from Paris that the Jackal was dead, and five landlords of isolated taverns in the far north of Sutherland County, Scotland, had testified that Charles Calthrop had indeed spent the previous three weeks indulging his passion for climbing and fishing, and had stayed at their establishments.

"If the Jackal wasn't Calthrop," said Thomas after Calthrop had finally walked out of the door a free man, "then who the hell was he?"

"There can be no question, of course," said the Commissioner of Metropolitan Police the next day to Assistant Commissioner Dixon and Superintendent Thomas, "of Her Majesty's Government ever conceding that this Jackal fellow was an Englishman at all. So far as one can see there was a period when a certain Englishman came under suspicion. He has now been cleared. We also know that for a period of his—er—assignment in France, the Jackal feller masqueraded as an Englishman under a falsely issued English passport. But he also masqueraded as a Dane, an American, and a Frenchman, under two stolen passports and one set of forged French papers. As far as we are concerned, our enquiries established that the assassin was travelling in France under a false passport in the name of Duggan, and in this name he was traced to—er—this place Gap. That's all. Gentlemen, the case is closed."

The following day the body of a man was buried in an unmarked grave at Père Lachaise cemetery in Paris. The death certificate showed the body to be that of an unnamed foreign tourist, killed on Sunday, August 25, 1963, in a hit-and-run accident on the motorway outside the city. Present were a priest, a policeman, a registrar, and two gravediggers. Nobody present showed any interest as the plain deal coffin was lowered into the grave, except the single other person who attended. When it was all over he turned round, declined to give his name, and walked back down the cemetery path, a solitary little figure, to return home to his wife and children.

The day of the Jackal was over.

The Odessa File

AUTHOR'S NOTE

It is customary for authors to thank those who have helped them to compile a book, particularly on a difficult subject, and in doing so to name them. All those who helped me, in however small a way, by assisting me to get the information I needed to write *The Odessa File* are entitled to my heartfelt thanks, and if I do not name them it is for three reasons.

Some, being former members of the SS, were not aware at the time either whom they were talking to, or that what they said would end up in a book. Others have specifically asked that their names never be mentioned as sources of information about the SS. In the case of others still, the decision not to mention their names is mine alone, and taken, I hope, for their sakes rather than for mine.

Throughout the book there occur the names of places and organizations and the titles and ranks of various people, most of which in the original language would be in German. To assist those who do not read German and find the longer words unpronounceable, I have taken the liberty of translating the majority into English. Those with a knowledge of German, who will no doubt recognize the original form, are asked to forgive the translations.

F. F.

FOREWORD

The ODESSA of the title is neither the city in southern Russia nor the smaller city in Texas. It is a word composed of six initial letters, which in German stand for *Organisation der ehemaligen SS-Angehörigen*. In English this means "Organization of Former Members of the SS."

The SS, as most readers will know, was the army within an army, the state within a state, devised by Adolf Hitler, commanded by Heinrich Himmler, and charged with special tasks under the Nazis who ruled Germany from 1933 to 1945. These tasks were supposedly concerned with the security of the Third Reich; in effect they included the carrying out of Hitler's ambition to rid Germany and Europe of all elements he considered to be "unworthy of life," to enslave in perpetuity the "subhuman races of the Slavic lands," and to exterminate every Jew, man, woman, and child, on the face of the Continent.

In carrying out these tasks the SS organized and executed the murder of some fourteen million human beings, comprising roughly six million Jews, five million Russians, two million Poles, half a million gypsies, and half a million mixed others, including, though it is seldom mentioned, close to two hundred thousand non-Jewish Germans and Austrians. These were either mentally or physically handicapped unfortunates, or so-called enemies of the Reich, such as Communists, Social Democrats, liberals, editors, reporters, and priests who spoke out too inconveniently, men of conscience and courage, and later Army officers suspected of lack of loyalty to Hitler.

Before it had been destroyed the SS had made the two initials of its name, and the twin-lightning symbol of its standard, synonymous with inhumanity in a way that no other organization before or since has been able to do.

Before the end of the war its most senior members, quite aware the war was lost and under no illusions as to how civilized men would regard their actions when the reckoning came, made secret provision to disappear to a new life, leaving the entire German people to carry and share the blame for the vanished culprits. To this end vast sums of SS gold were smuggled out and deposited in numbered bank accounts, false identity papers were prepared, escape channels opened up. When the Allies finally conquered Germany, the bulk of the mass-murderers had gone.

The organization which they formed to effect their escape was the Odessa. When the first task of ensuring the escape of the killers to more hospitable climes had been achieved, the ambitions of these men developed. Many never left Germany at all, preferring to remain under cover with false names and papers while the Allies ruled; others came back, suitably protected by a new identity. The few very top men remained abroad to manipulate the organization from the safety of a comfortable exile.

The aim of the Odessa was and remains fivefold: to rehabilitate former SS men *into the professions of* the new Federal Republic created in 1949 by the Allies, to infiltrate at least the lower echelons of political party activity, to pay for the very best legal defense for any SS killer hauled before a court and in every way possible to stultify the course of justice in West Germany when it operates against a former *Kamerad*, to see that former SS men established themselves in commerce and industry in time to take advantage of the economic miracle that has rebuilt the country since 1945, and finally to propagandize the German people to the viewpoint that the SS killers were in fact none other than ordinary patriotic soldiers doing their duty to the Fatherland, and in no way deserving of the persecution to which justice and conscience have ineffectually subjected them.

In all these tasks, backed by its considerable funds, it has been measurably successful, and in none more so than in reducing official retribution through the West German courts to a mockery. Changing its name several times, the Odessa has sought to deny its own existence as an organization, with the result that many Germans are inclined to say the Odessa does not exist. The short answer is: it exists, and the *Kameraden* of the Death's Head insignia are still linked within it.

Despite its successes in almost all its objectives, the Odessa does occasionally take a defeat. The worst it ever suffered occurred in the early spring of 1964, when a package of documents arrived unannounced and anonymously at the Ministry of Justice in Bonn. To the very few officials who ever saw the list of names on these sheets, the package became known as "The Odessa File."

PUBLISHERS' NOTE

As in the case of Mr. Forsyth's first novel, *The Day of the Jackal*, many characters in *The Odessa File* are real people. Some will be immediately recognized by the reader; others may puzzle the reader as to whether they are true or fictional, and the publishers do not wish to elucidate further because it is in this ability to perplex the reader as to how much is true and how much false that much of the grip of the story lies.

Nevertheless, the publishers feel the reader may be interested or assisted to know that the story of former SS Captain Eduard Roschmann, the commandant of the concentration camp at Riga from 1941 to 1944, from his birth in Graz, Austria, in 1908 to his present exile in South America, is completely factual and drawn from SS and West German records.

New York 1972

ONE

There was a thin robin's-egg-blue dawn coming up over Tel Aviv when the intelligence analyst finished typing his report. He stretched the cramped muscles of his shoulders, lit another filter-tipped Time, and read the concluding paragraphs.

The man on whose debriefing the report was based stood at the same hour in prayer fifty miles to the east at a place called Yad Vashem, but the analyst did not know this. He did not know precisely how the information in his report had been obtained, or how many men had died before it reached him. He did not need to know. All he needed was to be assured the information was accurate and that his forward-analysis was soundly and logically arrived at.

> Corroborative details arriving in this office indicate the substantial accuracy of the named agent's claim with regard to the location of the factory. If the appropriate action is taken, it may safely be assumed the West German authorities will concern themselves with its dismantlement.
>
> It is recommended that the substantial record of the facts be placed soon in the hands of these authorities. It is felt by this agency that this would be the best way of ensuring an attitude at the highest level in Bonn that will ensure the continuance of the Waldorf deal.
>
> To all intents and purposes therefore the Right Honourable members of the Committee may be assured the project known as Vulkan is in the process of being dismantled. Consequent on this, our best authorities assure us the rockets can never fly in time. Finally, that being so, it may be concluded that if and when war with Egypt comes, that war will be fought and won by conventional weapons, which is to say by the Republic of Israel.

The analyst signed the foot of the document and dated it: February 23, 1964. Then he pressed a bell to summon a dispatch rider who would take it to the office of the Prime Minister.

Everyone seems to remember with great clarity what he was doing on November 22, 1963, at the precise moment he heard President Kennedy was dead. Kennedy was hit at twelve-thirty in the afternoon, Dallas time, and the announcement that he was dead came at about half past one in the same time zone. It was two-thirty in New York, seven-thirty in the evening in London, and eight-thirty on a chilly, sleet-swept night in Hamburg.

Peter Miller was driving back into the town center after visiting his mother at her home in Osdorf, one of the outer suburbs of the city. He always visited her on Friday evenings, partly to see if she had everything she needed for the weekend and partly because he felt he had to visit her once a week. He would have telephoned her if she had a telephone, but as she had none, he drove out to see her. That was why she refused to have a telephone.

As usual, he had the radio on, and was listening to a music show being broadcast by Northwest German Radio. At half past eight he was in the Osdorf Way, ten minutes from his mother's flat, when the music stopped in the middle of a bar and the voice of the announcer came through, taut with tension.

"*Achtung, Achtung.* Here is an announcement. President Kennedy is dead. I repeat, President Kennedy is dead."

Miller took his eyes off the road and stared at the dimly illuminated band of frequencies along the upper edge of the radio, as if his eyes would be able to deny what his ears had heard, assure him he was tuned in to the wrong radio station, the one that broadcast nonsense.

"Jesus," he breathed quietly, eased down on the brake pedal, and swung to the right-hand side of the road. He glanced up. Right down the long, broad, straight highway through Altona toward the center of Hamburg, other drivers had heard the same broadcast and were pulling in to the side of the road as if driving and listening to the radio had suddenly become mutually exclusive, which in a way they had.

Along his own side he could see the brake lights glowing on as the drivers ahead swung to the right to park at the curb and listen to the supplementary information pouring from their radios. On the left the headlights of the cars heading out of town wavered wildly as they too swung away toward the pavement. Two cars overtook him, the first hooting angrily, and he caught a glimpse of the driver tapping his forehead in Miller's direction in the usual rude sign, indicating lunacy, that one German driver makes to another who has annoyed him.

He'll learn soon enough, thought Miller.

The light music on the radio had stopped, replaced by the "Funeral March," which was evidently all the disk jockey had on hand. At intervals he read snippets of further information straight off the teleprinter, as they were brought in from the newsroom. The details began to fill in: the open-car ride into Dallas, the rifleman in the window of the School Book Depository. No mention of an arrest.

The driver of the car ahead of Miller climbed out and walked back towards him. He approached the left-hand window, then realized that the driver's seat was inexplicably on the right and came round the car. He wore a nylon-fur-collared jacket. Miller wound down his window.

"You heard it?" asked the man, bending down to the window.

"Yeah," said Miller.

"Absolutely fantastic," said the man. All over Hamburg, Europe, the world, people were walking up to complete strangers to discuss the event.

"You reckon it was the Communists?" asked the man.

"I don't know."

"It could mean war, you know, if it was them," said the man.

"Maybe," said Miller. He wished the man would go away. As a reporter he could imagine the chaos sweeping across the newspaper offices of the country as every staff man was called back to help put out a crash edition for the morning breakfast tables. There would be obituaries to prepare, the thousands of instant tributes to correlate and typeset, the telephone lines jammed with yelling men seeking more and ever more details because a man with his head shattered lay dead in a city in Texas.

He wished in a way he were back on the staff of a daily newspaper, but since he had become a freelance three years earlier he had specialized in news features inside Germany, mainly connected with crime, the police, the underworld. His mother hated the job, accusing him of mixing with "nasty people," and his arguments that he was becoming one of the most sought-after reporter-investigators in the country availed nothing in persuading her that a reporter's job was worthy of her only son.

As the reports from the radio came through, his mind was racing, trying to think of another "angle" that could be chased up inside Germany and might make a sidebar story to the main event. The reaction of the Bonn government would be covered out of Bonn by the staff men; the memories of Kennedy's visit to Berlin the previous June would be covered from there. There didn't seem to be a good pictorial feature he could ferret out to sell to any of the score of German picture magazines that were the best customers of his kind of journalism.

The man leaning on the window sensed that Miller's attention was elsewhere and assumed it was out of grief for the dead President. Quickly he dropped his talk of world war and adopted the same grave demeanor. "*Ja, ja, ja,*" he murmured with sagacity, as if he had seen it coming all along. "Violent people, these Americans, mark my words, violent people. There's a streak of violence in them that we over here will never understand."

"Sure," said Miller, his mind still miles away.

The man took the hint at last. "Well, I must be getting home," he said, straightening up. "*Grüss Gott.*" He started to walk back to his own car.

Miller became aware he was going. "*Ja, gute Nacht,*" he called out of the open window, then wound it up against the sleet whipping in off the Elbe River. The music on the radio continued in funereal vein, and the announcer said there would be no more light music that night, just news bulletins interspersed with suitable music.

Miller leaned back on the comfortable leather upholstery of his Jaguar and lit up a Roth-Händl, a filterless black-tobacco cigarette with a foul smell, another thing that his mother complained about in her disappointing son.

It is always tempting to wonder what would have happened if . . . or if not. Usually it is a futile exercise, for what might have been is the greatest of all the mysteries. But it is probably accurate to say that if Miller had not had his radio on that night he would not have pulled in to the side of the road for half an hour. He would not have seen the ambulance, or heard of Salomon Tauber or Eduard Roschmann, and forty months later the republic of Israel would probably have ceased to exist.

He finished his cigarette, still listening to the radio, wound down the window, and threw the stub away. At a touch of the button the 3.8-liter engine beneath the long sloping bonnet of the Jaguar XK 150 S thundered once and settled down to its habitual and comforting rumble, like an angry animal trying to get out of a cage. Miller flicked on the two headlights, checked behind, and swung out into the growing traffic stream along Osdorf Way.

He had got as far as the traffic lights on Stresemannstrasse, and they were standing at red, when he heard the clamor of the ambulance behind him. It came past him on the left, the wail of the siren rising and falling, slowed slightly before heading into the road junction against the red light, then swung across Miller's nose and down to the right into Daimlerstrasse. Miller reacted on reflexes alone. He let in the clutch, and the Jaguar surged after the ambulance, twenty meters behind it.

As soon as he had done it he wished he had gone straight home. It was probably nothing, but one never knew. Ambulances meant trouble, and trouble could mean a story, particularly if one were first on the scene and the whole thing had been cleared up before the staff reporters arrived. It could be a major crash on the road, or a big wharf fire, a tenement building ablaze, with children trapped inside. It could be anything. Miller always carried a small Yashica with flash attachment in the glove compartment of his car because one never knew what was going to happen right in front of one's eyes.

He knew a man who had been waiting for a plane at Munich airport on February 6, 1958, and the plane carrying the Manchester United football team had crashed a few hundred meters from where he stood. The man was not even a professional photographer, but he had unslung the camera he was taking on a skiing holiday and snapped the first exclusive pictures of the burning aircraft. The pictorial magazines had paid more than 50,000 marks for them.

The ambulance twisted into the maze of small and mean streets of Altona, leaving the Altona railway station on the left and heading down toward the river. Whoever was driving the flat-snouted, high-roofed Mercedes ambulance knew his Hamburg and knew how to drive. Even with his greater acceleration and hard suspension, Miller could feel the back wheels of the Jaguar skidding across the cobbles slick with rain.

Miller watched Menck's auto-parts warehouse rush by, and two streets later his original question was answered. The ambulance drew up in a poor and sleazy street, ill lit and gloomy in the slanting sleet, bordered by crumbling tenements and rooming-houses. It stopped in front of one of these, where a police car already stood, its blue roof light twirling, the beam sending a ghostly glow across the faces of a knot of bystanders grouped round the door.

A burly police sergeant in a rain cape roared at the crowd to stand back and make a gap in front of the door for the ambulance. Into this the Mercedes slid. Its driver and attendant climbed down, ran round to the back, and eased out an empty stretcher. After a brief word with the sergeant, the pair hastened upstairs.

Miller pulled the Jaguar to the opposite curb twenty yards down the road and raised his eyebrows. No crash, no fire, no trapped children. Probably just a heart attack. He climbed out and strolled over to the crowd, which the sergeant was holding back in a semicircle around the door of the rooming-house.

"Mind if I go up?" asked Miller.

"Certainly do. It's nothing to do with you."

"I'm press," said Miller, proffering his Hamburg city press card.

"And I'm police," said the sergeant. "Nobody goes up. Those stairs are narrow enough as it is, and none too safe. The ambulance men will be down right away."

He was a big man, standing six feet three, and in his rain cape, with his arms spread wide to hold back the crowd, he looked as immovable as a barn door.

"What's up, then?" asked Miller.

"Can't make statements. Check at the station later on."

A man in civilian clothes came down the stairs and emerged onto the pavement. The turning light on top of the Volkswagen patrol car swung across his face, and Miller recognized him. They had been at school together at Hamburg Central High. The man was now a junior detective inspector in the Hamburg police, stationed at Altona Central.

"Hey, Karl."

The young inspector turned at the call of his name and scanned the crowd behind the sergeant. In the next swirl of the police-car light he caught sight of Miller and his raised right hand. His face broke into a grin, part of pleasure, part of exasperation. He nodded to the sergeant.

"It's all right, Sergeant. He's more or less harmless."

The sergeant lowered his arm, and Miller darted past. He shook hands with Karl Brandt.

"What are you doing here?'

"Followed the ambulance."

"Damned vulture. What are you up to these days?"

"Same as usual. Freelancing."

"Making quite a bundle out of it by the look of it. I keep seeing your name in the picture magazines."

"It's a living. Hear about Kennedy?"

"Yes. Hell of a thing. They must be turning Dallas inside out tonight. Glad it wasn't on my turf."

Miller nodded toward the dimly lit hallway of the rooming-house, where a low-watt naked bulb cast a yellow glare over peeling wallpaper.

"A suicide. Gas. Neighbors smelled it coming under the door and called us. Just as well no one struck a match; the place was reeking with it."

"Not a film star by any chance?" asked Miller.

"Yeah. Sure. They always live in places like this. No, it was an old man. Looked as if he had been dead for years anyway. Someone does it every night."

"Well, wherever he's gone now, it can't be worse than this."

The inspector gave a fleeting smile and turned as the two ambulance men negotiated the last seven steps of the creaking stairs and came down the hallway with their burden. Brandt turned around. "Make some room. Let them through."

The sergeant promptly took up the cry and pushed the crowd back even farther. The two ambulance men walked out onto the pavement and around to the open doors of the Mercedes. Brandt followed them, with Miller at his heels. Not that Miller wanted to look at the dead man, or even intended to. He was just following Brandt. As the ambulance men reached the door of the vehicle, the first one hitched his end of the stretcher into the runners and the second prepared to shove it inside.

"Hold it," said Brandt and flicked back the corner of the blanket above the dead man's face. He remarked over his shoulder, "Just a formality. My report has to say I accompanied the body to the ambulance and back to the morgue."

The interior lights of the Mercedes ambulance were bright, and Miller caught a single two-second look at the face of the suicide. His first and only impression was that he had never seen anything so old and ugly. Even given the effects of gassing, the dull mottling of the skin, the bluish tinge at the lips, the man in life could have been no beauty. A few strands of lank hair were plastered over the otherwise naked scalp. The eyes were closed. The face was hollowed out to the point of emaciation, and with the man's false teeth missing, each cheek seemed to be sucked inward till they almost touched inside the mouth, giving the effect of a ghoul in a horror film. The lips hardly existed, and both upper and lower were lined with vertical creases, reminding Miller of the shrunken skull from the Amazon basin he had once seen, whose lips had been sewn together by the natives. To cap the effect, the man seemed to have two pale and jagged scars running down his face, each from the temple or upper ear to the corner of the mouth.

After a quick glance, Brandt pulled the blanket back and nodded to the ambulance attendant behind him. He stepped back as the man rammed the stretcher into its berth, locked the doors, and went around to the cab to join his partner. The ambulance surged away. The crowd started to disperse accompanied by the sergeant's muted growls: "Come on, it's all over. There's nothing more to see. Haven't you got homes to go to?"

Miller looked at Brandt and raised his eyebrows. "Charming."

"Yes. Poor old guy. Nothing in it for you, though?"

Miller looked pained. "Not a chance. Like you say, there's one a night. People are dying all over the world tonight, and nobody's taking a bit of notice. Not with Kennedy dead."

Inspector Brandt laughed mockingly. "You lousy journalists."

"Let's face it. Kennedy's what people want to read about. They buy the newspapers."

"Yeah, Well, I must get back to the station. See you, Peter."

They shook hands again and parted. Miller drove back toward Altona station, picked up the main road back into the city center, and twenty minutes later swung the Jaguar into the underground garage off the Hansa Square, two hundred yards from the house where he had his penthouse apartment.

Keeping the car in an underground garage all winter was costly, but it was one of the extravagances he permitted himself. He liked his fairly expensive apartment because it was high and he could look down on the bustling boulevard of the Steindamm. Of his clothes and food he thought nothing, and at twenty-nine, just under six feet, with the rumpled brown hair and brown eyes that women go for, he didn't need expensive clothes. An envious friend had once told him, "You could pull broads in a monastery," and he had laughed but been pleased at the same time because he knew it was true.

The real passions of his life were sports cars, reporting, and Sigrid, though he sometimes shamefacedly admitted that if it came to a choice between Sigi and the Jaguar, Sigi would have to find her loving somewhere else.

He stood and looked at the Jaguar in the lights of the garage after he had parked it. He could seldom get enough of looking at that car. Even approaching it in the street, he would stop and admire it, occasionally joined by a passer-by who, not realizing it was Miller's, would stop also and remark, "Some motor, that."

Normally a young freelance reporter does not drive a Jaguar XK 150 S. Spare parts were almost impossible to come by in Hamburg, the more so as the XK series, of which the S model was the last ever made, had gone out of production in 1960. He maintained it himself, spending hours on Sunday in overalls beneath the chassis or half buried in the engine. The gas it used, with its three SU carburetors, was a major strain on his pocket, the more so because of the price of gas in Germany, but he paid it willingly. The reward was to hear the berserk snarl of the blown exhausts when he hit the accelerator on the open autobahn, to feel the thrust as it rocketed out of a turn on a mountain road. He had even hardened up the independent suspension on the two front wheels, and as the car had stiff suspension at the back, it took corners steady as a rock, leaving other drivers rolling wildly on their cushion springs if they tried to keep up with him. Just after buying it, he had had it resprayed black with a long wasp-yellow streak down each side. As it had been made in Coventry, England, and not as an export car, the driver's wheel was on the right, which caused an occasional problem in passing but allowed him to change gear with the left hand and hold the shuddering steering wheel in the right hand, which he had come to prefer.

Even now he wondered at the lucky stroke that had enabled him to buy it. Earlier that summer he had idly opened a pop magazine while waiting in a barber shop to have his hair cut. Normally he never read the gossip about pop stars, but there was nothing else to read. The center-page spread had been about the meteoric rise to fame and international stardom of four tousel-headed English youth. The face on the extreme right of the picture, the one with the big nose, meant nothing to him, but the other three faces rang a bell in his filing cabinet of a memory.

The names of the two disks that had brought the quartet to stardom, "Please, Please Me" and "Love Me, Do," meant nothing either, but three of the faces puzzled him for two days. Then he remembered them, more than a year earlier, in 1962, singing way down on the program at a small cabaret off the Reeperbahn. It took him another day to recall the name, for he had only once popped in for a drink to talk to an underworld figure from whom he needed information about the Sankt Pauli gang. The Star Club. He went down there and checked through the billings for 1962 and found them. They had been five then, the three he recognized and two others, Pete Best and Stuart Sutliffe.

From there he went to the photographer who had done the publicity photographs for the impresario Bert Kämpfert, and had bought right and title to every one he had. His story "How Hamburg Discovered the Beatles" had made almost every pop-music and picture magazine in Germany and a lot abroad. On the proceeds he had bought the Jaguar, which he had been in a car showroom, where it had been sold by a British Army officer whose wife had grown too pregnant to fit into it. He even bought some Beatles records out of gratitude, but Sigi was the only one who ever played them.

He left the car and walked up the ramp to the street and back to his flat. It was nearly midnight, and although his mother had fed him at six that evening with the usual enormous meal, he was hungry again. He made a plate of scrambled eggs and listened to the late-night news. It was all about Kennedy and heavily accented on the German angles, since there was little more news coming through from Dallas. The police were still searching for the killer. The announcer went to great lengths about Kennedy's love of Germany, his visit to Berlin the previous summer, and his statement in German, *"Ich bin ein Berliner."*

There was then a recorded tribute from the Governing Mayor of West Berlin, Willy Brandt, his voice choked with emotion, and other tributes were read from Chancellor Ludwig Erhard and the former Chancellor Konrad Adenauer, who had retired the previous October 15.

Peter Miller switched off and went to bed. He wished Sigi was home because he always wanted to snuggle up to her when he felt depressed, and then he got hard and then they made love, after which he fell into a dreamless sleep, much to her annoyance because it was after lovemaking that she always wanted to talk about marriage and children. But the cabaret at which she danced did not close till nearly four in the morning, often later on Friday nights, when the provincials and tourists were thick down the Reeperbahn, prepared to buy champagne at ten times its restaurant price for a girl with big tits and a low-cut dress, and Sigi had the biggest and the lowest.

So he smoked another cigarette and fell asleep alone at quarter to two to dream of the hideous face of the old gassed man in the slums of Altona.

While Peter Miller was eating his scrambled eggs at midnight in Hamburg, five men were sitting drinking in the comfortable lounge of a house attached to a riding school near the pyramids outside Cairo. The time there was one in the morning. The five men had dined well and were in a jovial mood, the cause being the news from Dallas they had heard almost four hours earlier.

Three of the men were Germans, the other two Egyptians. The wife of the host and proprietor of the riding school, a favorite meeting place of the cream of Cairo society and the several-thousand-strong German colony, had gone to bed, leaving the five men to talk into the small hours.

Sitting in the leather-backed easy chair by the shuttered window was Peter Bodden, formerly a Jewish expert in the Nazi Propaganda Ministry of Dr. Josef Goebbels. Having lived in Egypt since shortly after the end of the war, where he had been spirted by the Odessa, Bodden had taken the Egyptian name of El Gumra and worked as an expert on Jews in the Egyptian Ministry of Orientation. He held a glass of whisky. On his left was another former expert from Goebbels' staff, Max Bachmann, also working in the Orientation Ministry. He had in the meantime adopted the Moslem faith, made a trip to Mecca, and was called El Hadj. In deference to his new religion he held a glass of orange juice. Both men were still fanatical Nazis.

The two Egyptians were Colonel Shamseddin Badran, personal aide to

Marshal Abdel Hakim Amer, later to become Vice-President of Egypt before being accused of treason after the Six-Day War of 1967 and later committing suicide. The other was Colonel Ali Samir, head of the Moukhabarat, the Egyptian Secret Intelligence Service.

There had been a sixth guest at dinner, the guest of honor, who had rushed back to Cairo when the news came through at nine-thirty, Cairo time, that President Kennedy was dead. He was the Speaker of the Egyptian National Assembly, Anwar el Sadat, a close collaborator of President Nasser and later to become his successor.

Peter Bodden raised his glass toward the ceiling. "So Kennedy the Jew-lover is dead. Gentlemen, I give you a toast."

"But our glasses are empty," protested Colonel Samir.

Their host hastened to remedy the matter, filling the empty glasses from a bottle of Scotch from the sideboard.

The reference to Kennedy as Jew-lover baffled none of the five men in the room. On March 14, 1960, while Dwight Eisenhower was still President of the United States, the Premier of Israel, David Ben-Gurion, and the Chancellor of Germany, Konrad Adenauer, had met secretly at the Waldorf-Astoria hotel in New York, a meeting that ten years earlier would have been deemed impossible. What was deemed impossible even in 1960 was what happened at that meeting, which was why details of it took years to leak out and why even at the end of 1963 President Nasser refused to take seriously the information that the Odessa and the Moukhabarat of Colonel Samir placed on his desk.

The two statesmen had signed an agreement whereby West Germany agreed to open a credit account for Israel to the tune of fifty million dollars a year, without any strings attached. Ben-Gurion, however, soon discoverd that to have money was one thing, to have a secure and certain source of arms was quite another. Six months later the Waldorf agreement was topped off with another, signed by the Defense Ministers of Germany and Israel, Franz-Josef Strauss and Shimon Peres. Under its terms, Israel would be able to use the money from Germany to buy weapons in Germany.

Adenauer, aware of the vastly more controversial nature of the second agreement, delayed for months, until in 1961 he was in New York to meet the new President, John Fitzgerald Kennedy. Kennedy put the pressure on. He did not wish to have arms delivered directly from the United States to Israel, but he wanted them to arrive somehow. Israel needed fighters, transport planes, Howitzer 105-mm. artillery pieces, armored cars, armored personnel carriers, and tanks, but above all tanks.

Germany had all of them, mainly of American make, either bought from America to offset the cost of keeping American troops in Germany under the NATO agreement, or made under license in Germany.

Under Kennedy's pressure the Strauss-Peres deal was pushed through.

The first German tanks started to arrive at Haifa in late June 1963. It was difficult to keep the news secret for long; too many people were involved. The Odessa had found out in late 1962 and promptly informed the Egyptians, with whom its agents in Cairo had the closest links.

In late 1963 things started to change. On October 15, Konrad Adenauer, the Fox of Bonn, the Granite Chancellor, resigned and went into retirement. Adenauer's place was taken by Ludwig Erhard, a good vote-catcher as the father of the German economic miracle, but in matters of foreign policy weak and vacillating.

Even while Adenauer was in power there had been a vociferous group inside the West German cabinet in favor of shelving the Israeli arms deal and halting the supplies before they had begun. The old Chancellor had silenced them with a few terse sentences, and such was his power that they stayed silenced.

Erhard was quite a different man and already had earned himself the nickname of the Rubber Lion. As soon as he took the chair the anti-arms-deal group, based in the Foreign Ministry, ever mindful of its excellent and improving relations with the Arab world, opened up again. Erhard dithered. But behind them all was the determination of John Kennedy that Israel should get her arms via Germany.

And then he was shot. The big question in the small hours of the morning of November 23 was simply: would President Lyndon Johnson take the American pressure off Germany and let the indecisive Chancellor in Bonn renege on the deal? In fact he did not, but there were high hopes in Cairo that he would.

The host at the convivial meeting outside Cairo that night, having filled his guests' glasses, turned back to the sideboard to top up his own. His name was Wolfgang Lutz, born at Mannheim in 1921, a former major in the German Army, a fanatical Jew-hater, who had emigrated to Cairo in 1961 and started his riding academy. Blond, blue-eyed, hawk-faced, he was a top favorite among both the influential political figures of Cairo and the expatriate German and mainly Nazi community along the banks of the Nile.

He turned to face the room and gave a broad smile. If there was anything false about that smile, no one noticed it. But it was false. He had been born a Jew in Mannheim but had emigrated to Palestine in 1933 at the age of twelve. His name was Ze'ev, and he held the rank of *rav-seren* (major) in the Israeli Army. He was also the top agent of Israeli Intelligence in Egypt at that time. On February 28, 1965, after a raid on his home in which a radio transmitter was discovered in the bathroom scales, he was arrested. Tried on June 26, 1965, he was sentenced to hard labor in perpetuity. Released after the end of the 1967 war as part of an exchange against thousands of Egyptian prisoners of war, he and his wife stepped back onto the soil of home at Lod Airport on February 4, 1968.

But the night Kennedy died this was all in the future: the arrest, the tortures, the multiple rape of his wife. He raised his glass to the four smiling faces in front of him.

In fact, he could hardly wait for his guests to depart, for something one of them had said over dinner was of vital importance to his country, and he desperately wished to be alone, to go up to his bathroom, get the transmitter out of the bathroom scales, and send a message to Tel Aviv. But he forced himself to keep smiling.

"Death to the Jew-lovers," he toasted. "*Sieg Heil.*"

Peter Miller woke the next morning just before nine and shifted lux-uriously under the enormous feather cushion that covered the double bed. Even half awake, he could feel the warmth of the sleeping figure of Sigi seeping across the bed to him, and by reflex he snuggled closer so that her buttocks pushed into the base of his stomach. Automatically he began to erect.

Sigi, still fast asleep after only four hours in bed, grunted in annoyance and shifted away toward the edge of the bed. "Go away," she muttered without waking up.

Miller sighed, turned onto his back, and held up his watch, squinting at the face of it in the half-light. Then he slipped out of bed on the other side, pulled a toweling bathrobe around him, and padded through into the living room to pull back the curtains. The steely November light washed across the room, making him blink. He focused his eyes and looked down into the Steindamm. It was a Saturday morning, and traffic was light down the wet black tarmac. He yawned and went into the kitchen to brew the first of innumerable cups of coffee. Both his mother and Sigi reproached him with living almost entirely on coffee and cigarettes.

Drinking his coffee and smoking the first cigarette of the day in the kitchen, he considered whether there was anything particular he ought to do that day and decided there was not. For one thing, all the newspapers and the next issues of the magazines would be about President Kennedy, probably for days or weeks to come. And for another, there was no particular story he was chasing at the time. Besides which, Saturday and Sunday are bad days to get hold of people in their offices, and they seldom like being disturbed at home. He had recently finished a well-received series on the steady infiltration of Austrian, Parisian, and Italian gangsters into the gold mine of the Reeperbahn, Hamburg's half-mile of nightclubs, brothels, and vice, and had not yet been paid for it. He thought he might contact the magazine to which he had sold the series, then decided against it. It would pay in time, and he was not short of money for the moment. Indeed his bank statement, which had arrived three days earlier, showed he had more than 5000 marks to his credit, which he thought would keep him going for a while.

"The trouble with you, pal," he told his reflection in one of Sigi's brilliantly polished saucepans as he rinsed out the cup with his forefinger, "is that you are lazy."

He had been asked by a civilian-careers officer, at the end of his military service ten years earlier, what he wanted to be in life. He had replied, "An idle rich man," and at twenty-nine, although he had not achieved it and probably never would, he still thought it a perfectly reasonable ambition.

He carried the portable transistor radio into the bathroom, closed the door so Sigi would not hear it, and listened to the news while he showered and shaved. The main item was that a man had been arrested for the murder of President Kennedy. As he had supposed, there were no other items of news on the entire program but those connected with the Kennedy assassination.

After drying off he went back to the kitchen and made more coffee, this time two cups. He took them into the bedroom, placed them on the bedside table, slipped off his robe, and clambered back under the cushion beside Sigi, whose fluffy blond head was protruding onto the pillow.

She was twenty-two and at school had been a champion gymnast who, so she said, could have gone on to Olympic standing if her bust had not developed to the point where it got in the way and no leotard could safely contain it. On leaving school she became a teacher of physical training at a girls' school. The change to striptease dancer in Hamburg came a year later and for the very best and most simple of economic reasons. It earned her five times more than a teacher's salary.

Despite her willingness to take her clothes off to the buff in a nightclub, she was remarkably embarrassed by any lewd remarks made about her body by anyone whom she could see when the remarks were made.

"The point is," she once told an amused Peter Miller with great seriousness, "when I'm on the stage I can't see anything behind the lights, so I don't get embarrassed. If I could see them, I think I'd run offstage."

This did not stop her from later taking her place at one of the tables in the club when she was dressed again, and waiting to be invited for a drink by one of the customers. The only drink allowed was champagne, in half-bottles or preferably whole bottles. On these she collected a fifteen-per-cent commission. Although almost without exception the customers who invited her to drink champagne with them hoped to get much more than an hour of gazing in stunned admiration at the canyon between her breasts, they never did. She was a kindly and understanding girl, and her attitude to the pawing attentions of the customers was one of gentle regret rather than the contemptuous loathing that the other girls hid behind their neon smiles.

"Poor little men," she once said to Miller, "they ought to have a nice woman to go home to."

"What do you mean, poor little men?" protested Miller. "They're dirty old creeps with a pocketful of cash to spend."

"Well, they wouldn't be if they had someone to take care of them," retorted Sigi, and on this her feminine logic was unshakable.

Miller had seen her by chance on a visit to Madame Kokett's bar just below the Café Keese on the Reeperbahn, when he had gone to have a chat and a drink with the owner, an old friend and contact. She was a big girl, five feet, nine inches tall and with a figure to match, which, on a shorter girl, would have been out of proportion. She stripped to the music with the habitual supposedly sensual gestures, her face set in the usual bedroom pout of strippers. Miller had seen it all before and sipped his drink without batting an eyelid.

But when her brassière came off even he had to stop and stare, glass half-raised to his mouth. His host eyed him sardonically. "She's stacked, eh?" he said.

Miller had to admit she made *Playboy*'s Playmates of the Month look like severe cases of undernourishment. But she was so firmly muscled that her bosom stood outward and upward without a vestige of support.

At the end of her turn, when the applause started, the girl had dropped the bored poise of the professional dancer, bobbed a shy, half-embarrassed little bow to the audience, and given a big sloppy grin like a half-trained bird dog which against all the betting has just brought back a downed partridge. It was the grin that got Miller, not the dance routine or the figure. He asked if she would like a drink, and she was sent for.

As Miller was in the company of the boss, she avoided a bottle of champagne and asked for a gin fizz. To his surpirse, Miller found she was a very nice person to be around and asked if he might take her home after the show. With obvious reservations, she agreed. Playing his cards coolly, Miller made no pass at her that night. It was early spring, and she emerged from the cabaret, when it closed, clad in a most unglamorous duffel coat, which he presumed was intentional.

They just had coffee together and talked, during which she unwound from her previous tension and chatted gaily. He learned she liked pop music, art, walking along the banks of the Alster, keeping house, and children. After that they started going out on her one free night a week, taking in a dinner or a show, but not sleeping together.

After three months Miller took her to his bed and later suggested she might like to move in. With her single-minded attitude toward the important things of life, Sigi had already decided she wanted to marry Peter Miller, and the only problem was whether she should try to get him by not sleeping in his bed or the other way around. Sensing his ability to fill the other half of his mattress with other girls if the need arose, she decided to move in and make his life so comfortable that he would want to marry her. They had been together for six months by the end of November.

Even Miller, who was hardly house-trained, had to admit she kept a beautiful home, and she made love with a healthy and bouncing enjoyment. She never mentioned marriage directly but tried to get the message across in other ways. Miller feigned not to notice. Strolling in the sun by the Alster lake, she would sometimes make friends with a toddler under the benevolent eyes of its parent.

"Oh, Peter, isn't he an angel?"

Miller would grunt. "Yeah. Marvelous."

After that she would freeze him for an hour for having failed to take the hint. But they were happy together, especially Peter Miller, who was suited down to the ground by this arrangement of all the comforts of marriage, the delights of regular loving, without the ties of marriage.

After drinking half his coffee, Miller slithered down into the bed and put his arms around her from behind, gently caressing her crotch, which he knew would wake her up. After a few minutes she muttered with pleasure and rolled over onto her back. Still massaging, he leaned over and started to kiss her breasts. Still half asleep, she gave vent to a series of long mmmms, and her hands started to move drowsily over his back and buttocks. Ten minutes later they made love, squealing and shuddering with pleasure.

"That's a hell of a way to wake me up," she grumbled afterward.

"There are worse ways," said Miller.

"What's the time?"

"Nearly twelve," Miller lied, knowing she would throw something at him if she learned it was half past ten and she had had only five hours' sleep. "Never mind, you go back to sleep if you feel like it."

"Mmmm. Thank you, darling, you are good to me," said Sigi and fell asleep again.

Miller was halfway to the bathroom after drinking the rest of his coffee and Sigi's as well, when the phone rang. He diverted into the sitting room and answered it.

"Peter?"

"Yes, who's that?"

"Karl."

His mind was still fuzzed, and he did not recognize the voice. "Karl?"

The voice was impatient. "Karl Brandt. What's the matter? Are you still asleep?"

Miller recovered. "Oh, yes. Sure, Karl. Sorry, I just got up. What's the matter?"

"Look, it's about this dead Jew. I want to talk to you."

Miller was baffled. "What dead Jew?"

"The one who gassed himself last night in Altona. Can't you even remember that far back?"

"Yes, of course I remember last night," said Miller. "I didn't know he was Jewish. What about him?"

"I want to talk to you," said the police inspector. "But not on the phone. Can we meet?"

Miller's reporter's mind clicked into gear immediately. Anyone who has got something to say but does not wish to say it over the phone must think it important. In the case of Brandt, Miller could hardly suspect a police detective would be so cagy about something ridiculous.

"Sure," he said. "Are you free for lunch?"

"I can be," said Brandt.

"Good. I'll buy it if you think it's something worth while." He named a small restaurant on the Goose Market for one o'clock and replaced the receiver. He was still puzzled, for he couldn't see a story in the suicide of an old man, Jewish or not, in a slum tenement in Altona.

Throughout the lunch the young detective seemed to wish to avoid the subject about which he had asked for the meeting, but when the coffee came he said simply, "The man last night."

"Yes," said Miller. "What about him?"

"You must have heard, as we all have, about what the Nazis did to the Jews during the war and even before it?"

"Of course. They rammed it down our throats at school, didn't they?" Miller was puzzled and embarrassed. Like most young Germans, he had been told at school when he was twelve or so that he and the rest of his countrymen had been guilty of massive war crimes. At the time he had accepted it without even knowing what was being talked about.

Later it had been difficult to find out what the teachers had meant in the immediate postwar period. There was nobody to ask, nobody who wanted to talk—not the teachers, not the parents. Only with coming manhood had he been able to read a little about it, and although what he read disgusted him, he could not feel it concerned him. It was another time, another place, a long way away. He had not been there when it happened, his father had not been there, his mother had not been there. Something inside him had persuaded him it was nothing to do with Peter Miller, so he had asked for no names, dates, details. He wondered why Brandt should be bringing the subject up.

Brandt stirred his coffee, himself embarrassed, not knowing how to go on.

"That old man last night," he said at length. "He was a German Jew. He was in a concentration camp."

Miller thought back to the death's head on the stretcher the previous evening. Was that what they ended up like? It was ridiculous. The man must have been liberated by the Allies eighteen years earlier and had lived on to die of old age. But the face kept coming back. He had never seen anyone who had been in a camp before—at least, not knowingly. For that matter he had never met one of the SS mass-killers, he was sure of that. One would notice, after all.

His mind strayed back to the publicity surrounding the Eichmann trial in Jerusalem two years earlier. The papers had been full of it for weeks on end. He thought of the face in the glass booth and remembered that his impression at the time had been how ordinary that face was, so depressingly ordinary. It was in reading the press coverage of the trial that for the first time he had gained an inkling of how the SS had done it, how they had got away with it. But these had all been about things in Poland, Russia, Hungary, Czechoslovakia, far away and a long time back. He could not make them personal.

He brought his thoughts back to the present and the sense of unease Brandt's line of talk aroused in him.

"What about it?" he asked the detective.

For answer Brandt took a brown-paper-wrapped parcel out of his attaché case and pushed it across the table. "The old man left a diary. Actually, he wasn't so old. Fifty-six. It seems he wrote notes at the time and stored them in his foot-wrappings. After the war he transcribed them all. They make up the diary."

Miller looked at the parcel with scant interest. "Where did you find it?"

"It was lying next to the body, I picked it up and took it home. I read it last night."

Miller looked at his former school friend quizzically. "It was bad?"

"Horrible. I had no idea it was that bad—the things they did to them."

"Why bring it to me?"

Now Brandt was embarrassed. He shrugged. "I thought it might make a story for you."

"Who does it belong to now?"

"Technically, Tauber's heirs. But we'll never find them. So I suppose it belongs to the Police Department. But they'd just file it. You can have it, if you want it. Just don't let on that I gave it to you. I don't need any trouble in the department."

Miller paid the bill, and the pair walked outside.

"All right. I'll read it. But I don't promise to get steamed up about it. It might make an article for a magazine."

Brandt turned to him with a half-smile. "You're a cynical bastard," he said.

"No," said Miller, "it's just that, like most people, I'm concerned with the here and now. What about you? After ten years in the police I'd have thought you'd be a tough cop. This thing really upset you, didn't it?"

Brandt was serious again. He looked at the parcel under Miller's arm and nodded slowly. "Yes. Yes, it did. I just never thought it was that bad. And by the way, it's not all past history. That story ended here in Hamburg last night. Good-by, Peter."

The detective turned and walked away, not knowing how wrong he was.

TWO

Peter Miller took the brown-paper parcel home and arrived there just after three. He threw the package onto the living-room table and went to make a large pot of coffee before sitting down to read it.

Settled in his favorite armchair with a cup of coffee at his elbow and a cigarette going, he opened it. The diary was in the form of a looseleaf folder with stiff covers of cardboard bound in a dull black vinyl, and a series of clips down the spine so that the leaves of the book could be extracted, or further leaves inserted if necessary.

The contents consisted of a hundred and fifty pages of typewritten script, apparently banged out on an old machine, for some of the letters were above the line, others below it, and some either distorted or faint. The bulk of the pages seemed to have been written years before, or over a period of years, for most of them, although neat and clean, bore the unmistakable tint of white paper several years old. But at the front and back were a number of fresh sheets, evidently written barely a few days previously. There was a preface of some new pages at the front of the typescript, and there was a sort of epilogue at the back. A check of the dates on the preface and the epilogue showed both to have been written on November 21, two days previously. Miller supposed the dead man had written them after he had made the decision to end his life.

A quick glance at some of the paragraphs on the first page surprised him, for the language was clear and precise German, the writing of a well-educated and cultured man. On the outside of the front cover a square of white paper had been pasted, and over it a larger square of cellophane to keep it clean. On the square of paper had been written in large block capitals in black ink: THE DIARY OF SALOMON TAUBER.

Miller settled himself deeper in his chair, turned to the first page, and began to read.

TAUBER'S DIARY: PREFACE

My name is Salomon Tauber, I am a Jew and about to die. I have decided to end my own life because it has no more value, nor is there anything left for me to do. Those things that I have tried to do with my life have come to nothing, and my efforts have been unavailing. For the evil that I have seen has survived and flourished, and only the good has departed in dust and mockery. The friends that I have known, the sufferers and the victims, are all dead, and only the persecutors are all around me. I see their faces on the streets in the daytime, and in the night I see the face of my wife, Esther, who died long ago. I have stayed alive this long only because there was one more thing I wished to do, one thing I wanted to see, and now I know I never shall.

I bear no hatred or bitterness toward the German people, for they are a good people. Peoples are not evil; only individuals are evil. The English philosopher Burke was right when he said, "I do not know the means for drawing up the indictment of an entire nation." There is no collective guilt, for the Bible relates how the Lord wished to destroy Sodom and Gomorrah for the evil of the men who lived in them, with their women and children, but how there was living among them one righteous man, and because he was righteous he was spared. Therefore guilt is individual, like salvation.

When I came out of the concentration camps of Riga and Stutthof, when I survived the Death March to Magdeburg, when the British soldiers liberated my body there in April 1945, leaving only my soul in chains, I hated the world. I hated the people, and the trees and the rocks, for they had conspired against me and made me suffer. And above all I hated the Germans. I asked then, as I had asked many times over the previous four years, why the Lord did not strike them down, every last man, woman, and child, destroying their cities and their houses forever from the face of the earth. And when He did not, I hated Him too, crying that He had deserted me and my people, whom He had led to believe they were His chosen people, and even saying that He did not exist.

But with the passing of the years I have learned again to love; to love the rocks and the trees, the sky above and the river flowing past the city, the stray dogs and the cats, the weeds growing between the cobblestones, and the children who run away from me in the street because I am so ugly. They are not to blame. There is a French adage, "To understand everything is to forgive everything." When one can understand the people, their gullibility and their fear, their greed and their lust for power, their ignorance and their docility to the man who shouts the loudest, one can forgive. Yes, one can forgive even what they did. But one can never forget.

There are some men whose crimes surpass comprehension and therefore forgiveness, and here is the real failure. For they are still among us, walking through the cities, working in the offices, lunching in the canteens, smiling and shaking hands and calling decent men Kamerad. *That they should live on, not as outcasts but as cherished citizens, to smear a whole nation in perpetuity with their individual evil, this is the true failure. And in this we have failed, you and I, we have all failed, and failed miserably.*

Lastly, as time passed, I came again to love the Lord, and to ask His forgiveness for the things I have done against His Laws, and they are many.

Shema Yisroel, Adonai elohenu, Adonai ehad.
[The diary began with twenty pages during which Tauber described his birth and boyhood in Hamburg, his working-class war-hero father, and the death of his parents shortly after Hitler came to power in 1933. By the late thirties he was married to a girl called Esther and was working as an

architect. He was spared being rounded up before 1941 owing to the intervention of his employer. Finally he was taken, in Berlin, on a journey to see a client. After a period in a transit camp he was packed with other Jews into a boxcar on a cattle train bound for the east.]

I cannot really remember the date the train finally rumbled to a halt in a railway station. I think it was six days and seven nights after we were shut up in the car in Berlin. Suddenly the train was stationary, the slits of white light told me it was daytime outside, and my head reeled and swam from exhaustion and the stench.

There were shouts outside, the sound of bolts being drawn back, and the doors were flung open. It was just as well I could not see myself, who had once been dressed in a white shirt and well-pressed trousers. (The tie and jacket had long since been dropped to the floor.) The sight of the others was bad enough.

As brilliant daylight rushed into the car, men threw arms over their eyes and screamed with the pain. Seeing the doors opening, I had squeezed my eyes shut to protect them. Under the pressure of bodies half the car emptied itself onto the platform in a tumbling mass of stinking humanity. As I had been standing at the rear of the car, to one side of the centrally placed doors, I avoided this and, risking a half-open eye despite the glare, I stepped down upright to the platform.

The SS guards who had opened the gates, mean-faced, brutal men who jabbered and roared in a language I could not understand, stood back with expressions of disgust. Inside the boxcar thirty-one men lay huddled and trampled on the floor. They would never get up again. The remainder, starved, half-blind, steaming and reeking from head to foot in their rags, struggled upright on the platform. From thirst, our tongues were gummed to the roofs of our mouths, blackened and swollen, and our lips were split and parched.

Down the platform forty other cars from Berlin and eighteen from Vienna were disgorging their occupants, about half of them women and children. Many of the women and most of the children were naked, smeared with excrement, and in much as bad shape as we were. Some women carried the lifeless bodies of their children in their arms as they stumbled out into the light.

The guards ran up and down the platform, clubbing the deportees into a sort of column, prior to marching us into the town. But what town? And what was the language these men were speaking? Later I was to discover that this town was Riga and the SS guards were locally recruited Latvians, as fiercely anti-Semitic as the SS from Germany, but of a much lower intelligence, virtually animals in human form.

Standing behind the guards was a cowed group in soiled shirts and slacks, each bearing a black square patch with a big J on the chest and back. This was a special commando from the ghetto, brought down to empty the cattle cars of the dead and bury them outside the town. They too were guarded by half a dozen men who also had the J on their chests and backs, but who wore armbands and carried pickax handles. These were Jewish Kapos, who got better food than the other internees for doing the job they did.

There were a few German SS officers standing in the shade of the station awning, distinguishable only when my eyes were accustomed to the light. One stood aloof on a packing crate, surveying the several thousand human skeletons who emptied themselves from the train with a thin but satisfied smile. He tapped a black riding quirt of plaited leather against one jackboot. He wore the green uniform with black and silver flashes of the SS as if it were designed for him and carried the twin-lightning strikes of the Waffen SS on the right collar. On the left his rank was indicated as captain.

He was tall and lanky, with pale blond hair and washed-out blue eyes. Later I was to learn he was a dedicated sadist, already known by the name that the Allies would also later use for him—the Butcher of Riga. It was my first sight of SS Captain Eduard Roschmann.

[At 5 a.m. on the morning of June 22, 1941, Hitler's 130 divisions, divided into three army groups, had rolled across the border to invade Russia. Behind each army group came the swarms of SS extermination squads, charged by Hitler, Himmler, and Heydrich with wiping out the Communist commissars and the rural-dwelling Jewish communities of the vast tracts of land the Army overran, and penning the large urban Jewish communities into the ghettos of each major town for later "special treatment."

The Army took Riga, capital of Latvia, on July 1, 1941, and in the middle of that month the first SS commandos moved in. The first onsite unit of the SD and SP sections of the SS established themselves in Riga on August 1, 1941, and began the extermination program that would make Ostland (as the three occupied Baltic states were renamed) Jew-free.

Then it was decided in Berlin to use Riga as the transit camp to death for the Jews of Germany and Austria. In 1938 there were 320,000 German Jews and 180,000 Austrian Jews, a round half-million. By July 1941 tens of thousands had been dealt with, mainly in the concentration camps within Germany and Austria, notably Sachsenhausen, Mauthausen, Ravensbrück, Dachau, Buchenwald, Belsen, and Theresienstadt in Bohemia. But they were getting overcrowded, and the obscure lands of the east seemed an excellent place to finish off the rest. Work was begun to expand or begin the six extermination camps of Auschwitz, Treblinka, Belzec, Sobibor, Chelmno, and Maidanek. Until they were ready, however, a place had to be found to exterminate as many as possible and "store" the rest. Riga was chosen.

Between August 1, 1941, and October 14, 1944, almost 200,000 exclusively German and Austrian Jews were shipped to Riga. Eighty thousand stayed there, dead; 120,000 were shipped onward to the six extermination camps of southern Poland already mentioned; and 400 came out alive, half of them to die at Stutthof or on the Death March back to Magdeburg. Tauber's transport was the first into Riga from the German Reich, and reached there at 3:45 in the afternoon of August 18, 1941.]

The Riga ghetto was an integral part of the city and had formerly been the home of the Jews of Riga, of whom only a few hundred existed by the time I got there. In less than three weeks Roschmann and his deputy, Krause, had overseen the extermination of most of them, as per orders.

The ghetto lay at the northern edge of the city, with open country-side to the north. There was a wall along the south face; the other three were sealed off with rows of barbed wire. There was one gate, on the northern face, through which all exits and entries had to be made. It was guarded by two watchtowers manned by Latvian SS. From this gate, running clear down the center of the ghetto to the south wall, was Mase Kalnu Iela, or Little Hill Street. To the right-hand side of this (looking from south to north toward the main gate) was the Blech Platz, or Tin Square, where selections for execution took place, along with roll call, selection of slave-labor parties, floggings, and hangings. The gallows with its eight steel hooks and permanent nooses swinging in the wind stood in the center of this. It was occupied every night by at least six unfortunates, and frequently several shifts had to be processed by the eight hanging hooks before Roschmann was satisfied with his day's work.

The whole ghetto must have been just under two square miles, a township that had once housed 12,000 to 15,000 people. Before our arrival the Riga Jews, at least the 2000 of them left, had done the bricking-off work, so the area left to our transport of just over 5000 men, women, and children was spacious. But after we arrived transports continued to come day after day until the population of our part of the ghetto soared to 30,000 to 40,000, and with the arrival of each new transport a number of the existing inhabitants equal to the number of surviving new arrivals had to be executed to make room for the newcomers. Otherwise the overcrowding would have become a menace to the health of the workers among us, and that Roschmann would not have.

So on that first evening we settled ourselves in, taking the best-constructed houses, one room per person, using curtains and coats for blankets and sleeping on real beds. After drinking his fill from a water butt, my room neighbor remarked that perhaps it would not be too bad after all. We had not yet met Roschmann.

As summer merged into autumn and autumn into winter, the conditions in the ghetto grew worse. Each morning the entire population—mainly men, for the women and children were exterminated on arrival in far greater percentages than the work-fit males—was assembled on Tin Square, pushed and shoved by the rifle butts of the Latvians, and roll call took place. No names were called; we were counted and divided into work groups. Almost the whole population, men, women, and children, left the ghetto each day in columns to work twelve hours at forced labor in the growing host of workshops nearby.

I had said earlier that I was a carpenter, which was not true, but as an architect I had seen carpenters at work and knew enough to get by. I guessed, correctly, that there would always be a need for carpenters, and I was sent to work in a nearby lumber mill where the local pines were sawed up and made into prefabricated hutments for the troops.

The work was backbreaking, enough to ruin the constitution of a healthy man, for we worked, summer and winter, mainly outside in the cold and damp of the low-lying regions near the coast of Latvia.

Our food rations were a half-liter apiece of so-called soup, mainly tinted water, sometimes with a knob of potato in it, before marching to work in the mornings, and another half-liter, with a slice of black bread and a moldy potato, on return to the ghetto at night.

Bringing food into the ghetto was punishable by immediate hanging before the assembled population at evening roll call on Tin Square. Nevertheless, to take that risk was the only way to stay alive.

As the columns trudged back through the main gate each evening, Roschmann and a few of his cronies used to stand by the entrance, doing spot checks on those passing through. They would call to a man or a woman or a child at random, ordering the person out of the column to strip by the side of the gate. If a potato or a piece of bread was found, the person would wait behind while the others marched through toward Tin Square for evening roll call.

When they were all assembled, Roschmann would stalk down the road, followed by the other SS guards and the dozen or so condemned people. The males among them would mount the gallows platform and wait with the ropes around their necks while roll call was completed. Then Roschmann would walk along the line, grinning up at the faces above him and kicking the chairs out from under one by one. He liked to do this from the front, so the person about to die would see him. Sometimes he would pretend to kick the chair away, only to pull his foot back in time. He would laugh uproariously to see the man on the chair tremble, thinking he was already swinging at the rope's end, only to realize the chair was still beneath him.

Sometimes the condemned men would pray to the Lord; sometimes they would cry for mercy. Roschmann liked to hear this. He would pretend he was slightly deaf, cocking an ear and asking, "Can you speak up a little? What was that you said?"

When he had kicked the chair away—it was more like a wooden box, really—he would turn to his cronies and say, "Dear me, I really must get a hearing aid."

Within a few months Eduard Roschmann had become the Devil incarnate to us prisoners. There was little that he did not succeed in devising.

When a woman was caught bringing food into the camp, she was made to watch the hangings of the men first, especially if one was her husband or brother. Then Roschmann made her kneel in front of the rest of us, drawn up around three sides of the square, while the camp barber shaved her bald.

After roll call she would be taken to the cemetery outside the wire and made to dig a shallow grave, then kneel beside it while Roschmann or one of the others fired a bullet from his Luger pointblank into the base of the skull. No one was allowed to watch these executions, but word seeped through from the Latvian guards that he would often fire past the ear of the woman to make her fall into the grave with shock, then climb out again and kneel in the same position. Other times he would fire from an empty chamber, so there was just a click when the woman thought she was about to die. The Latvians were brutes, but Roschmann managed to amaze them for all that.

There was one certain girl at Riga who helped the prisoners at her own risk. She was Olli Adler—from Munich, I believe. Her sister Gerda had already been shot in the cemetery for bringing in food. Olli was a girl of surpassing beauty and took Roschmann's fancy. He made her his concubine—the official term was housemaid, because relations between an SS man and a Jewish girl were banned. She used to smuggle medicines into the ghetto when she was allowed to visit it, having stolen them from the SS stores. This, of course, was punishable by death. The last I saw of her was when we boarded the ship at Riga docks.

By the end of that first winter I was certain I could not survive much longer. The hunger, the cold, the damp, the overwork, the constant brutalities had whittled my formerly strong frame down to a mass of skin and bones. Looking in the mirror, I saw staring back at me a haggard, stubbled old man with red-rimmed eyes and hollow cheeks. I had just turned thirty-five, and I looked double that. But so did everyone else.

I had witnessed the departure of tens of thousands to the forest of the mass graves, the deaths of hundreds from cold, exposure, and overwork, and of scores from hanging, shooting, flogging, and clubbing. Even after surviving five months, I had outlived my time. The will to live that I had begun to show in the train had dissipated, leaving nothing but a mechanical routine of going on living that sooner or later had to break. And then something happened in March that gave me another year of will power.

I remember the date even now. It was March 3, 1942, the day of the second Dünamünde convoy. About a month earlier we had seen for the first time the arrival of a strange van. It was about the size of a long single-decker bus, painted steel-gray, and without windows. It parked just outside the ghetto gates, and at morning roll call

Roschmann said he had an announcement to make. He said there was a new fish-pickling factory just started at the town of Dünamünde, situated on the Düna River, about eighty miles from Riga. It offered light work, he said, good food, and good living conditions. Because the work was so light the opportunity was open only to old men and women, the frail, the sick, and the small children.

Naturally, many were eager to go to such a comfortable kind of labor. Roschmann walked down the lines, selecting those to go, and this time, instead of the old and sick hiding themselves at the back to be dragged screaming and protesting forward to join the forced marches to Execution Hill, they seemed eager to show themselves. Finally more than a hundred were selected, and all climbed into the van. Then the doors were slammed shut, and the watchers noticed how tight they fitted together. The van rolled away, emitting no exhaust fumes. Later, word filtered back what the van was. There was no fish-pickling factory at Dünamünde; the van was a gassing van. In the parlance of the ghetto the expression "Dünamünde convoy" henceforward came to mean death by gassing.

On March 3 the whisper went around the ghetto that there was to be another Dünamünde convoy, and sure enough, at morning roll call Roschmann announced it. But there was no pressing forward to volunteer, so with a wide grin Roschmann began to stroll along the ranks, tapping on the chest with his quirt those who were to go. Astutely, he started at the fourth and rear rank, where he expected to find the weak, the old, and the unfit-for-work.

There was one old woman who had foreseen this and stood in the front rank. She must have been close to sixty-five, but in an effort to stay alive she had put on high-heeled shoes, a pair of black silk stockings, a short skirt even above her knees, and a saucy hat. She had rouged her cheeks, powdered her face, and painted her lips carmine. In fact she would have stood out among any group of ghetto prisoners, but she thought she might be able to pass for a young girl.

Reaching her as he walked by, Roschmann stopped, stared, and looked again. Then a grin of joy spread over his face.

"Well, what have we here?" he cried, pointing to her with his quirt to draw the attention of his comrades in the center of the square guarding the hundred already chosen. "Don't you want a nice little ride to Dünamünde, young lady?"

Trembling with fear, the old woman whispered, "No, sir."

"And how old are you, then?" boomed Roschmann as his SS friends began to giggle. "Seventeen? Twenty?"

The old woman's knobbly knees began to tremble. "Yes, sir," she whispered.

"How marvelous," cried Roschmann. "Well, I always like a pretty girl. Come out into the center so we can all admire your youth and beauty."

So saying, he grabbed her by the arm and hustled her toward the center of Tin Square. Once there, he stood her out in the open and said, "Well now, little lady, since you're so young and pretty, perhaps you'd like to dance for us, eh?"

She stood there, shivering in the bitter wind, shaking with fear as well. She whispered something we could not hear.

"What's that?" shouted Roschmann. "You can't dance? Oh, I'm sure a nice young thing like you can dance, can't you?"

His cronies of the German SS were laughing to bust. The Latvians could not understand but started to grin. The old woman shook her head.

Roschmann's smile vanished. "Dance," he snarled.

She made a few little shuffling movements, then stopped. Roschmann drew his Luger, eased back the hammer, and fired it into the sand an inch from her feet. She jumped a foot in the air from fright.

"Dance . . . dance . . . dance for us you hideous Jewish bitch," he shouted, firing a bullet into the sand beneath her feet each time he said, "Dance."

Smacking in one spare magazine after another until he had used up the three in his pouch, he made her dance for half an hour, leaping even higher and higher, her skirts flying round her hips with each jump, until at last she fell to the sand unable to rise whether she lived or died. Roschmann fired his last three slugs into the sand in front of her face, blasting the sand up into her eyes. Between the crash of each shot came the old woman's rattling wheeze that could be heard across the parade square.

When he had no more ammunition left he shouted, "Dance," again and slammed his jackboot into her belly. All this had happened in complete silence from us, until the man next to me started to pray. He was a Hasid, small and bearded, still wearing the rags of his long black coat; despite the cold which forced most of us to wear ear-muffs on our caps, he had the broad-brimmed hat of his sect. He began to recite the Shema, *over and over again, in a quavering voice that grew steadily louder. Knowing that Roschmann was in his most vicious mood, I too began to pray silently that the Hasid would be quiet. But he would not.*

"Shema Yisroel . . ." (Hear, O Israel . . .)

"Shut up," I hissed out of the corner of my mouth.

"Adonai elohenu . . ." (the Lord is our God . . .)

"Will you be quiet! You'll get us all killed."

"Adonai eha-a-a-ad." (The Lord is One.)

Like a cantor, he drew out the last syllable in the traditional way, as Rabbi Akiba had done as he died in the amphitheater at Caesarea on the orders of Tinius Rufus. It was just at that moment that Roschmann stopped screaming at the old woman. He lifted his head like an animal scenting the wind and turned toward us. As I stood a head taller than the Hasid, he looked at me.

"Who was that talking?" he screamed, striding toward me across the sand. "You—step out of line." There was no doubt he was

pointing at me. I thought: This is the end, then. So what? It doesn't matter; it had to happen, now or some other time. I stepped forward as he arrived in front of me.

He did not say anything, but his face was twitching like a maniac's. Then it relaxed and he gave his quiet, wolfish smile that struck terror into everyone in the ghetto, even the Latvian SS men.

His hand moved so quickly no one could see it. I felt only a sort of thump down the left side of my face, simultaneous with a tremendous bang as if a bomb had gone off next to my eardrum. Then the quite distinct but detached feeling of my own skin splitting like rotten calico from temple to mouth. Even before it had started to bleed, Roschmann's hand moved again, the other way this time, and his quirt ripped open the other side of my face with the same loud bang in the ear and the feeling of something tearing. It was a two-foot quirt, sprung with whippy steel core at the handle end, the remaining foot-length being of plaited leather thongs without the core, and when drawn across and down human skin at the same time, the plaiting could split the hide like tissue paper. I had seen it done.

Within a matter of seconds I felt the trickle of warm blood beginning to flow down the front of my jacket, dripping off my chin in two little red fountains. Roschmann swung away from me, then back, pointing to the old woman still sobbing in the center of the square.

"Pick up that old hag and take her to the van," he barked.

And so, a few minutes ahead of the arrival of the other hundred victims, I picked up the old woman and carried her down Little Hill Street to the gate and the waiting van, pouring blood onto her from my chin. I set her down in the back of the van and made to leave her there. As I did so, she gripped my wrist in withered fingers with a strength I would not have thought she still possessed. She pulled me down toward her, squatting on the floor of the death van, and with a small cambric handkerchief that must have come from better days stanched some of the still flowing blood.

She looked up at me from a face streaked with mascara, rouge, tears, and sand, but with dark eyes bright as stars.

"Jew, my son," she whispered, "you must live. Swear to me that you will live. Swear to me you will get out of this place alive. You must live, so that you can tell them, them outside in the other world, what happened to our people here. Promise me, swear it by the Torah."

And so I swore that I would live, somehow, no matter what the cost. Then she let me go. I stumbled back down the road into the ghetto, and halfway down I fainted.

Shortly after returning to work I made two decisions. One was to keep a secret diary, nightly tattooing words and dates with a pin and black ink into the skin of my feet and legs, so that one day I would be able to transcribe all that had happened in Riga and give precise evidence against those responsible.

The second decision was to become a Kapo, a member of the Jewish police.

The decision was hard, for these were men who herded their fellow Jews to work and back, and often to the place of execution. Moreover, they carried pickax handles and occasionally, when under the eyes of a German SS officer, used them liberally to beat their fellow Jews so they would work harder. Nevertheless, on April 1, 1942, I went to the chief of the Kapos and volunteered, thus becoming an outcast from the company of my fellow Jews. There was always room for an extra Kapo, for despite the better rations, living conditions, and release from slave labor, very few agreed to become Kapos.

I should here describe the method of execution of those unfit for labor, for in this manner between 70,000 and 80,000 Jews were exterminated under the orders of Eduard Roschmann at Riga. When the cattle train arrived at the station with a new consignment of prisoners, usually about 5000 strong, there were always close to a thousand already dead from the journey. Only occasionally was the number as low as a few hundred, scattered among fifty cars.

When the new arrivals were lined up in Tin Square, the selections for extermination took place, not merely among the new arrivals but among us all. That was the point of the head-count each morning and evening. Among the new arrivals, those weak or frail, old or diseased, most of the women, and almost all the children, were singled out as being unfit for work. These were set to one side. The remainder were then counted. If they totaled 2000, then 2000 of the existing inmates were also picked out, so that 5000 had arrived and 5000 went to Execution Hill. That way there was no overcrowding. A man might survive six months of slave labor, seldom more; then, when his health was reduced to ruins, Roschmann's quirt would tap him on the chest one day, and he would go to join the ranks of the dead.

At first these victims were marched in column to a forest outside the town. The Latvians called it Bickernicker Forest, and the Germans renamed it the Hochwald or High Forest. Here, in clearings between the pines, enormous open ditches had been dug by the Riga Jews before they died. And here the Latvian SS guards, under the eye and orders of Eduard Roschmann, mowed them down so that they fell into the ditches. The remaining Riga Jews then filled in enough earth to cover the bodies, adding one more layer of corpses to those underneath until the ditch was full. Then a new one was started.

From the ghetto we could hear the chattering of the machine guns when each new consignment was liquidated, and watch Roschmann riding back down the hill and through the ghetto gates in his open car when it was over.

After I became a Kapo all social contact between me and the other internees ceased. There was no point in explaining why I had done it, that one Kapo more or less would make no difference, not increasing the death toll by a single digit, but that one single surviving witness might make all the difference, not to save the Jews of Germany, but to avenge them. This at least was the argument I repeated to myself, but was it the real reason? Or was I just afraid to die? Whatever it was, fear soon ceased to be a factor, for in August that year something happened that caused my soul to die inside my body, leaving only the husk struggling to survive.

In July 1942 a big new transport of Austrian Jews came through from Vienna. Apparently they were marked without exception for "special treatment," for the entire shipment never came to the ghetto. We did not see them, for they were all marched from the station to High Forest and machine-gunned. Later that evening, down the hill rolled four trucks full of clothes, which were brought to the Tin Square for sorting. They made a mound as big as a house until they were sorted out into piles of shoes, socks, underpants, trousers, dresses, jackets, shaving brushes, spectacles, dentures, wedding rings, signet rings, caps, and so forth.

Of course this was standard procedure for executed deportees. All those killed on Execution Hill were stripped at the graveside and their effects brought down later. These were then sorted and sent back to the Reich. The gold, silver, and jewelry were taken in charge by Roschmann personally.

In August 1942 there was another transport, from Theresienstadt, a camp in Bohemia where tens of thousands of German and Austrian Jews were held before being sent eastward to extermination. I was standing at one side of the Tin Square, watching Roschmann as he went around making his selections. The new arrivals were already shaved bald, which had been done at their previous camp, and it was not easy to tell the men from the women, except for the shift dresses the women mainly wore. There was one woman across on the other side of the square who caught my attention. There was something about her cast of features that rang a bell in my mind, although she was emaciated, thin as a rake, and coughing continuously.

Arriving opposite her, Roschmann tapped her on the chest and passed on. The Latvians following him at once seized her arms and pushed her out of line to join the others in the center of the square. There were many from that transport who were not work-fit, and the list of selections was long. That meant fewer of us would be selected to make up the numbers, though for me the question was academic. As a Kapo I wore an armband and carried a club, and the extra food rations had increased my strength a little. Although Roschmann had seen my face, he did not seem to remember it. He had slashed so many across the face that one more or less would not attract his attention.

Most of those selected that summer evening were formed into a column and marched to the ghetto gates by the Kapos. The column was then taken over by the Latvians for the last four miles to High Forest and death.

But as there was a gassing van standing by also at the gates, a group of about a hundred of the frailest of the selected ones was detached from the crowd. I was about to escort the other condemned men and women to the gates when SS Lieutenant Krause pointed to five of us Kapos. "You," he shouted, "take these to the Dünamünde convoy."

After the others had left, we five escorted the last hundred, most of them limping, crawling, coughing, to the gates where the van waited. The thin woman was among them, her chest racked by tuberculosis. She knew where she was going—they all did—but like the rest she stumbled with resigned obedience to the rear of the van. She was too weak to get up, for the tailboard was high off the ground, so she turned to me for help. We stood and looked at each other in stunned amazement.

I heard somebody approach behind me, and the other Kapos at the tailboard straightened to attention, scraping their caps off. Realizing it must be an SS officer, I did the same. The woman just stared at me, unblinking. The man behind me came forward. It was Captain Roschmann. He nodded to the other Kapos to carry on, and stared at me with those pale blue eyes. I thought he could only mean I would be flogged that evening for being slow to take my cap off.

"What's your name?" he asked softly.

"Tauber, Herr Kapitän," I said, still ramrod at attention.

"Well, Tauber, you seem to be a little slow. Do you think we ought to liven you up a little this evening?"

There was no point in saying anything. The sentence was passed. Roschmann's eyes flickered to the woman and narrowed as if he were suspecting something; then his slow, wolfish smile spread across his face.

"Do you know this woman?" he asked.

"Yes, Herr Kapitän," I answered.

"Who is she?" he asked. I could not reply. My mouth was gummed together as if by glue.

"Is she your wife?" he went on.

I nodded dumbly.

He grinned even more widely. "Well, now, my dear Tauber, where are your manners? Help the lady up into the van."

I still stood there, unable to move. He put his face closer to mine and whispered, "You have ten seconds to pack her in, or you will go yourself."

Slowly I held out my arm and Esther leaned upon it. With this assistance she climbed into the van. The other Kapos waited to slam the doors shut. When she was up, she looked down at me, and two tears came, one from each eye, and rolled down her cheeks. She did not say anything to me; we never spoke throughout. Then the doors were slammed shut and the van rolled away. The last thing I saw was her eyes looking at me.

I have spent twenty years trying to understand the look in her eyes. Was it love or hatred, contempt or pity, bewilderment or understanding? I shall never know.

When the van had gone, Roschmann turned to me, still grinning. "You may go on living until it suits us to finish you off, Tauber," he said. "But you are dead as of now."

And he was right. That was the day my soul died inside me. It was August 29, 1942.

After August that year I became a robot. Nothing mattered any more. There was no feeling of cold or of pain, no sensation of any kind at all. I watched the brutalities of Roschmann and his fellow SS men without batting an eyelid. I was inured to everything that can touch the human spirit and most things that can touch the body. I just noted everything, each tiny detail, filing them away in my mind or pricking the dates into the skin of my legs. The transports came, their occupants marched to Execution Hill or to the vans, died, and were buried. Sometimes I looked into their eyes as they went, walking beside them to the gates of the ghetto with my armband and club. It reminded me of a poem I had once read by an English poet, which described how an ancient mariner, condemned to live, had looked into the eyes of his crewmates as they died of thirst, and read the curse in them. But for me there was no curse, for I was immune even to the feeling of guilt. That was to come years later. There was only the emptiness of a dead man still walking upright. . . .

[Peter Miller read on late into the night. The effect of the narration of the atrocities on him was at once monotonous and mesmerizing. Several times he sat back in his chair and breathed deeply for a few minutes to regain his calm. Then he read on.

Once, close to midnight, he laid the book down and made more coffee. He stood at the window before drawing the curtains, looking down into the street. Farther down the road the brilliant neon light of the Café Chérie blazed across the Steindamm, and he saw one of the part-time girls who frequent it to supplement their incomes emerge on the arm of a businessman. They disappeared into a *pension* a little farther down, where the businessman would be relieved of 100 marks for half an hour of copulation.

Miller pulled the curtains across, finished his coffee, and returned to Salomon Tauber's diary.]

In the autumn of 1943 the order came through Berlin to dig up the tens of thousands of corpses in the High Forest and destroy them more permanently, with either fire or quicklime. The job was easier said than done, with winter coming on and the ground about to freeze hard. It put Roschmann in a foul temper for days, but the administrative details of carrying out the order kept him busy enough to stay away from us.

Day after day the newly formed labor squads were seen marching up the hill into the forest with their pickaxes and shovels, and day

*after day the columns of black smoke rose above the forest. For fuel
they used the pines of the forest, but largely decomposed bodies do not
burn easily, so the job was slow. Eventually they switched to quicklime, covered each layer of corpses with it, and in the spring of 1944,
when the earth softened, filled them in.**

*The gangs who did the work were not from the ghetto. They were
totally isolated from all other human contact. They were Jewish, but
were kept imprisoned in one of the worst camps in the neighborhood,
Salas Pils, where they were later exterminated by being given no
food at all until they died of starvation, despite the cannibalism to
which many resorted.*

*When the work was more or less completed in the spring of 1944,
the ghetto was finally liquidated. Most of its 30,000 inhabitants
were marched toward the forest to become the last victims that
pinewood was destined to receive. About 5000 of us were transferred to the camp of Kaiserwald, while behind us the ghetto was
fired and then the ashes were bulldozed. Of what had once been
there, nothing was left but an area of flattened ashes covering
hundreds of acres.†*

[For a further twenty pages of typescript Tauber's diary described the
struggle to survive in Kaiserwald concentration camp against the onslaught
of starvation, disease, overwork, and the brutality of the camp's guards.
During this time no sign was seen of SS Captain Eduard Roschmann. But
apparently he was still in Riga. Tauber described how in early October of
1944 the SS officers, by now panic-stricken at the thought they might be
taken alive by the vengeful Russians, prepared for a desperate evacuation of
Riga by sea, taking along a handful of the last surviving prisoners as their
passage ticket back to the Reich in the west. This became fairly common
practice for the SS staff of the concentration camps as the Russian advance
swept on. So long as they could still claim they had a task to perform,
important to the Reich, they could continue to outrank the Wehrmacht and
avoid the terrible prospect of being required to face Stalin's divisions in
combat. This "task," which they allotted to themselves, was the escorting
back into the still safe heart of Germany of the few remaining wretches from
the camps they had run. Sometimes the charade became ridiculous, as when
the SS guards outnumbered their tottering charges by as many as ten to one.]

*This procedure badly burned the corpses but did not destroy the bones. The Russians later
uncovered these 80,000 skeletons.

†The Russian spring offensive of 1944 carried the tide of war so far westward that the Soviet
troops pushed south of the Baltic States and through to the Baltic Sea to the west of them. This
cut off the whole of Ostand from the Reich and led to a blazing quarrel between Hitler and his
generals. They had seen it coming and had pleaded with Hitler to pull back the forty-five
divisions inside the enclave. He had refused, reiterating his parrot-cry, "Death or Victory." All
he offered those 500,000 soldiers inside the enclave was death. Cut off from resupply, they
fought with dwindling ammunition to delay a certain fate, and eventually surrendered. Of the
majority, made prisoners and transported in the winter of 1944-1945 to Russia, few returned
ten years later to Germany.

It was in the afternoon of October 11 that we arrived, by now barely 4000 strong, at the town of Riga, and the column went straight down to the docks. In the distance we could hear a strange crump, as if of thunder, along the horizon. For a while it puzzled us, for we had never heard the sound of shells or bombs. Then it filtered through to our minds, dazed by hunger and cold—there were Russian mortar shells landing in the suburbs of Riga.

When we arrived at the dock area it was crawling with officers and men of the SS. I had never seen so many in one place at the same time. There must have been more of them than there were of us. We were lined up in rows against one of the warehouses, and again most of us thought that this was where we would die under the machine guns. But this was not to be.

Apparently the SS troops were going to use us, the last remainder of the hundreds of thousands of Jews who had passed through Riga, as their alibi to escape from the Russian advance, their passage back to the Reich. The means of travel was berthed alongside Quay Six—a freighter, the last one out of the encircled enclave. As we watched, the loading began of some of the hundreds of German Army wounded who were lying on stretchers in two of the warehouses farther along the quay.

It was almost dark when Captain Roschmann arrived, and he stopped short when he saw how the ship was being loaded. When he had taken in the sight of the German Army wounded being put onto the ship he turned around and shouted to the medical orderlies bearing the stretchers, "Stop that."

He strode toward them across the quay and slapped one of the orderlies in the face. He whirled around on the ranks of us prisoners and roared, "You scum. Get up on that ship and get these men off. Bring them back down here. That ship is ours."

Under the prodding of the gun barrels of the SS men who had come down with us, we started to move toward the gangplank. Hundreds of other SS men, privates and NCOs, who till then had been standing back watching the loading, surged forward and followed the prisoners up onto the ship. When the first got on the deck, they began picking up the stretchers and carrying them back to the quay. Rather, they were about to, when another shout stopped us.

I had reached the foot of the gangway and was about to start up, when I heard the shout and turned to see what was happening.

An Army captain was running down the quay, and he came to a stop quite close to me by the gangway. Staring up at the men above, bearing stretchers they were about to unload, the captain shouted "Who ordered these men to be offloaded?"

Roschmann walked up behind him and said, "I did. This boat is ours." The captain spun around. He delved in his pocket and produced a piece of paper. "This ship was sent to pick up Army wounded," he said. "And Army wounded is what it will take."

With that he turned to the Army orderlies and shouted to them to resume the loading. I looked across at Roschmann. He was standing trembling, I thought with anger. Then I saw he was scared. He was frightened of being left to face the Russians. Unlike us, they were armed.

He began to scream at the orderlies, "Leave them alone! I have commandeered this ship in the name of the Reich." The orderlies ignored him and obeyed the Wehrmacht captain. I noticed his face, as he was only two meters away from me. It was gray with exhaustion, with dark smudges under the eyes. There were lines down each side of the nose and several weeks of stubble on his chin. Seeing the loading work begin again, he made to march past Roschmann to supervise his orderlies. From among the crowded stretchers in the snow of the quay I heard a voice shout in the Hamburg dialect, "Good for you, Captain. You tell the swine."

As the Wehrmacht captain was abreast of Roschmann, the SS officer grabbed his arm, swung him around, and slapped him across the face with his gloved hand. I had seen him slap men a thousand times, but never with the same result. The captain took the blow, shook his head, bunched his fist, and landed a haymaker of a rightfisted punch on Roschmann's jaw. Roschmann flew back several feet and went flat on his back in the snow, a small trickle of blood coming from his mouth. The captain moved toward his orderlies.

As I watched, Roschmann drew his SS officer's Luger from its holster, took careful aim, and fired between the captain's shoulders. Everything stopped at the crash from the pistol. The Army captain staggered and turned. Roschmann fired again, and the bullet caught the captain in the throat. He spun over backward and was dead before he hit the quay. Something he had been wearing around his neck flew off as the bullet struck, and when I passed it, after being ordered to carry the body and throw it into the water, I saw that the object was a medal on a ribbon. I never knew the captain's name, but the medal was the Knight's Cross with Oak Leaf Cluster.

[Miller read this page of the diary with growing astonishment gradually turning to disbelief, doubt, belief again, and finally a deep anger. He read the page a dozen times to make sure there was no doubt, then resumed reading the diary.]

After this we were ordered to start unloading the Wehrmacht wounded and told to lay them back in the gathering snow on the quayside. I found myself helping one young soldier back down the gangplank onto the quay. He had been blinded, and around his eyes was wrapped a dirty bandage torn from a shirttail. He was half delirious and kept asking for his mother. I suppose he must have been about eighteen.

*Finally they were all taken off, and we prisoners were ordered on
board. We were all taken down into the two holds, one forward and
one aft, until we were so cramped we could hardly move. Then the
hatches were battened down and the SS began to come aboard. We
sailed just before midnight, the captain evidently wishing to be well
out into the Gulf of Latvia before dawn came, to avoid the chance of
being spotted and bombed by the patrolling Russian Stormoviks.*

*It took three days to reach Danzig, well behind German lines.
Three days in a pitching, tossing hell below decks, without food or
water, during which a quarter of the four thousand prisoners died.
There was no food to vomit, and yet everyone was retching dry from
seasickness. Many died from the exhaustion of vomiting, others from
hunger or cold, others from suffocation, others because they simply
lost the will to live, lay back, and surrendered to death. And then the
ship was berthed again, the hatches were opened, and gusts of
ice-cold winter air came rushing into the fetid, stinking holds.*

*When we were unloaded onto the quay at Danzig, the dead bodies
were laid out in rows alongside the living, so that the numbers
should tally with those that had been taken on board at Riga. The SS
was always very precise about numbers.*

*We learned later that Riga had fallen to the Russians on October
14, while we were still at sea.*

[Tauber's pain-wracked Odyssey was reaching its end. From Danzig the
surviving inmates were taken by barge to the concentration camp of Stutthof, outside Danzig, and until the first weeks of 1945 he worked daily in the
submarine works of Burggraben by day and lived in the camp by night.
Thousands more at Stutthof died of malnutrition. He watched them all die,
but somehow stayed alive.

In January 1945, as the advancing Russians closed on Danzig, the survivors of Stutthof camp were driven westward on the notorious Death March
through the winter snow toward Berlin. All across eastern Germany these
columns of wraiths, used as a ticket to safety in Western hands by their SS
guards, were being herded westward. Along the route, in snow and frost,
they died like flies.

Tauber survived even this, and finally the remnant of his column reached
Magdeburg, west of Berlin, where the SS men finally abandoned them and
sought their own safety. Tauber's group was lodged in Magdeburg prison, in
the charge of the bewildered and helpless old men of the local Home Guard.
Unable to feed their prisoners, terrified of what the advancing Allies would
say when they found them, the Home Guard permitted the fittest of them to
go scrounging for food in the surrounding countryside.]

*The last time I had seen Eduard Roschmann was when we were
being counted on Danzig quayside. Warmly wrapped against the
winter cold, he was climbing into a car. I thought it would be my last*

glimpse of him, but I was to see him one last time. It was April 3, 1945.

I had been out that day toward Gardelegen, a village east of the city, and had gathered a small sackful of potatoes with three others. We were trudging back with our booty when a car came up behind us, heading west. It paused to negotiate a horse and cart on the road, and I glanced around with no particular interest to see the car pass. Inside were four SS officers, evidently making their escape toward the west. Sitting beside the driver, pulling on the uniform jacket of an Army corporal, was Eduard Roschmann.

He did not see me, for my head was largely covered by a hood cut from an old potato sack, a protection against the cold spring wind. But I saw him. There was no doubt about it.

All four men in the car were apparently changing their uniforms even as the vehicle headed west. As it disappeared down the road a garment was thrown from one window and fluttered into the dust. We reached the spot where it lay a few minutes later and stooped to examine it. It was the jacket of an SS officer, bearing the silver twin-lightning symbols of the Waffen SS and the rank of captain. Roschmann of the SS had disappeared.

Twenty-four days after this came the liberation. We had ceased to go out at all, preferring to stay hungry in the prison than venture along the streets, where complete anarchy was loose. Then on the morning of April 27 all was quiet in the town. Toward midmorning I was in the courtyard of the prison, talking to one of the old guards, who seemed terrified and spent nearly an hour explaining that he and his colleagues had nothing to do with Adolf Hitler and certainly nothing to do with the persecution of the Jews.

I heard a vehicle drive up outside the locked gates, and there was a hammering on them. The old Home Guard man went to open them. The man who stepped through, cautiously, with a revolver in his hand, was a soldier in full battle uniform, one that I had never seen before.

He was evidently an officer, for he was accompanied by a soldier in a flat round tin hat who carried a rifle. They just stood there in silence, looking around at the courtyard of the prison. In one corner were stacked about fifty corpses, those who had died in the past two weeks and whom no one had the strength to bury. Others, half alive, lay around the walls, trying to soak up a little of the spring sunshine, their sores festering and stinking.

The two men looked at each other, then at the seventy-year-old Home Guard. He looked back, embarrassed. Then he said something he must have learned in the First World War. He said, "Hello, Tommy."

The officer looked back at him, looked again around the courtyard, and said quite clearly in English, "You fucking Kraut pig."

And suddenly I began to cry.

I do not really know how I made it back to Hamburg, but I did. I think I wanted to see if there was anything left of the old life. There wasn't. The streets where I was born and grew up had vanished in the great firestorm of the Allied bombing raids; the office where I had worked was gone, my apartment, everything.

The English put me in the hospital in Magdeburg for a while, but I left of my own accord and hitchhiked back home. But when I got there and saw there was nothing left, I finally, belatedly collapsed completely. I spent a year in the hospital as a patient, along with others, who had come out of a place called Bergen-Belsen, and then another year working in the hospital as an orderly, looking after those who were worse than I had been.

When I left there, I went to find a room in Hamburg, the place of my birth, to spend the rest of my days.

[The book ended with two more clean, white sheets of paper, evidently recently typed, which formed the epilogue.]

I have lived in this little room in Altona since 1947. Shortly after I came out of the hospital I began to write the story of what happened to me and to the others at Riga.

But long before I had finished it, it became clear that others had also survived the holocaust. My original intent—believing, as others had done elsewhere in their isolation, that I might be the only survivor—had been to bear witness, to tell the world what had happened. It is clear now that this has already been done. So I did not submit my diary for publication. I kept it and the notes in the hope that one day I might at least bear witness to what happened in the small arena of Riga. I never even let anyone else read it.

Looking back, it was all a waste of time and energy, the battle to survive and to be able to write down the evidence, when others have already done it so much better. I wish now I had died in Riga with Esther.

Even the last wish, to see Eduard Roschmann stand before a court, and to give evidence to that court about what he did, will never be fulfilled. I know this now.

I walk through the streets sometimes and remember the old days here, but it can never be the same. The children laugh at me and run away when I try to be friends. Once I got talking to a little girl who did not run away, but her mother came up screaming and dragged her away. So I do not talk to many people.

Once a woman came to see me. She said she was from the Reparations Office and that I was entitled to money. I said I did not want any money. She was very put out, insisting that it was my right to be recompensed for what was done. I kept on refusing. They sent someone else to see me, and I refused again. He said it was very irregular to refuse to be recompensed. I sensed he meant it would upset their books. But I only take from them what is due to me.

When I was in the British hospital one of the doctors asked me why I did not emigrate to Israel, which was soon to have its indepen-

dence. How could I explain to him? I could not tell him that I can never go up to the Land, not after what I did to Esther, my wife. I think about it often and dream about what it must be like, but I am not worthy to go.

*   But if ever these lines should be read in the Land of Israel, which I shall never see, will someone there please say Kaddish for me?*

Salomon Tauber,
Altona, Hamburg,
November 21, 1963

Peter Miller put the diary down and lay back in his chair for a long time, staring at the ceiling and smoking. Just before five in the morning he heard the flat door open, and Sigi came in from work. She was startled to find him still awake.

"What are you doing up so late?" she asked.

"Been reading," said Miller.

Later they lay in bed as the first glint of dawn picked out the spire of Sankt Michaelis, Sigi drowsy and contented, like a young woman who has just been loved, Miller staring up at the ceiling silent and preoccupied.

"Penny for them," said Sigi after a while.

"Just thinking."

"I know. I can tell that. What about?"

"The next story I'm going to cover."

She shifted and looked across at him. "What are you going to do?" she asked.

Miller leaned over and stubbed out his cigarette. "I'm going to track a man down," he said.

THREE

While Peter Miller and Sigi were asleep in each other's arms in Hamburg, a giant Argentine Coronado airliner swung over the darkened hills of Castile and entered final approach for a landing at Barajas Airport, Madrid.

Sitting in a window seat in the third row of the first-class passenger section was a man in his early sixties with iron-gray hair and a trim mustache.

Only one photograph had ever existed of the man, in his early forties, showing him with close-cropped hair, no mustache to cover the rattrap mouth, and a razor-straight parting along the left side of his head. Hardly any one of the small group of men who had ever seen that photograph would recognize the man in the airliner, his hair now growing thickly back from the forehead, without a parting. The photograph in his passport matched his new appearance.

The name in that same passport identified him as Señor Ricardo Suertes, citizen of Argentina, and the name itself was his own grim joke against the world. For *suerte* in Spanish means "luck," and "luck" in German is *Glück*. The airline passenger that January night had been born Richard Glücks, later to become full general of the SS, head of the Reich Economic Administration Main Office, and Hitler's Inspector General of Concentration Camps. On the wanted lists of West Germany and Israel, he was number three after Martin Bormann and the former chief of the Gestapo, Heinrich Müller. He ranked higher even than Dr. Josef Mengele, the Devil Doctor of Auschwitz. In the Odessa he ranked number two—direct deputy of Martin Bormann, on whom the mantle of the Führer had fallen after 1945.

The role Richard Glücks had played in the crimes of the SS was unique and matched only by the manner in which he managed to effect his own complete disappearance on May 1945. Glücks had surpassed even Adolf Eichmann as one of the master minds of the holocaust, and yet he had never pulled a trigger.

Had an uninformed passenger been told who the man sitting next to him was, he might well have wondered why the former head of an economic administration office should be so high on the wanted list.

Had he asked, he would have learned that of the crimes against humanity committed on the German side between 1933 and 1945, probably 95 per cent can accurately be laid at the door of the SS. Of these, probably 80 to 90 per cent can be attributed to two departments within the SS. These were the Reich Security Main Office and the Reich Economic Administration Main Office.

If the idea of an economic bureau being involved in mass murder strikes a strange note, one must understand how it was intended that the job should be done. Not only was it intended to exterminate every Jew on the face of Europe, and most of the Slavic races also, but it was intended that the victims should pay for the privilege. Before the gas chambers opened, the SS had already carried out the biggest robbery in history.

In the case of the Jews, the payment was in three stages. First they were robbed of their businesses, houses, factories, bank accounts, furniture, cars, and clothes. They were shipped eastward to the slave-labor camps and the death camps, assured they were destined for resettlement and mainly believing it, with what they could carry, usually two suitcases. On the camp square these were also taken from them, along with the clothes they wore.

Out of this baggage of six million people millions of dollars' worth of booty was extracted, for the European Jews of the time habitually traveled with their wealth upon them, particularly those from Poland and the eastern lands. From the camps entire trainloads of gold trinkets, diamonds, sapphires, rubies, silver ingots, louis d'or, gold dollars, and banknotes of every kind and description were shipped back to the SS headquarters inside Germany. Throughout its history the SS made a profit on its operations. A part of this profit, in the form of gold bars stamped with the eagle of the Reich and the twin-lightning symbol of the SS, was deposited toward the end of the war in the banks of Switzerland, Liechtenstein, Tangier, and Beirut to form the fortune on which the Odessa was later based. Much of this gold still lies beneath the streets of Zurich, guarded by the complacent and self-righteous bankers of that city.

The second stage of the exploitation lay in the living bodies of the victims. They had calories of energy in them, and these could profitably be used. At this point the Jews came onto the same level as the Russians and the Poles, who had been captured penniless in the first place. Those in all categories unfit for work were exterminated as useless. Those able to work were hired out, either to the SS's own factories or to German industrial concerns such as Krupp, Thyssen, von Opel, and others at three marks a day for unskilled workers, four marks for artisans. The phrase "per day" meant as much work as could be extracted from the living body for as little food as possible during a twenty-four-hour period. Hundreds of thousands died at their places of work in this manner.

The SS was a state within a state. It had its own factories, workshops, engineering division, construction section, repair and maintenance shops, and clothing department. It made for itself almost everything it could ever need, and used the slave laborers, which by Hitler's decree were the property of the SS, to do the work.

The third stage of the exploitation lay in the corpses of the dead. These went naked to death, leaving behind wagonloads of shoes, socks, shaving brushes, spectacles, jackets, and trousers. They also left their hair, which was shipped back to the Reich to be turned into felt boots for the winter fighting, and their gold teeth-fillings, which were yanked out of the corpses with pliers and later melted down to be deposited as gold bars in Zurich. Attempts were made to use the bones for fertilizer and render the body fats down for soap, but these were found to be uneconomical.

In charge of the entire economic or profit-making side of the extermination of fourteen million people was the Reich Economic Administration Main Office of the SS, headed by the man in seat 3B on the airliner that night.

Glücks was one who preferred not to risk his neck, or his lifelong liberty, by returning to Germany after his escape. He had no need to. Handsomely provided for out of the secret funds, he could live out his days comfortably in South America, and still does. His dedication to the Nazi ideal remained unshaken by the events of 1945, and this, coupled with his former eminence, secured him a high and honored place among the fugitive Nazis of Argentina, from whence the Odessa was ruled.

The plane landed uneventfully, and the passengers cleared customs with no problems. The fluent Spanish of the first-class passenger from row 3 had long enabled him to pass for a South American.

Outside the terminal building he took a cab and from long habit gave an address a block away from the Zurburán Hotel. After paying off the cab in the center of Madrid, he took his grip and walked the remaining two hundred yards to the hotel.

His reservation assured by Telex, he checked in and went up to his room to shower and shave. It was at nine o'clock on the dot that three soft knocks, followed by a pause and two more, sounded at his door. He opened it himself and stood back when he recognized the visitor.

The new arrival closed the door behind him, snapped to attention, and flashed up his right arm, palm downward, in the old salute.

"*Sieg Heil,*" said the man.

General Glücks gave the younger man an approving nod and raised his own right hand. "*Sieg Heil,*" he said more softly. He waved his visitor to a seat.

The man facing him was another German, a former officer of the SS and at that time the chief of the Odessa network inside West Germany. He felt very keenly the honor of being summoned to Madrid for a personal confer- ence with a senior officer of such eminence, and suspected it had something to do with the death of President Kennedy thirty-six hours earlier. He was not wrong.

General Glücks poured himself and his visitor cups of coffee from the breakfast tray on the table beside him and carefully lit a large Corona.

"You have probably guessed the reason for this sudden and somewhat hazardous visit by me to Europe," he said. "As I dislike remaining on this continent longer than necessary, I will get to the point and be brief."

The subordinate from Germany sat forward expectantly.

"Kennedy is now dead, for us a remarkable stroke of good fortune," the general went on. "There must be no failure to extract the utmost advantage from this event. Do you follow me?"

"Certainly, in principle, General," the younger man replied eagerly, "but in what specific form?"

"I am referring to the secret arms deal between the rabble of traitors in Bonn and the pigs in Tel Aviv. You know about the arms deal? The tanks, guns, and other weaponry even now flowing from Germany to Israel?"

"Yes, of course."

"And you know also that our organization is doing everything in its power to assist the Egyptian cause so that it may one day prove completely victo- rious in the coming struggle?"

"Certainly. We have already organized the recruiting of numerous Ger- man scientists to that end."

General Glücks nodded. "I'll return to that later. What I was referring to was our policy of keeping our Arab friends as closely informed as possible about the details of this treacherous deal, so that they may make the strongest representations to Bonn through diplomatic channels. These Arab protests have led to the formation of a group in Germany strongly opposed to the arms deal on political grounds, because the deal upsets the Arabs. This group, mainly unwittingly, is playing our game for us, bringing pressure on the fool Erhard, even as high as cabinet level, to call off the arms deal."

"Yes. I follow you, General."

"Good. So far Erhard has not called off the arms shipments, but he has wavered several times. For those who wish to see the German-Israeli arms deal completed, the main argument to date has been that the deal is sup- ported by Kennedy, and what Kennedy wants, Erhard gives him."

"Yes. That's true."

"But Kennedy is now dead."

The younger man from Germany sat back, his eyes alight with enthu- siasm, as the new state of affairs opened up its perspectives to his mind. The SS general flicked an inch of ash from the cigar into the coffee cup and jabbed the glowing tip at his subordinate.

"For the rest of this year, therefore, the main plank of political action within Germany that our friends and supporters must undertake will be to whip up public opinion on as wide a scale as possible against this arms deal and in favor of Germany's true and traditional friends, the Arabs."

"Yes, yes, that can be done." The younger man was smiling broadly.

"Certain contracts we have in the government in Cairo will ensure a constant stream of diplomatic protests through their own and other embassies," the general continued. "Other Arab friends will ensure demonstrations by Arab students and German friends of the Arabs. Your job will be to coordinate press publicity through the various pamphlets and magazines we secretly support, advertisements taken in major newspapers and magazines, lobbying of civil servants close to government and politicians who must be persuaded to join the growing weight of opinion against the arms deal."

The younger man's brow furrowed. "It's very difficult to promote feelings against Israel in Germany today," he murmured.

"There need be no question of that," said the other tartly. "The angle is simple: for practical reasons Germany must not alienate eighty million Arabs with these foolish, supposedly secret arms shipments. Many Germans will listen to that argument, particularly diplomats. Known friends of ours in the Foreign Office can be enlisted. Such a practical viewpoint is wholly permissible. Funds, of course, will be made available. The main thing is, with Kennedy dead and Johnson unlikely to adopt the same internationalist, pro-Jewish outlook, Erhard must be subjected to constant pressure at every level, including his own cabinet, to shelve this arms deal. If we can show the Egyptians that we have caused foreign policy in Bonn to change course, our stock in Cairo must inevitably rise sharply."

The man from Germany nodded several times, already seeing his plan of campaign taking shape before him. "It shall be done," he said.

"Excellent," replied General Glücks.

The man in front of him looked up. "General, you mentioned the German scientists now working in Egypt. . . ."

"Ah yes, I said I would return to them later. They represent the second prong in our plan to destroy the Jews once and for all. You know about the rockets of Helwan, of course?"

"Yes, sir. At least, the broad details."

"But not what they are really for?"

"Well, I assumed, of course—"

"That they would be used to throw a few tons of high explosive onto Israel?" General Glücks smiled broadly. "You could not be more wrong. However, I think the time is ripe to tell you why these rockets and the men who build them are in truth so vitally important."

General Glücks leaned back, gazed at the ceiling, and told his subordinate the *real* story behind the rockets of Helwan.

In the aftermath of the war, when King Farouk still ruled Egypt, thousands of Nazis and former members of the SS had fled from Europe and found a sure refuge along the sands of the Nile. Among those who came were a number of scientists. Even before the *coup d'état* that dislodged Farouk, two German scientists had been charged by Farouk with the first studies for the eventual setting up of a factory to manufacture rockets. This was in 1952, and the two professors were Paul Görke and Rolf Engel.

The project went into abeyance for a few years after Naguil and then Nasser took power, but after the military defeat of the Egyptian forces in the 1956 Sinai campaign, the new dictator of Egypt swore an oath. He vowed that one day Israel would be totally destroyed.

In 1961, when he got Moscow's final "No" to his requests for heavy rockets, the Görke-Engel project for an Egyptian rocket factory was revitalized with a vengeance, and during this year, working against the clock and without rein on their expenditure of money, the German professors and the Egyptians built and opened Factory 333, at Helwan, north of Cairo.

To open a factory is one thing; to design and build rockets is another. Long since, the senior supporters of Nasser, mostly with pro-Nazi backgrounds stretching back to the Second World War, had been in close contact with the Odessa representatives in Egypt. From these came the answer to the Egyptians' main problem—that of acquiring the scientists necessary to make the rockets.

Neither Russia, America, Britain, nor France would supply a single man to help. But the Odessa pointed out that the kind of rockets Nasser needed were remarkably similar in size and range to the V-2 rockets that Wernher von Braun and his team had once built at Peenemünde to pulverize London. And many of his former team were still available.

In late 1961 the recruiting of German scientists started. Many of these were employed at the West German Institute for Aerospace Research at Stuttgart. But they were frustrated because the Paris Treaty of 1954 forbade Germany to indulge in research or manufacture in certain realms, notably nuclear physics and rocketry. They were also chronically short of research funds. To many of these scientists the offer of a place in the sun, plenty of research money, and the chance to design real rockets was too tempting.

The Odessa appointed a chief recruiting officer in Germany, and he in turn employed as his legman a former SS sergeant, Heinz Krug. Together they scoured Germany, looking for men prepared to go to Egypt and build Nasser's rocket for him.

With the salaries they could offer, they were not short of choice recruits. Notable among them were Professor Wolfgang Pilz, who had been recruited from postwar Germany by the French and had later become the father of the French Véronique rocket, itself the foundation of De Gaulle's aerospace program. Professor Pilz left for Egypt in early 1962. Dr. Eugen Sänger and his wife Irene, both formerly on the Von Braun V-2 team, also went along, as did Dr. Josef Eisig and Dr. Kirmayer, all experts in propulsions fuels and techniques.

The world saw the first results of their labors at a parade through the streets of Cairo on July 23, 1962, to mark the eighth anniversary of the Egyptian republic. Two rockets, the El Kahira and the El Zafira, respectively with ranges of 500 and 300 kilometers, were trundled past the screaming crowds. Although these rockets were only the casings, without warheads or fuel, they were destined to be the first of four hundred such weapons that would one day be launched against Israel.

General Glücks paused, drew on his cigar, and returned to the present.

"The problem is that, although we solved the matter of making the casings, the warheads, and the fuel, the key to a guided missile lies in the teleguidance system." He stabbed his cigar in the direction of the West German. "And *that* was what we were unable to furnish to the Egyptians," he went on.

"By ill luck, although there were scientists and experts in guidance systems working at Stuttgart and elsewhere, we could not persuade one of them of any value to emigrate to Egypt. All the experts sent out there were specialists in aerodynamics, propulsion, and the design of warheads.

"But we had promised Egypt that she would have her rockets, and have them she will. President Nasser is determined there will one day be another war between Egypt and Israel, and war there will be. He believes his tanks and soldiers alone will win for him. Our information is not so optimistic. They might not, despite their numerical superiority. But just think what our position would be if, when all the Soviet weaponry, bought at a cost of billions of dollars, had failed, it turned out to be the rockets, provided by the scientists recruited through our network, which won the war. Our position would be unassailable. We would have achieved the double *coup* of ensuring an eternally grateful Middle East, a safe and sure home for our people for all time, and of achieving the final and utter destruction of the Jew-pig state, thus fulfilling the last wish of the dying Führer. It is a mighty challenge, and one in which we must not and will not fail."

The subordinate watched his senior officer pacing the room, with awe and some puzzlement. "Forgive me, General, but will four hundred medium warheads really finish off the Jews once and for all? A massive amount of damage, yes, but total destruction?

Glücks spun around and gazed down at the younger man with a triumphant smile.

"But what warheads!" he exclaimed. "You do not think we are going to waste mere high explosive on these swine? We have proposed to President Nasser, and he has accepted with alacrity, that these warheads on the Kahiras and Zafiras be of a different type. Some will contain concentrated cultures of bubonic plague, and the others will explode high above the ground, showering the entire territory of Israel with irradiated cobalt-sixty. Within hours they will all be dying of the pest or of gamma-ray sickness. *That* is what we have in store for them.

The other gazed at him, open-mouthed. "Fantastic," he breathed. "Now I recall reading something about a trial in Switzerland last summer—just rumors, so much of the evidence was *in camera*. Then it's true. But, General, it's brilliant."

"Brilliant, yes, and inevitable, provided we of the Odessa can equip those rockets with the teleguidance systems necessary to direct them not merely in the right direction but to the exact locations where they must explode. The man who controls the entire research operation aimed at devising a teleguidance system for those rockets is now working in West Germany. His code name is Vulkan. You may recall that in Greek mythology Vulkan was the smith who made the thunderbolts of the gods."

"He is a scientist?" asked the West German in bewilderment.

"No, certainly not. When he was forced to disappear in 1955 he would normally have returned to Argentina. But your predecessor was required by us to provide him immediately with a false passport to enable him to stay in Germany. He was then funded out of Zurich with one million American dollars with which to start a factory in Germany. The original purpose was to use the factory as a front for another type of research in which we were interested at the time, but which has now been shelved in favor of the guidance systems for the rockets of Helwan.

"The factory Vulkan now runs manufactures transistor radios. But this is a front. In the research department of the factory a group of scientists is even now in the process of devising the teleguidance systems that will one day be fitted to the rockets of Helwan."

"Why don't they simply go to Egypt?" asked the other.

Glücks smiled again and continued pacing. "That is the stroke of genius behind the whole operation. I told you that there were men in Germany capable of producing such rocket-guidance systems, but none could be persuaded to emigrate. The group of them who now work in the research department of Vulkan's factory actually believe they are working on a contract, in conditions of top secrecy, of course, for the Defense Ministry in Bonn."

This time the subordinate got out of his chair, his coffee spilling on the carpet. "God in Heaven. How on earth was that arranged?"

"Basically quite simple. The Paris Treaty forbids Germany to do research into rockets. The men under Vulkan were sworn to secrecy by a genuine official of the Defense Ministry in Bonn, who also happens to be one of us. He was accompanied by a general whose face the scientists could recognize from the last war. They are all men prepared to work for Germany, even against the terms of the Paris Treaty, but not necessarily prepared to work for Egypt. Now they believe they *are* working for Germany.

"Of course, the cost is stupendous. Normally, research of this nature can only be undertaken by a major power. This entire program has made enormous inroads into our secret funds. Now do you understand the importance of Vulkan?"

"Of course," replied the Odessa chief from Germany. "But if anything happened to him, could not the program go on?"

"No. The factory and the company are owned and run by him alone. He is chairman and managing director, sole shareholder and paymaster. He alone can continue to pay the salaries of the scientists and the enormous research costs involved. None of the scientists ever has anything to do with anyone else in the firm, and no one else in the firm knows the true nature of the overlarge research section. The other workers believe the men in the closed-off section are working on microwave circuits with a view to making a breakthrough in the transistor market. The secrecy is explained as a precaution against industrial espionage. The only link man between the two sections is Vulkan. If he went, the entire project would collapse."

"Can you tell me the name of the factory?"

General Glücks considered for a moment, then mentioned a name.

The other man stared at him in astonishment. "But I know those radios," he protested.

"Of course. It's a bona fide firm and makes bona fide radios."

"And the managing director—he is . . . ?

"Yes. He is Vulkan. Now you see the importance of this man and what he is doing. For that reason there is one other instruction to you. Here." General Glücks took a photograph from his breast pocket and handed it to the man from Germany.

After a long, perplexed gaze at the face, he turned it over and read the name on the back. "Good God, I thought he was in South America."

Glücks shook his head. "On the contrary. He is Vulkan. At the present time his work has reached a most crucial stage. If by any chance, therefore, you should get a whisper of anyone asking inconvenient questions about this man, that person should be—discouraged. One warning, and then a permanent solution. Do you follow me, *Kamerad*? No one, repeat, no one is to get anywhere near exposing Vulkan for who he really is."

The SS general rose. His visitor did likewise.

"That will be all," said Glücks. "You have your instructions."

FOUR

"But you don't even know if he's alive."

Peter Miller and Karl Brandt were sitting side by side in Miller's car outside the house of the detective inspector, where Miller had found him over Sunday lunch on his day off.

"No, I don't. So that's the first thing I have to find out. If Roschmann's dead, obviously that's the end of it. Can you help me?"

Brandt considered the request, then slowly shook his head. "No, sorry, I can't."

"Why not?"

"Look, I gave you that diary as a favor. Just between us. Because it shocked me, because I thought it might make a story for you. But I never thought you were going to try and track Roschmann down. Why can't you just make a story out of the finding of the diary?"

"Because there's no story in it," said Miller. "What am I supposed to say? 'Surprise, surprise, I've just found a looseleaf folder in which an old man who just gassed himself describes what he went through during the war'? You think any editor's going to buy that? I happen to think it's a horrifying document, but that's just my opinion. There have been hundreds of memoirs written since the war. The world's getting tired of them. Just the diary alone won't sell to any editor in Germany."

"So what are you going on about?" asked Brandt.

"Simply this. Get a major police hunt started for Roschmann on the basis of the diary, and I've got a story."

Brandt tapped his ash slowly into the dashboard tray. "There won't be a major police hunt," he said. "Look, Peter, you may know journalism, but I know the Hamburg police. Our job is to keep Hamburg crime-free now, in nineteen sixty-three. Nobody's going to start detaching overworked detectives to hunt a man for what he did in Riga twenty years ago. It's not going to happen."

"But you could at least raise the matter?" asked Miller.

Brandt shook his head. "No. Not me."

"Why not? What's the matter?"

"Because I don't want to get involved. You're all right. You're single, unattached. You can go off chasing will-o'-the-wisps if you want to. I've got a wife and two kids and a good career, and I don't intend to jeopardize that career."

"Why should this jeopardize your career with the police? Roschmann's a criminal, isn't he? Police forces are supposed to hunt criminals. Where's the problem?"

Brandt crushed out his stub. "It's difficult to put your finger on. But there's a sort of attitude in the police, nothing concrete, just a feeling. And that feeling is that to start probing too energetically into the war crimes of the SS can do a young policeman's career no good. Nothing comes of it anyway. The request would simply be denied. But the fact that it was made goes into a file. Then bang goes your chance of promotion. Nobody mentions it, but everyone knows it. So if you want to make a big issue out of this, you're on your own. Count me out."

Miller sat and stared through the windshield. "All right. If that's the way it is," he said at length. "But I've got to start somewhere. Did Tauber leave anything else behind when he died?"

"Well, there was a brief note. I had to take it and include it in my report on the suicide. By now it will have been filed away. And the file's closed."

"What did he say in it?" asked Miller.

"Not much," said Brandt. "He just said he was committing suicide. Oh, there was one thing; he said he left his effects to a friend of his, a Herr Marx."

"Well, that's a start. Where's this Marx?"

"How the hell should I know?" said Brandt.

"You mean to say that's all the note said? Just Herr Marx? No address?"

"Nothing," said Brandt. "Just Marx. No indication where he lives."

"Well, he must be around somewhere. Didn't you look for him?"

Brandt sighed. "Will you get this through your head? We are very busy in the police force. Have you any idea how many Marxes there are in Hamburg? Hundreds in the telephone directory alone. We can't spend weeks looking for this particular Marx. Anyway, what the old man left wasn't worth ten pfennigs."

"That's all, then?" asked Miller. "Nothing else?"

"Not a thing. If you want to find Marx, you're welcome to try."

"Thanks. I will," said Miller. The two men shook hands, and Brandt returned to his family lunch table.

Miller started the next morning by visiting the house where Tauber had lived. The door was opened by a middle-aged man wearing a pair of stained trousers supported by string, a collarless shirt open at the neck, and three days' stubble around his chin.

"Morning. Are you the landlord?"

The man looked Miller up and down and nodded. He smelled of cabbage.

"There was a man gassed himself here a few nights back," said Miller.

"Are you from the police?"

"No. The press." Miller showed the man his press card.

"I ain't got nothing to say."

Miller eased a ten-mark note without too much trouble into the man's hand. "I only want to look at his room."

"I've rented it."

"What did you do with his stuff?"

"It's in the back yard. Nothing else I could do with it."

The pile of junk was lying in a heap under the thin rain. It still smelled of gas. There were a battered old typewriter, two scuffed pairs of shoes, an assortment of clothes, a pile of books, and a fringed white silk scarf that Miller assumed must be something to do with the Jewish religion. He went through everything in the pile, but there was no indication of an address book and nothing addressed to Marx.

"Is that all?" he asked.

"That's all," said the man, regarding him sourly from the shelter of the back door.

"Do you have any tenant by the name of Marx?"

"Nope."

"Do you know of any Marx?"

"Nope."

"Did old Tauber have any friends?"

"Not that I knew of. Kept himself to himself. Came and went at all hours, shuffling about up there. Crazy, if you ask me. But he paid his rent regular. Didn't cause no trouble."

"Ever see him with anybody? Out in the street, I mean."

"No, never. Didn't seem to have any friends. Not surprised, the way he kept mumbling to himself. Crazy."

Miller left and started asking up and down the street. Most people remembered seeing the old man shuffling along, head down, wrapped in an ankle-length overcoat, head covered by a woolen cap, hands in woolen gloves, from which the fingertips protruded.

For three days he quartered the area of streets where Tauber lived, checking through the dairy, the grocer, the butcher, the hardware store, the bar, the tobacconist, intercepting the milkman and the postman. It was Wednesday afternoon when he found the group of urchins playing football up against the warehouse wall.

"What, that old Jew? Mad Solly?" said the leader of the group in answer to his question. The rest gathered around.

"That's the one," said Miller. "Mad Solly."

"He was crazy," said one of the crowd. "He used to walk like this."

The boy hunched his head into his shoulders, hands clutching his jacket around him, and shuffled forward a few paces, muttering to himself and casting his eyes about. The others dissolved in laughter, and one gave the impersonator a hefty shove which sent him sprawling.

"Anyone ever see him with anyone else?" asked Miller. "Talking with anyone else? Another man?"

"Whatcher want to know for?" asked the leader suspiciously. "We didn't do him no harm."

Miller flicked a five-mark coin idly up and down in one hand. Eight pairs of eyes watched the silver glitter of the spinning coin. Eight heads shook slowly. Miller turned and walked away.

"Mister."

He stopped and turned around. The smallest of the group had caught up with him.

"I seen him once with a man. Talking, they was. Sitting and talking."

"Where was that?"

"Down by the river. On the grass bank along the river. There are some benches there. They was sitting on a bench, talking."

"How old was he, the other one?"

"Very old. Lot of white hair."

Miller tossed him the coin, convinced it had been a wasted gesture. But he walked to the river and stared down the length of the grass bank in both directions. There were a dozen benches along the bank, all of them empty. In summer there would be plenty of people sitting along the Elbe Chaussee watching the great liners come in and out, but not at the end of November.

To his left along the near bank lay the fishing port, with half a dozen North Sea trawlers drawn up at the wharfs, discharging their loads of fresh-caught herring and mackerel or preparing for the sea again.

As a boy, Peter had returned to the shattered city from a farm in the country where he had been evacuated during the bombing, and had grown up amid the rubble and the ruins. His favorite playing place had been this fishing port along the river at Altona.

He liked the fishermen, gruff, kindly men who smelled of tar and salt and shag tobacco. He thought of Eduard Roschmann in Riga and wondered how the same country could have produced them both.

His mind came back to Tauber and went over the problem again. Where could he possibly have met his friend Marx? Miller knew there was something missing but could not put his finger on it. It was not until he was back in his car and had stopped for gas close to Altona railway station that the answer came. As so often, it was a chance remark. The pump attendant pointed out there had been a price increase in top-grade gasoline and added, just to make conversation with his customer, that money went less and less far these days. He went to get the change and left Miller staring at the open wallet in his hand.

Money. Where did Tauber get his money? He didn't work. He refused to accept any compensation from the German state. Yet he paid his rent regularly and must have had something left over with which to eat. He was fifty-six years old, so he could not have had an old-age pension, but he could well have had a disability pension. Probably did.

Miller pocketed his change, gunned the Jaguar to life, and drove to the Altona post office. He approached the window marked PENSIONS.

"Can you tell me when the pensioners collect their money?" he asked the fat lady behind the grille.

"Last day of the month, of course," she said.

"That will be Saturday, then?"

"Except on weekends. This month it will be Friday, the day after tomorrow."

"Does that include those with disability pensions?" he asked.

"Everyone who's entitled to a pension collects it on the last day of the month."

"Here, at this window?"

"If the person lives in Altona, yes," replied the woman.

"At what time?"

"From opening time onward."

"Thank you."

Miller was back on Friday morning, watching the queue of old men and women begin to filter through the doors of the post office when it opened. He positioned himself against the wall opposite, watching the directions they took as they departed. Many had white hair, but most wore hats against the cold. The weather had turned dry again, sunny but chill. Just before eleven an old man with a shock of white hair like candy floss came out of the post office, counted his money to make sure it was all there, put it in his inside pocket, and looked around as if searching for someone. After a few minutes he turned and began to walk slowly away. At the corner he looked up and down again, then turned down Museum Street in the direction of the riverbank. Miller eased himself off the wall and followed him.

It took the old man twenty minutes to get the half-mile to the Elbe Chaussee; then he turned up the bank, crossed the grass, and settled himself on a bench. Miller approached slowly from behind.

"Herr Marx?"

The old man turned as Miller came around the end of the bench. He showed no surprise, as though he were often recognized by complete strangers.

"Yes," he said gravely, "I am Marx."

"My name is Miller."

Marx inclined his head gravely in acceptance of this news.

"Are you—er—waiting for Herr Tauber?"

"Yes, I am," said the old man without surprise.

"May I sit down?"

"Please."

Miller sat beside him, so they both faced toward the Elbe River. A giant dry-cargo ship, the *Kota Maru* out of Yokohama, was easing downriver on the tide.

"I'm afraid Herr Tauber is dead."

The old man stared at the passing ship. He showed neither grief nor surprise, as if such news was brought frequently. Perhaps it was.

"I see," he said.

Miller told him briefly about the events of the previous Friday night. "You don't seem surprised. That he killed himself."

"No," said Marx, "he was a very unhappy man."

"He left a diary, you know."

"Yes, he told me once about that."

"Did you ever read it?" asked Miller.

"No, he never let anybody read it. But he told me about it."

"It described the time he spent in Riga during the war."

"Yes, he told me he was in Riga."

"Were you in Riga too?"

The man turned and looked at him with sad old eyes. "No, I was in Dachau."

"Look, Herr Marx, I need your help. In his diary your friend mentioned a man, an SS officer, called Roschmann. Captain Eduard Roschmann. Did he ever mention him to you?"

"Oh, yes. He told me about Roschmann. That was really what kept him alive. Hoping one day to give evidence against Roschmann."

"That's what he said in his diary. I read it after his death. I'm a press reporter. I want to try and find Roschmann. Bring him to trial. Do you understand?"

"Yes."

"But there's no point if Roschmann is already dead. Can you remember if Herr Tauber ever learned whether Roschmann was still alive and free?"

Marx stared out at the disappearing stern of the *Kota Maru* for several minutes.

"Captain Roschmann is alive," he said simply, "and free."

Miller leaned forward earnestly. "How do you know?"

"Because Tauber saw him."

"Yes I read that. It was in early April nineteen forty-five."

Marx shook his head slowly. "No, it was last month."

For several more minutes there was silence as Miller stared at the old man and Marx stared out at the water.

"Last month?" repeated Miller at length. "Did he say how he saw him?"

Marx sighed, then turned to Miller. "Yes. He was walking late at night, as he often used to do when he could not sleep. He was walking back home past the State Opera House just as a crowd of people started to come out. He stopped as they came to the pavement. He said they were wealthy people, the men in dinner jackets, the women in furs and jewels. There were three taxis lined up at the curb waiting for them. The doorman held the passers-by back so they could climb in. And then he saw Roschmann."

"In the crowd of opera-goers?"

"Yes. He climbed into a taxi with two others, and they drove off."

"Now listen, Herr Marx, this is very important. Was he absolutely sure it was Roschmann?"

"Yes, he said he was."

"But it was almost nineteen years since he last saw him. He must have changed a lot. How could he be so sure?"

"He said he smiled."

"He what?"

"He smiled. Roschmann smiled."

"That is significant?"

Marx nodded several times. "He said once you had seen Roschmann smile that way, you never forgot it. He could not describe the smile but just said he would recognize it among a million others, anywhere in the world."

"I see. Do you believe him?"

"Yes. Yes, I believe he saw Roschmann."

"All right. Let's accept that I do too. Did he get the number of the taxi?"

"No. He said his mind was so stunned he just watched it drive away."

"Damn," said Miller. "It probably drove to a hotel. If I had the number I could ask the driver where he took that party. When did Herr Tauber tell you all this?"

"Last month, when we picked up our pensions. Here, on this bench."

Miller stood up and sighed. "You must realize that nobody would ever believe his story?"

Marx shifted his gaze off the river and looked up at the reporter. "Oh yes," he said softly. "He knew that. You see, that was why he killed himself."

That evening Peter Miller paid his usual weekend visit to his mother, and as usual she fussed over whether he was eating enough, the number of cigarettes he smoked in a day, and the state of his laundry. She was a short, plump, matronly person in her early fifties who had never quite resigned herself to the idea that all her only son wanted to be was a reporter.

During the course of the evening she asked him what he was doing at the moment. Briefly he told her, mentioning his intention to try to track down the missing Eduard Roschmann. She was aghast.

Peter ate away stolidly, letting the tide of reproach and recrimination flow over his head.

"It's bad enough that you always have to go around covering the doings of those nasty criminals and people," she was saying, "without going and getting mixed up with those Nazi people. I don't know what your dear father would have thought, I really don't."

A thought struck him. "Mother."

"Yes, dear?"

"During the war—those things that the SS did to people . . . in the camps. Did you ever suspect—did you ever think that it was going on?"

She busied herself furiously, tidying up the table. After a few seconds she spoke. "Horrible things. Terrible things. The British made us look at the films after the war. I don't want to hear any more about it."

She bustled out. Peter rose and followed her into the kitchen. "You remember in nineteen fifty when I was sixteen and I went to Paris with a school party?"

She paused, filling the sink for the dishwashing. "Yes, I remember."

"And we were taken to see a church called the Sacré Coeur. And there was a service just finishing, a memorial service for a man called Jean Moulin. Some people came out, and they heard me speaking German to another boy. One of the group turned and spat at me. I remember the spittle running down my jacket. I remember I came home later and told you about it. Do you remember what you said?"

Mrs. Miller was furiously scouring a dinner plate.

"You said the French were like that. Dirty habits, you said."

"Well, they have. I never did like them."

"Look, Mother, do you know what we did to Jean Moulin before he died? Not you, not Father, not me. But us, the Germans, or rather the Gestapo, which for millions of foreigners seems to be the same thing."

"I don't want to hear. Now, that's enough of that."

"Well, I can't tell you, because I don't know. Doubtless it's recorded somewhere. But the point is, I was spat on not because I was in the Gestapo, but because I'm a German."

"And you should be proud of it."

"Oh, I am, believe me, I am. But that doesn't mean I've got to be proud of the Nazis and the SS and the Gestapo."

"Well, nobody is, but there's no point in keeping talking about it."

She was flustered, as always when he argued with her, drying her hands on the dishtowel before bustling back into the living room. He trailed after her.

"Look, Mother, try to understand. Until I read that diary I never even asked precisely what it was we were all supposed to have done. Now at least I'm beginning to understand. That's why I want to find this man, this monster, if he's still around. It's right that he should be brought to trial."

She sat on the settee, close to tears. "Please, Peterkin, leave them alone. Just don't keep probing into the past. It won't do any good. It's over now, over and done with. It's best forgotten."

Peter Miller was facing the mantelpiece, which was dominated by the clock and the photograph of his dead father, who was wearing his Army captain's uniform, staring out of the frame with the kind, rather sad smile that Miller remembered. It was taken before he returned to the front after his last leave.

Peter remembered his father with startling clarity, looking at his photograph nineteen years later as his mother asked him to drop the Roschmann inquiry. He could remember before the war, when he was five years old, and his father had taken him to Hagenbeck's zoo and pointed out all the animals to him, one by one, patiently reading the details off the little tin plaques in front of each cage to reply to the endless flow of questions from the boy.

He could remember how his father came home after enlisting in 1940, and how his mother had cried and how he had thought how stupid women are to cry over such a wonderful thing as having a father in uniform. He recalled the day in 1944 when he was ten years old, and an Army officer had come to the door to tell his mother that her war-hero husband had been killed on the Eastern Front.

"Besides, nobody wants these awful exposés any more. Nor these terrible trials that we keep having, with everything dragged out into the open again. Nobody's going to thank you for it, even if you do find him. They'll just point to you in the street; I mean, they don't want any more trials. Not now, it's too late. Just drop it, Peter, please, for my sake."

He remembered the black-edged column of names in the newspaper, the same length as every day, but different that day in late October, for halfway down was the entry: "Fallen for Führer and Fatherland. Miller, Erwin, Captain, on October 11. In Ostland."

And that was it. Nothing else. No hint of where, or when, or why. Just one of tens of thousands of names pouring back from the east to fill the ever-lengthening black-edged columns, until the government had ceased to print them because they destroyed morale.

"I mean," said his mother behind him, "you might at least think of your father's memory. You think he'd want his son digging around into the past, trying to drag up another war-crimes trial? Do you think that's what he'd want?"

Miller spun around and walked across the room to his mother, placed both hands on her shoulders, and looked down into her frightened china-blue eyes. He stooped and kissed her lightly on the forehead.

"Yes, Mutti," he said. "I think that's exactly what he'd want."

He let himself out, climbed into his car, and headed back into Hamburg, his anger seething inside him.

Everyone who knew him and many who did not agreed Hans Hoffmann looked the part. He was in his late forties, boyishly handsome with carefully styled graying hair cut in the latest trendy fashion, and manicured fingers. His medium-gray suit was from Savile Row, his heavy silk tie was from Cardin. There was an air of expensive good taste of the kind money can buy about him.

If looks had been his only asset he would not have been one of West Germany's wealthiest and most successful magazine-publishers. Starting after the war with a hand-operated press, turning out handbills for the British Occupation authorities, he had founded in 1949 one of the first weekly picture magazines. His formula was simple—tell it in words and make it shocking, then back it up with pictures that make all competitors look like novices with their first box Brownies. It worked. His chain of eight magazines ranging from love stories for teenagers to the glossy chronicle of the doings of the rich and sexy had made him a multimillionaire. But *Komet,* the news and current-affairs magazine, was still his favorite, his baby.

The money had bought him a luxurious ranch-style house at Othmarschen, a chalet in the mountains, a villa by the sea, a Rolls-Royce, and a Ferrari. Along the way he had picked up a beautiful wife, whom he dressed from Paris, and two handsome children he seldom saw. The only millionaire in Germany whose succession of young mistresses, discreetly maintained and frequently exchanged, were never photographed in his gossip magazine was Hans Hoffmann. He was also very astute.

That Wednesday after he closed the cover of the diary of Salomon Tauber after reading the beginning, leaned back, and looked at the young reporter opposite.

"All right. I can guess the rest. What do you want?"

"I think that's a great document," said Miller. "There's a man mentioned throughout the diary called Eduard Roschmann. Captain in the SS. Commandant of Riga ghetto throughout. Killed eighty thousand men, women, and children. I believe he's alive and here in West Germany. I want to find him."

"How do you know he's alive?"

Miller told him briefly.

Hoffmann pursed his lips. "Pretty thin evidence."

"True. But worth a second look. I've brought home stories that started on less."

Hoffmann grinned, recalled Miller's talent for ferreting out stories that hurt the Establishment. Hoffmann had been happy to print them, once they were checked out as accurate. They sent circulation soaring.

"Then presumably this man—what do you call him, Roschmann? Presumably he's already on the wanted list. If the police can't find him, what makes you think you can?"

"Are the police really looking?" asked Miller.

Hoffman shrugged. "They're supposed to. That's what we pay them for."

"It wouldn't hurt to help a little, would it? Just check out whether he's really alive, whether he was ever picked up; if so, what happened to him?"

"So what do you want from me?" asked Hoffmann.

"A commission to give it a try. If nothing comes of it, I drop it."

Hoffmann swung in his chair, spinning around to face the picture windows looking out over the sprawling docks, mile after mile of cranes and wharfs spread out twenty floors below and a mile away.

"It's a bit out of your line, Miller. Why the sudden interest?"

Miller thought hard. Trying to sell an idea was always the hardest part. A freelance reporter has to sell the story, or the idea of the story, to the publisher or the editor first. The public comes much later.

"It's a good human-interest story. If *Komet* could find the man where the police forces of the country had failed, it would be a scoop. Something people want to know about."

Hoffmann gazed out at the December skyline and slowly shook his head. "You're wrong. That's why I'm not giving you a commission for it. I should think it's the last thing people want to know about."

"But look, Herr Hoffmann, this is different. These people Roschmann killed—they weren't Poles and Russians. These were Germans—all right, German Jews, but they *were* Germans. Why wouldn't people want to know about it?"

Hoffmann spun back from the window, put his elbows on the desk, and rested his chin on his knuckles. "Miller, you're a good reporter. I like the way you cover a story; you've got style. And you're a ferret. I can hire twenty, fifty, a hundred men in this city by picking up the phone, and they'll all do what they're told, cover the stories they're sent to cover. But they can't dig out a story for themselves. You can. That's why you get a lot of work from me and will get a lot more in the future. But not this one."

"But why? It's a good story."

"Listen, you're young. I'll tell you something about journalism. Half of journalism is about writing good stories. The other half is about selling them. You can do the first bit, but I can do the second. That's why I'm here and you're there. You think this is a story everyone will want to read because the victims of Riga were German Jews. I'm telling you that's exactly why *no one* will want to read the story. It's the last story in the world they'll want to read. And until there's a law in this country forcing people to buy magazines and read what's good for them, they'll go on buying magazines to read what they want to read. And that's what I give them. What they want to read."

"Then why not about Roschmann?"

"You still don't get it? Then I'll tell you. Before the war just about everyone in Germany knew at least one Jew. The fact is, before Hitler started, nobody hated the Jews in Germany. We had the best record of treatment of our Jewish minority of any country in Europe. Better than France, better than Spain, infinitely better than Poland and Russia, where the pogroms were fiendish.

"Then Hitler started. Telling people the Jews were to blame for the First War, the unemployment, the poverty, and everything else that was wrong. People didn't know what to believe. Almost everyone knew one Jew who was a nice guy. Or just harmless. People had Jewish friends, good friends; Jewish employers, good employers; Jewish employees, hard workers. They obeyed the laws; they didn't hurt anyone. And here was Hitler saying they were to blame for everything.

"So when the vans came and took them away, people didn't do anything.

They stayed out of the way, they kept quiet. They even got to believing the voice that shouted the loudest. Because that's the way people are, particularly the Germans. We're a very obedient people. It's our greatest strength and our greatest weakness. It enables us to build an economic miracle while the British are on strike, and it enables us to follow a man like Hitler into a great big mass grave.

"For years people haven't asked what happened to the Jews of Germany. They just disappeared—nothing else. It's bad enough to read at every war-crimes trial what happened to the faceless, anonymous Jews of Warsaw, Lublin, Bialystok—nameless, unknown Jews from Poland and Russia. Now you want to tell them, chapter and verse, what happened to their next-door neighbors. Now can you understand it? These Jews"—he tapped the diary— "these people they knew, they greeted them in the street, they bought in their shops, and they stood around while they were taken away for your Herr Roschmann to deal with. You think they want to read about that? You couldn't have picked a story that people in Germany want to read about less."

Having finished, Hans Hoffmann leaned back, selected a fine panatela from a humidor on the desk, and lit it from a rolled-gold Dupont. Miller sat and digested what he had not been able to work out for himself.

"That must have been what my mother meant," he said at length.

Hoffmann grunted. "Probably."

"I still want to find that bastard."

"Leave it alone, Miller. Drop it. No one will thank you."

"That's not the only reason, is it? The public reaction. There's another reason, isn't there?"

Hoffmann eyed him keenly through the cigar smoke. "Yes," he said shortly.

"Are you afraid of them—still?" asked Miller.

Hoffmann shook his head. "No. I just don't go looking for trouble, that's all."

"What kind of trouble?"

"Have you ever heard of a man called Hans Habe?" asked Hoffmann.

"The novelist? Yes, what about him?"

"He used to run a magazine in Munich once. Back in the early fifties. A good one too—he was a damn good reporter, like you. *Echo of the Week*, it was called. He hated the Nazis, so he ran a series of exposés of former SS men living in freedom in Munich."

"What happened to him?"

"To him, nothing. One day he got more mail than usual. Half the letters were from his advertisers, withdrawing their custom. Another was from his bank, asking him to drop around. When he did, he was told the bank was foreclosing on the overdraft, as of that minute. Within a week the magazine was out of business. Now he writes novels, good ones too. But he doesn't run a magazine any more."

"So what do the rest of us do? Keep running scared?"

Hoffmann jerked his cigar out of his mouth. "I don't have to take that from you, Miller," he said, his eyes snapping. "I hated the bastards then and I hate them now. But I know my readers. And they don't want to know about Eduard Roschmann."

"All right. I'm sorry. But I'm still going to cover it."

"You know, Miller, if I didn't know you, I'd think there was something personal behind it. Never let journalism get personal. It's bad for reporting, and it's bad for the reporter. Anyway, how are you going to finance yourself?"

"I've got some savings." Miller rose to go.

"Best of luck," said Hoffmann, rising and coming around the desk. "I tell you what I'll do. The day Roschmann is arrested and imprisoned by the West German police, I'll commission you to cover the story. That's straight news, so it's public property. If I decide not to print, I'll buy it out of my pocket. That's as far as I'll go. But while you're digging for him, you're not carrying the letterhead of my magazine around as your authority."

Miller nodded. "I'll be back," he said.

FIVE

Wednesday morning was also the time of the week when the heads of the five branches of the Israeli Intelligence apparat met for their informal weekly discussion.

In most countries the rivalry between the various separate Intelligence services is legendary. In Russia the KGB hates the guts of the GRU; in America the FBI will not cooperate with the CIA. The British Security Service regards Scotland Yard's Special Branch as a crowd of flat-footed coppers, and there are so many crooks in the French SDECE that experts wonder whether the French Intelligence service is part of the government or the underworld.

But Israel is fortunate. Once a week the chiefs of the five branches meet for a friendly chat without interdepartmental friction. It is one of the dividends of being a nation surrounded by enemies. At these meetings coffee and soft drinks are passed around, those present use first names to each other, the atmosphere is relaxed, and more work gets done than could be effected by a torrent of written memoranda.

It was to this meeting that the Controller of the Mossad and chief of the joint five branches of Israeli Intelligence, General Meir Amit, was traveling on the morning of December 4. Beyond the windows of his long black chauffeur-driven limousine a fine dawn was beaming down on the whitewashed sprawl of Tel Aviv. But the general's mood failed to match it. He was a deeply worried man.

The cause of his worry was a piece of information that had reached him in the small hours of the morning. A small fragment of knowledge to be added to the immense file in the archives, but vital, for the file into which that dispatch from one of his agents in Cairo would be added was the file on the rockets of Helwan.

The forty-two-year-old general's poker face betrayed nothing of his feelings as the car swung around the Zina Circus and headed toward the northern suburbs of the capital. He leaned back on the upholstery of his seat and considered the long history of those rockets being built north of Cairo, which had already cost several men their lives and had cost his predecessor, General Issar Harel, his job. . . .

During the course of 1961, long before Nasser's two rockets went on public display in the streets of Cairo, the Israeli Mossad had learned of their existence. From the moment the first dispatch came through from Egypt, it had kept Factory 333 under constant surveillance.

It was perfectly well aware of the large-scale recruitment by the Egyptians, through the good offices of the Odessa, of German scientists to work on the rockets of Helwan. It was a serious matter then; it became infinitely more serious in the spring of 1962.

In May that year Heinz Krug, the German recruiter of the scientists, first made approaches to the Austrian physicist Dr. Otto Yoklek in Vienna. Instead of allowing himself to be recruited, the Austrian professor made contact with the Israelis. What he had to say electrified Tel Aviv. He told the agent of the Mossad who was sent to interview him that the Egyptians intended to arm their rockets with warheads containing irradiated nuclear waste and cultures of bubonic plague.

So important was the news that the Controller of the Mossad, General Issar Harel, the man who had personally escorted the kidnaped Adolf Eichmann back from Buenos Aires to Tel Aviv, flew to Vienna to talk to Yoklek himself. He was convinced the professor was right, a conviction corroborated by the news that the Cairo government had just purchased through a firm in Zurich a quantity of radioactive cobalt equivalent to twenty-five times Egypt's possible requirement for medical purposes.

On his return from Vienna, Issar Harel went to see Premier David Ben-Gurion and urged that he be allowed to begin a campaign of reprisals against the German scientists who were either working in Egypt or about to go there. The old Premier was in a quandary. On the one hand he realized the hideous danger the new rockets and their genocidal warheads presented to his people; on the other, he recognized the value of the German tanks and guns due to arrive at any moment. Israeli reprisals on the streets of Germany might just be enough to persuade Chancellor Adenauer to listen to his Foreign Ministry faction and shut off the arms deal.

Inside the Tel Aviv cabinet there was a split developing similar to the split inside the Bonn cabinet over the arms sales. Issar Harel and the Foreign Minister, Madame Golda Meir, were in favor of a tough policy against the German scientists; Shimon Peres and the Army were terrified by the thought they might lose their precious German tanks. Ben-Gurion was torn between the two.

He hit on a compromise; he authorized Harel to undertake a muted, discreet campaign to discourage German scientists from going to Cairo to help Nasser build his rockets. But Harel, with his burning gut-hatred of Germany and all things German, went beyond his brief.

On September 11, 1962, Heinz Krug disappeared. He had dined the previous evening with Dr. Kleinwachter, the rocket-propulsion expert he was going to recruit, and an unidentified Egyptian. On the morning of the eleventh, Krug's car was found abandoned close to his home in a suburb of

Munich. His wife immediately claimed he had been kidnaped by Israeli agents, but the Munich police found not a trace either of Krug or of evidence as to his kidnapers. In fact, he had been abducted by a group of men led by a shadowy figure called Leon, and his body dumped in the Starnberg lake, assisted to the weedbed by a corset of heavy-link chain.

The campaign then turned against the Germans in Egypt already. On November 27 a registered package, mailed in Hamburg and addressed to Professor Wolfgang Pilz, the rocket scientist who had worked for the French, arrived in Cairo. It was opened by his secretary, Miss Hannelore Wenda. In the ensuing explosion the girl was maimed and blinded for life.

On November 28 another package, also mailed in Hamburg, arrived at Factory 333. By this time the Egyptians had set up a security screen for arriving parcels. It was an Egyptian official in the mail room who cut the cord. Five dead and ten wounded. On November 29 a third package was defused without an explosion.

By February 20, 1963, Harel's agents had turned their attention once again to Germany. Dr. Heinz Kleinwachter, still undecided whether to go to Cairo or not, was driving back home from his laboratory at Lörrach, near the Swiss frontier, when a black Mercedes barred his route. He threw himself to the floor as a man emptied his automatic through the windshield. Police subsequently discovered the black Mercedes abandoned. It had been stolen earlier in the day. In the glove compartment was an identity card in the name of Colonel Ali Samir. Inquiries revealed this was the name of the chief of the Egyptian Secret Service. Issar Harel's agents had got their message across, with a touch of black humor for good measure.

By now the reprisal campaign was making headlines in Germany. It became a scandal with the Ben-Gal affair. On March 2, young Heidi Görke, daughter of Professor Paul Görke, pioneer of Nasser's rockets, received a telephone call at her home in Freiburg, Germany. A voice suggested she meet the caller at the Three Kings Hotel in Basel, Switzerland, just over the border.

Heidi informed the German police, who tipped off the Swiss. They planted a bugging device in the room that had been reserved for the meeting. During the meeting, two men in dark glasses warned Heidi Görke and her young brother to persuade their father to get out of Egypt if he valued his life. Tailed to Zurich and arrested the same night, the two men went on trial at Basel on June 10, 1963. It was an international scandal. The chief of the two agents was Yosef Ben-Gal, Israeli citizen.

The trial went well. Professor Yoklek testified as to the warheads of plague and radioactive waste, and the judges were scandalized. Making the best of a bad job, the Israeli government used the trial to expose the Egyptian intent to commit genocide. Shocked, the judges acquitted the two accused.

But back in Israel there was a reckoning. Although the German Chancellor Adenauer had personally promised Ben-Gurion he would try to stop German scientists from taking part in the Helwan rocket-building, Ben-Gurion was humiliated by the scandal. In a rage, he rebuked General Issar Harel for the lengths to which he had gone in his campaign of intimidation. Harel responded with vigor and handed in his resignation. To his surprise, Ben-Gurion accepted it, proving the point that no one in Israel is indispensable, not even the Chief of Intelligence.

That night, June 20, 1963, Issar Harel had a long talk with his close friend, General Meir Amit, then the head of Military Intelligence. General Amit could remember the conversation clearly, the taut, angry face of the Russian-born fighter, nicknamed Issar the Terrible.

"I have to inform you, my dear Meir, that as from now Israel is no longer in the retribution business. The politicians have taken over. I have tendered my resignation, and it has been accepted. I have asked that you be named my successor, and I believe they will agree."

The ministerial committee that in Israel presides over the activities of the Intelligence networks agreed. At the end of June, General Meir Amit became Chief of Intelligence.

The knell had also sounded, however, for Ben-Gurion. The hawks of his cabinet, headed by Levi Eshkol and his own Foreign Minister, Golda Meir, forced his resignation, and on June 26, 1963, Levi Eshkol was named Prime Minister. Ben-Gurion, shaking his snowy head in anger, went down to his kibbutz in the Negev in disgust. But he remained a member of the Knesset.

Although the new government had ousted David Ben-Gurion, it did not reinstate Issar Harel. Perhaps it felt that Meir Amit was a general more likely to obey orders than the choleric Harel, who had become a legend in his own lifetime among the Israeli people and relished it.

Nor were Ben-Gurion's last orders rescinded. General Amit's instructions remained the same—to avoid any more scandals in Germany over the rocket scientists. With no alternative, he turned the terror campaign against the scientists already inside Egypt.

These Germans lived in the suburb of Meadi, seven miles south of Cairo on the bank of the Nile—a pleasant suburb, except that it was ringed by Egyptian security troops and its German inhabitants were almost prisoners in a gilded cage. To get at them, Meir Amit used his top agent inside Egypt, the riding-school-owner Wolfgang Lutz, who found himself from September 1963 onward forced to take suicidal risks, which sixteen months later would lead to his undoing.

For the German scientists, already shaken badly by the series of bomb parcels sent from Germany, the autumn of 1963 became a nightmare. In the heat of Meadi, ringed by Egyptian security guards, they began to get letters threatening their lives, mailed from Cairo.

Dr. Josef Eisig received one which described his wife, his two children, and the type of work he was engaged in with remarkable precision, then told him to get out of Egypt and go back to Germany. All the other scientists got the same kind of letter. On September 27 a letter blew up in the face of Dr. Kirmayer. For some of the scientists this was the last straw. At the end of September, Dr. Pilz left Cairo for Germany, taking the unfortunate Fräulein Wenda with him.

Others followed, and the furious Egyptians were unable to stop them, for they could not protect them from the threatening letters.

The man in the back of the limousine that bright winter morning in 1963 knew that his own agent, the supposedly pro-Nazi German Lutz, was the writer of the letters and the sender of the explosives.

But he also knew the rocket program was not being halted. The information he had just received proved it. He flicked his eye over the decoded message once again. It confirmed simply that a virulent strain of bubonic bacillus had been isolated in the contagious-diseases laboratory of Cairo Medical Institute, and that the budget of the department involved had been increased tenfold. The information left no doubt that, despite the adverse publicity Egypt had received over the Ben-Gal trial in Basel the previous summer, the government was going ahead with the genocide program.

Had Hoffmann been watching, he would have been forced to give Miller full marks for cheek. After leaving the penthouse office, he took the elevator down to the fifth floor and dropped in to see Max Dorn, the magazine's legal-affairs correspondent.

"I've just been up to see Herr Hoffmann," he said, dropping into a chair in front of Dorn's desk. "Now I need some background. Mind if I pick your brains?"

"Go ahead," said Dorn, assuming Miller had been commissioned to do a story for *Komet*.

"Who investigates war crimes in Germany?"

The question took Dorn aback. "War crimes?"

"Yes. War crimes. Which authorities are responsible for investigating what happened in all the various countries we overran during the war, and finding and prosecuting the individuals guilty of mass murder?"

"Oh, I see what you mean. Well, basically it's the various attorney generals' offices of the provinces of West Germany."

"You mean they *all* do it?"

Dorn leaned back in his chair, at home in his own field of expertise. "There are sixteen provinces in West Germany. Each has a state capital and a state attorney general. Inside each SAG's office there is a department responsible for investigation into what are called 'crimes of violence committed during the Nazi era.' Each state capital is allocated in an area of the former Reich or of the occupied territories as its special responsibility."

"Such as?" asked Miller.

"Well, for example, all crimes committed by the Nazis and the SS in Italy, Greece, and Polish Galicia are investigated by Stuttgart. The biggest extermination camp of all, Auschwitz, comes under Frankfurt. You may have heard there's a big trial coming up in Frankfurt next May of twenty-two former guards from Auschwitz. Then the extermination camps of Treblinka, Chelmno, Sobibor, and Maidanek are investigated by Düsseldorf-Cologne. Munich is responsible for Belzec, Dachau, Buchenwald, and Flosenburg. Most crimes in the Soviet Ukraine and the Lódz area of former Poland come under Hanover. And so on."

Miller noted the information, nodding. "Who is supposed to investigate what happened in the three Baltic States?" he asked.

"Hamburg," said Dorn promptly, "along with crimes in the areas of Danzig and the Warsaw sector of Poland."

"Hamburg?" said Miller. "You mean it's right here in Hamburg?"

"Yes. Why?"

"Well, it's Riga I'm interested in."

Dorn grimaced. "Oh, I see. The German Jews. Well, that's the pigeon of the SAG's office right here."

"If there had ever been a trial, or even an arrest, of anyone who had been guilty of crimes in Riga, it would have been here in Hamburg?"

"The trial would have been," said Dorn. "The arrest could have been made anywhere."

"What's the procedure with arrests?"

"Well, there's a book called the Wanted Book. In it is the name of every wanted war criminal, with surname, first names, and date of birth. Usually the SAG's office covering the area where the man committed the crimes spends years preparing the case against him before arrest. Then, when it's ready, it requests the police of the state in which the man is living to arrest him. A couple of detectives go there and bring him back. If a very much wanted man is discovered, he can be arrested wherever he's discovered, and the appropriate SAG's office informed that he's being held. Then they go and bring him back. The trouble is, most of the big SS men are not living under their own names."

"Right," said Miller. "Has there ever been a trial in Hamburg of anyone guilty of crimes committed in Riga?"

"Not that I remember," said Dorn.

"Would it be in the clippings library?"

"Sure. If it happened since 1950, when we started the clippings library, it'll be there."

"Mind if we look?" asked Miller.

"No problem."

The library was in the basement, tended by five archivists in gray smocks. It was almost half an acre in size, filled by row upon row of gray steel shelves on which reposed reference books of every kind and description. Around the walls, from floor to ceiling, were steel filing cabinets, the doors of each drawer indicating the contents of the files within.

"What do you want?" asked Dorn as the chief librarian approached.

"Roschmann, Eduard," said Miller.

"Personal index section, this way," said the librarian and led the way along one wall. He opened a cabinet door labeled ROA-ROZ, and flicked through it.

"Nothing on Roschmann, Eduard," he said.

Miller thought. "Do you have anything on war crimes?" he asked.

"Yes," said the librarian. "War crimes and war trials section, this way."

They went along another hundred yards of cabinets.

"Look under Riga," said Miller.

The librarian mounted a stepladder and foraged. He came back with a red folder. It bore the label RIGA—WAR CRIMES TRIAL. Miller opened it. Two pieces of newsprint the size of large postage stamps fluttered out. Miller picked them up. Both were from the summer of 1950. One recorded that three SS privates had gone on trial for brutalities committed at Riga between 1941 and 1944. The other recorded that they had all three been sentenced to long terms of imprisonment. Not long enough: they would all be free by late 1963.

"Is that it?" asked Miller.

"That's it," said the librarian.

"Do you mean to say," said Miller, turning to Dorn, "that a section of the State Attorney General's office has been beavering away for fifteen years on my tax money, and all it's got to show for it is two postage stamps?"

Dorn was a rather Establishment figure. "I'm sure they're doing their best," he said huffily.

"I wonder," said Miller.

They parted in the main hall two floors up, and Miller went out into the rain.

The building in the northern suburbs of Tel Aviv that houses the headquarters of the Mossad excites no attention, even from its nearest neighbors. The entrance to the underground garage of the office building is flanked by quite ordinary shops. On the ground floor is a bank, and in the entrance hall, before the plate-glass doors that lead into the bank, are an elevator, a board stating the business of the firms on the floors above, and a porter's desk for inquiries.

The board reveals that in the building are the offices of several trading companies, two insurance firms, an architect, an engineering consultant, and an import-export company on the top floor. Inquiries for any of the firms below the top floor will be met courteously. Questions asked about the top-floor company are politely refused an answer. The company on the top floor is the front for the Mossad.

The room where the chiefs of Israeli Intelligence meet is bare and cool, white-painted, with a long table and chairs around the walls. At the table sit the five men who control the branches of Intelligence. Behind them on the chairs sit clerks and stenographers. Other nonmembers can be invited for a hearing if required, but this is seldom done. The meetings are classified top secret, for all confidences may be aired.

At the head of the table sits the Controller of the Mossad. Founded in 1937, its full name Mossad Aliyah Beth, or Organization for the Second Immigration, the Mossad was the first Israeli Intelligence organ. Its first job was to get Jews from Europe to a safe berth in Palestine.

After the founding of the state of Israel in 1948, it became the senior of all Intelligence organs, its controller automatically the head of all the five.

To the Controller's right sits the Chief of the Aman, the Military Intelligence unit whose job is to keep Israel informed of the state of war-readiness of her enemies. The man who held the job at that time was General Aharon Yaariv.

To the left sits the Chief of the Shabak, sometimes wrongly referred to as the Shin Beth. These letters stand for Sherut Bitachon, the Hebrew for "Security Service." The full title of the organ that watches over Israel's internal security, and *only* internal security, is Sherut Bitachon Klali, and it is from these three words that the abbreviation Shabak is taken.

Beyond these two men sit the last two of the five. One is the Director General of the research division of the Foreign Ministry, charged specifically with the evaluation of the political situation in Arab capitals, a matter of vital importance to the security of Israel. The other is the director of a service solely occupied with the fate of Jews in the "countries of persecution." These countries include all the Arab countries and all the Communist countries. So that there shall be no overlapping of activities, the weekly meetings enable each chief to know what the other departments are doing.

Two other men are present as observers, the Inspector General of police, and the head of the Special Branch, the executive arms of the Shabak in the fight against terrorism inside the country.

The meeting on that day was quite normal. Meir Amit took his place at the head of the table, and the discussion began. He saved his bombshell until last. When he had made his statement, there was silence as the men present, including the aides scattered around the walls, had a mental vision of their country dying as the radioactive and plague warheads slammed home.

"The point surely is," said the head of the Shabak at last, "that those rockets must never fly. If we cannot prevent them from making warheads, we have to prevent the warheads from ever taking off."

"Agreed," said Amit, taciturn as ever, "but how?"

"Hit them," growled Yaariv. "Hit them with everything we've got. Ezer Weizmann's jets can take out Factory 333 in one raid."

"And start a war with nothing to fight with," replied Amit. "We need more planes, more tanks, more guns before we can take Egypt. I think we all know, gentlemen, that war is inevitable. Nasser is determined on it, but he will not fight until he is ready. But if we force it on him now, the simple answer is that he, with his Russian weaponry, is more ready than we are."

There was silence again. The head of the Foreign Ministry Arab section spoke.

"Our information from Cairo is that they think they will be ready in early nineteen sixty-seven, rockets and all."

"We will have our tanks and guns by then, and our new French jets," replied Yaariv.

"Yes, and they will have those rockets from Helwan. Four hundred of them. Gentlemen, there is only one answer. By the time we are ready for Nasser, those rockets will be in silos all over Egypt. They'll be unreachable. For, once they are in their silos and ready to fire, we must not simply take out ninety per cent of them but all of them. And not even Ezer Weizmann's fighter pilots can take them all, without exception."

"Then we have to take them in the factory at Helwan," said Yaariv with finality.

"Agreed," said Amit, "but without a military attack. We shall just have to try to force the German scientists to resign before they have finished their work. Remember, the research stage is almost at an end. We have six months. After that the Germans won't matter any more. The Egyptians can build the rockets, once they are designed down to the last nut and bolt. Therefore I shall step up the campaign against the scientists in Egypt and keep you informed."

For several seconds there was silence again as the unspoken question ran through the minds of all those present. It was one of the men from the Foreign Ministry who finally voiced it.

"Couldn't we discourage them inside Germany again?"

General Amit shook his head. "No. That remains out of the question in the prevailing political climate. The orders from our superiors remain the same:

no more muscle tactics inside Germany. For us from henceforth the key to the rockets of Helwan lies inside Egypt."

General Meir Amit, Controller of the Mossad, was not often wrong. But he was wrong that time. For the key to the rockets of Helwan lay in a factory inside West Germany.

SIX

It took Miller a week before he could get an interview with the chief of section in the department of the Hamburg Attorney General's office responsible for investigation into war crimes. He suspected Dorn had found out he was not working at Hoffmann's behest and had reacted accordingly.

The man he confronted was nervous, ill at ease. "You must understand I have only agreed to see you as a result of your persistent inquiries," he began.

"That's nice of you all the same," said Miller ingratiatingly. "I want to inquire about a man whom I assume your department must have under permanent investigation, called Eduard Roschmann."

"Roschmann?" said the lawyer.

"Roschmann," repeated Miller. "Captain of the SS. Commandant of Riga ghetto from nineteen forty-one to nineteen forty-four. I want to know if he's alive; if not, where he's buried. If you have found him, if he has ever been arrested, and if he has ever been on trial. If not, where he is now."

The lawyer was shaken. "Good Lord, I can't tell you that," he said.

"Why not? It's a matter of public interest. Enormous public interest."

The lawyer had recovered his poise. "I hardly think so," he said smoothly. "Otherwise we would be receiving constant inquiries of this nature. Actually, so far as I can recall, yours is the first inquiry we've ever had from . . . a member of the public."

"Actually, I'm a member of the press," said Miller.

"Yes, that may be. But I'm afraid as regards this kind of information that only means you are entitled to as much as one would give a member of the public."

"How much is that?" asked Miller.

"I'm afraid we are not empowered to give information regarding the progress of our inquiries."

"Well, that's not right, to start with," said Miller.

"Oh, come now, Herr Miller, you would hardly expect the police to give you information about the progress of *their* inquiries in a criminal case."

"I would. In fact, that's just what I do. The police are customarily very helpful in issuing bulletins on whether an early arrest may be expected. Certainly they'd tell a journalist if their main suspect was, to their knowledge, alive or dead. It helps their relations with the public."

The lawyer smiled thinly. "I'm sure you perform a very valuable function in that regard," he said. "But from this department no information may be issued on the state of progress of our work." He seemed to hit on a point of argument. "Let's face it: if wanted criminals knew how close we were to completing the case against them, they'd disappear."

"That may be so," answered Miller. "But the records show your department has only put on trial three privates who were guards in Riga. And that was in nineteen fifty, so the men were probably in pretrial detention when the British handed them over to your department. So the wanted criminals don't seem to be in much danger of being forced to disappear."

"Really, that's a most unwarranted suggestion."

"All right. So your inquiries are progressing. It still wouldn't harm your case if you were to tell me quite simply whether Eduard Roschmann is under investigation, and where he is now."

"All I can say is that all matters concerning the area of responsibility of my department are under constant inquiry. I repeat, constant inquiry. And now I really think, Herr Miller, there is nothing more I can do to help you."

He rose, and Miller followed suit. "Don't bust a gut," he said as he walked out.

It was another week before Miller was ready to move. He spent it mainly at home, reading six books concerned in whole or in part with the war along the Eastern Front and the things that had been done in the camps in the occupied eastern territories. It was the librarian at his local library who mentioned the Z Commission.

"It's in Ludwigsburg," he told Miller. "I read about it in a magazine. Its full name is the Central Federal Agency for the Elucidation of Crimes of Violence Committed during the Nazi Era. That's a bit of a mouthful, so people call it the Zentrale Stelle for short. Even shorter, the Z Commission. It's the only organization in the country that hunts Nazis on a nationwide, even an international level."

"Thanks," said Miller as he left. "I'll see if they can help me."

Miller went to his bank the next morning, made out a check to his landlord for three months' rent to cover January through March, and drew the rest of his bank balance in cash, leaving a 10-mark note to keep the account open.

He kissed Sigi before she went off to work at the club, telling her he would be gone for a week, maybe more. Then he took the Jaguar from its underground home and headed south toward the Rhineland.

The first snows had started, whistling in off the North Sea, slicing in flurries across the wide stretches of the autobahn as it swept south of Bremen and into the flat plain of Lower Saxony.

He paused once for coffee after two hours, then pressed on across North Rhine—Westphalia. Despite the wind and the descending darkness, he enjoyed driving down the autobahn in bad weather. Inside the XK 150 S he had the impression of being in the cockpit of a fast plane, the dashboard lights glowing dully under the facia, and outside the descending darkness of a winter's night, the icy cold, the slanting flurries of snow caught for a moment in the harsh beam of the headlights, whipping past the windshield and back into nothingness again.

He stuck to the fast lane as always, pushing the Jag to close to 100 miles an hour, watching the growling hulks of the heavy trucks swish past to his right as he passed them.

By six in the evening he was beyond the Hamm Junction, and the glowing lights of the Ruhr began to be dimly discernible to his right through the darkness. He never ceased to be amazed by the Ruhr, mile after mile after mile of factories and chimneys, towns and cities so close as to be in effect one gigantic city a hundred miles long and fifty broad. When the autobahn went into an overpass he could look down to the right and see it stretching away into the December night, thousands of hectares of lights and mills, aglow from a thousand furnaces churning out the wealth of the economic miracle. Fourteen years ago, as he traveled through it by train toward his school holiday in Paris, it had been rubble, and the industrial heart of Germany was hardly even beating. Impossible not to feel proud of what his people had done since then.

Just so long as I don't have to live in it, he thought as the giant signs of the Cologne Ring began to come up in the light of the headlights. From Cologne he ran southeast, past Wiesbaden and Frankfurt, Mannheim and Heilbronn, and it was late that evening when he cruised to a halt in front of a hotel in Stuttgart, the nearest city to Ludwigsburg, where he spent the night.

Ludwigsburg is a quiet and inoffensive little market town set in the rolling pleasant hills of Württemberg, fifteen miles north of the state capital of Stuttgart. Set in a quiet road off the High Street, to the extreme embarrassment of the town's upright inhabitants, is the home of the Z Commission, a small understaffed, underpaid, overworked group of men whose job and dedication in life is to hunt down the Nazis and the SS guilty during the war of the crimes of mass murder. Before the Statute of Limitations eliminated all SS crimes with the exception of murder and mass murder, those being sought might have been guilty only of extortion, robbery, grievous bodily harm including torture, and a variety of other forms of unpleasantness.

Even with murder as the only remaining charge able to be brought, the Z Commission still had 170,000 names in its files. Not unnaturally, the main effort had been and still is to trackdown the worst few thousand of the mass-murderers, if and where possible.

Deprived of any powers of arrest, able only to request the police of the various states of Germany to make an arrest when positive identification has already been made, unable to squeeze more than a pittance each year out of the federal government in Bonn, the men of Ludwigsburg worked solely because they were dedicated to the task.

There were eighty detectives on the staff, and fifty investigating attorneys. Of the former groups, all were young, below the age of thirty-five, so that none could possibly have had any implication in the matters under examination. The lawyers were mainly older, but vetted to ensure they too were uninvolved with events prior to 1945.

The lawyers were mainly taken from private practice, to which they would one day return. The detectives knew their careers were finished. No police force in Germany wanted to see on its staff a detective who had once served a term at Ludwigsburg. For detectives prepared to hunt the SS in West Germany, promotion was finished in any other police force in the country.

Quite accustomed to seeing their requests for cooperation ignored in over half the states, to seeing their loaned files unaccountably become missing, to see the quarry suddenly disappear after an anonymous tip-off, the Z men worked on as best they might at a task they realized was not in accordance with the wishes of the majority of their fellow countrymen.

Even on the streets of the smiling town of Ludwigsburg, the men on the staff of the Z Commission went ungreeted and unacknowledged by the citizens, to whom their presence brought an undesired notoriety.

Peter Miller found the commission at 58 Schorndorferstrasse, a large former private house set inside an eight-foot-high wall. Two massive steel gates barred the way to the drive. At one side was a bell handle, which he pulled. A steel shutter slid back, and a face appeared. The inevitable gatekeeper.

"Please?"

"I would like to speak to one of your investigating attorneys," said Miller.

"Which one?" said the face.

"I don't know any names," said Miller. "Anyone will do. Here is my card."

He thrust his press card through the aperture, forcing the man to take it. Then at least he knew it would go inside the building. The man shut the hatch and went away. When he came back, it was to open the gate. Miller was shown up the five stone steps to the front door, which was closed against the clear but icy winter air.

Inside, it was stuffily hot from the central heating. Another porter emerged from a glass-fronted booth to his right and showed him into a small waiting room. "Someone will be with you right away," he said and shut the door.

The man who came three minutes later was in his early fifties, mild-mannered and courteous. He handed Miller back his press card and asked, "What can I do for you?"

Miller started at the beginning, explaining briefly about Tauber, the diary, his inquiries into what had happened to Eduard Roschmann.

The lawyer listened intently. "Fascinating," he said at last.

"The point is, can you help me?"

"I wish I could," said the man, and for the first time since he had started asking questions about Roschmann in Hamburg, Miller believed he had met an official who genuinely would like to help him. "But the point is, although I am prepared to accept your inquiries as completely sincere, I am bound hand and foot by the rules that govern our continued existence here. Which are in effect that no information may be given out about any wanted SS criminal to anyone other than a person supported by the official backing of one of a specific number of authorities."

"In other words, you can tell me nothing?" said Miller.

"Please understand," said the lawyer, "this office is under constant attack. Not openly—no one would dare. But privately, within the corridors of power, we are incessantly being sniped at—our budget, such powers as we have, our terms of reference. We are allowed no latitude where the rules are concerned. Personally, I would like to engage the alliance of the press of Germany to help, but it's forbidden."

"I see," said Miller. "Do you then have any newspaper-clippings reference library?"

"No, we don't."

"Is there in Germany at all a newspaper-clippings reference library that is open to an inquiry by a member of the public?"

"No. The only newspaper-clippings libraries in the country are compiled and held by the various newspapers and magazines. The most comprehensive is reputed to be that of *Der Spiegel* magazine. After that, *Komet* has a very good one."

"I find this rather odd," said Miller. "Where in Germany today does a citizen inquire about the progress of investigation into war crimes, and for background material on wanted SS criminals?"

The lawyer looked slightly uncomfortable. "I'm afraid the ordinary citizen can't do that," he said.

"All right," said Miller. "Where are the archives in Germany that refer to the men of the SS?"

"There's one set here, in the basement," said the lawyer. "And ours is all composed of photostats. The originals of the entire card index of the SS were captured in nineteen forty-five by an American unit. At the last minute a small group of the SS stayed behind at the castle where they were stored in Bavaria and tried to burn the records. They got through about ten per cent before the American soldiers rushed in and stopped them. The rest were all mixed up. It took the Americans, with some German help, two years to sort out the rest.

"During those two years a number of the worst SS men escaped after being temporarily in Allied custody. Their dossiers could not be found in the mess. Since the final classification the entire SS index has remained in Berlin, still under American ownership and direction. Even we have to apply to them if we want something more. Mind you, they're very good about it; no complaints at all about cooperation from that quarter."

"And that's it?" asked Miller. "Just two sets in the whole country?"

"That's it," said the lawyer. "I repeat, I wish I could help you. Incidentally, if you should get anything on Roschmann, we'd be delighted to have it."

Miller thought. "If I find anything, there are only two authorities that can do anything with it. The Attorney General's office in Hamburg, and you. Right?"

"Yes, that's all," said the lawyer.

"And you're more likely to do something positive with it than Hamburg." Miller made it a flat statement.

The lawyer gazed fixedly at the ceiling. "Nothing that comes here that is of real value gathers dust on a shelf," he observed.

"Okay. Point taken," said Miller and rose. "One thing, between ourselves, are you still looking for Eduard Roschmann?"

"Between ourselves, yes, very much."

"And if he were caught, there'd be no problems about getting a conviction?"

"None at all," said the lawyer. "The case against him is tied up solid. He'd get hard labor for life without the option."

"Give me your phone number," said Miller.

The lawyer wrote it down and handed Miller the piece of paper. "There's my name and two phone numbers. Home and office. You can get me any time, day or night. If you get anything new, just call me from any phone box on direct-dial. In every state police force there are men I can call and know get action if necessary. There are others to avoid. So call me first, right?"

Miller pocketed the paper. "I'll remember that," he said as he left.

"Good luck," said the lawyer.

It's a long drive from Stuttgart to Berlin, and it took Miller most of the following day. Fortunately it was dry and crisp and the tuned Jaguar ate the miles northward past the sprawling carpet of Frankfurt, past Kassel and Göttingen to Hanover. Here he followed the branch-off to the right from autobahn E4 to E8 and the border with East Germany.

There was an hour's delay at the Marienborn Checkpoint while he filled out the inevitable currency-declaration forms and transit visas to travel through 110 miles of East Germany to West Berlin; and while the blue-uniformed customs man and the green-coated People's Police, fur-hatted against the cold, poked around in and under the Jaguar. The customs man seemed torn between the frosty courtesy required of a servant of the German Democratic Republic towards a national of revanchist West Germany, and one young man's desire to examine another's sports car.

Twenty miles beyond the border, the great motorway bridge reared up to cross the Elbe, where in 1945 the British, honorably obeying the rules laid down at Yalta, had halted their advance on Berlin. To his right, Miller looked down at the sprawl of Magdeburg and wondered if the old prison still stood. There was a further delay at the entry into West Berlin, where again the car was searched, his overnight case emptied onto the customs bench, and his wallet opened to see he had not given all his Westmarks away to the people of the worker's paradise on his progress down the road. Eventually he was through and the Jaguar roared past the Avus circuit toward the glittering ribbon of the Kurfürstendamm, brilliant with Christmas decorations. It was the evening of December 17.

He decided not to go blundering into the American Document Center the same way he had into the Attorney General's office in Hamburg or the Z Commission in Ludwigsburg. Without official backing, he had come to realize, no one got anywhere with Nazi files in Germany.

The following morning he called Karl Brandt from the main post office.

Brandt was aghast at his request. "I can't," he said into the phone. "I don't know anyone in Berlin."

"Well, think. You must have come across someone from the West Berlin force at one of the colleges you attended. I need him to vouch for me when I get there," shouted Miller back.

"I told you I didn't want to get involved."

"Well, you are involved." Miller waited a few seconds before putting in the body blow. "Either I get a look at that archive officially, or I breeze in and say you sent me."

"You wouldn't do that," said Brandt.

"I damn well would. I'm fed up with being pushed from pillar to post around this lousy country. So find somebody who'll get me in there officially. Let's face it, the request will be forgotten within the hour, once I've seen those files."

"I'll have to think," said Brandt, stalling for time.

"I'll give you an hour," said Miller. "Then I'm calling back."

He slammed down the receiver. An hour later Brandt was as angry as ever and more than a little frightened. He heartily wished he had kept the diary to himself and thrown it away.

"There's a man I was at detective college with," he said into the phone. "I didn't know him well, but he's now with Bureau One of the West Berlin force. That deals with the same subject."

"What's his name?"

"Schiller. Volkmar Schiller, detective inspector."

"I'll get in touch with him," said Miller.

"No, leave him to me. I'll call him today and introduce you to him. Then you can go and see him. If he doesn't agree to get you in, don't blame me. He's the only one I know in Berlin."

Two hours later Miller called Brandt back. Brandt sounded relieved. "He's away on leave," he said. "They tell me he's doing Christmas duty, so he's away until Monday."

"But it's only Wednesday," said Miller. "That gives me four days to kill."

"I can't help it. He'll be back on Monday morning. I'll ring him then."

Miller spent four boring days hanging around West Berlin, waiting for Schiller to come back from leave. Berlin was completely involved, as the Christmas of 1963 approached, with the issue by the East Berlin authorities, for the first time since the Wall had been built in August 1961, of passes enabling West Berliners to go through the Wall and visit relatives living in the eastern sector. The progress of the negotiations between the two sides of the city had held the headlines for days. Miller spent one of his days that weekend by going through the Heinestrasse Checkpoint into the eastern half of the city (as a West German citizen was able to do on the strength of his passport alone) and dropped in on a slight acquaintance, the Reuters correspondent in East Berlin. But the man was up to his neck in work on the Wall-passes story, so after a cup of coffee he left and returned to the west.

On Monday morning he went to see Detective Inspector Volkmar Schiller. To his great relief the man was about his own age and seemed, unusually for an official of any kind in Germany, to have his own cavalier attitude to red tape. Doubtless he would not get far, thought Miller, but that was his problem. He explained briefly what he wanted.

"I don't see why not," said Schiller. "The Americans are pretty helpful to us in Bureau One. Because we're charged by Willy Brandt with investigating Nazi crimes, we're in there almost every day."

They took Miller's Jaguar and drove out to the suburbs of the city, to the forests and the lakes, and at the bank of one of the lakes arrived at Number 1, Wasserkäferstieg, in the suburb of Zehlendorf, Berlin 37.

The building was a long, low, single-story affair set amid the trees.

"Is that it?" said Miller incredulously.

"That's it," said Schiller. "Not much, is it? The point is, there are eight floors below ground level. That's where the archives are stored, in fireproof vaults."

They went through the front door to find a small waiting room with the inevitable porter's lodge on the right. The detective approached it and proffered his police card. He was handed a form, and the two of them repaired to a table and filled it out.

The detective filled in his name and rank, then asked, "What was the chap's name again?"

"Roschmann," said Miller. "Eduard Roschmann."

The detective filled it in and handed the form back to the clerk in the front office.

"It takes about ten minutes," said the detective. They went into the larger room set out with rows of tables and chairs. After a quarter of an hour another clerk quietly brought them a file and laid it on the desk. It was about an inch thick, stamped with the single title: ROSCHMANN, EDUARD.

Volkmar Schiller rose. "If you don't mind, I'll be on my way," he said. "I'll find my own way back. Mustn't stay away too long after a week's leave. If you want anything photostated, ask the clerk." He gestured to a clerk sitting on a dais at the other end of the reading room, no doubt to ensure that no visitors tried to remove pages from the files.

Miller rose and shook hands. "Many thanks."

"Not at all."

Ignoring the other three or four readers hunched over their desks, Miller put his head between his hands and started to peruse the SS's own dossier on Eduard Roschmann.

It was all there. Nazi Party number, SS number, application form for each, filled out and signed by the man himself, result of his medical check, evaluation of him after his training period, self-written curriculum vitae, transfer papers, officer's commission, promotion certificates, right up to April 1945. There were also two photographs, taken for the SS records, one full-face, one profile. They showed a man of six feet, one inch, hair shorn close to the head with a parting on the left, staring at the camera with a grim expression, a pointed nose, and a lipless slit of a mouth. Miller began to read.
. . .

Eduard Roschmann was born on August 25, 1908, in the Austrian town of Graz, a citizen of Austria, son of a highly respectable brewery worker. He attended kindergarten, school, and high school in Graz. He attended college to try to become a lawyer, but failed. In 1931, at the age of twenty-three, he began work in the brewery where his father had a job and in 1937 was transferred to the administrative department from the brewery floor. The same year he joined the Austrian Nazi Party and the SS, both at that time banned organizations in neutral Austria. A year later Hitler annexed Austria and rewarded the Austrian Nazis with swift promotions all around.

In 1939, at the outbreak of war, he volunteered for the Waffen SS, was sent to Germany, trained during the winter of 1939 and the spring of 1940, and served in a Waffen SS unit in the overruning of France. In December 1940 he was transferred back from France to Berlin—here somebody had handwritten in the margin the word "Cowardice?"—and in January 1941 was assigned to the SD, Amt Three of the RSHA.

In July 1941 he set up the first SD post in Riga, and the following month became commandant of Riga ghetto. He returned to Germany by ship in October 1944 and, after handing over the remainder of the Jews of Riga to the SD of Danzig, returned to Berlin to report. He returned to his desk in Berlin headquarters of the SS and remained there awaiting reassignment.

The last document in the file was evidently never completed, presumably because the meticulous little clerk in Berlin SS headquarters reassigned himself rather quickly in May 1945.

Attached to the back of the bunch of documents was one last one apparently affixed by an American hand since the end of the war. It was a single sheet bearing the typewritten words: "Inquiry made about this file by the British Occupation authorities in December 1947."

Beneath this was the scrawled signature of some GI clerk long since forgotten, and the date December 21, 1947.

Miller gathered the file and eased out of it the self-written life story, the two photographs, and the last sheet. With these he approached the clerk at the end of the room.

"Could I have these photocopied please?"

"Certainly." The man took the file back and placed it on his desk to await the return of the three missing sheets after copying. Another man also tendered a file and two sheets of its contents for copying. The clerk took these also and placed them all in a tray behind him, when the sheets were whisked away through an aperture by an unseen hand.

"Please wait. It will take about ten minutes," the clerk told Miller and the other man. The pair retook their seats and waited, Miller wishing he could smoke a cigarette, which was forbidden; the other man, neat and gray in a charcoal winter coat, sitting with hands folded in his lap.

Ten minutes later there was a rustle behind the clerk, and two envelopes slid thrugh the aperture. He held them up. Both Miller and the middle-aged man rose and went forward to collect.

The clerk glanced quickly inside one of the envelopes. "The file on Eduard Roschmann?" he queried.

"For me," said Miller and extended his hand.

"These must be for you," the clerk said to the other man, who was glancing sideways at Miller.

The gray-coated man took his own envelope, and side by side they walked to the door. Outside, Miller ran down the steps and climbed into the Jaguar, slipped away from the curb, and headed back toward the center of the city.

An hour later he rang Sigi. "I'm coming home for Christmas," he told her.

Two hours later he was on his way out of West Berlin. As his car headed toward the first checkpoint at Drei Linden, the man with the gray coat was sitting in his neat and tidy flat off Savigny Platz, dialing a number in West Germany. He introduced himself briefly to the man who answered.

"I was in the Document Center today. Just normal research, you know the sort I do. There was another man in there. He was reading through the file of Eduard Roschmann. Then he had three sheets photocopied. After the message that went around recently, I thought I'd better tell you."

There was a burst of questions from the other end.

"No, I couldn't get his name. He drove away afterward in a long black sports car. Yes, yes, I did. It was a Hamburg number plate."

He recited it slowly while the man at the other end took it down.

"Well, I thought I'd better. I mean, one never knows with these snoopers. Yes, thank you, very kind of you.... Very well, I'll leave it with you.... Merry Christmas, *Kamerad*."

SEVEN

Christmas Day was on the Wednesday of that week, and it was not until after the Christmas period that the man in West Germany who had received the news from Berlin about Miller passed it on. When he did so, it was to his ultimate superior.

The man who took the call thanked his informant, put the office phone down, leaned back in his comfortable leather-padded executive chair, and gazed out of the window at the snow-covered rooftops of the Old Town.

"*Verdammt* and once again *verdammt*," he whispered. "Why now, of all times? Why now?"

To all the citizens of his city who knew him, he was a clever and brilliantly successful lawyer in private practice. To the score of his senior executive officers scattered across West Germany and West Berlin, he was the chief executive inside Germany of the Odessa. His telephone number was unlisted, and his code name was the Werwolf.

Unlike the monster-figure of the mythology of Hollywood and the horror films of Britain and America, the German *Werwolf* is not an odd man who grows hairs on the backs of his hands during the full moon. In old Germanic mythology the *Werwolf* is a patriotic figure who stays behind in the homeland when the Teuton warrior-heroes have been forced to flee into exile by the invading foreigner, and who leads the resistance against the invader from the shadows of the great forests, striking by night and disappearing, leaving only the spoor of the wolf in the snow.

At the end of the war a group of SS officers, convinced that the destruction of the invading Allies was merely a matter of months, trained and briefed a score of groups of ultrafanatical teenage boys to remain behind and sabotage the Allied occupiers. They were formed in Bavaria, then being overrun by the Americans. These were the original Werwolves. Fortunately for them, they never put their training into practice, for after discovering Dachau the GIs were just waiting for someone to start something.

When the Odessa began in the late forties to reinfiltrate West Germany, its first chief executive had been one of those who had trained the teenage Werwolves of 1945. He took the title. It had the advantage of being anonymous, symbolic, and sufficiently melodramatic to satisfy the eternal German lust for play-acting. But there was nothing theatrical about the ruthlessness with which the Odessa dealt with those who crossed its plans.

The Werwolf of late 1963 was the third to hold the title and position. Fanatic and astute, constantly in touch with his superiors in Argentina, the man watched over the interests of all former members of the SS inside West Germany, but particularly those formerly of high rank or those high on the wanted list.

He stared out of his office window and thought back to the image of SS General Glücks facing him in a Madrid hotel room more than thirty days earlier, and to the general's warning about the vital importance of maintaining at all costs the anonymity and security of the radio-factory-owner now preparing, under the code name Vulkan, the guidance systems for the Egyptian rockets. Alone in Germany, he also knew that in an earlier part of his life Vulkan had been better known under his real name of Eduard Roschmann.

He glanced down at the jotting pad on which he had scribbled the number of Miller's car and pressed a buzzer on his desk. His secretary's voice came through from the next room.

"Hilda, what was the name of that private investigator we employed last month on the divorce case?"

"One moment." There was a sound of rustling papers as she looked up the file. "It was Memmers, Heinz Memmers."

"Give me the telephone number, will you? No, don't call him, just give me the number."

He noted it down beneath the number of Miller's car, then took his finger off the intercom key.

He rose and crossed the room to a wall-safe set in a block of concrete, a part of the wall of the office. From the safe he took a thick, heavy book and went back to his desk. Flicking through the pages, he came to the entry he wanted. There were only two Memmers listed, Heinrich and Walter. He ran his finger along the page opposite Heinrich, usually shortened to Heinz. He noted the date of birth, worked out the age of the man in late 1963, and recalled the face of the private investigator. The ages fitted. He jotted down two other numbers listed against Heinz Memmers, picked up the telephone, and asked Hilda for an outside line.

When the dialing tone came through, he dialed the number she had given him. The telephone at the other end was picked up after a dozen rings. It was a woman's voice. "Memmers Private Inquiries."

"Give me Herr Memmers personally," said the lawyer.

"May I say who's calling?" asked the secretary brightly.

"No, just put him on the line. And hurry."

There was a pause. The tone of voice took its effect. "Yes, sir," she said. A minute later a gruff voice said, "Memmers."

"Is that Herr Heinz Memmers?"

"Yes, who is that speaking?"

"Never mind my name. It is not important. Just tell me, does the number 245.718 mean anything to you?"

There was dead silence on the phone, broken only by a heavy sigh as Memmers digested the fact that his SS number had just been quoted to him. The book now lying open on the Werwolf's desk was a list of every former member of the SS.

Memmers' voice came back, harsh with suspicion. "Should it?"

"Would it mean anything to you if I said that my own corresponding number had only five figures in it—*Kamerad*?"

The change was electric. Five figures meant a very senior officer. "Yes, sir," said Memmers down the line.

"Good," said the Werwolf. "There's a small job I want you to do. Some snooper has been inquiring into one of the *Kameraden*. I need to find out who he is."

"*Zu Befehl*"—At your command—came over the phone.

"Excellent. But between ourselves *Kamerad* will do. After all, we are all comrades in arms."

Memmers' voice came back, evidently pleased by the flattery. "Yes, *Kamerad*."

"All I have about the man is his car number. A Hamburg registration." The Werwolf read it slowly into the telephone. "Got that?"

"Yes, *Kamerad*."

"I'd like you to go to Hamburg personally. I want to know the name and address, profession, family and dependents, social standing—you know, the normal rundown. How long would that take you?"

"About forty-eight hours," said Memmers.

"Good, I'll call you back forty-eight hours from now. One last thing. There is to be no approach made to the subject. If possible it is to be done in such a way that he does not know any inquiry has been made. Is that clear?"

"Certainly. It's no problem."

"When you have finished, prepare your account and give it to me over the phone when I call you. I will send you the cash by post."

Memmers expostulated. "There will be no account, *Kamerad*. Not for a matter concerning the Comradeship."

"Very well, then. I'll call you back in two days."

The Werwolf put the phone down.

Miller set off from Hamburg the same afternoon, taking the same autobahn he had traveled two weeks earlier, past Bremen, Osnabrück, and Münster toward Cologne and the Rhineland. This time his destination was Bonn, the small and boring town on the river's edge that Konrad Adenauer had chosen as the capital of the Federal Republic, because he came from it.

Just south of Bremen his Jaguar crossed Memmers' Opel speeding north to Hamburg. Oblivious of each other, the two men flashed past on their separate missions.

It was dark when he entered the single long main street of Bonn and, seeing the white-topped peaked cap of a traffic policeman, he drew up beside him.

"Can you tell me the way to the British Embassy?" he asked the policeman.

"It will be closed in an hour," said the policeman, a true Rhinelander.

"Then I'd better get there all the quicker," said Miller. "Where is it?"

The policeman pointed straight down the road toward the south. "Keep straight on down here, follow the tramlines. This street becomes Friedrich Ebert Allee. Just follow the tramlines. As you are about to leave Bonn and enter Bad Godesberg, you'll see it on your left. It's lit up and it's got the British flag flying outside it."

Miller nodded his thanks and drove on. The British Embassy was where the policeman had said, sandwiched between a building site on the Bonn side and a football field on the other, both a sea of mud in the December fog rolling up off the river behind the embassy.

It was a long, low gray concrete building, built back-to-front, referred to by British newspaper correspondents in Bonn since it was built as "the vacuum-cleaner factory." Miller swung off the road and parked in one of the slots provided for visitors.

He walked through the wooden-framed glass doors and found himself in a small foyer with a desk on his left, behind which sat a middle-aged receptionist. Beyond her was a small room inhabited by two blue-serge-suited men who bore the unmistakable stamp of former Army sergeants.

"I would like to speak with the press attaché, please," said Miller, using his halting school English.

The receptionist looked worried. "I don't know if he's still here. It is Friday afternoon, you know."

"Please try," said Miller, and proffered his press card.

The receptionist looked at it and dialed a number on her house telephone. Miller was in luck. The press attaché was just about to leave. He evidently asked for a few minutes to get his hat and coat back off again. Miller was shown into a small waiting room adorned by several Rowland Hilder prints of the Cotswolds in autumn. On a table lay several back copies of the *Tatler* and brochures depicting the onward march of British industry. Within seconds, however, he was summoned by one of the ex-sergeants and led upstairs and along a corridor and shown into a small office.

The press attaché, he was glad to see, was in his mid-thirties and seemed eager to help. "What can I do for you?" he asked.

Miller decided to go straight into the matter. "I am investigating a story for a news magazine," he lied. "It's about a former SS captain, one of the worst, a man still sought by our own authorities. I believe he was also on the wanted list of the British authorities when this part of Germany was under British administration. Can you tell me how I can check whether the British ever captured him, and if so what happened to him?"

The young diplomat was perplexed. "Good Lord, I'm sure I don't know. I mean, we handed over all our records and files to your government in nineteen forty-nine. They took over where our chaps left off. I suppose they would have all these things now."

Miller tried to avoid mentioning that the German authorities had all declined to help. "True," he said. "Very true. However, all my inquiries so far indicate he has never been put on trial in the Federal Republic since nineteen forty-nine. That would indicate he had not been caught since nineteen forty-nine. However, the American Document Center in West Berlin reveals that a copy of the man's file was requested from them by the British in nineteen forty-seven. There must have been a reason for that, surely?"

"Yes, one would indeed suppose so," said the attaché. He had evidently taken in the reference to Miller's having procured the cooperation of the American authorities in West Berlin, and furrowed his brow in thought.

"So who on the British side would be the investigating authority during the Occupation—I mean, the administration period?"

"Well, you see, it would have been the Provost Marshal's office of the Army at that time. Apart from Nuremberg, which were the major war-crimes trials, the separate Allies were investigating individually, although obviously we cooperated with each other. Except the Russians. These investigations led to some zonal war-crimes trials—do you follow me?"

"Yes."

"The investigations were carried out by the Provost Marshal's department, that's the military police, you know, and the trials were prepared by the Legal Branch. But the files of both were handed over in nineteen forty-nine. Do you see?"

"Well, yes," said Miller, "but surely copies must have been kept by the British?"

"I suppose they were," said the attaché. "But they'd be filed away in the archives of the Army by now."

"Would it be possible to look at them?"

The attaché appeared shocked. "Oh, I very much doubt it. I don't think so. I suppose bona fide research scholars might be able to make an application to see them, but it would take a long time. And I don't think a reporter would be allowed to see them—no offense meant, you understand?"

"I understand," said Miller.

"The point is," resumed the attaché earnestly, "that, well, you're not exactly *official*, are you? And one doesn't wish to upset the German authorities, does one?"

"Certainly not."

The attaché rose. "I don't think there's really much the embassy can do to help you."

"Okay. One last thing. Was there anybody here then who is still here now?"

"On the embassy staff? Oh, dear me, no. No, they've all changed many times." He escorted Miller to the door. "Wait a minute, there's Cadbury. I think he was here then. He's been here for ages, I do know that."

"Cadbury?" said Miller.

"Anthony Cadbury. The foreign correspondent. He's the sort of senior British press chap here. Married a German girl. I think he was here after the war, just after. You might ask him."

"Fine," said Miller. "I'll try him. Where do I find him?"

"Well, it's Friday now," said the attaché. "He'll probably be at his favorite place by the bar in the Cercle Français later on. Do you know it?"

"No, I've never been here before."

"Ah, yes, well, it's a restaurant, run by the French, you know. Jolly good food, too. It's very popular. It's in Bad Godesberg, just down the road."

Miller found it, a hundred yards from the bank of the Rhine on a road called Ann Schwimmbad. The barman knew Cadbury well but had not seen him that evening. He told Miller if the doyen of the British foreign correspondents' corps in Bonn was not in that evening, he would almost certainly be there for prelunch drinks the following day.

Miller checked into the Dreesen Hotel down the road, a great turn-of-the-century edifice that had formerly been Adolf Hitler's favorite hotel in Germany, the place he had picked to meet Neville Chamberlain of Britain for their first meeting in 1938. He dined at the Cercle Français and dawdled over his coffee, hoping Cadbury would turn up. But by eleven the Englishman had not put in an appearance, so he went back to the hotel to sleep.

Cadbury walked into the bar of the Cercle Français a few minutes before twelve the following morning, greeted a few acquaintances, and seated himself on his favorite corner stool at the bar. When he had taken his first sip of his Ricard, Miller rose from his table by the window and came over.

"Mr. Cadbury?"

The Englishman turned and surveyed him. He had smooth-brushed white hair coming back from what had evidently once been a very handsome face. The skin was still healthy, with a fine tracery of tiny veins on the surface of each cheek. The eyes were bright blue under shaggy gray eyebrows. He surveyed Miller warily. "Yes."

"My name is Miller. Peter Miller. I am a reporter from Hamburg. May I talk with you a moment, please?"

Anthony Cadbury gestured to the stool beside him. "I think we had better talk in German, don't you?" he said, dropping into the language. Miller was relieved that he could go back to his own language, and it must have showed. Cadbury grinned. "What can I do for you?"

Miller glanced at the shrewd eyes and backed a hunch. Starting at the beginning, he told Cadbury the story from the moment of Tauber's death. The London man was a good listener. He did not interrupt once. When Miller had finished he gestured to the barman to fill his own Ricard and bring another beer for Miller.

"Spätenbräu, wasn't it?" he asked.

Miller nodded and poured the fresh beer to a foaming head on top of the glass.

"Cheers," said Cadbury. "Well, now, you've got quite a problem. I must say I admire your nerve."

"Nerve?" said Miller.

"It's not quite the most popular story to investigate among your country-men in their present state of mind," said Cadbury, "as you will doubtless find out in course of time."

"I already have," said Miller.

"Mmm. I thought so," said the Englishman and grinned suddenly. "A spot of lunch? My wife's away for the day."

Over lunch Miller asked Cadbury if he had been in Germany at the end of the war.

"Yes, I was a war correspondent. Much younger then, of course. About your age. I came in with Montgomery's army. Not to Bonn, of course. No one had heard of it then. The headquarters was at Lüneburg. Then I just sort of stayed on. Covered the end of the war, signature of the surrender and all that; then the paper asked me to remain."

"Did you cover the zonal war-crimes trials?" asked Miller.

Cadbury transferred a mouthful of fillet steak and nodded while he chewed. "Yes. All the ones held in the British Zone. We had a specialist come over for the Nuremberg Trials. That was the American Zone, of course. The star criminals in our zone were Josef Kramer and Irma Grese. Heard of them?"

"No, never."

"Well, they were called the Beast and Beastess of Belsen. I invented the titles, actually. They caught on. Did you hear about Belsen?"

"Only vaguely," said Miller. "My generation wasn't told much about all that. Nobody wanted to tell us anything."

Cadbury shot him a shrewd glance under his busy eyebrows. "But you want to know now?"

"We have to know sooner or later. May I ask you something? Do you hate the Germans?"

Cadbury chewed for a few minutes, considering the question seriously.

"Just after the discovery of Belsen, a crowd of journalists attached to the British Army went up for a look. I've never been so sickened in my life, and in war you see a few terrible things. But nothing like Belsen. I think at that moment, yes, I hated them all."

"And now?"

"No. Not any longer. Let's face it, I married a German girl in nineteen forty-eight. I still live here. I wouldn't if I still felt the way I did in nineteen forty-five. I'd have gone back to England long ago."

"What caused the change?"

"Time. The passage of time. And the realization that not all Germans were Josef Kramers. Or—what was his name, Roschmann? Or Roschmanns. Mind you, I still can't get over a sneaking sense of mistrust for people of my own generation among your nation."

"And my generation?" Miller twirled his wineglass and gazed at the light refracting through the red liquid.

"They're better," said Cadbury. "Let's face it, you have to be better."

"Will you help me with the Roschmann inquiry? Nobody else will."

"If I can," said Cadbury. "What do you want to know?"

"Do you recall him being put on trial in the British Zone?"

Cadbury shook his head. "No. Anyway, you said he was Austrian by birth. Austria was also under four-power occupation at the time. But I'm certain there was no trial against Roschmann in the British Zone of Germany. I'd remember the name if there were."

"But why would the British authorities request a photocopy of his career from the Americans in Berlin?"

Cadbury thought for a moment. "Roschmann must have come to the attention of the British in some way. At that time nobody knew about Riga. The Russians were at the height of their obstinacy in the late forties. They didn't give us any information from the east. Yet that was where the over-whelming majority of the worst crimes of mass murder took place. So we were in the odd position of having about eighty per cent of the crimes against humanity committed east of what is now the Iron Curtain, and the ones responsible for them were about ninety per cent in the three western zones. Hundreds of guilty men slipped through our hands because we knew nothing about what they had done a thousand miles to the east.

"But if an inquiry was made about Roschmann in nineteen forty-seven, he must have come to our attention somehow."

"That's what I thought," said Miller. "Where would one start to look, among the British records?"

"Well, we can start with my own files. They're back at my house. Come on, it's a short walk."

Fortunately, Cadbury was a methodical man and kept every one of his dispatches from the end of the war onward. His study was lined with file boxes along two walls. Besides these, there were two gray filing cabinets in one corner.

"I run the office from my home," he told Miller as they entered the study. "This is my own filing system, and I'm about the only one who understands it. Let me show you." He gestured to the filing cabinets. "One of these is stuffed with files on people, listed under the names in alphabetical order. The other concerns subjects, listed under subject headings, alphabetically.

We'll start with the first one. Look under Roschmann."

It was a brief search. There was no folder with Roschmann's name on it.

"All right," said Cadbury. "Now let's try subject headings. There are four that might help. There's one called Nazis, another labeled SS. Then there's a very large section headed Justice, which has subsections, one of which contains clippings about trials that have taken place. But they're mostly criminal trials that have taken place in West Germany since nineteen forty-nine. The last one that might help is about war crimes. Let's start going through them."

Cadbury read faster than Miller, but it took them until nightfall to wade through the hundreds of clippings in all four files. Eventually Cadbury rose with a sigh, closed the War Crimes file, and replaced it in its proper place in the filing cabinet.

"I'm afraid I have to go out to dinner tonight," he said. "The only things left to look through are these." He gestured to the box files on shelves along two of the walls.

Miller closed the file he had been searching. "What are those?"

"Those," said Cadbury, "are nineteen years of dispatches from me to the paper. That's the top row. Below them are nineteen years of clippings from the paper of news stories and articles about Germany and Austria. Obviously a lot in the first set are repeated in the second. Those are my pieces that were printed. But there are other pieces in the second set that were not from me. After all, other contributors have had pieces printed in the paper as well. And some of the stuff I sent was not used.

"There are about six boxes of clippings per year. That's quite a lot to get through. Fortunately it's Sunday tomorrow, so we can use the whole day if you like."

"It's very kind of you to take so much trouble," said Miller.

Cadbury shrugged. "I had nothing else to do this weekend. Anyway, weekends in late December in Bonn are hardly full of gaiety. My wife's not due back till tomorrow evening. Meet me for a drink in the Cercle Français about eleven-thirty."

It was in the middle of Sunday afternoon that they found it. Anthony Cadbury was nearing the end of the box file labeled November–December 1947 of the set that contained his own dispatches. He suddenly shouted, "Eureka," eased back the spring clip, and took out a single sheet of paper, long since faded, typewritten and headed "December 23, 1947."

"No wonder it wasn't used in the paper," he said. "No one would have wanted to know about a captured SS man just before Christmas. Anyway, with the shortage of newsprint in those days, the Christmas Eve edition must have been tiny."

He laid the sheet on the writing desk and shone the Anglepoise lamp onto it. Miller leaned over to read it.

> *British Military Government, Hanover, 23rd Dec.*—A former captain of the notorious SS has been arrested by British military authorities at Graz, Austria, and is being held pending further investigation, a spokesman at BMG headquarters said here today.

The man, Eduard Roschmann, was recognized on the streets of the Austrian town by a former inmate of a concentration camp, who alleged Roschmann had been the commandant of the camp in Latvia. After identification at the house to which the former camp inmate followed him, Roschmann was arrested by members of the British Field Security Service in Graz.

A request has been made to Soviet Zonal headquarters at Potsdam for further information about the concentration camp in Riga, Latvia, and a search for further witnesses is under way, the spokesman said. Meanwhile the captured man has been positively identified as Eduard Roschmann from his personal file, stored by the American authorities in their SS Index in Berlin. endit. Cadbury.

Miller read the brief dispatch four or five times. "Christ," he breathed. "You got him."

"I think this calls for a drink," said Cadbury.

When he had made the call to Memmers on Friday morning, the Werwolf had overlooked the fact that forty-eight hours later it would be Sunday. Despite this, he tried to call to Memmers' office from his home on Sunday, just as the two men in Bad Godesberg made their discovery. There was no reply.

But Memmers was in the office the following morning at nine sharp. The call from the Werwolf came through at half past.

"So glad you called, *Kamerad*," said Memmers. "I got back from Hamburg late last night."

"You have the information?"

"Certainly. If you would like to note it?"

"Go ahead," said the voice on the phone.

In his office Memmers cleared his throat and began to read from his notes.

"The owner of the car is a freelance reporter, one Peter Miller. Description: aged twenty-nine, just under six feet tall, brown hair, brown eyes. Has a widowed mother who lives in Osdorf, just outside Hamburg. He himself lives in an apartment close to the Steindamm in central Hamburg." Memmers read off Miller's address and telephone number. "He lives there with a girl, a striptease dancer, Miss Sigrid Rahn. He works mainly for the picture magazines. Apparently does very well. Specializes in investigative journalism. Like you said, *Kamerad*, a snooper."

"Any idea who commissioned him on his latest inquiry?" asked the Werwolf.

"No, that's the funny thing. Nobody seems to know what he is doing at the moment. Or for whom he is working. I checked with the girl, claiming to be from the editorial office of a big magazine. Only by phone, you understand. She said she did not know where he was, but she expected a call from him this afternoon, before she goes to work."

"Anything else?"

"Just the car. It's very distinctive. A black Jaguar, British model, with a yellow strip down the side. A sports car, two-seater, fixed-head coupe, called the XK one-fifty. I checked his local garage."

The Werwolf digested this. "I want to try and find out where he is now," he said at length.

"He's not in Hamburg now," said Memmers hastily. "He left on Friday about lunchtime, just as I was arriving. He spent Christmas there. Before that he was away somewhere else."

"I know," said the Werwolf.

"I could find out what story he is inquiring about," said Memmers helpfully. "I did not inquire too closely, because you said you did not want him to discover he was being asked about."

"I know what story he is working on. Exposing one of our comerades." The Werwolf thought for a minute. "Could you find out where he is now?" he asked.

"I think so," said Memmers. "I could call the girl back this afternoon, pretend I was from a big magazine and needed to contact Miller urgently. She sounded a simple girl on the phone."

"Yes, do that," said the Werwolf. "I'll call you at four this afternoon."

That Monday morning Cadbury was down in Bonn, where a ministerial press conference was scheduled. He rang Miller at the Dreesen Hotel at ten-thirty.

"Glad to get you before you left," he told the German. "I've got an idea. It might help you. Meet me at the Cercle Français this afternoon around four."

Just before lunch Miller rang Sigi and told her he was at the Dreesen.

When they met, Cadbury ordered tea. "I had an idea while not listening to that wretched conference this morning," he told Miller. "If Roschmann was captured and identified as a wanted criminal, his case would have come under the eyes of the British legal officials in our zone of Germany at the time. All files were copied and passed between the British, French, and Americans in both Germany and Austria at that time. Have you ever heard of a man called Lord Russell of Liverpool?"

"No, never," said Miller.

"He was the Legal Adviser to the British Military Governor during the occupation. Later he wrote a book called *The Scourge of the Swastika.* You can imagine what it was about. Didn't make him terribly popular in Germany, but it was quite accurate. About atrocities."

"He's a lawyer?" asked Miller.

"He was," said Cadbury. "A very brilliant one. He's retired now, lives in Wimbledon. I don't know if he'd remember me, but I could give you a letter of introduction."

"Would he remember so far back?"

"He might. He's not a young man any more, but he was reputed to have a memory like a filing cabinet. If the case of Roschmann was ever referred to him to prepare a prosecution, he'd remember every detail of it. I'm sure of that."

Miller nodded and sipped his tea. "Yes, I could fly to London to talk to him."

Cadbury reached into his pocket and produced an envelope. "I've written the letter already." He handed Miller the letter of introduction and stood up. "Good luck."

Memmers had the information for the Werwolf when the latter called just after four.

"His girl friend got a call from him," said Memmers. "He's in Bad Godesberg, staying at the Dreesen Hotel."

The Werwolf put the phone down and thumbed through an address book. Eventually he fixed on a name, picked up the phone again, and called a number in the Bonn-Bad Godesberg area.

Miller went back to the hotel to call Cologne airport and book a flight to London for the following day, Tuesday, December 31. As he reached the reception desk the girl behind the counter smiled brightly and pointed to the open seating area in the bay window overlooking the Rhine.

"There's a gentleman to see you, Herr Miller."

He glanced toward the groups of tapestry-backed chairs set around various tables in the window alcove. In one of them a middle-aged man in a black winter coat, holding a black Homburg and a rolled umbrella, sat waiting. Miller strolled over, puzzled as to who could have known he was there.

"You wanted to see me?" Miller asked.

The man sprang to his feet. "Herr Miller?"

"Yes."

"Herr Peter Miller?"

"Yes."

The man inclined his head in the short, jerky bow of old-fashioned Germans. "My name is Schmidt. Doctor Schmidt."

"What can I do for you?"

Dr. Schmidt smiled deprecatingly and gazed out of the windows where the black, bleak mass of the Rhine flowed under the fairy lights of the deserted terrace.

"I am told you are a journalist. Yes? A freelance journalist. A very good one." He smiled brightly. "You have a reputation for being very thorough, very tenacious."

Miller remained silent, waiting for him to get to the point.

"Some friends of mine heard you are presently engaged on an inquiry into events that happened—well, let us say, a long time ago. A very long time ago."

Miller stiffened and his mind raced, trying to work out who the "friends" were and who could have told them. Then he realized he had been asking questions about Roschmann all over the country.

"An inquiry about a certain Eduard Roschmann." And he said tersely, "So?"

"Ah yes, about Captain Roschmann. I just thought I might be able to help you." The man swiveled his eyes back from the river and fixed them kindly on Miller. "Captain Roschmann is dead."

"Indeed?" said Miller. "I didn't know."

Dr. Schmidt seemed delighted. "Of course not. There's no reason why you should. But it is true nevertheless. Really, you are wasting your time."

Miller looked disappointed. "Can you tell me when he died?" he asked the doctor.

"You have not discovered the circumstances of his death?" the man asked.

"No. The last trace of him I can find was in late April nineteen forty-five. He was seen alive then."

"Ah yes, of course." Dr. Schmidt seemed happy to oblige. "He was killed, you know, shortly after that. He returned to his native Austria and was killed fighting against the Americans in early nineteen forty-five. His body was identified by several people who had known him in life."

"He must have been a remarkable man," said Miller.

Dr. Schmidt nodded in agreement. "Well, yes, some thought so. Yes indeed, some of us thought so."

"I mean," continued Miller as if the interruption had not occurred, "he must have been remarkable to be the first man since Jesus Christ to have risen from the dead. He was captured alive by the British on December twentieth, nineteen forty-seven, at Graz in Austria."

The doctor's eyes reflected the glittering snow along the balustrade outside the window. "Miller, you are being very foolish. Very foolish indeed. Permit me to give you a word of advice, from an older man to a much, much younger one. Drop this inquiry."

Miller eyed him. "I suppose I ought to thank you," he said without gratitude.

"If you will take my advice, perhaps you ought," said the doctor.

"You misunderstand me again," said Miller. "Roschmann was also seen alive in mid-October this year in Hamburg. The second sighting was not confirmed. Now it is. You just confirmed it."

"I repeat, you are being very foolish if you do not drop this inquiry." The doctor's eyes were as cold as ever, but there was a hint of anxiety in them. There had been a time when people did not reject his orders, and he had never quite got used to the change.

Miller began to get angry, a slow glow of anger working up from his collar to his face. "You make me sick, *Herr Doktor*," he told the older man. "You and your kind, your whole stinking gang. You have a respectable façade, but you are filth on the face of my country. So far as I am concerned, I'll go on asking questions till I find him."

He turned to go, but the elder man grabbed his arm. They stared at each other from a range of two inches.

"You're not Jewish, Miller. You're Aryan. You're one of us. What did we ever do to you, for God's sake, what did we ever do to you?"

Miller jerked his arm free. "If you don't know yet, *Herr Doktor*, you'll never understand."

"*Ach*, you people of the younger generation, you're all the same. Why can you never do what you're told?"

"Because that's the way we are. Or at least it's the way *I* am."

The older man stared at him with narrowed eyes. "You're not stupid, Miller. But you're behaving as if you were. As if you were one of these ridiculous creatures constantly governed by what they call their conscience. But I'm beginning to doubt that. It's almost as if you had something personal in this matter."

Miller turned to go. "Perhaps I have," he said and walked away across the lobby.

EIGHT

Miller found the house, in a quiet residential street off the main road of the London borough of Wimbledon, without difficulty. Lord Russell himself answered the ring at the door, a man in his late sixties wearing a woolen cardigan and a bow tie. Miller introduced himself.

"I was in Bonn yesterday," he told the peer, "lunching with Mr. Anthony Cadbury. He gave me your name and a letter of introduction to you. I hoped I might have a talk with you, sir."

Lord Russell gazed down at him from the step with perplexity. "Cadbury? Anthony Cadbury? I can't seem to remember . . . "

"A British newspaper correspondent," said Miller. "He was in Germany just after the war. He covered the war-crimes trials. Josef Kramer and the others from Belsen. You recall those trials."

"Course I do. Course I do. Yes, Cadbury, yes, newspaper chap. I remember him now. Haven't seen him in years. Well, don't let's stand here. It's cold and I'm not as young as I was. Come in, come in."

Without waiting for an answer he turned and walked back down the hall. Miller followed, closing the door on the chill wind of the last day of 1963. He hung his coat on a hook in the hall at Lord Russell's bidding and followed him through into the back of the house, where a welcoming fire burned in the sitting-room grate.

Miller held out the letter from Cadbury. Lord Russell took it, read it quickly, and raised his eyebrows.

"Humph. Help in tracking down a Nazi? Is that what you came about?" He regarded Miller from under his eyebrows. Before the German could reply, Lord Russell went on, "Well, sit down, sit down. No good standing around."

They sat in flower-print-covered armchairs on either side of the fire.

"How come a young German reporter is chasing Nazis?" asked Lord Russell without preamble. Miller found his gruff directness disconcerting.

"I'd better explain from the beginning," said Miller.

"I think you better had," said the peer, leaning forward to knock out the dottle of his pipe on the side of the grate. While Miller talked he refilled the pipe, lit it, and was puffing contentedly away when the German had finished.

"I hope my English is good enough," said Miller at last, when no reaction seemed to be coming from the retired prosecutor.

Lord Russell seemed to wake from a private reverie. "Oh, yes, yes, better than my German after all these years. One forgets, you know."

"This Roschmann business—" began Miller.

"Yes, interesting, very interesting. And you want to try and find him. Why?"

The last question was shot at Miller and he found the old man's eyes gazing keenly from under the eyebrows.

"Well, I have my reasons," he said stiffly. "I believe the man should be found and brought to trial."

"Humph. Don't we all? The question is, will he be? Will he ever be?"

Miller played it straight back. "If I can find him, he will be. You can take my word on that."

The British peer seemed unimpressed. Little smoke signals shot out of the pipe as he puffed, rising in perfect series toward the ceiling. The pause lengthened.

"The point is, my Lord, do you remember him?"

Lord Russell seemed to start. "Remember him? Oh yes, I remember him. Or at least the name. Wish I could put a face to the name. An old man's memory fades with the years, you know. And there were so many of them in those days."

"Your Military Police picked him up on December twentieth, nineteen forty-seven, in Graz," Miller told him.

He took the two photocopies of Roschmann's picture from his breast pocket and passed them over. Lord Russell gazed at the two pictures, full-face and profile, rose and began to pace the sitting room, lost in thought.

"Yes," he said at last, "I've got him. I can see him now. Yes, the file was sent on from Graz Field Security to me in Hanover a few days later. That would be where Cadbury got his dispatch from. Our office in Hanover."

He paused and swung around on Miller. "You say your man Tauber last saw him on April third, nineteen forty-five, driving west through Magdeburg in a car with several others?"

"That's what he said in his diary."

"Mmmm. Two and a half years before we got him. And do you know where he was?"

"No," said Miller.

"In a British prisoner-of-war camp. Cheeky. All right, young man, I'll fill in what I can."

The car carrying Eduard Roschmann and his colleagues from the SS passed through Magdeburg and immediately turned south toward Bavaria and Austria. They made it as far as Munich before the end of April, then split up. Roschmann by this time was in the uniform of a corporal of the German Army, with papers in his own name but describing him as an Army man.

South of Munich the American Army columns were sweeping through Bavaria, mainly concerned not with the civilian population, which had become merely an administrative headache, but with rumors that the Nazi hierarchy intended to shut themselves up in a mountain fortress in the Bavarian Alps around Hitler's home at Berchtesgaden and fight it out to the last man. The hundreds of unarmed, wandering German soldiers were paid scant attention as Patton's columns rolled through Bavaria.

Traveling by night across country, hiding by day in woodsmen's huts and barns, Roschmann crossed the Austrian border that had not even existed since the annexation of 1938 and headed south and onward for Graz, his home town. In and around Graz he knew people on whom he could count to shelter him.

He passed around Vienna and had almost made it when he was challenged by a British patrol on May 6. Foolishly he tried to run for it. As he dived into the undergrowth by the roadside a hail of bullets cut through the brushwood, and one passed clean through his chest, piercing one lung. After a quick search in the darkness, the British tommies passed on, leaving him wounded and undiscovered in a thicket. From here he crawled to a farmer's house half a mile away.

Still conscious, he told the farmer the name of a doctor he knew in Graz, and the man cycled through the night and the curfew to fetch him. For three months he was tended by his friends, first at the farmer's house, later at another house in Graz itself. When he was fit enough to walk, the war was three months over and Austria under four-power occupation. Graz was in the heart of the British Zone.

All German soldiers were required to do two years in a prisoner-of-war camp, and Roschmann, deeming it the safest place to be, gave himself up. For two years, from August 1945 to August 1947, while the hunt for the worst of the wanted SS murderers went on, Roschmann remained at ease in the camp. For on giving himself up he had used another name, that of a former friend who had gone into the Army and had been killed in North Africa.

There were so many tens of thousands of German soldiers wandering about without any identity papers at all that the name given by the man himself was accepted by the Allies as genuine. They had neither the time nor the facilities to conduct a probing examination of Army corporals. In the summer of 1947 Roschmann was released and felt it safe to leave the custody of the camp. He was wrong.

One of the survivors of Riga camp, a native of Vienna, had sworn his own vendetta against Roschmann. This man haunted the streets of Graz, waiting for Roschmann to return to his home, the parents he had left in 1939, and the wife he had married while on leave in 1943, Hella Roschmann. The old man roamed from the house of the parents to the house of the wife, waiting for the SS man to return.

After release, Roschmann remained in the countryside outside Graz, working as a laborer in the fields. Then, on December 20, 1947, he went home to spend Christmas with his family. The old man was waiting. He hid behind a pillar when he saw the tall, lanky figure with the pale blond hair and cold blue eyes approach his wife's house, glance around a few times, then knock and enter.

Within an hour, led by the former inmate of the camp at Riga, two hefty British sergeants of the Field Security Service, puzzled and skeptical, arrived at the house and knocked. After a quick search Roschmann was discovered under a bed. Had he tried to brazen it out, claiming mistaken identity, he might have made the sergeants believe the old man was wrong. But hiding under a bed was the giveaway. He was led off to be interviewed by Major Hardy of the FSS, who promptly had him locked up in a cell while a request went off to Berlin and the American index of the SS.

Confirmation arrived in forty-eight hours, and the balloon went up. Even while the request was in Potsdam, asking for Russian help in establishing the dossier on Riga, the Americans asked for Roschmann to be transferred to Munich on a temporary basis, to give evidence at Dachau, where the Americans were putting on trial other SS men who had been active in the complex of camps around Riga. The British agreed.

At six in the morning of January 8, 1948, Roschmann, accompanied by a sergeant of the Royal Military Police and another from Field Security, was put on a train at Graz, bound for Salzburg and Munich.

Lord Russell paused in his pacing, crossed to the fireplace, and knocked out his pipe.

"Then what happened?" asked Miller.

"He escaped," said Lord Russell.

"He *what?*"

"He escaped. He jumped from the lavatory window of the moving train, after complaining the prison diet had given him diarrhea. By the time his two escorts had smashed in the lavatory door, he was gone into the snow. They never found him. A search was mounted, of course, but he had gone, evidently through the snowdrifts, to make contact with one of the organizations prepared to help ex-Nazis escape. Sixteen months later, in May nineteen forty-nine, your new republic was founded, and we handed over all our files to Bonn."

Miller finished writing and laid his notebook down. "Where does one go from here?" he asked.

Lord Russell blew out his cheeks. "Well, now, your own people, I suppose. You have Roschmann's life from birth to the eighth of January nineteen forty-eight. The rest is up to the German authorities."

"Which ones?" asked Miller, fearing what the answer would be.

"As it concerns Riga, the Hamburg Attorney General's office, I suppose," said Lord Russell.

"I've been there."

"They didn't help much?"

"Not at all."

Lord Russell grinned. "Not surprised, not surprised. Have you tried Ludwigsburg?"

"Yes. They were nice, but not very helpful. Against the rules," said Miller.

"Well, that exhausts the official lines of inquiry. There's only one other man. Have you ever heard of Simon Wiesenthal?"

"Wiesenthal? Yes, vaguely. The name rings a bell, but I can't place it."

"He lives in Vienna. Jewish chap, came from Polish Galicia originally. Spent four years in a series of concentration camps, twelve in all. Decided to spend the rest of his days tracking down wanted Nazi criminals. No rough stuff, mind you. He just keeps collating all the information about them he can get; then, when he's convinced he has found one, usually living under a false name—not always—he informs the police. If they don't act, he gives a press conference and puts them in a spot. Needless to say, he's not terribly popular with officialdom in either Germany or Austria. He reckons they are not doing enough to bring down Nazi murderers to book, let alone chase the hidden ones. The former SS hate his guts and have tried to kill him a couple of times; the bureaucrats wish he would leave them alone, and a lot of other people think he's a great chap and help him where they can."

"Yes, the name rings a bell now. Wasn't he the man who found Adolf Eichmann?" asked Miller.

Lord Miller nodded. "He identified him as Ricardo Klement, living in Buenos Aires. The Israelis took over from there. He's also traced several hundred other Nazi criminals. If anything more is known about your

Eduard Roschmann, he'll know it."

"Do you know him?" asked Miller.

Lord Russell nodded. "I'd better give you a letter. He gets a lot of visitors wanting information. An introduction would help."

He went to the writing desk, swiftly wrote a few lines on a sheet of headed notepaper, folded the sheet into an envelope, and sealed it.

"Good luck, you'll need it," he said as he showed Miller out.

The following morning Miller took the BEA flight back to Cologne, picked up his car, and set off on the two-day run through Stuttgart, Munich, Salzburg, and Linz to Vienna.

He spent the night at Munich, having made slow time along the snow-encrusted autobahns frequently narrowed down to one lane while a snow-plow or sanding truck tried to cope with the steadily falling snow. The following day he set off early and would have made Vienna by lunchtime had it not been for the long delay at Bad Tolz just south of Munich.

The autobahn was passing through dense pine forests when a series of SLOW signs brought the traffic to a halt. A police car, blue light spinning a warning, was parked at the edge of the road, and two white-coated patrolmen were standing across the road, holding back the traffic. In the left-hand, northbound lane the procedure was the same. To the right and left of the autobahn a drive cut into the pine forests, and two soldiers in winter clothing, each with a battery-powered illuminated baton, stood at the entrance to each, waiting to summmon something hidden in the forests across the road.

Miller fumed with impatience and finally wound down his window to call to one of the policemen. "What's the matter? What's the hold-up?"

The patrolman walked slowly over and grinned. "The Army," he said shortly. "They're on maneuvers. There's a column of tanks coming across in a minute."

Fifteen minutes later the first one appeared, a long gun barrel poking out of the pine trees, like a pachyderm scenting the air for danger; then with a rumble the flat armored bulk of the tank eased out of the trees and clattered down to the road.

Top Sergeant Ulrich Frank was a happy man. At the age of thirty he had already fulfilled his life's ambition, to command his own tank. He could remember to the day when his life's ambition had been born in him. It was January 1945 when, as a small boy in the city of Mannheim, he had been taken to the cinema. The screen during the newsreels was full of the spectacle of Hasso von Manteuffel's King Tiger tanks rolling forward to engage the Americans and British.

He stared in awe at the muffled figures of the commanders, steel-helmeted and goggled, gazing forward out of the turrets. For Ulrich Frank, eleven years old, it was a turning point. When he left the cinema he had made a vow, that one day he would command his own tank.

It took him nineteen years, but he made it. On those winter maneuvers in the forests around Bad Tolz, Top Sergeant Ulrich Frank commanded his first tank, an American-built M-48 Patton.

It was his last maneuver with the Patton. Waiting for the troop back at camp was a row of shining, brand-new French AMX-13s with which the unit was being re-equipped. Faster, more heavily armed than the Patton, the AMX would become his in another week.

He glanced down at the black cross of the new German Army on the side of the turret, and the tank's personal name stenciled beneath it, and felt a touch of regret. Though he had commanded it for only six months, it would always be his first tank, his favorite. He had named it Drachenfels, the Dragon Rock, after the rock overlooking the Rhine. After the re-equipment, he supposed the Patton would go for scrap.

With a last pause on the far side of the autobahn, the Patton and its crew breasted the rise and vanished into the forest.

Miller finally made it to Vienna in midafternoon of that day, January 3. Without checking into a hotel, he drove straight into the city center and asked his way to Rudolf Square.

He found number 7 easily enough and glanced at the list of tenants. Against the third floor was a card saying DOCUMENTATION CENTER. He mounted and knocked at the cream-painted wooden door. From behind it someone looked through the peephole before he heard the lock being drawn back. A pretty blond girl stood in the doorway.

"Please?"

"My name is Miller. Peter Miller. I would like to speak with Herr Wiesenthal. I have a letter of introduction."

He produced his letter and gave it to the girl. She looked uncertainly at it, smiled briefly, and asked him to wait.

Several minutes later she reappeared at the end of the corridor onto which the door gave access, and beckoned him. "Please come this way."

Miller closed the front door behind him and followed her down the passage, around a corner, and to the end of the apartment. On the right was an open door. As he entered, a man rose to greet him.

"Please come in," said Simon Wiesenthal.

He was bigger than Miller had expected, a burly man over six feet tall, wearing a thick tweed jacket, stooping as if permanently looking for a mislaid piece of paper. He held Lord Russell's letter in his hand.

The office was small to the point of being cramped. One wall was lined from end to end and ceiling to floor in shelves, each crammed with books. The wall facing was decorated with illuminated manuscripts and testimonials from a score of organizations of former victims of the SS. The back wall contained a long sofa, also stacked with books, and to the left of the door was a small window looking down on a courtyard. The desk stood away from the window, and Miller took the visitor's chair in front of it. The Nazi-hunter of Vienna seated himself behind it and reread Lord Russell's letter.

"My friend Lord Russell tells me you are trying to hunt down a former SS killer," he began without preamble.

"Yes, that's true."

"May I have his name?"

"Roschmann. Captain Eduard Roschmann."

Simon Wiesenthal raised his eyebrows and exhaled his breath in a whistle.

"You've heard of him?" asked Miller.

"The Butcher of Riga? One of my top fifty wanted men," said Wiesenthal. "May I ask why you are interested in him?"

Miller began to explain briefly.

"I think you'd better start at the beginning," said Wiesenthal. "What's all this about a diary?"

With the man in Ludwigsburg, Cadbury, and Lord Russell, this made the fourth time Miller had had to relate the story. Each time it grew a little longer as another period had been added to his knowledge of Roschmann's life story. He began again and went through until he had described the help given by Lord Russell.

"What I have to know now," he ended, "is where did he go when he jumped from the train?"

Simon Wiesenthal was gazing out into the court of the apartment house, watching the snowflakes dropping down the narrow shaft to the ground three floors below.

"Have you got the diary?" he asked at length. Miller reached down, took it out of his briefcase, and laid it on the desk.

Wiesenthal eyed it appreciatively. "Fascinating," he said. He looked up and smiled. "All right, I accept the story," he said.

Miller raised his eyebrows. "Was there any doubt?"

Simon Wiesenthal eyed him keenly. "There is always a little doubt, Herr Miller," he said. "Yours is a very strange story. I still cannot follow your motive for wanting to track Roschmann down."

Miller shrugged. "I'm a reporter. It's a good story."

"But not one you will ever sell to the press, I fear. And hardly worth your own money. Are you sure there's nothing personal in this?"

Miller ducked the question. "You're the second person who has suggested that. Hoffmann suggested the same at *Komet*. Why should there be? I'm only twenty-nine years old. All this was before my time."

"Of course." Wiesenthal glanced at his watch and rose. "It is five o'clock, and I like to get home to my wife these winter evenings. Would you let me read the diary over the weekend?"

"Yes, of course," said Miller.

"Good. Then please come back on Monday morning, and I will fill in what I know of the Roschmann story."

Miller arrived on Monday at ten and found Simon Wiesenthal attacking a pile of letters. He looked up as the German reporter came in and gestured him to a seat. There was silence for a while as the Nazi-hunter carefully snipped the edges off the sides of his envelopes before sliding the contents out.

"I collect the stamps," he said, "so I don't like to damage the envelopes." He worked away for a few more minutes. "I read the diary last night at home. Remarkable document."

"Were you surprised?" asked Miller.

"Surprised? No, not by the contents. We all went through much the same sort of thing. With variations, of course. But so precise. Tauber would have made a perfect witness. He noticed everything, even the small details. And noted them—at the time. That is very important to get a conviction before German or Austrian courts. And now he's dead."

Miller considered for a while. He looked up. "Herr Wiesenthal, so far as I know, you're the first Jew I have ever really had a long talk with, who went through all that. One thing Tauber said in his diary surprised me: he said there was no such thing as collective guilt. But we Germans have been told for twenty years that we are all guilty. Do you believe that?"

"No," said the Nazi-hunter flatly. "Tauber was right."

"How can you say that, if we killed fourteen million people?"

"Because you, personally, were not there. You did not kill anyone. As Tauber said, the tragedy is that the specific murderers have not been brought to justice."

"Then who," asked Miller, "really did kill those people?"

Simon Wiesenthal regarded him intently. "Do you know about the various branches of the SS? About the sections within the SS that really were responsible for killing those millions?" he asked.

"No."

"Then I'd better tell you. You've heard about the Reich Economic Administration Main Office, charged with exploiting the victims before they died?"

"Yes, I read something about it."

"Its job was in a sense the middle section of the operation," said Herr Wiesenthal. "That left the business of identifying the victims among the rest of the population, rounding them up, transporting them, and, when the economic exploitation was over, finishing them off. This was the task of the RSHA, the Reich Security Main Office, which actually killed the fourteen million already mentioned. The rather odd use of the word 'Security' in the title of this office stems from the quaint Nazi idea that the victims posed a threat to the Reich, which had to be made secure against them. Also in the functions of the RSHA were the tasks of rounding up, interrogating, and incarcerating in concentration camps other enemies of the Reich like Communists, Social Democrats, Liberals, editors, reporters, and priests who spoke out too inconveniently, resistance fighters in the occupied countries, and later Army officers like Field Marshal Erwin Rommel and Admiral Wilhelm Canaris, both murdered for suspicion of harboring anti-Hitler sentiments.

"The RSHA was divided into six departments, each called an Amt. Amt One was for administration and personnel; Amt Two was equipment and finance. Amt Three was the dreaded Security Service and Security police, headed by Reinhardt Heydrich, assassinated in Prague in 1942, and later by Ernst Kaltenbrunner, executed by the Allies. Theirs were the teams who devised the tortures used to make suspects talk, both inside Germany and in the occupied countries.

"Amt Four was the Gestapo, headed by Heinrich Müller (still missing), whose Jewish Section, department B4, was headed by Adolf Eichmann, executed by the Israelis in Jerusalem after being kidnaped from Argentina. Amt Five was the Criminal Police, and Amt Six the Foreign Intelligence Service.

"The two successive heads of Amt Three, Heydrich and Kaltenbrunner, were also the over-all chiefs of the whole RSHA, and throughout the reigns of both men the head of Amt One was their deputy. He is Lieutenant General of the SS Bruno Streckenbach, who today has a well-paid job with a department store in Hamburg and lives in Vogelweide.

"If one is going to specify guilt, therefore, most of it rests on these two departments of the SS, and the numbers involved are thousands, not the millions who make up contemporary Germany. The theory of the collective guilt of sixty million Germans, including millions of small children, women, old-age pensioners, soldiers, sailors, and airmen, who had nothing to do with the holocaust, was originally conceived by the Allies, but has since suited the former members of the SS extremely well. The theory is the best ally they have, for they realize, as few Germans seem to do, that so long as the collective-guilt theory remains unquestioned nobody will start to look for specific murderers—at least, look hard enough. The specific murderers of the SS therefore hide even today behind the collective-guilt theory."

Miller digested what he had been told. Somehow the very size of the figures involved baffled him. It was not possible to consider fourteen million people as each and every one an individual. It was easier to think of one man, dead on a stretcher under the rain in a Hamburg street.

"The reason Tauber apparently had for killing himself," Miller asked, "do you believe it?"

Herr Wiesenthal studied a beautiful pair of African stamps on one of the envelopes. "I believe he was right in thinking no one would believe that he saw Roschmann on the steps of the Opera. If that's what he believed, then he was right."

"But he didn't even go to the police," said Miller.

Simon Weisenthal snipped the edge off another envelope and scanned the letter inside. After a pause he replied, "No. Technically he should have. I don't think it would have done any good. Not in Hamburg, at any rate."

"What's wrong with Hamburg?"

"You went to the State Attorney General's office there?" asked Wiesenthal mildly.

"Yes, I did. They weren't terribly helpful."

Wiesenthal looked up. "I'm afraid the Attorney General's department in Hamburg has a certain reputation in this office," he said. "Take for example the man mentioned by me just now, SS General Bruno Streckenbach. Remember the name?"

"Of course," said Miller. "What about him?"

For answer Simon Wiesenthal riffled through a pile of papers on his desk, abstracted one, and gazed at it. "Here he is," he said. "Known to West German justice as Document 141 JS 747/61. Want to hear about him?"

"I have time," said Miller.

"Right. Here goes. Before the war Gestapo chief in Hamburg. Climbed rapidly from then on to a top position in the SD and SP, the Security Service and Security Police sections of the RSHA. In 1939 he led an extermination squad in Nazi-occupied Poland. At the end of 1940 he was head of the SD and SP sections of the SS for the whole of Poland, the so-called General Government, sitting in Cracow. Thousands were exterminated by SD and SP units in Poland during that period, mainly through Operation AB.

"At the start of 1941 he came back to Berlin, promoted to Chief of Personnel for the SD. That was Amt Three of the RSHA. His chief was Reinhardt Heydrich, and he became his deputy. Just before the invasion of Russia he helped to organize the extermination squads that went in behind the Army. As head of staffing he picked the personnel himself, for they were all from the SD branch.

"Then he was promoted again, this time to head of personnel for the entire six branches of the RSHA, and remained deputy chief of the RSHA under first Heydrich, who was killed by Czech partisans in Prague in 1942—that was the killing that led to the reprisal at Lidice—and then under Ernst Kaltenbrunner. As such he had all-embracing responsibility for the choice of personnel of the roving extermination squads and the fixed SD units throughout the Nazi-occupied eastern territories until the end of the war."

Miller looked stunned. "They haven't arrested him?" he asked.

"Who?"

"The police of Hamburg, of course."

For answer Simon Wiesenthal rummaged in a drawer and produced another sheet of paper. He folded it neatly down the center from top to bottom and laid it in front of Miller so that only the left side of the sheet was facing upward.

"Do you recognize those names?" he asked.

Miller scanned the list of ten names with a frown. "Of course. I've been a police reporter in Hamburg for years. These are all senior police officers of the Hamburg force. Why?"

"Spread the paper out," said Wiesenthal.

Miller did so. Fully expanded, the sheet read:

Name	Nazi Pty. No	SS No.	Rank	Promotion Date
A.	———	455,336	Capt.	1.3.43
B.	5,451,195	429,339	1st. Lt.	9.11.42
C.	———	353,004	1st. Lt.	1.11.41
D.	7,039,564	421,176	Capt.	21.6.44
E.	———	421,445	1st. Lt.	9.11.42
F.	7,040,308	174,902	Major	21.6.44
G.	———	426,553	Capt.	1.9.42
H.	3,138,798	311,870	Capt.	30.1.42
I.	1,867,976	424,361	1st Lt.	20.4.44
J.	5,063,331	309,825	Major	9.11.43

Miller looked up. "Christ," he said.

"Now do you begin to understand why a lieutenant general of the SS is walking around Hamburg today? They can't arrest him. He was their commanding officer once."

Miller looked at the list in disbelief. "That must have been what Brandt meant about inquiries into the former SS not being very popular in the Hamburg police."

"Probably," said Wiesenthal. "Nor is the Attorney General's office the most energetic in Germany. There's one lawyer on the staff at least who is trying, but certain interested parties have tried to have him dismissed several times."

The pretty secretary poked her head around the door. "Tea or coffee?" she asked.

After a lunchtime break, Miller returned to the office. Simon Wiesenthal had in front of him a number of sheets spread out, extracts from his own Roschmann file. Miller settled himself in front of the desk, got out his notebook, and waited.

Simon Wiesenthal began to relate the Roschmann story from January 8, 1948.

It had been agreed between the British and American authorities that after Roschmann had testified at Dachau he would be moved on to the British Zone of Germany, probably Hanover, to await his own trial and almost certain hanging. Even while in prison in Graz he had begun to plan his escape.

He had made contact with a Nazi escape organization working in Austria called the Six-Point Star, nothing to do with the Jewish symbol of the six-pointed star, but so called because the Nazi organization had its tentacles in six major Austrian cities, mainly in the British Zone.

At 6:00 a. m. on the eighth, Roschmann was awakened and taken to the train waiting at Graz station. Once he was in the compartment, an argument started between the Military Police sergeant, who wanted to keep the handcuffs on Roschmann throughout the journey, and the Field Security sergeant, who suggested taking them off.

Roschmann influenced the argument by claiming that he had diarrhea from the prison diet and wished to go to the lavatory. He was taken, the handcuffs were removed, and one of the sergeants waited outside the door until he had finished. As the train chugged through the snowbound landscape Roschmann made three requests to go to the lavatory. Apparently during this time he prized the window in the lavatory open, so that it slid easily on its runners.

Roschmann knew he had to get out before the Americans took him over at Salzburg for the last run by car to their own prison at Munich, but station after station went by, and still the train was going too fast. It stopped at Hallein, and one of the sergeants went to buy some food on the platform. Roschmann again said he wanted to go to the lavatory. It was the more easygoing FSS sergeant who accompanied him, warning him not to use the toilet while the train was stationary. As the train moved slowly out of Hallein, Roschmann jumped from the window into the snowdrifts. It was ten minutes before the sergeants beat down the door, and by then the train was running fast down the mountains toward Salzburg.

He staggered through the snow as far as a peasant's cottage and took refuge there. The following day he crossed the border from Upper Austria into Salzburg province and contacted the Six-point Star organization. It brought him to a brick factory, where he passed as a laborer, while contact was made with the Odessa for a passage to the south and Italy.

At that time the Odessa was in close contact with the recruitment section of the French Foreign Legion, into which scores of former SS soldiers had fled. Four days after contact was made, a car with French number plates was waiting outside the town of Ostermieting and took on board Roschmann and five other Nazi escapers. The Foreign Legion driver, equipped with papers that enabled the car to cross borders without being searched, brought the six SS men over the Italian border to Merano and was paid in cash by the Odessa representative there, a hefty sum per head of his passengers.

From Merano, Roschmann was taken down to an Italian displaced-persons camp at Rimini. Here, in the camp hospital, he had the five toes of his right foot amputated, for they were rotten with frostbite he had picked up while wandering through the snow after escaping from the train. Since then he had worn an orthopedic shoe.

His wife in Graz got a letter from him in October 1948 from the camp at Rimini. For the first time he used the new name he had been given, Fritz Bernd Wegener.

Shortly afterward he was transferred to the Franciscan Monastery in Rome, and when his papers were finalized he set sail from the harbor at Naples for Buenos Aires. Throughout his stay at the monastery in the Via Sicilia he had been among scores of comrades of the SS and the Nazi Party and under the personal supervision of Bishop Alois Hudal, who ensured that they lacked nothing.

In the Argentinian capital he was received by the Odessa and lodged with a German family called Vidmar in the Calle Hipolito Irigoyen. Here he lived for months in a furnished room. Early in 1949 he was advanced the sum of 50,000 American dollars out of the Bormann funds in Switzerland and went into business as an exporter of South American hardwood timber to Western Europe. The firm was called Stemmler and Wegener, for his false papers from Rome firmly established him as Fritz Bernd Wegener, born in the South Tirol province of Italy.

He also engaged a German girl as his secretary, Irmtraud Sigrid Müller, and in early 1955 he married her, despite his wife Hella, still living in Graz. But Roschmann was becoming nervous. In July 1952 Eva Perón, wife of the dictator of Argentina and the power behind the throne, had died of cancer. Three years later the writing was on the wall for the Perón regime, and Roschmann spotted it. If Perón fell, much of the protection accorded by him to ex-Nazis might be removed by his successors. With his new wife, Roschmann left for Egypt.

He spent three months there in the summer of 1955 and came to West Germany in the autumn. Nobody would have known a thing but for the anger of a woman betrayed. His first wife, Hella Roschmann, wrote to him from Graz, care of the Vidmar family in Buenos Aires, during that summer. The Vidmars, having no forwarding address for their former lodger, opened the letter and replied to the wife in Graz, telling her that he had gone back to Germany but had married his secretary.

Furious, the wife informed the police of his new name, Fritz Wegener, and asked for a warrant for his arrest on a charge of bigamy.

Immediately a lookout was posted for a man calling himself Fritz Bernd Wegener in West Germany.

"Did they get him?' asked Miller.

Wiesenthal looked up and shook his head. "No, he disappeared again. Almost certainly under a new set of false papers, and almost certainly in Germany. You see, that's why I believe Tauber could have seen him. It all fits with the known facts."

"Where's the first wife, Hella Roschmann?" asked Miller.

"She still lives in Graz."

"Is it worth contacting her?"

Wiesenthal shook his head. "I doubt it. The moment she learned of the bigamy, she spilled the beans to the police as far as she knew anything. There's nothing more she knows beyond what she has said, for she now hates him like poison and wants him arrested. Needless to say, after being 'blown,' Roschmann is not likely to reveal his whereabouts to her again. Or his new

name. For him it must have been quite an emergency when his identity of
Wegener was exposed. He must have acquired his new papers in a devil of a
hurry."

"Who would have got them for him?" asked Miller.

"The Odessa, certainly."

"Just what is the Odessa? You've mentioned it several times in the course
of the Roschmann story."

"You've never heard of them?" asked Wiesenthal.

"No. Not until now."

Simon Wiesenthal glanced at his watch. "You'd better come back in the
morning. I'll tell you all about them."

NINE

Peter Miller returned to Simon Wiesenthal's office the following morning.

"You promised to tell me about the Odessa," he said. "I remembered
something overnight that I forgot to tell you yesterday."

He recounted the incident of Dr. Schmidt, who had accosted him at the
Dreesen Hotel and warned him off the Roschmann inquiry.

Wiesenthal pursed his lips and nodded. "You're up against them, all
right," he said. "It's most unusual for them to take such a step as to warn a
reporter in that way, particularly at such an early stage. I wonder what
Roschmann is up to that could be so important."

Then for two hours the Nazi-hunter told Miller about the Odessa, from its
start as an organization for getting wanted SS criminals to a place of safety to
its development into an all-embracing free-masonry among those who had
once worn the black-and-silver collars, their aiders and abettors.

When the Allies stormed into Germany in 1945 and found the concentration camps with their hideous contents, they not unnaturally rounded on the
German people to demand who had carried out the atrocities. The answer
was "The SS"—but the members of the SS were nowhere to be found.

Where had they gone? They had either gone underground inside Germany and Austria, or fled abroad. In both cases their disappearance was no
spur-of-the-moment flight. What the Allies failed to realize until much later
was that each had meticulously prepared his disappearance beforehand.

It casts an interesting light on the so-called patriotism of the SS that,
starting at the top with Heinrich Himmler, each tried to save his own skin at
the expense of the suffering German people. As early as November 1944
Heinrich Himmler tried to negotiate his own safe conduct through the
offices of Count Bernadotte of the Swedish Red Cross. The Allies refused to
consider letting him off the hook. While the Nazis and the SS screamed at
the German people to fight on until the wonder weapons waiting around the
corner were delivered, they themselves prepared for their departure to a
comfortable exile elsewhere. They at least knew there were no wonder
weapons, and that the destruction of the Reich and, if Hitler had anything to
do with it, of the entire German nation, was inevitable.

On the Eastern Front the German Army was bullied into battle against the Russians to take unbelievable casualties, not to produce victory but to produce a delay while the SS finalized its escape plans. Behind the Army stood the SS, shooting and hanging some of the Army men who took a step backward after already taking more punishment than military flesh and blood is usually expected to stand. Thousands of officers and men of the Wehrmacht died in SS nooses in this way.

Just before the final collapse, delayed six months after the chiefs of the SS knew defeat was inevitable, the leaders of the SS disappeared. From one end of the country to the other they quit their posts, changed into civilian clothes, stuffed their beautifully (and officially) forged personal papers into their pockets, and vanished into the chaos that was Germany in May 1945. They left the old men of the Home Guard to meet the British and the Americans at the gates of the concentration camps, the exhausted Wehrmacht to go into prison-of-war camps, and the women and children to live or die under Allied rule in the coming bitter winter of 1945.

Those who knew they were too well known to escape detection for long fled abroad. This was where the Odessa came in. Formed just before the end of the war, it was designed to get wanted SS men out of Germany to safety. Already it had established close and friendly links with Juan Perón's Argentina, which had issued seven thousand Argentinian passports "in blank" so that the refugee merely had to fill in a false name and his own photograph, get it stamped by the ever-ready Argentine consul, and board ship for Buenos Aires or the Middle East.

Thousands of SS murderers poured southward through Austria and into the South Tirol province of Italy. They were shuttled from safe house to safe house along the route, thence mainly to the Italian port of Genoa or farther south to Rimini and Rome. A number of organizations, some supposed to be concerned with charitable work among the truly dispossessed, took it upon themselves, for reasons best known to themselves, to decide, on some evidence of their own imagining, that the SS refugees were being overharshly persecuted by the Allies.

Among the chief Scarlet Pimpernels of Rome who spirited thousands away to safety was Bishop Alois Hudal, the German Bishop in Rome. The main hiding-out station for the SS killers was the enormous Franciscan monastery in Rome, where they were hidden and boarded until papers could be arranged, along with a passage to South America. In some cases the SS men traveled on Red Cross travel documents, issued through the intervention of the Vatican and in many cases the charitable organization Caritas paid for their tickets.

This was the first task of Odessa, and it was largely successful. Just how many thousands of SS murderers who would have died for their crimes, had they been caught by the Allies, passed to safety will never be known, but they were well over eighty per cent of those meriting the death sentence.

Having established itself comfortably on the proceeds of mass murder, transferred from the Swiss banks, the Odessa sat back and watched the deterioration of relations between the Allies of 1945. The early ideas of the quick establishment of a Fourth Reich were discarded in the course of time by the leaders of the Odessa in South America as impractical, but with the establishment in May 1949 of a new Republic of West Germany, those leaders of the Odessa set themselves five new tasks.

The first was the reinfiltration of former members of the SS into every facet of life in the new Germany. Throughout the late forties and fifties former members of the SS slipped into the civil service at every level, back into lawyers' offices, onto judges' benches, into the police forces, local government, and doctors' surgeries. From these positions, however lowly, they were able to protect each other from investigation and arrest, advance each other's interests, and generally ensure that investigation and prosecution of former comrades—they called each other *Kamerad*—went forward as slowly as possible, if at all.

The second task was to infiltrate the mechanisms of political power. Avoiding the high levels, former Nazis slipped into the grassroots organization of the ruling party at ward and constituency level. Again, there was no law to forbid a former member of the SS from joining a political party. It may be a coincidence, but unlikely, that no politician with a known record of calling for increased vigor in the investigation and prosecution of SS crimes has ever been elected in the CDU or the CSU, either at federal level or at the equally important level of the very powerful provincial parliaments. One politician expressed it with crisp simplicity: "It's a question of election mathematics. Six million dead Jews don't vote. Five million former Nazis can and do, at every election."

The main aim of both these programs was simple. It was and is to slow down, if not to stop, the investigation and prosecution of former members of the SS. In this the Odessa had one other great ally. This was the secret knowledge in the minds of hundreds of thousands that they had either helped in what was done, albeit in a small way, or had known at the time what was going on and had remained silent. Years later, established and respected in their communities and professions, they could hardly relish the idea of energetic investigation into past events, let alone the mention of their names in a faraway courtroom where an SS man was on trial.

The third task the Odessa set itself in postwar Germany was to reinfiltrate business, commerce, and industry. To this end certain former SS men were established in businesses of their own in the early fifties, bankrolled by funds from the Zurich deposits. Any reasonably well-administered concern founded with plenty of liquidity in the early fifties could take full advantage of the staggering economic miracle of the fifties and sixties, to become in turn a large and flourishing business. The point of this was to use funds out of the profits from these businesses to influence press coverage of the SS crimes through advertising revenue, to assist financially the crop of SS-oriented propaganda sheets that have come and gone in postwar Germany, to keep alive some of the ultra-Right Wing publishing houses, and to provide jobs for former *Kameraden* fallen on hard times.

The fourth task was and still is to provide the best possible legal defense for any SS man forced to stand trial. In every case where an SS murderer has come before a court, his defense lawyers have been among the most brilliant and the most expensive in Germany. But no one ever asks who pays them when their client is a poor man, and they would be the first to deny that they do their work for SS men for free.

The fifth task is propaganda. This takes many forms, from encouraging the dissemination of Right Wing pamphlets to lobbying for a final ratification of the Statute of Limitations, under whose terms an end would be put to all culpability in law of the SS. Efforts are made to assure the Germans of today that the death figures of the Jews, Russians, Poles, and others were but a tiny fraction of those quoted by the Allies—100,000 dead Jews is the usual figure mentioned—and to point out that the Cold War between the West and the Soviet Union in some way proves Hitler to have been right.

But the mainstay of the Odessa propaganda is to persuade the seventy million Germans of today—and with a large degree of success—that the SS men were in fact patriotic soldiers like the Wehrmacht and that solidarity among former comrades must be upheld. This is the weirdest ploy of them all.

During the war the Wehrmacht kept its distance from the SS, which it regarded with repugnance, while the SS treated the Wehrmacht with contempt. At the end, millions of young Wehrmacht men were hurled into death or captivity at Russian hands, from which only a small proportion returned, and this so that the SS men could live prosperously elsewhere. Thousands more were executed by the SS, incuding five thousand in the aftermath of the July 1944 plot against Adolf Hitler, in which fewer than fifty men were implicated.

How former members of the German Army, Navy, and Air Force can conceivably regard ex-SS men as meriting from them the salutation *Kamerad*, let alone their solidarity and protection from prosecution, is a mystery. Yet herein lies the real success of the Odessa.

By and large the Odessa has succeeded in its tasks of stultifying West German efforts to hunt down and bring to trial the SS murderers. It has succeeded by virtue of its own ruthlessness, occasionally against its own kind if they seem likely to make full confessions to the authorities, of Allied mistakes between 1945 and 1949, of the Cold War, and of the usual German cowardice when faced with a moral problem, in stark contrast to German courage when faced with a military task or a technical issue like the reconstruction of postwar Germany.

When Simon Wiesenthal had finished, Miller laid down the pencil with which he had made copious notes and sat back.

"I hadn't the faintest idea," he said.

"Very few Germans have," conceded Wiesenthal. "In fact, very few people know much about the Odessa at all. The word is hardly ever mentioned in Germany and just as certain members of the American underworld will stoutly deny the existence of the Mafia, so any former member of the SS will deny the existence of the Odessa. To be perfectly frank, the term is not used as much nowadays as formerly. The new word is 'the Comradeship,' just as the Mafia in America is called *Cosa Nostra*. But what's in a name? The Odessa is still there, and will be while there is an SS criminal to protect."

"And you think these are the men I'm up against?" asked Miller.

"I'm sure of it. The warning you were given in Bad Godesberg could not have come from anyone else. Do be careful; these men can be dangerous."

Miller's mind was on something else. "When Roschmann disappeared, after his wife had given away his new name, you said he would need a fresh passport?"

"Certainly."

"Why the passport particularly?"

Simon Wiesenthal leaned back in his chair and nodded. "I can understand why you are puzzled. Let me explain. After the war in Germany, and here in Austria, there were tens of thousands wandering about with no identification papers. Some had genuinely lost them; others had thrown them away for good reason.

"To obtain new ones, it would normally be necessary to produce a birth certificate. But millions had fled from the former German territories overrun by the Russians. Who was to say if a man was, or was not, born in a small village in East Prussia, now miles behind the Iron Curtain? In other cases the buildings in which the certificates were stored had been destroyed by bombing.

"So the process was very simple. All one needed were two witnesses to swear that one was who one said, and a fresh personal ID card was issued. In the case of prisoners-of-war, they often had no papers either. On their release from camp, the British and American camp authorities would sign a release paper to the effect that Corporal Johann Schumann was certified as released from prisoner camp. These papers were then taken by the soldier to the civilian authorities, who issued an ID card in the same name. But often the man had only told the Allies his name was Johann Schumann. It could have been something else. No one checked. And so he got a new identity.

"That was all right in the immediate aftermath of the war, which was when most of the SS criminals were getting their new identities. But what happens to a man who is blown wide open in 1955, as was Roschmann? He can't go to the authorities and say he lost his papers during the war. They would be bound to ask how he had got by during the ten-year interim period. So he needs a passport."

"I understand so far," said Miller. "But why a passport? Why not a driving license or an ID card?"

"Because shortly after the founding of the republic the German authorities realized there must be hundreds or thousands wandering about under false names. There was a need for one document that was so well researched that it could act as the yardstick for all the others. They hit on the passport. Before you get a passport in Germany, you have to produce a birth certificate, several references, and a host of other documentation. These are thoroughly checked before the passport is issued.

"By contrast, once you have a passport, you can get anything else on the strength of it. Such is bureaucracy. The production of the passport convinces the civil servant that, since previous bureaucrats must have checked out the passport-holder thoroughly, no further checking is necessary. With a new passport, Roschmann could quickly build up the rest of the identity—driving license, back accounts, credit cards. The passport is the Open Sesame to every other piece of necessary documentation in present-day Germany."

"Where would the passport come from?"

"From the Odessa. They must have a forger somewhere who can turn them out," Wiesenthal said.

Miller thought for a while. "If one could find the passport-forger, one might find the man who could identify Roschmann today?" he suggested.

Wiesenthal shrugged. "One might. But it would be a long shot. And to do that one would have to penetrate the Odessa. Only an ex-SS man could do that."

"Then where do I go from here?" said Miller.

"I should think your best bet would be to try and contact some of the survivors of Riga. I don't know whether they would be able to help you further, but they'd certainly be willing. We are all trying to find Roschmann. Look." He flicked open the diary on his desk. "There's reference here to a certain Olli Adler from Munich, who was in Roschmann's company during the war. It may be she survived and came home to Munich."

Miller nodded. "If she did, where would she register?"

"At the Jewish Community Center. It still exists. It contains the archives of the Jewish community of Munich—since the war, that is. Everything else was destroyed. I'd try there."

"Do you have the address?"

Simon Wiesenthal checked through an address book. "Reichenbach-strasse, number twenty-seven, Munich," he said. "I suppose you want the diary of Salomon Tauber back?"

"Yes, I'm afraid I do."

"Too bad. I'd like to have kept it. A remarkable diary."

He rose and escorted Miller to the front door. "Good luck," he said, "and let me know how you get on."

Miller had dinner that evening in the House of the Golden Dragon, which had been in business as a beer house and restaurant in the Steindelgasse without a break from 1566, and thought over the advice. He had little hope of finding more than a handful of survivors of Riga still in Germany or Austria, and even less hope that any might help him track Roschmann beyond November 1955. But it was a hope, a last hope.

He left the next morning for the drive back to Munich.

TEN

Miller drove into Munich at midmorning of January 9 and found 27 Reichenbachstrasse from a map of Munich bought at a newspaper kiosk in the outskirts. Parking down the road, he surveyed the Jewish Community Center before entering. It was a flat-fronted five-story building. The façade of the ground floor was of uncovered stone blocks; above this the façade was of gray cement over brick. The fifth and top floor was marked by a row of mansard windows set in the red tile roof. At ground level there was a double door of glass panels at the extreme left end of the building.

The building contained a kosher restaurant, the only one in Munich, on the ground floor, the leisure rooms of the old people's home on the one above. The third floor contained the administration and records department, and the upper two housed the guest rooms and sleeping quarters of the inmates of the old people's home. At the back was a synagogue.

He went up to the third floor and presented himself at the inquiry desk. While he waited he glanced around the room. There were rows of books, all new, for the original library had long since been burned by the Nazis. Between the library shelves were portraits of some of the leaders of the Jewish community, stretching back hundreds of years, teachers and rabbis, gazing out of their frames above luxuriant beards, like the figures of the prophets he had seen in his Scripture textbooks at school. Some wore phylacteries bound to their foreheads, and all were hatted.

There was a rack of newspapers, some in German, others in Hebrew. He presumed the latter were flown in from Israel. A short dark man was scanning the front page of one of these.

"Can I help you?"

He looked around to the inquiry desk to find it now occupied by a dark-eyed woman in her mid-forties. There was a strand of hair falling over her eyes, which she nervously brushed back into place several times a minute.

Miller made his request: any trace of Olli Adler, who might have reported back to Munich after the war?

"Where would she have returned from?" asked the woman.

"From Magdeburg. Before that, Stutthof. Before that, from Riga."

"Oh dear, Riga," said the woman. "I don't think we have anyone on the lists who came back here from Riga. They all disappeared, you know. But I'll look."

She went into a back room, and Miller could see her going steadily through an index of names. It was not a big index. She returned after five minutes.

"I'm sorry. Nobody of that name reported back here after the war. It is a common name. But there is nobody listed."

Miller nodded. "I see. That looks like it, then. Sorry to have troubled you."

"You might try the International Tracing Service," said the woman. "It's really their job to find people who are missing. They have lists from all over Germany, whereas we only have the lists of those originating in Munich who came back."

"Where is the Tracing Service?" asked Miller.

"It's at Arolsen-in-Waldeck. That's just outside Hanover, Lower Saxony. It's run by the Red Cross, really."

Miller thought for a minute. "Would there be anybody else left in Munich who was at Riga? The man I'm really trying to find is the former commandant."

There was silence in the room. Miller sensed the man by the newspaper rack turn around to look at him. The woman seemed subdued.

"It might be possible there are a few left who were at Riga and now live in Munich. Before the war there were twenty-five thousand Jews in Munich. About a tenth came back. Now we are about five thousand again, half of them children born since nineteen forty-five. I might find someone who was at Riga. But I'd have to go through the whole list of survivors. The camps they were in are marked against the names. Could you come back tomorrow?"

Miller thought for a moment, debating whether to give up and go home. The chase was getting pointless.

"Yes," he said at length. "I'll come back tomorrow. Thank you."

He was back in the street, reaching for his car keys, when he felt a step behind him.

"Excuse me," said a voice. He turned. The man behind him was the one who had been reading the newspapers.

"You are inquiring about Riga?" asked the man. "About the commandant of Riga? Would that be Captain Roschmann?"

"Yes, it would," said Miller. "Why?"

"I was at Riga," said the man. "I knew Roschmann. Perhaps I can help you."

The man was short and wiry, somewhere in his mid-forties, with button-bright brown eyes and the rumpled air of a damp sparrow.

"My name is Mordecai," he said. "But people call me Motti. Shall we have coffee and talk?"

They adjourned to a nearby coffee shop. Miller, melted slightly by his companion's chirpy manner, explained his hunt so far, from the back streets of Altona to the Community Center of Munich.

The man listened quietly, nodding occasionally. "Mmmm. Quite a pilgrimage. Why should you, a German, want to track down Roschmann?"

"Does it matter? I've been asked that so many times I'm getting tired of it. What's so strange about a German being angry at what was done years ago?"

Motti shrugged. "Nothing," he said. "It's unusual for a man to go to such lengths, that's all. About Roschmann's disappearance in nineteen fifty-five. You really think his new passport must have been provided by the Odessa?"

"That's what I've been told," replied Miller. "And it seems the only way to find the man who forged it would be to penetrate the Odessa."

Motti considered the young German in front of him for some time. "What hotel are you staying at?" he asked at length.

Miller told him he had not checked into any hotel yet, as it was still early afternoon. But there was one he knew, that he had stayed in before. At Motti's request he went to the coffee-shop telephone and called the hotel for a room.

When he got back to the table, Motti had gone. There was a note under the coffee cup. It said: "Whether you get a room there or not, be in the residents' lounge at eight tonight."

Miller paid for the coffees and left.

The same afternoon, in his lawyer's office, the Werwolf read once again the written report that had come in from his colleague in Bonn, the man who had introduced himself to Miller a week earlier as Dr. Schmidt.

The Werwolf had had the report already for five days, but his natural caution had caused him to wait and reconsider before taking direct action.

The last words his superior, General Glücks, had spoken to him in Madrid in late November virtually robbed him of any freedom of action, but like most desk-bound men he found comfort in delaying the inevitable. "A permanent solution" had been the way his orders were expressed, and he knew what that meant. Nor did the phraseology of "Dr. Schmidt" leave him any more room for maneuver.

"A stubborn young man, truculent and headstrong, probably obstinate, and with an undercurrent of genuine and personal hatred in him for the

Kamerad in question, Eduard Roschmann, for which no explanation seems to exist. Unlikely to listen to reason, even in the face of personal threat. . . . "

The Werwolf read the doctor's summing up again and sighed. He reached for the phone and asked his secretary, Hilda, for an outside line. When he had it he dialed a number in Düsseldorf.

After several rings it was answered, and a voice said simply, "Yes."

"There's a call for Herr Mackensen," said the Werwolf.

The voice from the other end said simply, "Who wants him?"

Instead of answering the question directly, the Werwolf gave the first part of the identification code. "Who was greater than Frederick the Great?"

The voice from the other end replied, "Barbarossa." There was a pause, then: "This is Mackensen," said the voice.

"Werwolf," replied the chief of the Odessa in West Germany. "The holiday is over, I'm afraid. There is work to be done. Get over here by tomorrow morning."

"When?" replied Mackensen.

"Be here at ten," said the Werwolf. "Tell my secretary your name is Keller. I will ensure you have an appointment in that name."

He put the phone down. In Düsseldorf, Mackensen rose and went into the bathroom of his flat to shower and shave. He was a big, powerful man, a former sergeant of the Das Reich division of the SS, who had learned his killing when hanging French hostages in Tulle and Limoges, back in 1944.

After the war he had driven a truck for the Odessa, running human cargoes south through Germany and Austria into the South Tirol province of Italy. In 1946, stopped by an overly suspicious American patrol, he had slain all four occupants of the jeep, two of them with his bare hands. From then on, he too was on the run.

Employed later as a bodyguard for senior men of the Odessa, he had been saddled with the nickname "Mack the Knife," although, oddly, he never used a knife, preferring the strength of his butcher's hands to strangle or break the necks of his "assignments."

Rising in the esteem of his superiors, he had become in the mid-fifties the executioner of the Odessa, the man who could be relied on to cope quietly and discreetly with those who came too close to the top men of the organization, or those from within who elected to squeal on their comrades. By January 1964 he had fulfilled twelve assignments of this kind.

The call came on the dot of eight. It was taken by the reception clerk, who put his head around the corner of the residents' lounge, where Miller sat watching television.

He recognized the voice on the end of the phone.

"Herr Miller? It's me, Motti. I think I may be able to help you. Rather, some friends may be able to. Would you like to meet them?"

"I'll meet anybody who can help me," said Miller, intrigued by the maneuvers.

"Good," said Motti. "Leave your hotel and turn left down Schillerstrasse. Two blocks down on the same side is a cake and coffee shop called Lindemann. Meet me in there."

"When? Now?" asked Miller.

"Yes. Now. I would come to the hotel, but I'm with my friends here. Come right away."

He hung up. Miller took his coat and walked out through the doors. He turned left and headed down the pavement. Half a block from the hotel something hard was jabbed into his ribs from behind, and a car slid up to the curb.

"Get into the back seat, Herr Miller," said a voice in his ear.

The door beside him swung open and with a last dig in the ribs from the man behind, Miller ducked his head and entered the car. The driver was up front; the back seat contained another man, who slid over to make room for him. He felt the man behind him enter the car also; then the door slammed and the car slid from the curb.

Miller's heart was thumping. He glanced at the three men in the car with him, but recognized none of them.

The man to his right, who had opened the door for him to enter, spoke first. "I am going to bind your eyes," he said simply, producing a sort of black sock. "We would not want you to see where you are going."

Miller felt the sock being pulled over his head until it covered his nose. He remembered the cold blue eyes of the man in the Dreesen Hotel and recalled what the man in Vienna had told him. "Do be careful, these men can be dangerous." Then he remembered Motti and wondered how one of them could have been reading a Hebrew newspaper in the Jewish Community Center.

The car drove for twenty-five minutes, then slowed and stopped. He heard some gates being opened; the car surged forward again and stopped finally. He was eased out of the back seat, and with a man on each side he was helped across a courtyard. For a moment he felt the cold night air on his face; then he was back inside again. A door slammed behind him, and he was led down some steps into what seemed to be a cellar. But the air was warm and the chair into which he was lowered was well upholstered.

He heard a voice say, "Take off the bandage," and the sock over his head was removed. He blinked as his eyes got used to the light.

The room he was in was evidently below ground, for it had no windows. But an air extractor hummed high on one wall. It was well decorated and comfortable, evidently a form of committee room, for there was a long table with eight chairs ranged close to the far wall. The remainder of the room was an open space, fringed by five armchairs. In the center were a circular carpet and a coffee table.

Motti was standing, smiling quietly, almost apologetically, beside the committee table. The two men who had brought Miller, both well built and in early middle age, were perched on the arms of the armchairs to his left and right. Directly opposite him, across the coffee table, was a fourth man. Miller supposed the car driver had remained upstairs to lock up.

The fourth man was evidently in command. He sat at ease in his chair while his three lieutenants stood or perched around him. Miller judged him to be about sixty, lean and bony, with a hollow-cheeked, hook-nosed face. The eyes worried Miller. They were brown and deep-sunk into the sockets, but bright and piercing, the eyes of a fanatic. It was he who spoke.

"Welcome, Herr Miller. I must apologize for the strange way in which you were brought to my home. The reason for it was that if you decide you wish to turn down my proposal to you, you can be returned to your hotel and will never see any of us again.

"My friend here"—he gestured to Motti—"informs me that for reasons of your own you are hunting a certain Eduard Roschmann. And that to get closer to him you might be prepared to attempt to penetrate the Odessa. To do that you would need help. A lot of help. However, it might suit our interests to have you inside the Odessa. Therefore we might be prepared to help you. Do you follow me?"

Miller stared at him in astonishment. "Let me get one thing straight," he said at length. "Are you telling me you are not from the Odessa?"

The man raised his eyebrows. "Good heavens, you *have* got hold of the wrong end of the stick." He leaned forward and drew back the sleeve of his left wrist. On the forearm was tattooed a number in blue ink.

"Auschwitz," said the man. He pointed to the two men at Miller's sides. "Buchenwald and Dachau." He pointed at Motti. "Riga and Treblinka." He replaced his sleeve.

"Herr Miller, there are some who think the murderers of our people should be brought to trial. We do not agree. Just after the war I was talking with a British officer, and he told me something that has guided my life ever since. He said to me, 'If they had murdered six million of my people, I too would build a monument of skulls. Not the skulls of those who died in the concentration camps but of those who put them there.' Simple logic, Herr Miller, but persuasive. I and my group are men who decided to stay on inside Germany after nineteen forty-five with one object, and one only, in mind. Revenge, revenge pure and simple. We don't arrest them, Herr Miller; we kill them like the swine they are. My name is Leon."

Leon interrogated Miller for four hours before he was satisfied of the reporter's genuineness. Like others before him, he was puzzled about the motivation but had to concede it was possible Miller's reason was the one he gave, indignation at what had been done by the SS during the war. When he had finished, Leon leaned back in his chair and surveyed the younger man for a long time.

"Are you aware how risky it is to try and penetrate the Odessa, Herr Miller?" he asked.

"I can guess," said Miller. "For one thing, I'm too young."

Leon shook his head. "There's no question of your trying to persuade former SS men you are one of them under your own name. For one thing, they have lists of former SS men, and Peter Miller is not on that list. For another, you have to age ten years at the least. It can be done, but it involves a complete new identity, and a real identity. The identity of a man who really existed and was in the SS. That alone means a lot of research by us, and the expenditure of a lot of time and trouble."

"Do you think you can find such a man?" asked Miller.

Leon shrugged. "It would have to be a man whose death cannot be checked out," he said. "Before the Odessa accepts a man at all, it checks him out. You have to pass all the tests. That also means you will have to live for five or six weeks with a genuine former SS man who can teach you the folklore, the technical terms, the phraseology, the behavior patterns. Fortunately, we know such a man."

Miller was amazed. "Why should he do such a thing?"

"The man I have in mind is an odd character. He is a genuine SS captain who sincerely regretted what was done. He experienced remorse. Later he was inside the Odessa and passed information about wanted Nazis to the authorities. He would be doing so still, but he was 'shopped' and was lucky to escape with his life. Now he lives under a new name, in a house outside Bayreuth."

"What else would I have to learn?"

"Everything about your new identity. Where he was born, his date of birth, how he got into the SS, where he trained, where he served, his unit, his commanding officer, his entire history from the end of the war onward. You will also have to be vouched for by a guarantor. That will not be easy. A lot of time and trouble will have to be spent on you, Herr Miller. Once you are in, there will be no pulling back."

"What's in this for you?" asked Miller suspiciously.

Leon rose and paced the carpet. "Revenge," he said simply. "Like you, we want Roschmann. But we want more. The worst of the SS killers are living under false names. We want those names. That's what's in it for us."

"That sounds like information that might be of use to Israeli Intelligence," said Miller.

Leon glanced at him shrewdly. "It is," he said shortly. "We occasionally cooperate with them, though they do not own us."

"Have you ever tried to get your own men inside the Odessa?" asked Miller.

Leon nodded. "Twice," he said.

"What happened?"

"The first was found floating in a canal without his fingernails. The second disappeared without trace. Do you still want to go ahead?"

Miller ignored the question. "If your methods are so efficient, why were they caught?"

"They were both Jewish," said Leon shortly. "We tried to get the tattoos from the concentration camps off their arms, but they left scars. Besides, they were both circumcised. That was why, when Motti reported to me on a genuine Aryan German with a grudge against the SS, I was interested. By the way, are you circumcised?"

"Does it matter?" inquired Miller.

"Of course. If a man is circumcised it does not prove he's a Jew. Many Germans are circumcised as well. But if he is not, it more or less proves he is not a Jew."

"I'm not," said Miller shortly.

Leon nodded with pensive satisfaction. "Certainly that improves your chances. That just leaves the problem of changing your appearance and training you to play a very dangerous role."

It was long past midnight. Leon looked at his watch. "Have you eaten?" he asked Miller. The reporter shook his head.

"Motti, I think a little food for our guest."

Motti grinned and nodded. He disappeared through the door of the cellar room and went up into the house.

"You'll have to spend the night here," said Leon to Miller. "We'll bring a bedroll down to you. Don't try to leave, please. The door has three locks, and all will be shut on the far side. Give me your car keys, and I'll have your car brought around here. It will be better out of sight for the next few weeks. Your hotel bill will be paid and your luggage brought around here too. In the morning you will write letters to your mother and girl friend, explaining that you will be out of contact for several weeks, maybe months. Understood?"

Miller nodded and handed over his car keys. Leon gave them to one of the other two men, who quietly left.

"In the morning we will drive you to Bayreuth, and you will meet our SS officer. His name is Alfred Oster. He's the man you will live with. I will arrange it. Meanwhile, excuse me. I have to start looking for a new name and identity for you."

He rose and left. Motti soon returned with a plate of food and half a dozen blankets, leaving Miller to his cold chicken, potato salad, and growing doubts.

Far away to the north, in the General Hospital of Bremen, a ward orderly was patrolling his ward in the small hours of the morning. Around a bed at the end of the room was a tall screen that shut off the occupant from the rest of the ward.

The orderly, a middle-aged man called Hartstein, peered around the screen at the man in the bed. He lay very still. Above his head a dim light was burning through the night. The orderly entered the screened-off area and checked the patient's pulse. There was none.

He looked down at the ravaged face of the cancer victim, and something the man had said in delirium three days earlier caused the orderly to lift the left arm of the dead man out of the blankets. Inside the man's armpit was tattooed a number. It was the dead man's blood group, a sure sign that the patient had once been in the SS. The reason for the tattoo was that SS men were regarded in the Reich as more valuable than ordinary soldiers, so when wounded they always had first chance at any available plasma. Hence the tattooed blood group.

Orderly Hartstein covered the dead man's face and glanced into the drawer of the bedside table. He drew out the driving license that had been placed there along with the other personal possessions when the man had been brought in after collapsing in the streeet. It showed a man of about thirty-nine, date of birth June 18, 1925, and the name of Rolf Gunther Kolb.

The orderly slipped the driving license into the pocket of his white coat and went off to report the death to the night physician.

ELEVEN

Peter Miller wrote his letters to his mother and Sigi under the watchful eye of Motti, and finished by midmorning. His luggage had arrived from his hotel, the bill had been paid, and shortly before noon the two of them, accompanied by the driver of the previous night, set off for Bayreuth.

With a reporter's instinct he flashed a glance at the number plates of the blue Opel which had taken the place of the Mercedes that had been used the night before. Motti, at his side, noticed the glance and smiled. "Don't bother," he said. "It's a hired car, taken out in a false name."

"Well, it's nice to know one is among professionals," said Miller.

Motti shrugged. "We have to be. It's one way of staying alive when you're up against the Odessa."

The garage had two berths, and Miller noticed his own Jaguar in the second slot. Half-melted snow from the previous night had formed puddles beneath the wheels, and the sleek black bodywork gleamed in the electric light.

Once he was in the back of the Opel, the black sock was again pulled over his head, and he was pushed down to the floor as the car eased out of the garage, through the gates of the courtyard, and into the street. Motti kept the blindfold on him until they were well clear of Munich and heading north up autobahn E 6 toward Nuremberg and Bayreuth.

When Miller finally lost the blindfold he could see there had been another heavy snowfall overnight. The rolling forest countryside where Bavaria ran into Franconia was clothed in a coat of unmarked white, giving a chunky roundness to the leafless trees of the beech forests along the road. The driver was slow and careful, the windshield wipers working constantly to clear the glass of the fluttering flakes and the mush thrown up by the trucks they passed.

They lunched at a wayside inn at Ingolstadt, pressed on to skirt Nuremberg to the east, and were at Bayreuth an hour later.

Set in the heart of one of the most beautiful areas of Germany, nicknamed the Bavarian Switzerland, the small country town of Bayreuth has only one claim to fame, its annual festival of Wagner music. In earlier years the town had been proud to play host to almost the whole Nazi hierarchy as it descended in the wake of that keen Wagnerite, Adolf Hitler.

In January it is a quiet little town, blanketed by snow, the holly wreaths only a few days since removed from the door knockers of its neat and well-kept houses. They found the cottage of Alfred Oster on a quiet byroad a mile beyond the town, and there was not another car on the road as the small party went to the front door.

The former SS officer was expecting them—a big bluff man with blue eyes and a fuzz of ginger hair spreading over the top of his cranium. Despite the season, he had the healthy tan of men who spend their time in the mountains among wind and sun and unpolluted air.

Motti made the introductions and handed Oster a letter from Leon. The Bavarian read it and nodded, glancing sharply at Miller.

"Well, we can always try," he said. "How long can I have him?"

"We don't know yet," said Motti. "Obviously, until he's ready. Also, it will be necessary to devise a new identity for him. We will let you know."

A few minutes later he was gone.

Oster led Miller into the living room and drew the curtains against the descending dusk before he put on the light. "So, you want to be able to pass as a former SS man, do you?" he asked.

Miller nodded. "That's right," he said.

Oster turned on him. "Well, we'll start by getting a few basic facts right. I don't know where you did your military service, but I suspect it was in that ill-disciplined, democratic, wet-nursing shambles that calls itself the new German Army. Here's the first fact. The new German Army would have lasted exactly ten seconds against any crack regiment of the British, Americans, or Russians during the last war. Whereas the Waffen SS, man for man, could beat the shit out of five times their own number of Allies of the last war.

"Here's the second fact. The Waffen SS were the toughest, best-trained, best-disciplined, smartest, fittest bunch of soldiers who ever went into battle in the history of this planet. Whatever they did can't change that. So SMARTEN UP, MILLER. So long as you are in this house, this is the procedure.

"When I walk into a room, you leap to attention. And I mean LEAP. When I walk past, you smack those heels together and remain at attention until I am five paces beyond you. When I say something to you that needs an answer, you reply, 'JAWOHL, *Herr Hauptsturmführer.*' And when I give an order or an instruction, you reply, 'ZU BEFEHL, *Herr Hauptsturmführer.*' Is that clearly understood?"

Miller nodded in amazement.

"Heels together," roared Oster. "I want to hear the leather smack. All right, since we may not have much time, we'll press on, starting from tonight. Before supper we'll tackle the ranks, from private up to full general. You'll learn the titles, mode of address, and collar insignia of every SS rank that ever existed. Then we'll go on to the various types of uniform used, the differing branches of the SS and their different insignia, the occasions when gala uniform, full-dress uniform, walking-out uniform, combat uniform, and fatigue dress would be worn.

"After that I'll put you through the full political-ideological course that you would have undergone at Dachau SS training camp, had you been there. Then you'll learn the marching songs, the drinking songs, and the various unit songs.

"I can get you as far as your departure from training camp for your first posting. After that Leon has to tell me what unit you were supposed to have joined, where you worked, under which commanding officer, what happened to you at the end of the war, how you have passed your time since nineteen forty-five. However, the first part of the training will take from two to three weeks, and that's a crash course.

"By the way, don't think this is a joke. If you are once inside the Odessa, knowing who the top men are, and you make one slip in procedure, you'll end up in a canal. Believe me, I'm no milksop, and after betraying the Odessa, even I'm running scared of them. That's why I live here under a new name."

For the first time since he had set off on his one-man hunt for Eduard Roschmann, Miller wondered if he had not already gone too far.

Mackensen reported to the Werwolf on the dot of ten. When the door to the room where Hilda worked was safely shut, the Werwolf seated the executioner in the client's chair opposite the desk and lit a cigar.

"There is a certain person, a newspaper reporter, inquiring about the whereabouts and the new identity of one of our comrades," he began. The liquidator nodded with understanding. Several times before, he had heard one of his briefings begin in the same way.

"In the normal course of events," resumed the Werwolf, "we would be prepared to let the matter rest, either convinced that the reporter would eventually give up for lack of progress, or because the man being sought was not worth our while making an expensive and hazardous effort to save."

"But this time—it's different?" ask Mackensen softly.

The Werwolf nodded with what might have been genuine regret. "Yes. Through bad luck, ours on the grounds of the inconvenience involved, his on the grounds it will cost him his life, the reporter has unwittingly touched a nerve. For one thing, the man he is seeking is a man of vital, absolutely vital, importance to us and to our long-term planning. For another, the reporter himself seems to be an odd character—intelligent, tenacious, ingenious, and I regret, wholly committed to extracting a sort of personal vengeance from the *Kamerad.*"

"Any motive?" ask Mackensen.

The Werwolf's puzzlement showed in his frown. He tapped ash from his cigar before replying. "We cannot understand why there should be, but evidently there is," he murmured. "The man he is looking for undoubtedly has a background which might excite certain dislike among such as the Jews and their friends. He commanded a ghetto in Ostland. Some, mainly foreigners, refuse to acknowledge our justification for what was done there. The odd thing about this reporter is that he is neither foreign, nor Jewish, nor a noted Left-Winger, nor one of the well-known type of conscience-cowboy—who, in any case, seldom get beyond giving vent to a lot of piss and wind, but nothing else.

"But this man seems different. He's a young German, Aryan, son of a war hero, nothing in his background to suggest such a depth of hatred toward us, nor such an obsession with tracing one of our *Kameraden,* despite a firm and clear warning to stay off the matter. It gives me some regret to order his death. Yet he leaves me no alternative. That is what I must do!"

"Kill him?" asked Mack the Knife.

"Kill him," confirmed the Werwolf.

"Whereabouts?"

"Not known." The Werwolf flicked two sheets of foolscap paper covered with typed words across the desk. "That's the man. Peter Miller, reporter and investigator. He was last seen at the Dreesen Hotel in Bad Godesberg. He's certainly gone from there by now, but it's a good enough place to start.

The other place would be his own flat, where his girl friend lives with him. You should represent yourself as a man sent by one of the major magazines for which he normally works. That way, the girl will probably talk to you, if she knows his whereabouts. He drives a noticeable car. You'll find all the details of it there."

"I'll need money," said Mackensen. The Werwolf had foreseen the request. He pushed a wad of 10,000 marks across the desk.

"And the orders?" asked the killer.

"Locate and liquidate," said the Werwolf.

It was January 13 before the news of the death in Bremen five days earlier of Rolf Günther Kolb reached Leon in Munich. The letter from his North German representative enclosed the dead man's driving license.

Leon checked the man's rank and number on his list of former SS men, checked the West German wanted list and saw that Kolb was not on it, spent some time gazing at the face on the driving license, and made his decision.

He called Motti, who was on duty at the telephone exchange where he worked, and the assistant reported to Leon when he had finished his shift.

Leon laid Kolb's driving license in front of him. "That's the man we need," he said. "He was a staff sergeant at the age of nineteen, promoted just before the war ended. They must have been very short of material. Kolb's face and Miller's don't match, even if Miller were made up, which is a procedure I don't like anyway. It's too easy to see through at close range. But the height and build fit with Miller. So we'll need a new photograph. That can wait. To cover the photograph we'll need a replica of the stamp of the Bremen Police Traffic Department. See to it."

When Motti had gone, Leon dialed a number in Bremen and gave further orders.

"All right," said Alfred Oster to his pupil. "Now we'll start on the songs. You've heard of the 'Horst Wessel Song'?"

"Of course," said Miller. "It was the Nazi marching song."

Oster hummed the first few bars.

"Oh, yes, I remember hearing it now. But I can't remember the words."

"Okay," said Oster. "I'll have to teach you about a dozen songs. Just in case you are asked. But this is the most important. You may even have to join in a singsong, when you're among the *Kameraden*. Not to know it would be a death sentence. Now, after me:

> "The flags are high,
> The ranks are tightly closed. . . . "

It was January 18.

Mackensen sat and sipped a cocktail in the bar of the Schweizerhof Hotel in Munich and considered the source of his puzzlement: Miller, the reporter whose personal details and face were etched in his mind. A thorough man, Mackensen had even contacted the main Jaguar agents for West Germany and obtained from them a series of publicity photographs of the Jaguar XK 150 sports car, so he knew what he was looking for. His trouble was he could not find it.

The trail at Bad Godesberg had quickly led to Cologne Airport and the answer that Miller had flown to London and back within thirty-six hours over the New Year. Then he and his car had vanished.

Inquiries at his flat led to a conversation with his handsome and cheerful girl friend, but she had only been able to produce a letter postmarked from Munich, saying Miller would be staying there for a while.

For a week Munich had proved a dead lead. Mackensen had checked every hotel, public and private parking space, servicing garage, and gas station. There was nothing. The man he sought had disappeared as if from the face of the earth.

Finishing his drink, Mackensen eased himself off his bar stool and went to the telephone to report to the Werwolf. Although he did not know it, he stood just twelve hundred meters from the black Jaguar with the yellow stripe, which was parked inside the walled courtyard of the antique shop and private house where Leon lived and ran his small and fanatic organization.

In Bremen General Hospital a man in a white coat strolled into the registrar's office. He had a stethoscope around his neck, almost the badge of office of a new intern.

"I need a look at the medical file on one of our patients, Rolf Günther Kolb," he told the receptionist and filing clerk.

The woman did not recognize the intern, but that meant nothing. There were scores of them working in the hospital. She ran through the names in the filing cabinet, spotted the name of Kolb on the edge of a dossier, and handed it to the intern. The phone rang, and she went to answer it.

The intern sat on one of the chairs and flicked through the dossier. It revealed simply that Kolb had collapsed in the street and been brought in by ambulance. An examination had diagnosed cancer of the intestine in a virulent and terminal form. A decision had later been made not to operate. The patient had been put on a series of drugs, without any hope, and later on pain-killers. The last sheet in the file stated simply: "Patient deceased on the night of January 8/9. Cause of death: carcinoma of the main intestine. No next of kin. Corpus delicti delivered to the municipal mortuary January 10." It was signed by the doctor in charge of the case.

The new intern eased the last sheet out of the file and inserted in place one of his own. The new sheet read: "Despite serious condition of patient on admission, the carcinoma responded to a treatment of drugs and went into recession. Patient was adjudged fit to be transferred on January 16. At his own request he was transferred by ambulance for convalescence at the Arcadia Clinic, Delmenhorst." The signature was an illegible scrawl.

The intern gave the file back to the filing clerk, thanked her with a smile, and left. It was January 22.

Three days later Leon received a piece of information that filled in the last section of his private jigsaw puzzle. A clerk in a ticket agency in North Germany sent a message to say a certain bakery proprietor in Bremerhaven had just confirmed bookings on a winter cruise for himself and his wife. The pair would be touring the Caribbean for four weeks, leaving from Bremerhaven on Sunday, February 16. Leon knew the man to have been a colonel of the SS during the war, and a member of Odessa after it.

He ordered Motti to go out and buy a book of instructions on the art of making bread.

The Werwolf was puzzled. For nearly three weeks he had had his representatives in the major cities of Germany on the lookout for a man called Miller and a black Jaguar sports car. The apartment and the garage in Hamburg had been watched, a visit had been made to a middle-aged woman in Osdorf, who had said only that she did not know where her son was. Several telephone calls had been made to a girl called Sigi, purporting to come from the editor of a major picture magazine with an urgent offer of very lucrative employment for Miller, but the girl had also said she did not know where her boy friend was.

Inquiries had been made at his bank in Hamburg, but he had not cashed any checks since November. In short, he had disappeared. It was already January 30, and against his wishes the Werwolf felt obliged to make a phone call. With regret, he lifted his receiver and made it.

Far away, high in the mountains, a man put down his telephone half an hour later and swore softly and violently for several minutes. It was a Friday evening, and he had barely returned to his weekend manor for two days of rest when the call had come through.

He walked to the window of his elegantly appointed study and looked out. The light from the window spread out across the thick carpet of snow on the lawn, the glow reaching away toward the pine trees that covered most of the estate.

He had always wanted to live like this, in a fine house on a private estate in the mountains, since, as a boy, he had seen during the Christmas vacation the houses of the rich in the mountains around Graz. Now he had it, and he liked it.

It was better than the house of a brewery worker, where he had been brought up; better than the house in Riga where he had lived for four years; better than a furnished room in Buenos Aires or a hotel room in Cairo. It was what he had always wanted.

The call he had taken disturbed him. He had told the caller there had been no one spotted near his house, no one hanging around his factory, no one asking questions about him. But he was worried. Miller? Who the hell was Miller? The assurances on the phone that the reporter would be taken care of only partly assuaged his anxiety. The seriousness with which the caller and his colleagues took the threat posed by Miller was indicated by the decision to send him a personal bodyguard the next day to act as his chauffeur and stay with him until further notice.

He drew the curtains of the study, shutting out the winter landscape. The thickly padded door cut out all sounds from the rest of the house. The only sound in the room was the crackle of fresh pine logs on the hearth; the cheerful glow was framed by the great cast-iron fireplace with its wrought vine leaves and curlicues, one of the fittings he had kept when he bought and modernized the house.

The door opened, and his wife put her head around it. "Dinner's ready," she said.

"Coming, dear," said Eduard Roschmann.

The next morning, Saturday, Oster and Miller were disturbed by the arrival of a party from Munich. The car contained Leon and Motti, the driver, and another man, who carried a black bag.

When they reached the living room, Leon said to the man with the bag, "You'd better get up to the bathroom and set out your gear."

The man nodded and went upstairs. The driver had remained in the car.

Leon sat at the table and bade Oster and Miller take their places. Motti remained by the door, a camera with flash attachment in his hand.

Leon passed a driving license over to Miller. Where the photograph had been was a blank.

"That's who you are going to become," said Leon. "Rolf Günther Kolb, born June eighteenth, nineteen twenty-five. That would make you nineteen at the end of the war, almost twenty. And thirty-eight years old now. You were born and brought up in Bremen. You joined the Hitler Youth at the age of ten in nineteen thirty-five, and the SS in January nineteen forty-four, at the age of eighteen. Both your parents are dead. They were killed in an air raid on Bremen docks in nineteen forty-four."

Miller stared down at the driving license in his hand.

"What about his career in the SS?" asked Oster. "At the moment we have reached something of a dead end."

"How is he so far?" asked Leon. Miller might as well not have been there.

"Pretty good," said Oster. "I gave him a two-hour interrogation yesterday, and he could pass. Until someone starts asking for specific details of his career. Then he knows nothing."

Leon nodded for a while, examining some papers he had taken from his attaché case. "We don't know Kolb's career with the SS," he said. "It couldn't have been very much, for he's not on any wanted list and nobody has ever heard of him. In a way that's just as well, for the chances are the Odessa has never heard of him either. But the disadvantage is, he has no reason to seek refuge and help from the Odessa unless he is being pursued. So we have invented a career for him. Here it is."

He passed the sheets over to Oster, who began to read them. When he had finished he nodded. "It's good," he said. "It all fits with the known facts. And it would be enough to get him arrested if he were exposed."

Leon grunted with satisfaction. "That's what you have to teach him. Incidentally, we have found a guarantor for him. A man in Bremerhaven, a former SS colonel, is going on a sea cruise, starting February sixteenth, he will have a letter from this man assuring the Odessa that Kolb, his employee, is genuinely a former SS man and genuinely in trouble. By that time the bakery-owner will be on the high seas and uncontactable. By the way"—he turned to Miller and passed a book across to him—"you can learn baking as well. That's what you have been since nineteen forty-five, an employee in a bakery."

He did not mention that the bakery-owner would be away for only four weeks, and that after that period Miller's life would hang by a thread.

"Now my friend the barber is going to change your appearance somewhat," Leon told Miller. "After that we'll take a new photograph for the driving license."

In the upstairs bathroom the barber gave Miller one of the shortest haircuts he had ever had. The white scalp gleamed through the stubble almost up to the crown of the head by the time he had finished. The rumpled look was gone, but he also looked older. A ruler-straight parting was scraped in the short hair on the left side of his head. His eyebrows were plucked until they almost ceased to exist.

"Bare eyebrows don't make a man look older," said the barber chattily, "but they make the age almost unguessable within six or seven years. There's one last thing. You're to grow a mustache. Just a thin one, the same width as your mouth. It adds years, you know. Can you do that in a couple of weeks?"

Miller knew the way the hair on his upper lip grew. "Sure," he said. He gazed back at his reflection. He looked in his mid-thirties. The mustache would add another four years.

When they got downstairs, Miller was stood up against a white sheet held in place by Oster and Leon, and Motti took several full-face portraits of him.

"That'll do," he said. "I'll have the driving license ready within three days."

The party left, and Oster turned to Miller. "Right, Kolb," he said, having ceased to refer to him in any other way, "you were trained at Dachau SS training camp, seconded to Flossenburg concentration camp in July nineteen forty-four, and in April nineteen forty-five you commanded the squad that executed Admiral Canaris, chief of the Abwehr. You also helped kill a number of the other Army officers suspected by the Gestapo of complicity in the July nineteen forty-four assassination attempt on Hitler. No wonder the authorities today would like to arrest you. Admiral Canaris and his men were not Jews. There can be no overlooking that. Okay, let's get down to work, Staff Sergeant."

The weekly meeting of the Mossad had reached its end when General Amit raised his hand and said, "There is just one last matter, though I regard it as of comparatively low importance. Leon has reported from Munich that he has for some time had under training a young German, an Aryan, who for some reason of his own has a grudge against the SS and is being prepared to infiltrate the Odessa."

"His motive?" asked one of the men suspiciously.

General Amit shrugged. "For reasons of his own, he wants to track down a certain former SS captain called Roschmann."

The head of the Office for the Countries of Persecution, a former Polish Jew, jerked his head up. "Eduard Roschmann? The Butcher of Riga?"

"That's the man."

"Phew. If we could get him, that would be an old score settled."

General Amit shook his head. "I have told you before, Israel is no longer in the retribution business. My orders are absolute. Even if the man finds Roschmann, there is to be no assassination. After the Ben-Gal affair, it would be the last straw on Erhard's back. The trouble now is that if any ex-Nazi dies in Germany, Israeli agents get the blame."

"So what about this young German?" asked the Shabak chief.

"I want to try and use him to identify any more Nazi scientists who might be sent out to Cairo this year. For us that is priority number one. I propose to send an agent over to Germany, simply to put the young man under surveillance. Just a watching brief, nothing else."

"You have such a man in mind?"

"Yes," said General Amit. "He's a good man, reliable. He'll just follow the German and watch him, reporting back to me personally. He can pass for a German. He's a Yekke. He came from Karlsruhe."

"What about Leon?" asked someone else. "Will he not try to settle accounts on his own?"

"Leon will do what he's told," said General Amit angrily. "There is to be no more settling of accounts."

In Bayreuth that morning, Miller was being given another grilling by Alfred Oster.

"Okay," said Oster, "what are the words engraved on the hilt of the SS dagger?"

"Blood and Honor," replied Miller.

"Right. When is the dagger presented to an SS man?"

"At his passing-out parade from training camp," replied Miller.

"Right. Repeat to me the oath of loyalty to the person of Adolf Hitler." Miller repeated it, word for word.

"Repeat the blood oath of the SS." Miller complied.

"What is the significance of the emblem of the death's head?"

Miller closed his eyes and repeated what he had been taught. "The sign of the death's head comes from distant Germanic mythology. It is the emblem of those groups of Teuton warriors who have sworn fealty to their leader and to each other, unto the grave and even beyond, into Valhalla. Hence the skull and the crossbones, signifying the world beyond the grave."

"Right. Were all SS men automatically members of death's-head units?"

"No."

Oster rose and stretched. "Not bad," he said. "I can't think of anything else you might be asked in general terms. Now let's get on to specifics. This is what you would have to know about Flossenburg Concentration Camp, your first and only posting. . . . "

The man who sat in the window seat of the Olympic Airways flight from Athens to Munich seemed quiet and withdrawn.

The German businessman next to him, after several attempts at conversation, took the hint and confined himself to reading *Playboy* magazine. His next-door neighbor stared out of the window as the Aegean Sea passed beneath them and the airliner left the sunny spring of the eastern Mediterranean for the snow-capped peaks of the Dolomites and the Bavarian Alps.

The businessman had at least elicited one thing from his companion. The traveler in the window seat was undoubtedly a German, his grasp of the language fluent and familiar, his knowledge of the country without fault. The businessman, traveling home after a sales mission to the Greek capital, had not the slightest doubt that he was seated next to a fellow countryman.

He could hardly have been more wrong. The man next to him had been born in Germany thirty-three years earlier, under the name of Josef Kaplan, son of a Jewish tailor, in Karlsruhe. He had been three years old when Hitler came to power, seven when his parents had been taken away in a black van; he had been hidden in an attic for another three years until, at the age of ten in 1940, he too had been discovered and taken away in a van. His early teens had been spent using the resilience and the ingenuity of youth to survive in a series of concentration camps until in 1945, with the suspicion of a wild animal burning in his eyes, he had snatched a thing called a Hershey bar from the outstretched hand of a man who spoke to him in a foreign language through his nose, and had run away to eat the offering in a corner of the camp before it could be taken away from him.

Two years later, weighing a few pounds more, aged seventeen and hungry as a rat, with that creature's suspicion and mistrust of everyone and everything, he had come on a ship called the *President Warfield*, alias the *Exodus*, to a new shore many miles from Karlsruhe and Dachau.

The passing years had mellowed him, matured him, taught him many things, given him a wife and two children, a commission in the army, but never eliminated the hatred he felt for the country to which he was traveling that day. He had agreed to go, to swallow his feelings, to take up again, as he had done twice before in the previous ten years, the façade of amiability and bonhomie that was necessary to effect his transformation back into a German.

The other requirements had been provided by the service: the passport in his breast pocket, the letters, cards, and documentary paraphernalia of a citizen of a West European country, the underclothes, shoes, suits, and luggage of a German commercial traveler in textiles.

As the heavy and freezing clouds of Europe engulfed the plane he reconsidered his mission, fed into him in days and nights of briefing by the quiet-spoken colonel on the kibbutz that produced so little fruit and so many Israeli agents. To follow a man, to keep an eye on him, a young German four years his junior, while that man sought to do what several had tried and failed to do—infiltrate the Odessa. To observe him and measure his success, to note the persons he contacted and was passed on to, check on his findings, ascertain if the German could trace the recruiter of the new wave of German scientists headed for Egypt to work on the rockets. Never to expose himself, never to take matters into his own hands. Then to report back with the sum total of what the young German had found out before he was "blown" or discovered, one of which was bound to happen.

He would do it; he did not have to enjoy doing it, that was not part of the requirement. Fortunately, no one required that he like becoming a German again. No one asked him to enjoy mixing with Germans, speaking their language, smiling and joking with them. Had this been asked, he would have refused the job. For he hated them all, the young reporter he was ordered to follow included. Nothing, he was certain, would ever change that.

The following day Oster and Miller had their last visit from Leon. Apart from Leon and Motti, there was a new man, sun-tanned and fit-looking, much younger than the others. Miller adjudged the new man to be in his mid-thirties. He was introduced simply as Josef. He said nothing throughout.

"By the way," Motti told Miller, "I drove your car up here today. I've left it in a public parking lot down in the town, by the market square."

He tossed Miller the keys, adding, "Don't use it when you go to meet the

Odessa. For one thing, it's too noticeable; for another, you're supposed to be a bakery worker on the run after being spotted and identified as a former camp guard. Such a man would not have a Jaguar. When you go, travel by rail."

Miller nodded his agreement, but privately he regretted being separated from his beloved Jaguar.

"Right. Here is your driving license, complete with your photograph as you now look. You can tell anyone who asks that you drive a Volkswagen but you have left it in Bremen, as the number could identify you to the police."

Miller scanned the driving license. It showed himself with his short hair but no mustache. The one he now had could simply be explained as a precaution, grown since he was identified.

"The man who, unknown to him, is your guarantor, left from Bremerhaven on a cruise ship on the morning tide. This is the former SS colonel, now a bakery-owner and your former employer. His name is Joachim Eberhardt. Here is a letter from him to the man you are going to see. The paper is genuine, taken from his office. The signature is a perfect forgery. The letter tells its recipient that you are a good former SS man, reliable, now fallen on misfortune after being recognized, and it asks the recipient to help you acquire a new set of papers and a new identity."

Leon passed the letter across to Miller. He read it and put it back in its envelope.

"Now seal it," said Leon.

Miller did so. "Who's the man I have to present myself to?" he asked.

Leon held out a sheet of paper with a name and address on it. "This is the man" he said. "He lives in Nuremberg. We're not certain what he was in the war, for he almost certainly has a new name. However, of one thing we are quite certain. He is very high up in the Odessa. He may have met Eberhardt, who is a big wheel in the Odessa in North Germany. So here is a photograph of Eberhardt the baker. Study it, in case your man asks for a description of him from you. Got that?"

Miller looked at Eberhardt's photograph and nodded.

"When you are ready, I suggest a wait of a few days until Eberhardt's ship is beyond the reach of ship-to-shore radio-telephone. We don't want the man you will see to get through a telephone call to Eberhardt while the ship is still off the German coast. Wait till it's in mid-Atlantic. I think you should probably present yourself on next Thursday morning."

Miller nodded.

"All right. Thursday it is."

"Two last things," said Leon. "Apart from trying to trace Roschmann, which is your desire, we also would like some information. We want to know who is now recruiting scientists to go to Egypt and develop Nasser's rockets for him. The recruiting is being done by the Odessa, here in Germany. We need to know specifically who the new chief recruiting officer is. Secondly, stay in touch. Use public telephones and phone this number." He passed a piece of paper across to Miller. "The number will always be manned, even if I am not there. Report in whenever you get anything."

Twenty minutes later, the group was gone.

In the back seat of the car on their way back to Munich, Leon and Josef sat side by side, the Israeli agent hunched in his corner and silent. As they left the twinkling lights of Bayreuth behind them Leon nudged Josef with his elbow. "Why so gloomy?" he asked. "Everything is going fine."

Josef glanced at him. "How reliable do you reckon this man Miller?" he asked.

"Reliable? He's the best chance we have ever had for penetrating the Odessa. You heard Oster. He can pass for a former SS man in any company, provided he keeps his head."

Josef retained his doubts. "My brief was to watch him at all times," he grumbled. "I ought to be sticking to him when he moves, keeping an eye on him, reporting back on the men he is introduced to and their position in the Odessa. I wish I'd never agreed to let him go off alone and check in by phone when he sees fit. Supposing he doesn't check in?"

Leon's anger was barely controlled. It was evident they had been through this argument before. "Now, listen one more time. This man is my discovery. His infiltration into the Odessa was my idea. He's my agent. I've waited years to get someone where he is now—a non-Jew. I'm not having him exposed by someone tagging along behind him."

"He's an amateur. I'm a pro," growled the agent.

"He's also an Aryan," riposted Leon. "By the time he's outlived his usefulness, I hope he'll have given us the names of the top ten Odessa men in Germany. Then we go to work on them one by one. Among them, one must be the recruiter of the rocket scientists. Don't worry, we'll find him, and the names of the scientists he intends to send to Cairo."

Back in Bayreuth, Miller stared out of the window at the falling snow. Privately he had no intention of checking in by phone, for he had no interest in tracing recruited rocket scientists. He still had only one objective— Eduard Roschmann.

TWELVE

It was actually on the evening of Wednesday, February 19, that Peter Miller finally bade farewell to Alfred Oster in his cottage in Bayreuth and headed for Nuremberg.

The former SS officer shook him by the hand on the doorstep. "Best of luck, Kolb. I've taught you everything I know. Let me give you a last word of advice. I don't know how long your cover can hold. Probably not long. If you ever spot anyone who you think has seen through your cover, don't argue. Get out and revert to your real name."

As the young reporter walked down the drive, Oster muttered to himself, "Craziest idea I ever heard," shut the door, and went back to his hearth.

Miller walked the mile to the railway station, going steadily downhill and passing the public parking lot. At the small station, with its Bavarian eaves and gables, he bought a single ticket to Nuremberg.

It was only as he passed through the ticket barrier toward the windswept platform that the collector told him, "I'm afraid you'll have quite a wait, sir. The Nuremberg train will be late tonight."

Miller was surprised. German railroads make a point of honor of running on time. "What's happened?" he asked.

The ticket collector nodded up the line, where the track disappeared into close folds of hills and valleys heavy-hung with fresh snow. "There's been a large snowfall down the track. Now we've just heard the snow plow's gone on the blink. The engineers are working on it."

Years in journalism had given Miller a deep loathing of waiting rooms. He had spent too long in them, cold, tired, and uncomfortable. In the small station café he sipped a cup of coffee and looked at his ticket. It had already been clipped. His mind went back to his car parked up the hill.

Surely, if he parked it on the other side of Nuremberg, several miles from the address he had been given . . .? If, after the interview, they sent him on somewhere else by another means of transport, he would leave the Jaguar in Munich. He could even park it in a garage, out of sight. No one would ever find it. Not before the job was done. Besides, he reasoned, it wouldn't be a bad thing to have another way of getting out fast if the occasion required. There was no reason for him to think anyone in Bavaria had ever heard of him or his car.

He thought of Motti's warning about its being too noticeable, but then he recalled Oster's tip an hour earlier about getting out in a hurry. To use it was a risk, of course, but then so was to be stranded on foot. He gave the prospect another five minutes, then left his coffee, walked out of the station and back up the hill. Within ten minutes he was behind the wheel of the Jaguar and heading out of town.

It was a short trip to Nuremberg. When he arrived, Miller checked into a small hotel near the main station, parked his car in a side street two blocks away, and walked through the King's Gate into the old walled medieval city of Albrecht Dürer.

It was already dark, but the lights from the streets and windows lit up the quaint pointed roofs and decorated gables of the walled town. It was almost possible to think oneself back in the Middle Ages, when the Kings of Franconia had ruled over Nuremberg, one of the richest merchant cities of the Germanic states. It was hard to recall that almost every brick and stone of what he saw around him had been built since 1945, meticulously reconstructed from the actual architects' plans of the original town, which had been reduced with its cobbled streets and timbered houses to ashes and rubble by the Allied bombs of 1943.

He found the house he was looking for two streets from the square of the main market, almost under the twin spires of Saint Sebald's Church. The name on the doorplate checked with the one typed on the letter he carried, the forged introduction supposedly from former SS Colonel Joachim Eberhardt of Bremen. As he had never met Eberhardt, he could only hope the man in the house in Nuremberg had not met him either.

He walked back to the market square, looking for a place to have supper. After strolling past two or three traditional Franconian eating houses, he noticed smoke curling up into the frosty night sky from the red-tiled roof of the small sausage house in the corner of the square, in front of the doors of

Saint Sebald's. It was a pretty little place, fronted by a terrace fringed with boxes of purple heather, from which a careful owner had brushed the morning's snow.

Inside, the warmth and good cheer hit him like a wave. The wooden tables were almost all occupied, but a couple from a corner table were leaving, so he took it, bobbing and smiling back as the couple, on their way out, wished him a good appetite. He ordered the specialty of the house, the small spiced Nuremberg sausages, a dozen on one plate, and treated himself to a bottle of the local wine to wash them down.

After his meal he sat back and dawdled over his coffee and chased the black liquid home with two Asbachs. He didn't feel like bed, and it was pleasant to sit and gaze at the logs flickering in the open fire, to listen to the crowd in the corner roaring out a Franconian drinking song, locking arms and swinging from side to side to the music, voices and wine tumblers raised high each time they reached the end of a stanza.

For a long time he wondered why he should bother to risk his life in the quest for a man who had committed crimes twenty years before. He almost decided to let the matter drop, to shave off his mustache, grow his hair again, go back to Hamburg and the bed warmed by Sigi.

The waiter came over, bowed, deposited the bill on the table with a cheerful *"Bitte schön."*

He reached into his pocket for his wallet, and his fingers touched a photograph. He pulled it out and gazed at it for a while. The pale red-rimmed eyes and the rattrap mouth stared back at him above the collar with the black tabs and the silver lightning symbols. After a while he muttered, "You shit," and held the corner of the photograph above the candle on his table. When the picture had been reduced to ashes he crumpled them in the copper tray. He would not need it again. He could recognize the face when he saw it.

Peter Miller paid for his meal, buttoned his coat about him, and walked back to his hotel.

Mackensen was confronting an angry and baffled Werwolf at about the same time.

"How the hell *can* he be missing?" snapped the Odessa chief. "He can't vanish off the face of the earth, he can't disappear into thin air. His car must be one of the most distinctive in Germany, visible half a mile off. Six weeks of searching, and all you can tell me is that he hasn't been seen. . . ."

Mackensen waited until the outburst of frustration had spent itself. "Nevertheless, it's true," he pointed out at length. "I've had his apartment in Hamburg checked out, his girl friend and mother interviewed by supposed friends of Miller, his colleagues contacted. They all know nothing. His car must have been in a garage somewhere all this time. He must have gone to ground. Since he was traced leaving the airport parking lot in Cologne, after returning from London, and driving south, he has gone."

"We have to find him," repeated the Werwolf. "He must not get near this *Kamerad*. It would be a disaster."

"He'll show up," said Mackensen with conviction. "Sooner or later he has to break cover. Then we'll have him."

The Werwolf considered the patience and logic of the professional hunter. He nooded slowly. "Very well. Then I want you to stay close to me. Check into a hotel here in town, and we'll wait it out. If you're nearby, I can get you easily."

"Right, sir. I'll get into a hotel downtown and call you to let you know. You can get me there any time." He bade his superior good night and left.

It was just before nine the following morning that Miller presented himself at the house and rang the brilliantly polished bell. He wanted to get the man before he left for work. The door was opened by a maid, who showed him into the living room and went to fetch her employer.

The man who entered the room ten minutes later was in his mid-fifties with medium-brown hair and silver tufts at each temple, self-possessed and elegant. The furniture and decor of his room also spelled elegance and a substantial income.

He gazed at his unexpected visitor without curiosity assessing at a glance the inexpensive trousers and jacket of a working-class man. "And what can I do for you?" he inquired calmly.

The visitor was plainly embarrassed and ill at ease among the opulent surroundings of the room. "Well, *Herr Doktor,* I was hoping you might be able to help me."

"Come now," said the Odessa man, "I'm sure you know my office is not far from here. Perhaps you should go there and ask my secretary for an appointment."

"Well, it's not actually professional help I need," said Miller. He had dropped into the vernacular of the Hamburg and Bremen area, the language of working people. He was obviously embarrassed. At a loss for words, he produced a letter from his inside pocket and held it out. "I brought a letter of introduction from the man who suggested I come to you, sir."

The Odessa man took the letter without a word, slit it open, and cast his eyes quickly down it. He stiffened slightly and gazed narrowly across the sheet of paper at Miller. "I see, Herr Kolb. Perhaps you had better sit down."

He gestured toward an upright chair, while he himself took an easy chair. He spent several minutes looking speculatively at his guest, a frown on his face. Suddenly he snapped, "What did you say your name was?"

"Kolb, sir."

"First names?"

"Rolf Günther, sir."

"Do you have any identification on you?"

Miller looked nonplused. "Only my driving license."

"Let me see it, please."

The lawyer—for that was his profession—stretched out a hand, forcing Miller to rise from his seat and place the driving license in the outstretched palm. The man took it, flicked it open, and digested the details inside. He glanced over it at Miller, comparing the photograph and the face. They matched.

"What is your date of birth?" he snapped suddenly.

"My birthday? Oh—er—June eighteenth, sir."

"The year, Kolb?"

"Nineteen twenty-five, sir."

The lawyer considered the driving license for another few minutes. "Wait here," he said suddenly, got up, and left.

He traversed the house and entered the rear portion of it, an area that served as his office and was reached by clients from a street at the back. He went straight into the office and opened the wall safe. From it he took a thick book and thumbed through it.

By chance he knew the name of Joachim Eberhardt but had never met the man. He was not completely certain of Eberhardt's last rank in the SS. The book confirmed the letter. Joachim Eberhardt, promoted colonel of the Waffen SS on January 10, 1945. He flicked over several more pages and checked against Kolb. There were seven such names, but only one Rolf Günther. Staff Sergeant as of April 1945. Date of birth 18/6/25. He closed the book, replaced it, and locked the safe. Then he returned through the house to the living room. His guest was still sitting awkwardly on the upright chair.

He settled himself again. "It may not be possible for me to help you. You realize that, don't you?"

Miller bit his lip and nodded. "I've nowhere else to go, sir. I went to Herr Eberhardt for help when they started looking for me, and he gave me the letter and suggested I come to you. He said if you couldn't help me no one could."

The lawyer leaned back in his chair and gazed at the ceiling. "I wonder why he didn't call me if he wanted to talk to me," he mused. Then he evidently waited for an answer.

"Maybe he didn't want to use the phone on a matter like this," Miller suggested hopefully.

The lawyer shot him a scornful look. "It's possible," he said shortly. "You'd better tell me how you got into this mess in the first place."

"Oh, yes. Well, sir—I mean I was recognized by this man, and then they said they were coming to arrest me. So I got out, didn't I? I mean, I had to."

The lawyer sighed. "Start at the beginning," he said wearily. "Who recognized you, and as what?"

Miller drew a deep breath. "Well, sir, I was in Bremen. I live there, and I work—well, I worked, until this happened, for Herr Eberhardt. In the bakery. Well, I was walking in the street one day about four months back, and I suddenly got very sick. I felt terribly ill, with stomach pains. Anyway, I must have passed out. I fainted on the pavement. So they took me away to the hospital."

"Which hospital?"

"Bremen General, sir. They did some tests and they said I had cancer. In the intestine. I thought that was it, see?"

"It usually is it," observed the lawyer dryly.

"Well, that's what I thought, sir. Only apparently it was caught at an early stage. Anyway, they put me on a course of drugs instead of operating, and after some time the cancer went into a remission."

"So far as I can see, you're a lucky man. What's all this about being recognized?"

"Yes, well, it was this hospital orderly, see? He was Jewish, and he kept staring at me. Every time he was on duty he kept staring at me. It was a funny sort of look, see? And it got me worried. The way he kept looking at me. With a sort of 'I know you' look on his face. I didn't recognize him, but I got the impression he knew me."

"Go on." The lawyer was showing increasing interest.

"So about a month ago they said I was ready to be transferred, and I was taken away and put in a convalescent clinic. It was the employees' insurance plan at the bakery that paid for it. Well, before I left the Bremen General, I remembered him. The Jew-boy I mean. It took me weeks; then I got it. He was an inmate at Flossenburg."

The lawyer jackknifed upright. "You were at Flossenburg?"

"Yes, I was getting around to telling you that, wasn't I? I mean, sir. And I remembered this hospital orderly from then. I got his name in the Bremen hospital. But at Flossenburg he had been in the party of Jewish inmates that we used to burn the bodies of Admiral Canaris and the other officers we hanged for their part in the assassination attempt on the Führer."

The lawyer stared at him again. "You were one of those who executed Canaris and the others?" he asked.

Miller shrugged. "I commanded the execution squad," he said simply. "Well, they were traitors, weren't they? They tried to kill the Führer."

The lawyer smiled. "My dear fellow, I'm not reproaching you. Of course they were traitors. Canaris had even been passing information to the Allies. They were all traitors, those Army swine, from the generals down. I just never thought to meet the man who killed them."

Miller grinned weakly. "The point is, the police would like to get their hands on me for that. I mean, knocking off Jews is one thing, but now there's a lot of them saying Canaris and that crowd—saying they were sort of heroes."

The lawyer nodded. "Yes, certainly that would get you into bad trouble with the present authorities in Germany. Go on with your story."

"I was transferred to this clinic, and I didn't see the Jewish orderly again. Then last Friday I got a telephone call at the convalescent clinic. I thought it must be the bakery calling, but the man wouldn't give his name. He just said he was in a position to know what was going on, and that a certain person had informed those swine at Ludwigsburg who I was, and there was a warrant being prepared for my arrest. I didn't know who the man could be, but he sounded as if he knew what he was talking about. Sort of official-sounding voice, if you know what I mean, sir?"

The lawyer nodded understandingly. "Probably a friend on the police force of Bremen. What did you do?"

Miller looked surprised. "Well, I got out, didn't I? I discharged myself. I didn't know what to do. I didn't go home in case they were waiting for me there. I didn't even go and pick up my Volkswagen, which was still parked in front of my house. I slept out Friday night; then on Saturday I had an idea. I went to see the boss, Herr Eberhardt, at his house. He was in the telephone book. He was real nice to me. He said he was leaving with Frau Eberhardt for a winter cruise the next morning, but he'd try and see that I was all right. So he gave me the letter and told me to come to you."

"What made you suspect Herr Eberhardt would help you?"

"Well, you see I didn't know what he had been in the war. But he was always real nice to me at the bakery. Then about two years back we were having the staff party. We all got a little drunk, and I went to the men's room. There was Herr Eberhardt washing his hands. And singing. He was singing the 'Horst Wessel Song.' So I joined in. There we were, singing it in the men's room. Then he clapped me on the back, and said, 'Not a word, Kolb,' and went out. I didn't think any more about it till I got into trouble. Then I thought—well, he might have been in the SS like me. So I went to him for help."

"And he sent you to me?"

Miller nodded.

"What was the name of this Jewish orderly?"

"Hartstein, sir."

"And the convalescent clinic you were sent to?"

"The Arcadia Clinic, at Delmenhorst, just outside Bremen."

The lawyer nodded again, made a few notes on a sheet of paper taken from a desk, and rose. "Stay here," he said and left again.

He crossed the passage and entered his study. From the telephone information operator he elicited the numbers of the Eberhardt Bakery, the Bremen General Hospital, and the Arcadia Clinic at Delmenhorst. He called the bakery first.

Eberhardt's secretary was most helpful. "I'm afraid Herr Eberhardt is away, sir. No, he can't be contacted, he has taken his usual winter cruise to the Caribbean with Frau Eberhardt. He'll be back in four weeks. Can I be of any assistance?"

The lawyer assured her she could not and hung up. Next he dialed the Bremen General and asked for Personnel and Staff.

"This is the Department of Social Security, Pensions Section," he said smoothly. "I just wanted to confirm that you have a ward orderly on the staff by the name of Hartstein."

There was a pause while the girl at the other end went through the staff file. "Yes, we do," she said. "David Hartstein."

"Thank you," said the lawyer in Nuremberg and hung up. He dialed the same number again and asked for the registrar's office.

"This is the secretary of the Eberhardt Baking Company," he said. "I just wanted to check on the progress of one of our staff who has been in your hospital with a tumor in the intestine. Can you tell me of his progress? Rolf Günther Kolb."

There was another pause. The girl filing clerk got out the file on Rolf Günther Kolb and glanced at the last page.

"He's been discharged," she told the caller. "His condition improved to a point where he could be transferred to a convalescent clinic."

"Excellent," said the lawyer. "I've been away on my annual skiing vacation, so I haven't caught up yet. Can you tell me which clinic?"

"The Arcadia, at Delmenhorst," said the girl.

The lawyer hung up again and dialed the Arcadia Clinic. A girl answered. After listening to the request, she turned to the doctor by her side. She covered the mouthpiece. "There's a question about that man you mentioned to me, Kolb," she said.

The doctor took the telephone. "Yes," he said. "This is the Chief of the Clinic. I am Doctor Braun. Can I help you?"

At the name of Braun the secretary shot a puzzled glance at her employer. Without batting an eyelid, he listened to the voice from Nuremberg and replied smoothly, "I'm afraid Herr Kolb discharged himself last Friday afternoon. Most irregular, but there was nothing I could do to prevent him. Yes, that's right, he was transferred here from the Bremen General. A tumor, well on the way to recovery."

He listened a moment, then said, "Not at all. Glad I could be of help to you."

The doctor, whose real name was Rosemayer, hung up and then dialed a Munich number. Without preamble he said, "Someone's been on the phone asking about Kolb. The checking up has started."

Back in Nuremberg, the lawyer replaced the phone and returned to the living room. "Right, Kolb, you evidently are who you say you are."

Miller stared at him in astonishment.

"However, I'd like to ask you a few more questions. You don't mind?"

Still amazed, the visitor shook his head. "No, sir."

"Good. Are you circumcised?"

Miller stared back blankly. "No, I'm not," he said dumbly.

"Show me," said the lawyer calmly. Miller just sat in his chair and stared at him.

"Show me, Staff Sergeant," snapped the lawyer.

Miller shot out of his chair, ramrodding to attention. "*Zu Befehl,*" he responded, quivering at attention. He held the attention position, thumbs down the seams of his trousers, for three seconds, then unzipped his fly. The lawyer glanced at him briefly, then nodded that he could zip his fly up again.

"Well, at least you're not Jewish," he said amiably.

Back in his chair Miller stared at him, open-mouthed. "Of course I'm not Jewish," he blurted.

The lawyer smiled. "Nevertheless, there have been cases of Jews trying to pass themselves off as one of the *Kameraden.* They don't last long. Now you'd better tell me your story, and I'm going to shoot questions at you. Just checking up, you understand. Where were you born?"

"Bremen, sir."

"Right. Place of birth is in your SS records. I just checked. Were you in the Hitler Youth?"

"Yes, sir. Entered at the age of ten in nineteen thirty-five, sir."

"Your parents were good National Socialists?"

"Yes, sir, both of them."

"What happened to them?"

"They were killed in the great bombing of Bremen."

"When were you inducted into the SS?"

"Spring nineteen forty-four, sir. Age eighteen."

"Where did you train?"

"Dachau SS training camp, sir."

"You had your blood group tattooed under your right armpit?"

"No, sir. And it would have been the left armpit."

"Why weren't you tattooed?"

"Well, sir, we were due to pass out of training camp in August nineteen forty-four and go to our first posting in a unit of the Waffen SS. Then in July a large group of officers involved in the plot against the Führer was sent down to Flossenburg camp. Flossenburg asked for immediate troops from Dachau training camp to increase the staff at Flossenburg. I and about a dozen others were singled out as cases of special aptitude and sent straight there. We missed our tattooing and the formal passing-out parade of our draft. The commandant said the blood group was not necessary, as we would never get to the front, sir."

The lawyer nodded. No doubt the commandant had also been aware in July 1944 that, with the Allies well into France, the war was drawing to a close.

"Did you get your dagger?"

"Yes, sir. From the hands of the commandant."

"What are the words on it?"

"Blood and Honor, sir."

"What kind of training did you get at Dachau?"

"Complete military training, sir, and political-ideological training to supplement that of the Hitler Youth."

"Did you learn the songs?"

"Yes sir."

"What was the book of marching songs from which the 'Horst Wessel Song' was drawn?"

"The album *Time of Struggle for the Nation,* sir."

"Where was Dachau training camp?"

"Ten miles north of Munich, sir. Three miles from the concentration camp of the same name."

"What was your uniform?"

"Gray-green tunic and breeches, jackboots, black collar lapels, rank on the left one, black leather belt, and gunmetal buckle."

"The motto on the buckle?"

"A swastika in the center, ringed with the words 'My honor is loyalty,' sir."

The lawyer rose and stretched. He lit up a cigar and strolled to the window. "Now you'll tell me about Flossenburg Camp, Staff Sergeant Kolb. Where was it?"

"On the border of Bavaria and Thuringia, sir."

"When was it opened?"

"In nineteen thirty-four, sir. One of the first for the pigs who opposed the Führer."

"How large was it?"

"When I was there, sir, three hundred meters by three hundred. It was ringed by nineteen watchtowers with heavy and light machine guns mounted. It had a roll-call square one-twenty meters by one-forty. God, we had some fun there with them Yids—"

"Stick to the point," snapped the lawyer. "What were the accommodations?"

"Twenty-four barracks, a kitchen for the inmates, a washhouse, a sanatorium, and various workshops."

"And for the SS guards?"

"Two barracks, a shop, and a bordello."

"How were the bodies of those who died disposed of?"

"There was a small crematorium outside the wire. It was reached from inside the camp by an underground passage."

"What was the main kind of work done?"

"Stone-breaking in the quarry, sir. The quarry was also outside the wire, surrounded by barbed wire and watchtowers of its own."

"What was the population in late nineteen forty-four?"

"Oh, about sixteen thousand inmates, sir."

"Where was the commandant's office?"

"Outside the wire, sir, halfway up a slope overlooking the camp."

"Who were the successive commandants?"

"Two were before I got there, sir. The first was SS Major Karl Kunstler. His successor was SS Captain Karl Fritsch. The last one was SS Lieutenant Colonel Max Kögel."

"Which was the number of the political department?"

"Department Two, sir."

"Where was it?"

"In the commandant's block."

"What were its duties?"

"To ensure that requirements from Berlin that certain prisoners receive special treatment were carried out."

"Canaris and the other plotters were so indicated?"

"Yes, sir. They were all designated for special treatment."

"When was this carried out?"

"April twentieth, nineteen forty-five, sir. The Americans were moving up through Bavaria, so the orders came to finish them off. A group of us was designated to do the job. I was then a newly promoted staff sergeant, although I had arrived at the camp as a private. I headed the detail for Canaris and five others. Then we had a burial party of Jews bury the bodies. Hartstein was one of them, damn his eyes. After that we burned the camp documents. Some time later we were ordered to march the prisoners northward. On the way we heard the Führer had killed himself. Well, sir, the officers left us then. The prisoners started running off into the woods. We shot a few, us sergeants, but there didn't seem much point in marching on. I mean the Yanks were all over the place."

"One last question about the camp, Staff Sergeant. When you looked up, from anywhere in the camp, what did you see?"

Miller looked puzzled. "The sky," he said.

"Fool, I mean what dominated the horizon?"

"Oh, you mean the hill with the ruined castle keep on it?"

The lawyer nodded and smiled. "Fourteenth century, actually," he said. "All right, Kolb, you were at Flossenburg. Now, how did you get away?"

"Well, sir, it was on the march. We all broke up. I found an Army private wandering around, so I hit him on the head and took his uniform. The Yanks caught me two days later. I did two years in a prisoner-of-war camp, but just told them I was an Army private. Well, you know how it was, sir, there were rumors floating about that the Yanks were shooting SS men out of hand. So I said I was in the Army."

The lawyer exhaled a draft of cigar smoke. "You weren't alone in that. Did you change your name?"

"No, sir. I threw my papers away, because they identified me as SS. But I didn't think to change the name. I didn't think anyone would look for a staff sergeant. At the time the business with Canaris didn't seem very important. It was only much later people started making a fuss over those Army officers, and made a shrine of the place in Berlin where they hanged the ringleaders. But then I had papers from the Federal Republic in the name of Kolb. Anyway, nothing would have happened if that orderly hadn't spotted me, and after that it wouldn't have mattered what I called myself."

"True. Right, now we'll go on to a little of the things you were taught. Start by repeating to me the oath of loyalty to the Führer," said the lawyer.

It went on for another three hours. Miller was sweating, but was able to say he had left the hospital prematurely and had not eaten all day. It was past lunchtime when at last the lawyer professed himself satisfied.

"Just what do you want?" he asked Miller.

"Well, the thing is, sir, with them all looking for me, I'm going to need a set of papers showing I am not Rolf Günther Kolb. I can change my appearance, grow my hair, let the mustache grow longer, and get a job in Bavaria or somewhere. I mean, I'm a skilled baker, and people need bread, don't they?"

For the first time in the interview the lawyer threw back his head and laughed. "Yes, my good Kolb, people need bread. Very well. Listen. Normally people of your standing in life hardly merit a lot of expensive time and trouble being spent on them. But as you are evidently in trouble through no fault of your own, obviously a good and loyal German, I'll do what I can. There's no point in your getting simply a new driving license. That would not enable you to get a social-security card without producing a birth certificate, which you haven't got. But a new passport would get you all these things. Have you got any money?"

"No, sir. I'm dead broke. I've been hitchhiking south for the past three days."

The lawyer gave him a hundred-mark note. "You can't stay here, and it will take at least a week before your new passport comes through. I'll send you to a friend of mine who will acquire the passport for you. He lives in Stuttgart. You'd better check into a commercial hotel and go and see him. I'll tell him you're coming, and he'll be expecting you."

The lawyer wrote on a piece of paper. "He's called Franz Bayer, and here's his address. You'd better take the train to Stuttgart, find a hotel, and go straight to him. If you need a little more money, he'll help you out. But don't go spending a lot. Stay under cover and wait until Bayer can fix you up with a new passport. Then we'll find you a job in southern Germany, and no one will ever trace you."

Miller took the hundred marks and the address of Bayer with embarrassed thanks. "Oh, thank you, *Herr Doktor,* you're a real gentleman."

The maid showed him out, and he walked back toward the station, his hotel, and his parked car. An hour later he was speeding toward Stuttgart, while the lawyer rang Bayer and told him to expect Rolf Günther Kolb, refugee from the police, in the early evening.

There was no autobahn between Nuremberg and Stuttgart in those days,

and on a bright sunny day the road leading across the lush plain of Franconia and into the wooded hills and valleys of Württemberg would have been
picturesque. On a bitter February afternoon, with ice glittering in the dips of
the road surface and mist forming in the valleys, the twisting ribbon of
tarmac between Ansbach and Crailsheim was murderous. Twice the heavy
Jaguar almost slithered into a ditch, and twice Miller had to tell himself there
was no hurry. Bayer, the man who knew how to get false passports, would
still be there.

He arrived after dark and found a small hotel in the outer city that
nevertheless had a night porter for those who preferred to stay out late, and
a garage at the back for the car. From the hall porter he got a town plan and
found Bayer's street in the suburb of Ostheim, a well-set-up area not far
from the Villa Berg, in whose gardens the Princess of Württemberg and
their ladies had once disported themselves on summer nights.

Following the map, he drove the car down into the bowl of hills that
frames the center of Stuttgart, along which the vineyards come up to the
outskirts of the city, and parked his car a quarter of a mile from Bayer's
house. As he stooped to lock the driver's-side door, he failed to notice a
middle-aged lady coming home from her weekly meeting of the Hospital
Visitors Committee at the nearby Villa Hospital.

It was at eight that evening that the lawyer in Nuremberg thought he had
better ring Bayer and make sure the refugee Kolb had arrived safely. It was
Bayer's wife who answered.

"Oh, yes, the young man. He and my husband have gone out to dinner
somewhere."

"I just rang to make sure he had arrived safe and sound," said the lawyer
smoothly.

"Such a nice young man," burbled Frau Bayer cheerfully. "I passed him as
he was parking his car. I was just on my way home from the Hospital Visitors
Committee meeting. But miles away from the house. He must have lost his
way. It's very easy, you know, in Stuttgart, so many dead ends and one-way
streets—"

"Excuse me, Frau Bayer," the lawyer cut in. "The man did not have his
Volkswagen with him. He came by train."

"No, no," said Frau Bayer, happy to be able to show superior knowledge.
"He came by car. Such a nice young man, and such a lovely car. I'm sure he's
a success with all the girls with a—"

"Frau Bayer, listen to me. Carefully, now. What kind of a car was it?"

"Well, I don't know the make, of course. But a sports car. A long black one,
with a yellow stripe down the side—"

The lawyer slammed down the phone, then raised it and dialed a number
in Nuremberg. He was sweating slightly. When he got the hotel he wanted he
asked for a room number. The phone extension was lifted, and a familiar
voice said, "Hello."

"Mackensen," barked the Werwolf, "get over here fast. We've found
Miller."

THIRTEEN

Franz Bayer was as fat and round and jolly as his wife. Alerted by the Werwolf to expect the fugitive from the police, he welcomed Miller on his doorstep when he presented himself just before eight o'clock.

Miller was introduced briefly to his wife in the hallway before she bustled off to the kitchen.

"Well, now," said Bayer, "have you ever been in Württemberg before, my dear Kolb?"

"No, I confess I haven't."

"Ha, well, we pride ourselves here on being very hospitable people. No doubt you'd like some food. Have you eaten yet today?"

Miller told him he had had neither breakfast nor lunch, having been on the train all afternoon.

Bayer seemed most distressed. "Good heavens, how awful. You must eat. Tell you what, we'll go into town and have a really good dinner. . . . Nonsense, my boy, the least I can do for you."

He waddled off into the back of the house to tell his wife he was taking their guest out for a meal in downtown Stuttgart, and ten minutes later they were heading in Bayer's car toward the city center.

It is at least a two-hour drive from Nuremberg to Stuttgart along the old E12 highroad, even if one pushes the car hard. And Mackensen pushed his car that night. Half an hour after he received the Werwolf's call, fully briefed and armed with Bayer's address, he was on the road. He arrived at half past ten and went straight to Bayer's house.

Frau Bayer, alerted by another call from the Werwolf that the man calling himself Kolb was not what he seemed to be and might indeed be a police informer, was a trembling and frightened woman when Mackensen arrived. His terse manner was hardly calculated to put her at her ease.

"When did they leave?"

"About a quarter to eight," she quavered.

"Did they say where they were going?"

"No. Franz just said the young man had not eaten all day and he was taking him into town for a meal at a restaurant. I said I could make something here at home, but Franz just loves dining out. Any excuse will do—"

"This man Kolb. You said you saw him parking his car. Where was this?"

She described the street where the Jaguar was parked, and how to get to it from her house.

Mackensen thought deeply for a moment. "Have you any idea which restaurant your husband might have taken him to?" he asked.

She thought for a while. "Well, his favorite eating place is the Three Moors restaurant on Friedrichstrasse," she said. "He usually tries there first."

Mackensen left the house and drove the half-mile to the parked Jaguar. He examined it closely, certain that he would recognize it again whenever he saw it. He was of two minds whether to stay with it and wait for Miller's return. But the Werwolf's orders were to trace Miller and Bayer, warn the Odessa man and send him home, then take care of Miller. For that reason he had not telephoned the Three Moors. To warn Bayer now would be to alert Miller to the fact that he had been uncovered, giving him the chance to disappear again.

Mackensen glanced at his watch. It was ten to eleven. He climbed back into his Mercedes and headed for the center of town.

In a small and obscure hotel in the back streets of Munich, Josef was lying awake on his bed when a call came from the reception desk to say a cable had arrived for him. He went downstairs and brought it back to his room.

Seated at the rickety table, he slit the buff envelope and scanned the lengthy contents. It began:

Celery:	481 marks, 53 pfennigs.
Melons:	362 marks, 17 pfennigs.
Oranges:	627 marks, 24 pfennigs.
Grapefruit:	313 marks, 88 pfennigs. . . .

The list of fruit and vegetables was long, but all the articles were those habitually exported by Israel, and the cable read like the response to an inquiry by the German-based representative of an export company for price quotations. Using the public international cable network was not secure, but so many commercial cables pass through Western Europe in a day that checking them all would need an army of men.

Ignoring the words, Josef wrote down the figures in a long line. The five-figure groups into which the marks and pfennigs were divided disappeared. When he had them all in a line, he split them up into groups of six figures. From each six-figure group he subtracted the date, February 20, 1964, which he wrote as 20264. In each case the result was another six-figure group.

It was a simple book code, based on the paperback edition of Webster's New World Dictionary as published by Popular Library of New York. The first three figures in the group represented the page in the dictionary; the fourth figure could be anything from one to nine. An odd number meant column one, an even number column two. The last two figures indicated the number of words down the column from the top. He worked steadily for half an hour, then read the message through and slowly held his head in his hands.

Thirty minutes later he was with Leon in the latter's house. The revenge-group leader read the message and swore. "I'm sorry," he said at last. "I couldn't have known."

Unknown to either man, three tiny fragments of information had come into the possession of the Mossad in the previous six days. One was from the resident Israeli agent in Buenos Aires to the effect that someone had authorized the payment of a sum equivalent to one million German marks to a figure called Vulkan "to enable him to complete the next stage of his research project."

The second was from a Jewish employee of a Swiss bank known habitually

to handle currency transfers from secret Nazi funds elsewhere to pay off
Odessa men in Western Europe; it was to the effect that one million marks
had been transferred to the bank from Beirut and collected in cash by a man
operating an account at the bank for the previous ten years in the name of
Fritz Wegener.

The third was from an Egyptian colonel in a senior position in the security
apparat around Factory 333, who, for a substantial consideration in money
to help him prepare a comfortable retirement, had talked with a man from
the Mossad for several hours in a Rome hotel. What the man had to say was
the the rocket project was lacking only the provision of a reliable teleguidance system, which was being researched and constructed in a factory in
West Germany, and that the project was costing the Odessa millions of
marks.

The three fragments, among thousands of others, had been processed in
the computer banks of Professor Youvel Neeman, the Israeli genius who
had first harnessed science in the form of the computer to intelligence
analysis, and who later went on to become the father of the Israeli atomic
bomb. Where a human memory might have failed, the whirring microcir-
cuits had linked the three items, recalled that up to his exposure by his wife
in 1955 Roschmann had used the name of Fritz Wegener, and reported
accordingly.

Josef rounded on Leon in their underground headquarters. "I'm staying
here from now on. I'm not moving out of range of that telephone. Get me a
powerful motorcycle and protective clothing. Have both ready within the
hour. If and when your precious Miller checks in, I'll have to get to him fast."

"If he's exposed, you won't get there fast enough," said Leon. "No wonder
they warned him to stay away. They'll kill him if he gets within a mile of his
man."

As Leon left the cellar Josef ran his eye over the cable from Tel Aviv once
again. It said:

RED ALERT NEW INFORMATION INDICATES VITAL KEY ROCKET
SUCCESS GERMAN INDUSTRIALIST OPERAT(ING) YOUR TERRI-
TORY STOP CODE NAME VULCAN STOP PROBABLE IDENTIFICA-
TION ROSH MAN STOP USE MILLER INSTANTLY STOP TRACE AND
ELIMINATE TOP CORMORANT

Josef sat at the table and meticulously began to clean and arm his Walther
PPK automatic. From time to time he glanced at the silent telephone.

Over dinner Bayer had been the genial host, roaring with laughter in
great gusts as he told his own favorite jokes. Miller tried several times to get
the talk around to the question of a new passport for himself.

Each time Bayer clapped him soundly on the back, told him not to worry,
and added, "Leave it to me, old boy, leave it to old Franz Bayer."

He tapped the right-hand side of his nose with his forefinger, winked
broadly, and dissolved into gales of merriment.

One thing Miller had inherited from eight years as a reporter was the
ability to drink and keep a clear head. He was not used to the white wine of

which copious drafts were to wash down the meal. But white wine has one advantage if one is trying to get another man drunk. It comes in buckets of ice and cold water, to keep it chilled, and three times Miller was able to tip his entire glass into the ice bucket when Bayer was looking the other way.

By the dessert course they had demolished two bottles of excellent cold hock, and Bayer, squeezed into his tight horn-buttoned jacket, was perspiring in torrents. The effect was to enhance his thirst, and he called for a third bottle of wine.

Miller feigned to be worried that it would prove impossible to obtain a new passport for him, and that he would be arrested for his part in the events at Flossenburg in 1945.

"You'll need some photographs of me, won't you?" he asked with concern.

Bayer guffawed. "Yes, a couple of photographs. No problem. You can get them taken in one of the automatic booths at the station. Wait till your hair's a little longer, and the mustache a little fuller, and no one will ever know it's the same man."

"What happens then?" asked Miller, agog.

Bayer leaned over and placed a fat arm around his shoulders. Miller smelled the stench of wine as the fat man chuckled in his ear. "Then I send them away to a friend of mine, and a week later back comes the passport. With the passport we get you a driving license—you'll have to pass the test, of course—and a social-security card. So far as the authorities are concerned, you've just arrived back home after fifteen years abroad. No problem, old chap, stop worrying."

Although Bayer was getting drunk, he was still in command of his tongue. He declined to say more, and Miller was afraid to push him too far in case he suspected something was amiss with his young guest and closed up completely.

Although he was dying for coffee, Miller declined, in case the coffee should begin to sober up Franz Bayer. The fat man paid for the meal from a well-stuffed wallet, and they headed for the coat-check counter. It was half past ten.

"It's been a wonderful evening, Herr Bayer. Thank you very much."

"Franz, Franz," wheezed the fat man as he struggled into his coat.

"I suppose that's the end of what Stuttgart has to offer in the way of night life," observed Miller as he slipped into his own.

"Ha, silly boy. That's all you know. We have a great little city here, you know. Half a dozen good cabarets. You'd like to go on to one?"

"You mean there are cabarets, with stripteases and everything?" asked Miller, pop-eyed.

Bayer wheezed with mirth. "Are you kidding? I wouldn't be against the idea of watching some of the little ladies take their clothes off." Bayer tipped the coat-check girl handsomely and waddled outside.

"What nightclubs are there in Stuttgart?" asked Miller innocently.

"Well, now, let's see. There's the Moulin Rouge, the Balzac, the Imperial, and the Sayonara. Then there's the Madeleine in Eberhardtstrasse—"

"Eberhardt? Good Lord, what a coincidence. That was my boss in Bremen, the man who got me out of this mess and passed me on to the lawyer in Nuremberg," exclaimed Miller.

"Good. Good. Excellent. Let's go there, then," said Bayer and led the way to his car.

Mackensen reached the Three Moors at quarter past eleven. He inquired of the headwaiter, who was supervising the departure of the last guests.

"Herr Bayer? Yes, he was here tonight. Left about half an hour ago."

"He had a guest with him? A tall man with short brown hair and a mustache."

"That's right. I remember them. Sitting at the corner table over there."

Mackensen slipped a twenty-mark note into the man's hand without difficulty. "It's vitally important that I find him. It's an emergency. His wife, you know, a sudden collapse . . ."

The headwaiter's face puckered with concern. "Oh dear, how terrible!"

"Do you know where they went from here?"

"I confess I don't," said the headwaiter. He called to one of the junior waiters. "Hans, you served Herr Bayer and his guest at the corner table. Did they mention if they were going on anywhere?"

"No," said Hans. "I didn't hear them say anything about going on anywhere."

"You could try the hat-check girl," suggested the headwaiter. "She might have heard them say something."

Mackensen asked the girl. Then he asked for a copy of the tourist booklet, *What's Going on in Stuttgart*. In the section for cabarets were half a dozen names. In the middle pages of the booklet was a street map of the city center. He walked back to his car and headed for the first name on the list of cabarets.

Miller and Bayer sat at a table for two in the Madeleine nightclub. Bayer, on his second large tumbler of whisky, stared with pop eyes at a generously endowed young woman gyrating her hips in the center of the floor while her fingers unhooked the fasteners of her brassière. When it finally came off, Bayer jabbed Miller in the ribs with his elbow. He was quivering with mirth.

"What a pair, eh, lad, what a pair?" he chuckled. It was well after midnight, and he was becoming very drunk.

"Look, Herr Bayer, I'm worried," whispered Miller. "I mean, it's me who's on the run. How soon can you make this passport for me?"

Bayer draped his arm around Miller's shoulders. "Look, Rolf, old buddy, I've told you. You don't have to worry, see? Just leave it to old Franz." He winked broadly. "Anyway, I don't make the passports. I just send off the photographs to the chap who makes them, and a week later, back they come. No problem. Now, have a drink with old pal Franz." He raised a pudgy hand and flapped it in the air. "Waiter, another round."

Miller leaned back and considered. If he had to wait until his hair grew before the passport photographs could be taken, he might wait weeks. Nor was he going to get the name and address of the Odessa passport-maker from Bayer by guile. Drunk the man might be, but not so drunk he would give away his contact in the forging business by a slip of the tongue.

He could not get the fat Odessa man away from the club before the end of the first floor show. When they finally made it back to the cold night air outside, it was after one in the morning. Bayer was unsteady on his feet, one arm slung around Miller's shoulders, and the sudden shock of the cold air made him worse.

"I'd better drive you home," Miller told him as they approached the car parked by the curb. He took the car keys from Bayer's coat pocket and helped the unprotesting fat man into the passenger seat. After slamming the door on him, he walked around to the driver's side and climbed in. At that moment a gray Mercedes slewed around the corner behind them and jammed on its brakes to stop twenty yards up the road.

Behind the windshield Mackensen, who had already visited five night-clubs, stared at the number plate of the car moving away from the curb outside the Madeleine. It was the number Frau Bayer had given him. Her husband's car. Letting in the clutch, he followed it.

Miller drove carefully, fighting his own alcohol level. The last thing he wanted was to be stopped by a patrol car and tested for drunkenness. He drove not back to Bayer's house, but to his own hotel. On the way Bayer dozed, his head nodding forward, spreading out his multiple chins into an apron of fat over his collar and tie.

Outside the hotel, Miller nudged him awake. "Come on," he said, "come on, Franz, old pal, let's have a nightcap."

The fat man stared about him. "Must get home," he mumbled. "Wife waiting."

"Come on, just a little drink to finish the evening. We can have a noggin in my room and talk about the old times."

Bayer grinned drunkenly. "Talk about the old times. Great times we had in those days, Rolf."

Miller climbed out and came around to the passenger door to help the fat man to the pavement.

"Great times," he said as he helped Bayer across the pavement and through the door. "Come and have a chat about old times."

Down the street the Mercedes had doused its lights and merged with the gray shadows of the street.

Miller had kept his room key in his pocket. Behind his desk the night porter dozed. Bayer started to mumble.

"Ssssh," said Miller, "got to be quiet."

"Got to be quiet," repeated Bayer, tiptoeing like an elephant toward the stairs. He giggled at his own play-acting. Fortunately for Miller, his room was on the second floor, or Bayer would never have made it. He eased open the door, flicked on the light, and helped Bayer into the only armchair in the room, a hard upright affair with wooden arms.

Outside in the street, Mackensen stood across from the hotel and watched the blacked-out façade. At two in the morning there were no lights burning. When Miller's light came on, he noted it was on the second floor, to the right of the hotel as he faced it.

He debated whether to go straight up and hit Miller as he opened his bedroom door. Two things decided him against it. Through the glass door of the lobby he could see that the night porter, waked by the heavy tread of Bayer past his desk, was puttering around the inside of the foyer. He would undoubtedly notice a nonresident heading up the stairs at two in the morning, and later give a good description to the police. The other thing that dissuaded him was Bayer's condition. He had watched the fat man being helped across the pavement, and knew he could never get him out of the hotel in a hurry after killing Miller. If the police got Bayer, there would be trouble with the Werwolf. Despite appearances, Bayer was a much-wanted man under his real name, and important inside the Odessa.

One last factor persuaded Mackensen to go for a window-shot. Across from the hotel was a building halfway through construction. The frame and the floors were in place, with a rough concrete stairway leading up to the second and third floors. He could wait; Miller was not going anywhere. He walked purposefully back to his car and the hunting rifle locked in the trunk.

Bayer was taken completely by surprise when the blow came. His reactions, slowed by drink, gave him no chance to duck in time. Miller, pretending to search for his bottle of whisky, opened the wardrobe door and took out his spare tie. The only other one he had was around his neck. He took this off too.

He had never had occasion to use the blows he and his fellow rookies had practiced in the gymnasium of their Army training camp ten years before and was not entirely certain how effective they were. The vast bulk of Bayer's neck, like a pink mountain when seen from behind as the man sat in the chair muttering, "Good old times, great old times . . ." caused him to hit as hard as he could.

It was not even a knockout blow, for the edge of his hand was soft and inexperienced, and Bayer's neck was insulated by layers of fat. But it was enough. By the time the Odessa contact man had cleared the dizziness from his brain, both his wrists were lashed tightly to the arms of the wooden chair.

"What the shit?" he growled thickly, shaking his head to clear the muzziness. His own tie came off and secured his left ankle to the foot of the chair, and the telephone cord secured the right one.

He looked up owlishly at Miller as comprehension began to dawn in his button eyes. Like all of his kind, Bayer had one nightmare that never quite left him.

"You can't get me away from here," he said. "You'll never get me to Tel Aviv. You can't prove anything. I never touched you people—"

The words were cut off as a rolled-up pair of socks was stuffed in his mouth and a woolen scarf, a present to Miller from his ever-solicitous mother, was wound around his face. From above the patterned knitting his eyes glared balefully out.

Miller drew up the other chair in the room, reversed it, and sat astride, his face two feet away from that of his prisoner.

"Listen, you fat slug. For one thing, I'm not an Israeli agent. For another, you're not going anywhere. You're staying right here, and you're going to talk right here. Understand?"

For answer Franz Bayer stared back above the scarf. The eyes no longer twinkled with merriment. They were red-tinged, like those of an angry boar in a thicket.

"What I want, and what I'm going to have before this night is through, is the name and address of the man who makes the passports for the Odessa."

Miller looked around, spotted the lamp on the bedside table, unhooked the wall socket, and brought it over.

"Now, Bayer, or whatever your name is, I'm going to take the gag off. You are going to talk. If you attempt to yell, you get this right across the head. I don't really care if I crack your head or not. Got it?"

Miller was not telling the truth. He had never killed a man before and had no desire to start now.

Slowly he eased off the scarf and pulled the rolled socks out of Bayer's mouth, keeping the lamp poised in his right hand, high over the fat man's head.

"You bastard," whispered Bayer. "You're a spy. You'll get nothing out of me."

He hardly got the words out before the socks went back into his bulging cheeks. The scarf was replaced.

"No?" said Miller. "We'll see. I'll start on your fingers and see how you like it."

He took the little finger and ring finger of Bayer's right hand and bent them backward until they were almost vertical. Bayer threw himself about in the chair so that it almost fell over. Miller steadied it and eased the pressure on the fingers.

He took off the gag again. "I can break every finger on both your hands, Bayer," he whispered. "After that I'll take the bulb out of the table lamp, switch it on, and stuff your prick down the socket."

Bayer closed his eyes, and sweat rolled in torrents off his face. "No, not the electrodes. No, not the electrodes. Not there," he mumbled.

"You know what it's like, don't you?" said Miller, his mouth a few inches from Bayer's ear.

Bayer closed his eyes and moaned softly. He knew what it was like. Twenty years before, he had been one of the men who had pounded the White Rabbit, Wing Commander Yeo-Thomas, to a maimed pulp in the cellars beneath Fresnes Jail in Paris. He knew too well what it was like, but not on the receiving end.

"Talk," whispered Miller. "The forger, his name and address."

Bayer slowly shook his head. "I can't," he whispered. "They'll kill me."

Miller replaced the gag. He took Bayer's little finger, closed his eyes, and jerked once. The bone snapped at the knuckle. Bayer heaved in his chair and vomited into the gag.

Miller whipped it off before he could drown. The fat man's head jerked forward, and the evening's highly expensive meal, accompanied by two bottles of wine and several double Scotches, poured down his cheek into his lap.

"Talk," said Miller. "You've got seven more fingers to go."

Bayer swallowed, eyes closed. "Winzer," he said.

"Who?"

"Winzer. Klaus Winzer. He makes the passports."

"He's a professional forger?"

"He's a printer."

"Where? Which town?"

"They'll kill me."

"I'll kill you if you don't tell me. Which town?"

"Osnabrück," whispered Bayer.

Miller replaced the gag across Bayer's mouth and thought. Klaus Winzer, a printer in Osnabrück. He went to his attaché case, which contained the diary of Salomon Tauber and various maps, and took out a road map of Germany.

The autobahn to Osnabrück, far away to the north in Nord Rhine/Westphalia, led through Mannheim, Frankfurt, Dortmund, and Münster. It was a four- to five-hour drive, depending on road conditions. It was already near three in the morning of February 21.

Across the road Mackensen shivered in his niche on the third floor of the half-completed building. The light still shone in the room over the road, the second-floor front. He flicked his eyes constantly from the illuminated window to the front door. If only Bayer would come out, he thought, he could take Miller alone. Or if Miller came out, he could take him farther down the street. Or if someone opened the window for a breath of fresh air . . . . He shivered again and clasped the heavy Remington .300 rifle. At a range of thirty yards there would be no problems with such a gun. Mackensen could wait; he was a patient man.

In his room Miller quietly packed his things. He needed Bayer to remain quiescent for at least six hours. Perhaps the man would be too terrified to warn his chiefs that he had given away the secret of the forger. But Miller couldn't count on it.

He spent a last few minutes tightening the bonds and the gag that held Bayer immobile and silent, then eased the chair onto its side so the fat man could not raise an alarm by rolling the chair over with a crash. The telephone cord was already ripped out. He took a last look around the room and left, locking the door behind him.

He was almost at the top of the stairs when a thought came to him. The night porter might have seen them both mount the stairs. What would he think if only one came down, paid his bill, and left? Miller retreated and headed toward the back of the hotel. At the end of the corridor was a window looking out onto the fire-escape. He slipped the catch and stepped out onto the escape ladder. A few seconds later he was in the rear courtyard, where the garage was situated. A back entrance led to a small alley behind the hotel.

Two minutes later he was striding the three miles to where he had parked his Jaguar, half a mile from Bayer's house. The effect of the drink and the night's activities combined to make him feel desperately tired. He needed sleep badly but realized he had to reach Winzer before the alarm was raised.

It was almost four in the morning when he climbed into the Jaguar, and half past the hour before he had made his way back to the autobahn leading north for Heilbronn and Mannheim.

Almost as soon as he had gone, Bayer, by now completely sober, began to struggle to get free. He tried to lean his head forward far enough to use his teeth, through the sock and the scarf, on the knots of the ties that bound his wrists to the chair. But his fatness prevented his head from getting low enough, and the sock in his mouth forced his teeth apart. Every few minutes he had to pause to take deep breaths through his nose.

He tugged and pulled at his ankle bonds, but they held. Finally, despite the pain from his broken and swelling little finger, he decided to wriggle his wrists free.

When this did not work, he spotted the table lamp lying on the floor. The bulb was still in it, but a crushed light bulb leaves enough slivers of glass to cut a single necktie.

It took him an hour to inch the overturned chair across the floor and crush the light bulb.

It may sound easy, but it isn't, to use a piece of broken glass to cut wrist-bonds. It takes hours to get through a single strand of cloth. Bayer's wrists poured sweat, dampening the cloth of the neckties and making them even tighter around his fat wrists. It was seven in the morning, and light was beginning to filter over the roofs of the town, before the first strands binding his left wrist parted from the effects of being rubbed on a piece of broken glass. It was nearly eight when his left wrist came free.

By that time Miller's Jaguar was boring around the Cologne Ring to the east of the city with another hundred miles before Osnabrück. It had started to rain, an evil sleet running in curtains across the slippery autobahn, and the mesmeric effect of the windshield wipers almost sent him to sleep.

He slowed down to a steady cruise at eighty m.p.h., rather than risk running off the road into the muddy fields on either side.

With his left hand free, Bayer took only a few minutes to rip off his gag, then lay for several minutes, whooping in great gulps of air. The smell in the room was appalling, a mixture of sweat, fear, vomit, and whisky. He un-picked the knots on his right wrist, wincing as the pain from the snapped finger shot up his arm, then released his feet.

His first thought was the door, but it was locked. He tried the telephone, lumbering about on feet long since devoid of feeling from the tightness of the bindings. Finally he staggered to the window, ripped back the curtains, and jerked the windows inward and open.

In his shooting niche across the road, Mackensen was almost dozing despite the cold, when he saw the curtains of Miller's room pulled back. Snapping the Remington up into the aiming position, he waited until the figure behind the net curtains jerked the windows inward, then fired straight into the face of the figure.

The bullet hit Bayer in the base of the throat, and he was dead before his reeling bulk tumbled backward to the floor. The crash of the rifle might be put down to a car backfiring for a minute, but not longer. Within less than a minute, even at that hour of the morning, Mackensen knew someone would investigate.

Without waiting to cast a second look into the room across the road, he was out of the third floor and running down the concrete steps of the building toward the ground. He left by the back, dodging two cement-mixers and a pile of gravel in the rear yard. He regained his car within sixty seconds of firing, stowed the gun in the trunk, and drove off.

He knew as he sat at the wheel and inserted the ignition key that all was not right. He suspected he had made a mistake. The man the Werwolf had briefed him to kill was tall and lean. The mind's-eye impression of the figure at the window was of a fat man. From what he had seen the previous evening, he was sure it was Bayer he had hit.

Not that it was too serious a problem. Seeing Bayer dead on his carpet, Miller would be bound to flee as fast as his legs would carry him. Therefore he would return to his Jaguar, parked three miles away. Mackensen headed the Mercedes back to where he had last seen the Jaguar. He only began to worry badly when he saw the space between the Opel and the Benz truck where the Jaguar had stood the previous evening in the quiet residential street.

Mackensen would not have been the chief executioner for the Odessa if he had been the sort who panics easily. He had been in too many tight spots before. He sat at the wheel of his car for several minutes before he reacted to the prospect of Miller's now being hundreds of miles away.

If Miller had left Bayer alive, he reasoned, it could only be because he had got nothing from him or he had got something. In the first case, there was no harm done; he could take Miller later. There was no hurry. If Miller had got something from Bayer, it could only be information. The Werwolf alone would know what kind of information Miller had been seeking, that Bayer had to give. Therefore, despite his fear of the Werwolf's rage, he would telephone him.

It took him ten minutes to find a public telephone. He always kept a pocketful of one-mark pieces for long-distance calls.

When he took the call in Nuremberg and heard the news, the Werwolf went into a transport of rage, mouthing abuse down the line at his hired killer. It took several seconds before he could calm down. "You'd better find him, you oaf, and quickly. God knows where he's gone now."

Mackensen explained to his chief he needed to know what kind of information Bayer could have supplied to Miller before he died.

At the other end of the line the Werwolf thought for a while. "Dear God," he breathed, "the forger. He's got the name of the forger."

"What forger, Chief?" asked Mackensen.

The Werwolf pulled himself together. "I'll get on to the man and warn him," he said crisply. "This is where Miller has gone." He dictated an address to Mackensen and added, "You get the hell up to Osnabrück like you've never moved before. You'll find Miller at that address, or somewhere in the town. If he's not at the house, keep searching the town for the Jaguar. And this time, don't leave the Jaguar. It's the one place he always returns."

He slammed down the phone, then picked it up again and asked for Information. When he had the number he sought, he dialed a number in Osnabrück.

In Stuttgart, Mackensen was left holding a buzzing receiver. With a shrug he replaced it and went back to his car, facing the prospect of a long, wearying drive followed by another "job." He was almost as tired as Miller, by then twenty miles short of Osnabrück. Neither man had slept for twenty-four hours, and Mackensen had not even eaten since the previous lunch.

Chilled to the marrow from his night's vigil, longing for piping-hot coffee and a Steinhäger to chase it, he got back into the Mercedes and headed it north on the road to Westphalia.

FOURTEEN

To look at him, there was nothing about Klaus Winzer to suggest he had ever been in the SS. For one thing, he was well below the required height of six feet; for another, he was nearsighted. At the age of forty, he was plump and pale, with fuzzy blond hair and a diffident manner.

In fact he had had one of the strangest careers of any man to have worn the uniform of the SS. Born in 1924, he was the son of a certain Johann Winzer, a pork butcher of Wiesbaden, a large, boisterous man who from the early twenties onward was a trusting follower of Adolf Hitler and the Nazi Party. From his earliest days Klaus could remember his father coming home from street battles with the Communists and Socialists.

Klaus took after his mother, and to his father's disgust grew up small, weak, shortsighted, and peaceful. He hated violence, sports, and belonging to the Hitler Youth. At only one thing did he excel: from his early teens he fell completely in love with the art of handwriting and the preparation of illuminated manuscripts, an activity his disgusted father regarded as an occupation for sissies.

With the coming of the Nazis, the pork butcher flourished, obtaining as a reward for his earlier services to the Party the exclusive contract to supply meat to the local SS barracks. He mightily admired the strutting SS youths and devoutly hoped he might one day see his own son wearing the black and silver of the *Schutzstaffel*.

Klaus showed no such inclination, preferring to spend his time poring over his manuscripts, experimenting with colored inks and beautiful lettering.

The war came, and in the spring of 1942 Klaus turned eighteen, the draft age. In contrast to his ham-fisted, brawling, Jew-hating father, he was small, pallid, and shy. Failing even to pass the medical then required for a desk job with the Army, Klaus was sent home from the draft board. For his father it was the last straw.

Johann Winzer took the train to Berlin to see an old friend from his street-fighting days who had since risen high in the ranks of the SS, in the hopes the man might intercede for his son and obtain an entry into some branch of service to the Reich. The man was as helpful as he could be, which was not much, and asked if there was anything the young Klaus could do well. Shamefacedly his father admitted he could write illuminated manuscripts.

The man promised he would do what he could, but meanwhile he asked if Klaus would prepare an illuminated address on parchment in honor of a certain SS Major Fritz Suhren.

Back in Wiesbaden, the young Klaus did as he was asked, and at a ceremony in Berlin a week later this manuscript was presented to Suhren by his colleagues. Suhren, then the commandant of Sachsenhausen concentration camp, was being sent to take over command of the even more notorious Ravensbrück.

Suhren was executed by the French in 1945.

At the handing-over ceremony in the RSHA headquarters in Berlin, everyone admired the beautifully prepared manuscript, and not least a certain SS Lieutenant Alfred Naujocks. This was the man who had carried out the mock attack on Gleiwitz radio station on the German-Polish border in August 1939, leaving the bodies of concentration-camp inmates in German Army uniforms as "proof" of the Polish attack on Germany, Hitler's excuse for invading Poland the following week.

Naujocks asked who had done the manuscript, and, on being told, he requested the young Klaus Winzer be brought to Berlin.

Before he knew what was happening, Klaus Winzer was inducted into the SS, without any formal training period, made to swear the oath of loyalty and another oath of secrecy, and told he would be transferred to a top-secret Reich project. The butcher of Wiesbaden, bewildered, was in seventh heaven.

The project involved was then being carried out under the auspices of the RSHA, Amt Six, Section F, in a workshop in Delbrückstrasse, Berlin. Basically it was quite simple. The SS was trying to forge hundreds of thousands of British £5 notes and American $100 bills. The paper was being made in the Reich banknote-paper factory at Spechthausen, outside Berlin, and the job of the workshop in Delbrückstrasse was to try and get the right watermarks for British and American currency. It was for his knowledge of papers and inks that they wanted Klaus Winzer.

The idea was to flood Britain and America with phony money, thus ruining the economies of both countries. In early 1943, when the watermark for the British fivers had been achieved, the project of making the printing plates was transferred to Block 19, Sachsenhausen concentration camp, where Jewish and non-Jewish graphologists and graphic artists worked under the direction of the SS. The job of Winzer was quality control, for the SS did not trust its prisoners not to make a deliberate error in their work.

Within two years Klaus Winzer had been taught by his charges everything they knew, and that was enough to make him a forger extraordinary. Toward the end of 1944 the project in Block 19 was also being used to prepare forged identity cards for the SS officers to use after the collapse of Germany.

In the early spring of 1945 the private little world, happy in its way when contrasted with the devastation then overtaking Germany, was brought to an end.

The whole operation, commanded by a certain SS Captain Bernhard Krüger, was ordered to leave Sachsenhausen and transfer itself into the remote mountains of Austria and continue the good work. The group drove south and set up the forgery again in the deserted brewery of Redl-Zipf in Upper Austria. A few days before the end of the war, a brokenhearted Klaus Winzer stood weeping on the edge of a lake as millions of pounds and billions of dollars in his beautiful forged currency were dumped into the lake.

He went back to Wiesbaden and home. To his astonishment, having never lacked for a meal in the SS, he found the German civilians almost starving in that summer of 1945. The Americans now occupied Wiesbaden, and although they had plenty to eat, the Germans were nibbling at crusts. His father, by now a lifelong anti-Nazi, had come down in the world. Where once his shop had been stocked with hams, only a single string of sausages hung from the rows of gleaming hooks.

Klaus's mother explained to him that all food had to be bought on ration cards issued by the Americans. In amazement Klaus looked at the ration cards, noted they were locally printed on fairly cheap paper, took a handful, and retired to his room for a few days. When he emerged, it was to hand over to his astonished mother sheets of American ration cards, enough to feed them all for six months.

"But they're forged," gasped his mother.

Klaus explained patiently what by then he sincerely believed: they were not forged, just printed on a different machine.

His father backed Klaus. "Are you saying, foolish woman, that our son's ration cards are inferior to the Yankee ration cards?"

The argument was unanswerable, the more so when they sat down to a four-course meal that night.

A month later Klaus Winzer met Otto Klops, flashy, self-assured, the king of the black market of Wiesbaden, and they were in business. Winzer turned out endless quantities of ration cards, gasoline coupons, zonal border passes, driving licenses, United States military passes, PX cards; Klops used them to buy food, gasoline, truck tires, nylon stockings, soap, cosmetics, and clothing, keeping a part of the booty to enable him and the Winzers to live well, selling the rest at black-market prices. Within thirty months, by the summer of 1948, Klaus Winzer was a rich man. In his bank account reposed five million Reichsmarks.

To his horrified mother he explained his simple philosophy. "A document is not either genuine or forged; it is either efficient or inefficient. If a pass is supposed to get you past a checkpoint, and it gets you past the checkpoint, it is a good document."

In October 1948 came the second dirty trick played on Klaus Winzer. The authorities reformed the currency, substituting the new Deutschmark for the old Reichsmark. But instead of giving one for one, they simply abolished the Reichsmark and gave everyone the flat sum of 1000 new marks. He was ruined. Once again his fortune was mere useless paper.

The populace, no longer needing the black-marketeers as goods came on the open market, denounced Klops, and Winzer had to flee. Taking one of his own zonal passes, he drove to the headquarters of the British Zone at Hanover and applied for a job in the passport office of the British Military Government.

His references from the United States authorities at Wiesbaden, signed by a full colonel of the USAF, were excellent. They should have been; he had written them himself. The British major who interviewed him for the job put down his cup of tea and told the applicant, "I do hope you realize the importance of people having proper documentation on them at all times."

With complete sincerity Winzer assured the major that he did indeed. Two months later came his lucky break. He was alone in a beer hall, sipping a beer, when a man got into conversation with him. The man's name was Herbert Molders. He confided to Winzer he was being sought by the British for war crimes and needed to get out of Germany. But only the British could supply passports to Germans, and he dared not apply. Winzer murmured that it might be arranged but would cost money.

To his amazement, Molders produced a genuine diamond necklace. He explained that he had been in a concentration camp, and one of the Jewish inmates had tried to buy his freedom with the family jewelry. Molders had taken the jewelry, ensured that the Jew was in the first party to the gas chambers, and against orders had kept the booty.

A week later, armed with a photograph of Molders, Winzer prepared the passport. He did not even forge it. He did not need to.

The system at the passport office was simple. In Section One, applicants turned up with all their documentation and filled out forms. Then they went away, leaving their documents for study. Section Two examined the birth certificates, ID cards, driving licenses, etc., for possible forgery, checked the war criminals wanted list, and, if the application was approved, passed the documents, accompanied by a signed approval from Head of Department, to Section Three. Section Three, on receipt of the note of approval from Section Two, took a blank passport from the safe where it was stored, filled it out, stuck in the applicant's photograph, and gave the passport to the applicant, who presented himself a week later.

Winzer got himself transferred to Section Three. Quite simply, he filled out an application form for Molders in a new name, wrote out an "Application Approved" slip from the head of Section Two, and forged that British officer's signature.

He walked through into Section Two and picked up the nineteen application forms and approval slips waiting for collection, slipped the Molders application form and approval slip among them, and took the sheaf to Major Johnstone. Johnstone checked that there were twenty approval slips, went to his safe, took out twenty blank passports, and handed them to Winzer. Winzer duly filled them out, gave them the official stamp, and handed nineteen to the waiting nineteen happy applicants. The twentieth went into his pocket. Into the filing cabinet went twenty application forms to match the twenty issued passports.

That evening he handed Molders his new passport and took the diamond necklace. He had found his new métier.

In May 1949 West Germany was founded, and the passport office was handed over to the state government of Lower Saxony, capital city Hanover. Winzer stayed on. He did not have any more clients. He did not need them. Each week, armed with a full-face portrait of some nonentity bought from a studio photographer, Winzer carefully filled out a passport-application form, attached the photograph to the form, forged an approval slip with the signature of the head of Section Two (by now a German), and went to see the head of Section Three with a sheaf of application forms and approval slips. So long as the numbers tallied, he got a bunch of blank passports in return. All but one went to the genuine applicants. The last blank passport went into his pocket. Apart from that, all he needed was the official stamp. To steal it would have aroused suspicion. He took it for one night and by morning had a casting of the stamp of the passport office of the state government of Lower Saxony.

In sixty weeks he had sixty blank passports. He resigned his job, blushingly acknowledged the praise of his superiors for his careful, meticulous work as a clerk in their employ, left Hanover, sold the diamond necklace in Antwerp, and started a nice little printing business in Osnabrück, at a time when gold and dollars could buy anything well below market price.

He would never have got involved with the Odessa if Molders had kept his mouth shut. But once arrived in Madrid and among friends, Molders boasted of his contact who could provide genuine West German passports in a false name to anyone who asked.

In late 1950 a "friend" came to see Winzer, who had just started work as a printer in Osnabrück. There was nothing Winzer could do but agree. From then on, whenever an Odessa man was in trouble, Winzer supplied the new passport.

The system was perfectly safe. All Winzer needed was a photograph of the man and his age. He had kept a copy of the personal details written into each of the application forms by then reposing in the archive in Hanover. He would take a blank passport and fill in the personal details already written on one of those application forms from 1949. The name was usually a common one, the place of birth usually by then far behind the Iron Curtain, where no one would check, the date of birth would almost correspond to the real age of the SS applicant, and then he would stamp it with the stamp of Lower Saxony. The recipient would sign his new passport in his own handwriting with his new name when he received it.

Renewals were easy. After five years the wanted SS man would simply apply for renewal at the state capital of any state other than Lower Saxony. The clerk in Bavaria, for example, would check with Hanover: "Did you issue a passport number so-and-so in nineteen fifty to one Walter Schumann, place of birth such and date of birth such?" In Hanover another clerk would check the records in the files and reply, "Yes." The Bavarian clerk, reassured by his Hanoverian colleague that the original passport was genuine, would issue a new one, stamped by Bavaria.

So long as the face on the application form in Hanover was not compared with the face in the passport presented in Munich, there could be no problem. And comparison of faces never took place. Clerks rely on forms correctly filled in, correctly approved, and passport numbers, not faces.

Only after 1955, more than five years after the original issuing of the Hanover passport, would immediate renewal be necessary for the holder of a Winzer passport. Once the passport was obtained, the wanted SS man could acquire a fresh driving license, social-security card, bank account, credit card, in short an entire new identity.

By the spring of 1964 Winzer had supplied forty-two passports out of his stock of sixty originals.

But the cunning little man had taken one precaution. It occurred to him that one day the Odessa might wish to dispose of his services, and of him. So he kept a record. He never knew the real names of his clients; to make out a false passport in a new name, it was not necessary. The point was immaterial. He took a copy of every photograph sent to him, pasted the original in the passport he was sending back, and kept the copy. Each photograph was pasted onto a sheet of cartridge paper. Beside it was typed the new name, the address (addresses are required on German passports), and the new passport number.

These sheets were kept in a file. The file was his life insurance. There was one in his house, and a copy with a lawyer in Zurich. If his life were ever threatened by the Odessa, he would tell them about the file and warn them that if anything happened to him the lawyer in Zurich would send the copy to the German authorities.

The West Germans, armed with a photograph, would soon compare it with their rogues' gallery of wanted Nazis. The passport number alone, checked quickly with each of the sixteen state capitals, would reveal the domicile of the holder. Exposure would take no more than a week. It was a foolproof scheme to ensure that Klaus Winzer stayed alive and in good health.

This, then, was the man who sat quietly munching his toast and jam, sipping his coffee, and glancing through the front page of the Osnabrück *Zeitung* over breakfast at half past eight that Friday morning, when the phone rang. The voice at the other end was first peremptory, then reassuring.

"There is no question of your being in any trouble with us at all," the Werwolf assured him. "It's just this damn reporter. We have a tip that he's coming to see you. It's perfectly all right. We have one of our men coming up behind him, and the whole affair will be taken care of within the day. But you must get out of there within ten minutes. Now here's what I want you to do
. . . ."

Thirty minutes later a very flustered Klaus Winzer had a small bag packed, cast an undecided glance in the direction of the safe where the file was kept, came to the conclusion he would not need it, and explained to a startled housemaid, Barbara, that he would not be going to the printing plant that morning. On the contrary, he had decided to take a brief vacation in the Austrian Alps. A breath of fresh air—nothing like it to tone up the system.

Barbara stood on the doorstep open-mouthed as Winzer's Kadett shot backward down the drive, swung out into the residential road in front of his house, and drove off. Ten minutes after nine o'clock he had reached the cloverleaf four miles west of the town, where the road climbed up to join the autobahn. As the Kadett shot up the incline to the motorway on one side, a black Jaguar was coming down the other side, heading into Osnabrück.

Miller found a filling station at the Saar Platz at the western entrance to the town. He pulled up by the pumps and climbed wearily out. His muscles ached and his neck felt as if it were locked solid. The wine he had drunk the evening before gave his mouth a taste like parrot droppings.

"Fill her up. Super," he told the attendant. "Have you got a pay phone?"

"In the corner," said the boy.

On the way over, Miller noticed a coffee machine and took a steaming cup into the phone booth with him. He flicked through the phone book for Osnabrück. There were several Winzers, but only one Klaus. The name was repeated twice. Against the first entry was the word "Printer." The second Klaus Winzer had the abbreviation "res." for residence against it. It was nine-twenty. Working hours. He rang the printing plant.

The man who answered was evidently the foreman. "I'm sorry, he's not in yet," said the voice. "Usually he's here at nine sharp. He'll no doubt be along soon. Call back in half an hour."

Miller thanked him and considered dialing the house. Better not. If Winzer was at home, Miller wanted him personally. He noted the address and left the booth.

"Where's Westerberg?" he asked the pump attendant as he paid for the gas, noting that he had only 500 marks left of his savings. The boy nodded across to the north side of the road.

"That's it. The posh suburb. Where all the rich people live."

Miller bought a town plan as well and traced the street he wanted. It was barely ten minutes away.

The house was obviously prosperous, and the whole area spoke of well-to-do professional people living in comfortable surroundings. He left the Jaguar at the end of the drive and walked to the front door.

The maid who answered it was in her late teens and very pretty. She smiled brightly at him.

"Good morning. I've come to see Herr Winzer," he told her.

"Oooh, he's left, sir. You just missed him by about twenty minutes."

Miller recovered. Doubtless Winzer was on his way to the printing plant and had been held up.

"Oh, what a pity. I'd hoped to catch him before he went to work," he said.

"He hasn't gone to work, sir. Not this morning. He's gone off on vacation," replied the girl helpfully.

Miller fought down a rising feeling of panic. "Vacation? That's odd at this time of year. Besides"—he invented quickly—"we had an appointment this morning. He asked me to come here especially."

"Oh, what a shame," said the girl, evidently distressed. "He went off very suddenly. He got this phone call in the library; then he went upstairs. 'Barbara,' he said—that's my name—'Barbara, I'm going on a vacation in Austria. Just for a week,' he said. Well, I hadn't heard any plans for a vacation. He told me to call the plant and say he's not coming in for a week. Then off he went. That's not like Herr Winzer at all. He's usually so quiet."

Inside Miller, the hope began to die. "Did he say where he was going?" he asked.

"No. Nothing. Just said he was going to the Austrian Alps."

"No forwarding address? No way of getting in touch with him?"

"No, that's what's so strange. I mean, what about the printing plant? I just called them before you came. They were very surprised, with all the orders they had to be completed."

Miller calculated fast. Winzer had a half-hour's start on him. Driving at eighty miles an hour, he would have covered forty miles. Miller could keep up a hundred, overtaking at twenty miles an hour. That would mean two hours before he saw the tail of Winzer's car. Too long. Winzer could be anywhere in two hours. Besides, there was no proof he was heading south to Austria.

"Then could I speak to Frau Winzer, please?" he asked.

Barbara giggled and looked at him archly. "There isn't any Frau Winzer," she said. "Don't you know Herr Winzer at all?"

"No, I never met him."

"Well, he's not the marrying kind, really. I mean very nice, but not really interested in women, if you know what I mean."

"So he lives here alone, then?"

"Well, except for me. I mean, I live in. It's quite safe. From that point of view." She giggled.

"I see. Thank you," said Miller and turned to go.

"You're welcome," said the girl, and watched him go down the drive and climb into the Jaguar, which had already caught her attention. What with Herr Winzer being away, she wondered if she might be able to ask a nice young man home for the night before her employer got back. She watched the Jaguar drive away with a roar of exhaust, sighed for what might have been, and closed the door.

Miller felt the weariness creeping over him, accentuated by the last and, so far as he was concerned, final disappointment. He surmised Bayer had wriggled free from his bonds and used the hotel telephone in Stuttgart to call Winzer and warn him. He had got so close, fifteen minutes from his target, and almost made it. Now he felt only the need for sleep.

He drove past the medieval wall of the old city, followed the map to the Theodor Heuss Platz, parked the Jaguar in front of the station, and checked into the Hohenzollern Hotel across the square.

He was lucky; they had a room available at once, so he went upstairs, undressed, and lay on the bed. There was something nagging in the back of his mind, some point he had not covered, some tiny detail of a question he had left unasked. It was still unsolved when he fell asleep at half past ten.

Mackensen made it to the center of Osnabrück at half past one. On the way into town he had checked the house in Westerberg, but there was no sign of a Jaguar. He wanted to call the Werwolf before he went there, in case there was more news.

By chance the post office in Osnabrück flanks one side of the Theodor Heuss Platz. A whole corner and one side of the square is taken up by the main railway station, and a third side is occupied by the Hohenzollern Hotel. As Mackensen parked by the post office, his face split in a grin. The Jaguar he sought was in front of the station.

The Werwolf was in a better mood. "It's all right. Panic over for the moment," he told the killer. "I reached the forger in time, and he got out of town. I just phoned his house again. It must have been the maid who answered. She told me her employer had left barely twenty minutes before a young man with a black sports car came inquiring after him."

"I've got some news too," said Mackensen. "The Jaguar is parked right here on the square in front of me. Chances are he's sleeping it off in the hotel. I can take him right here in the hotel room. I'll use the silencer."

"Hold it, don't be in too much of a hurry," warned the Werwolf. "I've been thinking. For one thing, he must not get it inside Osnabrück town. The maid has seen him and his car. She would probably report to the police. That would bring attention to our forger, and he's the panicking kind. I can't have him involved. The maid's testimony would cast a lot of suspicion on him. First he gets a phone call, then he dashes out and vanishes, then a young man calls to see him, then the man is shot in a hotel room. It's too much."

Mackensen's brow was furrowed. "You're right," he said at length. "I'll have to take him when he leaves."

"He'll probably stick around for a few hours, checking for a lead on the forger. He won't get one. There's one other thing. Does Miller carry a document case?"

"Yes," said Mackensen. "He had it with him as he left the cabaret last night. And took it with him when he went back to his hotel room."

"So why not leave it locked in the trunk of his car? Why not in his hotel room? Because it's important to him. You follow me?"

"Yes," said Mackensen.

"The point is," said the Werwolf, "he has now seen me and knows my name and address. He knows of the connection with Bayer and the forger. And reporters write things down. That document case is now vital. Even if Miller dies, the case must not fall into the hands of the police."

"I've got you. You want the case as well?"

"Either get it or destroy it," said the voice from Nuremberg.

Mackensen thought for a moment. "The best way to do both would be for me to plant a bomb in the car. Linked to the suspension, so it will detonate when he hits a bump at high speed on the autobahn."

"Excellent," said the Werwolf. "Will the case be destroyed?"

"With the bomb I have in mind, the car, Miller, and the case will go up in flames and be completely gutted. Moreover, at high speed it looks like an accident. The gas tank exploded, the witnesses will say. What a pity."

"Can you do it?" asked the Werwolf.

Mackensen grinned. The killing kit in the trunk of his car was an assassin's dream. It included nearly a pound of plastic explosive and two electric detonators.

"Sure," he growled, "no problem. But to get at the car I'll have to wait until dark."

He stopped talking, gazed out of the window of the post office, and barked into the phone, "Call you back."

He called back in five minutes. "Sorry about that. I just saw Miller, attaché case in hand, climbing into his car. He drove off. I checked the hotel, and he's registered there all right. He's left his traveling bags, so he'll be back. No panic, I'll get on with the bomb and plant it tonight."

Miller had waked up just before one, feeling refreshed and somewhat elated. In sleeping he had remembered what was troubling him. He drove back to Winzer's house.

The maid was plainly pleased to see him. "Hello. You again?" She beamed.

"I was just passing on my way back home," said Miller, "and I wondered, how long have you been in service here?"

"Oh, about ten months. Why?"

"Well, with Herr Winzer not being the marrying kind, and you being so young, who looked after him before you came?"

"Oh, I see what you mean. His housekeeper. Fräulein Wendel."

"Where is she now?"

"Oh, in the hospital. I'm afraid she's dying. Cancer of the breast, you know. Terrible thing. That's what makes it so funny that Herr Winzer dashed off like that. He goes to visit her every day. He's devoted to her. Not that they ever—well, you know—*did* anything but she was with him for a long time, since nineteen fifty, I think, and he thinks the world of her. He's always saying to me, 'Fräulein Wendel did it this way,' and so on."

"What hospital is she in?" asked Miller.

"I forget now. No, wait a minute. It's on the telephone notepad. I'll get it."

She was back in two minutes and gave him the name of the clinic, an exclusive private sanatorium just beyond the outskirts of the town.

Finding his way by the map, Miller presented himself at the clinic just after three in the afternoon.

Mackensen spent the early afternoon buying the ingredients for his bomb. "The secret of sabotage," his instructor had once told him, "is to keep the requirements simple. The sort of thing you can buy in any shop."

From a hardware store he bought a soldering iron and a small stick of solder; a roll of black insulating tape; a yard of thin wire and a pair of cutters; a one-foot hacksaw blade and a tub of instant glue. In an electrician's he acquired a nine-volt transistor battery; a small bulb, one inch in diameter; and two lengths of fine single-strand, five-amp plastic-coated wire, each three yards long, one colored red and the other blue. He was a neat man and liked to keep positive and negative terminals distinct. A stationer's supplied him with five erasers of the large kind, one inch wide, two inches long, and a quarter of an inch thick. In a drugstore he bought two packages of condoms,; each contaning three rubber sheaths, and from a high-class grocer he got a canister of fine tea. It was a 250-gram can with a tight-fitting lid. As a good workman, he hated the idea of his explosives getting wet, and the tea can's lid would keep out the air, let alone the moisture.

With his purchases made, he took a room in the Hohenzollern Hotel overlooking the square, so that he could keep an eye on the parking area, to which he was certain Miller would return, while he worked.

Before entering the hotel, he took from his trunk a pound of the plastic explosive, squashy stuff like children's plasticene, and one of the electronic detonators.

Seated at the table in front of the window, keeping half an eye on the square, with a pot of strong black coffee to stave off his tiredness, he went to work.

It was a simple bomb he made. First he emptied the tea down the toilet and kept the can only. In the lid he jabbed a hole with the handle of the wire clippers. He took the nine-foot length of red wire and cut a ten-inch length off it.

One end of this short length of red-coated wire he spot-soldered to the positive terminal of the battery. To the negative terminal he soldered one end of the long, blue-colored wire. To ensure that these wires never touched each other, he drew one down each side of the battery and whipped both wires and battery together with insulating tape.

The other end of the short red wire was twirled around the contact point on the detonator. To the same contact point was fixed one end of the other, eight-foot piece of red wire.

He deposited the battery and its wires in the base of the square tea can, embedded the detonator deep into the plastic explosive, and smoothed the explosive into the can on top of the battery until the can was full.

A near-circuit had now been set up. A wire went from the battery to the detonator. Another went from the detonator to nowhere, its bare end in space. But when these two exposed ends, one of the eight-foot-long red wire, the other of the blue wire, touched each other, the circuit would be complete. The charge from the battery would fire the detonator, which would explode with a sharp crack. But the crack would be lost in the roar as the plastic went off, enough to demolish two or three of the hotel's bedrooms.

The remaining device was the trigger mechanism. For this he wrapped his hands in handkerchiefs and bent the hacksaw blade until it snapped in the middle, leaving him with two six-inch lengths, each one perforated at one end by the small hole that usually fixes a hacksaw blade to its frame.

He piled the five erasers one on top of another so that together they made a block of rubber. Using this to separate the halves of the blade, he bound them along the upper and lower side of the block of rubber, so that the six-inch lengths of steel stuck out, parallel to each other and one and a quarter inches apart. In outline they looked rather like the jaws of a crocodile. The rubber block was at one end of the lengths of steel, so four inches of the blades were separated only by air. To make sure there was a little more resistance than air to prevent their touching, Mackensen lodged the light bulb between the open jaws, fixing it in place with a generous blob of glue. Glass does not conduct electricity.

He was almost ready. He threaded the two lengths of wire, one red and one blue, which protruded from the can of explosive through the hole in the lid and replaced the lid on the can, pushing it firmly back into place. Of the two pieces of wire, he soldered the end of one to the upper hacksaw blade, the other to the lower blade. The bomb was now live.

Should the trigger ever be trodden on, or subjected to sudden pressure, the bulb would shatter, the two lengths of sprung steel would close together, and the electric circuit from the battery would be complete. There was one last precaution. To prevent the exposed hacksaw blades from ever touching the same piece of metal at the same time, which would also complete the circuit, he smoothed all six condoms over the trigger, one on top of another, until the device was protected from outside detonation by six layers of thin but insulating rubber. That at least would prevent accidental detonation.

His bomb complete, he stowed it in the bottom of the wardrobe, along with the binding wire, the clippers and the rest of the sticky tape, which he would need to fix it to Miller's car. Then he ordered more coffee to stay awake, and settled down at the window to wait for Miller's return to the parking lot in the center of the square.

He did not know where Miller had gone, nor did he care. The Werwolf had assured him there were no leads he could pick up to give him the whereabouts of the forger, and that was that. As a good technician, Mackensen was prepared to do his job and leave the rest to those in charge. He was prepared to be patient. He knew Miller would return sooner or later.

FIFTEEN

The doctor glanced with little favor at the visitor. Miller, who hated collars and ties and avoided wearing them whenever he could, had on a white nylon turtle-necked sweater and over it a black pullover with a crew neck. Over the two pullovers he wore a black blazer. For hospital-visiting, the doctor's expression clearly said, a collar and tie would be more appropriate.

"Her nephew?" he repeated with surprise. "Strange, I had no idea Fräulein Wendel had a nephew."

"I believe I am her sole surviving relative," said Miller. "Obviously I would have come far sooner, had I known of my aunt's condition, but Herr Winzer only called me this morning to inform me, and asked me to visit her."

"Herr Winzer is usually here himself about this hour," observed the doctor.

"I understand he's been called away," said Miller blandly. "At least, that was what he told me on the phone this morning. He said he would not be back for some days, and asked me to visit in his stead."

"Gone away? How extraordinary. How very odd." The doctor paused for a moment, irresolute, and then added, "Would you excuse me?"

Miller saw him go back from the entrance hall where they had been talking to a small office to one side. From the open door he heard snatches of conversation as the clinic doctor rang Winzer's house.

"He has indeed gone away? . . . This morning? . . . Several days? . . . Oh, no, thank you, Fräulein, I just wanted to confirm that he will not be visiting this afternoon."

The doctor hung up and came back to the hall. "Strange," he murmured. "Herr Winzer has been here, as regular as clockwork, since Fräulein Wendel was brought in. Evidently a most devoted man. Well, he had better be quick if he wishes to see her again. She is very far gone, you know."

Miller looked sad. "So he told me on the phone," he lied. "Poor Auntie."

"As her relative, of course you may spend a short time with her. But I must warn you, she is hardly coherent, so I must ask you to be as brief as you can. Come this way."

The doctor led Miller down several passages of what had evidently once been a large private house, now converted into a clinic, and stopped at a bedroom door.

"She's in here," he said and showed Miller in, closing the door after him. Miller heard his footsteps retreating down the passage.

The room was in semi-darkness and until his eyes had become accustomed to the dull light from the wintry afternoon that came through the gap in the slightly parted curtains, he failed to distinguish the shriveled form of the woman in the bed. She was raised on several pillows under her head and shoulders, but so pale was her nightgown and the face above it that she almost merged with the bedclothes. Her eyes were closed. Miller had few hopes of obtaining from her the likely bolt-hole of the vanished forger.

He whispered, "Fräulein Wendel," and the eyelids fluttered and opened.

She stared at him without a trace of expression in the eyes, and Miller doubted if she could even see him. She closed her eyes again and began to mutter incoherently. He leaned closer to catch the phrases coming in a monotonous jumble from the gray lips.

They meant very little. There was something about Rosenheim, which he knew to be a small village in Bavaria, perhaps the place she had been born. Something else about "all dressed in white, so pretty, so very pretty." Then there was another jumble of words that meant nothing.

Miller leaned closer. "Fräulein Wendel, can you hear me?"

The dying woman was still muttering. Miller caught the words " . . . each carrying a prayer book and a posy, all in white, so innocent then."

Miller frowned in thought before he understood. In delirium she was trying to recall her First Communion. Like himself, she had once been a practicing Roman Catholic.

"Can you hear me, Fräulein Wendel?" he repeated, without any hope of getting through. She opened her eyes again and stared at him, taking in the white band around his neck, the black material over his chest, and the black jacket. To his astonishment she closed her eyes again, and her flat torso heaved in spasm. Miller was worried. He thought he had better call the doctor. Then two tears, one from each closed eye, rolled down the parchment cheeks.

On the coverlet one of her hands crawled slowly toward his wrist, where he had supported himself on the bed while leaning over her. With surprising strength, or simply desperation, her hand gripped his wrist possessively. Miller was about to detach himself and go, convinced she could tell him nothing about Klaus Winzer, when she said quite distinctly, "Bless me, Father, for I have sinned."

For a few seconds Miller failed to understand, then a glance at his own chest-front made him realize the mistake the woman had made in the dim light. He debated for two minutes whether to leave her and go back to Hamburg, or whether to risk his soul and have one last try at locating Eduard Roschmann through the forger.

He leaned forward again. "My child, I am prepared to hear your confession."

Then she began to talk. In a tired, dull monotone, her life story came out. Once she had been a girl, born and brought up amid the fields and forests of Bavaria. Born in 1910, she remembered her father going away to the First War and returning three years later after the Armistice of 1918, angry and bitter against the men in Berlin who had capitulated.

She remembered the political turmoil of the early twenties and the attempted *Putsch* in nearby Munich when a crowd of men headed by a streetcorner rabble-rouser called Adolf Hitler had tried to overthrow the government. Her father had later joined the man and his party, and by the time she was twenty-three the rabble-rouser and his party had become the government of Germany. There were the summer outings of the Union of German Maidens, the secretarial job with the Gauleiter of Bavaria, and the dances with the handsome blond young men in their black uniforms.

But she had grown up ugly, tall, bony, and angular, with a face like a horse and hair along her upper lip. Her mousy hair tied back in a bun, in heavy clothes and sensible shoes, she had realized in her late twenties there would be no marriage for her, as for the other girls in the village. By 1939 she had been posted, an embittered and hate-filled woman, as a wardress in a camp called Ravensbrück.

She told of the people she had beaten and clubbed, the days of power and cruelty in the camp in Brandenburg, the tears rolling quietly down her cheeks, her fingers gripping Miller's wrist lest he should depart in disgust before she had done.

"And after the war?" he asked softly.

There had been years of wandering—abandoned by the SS, hunted by the Allies, working in kitchens as a scullery maid, washing dishes and sleeping in Salvation Army hostels. Then in 1959 she met Winzer staying in a hotel in Osnabrück while he looked for a house to buy. She had been a waitress. He bought his house, the little neuter man, and suggested she come and keep house for him.

"Is that all?" asked Miller when she stopped.

"Yes, Father."

"My child, you know I cannot give you absolution if you have not confessed all your sins."

"That is all, Father."

Miller drew a deep breath. "And what about the forged passports? The ones he made for the SS men on the run?"

She was silent for a while, and he feared she had passed into unconsciousness.

"You know about that, Father?"

"I know about it."

"I did not make them," she said.

"But you knew about them, about the work Klaus Winzer did."

"Yes." The word was a low whisper.

"He has gone now. He has gone away," said Miller.

"No. Not gone. Not Klaus. He would not leave me. He will come back."

"Do you know where he has gone?"

"No, Father."

"Are you sure? Think, my child. He has been forced to run away. Where would he go?"

The emaciated head shook slowly against the pillow. "I don't know, Father. If they threaten him, he will use the file. He told me he would."

Miller started. He looked down at the woman, her eyes now closed as if in sleep. "What file, my child?"

They talked for another five minutes. Then there was a soft tap on the door. Miller eased the woman's hand off his wrist and rose to go.

"Father . . . " The voice was plaintive, pleading. He turned. She was staring at him, her eyes wide open. "Bless me, Father."

The tone was imploring. Miller sighed. It was a mortal sin. He hoped somebody somewhere would understand. He raised his right hand and made the sign of the cross.

"*In nomine Patris, et Filii, et Spiritus Sancti, ego te absolvo a peccatis tuis.*"

The woman sighed deeply, closed her eyes, and passed into unconsciousness.

Outside in the passage, the doctor was waiting. "I really think that is long enough," he said.

Miller nodded. "Yes, she is sleeping," he said, and, after a glance around the door, the doctor escorted him back to the entrance hall.

"How long do you think she has?" asked Miller.

"Very difficult to say. Two days, maybe three. Not more. I'm very sorry."

"Yes, well, thank you for letting me see her," said Miller. The doctor held open the front door for him. "Oh, there is one last thing, Doctor. We are all Catholics in our family. She asked me for a priest. The last rites, you understand?"

"Yes, of course."

"Will you see to it?"

"Certainly," said the doctor. "I didn't know. I'll see to it this afternoon. Thank you for telling me. Good-by."

It was late afternoon and dusk was turning into night when Miller drove back into the Theodor Heuss Platz and parked the Jaguar twenty yards from the hotel. He crossed the road and went up to his room. Two floors above, Mackensen had watched his arrival. Taking his bomb in his suitcase, he descended to the foyer, paid his bill for the coming night, explaining that he would be leaving very early in the morning, and went out to his car. He maneuvered it into a place where he could watch the hotel entrance and the Jaguar, and settled down to another wait.

There were still too many people in the area for him to go to work on the Jaguar, and Miller might come out of the hotel any second. If he drove off before the bomb could be planted, Mackensen would take him on the open highway, several miles from Osnabrück, and steal the document case. If Miller slept in the hotel, Mackensen would plant the bomb in the small hours, when no one was about.

In his room, Miller was racking his brains for a name. He could see the man's face, but the name still escaped him.

It had been just before Christmas 1961. He had been in the press box in the Hamburg provincial court, waiting for a case in which he was interested. He had caught the tail end of the preceding case. There was a little ferret of a man standing in the dock, and defending counsel was asking for leniency, pointing out that it was just before the Christmas period and his client had a wife and five children.

Miller remembered glancing at the well of the court, and noting the tired, harassed face of the convicted man's wife. She had covered her face with her hands in utter despair when the judge, explaining the sentence would have been longer but for the defending counsel's plea for leniency, sentenced the man to eighteen months in jail. The prosecution had described the prisoner as one of the most skillful safecrackers in Hamburg.

Two weeks later, Miller had been in a bar not two hundred yards from the Reeperbahn, having a Christmas drink with some of his underworld contacts. He was flush with money, having been paid for a big picture feature that day. There was a woman scrubbing the floor at the far end. He had recognized the worried face of the wife of the cracksman who had been sentenced two weeks earlier. In a fit of generosity which he regretted the next morning, he had pushed a 100-mark note into her apron pocket and left.

In January he had got a letter from Hamburg Jail. It was hardly literate.

The woman must have asked the barman for his name and told her husband. The letter had been sent to a magazine for which he sometimes worked. They had passed it on to him.

> Dear Herr Miller,
>   My wife wrote me about what you done just before Christmas. I never met you, and I don't know why you done it, but I want to thank you very much. You are a real good guy. The money helped Marta and the kids have a real good time over Christmas and the New Year. If ever I can do you a good turn back, just let me know. Yours with respects . . .

But what was the name on the bottom of that letter? Koppel. That was it. Viktor Koppel. Praying that he had not got himself back inside prison again, Miller took out his little book of contacts' names and telephone numbers, dragged the hotel telephone onto his knees, and started calling friends in the underworld of Hamburg.

He found Koppel at half past seven. As it was a Friday evening, he was in a bar with a crowd of friends, and Miller could hear the jukebox in the background. It was playing the Beatles' "I Want to Hold Your Hand," which had almost driven him mad that winter, so frequently had it been played.

With a little prompting, Koppel remembered him, and the present he had given to Marta two years earlier. Koppel had evidently had a few drinks.

"Very nice of you that was, Herr Miller, very nice thing to do."

"Look, you wrote me from prison saying if there was ever anything you could do for me, you'd do it. Remember?"

Koppel's voice was wary. "Yeah, I remember."

"Well, I need a bit of help. Not much. Can you help me out?" said Miller.

The man in Hamburg was still wary. "I ain't got much on me, Herr Miller."

"I don't want a loan," said Miller. "I want to pay you for a job. Just a small one."

Koppel's voice was full of relief. "Oh, I see, yes, sure. Where are you?"

Miller gave him his instructions. "Just get down to Hamburg station and grab the first train to Osnabrück. I'll meet you at the station. One last thing: bring your working tools with you."

"Now look, Herr Miller, I don't work off my turf. I don't know about Osnabrück."

Miller dropped into the Hamburg slang. "It's a walkover, Koppel. Empty, owner gone away, and a load of gear inside. I've cased it, and there's no problem. You can be back in Hamburg for breakfast, with a bagful of loot and no questions asked. The man will be away for a week. You can unload the stuff before he's back, and the cops down here will think it was a local job."

"What about my train fare?" asked Koppel.

"I'll give it to you when you get here. There's a train at nine out of Hamburg. You've got an hour. So get moving."

Koppel sighed deeply. "All right, I'll be on the train."

Miller hung up, asked the hotel switchboard operator to call him at eleven, and dozed off.

Outside, Mackensen continued his lonely vigil. He decided to start on the

Jaguar at midnight if Miller had not emerged.

But Miller walked out of the hotel at quarter past eleven, crossed the square, and entered the station. Mackensen was surprised. He climbed out of the Mercedes and went to look through the entrance hall. Miller was on the platform, standing waiting for a train.

"What's the next train from this platform?" Mackensen asked a porter.

"Eleven thirty-three to Münster," said the porter.

Mackensen wondered idly why Miller should want to take a train when he had a car. Still puzzled, he returned to his Mercedes and resumed his wait.

At eleven thirty-five his problem was solved. Miller came back out of the station, accompanied by a small, shabby man carrying a black leather bag. They were in deep conversation. Mackensen swore. The last thing he wanted was for Miller to drive off in the Jaguar with company. That would complicate the killing to come. To his relief, the pair approached a waiting taxi, climbed in, and drove off. He decided to give them twenty minutes and then start on the Jaguar, still parked twenty yards away from him.

At midnight the square was almost empty. Mackensen slipped out of his car, carrying a pencil-flashlight and three small tools, crossed to the Jaguar, cast a glance around, and slid underneath it.

Amid the mud and snow-slush of the square, his suit, he knew, would be wet and filthy within seconds. That was the least of his worries. Using the flashlight beneath the front end of the Jaguar, he located the locking switch for the hood. It took him twenty minutes to ease it free. The hood jumped upward an inch when the catch was released. Simple pressure from on top would relock it when he had finished. At least he had no need to break into the car to release the catch from inside.

He went back to the Mercedes and brought the bomb over to the sports car. A man working under the hood of a car attracts little or no attention. Passers-by assume he is tinkering with his own car.

Using the binding wire and the pliers, he lashed the explosive charge to the inside of the engine compartment, fixing it to the wall directly in front of the driving position. It would be barely three feet from Miller's chest when it went off. The trigger mechanism, connected to the main charge by two wires eight feet long, he lowered through the engine area to the ground beneath.

Sliding back under the car, he examined the front suspension by the light of his flashlight. He found the place he needed within five minutes and tightly wired the rear end of the trigger to a handy bracing-bar. The open jaws of the trigger, sheathed in rubber and held apart by the glass bulb, he jammed between two of the coils of the stout spring that formed the front near-side suspension.

When it was firmly in place, unable to be shaken free by normal jolting, he came back out from under. He estimated the first time the car hit a bump or a normal pothole at speed, the retracing suspension on the front near-side wheel would force the open jaws of the trigger together, crushing the frail glass bulb that separated them and make contact between the two lengths of electrically charged hacksaw blade. When that happened, Miller and his incriminating documents would be blown to pieces.

Finally Mackensen gathered up the slack in the wires connecting the charge and the trigger, made a neat loop of them, and taped them out of the way at the side of the engine compartment, so they would not trail on the

ground and be rubbed through by abrasion against the road surface. This
done, he closed the hood and snapped it shut. Then he returned to the back
seat of the Mercedes, curled up, and dozed. He had done, he thought, a
good night's work.

Miller ordered the taxi-driver to take them to the Saarplatz, paid him, and
dismissed him. Koppel had had the good sense to keep his mouth shut
during the ride, and it was only when the taxi was disappearing back into
town that he opened it again.

"I hope you know what you're doing, Herr Miller. I mean, it's strange you
being on a caper like this, you being a reporter."

"Koppel, there's no need to worry. What I'm after is a bunch of documents
kept in a safe inside the house. I'll take them. You get anything else there is
on hand. Okay?"

"Well, since it's you, all right. Let's get it over with."

"There's one last thing. The place has a live-in maid," said Miller.

"You said it was empty," protested Koppel. "If she comes down, I'll split. I
don't want no part of violence."

"We'll wait until two in the morning. She'll be fast asleep."

They walked the mile to Winzer's house, cast a quick look up and down the
road, and darted through the gate. To avoid the gravel, both men walked up
the grass edge along the driveway, then crossed the lawn to hide in the
rhododendron bushes facing the windows of what looked like the study.

Koppel, moving like a furtive little animal through the undergrowth,
made a tour of the house, leaving Miller to watch the bag of tools. When he
came back he whispered, "The maid's still got her light on. Window at the
back under the eaves."

Not daring to smoke, they sat for an hour, shivering beneath the fat
evergreen leaves of the bushes. At one in the morning Koppel made another
tour and reported the girl's bedroom light was out.

They sat for another ninety minutes before Koppel squeezed Miller's
wrist, took his bag, and padded across the stretch of moonlight on the lawn
toward the study windows. Somewhere down the road a dog barked, and
farther away a car tire squealed as a motorist headed home.

Fortunately for them, the area beneath the study windows was in shadow,
the moon not having come around the side of the house. Koppel flicked on a
pencil-flashlight and ran it around the window frame, then along the bar
dividing the upper and lower sections. There was a good burglar-proof
window catch but no alarm system. He opened his bag and bent over it for a
second, straightening up with a roll of sticky tape, a suction pad on a stick, a
diamond-tipped glass-cutter like a fountain pen, and a rubber hammer.

With remarkable skill he cut a perfect circle on the surface of the glass just
below the window catch. For double insurance he taped two lengths of sticky
tape across the disk, with the ends of each tape pressed to the uncut section
of window. Between the tapes he pressed the sucker, well licked, so that a
small area of glass was visible on either side of it.

Using the rubber hammer, holding the stick from the sucker in his left
hand, he gave the exposed area of the cut circle of window pane a sharp tap.

At the second tap there was a crack, and the disk fell inward toward the
room. They both paused and waited for reaction, but no one had heard the

sound. Still gripping the end of the sucker, to which the glass disk was attached inside the window, Koppel ripped away the two pieces of sticky tape. Glancing through the window, he spotted a thick rug five feet away, and with a flick of the wrist tossed the disk of glass and the sucker inward, so they fell soundlessly on the rug.

Reaching through the hole, he unscrewed the burglar catch and eased up the lower window. He was over it as nimbly as a fly, and Miller followed more cautiously. The room was pitch-black by contrast with the moonlight on the lawn, but Koppel seemed to be able to see perfectly well.

He whispered, "Keep still," to Miller, who froze, while the burglar quietly closed the window and drew the curtains across it. He drifted through the room, avoiding the furniture by instinct, closed the door that led to the passage, and only then flicked on his flashlight.

It swept around the room, picking out a desk, a telephone, a wall of bookshelves, and a deep armchair, and finally settled on a handsome fireplace with a large surround of red brick.

He materialized at Miller's side. "This must be the study. There can't be two rooms like this, and two brick fireplaces, in one house. Where's the lever that opens the brickwork?"

"I don't know," muttered Miller back, imitating the low murmur of the burglar, who had learned the hard way that a murmur is far more difficult to detect than a whisper. "You'll have to find it."

"God, it could take ages," said Koppel.

He sat Miller in the chair, warning him to keep his string-backed driving gloves on at all times. Taking his bag, Koppel went over to the fireplace, slipped a headband around his head, and fixed the flashlight into a bracket so that it pointed forward. Inch by inch, he went over the brickwork, feeling with sensitive fingers for bumps or lugs, indentations or hollow areas. Abandoning this when he had covered it all, he started again with a palette knife probing for cracks. He found it at half past three.

The knife blade slipped into a crack between two bricks, and there was a low click. A section of bricks, two feet by two feet in size, swung an inch outward. So skillfully had the work been done that no naked eye could spot the square area among the rest of the surround.

Koppel eased the door open; it was hinged on the left side by silent steel hinges. The four-square-foot area of brickwork was set in a steel tray that formed a door. Behind the door, the thin beam of Koppel's headlamp picked out the front of a small wall safe.

He kept the light on but slipped a stethoscope around his neck and fitted the earpieces. After five minutes spent gazing at the four-disk combination lock, he held the listening end where he judged the tumblers would be and began to ease the first ring through its combinations.

Miller, from his seat ten feet away, gazed at the work and became increasingly nervous. Koppel, by contrast, was completely calm, absorbed in his work. Apart from this, he knew that both men were unlikely to cause anyone to investigate the study so long as they remained completely immobile. The entry, the moving about, and the exit were the danger periods.

It took him forty minutes until the last tumbler fell over. Gently he eased the safe door back and turned to Miller, the beam from his head darting over a table containing a pair of silver candlesticks and a heavy old snuffbox.

Without a word, Miller rose and went to join Koppel by the safe. He reached up, took the light from Koppel's head bracket, and used it to probe the interior. There were several bundles of banknotes, which he pulled out and passed to the grateful burglar, who uttered a low whistle that carried no more than several feet.

The upper shelf in the safe contained only one object, a buff manila folder. Miller pulled it out, flicked it open, and riffled through the sheets inside. There were about forty of them. Each contained a photograph and several lines of type. At the eighteenth he paused and said out loud, "Good God."

"Quiet," muttered Koppel with urgency.

Miller closed the file, handed the flashlight back to Koppel, and said, "Close it."

Koppel slid the door back into place and twirled the dial not merely until the door was locked, but until the figures were in the same order in which he had found them. When he was done he eased the brickwork across the area and pressed it firmly home. It gave another soft click and locked into place.

He had stuffed the banknotes in his pocket, the cash proceeds of Winzer's last four passports, and he remained only to lay the candlesticks and snuff-box gently into his black leather bag.

After switching off his light, he led Miller by the arm to the window, slipped the curtains back to right and left, and took a good look out through the glass. The lawn was deserted, and the moon had gone behind cloud. Koppel eased up the window, hopped over it, bag and all, and waited for Miller to join him. He pulled the window down and headed for the shrubbery, followed by the reporter, who had stuffed the file inside his polo-necked sweater.

They kept to the bushes until close to the gate, then emerged onto the road. Miller had an urge to run.

"Walk slowly," said Koppel in his normal talking voice. "Just walk and talk like we were coming home from a party."

It was three miles back to the railway station, and already it was close to five o'clock. The streets were not wholly deserted, although it was Saturday, for the German working man rises early to go about his business. They made it to the station without being stopped and questioned.

There was no train to Hamburg before seven, but Koppel said he would be glad to wait in the café and warm himself with coffee and a double whisky.

"A very nice little job, Herr Miller," he said. "I hope you got what you wanted."

"Oh, yes, I got it all right," said Miller.

"Well, mum's the word. By-by, Herr Miller."

The little burglar nodded and strolled toward the station café. Miller turned back and crossed the square to the hotel, unaware of the red-rimmed eyes that watched him from the back of a parked Mercedes.

It was too early to make the inquiries Miller needed to make, so he allowed himself three hours of sleep and asked to be waked at nine-thirty.

The phone shrilled at the exact hour, and he ordered coffee and rolls, which arrived just as he had finished a piping-hot shower. Over coffee he sat and studied the file of papers, recognizing about half a dozen of the faces but none of the names. The names, he had to tell himself, were meaningless.

Sheet eighteen was the one he came back to. The man was older, the hair longer, a sporting mustache covered the upper lip. But the ears were the same—the part of a face that is more individual to each owner than any other feature, yet which are always overlooked. The narrow nostrils were the same, the tilt of the head, the pale eyes.

The name was a common one; what fixed his attention was the address. From the postal district, it had to be the center of the city, and that would probably mean an apartment.

Just before ten o'clock he called the telephone Information department of the city named on the sheet of paper. He asked for the number of the superintendent for the apartment house at that address. It was a gamble, and it came off. It *was* an apartment house, and an expensive one.

He called the superintendent and explained that he had repeatedly called one of the tenants but could get no reply, which was odd because he had specifically been asked to call the man at that hour. Could the superintendent help him? Was the phone out of order?

The man at the other end was most helpful. The *Herr Direktor* would probably be at the factory, or perhaps at his weekend house in the country. What factory was that? Why, his own, of course. The radio factory. Oh, yes, of course, how stupid of me, said Miller and rang off. Information gave him the number of the factory. The girl who answered passed him to the boss's secretary, who told the caller the *Herr Direktor* was spending the weekend at his country house and would be back on Monday morning. The private house number was not to be divulged from the factory. A question of privacy. Miller thanked her and hung up.

The man who finally gave him the private number and address of the owner of the radio factory was an old contact, the industrial and business affairs correspondent of a large newspaper in Hamburg. He had the man's address in his private address book.

Miller sat and stared at the face of Roschmann, the new name, and the private address scribbled in his notebook. Now he remembered hearing of the man before, an industrialist from the Ruhr; he had even seen the radios in the stores. He took out his map of Germany and located the country villa on its private estate, or at least the area of villages where it was situated.

It was past twelve o'clock when he packed his bags, descended to the hall, and settled his bill. He was famished, so he went into the hotel dining room, taking only his document case, and treated himself to a large steak.

Over his meal he decided to drive the last section of the chase that afternoon and confront his target the next morning. He still had the slip of paper with the private telephone number of the lawyer with the Z Commission in Ludwigsburg. He could have called him then, but he wanted, was determined, to face Roschmann first. He feared if he tried that evening, the lawyer might not be at home when he called him to ask for a squad of policemen within thirty minutes. Sunday morning would be fine, just fine.

It was nearly two when he finally emerged, stowed his suitcase in the trunk of the Jaguar, tossed the document case onto the passenger seat, and climbed behind the wheel.

He failed to notice the Mercedes that tailed him to the edge of Osnabrück. The car behind him came onto the main autobahn after him, paused for a few seconds as the Jaguar accelerated fast down the southbound lane, then left the main road twenty yards farther on and drove back into town.

From a telephone booth by the roadside, Mackensen phoned the Werwolf in Nuremberg.

"He's on his way," he told his superior. "I just left him going down the southbound lane like a bat out of hell."

"Is your device accompanying him?"

Mackensen grinned. "Right. Fixed to the front near-side suspension. Within fifty miles he'll be in pieces you couldn't identify."

"Excellent," purred the man in Nuremberg. "You must be tired, my dear *Kamerad.* Go back into town and get some sleep."

Mackensen needed no second bidding. He had not slept a full night since Wednesday.

Miller made those fifty miles, and another hundred. For Mackensen had overlooked one thing. His trigger device would certainly have detonated quickly if it had been jammed into the cushion suspension system of a Continental saloon car. But the Jaguar was a British sports car, with a far harder suspension system. As it tore down the autobahn toward Frankfurt, the bumping caused the heavy springs above the front wheels to retract slightly, crushing the small bulb between the jaws of the bomb trigger to fragments of glass. But the electrically charged lengths of steel failed to touch each other. On the hard bumps they flickered to within a millimeter of each other before springing apart.

Unaware of how close to death he was, Miller made the trip past Münster, Dortmund, Wetzlar, and Bad Homburg to Frankfurt in just under three hours, then turned off the ring road toward Königstein and the wild, snow-thick forests of the Taunus Mountains.

<u>SIXTEEN</u>

It was already dark when the Jaguar slid into the small spa town in the eastern foothills of the mountain range. A glance at his map told Miller he was less than twenty miles from the private estate he sought. He decided to go no farther that night, but to seek a hotel and wait until morning.

To the north lay the mountains, straddled by the road to Limburg, lying quiet and white under the thick carpet of snow that muffled the rocks and shrouded the miles and miles of pine forest. There were lights twinkling down the main street of the small town, and the glow of them picked out the skeletal frame of the ruined castle brooding on its hill, once the fortress home of the Lords of Falkenstein. The sky was clear, but an icy wind gave promise of more snow to come during the night.

At the corner of Hauptstrasse and Frankfurtstrasse he found a hotel, the Park, and asked for a room. In a spa town in February the cold-water cure has hardly the same charm as in the summer months. There was plenty of room.

The porter directed him to put his car in the small lot at the back of the hotel, fringed by trees and bushes. He had a bath and went out for supper, picking the Grüne Baum hostelry in the Hauptstrasse, one of the dozen old, beamed eating houses the town had to offer.

It was over his meal that the nervousness set in. He noticed his hands were shaking as he raised his wineglass. Part of the condition was exhaustion, the lack of sleep in the past four days, the catnapping for one and two hours at a time.

Part was delayed reaction from the tension of the break-in with Koppel, and part the sense of astonishment at the luck that had rewarded his instinct to go back to Winzer's house after the first visit and ask the maid who had looked after the bachelor forger all these years.

But most, he knew, was the sense of the impending end of the chase, the confrontation with the man he hated and had sought through so many unknown byways of inquiry, coupled with the fear that something might still go wrong.

He thought back to the anonymous doctor in the hotel in Bad Godesberg who had warned him to stay away from the men of the Comradeship; and the Jewish Nazi-hunter of Vienna who had told him, "Be careful; these men can be dangerous." Thinking back, he wondered why they had not struck at him yet. They knew his name as Miller—the Dreesen Hotel visit proved that; and as Kolb—the beating of Bayer in Stuttgart would have blown that cover. Yet he had seen no one. One thing they could not know, he was sure, was that he had got as far as he had. Perhaps they had lost him, or decided to leave him alone, convinced, with the forger in hiding, he would end up by going in circles.

And yet he had the file, Winzer's secret and explosive evidence, and with it the greatest news story of the decade in West Germany. He grinned to himself, and the passing waitress thought it was for her. She swung her bottom as she passed his table next time, and he thought of Sigi. He had not called her since Vienna, and the letter he wrote in early January was the last she had had, six weeks back. He felt now that he needed her as he never had before.

Funny, he thought, how men always need women more when they are afraid. He had to admit he *was* frightened, partly of what he had done, partly of the mass-murderer who waited, unknowing, for him in the mountains.

He shook his head to shake off the mood and ordered another half-bottle of wine. This was no time for melancholy; he had pulled off the greatest journalistic coup he had ever heard of and was about to settle a score as well.

He ran over his plan as he drank the second portion of wine. A simple confrontation, a telephone call to the lawyer at Ludwigsburg, the arrival thirty minutes later of a police van to take the man away for imprisonment, trial, and a life sentence. If Miller had been a harder man, he would have wanted to kill the SS captain himself.

He thought it over and realized he was unarmed. Supposing Roschmann had a bodyguard? Would he really be alone, confident his new name would protect him from discovery? Or would there be a strong-arm retainer in case of trouble?

During Miller's military service, one of his friends, spending a night in the guardroom for being late back into camp, had stolen a pair of handcuffs from the Military Police. Later he had become worried by the thought they might be found in his kitbag and had given them to Miller. The reporter had kept them, simply as a trophy of a wild night in the Army. They were at the bottom of a trunk in his Hamburg flat.

He also had a gun, a small Sauer automatic, bought quite legally when he had been covering an exposé of Hamburg's vice rackets in 1960 and had been threatened by Little Pauli's mobsters. That was locked in a desk drawer, also in Hamburg.

Feeling slightly dizzy from the effects of his wine, a double brandy, and tiredness, he rose, paid his bill, and went back to the hotel. He was just about to enter to make his phone call, when he saw two public booths almost at the hotel door. Safer to use these.

It was nearly ten o'clock, and he found Sigi at the club where she worked. Above the clamor of the band in the background, he had to shout to make her hear him.

Miller cut short her stream of questions about where he had been, why he had not got in touch, where he was now, and told her what he wanted. She protested she couldn't get away, but something in his voice stopped her.

"Are you all right?" she shouted over the line.

"Yes, I'm fine. But I need your help. Please, darling, don't let me down. Not now, not tonight."

There was a pause; then she said simply, "I'll come. I'll tell them it's an emergency. Close family or something."

"Do you have enough to rent a car?"

"I think so. I can borrow something off one of the girls."

He told her the address of an all-night car-rental firm he had used before, and stressed she should mention his name, as he knew the proprietor.

"How far is it?" she asked.

"From Hamburg, five hundred kilometers. You can make it in five hours. Say six hours from now. You'll arrive about five in the morning. And don't forget to bring the things."

"All right, you can expect me then." There was a pause, then: "Peter, darling . . ."

"What?"

"Are you afraid of something?"

The time signal started, and he had no more one-mark pieces.

"Yes," he said and put down the receiver as they were cut off.

In the foyer of the hotel he asked the night porter if he could have a large envelope, and after some hunting beneath the counter the man obligingly produced a stiff brown one large enough to take a quarto-sized sheet of paper. Miller also bought enough stamps to cover the cost of sending the envelope by first-class mail with a lot of contents, emptying the porter's stock of stamps, which were usually needed only when a guest wished to send a postcard.

Back in his room he took his document case, which he had carried throughout the evening, laid it on the bed, and took out Salomon Tauber's diary, the sheaf of papers from Winzer's safe, and two photographs. He read again the two pages in the diary that had originally sent him on his hunt for a man he had never heard of, and studied the two photographs side by side.

Finally he took a sheet of plain paper from his case and wrote on it a brief but clear message, explaining to any reader what the sheaf of documents enclosed really was. The note, along with the file from Winzer's safe and one of the photographs, he placed inside the envelope, addressed it, and stuck on all the stamps he had bought.

The other photograph he put into the breast pocket of his jacket. The sealed envelope and the diary went back into his attaché case, which he slid under the bed.

He carried a small flask of brandy in his suitcase, and he poured a measure into the glass above the washbasin. He noticed his hands were trembling, but the fiery liquid relaxed him. He lay down on the bed, his head spinning slightly, and dozed off.

In the underground room in Munich, Josef paced the floor, angry and impatient. At the table, Leon and Motti gazed at their hands. It was forty-eight hours since the cable had come from Tel Aviv.

Their own attempts to trace Miller had brought no result. At their request by telephone, Alfred Oster had been to the parking lot in Bayreuth and later called back to tell them the car was gone.

"If they spot that car, they'll know he can't be a bakery worker from Bremen," growled Josef when he heard the news, "even if they don't know the car-owner is Peter Miller."

Later a friend in Stuttgart had informed Leon the local police were looking for a young man in connection with the murder in a hotel room of a citizen called Bayer. The description fitted Miller in his disguise as Kolb too well for it to be any other man, but fortunately the name from the hotel register was neither Kolb nor Miller, and there was no mention of a black sports car.

"At least he had the sense to register in a false name," said Leon.

"That would be in character with Kolb," Motti pointed out. "Kolb was supposed to be on the run from the Bremen police for war crimes."

But it was scant comfort. If the Stuttgart police could not find Miller, neither could the Leon group, and the latter could only fear the Odessa would by now be closer than either.

"He must have known, after killing Bayer, that he had blown his cover, and therefore reverted to the name of Miller," reasoned Leon. "So he has to abandon the search for Roschmann, unless he got something out of Bayer that took him to Roschmann."

"Then why the hell doesn't he check in?" snapped Josef. "Does the fool think he can take Roschmann on his own?"

Motti coughed quietly. "He doesn't know Roschmann has any real importance to the Odessa," he pointed out.

"Well, if he gets close enough, he'll find out," said Leon.

"And by then he'll be a dead man, and we'll all be back to square one," snapped Josef. "Why doesn't the idiot call in?"

But the phone lines were busy elsewhere that night, for Klaus Winzer had called the Werwolf from a small mountain chalet in the Regensburg region. The news he got was reassuring.

"Yes, I think it's safe for you to return home," the Odessa chief had answered in reply to the forger's question. "The man who was trying to interview you has by now certainly been taken care of."

The forger had thanked him, settled his overnight bill, and set off through the darkness for the north and the familiar comfort of his large bed at home in Westerberg, Osnabrück. He expected to arrive in time for a hearty breakfast, a bath, and a long sleep. By Monday morning he would be back in his printing plant, supervising the handling of the business.

Miller was waked by a knock at the bedroom door. He blinked, realizing the light was still on, and opened. The night porter stood there, Sigi behind him.

Miller quieted his fears by explaining the lady was his wife, who had brought him some important papers from home for a business meeting the following morning. The porter, a simple country lad with an indecipherable Hessian accent, took his tip and left.

Sigi threw her arms around him as he kicked the door shut. "Where have you been? What are you doing here?"

He shut off the questions in the simplest way, and by the time they parted Sigi's cold cheeks were flushed and burning and Miller was feeling like a fighting rooster.

He took her coat and hung it on the hook behind the door. She started to ask more questions.

"First things first," he said and pulled her down onto the bed, still warm under the thick feather cushion, where he had lain dozing.

She giggled. "You haven't changed."

She was still wearing her hostess dress from the cabaret, low-cut at the front, with a skimpy sling-bra beneath it. He unzipped the dress down the back and eased the thin shoulder-straps off.

"Have you?" he asked quietly.

She took a deep breath and lay back as he bent over her, pushing herself toward his face. She smiled. "No," she murmured, "not at all. You know what I like."

"And you know what I like," muttered Miller indistinctly.

She squealed. "Me first. I've missed you more than you've missed me."

There was no reply, only silence disturbed by Sigi's rising sighs and groans.

It was an hour before they paused, panting and happy, and Miller filled the glass with brandy and water. Sigi sipped a little, for she was not a heavy drinker, despite her job, and Miller took the rest.

"So," said Sigi teasingly, "first things having been dealt with—"

"For a while," interjected Miller.

She giggled. "For a while. Would you mind telling me why the mysterious letter, why the six-week absence, why that awful skin-head haircut, and why this small room in an obscure hotel in Hesse?"

Miller grew serious. At length he rose, still naked, crossed the room, and came back with his document case. He seated himself on the edge of the bed.

"You're going to learn pretty soon what I've been up to," he said. "So I may as well tell you now."

He talked for nearly an hour, starting with the discovery of the diary, which he showed her, and ending with the break into the forger's house. As he talked, she grew more and more horrified.

"You're mad," she said when he had finished. "You're stark, staring, raving mad. You could have got yourself killed or imprisoned or a hundred things."

"I had to do it," he said, bereft of an explanation for things that now seemed to him to have been crazy.

"All this for a rotten old Nazi? You're nuts. It's over, Peter, all that is over. What do you want to waste your time on them for?" She was staring at him in bewilderment.

"Well, I have," he said defiantly.

She sighed heavily and shook her head to indicate her failure to under-stand. "All right," she said, "so now it's done. You know who he is and where he is. You just come back to Hamburg, pick up the phone, and call the police. They'll do the rest. That's what they're paid for."

Miller did not know how to answer her. "It's not that simple," he said at last. "I'm going up there later this morning."

"Going up where?"

He jerked his thumb toward the window and the still-dark range of mountains beyond it. "To his house."

"To his house? What for?" Her eyes widened in horror. "You're not going in to see him?"

"Yes. Don't ask me why, because I can't tell you. It's just something I have to do."

Her reaction startled him. She sat up with a jerk, turned onto her knees, and glared at where he lay smoking, his head propped up by a pillow.

"That's what you wanted the gun for," she threw at him, her breasts rising and falling in her growing anger. "You're going to kill him—"

"I'm not going to kill him—"

"Well, then, he'll kill you. And you're going up there alone with a gun against him and his mob. You bastard, you rotten, stinking, horrible—"

Miller was staring at her in amazement. "What have you got so het up for? Over Roschmann?"

"I'm not het up about that horrid old Nazi. I'm talking about me. About me and you, you stupid dumb oaf. You're going to risk getting yourself killed up there, all to prove some silly point and make a story for your idiotic magazine readers. You don't even think for a minute about me."

She had started crying as she talked, the tears making tracks of mascara down each cheek like black railway lines.

"Look at me—just damn well look at me. What do you think I am, just another good screw? You really think I want to give myself every night to some randy reporter so he can feel pleased with himself when he goes off to chase some idiot story that could get him killed? You really think that? Listen, you moron, I want to get married. I want to be Frau Miller. I want to have babies. And you're going to get yourself killed. Oh, God . . ."

She jumped off the bed, ran into the bathroom, slammed the door behind her, and locked it.

Miller lay on the bed, open-mouthed, the cigarette burning down to his fingers. He had never seen her so angry, and it had shocked him. He thought over what she had said as he listened to the tap running in the bathroom.

Stubbing out the cigarette, he crossed the room to the bathroom door. "Sigi."

There was no answer.

"Sigi."

The tap was turned off. "Go away."

"Sigi, please open the door. I want to talk to you."

There was a pause; then the door was unlocked. She stood there, naked and looking sulky. She had washed the mascara streaks off her face.

"What do you want?" she asked.

"Come over to the bed. I want to talk to you. We'll freeze standing here."

"No, you just want to start making love again."

"I won't. Honestly. I promise you I won't. I just want to talk."

He took her hand and led her back to the bed and the warmth it offered.

Her face looked up warily from the pillow. "What do you want to talk about?" she asked suspiciously.

He climbed in beside her and put his face close to her ear. "Sigrid Rahn, will you marry me?"

She turned to face him. "Do you mean it?" she asked.

"Yes, I do. I never really thought of it before. But then, you never got angry before."

"Gosh." She sounded as if she couldn't believe her ears. "I'll have to get angry more often."

"Do I get an answer?" he asked.

"Oh yes, Peter, I will. We'll be so good together."

He began caressing her again, becoming aroused as he did so.

"You said you weren't going to start that again," she accused him.

"Well, just this once. After that I promise I'll leave you strictly alone for the rest of time."

She swung her thigh across him and slid her hips on top of his lower belly. Looking down at him, she said, "Peter Miller, don't you dare."

Miller reached up and pulled the toggle that extinguished the light, as she started to make love to him. . . .

Outside in the snow there was a dim light breaking over the eastern horizon. Had Miller glanced at his watch, it would have told him the time was ten minutes before seven on the morning of Sunday, February 23. But he was already asleep.

Half an hour later Klaus Winzer rolled up the drive of his house, stopped before the closed garage door, and climbed out. He was stiff and tired, but glad to be home.

Barbara was not yet up, taking advantage of her employer's absence to sleep longer than usual. When she did appear, after Winzer had let himself in and called from the hallway, it was in a nightgown that would have set another man's pulses bounding. Instead, Winzer required fried eggs, toast and jam, a pot of coffee, and a bath. He got none of them.

She told him, instead, of her discovery on Saturday morning, on entering the study to dust, of the broken window and the missing silverware. She had called the police, and they had been positive the neat circular hole was the work of a professional burglar. She had had to tell them the house-owner was away, and they said they wanted to know when he returned, just for routine questions about the missing items.

Winzer listened in absolute quiet to the girl's chatter, his face paling, a single vein throbbing steadily in his temple. He dismissed her to the kitchen to prepare coffee, went into his study, and locked the door. It took him thirty seconds and frantic scratching inside the empty safe to convince himself that the file of forty Odessa criminals was gone.

As he turned away from the safe, the phone rang. It was the doctor from the clinic to inform him Fräulein Wendel had died during the night.

For two hours Winzer sat in his chair before the unlit fire, oblivious of the cold seeping in through the newspaper-stuffed hole in the window, aware only of the cold fingers worming around inside himself as he tried to think what to do. Barbara's repeated calls from outside the locked door that breakfast was ready went unheeded. Through the keyhole she could hear him muttering occasionally, "Not my fault, not my fault at all."

Miller had forgotten to cancel the morning call he had ordered the previous evening. The bedside phone shrilled at nine. Bleary-eyed, he answered it, grunted his thanks, and climbed out of bed. He knew if he did not, he would fall asleep again. Sigi was still fast asleep, exhausted by her drive from Hamburg, their lovemaking, and the contentment of being engaged at last.

Miller showered, finishing off with several minutes under the ice-cold spray, rubbed himself briskly with the towel he had left over the radiator all night, and felt like a million dollars. The depression and anxiety of the night before had vanished. He felt fit and confident.

He dressed in ankle boots and slacks, a thick roll-neck pullover, and his double-breasted blue duffel overjacket, a German winter garment called a *Joppe*, halfway between a jacket and a coat. It had deep slit pockets at each side, capable of taking the gun and the handcuffs, and an inside breast pocket for the photograph. He took the handcuffs from Sigi's bag and examined them. There was no key, and the manacles were self-locking, which made them useless for anything other than locking a man up until he was released by the police or a hacksaw blade.

The gun he opened and examined. He had never fired it, and it still had the maker's grease on the interior. The magazine was full; he kept it that way. To familiarize himself with it once again, he worked the breech several times, made sure he knew which positions of the safety catch were the "On" and "Fire," smacked the magazine into the grip, pushed a round into the chamber, and set the safety catch to "On." He stuffed the telephone number of the lawyer in Ludwigsburg into his trouser pocket.

He took his attaché case out from under the bed, and on a plain sheet from it wrote a message for Sigi to read when she awoke. It said: "My darling. I am going now to see the man I have been hunting. I have a reason for wanting to look into his face and be present when the police take him away in handcuffs. It is a good one, and by this afternoon I will be able to tell you. But just in case, here is what I want you to do. . . ."

The instructions were precise and to the point. He wrote down the telephone number in Munich she was to call, and the message she was to give the man at the other end. He ended: "Do not under any circumstances follow me up the mountain. You could only make matters worse, whatever the situation. So if I am not back by noon, or have not called you in this room by then, call that number, give that message, check out of the hotel, mail the envelope at any box in Frankfurt, then drive back to Hamburg. Don't get engaged to anyone else in the meantime. All my love, Peter."

He propped the note on the bedside table by the telephone, along with the large envelope containing the Odessa file, and three 50-mark bills. Tucking Salomon Tauber's diary under his arm, he slipped out of the bedroom and headed downstairs. Passing the reception desk, he ordered the porter to give his room another morning call at eleven-thirty.

He came out of the hotel doorway at nine-thirty and was surprised at the amount of snow that had fallen during the night.

Miller walked around to the back, climbed into the Jaguar, gave full choke, and pressed the starter. It took several minutes before the engine caught. While it was warming up he took a hand-brush from the trunk and brushed the thick carpet of snow off the hood, roof, and windshield.

Back behind the wheel, he slipped into gear and drove out onto the main road. The thick layer of snow over everything acted as a sort of cushion, and he could hear it crunching under the wheels. After a glance at the ordnance survey map he had bought the previous evening just before closing time, he set off down the road toward Limburg.

SEVENTEEN

The morning had turned out gray and overcast after a brief and brilliant dawn which he had not seen. Beneath the clouds the snow glittered under the trees and a wind keened off the mountains.

The road led upward, winding out of town and immediately becoming lost in the sea of trees that make up the Romberg Forest. After he had cleared town, the carpet of snow along the road was almost virgin, only one set of tracks running parallel through it, where an early-morning visitor to König-stein for church service had headed an hour before.

Miller took the branch-off toward Glashütten, skirted the flanks of the towering Feldberg mountain, and took a road signposted as leading to the village of Schmitten. On the flanks of the mountain the wind howled through the pines, its pitch rising to a near-scream among the snow-clogged boughs.

Although Miller had never bothered to think about it, it was once out of these and other oceans of pine and beech that the old Germanic tribes had swarmed to be checked by Caesar at the Rhine. Later, converted to Christianity, they had paid lip service by day to the Prince of Peace, dreaming only in the dark hours of the ancient gods of strength and lust and power. It was this ancient atavism, the worship in the dark of the private gods of screaming endless trees, that Hitler had ignited with a magic touch.

After another twenty minutes of careful driving, Miller checked his map again and began to look for a gateway off the road onto a private estate. When he found it, it was a barred gate held in place by a steel catch, with a notice board to one side saying: PRIVATE PROPERTY, KEEP OUT.

Leaving the engine running, he climbed out and swung the gate inward.

Miller entered the estate and headed up the driveway. The snow was untouched, and he kept in low gear, for there was only frozen sand beneath the snow.

Two hundred yards up the track, a branch from a massive oak tree had come down in the night, overladen with half a ton of snow. The branch had crashed into the undergrowth to the right, and some of its twigs lay on the track. It had also brought down a thin black pole that had stood beneath it, and this lay square across the drive.

Rather than get out and move it, he drove carefully forward, feeling the bump as the pole passed under the front and then the rear wheels.

Clear of the obstruction, he moved on toward the house and emerged into a clearing, which contained the villa and its gardens, fronted by a circular area of gravel. He halted the car in front of the main door, climbed out, and rang the bell.

While Miller was climbing out of his car, Klaus Winzer made his decision and called the Werwolf. The Odessa chief was brusque and irritable, for it was long past the time he should have heard on the news of a sports car being blown to pieces, apparently by an exploding gas tank, on the autobahn south of Osnabrück. But as he listened to the man on the other end of the telephone, his mouth tightened in a thin, hard line.

"You did what? You fool, you unbelievable, stupid little cretin. Do you know what's going to happen to you if that file is not recovered? . . ."

Alone in his study in Osnabrück, Klaus Winzer replaced the receiver after the last sentences from the Werwolf came over the wire, and went back to his desk. He was quite calm. Twice already life had played him the worst of tricks: first the destruction of his war work in the lakes; then the ruin of his paper fortune in 1948. And now this. Taking an old but serviceable Luger from the bottom drawer, he placed the end in his mouth and shot himself. The lead slug that tore his head apart was not a forgery.

The Werwolf sat and gazed in something close to horror at the silent telephone. He thought of the men for whom it had been necessary to obtain passports through Klaus Winzer, and the fact that each of them was a wanted man on the list of those destined for arrest and trial if caught. The exposure of the dossier would lead to a welter of prosecutions that could only jerk the population out of its growing apathy toward the question of continuing pursuit of wanted SS men, regalvanize the hunting agencies. . . . The prospect was appalling.

But his first priority was the protection of Roschmann, one of those he knew to be on the list taken from Winzer. Three times he dialed the Frankfurt area code, followed by the private number of the house on the hill, and three times he got a busy signal. Finally he tried through the operator, who told him the line must be out of order.

Instead, he rang the Hohenzollern Hotel in Osnabrück and caught Mackensen about to leave. In a few sentences he told the killer of the latest disaster, and where Roschmann lived.

"It looks as if your bomb hasn't worked," he told him. "Get down there faster than you've ever driven," he said. "Hide your car and stick close to Roschmann. There's a bodyguard called Oskar as well. If Miller goes straight to the police with what he's got, we've all had it. But if he comes to Roschmann, take him alive and make him talk. We must know what he's done with those papers before he dies."

Mackensen glanced at his road map inside the phone booth and estimated the distance.

"I'll be there at one o'clock," he said.

The door opened at the second ring, and a gust of warm air flowed out of the hall. The man who stood in front of Miller had evidently come from his study, the door of which Miller could see standing open and leading off the hallway.

Years of good living had put weight on the once lanky SS officer. His face had a flush, either from drinking or from the country air, and his hair was gray at the sides. He looked the picture of middle-aged, upper-middle-class, prosperous good health. But although different in detail, the face was the same Tauber had seen and described.

The man surveyed Miller without enthusiasm. "Yes?" he said.

It took Miller another ten seconds before he could speak. What he had rehearsed just went out of his head.

"My name is Miller, he said, "and yours is Eduard Roschmann."

At the mention of both names, something flickered through the eyes of the man in front of him, but iron control kept his face muscles straight. "This is preposterous," he said at length. "I've never heard of the man you are talking about."

Behind the façade of calm, the former SS officer's mind was racing. Several times in his life since 1945 he had survived through sharp thinking in a crisis. He recognized the name of Miller well enough and recalled his conversation with the Werwolf weeks before. His first instinct was to shut the door in Miller's face, but he overcame it.

"Are you alone in the house?" asked Miller.

"Yes," said Roschmann truthfully.

"We'll go into your study," said Miller flatly.

Roschmann made no objection, for he realized he was now forced to keep Miller on the premises and stall for time, until . . .

He turned on his heel and strode back across the hallway. Miller slammed the front door after him and was at Roschmann's heels as they entered the study. It was a comfortable room, with a thick, padded door, which Miller closed behind him, and a log fire burning in the grate.

Roschmann stopped in the center of the room and turned to face Miller.

"Is your wife here?" asked Miller.

Roschmann shook his head. "She has gone away for the weekend to visit relatives," he said. This much was true. She had been called away the

previous evening at a moment's notice and had taken the second car. The
first car owned by the pair was, by ill luck, in the garage for repairs. She was
due back that evening.

What Roschmann did not mention, but what occupied his racing mind,
was that his bulky, shaven-headed chauffeur-bodyguard, Oskar, had bicy-
cled down to the village half an hour earlier to report that the telephone was
out of order. He knew he had to keep Miller talking until the man returned.

When he turned to face Miller, the young reporter's right hand held an
automatic pointed straight at his belly.

Roschmann was frightened but covered it with bluster. "You threaten me
with a gun in my own house?"

"Then call the police," said Miller, nodding at the telephone on the writing
desk. Roschmann made no move toward it.

"I see you still limp a little," remarked Miller. "The orthopedic shoe almost
disguises it, but not quite. The missing toes, lost in an operation in Rimini
camp. The frostbite you got wandering through the fields of Austria caused
that, didn't it?"

Roschmann's eyes narrowed slightly, but he said nothing.

"You see, if the police come, they'll identify you, *Herr Direktor.* The face is
still the same, the bullet wound in the chest, the scar under the left armpit
where you tried to remove the Waffen SS blood-group tattoo, no doubt. Do
you really want to call the police?"

Roschmann let out the air in his lungs in a long sigh. "What do you want,
Miller?"

"Sit down," said the reporter. "Not at the desk, there in the armchair,
where I can see you. And keep your hands on the armrests. Don't give me an
excuse to shoot, because, believe me, I'd dearly love to."

Roschmann sat in the armchair, his eyes on the gun.

Miller perched on the edge of the desk, facing him. "So now we talk," he
said.

"About what?"

"About Riga. About eighty thousand people, men, women, and children,
whom you had slaughtered up there."

Seeing he did not intend to use the gun, Roschmann began to regain his
confidence. Some of the color returned to his face. He switched his gaze to
the face of the younger man in front of him.

"That's a lie. There were never eighty thousand disposed of in Riga."

"Seventy thousand? Sixty?" asked Miller. "Do you really think it matters
precisely how many thousand you killed."

"That's the point," said Roschmann eagerly. "It doesn't matter—not now,
not then. Look, young man, I don't know why you've come after me. But I
can guess. Someone's been filling your head with a lot of sentimental clap-
trap about so-called war crimes and suchlike. It's all nonsense. Absolute
nonsense. How old are you?"

"Twenty-nine."

"Then you were in the Army for military service?"

"Yes. One of the first national servicemen of the postwar army. Two years
in uniform."

"Well, then, you know what the Army is like. A man's given orders; he obeys those orders. He doesn't ask whether they are right or wrong. You know that as well as I do. All I did was to obey my orders."

"Firstly, you weren't a soldier," said Miller quietly. "You were an executioner. Put more bluntly, a murderer, and a mass-murderer. So don't compare yourself with a soldier."

"Nonsense," said Roschmann earnestly. "It's all nonsense. We were soldiers just like the rest. We obeyed our orders just like the rest. You young Germans are all the same. You don't want to understand what it was like then."

"So tell me, what was it like?"

Roschmann, who had leaned forward to make his point, leaned back in the chair, almost at ease, the immediate danger past.

"What was it like? It was like ruling the world. Because we did rule the world, the Germans. We had beaten every army they could throw at us. For years they had looked down on us, we poor Germans, and we had shown them, yes, all of them, that we were a great people. You youngsters today don't realize what it is to be proud of being a German.

"It lights a fire inside you. When the drums beat and the bands played, when the flags were waving and the whole nation was united behind one man, we could have marched to the ends of the world. That is greatness, young Miller, greatness your generation has never known and never will know. And we of the SS were the elite, still are the elite. Of course they hunt us down now, first the Allies and then the wishy-washy old women of Bonn. Of course they want to crush us. Because they want to crush the greatness of Germany, which we represented and still do.

"They say a lot of stupid things about what happened then in a few camps a sensible world would long since have forgotten about. They make a big fuss because we had to clean up Europe from the pollution of this Jewish filth that impregnated every facet of German life and kept us down in the mud with them. We had to do it, I tell you. It was a mere sideshow in the great design of a Germany and a German people, pure in blood and ideals, ruling the world as is their right, *our* right, Miller, *our* right and our destiny, if those hell-damned Britishers and the eternally stupid Americans had not stuck their prissy noses in. For make no bones about it, you may point that thing at me, but we are on the same side, young man, a generation between us, but still on the same side. For we are Germans, the greatest people in the world. And you would let your judgment of all this, of the greatness that once was Germany's—and will be again one day—of the essential unity of us, all of us, the German people, you will let your judgment of all this be affected by what happened to a few miserable Jews? Can't you see, you poor misled young fool, that we are on the same side, you and me, the same side, the same people, the same destiny?"

Despite the gun, he rose from his chair and paced the carpet between the desk and the window.

"You want proof of our greatness? Look at Germany today. Smashed to rubble in nineteen forty-five, utterly destroyed and prey to the barbarians from the east and the fools in the west. And now? Germany is rising again, slowly and surely, still lacking the essential discipline that we were able to give her, but increasing each year in her industrial and economic power. Yes, and military power. One day, when the last vestiges of the influence of the Allies of nineteen forty-five have been shaken off, we will be as mighty again as we ever were. It will take time, and a new leader, but the ideas will be the same, and the glory—yes, that will be the same too.

"And you know what brings this about? I will tell you, yes, I will tell you, young man. It's discipline and management. Harsh discipline, the harsher the better, and management, *our* management, the most brilliant quality after courage that we possess. For we can manage things; we have shown that. Look at all this—you see all this? This house, this estate, the factory down in the Ruhr, mine and thousands like it, tens, hundreds of thousands, churning out power and strength each day, with each turn of the wheel another ounce of might to make Germany mighty once again.

"And who do you think did all this? You think people prepared to spend time mouthing platitudes over a few miserable Yids did all this? You think cowards and traitors trying to persecute good honest, patriotic German soldiers did all this? *We* did this, we brought this prosperity back to Germany, the same men as we had twenty, thirty years ago."

He turned from the window and faced Miller, his eyes alight. But he also measured the distance from the farthest point of his pacing along the carpet to the heavy iron poker by the fire. Miller had noticed the glances.

"Now, you come here, a representative of the young generation, full of your idealism and your concern, and point a gun at me. Why not be idealistic for Germany, your own country, your own people? You think you represent the people, coming to hunt me down? You think that's what they want, the people of Germany?"

Miller shook his head. "No, I don't," he said shortly.

"Well, there you are, then. If you call the police and turn me in to them, they might make a trial out of it—I say only 'might' because even that is not certain, so long afterward, with all the witnesses scattered or dead. So put your gun away and go home. Go home and read the true history of those days, learn that Germany's greatness then and her prosperity today stem from patriotic Germans like me."

Miller had sat through the tirade mute, observing with bewilderment and rising disgust the man who paced the carpet in front of him, seeking to convert him to the old ideology. He had wanted to say a hundred, a thousand things about the people he knew and the millions beyond them who did not want or see the necessity of purchasing glory at the price of slaughtering millions of other human beings. But the words did not come. They never do when one needs them. So he just sat and stared until Roschmann had finished.

After some seconds of silence Miller asked, "Have you ever heard of a man called Tauber?"

"Who?"

"Salomon Tauber. He was a German too. Jewish. He was in Riga from the beginning to the end."

Roschmann shrugged. "I can't remember him. It was a long time ago. Who was he?"

"Sit down," said Miller. "And this time stay seated."

Roschmann shrugged impatiently and went back to the armchair. With his rising conviction that Miller would not shoot, his mind was concerned with the problem of trapping him before he could get away, rather than with an obscure and long-dead Jew.

"Tauber died in Hamburg on November twenty-second last year. He gassed himself. Are you listening?"

"Yes. If I must."

"He left behind a diary. It was an account of his story, what happened to him, what you and others did to him, in Riga and elsewhere. But mainly in Riga. But he survived, he came back to Hamburg, and he lived for eighteen years, because he was convinced you were alive and would never stand trial. I got hold of his diary. It was my starting point in finding you today, here, under your new name."

"The diary of a dead man's not evidence," growled Roschmann.

"Not for a court, but enough for me."

"And you really came here to confront me over the diary of a dead Jew?"

"No, not at all. There's a page of that diary I want you to read."

Miller opened the diary at a certain page and pushed it into Roschmann's lap. "Pick it up," he ordered, "and read it—aloud."

Roschmann unfolded the sheet and began to read it. It was the passage in which Tauber described the murder by Roschmann of an unnamed German Army officer wearing the Knight's Cross with Oak Leaf Cluster.

Roschmann reached the end of the passage and looked up. "So what?" he said, puzzled. "The man struck me. He disobeyed orders. I had the right to commandeer that ship to bring the prisoners back."

Miller tossed a photograph onto Roschmann's lap. "Is that the man you killed?"

Roschmann looked at it and shrugged. "How should I know? It was twenty years ago."

There was a slow *ker-lick* as Miller thumbed the hammer back and pointed the gun at Roschmann's face. "Was that the man?"

Roschmann looked at the photograph again. "All right. So that was the man. So what?"

"That was my father," said Miller.

The color drained out of Roschmann's face as if a plug had been pulled. His mouth dropped open; his gaze dropped to the gun barrel two feet from his face, and the steady hand behind it.

"Oh, dear God," he whispered, "you didn't come about the Jews at all."

"No. I'm sorry for them, but not that sorry."

"But how could you know, how could you possibly know from that diary that the man was your father? I never knew his name. This Jew who wrote the diary never knew. How did you know?"

"My father was killed on October eleventh, nineteen forty-four, in Ostland," said Miller. "For twenty years that was all I knew. Then I read the diary. It was the same day, the same area, the two men had the same rank. Above all, both men wore the Knight's Cross with Oak Leaf Cluster, the highest award for bravery in the field. There weren't all that many of those awarded, and very few to mere Army captains. It would have been millions to one against two similar officers dying in the same area on the same day."

Roschmann knew he was up against a man whom no argument could influence. He stared, as if mesmerized, at the gun. "You're going to kill me. You mustn't do that, not in cold blood. You wouldn't do that. Please, Miller, I don't want to die."

Miller leaned forward and began to talk. "Listen to me, you repulsive piece of dogshit. I've listened to you and your twisted mouthings till I'm sick to my guts. Now you're going to listen to me while I make up my mind whether you die here or rot in some jail for the rest of your days.

"You had the nerve, the damned crass nerve, to tell me that you, you of all people, were a patriotic German. I'll tell you what you are. You and your kind were and are the filthiest crap that was ever elevated from the gutters of this country to positions of power. And in twelve years you smeared my country with your dirt in a way that has never happened throughout our history.

"What you did sickened and revolted the whole of civilized mankind and left my generation a heritage of shame to live down that's going to take us all the rest of our lives. You spat on Germany throughout your lives. You bastards used Germany and the German people until they could not be used any more, and then you quit while the going was good. You brought us so low it would have been inconceivable before your crew came along—and I don't mean in terms of bomb damage.

"You weren't even brave. You were the most sickening cowards ever produced in Germany or Austria. You murdered millions for your own profit and in the name of your maniac power-lust, and then you got out and left the rest of us in the shit. You ran away from the Russians, hanged and shot Army men to keep them fighting, and then disappeared and left me to carry the can back.

"Even if there could be any oblivion about what you did to the Jews and the others, there can never be any forgetting that your bunch ran and hid like the dogs you are. You talk of patriotism; you don't even know the meaning of the word. And as for daring to call Army soldiers and others who fought, really fought, for Germany, *Kamerad,* it's a damned obscenity.

"I'll tell you one other thing, as a young German of the generation you so plainly despise. This prosperity we have today—it's got nothing to do with you. It's got a lot to do with millions who do a hard day's work and never murdered anyone in their lives. And as for murderers like you who may still be among us, as far as I and my generation are concerned, we would put up with a little less prosperity if we could be sure scum like you were not still around. Which, incidentally, you are not going to be for very long."

"You're going to kill me," mumbled Roschmann.

"As a matter of fact, I'm not." Miller reached behind him and pulled the telephone over toward where he sat on the desk. He kept his eyes on Roschmann and the gun pointed. He took the receiver off the cradle, slid it onto the desk, and dialed. When he had finished, he picked up the receiver.

"There's a man in Ludwigsburg who wants to have a chat with you," he said and put the telephone to his ear. It was dead.

He laid it back in the cradle, took it off again, and listened for the dial tone. There was none.

"Have you cut this off?" he asked.

Roschmann shook his head.

"Listen, if you've pulled the connection out, I'll drill you here and now."

"I haven't. I haven't touched the phone this morning. Honestly."

Miller remembered the fallen branch of the oak tree and the pole lying across the track to the house. He swore softly.

Roschmann gave a small smile. "The lines must be down," he said. "You'll have to go into the village. What are you going to do now?"

"I'm going to put a bullet through you unless you do as you're told," Miller snapped back. He dragged the handcuffs he had thought to use on a bodyguard out of his pocket.

He tossed the bracelets over to Roschmann. "Walk over to the fireplace," he ordered and followed the man across the room.

"What are you going to do?"

"I'm going to handcuff you to the fireplace, then go and phone from the village," said Miller.

He was scanning the wrought-iron scrollwork that composed the surround of the fireplace when Roschmann dropped the handcuffs at his feet. The SS man bent to pick them up, and Miller was almost caught unawares when Roschmann instead gripped a heavy poker and swung it viciously at Miller's kneecaps. The reporter stepped back in time, the poker swished past, and Roschmann was off balance.

Miller stepped in, whipped the barrel of the pistol across the bent head, and stepped back. "Try that again, and I'll kill you," he said.

Roschmann straightened up, wincing from the blow to the head.

"Clip one of the bracelets around your right wrist," Miller commanded, and Roschmann did as he was told. "You see that vine-leaf ornament in front of you? At head height? There's a branch next to it that comes out of the metalwork and rejoins it again. Lock the other bracelet onto that."

When Roschmann had snapped the second link home, Miller walked over and kicked the fire-tongs and poker out of reach. Keeping his gun against Roschmann's jacket, he frisked him and cleared the area around the chained man of all objects which he could throw to break the window.

Outside in the driveway, the man called Oskar pedaled toward the door, his errand to report the broken phone line accomplished. He paused in surprise on seeing the Jaguar, for his employer had assured him before he went that no one was expected.

He leaned the bicycle against the side of the house and quietly let himself in by the front door. In the hallway he stood irresolute, hearing nothing through the padded door to the study and not being heard himself by those inside.

Miller took a last look around and was satisfied. "Incidentally," he told the glaring Roschmann, "it wouldn't have done you any good if you had managed to hit me. It's eleven o'clock now, and I left the complete dossier of evidence on you in the hands of my accomplice, to drop into the mailbox, addressed to the right authorities, if I have not returned or phoned by noon. As it is, I'm going to phone from the village. I'll be back in twenty minutes. You won't be out of there in twenty minutes, even with a hacksaw. When I get back, the police will be thirty minutes behind me."

As he talked, Roschmann's hopes began to flicker. He knew he had only one chance left—for the returning Oskar to take Miller alive so that he could be forced to make the phone call from a phone in the village at their demand and keep the documents from reaching the mailbox.

Miller swung open the door at the other side of the room and walked through it. He found himself staring at the roll-neck pullover worn by a man a full head taller than he was. From his place by the fire Roschmann recognized Oskar and screamed, *"Hold him."*

Miller stepped back into the room and jerked up the gun he had been replacing in his pocket. He was too slow. A swinging left backhander from Oskar's paw swept the automatic out of his grasp, and it flew across the room. At the same time Oskar thought his employer cried, *"Hit him."* He crashed a right hand into Miller's jaw. The reporter weighed 170 pounds, but the blow lifted him off his feet and threw him backward. His feet caught in a low newspaper rack, and as he went over, his head slammed into the corner of a mahogany bookcase. Crumpling like a rag doll, his body slid to the carpet and rolled onto one side.

For several seconds there was silence as Oskar took in the spectacle of his employer manacled to the fireplace, and Roschmann stared at the inert figure of Miller, from the back of whose head a trickle of blood flowed onto the floor.

"You fool," yelled Roschmann when he had taken in what had happened. Oskar looked baffled. "Get over here."

The giant lumbered across the room and stood waiting for orders.

Roschmann thought fast. "Try and get me out of these handcuffs," he commanded. "Use the fire-irons."

But the handcuffs had been made in an age when craftsmen intended their handiwork to last for a long time. The result of Oskar's efforts was a curly poker and a pair of wriggly tongs.

"Bring him over here," he told Oskar at last. While Oskar held Miller up, Roschmann looked under the reporter's eyelids and felt his pulse. "He's still alive, but out cold," he said. "He'll need a doctor to come around in less than an hour. Bring me a pencil and paper."

Writing with his left hand, he scribbled two phone numbers on the paper while Oskar brought a hacksaw blade from the tool chest under the stairs. When he returned, Roschmann gave him the sheet of paper.

"Get down to the village as fast as you can," he told Oskar. "Ring this Nuremberg number and tell the man who answers it what has happened. Ring this local number and get the doctor up here immediately. You understand? Tell him it's an emergency. Now hurry."

As Oskar ran from the room, Roschmann glanced at the clock again. Ten-fifty. If Oskar could make the village by eleven, and he and the doctor could be back by eleven-fifteen, they might bring Miller around in time to get to a phone and delay the accomplice, even if the doctor would only work at gunpoint. Urgently, Roschmann began to saw at his handcuffs.

In front of the door Oskar grabbed his bicycle, then paused and glanced at the parked Jaguar. He peered through the driver's window and saw the key in the ignition. His master had told him to hurry, so he dropped the bicycle, climbed behind the wheel of the car, gunned it into life, and spurted gravel in a wide arc as he slid the sports car out of the forecourt into the driveway.

He had got up into third gear and was boring down the slippery track as fast as he could take it when he hit the snow-covered telegraph pole lying across the road.

Roschmann was still sawing at the chain linking the two bracelets when the shattering roar in the pine forest stopped him. Straining to one side, he could peer through the French windows, and although the car and the driveway were out of sight, the plume of smoke drifting across the sky told him at least that the car had been destroyed by an explosion. He recalled the assurance he had been given that Miller would be taken care of. But Miller was on the carpet a few feet away from him, his bodyguard was certainly dead, and time was running out without hope of reprieve. He leaned his head against the chill metal of the fire-surround and closed his eyes.

"Then it's over," he murmured quietly. After several minutes he continued sawing. It was over an hour before the specially hardened steel of the military handcuffs parted to the now blunt hacksaw. As he stepped free, with only a bracelet around his right wrist, the clock chimed twelve.

If he had had time, he might have paused to kick the body on the carpet, but he was a man in a hurry. From the wall safe he took a passport and several fat bundles of new, high-denomination bank-notes. Twenty minutes later, with these and a few clothes in a bag, he was bicycling down the track, around the shattered hulk of the Jaguar and the still-smoldering body lying face down in the snow, past the scorched and broken pines, toward the village.

From there he called a taxi and ordered it to take him to Frankfurt international airport. He walked to the flight-information desk and inquired, "What time is the next flight out of here for Argentina—preferably within an hour? Failing that, for Madrid."

EIGHTEEN

It was ten past one when Mackensen's Mercedes turned off the country road into the gate of the estate. Halfway up the drive to the house he found the way blocked.

The Jaguar had evidently been blown apart from inside, but its wheels had not left the road. It was still upright, slewed slantwise across the drive. The forward and rear sections were recognizable as those of a car, still held together by the tough steel girders that formed the chassis. But the center section, including the cockpit, was missing from floor to roof. Bits of this section were scattered in an area around the wreckage.

Mackensen surveyed the skeleton with a grim smile and walked over to the bundle of scorched clothes and their contents on the ground twenty feet away. Something about the size of the corpse caught his attention, and he stooped over it for several minutes. Then he straightened and ran at an easy lope up the rest of the drive toward the house.

He avoided ringing the front doorbell but tried the handle. The door opened, and he went into the hallway. For several seconds he listened, poised like a carnivorous animal by a water hole, sensing the atmosphere for danger. There was no sound. He reached under his left armpit and brought out a long-barreled Luger automatic, flicked off the safety catch, and started to open the doors leading off the hall.

The first was to the dining room, the second to the study. Although he saw the body on the hearthrug at once, he did not move from the half-open door before he had covered the rest of the room. He had known two men to fall for that trick—the obvious bait and the hidden ambush. Before entering, he glanced through the crack between the door's hinges to make sure no one waited behind it, then entered.

Miller was lying on his back with his head turned to one side. For several seconds Mackensen stared down into the chalky white face, then bent to listen to the shallow breathing. The matted blood on the back of the head told him roughly what had happened.

He spent ten minutes scouring the house, noting the open drawers in the master bedroom, the missing shaving gear from the bathroom. Back in the study, he glanced into the yawning and empty wall safe, then sat himself at the desk and picked up the telephone.

He sat listening for several seconds, swore under his breath, and replaced the receiver. There was no difficulty in finding the tool chest under the stairs, for the cupboard door was still open. He took what he needed and went back down the drive, passing through the study to check on Miller and leaving by the French windows.

It took him almost an hour to find the parted strands of the telephone line, sort them out from the entangling undergrowth, and splice them back together. When he was satisfied with his handiwork he walked back to the house, sat at the desk, and tried the phone. He got the dial tone and called his chief in Nuremberg.

He had expected the Werwolf to be eager to hear from him, but the man's voice coming down the wire sounded tired and only half-interested. Like a good sergeant, he reported what he had found: the car, the corpse of the bodyguard, the half-handcuff still linked to the scrollwork by the fire, the blunt hacksaw blade on the carpet, Miller unconscious on the floor. He finished with the absent owner.

"He hasn't taken much, Chief. Overnight things, probably money from the open safe. I can clear up here; he can come back if he wants to."

"No, he won't come back," the Werwolf told him. "Just before you called, I put the phone down. He called me from Frankfurt airport. He's got a reservation on a flight to Madrid, leaving in ten minutes. Connection this evening to Buenos Aires—"

"But there's no need," protested Mackensen. "I'll make Miller talk, we can find where he left his papers. There was no document case in the wreckage of the car, and nothing on him, except a sort of diary lying on the study floor. But the rest of his stuff must be somewhere not far away."

"Far enough," replied the Werwolf. "In a mailbox."

Wearily he told Mackensen what Miller had stolen from the forger, and what Roschmann had just told him on the phone from Frankfurt. "Those papers will be in the hands of the authorities in the morning, or Tuesday at the latest. After that everyone on that list is on borrowed time. That includes

Roschmann, the owner of the house you're in, and me. I've spent the whole morning trying to warn everyone concerned to get out of the country inside twenty-four hours."

"So where do we go from here?" asked Mackensen.

"You get lost," replied his chief. "You're not on that list. I am, so I have to get out. Go back to your flat and wait until my successor contacts you. For the rest, it's over. Vulkan has fled and won't come back. With his departure his whole operation is going to fall apart unless someone new can come in and take over the project."

"What Vulkan? What project?"

"Since it's over, you might as well know. Vulkan was the name of Roschmann, the man you were supposed to protect from Miller. . . . " In a few sentences the Werwolf told the executioner why Roschmann had been so important, why his place in the project and the project itself were irreplaceable.

When he had finished, Mackensen uttered a low whistle and stared across the room at the form of Peter Miller. "That little boy sure fucked things up for everyone," he said.

The Werwolf seemed to pull himself together, and some of his old authority returned to his voice. "*Kamerad,* you must clear up the mess over there. You remember that disposal squad you used once before?"

"Yes, I know where to get them. They're not far from here."

"Call them up, bring them over. Have them leave the place without a trace of what happened. The man's wife must be coming back late tonight; she must never know what happened. Understand?"

"It'll be done," said Mackensen.

"Then make yourself scarce. One last thing. Before you go, finish that bastard Miller. Once and for all."

Mackensen looked across at the unconscious reporter with narrowed eyes. "It'll be a pleasure," he grated.

"Then good-by and good luck."

The phone went dead. Mackensen replaced it, took out an address book, thumbed through it, and dialed a number. He introduced himself to the man who answered and reminded him of the previous favor the man had done for the Comradeship. He told him where to come and what he would find.

"The car and body beside it have to go into a deep gorge off a mountain road. Plenty of gasoline over it, a real big blaze. Nothing identifiable about the man—go through his pockets and take everything, including his watch."

"Got it," said the voice on the phone. "I'll bring a trailer and winch."

"There's one last thing. In the study of the house you'll find another stiff on the floor and a bloodstained hearthrug. Get rid of them. Not in the car—a long, cold drop to the bottom of a long, cold lake. Well weighted. No traces. Okay?"

"No problem. We'll be there by five and gone by seven. I don't like to move that kind of cargo in daylight."

"Fine," said Mackensen. "I'll be gone before you get here. But you'll find things like I said."

He hung up, slid off the desk, and walked over to Miller. He pulled out his

Luger and automatically checked the breech, although he knew it was loaded.

"You little shit," he told the body and held the gun at arm's length pointing downward, lined up on the forehead.

Years of living like a predatory animal and surviving where others, victims and colleagues, had ended on a pathologist's slab had given Mackensen the senses of a leopard. He didn't see the shadow that fell onto the carpet from the open French window; he felt it and spun around, ready to fire. But the man was unarmed.

"Who the hell are you?" growled Mackensen, keeping him covered.

The man stood in the French window, dressed in the black leather leggings and jacket of a motorcyclist. In his left hand he carried his crash helmet, gripped by the short peak and held across his stomach. The man flicked a glance at the body at Mackensen's feet and the gun in his hand.

"I was sent for," he said innocently.

"Who by?" said Mackensen.

"Vulkan," replied the man. "My *Kamerad*, Roschmann."

Mackensen grunted and lowered the gun. "Well, he's gone."

"Gone?"

"Fucked off. Heading for South America. The whole project's off. And all thanks to this little bastard reporter." He jerked the gun barrel toward Miller.

"You going to finish him?" asked the man.

"Sure. He screwed up the project. Identified Roschmann and mailed the information to the police, along with a pile of other stuff. If you're in that file, you'd better get out too."

"What file?"

"The Odessa file."

"I'm not in it," said the man.

"Neither am I," growled Mackensen. "But the Werwolf is, and his orders are to finish this one off before we quit."

"The Werwolf?"

Something began to sound a small alarm inside Mackensen. He had just been told that in Germany no one apart from the Werwolf and himself knew about the Vulkan project. The others were in South America, from where he assumed the new arrival had come. But such a man would know about the Werwolf. His eyes narrowed slightly.

"You're from Buenos Aires?" he asked.

"No."

"Where from, then?"

"Jerusalem."

It took half a second before the meaning of the name made sense to Mackensen. Then he swung up his Luger to fire. Half a second is a long time, long enough to die.

The foam rubber inside the crash helmet was scorched when the Walther went off. But the nine-millimeter parabellum slug came through the fiberglass without a pause and took Mackensen high in the breastbone with the force of a kicking mule. The helmet dropped to the ground to reveal the agent's right hand, and from inside the cloud of blue smoke the PPK fired again.

Mackensen was a big man and a strong one. Despite the bullet in the chest he would have fired, but the second slug, entering his head two finger-widths above the right eyebrow, spoiled his aim. It also killed him.

Miller awoke on Monday afternoon in a private ward in Frankfurt General Hospital. He lay for half an hour, becoming slowly aware that his head was swathed in bandages and contained a pair of energetic artillery units. He found a buzzer and pressed it, but the nurse who came told him to lie quietly because he had a severe concussion.

So he lay and, piece by piece, recollected the events of the previous day until the middle of the morning. After that there was nothing. He dozed off and when he woke it was dark outside and a man was sitting by his bed. The man smiled.

Miller stared at him. "I don't know you," he said.

"Well, I know you," said the visitor.

Miller thought. "I've seen you," he said at length. "You were in Oster's house. With Leon and Motti."

"That's right. What else do you remember?"

"Almost everything. It's coming back."

"Roschmann?"

"Yes. I talked with him. I was going for the police."

"Roschmann's gone. Fled back to South America. The whole affair's over. Complete. Finished. Do you understand?"

Miller slowly shook his head. "Not quite. I've got one hell of a story. And I'm going to write it."

The visitor's smile faded. He leaned forward. "Listen, Miller. You're a lousy amateur, and you're lucky to be alive. You're going to write nothing. For one thing, you've got nothing to write. I've got Tauber's diary, and it's going back home with me, where it belongs. I read it last night. There was a photograph of an Army captain in your jacket pocket. Your father?"

Miller nodded.

"So that was what it was really all about?" asked the agent.

"Yes."

"Well, in a way I'm sorry. About your father, I mean. I never thought I'd say that to a German. Now about the file. What was it?"

Miller told him.

"Then why the hell couldn't you let us have it? You're an ungrateful man. We took a lot of trouble getting you in there, and when you get something you hand it over to your own people. We could have used that information to best advantage."

"I had to send it to someone, through Sigi. That meant by mail. You're so clever, you never let me have Leon's address."

Josef nodded. "All right. But either way, you have no story to tell. You have no evidence. The diary's gone, the file is gone. All that remains is your personal word. If you insist on talking, nobody will believe you except the Odessa, and they'll come for you. Or rather, they'll probably hit Sigi or your mother. They play rough, remember?"

Miller thought for a while. "What about my car?"

"You don't know about that. I forgot."

Josef told Miller about the bomb in it, and the way it went off. "I told you they play rough. The car has been found gutted by fire in a ravine. The body in it is unidentified, but not yours. Your story is that you were flagged down by a hitchhiker, he hit you with an iron bar and went off in it. The hospital will confirm you were brought in by a passing motorcyclist who called an ambulance when he saw you by the roadside. They won't recognize me again; I was in a helmet and goggles at the time. That's the official version, and it will stay. To make sure, I rang the German press agency two hours ago, claiming to be the hospital, and gave them the same story. You were the victim of a hitchhiker who later crashed and killed himself."

Josef stood up and prepared to leave. He looked down at Miller. "You're a lucky bastard, though you don't seem to realize it. I got the message your girl friend passed me, presumably on your instructions, at noon yesterday, and by riding like a maniac I made it from Munich to the house on the hill in two and a half hours dead. Which was what you almost were—dead. They had a guy who was going to kill you. I managed to interrupt him in time."

He turned, hand on the doorknob. "Take a word of advice. Claim the insurance on your car, get a Volkswagen, go back to Hamburg, marry Sigi, have kids, and stick to reporting. Don't tangle with professionals again."

Half an hour after he had gone, the nurse came back. "There's a phone call for you," she said.

It was Sigi, crying and laughing on the line. She had received an anonymous call telling her Peter was in Frankfurt General. "I'm on my way down right this minute," she said and hung up.

The phone rang again. "Miller? This is Hoffmann. I just saw a piece on the agency tapes. You got a bang on the head. Are you all right?"

"I'm fine, Herr Hoffmann," said Miller.

"Great. When are you going to be fit?"

"In a few days. Why?"

"I've got a story that's right up your alley. A lot of daughters of wealthy papas in Germany are going to the ski slopes and getting screwed by these handsome young ski-instructors. There's a clinic in Bavaria that gets them back out of trouble—for a fat fee and no word to Daddy about it. Seems some of the young studs take a rake-off from the clinic. A great little story. Sex amid the Snow, Orgies in Oberland. When can you start?"

Miller thought. "Next week."

"Excellent. By the way, that thing you were on. Nazi-hunting. Did you get the man? Is there a story at all?"

"No, Herr Hoffmann," said Miller slowly. "No story."

"Didn't think so. Hurry up and get well. See you in Hamburg."

Josef's plane from Frankfurt via London came into Lod Airport, Tel Aviv, as dusk was settling on Tuesday evening. He was met by two men in a car and taken to headquarters for debriefing by the colonel who had signed the cable from Cormorant. They talked until almost two in the morning, a stenographer noting it all down. When it was over, the colonel leaned back, smiled, and offered his agent a cigarette.

"Well done," he said simply. "We've checked on the factory and tipped off the authorities—anonymously, of course. The research section will be dismantled. We'll see to that, even if the German authorities don't. But they will. The scientists apparently didn't know whom they were working for. We'll approach them all privately, and most will agree to destroy their records. They know, if the story broke, the weight of opinion in Germany today is pro-Israeli. They'll get other jobs in industry and keep their mouths shut. So will Bonn, and so will we. What about Miller?"

"He'll do the same. What about those rockets?"

The colonel blew a column of smoke and gazed at the stars in the night sky outside. "I have a feeling they'll never fly now. Nasser has to be ready by the summer of 'sixty-seven at the latest, and if the research work in that Vulkan factory is destroyed, they'll never mount another operation in time to fit the guidance systems to the rockets before the summer of 'sixty-seven."

"Then the danger's over," said the agent.

The colonel smiled. "The danger's never over. It just changes shape. This particular danger may be over. The big one goes on. We're going to have to fight again, and maybe after that, before it's over. Anyway, you must be tired. You can go home now."

He reached into a drawer and produced a polyethylene bag of personal effects, while the agent deposited on the desk his false German passport, money, wallet, and keys. In a side room he changed clothes, leaving the German clothes with his superior.

At the door the colonel looked the figure up and down with approval and shook hands. "Welcome home, Major Uri Ben-Shaul."

The agent felt better back in his own identity, the one he had taken in 1947 when he first came to Israel and enlisted in the Palmach. He took a taxi back home to his flat in the suburbs and let himself in with the key that had just been returned to him with his other effects.

In the darkened bedroom he could make out the sleeping form of Rivka, his wife, the light blanket rising and falling with her breathing. He peeked into the children's room and looked down at their two boys: Shlomo, who was six, and the two-year-old baby, Dov.

He wanted badly to climb into bed beside his wife and sleep for several days, but there was one more job to be done. He set down his case and quietly undressed, taking off even the underclothes and socks. He dressed in fresh ones taken from the clothes chest, and Rivka slept on, undisturbed.

From the closet he took his uniform trousers, cleaned and pressed as they always were when he came home, and laced up the gleaming black calf-boots over them. His khaki shirts and ties were where they always were, with razor-sharp creases down the shirt where the hot iron had pressed. Over them he slipped his battle jacket, adorned only with the glinting steel wings of a paratroop officer and the five campaign ribbons he had earned in Sinai and in raids across the borders.

The final article was his red beret. When he had dressed he took several articles and stuffed them into a small bag. There was already a dim glint in the east when he got back outside and found his small car still parked where he had left it a month before in front of the apartment house.

Although it was only February 26, three days before the end of the last month of winter, the air was mild again and gave promise of a brilliant spring.

He drove eastward out of Tel Aviv and took the road to Jerusalem. There was a stillness about the dawn that he loved, a peace and a cleanness that never ceased to cause him wonder. He had seen it a thousand times on patrol in the desert, the phenomenon of a sunrise, cool and beautiful, before the onset of a day of blistering heat and sometimes of combat and death. It was the best time of the day.

The road led across the flat, fertile countryside of the littoral plain toward the ocher hills of Judea, through the waking village of Ramleh. After Ramleh there was in those days a detour around the Latroun Salient, five miles to skirt the front positions of the Jordanian forces. To his left he could see the morning breakfast fires of the Arab Legion sending up thin plumes of blue smoke.

There were a few Arabs awake in the village of Abu Gosh, and when he had climbed up the last hills to Jerusalem the sun had cleared the eastern horizon and glinted off the Dome of the Rock in the Arab section of the divided city.

He parked his car a quarter of a mile from his destination, the mausoleum of Yad Vashem, and walked the rest, down the avenue flanked by trees planted in memory of the gentiles who had tried to help, and to the great bronze doors that guarded the shrine to six million of his fellow Jews who had died in the holocaust.

The old gatekeeper told him it was not open so early in the morning, but he explained what he wanted, and the man let him in. He passed through into the Hall of Remembrance and glanced about him. He had been there before to pray for his own family, and still the massive gray granite blocks of which the hall was built overawed him.

He walked forward to the rail and gazed at the names written in black on the gray stone floor, in Hebrew and Roman letters. There was no light in the sepulcher but that from the Eternal Flame, flickering above the shallow black bowl from which it sprang.

By its light he could see the names across the floor, score upon score: Auschwitz, Treblinka, Belsen, Ravensbrück, Buchenwald. . . . There were too many to count, but he found the one he sought. Riga.

He did not need a yarmulka to cover himself, for he still wore his red beret, which would suffice. From his bag he took a fringed silk shawl, the tallith, the same kind of shawl Miller had found among the effects of the old man in Altona and had not understood. This he draped around his shoulders.

He took a prayer book from his bag and opened it at the right page. He advanced to the brass rail that separates the hall into two parts, gripped it with one hand, and gazed across it at the flame in front of him. Because he was not a religious man, he had to consult his prayer book frequently, as he recited the prayer already five thousand years old.

> *"Yitgaddal,*
> *Veyitkaddash,*
> *Shemay rabbah . . . "*

And so it was that, twenty-one years after it had died in Riga, a major of paratroops of the Army of Israel, standing on a hill in the Promised Land, finally said Kaddish for the soul of Salomon Tauber.

It would be agreeable if things in this world always finished with all the ends neatly tied up. That is very seldom the case. People go on, to live and die in their own appointed time and place. So far as it has been possible to establish, this is what happened to the main characters.

Peter Miller went home, married, and stuck to reporting the sort of things that people want to read over breakfast and in the hairdresser's. By the summer of 1970 Sigi was carrying their third child.

The men of the Odessa scattered. Eduard Roschmann's wife returned home and later received a cable from her husband telling her he was in Argentina. She refused to follow him. In the summer of 1965 she wrote to him at their old address, the Villa Jerbal, to ask him for a divorce before the Argentinian courts.

The letter was forwarded to his new address, and she got a reply consenting to her request, but stipulating the German courts, and enclosing a legal document agreeing to a divorce. She was awarded this in 1966. She still lives in Germany but has retaken her maiden name of Müller, of which there are tens of thousands in Germany. The man's first wife, Hella, still lives in Austria.

The Werwolf finally made his peace with his furious superiors in Argentina and settled on a small estate he bought with the money realized from the sale of his effects, on the Spanish island of Formenteria.

The radio factory went into liquidation. The scientists working on the guidance systems for the rockets of Helwan all found jobs in industry or the academic world. The project on which they had unwittingly been working for Roschmann, however, collapsed.

The rockets at Helwan never flew. The fuselages were ready, along with the rocket fuel. The warheads were under production. Those who may doubt the authenticity of those warheads should examine the evidence of Professor Otto Yoklek, given at the trial of Yossef ben Gal, June 10 to June 26, 1963, Basel Provincial Court, Switzerland. The forty preproduction rockets, helpless for want of the electronic systems necessary to guide them to their targets in Israel, were still standing in the deserted factory at Helwan when they were destroyed by bombers during the Six-Day War. Before that the German scientists had disconsolately returned to Germany.

The exposure to the authorities of Klaus Winzer's file upset a lot of Odessa applecarts. The year which began so well ended for them disastrously. So much so that years later a lawyer and investigator of the Z Commission in Ludwigsburg was able to say, "Nineteen sixty-four was a good year for us, yes, a very good year."

At the end of 1964 Chancellor Erhard, shaken by the exposures, issued a nationwide and international appeal for all those having knowledge of the whereabouts of wanted SS criminals to come forward and tell the authorities. The response was considerable, and the work of the men of Ludwigsburg received an enormous boost which continued for several more years.

Of the politicians behind the arms deal between Germany and Israel,

Chancellor Adenauer of Germany lived in his villa at Rhöndorf, above his beloved Rhine and close to Bonn, and died there on April 19, 1967. The Israeli Premier David Ben-Gurion stayed on as a member of the Knesset (Parliament) until 1970, then finally retired to his home on the kibbutz of Sede Boker, in the heart of the brown hills of the Negev, on the road from Beersheba to Eilat. He likes to receive visitors and talks with animation about many things, but not about the rockets of Helwan and the reprisal campaign against the German scientists who worked on them.

Of the secret-service men in the story, General Amit remained Controller until September 1968, and on his shoulders fell the massive responsibility of ensuring that his country was provided with pinpoint information in time for the Six-Day War. As history records, he succeeded brilliantly.

On his retirement he became chairman and managing director of the labor-owned Koor Industries of Israel. He still lives very modestly, and his charming wife, Yona, refuses, as ever, to employ a maid, preferring to do all her own housework.

His successor, who still holds the post, is General Zvi Zamir.

Major Uri Ben-Shaul was killed on Wednesday, June 7, 1967, at the head of a company of paratroops fighting their way into Old Jerusalem. He took a bullet in the head from an Arab Legionary and went down four hundred yards east of the Mandelbaum Gate.

Simon Wiesenthal still lives and works in Vienna, gathering a fact here, a tip there, slowly tracking down the whereabouts of wanted SS murderers, and each month and year brings him a crop of successes.

Leon died in Munich in 1968, and after his death the group of men he had led on his personal crusade of vengeance lost heart and split up.

And last, Top Sergeant Ulrich Frank, the tank commander who crossed Miller's path on the road to Vienna. He was wrong about the fate of his tank, the Dragon Rock. It did not go to the scrap heap. It was taken away on a low-loader, and he never saw it again. Forty months later he would not have recognized it anyway.

The steel-gray of its body had been painted out and covered with paint the color of dust-brown to merge with the landscape of the desert. The black cross of the German Army was gone from the turret and replaced by the pale blue six-pointed Star of David. The name he had given it was gone too, and it had been renamed *The Spirit of Masada*.

It was still commanded by a top sergeant, a hawk-nosed blackbearded man called Nathan Levy. On June 5, 1967, the M-48 began its first and only week of combat since it had rolled from the workshops of Detroit, Michigan, ten years before. It was one of those tanks that General Israel Tal hurled into the battle for the Mitla Pass two days later, and at noon on Saturday, June 10, caked with dust and oil, scored by bullets, its tracks worn to wafers by the rocks of Sinai, the old Patton rolled to a stop on the eastern bank of the Suez Canal.

The Dogs of War

For Giorgio, and Christian and Schlee,
And Big Marc and Black Johnny,
And the others in the unmarked graves.
At least we tried.

Cry "Havoc!" and let slip the dogs of war.

—William Shakespeare, *Julius Caesar*

That . . . be not told of my death,
Or made to grieve on account of me,
And that I be not buried in consecrated ground,
And that no sexton be asked to toll the bell,
And that nobody is wished to see my dead body,
And that no mourners walk behind me at my funeral,
And that no flowers be planted on my grave,
And that no man remember me,
To this I put my name.

—Thomas Hardy

PART I
The Crystal Mountain

ONE

There were no stars that night on the bush airstrip, nor any moon; just the West African darkness wrapping round the scattered groups like warm, wet velvet. The cloud cover was lying hardly off the tops of the iroko trees, and the waiting men prayed it would stay a while longer to shield them from the bombers.

At the end of the runway the battered old DC-4, which had just slipped in for a landing by runway lights that stayed alight for just the last fifteen seconds of final approach, turned and coughed its way blindly toward the palm-thatch huts.

Between two of them, five white men sat crouched in a Land Rover and stared toward the incoming aircraft. They said nothing, but the same thought was in each man's mind. If they did not get out of the battered and crumbling enclave before the forces of the central government overran the last few square miles, they could not get out alive. Each man had a price on his head and intended to see that no man collected it. They were the last of the mercenaries who had fought on contract for the side that had lost. Now it was time to go. So they watched the incoming and unexpected cargo plane with silent attention.

A Federal MIG-17 night fighter, probably flown by one of the six East German pilots sent down over the past three months to replace the Egyptians, who had a horror of flying at night, moaned across the sky to the west. It was out of sight above the cloud layers.

The pilot of the taxiing DC-4, unable to hear the scream of the jet above him, flicked on his own lights to see where he was going, and from the darkness a voice cried uselessly, "Kill de lights!" When the pilot had got his bearings, he turned them off anyway, and the fighter above was miles away. To the south there was a rumble of artillery where the front had finally crumbled as men who had had neither food nor bullets for two months threw down their guns and headed for the protecting bush forest.

The pilot of the DC-4 brought his plane to a halt twenty yards from the Superconstellation already parked on the apron, killed the engines, and climbed down to the concrete. An African ran over to him and there was a muttered conversation. The two men walked through the dark toward one of the larger groups of men, a blob of black against the darkness of the palm forest. The group parted as the two from the tarmac approached, until the white man who had flown in the DC-4 was face to face with the one who stood in the center. The white man had never seen him before, but he knew of him, and even in the darkness dimly illumined by a few cigarettes, he could recognize the man he had come to see.

The pilot wore no cap, so instead of saluting he inclined his head slightly. He had never done that before, not to a black, and could not have explained why he did it.

"My name is Captain Van Cleef," he said in English accented in the Afrikaner manner.

The African nodded his acknowledgment, his bushy black beard brushing the front of his striped camouflage uniform as he did so.

"It's a hazardous night for flying, Captain Van Cleef," he remarked dryly, "and a little late for more supplies."

His voice was deep and slow, the accent more like that of an English public-school man, which he was, than like an African. Van Cleef felt uncomfortable and again, as a hundred times during his run through the cloudbanks from the coast, asked himself why he had come.

"I didn't bring any supplies, sir. There weren't any more to bring."

Another precedent set. He had sworn he would not call the man "sir." Not a kaffir. It had just slipped out. But they were right, the other mercenary pilots in the hotel bar in Libreville, the ones who had met him. This one was different.

"Then why have you come?" asked the general softly. "The children perhaps? There are a number here the nuns would like to fly out to safety, but no more Caritas planes will come in tonight."

Van Cleef shook his head, then realized no one could see the gesture. He was embarrassed, and thankful that the darkness hid it. Around him the bodyguards clutched their submachine carbines and stared at him.

"No. I came to collect you. If you want to come, that is."

There was a long silence. He could feel the African staring at him through the gloom, occasionally caught a flash of eye-white as one of the attendants raised his cigarette.

"I see. Did your government instruct you to come in here tonight?"

"No," said Van Cleef. "It was my idea."

There was another long pause. The bearded head was nodding slowly in what could have been comprehension or bewilderment.

"I am very grateful," said the voice. "It must have been quite a trip. Actually I have my own transport. The Constellation. Which I hope will be able to take me away to exile."

Van Cleef felt relieved. He had no idea what the political repercussions would have been if he had flown back to Libreville with the general.

"I'll wait till you're off ground and gone," he said and nodded again. He felt like holding out his hand to shake, but did not know whether he ought. If he had but known it, the African general was in the same quandary. So he turned and walked back to his aircraft.

There was a silence for a while in the group of black men after he had left.

"Why does a South African, and an Afrikaner, do a thing like that, General?" one of them asked.

There was a flash of teeth as the general smiled briefly. "I don't think we shall ever understand that," he said.

A match spluttered as another cigarette was lit, the glow setting for a parting instant into sharp relief the faces of the men in the group. At the center was the general, taller than all but two of the guards, heavily built with burly chest and shoulders, distinguishable from others at several hundred yards by the bushy black beard that half the world had come to recognize.

In defeat, on the threshold of an exile he knew would be lonely and humiliating, he still commanded. Surrounded by his aides and several ministers, he was as always slightly aloof, withdrawn. To be alone is one of the prices of leadership; with him it was also a state of relax.

For two and a half years, sometimes by sheer force of personality when there was nothing else to employ, he had kept his millions of people together and fighting against the central Federal Government. All the experts had told the world they would have to collapse in a few weeks, two months at most. The odds were insuperable against them. Somehow they had kept fighting, surrounded, besieged, starving but defiant.

His enemies had refuted his leadership of his people, but few who had been there had any doubts. Even in defeat, as his car passed through the last village before the airstrip, the villagers had lined the mud road to chant their loyalty. Hours earlier, at the last meeting of the cabinet, the vote had asked him to leave. There would be reprisals in defeat, the spokesman for the caucus said, but a hundred times worse if he remained. So he was leaving, the man the Federal Goverment wanted dead by sunrise.

By his side stood one of his confidants, one of those whose loyalty had not been changed. A small, graying professor, he was called Dr. Okoye. He had decided to remain behind, to hide in the bush until he could return quietly to his home when the first wave of reprisals had ended. The two men had agreed to wait six months before making the first steps to contact each other.

Farther up the apron, the five mercenaries sat and watched the dim figure of the pilot return to his plane. The leader sat beside the African driver, and all five were smoking steadily.

"It must be the South African plane," said the leader and turned to one of the four other whites crouched in the Land Rover behind him. "Janni, go and ask the skipper if he'll make room for us."

A tall, rawboned, angular man climbed out of the rear of the vehicle. Like the others, he was dressed from head to foot in predominantly green jungle camouflage uniform, slashed with streaks of brown. He wore green canvas jackboots on his feet, the trousers tucked into them. From his belt hung a water bottle and a Bowie knife, three empty pouches for magazines for the FAL carbine over his shoulder. As he came round to the front of the Land Rover the leader called him again.

"Leave the FAL," he said, stretching out an arm to take the carbine, "and, Janni, make it good, huh? Because if we don't get out of here in that crate, we could get chopped up in a few days."

The man called Janni nodded, adjusted the beret on his head, and ambled toward the DC-4. Captain Van Cleef did not hear the rubber soles moving up behind him.

"*Naand, meneer.*"

Van Cleef spun round at the sound of the Afrikaans and took in the shape and size of the man beside him. Even in the darkness he could pick out the black and white skull-and-crossbones motif on the man's left shoulder. He nooded warily.

"*Naand. Jy Afrikaans?*"

The man nodded. "Jan Dupree," he said and held out his hand.

"Kobus Van Cleef," said the airman and shook.

"*Waar gaan-jy nou?*" asked Dupree.

"To Libreville. As soon as they finish loading. And you?"

Janni Dupree grinned. "I'm a bit stuck, me and my mates. We'll get the chop for sure if the Federals find us. Can you help us out?"

"How many of you?" asked Van Cleef.

"Five in all."

As a fellow mercenary, Van Cleef did not hesitate. Outlaws sometimes need each other.

"All right, get aboard. But hurry up. As soon as that Connie is off, so are we."

Dupree nodded his thanks and jog-trotted back to the Land Rover. The four other whites were standing in a group round the hood.

"It's okay, but we have to get aboard," the South African told them.

"Right, dump the hardware in the back and let's get moving," said the group leader. As the rifles and ammunition pouches thumped into the back of the vehicle, he leaned over to the black officer with second lieutenant's tabs who sat at the wheel.

"We have to go now," he said. "Take the Land Rover and dump it. Bury the guns and mark the spot. Leave your uniform and go for bush. Understand?"

The lieutenant, who had been in his last term of high school when he volunteered to fight and had been with the mercenary-led commando unit for the past year, nodded somberly, taking in the instructions.

"G'by, Patrick," the mercenary said. "I'm afraid it's over now."

The African looked up. "Perhaps," he said. "Perhaps it is over."

"Don't go on fighting," urged the white man. "There's no point."

"Not now," the lieutenant agreed. He nodded toward the steps of the Constellation, where the leader and his group were saying good-by. "But he is leaving for safety. That is good. He is still the leader. While he lives, we will not forget. We will say nothing, do nothing, but we will remember."

He started the engine of the Land Rover and swung the vehicle into a turn. "Good-by," he called.

The four other mercenaries called good-by and walked toward the DC-4.

The leader was about to follow them when two nuns fluttered up to him from the darkness of the bush behind the parking apron.

"Major."

The mercenary turned and recognized the first of them as the sister he had met months earlier, when fighting had raged in the zone where she ran a hospital and he had been forced to evacuate the whole complex.

"Sister Mary Joseph! What are you doing here?"

The elderly Irish nun began talking earnestly, holding the stained uniform sleeve of his jacket.

He nodded, "I'll try, I can do no more than that," he said when she had finished.

He walked across the apron to where the South African pilot was standing under the wing of his DC-4, and the two of them talked for several minutes. Finally the man in uniform came back to the waiting nuns.

"He says yes, but you must hurry, Sister. He wants to get this crate off the ground as soon as he can."

"God bless you," said the figure in the white habit and gave hurried orders to her companion. The latter ran to the rear of the aircraft and began to climb the short ladder to the passenger door. The other scurried back to the shade of a patch of palms behind the parking apron, from which a file of men soon emerged. Each carried a bundle in his arms. At the DC-4 the bundles were passed up to the waiting nun at the top of the steps. Behind her the co-pilot watched her lay the first three side by side in the beginning of a row down the aircraft's hull, then began gruffly to help, taking the bundles from the stretching hands beneath the aircraft's tail and passing them inside.

"God bless you," whispered the Irish nun.

One of the bundles deposited a few ounces of liquid green excrement onto the co-pilot's sleeve. "Bloody hell," he muttered and went on working.

Left alone, the leader of the group of mercenaries glanced toward the Superconstellation. A file of refugees, mainly the relations of the leaders of the defeated people, was climbing up the rear steps. In the dim light from the airplane's door he caught sight of the man he wanted to see. As he approached, the man was about to mount the steps while others waited to pull them away. One of them called to him.

"Sah. Major Shannon come."

The general turned as Shannon approached, and even at this hour he managed a grin.

"So, Shannon, do you want to come along?"

Shannon stepped in front of him and brought up a salute. The general acknowledged it.

"No thank you, sir. We have transport to Libreville. I just wanted to say good-by."

"Yes. It was a long fight. Now it's over, I'm afraid. For some years, at any rate. I find it hard to believe my people will continue to live in servitude forever. By the way, have you and your colleagues been paid up to contract?"

"Yes, thank you, sir. We're all up to date," replied the mercenary. The African nodded somberly.

"Well, good-by, then. And thank you for all you were able to do." He held out his hand, and the two men shook.

"There's one more thing, sir," said Shannon. "Me and the boys, we were talking things over, sitting in the jeep. If there's ever any time— Well, if you should ever need us, you only have to let us know. We'll all come. You only have to call. The boys want you to know that."

The general stared at him for several seconds. "This night is full of surprises," he said slowly. "You may not know it yet, but half my senior advisers and all of the wealthy ones are crossing the lines tonight to ingratiate themselves with the enemy. Most of the others will follow suit within a month. Thank you for your offer, Mr. Shannon. I will remember it. But how about yourself? What do the mercenaries do now?"

"We'll have to look around for more work."

"Another fight, Major Shannon?"

"Another fight, sir."

"But always somebody else's."

"That's our way of life," said Shannon.

"And you think you will fight again, you and your men?"

"Yes. We'll fight again."

The general laughed softly. " 'Cry "Havoc!" and let slip the dogs of war,' " he murmured.

"Sir?"

"Shakespeare, Mr. Shannon, just a bit of Shakespeare. Well, now, I must go. The pilot is waiting. Good-by again, and good luck."

He turned and walked up the steps into the dimly lit interior of the Superconstellation just as the first of the four engines coughed into life. Shannon stepped back and gave the man who had employed his services for a year and a half a last salute.

"Good luck to you," he said, half to himself. "You'll need it."

He turned and walked back to the waiting DC-4. When the door had closed, Van Cleef kept the aircraft on the apron, engines turning, as he watched the dim droop-nosed shape of the Super Connie rumble down the runway through the gloom past his nose, and finally lift off. Neither plane carried any lights, but from the cockpit of the Douglas the Afrikaner could make out the three fins of the Constellation vanishing over the palm trees to the south and into the welcoming clouds. Only then did he ease the DC-4 forward to the take-off point.

It was close to an hour before Van Cleef ordered his co-pilot to switch on the cabin lights, an hour of jinking from cloudbank to cloudbank, breaking cover and scooting across low racks of altostratus to find cover again with another, denser bank, always seeking to avoid being caught out in the moonlit white plains by a roving MIG. Only when he knew he was as far out over the gulf, with the coast many miles astern, did he allow the lights on.

Behind him they lit up a weird spectacle which could have been drawn by Doré in one of his blacker moods. The floor of the aircraft was carpeted with sodden and fouled blankets. Their previous contents lay writhing in rows down both sides of the cargo space, forty small children, shrunken, wizened, deformed by malnutrition. Sister Mary Joseph rose from her crouch behind the cabin door and began to move among the starvelings, each of whom had a piece of sticking plaster stuck to his or her forehead, just below the line of the hair long since turned to an ocher red by anemia. The plaster bore in ball-point letters the relevant information for the orphanage outside Libreville. Just name and number; they don't give rank to losers.

In the tail of the plane the five mercenaries blinked in the light and glanced at their fellow passengers. They had seen it all before, many times, over the past months. Each man felt some disgust, but none showed it. You can get used to anything eventually. In the Congo, Yemen, Katanga, Sudan. Always the same story, always the kids. And always nothing you can do about it. So they reasoned, and pulled out their cigarettes.

The cabin lights allowed them to see one another properly for the first time since sundown the previous evening. The uniforms were stained with sweat and the red earth, and the faces drawn with fatigue. The leader sat with his back to the washroom door, feet straight out, facing up the fuselage toward the pilot's cabin. Carlo Alfred Thomas Shannon, thirty-three, blond hair cropped to a ragged crew-cut. Very short hair is more convenient in the tropics because the sweat runs out easier and the bugs can't get in. Nicknamed Cat Shannon, he came originally from County Tyrone in the province of Ulster. Sent by his father to be educated at a minor English public school, he no longer carried the distinctive accent of Northern Ireland.

After five years in the Royal Marines, he had left to try his hand at civilian life and six years ago had found himself working for a London-based trading company in Uganda. One sunny morning he quietly closed his accounts ledgers, climbed into his Land Rover and drove westward to the Congolese border. A week later he signed on as a mercenary in Mike Hoare's Fifth Commando at Stanleyville.

He had seen Hoare depart and John-John Peters take over, had quarreled with Peters and driven north to join Denard at Paulis, had been in the Stanleyville mutiny two years later and, after the Frenchman's evacuation to Rhodesia with head wounds, had joined Black Jacques Schramme, the Belgian planter-turned-mercenary, on the long march to Bukavu and thence to Kigali. After repatriation by the Red Cross, he had promptly volunteered for another African war and had finally taken command of his own battalion. But too late to win, always too late to win.

He lay with his back against the washroom door as the DC-4 droned on toward Libreville and let his mind range back over the past year and a half. Thinking of the future was harder, for his claim to the general that he and his men would go to another war was based more on optimism than on foreknowledge. In fact he had no idea where the next job would come from. But although he could not know it that night in the plane, he and his men would fight again and would shake some mighty citadels before they finally went down.

To his immediate left sat the man who was arguably the best mortarman north of the Zambesi. Big Jan Dupree was twenty-eight and came from Paarl in Cape Province, a descendant of impoverished Huguenots whose ancestors had fled to the Cape of Good Hope from the wrath of Mazarin more than three hundred years ago. His hatchet face, dominated by a curved beak of a nose above a thin-lipped mouth, looked even more haggard than usual, his exhaustion furrowing deep lines down each cheek. The eyelids were down over the pale blue eyes, the sandy eyebrows and hair were smudged with dirt. He glanced down at the children lying along the aisle of the plane, muttered "*Bliksems*" (bastards) at the world of possession and privilege he held responsible for the ills of this planet, and tried to get to sleep.

By his side sprawled Marc Vlaminck, Tiny Marc, so called because of his vast bulk. A Fleming from Ostend, he stood 6 feet 3 inches in his socks, when he wore any, and weighed 250 pounds. Some people thought he might be fat. He was not. He was regarded with trepidation by the police of Ostend, for the most part peaceable men who would rather avoid problems than seek them out, and was viewed with kindly appreciation by the glaziers and carpenters of that city for the work he provided them. They said you could tell a bar where Tiny Marc had become playful by the number of artisans it needed to put it back together again.

An orphan, he had been brought up in an institution run by priests, who had tried to beat some sense of respect into the overgrown boy, and so repeatedly that even Marc had finally lost patience and, at the age of thirteen, laid one of the cane-wielding holy fathers cold along the flagstones with a single punch.

After that it had been a series of reformatories, then approved school, a dose of juvenile prison, and an almost communal sigh of relief when he enlisted in the paratroops. He had been one of the five hundred men who dropped onto Stanleyville with Colonel Laurent to rescue the missionaries whom the local Simba chief, Christophe Gbenye, threatened to roast alive in the main square.

Within forty minutes of hitting the airfield, Tiny Marc had found his vocation in life. After a week he went AWOL to avoid being repatriated to barracks in Belgium, and joined the mercenaries. Apart from his fists and shoulders, Tiny Marc was extremely useful with a bazooka, his favorite weapon, which he handled with the easy nonchalance of a boy with a peashooter.

The night he flew out of the enclave toward Libreville he was just thirty.

Across the fuselage from the Belgian sat Jean-Baptiste Langarotti, thirty-one. Short, compact, lean, and olive-skinned, he was a Corsican, born and raised in the town of Calvi. At the age of eighteen he had been called up by France to go and fight as one of the hundred thousand "appelés" in the Algerian war. Halfway through his eighteen months he had signed on as a regular and later had transferred to the 10th Colonial Paratroops, the dreaded red berets commanded by General Massu and known simply as *les paras*. He was twenty-one when the crunch came and some units of the professional French colonial army rallied to the cause of an eternally French Algeria, a cause embodied for the moment in the organization of the OAS. Langarotti went with the OAS, deserted, and after the failure of the April 1961 putsch, went underground. He was caught in France three years later, living under a false name, and spent four years in prison, eating his heart out in the dark and sunless cells of first the Santé in Paris, then Tours, and finally the Ile de Ré. He was a bad prisoner, and two guards would carry the marks to prove it until they died.

Beaten half to death several times for attacks on guards, he had served his full time without remission, and emerged in 1968 with only one fear in the world, the fear of small enclosed spaces, cells and holes. He had long since vowed never to return to one, even if staying out cost him his life, and to take half a dozen men with him if "they" ever came for him again. Within three months of release he had flown down to Africa by paying his own way, talked himself into a war, and joined Shannon as a professional mercenary. Since being released from prison he had practiced steadily with the weapon he had learned to use first as a boy in Corsica and with which he had later made himself a reputation in the back streets of Algiers. Round his left wrist he wore a broad leather razor strop, which was held in place by two press-studs. In moments of idleness he would take it off, turn it over to the side unmarked by the studs, and wrap it round his left fist. That was where it was as he whiled away the time to Libreville. In his right hand was the knife, the six-inch-bladed bone-handled weapon that he could use so fast it was back in its sleeve-sheath before the victim knew he'd been cut. In steady rhythm the blade, already razor-sharp, moved backward and forward across the tense leather of the strop, becoming with each stroke a mite sharper. The movement soothed his nerves. It also annoyed everybody else, but no one ever complained. Nor did those who knew him ever quarrel with the soft voice or the sad half-smile of the little man.

Sandwiched between Langarotti and Shannon was the oldest man in the party, a German. Kurt Semmler was forty, and it was he who, in the early days back in the enclave, had devised the skull-and-crossbones motif that the mercenaries and their African trainees wore. It was also he who had cleared a five-mile sector of Federal soldiers by marking out the front line with stakes, each bearing the head of one of the previous day's Federal casualties. For a month after that, his was the quietest sector of the campaign. Born in 1930, he had been brought up in Hitler's Germany, the son of a Munich engineer who had later died on the Russian front with the Todt Organisation.

At the age of fifteen, a fervent Hitler Youth graduate, as indeed was almost the entire youth of the country after twelve years of Hitler, he had commanded a small unit of children younger than himself and old men over seventy. His mission, armed with one Panzerfaust and three bolt-action rifles, had been to stop the columns of General George Patton's tanks. Not surprisingly, he had failed, and spent his adolescence in Bavaria under American occupation, which he hated. He had little time for his mother, a religious fanatic who wanted him to become a priest. At seventeen he ran away, crossed the French frontier at Strasbourg, and signed on in the Foreign Legion at the recruiting office sited in Strasbourg for the purpose of picking up runaway Germans and Belgians. After a year in Sidi-bel-Abbès, he went with the expeditionary force to Indochina. Eight years and Dien Bien Phu later, with a lung removed by surgeons at Tourane (Danang), fortunately unable to watch the final humiliation in Hanoi, he was flown back to France. After recuperation he was sent to Algeria in 1958 as a top sergeant in the elite of the elite of the French colonial army, the 1ᵉʳ Régiment Etranger Parachutiste. He was one of a handful who had already survived the utter destruction of the 1ᵉʳ REP twice in Indochina, when it was at battalion size and later at regiment size. He revered only two men, Colonel Roger Faulques, who had been in the original Compagnie Etrangère Parachutiste when, at company strength, it had been wiped out the first time, and Commandant le Bras, another veteran, who now commanded the Garde Républicaine of the Republic of Gabon and kept that uranium-rich state safe for France. Even Colonel Mark Rodin, who had once commanded him, had lost his respect when the OAS finally crumbled.

Semmler had been in the 1ᵉʳ REP when it marched to a man into perdition in the putsch of Algiers and was later disbanded permanently by Charles de Gaulle. He had followed where his French officers had led, and later, picked up just after Algerian independence in Marseilles in September 1962, had served two years in prison. His four rows of campaign ribbons had saved him from worse. A civilian for the first time in twenty years in 1964, he had been contacted by a former cellmate with a proposition—to join him in a smuggling operation in the Mediterranean. For three years, apart from one spent in an Italian jail, he had run spirits, gold, and occasionally arms from one end of the Meditarranean to the other. He had been making a fortune on the Italy-Yugoslavia cigarette run when his partner had double-crossed the buyers and the sellers at the same time, pointed the finger at Semmler, and vanished with the money. Wanted by a lot of belligerent gentlemen, Semmler had hitched a lift by sea to Spain, ridden a series of buses to Lisbon, contacted an arms-dealer friend, and taken passage to the African war, about which he had read in the papers. Shannon had taken him like a shot, for with sixteen years of combat he was more experienced than all of them in jungle warfare. He too dozed on the flight to Libreville.

It was two hours before dawn when the DC-4 began to circle the airport. Above the mewling of the children, another sound could be made out, the sound of a man whistling. It was Shannon. His colleagues knew he always whistled when he was going into action or coming out of it. They also knew from Shannon that the tune was called "Spanish Harlem."

The DC-4 circled the airport at Libreville twice while Van Cleef talked to ground control. As the old cargo plane rolled to a halt at the end of a runway, a military jeep carrying two French officers swerved up in front of the nose; they beckoned Van Cleef to follow them round the taxi track.

They led him away from the main airport buildings to a cluster of huts on the far side of the airport, and it was here that the DC-4 ws signaled to halt but keep its engines running. Within seconds a set of steps was up against the rear of the airplane, and from the inside the co-pilot heaved open the door. A *képi* poked inside and surveyed the interior, the nose beneath it wrinkling in distaste at the smell. The French officer's eyes came to rest on the five mercenaries, and he beckoned them to follow him down the tarmac. When they were on the ground the officer gestured to the co-pilot to close the door, and without more ado the DC-4 moved forward again to roll around the airport to the main buildings, where a team of French Red Cross nurses and doctors was waiting to receive the children. As the aircraft swung past them, the five mercenaries waved their thanks to Van Cleef up in his flight deck and turned to follow the French officer.

They had to wait an hour in one of the huts, perched uncomfortably on upright wooden chairs, while several other young French servicemen peeked in through the door to take a look at *les affreux*, the terrible ones. Finally a jeep squealed to a halt outside and there was the smack of feet coming to attention in the corridor. When the door opened it was to admit a tanned, hard-faced senior officer in tropical fawn uniform and a *képi* with gold braid ringing the peak. Shannon took in the keen, darting eyes, the iron-gray hair cropped short beneath the *képi*, the parachutist's wings pinned above the five rows of campaign ribbons, and the sight of Semmler leaping to ramrod attention, chin up, five fingers pointing straight down what had once been the seams of his combat trousers. Shannon needed no more to tell him who the visitor was—the legendary Le Bras.

The Indochina/Algeria veteran shook hands with each, pausing in front of Semmler longer.

"*Alors,* Semmler?" he said softly, with a slow smile. "Still fighting. But not an adjutant any more. A captain now, I see."

Semmler was embarrassed. "*Oui, mon commandant—pardon, mon colonel.* Just temporary."

Le Bras nodded pensively several times. Then he addressed them all. "I will have you quartered comfortably. No doubt you will appreciate a bath, a shave, and some food. Apparently you have no other clothes; some will be provided. I am afraid for the time being you will have to remain confined to your quarters. This is solely a precaution. There are a lot of newspapermen in town, and all forms of contact with them must be avoided. As soon as it is feasible, we will arrange to fly you back to Europe."

He had said all he came to say. Raising his right hand to his *képi* brim, he left.

An hour later, after a journey in a closed truck and entrance by the back door, the men were in their quarters, the five bedrooms of the top floor of the Gamba Hotel, a new construction situated only five hundred yards from the airport building across the road and therefore miles from the center of town. The young officer who accompanied them told them they would have to take their meals in their rooms and remain there until further notice. He provided them with towels, razors, toothpaste and brushes, soap, and sponges. A tray of coffee had already arrived, and each man sank gratefully into a deep, steaming, soap-smelling bath, the first in more than six months.

At noon an army barber came, and a corporal with piles of slacks and shirts, underwear and socks, pajamas and canvas shoes. They tried them on and selected the ones they wanted, and the corporal retired with the surplus. The officer was back at one with four waiters bearing lunch, and told them they must stay away from the balconies. If they wanted to exercise in their confinement they would have to do it in their rooms. He would return that evening with a selection of books and magazines, though he could not promise English or Afrikaans.

After eating as they never had in the previous six months, since their last leave period from the fighting, the five men rolled into bed and slept. While they snored on unaccustomed mattresses between unbelievable sheets, Van Cleef lifted his DC-4 off the tarmac in the dusk, flew a mile away past the windows of the Gamba Hotel, and headed south for Caprivi and Johannesburg. His job was done.

The five mercenaries spent four weeks on the top floor of the hotel, while press interest in them died down and the reporters were all called back to their head offices by editors who saw no point in keeping men in a city where there was no news to be had. One evening, without warning, a captain on the staff of Commandant Le Bras came to see the men. He grinned broadly.

"Messieurs, I have news for you. You are flying out tonight. To Paris. You are all booked on the Air Afrique flight at twenty-three-thirty hours."

The five men, bored to distraction by their prolonged confinement, cheered.

The flight to Paris took ten hours, with stops at Douala and Nice. Just before ten the following day they emerged into the blustery cold of Le Bourget airport on a mid-February morning. In the airport coffee lounge they said their good-bys. Dupree elected to take the transit coach to Orly and buy himself a single ticket on the next SAA flight to Johannesburg and Cape Town. Semmler opted to go too, but first he would return to Munich for a visit. Vlaminck said he would head for the Gare du Nord and take the first express to Brussels and connect for Ostend. Langarotti was going to the Gare de Lyon to take the train to Marseilles.

They agreed to stay in touch and looked to Shannon. He was their leader; it would be up to him to look for work, another contract, another war. Similarly, if any of them heard of anything that involved a group, he would want to contact one of the group, and Shannon was the obvious one.

"I'll stay in Paris for a while," said Shannon. "There's more chance of an interim job here than in London."

So they exchanged addresses—*poste restante* addresses, or cafés where the barman would pass on a message or keep a letter until the addressee dropped in for a drink. And then they parted and went their separate ways.

The security surrounding their flight back from Africa had been tight, and there were no waiting newspapermen at Le Bourget. But someone had heard of their arrival, for he was waiting for Shannon when, after the others had left, the group's leader came out of the terminal building.

"Shannon." The voice pronounced the name in the French way, and the tone was not friendly. Shannon turned, and his eyes narrowed fractionally as he saw the figure standing ten yards from him. The man was burly, with a down-turned mustache. He wore a heavy coat against the winter cold and walked forward until the two men faced each other at two feet. To judge by the way they surveyed each other, there was no love lost between them.

"Roux," said Shannon.

"So you're back," snarled the Frenchman.

"Yes. We're back."

The man called Roux sneered. "And you lost."

"We didn't have much choice," said Shannon.

"A word of advice, my friend," snapped Roux. "Go back to your own country. Do not stay here. It would be unwise. This is my city. If there is any contract to be found here, I will hear first news of it, I will conclude it. And I will select those who share in it."

For answer Shannon walked to the first taxi waiting at the curb and humped his bag into the back. Roux walked after him, his face mottling with anger.

"Listen to me, Shannon. I'm warning you—"

The Irishman turned to face him again. "No, you listen to me, Roux. I'll stay in Paris just as long as I want. I was never impressed by you in the Congo, and I'm not now. So get stuffed."

As the taxi moved away, Roux stared after it angrily. He was muttering to himself as he strode toward the parking lot and his own automobile.

He switched on the engine, slipped into gear, and sat for a few moments staring through the windscreen. "One day I'll kill that bastard," he murmured to himself. But the thought hardly put him in a better mood.

TWO

Jack Mulrooney shifted his bulk on the canvas-and-frame cot beneath the mosquito netting and watched the slow lightening of the darkness above the trees to the east. A faint paling, enough to make out the trees towering over the clearing. He drew on his cigarette and cursed the primeval jungle which surrounded him, and, like all old Africa hands, asked himself once again why he ever returned to the pestiferous continent.

If he had really tried to analyze himself, he would have admitted he could not live anywhere else, certainly not in London or even Britain. He couldn't take the cities, the rules and regulations, the taxes, the cold. Like all old hands, he alternately loved and hated Africa but conceded it had got into his blood over the past quarter-century, along with the malaria, the whisky, and the million insect stings and bites.

He had come out from England in 1945 at the age of twenty-five, after five years as a fitter in the Royal Air Force, part of them at Takoradi, where he had assembled crated Spitfires for onward flight to East Africa and the Middle East the long way around. That had been his first sight of Africa, and on demobilization he had taken his discharge pay, bidden good-by to frozen, rationed London in December 1945, and taken ship for West Africa. Someone had told him there were fortunes to be made in Africa.

He had found no fortunes but after wandering the continent had got himself a small tin concession in the Benue Plateau, eighty miles from Jos in Nigeria. Prices had been good while the Malay emergency was on. He had worked alongside his Tiv laborers, and at the English club where the colonial ladies gossiped away the last days of the empire they said he had "gone native" and it was a damned bad show. The truth was, Mulrooney really preferred the African way of life. He liked the bush; he liked the Africans, who did not seem to mind that he swore and roared and cuffed them to get more work done. He also sat and took palm wine with them and observed the tribal taboos. He did not patronize them. His tin concession ran out in 1960, around the time of independence, and he went to work as a charge hand for a company running a larger and more efficient concession nearby. It was called Manson Consolidated, and when that concession also was exhausted, in 1962, he was signed on the staff.

At fifty he was still a big, powerful man, large-boned and strong as an ox. His hands were enormous, chipped and scarred by years in the mines. He ran one of them through his wild, crinkly gray hair and with the other stubbed out the cigarette in the damp red earth beneath the cot. It was lighter now; soon it would be dawn. He could hear his cook blowing on the beginnings of a fire on the other side of the clearing.

Mulrooney called himself mining engineer, although he had no degree in mining or engineering. He had taken a course in both and added what no university could ever teach—twenty-five years of hard experience. He had burrowed for gold on the Rand and copper outside Ndola; drilled for precious water in Somaliland, grubbed for diamonds in Sierra Leone. He could tell an unsafe mineshaft by instinct, and the presence of an ore deposit by the smell. At least that was his claim, and after he had drunk his habitual twenty bottles of beer in the shanty town of an evening, no one was going to argue with him. In reality, he was one of the last of the old prospectors. He knew ManCon gave him the little jobs, the ones in the deep bush, the wild country that was miles from civilization and still had to be checked out, but he liked it that way. He preferred to work alone; it was his way of life.

The latest job had certainly fulfilled these conditions. For three months he had been prospecting in the foothills of the range called the Crystal Mountains in the hinterland of the republic of Zangaro, a tiny enclave on the coast of West Africa.

He had been told where to concentrate his survey, around the Crystal Mountain itself. The chain of large hills, curved hummocks rising to two or three thousand feet, ran in a line from one side of the republic to the other, parallel to the coast and forty miles from it. The range divided the coastal plain from the hinterland. There was only one gap in the chain, and through it ran the only access to the interior, a narrow dirt road, baked like concrete in summer, a quagmire in winter. Beyond the mountains, the natives were the Vindu, a tribe of almost Iron Age development, except that their implements were of wood. He had been in some wild places but vowed he had never seen anything as backward as the hinterland of Zangaro.

Set on the farther side of the range of hills was the single mountain that gave its name to the rest. It was not even the biggest of them. Forty years earlier a lone missionary, penetrating the hills into the interior, branched to the south after following the gap in the range and after twenty miles glimpsed a hill set aside from the rest. It had rained the previous night, a torrential downpour, one of the many that gave the area its annual rainfall of three hundred inches during five soaking months. As the priest looked, he saw that the mountain seemed to be glittering in the morning sun, and he called it the Crystal Mountain. He noted this in his diary. Two days later he was clubbed and eaten. The diary was found by a patrol of colonial soldiers a year later, being used as a juju by a local village. The soldiers did their duty and wiped out the village, then returned to the coast and handed the diary to the mission society. Thus the name the priest had given to the mountain lived on, even if nothing else he did for an ungrateful world was remembered. Later the same name was given to the entire range of hills.

What the man had seen in the morning light was not crystal but a myriad of streams caused by the water of the night's rain cascading off the mountain. Rain was also cascading off all the other mountains, but the sight of it was hidden by the dense jungle vegetation that covered them all, like a chunky green blanket when seen from afar, which proved to be a steaming hell when penetrated. The one that glittered with a thousand rivulets did so because the vegetation was substantially thinner on the flanks of this hill. It never occurred to the missionary, or to any of the other dozen white men who had ever seen it, to wonder why.

After three months living in the steaming hell of the jungles that surrounded Crystal Mountain, Mulrooney knew why.

He had started by circling the entire mountain and had discovered that there was effectively a gap between the seaward flank and the rest of the chain. This set the Crystal Mountain eastward of the main chain, standing on its own. Because it was lower than the highest peaks to seaward, it was invisible from the other side. Nor was it particularly noticeable in any other way, except that it had more streams running off it per mile of hillside than ran off the other hills, to north and south.

Mulrooney counted them all, both on the Crystal Mountain and on its companions. There was no doubt of it. The water ran off the other mountains after rain, but a lot of water was soaked up in the soil. The other mountains had twenty feet of topsoil over the basic rock structure beneath, the Crystal Mountain hardly any. He had his native workers, locally recruited Vindu, bore a series of holes with the augur he had with him, and confirmed the difference in depth of the topsoil in twenty places. From these he would work out why.

Over millions of years the earth had been formed by the decomposition of the rock and by dust carried on the wind, and although each rainfall had eroded some of it down the slopes into the streams, and from the streams to the rivers and then to the shallow, silted estuary, some earth had also remained, lodged in little crannies, left alone by the running water which had bored its own holes in the soft rock. And these holes had become drains, so that part of the rainfall ran off the mountain, finding its own channels and wearing them deeper and deeper, and some had sunk into the mountain, both having the effect of leaving part of the topsoil intact. Thus the earth layer had built up and up, a little thicker each century or millennium. The birds and the wind had brought seeds, which had found niches of earth and flourished there, their roots contributing to the process of retaining the earth on the hill slopes. When Mulrooney saw the hills, there was enough rich earth to sustain mighty trees and tangled vines which covered the slopes and the summits of all the hills. All except one.

On this one the water could not burrow channels that became streams, nor could it sink into the rock face, especially on the steepest face, which was to the east, toward the hinterland. Here the earth had collected in pockets, and the pockets had produced clumps of bush, grass, and fern. From niche to niche the vegetation had reached out to itself, linking vines and tendrils in a thin screen across bare patches of rock regularly washed clean by the falling water of the rain season. It was these patches of glistening wet amid the green that the missionary had seen before he died. The reason for the change was simple: the separate hill was of a different rock from the main range, an ancient rock, hard as granite as compared to the soft, more recent rock of the main chain of hills.

Mulrooney had completed his circuit of the mountain and established this beyond a doubt. It took him fortnight to do it and to establish that no less than seventy streams ran off the Crystal Mountain. Most of them joined up into three main streams that flowed away eastward out of the foothills into the deeper valley. He noticed something else. Along the banks of the streams that came off this mountain, the soil color and the vegetation were different. Some plants appeared unaffected; others were stunted or nonexistent, although they flourished on the other mountains and beside the other streams.

Mulrooney set about charting the seventy streams, drawing his map as he went. He also took samples of the sand and gravel along the beds of the streams, starting with the surface gravel, then working down to bedrock.

In each case he took two buckets full of gravel, poured them out onto a tarpaulin, and coned and quartered. This is a process of sample-taking. He piled the gravel into a cone, then quartered it with a shovel blade, took the two opposite quarters of his choice, remixed them, and made another cone. Then he quartered that one, working down till he had a cross-section of the sample weighing two to three pounds. Then this went into a polyethylene-lined canvas bag after drying; the bag was sealed and carefully labeled. In a month he had fifteen hundred pounds of sand and gravel in six hundred bags from the beds of the seventy streams. Then he started on the mountain itself.

He already believed his sacks of gravel would prove to contain, under laboratory examination, quantities of alluvial tin, minute particles washed down from the mountain over tens of thousand of years, showing that there was cassiterite, or tin ore buried in the Crystal Mountain.

He divided the mountain faces into sections, seeking to identify the birthplaces of the streams and the rock faces that fed them in the wet season. By the end of the week he knew there was no mother lode of tin inside the rock, but suspected what geologists called a disseminated deposit. The signs of mineralization were everywhere. Beneath the trailing tendrils of vegetation he found faces of rock shot through with stringers, half-inch-wide veins like the capillaries in a drinker's nose, of milky-white quartz, lacing yard after yard of bare rock face.

Everything he saw about him said "tin." He went right around the mountain again three times, and his observations confirmed the disseminated deposit, the ever-present stringers of white in the dark gray rock. With hammer and chisel he smashed holes deep in the rock, and the picture was still the same. Sometimes he thought he saw dark blurs in the quartz, confirming the presence of tin.

Then he began chipping in earnest, marking his progress as he went. He took samples of the pure white stringers of quartz, and to be on the safe side he also took samples of the country rock, the rock between the veins. Three months after he had entered the primeval forest east of the mountains, he was finished. He had another fifteen hundred pounds of rock to carry back to the coast with him. The whole ton and a half of rock and alluvial samples had been carried in portions every three days back from his working camp to the main camp, where he now lay waiting for dawn, and stacked in cones under tarpaulins.

After coffee and breakfast the bearers, whose terms he had negotiated the previous day, would come from the village and carry his trophies back to the track that called itself a road and linked the hinterland with the coast. There, in a roadside village, lay his two-ton truck, immobilized by the absence of the key and distributor rotor that lay in his knapsack. It should still work, if the natives had not hacked it to bits. He had paid the village chief enough to look after it. With his samples aboard the truck and twenty porters walking ahead to pull the lurching vehicle up the gradients and out of the ditches, he would be back in the capital in three days. After a cable to London, he would have to wait several days for the company's chartered ship to come and take him off. He would have preferred to turn north at the coast highway and drive the extra hundred miles into the neighboring republic, where there was a good airport, and freight his samples home. But the agreement between ManCon and the Zangaran government specified that he would take them back to the capital.

Jack Mulrooney heaved himself out of his cot, swung aside the netting, and roared at his cook, "Hey, Dingaling, where's my bloody coffee?"

The Vindu cook, who did not understand a word except "coffee," grinned from beside the fire and waved happily. Mulrooney strode across the clearing toward his canvas washbucket and began scratching as the mosquitoes descended on his sweating torso.

"Bloody Africa," he muttered as he doused his face. But he was content that morning. He was convinced he had found both alluvial tin and tin-bearing rock. The only question was how much tin per rock-ton. With tin standing at about $3300 per ton, it would be up to the analysts and mining economists to work out if the quantity of tin per ton of rock merited establishing a mining camp with its complex machinery and teams of workers, not to mention improved access to the coast by a narrow-gauge railway that would have to be built from scratch. And it was certainly a godforsaken and inaccessible place. As usual, everything would be worked out, taken up or thrown away, on the basis of pounds, shillings, and pence. The was the way of the world. He slapped another mosquito off his upper arm and pulled on his T-shirt.

Six days later Jack Mulrooney leaned over the rail of a small coaster chartered by his company and spat over the side as the coast of Zangaro slid away.

"Bloody bastards," he muttered savagely. He carried a series of livid bruises about his chest and back, and a raw graze down one cheek, the outcome of swinging rifle butts when the troops had raided the hotel.

It had taken him two days to bring his samples from the deep bush to the track, and another grunting, sweating day and night to haul the truck along the pitted and rutted earth road from the interior to the coast. In the wet he would never had made it, and in the dry season, which had another month to run, the concrete-hard mud ridges had nearly smashed the Mercedes to pieces. Three days earlier he had paid and dismissed his Vindu workers and trundled the creaking truck down the last stretch to the blacktop road which started only fourteen miles from the capital. From there it had been an hour to the city and the hotel.

Not that "hotel" was the right word. Since independence, the town's main hostelry had degenerated into a flophouse, but it had a parking lot, and here he had parked and locked the truck, then sent his cable. He had only just been in time. Six hours after he sent it, all hell broke loose, and the port, airport, and all other communications had been closed by order of the President.

The first he had known about it was when a group of soldiers, dressed like tramps and wielding rifles by the barrels, had burst into the hotel and started to ransack the rooms. There was no point in asking what they wanted, for they only screamed back in a lingo that meant nothing to him, though he thought he recognized the Vindu dialect he had heard his workers using over the past three months.

Being Mulrooney, he had taken two clubbings from rifle butts, then swung a fist. The blow carried the nearest soldier halfway down the hotel corridor on his back, and the rest of the pack had gone wild. It was only by the grace of God no shots were fired, and also owing to the fact that the soldiers preferred to use their guns as clubs rather than search for complicated mechanisms like triggers and safety catches.

He had been dragged to the nearest police barracks and had been alternately screamed at and ignored in a subterranean cell for two days. He had been lucky. A Swiss businessman, one of the rare foreign visitors to the republic, had witnessed his departure and feared for his life. The man had looked through Mulrooney's belongings and contacted the Swiss embassy, one of the only six European and North American embassies in the town, and it had contacted ManCon.

Two days later the called-for coaster had arrived from farther up the coast, and the Swiss consul had negotiated Mulrooney's release. No doubt a bribe had been paid, and no doubt ManCon would foot the bill. Jack Mulrooney was still aggrieved. On release he had found his truck broken open and his samples strewn all over the parking lot. The rocks had all been marked and could be reassembled, but the sand, gravel, and chippings were mixed up. Fortunately each of the slit bags, about fifty in all, had half its contents intact, so he had resealed them and taken them to the boat. Even here the customs men, police, and soldiers had searched the boat from stem to stern, screamed and shouted at the crew, and all without saying what they were looking for.

The terrified official from the Swiss consulate who had taken Mulrooney back from the barracks to his hotel had told him there had been rumors of an attempt on the President's life and the troops were looking for a missing senior officer who was presumed to be responsible.

Four days after leaving the port of Clarence, Jack Mulrooney, still nurse-maiding his rock samples, arrived back at Luton, England, aboard a chartered aircraft. A truck took his samples away for analysis at Watford, and after a checkout by the company doctor he was allowed to start his three weeks' leave. He went to spend it with his sister in Dulwich and within a week was thoroughly bored.

Exactly three weeks later to the day, Sir James Manson, Knight of the British Empire, chairman and managing director of Manson Consolidated Mining Company Limited, leaned back in his leather armchair in the penthouse office suite on the tenth floor of his company's London headquarters, glanced once more at the report in front of him and breathed, "Jesus Christ."

He rose from behind the broad desk, crossed the room to the picture windows on the south face, and gazed down at the sprawl of the City of London, the inner square mile of the ancient capital and heart of a financial empire that was still worldwide, despite what its detractors said. To some of the scuttling beetles in somber gray, topped by black bowler hats, it was perhaps a place of employment only, boring, wearisome, exacting its toll of a man, his youth, his manhood, his middle age, until final retirement. For others, young and hopeful, it was a palace of opportunity, where merit and hard work were rewarded with the prizes of advancement and security. To romantics it was no doubt the home of the houses of the great merchant-adventurers, to a pragmatist the biggest market in the world, and to a left-wing trade unionist a place where the idle and worthless rich, born to wealth and privilege, lolled at ease in luxury. James Manson was a cynic and a realist. He knew what the City was; it was a jungle pure and simple, and in it he was one of the panthers.

A born predator, he had nevertheless realized early that there were certain rules that needed to be publicly revered and privately ripped to shreds; that, as in politics, there was only one commandment, the eleventh, "Thou shalt not be found out." It was by obeying the first requirement that he had acquired his knighthood in the New Year's Honours List a month before. This had been proposed by the Conservative Party (ostensibly for services to industry, but in reality for secret contributions to party funds for the general election), and accepted by the Wilson government because of his support for its policy on Nigeria. And it was by fulfilling the second require-ment that he had made his fortune and now, holding twenty-five per cent of the stock of his own mining corporation and occupying the penthouse floor, was a millionaire several times over.

He was sixty-one, short, aggressive, built like a tank, with a thrusting vigor and a piratical ruthlessness that women found attractive and competitors feared. He had enough cunning to pretend to show respect for the establishments of both the City and the realm, of commercial and political life, even though he was aware that both organs were rife with men of almost complete moral unscrupulousness behind the public image. He had collected a few on his board of directors, including two former ministers in Conservative administrations. Neither was averse to a fat supplementary fee over and above directors' salary, payable in the Cayman Islands or Grand Bahama—and one, to Manson's knowledge, enjoyed the private diversion of waiting at table upon three or four leather-clad tarts, himself dressed in a maid's cap, a pinafore, and a bright smile. Manson regarded both men as useful, possessing the advantage of considerable influence and superb connections without the inconvenience of integrity. The rest of the public knew both men as distinguished public servants. So James Manson was respectable within the set of rules of the City, a set of rules that had nothing whatever to do with the rest of humanity.

It had not always been so, which was why inquirers into his background found themselves up against one blank wall after another. Very little was known of his start in life, and he knew enough to keep it that way. He would let it be known that he was the son of a Rhodesian train-driver, brought up not far from the sprawling copper mines of Ndola, Northern Rhodesia, now Zambia. He would even let it be known that he had started work at the minehead as a boy and later had made his first fortune in copper. But never how he had made it.

In fact he had quit the mines quite early, before he was twenty, and had realized that the men who risked their lives below ground amid roaring machinery would never make money, not big money. That lay above ground, and not even in mine management. As a teenager he had studied finance, the using and manipulating of money, and his nightly studies had taught him that more was made in shares in copper in a week than a miner made in his whole life.

He had started as a share-pusher on the Rand, had peddled a few illicit diamonds in his time, started a few rumors that sent the punters reaching into their pockets, and sold a few worked-out claims to the gullible. That was where the first fortune came from. Just after the Second World War, at thirty-five, he was in London with the right connections for a copper-hungry Britain trying to get its industries back to work, and in 1948 had founded his own mining company. It had gone public in the mid-fifties and in fifteen years had developed worldwide interests. He was one of the first to see Harold Macmillan's wind of change blowing through Africa as independence for the black republics approached, and he took the trouble to meet and know most of the new power-hungry African politicians while most city businessmen were still deploring independence in the former colonies.

When he met the new men, it was a good match. They could see through his success story, and he could see through their professed concern for their fellow blacks. They knew what he wanted, and he knew what they wanted. So he fed their Swiss bank accounts, and they gave Manson Consolidated mining concessions at prices below par for the course. ManCon prospered.

James Manson had also made several fortunes on the side. His latest was in the shares of the nickel-mining company in Australia called Poseidon. When Poseidon shares in late summer 1969 had been standing at four shillings, he had got a whisper that a survey team in central Australia might have found something on a stretch of land whose mining rights were owned by Poseidon. He had taken a gamble and paid out a very hefty sum to have a sneak preview of the first reports coming out of the interior. Those reports said nickel, and lots of it. In fact nickel was not in shortage on the world market, but that never deterred the punters, and it was they who sent share prices spiraling, not investors.

He contacted his Swiss bank, an establishment so discreet that its only way of announcing its presence in the world was a small gold plate no larger than a visiting card, set into the wall beside a solid oak door in a small street in Zurich. Switzerland has no stockbrokers; the banks do all the investments. Manson instructed Dr. Martin Steinhofer, the head of the investments section of the Zwingli Bank, to buy on his behalf five thousand Poseidon shares. The Swiss banker contacted the prestigious London firm of Joseph Sebag & Co., in the name of Zwingli, and placed the order. Poseidon stood at five shillings a share when the deal was concluded.

The storm broke in late September when the size of the Australian nickel deposit became known. The shares began to rise, and assisted by helpful rumors, the rising spiral became a rush. Sir James Manson had intended to start to sell when they reached £50 a share, but so vast was the rise that he held on. Finally he estimated that the peak would be £115 and ordered Dr. Steinhofer to start selling at £100 a share. This the discreet Swiss banker did and cleared the lot at an average of £103 for each share. In fact the peak was reached at £120 a share, before common sense began to prevail and the shares slide back to £10. Manson did not mind the extra £20, for he knew the time to sell was just before the peak, when buyers are still plentiful. With all fees paid, he netted a cool £500,000, which was still stashed in the Zwingli Bank.

It happens to be illegal for a British citizen and resident to have a foreign bank account without informing the Treasury, and also to make half a million sterling profit in sixty days without paying capital gains tax on it. But Dr. Steinhofer was a Swiss resident, and Dr. Steinhofer would keep his mouth shut. That was what Swiss banks were for.

On that mid-February afternoon Sir James Manson strolled back to his desk, sat back in the lush leather chair behind it, and glanced again at the report that lay on the blotter. It had arrived in a large envelope, sealed with wax and marked for his eyes only. It was signed at the bottom by Dr. Gordon Chalmers, the head of ManCon's Department of Study, Research, Geo-Mapping, and Sample Analysis, situated outside London. It was the analyst's report on tests conducted on the samples a man called Mulrooney had apparently brought back from a place called Zangaro three weeks earlier.

Dr. Chalmers did not waste words. The summary of the report was brief and to the point. Mulrooney had found a mountain, or a hill, some 1800 feet high above ground level and close to 1000 yards across the base. It was set slightly apart from a range of such mountains in the hinterland of Zangaro. The hill contained a widely disseminated deposit of mineral in apparently evenly consistent presence throughout the rock, which was of igneous type and millions of years older than the sandstone and ragstone of the mountains that surrounded it.

Mulrooney had found numerous and ubiquitous stringers of quartz and had predicated the presence of tin. He had returned with samples of the quartz, the country rock surrounding it, and shingle from the beds of the streams surrounding the hill. The quartz stringers did indeed contain small quantities of tin. But it was the country rock that was interesting. Repeated and varied tests showed that this country rock, and the gravel samples, contained minor quantities of low-grade nickel. They also contained remarkable quantities of platinum. It was present in all the samples and was fairly evenly distributed. The richest rock in platinum known in this world was in the Rustenberg mines in South Africa, where concentrations or "grades" ran as high as Point Two Five of a Troy ounce per rock ton. The average concentration in the Mulrooney samples was Point Eight One. I have the honor to remain, Sir, Yours, etc. . . .

Sir James Manson knew as well as anyone in mining that platinum was the third most precious metal in the world, and stood at a market price of $130 a Troy ounce as he sat in his chair. He was also aware that, with the growing world hunger for the stuff, it had to rise to at least $150 an ounce over the next three years, probably to $200 within five years. It would be unlikely to rise to the 1968 peak price of $300 again, because that was ridiculous.

He did some calculations on a scratch pad. Two hundred and fifty million cubic yards of rock at two tons per cubic yard was five hundred million tons. At even half an ounce per rock ton, that was two hundred and fifty million ounces. If the revelation of a new world source dragged the price down to ninety dollars an ounce, and even if the inaccessibility of the place meant a cost of fifty dollars an ounce to get it out and refined, that still meant . . .

Sir James Manson leaned back in his chair again and whistled softly.

"Jesus Christ. A ten-billion-dollar mountain."

THREE

Platinum is a metal and, like all metals, it has its price. The price is basically controlled by two factors. These are the indispensability of the metal in certain processes that the industries of the world would like to complete, and the rarity of the metal. Platinum is very rare. Total world production each year, apart from stockpiled production, which is kept secret by the producers, is a shade over one and a half million Troy ounces.

The overwhelming majority of it, probably more than ninety-five per cent, comes from three sources: South Africa, Canada, and Russia. Russia, as usual, is the uncooperative member of the group. The producers would like to keep the world price fairly steady so as to be able to make long-term plans for investment in new mining equipment and development of new mines in the confidence that the bottom will not suddenly drop out of the market should a large quantity of stockpiled platinum suddenly be released. The Russians, by stockpiling unknown quantities and being able to release large quantities any time they feel like it, keep tremors running through the market whenever they can.

Russia releases on the world each year about 350,000 Troy ounces out of the 1,500,000 that reach the same market. This gives her between 23 and 24 per cent of the market, enough to ensure her a considerable degree of influence. Her supplies are marketed through Soyuss Prom Export. Canada puts on the market some 200,000 ounces a year, the whole production coming from the nickel mines of International Nickel, and just about the whole of this supply is bought up each year by the Engelhard Industries of the United States. But should the United States need for platinum suddenly rise sharply, Canada might well not be able to furnish the extra quantity.

The third source is South Africa, turning out close to 950,000 ounces a year and dominating the market. Apart from the Impala mines, which were just opening when Sir James Manson sat considering the world position of platinum, and have since become very important, the giants of platinum are the Rustenberg mines, which account for well over half the world's production. These are controlled by Johannesburg Consolidated, which had a big enough slice of the stock to be sole manager of the mines. The world refiner and marketer of Rustenberg's supply was and is the London-based firm of Johnson-Matthey.

James Manson knew this as well as anyone else. Although he was not into platinum when Chalmers' report hit his desk, he knew the position as well as a brain surgeon knows how a heart works. He also knew why, even at that time, the boss of Engelhard Industries of America, the colorful Charlie Engelhard, better known to the populace as the owner of the fabulous racehorse Nijinsky, was buying into South African platinum. It was because America would need much more than Canada could supply for the mid-seventies. Manson was certain of it.

And the particular reason why American consumption of platinum was almost certain to rise, even triple, by the mid- to late seventies, lay in that simple piece of metal the car exhaust pipe and in those dire words "air pollution."

With legislation already passed in the United States projecting ever more stringent controls, and with little likelihood that any nonprecious-metal car exhaust-control device would be marketed before 1980, there was a strong probability that every American car would soon require one-tenth of an ounce of pure platinum. This meant that the Americans would need one and a half million ounces of platinum every year, an amount equal to the present world production, and they would not know where to get it.

James Manson thought he had an idea where. They could always buy it from him. And with the absolute indispensability of a platinum-based anti-pollutant catalyst in every fume-control device established for a decade, and world demand far outstripping supply, the price would be nice, very nice indeed.

There was only one problem. He had to be absolutely certain that he, and no one else, would control all mining rights to the Crystal Mountain. The question was, how?

The normal way would be to visit the republic where the mountain was situated, seek an interview with the President, show him the survey report, and propose to him a deal whereby ManCon secured the mining rights, the government secured a profit-participation clause that would fill the coffers of its treasury, and the President would secure a fat and regular payment into his Swiss account. That would be the normal way.

But apart from the fact that any other mining company in the world, if advised of what lay inside the Crystal Mountain, would counterbid for the same mining rights, sending the government's share up and Manson's down, there were three groups who more than any other would want to take control, either to begin production or to stop it forever. These were the South Africans, the Canadians, and most of all the Russians. For the advent on the world market of a massive new supply source would cut the Soviet slice of the market back to the level of the unnecessary, removing from the Russians their power, influence, and money-making capacity in the platinum field.

Manson had a vague recollection of having heard the name of Zangaro, but it was such an obscure place he realized he knew nothing about it. The first requirement was evidently to learn more. He leaned forward and depressed the intercom switch.

"Miss Cooke, would you come in, please?"

He had called her Miss Cooke throughout the seven years she had been his personal and private secretary, and even in the ten years before that, when she had been an ordinary company secretary, rising from the typing pool to the tenth floor, no one had ever suggested she might have a first name. In fact she had. It was Marjory. But she just did not seem the sort of person one called Marjory.

Certainly men had once called her Marjory, long ago, before the war, when she was a young girl. Perhaps they had even tried to flirt with her, pinch her bottom, those long thirty-five years ago. But that was then. Five years of war, hauling an ambulance through burning rubble-strewn streets, trying to forget a Guardsman who never came back from Dunkirk, and twenty years of nursing a crippled and whining mother, a bedridden tyrant who used tears for weapons, had taken away the youth and the pinchable qualities of Miss Marjory Cooke. At fifty-four, she was tailored, efficient, and severe; her work at ManCon was almost all her life, the tenth floor her fulfillment, and the terrier who shared her neat apartment in suburban Chigwell and slept on her bed, her child and lover.

So no one ever called her Marjory. The young executives called her a shriveled apple, and the secretary birds "that old bat." The others, including her employer, Sir James Manson, about whom she knew more than she would ever tell him or anyone else, called her Miss Cooke.

She entered through the door set in the beech-paneled wall which, when closed, looked like part of the wall.

"Miss Cooke, it has come to my attention that we have had, during the past few months, a small survey—one man, I believe—in the republic of Zangaro."

"Yes, Sir James. That's right."

"Oh, you know about it."

Of course she knew about it. Miss Cooke never forgot anything that had crossed her desk.

"Yes, Sir James."

"Good. Then please find out for me who secured that government's permission for us to conduct the survey."

"It will be on file, Sir James. I'll go and look."

She was back in ten minutes, having first checked in her daily diary appointment books, which were cross-indexed into two indices, one under personal names and the other under subject headings, and then confirmed with Personnel.

"It was Mr. Bryant, Sir James." She consulted a card in her hand. "Richard Bryant, of Overseas Contracts."

"He submitted a report, I suppose?" asked Sir James.

"He must have done, under normal company procedure."

"Send me in his report, would you, Miss Cooke?"

She was gone again, and the head of ManCon stared out through the plate-glass windows across the room from his desk at the mid-afternoon dusk settling over the City of London. The lights were coming on in the middle-level floors—they had been on all day in the lowest ones—but at skyline level there was still enough winter daylight to see by. But not to read by. Sir James Manson flicked on the reading lamp on his desk as Miss Cooke returned, laid the report he wanted on his blotter, and receded back into the wall.

The report Richard Bryant had submitted was dated six months earlier and was written in the terse style favored by the company. It recorded that, according to instructions from the head of Overseas Contracts, he had flown to Clarence, the capital of Zangaro, and there, after a frustrating week in a hotel, had secured an interview with the Minister of Natural Resources. There were three separate interviews, spaced over six days, and at length an agreement had been reached that a single representative of ManCon might enter the republic to conduct a survey for minerals in the hinterland beyond the Crystal Mountains. The area to be surveyed was deliberately left vague by the company, so that the survey team could travel more or less where it wished. After further haggling, during which it was made plain to the Minister that he could forget any idea that the company was prepared to pay the sort of fee he seemed to expect, and that there were no indications of mineral presence to work on, a sum had been agreed on between Bryant and the Minister. Inevitably, the sum on the contract was just over half the total that changed hands, the balance being paid into the Minister's private account.

That was all. The only indication of the character of the place was in the reference to a corrupt minister. So what? thought Sir James Manson. Nowadays Bryant might have been in Washington. Only the going rate was different.

He leaned forward to the intercom again. "Tell Mr. Bryant of Overseas Contracts to come up and see me, would you, Miss Cooke?"

He lifted the switch and pressed another one. "Martin, come in a minute, please."

It took Martin Thorpe two minutes to come from his office on the ninth floor. He did not look the part of a financial whiz-kid and protégé of one of the most ruthless go-getters in a traditionally ruthless and go-getting industry. He looked more like the captain of the Rugby team from a good public school—charming, boyish, clean-cut, with dark wavy hair and deep blue eyes. The secretaries called him dishy, and the directors, who had seen stock options they were certain of whisked out from under their noses or found their companies slipping into control of a series of nominee shareholders fronting for Martin Thorpe, called him something not quite so nice.

Despite the looks, Thorpe had never been either a public-school man or an athlete. He could not differentiate between a batting average and the ambient air temperature, but he could retain the hourly movement of share prices across the range of ManCon's subsidiary companies in his head throughout the day. At twenty-nine he had ambitions and the intent to carry them out. ManCon and Sir James might provide the means, so far as he was concerned, and his loyalty depended on his exceptionally high salary, the contracts throughout the City that his job under Manson could bring him, and the knowledge that where he was constituted a good vantage point for spotting what he called "the big one."

By the time he entered, Sir James had slipped the Zangaro report into a drawer, and the Bryant report alone lay on his blotter. He have his protégé a friendly smile.

"Martin, I've got a job I need done with some discretion. I need it done in a hurry, and it may take half the night."

It was not Sir James's way to ask if Thorpe had any engagements that evening. Thorpe knew that; it went with the salary.

"That's okay, Sir James. I had nothing on that a phone call can't kill."

"Good. Look, I've been going over some old reports and came across this one. Six months ago one of our men from Overseas Contracts was sent out to a place called Zangaro. I don't know why, but I'd like to. The man secured that government's go-ahead for a small team from here to conduct a survey for any possible mineral depostis in unchartered land beyond the mountain range called the Crystal Mountains. Now, what I want to know is this: Was it ever mentioned in advance or at the time, or since that visit six months ago, to the board?"

"To the board?"

"That's right. Was it ever mentioned to the board of directors that we were doing any such survey? That's what I want to know. It may not necessarily be on the agenda. You'll have to look at the minutes. And in case it got a passing mention under 'any other business,' check through the documents of all board meetings over the past twelve months. Secondly, find out who authorized the visit by Bryant six months ago and why, and who sent the survey engineer down there and why. The man who did the survey is called Mulrooney. I also want to know something about him, which you can get from his file in Personnel. Got it?"

Thorpe was surprised. This was way out of his line of country.

"Yes, Sir James, but Miss Cooke could do that in half the time, or get somebody to do it—"

"Yes, she could. But I want you to do it. If you look at a file from Personnel, or boardroom documents, it will be assumed it has something to do with finance. Therefore it will remain discreet."

The light began to dawn on Martin Thorpe. "You mean . . . they found something down there, Sir James?"

Manson stared out at the now inky sky and the blazing lights below him as the brokers and traders, clerks and merchants, bankers and assessors, insurers and jobbers, buyers and sellers, lawyers and, in some offices no doubt, lawbreakers, worked on through the winter afternoon toward the witching hour of five-thirty.

"Never mind," he said gruffly to the young man behind him. "Just do it."

Martin Thorpe was grinning as he slipped through the back entrance of the office and down the stairs to his own premises. "Cunning bastard," he said to himself on the stairs.

"Mr. Bryant is here, Sir James."

Manson crossed the room and switched on the main lights. Returning to his desk, he depressed the intercom button. "Send him in, Miss Cooke."

There were three reasons why middle-level executives had occasion to be summoned to the sanctum on the tenth floor. One was to hear instructions or deliver a report that Sir James wanted to issue or hear personally, which was business. One was to be chewed into a sweat-soaked rag, which was hell. The third was that the chief executive had decided he wanted to play favorite uncle to his cherished employees, which was reassuring.

On the threshold Richard Bryant, at thirty-nine a middle-level executive who did his work competently and well but needed his job, was plainly aware that the first reason of the three could not be the one that brought him here. He suspected the second and was immensely relieved to see it had to be the third.

From the center of the office Sir James walked toward him with a smile of welcome. "Ah, come in, Bryant. Come in."

As Bryant entered, Miss Cooke closed the door behind him and retired to her desk.

Sir James Manson gestured to his employee to take one of the easy chairs set well away from the desk in the conference area of the spacious office. Bryant, still wondering what it was all about, took the indicated chair and sank into its brushed suede cushions. Manson advanced toward the wall and opened two doors, revealing a well-stocked bar cabinet.

"Take a drink, Bryant? Sun's well down, I think."

"Thank you, sir—er—scotch, please."

"Good man. My own favorite poison. I'll join you."

Bryant glanced at his watch. It was quarter to five, and the tropical maxim about taking a drink after the sun has gone down was hardly coined for London winter afternoons. But he recalled an office party at which Sir James had snorted his derision of sherry-drinkers and the like and spent the evening on scotch. It pays to watch things like that, Bryant reflected, as his chief poured his special Glenlivet into two fine old crystal glasses. Of course he left the ice bucket strictly alone.

"Water? Dash of soda?" he called from the bar.

Bryant craned around and spotted the bottle. "Is that a single malt, Sir James? No, thank you, straight as it comes."

Manson nodded several times in approval and brought the glasses over. They "Cheers"ed each other and savored the whisky. Bryant was still waiting for the conversation to start. Manson noted this and gave him the gruff-uncle look.

"No need to worry about me having you up here like this," he began. "I was just going through a sheaf of old reports in the desk drawers and came across yours, or one of them. Must have read it at the time and forgotten to give it back to Miss Cooke for filing."

"My report?" queried Bryant.

"Eh? Yes, yes, the one you filed after your return from that place—what's it called again? Zangaro? Was that it?"

"Oh, yes, sir. Zangaro. That was six months ago."

"Yes, quite so. Six months, of course. Noticed as I reread it that you'd had a bit of a rough time with that Minister fellow."

Bryant began to relax. The room was warm, the chair extremely comfortable, and the whisky like an old friend. He smiled at the memory. "But I got the contract for survey permission."

"Damn right you did," congratulated Sir James. He smiled as if at fond memories. "I used to do that in the old days, y'know. Went on some rough missions to bring home the bacon. Never went to West Africa, though. Not in those days. Went later, of course. But after all this started."

To indicate "all this" he waved his hand at the luxurious office.

"So nowadays I spend too much time up here, buried in paperwork," Sir James continued. "I even envy you younger chaps going off to clinch deals in the old way. So tell me about your Zangaro trip."

"Well, that really was doing things the old way. One look, and I half expected to find people running around with bones through their noses," said Bryant.

"Really? Good Lord. Rough place is it, this Zangaro?" Sir James Manson's head had tilted back into the shadows, and Bryant was sufficiently comfortable not to catch the gleam of concentration in the eye that belied the encouraging tone of voice.

"Too right, Sir James. It's a bloody shambles of a place, moving steadily backward into the Middle Ages since independence five years ago." He recalled something else he had heard his chief say once in an aside remark to a group of executives. "It's a classic example of the concept that most of the African republics today have thrown up power groups whose performance in power simply cannot justify their entitlement to leadership of a town dump. As a result, of course, it's the ordinary people who suffer."

Sir James, who was as capable as the next man of recognizing his own words when he heard them played back at him, smiled quietly, rose, and walked to the window to look down at the teeming streets below.

"So who does run the show out there?" he asked quietly.

"The President. Or rather the dictator," said Bryant from his chair. His glass was empty. "A man called Jean Kimba. He won the first and only election, just before independence five years ago, against the wishes of the colonial power—some said by the use of terrorism and voodoo on the voters. They're pretty backward, you know. Most of them didn't know what a vote was. Now they don't need to know."

"Tough guy, is he, this Kimba?" asked Sir James.

"It's not that he's tough, sir. He's just downright mad. A raving megalomaniac, and probably a paranoid to boot. He rules completely alone, surrounded by a small coterie of political yes-men. If they fall out with him, or arouse his suspicions in any way, they go into the cells of the old colonial police barracks. Rumor has it Kimba goes down there himself to supervise the torture sessions. No one has ever come out alive."

"Hm, what a world we live in, Bryant. And they've got the same vote in the UN General Assembly as Britain or America. Whose advice does he listen to in government?"

"No one of his own people. Of course, he has his voices—so the few local whites say, those who've stuck it out by staying on."

"Voices?" queried Sir James.

"Yes, sir. He claims to the people he is guided by divine voices. He says he talks to God. He's told the people and the assembled diplomatic corps that in so many words."

"Oh dear, not another," mused Manson, still gazing down at the streets below. "I sometimes think it was a mistake to introduce the Africans to God. Half their leaders now seem to be on first-name terms with Him."

"Apart from that, he rules by a sort of mesmeric fear. The people think he has a powerful juju, or voodoo, or magic or whatever. He holds them in the most abject terror."

"What about the foreign embassies?" queried the man by the window.

"Well, sir, they keep themselves to themselves. It seems they are just as terrified of the excesses of this maniac as the natives. He's a bit like a cross between Sheikh Abeid Karume in Zanzibar, Papa Doc Duvalier in Haiti, and Sékou Touré in Guinea."

Sir James turned smoothly from the window and asked with deceptive softness, "Why Sékou Touré?"

"Well, Kimba's next best thing to a Communist, Sir James. The man he really worshiped all his political life was Lumumba. That's why the Russians are so strong. They have an enormous embassy, for the size of the place. To earn foreign currency, now that the plantations have all failed through maladministration, Zangaro sells most of its produce to the Russian trawlers that call. Of course the trawlers are electronic spy ships or supply ships for submarines. Again, the money they get from the sale doesn't go to the people; it goes into Kimba's bank account."

"It doesn't sound like Marxism to me," joked Manson.

Bryant grinned widely. "Money and bribes are where the Marxism stops," he replied. "As usual."

"But the Russians are strong, are they? Influential? Another whisky, Bryant?"

While Bryant replied, the head of ManCon poured two more glasses of Glenlivet.

"Yes, Sir James. Kimba has virtually no understanding of matters outside his immediate experience, which has been exclusively inside his own country and maybe a couple of visits to other African states nearby. So he sometimes consults on matters when dealing with outside concerns. Then he uses any one of three advisers, black ones, who come from his own tribe. Two Moscow-trained, and one Peking-trained. Or he contacts the Russians direct. I spoke to a trader in the bar of the hotel one night, a Frenchman. He said the Russian ambassador or one of his counselors was at the palace almost every day."

Bryant stayed for another ten minutes, but Manson had learned most of what he needed to know. At five-twenty he ushered Bryant out as smoothly as he had welcomed him. As the younger man left, Manson beckoned Miss Cooke in.

"We employ an engineer in mineral exploration work called Jack Mulrooney," he said. "He returned from a three-month sortie into Africa, living in rough bush conditions, three months ago, so he may be on leave still. Try and get him at home. I'd like to see him at ten tomorrow morning. Secondly, Dr. Gordon Chalmers, the chief survey analyst. You may catch him at

Watford before he leaves the laboratory. If not, reach him at home. I'd like him here at twelve tomorrow. Cancel any other morning appointments and leave me time to take Chalmers out for a spot of lunch. And you'd better book me a table at Wilton's in Bury Street. That's all, thank you. I'll be on my way in a few minutes. Have the car round at the front in ten minutes."

When Miss Cooke withdrew, Manson pressed one of the switches on his intercom and murmured, "Come up for a minute, would you, Simon?"

Simon Endean was as deceptive as Martin Thorpe but in a different way. He came from an impeccable background and, behind the veneer, had the morals of an East End thug. Going with the polish and the ruthlessness was a certain cleverness. He needed a James Manson to serve, just as James Manson, sooner or later on his way to the top or his struggle to stay there in big-time capitalism, needed the services of a Simon Endean.

Endean was the sort to be found by the score in the very smartest and smoothest of London's West End gambling clubs—beautifully spoken hatchet men who never leave a millionaire unbowed to or a showgirl unbruised. The difference was that Endean's intelligence had brought him to an executive position as aide to the chief of a very superior gambling club.

Unlike Thorpe, he had no ambitions to become a multimillionaire. He thought one million would do, and until then the shadow of Manson would suffice. It paid for the six-room pad, the Corvette, the girls.

He too came from the floor below and entered from the interior stairwell through the beech-paneled door across the office from the one Miss Cooke came and left by. "Sir James?"

"Simon, tomorrow I'm having lunch with a fellow called Gordon Chalmers. One of the back-room boys. The chief scientist and head of the laboratory out at Watford. He'll be here at twelve. Before then I want a rundown on him. The Personnel file, of course, but anything else you can find. The private man, what his home life is like, any failings; above all, if he has any pressing need for money over and above his salary. His politics, if any. Most of these scientific people are Left. Not all, though. You might have a chat with Errington in Personnel tonight before he leaves. Go through the file tonight and leave it for me to look at in the morning. Sharp tomorrow, start on his home environment. Phone me not later than eleven-forty-five. Got it? I know it's a short-notice job, but it could be important."

Endean took in the instructions without moving a muscle, filing the lot. He knew the score; Sir James Manson often needed information, for he never faced any man, friend or foe, without a personal rundown on the man, including the private life. Several times he had beaten opponents into submission by being better prepared. Endean nodded and left, making his way straight to Personnel.

As the chauffeur-driven Rolls-Royce slid away from the front of ManCon House, taking its occupant back to his third-floor apartment in Arlington House behind the Ritz, a long, hot bath, and a dinner sent up from the Caprice, Sir James Manson leaned back and lit his first cigar of the evening. The chauffeur handed him a late *Evening Standard,* and they were abreast of Charing Cross Station when a small paragraph in the "Stop Press" caught his eye. It was in among the racing results. He glanced back at it, then read it several times. He stared out at the swirling traffic and huddled pedestrians shuffling toward the station or plodding to the buses through the February drizzle, bound for their homes in Edenbridge and Sevenoaks after another exciting day in the City.

As he stared, a small germ of an idea began to form in his mind. Another man would have laughed and dismissed it out of hand. Sir James Manson was not another man. He was a twentieth-century pirate and proud of it. The nine-point-type headline above the obscure paragraph in the evening paper referred to an African republic. It was not Zangaro, but another one. He had hardly heard of the other one either. It had no known mineral wealth. The headline said:

NEW COUP D'ETAT IN AFRICAN STATE

FOUR

Martin Thrope was waiting in his chief's outer office when Sir James arrived at five past nine, and followed him straight in.

"What have you got?" demanded Sir James Manson, even while he was taking off his vicuña topcoat and hanging it in the closet. Thorpe flicked open a notebook he had pulled from his pocket and recited the result of his investigations of the night before.

"One year ago we had a survey team in the republic lying to the north and east of Zangaro. It was accompanied by an aerial reconnaissance unit hired from a French firm. The area to be surveyed was close to, and partly on the border with Zangaro. Unfortunately there are few topographical maps of that area, and no aerial maps at all. Without Decca or any other form of beacon to give him cross-bearings, the pilot used speed and time of flight to assess the ground he had covered.

"One day when there was a following wind stronger than forecast, he flew several times up and down the entire strip to be covered by aerial survey, to his own satisfaction, and returned to base. What he did not know was that on each downwind leg he had flown over the border and forty miles into Zangaro. When the aerial film was developed, it showed that he had overshot the survey area by a large margin."

"Who first realized it? The French company?" asked Manson.

"No, sir. They developed the film and passed it to us without comment, as per our contract with them. It was up to the men in our own aerial-survey department to identify the areas on the ground represented by the pictures they had. Then they realized that at the end of each run was a stretch of territory not in the survey area. So they discarded the pictures, or at any rate put them on one side. They had realized that in one section of pictures a range of hills was featured that could not be in our survey area because there were no hills in that part of the area.

"Then one bright spark had a second look at the surplus photographs and noticed a part of the hilly area, slightly to the east of the main range, had a variation in the density and type of the plant life. The sort of thing you can't see down on the ground, but an aerial picture from three miles up will show it up like a beermat on a billiard table."

"I know how it's done," growled Sir James. "Go on."

"Sorry, sir, I didn't know this. It was new to me. So, anyway, half a dozen photos were passed to someone in the Photo-Geology section, and he confirmed from a blow-up that the plant life was different over quite a small area involving a small hill about eighteen hundred feet high and roughly conical in shape. Both sections prepared a report, and that went to the head of Topographic section. He identified the range as the Crystal Mountains and the hill as probably the original Crystal Mountain. He sent the file to Overseas Contracts, and Willoughby, the head of O.C., sent Bryant down there to get permission to survey."

"He didn't tell me," said Manson, now seated behind his desk.

"He sent a memo, Sir James. I have it here. You were in Canada at the time and were not due back for a month. He makes plain he felt the survey of that area was only an off-chance, but since a free aerial survey had been presented to us, and since Photo-Geology felt there had to be some reason for the different vegetation, the expense could be justified. Willoughby also suggested it might serve to give his man Bryant a bit of experience to go it alone for the first time. Up till then he had always accompanied Willoughby."

"Is that it?"

"Almost. Bryant got visa-ed up and went in six months ago. He got permission and arrived back after three weeks. Four months ago Ground Survey agreed to detach an unqualified prospector-cum-surveyor called Jack Mulrooney from the diggings in Ghana and send him in to look over the Crystal Mountains, provided that the cost would be kept low. It was. He got back three weeks ago with a ton and a half of samples, which have been at the Watford laboratory ever since."

"Fair enough," said Sir James Manson after a pause. "Now, did the board ever hear about all this?"

"No, sir." Thorpe was adamant. "It would have been considered much too small. I've been through every board meeting for twelve months, and every document presented, including every memo and letter sent to the board members over the same period. Not a mention of it. The budget for the whole thing would simply have been lost in the petty cash anyway. And it didn't originate with Projects, because the aerial photos were a gift from the French firm and their ropy old navigator. It was just an *ad hoc* affair throughout and never reached board level."

James Manson nodded in evident satisfaction. "Right. Now, Mulrooney. How bright is he?"

For answer, Thorpe tended Jack Mulrooney's file from Personnel. "No qualifications, but a lot of practical experience, sir. An old sweat. A good African hand."

Manson flicked through the file on Jack Mulrooney, scanned the biography notes and the career sheet since the man had joined the company. "He's experienced all right," he grunted. "Don't underestimate the old Africa hands. I started out in the Rand, on a mining camp. Mulrooney just stayed at that level. But never condescend; such people are very useful. And they can be perceptive."

He dismissed Martin Thorpe and muttered to himself, "Now let's see how perceptive Mr. Mulrooney can be."

He depressed the intercom switch and spoke to Miss Cooke. "Is Mr. Mulrooney there yet, Miss Cooke?"

"Yes, Sir James, he's here waiting."

"Show him in, please."

Manson was halfway to the door when his employee was ushered in. He greeted him warmly and led him to the chairs where he had sat with Bryant the previous evening. Before she left, Miss Cooke was asked to produce coffee for them both. Mulrooney's coffee habit was in his file.

Jack Mulrooney in the penthouse suite of a London office building looked as out of place as Thorpe would have in the dense bush. His hands hung way out of his coat sleeves, and he did not seem to know where to put them. His gray hair was plastered down with water, and he had cut himself shaving. It was the first time he had ever met the man he called the gaffer. Sir James used all his efforts to put him at ease.

When Miss Cooke entered with a tray of porcelain cups, matching coffee pot, cream jug and sugar bowl, and an array of Fortnum and Mason biscuits, she heard her employer telling the Irishman, " . . . that's just the point, man. You've got what I or anyone else can't teach these boys fresh out of college, twenty-five years' hard-won experience getting the bloody stuff out of the ground and into the skips."

It is always nice to be appreciated, and Jack Mulrooney was no exception. He beamed and nodded. When Miss Cooke had gone, Sir James Manson gestured at the cups.

"Look at these poofy things. Used to drink out of a good mug. Now they give me thimbles. I remember back on the Rand in the late thirties, and that would be before your time, even . . . "

Mulrooney stayed for an hour. When he left he felt the gaffer was a damn good man despite all they said about him. Sir James Manson thought Mulrooney was a damn good man—at his job, at any rate, and that was and would always be chipping bits of rock off hills and asking no questions.

Just before he left, Mulrooney had reiterated his view. "There's tin down there, Sir James. Stake my life on it. The only thing is, whether it can be got out at an economical figure."

Sir James had slapped him on the shoulder. "Don't you worry about that. We'll know as soon as the report comes through from Watford. And don't worry, if there's an ounce of it that I can get to the coast below market value, we'll have the stuff. Now how about you? What's your next adventure?"

"I don't know, sir. I have three more days' leave yet; then I report back to the office."

"Like to go abroad again?" said Sir James expansively.

"Yes, sir. Frankly, I can't take this city and the weather and all."

"Back to the sun, eh? You like the wild places, I hear."

"Yes, I do. You can be your own man out there."

"You can indeed." Manson smiled. "You can indeed. I almost envy you. No, dammit, I *do* envy you. Anyway, we'll see what we can do."

Two minutes later Jack Mulrooney was gone. Manson ordered Miss Cooke to send his file back to Personnel, rang Accounts and instructed them to send Mulrooney a £1000 merit bonus and make sure he got it before the following Monday, and rang the head of Ground Survey.

"What surveys have you got pending in the next few days or just started?" he asked without preamble.

There were three, one of them in a remote stretch of the extreme north of Kenya, close to the Somaliland border, where the midday sun fries the brain like an egg in a pan, the nights freeze the bone marrow like Blackpool rock, and the shifta bandits prowl. It would be a long job, close to a year. The head of Ground Survey had nearly had two resignations trying to get a man to go there for so long.

"Send Mulrooney," said Sir James and hung up.

He glanced at the clock. It was eleven. He picked up the Personnel report on Dr. Gordon Chalmers, which Endean had left on his desk the previous evening.

Chalmers was a graduate with honors from the London School of Mining, which is probably the best of its kind in the world, even if Witwatersrand liked to dispute that claim. He had taken his degree in geology and later chemistry and gone on to a doctorate in his mid-twenties. After five years of fellowship work at the college he had joined Rio Tinto Zinc in its scientific section, and six years earlier ManCon had evidently stolen him from RTZ for a better salary. For the last four years he had been head of the company's Scientific Department situated on the outskirts of Watford in Hertfordshire, one of the counties abutting London to the north. The ID photograph in the file showed a man in his late thirties glowering at the camera over a bushy ginger beard. He wore a tweed jacket and a purple shirt. The tie was of knitted wool and askew.

At eleven-thirty-five the private phone rang and Sir James Manson heard the regular pips of a public coin box at the other end of the line. A coin clunked into the slot, and Endean's voice came on the line. He spoke concisely for two minutes from Watford station. When he had finished, Manson grunted his approval.

"That's useful to know," he said. "Now get back to London. There's another job I want you to do. I want a complete rundown on the republic of Zangaro. I want the lot. Yes, Zangaro." He spelled it out.

"Start back in the days when it was discovered, and work forward. I want the history, geography, lie of the land, economy, crops, mineralogy if any, politics, and state of development. Concentrate on the ten years prior to independence, and especially the period since. I want to know everything there is to know about the President, his cabinet, parliament if any, administration, executive, judiciary, and political parties. There are three things that are more important than all else. One is the question of Russian or Chinese involvement and influence, or local Communist influence, on the President. The second is that no one remotely connected with the place is to know any questions are being asked, so don't go there yourself. And thirdly, under no circumstances are you to announce you come from ManCon. So use a different name. Got it? Good. Well, report back as soon as you can, and not later than twenty days. Draw cash from Accounts on my signature alone, and be discreet. For the record, consider yourself on leave; I'll let you make it up later."

Manson hung up and called down to Thorpe to give further instructions. Within three minutes Thorpe came up to the tenth floor and laid the piece of paper his chief wanted on the desk. It was the carbon copy of a letter.

Ten floors down, Dr. Gordon Chalmers stepped out of his taxi at the corner of Moorgate and paid it off. He felt uncomfortable in a dark suit and topcoat, but Peggy had told him they were necessary for an interview and lunch with the Chairman of the Board.

As he walked the last few yards toward the steps and doorway of ManCon House, his eye caught a poster fronting the kiosk of a seller of the *Evening News* and *Evening Standard*: THALIDOMIDE PARENTS URGE SETTLE-MENT. He curled his lip in a bitter sneer, but he bought both papers.

The stories backed up the headline in greater detail, though they were not long. They recorded that after another marathon round of talks between representatives of the parents of the four-hundred-odd children in Britain who had been born deformed because of the thalidomide drug ten years earlier, and the company that had marketed the drug, a further impasse had been reached. So talks would be resumed "at a later date."

Gordon Chalmers' thoughts went back to the house outside Watford that he had left earlier that same morning, to Peggy, his wife, just turned thirty and looking forty, and to Margaret, legless, one-armed Margaret, coming up to nine years, who needed a special pair of legs and a specially built house, which they now lived in at long last, the mortgage on which was costing him a fortune.

"At a later date," he snapped to no one in particular and stuffed the newspapers into a trash basket. He seldom read the evening papers anyway. He preferred the *Guardian, Private Eye,* and the left-wing *Tribune.* After nearly ten years of watching a group of almost unmoneyed parents try to face down the giant distillers for their compensation, Gordon Chalmers harbored bitter thoughts about big-time capitalists. Ten minutes later he was facing one of the biggest.

Sir James Manson could not put Chalmers off his guard as he had Bryant and Mulrooney. The scientist clutched his glass of beer firmly and stared right back. Manson grasped the situation quickly and, when Miss Cooke had handed him his whisky and retired, he came to the point.

"I suppose you can guess what I asked you to come and see me about, Dr. Chalmers."

"I can guess, Sir James. The report on Crystal Mountain."

"That's it. Incidentally, you were quite right to send it to me personally in a sealed envelope. Quite right."

Chalmers shrugged. He had done it because he realized that all important analysis results had to go direct to the Chairman, according to company policy. It was routine, as soon as he had realized what the samples contained.

"Let me ask you two things, and I need specific answers," said Sir James. "Are you absolutely certain of these results? There could be no other possible explanation of the tests of the samples?"

Chalmers was neither shocked nor affronted. He knew the work of scientists was seldom accepted by laymen as being far removed from black magic, and that they therefore considered it imprecise. He had long since ceased trying to explain the precision of his craft.

"Absolutely certain. For one thing, there are a variety of tests to establish the presence of platinum, and these samples passed them all with unvarying regularity. For another, I not only did all the known tests on every one of the samples, I did the whole thing twice. Theoretically it is possible someone could have interfered with the alluvial samples, but not with the internal structures of the rocks themselves. The summary of my report is accurate beyond scientific dispute."

Sir James Manson listened to the lecture with head-bowed respect, and nodded in admiration. "And the second thing is, how many other people in your laboratory know of the results of the analysis of the Crystal Mountain samples?"

"No one," said Chalmers with finality.

"No one?" echoed Manson. "Come now, surely one of your assistants . . . "

Chalmers downed a swig of his beer and shook his head. "Sir James, when the samples came in they were crated as usual and put in store. Mulrooney's accompanying report predicated the presence of tin in unknown quantities. As it was a very minor survey, I put a junior assistant onto it. Being inexperienced, he assumed tin or nothing and did the appropriate tests. When they failed to show up positive, he called me over and pointed this out. I offered to show him how, and again the tests were negative. So I gave him a lecture on not being mesmerized by the prospector's opinion and showed him some more tests. These too were negative. The laboratory closed for the night, but I stayed on late, so I was alone in the place when the first tests came up positive. By midnight I knew the shingle sample from the stream bed, of which I was using less than half a pound, contained small quantities of platinum. After that I locked up for the night.

"The next day I took the junior off that assignment and put him on another. Then I went on with it myself. There were six hundred bags of shingle and gravel, and fifteen hundred pounds' weight on rocks—over three hundred separate rocks taken from different places on the mountain. From Mulrooney's photographs I could picture the mountain. The disseminated deposit is present in all parts of the formation. As I said in my report." With a touch of defiance he drained his beer.

Sir James Manson continued nodding, staring at the scientist with well-feigned awe.

"It's incredible," he said at length. "I know you scientists like to remain detached, impartial, but I think even you must have become excited. This could form a whole new world source of platinum. You know how often that happens with a rare metal? Once in a decade, maybe once in a lifetime."

In fact Chalmers had been excited by his discovery and had worked late into the night for three weeks to cover every single bag and rock from the Crystal Mountain, but he would not admit it. Instead he shrugged and said, "Well, it'll certainly be very profitable for ManCon."

"Not necessarily," said James Manson quietly. This was the first time he shook Chalmers.

"Not?" queried the analyst. "But surely it's a fortune?"

"A fortune in the ground, yes," replied Sir James, rising and walking to the window. "But it depends very much who gets it, if anyone at all. You see, there is a danger it could be kept unmined for years, or mined and stockpiled. Let me put you in the picture, my dear Doctor . . . "

He put Dr. Chalmers in the picture for thirty minutes, talking finance and politics, neither of which was the analyst's forte.

"So there you are," he finished. "The chances are it will be handed on a plate to the Russian government if we announce it immediately."

Dr. Chalmers, who had nothing in particular against the Russian government, shrugged slightly. "I can't change the facts, Sir James."

Manson's eyebrows shot up in horror. "Good gracious, Doctor, of course you can't." He glanced at his watch in surprise. "Close to one," he exclaimed. "You must be hungry. I know I am. Let's go and have a spot of lunch."

He had thought of taking the Rolls, but after Endean's phone call from Watford that morning and the information from the local news agent about the regular subscription to the *Tribune*, he opted for an ordinary taxi.

A spot of lunch proved to be pâté, truffled omelet, jugged hare in red-wine sauce, and trifle. As Manson had suspected, Chalmers disapproved of such indulgence but at the same time had a healthy appetite. And even he could not reverse the simple laws of nature, which are that a good meal produces a sense of repletion, contentment, euphoria, and a lowering of moral resistance. Manson had also counted on a beer-drinker's being unused to the fuller red wines, and two bottles of Côte du Rhône had encouraged Chalmers to talk about the subjects that interested him: his work, his family, and his views on the world.

It was when he touched on his family and their new house that Sir James Manson, looking suitably sorrowful, mentioned that he recalled having seen Chalmers in a television interview in the street a year back.

"Do forgive me," he said, "I hadn't realized before—I mean, about your little girl. What a tragedy."

Chalmers nodded and gazed at the tablecloth. Slowly at first, and then with more confidence, he began to tell his superior about Margaret.

"You wouldn't understand," he said at one point.

"I can try," replied Sir James quietly. "I have a daughter myself, you know. Of course, she's older."

Ten minutes later there was a pause in the talking. Sir James Manson drew a folded piece of paper from his inside pocket. "I don't really know how to put this," he said with some embarrassment, "but—well, I am as aware as any man how much time and trouble you put in for the company. I am aware you work long hours, and the strain of this personal matter must have its effect on you, and no doubt on Mrs. Chalmers. So I issued this instruction to my personal bank this morning."

He passed the carbon copy of the letter across to Chalmers, who read it. It was brief and to the point. It instructed the manager of Coutts Bank to remit by registered mail each month on the first day fifteen banknotes, each of value £10, to Dr. Gordon Chalmers at his home address. The remittances were to run for ten years unless further instructions were received.

Chalmers looked up. His employer's face was all concern, tinged with embarrassment.

"Thank you," said Chalmers softly.

Sir James's hand rested on his forearm and shook it. "Now come on, that's enough of this matter. Have a brandy."

In the taxi on the way back to the office, Manson suggested he drop Chalmers off at the station where he could take his train for Watford.

"I have to get back to the office and get on with this Zangaro business and your report," he said.

Chalmers was staring out of the cab window at the traffic moving out of

London that Friday afternoon. "What *are* you going to do about it?" he asked.

"Don't know, really. Of course, I'd like not to send it. Pity to see all that going into foreign hands, which is what must happen when your report gets to Zangaro. But I've got to send them something, sooner or later."

There was another long pause as the taxi swung into the station forecourt. "Is there anything I can do?" asked the scientist.

Sir James Manson breathed a long sigh. "Yes," he said in measured tones. "Junk the Mulrooney samples in the same way as you would junk any other rocks and bags of sand. Destroy your analysis notes completely. Take your copy of the report and make an exact copy, with one difference—let it show the tests prove conclusively that there exist marginal quantities of low-grade tin which could not be economically mined. Burn your own copy of the original report. And then never mention a word of it."

The taxi came to a halt, and as neither of his passengers moved, the cabbie poked his nose through the screen into the rear compartment. "This is it, guv."

"You have my solemn word," murmured Sir James Manson. "Sooner or later the political situation may well change, and when that happens, Man-Con will put in a tender for the mining concession exactly as usual and in accordance with normal business procedures."

Dr. Chalmers climbed out of the taxi and looked back at his employer in the corner seat. "I'm not sure I can do that, sir," he said. "I'll have to think it over."

Manson nodded. "Of course you will. I know it's asking a lot. Look, why don't you talk it over with your wife? I'm sure she'll understand."

Then he pulled the door to and told the cabbie to take him to the City.

Sir James dined with an official of the Foreign Office that evening and took him to his club. It was not one of the very uppercrust clubs of London, for Manson had no intention of putting up for one of the bastions of the old Establishment and finding himself blackballed. Besides, he had no time for social climbing and little patience with the posturing idiots one found at the top when one got there. He left the social side of things to his wife. The knighthood was useful, but that was an end to it.

He despised Adrian Goole, whom he reckoned for a pedantic fool. That was why he had invited him to dinner. That, and the fact that the man was in the Economic Intelligence section of the FO.

Years ago, when his company's activities in Ghana and Nigeria had reached a certain level, he had accepted a place on the inner circle of the City's West Africa Committee. This organ was and still is a sort of trade union of all major firms based in London and carrying on operations in West Africa. Concerned far more with trade, and therefore money, than, for example, the East Africa Committee, the WAC periodically reviewed events of both commerical and political interet in West Africa—and usually the two were bound to become connected in the long term—and tendered advice to the Foreign and Commonwealth Office on what would in its view constitute an advisable policy for British interests.

Sir Jame Manson would not have put it that way. He would have said the WAC was in existence to suggest to the government what to do in that part of the world to improve profits. He would have been right, too. He had been on the committee during the Nigerian civil war and heard the various representatives of banks, mines, oil, and trade advocate a quick end to the war, which seemed to be synonymous with a Federal victory in double time.

Predictably, the committee had proposed to the government that the Federal side be supported, provided it could show it was going to win and win quickly, and provided corroborative evidence from British sources on the spot confirmed this. The committee then sat back and watched the government, on Foreign Office advice, make another monumental African cock-up. Instead of lasting six months, the war had lasted thirty. But the businessmen were sick to their teeth at the whole mess and would, with hindsight, have preferred a negotiated peace at month three rather than thirty months of war. But Harold Wilson, once committed to a policy, was no more going to concede that his minions might have made a mistake on his behalf than fly to the moon.

Manson had lost a lot in revenue from his disrupted mining interests and because of the impossibility of shipping the stuff to the coast on crazily running railways throughout the period, but MacFazdean of Shell-BP had lost a lot more in oil production.

Adrian Goole had been the FO's liaison officer on the committee for most of the time. Now he sat opposite James Manson in the alcove dining recess, his cuffs shot the right inch and a quarter, his face registering earnest intent.

Manson told him some of the truth but kept the reference to platinum out of it. He stuck to a tale of tin but increased the quantities. It would have been viable to mine it, of course, but quite frankly he'd been scared off by the close dependence of the President on the Russian advisers. The profit-particiation of the Zangaran government could well have made it a tidy sum, and since the despot was almost a puppet of the Russkies, who wanted to increase the republic's power and influence through wealth? Goole took it all in. His face wore a solemn expression of deep concern.

"Damnably difficult decision," he said with sympathy. "Mind you, I have to admire your political sense. At the moment Zangaro is bankrupt and obscure. But if it became rich—Yes, you're quite right. A real dilemma. When do you have to send them the survey report and analysis?"

"Sooner or later," grunted Manson. "The question is, what do I do about it? If they show it to the Russians at the embassy, the trade counselor is bound to realize the tin deposits are viable. Then it will go out for tender. So someone else will get it, still help to make the dictator rich, and then who knows what problems he'll make for the West? One is back to square one."

Goole thought it over for a while.

"I just thought I ought to let you chaps know," said Manson.

"Yes, yes, thank you." Goole was absorbed. "Tell me," he said at length, "what would happen if you halved the figures showing the quantity of tin per rock-ton in the report?"

"Halved them?"

"Yes. Halved the figures, showing a purity figure of tin per rock-ton of fifty per cent the figure shown by your rock samples?"

"Well, the quantity of tin present would be shown to be economically unviable."

"And the rock samples could have come from another area, a mile away, for example?" asked Goole.

"Yes, I suppose they could. But my surveyor found the richest rock samples."

"But if he had not done so," pursued Goole. "If he had taken his samples from a mile from where he actually operated. The content could be down by fifty per cent?"

"Yes, it could. They probably would, probably would show even less than fifty per cent. But he operated where he did."

"Under supervision?" asked Goole.

"No. Alone."

"And there are no real traces of where he worked?"

"No," replied Manson. "Just a few rock chippings, long since overgrown. Besides, no one goes up there. It's miles from anywhere."

He paused for a few instants to light a cigar. "You know, Goole, you're a damnably clever fellow. Steward, another brandy, if you please."

They parted with mutual jocularity on the steps of the club. The doorman hailed a taxi for Goole to go back to Mrs. Goole in Holland Park.

"One last thing," said the FO man by the taxi door. "Not a word to anyone else about this. I'll have to file it, well classified, at the department, but otherwise it remains just between you and us at the FO."

"Of course," said Manson.

"I'm very grateful you saw fit to tell me all this. You have no idea how much easier it makes our job on the economic side to know what's going on. I'll keep a quiet eye on Zangaro, and if there should be any change in the political scene there, you'll be the first to know. Good night."

Sir James Manson watched the taxi head down the road and signaled to his Rolls-Royce waiting up the street.

"You'll be the first to know," he mimicked. "Too bloody right I will, boy. 'Cause I'm going to start it."

He leaned through the passenger-side window and observed to Craddock, his chauffeur, "If pisswilly little buggers like that had been in charge of building our empire, Craddock, we might by now just about have colonized the Isle of Wight."

"You're absolutely right, Sir James," said Craddock.

When his employer had climbed into the rear, the chauffeur slid open the communicating panel. "Gloucestershire, Sir James?"

"Gloucestershire, Craddock."

It was starting to drizzle again as the sleek limousine swished down Piccadilly and up Park Lane, heading for the A40 and the West Country, carrying Sir James Manson toward his ten-bedroom mansion bought three years earlier for him by a grateful company for £250,000. It also contained his wife and nineteen-year-old daughter, but these he had won himself.

An hour later Gordon Chalmers lay beside his wife, tired and angry from the row they had had for the past two hours. Peggy Chalmers lay on her back, looking up at the ceiling.

"I can't do it," Chalmers said for the umpteenth time. "I can't just go and falsify a mining report to help James Bloody Manson make more money."

There was a long silence. They had been over it all a score of times since Peggy had read Manson's letter to his banker and heard from her husband the conditions of future financial security.

"What does it matter?" she said in a low voice from the darkness beside him. "When all's said and done, what does it matter? Whether he gets the concession, or the Russians, or no one. Whether the price rises or falls. What does it matter? It's all pieces of rock and grains of metal."

Peggy Chalmers swung herself across her husband's torso and stared at the dim outline of his face. Outside, the night wind rattled the branches of the old elm close to which they had built the new house with the special fittings for their crippled daughter.

When Peggy Chalmers spoke again it was with passionate urgency. "But Margaret is not a piece of rock, and I am not a few grains of metal. We need that money, Gordon, we need it now and for the next ten years. Please, darling, please just one time forget the idea of a nice letter to *Tribune* or *Private Eye* and do what he wants."

Gordon Chalmers continued to stare at the slit of window between the curtains, which was half open to let in a breath of air.

"All right," he said at length.

"You'll do it?" she asked.

"Yes, I'll bloody do it."

"You swear it, darling? You give me your word?"

There was another long pause. "You have my word," said the low voice from the face above her.

She pillowed her head in the hair of his chest. "Thank you, darling. Don't worry about it. Please don't worry. You'll forget it in a month. You'll see."

Ten minutes later she was asleep, exhausted by the nightly struggle to get Margaret bathed and into bed, and by the unaccustomed quarrel with her husband.

Gordon Chalmers continued to stare into the darkness. "They always win," he said softly and bitterly after a while. "The bastards, they always bloody win."

The following day, Saturday, he drove the five miles to the laboratory and wrote out a completely new report for the republic of Zangaro. Then he burned his notes and the original report and trundled the core samples over to the scrap heap, where a local builder would remove them for concrete and garden paths. He mailed the fresh report, registered, to Sir James Manson at the head office, went home, and tried to forget it.

On Monday the report was received in London, and the instructions to the bankers in Chalmers' favor were mailed. The report was sent down to Overseas Contracts for Willoughby and Bryant to read, and Bryant was told to leave the next day and take it to the Minister of Natural Resources in Clarence. A letter from the company would be attached, expressing the appropriate regret.

On Tuesday evening Richard Bryant found himself in Number One Building at London's Heathrow Airport, waiting for a BEA flight to Paris, where he could get the appropriate visa and make a connecting flight by Air Afrique. Five hundred yards away, in Three Building, Jack Mulrooney humped his bag through Passport Control to catch the BOAC overnight Jumbo to Nairobi. He was not unhappy. He had had enough of London. Ahead lay Kenya, sun, bush, and the chance of a lion.

By the end of the week only two men had in their heads the knowledge of what really lay inside the Crystal Mountain. One had given his word to his wife to remain silent forever, and the other was plotting his next move.

FIVE

Simon Endean entered Sir James Manson's office with a bulky file containing his hundred-page report on the republic of Zangaro, a dossier of large photographs, and several maps. He told his chief what he had brought.

Manson nodded his approval. "No one learned while you were putting all this together who you were or who you worked for?" he asked.

"No, Sir James. I used a pseudonym, and no one questioned it."

"And no one in Zangaro could have learned that a file of data could have been put together about them?"

"No. I used existing archives, sparse though they are, some university libraries here and in Europe, standard works of reference, and the one tourist guide published by Zangaro itself, although in fact this is a leftover from colonial days and five years out of date. I always claimed I was simply seeking information for a graduate thesis on the entire African colonial and postcolonial situation. There will be no comebacks."

"All right," said Manson. "I'll read the report later. Give me the main facts."

For an answer Endean took one of the maps from the file and spread it across the desk. It showed a section of the African coastline, with Zangaro marked.

"As you see, Sir James, it's stuck like an enclave on the coast here, bordered on the north and east by this republic and on the short southern border by this one. The fourth side is the sea, here.

"It's shaped like a matchbox, the short edge along the seacoast, the longer sides stretching inland. The borders were completely arbitrarily drawn in the old colonial days during the scramble for Africa, and merely represent lines on a map. On the ground there are no effective borders, and due to the almost complete nonexistence of roads there is only one border-crossing point—here, on the road leading north to the neighbor country, Manandi. All land traffic enters and leaves by this road."

Sir James Manson studied the enclave on the map and grunted. "What about the eastern and southern borders?"

"No road, sir. No way in or out at all, unless you cut straight through the jungle, and in most places it is impenetrable bush.

"Now, in size it has seven thousand square miles, being seventy miles along the coast and a hundred miles deep into the hinterland. The capital, Clarence, named after the sea captain who first put in there for fresh water two hundred years ago, is here, in the center of the coast, thirty-five miles from the northern and southern borders.

"Behind the capital lies a narrow coastal plain which is the only cultivated area in the country, apart from the bush natives' tiny clearings in the jungle. Behind the plain lies the river Zangaro, then the foothills of the Crystal Mountains, the mountains themselves, and beyond that, miles and miles of jungle up to the eastern border."

"How about other communications?" asked Manson.

"There are virtually no roads at all," said Endean. "The river Zangaro flows from the northern border fairly close to the coast across most of the republic until it reaches the sea just short of the southern border. On the estuary there are a few jetties and a shanty or two which constitute a small port for the exporting of timber. But there are no wharves, and the timber businesses have virtually ceased since independence. The fact that the Zangaro River flows almost parallel to the coast, slanting in toward it, for sixty miles, in effect cuts the republic in two; there is this strip of coastal plain to the seaward side of the river, ending in mangrove swamps which make the whole coast unapproachable by shipping or small boats, and the hinterland beyond the river. East of the river are mountains, and beyond them the hinterland. The river could be used for barge traffic, but no one is interested. Manandi has a modern capital on the coast with a deep-water harbor, and the Zangaro River itself ends in a silted-up estuary."

"What about the timber-exporting operations? How were they carried out?"

Endean took a larger-scale map of the republic out of the file and laid it on the table. With a pencil he tapped the Zangaro estuary in the south of Zangaro.

"The timber used to be cut upcountry, either along the banks or in the western foothills of the mountains. There's still quite good timber there, but since independence no one is interested. The logs were floated downriver to the estuary and parked there. When the ships came they would anchor offshore and the log rafts were towed out to them by power boats. Then they hoisted the logs aboard by using their own derricks. It always was a tiny operation."

Manson stared intently at the large-scale map taking in the seventy miles of coast, the river running almost parallel to it twenty miles inland, the strip of impenetrable mangrove swamp between river and the sea, and the mountains behind the river. He could identify the Crystal Mountain but made no mention of it.

"What about the main roads? There must be some."

Endean warmed to his explanation. "The capital is stuck on the seaward end of a short, stubby peninsula here, midway down the coast. It faces toward the open sea. There's a small port, the only real one in the country, and behind the town the peninsula runs back to join the main landmass. There is one road which runs down the spine of the peninsula and six miles inland, going straight east. Then there is the junction—here. A road runs to the right, heading south. It is laterite for seven miles, then becomes an earth road for the next twenty. Then it peters out on the banks of the Zangaro estuary.

"The other branch turns left and runs north, through the plain west of the river and onward to the northern border. Here there is a crossing point manned by a dozen sleepy and corrupt soldiers. A couple of travelers told me they can't read a passport anyway, so they don't know whether there is a visa in it or not. You just bribe them a couple of quid to get through."

"What about the road into the hinterland?" asked Sir James.

Endean pointed with his finger. "It's not even marked, it's so small. Actually, if you follow the north-running road after the junction, go along it for ten miles, there is a turn-off to the right, toward the hinterland. It's an earth road. It crosses the remainder of the plain and then the Zangaro River, on a rickety wooden bridge—"

"So that bridge is the only communication between the two parts of the country on either side of the river?" asked Manson in wonderment.

Endean shrugged. "It's the only crossing for wheeled traffic. But there is hardly any wheeled traffic. The natives cross the Zangaro by canoe."

Manson changed the subject, though his eyes never left the map. "What about the tribes who live there?"

"There are two," said Endean. "East of the river and right back to the end of the hinterland is the country of the Vindu. For that matter, more Vindu live over the eastern border. I said the borders were arbitrary. The Vindu are practically in the Stone Age. They seldom, if ever, cross the river and leave their bush country. The plain to the west of the river and down to the sea, including the peninsula on which the capital stands, is the country of the Caja. They hate the Vindu, and vice versa."

"Population?"

"Almost uncountable in the interior. Officially put at two hundred and twenty thousand in the entire country. That is, thirty thousand Caja and an estimated one hundred and ninety thousand Vindu. But the numbers are a total guess—except probably the Caja can be counted accurately."

"Then how the hell did they ever hold an election?" asked Manson.

"That remains one of the mysteries of creation," said Endean. "It was a shambles, anyway. Half of them didn't know what a vote was or what they were voting for."

"What about the economy?"

"There is hardly any left," replied Endean. "The Vindu country produces nothing. The lot of them just about subsist on what they can grow in yam and cassava plots cut out of the bush by the women, who do any work there is to be done, which is precious little—unless you pay them well; then they will carry things. The men hunt. The children are a mass of malaria, trachoma, bilharzia, and malnutrition.

"In the coastal plain there were in colonial days plantations of low-grade cocoa, coffee, cotton, and bananas. These were run and owned by whites, who used native labor. It wasn't high-quality stuff, but it made enough, with a guaranteed European buyer, the colonial power, to make a bit of hard currency and pay for the minimal imports. Since independence, these have been nationalized by the President, who expelled the whites, and given to his party hacks. Now they're about finished, overgrown with weeds."

"Got any figures?"

"Yes, sir. In the last year before independence total cocoa output, that was the main crop, was thirty thousand tons,. Last year it was one thousand tons, and there were no buyers. It's still rotting on the ground."

"And the others—coffee, cotton, bananas?"

"Bananas and coffee virtually ground to a halt through lack of attention. Cotton got hit by a blight, and there were no insecticides."

"What's the economic situation now?"

"Total disaster. Bankrupt, money worthless paper, exports down to almost nothing, and nobody letting them have any imports. There have been gifts from the UN, the Russians, and the colonial powers, but as the government always sells the stuff elsewhere and pockets the cash, even these three have given up."

"A cheap tinhorn dictatorship, eh?" murmured Sir James.

"In every sense. Corrupt, vicious, brutal. They have seas off the coast rich in fish, but they can't fish. The two fishing boats they had were skippered by whites. One got beaten up by the army thugs, and both quit. Then the engines rusted up, and the boats were abandoned. So the locals have protein deficiency. There aren't even goats and chickens to go around."

"What about medicines?"

"There's one hospital in Clarence, which is run by the United Nations. That's the only one in the country."

"Doctors?"

"There were two Zangarans who were qualified doctors. One was arrested and died in prison. The other fled into exile. The missionaries were expelled by the President as imperialist influences. They were mainly medical missionaries as well as preachers and priests. The nuns used to train nurses, but they got expelled as well."

"How many Europeans?"

"In the hinterlands, probably none. In the coastal plain, a couple of agronomists, technicians sent by the United Nations. In the capital, about forty diplomats, twenty of them in the Russian embassy, the rest spread among the French, Swiss, American, West German, East German, Czech, and Chinese embassies, if you call the Chinese white. Apart from that, about five United Nations hospital staff, another five technicians manning the electrical generator, the airport control tower, the waterworks, and so on. Then there must be fifty others, traders, managers, businessmen who have hung on hoping for an improvement.

"Actually, there was a ruckus six weeks ago and one of the UN men was beaten half to death. The five nonmedical technicians threatened to quit and sought refuge in their respective embassies. They may be gone by now, in which case the water, electricity, and airport will soon be out of commission."

"Where is the airport?"

"Here, on the base of the peninsula behind the capital. It's not of international standards, so if you want to fly in you have to take Air Afrique to here, in Manandi, and take a connecting flight by a small two-engined plane that goes down to Clarence three times a week. It's a French firm that has the concession, though nowadays it's hardly economic."

"Who are the country's friends, diplomatically speaking?"

Endean shook his head. "They don't have any. No one is interested, it's such a shambles. Even the Organization of African Unity is embarrassed by the whole place. It's so obscure no one ever mentions it. No newsmen ever go, so it never gets publicized. The government is rabidly anti-white, so no one wants to send staff men down there to run anything. No one invests anything, because nothing is safe from confiscation by any Tom, Dick, or Harry wearing a party badge. There's a party youth organization that beats up anyone it wants to, and everyone lives in terror."

"What about the Russians?"

"They have the biggest mission and probably a bit of say over the President in matters of foreign policy, about which he knows nothing. His advisers are mainly Moscow-trained Zangarans, though he wasn't schooled in Moscow personally."

"Is there any potential at all down there?" asked Sir James.

Endean nodded slowly. "I suppose there is enough potential, well managed and worked, to sustain the population at a reasonable degree of prosperity. The population is small, the needs few; they could be self-sufficient in clothing, food, the basics of a good local economy, with a little hard currency for the necessary extras. It could be done, but in any case, the needs are so few the relief and charitable agencies could provide the total necessary, if it wasn't that their staffs are always molested, their equipment smashed or looted, and their gifts stolen and sold for the government's private profit."

"You say the Vindu won't work hard. What about the Caja?"

"Nor they either," said Endean. "They just sit about all day, or fade into the bush if anyone looks threatening. Their fertile plain has always grown enough to sustain them, so they are happy the way they are."

"Then who worked the estates in the colonial days?"

"Ah, the colonial power brought in about twenty thousand black workers from elsewhere. They settled and live there still. With their families, they are about fifty thousand. But they were never enfranchised by the colonial power, so they never voted in the election at independence. If there is any work done, they still do it."

"Where do they live?" asked Manson.

"About fifteen thousand still live in their huts on the estates, even though there is no more work worth doing, with all the machinery broken down. The rest have drifted toward Clarence and grub a living as best they can. They live in a series of shanty towns scattered down the road at the back of the capital, on the road to the airport."

For five minutes Sir James Manson stared at the map in front of him, thinking deeply about a mountain, a mad President, a coterie of Moscow-trained advisers, and a Russian embassy. Finally he sighed. "What a bloody shambles of a place."

"That's putting it mildly," said Endean. "They still have ritual public executions before the assembled populace in the main square. Death by being chopped to pieces with a machete. Quite a bunch."

"And who precisely has produced this paradise on earth?"

For answer, Endean produced a photograph and placed it on the map.

Sir James Manson found himself looking at a middle-aged African in a silk top hat, black frock coat, and checked trousers. It was evidently inauguration day, for several colonial officials stood in the background, by the steps of a large mansion. The face beneath the shining black silk was not round, but long and gaunt, with deep lines on each side of the nose. The mouth was twisted downward at each corner, so that the effect was of deep disapproval of something.

But the eyes held the attention. There was a glazed fixity about them, as one sees in the eyes of fanatics.

"That's the man," said Endean. "Mad as a hatter, and nasty as a rattlesnake. West Africa's own Papa Doc. Visionary, communicant with spirits, liberator from the white man's yoke, redeemer of his people, swindler, robber, police chief and torturer of the suspicious, extractor of confessions, hearer of voices from the Almighty, seer of visions, Lord High Everything Else, His Excellency, President Jean Kimba."

Sir James Manson stared longer at the face of the man who, unbeknownst to himself, was sitting in control of ten billion dollars' worth of platinum. I wonder, he thought to himself, if the world would really notice his passing on.

He said nothing, but, after he had listened to Endean, that event was what he had decided to arrange.

Six years earlier the colonial power ruling the enclave now called Zangaro, increasingly conscious of world opinion, had decided to grant independence. Overhasty preparations were made among a population wholly inexperienced in self-government, and a general election and independence were fixed for the following year.

In the confusion, five political parties came into being. Two were wholly tribal, one claiming to look after the interests of the Vindu, the other of the Caja. The other three parties devised their own political platforms and pretended to make appeal through the tribal division of the people. One of these parties was the conservative group, led by a man holding office under the colonialists and heavily favored by them. He pledged he would continue the close links with the mother country, which, apart from anything else, guaranteed the local paper money and bought the exportable produce. The second party was centrist, small and weak, led by an intellectual, a professor who had studied in Europe. The third was radical and led by a man who had served several prison terms under a security classification. This was Jean Kimba.

Long before the elections, two of his aides, men who during their time as students in Europe had been contacted by the Russians (who had noticed their presence in anti-colonial street demonstrations) and who had accepted scholarships to finish their schooling at the Patrice Lumumba University outside Moscow, left Zangaro secretly and flew to Europe. There they met emissaries from Moscow and, as a result of their conversations, received a sum of money and considerable advice of a very practical nature.

Using the money, Kimba and his men formed squads of political thugs from among the Vindu and completely ignored the small minority of Caja. In the unpoliced hinterland the political squads went to work. Several agents of the rival parties came to very sticky ends, and the squads visited all the clan chiefs of the Vindu.

After several public burnings and eye-gougings, the clan chiefs got the message. When the elections came, acting on the simple and effective logic that you do what the man with the power to extract painful retribution tells you, and ignore or mock the weak and the powerless, the chiefs ordered their people to vote for Kimba. He won the Vindu by a clear majority, and the total votes cast for him swamped the combined opposition and the Caja votes. He was aided by the fact that the number of the Vindu votes had been almost doubled by the persuasion of every village chief to increase the number of people he claimed lived in his village. The rudimentary census taken by the colonial officials was based on affidavits from each village chief as to the population of his village.

The colonial power had made a mess of it. Instead of taking a leaf from the French book and ensuring that the colonial protégé won the first, vital election and then signed a mutual defense treaty to ensure that a company of white paratroops kept the pro-Western president in power in perpetuity, the colonials had allowed their worst enemy to win. A month after the election, Jean Kimba was inaugurated as first President of Zangaro.

What followed was along traditional lines. The four other parties were banned as "divisive influences," and later the four party leaders were arrested on trumped-up charges. They died under torture in prison, after making over the party funds to the liberator, Kimba. The colonial army and police officers were dismissed as soon as a semblance of an exclusively Vindu army had been brought into being. The Caja soldiers, who had constituted most of the gendarmerie under the colonists, were dismissed at the same time, and trucks were provided to take them home. After leaving the capital, the six trucks headed for a quiet spot on the Zangaro River, and here the machine guns opened up. That was the end of the trained Caja.

In the capital, the police and customs men, mainly Caja, were allowed to stay on, but their guns were emptied and all their ammunition was taken away. Power passed to the Vindu army, and the reign of terror started. It had taken eighteen months to achieve this. The confiscation of the estates, assets, and businesses of the colonists began, and the economy ran steadily down. There were no Vindu trained to take over who could run the republic's few enterprises with even moderate efficiency, and the estates were in any case given to Kimba's party supporters. As the colonists left, a few UN technicians came in to run the basic essentials, but the excesses they witnessed caused most sooner or later to write home to their governments insisting they be removed.

After a few short, sharp examples of terror, the timorous Caja were subdued into absolute submission, and even across the river in Vindu country several savage examples were made of chiefs who mumbled something about the pre-election promises. After that the Vindu simply shrugged and went back to their bush. What happened in the capital had never affected them anyway in living memory, so they could afford to shrug. Kimba and his group of supporters, backed by the Vindu army and the unstable and highly dangerous teenagers who made up the party's youth movement, continued to rule from Clarence entirely for their own benefit and profit.

Some of the methods used to obtain the latter were mindboggling. Simon Endean's report contained documentation of an instance where Kimba, frustrated over the nonarrival of his share of a business deal, arrested the European businessman involved and imprisoned him, sending an emissary to his wife with the pledge that she would receive her husband's toes, fingers, and ears by post unless a ransom were paid. A letter from her imprisoned husband confirmed this, and the woman raised the necessary half-million dollars from his business partners and paid. The man was released, but his government, terrified of black African opinion at United Nations, urged him to remain silent. The press never heard about it. On another occasion two nationals of the colonial power were arrested and beaten in the former colonial police barracks, since converted into the army barracks. They were released after a handsome bribe was paid to the Minister of Justice, of which a part evidently went to Kimba. Their offense was failing to bow as Kimba's car went past.

In the previous five years since independence, all conceivable opposition to Kimba had been wiped out or driven into exile, and those who suffered the latter were the lucky ones. As a result there were no doctors, engineers, or other qualified people left in the republic. There had been few enough in the first place, and Kimba suspected all educated men as possible opponents.

Over the years he had developed a psychotic fear of assassination and never left the country. He seldom left the palace and, when he did, it was under a massive escort. Firearms of every kind and description had been rounded up and impounded, including hunting rifles and shotguns, so that scarcity of protein food increased. Import of cartridges and black powder was halted, so eventually the Vindu hunters of the interior, coming to the coast to buy the powder they needed to hunt game, were sent back empty-handed and hung up their useless dane guns in their huts. Even the carrying of machetes within the city limits was forbidden. The carrying of any of these items was punishable by death.

When he had finally digested the lengthy report, studied the photographs of the capital, the palace, and Kimba, and pored over the maps, Sir James Manson sent again for Simon Endean.

The latter was becoming highly curious about his chief's interest in this obscure republic and had asked Martin Thorpe in the adjoining office on the ninth floor what it was about. Thorpe had just grinned and tapped the side of his nose with a rigid forefinger. Thorpe was not completely certain either, but he suspected he knew. Both men knew enough not to ask questions when their employer had got an idea in his head and needed information.

When Endean reported to Manson the following morning, the latter was standing in his favorite position by the plate-glass windows of his penthouse, looking down into the street, where pygmies hurried about their business.

"There are two things I need to know more about, Simon," Sir James Manson said without preamble and walked back to his desk, where the Endean report was lying. "You mention here a ruckus in the capital about six to seven weeks ago. I heard another report about the same upset from a man who was there. He mentioned a rumor of an attempted assassination of Kimba. What was it all about?"

Endean was relieved. He had heard the same story from his own sources but had thought it too small to include in the report.

"Every time the president has a bad dream there are arrests and rumors of an attempt on his life," said Endean. "Normally it just means he wants justification to arrest and execute somebody. In this case, in late January, it was the commander of the army, Colonel Bobi. I was told, on the quiet, the quarrel between the two men was really about Kimba's not getting a big enough cut in the rake-off from a deal Bobi put through. A shipment of drugs and medicines had arrived for the UN hospital. The army impounded them at the quayside and stole half. Bobi was responsible, and the stolen portion of the cargo was sold elsewhere on the black market. The proceeds of the sale should have passed to Kimba. Anyway, the head of the UN hospital, when making his protest to Kimba and tendering his resignation, mentioned the true value of the missing stuff. It was a lot more than Bobi had admitted to Kimba.

"The President went mad and sent some of his own guards out looking for Bobi. They ransacked the town, arresting anyone who got in the way or took their fancy."

"What happened to Bobi?" asked Manson.

"He fled. He got away in a jeep and made for the border. He got across by abandoning his jeep and walking through the bush round the border control point."

"What tribe is he?"

"Oddly enough, a halfbreed. Half Vindu and half Caja, probably the outcome of a Vindu raid on a Caja village forty years ago."

"Was he one of Kimba's new army, or the old colonial one?" asked Manson.

"He was corporal in the colonial gendarmerie, so presumably he had some form of rudimentary training. Then he was busted, before independence, for drunkenness and insubordination while drunk. When Kimba came to power he took him back in the early days because he needed at least one man who could tell one end of a gun from the other. In the colonial days Bobi styled himself a Caja, but as soon as Kimba came to power he swore he was a true Vindu."

"Why did Kimba keep him on? Was he one of his original supporters?"

"From the time Bobi saw which way the wind was blowing, he went to Kimba and swore loyalty to him. Which was smarter than the colonial governor, who couldn't believe Kimba had won the election until the figures proved it. Kimba kept Bobi on and even promoted him to command the army, because it looked better for a half-Caja to carry out the reprisals against the Caja opponents of Kimba."

"What's he like?" asked Manson pensively.

"A big thug," said Simon. "A human gorilla. No brains as such, but a certain low animal cunning. The quarrel between the two men was only a question of thieves falling out."

"But Western-trained? Not Communist?" insisted Manson.

"No, sir. Not a Communist. Not anything politically."

"Bribable? Cooperate for money?"

"Certainly. He must be living pretty humbly now. He couldn't have stashed much away outside Zangaro. Only the President could get the big money."

"Where is he now?" asked Manson.

"I don't know, sir. Living somewhere in exile."

"Right," said Manson. "Find him, wherever he is."

Endean nodded. "Am I to visit him?"

"Not yet," said Manson. "There was one other matter. The report is fine, very comprehensive, except in one detail. The military side. I want to have a complete breakdown of the military security situation in and around the President's palace and the capital. How many troops, police, any special presidential bodyguards, where they are quartered, how good they are, level of training and experience, the amount of fight they would put up if under attack, what weapons they carry, can they use them, what reserves are there, where the arsenal is situated, whether they have guards posted overall, if there are armored cars or artillery, if the Russians train the army, if there are strike-force camps away from Clarence—in fact, the whole lot."

Endean stared at his chief in amazement. The phrase "if under attack" stuck in his mind. What on earth was the old man up to? he wondered, but his face remained impassive.

"That would mean a personal visit, Sir James."

"Yes, I concede that. Do you have a passport in another name?"

"No, sir. In any case, I couldn't furnish that information. It requires a sound judgment of military matters, and a knowledge of African troops as well. I was too late for National Service. I don't know a thing about armies or weapons."

Manson was back at the window, staring across the City. "I know," he said softly. "It would need a soldier to produce that report."

"Well, Sir James, you would hardly get an army man to go and do that sort of mission. Not for any money. Besides, a soldier's passport would have his profession on it. Where could I find a military man who would go down to Clarence and find that sort of information?"

"There is a kind," said Manson. "The mercenaires. They fight for whoever pays them and pays them well. I'm prepared to do that. So go and find me a mercenary with initiative and brains. The best in Europe.

Cat Shannon lay on his bed in the small hotel in Montmartre and watched the smoke from his cigarette drifting up toward the ceiling. He was bored. In the weeks that had passed since his return from Africa he had spent most of his saved pay traveling around Europe trying to set up another job.

In Rome he had seen an order of Catholic priests he knew, with a view to going to South Sudan on their behalf to set up in the interior an airstrip into which medical supplies and food could be ferried. He knew there were three separate groups of mercenaries operating in South Sudan, helping the Christian blacks in their civil war against the Arab North. In Bahr-el-Gazar two other British mercenaries, Ron Gregory and Rip Kirby, were leading a small operation of Dinka tribesmen, laying mines along the roads used by the Sudanese army in an attempt to knock out their British Saladin armored cars. In the south, in Equatoria Province, Rolf Steiner had a camp that was supposed to be training the locals in the arts of war, but nothing had been heard of him for months. In Upper Nile, to the East, there was a much more efficient camp, where four Israelis were training the tribesmen and equipping them with Soviet weaponry from the vast stocks the Israelis had taken from the Egyptians in 1967. The warfare in the three provinces of South Sudan kept the bulk of the Sudanese army and air force pinned down there, so that five squadrons of Egyptian fighters were based around Khartoum and thus not available to confront the Israelis on the Suez Canal.

Shannon had visited the Israeli embassy in Paris and talked for forty minutes to the military attaché. The latter had listened politely, thanked him politely, and just as politely ushered him out. The only thing the officer would say was that there were no Israeli advisers on the rebel side in South Sudan, and therefore he could not help. Shannon had no doubts the conversation had been tape-recorded and sent to Tel Aviv, but doubted he would hear any more. He conceded the Israelis were first rate as fighters and good at intelligence, but he thought they knew nothing about black Africa and were heading for a fall in Uganda and probably elsewhere.

Apart from Sudan, there was little else being offered. Rumors abounded that the CIA was hiring mercenaries for training anti-Communist Meos in Cambodia, and that some Persian Gulf sheiks were getting fed up with their dependence on British military advisers and were looking for mercenaries who would be entirely their own dependents. The story was that there were jobs going for men prepared to fight for the sheiks in the hinterland or take charge of palace security. Shannon doubted all these stories; for one thing he wouldn't trust the CIA as far as he could spit, and the Arabs were not much better when it came to making up their minds.

Outside of the Gulf, Cambodia, and Sudan, there was little scope and there were no good wars. In fact he foresaw in the offing a very nasty outbreak of peace. That left the chance of working as a bodyguard for a European arms dealer, and he had had one approach from such a man in Paris who felt himself threatened and needed someone good to give him cover.

Hearing Shannon was in town and knowing his skill and speed, the arms dealer had sent an emissary with the proposition. Without actually turning it down, the Cat was not keen. The dealer was in trouble through his own stupidity: a small matter of sending a shipment of arms to the Provisional IRA and then tipping off the British as to where it would be landed. There had been a number of arrests, and the Provos were furious. Having Shannon giving gun-cover would send most professionals back home while still alive, but the Provos were mad dogs and probably did not know enough to stay clear. So there would be a gunfight, and the French police would take a dim view of one of their streets littered with bleeding Fenians. Morover, as he was an Ulster Protestant, they would never believe Shannon had just been doing his job. Still, the offer was open.

The month of March had opened and was ten days through, but the weather remained dank and chill, with daily drizzle and rain, and Paris was unwelcoming. Outdoors meant fine weather in Paris, and indoors cost a lot of money. Shannon was husbanding his remaining resources of dollars as best he could. So he left his telephone number with the dozen or so people he thought might hear something to interest him and read several paperback novels in his hotel room.

He lay staring at the ceiling and thinking of home. Not that he really had a home any more, but for want of a better word he still thought of the wild sweep of turf and stunted trees that sprawls across the border of Tyrone and Donegal as the place that he came from.

He had been born and brought up close to the small village of Castlederg, situated inside County Tyrone but lying on the border with Donegal. His parents' house had been set a mile from the village on a slope looking out to the west across Donegal.

They called Donegal the county God forgot to finish, and the few trees were bent toward the east, curved over by the constant beating of the winds from the North Atlantic.

His father had owned a flax mill that turned out fine Irish linen and had been in a small way the squire of the area. He was Protestant, and almost all the workers and local farmers were Catholic, and in Ulster never the twain shall meet, so the young Carlo had no other boys to play with. He made his friends among the horses instead, and this was horse country. He could ride before he could mount a bicycle, and had a pony of his own when he was five, and he could still remember riding the pony into the village to buy a halfpennyworth of sherbet powder from the sweetshop of old Mr. Sam Gailey.

At eight he had been sent to boarding school in England at the urging of his mother, who was English and came from moneyed people. So for the next ten years he had learned to be an Englishman and had to all intents and purposes lost the stamp of Ulster in both speech and attitudes. During the holidays he had gone home to the moors and the horses, but he knew no contemporaries near Castlederg, so the vacations were lonely if healthy, consisting of long, fast gallops in the wind.

It was while he was a sergeant in the Royal Marines at twenty-two that his parents had died in a car crash on the Belfast Road. He had returned for the funeral, smart in his black belt and gaiters, topped by the green beret of the Commandos. Then he had accepted an offer for the run-down, nearly bankrupt mill, closed up the house, and returned to Portsmouth.

That was eleven years ago. He had served the remainder of his five-year contract in the Marines, and on returning to civilian life had pottered from job to job until taken on as a clerk by a London merchant house with widespread African interest. Working his probationary year in London, he had learned the intricacies of company structure, trading and banking the profits, setting up holding companies, and the value of a discreet Swiss account. After a year in London he had been posted as assistant manager of the Uganda branch office, from which he had walked out without a word and driven into the Congo. So for the last six years he had lived as a mercenary, often as outlaw, at best regarded as a soldier for hire, at worst as a paid killer. The trouble was, once he was known as a mercenary, there was no going back. It was not a question of being unable to get a job in a business house; that could be done at a pinch, or even by giving a different name. Even without going to these lengths, one could always get hired as a truck-driver, as a security guard, or for some manual job if the worst came to the worst. The real problem was being able to stick it out, to sit in an office under the orders of a wee man in a dark gray suit and look out of the window and recall the bush country, the waving palms, the smell of sweat and cordite, the grunts of the men hauling the jeeps over the river crossings, the copper-tasting fears just before the attack, and the wild, cruel joy of being alive afterward. To remember, and then to go back to the ledgers and the commuter train, that was what was impossible. He knew he would eat his heart out if it ever came to that. For Africa bites like a tse-tse fly, and once the drug is in the blood it can never be wholly exorcised.

So he lay on his bed and smoked some more and wondered where the next job was coming from.

SIX

Simon Endean was aware that somewhere in London there had to exist the wherewithal to discover just about any piece of knowledge known to man, including the name and address of a first-class mercenary. The only problem sometimes is to know where to start looking and whom to start asking.

After a reflective hour drinking coffee in his office, he left and took a taxi down to Fleet Street. Through a friend on the city desk of one of London's biggest daily papers, he got access to that paper's morgue and to virtually every newspaper clipping in Britain over the previous ten years concerning mercenaries. There were articles about Katanga, the Congo, Yemen, Vietnam, Cambodia, Laos, Sudan, Nigeria, and Rwanda; news items, commentaries, editorial feature articles, and photographs. He read them all and paid special attention to the names of the writers.

At this stage he was not looking for the name of a mercenary. There were in any case too many names—pseudonyms, noms de guerre, nicknames— and he had little doubt some of them were false. He was looking for the name of an expert on mercenaries, a writer or reporter whose articles seemed to be authoritative enough to indicate that the journalist knew his subject well, who could find his way around the bewildering labyrinth of rival claims and alleged exploits and give a balanced judgment. At the end of two hours he had secured the name he was looking for, although he had never heard of the man before.

There were three articles over the previous three years carrying the same byline, apparently that of an Englishman or American. The writer seemed to know what he was talking about, and he mentioned mercenaries from half a dozen different nationalities, neither overpraising them nor sensationalizing their careers to set spines atingling. Endean noted the name and the three newspapers in which the articles had appeared, a fact which seemed to indicate that the writer was freelancing. A second phone call to his newspaper friend eventually produced the writer's address. It was a small flat in North London.

Darkness had already fallen when Endean left ManCon House, and, having taken his Corvette from the underground parking lot, he drove northward to find the journalist's flat. The lights were off when he got there, and there was no answer to the doorbell. Endean hoped the man was not abroad, and the woman in the basement flat confirmed that he was not. He was glad to see the house was not large or smart and hoped the reporter might be hard up for a little extra cash, as freelances usually are. He decided to come back in the morning.

Simon Endean pressed the bell next to the writer's name just after eight the following morning, and half a minute later a voice tinkled "Yes" at him from the metal grill set in the woodwork.

"Good morning," said Endean into the grill. "My name is Harris. Walter Harris. I'm a businessman. I wonder if I might have a word with you?"

The door opened, and he mounted to the fourth floor, where a door stood open onto the landing. Framed in it was the man he had come to see. When they were seated in the sitting room, Endean came straight to the point.

"I am a businessman in the City," he lied smoothly. "I am here, in a sense, representing a consortium of friends, all of whom have this in common: that we all have business interests in a state in West Africa."

The writer nodded warily and sipped his coffee.

"Recently there have been increasing reports of the possibility of a coup d'état. The President is a moderate and reasonably good man, as things go down there, and very popular with his people. One of my business friends was told by one of his workers that the coup, if and when it came, could well be Communist-backed. Do you follow me?"

"Yes. Go on."

"Well now, it is felt that no more than a small portion of the army would support a coup unless the speed of it threw them into confusion and left them leaderless. In other words, if it were a *fait accompli,* the bulk of the army might agree to go along in any case, once they realized the coup had succeeded. But if it came and half failed, the bulk of the army would, we all feel sure, support the President. As you may know, experience shows the twenty hours following the strike are the vital ones."

"What has this to do with me?" asked the writer.

"I'm coming to that," said Endean. "The general feeling is that, for the coup to succeed, it would be necessary for the plotters first to assassinate the President. If he remained alive, the coup would fail, or might not even be tried, and all would be well. Therefore the question of palace security is vital and becoming more so. We have been in touch with some friends in the Foreign Office, and they feel it is out of the question to send a professional British officer to advise on security in and around the palace."

"So?" The writer sipped more coffee and lit a cigarette. He reckoned his visitor was too smooth, too smooth by half.

"So the President would be prepared to accept the services of a professional soldier to advise, on the basis of a contract, on all security matters regarding the person of the President. What he is seeking is a man who could go down there, make a complete and thorough survey of the palace and all its security arrangements, and plug any loopholes in the existing security measures surrounding the President."

The freelance nodded several times. He had few doubts that the story of the man who called himself Harris was some way from true. For one thing, if palace security was really what was sought, the British government would not be against providing the expert to advise on its improvement. For another, there was a perfectly capable firm at 22 Sloane Street, London, called Watchguard International, whose specialty was precisely that. In a few sentences he pointed this out to Harris.

Endean was not fazed in the slightest. "Ah," he said, "evidently I have to be a little more candid."

"It would help," said the writer.

"The point is, you see, that HMG might agree to send an expert merely to advise, but if the advice was that the palace security troops needed extensive further training—and a crash course, at that—politically speaking a Britisher sent by the government could not do that. And if the President wished to offer the man a longer-term post on his staff, the same would apply. As for Watchguard, one of their ex-Special Air Service men would be fine, but if he were on the staff of the palace guard and a coup were tried despite his presence, there might be a question of combat. Now you know what the rest of Africa would think about a staff man from Watchguard, which most of these blacks regard as being linked to the Foreign Office in some way, doing that. But a pure outsider, although not respectable, would at least be understandable, without exposing the President to the sneer of being a tool of the dirty old imperialists."

"So what do you want?" asked the writer.

"The name of a good mercenary soldier," said Endean. "One with brains and initiative, who'll do a workmanlike job for his money."

"Why come to me?"

"Your name was recalled by one of our group from an article you wrote several months ago. It seemed very authoritative."

"I write for my living," said the freelance.

Endean gently withdrew £200 in £10 notes from his pocket and laid them on the table. "Then write for me."

"What? An article?"

"No, a memorandum. A list of names and track records. Or you can talk if you like."

"I'll write," said the freelance. He walked to a corner, where his desk, a typewriter, and a stack of white paper comprised the working area of the open-plan flat. Having run a sheet into his machine, he wrote steadily for fifty minutes, consulting occasionally from a set of files beside his desk. When he rose, he walked over to the waiting Endean with three sheets of quarto paper and held them out.

"These are the best around today, the older generation of the Congo six years ago and the new up-and-comers. I haven't bothered with men who couldn't command a platoon well. Mere heavies would be no use to you."

Endean took the sheets and studied them intently.

The contents were:

COLONEL LAMOULINE. Belgian, probably government man. Came into Congo in 1964 under Moïse Tshombe. Probably with full approval of Belgian government. First-class soldier, not really a mercenary in full sense of the word. Set up Sixth Commando (French-speaking) and commanded until 1965, when he handed over command to Denard and left.

ROBERT DENARD. Frenchman. Police background, not army. Was in Katanga secession in 1961–62, probably as gendarmerie adviser. Left after failure of secession and exile of Tshombe. Commanded French mercenary operation in Yemen for Jacques Foccart. Returned Congo 1964, joined Lamouline. Commanded Sixth after Lamouline and up till 1967. Took part, halfheartedly, in second Stanleyville revolt (the mercenaries' mutiny) in 1967. Wounded badly in head by ricocheting bullet from own side. Flown out of Rhodesia for treatment. Tried to return by mounting

November 1967 mercenary invasion of Congo from the
south at Dilolo. Operation delayed, some said as a result of
CIA bribes, was a fiasco when it happened. Since lived in
Paris.

JACQEUS SCHRAMME. Belgian. Planter-turned-mercenary.
Nicknamed Black Jacques. Formed own unit of Katangese
early in 1961 and was prominent in Katangese secession
attempt. One of the last to flee into Angola on defeat of the
secession. Took his Katangese with him. Waited in Angola
until return of Tshombe, then marched back into Katanga.
Through the 1964–65 war against the Simba rebels, his 10th
Codo was more or less independent. Sat out the first Stanleyville revolt of 1966 (the Katangese mutiny), and his
mixed mercenary/Katangese force was left intact. Launched 1967 Stanleyville mutiny, in which Denard later
joined. Took joint command after wounding of Denard and
led the march to Bukavu. Repatriated 1968, no further
mercenary work since.

ROGER FAULQUES. Much-decorated French professional
officer. Sent, probably by French govt., into Katanga during
secession. Later commanded Denard, who ran the French
operation in the Yemen. Was not involved in Congolese
mercenary operations. Mounted small operation at French
behest in Nigerian civil war. Ferociously brave but now
nearly crippled by combat wounds.

MIKE HOARE. British-turned-South African. Acted as
mercenary adviser in Katanga secession, became close personal friend of Tshombe. Invited back to Congo in 1964,
when Tshombe returned to power, and formed English-
speaking Fifth Commando. Commanded through bulk of
anti-Simba war, retired in December 1965 and handed over
to Peters. Well off and semi-retired.

JOHN PETERS. Joined Hoare in 1964 in first mercenary
war. Rose to become deputy commander. Fearless and totally ruthless. Several officers under Hoare refused to serve
under Peters and transferred or left 5th Codo. Retired
wealthy late 1966.

N.B. The above six count as "the older generation," in-
asmuch as they were the originals who came to prominence
in the Katanga and Congolese wars. The following five are
younger in age, except Roux, who is now in his mid-forties,
but may be considered the "younger" generation because
they had junior commands in the Congo or came to prominence since the Congo.

ROLF STEINER. German. Began first mercenary operation

under Faulques-organized group that went into Nigerian civil war. Stayed on and led the remnants of the group for nine months. Dismissed. Signed on for South Sudan.

GEORGE SCHROEDER. South African. Served under Hoare and Peters in 5th Codo in the Congo. Prominent in the South African contingent in that unit. Their choice as a leader after Peters. Peters conceded and gave him the command. 5th Codo disbanded and sent home a few months later. Not heard of since. Living in South Africa.

CHARLES ROUX. French. Very junior in Katangese secession. Quit early and went to South Africa via Angola. Stayed there and returned with South Africans to fight under Hoare in 1964. Quarreled with Hoare and went to join Denard. Promoted and transferred to 6th Codo subsidiary unit, the 14th Codo, as second-in-command. Took part in 1966 Katangese revolt in Stanleyville, in which his unit was nearly wiped out. Was smuggled out of the Congo by Peters. Returned by air with several South Africans and joined Schramme, May 1967. Took part in 1967 Stanleyville revolt as well. After wounding of Denard, proposed for overall command of 10th and 6th Commandos, now merged. Failed. Wounded at Bukavu in a shoot-out, quit, and returned home via Kigali. Not in action since. Lives in Paris.

CARLO SHANNON. British. Served under Hoare in 5th, 1964. Declined to serve under Peters. Transferred to Denard 1966, joined the 6th. Served under Schramme on march to Bukavu. Fought throughout siege. Repatriated among the last in April 1968. Volunteered for Nigerian civil war, served under Steiner. Took over remnants after Steiner's dismissal, November 1968. Commanded till the end. Believed staying in Paris.

LUCIEN BRUN. Alias Paul Leroy. French, speaks fluent English. Served as enlisted officer French Army, Algerian war. Normal discharge. Was in South Africa 1964, volunteered for Congo. Arrived 1964 with South African unit, joined Hoare's 5th Commando. Fought well, wounded late 1964. Returned 1965. Refused to serve under Peters, transferred to Denard and the 6th in early 1966. Left Congo May 1966, sensing forthcoming revolt. Served under Faulques in Nigerian civil war. Wounded and repatriated. Returned and tried for his own command. Failed. Repatriated 1968. Lives in Paris. Highly intelligent, also very politically minded.

When he had finished, Endean looked up. "These men would all be available for such a job?" he asked.

The writer shook his head. "I doubt it," he said. "I included all those who could do such a job. Whether they would want to is another matter. It would depend on the size of the job, the number of men they would command. For the older ones there is a question of the prestige involved. There is also the question of how much they need the work. Some of the older ones are more or less retired and comfortably off."

"Point them out to me," invited Endean.

The writer leaned over and ran his finger down the list. "First the older generation. Lamouline you'll never get. He was always virtually an extension of Belgian government policy, a tough veteran and revered by his men. He's retired now. The other Belgian, Black Jacques Schramme, is now retired and runs a chicken farm in Portugal. Of the French, Roger Faulques is perhaps the most decorated ex-officer of the French Army. He also is revered by the men who fought under him, in and out of the Foreign Legion, and regarded as a gentleman by others. But he's also crippled with wounds, and the last contract he got was a failure because he delegated the command to a subordinate who failed.

"Denard was good in the Congo but got a very bad head wound at Stanleyville. Now he's past it. The French mercenaries still stay in contact with him, looking for a bite, but he hasn't been given a command or a project to set up since the fiasco at Dilolo. And little wonder.

Of the Anglo-Saxons, Mike Hoare is retired and comfortably off. He might be tempted by a million-pound project, but even that's not certain. His last foray was into Nigeria, where he proposed a project to each side, costed at half a million pounds. They both turned him down. John Peters is also retired and runs a factory in Singapore. All six made a lot of money in the heyday, but none has adapted to the smaller, more technical mission that might be called for nowadays, some because they don't wish to, or because they can't!"

"What about the other five?" asked Endean.

"Steiner was good once, but deteriorated. The press publicity got to him, and that's always bad for a mercenary. They begin to believe they are as fearsome as the Sunday papers say they are. Roux became bitter when he failed to get the Stanleyville command after Denard's wounding and claims leadership over all French mercenaries, but he hasn't been employed since Bukavu. The last two are better; both in their thirties, intelligent, educated, and with enough guts in combat to be able to command other mercs. Incidentally, mercs only fight under a leader they choose themselves. So hiring a bad mercenary to recruit others serves no purpose, because no one else wants to know about serving under a guy who once ran out. So the combat record is important.

"Lucien Brun, alias Paul Leroy, could do this job. Trouble is, you would never be quite sure if he was not passing stuff to French intelligence, the SDECE. Does that matter?"

"Yes, very much," said Endean shortly. "You left out Schroeder, the South African. What about him? You say he commanded Fifth Commando in the Congo?"

"Yes," said the writer. "At the end, the very end. It also broke up under his command. He's a first-class soldier, within his limitations. For example, he would command a battalion of mercenaries excellently, providing it were within the framework of a brigade with a good staff. He's a good combat man, but conventional. Very little imagination, not the sort who could set up his own operation starting from scratch. He'd need staff officers to take care of the admin."

"And Shannon? He's British?"

"Anglo-Irish. He's new; he got his first command only a year ago, but he did well. He can think unconventionally and has a lot of audacity. He can also organize down to the last detail."

Endean rose to go. "Tell me something," he said at the door. "If you were mounting an—seeking a man to go on a mission and assess the situation, which would you choose?"

The writer picked up the notes on the breakfast table. "Cat Shannon," he said without hesitation. "If I were doing that, or mounting an operation, I'd pick the Cat."

"Where is he?" asked Endean.

The writer mentioned a hotel and a bar in Paris. "You could try either of those," he said.

"And if this man Shannon was not available, or for some other reason could not be employed, who would be second on the list?"

The writer thought for a while. "If not Lucien Brun, then the only other one who would almost certainly be available and has the experience would be Roux," he said.

"You have his address?" asked Endean.

The writer flicked through a small notebook that he took from a drawer in his desk.

"Roux has a flat in Paris," he said and gave Endean the address. A few seconds later he heard the clump of Endean's feet descending the stairs. He picked up the phone and dialed a number. "Carrie? Hi, it's me. We're going out tonight. Somewhere expensive. I just got paid for a feature article."

Cat Shannon walked slowly and pensively up the rue Blanche toward the Place Clichy. The little bars were already open on both sides of the street, and from the doorways the hustlers tried to persuade him to step inside and see the most beautiful girls in Paris. The latter, who, whatever else they were, most certainly were not that, peered through the lace curtains at the darkened street. It was just after five o'clock on a mid-March evening, with a cold wind blowing. The weather matched Shannon's mood.

He crossed the square and ducked up another side street toward his hotel, which had few advantages but a fine view from its top floors, since it was close to the summit of Montmartre. He was thinking about Dr. Dunois, whom he had visited for a general checkup a week earlier. A former paratrooper and army doctor, Dunois had become a mountaineer and gone on two French expeditions to the Himalayas and the Andes as the team medico.

He had later volunteered for several tough medical missions in Africa, on a temporary basis and for the duration of the emergency, working for the French Red Cross. There he had met the mercenaries and had patched up several of them after combat. He had become known as the mercenaries' doctor, even in Paris, and had sewn up a lot of bullet holes, removed many splinters of mortar casing from their bodies. If they had a medical problem or needed a checkup, they usually went to him at his Paris surgery. If they were well off, flush with money, they paid on the nail in dollars. If not, he forgot to send his bill, which is unusual in French doctors.

Shannon turned into the door of his hotel and crossed to the desk for his key. The old man was on duty behind the desk.

"Ah, monsieur, one has been calling you from London. All day. He left a message."

The old man handed Shannon the slip of paper in the key aperture. It was written in the old man's scrawl, evidently dictated letter by letter. It said simply "Careful Harris," and was signed with the name of a freelance writer he knew from his African wars and who lived in London.

"There is another, m'sieur. He is waiting in the salon."

The old man gestured toward the small room set aside from the lobby, and through the archway Shannon could see a man about his own age, dressed in the sober gray of a London businessman, watching him as he stood by the desk. There was little of the London businessman in the ease with which the visitor came to his feet as Shannon entered the salon, or about the build of the shoulders. Shannon had seen men like him before. They always represented older, richer men.

"Mr. Shannon?"

"Yes."

"My name is Harris, Walter Harris."

"You wanted to see me?"

"I've been waiting a couple of hours for just that. Can we talk here, or in your room?"

"Here will do. The old man understands no English."

The two men seated themselves facing each other. Harris relaxed and crossed his legs. He reached for a pack of cigarettes and gestured to Shannon with the pack. Shannon shook his head and reached for his own brand in his jacket pocket.

"I understand you are a mercenary, Mr. Shannon?"

"Yes."

"In fact you have been recommended to me. I represent a group of London businessmen. We need a job done. A sort of mission. It needs a man who has some knowledge of military matters, and who can travel to a foreign country without exciting any suspicions. Also a man who can make an intelligent report on what he saw there, analyze a military situation, and then keep his mouth shut."

"I don't kill on contract," said Shannon briefly.

"We don't want you to," said Harris.

"All right, what's the mission? And what's the fee?" asked Shannon. He saw no sense in wasting words. The man in front of him was unlikely to be shocked by a spade being called a spade.

Harris smiled briefly. "First, you would have to come to London for briefing. We would pay for your trip and expenses, even if you decided not to accept."

"Why London? Why not here?" asked Shannon.

Harris exhaled a long stream of smoke. "There are some maps and other papers involved," he said. "I don't want to bring them with me. Also, I have to consult my partners, report to them that you have accepted or not, as the case may be."

There was silence as Harris drew a wad of French 100-franc notes from his pockets.

"Fifteen hundred francs," he said. "About a hundred and twenty pounds. That's for your air ticket to London, single or return, whichever you wish to buy. And your overnight stay. If you decline the proposition after hearing it, you get another hundred for your trouble in coming. If you accept, we discuss the further salary."

Shannon nodded. "All right. I'll listen—in London. When?"

"Tomorrow," said Harris and rose to leave. "Arrive any time during the course of the day, and stay at the Post House Hotel on Haverstock Hill. I'll book your room when I get back tonight. At nine the day after tomorrow I'll phone you in your room and make a rendezvous for later that morning. Clear?"

Shannon nodded and picked up the francs. "Book the room in the name of Brown, Keith Brown," he said.

The man who called himself Harris left the hotel and headed downhill, looking for a taxi. He had not seen any reason to mention to Shannon that he had spent three hours earlier that afternoon talking with another mercenary, a man by the name of Charles Roux. Nor did he mention that he had decided, despite the Frenchman's evident eagerness, that Roux was not the man for the job; he had left the man's flat with a vague promise to get in touch again, with his decision.

Twenty-four hours later Shannon stood at his bedroom window in the Post House Hotel and stared out at the rain and the commuter traffic swishing up Haverstock Hill from Camden Town toward Hampstead and the commuter suburbs.

He had arrived that morning on the first plane, using his passport in the name of Keith Brown. Long since, he had had to acquire a false passport by the normal method used in mercenary circles. At the end of 1967 he had been with Black Jacques Schramme at Bukavu, surrounded and besieged for months by the Congolese army. Finally, undefeated but running out of ammunition, the mercenaries had vacated the Congolese lakeside city, walked across the bridge into neighboring Rwanda, and allowed themselves, with Red Cross guarantees which the Red Cross could not possibly fulfill, to be disarmed.

From then on, for nearly six months, they had sat idle in an internment camp at Kigali while the Red Cross and the Rwanda government hassled over their repatriation to Europe. President Mobutu of the Congo wanted them sent back to him for execution, but the mercenaries had threatened if that was the decision they would take the Rwandan army barehanded, recover their guns and find their own way home. The Rwandan government had believed, rightly, that they might do it.

When finally the decision was made to fly them back to Europe, the British consul had visited the camp and soberly told the six British mercenaries present that he would have to impound their passports. They had soberly told him they had lost everything across the lake in Bukavu. On being flown home to London, Shannon and the others had been told by the Foreign Office that each man owed £350 for the air fare and would receive no new passport ever again.

Before leaving the camp, the men had been photographed and finger-printed and had had their names taken. They also had to sign documents pledging never to set foot on the continent of Africa. These documents would be sent in copy to every African government.

The reaction of the mercenaries was predictable. Every one had a lush beard and mustache and hair left uncut after months in the camp, where no scissors were allowed in case they went on the warpath with them. The photographs were therefore unrecognizable. Each man then submitted his own fingerprints for another man's prints, and they all exchanged names. The result was that every identity document contained one man's name, another man's fingerprints, and a third man's photograph. Finally, they signed the pledge to leave Africa forever with names like Sebastian Weetabix and Neddy Seagoon.

Shannon's reaction to the Foreign Office demand was no less unhelpful. As he still had his "lost" passport, he kept it and traveled where he wished until it expired. Then he took the neccessary steps to secure another one, issued by the Passport Office but based on a birth certificate, secured from the Registry of Births in Somerset House for the standard fee of five shillings, which referred to a baby who had died of meningitis in Yarmouth about the time Shannon was born.*

On arrival in London that morning, he had contacted the writer he had first met in Africa and learned how Walter Harris had found him. He thanked the man for recommending him and asked if he knew the name of a good agency of private inquirers. Later that afternoon he visited the agency and paid a deposit of £20, promising to phone the next morning with further instructions.

Harris called, as he had promised, on the dot of nine the following morning and was put through to Mr. Brown's room.

"There's a block of flats in Sloane Avenue called Chelsea Cloisters," he said without preamble. "I have booked flat three-seventeen for us to talk. Please be there at eleven sharp. Wait in the lobby until I arrive, as I have the key." Then he hung up.

Shannon checked the address in the telephone book under the bedside table and called the detective agency. "I want your man in the lobby of Chelsea Cloisters in Sloane Avenue at ten-fifteen," he said. "He had better have his own transport."

"He'll have a scooter," said the head of the agency.

An hour later Shannon met the man from the agency in the lobby of the apartment house. Rather to his surprise, the man was a youth in his late teens, with long hair.

Shannon surveyed him suspiciously. "Do you know your job?" he asked.

The boy nodded. He seemed full of enthusiasm, and Shannon only hoped it was matched by a bit of skill.

"Well, park that crash helmet outside on the scooter," he said. "People who come in here don't carry crash helmets. Sit over there and read a news-paper."

*For a more detailed explanation of this procedure, which was used by a would-be assassin of General de Gaulle, see *The Day of the Jackal* (New York: The Viking Press, 1971).

The youth did not have one, so Shannon gave him his own. "I'll sit on the other side of the lobby. At about eleven a man will come in, nod to me, and we'll go into the lift together. Note that man, so you will recognize him again. He should come out about an hour later. By then you must be across the road, astride the scooter, with the helmet on and pretending to be busy with a breakdown. Got it?"

"Yes. I've got it."

"The man will either take his own car from nearby, in which case grab the number of it. Or he'll take a taxi. In either case, follow him and note where he goes. Keep on his tail until he arrives at what looks like his final destination."

The youth drank in the instructions and took his place in the far corner of the lobby behind his newspaper.

The lobby porter frowned but left him alone. He had seen quite a few meetings take place in front of his reception desk.

Forty minutes later Simon Endean walked in. Shannon noticed that he dismissed a taxi at the door, and hoped the youth had noticed it as well. He stood up and nodded to the newcomer, but Endean strolled past him and pressed the summons button for the lift. Shannon joined him and remarked the youth peering over his newspaper.

For God's sake, thought Shannon and mentioned something about the foul weather lest the man who called himself Harris should glance round the lobby.

Settled into an easy chair in flat 317, Harris opened his briefcase and took out a map. Spreading it out on the bed, he told Shannon to look at it. Shannon gave it three minutes and had taken in all the details the map had to give. Then Harris began his briefing.

It was a judicious mixture of fact and fiction. He still claimed he represented a consortium of British businessmen, all of whom did some form of business with Zangaro and all of whose businesses, including some which were virtually out of business, had suffered as a result of President Kimba.

Then he went into the background of the republic from independence onward, and what he said was truthful, most of it out of his own report to Sir James Manson. The punch line came at the end.

"A group of officers in the army has got in touch with a group of local businessmen—who are, incidentally, a dying breed. They have mentioned that they are considering toppling Kimba in a coup. One of the local businessmen mentioned it to one of my group, and put their problem to us. It is basically that they are virtually untrained in military terms, despite their officer status, and do not know how to topple the man, because he spends too much time hidden inside the walls of his palace, surrounded by his guards.

"Frankly, we would not be sorry to see this Kimba go, and neither would his people. A new government would be good for the economy of the place and good for the country. We need a man to go down there and make a complete assessment of the military and security situation in and around the palace and the important institutions. We want a complete report on Kimba's military strength."

"So you can pass it on to your officers?" asked Shannon.

"They are not our officers. They are Zangaran officers. The fact is, if they are going to strike at all, they had better know what they are doing."

Shannon believed half of the briefing, but not the second half. If the officers, who were on the spot, could not assess the situation, they would be incompetent to carry out a coup. But he did not say so.

"I'll have to go in as a tourist," he said. "There's no other cover that would work."

"That's right."

"There must be precious few tourists that go there. Why cannot I go in as a company visitor to one of your friends' business houses?"

"That will not be possible," said Harris. "If anything went wrong, there would be all hell to pay."

If I get caught, you mean, thought Shannon, but kept silent. He was being paid, so he would take risks. That, and his knowledge, was what he was being paid for.

"There's the question of pay," he said shortly.

"Then you'll do it?"

"If the money's right, yes."

Harris nodded approvingly. "Tomorrow morning a round-trip ticket from London to the capital of the neighboring republic will be at your hotel," he said. "You have to fly back to Paris and get a visa for this republic. Zangaro is so poor there is only one embassy in Europe, and that's in Paris also. But getting a Zangaran visa there takes a month. In the next-door republic's capital there is a Zangaran consulate. There you can get a visa for cash, and within an hour if you tip the consul. You understand the procedure."

Shannon nodded. He understood it very well.

"So get visa-ed up in Paris, then fly down by Air Afrique. Get your Zangaran visa on the spot and take the connecting plane service from there to Clarence, paying cash. With the tickets at your hotel tomorrow will be three hundred pounds in French francs as expenses."

"I'll need five," said Shannon. "It'll be ten days at least, possibly more, depending on connections and how long the visas take to get. Three hundred leaves no margin for the occasional bribe or any delay."

"All right, five hundred in French francs. Plus five hundred for yourself," said Harris.

"A thousand," said Shannon.

"Dollars? I understand you people deal in U.S. dollars."

"Pounds," said Shannon. "That's twenty-five hundred dollars, or two months at flat salary if I were on a normal contract."

"But you'll only be away ten days," protested Harris.

"Ten days of high risk," countered Shannon. "If this place is half what you say it is, anyone getting caught on this kind of job is going to be very dead, and very painfully. You want me to take the risks rather than go yourself, you pay."

"Okay, a thousand pounds. Five hundred down and five hundred when you return."

"How do I know you'll contact me when I return?" said Shannon

"How do I know you'll even go there at all?" countered Harris.

Shannon considered the point. Then he nodded. "All right, half now, half later."

Ten minutes later Harris was gone, after instructing Shannon to wait five minutes before leaving himself.

At three that afternoon the head of the detective agency was back from his lunch. Shannon called at three-fifteen.

"Ah, yes, Mr. Brown," said the voice on the phone. "I have spoken to my man. He waited as you instructed, and when the subject left the building he recognized him and followed. The subject hailed a taxi from the curb, and my man followed him to the City. There he dismissed the taxi and entered a building."

"What building?"

"ManCon House. That's the headquarters of Manson Consolidated Mining."

"Do you know if he works there?" asked Shannon.

"It would seem he does," said the agency chief. "My man could not follow him into the building, but he noticed the commissionaire touched his cap to the subject and held the door open for him. He did not do that for a stream of secretaries and evidently junior executives who were emerging for lunch."

"He's brighter than he looks," conceded Shannon. The youth had done a good job. Shannon gave several further instructions and that afternoon mailed £50 by registered mail to the detective agency. He also opened a bank account and put down £10 deposit in it. The following morning he banked a further £500 and that evening flew to Paris.

Dr. Gordon Chalmers was not a drinking man. He seldom touched anything stronger than beer, and when he did he became talkative, as his employer, Sir James Manson, had found out for himself over their luncheon at Wilton's. The evening that Cat Shannon was changing planes at Le Bourget to catch the Air Afrique DC-8 to West Africa, Dr. Chalmers was having dinner with an old college friend, now also a scientist and working in industrial research.

There was nothing special about their meal. He had run into his former classmate in one of those coincidental meetings on the street a few days earlier, and they had agreed to have dinner together.

Fifteen years earlier they had been young undergraduates, single and working hard on their respective degrees, earnest and concerned as so many young scientists feel obliged to be. In the mid-1950s the concern had been the bomb and colonialism, and they had joined thousands of others marching for the Campaign for Nuclear Disarmament and the various movements that sought an instant end to empire, and world freedom now. Both had been indignant, serious, committed, and both had changed nothing. But in their indignation over the state of the world they had dabbled with the Young Communist movement. Chalmers had grown out of it, married, started his family, secured a mortgage for his house, and slowly merged into the salaried middle class.

The combination of worries that had come his way over the previous two weeks caused him to take more than his usual single glass of wine with dinner, considerably more. His friend, a kindly man with soft brown eyes, noticed his worry and asked if he could help.

It was over the brandy that Dr. Chalmers felt he had to confide his worries to someone, someone who, unlike his wife, was a fellow scientist and would understand the problem. Of course it was highly confidential, and his friend was solicitous and sympathetic.

When he heard about the crippled daughter and the need for the money to pay for her expensive equipment, the man's eyes clouded over with sympathy, and he reached across the table to grip Dr. Chalmers' forearm.

"Don't worry about it, Gordon. It's completely understandable. Anyone else would have done the same thing," he told him. Chalmers felt better when they left the restaurant and made their separate ways home. He was easier in his mind, his problem somehow shared.

Though he had asked his old friend how he had fared in the intervening years since their undergraduate days together, the man had been slightly evasive. Chalmers, bowed under his own worries and his observation blunted by wine, had not pressed for detail. Even had he done so, it was unlikely the friend would have told him that, far from merging into the bourgeoisie, he had remained a fully committed member of the Communist party.

<u>SEVEN</u>

The Convair 440 that ran the connecting air service into Clarence banked steeply over the bay and began its descent toward the airfield. Being intentionally on the left side of the plane, Shannon could look down toward the town as the aircraft overflew it. From a thousand feet he could see the capital of Zangaro occupying the end of the peninsula, surrounded on three sides by the palm-fringed waters of the gulf, and on the fourth side by the land, where the stubby peninsula, just eight miles long, ran back to join the main coastline.

The spit of land was three miles wide at its base, set in the mangrove swamps on the coastline, and a mile wide at the tip, where the town was situated. The flanks along each side were also composed of mangrove, and only at the end did the mangroves give way to some shingly beaches.

The town spanned the end of the peninsula from side to side and stretched about a mile back down the length of it. Beyond the fringes of the town at this end, a single road ran between cultivated patches the remaining seven miles to the main coast.

Evidently all the best buildings were set toward the seaward tip of the land, where the breezes would blow, for the aerial view showed the buildings to be set in their own plots of land, one to an acre. The landward side of the town was evidently the poorer section, where thousands of tin-roofed shanties intersected with narrow muddy alleys. He concentrated on the richer section of Clarence, where the colonial masters had once lived, for here would be the important buildings, and he would only have a few seconds to see them from this angle.

At the very end was a small port, formed where, for no geological reason, two long curving spits of shingle ran out into the sea like the antlers of a stag beetle or the pincers of an earwig. The port was set along the landward side of this bay. Outside the arms of the bay, Shannon could see the water ruffled by the breeze, while inside the three-quarter-circle enclosed within the arms, the water was a flat calm. No doubt it was this anchorage, tacked onto the end of the peninsula in one of nature's afterthoughts, which had attracted the first mariners.

The center of the port, directly opposite the opening to the high seas, was dominated by a single concrete quay without any ship tied up to it, and a warehouse of sorts. To the left of the concrete quay was evidently the natives' fishing area, a shingly beach littered with long canoes and nets laid out to dry, and to the right of the quay was the old port, a series of decrepit wooden jetties pointing toward the water.

Behind the warehouse there were perhaps two hundred yards of rough grass, ending with a road along the shore, and behind the road the buildings started. Shannon caught a glimpse of a white colonial-style church and what could have been the governor's palace in bygone days, surrounded by a wall. Inside the wall, apart from the main buildlings, was a large courtyard surrounded by lean-to hutments of evidently recent addition.

At this point the Convair straightened up, the town disappeared from view, and they were on final approach.

Shannon had already had his first experience of Zangaro the previous day when he had applied for his visa for a tourist visit. The consul in the neighboring capital had received him with some surprise, being unused to such applications. He had to fill out a five-page form giving his parents' first names (as he had no idea of Keith Brown's parents' names, he invented them) and every other conceivable piece of information.

His passport, when he handed it over, had a handsome banknote idly lying between the first and second pages. This went into the consul's pocket. The man then examined the passport from every angle, read every page, held it up to the light, turned it over, checked the currency allowances at the back. After five minutes of this, Shannon began to wonder if there was something wrong. Had the British Foreign Office made an error in this particular passport?

Then the consul looked at him and said, "You are an American."

With a sense of relief Shannon realized the man was illiterate. He had his visa in five minutes more. But at Clarence airport the fun stopped.

He had no luggage in the aircraft hold, just a hand grip. Inside the main (and only) passenger building the heat was overpowering, and the place buzzed with flies. About a dozen soldiers lounged about, and ten policemen. They were evidently of different tribes. The policemen were self-effacing, hardly speaking even to each other, leaning against the walls. It was the soldiers who attracted Shannon's attention. He kept half an eye on them as he filled in another immensely long form (the same one he had filled the previous day at the consulate) and penetrated Health and Passport Control, both manned by officials whom he took to be Caja, like the policemen.

It was when he got to customs that the trouble started. A civilian was waiting for him and instructed him with a curt gesture to go into a side room. As he did so, taking his bag with him, four soldiers swaggered in after him. Then he realized what it was about them that rang a bell in his memory. Long ago in the Congo he had seen the same attitude, the blank-eyed sense of menace conveyed by an African of almost primeval cultural level, armed with a weapon, in a state of power—wholly unpredictable, with reactions to a situation that were utterly illogical, ticking away like a moving time bomb. Just before the worst of the massacres he had seen launched by Congolese on Katangese, Simbas on missionaries, and Congolese army on Simbas, he had noticed this same menacing mindlessness, the sense of power without reason, that can suddenly and for no recollected explanation turn to frenetic violence. The Vindu soldiers of President Kimba had it.

The civilian customs officer ordered Shannon to put his bag on the rickety table and then began to go through it. The search looked thorough, as if for concealed weapons, until he spotted the electric shaver, took it from its case, examined it, tried the "on" switch. Being a Remington Lektronic and fully charged, it buzzed furiously. Without a trace of expression, the customs man put it in his pocket.

Finishing with the bag, he gestured to Shannon to empty his pockets onto the table. Out came the keys, handkerchief, coins, wallet, and passport. The customs man went for the wallet, extracted the travelers' checks, looked at them, grunted, and handed them back. The coins he swept into his hand and pocketed them. Of the banknotes, there were two 5000-French-African-franc notes and several 100s. The soldiers crowded nearer, still making no sound but for their breathing in the roasting atmosphere, gripping guns like clubs, but overcome with curiosity. The civilian behind the table pocketed the two 5000-franc notes, and one of the soldiers picked up the smaller denominations.

Shannon looked at the customs man. The man looked back. Then he lifted his singlet and showed the butt of a Browning 9-mm. short, or perhaps an 875, jammed into his trouser band. He tapped it.

"Police," he said, and kept staring. Shannon's fingers itched to smash the man in the face. Inside his head he kept telling himself: Keep cool, baby, absolutely cool.

He gestured slowly, very slowly, to what remained of his belongings on the table and raised his eyebrows. The civilian nodded, and Shannon began to pick them up and put them back. Behind him he felt the soldiers back off, though they still gripped their rifles with both hands, able to swing or butt-jab as the mood took them.

It seemed an age before the civilian nodded toward the door and Shannon left. He could feel the sweat running in a stream down the spine toward the waistband of his pants.

Outside in the main hall, the only other white tourist on the flight, an American girl, had been met by a Catholic priest, who, with his voluble explanations to the soldiers in coast pidgin, was having less trouble. He looked up and caught Shannon's eye. Shannon raised an eyebrow slightly. The father looked beyond Shannon at the room he had come from and nodded imperceptibly.

Outside, in the heat of the small square before the airport building, there was no transport. Shannon waited. Five minutes later he heard a soft Irish-American voice behind him.

"Can I give you a lift into town, my son?"

They traveled in the priest's car, a Volkswagen beetle, which he had hidden for safety in the shade of a palm grove several yards outside the gate. The American girl was shrill and outraged; someone had opened her handbag and gone through it. Shannon was silent, knowing how close they could all have come to a beating. The priest was with the UN hospital, combining the roles of chaplain, almoner, and doctor of medicine. He glanced across at Shannon with understanding.

"They shook you down."

"The lot," said Shannon. The loss of £15 was nothing but both men had recognized the mood of the soldiery.

"One has to be very careful here, very careful indeed," said the priest softly. "Have you a hotel?"

When Shannon told him he had not, the priest drove him to the Independence, the only hotel in Clarence where Europeans were permitted to stay.

"Gomez is the manager, he's a good enough sort," said the priest.

Usually when a new face arrives in an African city there are invitations from the other Europeans to visit the club, come back to the bungalow, have a drink, come to a party that evening. The priest, for all his helpfulness, issued no such offers. That was another thing Shannon learned quickly about Zangaro. The mood affected the whites as well. He would learn more in the days to come, much of it from Gomez.

It was that same evening that he came to know Jules Gomez, formerly proprietor and latterly manager of the Independence Hotel. Gomez was fifty and a *pied noir,* a Frenchman from Algeria. In the last days of French Algeria, almost ten years earlier, he had sold his flourishing business in agricultural machinery just before the final collapse, when one could not give a business away. With what he had made, he returned to France, but after a year found he could not live in the atmosphere of Europe any longer and looked around for another place to go. He had settled on Zangaro, five years before independence and before it was even in the offing. Taking his savings, he had bought the hotel and steadily improved it over the years.

After independence, things had changed. Three years before Shannon arrived, Gomez had been brusquely infomed that the hotel was to be nationalized and he would be paid in local currency. He never was, and it was worthless paper in any case. But he hung on as manager, hoping against hope that one day things might improve again and something would be left of his only asset on this planet to secure him in his old age. As manager, he ran the reception desk and the bar. Shannon found him at the bar.

It would have been easy to win Gomez' friendship by mentioning the friends and contacts Shannon had who were former OAS men, fighters in the Legion and the paras, who had turned up in the Congo. But that would have blown his cover as a simple English tourist who, with five days to kill, had flown down from the north, impelled only by curiosity to see the obscure republic of Zangaro. So he stuck to his role of tourist.

But later, after the bar closed, he suggested Gomez join him for a drink in his room. For no explicable reason, the soldiers at the airport had left him a bottle of whisky he had been carrying in his case. Gomez' eyes opened wide at the sight of it. Whisky was another import the country could not afford. Shannon made sure Gomez drank more than he. When he mentioned that he had come to Zangaro out of curiosity, Gomez snorted.

"Curiosity? Huh, it's curious, all right. It's bloody weird."

Although they were talking French, and alone in the room, Gomez lowered his voice and leaned forward as he said it. Once again Shannon got an impression of the extraordinary sense of fear present in everyone he had seen, except the bully-boy army thugs and the secret policeman who posed as a customs officer at the airport. By the time Gomez had sunk half the bottle, he had become slightly garrulous, and Shannon probed gently for information. Gomez confirmed much of the briefing Shannon had been given by the man he knew as Walter Harris, and added more anecdotal details of his own, some of them highly gruesome.

He confirmed that President Kimba was in town, that he hardly ever left it these days, except for the occasional trip to his home village across the river in Vindu country, and that he was in his presidential palace, the large, walled building Shannon had seen from the air.

By the time Gomez bade him good night and wove his way back to his own room at two in the morning, further nuggets of information had been culled. The three units known as the civilian police force, the gendarmerie, and the customs force, although all carried sidearms, had, Gomez swore, no ammunition in their weapons. Being Caja, they were not trusted to have any, and Kimba, with his paranoia about an uprising, kept them without one round of ammunition between the lot of them. He knew they would never fight for him and must not have the opportunity of fighting against him. The sidearms were just for show.

Gomez had also vouchsafed that the power in the city was exclusively in the hands of Kimba's Vindu. The dreaded secret police usually wore civilian clothes and carried automatics, the soldiers of the army had bolt-action rifles such as Shannon had seen at the airport, and the President's own Praetorian Guards had submachine guns. The latter lived exclusively in the palace grounds and were ultra-loyal to Kimba, and he never moved without at least a squad of them hemming him in.

The next morning Shannon went out for a walk. Within seconds he found a small boy of ten or eleven scampering by his side, sent after him by Gomez. Only later did he learn why. He thought Gomez must have sent the boy as a guide, though, as they could not exchange a word, there was not much point in that. The real purpose was different, a service Gomez offered to all his guests, whether they asked or not. If the tourist was arrested for whatever reason, and carted off, the small boy would speed away through the bushes and tell Gomez, who would slip the information to the Swiss or West German embassy so that someone could begin to negotiate the tourist's release before he was beaten half dead The boy's name was Boniface.

Shannon spent the morning walking, mile after mile, while the small boy trotted at his heels. As he expected, they were stopped by no one. Shannon knew that the sheer inefficiency of the place meant that no one would seriously question why a foreigner should spend a week as a tourist. Such countries even advertise for tourism in the waiting rooms of their embassies in Europe. Moreover, in the case of Zangaro there was a community of about a hundred whites in the capital, and no soldier was going to know that the white walking down the street was not a local one, or care, provided he was given a dollar for beer.

There was hardly a vehicle to be seen, and the streets in the residental area were mainly deserted. From Gomez, Shannon had obtained a small map of the town, a leftover from colonial days, and with this he tracked down the main buildings of Clarence. At the only bank, the only post office, half a dozen ministries, the port, and the UN hospital there were groups of six or seven soldiers lounging about the steps. Inside the bank, where he went to cash a travelers' check, he noticed bedrolls in the lobby, and in the lunch hour he twice saw pots of food being carried by a soldier to his colleagues. Shannon judged that the guard details lived on the premises of each building. Gomez confirmed this later the same evening.

He noticed a soldier in front of each of six embassies he passed, three of them asleep in the dust. By the lunch hour he estimated there were about a hundred soldiers scattered in twelve groups around the main area of the town. He noted what they were armed with. Each carried an old Mauser 7.92 bolt-action rifle, most of them looking rusted and dirty. The soldiers wore drab green trousers and shirts, canvas boots, webbing belts, and peaked caps rather like American baseball caps. Without exception they were shabby, unpressed, unwashed, and unprepossessing. He estimated their level of training, weapons familiarization, leadership, and fighting capacity at nil. They were a rabble, undisciplined thugs who could terrify the timorous Caja by their arms and their brutishness, but had probably never fired a shot in anger and certainly had never been fired at by people who knew what they were doing. Their purpose on guard duty seemed to be to prevent a civilian riot, but he estimated that in a real firefight they would quit and run.

The most interesting thing about them was the state of their ammunition pouches. They were pressed flat, empty of magazines. Each Mauser had its fixed magazines, of course, but Mausers hold only five shells.

That afternoon Shannon patrolled the port. Seen from the ground, it looked different. The two spits of sand running out across the water and forming the natural harbor were about twenty feet high at the base and six feet above the water at the tip. He walked down both until he reached the end. Each one was covered in knee-to-waist-high scrub vegetation, burned brown at the end of the long dry season, and invisible from the air. Each spit was about forty feet wide at the tip, forty yards wide at the base, where it left the shoreline. From the tip of each, looking back toward the port area, one had a panoramic view of the waterfront.

The concreted area was at dead center, backed by the warehouse. To the north of this stood the old wooden jetties, some long crumbled away, their supports sticking up like broken teeth above or below the water. To the south of the warehouse was the shingly beach where the fishing canoes lay. From the tip of one sandspit the President's palace was invisible, hidden behind the warehouse, but from the other spit the uppermost story of the palace was plainly visible. Shannon walked back to the port and examined the fishing beach. It was a good place for a landing, he thought idly, a gentle slope to the water's edge.

Behind the warehouse the concrete ended and a sloping bank of waist-high scrub, dissected by numerous footpaths and one laterite road for trucks, ran back toward the palace. Shannon took the road. As he breasted the top of the rise the full façade of the old colonial governor's mansion came into view, two hundred yards away. He continued another hundred yards and reached the lateral road running along the seashore. At the junction a group of soldiers waited, four in all, smarter, better dressed than the army, armed with Kalashnikov AK 47 assault rifles. They watched him in silence as he turned right along the road toward his hotel. He nodded, but they just stared back. The palace guards.

He glanced to his left as he walked and took in the details of the palace. Thirty yards wide, its ground-floor windows now bricked up and painted over the same off-white wash as the rest of the building, it was dominated at ground level by a tall, wide, bolt-studded timber door, almost certainly another new addition. In front of the bricked-up windows ran a terrace, now useless because there was no access from the building to it. On the second floor a row of seven windows ran from side to side of the façade, three left, three right, and one above the main entrance. The topmost floor had ten windows, all much smaller. Above these were the gutter and the red-tiled roof sloping away toward the apex.

He noticed more guards lounging around the front door, and that the second-floor windows had shutters which might have been of steel (he was too far away to tell) and were drawn down. Evidently no closer access to the front of the building than the road junction was permitted, except on official business.

He completed the afternoon just before the sun went down by making a tour of the palace from afar. At each side he saw that a new wall eight feet high ran from the main mansion toward the land for a distance of eighty yards, and the fourth wall joined them together at the rear. Interestingly, there were no other gates to the entire compound. The wall was uniformly eight feet high—he could tell by the height of a guard he saw walking near the wall—and topped by broken bottles. He knew he would never see inside, but he could retain the image from the air. It almost made him laugh.

He grinned at Boniface. "You know, kid, that bloody fool thinks he has protected himself with a big wall topped with glass and only one entrance. All he has really done is pin himself inside a brick trap, a great big closed-in killing ground."

The boy grinned widely, not understanding a word, and indicated he wanted to go home and eat. Shannon nodded, and they went back to the hotel, feet burning and legs aching.

Shannon made no notes or maps but retained every detail in his head. He returned Gomez' map and after dinner joined the Frenchman at the bar.

Two Chinese from the embassy sat quietly drinking beer at the back tables, so conversation between the Europeans was minimal. Besides, the windows were open. Later, however, Gomez, longing for company, took a dozen bottles of beer and invited Shannon up to his room on the top floor, where they sat on the balcony and looked out through the night at the sleeping town, mainly in darkness because of an electricity breakdown.

Shannon was of two minds whether to take Gomez into his confidence, but decided not to. He mentioned that he had found the bank and it had not been easy to change a £50 check.

Gomez snorted. "It never is," he said. "They don't see travelers' checks here, or much foreign currency for very long."

"They must see it at the bank, surely."

"Not for long. The entire treasure of the republic Kimba keeps locked up inside the palace."

Shannon was at once interested. It took two hours to learn, in dribs and drabs, that Kimba kept not only the national armory of ammunition in the old wine cellar of the governor's palace, under his own lock and key, but also the national radio-broadcasting station so that he could broadcast direct from his communications room to the nation and the world and no one else could take control of it from outside the palace. National radio stations always play a vital role in coups d'état. Shannon also learned he had no armored cars and no artillery, and that apart from the hundred soldiers scattered around the capital there were another hundred outside the town, a score in the native township on the airport road, and the rest dotted in the Caja villages beyond the peninsula toward the Zangaro River bridge. These two hundred were half the army. The other half were in the army barracks, which were not barracks in truth but the old colonial police lines four hundred yards from the palace—rows in low tin shanties inside a reed fence enclosure. The four hundred men constituted the entire army, and the personal palace guards numbered from forty to sixty, living in the lean-to sheds inside the palace courtyard walls.

On his third day in Zangaro, Shanon checked out the police lines, where the two hundred army men not on guard duty lived. They were, as Gomez had said, surrounded by a reed fence, but a visit to the nearby church enabled Shannon to slip unnoticed into the belltower, run up the circular brick staircase, and sneak a view from the belfry. The lines were two rows of shanties, adorned with some clothes hung out to dry. At one end was a row of low brick kilns, over which pots of stew bubbled. Twoscore men lounged around in various stages of boredom, and all were unarmed. Their guns might be in the hutments, but Shannon guessed they were more probably in the armory, a small stone pillbox set aside from the huts. The other facilities of the camp were primitive in the extreme.

It was that evening, when he had gone out without Boniface, that he met his soldier. He spent an hour circling the darkened streets, which fortunately for him had never seen lamplighting, trying to get close to the palace.

He had managed a good look at the back and sides and had assured himself there were no patrolling guards on these sides. Trying the front of the palace, he had been intercepted by two of the palace guards, who had brusquely ordered him on his way home. He had established that there were three of them sitting at the road junction halfway between the top of the rise from the port and the front gate of the palace. More importantly, he had also established that they could not see the harbor from where they stood. From that road junction the soldiers' eyeline, passing over the top of the rise, would meet the sea beyond the tips of the arms of the harbor, and without a brilliant moon they would not even see the water five hundred yards away, though undoubtedly they would see a light out there, if there were one.

In the darkness on the road junction, Shannon could not see the front gate of the palace a hundred yards inland, but assumed there were two other guards there as usual. He offered packets of cigarettes to the soldiers who had accosted him, and left.

On the road back to the Independence he passed several bars, lit inside by kerosene lamps, and then moved on down the darkened street. A hundred yards farther on, the soldier stopped him. The man was evidently drunk and had been urinating in a rain ditch by the roadside. He swayed up to Shannon, gripping his Mauser two-handed by the butt and barrel. In the moonlight Shannon could see him quite clearly as he moved toward him. The soldier grunted something Shannon failed to understand, though he assumed it was a demand for money.

He heard the soldier mutter, "Beer," several times and add some more indistinguishable words. Then, before Shannon could reach for money or pass on, the man snarled and jabbed the barrel of the gun toward him. From then on it was quick and silent. Shannon took the barrel in one hand and moved it away from his stomach, jerking hard and pulling the soldier off balance. The man was evidently surprised at the reaction, which was not what he was accustomed to. Recovering, he squealed with rage, reversed the gun, gripped it by the barrel, and swung it clubwise. Shannon stepped in close, blocked the swing by gripping the soldier by both biceps, and brought up his knee.

It was too late to go back after that. As the gun dropped he brought up his right hand, crooked into a ninety-degree angle, stiffarmed, and slammed the base of the hand under the soldier's jawbone. A stab of pain went up his arm and shoulder as he heard the neck crack, and he later found he had torn a shoulder muscle with the effort. The Zangaran went down like a sack.

Shannon looked up and down the road, but no one was coming. He rolled the body into the rain ditch and examined the rifle. One by one, he pumped the cartridges out of the magazine. At three they stopped coming. There had been nothing in the breech. He removed the bolt and held the gun to the moon, looking down the barrel. Several months' accumulation of grit, dirt, dust, grime, rust, and earth particles met his eye. He slipped the bolt back home, replaced the three cartridges where they had been, tossed the rifle onto the corpse, and walked home.

"Better and better," he murmured as he slipped into the darkened hotel and went to bed. He had few doubts there would be no effective police inquiry. The broken neck would be put down to a fall into the rain ditch, and tests for fingerprints were, he was sure, unheard of.

Nevertheless, the next day he pleaded a headache, stayed in, and talked to Gomez. On the following morning he left for the airport and took the Convair 440 back to the north. As he sat in the plane and watched the republic disappear beneath the port wing, something Gomez had mentioned in passing ran like a current through his head.

There were not, and never had been, any mining operations in Zangaro. Forty hours later he was back in London.

Ambassador Leonid Dobrovolsky always felt slightly uneasy when he had his weekly interview with President Kimba. Like others who had met the dictator, he had few doubts about the man's insanity. Unlike most of the others, Leonid Dobrovolsky had orders from his superiors in Moscow to make his utmost efforts to establish a working relationship with the unpredictable African. He stood in front of the broad mahogany desk in the President's study on the second floor of the palace and waited for Kimba to show some sort of reaction.

Seen close to, President Kimba was neither as large nor as handsome as his officials protraits indicated. Behind the enormous desk he seemed almost dwarfish, the more so as he held himself hunched in his chair in a state of total immobility. Dobrovolsky waited for the period of immobility to end. He knew it could end one of two ways. Either the man who ruled Zangaro would speak carefully and lucidly, in every sense like a perfectly sane man, or the almost catatonic stillness would give way to a screaming rage, during which the man would rant like someone possessed, which was in any case what he believed himself to be.

Kimba nodded slowly. "Please proceed," he said.

Dobrovolsky breathed a sigh of relief. Evidently the President was prepared to listen. But he knew the bad news was yet to come, and he had to give it. That could change things.

"I am informed by my government, Mr. President, that it has received information that a mining survey report recently sent to Zangaro by a British company may not be accurate. I am referring to the survey carried out several weeks ago by a firm called Manson Consolidated of London."

The President's eyes, slightly bulging, still stared at the Russian Ambassador without a flicker of expression. Nor was there any word from Kimba to indicate that he recalled the subject that had brought Dobrovolsky to his palace.

The Ambassador continued to describe the mining survey that had been delivered by a certain Mr. Bryant into the hands of the Minister for Natural Resources.

"In essence, then, Your Excellency, I am instructed to inform you that my government believes the report was not a true representation of what was really discovered in the area that was then under survey, specifically, the Crystal Mountain range."

He waited, aware that he could say little more. When Kimba finally spoke, it was calmly and cogently, and Dobrovolsky breathed again.

"In what way was this survey report inaccurate?" whispered Kimba.

"We are not sure of the details, Your Excellency, but it is fair to assume that since the British company has apparently not made any effort to secure from you a mining concession, the report it submitted must have indicated that there were no mineral deposits worth exploiting in that region. If the report was inaccurate, then it was probably in this respect. In other words, whatever the mining engineer's samples contained, it would appear there was more than the British were prepared to inform you."

There was another long silence, during which the Ambassador waited for the explosion of rage. It did not come.

"They cheated me," whispered Kimba.

"Of course, Your Excellency," cut in Dobrovolsky hurriedly, "the only way of being completely sure is for another survey party to examine the same area and take further samples of the rocks and the soil. To this end I am instructed by my government most humbly to ask Your Excellency to grant permission for a survey team from the Institute of Mining of Sverdlovsk to come to Zangaro and examine the same area as that covered by the British engineer."

Kimba took a long time digesting the proposal. Finally he nodded. "Granted," he said.

Dobrovolsky bowed. By his side Volkov, ostensibly Second Secretary at the embassy but more pertinently the resident of the KGB detachment, shot him a glance.

"The second matter is that of your personal security," said Dobrovolsky. At last he secured some reaction from the dictator. It was a subject that Kimba took extremely seriously. His head jerked up, and he shot suspicious glances around the room. Three Zangaran aides standing behind the two Russians quaked.

"My security?" said Kimba in his usual whisper.

"We would respectfully seek once again to reiterate the Soviet government's view of the paramount importance of Your Excellency's being able to continue to lead Zangaro on the path of peace and progress that Your Excellency has already so magnificently established," said the Russian. The flow of flattery caused no incongruous note; it was Kimba's habitual due and a regular part of any words addressed to him.

"To guarantee the continued security of the invaluable person of Your Excellency and in view of the recent and most dangerous treason by one of your army officers, we would respectfully once again propose that a member of my embassy staff be permitted to reside inside the palace and lend his assistance to Your Excellency's own personal security corps."

The reference to the "treason" of Colonel Bobi brought Kimba out of his trance. He trembled violently, though whether from rage or fear the Russians could not make out. Then he began to talk, slowly at first, in his usual whisper, then faster, his voice rising as he glared at the Zangarans across the room. After a few sentences he lapsed back into the Vindu dialect, which only the Zangarans understood, but the Russians already knew the gist: the ever-present danger of treason and treachery that Kimba knew himself to be in, the warnings he had received from the spirits telling him of plots in all corners, his complete awareness of the identity of all those who were not loyal and who harbored evil thoughts in their minds, his intention to root them out, all of them, and what would happen to them when he did. He went on for half an hour in this vein, before calming down and reverting to a European language the Russians could understand.

When they emerged into the sunlight and climbed into the embassy car, both men were sweating, partly from the heat, for the air-conditioning in the palace was broken yet again, partly because that was the effect Kimba usually had on them.

"I'm glad that's over," muttered Volkov to his colleague as they drove back toward the embassy. "Anyway, we got permission. I'll install my man tomorrow."

"And I'll get the mining engineers sent in as soon as possible," said Dobrovolsky. "Let's hope there really is something fishy about the British survey report. If there isn't, I don't know how I'll explain that to the President."

Volkov grunted. "Rather you than me," he said.

Shannon checked into the Lowndes Hotel off Knightsbridge, as he had agreed with Walter Harris to do before he left London. The agreement was that he would be away about ten days, and each morning at nine Harris would phone the hotel and ask for Mr. Keith Brown. Shannon arrived at noon to find the first call for him had been three hours earlier that morning. The news meant he had till the next day to himself.

One of his first calls after a long bath, a change, and lunch, was to the detective agency. The head of it recognized the name of Keith Brown after a few moments' thought, and Shannon heard him sorting out some files on his desk. Eventually he found the right one.

"Yes, Mr. Brown, I have it here. Would you like me to mail it to you?"

"Rather not," said Shannon. "Is it long?"

"No, about a page. Shall I read it over the phone?"

"Yes, please."

The man cleared his throat and began. "On the morning following the client's request, my operative waited close to the entrance of the underground parking lot beneath ManCon House. He was lucky, in that the subject, whom he had noted the day before arriving back there by taxi from his interview at Sloane Avenue with our client, arrived by car. The operative got a clear view of him as he swung into the parking lot tunnel entrance. It was beyond doubt the subject. He was at the wheel of a Chevrolet Corvette. The operative took the number as the car went down the ramp. Inquiries were later made with a contact at the Licensing Department at County Hall. The vehicle is registered in the name of one Simon John Endean, resident in South Kensington," The man paused. "Do you want the address, Mr. Brown?"

"Not necessarily," said Shannon. "Do you know what this man Endean does at ManCon House?"

"Yes," said the private agent. "I checked up with a friend who's a City journalist. He is the personal aide and right hand man of Sir James Manson, chairman and managing director of Manson Consolidated."

"Thank you," said Shannon and put the phone down.

"Curiouser and curiouser," he murmured as he left the hotel lobby and strolled down to Jermyn Street to cash a check and buy some shirts. It was the first of April, April Fool's Day; the sun was shining and daffodils covered the grass around Hyde Park Corner.

Simon Endean had also been busy while Shannon was away. The results of his labors he imparted to Sir James Manson that afternoon in the penthouse over Moorgate.

"Colonel Bobi," he told his chief as he entered the office.

The mining boss furrowed his brow. "Who?"

"Colonel Bobi. The former commander of the army of Zangaro. Now in exile, banished forever by President Jean Kimba. Who, incidentally, has sentenced him to death by presidential decree for high treason. You wanted to know where he was."

Manson was at his desk by this time, nodding in recollection. "All right, where is he?" he asked.

"In exile in Dahomey," said Endean. "It took a hell of a job to trace him without being too obvious about it. But he's taken up residence in the capital of Dahomey. Place called Cotonou. He must have a little money, but probably not much, or he'd be in a walled villa outside Geneva with all the other rich exiles. He has a small rented villa and lives very quietly, probably because it is the safest way of ensuring the Dahomey government doesn't ask him to leave. It's believed Kimba has asked for his extradition back home, but no one has done anything about it. Besides, he's far enough away from Kimba to assume he'll never present a threat."

"And Shannon, the mercenary?" asked Manson.

"Due back sometime today or tomorrow," said Endean. "I booked him into the Lowndes from yesterday onward to be on the safe side. He hadn't arrived this morning at nine. I'm due to try again tomorrow at the same time."

"Try now," said Manson.

The hotel confirmed to Endean that Mr. Brown had indeed arrived, but that he was out. Sir James Manson listened on the extension.

"Leave a message," he growled at Endean. "Ring him tonight at seven."

Endean left the message, and the two men put the phones down.

"I want his report as soon as possible," said Manson. "He should finish it at noon tomorrow. You meet him first and read the report. Make sure it covers every point I told you I wanted answered. Then bring it to me. Put Shannon on ice for two days to give me time to digest it."

Shannon got Endean's message just after five and was in his room to take the call at seven. He spent the rest of the evening between supper and bed making up his notes and the memorabilia he had brought back from Zangaro—a series of sketches done freehand on a pad of cartridge paper he had bought in the airport in Paris to while away the time, some scale-drawings done from measurements between fixed points in Clarence that he had paced out stride by stride, a local guidebook showing "points of interest," of which the only interesting one was titled "the residence of His Excellency the Governor of the Colony" and dated from 1959, and an official and highly flattering portrait of Kimba, one of the few items not in short supply in the republic.

The next day he strolled down Knightsbridge just as the shops opened, bought himself a typewriter and a pad of paper, and spent the morning writing his report. It covered three subjects: a straight narrative of his visit, including the episode of the soldier he had killed; a detailed description of the capital, building by building, accompanied by the diagrams; and an equally detailed description of the military situation. He mentioned the fact that he had seen no signs of either an air force or a navy, and Gomez' confirmation that neither existed. He did not mention his stroll down the peninsula to the native shanty towns, where he had seen the clustered shacks of the poorer Caja and beyond them the shanties of the thousands of immigrant workers and their families, who chattered to one another in their native tongue, brought with them from many miles away.

He finished the report with a summary:

> The essence of the problem of toppling Kimba has been simplified by the man himself. In all respects the majority of the republic's land area, the Vindu country beyond the river, is of nil political or economic value. If Kimba should ever lose control of the coastal plain producing the bulk of the nation's few resources, he must lose the country. To go one step further, he and his men could not hold this plain in the face of the hostility and hatred of the entire Caja population, which, although muted by fear, exists beneath the surface, if he had once lost the peninsula. Again, the peninsula is untenable by Vindu forces if once the town of Clar-

The Dogs of War 529

ence is lost. And lastly, he has no strength within the town of Clarence if he and his forces have lost the palace. In short, his policy of total centralization has reduced the number of targets necessary to be subdued for a take-over of the state to one—his palace complex, containing himself, his guards, the armory, treasury and radio station.

As to means of taking and reducing this palace and compound, they have been reduced to one, by virtue of the wall surrounding the entire place. It has to be stormed.

The main gate could perhaps be rammed down by a very heavy truck or bulldozer driven straight at it by a man prepared to die in the attempt. I saw no evidence of any such spirit among the citizenry or the army, nor signs of a suitable truck. Alternatively, self-sacrificing courage by hundreds of men with scaling ladders could overwhelm the palace walls and take the place. I saw no signs of such spirit either. More realistically, the palace and grounds could be taken with little life loss after being first pulverized with mortar fire. Against a weapon like this the encircling wall, far from being a protection, becomes a death-trap to those inside. The door could be taken apart by a bazooka rocket. I saw no signs of either of these weapons, nor any sign of one single person capable of using them. The unavoidable conclusion reached from the above has to be as follows:

Any section or faction within the republic seeking to topple Kimba and take over must destroy him and his Praetorian Guards inside the palace compound. To achieve this they would require expert assistance at a technical level they have not reached, and such assistance would have to arrive, complete with all necessary equipment, from outside the country. With these conditions fulfilled, Kimba could be destroyed and toppled in a firefight lasting no longer than one hour.

"Is Shannon aware that there is no faction inside Zangaro that has indicated it wants to topple Kimba?" asked Sir James Manson the following morning when he read the report.

"I haven't told him so," said Endean. "I briefed him as you told me. Just said there was an army faction inside, and that the group I represented, as interested businessmen, were prepared to pay for a military assessment of their chances of success. But he's no fool. He must have seen for himself there's no one there capable of doing the job anyway."

"I like the sound of this Shannon," said Manson, closing the military report. "He's obviously got nerve, to judge by the way he dealt with the soldier. He writes quite well; he's short and to the point. Question is, could he do the whole of this job himself?"

"He did mention something significant," interjected Endea. "He said when I was questioning him that the caliber of the Zangaran army was so low that any assisting force of technicians would have to do practically the whole job anyway, then hand over to the new men when it was done."

"Did he now? Did he?" Manson said musingly. "Then he suspects already the reason for his going down there was not the stated one."

He was still musing when Endean asked, "May I put a question, Sir James?"

"What is it?" asked Manson.

"Just this: What did he go down there for? Why do you need a military report on how Kimba could be toppled and killed?"

Sir James Manson stared out of the window for some time. Finally he said, "Get Martin Thorpe up here." While Thorpe was being summoned, Manson walked to the window and gazed down, as he usually did when he wanted to think hard.

He knew he had personally taken Endean and Thorpe as young men and promoted them to salaries and positions beyond their years. It was not simply because of their intelligence, although they had plenty of it. It was because he recognized an unscrupulousness in each of them that matched his own, a preparedness to ignore so-called moral principles in pursuit of the goal success. He had made them his team, his hatchetmen, paid by the company but serving him personally in all things. The problem was: Could he trust them with this one, the big one? As Thorpe entered the office, he decided he had to. He thought he knew how to guarantee their loyalty.

He bade them sit down and, remaining standing with his back to the window, he told them, "I want you two to think this one over very carefully, then give me your reply. How far would you be prepared to go to be assured of a personal fortune in a Swiss bank of five million pounds each?"

The hum of the traffic ten floors down was like a buzzing bee, accentuating the silence in the room.

Endean stared back at his chief and nodded slowly. "A very, very long way," he said softly.

Thorpe made no reply. He knew this was what he had come to the City for, joined Manson for, absorbed his encyclopedic knowledge of company business for. The big one, the once-in-a-decade grand slam. He nodded assent.

"How?" whispered Endean. For answer Manson walked to his wall safe and extracted two reports. The third, Shannon's, lay on his desk as he seated himself behind it.

Manson talked steadily for an hour. He started at the beginning and soon read the final six paragraphs of Dr. Chalmers' report on the samples from the Crystal Mountain.

Thorpe whistled softly and muttered, "Jesus."

Endean required a ten-minute lecture on platinum to catch the point; then he too breathed a long sigh.

Manson went on to relate the exiling of Mulrooney to northern Kenya, the suborning of Chalmers, the second visit of Bryant to Clarence, the acceptance of the dummy report by Kimba's Minister. He stressed the Russian influence on Kimba and the recent exiling of Colonel Bobi, who, given the right circumstances, could return as a plausible alternative in the seat of power.

For Thorpe's benefit he read much of Endean's general report on Zangaro and finished with the conclusion of Shannon's report.

"If it is to work at all, it must be a question of mounting two parallel, highly secret operations," Manson said finally. "In one, Shannon, stage-managed throughout by Simon, mounts a project to take and destroy that palace and all its contents, and for Bobi, accompanied by Simon, to take over the powers of state the following morning and become the new president. In the other, Martin would have to buy a shell company without revealing who had gained control or why."

Endean furrowed his brow. "I can see the first operation, but why the second?" he asked.

"Tell him, Martin," said Manson.

Thorpe was grinning, for his astute mind had caught Manson's drift. "A shell company, Simon, is a company, usually very old and without assets worth talking about, which has virtually ceased trading and whose shares are very cheap—say, a shilling each."

"So why buy one?" asked Endean, still puzzled.

"Say Sir James has control of a company, bought secretly through unnamed nominees, hiding behind a Swiss bank, all nice and legal, and the company has a million shares valued at one shilling each. Unknown to the other shareholders or the board of directors or the Stock Exchange, Sir James, via the Swiss bank, owns six hundred thousand of these million shares. Then Colonel—beg his pardon—President Bobi sells that company an exclusive ten-year mining franchise for an area of land in the hinterland of Zangaro. A new mining survey team from a highly reputable company specializing in mining goes out and discovers the Crystal Mountain. What happens to the shares of Company X when the news hits the stock market?"

Endean got the message. "They go up," he said with a grin.

"Right up," said Thorpe. "With a bit of help they go from a shilling to well over a hundred pounds a share. Now do your arithmetic. Six hundred thousand shares at a shilling each cost thirty thousand pounds to buy. Sell six hundred thousand shares at a hundred pounds each—and that's the minimum you'd get—and what do you bring home? A cool sixty million pounds, in a Swiss bank. Right, Sir James?"

"That's right." Manson nodded grimly. "Of course, if you sold half the shares in small packets to a wide variety of people, the control of the company owning the concession would stay in the same hands as before. But a bigger company might put in a bid for the whole block of six hundred thousand shares in one flat deal."

Thorpe nodded thoughtfully. "Yes, control of such a company bought at sixty million pounds would be a good market deal. But whose bid would you accept?"

"My own," said Manson.

Thorpe's mouth opened. "Your own?"

"ManCon's bid would be the only acceptable one. That way the concession would remain firmly British, and ManCon would have gained a fine asset."

"But," queried Endean, "surely you would be paying yourself sixty million quid?"

"No," said Thorpe quietly. "ManCon's shareholders would be paying Sir James sixty million quid, without knowing it."

"What's that called—in financial terms, of course?" asked Endean.

"There is a word for it on the Stock Exchange," Thorpe admitted.

Sir James Manson tendered them each a glass of whisky. He reached round and took his own. "Are you on, gentlemen?" he asked quietly.

Both younger men looked at each other and nodded.

"Then here's to the Crystal Mountain."

They drank.

"Report to me here tomorrow morning at nine sharp," Manson told them, and they rose to go.

At the door to the back stairs Thorpe turned. "You know, Sir James, it's going to be bloody dangerous. If one word gets out . . . "

Sir James Manson stood again with his back to the window, the westering sun slanting onto the carpet by his side. His legs were apart, his fists on his hips.

"Knocking off a bank or an armored truck" he said, "is merely crude. Knocking off an entire republic has, I feel, a certain style."

EIGHT

"What you are saying in effect is that there is no dissatisfied faction within the army that, so far as you know, has ever thought of toppling President Kimba?"

Cat Shannon and Simon Endean were sitting in Shannon's room at the hotel, taking midmorning coffee. Endean had phoned Shannon by agreement at nine and told him to wait for a second call. He had been briefed by Sir James Manson and had called Shannon back to make the eleven-o'clock appointment.

Endean nodded. "That's right. The information has changed in that one detail. I can't see what difference it makes. You yourself said the caliber of the army was so low that the technical assistants would have to do all the work themselves in any case."

"It makes a hell of a difference," said Shannon. "Attacking the palace and capturing it is one thing. Keeping it is quite another. Destroying the palace and Kimba simply creates a vacuum at the seat of power. Someone has to step in and take over that power. The mercenaries must not even be seen by daylight. So who takes over?"

Endean nodded again. He had not expected a mercenary to have any political sense at all.

"We have a man in view," he said cautiously.

"He's in the republic now, or in exile?"

"In exile."

"Well, he would have to be installed in the palace and broadcasting on the radio that he has conducted an internal coup d'état and taken over the country, by midday of the day following the night attack in the palace."

"That could be arranged."

"There's one more thing."

"What's that?" asked Endean.

"There must be troops loyal to the new regime, the same troops who ostensibly carried out the coup of the night before, visibly present and mounting the guard by sunrise of the day after the attack. If they don't show up, we would be stuck—a group of white mercenaries holed up inside the palace, unable to show themselves for political reasons, and cut off from retreat in the event of a counterattack. Now your man, the exile, does he have such a back-up force he could bring in with him when he comes? Or could he assemble them quickly once inside the capital?"

"I think you have to let us take care of that," said Endean stiffly. "What we are asking you for is a plan in military terms to mount the attack and carry it through."

"That I can do," said Shannon without hesitation. "But what about the preparations, the organization of the plan, getting the men, the arms, the ammo?"

"You must include that as well. Start from scratch and go right through to the capture of the palace and the death of Kimba."

"Kimba has to get the chop?"

"Of course," said Endean. "Fortunately he has long since destroyed anyone with initiative or brains to become a rival. Consequently, he is the only man who might regroup his forces and counterattack. With him dead, his ability to mesmerize the people into submission will also end."

"Yeah. The juju dies with the man."

"The what?"

"Nothing. You wouldn't understand."

"Try me," said Endean coldly.

"The man has a juju," said Shannon, "or at least the people believe he has. That's a powerful protection given him by the spirits, protecting him against his enemies, guaranteeing him invincibility, guarding him from attack, ensuring him against death. In the Congo the Simbas believed their leader, Pierre Mulele, had a similar juju. He told them he could pass it on to his supporters and make them immortal. They believed him. They thought bullets would run off them like water. So they came at us in waves, bombed out of their minds on dagga and whisky, died like flies, and still kept coming. It's the same with Kimba. So long as they think he's immortal, he is. Because they'll never lift a finger against him. Once they see his corpse, the man who killed him becomes the leader. He has the stronger juju."

Endean stared in surprise. "It's really that backward?"

"It's not so backward. We do the same with lucky charms, holy relics, the assumption of divine protection for our own particular cause. But we call it religion in us, savage superstition in them."

"Never mind," snapped Endean. "All the more reason why Kimba has to die."

"Which means he must be in that palace when we strike. If he's upcountry it's no good. No one will support your man if Kimba is still alive."

"He usually is in the palace, so I'm told."

"Yes," said Shannon, "but we have to guarantee it. There's one day he never misses. Independence Day. On the eve of Independence Day he will be sleeping in the palace, sure as eggs is eggs."

"When's that?"

"Three and a half months away."

"Could a project be mounted in that time?" asked Endean.

"Yes, with a bit of luck. I'd like at least a couple of weeks longer."

"The project has not been accepted yet," observed Endean.

"No, but if you want to install a new man in that palace, an attack from outside is the only way of doing it. Do you want me to prepare the whole project from start to finish, with estimated costings and time schedule?"

"Yes. The costing is very important. My—er—associates will want to know how much they are letting themselves in for."

"All right," said Shannon. "The report will cost you five hundred pounds."

"You've already been paid," said Endean coldly.

"I've been paid for a mission into Zangaro and a report on the military situation there," replied Shannon. "What you're asking for is a new report right outside the original briefing you gave me."

"Five hundred is a bit steep for a few sheets of paper with writing on them."

"Rubbish. You know perfectly well if your firm consults a lawyer, architect, accountant, or any other technical expert you pay him a fee. I'm a technical expert in war. What you pay for is the knowledge and the experience—where to get the best men, the best arms, how to ship them, et cetera. That's what costs five hundred pounds, and the same knowledge would cost you double if you tried to research it yourself in twelve months, which you couldn't anyway because you haven't the contacts."

Endean rose. "All right. It will be here this afternoon by special messenger. Tomorrow is Friday. My partners would like to read your report over the weekend. Please have it prepared by tomorrow afternoon at three. I'll collect it here."

He left, and as the door closed behind him Shannon raised his coffee cup in mock toast. "Be seeing you, Mr. Walter Harris oblique stroke Simon Endean," he said softly.

Not for the first time he thanked his stars for the amiable and garrulous hotelkeeper Gomez. During one of their long nightly conversations Gomez had mentioned the affair of Colonel Bobi, now in exile. He had also mentioned that, without Kimba, Bobi was nothing, being hated by the Caja for his army's cruelties against them on the orders of Kimba, and not able to command Vindu troops either. Which left Shannon with the problem of a back-up force with black faces to take over on the morning after.

Endean's brown manila envelope containing fifty £10 notes arrived just after three in a taxicab and was delivered to the reception desk of the Lowndes Hotel. Shannon counted the notes, stuffed them into the inside pocket of his jacket, and began work. It took him the rest of the afternoon and most of the night.

He worked at the writing desk in his room, poring over his own diagrams and maps of the city of Clarence, its harbor, port area, and the residential section that included the presidential palace and the army lines.

The classical military approach would have been to land a force on the side of the peninsula near the base with the main coastline, march the short distance inland, and take the road from Clarence to the interior, with guns covering the T-junction. That would have sealed off the peninsula and the capital from reinforcement. It would also have lost the element of surprise.

Shannon's talent was that he understood Africa and the African soldier, and his thinking was unconventional. Tactics suited to African terrain and opposition are almost the exact opposite of those that will work in a European situation.

Had Shannon's plans ever been considered by a European military mind thinking in conventional terms, they would have been styled as reckless and without hope of success. He was banking on Sir James Manson's not having been in the British army—there was no reference in *Who's Who* to indicate that he had—and accepting the plan. Shannon knew it was workable and the only one that was.

He based his plan on three facts about war in Africa that he had learned the hard way. One is that the European soldier fights well and with precision in the dark, provided he has been well briefed on the terrain he can expect, while the African soldier, even on his own terrain, is sometimes reduced to near helplessness by his fear of the hidden enemy in the surrounding darkness. The second is that the speed of recovery of the disoriented African soldier—his ability to regroup and counterattack—is slower than the European soldier's, exaggerating the normal effects of surprise. The third is that firepower and hence noise can bring African soldiers to fear, panic, and headlong flight, without consideration of the smallness of the actual numbers of their opponents.

So Shannon based his plan on a night attack of total surprise in conditions of deafening noise and concentrated firepower.

He worked slowly and methodically and, being a poor typist, tapped out the words with two forefingers. At two in the morning the occupant of the bedroom next door could stand no more and banged on the wall to ask plaintively for a bit of peace so that he could get to sleep. Shannon concluded what he was doing five minutes later and packed up for the night. There was one other sound that disturbed the man next door, apart from the clacking of the typewriter. As he worked, and later as he lay in bed, the writer kept whistling a plaintive little tune. Had the insomniac next door known more of music, he would have recognized "Spanish Harlem."

Martin Thorpe was also lying awake that night. He knew he had a long weekend ahead, two and a half days of monotonous and time-consuming poring over cards, each bearing the basic details of one of the forty-five hundred public companies registered at Companies House in the City of London.

There are two agencies in London which provide their subscribers with such an information service about British companies. These are Moodies and the Exchange Telegraph, know as Extel. In his office in ManCon House, Thorpe had the set of cards provided by Extel, the agency whose service ManCon took as a necessary part of its commercial activities. But for the business of searching for a shell company, Thorpe had decided to buy the Moodies service and have it sent to his home, partly because he thought Moodies did a better information job on the smaller companies registered in the United Kingdom, and partly for security reasons.

After his briefing from Sir James Manson on Thursday, he had gone straight to a firm of lawyers. Acting for him, and keeping his name to themselves, they had ordered a complete set of Moodies cards. He had paid the lawyer £260 for the cards, plus £50 for the three gray filing cabinets in which they would arrive, plus the lawyer's fee. He had also engaged a small moving firm to send a van around to Moodies, after being told the set of cards would be ready for pick-up on Friday afternoon.

As he lay in bed in his elegant detached house in Hampstead Garden Suburb, he too was planning his campaign—not in detail like Shannon, for he had too little information, but in general terms, using nominee shareholders and parcels of voting stock as Shannon used submachine guns and mortars. He had never met the mercenary and never would. But he would have understood him.

Shannon handed his completed project to Endean at three on Friday afternoon. It contained fourteen pages, four of them diagrams and two of them lists of equipment. He had finished it after breakfast and had enclosed it in a brown folder. He was tempted to put "For Sir James Manson's Eyes Only" on the cover, but had resisted. There was no need to blow the affair wantonly, and he could sniff a good contract in the offing if the mining baron offered the job to him.

So he continued to call Endean Harris and to refer to "your associates" instead of "your boss." After taking the folder, Endean told him to stay in town over the weekend and to be available from Sunday midnight onward.

Shannon went shopping during the rest of the afternoon, but his mind was on the references he had already seen in *Who's Who* to the man he now knew employed him, Sir James Manson, self-made millionaire and tycoon.

He had an urge, partly from curiosity, partly from the feeling that one day he might need the information, to learn more about Sir James Manson, about the man himself and about why he had hired a mercenary to make war in Zangaro on his behalf.

The reference from *Who's Who* that stuck in his mind was the mention of a daughter Manson had, a girl who would now be in her late teens or just turned twenty. In the middle of the afternoon he stepped into a phone booth off Jermyn Street and called the private inquiry agents who had traced Endean from their first meeting in Chelsea and identified him as Manson's aide.

The head of the agency was cordial when he heard his former client on the phone. Previously, he knew, Mr. Brown had paid promptly and in cash. Such customers were valuable. If he wished to remain on the end of a telephone, that was his affair.

"Do you have access to a fairly comprehensive newspaper cuttings library?" Shannon asked.

"I could have," the agency chief admitted.

"I wish to get a brief description of a young lady to whom there has probably at one time been a reference in society gossip columns somewhere in the London press. I need very little, simply what she does and where she lives. But I need it quickly."

There was a pause on the other end. "If there are such references, I could probably do it by phone," said the inquiry agent. "What is the name?"

"Miss Julia Manson, daughter of Sir James Manson."

The inquiry agent thought it over. He recalled that this client's previous assignment had concerned a man who turned out to be Sir James Manson's aide. He also knew he could find out what Mr. Brown wanted to know within an hour.

The two men agreed on the fee, a modest one, and Shannon promised to mail it in cash by registered mail within the hour. The inquiry agent decided to accept the promise and asked his client to call him back just before five.

Shannon completed his shopping and called back on the dot of five. Within a few seconds he had what he wanted. He was deep in thought as he walked back to his hotel and phoned the writer who had originally introduced him to "Mr. Harris."

"Hi," he said gruffly, "it's me, Cat Shannon."

"Oh, hello, Cat," came the surprised reply. "Where have you been?"

"Around," said Shannon. "I just wanted to say thanks for recommending me to that fellow Harris."

"Not at all. Did he offer you a job?"

Shannon was cautious. "Yeah, a few days' worth. It's over now. But I'm in funds. How about a spot of dinner?"

"Why not?" said the writer.

"Tell me," said Shannon, "are you still going out with that girl you used to be with when we met last?"

"Yeah. The same one. Why?"

"She's a model, isn't she?"

"Yes."

"Look," said Shannon, "you may think this crazy, but I very much want to meet a girl who's also a model but I can't get an introduction to. Name of Julie Manson. Could you ask your girl if she ever met her in the modeling world?"

The writer thought it over. "Sure. I'll call Carrie and ask her. Where are you now?"

"In a call box. I'll call you back in half an hour."

Shannon was lucky. The two girls had been at modeling school together. They were also handled by the same agency. It took another hour before Shannon, by then speaking directly to the writer's girlfriend, learned that Julie Manson had agreed to a dinner date, providing it was a foursome with Carrie and her boyfriend. They agreed to meet at Carrie's flat just after eight, and she would have Julie Manson there.

Shannon and the writer turned up within a few minutes of each other at Carrie's flat off Maida Vale, and the four of them went off to dinner. The writer had reserved a table at a small cellar restaurant called the Baker and Oven in Marylebone, and the meal was the kind Shannon liked, enormous portions of English roast meats and vegetables, washed down with two bottles of Piat de Beaujolais. He liked the food, and he liked Julie.

She was quite short, a little over five feet, and to give the impression of more height she wore high heels and carried herself well. She said she was nineteen, and she had a pert, round face that could be innocently angelic when she wanted, or extremely sexy when she thought no one else was looking.

She was evidently spoiled and too accustomed to getting things her own way—probably, Shannon estimated, the result of an overindulgent upbringing. But she was amusing and pretty, and Shannon had never asked more of a girl. She wore her dark brown hair loose so that it fell to her waist, and beneath her dress she evidently had a very curved figure. She also seemed to be intrigued by her blind date.

Although Shannon had asked his friend not to mention what he did for a living, Carrie had nevertheless let it slip that he was a mercenary. But the conversation managed to avoid the question during dinner. As usual Shannon did less talking than anyone, which was not difficult because Julie and the tall auburn-haired Carrie did enough for four between them.

As they left the restaurant and climbed back into the cool night air of the streets, the writer mentioned that he and his girlfriend were taking the car back to his flat. He hailed a taxi for Shannon asking him if he would take Julie home before going on to his hotel.

As the mercenary climbed in, the writer gave him a slow wink. "I think you're on," he whispered. Shannon grunted.

Outside her Mayfair flat Julie suggested he might like to come in for coffee, so he paid off the taxi and accompanied her up to the evidently expensive apartment. Only when they were seated on the settee drinking the appalling coffee Julie had prepared did she refer to the way he earned his living.

He was leaning back in the corner of the settee; she was perched on the edge of the seat, turned toward him.

"Have you killed people?" she asked.

"Yes."

"In battle?"

"Sometimes. Mostly."

"How many?"

"I don't know. I never counted."

She savored the information and swallowed several times. "I've never known a man who had killed people."

"You don't know that," countered Shannon. "Anyone who has been in a war has probably killed people."

"Have you got any scars from wounds?"

It was another of the usual questions. In fact Shannon carried over a score of marks on his back and chest, legacies of bullets, fragments of mortar, and shards of grenade. He nodded. "Some."

"Show me," she said.

"No."

"Go on, show me. Prove it." She stood up.

He grinned up at her. "I'll show you mine if you'll show me yours," he taunted, mimicking the old kindergarten challenge.

"I haven't got any," Julie said indignantly.

"Prove it," said Shannon shortly and turned to place his empty coffee cup on the table behind the sofa. He heard a rustle of cloth. When he turned back he nearly choked on the last mouthful of coffee. It had taken her less than a second to unzip her dress at the back and let it slip to a pool of crumpled cloth around her ankles. Beneath it she wore a thin gold waist-chain.

"See," she said softly, "not a mark anywhere."

She was right. Her small nubile teenager's body was an unblemished milky white from the floor to the mane of dark hair that hung round her shoulders and almost touched the waist-chain.

Shannon swallowed. "I thought you were supposed to be Daddy's sweet little girl," he said.

She giggled. "That's what they all think, especially Daddy," she said. "Now it's your turn."

Sir James Manson sat at the same hour in the library of his country mansion not far from the village of Notgrove in the rolling Gloucestershire countryside, Shannon's file on his knee and a brandy and soda at his elbow. It was close to midnight, and Lady Manson had long since gone up to bed. He had saved the Shannon project to read alone in his library, resisting the temptation to open it in the car on the way down or to slip away early from dinner. When he wanted to concentrate hard he preferred the night hours, and on this document he wanted to concentrate hard.

He flicked the cover open and set on one side the maps and sketches. Then he started on the narrative. It read:

> *Preamble.* The following plan has been prepared on the basis of the report on the republic of Zangaro prepared by Mr. Walter Harris, my own visit to Zangaro and my own report on that visit, and the briefing given by Mr. Harris on what it is desired to achieve. It cannot take into account elements known to Mr. Harris but undisclosed by him to me. Notable among these must be the aftermath of the attack and the installation of the successor government. Nevertheless, this aftermath may well require preparations built in to the planning of the attack, and these I have obviously not been able to make.
>
> *Object of the Exercise.* To prepare, launch, and carry out an attack on the presidential palace at Clarence, capital of Zangaro, to storm and capture that palace, and to liquidate the President and his personal guards living inside. Also, to take possession of the bulk of the weapons and armory of the republic, its national treasury and broadcasting radio station, also inside the palace. Lastly, to create such conditions that any armed survivors of the guard unit or the army are scattered outside the town and in no position to mount a viable counterattack.
>
> *Method of Attack.* After studying the military situation of Clarence, there is no doubt the attack must be from the sea, and launched directly from the sea at the palace itself. I have studied the idea of an airborne landing at the airport. It is not feasible. Firstly, the authorities at the airport of take-off would not permit the necessary quantity of arms and men to board a charter aircraft without suspecting the nature of the flight. Any authorities, even if they permitted such a take-off, would constitute a serious risk of arrest, or a breach of security.

Secondly, a land attack offers no extra advantages and many disadvantages. To arrive in an armed column over the northern border would only mean the men and arms would have to be smuggled into the neighboring republic, which has an efficient police and security system. The risk of premature discovery and arrest would be extremely high, unacceptably so. To land elsewhere on the coast of Zangaro and march to Clarence would be no more realistic. For one thing, most of the coast is of tangled mangrove swamp impenetrable by boats, and such tiny coves as there are would be unfindable in darkness. For another, being without motor transport, the attack force would have a long march to the capital, and the defenders would be forewarned. For a third, the paucity of the numbers of the attacking force would be visible in daylight, and would hearten the defenders to put up a stiff resistance.

Lastly, the idea was examined to smuggle the arms and the men into the republic clandestinely and hide them out until the night of attack. This too is unrealistic, partly because the quantity of weapons would be too great in weight terms, partly because such quantities and so many unaccustomed visitors would inevitably be spotted and betrayed, and partly because such a plan would require an assisting organization on the ground inside Zangaro, which does not exist.

In consequence it is felt the only realistic plan must be for an attack by light boats, departing from a larger vessel moored out at sea, straight into the harbor of Clarence, and an attack on the palace immediately on landing.

Requirements for the Attack. The force should be not less than a dozen men, armed with mortars, bazookas, and grenades, and all carrying as well submachine carbines for close-quarters use. The men should come off the sea between two and three in the morning, giving ample time for all in Clarence to be asleep, but sufficiently before dawn for no visible traces of white mercenaries to be available by sunrise of the same day.

The report continued for six more pages to describe exactly how Shannon proposed to plan the project and engage the necessary personnel; the arms and ammunition he would need, the ancillary equipment of radio sets, assault craft, outboard engines, flares, uniforms, webbing, food and supplies; how each item could be costed; and how he would destroy the palace and scatter the army.

On the question of the ship to carry the attacking force he said:

Apart from the arms, the acquisition of the ship will prove the most difficult part. On reflection I would be against chartering a vessel, since this involves crew who may turn out to be unreliable, a captain who could at any time change his mind, and the security hazard that vessels of a kind likely to undertake such a charter are probably notorious to the authorities of the countries bordering on the Mediterranean. I advocate spending more money to buy outright a small freighter, crew it with men paid by and loyal to the patrons and with a legal reputation in shipping circles. Such a boat would in any case be a returnable asset and might work out cheaper in the long run.

Shannon had also stressed the necessity of security at all times. He pointed out:

Since I am unware of the identity of the patrons, with the exception of Mr. Harris, it is recommended that, in the event of the project being accepted, Mr. Harris remain the sole link between the patrons and me. Payments of the necessary money should be made to me by Mr. Harris, and my accounting of expenditure returned the same way. Similarly, although I would need four subordinate operatives, none would know the nature of the project, and certainly not the destination, until all are well out to sea. Even the coastal charts should be handed over to the captain only after sailing. The above plan takes in the security angle, since wherever possible the purchases may be made legally on the open market, and only the arms an illegal purchase. At each stage there is a cut-out at which any investigator comes up against a blank wall, and also at each stage the equipment is being bought separately in different countries by different operatives. Only myself, Mr. Harris, and the patrons would know the whole plan, and in the worst event I could not identify the patrons, nor, probably, Mr. Harris.

Sir James Manson nodded and grunted in approval several times as he read. At one in the morning he poured himself another brandy and turned to the costings and timings, which were on separate sheets. These read:

		COMPLETED
Reconnaissance visit to Zangaro.		
Two reports	£	2,500
Project commander's fee	£	10,000
Engagement all other personnel and their salaries	£	10,000
Total administrative costs, traveling, hotels, etc., for CO and all subordinates	£	10,000
Purchase of arms	£	25,000
Purchase of vessel	£	30,000
Purchase of ancillary equipment	£	5,000
Reserve	£	2,500
TOTAL	£	100,000

The second sheet bore the estimated timings.

Preparatory Stage: Recruitment and assembly of personnel. Setting up of bank account. Setting up of foreign-based company to cover purchases.   20 days

Purchasing Stage: Period to cover purchase of all items in sections.   40 days

Assembly Stage: Assembly of equipment and personnel onto the vessel, culminating in sailing day.   20 days

Shipment Stage: Transporting entire project by sea from embarkation port to point off coast of Clarence.   20 days

Strike day would take place on Zangaran Independence Day, which in the above calendar, if set in motion not later than next Wednesday, would be Day 100.

Sir James Manson read the report twice and slowly smoked one of his Upmann Coronas while he stared at the rich paneling and Morocco-bound books that lined his walls. Finally he locked the project file in his wall safe and went upstairs to bed.

Cat Shannon lay on his back in the darkened bedroom and ran his hand idly over the girl's body that lay half across his own. It was a small but highly erotic body, as he had discovered during the previous hour, and whatever Julie had spent her time learning in the two years since she left school, it had not had much to do with shorthand and typing. Her appetite and taste for sexual variety were equaled only by her energy and almost constant stream of chatter between meals.

As he stroked her she stirred and began to play with him.

"Funny," he said reflectively, "it must be a sign of the times. We've been screwing half the night, and I don't know a thing about you."

She paused for a second, said, "Like what?" and resumed.

"Where your home is," he said. "Apart from this pad."

"Gloucestershire," she mumbled.

"What does your old man do?" he asked softly. There was no answer. He took a handful of her hair and pulled her face around to him.

"Ow, you're hurting. He's in the City. Why?"

"Stockbroker?"

"No, he runs some company to do with mining. That's his specialty, and this is mine. Now, watch."

Half an hour later she rolled off him and asked, "Did you like that, darling?"

Shannon laughed, and she caught a flash of teeth in the darkness as he grinned.

"Oh yes," he said softly, "I enjoyed that enormously. Tell me about your old man."

"Daddy? Oh he's a boring old businessman. Spends all his day in a stuffy office in the City."

"Some businessmen interest me. So tell me, what's he like?"

Sir James Manson was enjoying his midmorning coffee in the sun lounge on the south side of his country mansion that Saturday morning when the call came through from Adrian Goole. The Foreign Office official was speaking from his own home in Kent.

"I hope you won't mind my calling you over the weekend," he said.

"Not at all, my dear fellow," said Manson quite untruthfully. "Any time."

"I would have called at the office last night, but I got held up at a meeting. Recalling our conversation some time ago about the results of your mining survey down in that African place. You remember?"

Manson supposed Goole felt obliged to go through the security rigmarole on an open line.

"Yes indeed," he said. "I took up your suggestion made at that dinner. The figures concerned were slightly changed, so that the quantities revealed were quite unviable from a business standpoint. The report went off, was received, and I've heard no more about it."

Goole's next words jerked Sir James Manson out of his weekend relaxation.

"Actually, we have," said the voice on the phone. "Nothing really disturbing, but odd all the same. Our Ambassador in the area, although accredited to that country and three other small republics, doesn't live there, as you know. But he sends in regular reports, gleaned from a variety of sources, including normal liaison with other friendly diplomats. A copy of a section of his latest report, concerned with the economic side of things out there, landed on my desk yesterday at the office. It seems there's a rumor out there that the Soviet government has secured permission to send in a mining survey team of their own. Of course, they may not be concerned with the same area as your chaps. . . ."

Sir James Manson stared at the telephone as Goole's voice twittered. In his head a pulse began to hammer, close to his left temple.

"I was only thinking, Sir James, that if these Russian chaps go over the same area your man went over, their findings might be somewhat different. Fortunately, it's only a question of minor quantities of tin. Still, I thought you ought to know. Hello? Hello? Are you there?"

Manson jerked himself out of his reverie. With a massive effort he made his voice appear normal.

"Yes indeed. Sorry, I was just thinking. Very good of you to call me, Goole. I don't suppose they'll be in the same area as my man. But damn useful to know, all the same."

He went through the usual pleasantries before hanging up, and walked slowly back to the sun terrace, his mind racing. Coincidence? Could be, it just could be. If the Soviet survey team was going to cover an area miles away from the Crystal Mountain range, it would be purely a coincidence. On the other hand, if it went straight toward the Crystal Mountain without having done any aerial survey work to notice the differences in vegetation in that area, then that would be no coincidence. That would be bloody sabotage. And there was no way he could find out, no way of being absolutely certain, without betraying his own continuing interest. And that would be fatal.

He thought of Chalmers, the man he was convinced he had silenced with money. His teeth ground. Had he talked? Wittingly? Unwittingly? He had half a mind to let Endean take care of Dr. Chalmers, or one of Endean's friends. But that would change nothing. And there was no proof of a security leak.

He could shelve his plans at once and think no more of them. He considered this, then considered again the pot of pure gold at the end of this particular rainbow. James Manson was not where he was because he had the habit of backing down on account of risk.

He sat down in his deck chair next to the now cold coffeepot and thought hard. He intended to go forward as planned, but he had to assume the Russian mining team would touch on the area Mulrooney had visited, and he had to assume that it too would notice the vegetation changes. Therefore there was now a new element, a time limit. He did some mental calculation and came up with the figure of three months. If the Russians learned the content of the Crystal Mountain, there would be a "technical aid" team in there like a dose of salts. A big one at that, and half the members would be hard men from KGB.

Shannon's shortest schedule had been a hundred days, but he had originally told Endean that another fortnight added to the timetable would make the whole project that much more feasible. Now they did not have that fortnight. In fact, if the Russians moved faster than usual, they might not even have a hundred days.

He returned to the telephone and called Simon Endean. His own weekend had been disturbed; there was no reason why Endean should not start doing a bit of work.

Endean called Shannon at the hotel on Monday morning and set up a rendezvous for two that afternoon at a small apartment house in St. John's Wood. He had hired the flat on the instructions of Sir James Manson, after having had a long briefing at the country mansion on Sunday afternoon. He had taken the flat for a month in the name of Harris, paying cash and giving a fictitious reference which no one checked. The reason for the hiring was simple: the flat had a telephone that did not go through a switchboard.

Shannon was there on time and found the man he still called Harris already installed. The telephone was hung in a desk microphone set that would enable a telephone conference to be held between one or more people in the room and the person on the other end of the line.

"The chief of the consortium has read your report," he told Shannon, "and wants to have a word with you."

At two-thirty the phone rang. Endean threw the "speak" switch on the machine, and Sir James Manson's voice came on the line. Shannon already knew who it would be but gave no sign.

"Are you there, Mr. Shannon?" asked the voice.

"Yes, sir."

"Now, I have read your report, and I approve your judgment and conclusions. If offered this contract, would you be prepared to go through with it?"

"Yes, sir, I would," said Shannon.

"There are a couple of points I want to discuss. I notice in the budget you award yourself the sum of ten thousand pounds."

"Yes, sir. Frankly, I don't think anyone would do the job for less, and most would ask more. Even if a budget were prepared by another person which quoted a lower sum, I think that person would still pass a minimum of ten per cent to himself, simply by hiding the sum in the prices of purchases that could not be checked out."

There was a pause; then the voice said, "All right. I accept that. What does this salary buy me?"

"It buys you my knowledge, my contacts, my acquaintanceship with the world of arms dealers, smugglers, gun-runners, and mercenaries. It also buys my silence in the event of anything's going wrong. It pays me for three months' damned hard work, and the constant risk of arrest and imprisonment. Lastly, it buys the risk of my getting killed in the attack."

There was a grunt. "Fair enough. Now as regards financing. The sum of one hundred thousand pounds will be transferred into a Swiss account which Mr. Harris will open this week. He will pay you the necessary money in slices, as and when you need it over the forthcoming two months. For that purpose you will have to set up your own communications system with him. When the money is spent, he will either have to be present or to receive receipts."

"That will not always be possible, sir. There are no receipts in the arms business, least of all in black-market deals, and most of the men I shall be dealing with would not have Mr. Harris present. He is not in their world. I would suggest the extensive use of travelers' checks and credit transfers by banks. At the same time, if Mr. Harris has to be present to countersign every banker's draft or check for a thousand pounds, he must either follow me around everywhere, which I would not accept on grounds of my own security, or we could never do it all inside a hundred days."

There was another long pause. "What do you mean by your own security?" asked the voice.

"I mean, sir, that I don't know Mr. Harris. I could not accept that he be in a position to know enough to get me arrested in a European city. You have taken your security precautions. I have to take mine. These are that I travel and work alone and unsupervised."

"You're a cautious man, Mr. Shannon."

"I have to be. I'm still alive."

There was a grim chuckle. "And how do I know you can be trusted with large sums of money to handle on your own?"

"You don't, sir. Up to a point Mr. Harris can keep the sums low at each stage. But the payments for the arms have to be made in cash and by the buyer alone. The only alternatives are to ask Mr. Harris to mount the operation personally, or to hire another professional. And you would not know if you could trust him either."

"Fair enough, Mr. Shannon. Mr. Harris."

"Sir?" answered Endean immediately.

"Please return to see me at once after leaving where you are now. Mr. Shannon, you have the job. You have one hundred days, Mr. Shannon, to steal a republic. One hundred days."

PART 2
The Hundred Days

NINE

For several minutes after Sir James Manson had hung up, Simon Endean and Cat Shannon sat and stared at each other. It was Shannon who recovered first.

"Since we're going to have to work together," he told Endean, "let's get this clear. If anyone, anyone at all, gets to hear about this project, it will eventually get back to one or another of the secret services of one of the main powers. Probably the CIA, or at least the British SIS or maybe the French SDECE. And they will screw, but good. There'll be nothing you or I could do to prevent them ending the affair stone dead. So we keep security absolute."

"Speak for yourself," snapped Endean. "I've got a lot more tied up in this than you."

"Okay. First thing has to be money. I'll fly to Brussels tomorrow and open a new bank account somewhere in Belgium. I'll be back by tomorrow night. Contact me then, and I'll tell you where, in which bank and in what name. Then I shall need a transfer of credit to the tune of at least ten thousand pounds. By tomorrow night I'll have a complete list of where it has to be spent. Mainly, it will be in salary checks for my assistants, deposits, and so on."

"Where do I contact you?" asked Endean.

"That's point number two," said Shannon. "I'm going to need a permanent base, secure for telephone calls and letters. What about this flat? Is it traceable to you?"

Endean had not thought of that. He considered the problem. "It's hired in my name. Cash in advance for one month," he said.

"Does it matter if the name Harris is on the tenancy agreement?" asked Shannon.

"No."

"Then I'll take it over. That gives me a month's tenancy—seems a pity to waste it—and I'll take up the payments at the end of that time. Do you have a key?"

"Yes, of course. I let myself in by it."

"How many keys are there?"

For answer Endean reached into his pocket and brought out a ring with four keys on it. Two were evidently for the front door of the house and two for the flat door. Shannon took them from his hand.

"Now for communications," he said. "You can contact me by phoning here any time. I may be in, I may not. I may be away abroad. Since I assume you will not want to give me your phone number, set up a *poste restante* mailing address in London somewhere convenient to either your home or office, and check twice daily for telegrams. If I need you urgently, I'll telegraph the phone number of where I am, and a time to phone. Understood?"

"Yes. I'll have it by tomorrow night. Anything else?"

"Only that I'll be using the name of Keith Brown throughout the operation. Anything signed as coming from Keith is from me. When calling a hotel, ask for me as Keith Brown. If ever I reply by saying 'This is Mr. Brown,' get off the line fast. It means trouble. Explain that you have the wrong number, or the wrong Brown. That's all for the moment. You'd better get back to the office. Call me here at eight tonight, and I'll give you the progress to date."

A few minutes later Endean found himself on the pavements of St. John's Wood, looking for a taxi.

Luckily Shannon had not banked the £500 he had received from Endean before the weekend for his attack project, and he still had £450 of it left.

He rang BEA and booked an economy-class round trip on the morning flight to Brussels, returning at 1600 hours, which would get him back in his flat by six. Following that, he telephoned four telegrams abroad, one to Paarl, Cape Province, South Africa; one to Ostend; one to Marseilles; and one to Munich. Each said simply, "Urgent you phone me London 507-0041 any midnight over next three days. Shannon." Finally he summoned a taxi and had it take him back to the Lowndes Hotel. He checked out, paid his bill, and left as he had come, anonymously.

At eight Endean rang him as agreed, and Shannon told Manson's aide what he had done so far. They agreed Endean would ring again at ten the following evening.

Shannon spent a couple of hours exploring the block he was now living in, and the surrounding area. He spotted several small restaurants, including a couple not far away in St. John's Wood High Street, and ate a leisurely supper at one of them. He was back home by eleven.

He counted his money—there was more than £400 left—put £300 on one side for the air fare and expenses the following day, and checked over his effects. The clothes were unremarkable, all of them less than three months old, most bought in the last ten days in London. He had no gun to bother about, and for safety destroyed the typewriter ribbon he had used to type his reports, replacing it with one of his spares.

Though it was dark early in London that evening, it was still light on a warm, sunny summer evening in Cape Province as Janni Dupree gunned his car past Seapoint and on toward Cape Town. He too had a Chevrolet, older than Endean's, but bigger and flashier, bought second-hand with some of the dollars with which he had returned from Paris four weeks earlier. After spending the day swimming and fishing from a friend's boat at Simonstown, he was driving back to his home in Paarl. He always liked to come home to Paarl after a contract, but inevitably it bored him quickly, just as it had when he left it ten years before.

As a boy he had been raised in the Paarl Valley and had spent his preschool years scampering through the thin and poor vineyards owned by people like his parents. He had learned to stalk birds and shoot in the valley with Pieter, his klonkie, the black playmate a white boy is allowed to play with until he grows too old and learns what skin color is all about.

Pieter, with his enormous brown eyes, tangled mass of black curls, and mahogany skin, was two years older than Janni and had been supposed to look after him. In fact they had been the same size, for Janni was physically precocious and had quickly taken the leadership of the pair. On summer days like this one, twenty years ago, the two barefoot boys used to take the bus along the coast to Cape Agulhas, where the Atlantic and the Indian oceans finally meet, and fish for yellowtail, galjoen, and red steenbras off the point.

After Paarl Boys' High, Janni had been a problem—too big, aggressive, restless, getting into fights with those big scything fists and ending up twice in front of the magistrates. He could have taken over his parents' farm and tended with his father the stubby little vines that produced such thin wine. The prospect appalled him—of becoming old and bent trying to make a living from the smallholding, with only four black boys working with him. At eighteen he volunteered for the army, did his basic training at Potchefstroom, and transferred to the paratroops at Bloemfontein. It was here he had found the thing he wanted to do most in life, here and in the counterinsurgency training in the harsh bushveld around Pietersburg. The army had agreed with him about his suitability, except on one point: his propensity for going to war while pointing in the wrong direction. In one fistfight too many, Corporal Dupree had beaten a sergeant senseless, and the commanding officer had busted him to private.

Bitter, he went AWOL, was taken in a bar in East London, battered two MPs before they held him down, and did six months in the stockade. On release he saw an advertisement in an evening newspaper, reported to a small office in Durban, and two days later was flown out of South Africa to Kamina base in Katanga. He had become a mercenary at twenty-two, and that was six years ago.

As he drove along the winding road through Franshoek toward the Paarl Valley, he wondered if there would be a letter from Shannon or one of the boys, with news of a contract. But when he got there, nothing was waiting at the post office. Clouds were blowing up from the sea, and there was a hint of thunder in the air.

It would rain that evening, a nice cooling shower, and he glanced up toward the Paarl Rock, the phenomenon that had given the valley and the town its name long ago when his ancestors first came into the valley. As a boy he had stared in wonderment at the rock, which was a dull gray when dry but after rain glistened like an enormous pearl in the moonlight. Then it became a great glistening, gleaming thing, dominating the tiny town beneath it. Although the town of his boyhood could never offer him the kind of life he wanted, it was still home; and when he saw the Paarl Rock glistening in the light, he always knew he was back home again. That evening he wished he were somewhere else, heading toward another war.

Tiny Marc Vlaminck leaned on the bar counter and downed another foaming schooner of Flemish ale. Outside the front wondows of the place his girlfriend managed, the streets of Ostend's red-light district were almost empty. A chill wind was blowing off the sea, and the summer tourists had not started to arrive yet. He was bored already.

For the first month since his return from the tropics, it had been good to be back, good to take hot baths again, to chat with his friends who had dropped in to see him. Even the local press had taken an interest, but he had told them to get lost. The last thing he needed was trouble from the authorities, and he knew they would leave him alone if he did or said nothing to embarrass them with the African embassies in Brussels.

But after weeks the inactivity had palled. A few nights back it had been enlivened when he thumped a seaman who had tried to fondle Anna's bottom, an area he regarded as entirely his own preserve. The memory started a thought running through his mind. He could hear a low thump-thump from upstairs, where Anna was doing the housework in the small flat that they shared above the bar. He heaved himself off his barstool, drained the tankard, and called, "If anyone comes in, serve 'em yourself."

Then he lumbered up the back stairs. As he did so, the door opened and a telegram came in.

It was a clear spring evening with just a touch of chill in the air, and the water of the Old Port of Marseilles was like glass. Across its center, a few months ago a mirror for the surrounding bars and cafés, a single homecoming trawler cut a swathe of ripples that wandered across the harbor and died chuckling under the hulls of the fishing boats already moored. The cars were locked solid along the Canebière, smells of cooking fish emanated from a thousand windows, the old men sipped their anisette, and the heroin-sellers scuttled through the alleys on their lucrative missions. It was an ordinary evening.

In the multinational, multilingual caldron of seething humanity that called itself Le Panier, where only a policeman is illegal, Jean-Baptiste Langarotti sat at a corner table in a small bar and sipped a long, cool Ricard.

He was not as bored as Janni Dupree or Marc Vlaminck. Years in prison had taught him the ability to keep himself interested in even the smallest things, and he could survive long periods of inactivity better than most.

Moreover, he had been able to get himself a job and earn a living, so that his savings were still intact. He saved steadily, the results of his economies mounting up in a bank in Switzerland that no one knew about. One day they would buy him the little bar in Calvi that he wanted.

A month earlier a good friend of his from the Algerian days had been picked up for a small matter of a suitcase containing twelve former French army Colt .45s and from Les Baumettes had sent Jean-Baptiste a message asking him to "mind" the girl on whose earnings the imprisoned friend normally lived. He knew he could trust the Corsican not to cheat him. She was a good girl, a broad-beamed hoyden called Marie-Claire, who went under the name of Lola and did her nightly stint in a bar in the Tubano district. She had taken quite a fancy to Langarotti, perhaps because of his size, and her only complaint was that he did not knock her about the way her boyfriend in prison had done. Being small was no hindrance to being a "minder," because the rest of the underworld, who might have made a claim for Lola, needed no education about Langarotti.

So Lola was happy to be the best-minded girl in town, and Jean-Baptiste was content to while away the days until another contract to fight came up. He was in contact with a few people in the mercenary business but, being new to it, was relying more on Shannon to hear of something first. Shannon was more the sort clients would come to.

Shortly after returning to France, Langarotti had been contacted by Charles Roux in Paris, who had proposed that the Corsican sign on with him exclusively in exchange for first choice if and when a contract turned up. Roux had talked largely of the half-dozen projects he had brewing at the time, and the Corsican had remained noncommittal. Later he had checked up and found Roux was mostly talk, for he had set up no projects of his own since his return from Bukavu in the autumn of '67 with a hole through his arm.

With a sigh Langarotti glanced at his watch, finished his drink, and rose to go. It was time to fetch Lola from their apartment and escort her to the bar for work, and then drop in at the all-night post office to see if there was a telegram from Shannon offering a prospect of a new war.

In Munich it was even colder than in Marc Vlaminck's Ostend, and Kurt Semmler, his blood thinned by years in the Far East, Algeria, and Africa, shivered in his knee-length black leather coat as he headed toward the all-night post office. He made a regular check-call at the counter every morning and evening, and each time hoped for some letter or telegram bearing news or an invitation to meet someone for an interview for possible selection for a mercenary assignment.

The period since his return from Africa had been one of idleness and boredom. Like most army veterans, he disliked civilian life, wore the clothes badly, despised the politics, and longed again for some form of routine combined with action. The return to his birth city had not been encouraging. Everywhere he saw long-haired youths, sloppy and ill-disciplined, waving their banners and screaming their slogans. There seemed to be none of the sense of purpose, of commitment to the ideal of the greatness of the Fatherland and its leader, that had so completely absorbed his own childhood and youth, nor the sense of order that characterized army life.

Even the smuggling life in the Mediterranean, although it had been free and easy, at least could offer the sense of activity, the scent of danger, the feeling of a mission planned, executed, and accomplished. Easing a fast launch in toward the Italian coast with two tons of American cigarettes on board, he had at least been able to imagine himself back on the Mekong, going into action with the Legion against the Xoa Binh river priates.

Munich offered him nothing. He had drunk too much, smoked too much, whored a bit, and become thoroughly disgruntled.

At the post office there was nothing for him that evening.

At midnight Marc Vlaminck phoned in from Ostend. The Belgian telegram delivery service is excellent and delivers until ten at night. Shannon told Vlaminck simply to meet him in front of Brussels National Airport the following morning with a car, and gave him his flight number.

Belgium has, from the point of view of those wishing to operate a discreet but legal bank account, many advantages that outweigh those offered by the much better-publicized Swiss banking system. Not nearly as rich or powerful as Germany, not neutral like Switzerland, Belgium nevertheless offers the facility of permitting unlimited quantities of money to pass in and out without government control or interference. The banks are also just as discreet as those of Switzerland, which is why they and the banks of Luxembourg and Lichtenstein have been steadily increasing their volume of business at the expense of the Swiss.

It was to the Kredietbank in Brugge, seventy minutes' driving time from the Brussels airport, that Shannon had himself driven by Marc Vlaminck the following morning. The big Belgian was evidently full of curiosity, but he kept it to himself. When they were on the road to Brugge, Shannon mentioned briefly that he had been given a contract and there was room for four helpers. Was Vlaminck interested?

Tiny Marc indicated that of course he was. Shannon told him he could not say what the operation was, other than that it was a job that had to be not merely fought but set up from scratch. He was prepared to offer normal rates of $1250 a month, plus expenses, for the next three months, and the job, although not requiring absence from home until the third month, would require a few hours' risk in Europe. That, of course, was not strictly mercenary work, but it had to be done.

Marc grunted. "I'm not knocking off banks," he said. "Not for that kind of money."

"It's nothing like that. I need some guns taken on board a boat. We have to do it ourselves. After we sail, it's all set for Africa and a nice little firefight."

Marc grinned. "A long compaign, or a quick in-and-out job?"

"An attack," said Shannon. "Mind you, if it works there could be a long contract in the offing. Can't promise, but it looks like that. And a fat success bonus."

"Okay, I'm on," said Marc, and they drove into the main square at Brugge.

The Kredietbank head office is situated at number 25 in the Vlamingstraat, a narrow thoroughfare flanked by house after house in the distinctive style of eighteenth-century Flemish architecture, and all in a perfect state of preservation. Most of the ground floors have been converted into shops, but upward from the ground floors the façades resemble something from a painting by one of the old masters.

Inside the bank, Shannon introduced himself to the head of the foreign accounts' section, Mr. Goossens, and proved his identity as Keith Brown by tendering his passport. Within forty minutes he had opened a current account with a deposit of £100 sterling in cash, informed Mr. Goossens that a sum of £10,000 in the form of a transfer from Switzerland could be expected any day, and left instructions that of this sum £5000 was to be transferred at once to his account in London. He left several examples of his Keith Brown signature and agreed on a method of establishing his identity over the phone by reeling off the twelve numbers of his account in reverse order, followed by the previous day's date. On this basis oral instructions for transfers and withdrawals could be made without his coming to Brugge again. He signed an indemnity form protecting the bank from any risk in using this method of communication, and agreed to write his account number in red ink under his signature on any written instruction to the bank, again to prove authenticity.

By half past twelve he was finished and joined Vlaminck outside. They ate a lunch of solid food accompanied by the inevitable french-fried potatoes at the Café des Arts on the main square before the town hall, and then Vlaminck drove him back to Brussels airport. Before parting from the Fleming, Shannon gave him £50 in cash and told him to take the Ostend-Dover ferry the next day and be at the London flat at six in the evening. He had to wait an hour for his plane and was back in London by teatime.

Simon Endean had also had a busy day. He had caught the earliest flight of the day to Zurich and had landed at Kloten Airport by just after ten. Within an hour he was standing at the counter of the Handelsbank of Zurich's main office, at 58 Talstrasse, and opening a current account in his own name. He too left several specimen signatures and agreed with the bank official who interviewed him on a method signing all written communications to the bank simply by writing the account number at the bottom of the letter and under the day of the week on which the letter had been written. The day would be written in green ink, while the account number would invariably be in black. He deposited the £500 in cash that he had brought, and informed the bank the sum of £100,000 would be transferred into the account within the week. Last, he instructed the bank that as soon as the credit had been received they were to remit £10,000 to an account in Belgium which he would identify for them later by letter. He signed a long contract which exonerated the bank from anything and everything, including culpable negligence, and left him no protection whatever in law. Not that there was any point in contesting a Swiss bank before a Swiss court, as he well knew.

Taking a taxi from Talstrasse, he dropped a wax-sealed letter through the door of the Zwingli Bank and headed back to the airport.

The letter, which Dr. Martin Steinhofer had in his hand within thirty minutes, was from Sir James Manson. It was signed in the approved manner in which Manson signed all his correspondence with his Zurich bank. It requested Dr. Steinhofer to transfer £100,000 to the account of Mr. Simon Endean at the Handelsbank forthwith, and informed him that Sir James would be calling on him at his office the following day, Wednesday.

Endean was at London airport just before six.

Martin Thorpe was exhausted when he came into the office that Tuesday afternoon. He had spent the two days of the weekend and Monday going methodically through the 4500 cards in the Moodies index of companies quoted on the London Stock Exchange.

He had been concentrating on finding a suitable shell company and had sought out the small companies, preferably founded many years ago, largely run-down and with few assets, companies which over the past three years had traded at a loss, or broken even, or made a profit below £10,000. He also wanted a company with a market capitalization of under £200,000.

He had come up with two dozen companies that fitted the bill, and these names he showed to Sir James Manson. He had listed them provisionally in order from 1 to 24 on the basis of their apparent suitability.

He still had more to do, and by midafternoon he was at Companies House, in City Road, E.C.2.

He sent up to the archivists the list of his first eight companies and paid his statutory fee for each name on the list, giving him, as it would any other member of the public, the right to examine the full company documents. As he waited for the eight bulky folders to come back to the reading room, he glanced through the latest Stock Exchange Official List and noted with satisfaction that none of the eight was quoted at over three shillings a share.

When the files arrived he started with the first on his list and began to pore over the records. He was looking for three things not given in the Moodies cards, which are simply synopses. He wanted to study the distribution of the ownership of the shares, to ensure that the company he sought was not controlled by the combined board of directors, and to be certain there had not been a recent build-up of share holdings by another person or associated group, which would have indicated that another City predator was looking for a meal.

By the time Companies House closed for the evening, he had been through seven of the eight files. He could cover the remaining seventeen the following day. But already he was intrigued by the third on his list and mildly excited. On paper it looked great, from his point of view—even too good, and that was the rub. It looked so good he was surprised no one had snapped it up ages ago. There had to be a flaw somewhere, but Martin Thorpe's ingenuity might even find a way of overcoming it. If there was such a way—it was perfect.

Simon Endean phoned Cat Shannon at the latter's flat at ten that evening. Shannon reported what he had done, and Endean gave a résumé of his own day. He told Shannon the necessary £100,000 should have been transferred to his new Swiss account before closing time that afternoon, and Shannon told Endean to have the first £10,000 sent to him under the name of Keith Brown at the Kredietbank in Brugge, Belgium.

Within a few minutes of hanging up, Endean had written his letter of instruction to the Handelsbank, stressing that the transferred sum should be sent at once but that under no condition was the name of the Swiss account-holder to become known to the Belgian bank. The account number alone should be quoted on the transfer, which should be by Telex. He mailed the letter express rate from the all-night post office in Trafalgar Square just before midnight.

At eleven-forty-five the phone rang again in Shannon's flat. It was Semmler on the line from Munich. Shannon told him he had work for all of them if they wanted it, but that he could not come to Munich. Semmler should take a single ticket by air to London the following day and be there by six. He gave his address and promised to repay the German his expenses in any case, and pay his fare back to Munich if he declined the job. Semmler agreed to come, and Shannon hung up.

The next on the line was Langarotti from Marseilles. He had checked his *poste restante* box and found Shannon's telegram waiting for him. He would be in London by six and would report to the flat.

Janni Dupree's call was late, coming through at half past midnight. He too agreed to pack his bags and fly the eight thousand miles to London, though he could not be there for a day and a half. He would be at Shannon's flat on Thursday evening instead.

With the last call taken, Shannon read *Small Arms of the World* for an hour and switched off the light. It was the end of Day One.

Sir James Manson, first class on the businessman's Trident III to Zurich, ate a hearty breakfast that Wednesday morning. Shortly before noon he was ushered respectfully into the paneled office of Dr. Martin Steinhofer.

The two men had known each other for ten years, and during this time the Zwingli Bank had several times carried out business on Manson's behalf in situations where he had needed a nominee to buy shares which, had it become known that the name of Manson was behind the purchase, would have trebled in value. Dr. Steinhofer valued his client and rose to shake hands and usher the English knight to a comfortable armchair.

The Swiss offered cigars, and coffee was brought, along with small glasses of Kirschwasser. Only when the male secretary had gone did Sir James broach his business.

"Over the forthcoming weeks I shall be seeking to acquire a controlling interest in a small British company, a public company. At the moment I cannot give the name of it, because a suitable vehicle for my particular operation has not yet come to light. I hope to know it fairly soon."

Dr. Steinhofer nodded silently and sipped his coffee.

"At the start it will be quite a small operation, involving relatively little money. Later, I have reason to believe news will hit the Stock Exchange that will have quite an interesting effect on the share value of that company," Sir James went on.

There was no need for him to explain to the Swiss banker the rules that apply in share dealings on the London Stock Exchange, for Steinhofer was as familiar with them as Manson, as he was also with the rules of all the main exchanges and markets throughout the world.

Under British company law, any person acquiring 10 per cent or more of the shares of a public quoted company must identify himself to the directors within fourteen days. The aim of the law is to permit the public to know who owns what, and how much, of any public company.

For this reason, a reputable London stockbrokerage house, buying on behalf of a client, will also abide by the law and inform the directors of their client's name, unless the purchase is less than 10 per cent of the company's stock, in which case the buyer may remain anonymous.

One way around this rule for a tycoon seeking to gain secret control of a company is to use nominee buyers. But again, a reputable firm on the Stock Exchange will soon spot whether the real buyer of a big block of shares is in fact one man operating through nominees, and will obey the law.

But a Swiss bank, not bound by the laws of Britain, abiding by its own laws of secrecy, simply refuses to answer questions about who stands behind the names it presents as its clients, nor will it reveal anything else, even if it privately suspects that the front men do not exist at all.

Both of the men in Dr. Steinhofer's office that morning were well aware of all the finer points involved.

"In order to make the necessary acquisition of shares," Sir James went on, "I have entered into association with six partners. They will purchase the shares on my behalf. They have all agreed they would wish to open small accounts with the Zwingli Bank and to ask you to be so kind as to make the purchases on their behalf."

Dr. Steinhofer put down his coffee cup and nodded. As a good Swiss, he agreed there was no point in breaking rules where they could be legally bent, with the obvious proviso that they were not Swiss rules, and he could also see the point in not wantonly sending the share price upward, even in a small operation. One started by saving pfennigs, and one became rich after a lifetime of application.

"That presents no problem," he said carefully. "These gentlemen will be coming here to open their accounts?"

Sir James exhaled a stream of aromatic smoke. "It may well be they will find themselves too busy to come personally. I have myself appointed my financial assistant to stand in for me—to save time and trouble, you understand. It may well be the other six partners will wish to avail themselves of the same procedure. You have no objection to that?"

"Of course not," murmured Dr. Steinhofer. "Your financial assistant is who, please?"

"Mr. Martin Thorpe." Sir James Manson drew a slim envelope from his pocket and handed it to the banker. "This is my power of attorney, duly notarized and witnessed, and signed by me. You have my signature for comparison, of course. In here you will find Mr. Thorpe's full name and the number of his passport, by which he will identify himself. He will be visiting Zurich in the next week or ten days to finalize arrangements. From then on he will act in all matters on my behalf, and his signature will be as good as mine. Is that acceptable?"

Dr. Steinhofer scanned the single sheet in the envelope and nodded. "Certainly, Sir James. I see no problems."

Manson rose and stubbed out his cigar. "Then I'll bid you good-by, Dr. Steinhofer, and leave further dealings in the hands of Mr. Thorpe, who of course will consult with me on all steps to be taken."

They shook hands, and Sir James Manson was ushered down to the street. As the solid oak door clicked quietly shut behind him, he pulled up his coat collar against the still chilly air of the north Swiss town, stepped into the waiting hired limousine, and gave instructions for the Baur au Lac for lunch. One ate well there, he reflected, but otherwise Zurich was a dreary place. It did not even have a good brothel.

Assistant Under Secretary Sergei Golon was not in a good humor that morning. The mail had brought a letter to his breakfast table to notify him that his son had failed the entrance examination for the Civil Service Academy, and there had been a general family quarrel. In consequence, his perennial problem of acid indigestion had elected to ensure him a day of unrelenting misery, and his secretary was out sick.

Beyond the windows of his small office in the West Africa section of the Foreign Ministry, the canyons of Moscow's windswept boulevards were still covered with snow slush, a grimy gray in the dim morning light, waiting tiredly for the thaw of spring.

"Neither one thing nor the other," the attendant had remarked as he had berthed his Moskvitch in the parking lot beneath the ministry building.

Golon had grunted agreement and taken the elevator to his eighth-floor office to begin the morning's work. Devoid of a secretary, he had taken the pile of files brought for his attention from various parts of the building and started to go through them, an antacid tablet revolving slowly in his mouth.

The third file had been marked for his attention by the office of the Under

Secretary, and the same clerkish hand had written on the cover sheet: "Assess and Instigate Necessary Action." Golon perused it gloomily. He noted that the file had been started on the basis of an interdepartmental memorandum from Foreign Intelligence, that his ministry had, on reflection, given Ambassador Dobrovolsky certain instructions, and that, according to the latest cable from Dobrovolsky, they had been carried out. The request had been granted, the Ambassador reported, and he urged prompt action.

Golon snorted. Passed over for an ambassadorship, he held firmly to the view that men in diplomatic posts abroad were far too prone to believe their own parishes were of consummate importance.

"As if we have nothing else to bother about," he grunted. Already his eye had caught the folder beneath the one he was reading. He knew it concerned the Republic of Guinea, where the constant stream of telegrams from the Soviet Ambassador reported the growth of Chinese influence in Conakry. Now that, he mused, was something of concern. Compared to this, he could not see the importance of whether there was, or was not, tin in commercial quantities in the hinterland of Zangaro. Besides, the Soviet Union had enough tin.

Nevertheless, action had been authorized from above, and, as a good civil servant, he took it. To a secretary borrowed from the typing pool, he dictated a letter to the director of the Sverdlovsk Institute of Mining, requiring him to select a small team of survey geologists and engineers to carry out an examination of a suspected tin deposit in West Africa, and to inform the Assistant Under Secretary in due course that the team and its equipment were ready to depart.

Privately he thought he would have to tackle the question of transportation to West Africa through the appropriate directorate, but pushed the thought to the back of his mind. The painful burning in his throat subsided, and he observed that the scribbling stenographer had rather pretty knees.

Cat Shannon had a quiet day. He rose late and went into the West End to his bank, where he withdrew most of the £1000 his account contained. He was confident the money would be replaced, and more, when the transfer came through from Belgium.

After lunch he rang his friend the writer, who seemed surprised to hear from him. "I thought you'd left town."

"Why should I?" asked Shannon.

"Well, little Julie has been looking for you. You must have made an impression. Carrie says she has not stopped talking. But she rang the Lowndes, and they said you had left, address unknown."

Shannon promised he'd call. He gave his own phone number, but not his address. With the small talk over, he requested the information he wanted.

"I suppose I could," said the friend dubiously. "But honestly, I ought to ring him first and see if it's okay."

"Well, do that," said Shannon. "Tell him it's me, that I need to see him and am prepared to go down there for a few hours with him. Tell him I wouldn't trouble him if it wasn't important, in my opinion."

The writer agreed to put through the call and ring him back with the telephone number and address of the man Shannon wished to talk to, if the man agreed to speak to Shannon.

In the afternoon Shannon wrote a letter to Mr. Goossens at the Krediet-bank to tell him that he would in the future give two or three business partners the Kredietbank as his mailing address and would keep in contact by phone with the bank to check whether any mail was waiting for collection. He would also be sending some letters to business associates via the Krediet-bank, in which case he would mail an envelope to Mr. Goossens from wherever he happened to be. He requested Mr. Goossens to take the en-velope which would be enclosed, addressed but not stamped, and forward it from Brugge to its destination. Last, he bade Mr. Goossens deduct all postal and bank charges from his account.

At five that afternoon Endean called him at the flat, and Shannon gave him a progress report, omitting to mention his contact with his writer friend, whom he had never mentioned to Endean. He told him, however, that he expected three of his four chosen associates to be in London for their separate briefings that evening, and the fourth to arrive on Thursday evening at the latest.

Martin Thorpe had his fifth tiring day, but at least his search was over. He had perused the documents of another seventeen companies in the City Road, and had drawn up a second short list, this time of five companies. At the top of the list was the company that had caught his eye the previous day. He finished his reading by midafternoon and, as Sir James Manson had not returned from Zurich, decided to take the rest of the day off. He could brief his chief in the morning and later begin his private inquiries into the set-up of his chosen company, a series of inquiries to determine why such a prize was still available. By the late afternoon he was back in Hampstead Garden Suburb, mowing the lawn.

TEN

The first of the mercenaries to arrive at London's Heathrow Airport was Kurt Semmler, on the Lufthansa flight from Munich. He tried to reach Shannon by phone soon after clearing customs, but there was no reply. He was early for his check-in call, so he decided to wait at the airport and took a seat by the restaurant window overlooking the apron of Number Two building. He chain-smoked nervously as he sat over coffee and watched the jets leaving for Europe.

Marc Vlaminck phoned to check in with Shannon just after five. The Cat glanced down the list of three hotels in the neighborhood of his apartment and read out the name of one. The Belgian took it down in his Victoria Station phone booth, letter by letter. A few minutes later he hailed a taxi outside the station and showed the paper to the driver.

Semmler was ten minutes after Vlaminck. He too received from Shannon the name of a hotel, wrote it down, and took a minicab from the front of the airport building.

Langarotti was the last, checking in just before six from the air terminal in

Cromwell Road. He too hired a taxi to take him to his hotel.

At seven Shannon rang them all, one after the other, and bade them assemble at his flat within thirty minutes.

When they greeted one another, it was the first indication any of them had had that the others had been invited. Their broad grins came partly from the pleasure of meeting friends, partly from the knowledge that Shannon's investment in bringing them all to London with a guarantee of a reimbursed air fare could only mean he had money. If they wondered who the patron might be, they knew better than to ask.

Their first impression was strengthened when Shannon told them that he had instructed Dupree to fly in from South Africa on the same terms. A £500 air ticket meant Shannon was not playing games. They settled down to listen.

"The job I've been given," he told them, "is a project that has to be organized from scratch. It has not been planned, and the only way to set it up is to do it ourselves. The object is to mount an attack, a short, sharp attack, commando-style, on a town on the coast of Africa. We have to shoot the shits out of one building, storm it, capture it, knock off everyone in it, and pull back out again."

The reaction was what he had confidently expected. The men exchanged glances of approval. Vlaminck gave a wide grin and scratched his chest; Semmler muttered, "*Klasse,*" and lit a fresh cigarette from the stub of the old one. Langarotti remained deadpan, his eyes on Shannon, the knife blade slipping smoothly across the black leather around his left fist.

Shannon spread a map out on the floor in the center of the circle, and the men eyed it keenly. It was a hand-drawn map depicting a section of seashore and a series of buildings on the landward side. It was not accurate, for it excluded the two curving spits of shingle that were the identifying marks of the harbor of Clarence, but it sufficed to indicate the kind of operation required.

The mercenary leader talked for twenty minutes, outlining the kind of attack he had already proposed to his patron as the only feasible way of taking the objective, and the three men concurred. None of them asked the name of the destination. They knew he would not tell them and that they did not need to know. It was not a question of lack of trust, simply of security. If a leak were sprung in the secret, they did not want to be among the possible suspects.

Shannon spoke in strongly accented French, which he had picked up in the Sixth Commando in the Congo. He knew Vlaminck had a reasonable grasp of English, as a barman in Ostend must have, and that Semmler commanded a vocabulary of about two hundred words. But Langarotti knew very little indeed, so French was the common language, except when Dupree was present, when everything had to be translated.

"So that's it," said Shannon as he finished. "The terms are that you all go on a salary of twelve hundred and fifty dollars a month from tomorrow morning, plus expenses for living and traveling while in Europe. The budget is ample for the job. Only two of the tasks that have to be done in the preparation stages are illegal, because I've planned to keep the maximum strictly legal. Of these tasks, one is a border crossing from Belgium to France, the other a problem of loading some cases onto a ship somewhere in southern Europe. We'll all be involved in both jobs.

"You get three months' guaranteed salary, plus five thousand dollars' bonus each for success. So what do you say?"

The three men looked at each other. Vlaminck nodded. "I'm on," he said. "Like I said yesterday, it looks good."

Langarotti stropped his knife. "Is it against French interests?" he asked. "I don't want to be an exile."

"You have my word it is not against the French in Africa."

"*D'accord,*" said the Corsican simply.

"Kurt?" asked Shannon.

"What about insurance?" asked the German. "It doesn't matter for me, I have no relatives, but what about Marc?"

The Belgian nodded. "Yes, I don't want to leave Anna with nothing," he said.

Mercenaries on contract are usually insured by the contractor for $20,000 dollars for loss of life and $6000 for loss of a major limb.

"You have to take out your own, but it can be as high as you want to go. If anything happens to anyone, the rest swear blind he was lost overboard at sea by accident. If anyone gets badly hurt and survives, we all swear the injury was caused by shifting machinery on board. You all take out insurance for a sea trip from Europe to South Africa as passengers on a small freighter. Okay?"

The three men nodded.

"I'm on," said Semmler.

They shook on it, and that was enough. Then Shannon went into the jobs he wanted each man to do.

"Kurt, you'll get your first salary check and one thousand dollars for expenses on Friday. I want you to go down to the Mediterranean and start looking for a boat. I need a small freighter with a clean record. Get that: it must be clean. Papers in order, ship for sale. One hundred to two hundred tons, coaster or converted trawler, possibly converted navy vessel if need be, but not looking like an MTB. I don't want speed, but reliability. The sort that can pick up a cargo in a Mediterranean port without exciting attention, even an arms cargo. Registered as a general freighter owned by a small company or its own skipper. Price not over twenty-five thousand pounds, including the cost of any work that needs doing on it. Absolute latest sailing date, fully fueled and supplied for a trip to Cape Town, not later than sixty days from now. Got it?"

Semmler nodded and began to think at once of his contacts in the shipping world.

"Jean-Baptiste, which city do you know best in the Mediterranean?"

"Marseilles," said Langarotti without hesitation.

"Okay. You get salary and five hundred pounds on Friday. Get to Marseilles, set up in a small hotel, and start looking. Find me three large inflatable semi-rigid craft of the same kind as Zodiac makes. The sort developed for water sports from the basic design of the Marine Commando assault craft. Buy them from separate suppliers, then book them into the bonded warehouse of a respectable shipping agent for export to Morocco. Purpose, water-skiing and sub-aqua diving at a holiday resort. Color, black. Also three powerful outboard engines, battery-started. The boats should take up to a ton of payload. The engines should move such a craft and that weight at not less than ten knots, with a big reserve. You'll need about sixty horsepower. Very important: make sure they are fitted with underwater exhausts for silent running. If they can't be had in that condition, get a mechanic to make you three exhaust-pipe extensions with the necessary outlet valves, to fit the engines. Store them at the same export agent's bonded warehouse, for the same purpose as the dinghies: water sports in Morocco. You won't have enough money in the five hundred. Open a bank account and send me the name and number, by mail, to this address. I'll send the money by credit transfer. Buy everything separately, and submit me the price lists by mail here. Okay?"

Langarotti nodded and resumed his knife-stropping.

"Marc. You remember you mentioned once that you knew a man in Belgium had knocked off a German store of a thousand brand-new Schmeisser submachine pistols in nineteen-forty-five and still had half of them in store? I want you to go back to Ostend on Friday with your salary and five hundred pounds and locate that man. See if he'll sell. I want a hundred, and in first-class working order. I'll pay a hundred dollars each, which is way over the rate. Write me by letter only, here at this flat, when you have found the man and can set up a meeting between him and me. Got it?"

By nine-thirty they were through, the instructions memorized, noted, and understood.

"Right. What about a spot of dinner?" Shannon asked his colleagues.

He took them around the corner to the Paprika for a meal. They still spoke in French, but no one else took much notice, except to glance over when a loud burst of laughter came from the group of four. Evidently they were excited at something, though none of the diners could have surmised that what elated the group in the corner was the prospect of going once again to war under the leadership of Cat Shannon.

Across the Channel another man was thinking hard about Carlo Alfred Thomas Shannon, and his thoughts were not charitable. He paced the living room of his apartment on one of the residential boulevards near the Place de la Bastille and considered the information he had been gathering for the previous week, and the snippet from Marseilles that had reached him several hours earlier.

If the writer who had originally recommended Charles Roux to Simon Endean as a second possible mercenary for Endean's project had known more about the Frenchman, his description would not have been so complimentary. But he knew only the basic facts of the man's background and little about his character. Nor did he know, and thus was unable to tell Endean, of the vitriolic hatred that Roux bore for the other man he had recommended, Cat Shannon.

After Endean had left Roux, the Frenchman had waited a full fortnight for a second contact to be made. When it never came, he was forced to the conclusion either that the project in the mind of the visitor who had called himself Walter Harris had been abandoned, or that someone else had got the job.

Pursuing the latter line of inquiry, he had looked for anyone among the other possible selections that the English businessman could have made. It was while he was making these inquiries, or having them made for him, that he had learned Cat Shannon had been in Paris, staying under his own name at a small hotel in Montmartre. This had shaken Roux, for he had lost trace of Shannon after their parting at Le Bourget Airport and had thought the man had left Paris.

At this point, more than a week earlier, he had briefed one of the men he knew to be loyal to him to make intensive inquiries about Shannon. The man was called Henri Alain and was a former mercenary.

Alain had reported back within twenty-four hours that Shannon had left his Montmartre hotel and not reappeared. He had also been able to tell Roux two other things: that Shannon's disappearance had taken place the morning after Roux had received the London businessman in his own apartment, and that Shannon had also received a visitor the same afternoon. The hotel clerk, with a little currency persuasion, had been able to describe Shannon's visitor, and privately Roux had no doubt the visitor in Montmartre had been the same man who came to him.

So Mr. Harris from London had seen two mercenaries in Paris, although he needed only one. As a result, Shannon had disappeared while he, Roux, had been left on the shelf. That it was Shannon of all people who seemed to have got the contract made his rage even worse, for there was no one the man in the flat in the 11th *arrondissement* hated more.

He had had Henri Alain stake out the hotel for four days, but Shannon had not come back. Then he tried another tack. He recalled that newspaper reports had linked Shannon with the Corsican Langarotti in the fighting in the last days of the enclave. Presumably if Shannon was back in circulation, so was Langarotti. So he had sent Henri Alain to Marseilles to find the Corsican and discover where Shannon might be. Alain had just arrived back, bearing the news that Langarotti had left Marseilles that same afternoon. Destination, London.

Roux turned to his informant. "*Bon,* Henri. That's all. I'll contact you when I need you. Meantime, the clerk in the Montmartre place will let you know if Shannon returns?"

"Sure," said Alain as he rose to go.

"Then ring me immediately if you hear."

When Alain had gone, Roux thought things over. For him the disappearance of Langarotti to London of all places meant the Corsican had gone to join Shannon there. That in turn meant Shannon was recruiting, and that could only mean he had got a contract. Roux had no doubt it was Walter Harris's contract, one he felt he personally should have had. It was an impertinence, compounded by the recruiting of a Frenchman, and on French territory, which Roux regarded as being his own exclusive preserve.

There was another reason why he wanted the Harris contract. He had not worked since the Bukavu affair, and his ability to keep his hold over the French mercenary community was likely to slip unless he could produce some form of work for it. If Shannon was unable to continue, if for instance he were to disappear permanently, Mr. Harris would presumably have to come back to Roux and engage him, as he should have done in the first place.

Without further delay he made a local Paris phone call.

Back in London, the dinner was nearing its end. The men had drunk a lot of carafe wine, for, like most mercenaries, they preferred it. Tiny Marc raised his glass and proposed the often-heard toast of the Congo.

Vive la mort, vive la guerre,
vive le sacré mercenaire.

Sitting back in his chair, clear-headed while the rest got drunk, Cat Shannon wondered idly how much havoc would be wreaked when he let slip this group of dogs on Kimba's palace. Silently he raised his own glass and drank to the dogs of war.

Charles Roux was forty-eight, and several parts mad, although the two facts were quite unconnected. He could never have been certified insane, but most psychiatrists would at least have held him to be mentally unstable. The basis for such a diagnosis would have been the presence of a fair degree of megalomania, but this is present in many people outside lunatic asylums and is usually more kindly interpreted, at least when present in the rich and famous, as merely exaggerated egocentricity.

The same psychiatrists would probably have detected a tinge of paranoia, and a severe examiner might have gone so far as to suggest there was a streak of the psychopath in the French mercenary. But as Roux had never been examined by a skilled psychiatrist, and as his instability was usually well camouflaged beneath an exterior of some intelligence and considerable cunning, these questions were never raised.

The only exterior clues to his make-up lay in his capacity to impute a status and importance to himself that was wholly illusory, a self-pity that insisted he had never once been at fault but that all others who disagreed with him were wholly in the wrong, and the capacity for vicious hatred toward those he felt had wronged him.

Often the victims of his hatred had done little 'or nothing beyond frustrating Roux, but in Shannon's case there were at least grounds for the dislike.

Roux had been a top sergeant in the French army until his late thirties, when he was dismissed after an affair involving certain missing funds. In 1961, at a loose end, he had paid his own fare to Katanga and proposed himself as a well-qualified adviser to the secessionist movement of the then Katangese leader, Moïse Tshombe. That year was the height of the struggle to tear the mineral-rich province of Katanga out of the union with the sprawling, anarchic, and newly independent Congo. Several of the men who later became mercenary chieftains began their freelance careers in the imbroglio in Katanga. Hoare, Denard, and Schramme were among them. Despite his claims to greater things, Roux was permitted only a small role in the Katangese events, and when the mighty United Nations finally managed to vanquish the small bands of freebooting pistoleros—which had to be done politically, since it could not be done militarily—Roux was among those who got out.

That was in 1962. Two years later, with the Congo falling like a set of skittles to the Communist-backed Simbas, Tshombe was recalled from exile to take over not Katanga but the whole Congo. He in turn sent for Hoare, and Roux was among those who flew back to enter service under Hoare. As a Frenchman, he naturally would have been in the French-speaking Sixth Commando, but as he had been in South Africa at the time, it was to the Fifth that he went. Here he was put in charge of a company, and one of his section commanders six months later was a young Anglo-Irishman called Shannon.

Roux's break with Hoare came three months later. Already becoming convinced of his own superiority as a military commander, Roux was entrusted with the job of knocking out a Simba roadblock. He devised his own plan of attack, and it was a total disaster. Four white mercenaries were killed and more than a score of his Katangese levies. Part of the reason was the plan of attack, part the fact that Roux had been blind drunk. Behind the drunkenness was the secret certainty that, for all his bombast, Roux did not like combat.

Colonel Hoare called for a report from Roux and got it. Parts of it did not tally with the known facts. Hoare sent for the only surviving section commander, Carlo Shannon, and questioned him closely. From what emerged, he sent for Roux and dismissed him on the spot.

Roux went north and joined the Sixth Commando under Denard at Paulis, explaining his defection from the Fifth as being due to dislike of a superb French commander by the inferior British, a reason Denard found little difficulty in believing. He posted Roux as second-in-command of a smaller commando, nominally dependent on the Sixth but in fact almost independent. This was the Fourteenth Commando at Watsa, ruled by Commandant Tavernier.

By 1966 Hoare had retired and gone home, and Tavernier had left. The Fourteenth was commanded by Commandant Wautier—like Tavernier, a Belgian. Roux was still second-in-command and hated Wautier. Not that the Belgian had done anything; the reason for the loathing was that Roux had expected the command after Tavernier's departure. He had not got it. So he hated Wautier.

The Fourteenth, heavily staffed by Katangese levies, was the spearpoint of the 1966 mutiny against the Congolese government. This had been planned, and well so, by Wautier, and would probably have succeeded. Black Jacques Schramme was holding his own predominantly Katangese Tenth Commando in check only to see how things went. Had Wautier led the revolt, it might well have succeeded; Black Jacques would probably have brought his Tenth into the affair, had it been successful, and the Congolese government might well have fallen. To launch the revolt, Wautier had brought his Fourteenth to Stanleyville, where on the left bank of the Congo River the vast arsenal stood, containing enough munitions to enable anyone holding it to rule the central and eastern Congo for years.

Two hours before the attack, Commandant Wautier was shot dead, and although it was never proved, it was Roux who murdered him with a shot in the back of the head. A wiser man might have called off the attack. Roux insisted on taking command, and the mutiny was a disaster. His forces never got across the river to the left bank, the Congolese army rallied on learning the armory was still in its hands, and Roux's unit was wiped out to the last man. Schramme thanked his stars he had kept his own men out of the fiasco. On the run and terrified, Roux sought refuse with John Peters, new commander of the English-speaking Fifth, which was also not involved. Peters smuggled the desperate Roux, swathed in bandages and masquerading as an Englishman, out of the country.

The only plane out was heading for South Africa, and that was where Roux went. Ten months later, he flew back into the Congo, this time accompanied by five South Africans. He had got wind of the coming July 1967 revolt and came to join Schramme at the headquarters of the Tenth Commando near Kindu. He was in Stanleyville again when mutiny broke out, this time with Schramme and Denard participating. Within hours Denard was out of action, hit in the head by a ricochet bullet loosed off in error by one of his own men. At a crucial point the leader of the joint forces of the Sixth and Tenth was out of the fight. Roux, claiming that as a Frenchman he should take precedence over the Belgian Schramme, maintaining he was the best commander present and the only one who could command the mercenaries, put himself forward for overall command.

The choice fell on Schramme, not because he was the best man to command the whites but because he was the only man who could command the Katangese, and without these levies the small band of Europeans would have been too badly outnumbered.

Roux's claim failed on two fronts. The Katangese loathed and distrusted him, remembering the unit of their own people he had led to annihilation the previous year. And at the mercenaries' council, held the night Denard was flown out on a stretcher to Rhodesia, one of those who spoke against Roux's nomination was one of Denard's company commanders, Shannon, who had left the Fifth eighteen months earlier and joined the Sixth rather than serve under Peters.

A second time the mercenaries failed to take the arsenal, and Schramme opted for the long march from Stanleyville to Bukavu, a resort town on Lake Bukavu, abutting the neighboring republic of Rwanda and offering some form of retreat if things went wrong.

By this time Roux was gunning for Shannon, and to keep them apart Schramme gave Shannon's company the hazardous job of point unit, breaking trail up front as the column of mercenaries, Katangese, and thousands of camp followers fought their way through the Congolese toward the lake. Roux was given a job at the rear of the convoy, so the two never met on the march.

They finally met in Bukavu town after the mercenaries had settled in and the Congolese had surrounded them on all sides except the lake behind the town. It was September 1967, and Roux was drunk. Over a game of cards he lost through lack of concentration, he accused Shannon of cheating. Shannon replied that Roux made as big a mess of his poker as he had of attacks on Simba roadblocks and for the same reason—he had no nerve. There was dead silence among the group around the table as the other mercenaries edged back toward the walls. But Roux backed down. Glaring at Shannon, he let the younger man get up and walk toward the door. Only when the Irishman had his back turned did Roux reach for the Colt .45 he, like all of them, carried, and take aim.

Shannon, listening, heard the scrape of a chair and reacted first. He turned, pulled his own automatic, and fired down the length of the hall. The slug was a lucky one for a shot from the hip on a half-turn. It took Roux high in the right arm, tore a hole through the biceps, and left his arm hanging limp from his side, the fingers dripping blood onto the useless Colt on the floor by his side.

"There's one other thing I remember," Shannon called down the room. "I remember what happened to Wautier."

Roux was finished after the shoot-out. He evacuated himself across the bridge into Rwanda, had himself driven to Kigali, the capital, and flew back to France. Thus he missed the fall of Bukavu when finally the ammunition ran out in November, and the five months in an internment camp in Kigali. He also missed a chance to settle scores with Shannon.

Being the first back into Paris from Bukavu, Roux had given several interviews in which he spoke glowingly of himself, his battle wound, and his desire to get back and lead his men. The fiasco at Dilolo, when a recuperated Denard tried a badly planned invasion of the Congo from Angola in the south as a diversion to take the strain off his men in Bukavu, and the virtual retirement of the former leader of the Sixth, gave Roux the impression he had every right to claim leadership over the French mercenaries. He had made quite a lot of money from looting in the Congo and had salted it away.

With the money, he was able to make a splash among the barflies and streetcorner bums who like to style themselves mercenaries, and from them he still retained a certain degree of loyalty, but of the bought kind.

Henri Alain was one such, and so was Roux's next visitor, who came in answer to his telephoned summons. He was another mercenary, but of a different type.

Raymond Thomard was a killer by instinct and profession. He too had been in the Congo once, when on the run from the police, and Roux had used him as a hatchet man. For a few small handouts and in the mistaken view that Roux was a big shot, Thomard was as loyal as a paid man can ever be.

"I've got a job for you," Roux told him. "A contract worth five thousand dollars. Are you interested?"

Thomard grinned. "Sure, *patron*. Who's the bugger you want knocked off?"

"Cat Shannon."

Thomard's face dropped.

Roux went on before he could reply. "I know he's good. But you're better. Besides, he knows nothing. You'll be given his address when he checks into Paris next time. You just have to wait till he leaves, then take him at your own convenience. Does he know you by sight?"

Thomard shook his head. "We never met," he said.

Roux clapped him on the back. "Then you've got nothing to worry about. Stay in touch. I'll let you know when and where you'll find him."

ELEVEN

Simon Endean's letter sent on Tuesday night arrived at ten on Thursday morning at the Handelsbank in Zurich. According to the instructions the bank Telexed £10,000 to the account of Mr. Keith Brown at the Kredietbank in Brugge.

By noon Mr. Goossens had seen the Telex and wired £5000 to Mr. Brown's account in the West End of London. Shortly before four that afternoon, Shannon made a check call to his bank and learned the credit was there waiting for him. He asked the manager personally to give him drawing facilities in cash up to £3500 the following morning. He was told it would be available for collection by eleven-thirty.

Shortly after nine the same morning Martin Thorpe presented himself in Sir James Manson's office with his findings. The two men went over the short list together, studying the pages of photostat documents acquired at Companies House on Tuesday and Wednesday. When they finished, Manson sat back in his chair and gazed at the ceiling.

"There's no doubt you are right about Bormac, Martin," he said, "but why the hell hasn't the major stockholder been bought out long ago?"

It was the question Martin Thorpe had been asking himself all the previous night and day.

The Bormac Trading Company Limited had been founded in 1904 to exploit the output of a series of vast rubber plantations that had been created during the last years of the previous century on the basis of slave labor by Chinese coolies.

The founder of the estates had been an enterprising and ruthless Scot by the name of Ian Macallister, later created Sir Ian Macallister in 1921, and the estates were situated in Borneo, hence the name of the company.

More of a builder than a businessman, Macallister had agreed in 1903 to enter into partnership with a group of London businessmen, and the following year Bormac was created and floated with an issue of half a million ordinary shares. Macallister, who had married a seventeen-year-old girl the previous year, received 150,000 shares, a place on the board, and managership during his lifetime of the rubber estates.

Ten years after the company's founding, the London businessmen had clinched a series of lucrative contracts with companies supplying the British war effort with rubber, and the share price had climbed from its issue price of four shillings to more than two pounds. The war profiteers' boom lasted until 1918. There was a slump for the company just after the First World War, until the motor-car craze of the 1920s boosted the need for rubber tires, and again shares rose. This time there was a one-for-one new issue, raising the total amount of the company's shares on the market to 1 million and Sir Ian's block to 300,000. There had been no more share issues after that.

The slump of the Depression sent prices and shares down again, and they were recovering by 1937. In that year one of the Chinese coolies finally ran amok and performed an unpleasantness on the sleeping Sir Ian with a heavy-bladed parang. The under manager took over but lacked the drive of his dead master, and production fell as prices rose. The Second World War could have been a boon to the company, but the Japanese invasion of Borneo in 1941 disrupted supplies.

The death knell of the company was finally sounded by the Indonesian nationalist movement, which wrested control of the Dutch East Indies and Borneo from Holland in 1948. When the border between Indonesian Borneo and British North Borneo was finally drawn, the estates were on the Indonesian side and were promptly nationalized without compensation.

For more than twenty years the company had staggered on, its assets unrecoverable, fruitless lawsuits with President Sukarno's regime eating away at the cash, prices falling. By the time Martin Thorpe went over the company's books, the shares stood at a shilling each, and their highest price over the previous year had been one shilling and threepence.

The board was composed of five directors, and the company rules stipulated that two of them made a quorum for the purposes of passing a resolution. The company office's address was given and turned out to be the premises of an old-established firm of City solicitors, one of whose partners acted as company secretary and was also on the board. The original offices had long since been given up because of rising costs. Board meetings were rare and usually consisted of the chairman, an elderly man living in Sussex, who was the younger brother of Sir Ian's former under manager, who had died in Japanese hands during the war. Sitting with the chairman were the company secretary, the City solicitor, and occasionally one of the other three, who all lived a long way from London. There was seldom any business to discuss, and the company income consisted mainly of the occasional belated compensation payments now being made by the Indonesian government under General Suharto.

The combined five directors controlled no more than 18 per cent of the million shares, and 52 per cent was distributed among 6500 shareholders scattered across the country. There seemed to be a fair proportion of married women and widows. No doubt portfolios of long-forgotten shares sat in deed boxes and banks and solicitors' offices up and down the land and had done so for years.

But these were not what interested Thorpe and Manson. If they tried to acquire a controlling interest by buying through the market, first it would take years, and second, it would become quickly plain to other City-watchers that someone was at work on Bormac. Their interest was held by the one single block of 300,000 shares held by the widowed Lady Macallister.

The puzzle was why someone had not long since bought the entire block from her and taken on the shell of the once-flourishing rubber company. In every other sense it was ideal for the purpose, for its memorandum was widely drawn, permitting the company to operate in any field of exploitation of any country's natural assets outside the United Kingdom.

"She must be eighty-five if she's a day," said Thorpe at last. "Lives in a vast, dreary old block of flats in Kensington, guarded by a long-serving lady companion, or whatever they are called."

"She must have been approached," said Sir James musingly, "so why does she cling to them?"

"Perhaps she just doesn't want to sell," said Thorpe, "or didn't like the people who came to ask her to let them buy. Old people can be funny."

It is not simply old people who are illogical about buying and selling stocks and shares. Most stockbrokers have long since had the experience of seeing a client refuse to do business when proposed a sensible and advantageous offer, solely and simply for the reason that he did not like the stockbroker.

Sir James Manson shot forward in his chair and planted his elbows on the desk. "Martin, find out about the old woman. Find out who she is, where she is, what she thinks, what she likes and hates, what are her tastes, and above all, find out where her weak spot is. She has to have one, some little thing that would be too big a temptation for her and for which she would sell her holding. It may not be money, probably isn't, for she's been offered money before now. But there has to be something. Find it."

Thorpe rose to go. Manson waved him back to his chair. From his desk drawer he drew six printed forms, all identical and all application forms for numbered accounts at the Zwingli Bank in Zurich.

He explained briefly and concisely what he wanted done, and Thorpe nodded.

"Book yourself on the morning flight, and you can be back tomorrow night," said Manson as his aide left.

Simon Endean rang Shannon at his flat just after two and was given an up-to-date report on the arrangements the mercenary was making. Manson's assistant was pleased by the precision of Shannon's reporting, and he noted the details on a scratch pad so that he could later make up his own report for Sir James.

When he had finished, Shannon put forward his next requirements. "I want five thousand pounds Telexed direct from your Swiss bank to my credit as Keith Brown at the head office of the Banque de Luxembourg by next Monday noon," he told Endean, "and another five thousand Telexed direct to my credit at the head office of the Landesbank in Hamburg by Wednesday morning."

He explained tersely how the bulk of the £5000 he had imported to London was already spoken for and the other £5000 was needed as a reserve in Brugge. The two identical sums required in Luxembourg and Hamburg were mainly so that he could show his contacts there a certified check to prove his credit before entering into purchasing negotiations. Later, most of the money would be remitted to Brugge and the balance fully accounted for.

"In any case, I can write you out a complete accounting of money spent to date or committed for spending," he told Endean, "but I have to have your mailing address."

Endean gave him the name of a professional accommodation address where he had opened a box that morning in the name of Walter Harris, and promised to get the instructions off to Zurich within the hour to have both sums of £5000 awaiting collection by Keith Brown in Luxembourg and Hamburg.

Big Janni Dupree checked in from London airport at five. His had been the longest journey; from Cape Town to Johannesburg the previous day, and then the long SAA flight, through Luanda in Portuguese Angola and the Isla do Sol stopover, which avoided overflying the territory of any black African country. Shannon ordered him to take a taxi straight to the flat.

At six there was a second reunion when the other three mercenaries all came around to greet the South African. When he heard Shannon's terms, Janni's face cracked into a grin.

"We going to go fighting again, Cat? Count me in."

"Good man. So here's what I want from you. Stay here in London, find yourself a small bed-sitting-room flat. I'll help you do that tomorrow. We'll go through the *Evening Standard* and get you fixed up by nightfall.

"I want you to buy all our clothing. We need fifty sets of T-shirts, fifty sets of underpants, fifty pair of light nylon socks. Then a spare set for each man, making a hundred. I'll give you the list later. After that, fifty sets of combat trousers, preferably in jungle camouflage and preferably matching the jackets. Next, fifty combat blouses, zip-fronted and in the same jungle camouflage.

"You can get all these quite openly at camping shops, sports shops, and army surplus stores. Even the hippies are beginning to wear combat jackets about town, and so do people who go shooting in the country.

"You can get all the T-shirts, socks, and underpants at the same stockist, but get the trousers and blouses at different ones. Then fifty green berets and fifty pairs of boots. Get the trousers in the large size, we can shorten them later; get the blouses half in large size, half in medium. Get the boots from a camping-equipment shop. I don't want heavy British army boots, I want the green canvas jackboots with front lacing and waterproofed.

"Now for the webbing. I need fifty webbing belts, ammo pouches, knapsacks, and campers' haversacks, the ones with the light tubular frame to support them. These will carry the bazooka rockets with a bit of reshaping. Lastly, fifty light nylon sleeping bags. Okay? I'll give you the full written list later."

Dupree nodded. "Okay. How much will that lot cost?"

"About a thousand pounds. This is how you buy it. Take the Yellow Pages telephone directory, and under Surplus Stores you'll find over a dozen shops and stockists. Get the jackets, blouses, belts, berets, webbing harnesses, knapsacks, haversacks, and boots at different shops, placing one order at each. Pay cash and take the purchase away with you. Don't give your real name—not that anyone should ask it—and don't leave a real address.

"When you have bought the stuff, store it in a normal storage warehouse, have it crated for export, and contact four separate freight agents accustomed to handling export shipments. Pay them to send it in four separate consignments in bond to a shipping freight agent in Marseilles for collection by Mr. Jean-Baptiste Langarotti."

"Which agent in Marseilles?" asked Dupree.

"We don't know yet," said Shannon. He turned to the Corsican. "Jean, when you have the name of the shipping agent you intend to use for the export of the boats and engines, send the full name and address by mail to London, one copy to me here at the flat, and a second copy to Jan Dupree, Poste Restante, Trafalgar Square Post Office, London. Got it?"

Langarotti noted the address while Shannon translated the instructions for Dupree.

"Janni, go down there in the next few days and get yourself *poste restante* facilities. Then check in every week or so until Jean's letter arrives. Then instruct the freight agents to send the crates to the Marseilles agent in a bonded shipment for export by sea from Marseilles onward, in the ownership of Langarotti. Now for the question of money. I just heard the credit came through from Brussels."

The three Europeans produced slips of paper from their pockets while Shannon took Dupree's airline ticket stub. From his desk Shannon took four letters, each of them from him to Mr. Goossens at the Kredietbank. Each letter was roughly the same. It required the Kredietbank to transmit a sum of money in United States dollars from Mr. Keith Brown's account to another account for the credit of Mr. X.

In the blanks Shannon filled in the sum equivalent to the roundtrip air fare to and from London, starting at Ostend, Marseilles, Munich, and Cape

Town. The letters also bade Mr. Goossens transmit $1250 to each of the named men in the named banks on the day of receipt of the letter, and again on May 5 and again on June 5. Each mercenary dictated to Shannon the name of his bank—most were in Switzerland—and Shannon typed it in.

When he had finished, each man read his own letter and Shannon signed them at his desk, sealed them in separate envelopes, and gave each man his own envelope for mailing.

Last, he gave each £50 in cash to cover the forty-eight-hour stay in London and told them to meet him outside the door of his London bank at eleven the following morning.

When they had gone, he sat down and wrote a long letter to a man in Africa. He rang the writer, who, having checked by phone that it was in order to do so, gave him the African's mailing address. That evening Shannon mailed his letter, express rate, and dined alone.

Martin Thorpe got his interview with Dr. Steinhofer at the Zwingli Bank just before lunch. Having been previously announced by Sir James Manson, Thorpe received the same red-carpet treatment.

He presented the banker with the six application forms for numbered accounts. Each had been filled out in the required manner and signed. Separate cards carried the required two specimen signatures of the men seeking to open the accounts. They were in the names of Messrs. Adams, Ball, Carter, Davies, Edwards, and Frost.

Attached to each form were two other letters. One was a signed power of attorney, in which Messrs. Adams, Ball, Carter, Davies, Edwards, and Frost separately gave power of attorney to Mr. Martin Thorpe to operate the accounts in their names. The other was a letter signed by Sir James Manson, requesting Dr. Steinhofer to transfer to the accounts of each of his associates the sum of £50,000 from Sir James's account.

Dr. Steinhofer was neither so gullible nor so new to the business of banking as not to suspect that the fact the names of the six "business associates" began with the first six letters of the alphabet was a remarkable coincidence. But he was quite able to believe that the possible nonexistence of the six nominees was not his business. If a wealthy British businessman chose to get around the tiresome rules of his own Companies Act, that was his own business. Besides, Dr. Steinhofer knew certain things about quite a number of City businessmen that would have created enough Department of Trade inquiries to keep that London ministry occupied for the rest of the century.

There was another good reason why he should stretch out his hand and take the application forms from Thorpe. If the shares of the company Sir James was going to try to buy secretly shot up from their present level to astronomic heights—and Dr. Steinhofer could see no other reason for the operation—there was nothing to prevent the Swiss banker from buying a few of those shares for himself.

"The company we have our eye on is called Bormac Trading Company," Thorpe told him quietly. He outlined the position of the company, and the fact that old Lady Macallister held 300,00 shares, or 30 per cent of the company.

"We have reason to believe attempts may already have been made to persuade this old lady to sell her holding," he went on. "They appear to have been unsuccessful. We are going to have another try. Even should we fail, we will still go ahead and choose another shell company."

Dr. Steinhofer listened quietly as he smoked his cigar.

"As you know, Dr. Steinhofer, it would not be possible for one purchaser to buy these shares without declaring his identity. Therefore the four buyers will be Mr. Adams, Mr. Ball, Mr. Carter, and Mr. Davies, who will each acquire seven and a half per cent of the company. We would wish you to act on behalf of all four of them."

Dr. Steinhofer nodded. It was standard practice. "Of course, Mr. Thorpe."

"I shall attempt to persuade the old lady to sign the share-transfer certificates with the name of the buyer left out. This is simply because some people in England, especially old ladies, find Swiss banks rather—how shall I say?—secretive organizations."

"I am sure you mean sinister," said Dr. Steinhofer smoothly. "I completely understand. Let us leave it like this, then. When you have had an interview with this lady, we will see how best it can be arranged. But tell Sir James to have no fear. The purchase will be by four separate buyers, and the rules of the Companies Act will not be affronted."

As Sir James Manson had predicted, Thorpe was back in London by nightfall to begin his weekend.

The four mercenaries were waiting on the pavement when Shannon came out of his bank just before twelve. He had in his hand four brown envelopes.,

"Marc, here's yours. There's five hundred pounds in it. Since you'll be living at home, your expenses will be the smallest. So within that five hundred you have to buy a truck and rent a lock-up garage. There are other items to be bought. You'll find the list inside the envelope. Trace the man who has the Schmeissers for sale and set up a meeting between me and him. I'll be in touch with you by phone at your bar in about ten days."

The giant Belgian nodded and hailed a taxi at the curb to take him to Victoria Station and the boat train back to the Ostend ferry.

"Kurt, this is your envelope. There's a thousand inside it, because you'll have to do much more traveling. Find that ship, and inside forty days. Keep in touch by phone and cable, but be very discreet and brief when using either. You can be frank in written letters to my flat. If my mail is on intercept we're finished anyway.

"Jean-Baptiste, here's five hundred for you. It has to keep you for forty days. Stay out of trouble and avoid your old haunts. Find the boats and engines and let me know by letter. Open a bank account and tell me where it is. When I approve the type and price of the stuff, I'll transmit you the money. And don't forget the shipping agent. Keep it nice and legal all down the line."

The Frenchman and the German took their money and instructions and looked for a second taxi to get them to London airport, Semmler bound for Naples and Langarotti for Marseilles.

Shannon took Dupree's arm, and they strolled down Piccadilly together. Shannon passed Dupree his envelope.

"I've put fifteen hundred in there for you, Janni. A thousand should cover all the purchases and the storage, crating, and shipping costs to Marseilles, with something to spare. The five hundred should keep you easily for the next month to six weeks. I want you to get straight into the buying first thing Monday morning. Make your list of shops and warehouses with the Yellow Pages and a map over the weekend. You have to finish the buying in thirty days, because I want the stuff in Marseilles in forty-five."

He stopped and bought the *Evening Standard*, opened it at the "Properties to Let" page, and showed Dupree the columns of advertisements for flats and flatlets for rent, furnished and unfurnished. There were, as usual, about 300 flats to rent, ranging from £6 a week to £200.

"Find yourself a small flat by tonight and let me know the address tomorrow."

They parted just short of Hyde Park Corner.

Shannon spent the evening writing out a complete statement of accounts for Endean. He pointed out that the total had eaten up the bulk of the £5000 transferred from Brugge and that he would leave the few hundreds left over from that sum in the London account as a reserve.

Last, he pointed out that he had not taken any part of his own £10,000 fee for the job and proposed either that Endean transfer it straight from Endean's Swiss account into Shannon's Swiss account, or remit the money to the Belgian bank for credit to Keith Brown.

He mailed his letter that Friday evening.

The weekend was free, so he called Julie Manson and suggested taking her out to dinner. She had been about to set off for a weekend at her parents' country house, but called and told them she was not coming. As it was late by the time she was ready, she came to collect Shannon, looking pert and spoiled at the wheel of her red MGB.

"Have you booked anywhere?" she asked.

"Yes. Why?"

"Let's go and eat at one of my places," she suggested. "Then I can introduce you to some of my friends."

Shannon shook his head. "Forget it," he said. "That's happened to me before. I am not spending the whole evening being stared at like a zoo animal and asked damnfool questions about killing people. It's sick."

She pouted. "Please, Cat darling."

"Nope."

"Look, I won't say what you are and what you do. I'll just keep it secret. Come on. No one will know you by your face."

Shannon weakened. "One condition," he said. "My name is Keith Brown. Got it? Keith Brown. That's all. Nothing else do you say about me or where I come from. Nor about what I do. Understood?"

She giggled. "Great," she said. "Great idea. Mystery Man himself. Come on, then, Mr. Keith Brown."

She took him to Tramps, where she was evidently well known. Johnny Gold rose from his doorside table as they entered and greeted her effusively with kisses on both cheeks. He shook hands with Shannon as she introduced him. "Nice to see you, Keith. Have a good time."

They dined at the long row of tables running parallel to the bar, and started by ordering the house lobster cocktail in a hollowed-out pineapple. Seated facing the room, Shannon glanced around at the diners; most, from their long hair and casual dress, could be placed in show business or on its fringes. Others were evidently young-generation businessmen trying to be trendy or make a model or an actress. Among the latter he spotted a face he knew across the room, with a group, out of Julie's vision.

After the lobster Shannon ordered "bangers and mash" and, excusing himself, got up. He strolled slowly out of the door and into the center lobby as if on his way to the men's room. Within seconds a hand fell on his shoulder, and he turned to face Simon Endean.

"Are you out of your mind?" grated the City hard boy.

Shannon looked at him in mock surprise, a wide-eyed innocent. "No. I don't think so. Why?" he asked.

Endean was about to tell him, but checked himself in time. His face was white with anger. He knew his boss well enough to know how Manson doted on his supposedly innocent little girl, and knew roughly what his reaction would be should he ever hear about Shannon taking her out, let alone climbing into bed with her.

But he was checkmated. he assumed Shannon was still unaware of his own real name, and certainly of Manson's existence. To bawl him out for dining with a girl called Julie Manson would blow both his own concern and Manson's name, together with both their roles as Shannon's employer. Nor could he tell Shannon to leave her alone, for fear Shannon would consult the girl and she would tell him who Endean was. He choked back his anger.

"What are you doing here?" he asked lamely.

"Having dinner," said Shannon, appearing puzzled. "Look, Harris, if I want to go out and have dinner, that's my affair. There's nothing to be done over the weekend. I have to wait till Monday to fly to Luxembourg."

Endean was even angrier. He could not explain that Shannon's slacking on the job was not what concerned him. "Who's the girl?" he asked.

Shannon shrugged. "Name's Julie. Met her in a café two days ago."

"Picked her up?" asked Endean in horror.

"Yes, you might say that. Why?"

"Oh, nothing. But be careful about girls, all girls. It would be better if you left them alone for a while, that's all."

"Harris, don't worry about my security. There won't be any indiscretions, in bed or out. Besides, I told her my name was Keith Brown; I'm on leave in London and I'm in the oil business."

For answer Endean spun round, snapped at Paolo to tell the group he was with that he had been called away, and headed for the stairs to the street before Julie Manson could recognize him.

Shannon watched him leave. "Up yours," he said quietly, "with Sir Bloody James Manson's biggest drill."

On the pavement outside, Endean swore quietly. Apart from that, he could only pray that Shannon had been telling the truth about the Keith Brown business and that Julie Manson would not tell her father about her new boyfriend.

Shannon and his girl danced until shortly before three and had their first quarrel on the way back to Shannon's flat. He had told her it would be better if she did not tell her father she was going out with a mercenary, or even mention his name. "From what you have already told me about him, he seems to dote on you. He'd probably send you away somewhere, or have you made a ward of court."

Her response had been to start teasing, keeping a straight face and saying she would be able to handle her father, as she always had, and in any case being made a ward of court would be fun and would get her name in all the papers. Besides, she argued, Shannon could always come and get her, fight his way out, and elope with her.

Shannon was not sure how serious she was and thought he might have gone too far in provoking Endean that evening, although he had not planned on meeting him, anyway. They were still arguing when they reached the living room of his flat.

"Anyway, I'm not being told what I'll do and what I won't do." said the girl as she dropped her coat over the armchair.

"You will be by me," growled Shannon. "You'll just keep damn silent about me when you're with your father. And that's flat."

For answer the girl stuck her tongue out at him. 'I'll do what I damn well like," she insisted and, to emphasize her words, stamped her foot. Shannon got angry. He picked her up, spun her around, marched her to the armchair, sat down, and pulled her over his knee. For five minutes there were two conflicting sounds in the sitting room, the girl's protesting squeals and the crack of Shannon's hand. When he let her up she scuttled into the bedroom, sobbing loudly, and slammed the door.

Shannon shrugged. The die was cast one way or the other, and there was nothing he could do about it. He went into the kitchen, made coffee, and drank it slowly by the window, looking out at the backs of the houses across the gardens, almost all dark as the respectable folk of St. John's Wood slept.

When he entered the bedroom it was in darkness. In the far corner of the double bed was a small hump, but no sound, as if she were holding her breath. Halfway across the floor his foot scuffed her fallen dress, and two paces farther he kicked one of her discarded shoes. He sat on the edge of the bed and as his eyes grew accustomed to the darkness he made out her face on the pillow, eyes watching him.

"You're rotten," she whispered.

He leaned forward and slipped a hand into the angle of her neck and jaw, stroking slowly and firmly.

"No one's ever hit me before."

"That's why you've turned out the way you have," he murmured.

"How is that?"

"A spoiled little girl."

"I'm not." There was a pause. "Yes, I am."

He continued caressing her.

"Cat."

"Yes."

"Did you really think Daddy might take me away from you if I told him?"

"Yes. I still do."

"And do you think I'd really tell him?"

"I thought you might."

"Is that why you got angry?"

"Yes."

"Then you only smacked me because you love me?"

"I suppose so."

She turned her head, and he felt her tongue busily licking the inside of his palm.

"Get into bed, Cat, darling. I'm so randy I can't wait any more."

He was only half out of his clothes when she threw the bedsheets back and knelt on the mattress, running her hands over his chest and muttering, "Hurry, hurry," between kisses.

"Your're a lying bastard, Shannon," he thought as he lay on his back, feeling this avid and infatuated young girl go to work on him.

There was a light gray glow in the east over Camden Town when they lay still two hours later. Julie was curled up in the crook of his arm, her varied appetites for the moment satisfied.

"Tell me something," she said.

"What?"

"Why do you live the way you do? Why be a mercenary and go around making wars on people?'

"I don't make wars. The world we live in makes wars, led and governed by men who pretend they are creatures of morality and integrity, whereas most of them are self-seeking bastards. They make the wars, for increased profits or increased power. I just fight the wars because it's the way I like to live."

"But why for money? Mercenaries fight for money, don't they?"

"Not only the money. The bums do, but when it comes to a crunch the bums who style themselves mercenaries usually don't fight. They run away. Most of the best ones fight for the same reason I do; they enjoy the life, the hard living, the combat."

"But why do there have to be wars? Why can't they all live in peace?"

He stirred and in the darkness scowled at the ceiling. "Because there are only two kinds of people in this world: the predators and the grazers. And the predators always get to the top, because they're prepared to fight to get there and consume people and things that get in their way. The others haven't the nerve, or the courage, or the hunger or the ruthlessness. So the world is governed by the predators, who become the potentates. And the potentates are never satisfied. They must go on and on seeking more of the currency they worship.

"In the Communist world—and don't ever kid yourself into thinking the Communist leaders are peace-loving—the currency is power. Power, power, and more power, no matter how many people have to die so they can get it. In the capitalist world the currency is money. More and more money. Oil, gold, stocks and shares, more and more, are the goals, even if they have to lie, steal, bribe, and cheat to get it. These make the money, and the money buys the power. So really it all comes back to the lust for power. If they think there's enough of it to be taken, and it needs a war to grab it, you get a war. The rest, the so-called idealism, is a load of cock."

"Some people fight for idealism. The Vietcong do. I've read it in the papers."

"Yeah, some people fight for idealism, and ninety-nine out of a hundred of them are being conned. So are the ones back home who cheer for war. We're always right, and they're always wrong. In Washington and Peking,

London and Moscow. And you know what? They're being conned. Those GIs in Vietnam, do you think they die for life, liberty, and the pursuit of happiness? They die for the Dow Jones Index in Wall Street, and always have. And the British soldiers who died in Kenya, Cyprus, Aden. You really think they rushed into battle shouting for God, king, and country? They were in those lands because their colonel ordered them there, and he was ordered by the War Office, and that was ordered by the Cabinet, to keep British control over the economies. So what? They went back to the people who owned them in the first place, and who cared about the bodies the British army left behind? It's a big con, Julie Manson, a big con. The difference with me is that no one tells me to go and fight, or where to fight, or which side to fight on. That's why the politicians, the Establishments, hate mercenaries. It's not that we are more lethal than they are; in fact we're a damn sight less so. It's because they can't control us; we don't take their orders. We don't shoot the ones they tell us to shoot, and we don't start when they say, 'Start,' or stop when they say, 'Stop.' That's why we're outlaws; we fight on contract and we pick our own contracts."

Julie sat up and ran her hands over the hard, scarred muscles of his chest and shoulders. She was a conventionally raised girl and, like so many of her generation, could not understand even a tiny fraction of the world she saw about her.

"What about the wars when people fight for what they know is right?" she asked. "I mean, what about fighting against Hitler? That was right, wasn't it?"

Shannon sighed and nodded. "Yes, that was right. He was a bastard all right. Except that they, the big shots in the Western world, sold him steel up to the outbreak of war and then made more fortunes making more steel to crush Hitler's steel. And the Communists were no better. Stalin signed a pact with him and waited for capitalism and Nazism to destroy each other so he could take over the rubble. Only when Hitler struck Russia did the world's so idealistic Communists decide Nazism was naughty. Besides, it cost thirty million lives to kill Hitler. A mercenary could have done it with one bullet costing less than a shilling."

"But we won, didn't we? It was the right thing to do, and we won."

"We won, my little darling, because the Russians, British, and Americans had more guns, tanks, planes, and ships than Adolf. That's why, and that's the only reason why. If he had had more, he'd have won, and you know what? History would have written that he was right and we were wrong. Victors are always right. There's a nice little adage I heard once: 'God is on the side of the big battalions.' It's the gospel of the rich and powerful, the cynical and the gullible. Politicians believe in it, the so-called quality newspapers preach it. The truth is, the Establishment is on the side of the big battalions, because it created and armed them in the first place. It never seems to occur to the millions of readers of that garbage that maybe God, if there is one, has something to do with truth, justice, and compassion rather than sheer brute force, and that truth and justice might possibly be on the side of the little platoons. Not that it matters. The big battalions always win, and the 'serious' press always approves, and the grazers always believe it."

"You're a rebel, Cat," she murmured.

"Sure. Always have been. No, not always. Since I buried six of my mates in

Cyprus. That was when I began to question the wisdom and integrity of all our leaders."

"But, apart from killing people, you could die yourself. You could get killed in one of these futile wars."

"Yes, and I could live on, like a battery hen, in one of these futile cities. Filling in futile forms, paying futile taxes to enable futile politicians and state managers to fritter it away on electorally useful white elephants. I could earn a futile salary in a futile office and commute futilely on a train, morning and evening, until a futile retirement. I prefer to do it my way, live my way and die my way."

"Do you ever think of death?" she asked him.

"Of course. Often. Don't you?"

"Yes. But I don't want to die. I don't want to die."

"Death's not so bad. You get used to the idea when it has come very close and passed by many times. Let me tell you something. The other day I was clearing out the drawers in this place. There was some newspaper, a year old, at the bottom of one. I saw a piece of news and began to read it. It dated from the winter before last. There was this old man, see? He lived alone in a basement. They found him dead one day, a week or so after he died. The coroner was told no one ever came to see him and he couldn't get out much. The pathologist said he had been undernourished for at least a year. You know what they found in his throat? Bits of cardboard. He had been nibbling bits of cardboard from a cereal package to try and get nourishment. Well, not me, baby. When I go, I'll go my way. I'd prefer to go with a bullet in my chest and blood in my mouth and a gun in my hand; with defiance in my heart and shouting, 'Sod the lot of you,' than to flicker out in a damp basement with a mouth full of cardboard.

"Now go to sleep, love, it's dawn already."

TWELVE

Shannon arrived in Luxembourg just after one on the following Monday and from the airport took a taxi to the Banque de Crédit. He identified himself as Keith Brown by using his passport and asked for the £5000 that should be waiting for collection by him.

After a delay while the Telex room was checked, the credit was discovered. It had just come through from Zurich. Instead of drawing the whole sum in cash, Shannon took the equivalent in Luxembourg francs of £1000 and signed a form making over the balance of £4000 to the bank. In exchange for this he was given a certified bank check for the equivalent of £4000.

He had time for a quick lunch before making his way to the Hougstraat, where he had an appointment with the firm of accountants Lang and Stein.

Luxembourg, like Belgium and Lichtenstein, maintains a system of offering to the investor a highly discreet and even secretive service in banking and the operation of companies, into whose affairs a foreign police force has the greatest difficulty in trying to pry. By and large, unless a company registered in Luxembourg can be shown to have broken the laws of the grand duchy or can be proved beyond doubt to have been involved in international illegal activities of a highly unpleasant nature, foreign police inquiries as to who owns or controls such a company will be met with a stoic refusal to cooperate. It was this kind of facility that Shannon sought.

His interview, arranged by phone three days earlier, was with Mr. Emil Stein, one of the partners in the highly respectable firm. For the occasion Shannon wore a newly acquired charcoal-gray suit, white shirt, and school tie. He carried a briefcase and the *Times* under one arm. For some reason, the carrying of this newspaper always seems to impress Europeans with the idea that the bearer is a respectable Englishman.

"Over the forthcoming few months," he told the gray-haired Luxembourger, "a group of British associates, of whom I am one, wish to engage in commercial activities in the Mediterranean area, possibly Spain, France, and Italy. For this purpose we would like to establish a holding company in Luxembourg. As you may imagine, being British citizens and residents and doing business in several European countries with differing financial laws could prove very complicated. From a tax standpoint alone, a holding company in Luxembourg seems to be advisable."

Mr. Stein nodded, for the request was no surprise. Many such holding companies were already registered in his tiny country, and his firm received such requests every day.

"That should present no problem, Mr. Brown," he told his visitor. "You are aware of course that all the procedures required by the Grand Duchy of Luxembourg must be complied with. Once that is done, the holding company may hold the majority of shares in an array of other companies registered elsewhere, and after that the company affairs remain entirely private from foreign tax investigations."

"That's very kind of you. Perhaps you would outline the essentials of starting such a company in Luxembourg," said Shannon.

The accountant could reel off the requisites in a few seconds. "Unlike the situation in Britain, all limited liability companies in Luxembourg must have a minimum of seven shareholders and a minimum of three directors. However, quite often the accountant asked to help in setting the company up takes the chairmanship of the directors, his junior partners are the other two, and his staff become shareholders, each with a purely nominal number of shares. In this manner the person wishing to establish the company is merely the seventh shareholder, although by virtue of his greater number of shares he controls the company.

"Shares will normally be registered, and the names of the shareholders also, but there is the provision for the issue of bearer shares, in which case no registration of the identity of the majority holder is necessary. The snag to that is that the bearer shares are exactly what they mean, and the bearer of the majority controls the company. Should one man lose them, or have them stolen, the new owner would automatically become the controller without needing a vestige of proof as to how he acquired them. Do you follow me, Mr. Brown?"

Shannon nodded. This was the arrangement he hoped to establish, in order to have Semmler buy the boat behind the cover of an uncheckable company.

"A holding company," said Mr. Stein, "as its name implies, may not trade in any form. It may only hold stock in other companies. Does your group of associates hold shares in other companies which it would like to have taken over and held in Luxembourg?"

"No, not yet," said Shannon. "We hope to acquire existing companies in the area of chosen operations, or found other limited-liability companies and transfer the majority shareholdings to Luxembourg for safekeeping."

By the end of an hour the agreement had been reached. Shannon had shown Mr. Stein his £4000 banker's check to prove his solvency, and had paid a deposit of £500 in cash.

Mr. Stein had agreed to proceed at once with the foundation and registration of a holding company to be called Tyrone Holdings SA, after searching through the bulky lists of already registered companies to ensure that no such name existed on the register. The total share capital would be £40,000 of which only £1000 would be issued immediately, and this would be issued in 1000 bearer shares of £1 each. Mr. Stein would accept one share and the chairmanship of the board. One share each would go to his partner, Mr. Lang, and a junior partner in the firm. These three men would form the board. Three other staff members of the firm—they turned out later to be secretaries—would be issued with one bearer share each, and the remaining 994 shares would be held by Mr. Brown, who would thus control the company and whose wishes the board would have to implement.

A general meeting to float the company was fixed for twelve days thence, or any time after that, if Mr. Brown would let them know in writing when he could be in Luxembourg to attend it. On that note Shannon left.

Before closing time he was back at the bank, returned the check, and had the £4000 transferred to the account at Brugge. He checked into the Exelsior and spent the night in Luxembourg. He already had his reservation for Hamburg the next morning, and he had the hotel call to confirm it. It was to Hamburg that he flew the following morning. This time, he was looking for arms.

The trade in lethal weapons is the world's most lucrative, after narcotics, and, not surprisingly, the governments of the world are deeply involved in it. Since 1945 it has become almost a point of national prestige to have one's own native arms industry, and these industries have flourished and multiplied to the point where by the early 1970s it was estimated there existed one military firearm for every man, woman, and child on the face of the planet. Arms manufacture simply cannot be kept down to arms consumption except in case of war, and the logical response has to be either to export the surplus or encourage war, or both. As few governments want to be involved in a war themselves but also do not wish to run down their arms industries just in case, the accent has for years been on the exporting of arms. To this end, all the major powers operate highly paid teams of salesmen to trot the globe persuading any potentate with whom they can secure an interview that he does not have enough weapons, or that what he does possess are not modern enough and should be replaced.

It is of no concern to the sellers that 95 per cent of all the hardware on the face of, for example, Africa is used not to protect the owner-country from external aggression but to keep the populace in subjection to the dictator. Arms sales having logically started as a product of the profits rivalry between competing Western nations, the entry of Russia and China into the arms-manufacturing and -exporting business has logically transferred the sales-manship into an extension of the power rivalry.

The interaction of profit desirability and political desirability has produced a tangled web of calculations that continue daily in the capitals of the major world powers. One power will sell arms to republic A, but not to B. At which a rival power will rush to sell weapons to B but not to A. This is called establishing a power balance and therefore keeping the peace. The profit desirability of selling arms is permanent; it is always profitable. The only constraints are imposed by the political desirability of this or that country having certain arms in its possession at all, and from this shifting quicksand of expediency versus profit has evolved the intimate link between Foreign Affairs Departments and Defense Departments all over the world.

To establish an indigenous arms industry is not difficult, providing it is kept basic. It is relatively simple to manufacture rifles and submachine guns and ammunition for both, along with hand grenades and hand guns. The required level of technology is not high industrial development, and the variety of needed raw materials is not large. But the smaller countries usually buy their weaponry ready-made from the larger ones, because their internal requirements are too small to justify the necessary industrialization, and they know their technical level would not put them into the export market with a chance.

Nevertheless, a very large and growing number of medium-sized countries have in the past two decades gone ahead and established their own native, if basic, arms factories. The difficulties increase, and therefore the number of participating nations decreases, with the complexity of the weapon to be made. It is easy to make small arms, harder to make artillery, armored cars and tanks, very difficult to create an entire shipbuilding industry to build modern warships, and hardest of all to turn out modern jet fighters and bombers. The level of development of a local arms industry can be judged by the point at which local weaponry reaches its technical limits, and imports have to be made for anything above those limits.

The main world arms-makers and -exporters are the United States, Canada, Britain, France, Italy, West Germany (with certain banned manufactures under the 1954 Paris treaty), Sweden, Switzerland, Spain, Belgium, Israel, and South Africa in the Western world. Sweden and Switzerland are neutral but still make and export very fine weaponry, while Israel and South Africa built up their arms industries in light of their peculiar situations, because they did not wish to be dependent on anyone in the event of a crisis, and both export very little indeed. The others are all NATO countries and linked by a common defense policy. They also share an ill-defined degree of cooperation on foreign policy as it relates to arms sales, and an application for an arms purchase made to any of them habitually undergoes a close scrutiny before it is granted and the arms are sold. In the same vein, the small buyer country always has to sign a written undertaking not to pass weaponry sold to itself to another party without express written permission from the supplier. In other words, a lot of questions are asked, before a sale is agreed to, by the Foreign Affairs Office rather than the Weapons Sales Office, and sales are almost inevitably deals made government-to-government.

Communist arms are largely standardized and come mainly from Russia and Czechoslovakia. The newcomer, China, now also produces weaponry up to a sufficiently high level of sophistication for Mao's guerrilla-war theory's requirements. For Communists the sales policy is different. Political influence, not money, is the overriding factor, and many Soviet arms shipments are made as gifts to curry favor, not as commercial deals. Being committed to the adage that power grows out of the barrel of a gun, and obsessed with power, the Communist nations will not merely sell weapons to other sovereign governments, but also to "liberation" organizations that they politically favor. In most cases these are not sales, but gifts. Thus a Communist, Marxist, extreme Left-wing, or revolutionary movement almost anywhere in the world can be reasonably assured of not running short of the necessary hardware for guerrilla war.

In the middle, the neutral Swiss and Swedes have their own self-imposed inhibitions on whom they will sell to and thus curtail their arms export by their own volition on moral grounds. No one else does.

With the Russians selling or giving their hardware from governmental source to nongovernmental recipients, and the West being too shy to do so, the private arms dealer enters into the picture. The Russians have no private arms dealers, so this creature fills the gap for the West. He is a businessman who may be used as a source of weaponry by someone seeking to buy, but in order to stay in business he must liaise closely with the defense department of his own country, or the department will see that he goes out of business. It is in his interest to abide by his native country's wishes anyway; that country may be the source of his own purchases, which could be cut off if he causes displeasure, apart from his fear of being put out of business by other, less pleasant means.

Thus the licensed arms dealer, a national and resident usually of his native country, sells arms to buyers after consulting his own government to be sure that the sale is acceptable to them. Such dealers are usually large companies and hold stocks.

This is at the highest level of the private-enterprise arms business. Lower in the pond are more dubious fish. Next down the scale is the licensed dealer who does not hold a stock of weapons in a warehouse but is licensed to hold a franchise by one of the large, often government-owned or -controlled arms-manufacturing companies. He will negotiate a deal on behalf of a client and take his cut. His license depends on his toeing the line with the government whose franchise to operate he holds. This does not prevent some licensed arms dealers from occasionally pulling a fast one, though two well-established arms dealers have been put out of business by their governments when discovered doing it.

Down in the mud at the bottom sit the black-market arms dealers. These are self-styled, since they hold no license. They may not therefore legally hold any stocks of weapons at all. They remain in business by being of value to the secret buyer, a man or organization who, not being a government or representing one, cannot clinch an intergovernmental deal; who would not be tacitly approved of by a Western government as desirable to receive arms; who cannot persuade a Communist government to support his cause on the grounds of political ideology; but who needs arms.

The vital document in an arms deal is called the End User Certificate. This certifies that the weapons purchase is being made by, or on behalf of, the

End User, who almost without exception in the Western world has to be a sovereign government. Only in the case of a flat gift by a secret-service organization to an irregular army, or of a pure black-market deal, does the question of an End User Certificate not apply. Examples of the former were the arming, without payment, by the CIA of the anti-Castro forces of the Bay of Pigs, and the arming of the Congo mercenaries, also by the CIA. An example of the latter is the shipment to Ireland from various European and United States private sources of arms for the Provisional IRA.

The End User Certificate, being an international document, has no specific form, shape, or size, or specific wording. It is a written affirmation from a certified representative of a national government that either he, the bearer, or Mr. X, the dealer, is authorized to apply to the supplier government for permission to purchase *and export* a quantity of arms.

The vital point about the End User Certificate is that some countries carry out the most rigorous checks to ensure the authenticity of this document, while others come under the heading of "no questions asked" suppliers. Needless to say, End User Certificates, like anything else, can be forged. It was into this world that Shannon carefully entered when he flew to Hamburg.

He was aware that he could certainly not make a direct application for permission to buy arms to any European government with a chance of success. Nor would any Communist government be kind enough to donate the weapons; indeed, it would be totally opposed to the toppling of Kimba. By the same token, any direct application would surely blow the entire operation.

He was also not in a position, for the same reason, to approach one of the leading government-owned arms-makers, such as Fabrique Nationale of Belgium, for any request put to a government-owned combine in the arms-making and -selling business would be passed on to the government; similarly, he could not approach a large private arms dealer, such as Cogswell and Harrison of London or Parker Hale of Birmingham. In the same category, Bofors of Sweden, Oerlikon of Switzerland, CETME of Spain, Werner and others in Germany, Omnipol of Czechoslovakia, and Fiat of Italy were ruled out.

He also had his own peculiar buying circumstances to consider. The amount he had to spend was too small to interest the big legitimate licensed dealers who habitually dealt in millions. He could not have interested the erstwhile king of the private arms dealers, Sam Cummings of Interarmco, who for two decades after the war ran a private arms empire from his penthouse suite in Monaco and had retired to enjoy his wealth; nor Dr. Strakaty of Vienna, the licensee franchise holder for Omnipol across the border at Washington Street 11, Prague; nor Dr. Langenstein in Munich; nor Dr. Peretti in Rome; nor M. Cammermundt in Brussels; nor Herr Otto Schlueter in Hamburg.

He had to go farther down the scale, to the men who dealt in smaller sums and quantities. He knew the names of Günther Leinhauser, the German, former associate of Cummings; in Paris, of Pierre Lorez, Maurice Herscu, and Paul Favier. But on consideration he had decided to go and see two men in Hamburg.

The trouble with the packet of arms he sought was that it looked like what it was: a single packet of arms for a single job, and it would not need a keen military mind to realize that job had to be the taking of one building within a short period. There was not enough leeway in the quantities to kid any professional soldier that a Defense Ministry, even a small one, was behind the order.

Shannon had therefore decided to split the packet even smaller, so that at least the items sought from each dealer were consistent. A mixed package would be a giveaway.

From one of the men he was going to see he wanted 400,000 rounds of standard 9mm. ammunition, the kind that fits into automatic pistols and also submachine carbines. Such a consignment was too large and too heavy to be bought on the black market and shipped without a large amount of complicated smuggling to get it on board. But it could well be the kind of consignment needed by the police force of any small country, and was not suspicious in that there were no matching guns in the same packet and it could therefore pass under scrutiny as an order designed simply to replenish stock.

To get it, he needed a licensed arms dealer who could slip such a small order through the procedures among a batch of bigger orders. Although licensed to trade in arms, the dealer must nevertheless be prepared to do a bent deal with a forged End User Certificate. This was where an intimate knowledge of the no-questions-asked countries came in useful.

Ten years earlier there had been vast quantities of superfluous weaponry lying about Europe in private hands, "black," i.e. illegally held, arms, leftovers from colonial wars such as those of the French in Algeria and the Belgians in the Congo.

But a series of small irregular operations and wars throughout the 1960s, notably Yemen and Nigeria, had used them up. So he would have to find a man who would use a bent End User Certificate and present it to a supplier government that asked no or few questions. Only four years earlier the most noted of these was the Czech government, which, although Communist, had continued the old Czech tradition of selling arms to all comers. Four years earlier one could have walked into Prague with a suitcase full of dollars, gone to the Omnipol headquarters, selected one's hardware, and a few hours later have taken off from the airport in one's chartered plane with the stuff on board. It was that simple. But since the Soviet takeover in 1968 the KGB had taken to vetting all such applications, and far too many questions were being asked.

Two other countries had earned a reputation of asking few questions about where the presented End User Certificate really came from. One was Spain, traditionally interested in earning foreign currency, and whose CETME factories produced a wide range of weapons, which were then sold by the Spanish Army Ministry to almost all comers. The other, a newcomer, was Yugoslavia.

Yugoslavia had begun manufacturing her own arms only a few years earlier and inevitably had reached a point where her own armed forces were equipped with domestic arms. The next step was overproduction (because factories cannot be abandoned a few years after they have been most expensively started), and hence the desire to export. Being a newcomer to the arms market, with weapons of unknown quality, and eager for foreign currency,

Yugoslavia had adopted the "ask me no questions and I'll tell you no lies" attitude to applicants for weaponry. She produced a good light company mortar and a useful bazooka, the latter based heavily on the Czech RPG-7.

Because the goods were new, Shannon estimated a dealer could persuade Belgrade to sell a tiny quantity of these arms, consisting of two 60mm. mortar tubes and a hundred bombs, plus two bazooka tubes and forty rockets. The excuse could well be that the customer was a new one, wishing to make some tests with the new weaponry and then come back with a far larger order.

For the first of his orders (the 400,000 rounds of 9mm. ammunition), Shannon intended to go to a dealer licensed to trade with CETME in Madrid but known also not to be above putting through a phony End User Certificate. For the second, Shannon had heard the name of another man in Hamburg who had skillfully cultivated the baby Yugoslav arms-makers at an early stage and had established good relationships with them, although he was unlicensed.

Normally there is no point in going to an unlicensed dealer. Unless he can fulfill the order out of illegally held stocks of his own, which means no export license, his only use can be in securing a bent but plausible End User Certificate for those who cannot find their own, and then persuading a licensed dealer to accept this piece of paper. The licensed dealer can then fulfill it, with government approval, from his own legally held stocks and secure an export license—or put the phony certificate to a government, with his name and guarantee backing it up. But occasionally he has one other use which makes him employable: his intimate knowledge of the state of the market and where to go at any given moment with any given requirement to have the best chance of success. It was for this quality that Shannon was visiting the second man on his Hamburg list.

When he arrived in the Hansa city, Shannon stopped by the Landesbank to find his £5000 was there already. He took the whole sum in the form of a banker's check made out to himself and went on to the Atlantic Hotel, where his room was booked.

Johann Schlinker, whom Shannon confronted in his small and modest office that morning, was short, round, and jovial. His eyes sparkled with bonhomie and welcome, so much so that it took Shannon ten seconds to realize the man could be trusted as far as the door. The pair of them spoke in English but talked of dollars—the twin languages of the arms marketplace.

Shannon thanked the arms dealer for agreeing to see him and offered his passport in the name of Keith Brown as identification.

The German flicked through it and handed it back. "And what brings you here?" he asked.

"You were recommended to me, Herr Schlinker, as a businessman with a high reputation for reliability in the business of military and police hardware."

Schlinker smiled and nodded, but the flattery made no impression. "By whom, may I ask?"

Shannon mentioned the name of a man in Paris, closely associated with African affairs on behalf of a certain French governmental but clandestine service. The two had met during one of Shannon's previous African wars, and a month earlier Shannon had looked him up in Paris for old times' sake. A week ago Shannon had called the man again, and he had indeed recommended Schlinker to Shannon for the kind of merchandise he wanted. Shannon had told the man he would be using the name Brown.

Schlinker raised his eyebrows. "Would you excuse me a minute?" he asked and left the room. In an adjoining booth Shannon could hear the chatter of a Telex.

It was thirty minutes before Schlinker came back. He was smiling. "I had to call a friend of mine in Paris on a business matter," he said brightly. "Please go on."

Shannon knew perfectly well he had Telexed to another arms dealer in Paris, asking the man to contact the French agent and get a confirmation that Keith Brown was all right. Apparently the confirmation had just come back.

"I want to buy a quantity of nine-mm. ammunition," he said bluntly. "I know it is a small order, but I have been approached by a group of people in Africa who need this ammunition for their own affairs, and I believe if those affairs go well there would be further and much larger shipments in the future."

"How much would the order be?" asked the German.

"Four hundred thousand rounds."

Schlinker made a moue. "That is not very much," he said simply.

"Certainly. For the moment the budget is not large. One is hoping a small investment now might lead to greater things later on."

The German nodded. It had happened in the past. The first order is usually a small one. "Why did they come to you? You are not a dealer in arms or ammunition."

"They happened to have retained me as a technical adviser on military matters of all kinds. When the question of seeking a fresh supplier for their needs arose, they asked me to come to Europe for them," said Shannon.

"And you have no End User Certificate?" the German asked.

"No, I'm afraid not. I hoped that sort of thing could be arranged."

"Oh, yes, it can," said Schlinker. "No problem there. It takes longer and costs more. But it can be done. One could supply this order from stocks, but they are held in my Vienna office. That way there would be no requirement for an End User Certificate. Or one could obtain such a document and make the application normally through legal channels."

"I would prefer the latter," said Shannon. "The delivery has to be by ship, and to bring that sort of quantity through Austria and into Italy, then on board a ship, would be hazardous. It enters an area I am not familiar with. Moreover, interception could mean long terms in prison for those found in possession. Apart from that, the cargo might be identified as coming from your stocks."

Schlinker smiled. Privately he knew there would be no danger of that, but Shannon was right about the border controls. The newly emergent menace of the Black September terrorists had made Austria, Germany, and Italy highly nervous about strange cargoes passing through the borders.

Shannon, for his part, did not trust Schlinker not to sell them the ammunition one day and betray them the next. With a phony End User Certificate, the German would have to keep his side of the bargain; it would be he who presented the bent certificate to the authorities.

"I think you are perhaps right," Schlinker said at last. "Very well. I can offer you nine-mm. standard ball at sixty-five dollars per thousand. There would be a surcharge of ten per cent for the certificate, and another ten per cent free on board."

Shannon calculated hastily. Free on board meant a cargo complete with export license, cleared through customs and loaded onto the ship, with the ship itself clearing the harbor mouth. The price would be $26,000 for the ammunition, plus $5200 surcharge.

"How would payment be made?" he asked.

"I would need the fifty-two hundred dollars before starting work," said Schlinker. "That has to cover the certificate, which has to be paid for, plus all personal traveling and administrative costs. The full purchase price would have to be paid here in this office when I am able to show you the certificate, but before purchase. As a licensed dealer I would be buying on behalf of my client, the government named on the certificate. Once the stuff had been bought, the selling government would be extremely unlikely to take it back and repay the money. Therefore I would need total payment in advance. I would also need the name of the exporting vessel, to fill in the application for export permit. The vessel would have to be a scheduled liner or freighter, or a general frighter owned by a registered shipping company."

Shannon nodded. The terms were steep, but beggars cannot be choosers. If he had really represented a sovereign government, he would not be here in the first place.

"How long from the time I give you the money until shipment?" he asked.

"Madrid is quite slow in these matters. About forty days at the outside," said the German.

Shannon rose. He showed Schlinker the banker's check to prove his solvency, and promised to be back in an hour with 5200 United States dollars in cash, or the equivalent in German marks. Schlinker opted for German marks, and when Shannon returned, he gave him a standard receipt for the money.

While Schlinker was writing out the receipt, Shannon glanced through a series of brochures on the coffee table. They covered the items put on sale by another company, which evidently specialized in nonmilitary pyrotechnic goods of the kind that are not covered by the classification of "arms," and a wide variety of items used by security companies, including riot sticks, truncheons, walkie-talkies, riot-gas canisters and launchers, flares, rockets, and the like.

As Schlinker handed him his receipt, Shannon asked, "Are you associated with this company, Herr Schlinker?"

Schlinker smiled broadly. "I own it," he said. "It is what I am best known for to the general public."

And a damn good cover for holding a warehouse full of crates labeled "Danger of Explosion," thought Shannon. But he was interested. Quickly he wrote out a list of items and showed them to Schlinker. "Could you fulfill this order, for export, out of your stocks?" he asked.

Schlinker glanced at the list. It included two rocket-launching tubes of the type used by coast guards to send up distress flares, ten rockets containing magnesium flares of maximum intensity and duration attached to para-chutes, two penetrating foghorns powered by compressed-gas canisters, four sets of night binoculars, three fixed-crystal walkie-talkie sets with a range of not less than five miles, and five wrist compasses.

"Certainly," he said. "I stock all these things."

"I'd like to place an order for the list. As they are off the classification of arms, I assume there would be no problems with exporting them?"

"None at all. I can send them anywhere I want, particularly to a ship."

"Good," said Shannon. "How much would that lot cost, with freight in bond to an exporting agent in Marseilles?"

Schlinker went through his catalogue and priced the list, adding on 10 per cent for freight. "Four thousand, eight hundred dollars," he said.

"I'll be in touch with you in twelve days," said Shannon. "Please have the whole lot ready-crated for freighting. I will give you the name of the exporting agent in Marseilles, and mail you a banker's check in your favor for forty-eight hundred dollars. Within thirty days I expect to be able to give you the remaining twenty-six thousand dollars for the ammunition deal, and the name of the ship."

He met his second contact for dinner that night at the Atlantic. Alan Baker was an expatriate, a Canadian who had settled in Germany after the war and married a German girl. A former Royal Engineer during the war, he had got himself involved during the early postwar years in a series of border-crossing operations into and out of the Soviet Zone, running nylons, watches, and refugees. From there, he had drifted into arms-running to the scores of tiny nationalist or anti-Communist bands of *maquis* who, left over from the war, still ran their resistance movements in Central and Eastern Europe—with the sole difference that during the war they has been resisting the Germans, while after it they were resisting the Communists.

Most of them had been paid for by the Americans, but Baker was content to use his knowledge of German and commando tactics to slip quantities of arms to them and take a hefty salary check from the Americans for doing so. When these groups finally petered out, he found himself in Tangier in the early 1950s, using the smuggling talents he had learned in the war and after it to bring cargoes of perfume and cigarettes into Italy and Spain from the then international and free port on the north coast of Morocco. Finally put out of business by the bombing and sinking of his ship in a gangland feud, he had returned to Germany and gone into the business of wheeler-dealing in any commodity that had a buyer and a supplier. His most recent feat had been to negotiate a deal in Yugoslav arms on behalf of the Basques in northern Spain.

He and Shannon had met when Baker was running guns into Ethiopia and Shannon had been at a loose end after returning from Bukavu in April 1968. Baker knew Shannon under his real name.

The short, wiry man listened quietly while Shannon explained what he wanted, his eyes flickering from his food to the other mercenary.

"Yes, it can be done," he said when Shannon had finished. "The Yugoslavs would accept the idea that a new customer wanted a sample of two mortars and two bazookas for test purposes before placing a larger order if he was satisfied. It's plausible. There's no problem from my side in getting the stuff from them. My relations with the men in Belgrade are excellent. And they are quick. Just at the moment I have to admit I have one other problem, though."

"What's that?"

"End User Certificate," said Baker. "I used to have a man in Bonn, diplomat for a certain East African country, who would sign anything for a price and a few nice big German girls laid on at a party, the sort he liked. He was transferred back to his own country two weeks ago. I'm a bit stuck for a replacement at the moment."

"Are the Yugoslavs particular about End Users?"

Baker shook his head. "Nope. So long as the documentation is in order, they don't check further. But there has to be a certificate, and it must have the right governmental stamp on it. They can't afford to be too slack, after all."

Shannon thought for a moment. He knew of a man in Paris who had once boasted he had a contact in an embassy there who could make out End User Certificates.

"If I could get you one, a good one, from an African country? Would that work?" he asked.

Baker inhaled on his cigar. "No problem at all," he said. "As for the price, a sixty-mm. mortar tube would run you eleven hundred dollars each. Say, twenty-two hundred for the pair. The bombs are twenty-four dollars each. The only problem with your order is that the sums are really too small. Couldn't you up the number of mortar bombs from a hundred to three hundred? It would make things much easier. No one throws off just a hundred bombs, not even for test purposes."

"All right," said Shannon, "I'll take three hundred, but no more. Otherwise I'll go over budget, and that comes off my cut."

It did not come off his cut, for he had allowed a margin for overexpenditure, and his own salary was secure. But he knew Baker would accept the argument as final.

"Good," said Baker. "So that's seventy-two hundred dollars for the bombs. The bazookas cost a thousand dollars each, two thousand for the pair. The rockets are forty-two dollars and fifty cents each. The forty you want come out at . . . let's see . . . "

"Seventeen hundred dollars," said Shannon. "The whole packet comes out at thirteen thousand, one hundred dollars."

"Plus ten per cent for getting the stuff free on board your ship, Cat. Without the End User Certificate. If I could have got one for you, it would have been twenty per cent. Let's face it, it's a tiny order, but the traveling and out-of-pocket expenses for me are constants. I ought to charge you fifteen per cent for such a small order. So the total is fourteen thousand, four hundred dollars. Let's say fourteen and a half, eh?"

"We'll say fourteen four," said Shannon. "I'll get the certificate and mail it to you, along with a fifty-per-cent deposit. I'll pay another twenty-five per cent when I see the stuff in Yugoslavia crated and ready to go, and twenty-five per cent as the ship leaves the quay. Travelers' checks in dollars, okay?"

Baker would have liked it all in advance, but, not being a licensed dealer, he had no offices, warehouses, or business address as Schlinker had. He would act as broker, using another dealer he knew to make the actual purchase on his behalf. As a black-market man, he had to accept these terms, the lower cut, and less in advance.

One of the oldest tricks in the book is to promise to fulfill an arms order, show plenty of confidence, assure the customer of the broker's absolute integrity, take the maximum in advance, and disappear. Many a black and brown seeker after arms in Europe has had that trick played on him. Baker knew Shannon would never fall for it; besides, 50 per cent of $14,400 was too small a sum to disappear for.

"Okay. The moment I get your End User Certificate I'll get straight onto it."

They rose to leave.

"How long from the time you make your first approach until shipping date?" asked Shannon.

"About thirty to thirty-five days," said Baker. "By the way, have you got a ship?"

"Not yet. You'll need the name, I suppose. I'll let you have it with the certificate."

"If you haven't, I know a very good one for charter. Two thousand German marks a day and all found. Crew, food, the lot. Take you and the cargo anywhere, and discreet as you like."

Shannon thought it over. Twenty days in the Mediterranean, twenty days out to target, and twenty days back. A hundred and twenty thousand marks, or £15,000. Cheaper than buying one's own ship. Tempting. But he objected to the idea of one man outside the operation controlling part of the arms deal and the ship, and being aware of the target as well. It would involve making Baker, or the man he would have to go to for the charter, virtually a partner.

"Yes," he said cautiously. "What's she called?"

"The *San Andrea*," said Baker.

Shannon froze. He had heard Semmler mention that name. "Registered in Cyprus?" asked Shannon.

"That's right."

"Forget it," he said shortly.

As they left the dining room, Shannon caught a swift glimpse of Johann Schlinker dining in an alcove. For a moment he thought the German dealer might have followed him, but the man was dining with a second man, evidently a valued customer. Shannon averted his head and strode past.

On the doorstep of the hotel he shook hands with Baker. "You'll be hearing from me," he said. "And don't let me down."

"Don't worry, Cat. You can trust me," said Baker. He turned and hurried off down the street.

"In a pig's ear I can," muttered Shannon and went back into the hotel.

On the way up to his room the face of the man he had seen dining with the German arms merchant stayed in his memory. He had seen the face somewhere but could not place it. As he was falling asleep it came to him. The man was the chief of staff of Provisional IRA.

The next morning, Wednesday, he flew back to London. It was the start of Day Nine.

THIRTEEN

Martin Thorpe stepped into Sir James Manson's office about the time Cat Shannon was taking off from Hamburg.

"Lady Macallister," he said by way of introduction, and Sir James waved him to a seat.

"I've been into her with a fine-tooth comb," Thorpe went on. "As I suspected, she has twice been approached by people interested in buying her thirty-per-cent holding in Bormac Trading. It would seem each person used the wrong approach and got turned down. She's eighty-six, halfway senile, and very tetchy. At least, that's her reputation. She's also broad Scottish and has all her affairs handled by a solicitor up in Dundee. Here's my full report on her."

He handed Sir James a buff folder, and the head of Manson Consolidated read it within a few minutes. He grunted several times and muttered, "Bloody hell," once. When he had finished, he looked up. "I still want those three hundred thousand shares in Bormac," he said. "You say the others went about it the wrong way. Why?"

"She would appear to have one obsession in life, and it's not money. She's rich in her own right. When she married, she was the daughter of a Scottish laird with more land than ready cash. The marriage was no doubt arranged between the families. After her old man died she inherited the lot, mile after mile of desolate moorland. But over the past twenty years the fishing and hunting rights have brought in a small fortune from city-dwelling sportsmen, and parcels of land sold off for industry have made even more. It's been shrewdly invested by her broker, or whatever they call them up there. She has a nice income to live on. I suspect the other bidders offered a lot of money but nothing else. That would not interest her."

"Then what the hell would?" asked Sir James.

"Look at paragraph two on the second page, Sir James. See what I mean? The notices in *The Times* every anniversary, the attempt to have a statue erected, which was refused by the London County Council. The memorial she has put up in his home town. I think that's her obsession—the memory of the old slave-driver she married."

"Yes, yes, you may be right. So what do you propose?"

Thorpe outlined his idea, and Manson listened thoughtfully.

"It might work," he said eventually. "Stranger things have happened. The trouble is, if you try it and she still refuses, you can hardly go back again with another offer couched in a different vein. But then, I suppose a pure cash offer would in any case get the same reaction the previous two proposals met. All right, play it your way. Just get her to sell those shares."

With that, Thorpe was on his way.

Shannon was back in his London flat shortly after twelve. Lying on the mat was a cable from Langarotti in Marseilles. It was signed simply "Jean" and addressed to Keith Brown. Its message was an address, a hotel in a street a little way out of the center of the town, where the Corsican had checked in under the name of Lavallon. Shannon approved the precaution. Checking into a French hotel requires the filling out of a form which is later collected by the police. They might have wondered why their old friend Langarotti was staying so far out of town from his usual haunts.

Shannon spent ten minutes extracting the number of the hotel from Continental Directory Enquiries, and placed a call. When he asked the hotel for M. Lavallon, he was told the monsieur was out. He left a message asking M. Lavallon to call M. Brown in London on his return. He had already given each of the four his own telephone number and made them commit it to memory.

Still using the telephone, he sent a telegram to the *poste restante* address of Endean under the name of Walter Harris, advising the project manager that he was back in London and would like to discuss something. Another telegram went to Janni Dupree at his flat, instructing him to report to Shannon as soon as he received the telegram.

He rang his own Swiss bank and learned that of the salary for himself of £10,000, half that amount had been transferred to him, the credit having come from an unnamed account-holder at the Handelsbank. This he knew to be Endean. He shrugged. It was normal for half the salary only to be paid at this early date. He was confident, from the sheer size of ManCon and its evident eagerness to see Kimba fall from power, that the other £5000 would be his as the operation progressed.

Through the afternoon he typed out a full report of his Luxembourg and Hamburg trip, excluding the names of the firm of accountants in Luxembourg and the two arms dealers. To these sheets he attached a full statement of expenditure.

It was past four when he finished, and he had not eaten since the midmorning snack provided by Lufthansa on the flight from Hamburg. He found half a dozen eggs in the refrigerator, made a complete mess of an omelet, threw it away, and had a nap.

The arrival of Janni Dupree at the door just after six woke him, and five minutes later the phone rang. It was Endean, who had picked up the telegram in the post office.

Endean soon noticed that Shannon was not in a position to talk freely. "Is there someone with you?" he asked.

"Yes."

"Is it connected with business?"

"Yes."

"Do you want to meet?"

"I think we ought," said Shannon. "What about tomorrow morning?"

"Okay. About eleven suit you?"

"Sure," said Shannon.

"Your place?"

"Suits me fine."

"I'll be there at eleven," said Endean and hung up.

Shannon turned to the South African. "How are you getting on, Janni?" he asked.

Dupree had made a little progress in the three days he had been working. The hundred pairs of socks, T-shirts, and underpants were on order and would be ready for collection by Friday. He had found a supplier for the fifty combat tunics and had placed the order. The same firm could have provided trousers to match, but, according to his orders, Dupree was seeking another firm to supply the trousers, so that no one supplier would realize he was providing complete sets of uniforms. Dupree mentioned that no one seemed suspicious in any case, but Shannon decided nevertheless to stick to the original idea.

Janni said he had tried several footwear stores but had not found the canvas boots he was looking for. He would go on trying for the rest of the week and start searching for berets, haversacks, knapsacks, a variety of webbing, and sleeping bags next week. Shannon advised him to contact his first export agent and get the first consignment of underwear and tunics off to Marseilles as soon as possible. He promised Dupree to get from Langarotti the name and address of a consignee agent in Marseilles within the next forty-eight hours.

Before the South African left, Shannon typed out a letter to Langarotti and addressed it to him under his real name at the main post office of Marseilles. In the letter he reminded the Corsican of a conversation they had had six months earlier beneath the palm trees, when the talk had turned to the buying of arms. The Corsican had mentioned that he knew a man in Paris who could get End User Certificates from a diplomat in one of the Paris embassies of an African republic. Shannon needed to know the name of the man and where he could be contacted.

When he had finished he gave Dupree the letter and ordered him to post it, express rate, that same evening from Trafalgar Square. He explained he would have done it himself, but he had to wait in the flat for Langarotti to call from Marseilles.

He was getting very hungry by eight, when Langarotti finally called, his voice crackling over a telephone line that must have been created personally by the inventor of that antique masterpiece the French telephone network.

Shannon asked him, in guarded terms, how he had been getting on. Before any of the mercenaries had left him, he had warned them all that under no circumstances was a telephone line to be used to talk openly about what they were doing.

"I checked into a hotel and sent you a telegram with my address on it," said Langarotti.

"I know. I got it," shouted Shannon.

"I hired a scooter and toured all the shops that deal in the kind of merchandise we are looking for," came the voice. "There are three manufacturers in each category. I got the addresses and names of the three boatmakers and wrote off to each for their brochures. I should get them in a week or so. Then I can order the best-suited from the local dealers, quoting the maker's name and brand name of the article," said Langarotti.

"Good idea," said Shannon. "What about the second articles?"

"They depend on the kind we pick from the brochures I shall get. One depends on the other. But don't worry. On the second thing we need, there are thousands of every kind and description in the shops along this coast. With spring coming, every shop in every port is stocking up with the latest models."

"Okay. Fine," Shannon shouted. "Now listen. I need the name of a good export agent for shipping. I need it earlier than I thought. There will be a few crates to be sent from here in the near future, and another from Hamburg."

"I can get that easy enough," said Langarotti from the other end. "But I think it will be better in Toulon. You can guess why."

Shannon could guess. Langarotti could use another name at his hotel, but for exporting goods from the port on a small freighter he would have to show his identity card. Moreover, in the past year or so Marseilles police had tightened up considerably in their watch on the port and a new customs chief had been drafted in, who was believed to be a holy terror. The aim of both operations was to clamp down on the heroin traffic that made Marseilles the start of the French connection with New York, but a search of a boat for drugs could just as easily turn up arms instead. It would be the worst irony to be caught because of something one was not even involved in.

"Fair enough, you know that area best," said Shannon. "Cable me the name and address as soon as you have them. There is one other thing. I have sent a letter by express rate tonight, to you personally at the main post office in Marseilles. You'll see what I want when you read it. Cable me the man's name at once when you get the letter, which should be Friday morning."

"Okay," said Langarotti. "Is that all?"

"Yes, for the moment. Send me those brochures as soon as you get them, with your own comments and the prices. We must stay in budget."

"Right. By-by," called Langarotti, and Shannon hung up. He had a dinner alone at the Bois de St. Jean and slept early.

Endean arrived at eleven the next morning and spent an hour reading the report and accounts and discussing both with Shannon.

"Fair enough," he said at length. "How are things going?"

"Well," said Shannon, "it's early days yet, of course. I've only been on the job for ten days, but a lot of ground has been covered. I want to get all the orders placed by Day Twenty, which will leave forty days for them to be fulfilled. After that there must be an allowance of twenty days to collect all the component parts and get them safely and discreetly aboard the ship. Sailing date should be Day Eighty, if we are to strike on schedule. By the way, I shall need more money soon."

"You have three and a half thousand in London, and seven thousand in Belgium," objected Endean.

"Yes, I know. But there is going to be a spate of payments soon."

He explained he would have to pay Johann, the Hamburg arms dealer, the outstanding $26,000 within twelve days to allow him forty days to get the consignment through the formalities in Madrid and ready for shipment; then there would be $4800 dollars, also to Johann, for the ancillary gear he needed for the attack. When he had the End User Certificate in Paris, he would have to send it to Alan, along with a credit transfer of $7200, 50 per cent of the Yugoslav arms price.

"It all mounts up," he said. "The big payments, of course, are the arms and the boat. They form over half the total budget."

"All right," said Endean. "I'll consult and prepare a draft to your Belgian account for another twenty thousand pounds. Then the transfer can be made on a telephone call from me to Switzerland. In that way it will only take a matter of hours, when you need it." He rose to go. "Anything else?"

"No," said Shannon. "I'll have to go away again at the weekend for another trip. I should be away most of next week. I want to check on the search for the boat, the choice of dinghies and outboards in Marseilles, and the submachine guns in Belgium."

"Wire me at the usual address when you leave and when you get back," said Endean.

The drawing room in the sprawling apartment above Cottesmore Gardens, not far from Kensington High Street, was gloomy in the extreme, with heavy drapes across the windows to shut out the spring sunshine. A gap a few inches wide between them allowed a little daylight to filter in through thick net curtains. Between the four formally placed and overstuffed chairs, each of them late-Victorian pieces, myriad small tables bore assorted bric-àbrac. There were buttons from long-punctured uniforms, medals won in long-past skirmishes with long-liquidated heathen tribes. Glass paperweights nudged Dresden china dolls, cameos of once demure Highland beauties, and fans that had cooled faces at balls whose music was no longer played.

Around the walls of discolored brocade hung portraits of ancestors, Montroses and Monteagles, Farquhars and Frazers, Murrays and Mintoes. Surely such a gathering could not be the ancestors of one old woman? Still, you never knew, with the Scots.

Bigger than them all, in a vast frame above the fire that clearly was never lit, stood a man in a kilt, a painting evidently much more recent than the other blackened antiques, but still discolored by age. The face, framed by two bristling ginger muttonchop whiskers, glared down into the room as if its owner had just spotted a coolie impudently collapsing from overwork at the other end of the plantation. "Sir Ian Macallister, K.B.E.," read the plate beneath the portrait.

Martin Thorpe dragged his eyes back to Lady Macallister, who was slumped in a chair, fiddling as she constantly did with the hearing aid that hung on her chest. He tried to make out from the mumblings and ramblings, sudden digressions, and difficult accent, what she was saying.

"People have come before, Mr. Martin," she was saying; she insisted on calling him Mr. Martin, although he had introduced himself twice. "But I don't see why I should sell. It was my husband's company, don't you see. He founded all these estates that they make their money from. It was all his work. Now people come and say they want to take the company away and do other things with it—build houses and play around with other things. I don't understand it all, not at all, and I will not sell—"

"But Lady Macallister—"

She went on as if she had not heard him, which indeed she had not, for her hearing aid was up to its usual tricks because of her constant fiddling with it. Thorpe began to understand why other suitors had eventually gone elsewhere for their shell companies.

"You see, my dear husband, God rest his poor soul, was not able to leave me very much, Mr. Martin. When those dreadful Chinese killed him, I was in Scotland on furlough, and I never went back. I was advised not to go. But they told me the estates belonged to the company, and he had left me a large part of the company. So that was his legacy to me, don't you see. I could not sell his own legacy to me . . . "

Thorpe was about to point out that the company was worthless, but realized that would not be the right thing to say. "Lady Macallister—" he began again.

"You'll have to speak directly into the hearing aid. She's deaf as a post," said Lady Macallister's companion.

Thorpe nodded his thanks at her and really noticed her for the first time. In her late sixties, she had the careworn look of those who once had their own independence but who, through the strange turns of fortune, have fallen on harder times and to survive have to put themselves in bond to others, often to cantankerous, troublesome, exhausting employers whose money enables them to hire others to serve them.

Thorpe rose and approached the senile old woman in the armchair. He spoke closer to the hearing aid. "Lady Macallister, the people I represent do not want to change the company. On the contrary, they want to put a lot of money into it and make it rich and famous again. We want to start up the Macallister estates, just like when your husband ran them . . . "

For the first time since the interview had started an hour before, something like a glimmer of light awoke in the old woman's eyes. "Like when my husband ran them?" she queried.

"Yes, Lady Macallister," bawled Thorpe. He pointed up at the figure of the tyrant on the wall. "We want to create all his life's work again, just the way he would have wanted it, and make the Macallister estates a memorial to him and his work."

But she was gone again. "They never put up a memorial to him," she quavered. "I tried, you know. I wrote to the authorities. I said I would pay for the statue, but they said there was no room. No room. They put up lots of statues, but not to my Ian."

"They will put up a memorial to him if the estates and the company become rich again," Thorpe shouted into the hearing aid. "They'll have to. If the company was rich, it could insist on a memorial. It could found a scholarship, or a foundation, called the Sir Ian Macallister Trust, so that people would remember him."

He had already tried that ploy once, but no doubt she had not heard him or had not grasped what he was saying. But she heard him this time.

"It would cost a lot of money," she quavered. "I am not a rich woman." She was in fact extremely rich, but probably unaware of it.

"You don't have to pay for it, Lady Macallister," he said. "The company would pay for it. But the company would have to expand again. And that means money. The money would be put into the company by my friends."

"I don't know, I don't know," she wailed and began to sniff, reaching for a cambric handkerchief in her sleeve. "I don't understand these things. If only my dear Ian were here. Or Mr. Dalgleish. I always ask him what would be for the best. He always signs the papers for me. Mrs. Barton, I'd like to go back to my room."

"It's time enough," said the housekeeper-companion brusquely. "Now come along, it's time for your nap. And your medicine."

She helped the old woman to her feet and assisted her out of the sitting room and down the corridor. Through the open door Thorpe could hear her businesslike voice commanding her charge to get onto the bed, and the old woman's protests as she took the medicine.

After a while Mrs. Barton came back to the sitting room. "She's on the bed, she'll rest for a while," she said.

Thorpe smiled his most rueful smile. "It looks as if I've failed," he said sadly. "And yet, you know, the stock she holds is quite valueless unless the company is rejuvenated with fresh management and some hard cash, quite a lot of it, which my partners would be prepared to put in." He turned to the door. "I'm sorry if I put you to inconvenience," he said.

"I'm quite used to inconvenience," said Mrs. Barton, but her face softened. It had been a long time since anyone had apologized for putting her to trouble. "Would you care for a cup of tea? I usually make one at this hour."

Some instinct at the back of Thorpe's mind prompted him to accept. As they sat over a pot of tea in the back kitchen, which was the housekeeper-companion's domain, Martin Thorpe felt almost at home. His mother's kitchen in Battersea had not been dissimilar. Mrs. Barton told him about Lady Macallister, her whining and tantrums, her obstinacy and the constant strain of competing with her all-too-convenient deafness.

"She can't see all your fine arguments, Mr. Thorpe, not even when you offered to put up a memorial to that old ogre in the sitting room."

Thorpe was surprised. Evidently the tart Mrs. Barton had a mind of her own when her employer was not listening. "She does what you tell her," he said.

"Would you like another cup of tea?" she asked. As she poured it, she said quietly, "Oh, yes, she does what I tell her. She depends on me, and she knows it. If I went, she'd never get another companion. You can't nowadays. People aren't prepared to put up with that sort of thing these days."

"It can't be much of a life for you, Mrs. Barton."

"It's not," she said shortly, "but I have a roof over my head, and food and some clothes. I get by. It's the price one pays."

"For being a widow?" asked Thorpe gently.

"Yes."

There was a picture of a young man in the uniform of a pilot of the Royal Air Force propped on the mantelpiece next to the clock. He wore a sheepskin jacket, a polka-dotted scarf, and a broad grin. Seen from one angle, he looked not unlike Martin Thorpe.

"Your son?" said the financier, with a nod.

Mrs. Barton gazed at the picture. "Yes. Shot down over France in nineteen-forty-three."

"I'm sorry."

"It was a long time ago. One becomes accustomed."

"So he won't be able to look after you when she's dead and gone."

"No."

"Then who will?"

"I'll get by. She'll no doubt leave me something in her will. I've looked after her for sixteen years."

"Yes, of course she will. She'll see you are all right—no doubt of it."

He spent another hour in the back kitchen, and when he left he was a much happier man. It was nearly closing time for shops and offices, but from a corner phone booth he made a call to the head office of ManCon, and within ten minutes Endean had done what his colleague asked.

In the West End an insurance broker agreed to stay late in his office that night and receive Mr. Thorpe at ten the next morning.

That Thursday evening Johann Schlinker flew into London from Hamburg. He had arranged his appointment by telephone from Hamburg the same morning, phoning his contact at his home rather than at the office.

He met the diplomat from the Iraqi embassy for dinner at nine. It was an expensive dinner, even more so when the German arms dealer handed over an envelope containing the equivalent in German marks of £1000. In return he took an envelope from the Arab and checked the contents. They took the form of a letter on crested embassy notepaper. The letter was addressed to whom it might concern and stated that the undersigned, being a diplomat on the staff of the London embassy of the Republic of Iraq, had been required and requested by the Interior and Police Ministry of his country to authorize Herr Johann Schlinker to negotiate the purchase of 400,000 rounds of

standard 9mm. ball for shipment to Iraq to replenish the stocks of the police
forces of the country. It was signed by the diplomat and bore the stamp and
seal of the Republic of Iraq, which would normally be on the desk of the
Ambassador. The letter further stated that the purchase would be wholly
and exclusively for the use of the Republic of Iraq and would under no
circumstances be passed, in whole or in part, to any other party. It was an
End User Certificate.

When they parted, it was too late for the German to return home, so he
spent the night in London and left the following morning.

At eleven on Friday morning, Cat Shannon phoned Marc Vlaminck at his
flat above the bar in Ostend.

"Did you find that man I asked you to trace?" he inquired after introducing himself. He had already warned the Belgian to talk very carefully on the
telephone.

"Yes, I found him," replied Tiny Marc. He was sitting up in bed, while
Anna snored gently beside him. The bar usually closed between three and
four in the morning, so midday was the habitual rising time for both of them.

"Is he prepared to talk business about the merchandise?" asked Shannon.

"I think so," said Vlaminck. "I haven't raised the matter with him yet, but a
business friend here says he will normally do business after a suitable
introduction through a mutual acquaintance."

"He still has the goods I mentioned to you at our last meeting?"

"Yes," said the voice from Belgium, "he still has them."

"Fine," said Shannon. "Get a meeting and introduction with him yourself
first, and tell him you have a customer who has approached you and would
like to talk business. Ask him to be available for a meeting next weekend with
the customer. Tell him the customer is good and reliable and is an Englishman called Brown. You know what to say. Just get him interested in a
business deal. Tell him the customer would wish to examine one example of
the goods at the meeting, and if it is up to standard, discuss terms and
delivery. I'll ring you toward the weekend and let you know where I am and
when I could come to see you and him together. Understand?"

"Sure," said Marc. "I'll get on with it over the next couple of days and set
the meeting up for some time to be confirmed later, but during next
weekend."

They exchanged the usual good wishes and hung up.

At half past two a cable from Marseilles arrived at the flat. It bore the name
of a Frenchman and an address. Langarotti said he would telephone the
man and introduce Shannon with a personal recommendation. The cable
concluded by saying inquiries regarding the shipping agent were under way,
and he expected to be able to give Shannon a name and address within five
days.

Shannon picked up the phone and called the offices of UTA airlines in
Piccadilly to get himself a seat on the flight of the following Sunday midnight
to Africa from Le Bourget, Paris. From BEA he reserved a ticket to Paris on
the first flight the next morning, Saturday.

He put £2000 of the money he had brought back from Germany into an
envelope and slipped it into the lining at the bottom of his handgrip, for
London airport representatives of the Treasury by and large disapprove of

British citizens strolling out of the country with more than the permitted £25 in cash and £300 in travelers' checks.

Just after lunch Sir James Manson summoned Simon Endean to his office. He had finished reading Shannon's report and was agreeably surprised at the speed with which the mercenary's proposed plan of twelve days earlier was being carried out. He had checked the accounts and approved the expenditures. What pleased him even more was the long telephone call he had had from Martin Thorpe, who had spent half the night and most of the morning with an insurance broker.

"You say Shannon will be abroad for most of next week," he told Endean when his aide entered the office.

"Yes, Sir James."

"Good. There's a job that has to be done sooner or later, and it might as well be now. Get one of our standard contracts of employment, the kind we use for the engagement of African representatives. Paste over the name of ManCon with a strip of white paper and fill in the name of Bormac in its place. Make it out for a one-year engagement for the services as West African representative of Antoine Bobi at a salary of five hundred pounds a month. When you've got it done, show it to me."

"Bobi?" queried Endean. "You mean Colonel Bobi?"

"That's the one. I don't want the future president of Zangaro running off anywhere. Next week, starting Monday, you are going down to Cotonou to interview the colonel and persuade him that Bormac Trading Company, whose representative you are, has been so impressed by his mental and business acumen that it would like to engage his services as a West African consultant. Don't worry, he'll never check to see who or what Bormac is, or that you are its representative. If I know anything about these lads, the hefty salary will be what interests him. If he's short of the ready, it ought to be manna from heaven.

"You are to tell him his duties will be communicated to him later, but the sole condition of employment for the moment is that he remain where he is at his house in Dahomey for the next three months or until you visit him again. Persuade him there will be a bonus in salary if he waits where he is. Tell him the money will be transferred to his local account in Dahomean francs. On no account is he to receive any hard currency. He might vamoose. One last thing. When the contract is ready, have it photocopied to hide the traces of the change of name of the employing company, and only take with you photocopies. As for the date on it, make sure the last figure for the year is blurred. Smudge it yourself."

Endean absorbed the instructions and left to begin setting up the employment under false pretenses of Colonel Antoine Bobi.

That Friday afternoon, just after four, Thorpe emerged from the gloomy Kensington apartment with the four share-transfer deeds he needed, duly signed by Lady Macallister and witnessed by Mrs. Barton. He also bore a letter of authority signed by the old woman, instructing Mr. Dalgleish, her attorney in Dundee, to hand over to Mr. Thorpe the share certificates upon presentation of the letter and proof of identity and the necessary check.

The name of the recipient of the shares had been left blank on the transfer deeds, but Lady Macallister had not noticed. She had been too distraught at the thought of Mrs. Barton packing her bags and leaving. Before nightfall the name of the Zwingli Bank's nominee company acting on behalf of Messrs. Adams, Ball, Carter, and Davies would be written into the vacant space. After a visit to Zurich the following Monday, the bank stamp and countersignature of Dr. Steinhofer would complete the form, and four certified checks, one drawn against the account of each of the four nominees buying 7.5 per cent of the stock of Bormac, would be brought back from Switzerland.

It had cost Sir James Manson 2 shillings to buy each of the 300,000 shares, then quoted at 1 shilling and 1 penny on the Stock Exchange, or a total of £30,000. It had also cost him another £30,000, shunted that morning through three bank accounts, withdrawn once in cash and repaid into a fresh account an hour later, to purchase a life annuity which would assure a comfortable and worry-free end to her days for an elderly housekeeper-companion.

All in all, Thorpe reckoned it was cheap at the price. Even more important, it was untraceable. Thorpe's name appeared nowhere on any document; the annuity had been paid for by a solicitor, and solicitors are paid to keep their mouths shut. Thorpe was confident Mrs. Barton would have enough sense to do the same. And to cap it all, it was even legal.

FOURTEEN

Benoit Lambert, known to friends and police as Benny, was a small-fry member of the underworld and self-styled mercenary. In point of fact, his sole appearance in the mercenary-soldier field had occurred when, with the police looking for him in the Paris area, he had taken a plane for Africa and signed on in the Sixth Commando in the Congo under the leadership of Denard.

For some strange reason the mercenary leader had taken a liking to the timorous little man and had given him a job at headquarters, which kept him well away from combat. He had been useful in his job, because it enabled him to exercise to good effect the one talent he really did possess. He was a wizard at obtaining things. He seemed to be able to conjure up eggs where there were no chickens and whisky where there was no still. In the headquarters of any military unit, such a man is always useful, and most units have one. He had stayed with the Sixth Commando for nearly a year, until May 1967, when he spotted trouble brewing in the form of a pending revolt by Schramme's Tenth Commando against the Congolese government. He felt—rightly, as it turned out—that Denard and the Sixth might be drawn into this fracas and there would be an opportunity for all, including headquarters staff, to see some real combat. For Benny Lambert this was the moment to move briskly in the other direction.

To his surprise, he had been allowed to go.

Back in France, he had cultivated the notion of himself as a mercenary and later had called himself an arms dealer. The first he certainly was not, but as for arms, with his variety of contacts he had occasionally been able to provide an item of weaponry here and there, usually hand guns for the underworld, occasionally a case of rifles. He had also come to know an African diplomat who was prepared, for a price, to provide a moderately serviceable End User Certificate in the form of a letter from the Ambassador's personal desk, complete with embassy stamp. Eighteen months earlier he had mentioned this in a bar to a Corsican called Langarotti.

Nevertheless, he was surprised on Friday evening to hear the Corsican on the phone, calling long distance to tell him he would be visited at his home the next day or Sunday by Cat Shannon. He had heard of Shannon, but, even more, he was aware of the vitriolic hatred Charles Roux bore for the Irish mercenary, and he had long since heard on the grapevine that circulated among the mercenaries of Paris that Roux was prepared to pay money to anyone who would tip him off as to Shannon's whereabouts, should the Irishman ever turn up in Paris. After consideration, Lambert agreed to be at home to see Shannon.

"Yes, I think I can get that certificate," he said when Shannon had finished explaining what he wanted. "My contact is still in Paris. I deal with him fairly frequently, you know."

It was a lie, for his dealings were very infrequent, but he was sure he could swing the deal.

"How much?" asked Shannon shortly.

"Fifteen thousand francs," said Benny Lambert.

"*Merde,*" said Shannon. 'I'll pay you a thousand pounds, and that's over the rate."

Lambert calculated. The sum was just over eleven thousand francs at the current rate. "Okay," he said.

"You let out one word of this, and I'll slit your gizzard like a chicken," said Shannon. "Even better, I'll get the Corsican to do it, and he'll start at the knee."

"Not a word, honest," protested Benny. "A thousand pounds, and I'll get you the letter in four days. And not a word to anyone."

Shannon put down five hundred pounds. "You'll take it in sterling," he said. "Half now, half when I pick it up."

Lambert was about to protest but realized it would do no good. The Irishman did not trust him.

"I'll call you here on Wednesday," said Shannon. "Have the letter here, and I'll hand over the other five hundred."

When he had gone, Benny Lambert thought over what he would do. Finally he decided to get the letter, collect the remainder of his fee, and tell Roux later.

The following evening Shannon flew to Africa on the midnight flight and arrived at dawn on Monday morning.

It was a long drive upcountry. The taxi was hot and rattled abominably. It was still the height of the dry season, and the sky above the oil-palm plantations was robin's-egg blue, without a cloud. Shannon did not mind. It was good to be back in Africa again for a day and a half, even after a six-hour flight without sleep.

It was familiar to him, more so than the cities of Western Europe. Familiar were the sounds and the smells, the villagers walking along the edge of the road to market, columns of women in Indian file, their gourds and bundles of wares balanced on their heads, unwaveringly steady.

At each village they passed, the usual morning market was set out beneath the shade of the palm-thatch roofs of the rickety stalls, the villagers bargaining and chattering, buying and selling, the women tending the stalls while the men sat in the shade and talked of important matters that only they could understand, and the naked brown children scampering through the dust between the legs of their parents and the stalls.

Shannon had both windows open. He sat back and sniffed the moisture and the palms, the woodsmoke and the brown, stagnant rivers they crossed. From the airport he had already telephoned the number the writer had given him and knew he was expected. He arrived at the villa set back from the road in a private, if small, park just before noon.

The guards checked him at the gate, frisking him from ankles to armpits, before letting him pay off the taxi and enter the gate. Inside, he recognized a face, one of the personal attendants of the man he had come to see. The servant grinned broadly and bobbed his head. He led Shannon to one of the three houses in the grounds of the park and ushered him into an empty sitting room. Shannon waited alone for half an hour.

He was staring out of the windows, feeling the cool of the air-conditioner dry out his clothes, when he heard the creak of a door and the soft sound of a sandal on tiles behind him. He turned around.

The general was much the same as when they had last met on the darkened airstrip, the same luxuriant beard, the same deep bass voice.

"Well, Major Shannon, so soon. Couldn't you stay away?"

He was bantering, as he usually did. Shannon grinned as they shook hands.

"I've come down because I need something, sir. And because there is something I think we ought to talk over. An idea in the back of my head."

"There's not much that an impoverished exile can offer you," said the general, "but I'll always listen to your ideas. If I remember rightly, you used to have some fairly good ones."

Shannon said, "There's one thing you have, even in exile, that I could use. You still have your people's loyalty. And what I need is men."

The two men talked through the lunch hour and through the afternoon. They were still discussing when darkness fell, Shannon's freshly drawn diagrams spread out on the table. He had brought nothing with him but clean white paper and a variety of colored felt-tipped pens, just in case of a skin search at customs.

They reached agreement on the basic points by sundown and elaborated the plan through the night. Only at three in the morning was the car summoned to drive Shannon back to the coast and the airport for take-off on the dawn plane to Paris.

As they parted on the terrace above the waiting car and its sleepy chauffeur, they shook hands again.

"I'll be in touch, sir," said Shannon.

"And I'll have to send my emissaries immediately," replied the general. "But in sixty days the men will be there."

Shannon was dead tired. The strain of the constant traveling was beginning to tell; the nights without sleep, the endless succession of airports and hotels, negotiations and meetings, had left him drained. In the car driving to the south he slept for the first time in two days, and dozed again on the plane trip back to Paris. The flight stopped too many times to allow a real sleep: an hour at Ouagadougou, another at a godforsaken strip in Mauretania, and again at Marseilles. He reached Le Bourget just before six in the evening. It was the end of Day Fifteen.

While he was landing in Paris, Martin Thorpe was boarding the overnight sleeper train to Glasgow, Stirling, and Perth. From there he could take a connecting train to Dundee, where were situated the old-established offices of Dalgleish and Dalgleish, attorneys-at-law. He carried in his briefcase the document signed before the weekend by Lady Macallister and witnessed by Mrs. Barton, along with the checks issued by the Zwingli Bank of Zurich, four of them, each in the sum of £7500 and each enough to purchase 75,000 of Lady Macallister's shares in Bormac.

Twenty-four hours, he thought as he drew down the blinds of his first-class sleeping compartment, blotting out the sight of the scurrying on the platform of King's Cross station. Twenty-four hours should see it through, and they would be home and dry; and three weeks later a new director on the board, a nominee responding to the strings pulled by him and Sir James Manson. Settling himself on the bunk, his briefcase under the pillow, Martin Thorpe gazed up at the ceiling and enjoyed the feeling.

Later that Tuesday evening Shannon was settled into a hotel not far from the Madeleine in the heart of Paris's 8th arrondissement. He had had to forsake his regular Montmartre hideout, where he was known as Carlo Shannon, because he was now using the name of Keith Brown. But the Plaza-Surène was a good substitute. He had bathed and shaved and was about to go out for dinner. He had telephoned to reserve a table at his favorite eating place in the quarter, the Restaurant Mazagran, and Madame Michèle had promised him a filet mignon the way he like it, with a tossed-lettuce salad by the side and a Pot de Chirouble to wash it down.

The two person-to-person calls he had put in came through almost together. First on the line was a certain M. Lavallon from Marseilles.

"Do you have that shipping agent yet?" asked Shannon when they had exchanged greetings.

"Yes," said the Corsican. "It's in Toulon. A very good one, very respectable and efficient. They have their own bonded warehouse on the harbor."

"Spell it out," said Shannon. He had pencil and paper ready.

"Agence Maritime Duphot," spelled Langarotti and dictated the address. "Send the consignments to the agency, clearly marked as the property of Monsieur Langarotti."

Shannon hunt up, and the hotel operator came on the line immediately to say a Mr. Dupree was calling from London.

Shannon dictated the name and address of the Toulon agent to him, letter by letter.

"Fine," Janni said at length. "I've got the first of the four crates ready and bonded here. I'll tell the London agents to get the stuff on its way as soon as possible. Oh, by the way, I've found the boots."

"Good," said Shannon, "well done."

He placed one more call, this time to a bar in Ostend. There was a fifteen-minute delay before Marc's voice came through.

"I'm in Paris," said Shannon. "That man with the samples of merchandise I wanted to examine . . ."

"Yes," said Marc. "I've been in touch. He's prepared to meet you and discuss prices and terms."

"Good. I'll be in Belgium Thursday night or Friday morning. Tell him I propose Friday morning over breakfast in my room at the Holiday Inn near the airport."

"I know it," said Marc. "All right, I'll put it to him and call you back."

"Call me tomorrow between ten and eleven," said Shannon and hung up.

Only then did he slip on his jacket and head for a long-awaited dinner to be followed by a long-desired full night's sleep.

While Shannon slept, Simon Endean also was winging his way southward to Africa on the overnight flight. He had arrived in Paris by the first flight on Monday and taken a taxi immediately to the embassy of Dahomey in the Avenue Victor Hugo. Here he had filled out a lengthy pink form requesting a six-day tourist visa. It was ready for collection just before the closing of the consular office on the Tuesday afternoon, and he had caught the midnight flight to Cotonou via Niamey. Shannon would not have been particularly surprised to know that Endean was going to Africa, for he assumed the exiled Colonel Bobi had to play a part in Sir James Manson's scheme of things and that the former commander of the Zangaran army was cooling his heels somewhere along the mangrove coast. But if Endean had known Shannon had just returned from a secret visit to the general in the same area of Africa, it would have quite ruined his sleep aboard the UTA DC-8 that night, despite the pill he had taken to ensure an uninterrupted slumber.

Marc Vlaminck called Shannon at his hotel at ten-fifteen the next day. "He agrees to the meeting, and he'll bring the sample," said the Belgian. "Do you want me to come too?"

"Certainly," said Shannon. "When you get to the hotel, ask at reception for the room of Mr. Brown. One other thing. Have you bought that truck I asked you to get?"

"Yes, why?"

"Has this gentleman seen it yet?"

There was a pause while Vlaminck thought. "No."

"Then don't bring it to Brussels. Hire a car and drive yourself. Pick him up on the way. Understand?"

"Yes," said Vlaminck, still perplexed. "Anything you say."

Shannon, who was still in bed but feeling a sight better, rang for breakfast and had his habitual five minutes under the shower, four of them in steaming hot water and sixty seconds under a stream of ice-cold.

The coffee and rolls were on the side table when he emerged. He placed two calls from the bedside phone, to Benny Lambert in Paris and Mr. Stein of Lang and Stein in Luxembourg.

"Have you got that letter for me?" he asked Lambert.

The little crook's voice sounded strained. "Yes. I got it yesterday. Luckily my contact was on duty on Monday, and I saw him that night. He produced the letter of introduction yesterday evening. When do you want it?"

"This afternoon," said Shannon.

"All right. Have you got my fee?"

"Don't worry, I've got it right here."

"Then come to my place about three," said Lambert.

Shannon thought for a moment. "No, I'll meet you here," he said and gave

Lambert the name of his hotel. He preferred to meet the little man in a public place. Rather to his surprise, Lambert agreed to come to the hotel with what sounded like elation in his voice. There was something not quite right about this deal, but Shannon could not put his finger on it. He did not realize that he had given the Paris crook the information he would later sell to Roux.

Mr. Stein was engaged on the other phone when the call came, so, rather than wait, Shannon said he would ring back. This he did an hour later.

"About the meeting to launch my holding company, Tyrone Holdings," he began.

"Ah yes, Mr. Brown," said Stein's voice. "Everything is in order. When would you suggest?"

"Tomorrow afternoon," replied Shannon. It was agreed the meeting would be in Stein's office at three. Shannon got the hotel to reserve a seat on the express from Paris to Luxembourg just after nine the next morning.

"I must say, I find it all very strange, very strange indeed."

Mr. Duncan Dalgleish, Senior, in appearance and manner matched his office, and his office looked as if it had been the scene for the reading of the will of Sir Walter Scott.

He examined the four share-transfer deeds signed by Lady Macallister and witnessed by Mrs. Barton carefully and at length. He had muttered, "Aye," in sorrowful tones several times, and the glances he shot at the younger man from London were disapproving. He was evidently quite unused to handling certified checks from a bank in Zurich, and he had held them between forefinger and thumb as he read them. He was examining the four deeds again as he spoke.

"Ye'll understand, Lady Macallister has been approached before concerning the sale of these shares. In the past she has always seen fit to consult the firm of Dalgleish, and I have always seen fit to advise her against selling the stock," he went on.

Thorpe thought privately that no doubt other clients of Mr. Duncan Dalgleish were holding on to piles of valueless stock on the basis of his advice, but he kept his face polite.

"Mr. Dalgleish, you must agree the gentlemen whom I represent have paid Lady Macallister close to twice the face value of the stock. She, for her part, has freely signed the deeds and empowered me to collect the shares on presentation of check or checks totaling thirty thousand pounds. Which you now hold in your hand."

The old man sighed again. "It's just so strange that she should not have consulted me first," he said sadly. "I usually advise her on all her financial matters. For this I hold her general power of attorney."

"But her own signature is still perfectly valid," insisted Thorpe.

"Yes, yes, my power of attorney in no way invalidates her own power to sign on her behalf."

"Then I would be grateful if you would let me have the share certificates so that I can return to London," said Thorpe.

The old man rose slowly. "Would you excuse me, Mr. Thorpe?" he said with dignity and withdrew into an inner sanctum. Thorpe knew he was going to telephone London and prayed Lady Macallister's hearing aid would make it necessary for Mrs. Barton to interpret for the pair of them on the telephone. It was half an hour before the old attorney came back. He held a large wad of old and discolored share certificates in his hand.

"Lady Macallister has confirmed what you say, Mr. Thorpe. Not, of course, that I doubted your word, ye understand. I felt obliged to speak with my client before completing such a large transaction."

"Of course," said Thorpe, rose, and held out his hand. Dalgleish parted with the shares as if they had been his own.

An hour later Thorpe was in his train, rolling through the springlit countryside of Angus County on his way back to London.

Six thousand miles away from the heather-clad hills of Scotland, Simon Endean was seated with the hulking form of Colonel Bobi in a small rented villa in the residential district of Cotonou. He had arrived on the morning plane and checked into the Hotel du Port, whose Israeli manager had helped him trace the house where the Zangaran army officer lived in the straitened circumstances of exile.

Bobi was a lumbering giant of a man with a face of brooding brutishness and massive hands. The combination pleased Endean. It was of no consequence to him with what disastrous effects Bobi might rule Zangaro in succession to the equally disastrous Jean Kimba. What he had come to find was a man who would sign away the mineral rights of the Crystal Mountain range to Bormac Trading Company for a pittance and a hefty bribe to his personal account. He had found what he sought.

In exchange for a salary of £500 a month the colonel would be delighted to accept the post of West African consultant to Bormac. He had pretended to study the contract Endean had brought, but the Englishman noted with pleasure that when he turned to the second page, which Endean had stapled upside down between the first and third pages, Bobi's expression did not flicker. He was illiterate, or the next thing to it.

Endean explained the terms of the contract slowly in the mishmash of language they had been using, a mixture of basic French and Coast-pidgin English. Bobi nodded soberly, his small eyes, much flecked with bloodshot vessels around the whites, studying the contract intently. Endean stressed that Bobi was to remain in his villa or near it for the next two to three months, and that Endean would return to see him again in that time.

The Englishman elicited that Bobi still had a valid Zangaran diplomatic passport, a legacy of a visit he had once made outside Zangaro at the side of the Defense Minister, Kimba's cousin.

Shortly before sundown he scrawled what could pass for a signature on the bottom of the Bormac document. Not that a signature really mattered. Only later would Bobi be told that Bormac was putting him back into power in exchange for mining rights. Endean surmised that, if the price was right, Bobi would not quibble.

The following morning at dawn Endean was on another plane, heading back to Paris and London.

The meeting with Benny Lambert took place, as agreed, in the hotel. It was short and to the point. Lambert handed over an envelope, which Shannon flicked open. From it he took two pieces of paper, both identical and both bearing the printed crest and letterhead of the stationery of the Ambassador in Paris of the Republic of Togo.

One of the sheets was blank, except for a signature on the bottom and an embassy seal. The other sheet was a letter in which the writer stated that he had been authorized by his government to engage the services of——————to apply to the government of —————— for the purchase of the military weapons listed on the attached sheet. The letter concluded with the usual assurance that the weapons were intended solely for use by the armed forces of the Republic of Togo and would not be given or sold to any third party. This too was signed and decorated with the seal of the republic.

Shannon nodded. He was confident Alan Baker would be able to insert his own name as the authorized agent and the Federal Republic of Yugoslavia as the vendor government in such a way as to leave no trace of the insertion. He handed to Lambert the £500 he owed him, and the latter left.

Like most weak men, Lambert was indecisive. He had for three days been on the verge of calling Charles Roux and telling him that Shannon was in town and seeking an End User Certificate. He knew the French mercenary would be more than interested in the news, but he did not know why. He assumed it was because Roux regarded Paris and its resident mercenaries as his private preserve. He would not take kindly to a foreigner coming there to set up an operation in either arms or men without cutting Roux in on the deal as equal partner or, more desirable, as the *patron*, the boss of the project. It would never occur to Roux that no one would want to finance him to set up an operation because he had blown far too many already, taken too many bribes to kill a project, and cheated too many men of their salary.

But Lambert was afraid of Roux and felt he ought to tell him. He had been on the verge of doing so that afternoon, and would have if Shannon had not had the balance of £500 with him. But to have warned Roux in those circumstances would have cost the little crook that £500, and he was sure Roux would not have made up such a large sum to him simply for a tip-off. What Lambert did not know was that Roux had placed a killing contract on the Irishman. So in his state of ignorance he worked out another idea.

He could collect his full £1000 from Shannon and tell Roux the Irishman had approached him with a request for an End User Certificate, which he had promptly refused. There was just one snag. He had heard enough of Shannon to be afraid of him also, and he feared that if Roux was in contact with the Irishman too soon after Lambert's own meeting at the hotel, Shannon would guess from whom the tip-off came. He decided to wait until the following morning.

When he finally gave Roux the tip-off, it was too late. Roux telephoned the hotel at once under another name and asked if a Mr. Shannon was staying there. The chief desk clerk replied quite truthfully that there was no one of that name at the hotel.

Cross-examined, a thoroughly frightened Lambert claimed he had not actually visited the hotel but had simply received a call from Shannon, who had given that hotel as the place where he was staying.

Shortly after nine Roux's man Henri Alain was at the reception desk of the Plaza-Surène and established that the only Englishman or Irishman who had stayed in the hotel the previous night exactly corresponded in description to Cat Shannon, that his name and passport had been those of Keith Brown, and that he had reserved through the reception desk a ticket on the 9:00 a.m. express train to Luxembourg. Henri Alain learned two more things: of a meeting that M. Brown had had in the resident's lounge the previous afternoon, and a description of the Frenchman with whom he had been seen speaking. All this he reported back to Roux at midday.

In the French mercenary leader's flat, Roux, Henri Alain, and Raymond Thomard held a conference of war. Roux made the final decision.

"Henri, we've missed him this time, but the chances are that he still knows nothing about it. So he may well return to that hotel next time he has to overnight in Paris. I want you to get friendly, real friendly, with someone on the staff there. The next time that man checks in there, I want to know, but at once. Understand?"

Alain nodded. "Sure, *patron*. I'll have it staked out from the inside, and if he even calls to make a reservation, we'll know."

Roux turned to Thomard. "When he comes again, Raymond, you take the bastard. In the meantime, there's one other little job. That shit Lambert lied his head off. He could have tipped me off last night, and we'd have been finished with this affair. So he probably took money off Shannon, then tried to take some more off me for out-of-date information. Just make sure Benny Lambert doesn't do any walking for the next six months."

The floating of the company to be known as Tyrone Holdings was shorter than Shannon could have thought possible It was so quick it was over almost before it had begun. He was invited into Mr. Stein's private office, where Mr. Lang and a junior partner were already seated. Along one wall were three secretaries—as it turned out, the secretaries of the three accountants present. With the required seven stockholders on hand, Mr. Stein set up the company within five minutes. Shannon handed over the balance of £500, and the thousand shares were issued. Each person present received one and signed for it, then passed it to Mr. Stein, who agreed to keep it in the company safe. Shannon received 994 shares in a block constituted by one sheet of paper, and signed for them. His own shares he pocketed. The articles and memorandum of association were signed by the chairman and company secretary, and copies of each would later be filed with the Registrar of Companies for the Grand Duchy of Luxembourg. The three secretaries were then sent back to their duties, the board of three directors met and approved the aims of the company, the minutes were noted on one sheet of paper, read out by the secretary, and signed by the chairman. That was it. Tyrone Holdings SA existed in law.

The other two directors shook hands with Shannon, calling him Mr. Brown as they did so, and left. Mr. Stein escorted him to the door.

"When you and your associates wish to buy a company in the chosen field of operations, to be owned by Tyrone Holdings," he told Shannon, "you will then need to come here, present us with a check for the appropriate amount, and buy the new issue at one pound per share. The formalities you can leave to us."

Shannon understood. Any inquiries would stop at Mr. Stein as company chairman. Two hours later he caught the evening plane for Brussels, and he checked into the Holiday Inn just before eight.

The man who accompanied Tiny Marc Vlaminck when they knocked at Shannon's door the following morning just after ten was introduced as M. Boucher. The pair of them, standing on the threshold when he opened the door, looked like a comic turn. Marc was bulky, towering over his companion, and he was beefy in every place. The other man was fat, extremely fat—the sort of fatness associated with fairground sideshows. He seemed almost circular, balanced like one of those children's spherical plastic toys that cannot be overturned. Only on closer examination was it apparent there were two tiny feet in brilliantly polished shoes beneath the mass, and that the bulk constituting the lower half was divided into two legs. In repose, the man looked like one single unit.

M. Boucher's head appeared to be the only object to mar the contours of the otherwise uniformly globular mass. It was small at the top and flowed downward to engulf his collar and hide it from view, the flesh of the jowls resting thankfully on the shoulders. After several seconds Shannon conceded that he also had arms, one on each side, and that one held a sleek document case some five inches thick.

"Please come in," said Shannon and stepped back.

Boucher entered first, turning slightly sideways to slip through the door, like a large ball of gray worsted fabric on castors. Marc followed, giving Shannon a wink as he caught his eye. They all shook hands. Shannon gestured to an armchair, but Boucher chose the edge of the bed. He was wise and experienced. He might never have got out of the armchair.

Shannon poured them all coffee and went straight to business. Tiny Marc sat and stayed silent.

"Monsieur Boucher, my associate and friend may have told you that my name is Brown, I am English by nationality, and I am here representing a group of friends who would be interested in acquiring a quantity of submachine carbines or machine pistols. Monsieur Vlaminck kindly mentioned to me that he was in a position to introduce me to someone who might have a quantity of machine pistols for sale. I understand from him that these are Schmeisser nine-mm. machine pistols, of wartime manufacture but never used. I also understand and accept that there can be no question of obtaining an export license for them, but this is accepted by my people, and they are prepared to take all responsibility in this regard. Is that a fair assessment?"

Boucher nodded slowly. He could not not fast. "I am in a position to make available a quantity of these pieces," he said carefully. "You are right about the impossibility of an export license. For that reason the identity of my own people has to be protected. Any business arrangement we might come to would have to be on a cash basis, and with security arrangements for my own people."

He's lying, thought Shannon. There are no people behind Boucher. He is the owner of this stuff and works alone.

In fact M. Boucher in his younger and slimmer days had been a Belgian SS man and had worked as a cook in the SS barracks at Namur. His obsession with food had taken him into cooking, and before the war he had lost several jobs because he tasted more than he served through the hatch. In the starving conditions of wartime Belgium he had opted for the cookhouse of the Belgian SS unit, one of the several local SS groups the Nazis recruited in the occupied countries. In the SS, surmised the young Boucher, one could eat. In 1944, when the Germans pulled back from Namur toward the frontier, a truckload of unused Schmeissers from the armory had been on its way east when the truck broke down. There was no time to repair it, so the cargo was shifted into a nearby bunker and the entrance dynamited. Boucher watched it happen. Years later he had returned, shoveled away the rubble, and removed the thousand weapons.

Since then they had reposed beneath a trapdoor built into the floor of the garage of his country cottage, a building left him by his parents, who died in the mid-1950s. He had sold job lots of Schmeissers at various times and had "unloaded" half of his reserve.

"If these guns are in good working order, I would be interested in buying a hundred of them," said Shannon. "Of course, payment would be by cash, in any currency. All reasonable conditions imposed by you would be adhered to in the handing over of the cargo. We also would expect complete discretion."

"As for the condition, monsieur, they are all brand new. Still in their maker's grease and each still wrapped in its sachet of greaseproof paper with seals unbroken. As they came from the factory thirty years ago and, despite their age, still possibly the finest machine pistol ever made."

Shannon needed no lectures about the Schmeisser 9mm. Personally he would have said the Israeli Uzi was better, but it was heavy. The Schmeisser was much better than the Sten, and certainly as good as the much more modern British Sterling. He thought nothing of the American grease-gun and the Soviet and Chinese burp-guns. However, Uzis and Sterlings are almost unobtainable and never in mint condition.

"May I see?" he asked.

Wheezing heavily, Boucher pulled the black case he carried onto his knees and flicked open the catches after twirling the wheels of the combination lock. He lifted the lid and held the case forward without attempting to get up.

Shannon rose, crossed the room, and took the case from him. He laid it on the bedside table and lifted out the Schmeisser.

It was a beautiful piece of weaponry. Shannon slid his hands over the smooth blue-black metal, gripped the pistol grip, and felt the lightness of it. He pulled back and locked the folding stock and operated the breech mechanism several times and squinted down the barrel from the foresight end. The inside was untouched, unmarked.

"That is the sample model," wheezed Boucher. "Of course it has had the maker's grease removed and carries only a light film of oil. But the others are identical. Unused."

Shannon put it down.

"It takes standard nine-mm. ammunition, which is easy to come by," said Boucher helpfully.

"Thank you, I know," said Shannon. "What about magazines? They can't be picked up just anywhere, you know."

"I can supply five with each weapon," said Boucher.

"Five?" Shannon asked in feigned amazement. 'I need more than five. Ten at least."

The bargaining had begun, Shannon complaining about the arms dealer's inability to provide enough magazines, the Belgian protesting that was the limit he could provide for each weapon without beggaring himself. Shannon proposed $75 for each Schmeisser on a deal for 100 guns; Boucher claimed he could allow that price only for a deal of not less than 250 weapons, and that for 100 he would have to demand $125 each. Two hours later they settled for 100 Schmeissers at $100 each. They fixed time and place for the following Wednesday evening after dark, and agreed on the method for the handover. Shannon offered Boucher a lift back in Vlaminck's car to where he had come from, but the fat man chose to call a taxi and be taken to Brussels city center to make his own way home. He was not prepared to assume that the Irishman, who he was certain was from the IRA, would not take him somewhere quiet and work on him until he had learned the location of the secret hoard. Boucher was quite right. Trust is silly and superfluous weakness in the black-market arms business.

Vlaminck escorted the fat man with his lethal briefcase down to the lobby and saw him away in his taxi. When he returned, Shannon was packing.

"Do you see what I mean about the truck you bought?" he asked Tiny.

"No," said the other.

"We will have to use that truck for the pick-up on Wednesday," Shannon pointed out. "I saw no reason why Boucher should see the real number plates. Have a spare set ready for Wednesday night, will you? It's only for an hour, but if Boucher does want to tip off anyone, they'll have the wrong truck."

"Okay, Cat, I'll be ready. I got the lock-up garage two days ago. And the other stuff is on order. Is there anywhere I can take you? I have the hired car for the rest of the day."

Shannon had Vlaminck drive him westward to Brugge and wait in a café while Shannon went to the bank. Mr. Goossens was at lunch, so the pair ate their own lunch in the small restaurant on the main square and Shannon returned to the bank at two-thirty.

There was still £7000 in the Keith Brown account, but a debit of £2000 for the four mercenaries' salaries was due in nine days. He drew a banker's check in favor of Johann Schlinker and placed it in an envelope containing a letter from him to Schlinker that he had written in his hotel room late the previous night. It informed Schlinker that the enclosed check for $4800 was in full payment for the assorted marine and life-saving articles he had ordered a week earlier, and gave the German the name and address of the Toulon shipping agent to whom the entire consignment should be sent in bond for export, for collection by M. Jean-Baptiste Langarotti. Last, he informed Schlinker that he would be telephoning him the coming week to inquire if the End User Certificate for the ordered 9mm. ammunition was in order.

The other letter was to Alan Baker, addressed to his home in Hamburg. The check it contained was in Baker's name for $7200, and Shannon's letter stated that the sum was in full settlement of the required 50-per-cent advance for the purchase of the goods they had discussed over dinner at the Atlantic a week earlier. He included the End User Certificate from the government of Togo and the spare sheet from the same source. Last, he instructed Baker to get right on with the purchase and promised to be in touch by phone regularly to check on progress. Both letters were mailed from Brugge post office, express rate and registered.

Shannon had Vlaminck drive him from Brugge to Ostend, had a couple of beers with the Belgian in a local bar near the seaport, and bought himself a single ticket on the evening ferry to Dover.

The boat train deposited him at Victoria Station at midnight, and he was in bed and asleep by one in the morning of that Saturday. The last thing he did before sleeping was to send a telegram to Endean's *poste restante* address to say he was back and he felt they ought to meet.

The Saturday morning mail brought a letter mailed at express rate from Malaga in the south of Spain. It was addressed to Keith Brown but began "Dear Cat." It came from Kurt Semmler and stated briefly that he had found a boat, a converted motor fishing vessel built twenty years earlier in a British shipyard, owned by a British citizen, and registered in London. It flew a British flag, was 90 feet overall and 80 tons deadweight, with a large central hold amidships and a smaller one aft. It was classed as a private yacht but could be reregistered as a coaster.

Semmler went on to say the vessel was for sale at a price of £20,000 and that two of the crew would be worth engaging under the new management. He was certain he could find good replacements for the other two crew members.

He finished by saying he was staying at the Malaga Palacio Hotel and asked Shannon to contact him there with his own date of arrival to inspect the boat. Shannon cabled him he would arrive on Monday.

The boat was called the MV *Albatross*.

Endean phoned Shannon that afternoon after checking his mail and receiving the telegram. They met around dinnertime that evening at the flat, and Shannon presented Endean with his third lengthy progress report and statement of accounts and expenditures.

"You'll have to make further transfers of money if we are to move ahead in the forthcoming weeks," Shannon told him. "We are entering the areas of major expenditure now—the arms and the ship."

"How much do you need at once?" Endean asked.

Shannon said, "Two thousand for salaries, four thousand for boats and engines, four thousand for submachine guns, and over ten thousand for nine-mm. ammunition. That's over twenty thousand. Better make it thirty thousand, or I'll be back next week."

Endean shook his head. "I'll make it twenty thousand," he said. "You can always contact me if you need more. By the way, I would like to see some of this stuff. That will be fifty thousand you'll have gone through inside a month."

"You can't," said Shannon. "The ammunition is not yet bought, nor the boats, engines, and so forth. Nor are the mortars and bazookas, nor the submachine pistols. All these deals have to be put through cash on the barrelhead or in advance. I explained that in my first report to your associates."

Endean eyed him coldly. "There had better be some purchases being made with all this money," he grated.

Shannon stared him out. "Don't threaten me, Harris. A lot of people have tried it; it costs a fortune in flowers. By the way, what about the boat?"

Endean rose. "Let me know which boat and from whom it is being bought. I'll make the credit transfer direct from my Swiss account."

"Please yourself," said Shannon.

He dined alone and well that evening and had an early night. Sunday would be a free day, and he had found Julie Manson was already at home with her parents in Gloucestershire. Over his brandy and coffee he was lost in thought, planning the weeks ahead and trying to visualize the attack on the palace of Zangaro.

It was in the middle of Sunday morning that Julie Manson decided to call her new lover's flat in London and see if he was there. Outside, the spring rain fell in a steady curtain on the Gloucestershire countryside. She had hoped to be able to saddle up the handsome new gelding her father had given her a month earlier and gallop through the parkland surrounding the family mansion. She had hoped the ride would be a tonic to the feelings that flooded through her when she thought of the man she had fallen for. But the rain had washed out the idea of riding. Instead she was confined to wandering around the old house, listening to her mother's chitchat about charity bazaars and orphan-relief committees, or staring at the rain falling on the garden.

Her father had been working in his study, but she had seen him go out to the stables to talk to the chauffeur a few minutes earlier. As her mother was within earshot of the telephone in the hallway, she decided to use the extension in the study.

She had lifted the telephone beside the desk in the empty room when her eye caught the sprawl of papers lying across the blotter. On top of them was a single folder. She noted the title and idly lifted the cover to glance at the first page. A name on it caused her to freeze, the telephone still buzzing furiously in her ear. The name was Shannon.

Like most young girls, she had had her fantasies, seeing herself as she lay in the darkness of the dormitory at boarding school in the role of heroine of a hundred hazardous exploits, usually saving the man she loved from a terrible fate, to be rewarded by his undying devotion. Unlike most girls, she had never completely grown up. From Shannon's persistent questioning about her father she had already half managed to translate herself into the role of a girl agent on her lover's behalf. The trouble was, most of what she knew about her father was either personal, in his role of indulgent daddy, or very boring. Of his business affairs she knew nothing. And then here, on a rainy Sunday morning, lay her chance.

She flicked her eyes down the first page of the folder and understood nothing. There were figures, costings, a second reference to the name Shannon, a mention of several banks by name, and two references to a man called Clarence. She got no further. The turning of the door handle interrupted her.

With a start she dropped the cover of the folder, stood back a yard, and began to babble into the unhearing telephone. Her father stood in the doorway.

"All right, Christine, that will be marvelous, darling. I'll see you on Monday, then. 'By now," she chattered into the telephone and hung up.

Her father's set expression had softened as he saw the person in the room was his daughter, and he walked across the carpet to sit behind his desk. "Now what are you up to?" he said with mock gruffness.

For answer she twined her soft arms around his neck from behind and kissed him on the cheek. "Just phoning a friend in London, Daddy," she said in her small, little-girl voice. "Mummy was fussing about in the hall, so I came in here."

"Humph. Well, you've got a phone in your own room, so please use that for private calls."

"All right, Daddikins." She cast her glance over the papers lying under the folder on the desk, but the print was too small to read and was mostly columns of figures. She could make out the headings only. They concerned mining prices. Then her father turned to look up.

"Why don't you stop all this boring old work and come and help me saddle up Tamerlane?" she asked him. "The rain will stop soon, and I can go riding."

He smiled up at the girl who was the apple of his eye. "Because this boring old work happens to be what keeps us all clothed and fed," he said. "But I will, anyway. Give me a few more minutes, and I'll join you in the stable."

Outside the door, Julie Manson stopped and breathed deeply. Mata Hari, she was sure, could not have done better.

FIFTEEN

The Spanish authorities are far more tolerant to tourists than is generally thought. Bearing in mind the millions of Scandinavians, Germans, French, and British who pour into Spain each spring and summer, and since the law of averages must provide that a certain percentage of them are up to no good, the authorities have quite a lot to put up with. Irrelevant breaches of regulations such as importing two cartons of cigarettes rather than the permitted one carton, which would be pounced on at London airport, are shrugged off in Spain.

The attitude of the Spanish authorities has always tended to be that a tourist really has to work at it to get into trouble in Spain, but once he has made the effort, the Spaniards will oblige and make it extremely unpleasant for him. The four items they object to finding in passenger luggage are arms and/or explosives, drugs, pornography, and Communist propaganda. Other countries may object to two bottles of duty-free brandy but permit *Penthouse* magazine. Not Spain. Other countries have different priorities, but, as any Spaniard will cheerfully admit, Spain is different.

The customs officer at Malaga airport that brilliant Monday afternoon cast a casual eye over the bundle of £1000 in used £20 notes he found in Shannon's travel bag and shrugged. If he was aware that, to get it to Malaga, Shannon must have carried it with him through London airport customs, which is forbidden, he gave no sign. In any case, that was London's problem. He found no copies of *Sexy Girls* or *Soviet News* and waved the traveler on.

Kurt Semmler looked fit and tanned from his three weeks orbiting the Mediterranean looking for ships for sale. He was still rake-thin and chain-smoked nervously, a habit that belied his cold nerve when in action. But the suntan gave him an air of health and set off with startling clarity his close-cropped pale hair and icy blue eyes.

As they rode from the airport into Malaga, Semmler told Shannon he had been in Naples, Genoa, Valletta, Marseilles, Barcelona, and Gibraltar, looking up old contacts in the world of small ships, checking the lists of perfectly respectable shipping brokers and agents for ships for sale, and looking some of them over as they lay at anchor. He had seen a score, but none of them suitable. He had heard of another dozen in ports he had not visited, and had rejected them because he knew from the names of their skippers they must have suspect backgrounds. From all his inquiries he had drawn up a list of seven, and the *Albatross* was the third. Of her qualities, all he would say was that she looked right.

He had reserved Shannon a room in the Malaga Palacio in the name of Brown, and Shannon checked in there first. It was just after four when they strolled through the wide gates of the south face of the Acera de la Marina square and onto the docks.

The *Albatross* was drawn up alongside a quay at the far end of the port. She was as Semmler had described her, and her white paint glistened in the sun and heat. They went aboard, and Semmler introduced Shannon to the owner and captain, George Allen, who showed him over the vessel. Before very long Shannon had come to the conclusion that it was too small for his purposes. There were a master cabin to sleep two, a pair of single cabins, and a saloon where mattresses and sleeping bags could be laid on the floor.

The after hold could at a pinch be converted into a sleeping area for another six men, but with the crew of four and Shannon's five, they would be cramped. He cursed himself for not warning Semmler there were six more men expected who would also have to be fitted in.

Shannon checked the ship's papers, which appeared to be in order. She was registered in Britain, and her Board of Trade papers confirmed it. Shannon spent an hour with Captain Allen, discussing methods of payment, examining invoices and receipts showing the amount of work that had been done on the *Albatross* over recent months, and checking the ship's log. He left with Semmler just before six and strolled back to the hotel, deep in thought.

"What's the matter?" asked Semmler. "She's clean."

"It's not that," said Shannon. "She's too small. She's registered as a private yacht. She doesn't belong to a shipping company. The thing that bugs me is that she might not be accepted by the exporting authorities as a fit vessel to take on board a load of arms."

It was too late back at the hotel to make the calls he wanted to make, so they waited till the following morning. Shortly after nine Shannon called Lloyds of London and asked for a check of the Yacht List. The *Albatross* was there all right, listed as an auxiliary ketch of 74 tons NRT, with her home port given as Milford and port of residence as Hooe, both of them in Britain.

Then what the hell's she doing here? he wondered, and then recalled the method of payment that had been demanded. His second call, to Hamburg, clinched it.

"*Nein,* not a private yacht, please," said Johann Schlinker. "There would be too great a possibility she would not be accepted to carry freight on a commercial basis."

"Okay. When do you need to know the name of the ship?" asked Shannon.

"As soon as possible. By the way, I have received your credit transfer for the articles you ordered in my office. These will now be crated and sent in bond to the address in France you supplied. Secondly, I have the paperwork necessary for the other consignment, and as soon as I receive the balance of the money owing, I will go ahead and place the order."

"When is the latest you need to know the name of the carrying vessel?" Shannon bawled into the phone.

There was a pause while Schlinker thought. "If I receive your check within five days, I can make immediate application for permission to buy. The

618 The Dogs of War

ship's name is needed for the export license. In about fifteen days after that."

"You will have it," said Shannon and replaced the receiver. He turned to Semmler and explained what had happened.

"Sorry, Kurt. It has to be a registered company in the maritime freighting business, and it has to be a licensed freighter, not a private yacht. You'll have to keep on searching. But I want the name within twelve days and no later. I have to provide the man in Hamburg with the ship's name in twenty days or less."

The two men parted that evening at the airport, Shannon to return to London and Semmler to fly to Madrid and thence to Rome and Genoa, his next port of call.

It was late when Shannon reached his flat again. Before turning in, he called BEA and booked a flight on the noon plane to Brussels. Then he called Marc Vlaminck and asked him to be present at the airport to pick him up on arrival, to take him first to Brugge for a visit to the bank and then to the rendezvous with Boucher for the handover of the equipment.

It was the end of Day Twenty-two.

Mr. Harold Roberts was a useful man. Born sixty-two years earlier of a British father and a Swiss mother, he had been brought up in Switzerland after the premature death of his father, and retained dual nationality. After entering banking at an early age, he had spent twenty years in the Zurich head office of one of Switzerland's largest banks before being sent to their London branch as an assistant manager.

That had been just after the war, and over the second twenty-year period of his career he had risen to become the manager of the investment accounts section and later overall manager of the London branch, before retiring at the age of sixty. By then he had decided to take his retirement and his pension in Swiss francs in Britain.

Since retirement he had been available for several delicate tasks on behalf not only of his former employers but also of other Swiss banks. He was engaged on such a task that Wednesday afternoon.

It had taken a formal letter from the Zwingli Bank to the chairman and the secretary of Bormac to achieve the introduction to them of Mr. Roberts, and he had been able to present letters corroborating his engagement as agent of the Zwingli Bank in London.

Two further meetings had taken place between Mr. Roberts and the secretary of the company, the second one attended by the chairman, Major Luton, younger brother of the deceased under manager for Sir Ian Macallister in the Far East.

The extraordinary board meeting had been agreed on, and was called in the City offices of the secretary of Bormac. Apart from the solicitor and Major Luton, one other director had agreed to come to London for the meeting and was present. Although two directors made up a working board, three gave an outright majority. They considered the resolution put by the company secretary and the documents he placed before them. The four unseen shareholders whose interests were being looked after by the Zwingli Bank undoubtedly did now own between them 30 per cent of the stock of the company. They certainly had empowered the Zwingli Bank to act on their behalf, and the bank had incontrovertibly appointed Mr. Roberts to represent it.

The argument that clinched the discussion was the simple one that if a consortium of businessmen had agreed together to buy up such a large amount of Bormac stock, they could be believed when their bank said on their behalf that their intention was to inject fresh capital into the company and rejuvenate it. Such a course of action could not be had for the share price, and all three directors were shareholders. The resolution was proposed, seconded, and passed. Mr. Roberts was taken onto the board as a nominee director representing the interests of the Zwingli Bank. No one bothered to change the company rule stipulating that two directors constituted a quorum with power to pass resolutions, although there were now six and no longer five directors.

Mr. Keith Brown was becoming a fairly regular visitor to Brugge and a valued customer at the Kredietbank. He was received with the usual friendliness by Mr. Goossens, and the latter confirmed that a credit of £20,000 had arrived that morning from Switzerland. Shannon drew $10,000 in cash and a certified bank check for $26,000 in the name of Johann Schlinker of Hamburg.

From the nearby post office he mailed the check to Schlinker by registered mail, accompanied by a letter from himself asking the arms dealer to go ahead with the Spanish purchase.

He and Marc Vlaminck had nearly four hours to kill before the rendezvous with Boucher, and they spent two of them taking a leisurely pot of tea in a café in Brugge before setting off just before dusk.

There is a lonely stretch of road between Brugge and Ghent, which lies 44 kilometers to the east. Because the road twists and winds through flat farmland, most motorists prefer to take the new motorway E5, which also links the two Flemish towns as it runs from Ostend to Brussels. Halfway along the old road the two mercenaries found the abandoned farm that Boucher had described, or rather they found the faded notice board pointing down the track to the farm, which was hidden from view by a clump of trees.

Shannon drove on past the spot and parked, while Marc got out and went to check the farm over. He came back twenty minutes later to confirm the farm was indeed deserted and there were no signs that anyone had been there for quite a time. Nor were there any preparations in progress to provide an unpleasant reception for the two buyers.

"Anyone in the house or outbuildings?" asked Shannon.

"The house is locked front and back. No signs of interference. I checked out the barns and stables. No one there."

Shannon glanced at his watch. It was dark already, and there was still an hour to go. "Get back there and keep a watch from cover," he ordered. "I'll watch the front entrance from here."

When Marc had gone, Shannon checked the truck once again. It was old and rattled, but it was serviceable and the engine had been looked over by a good mechanic. Shannon took the two false number plates from the facia and whipped them onto the real number plates with sticky insulating tape. They could be ripped off easily enough once the truck was well away from the farm. On each side of the truck was a large publicity sticker that gave the vehicle a distinctive air but which could also come off in a hurry. In the back were the six large sacks of potatoes he had ordered Vlaminck to bring with him, and the broad wooden board sawn to make an internal tailgate when slotted into place. Satisfied, he resumed his vigil by the roadside.

The truck he was expecting turned up at five to eight. As it slowed and swung down the track to the farm, Shannon could make out the form of the driver hunched over the wheel and beside him the blob surmounted by a pimple of a head that could only be M. Boucher. The red taillights of the vehicle disappeared down the track and went out of sight behind the trees. Apparently Boucher was playing it straight.

Shannon gave him three minutes; then he too pulled his truck off the hard road and onto the track. When he got to the farmyard, Boucher's truck was standing with sidelights on the center. He cut his engine and climbed down, leaving his own sidelights on, the nose of his truck parked ten feet from the rear of Boucher's.

"Monsieur Boucher," he called into the gloom. He stood in darkness himself, well to one side of the glow of his own lights.

"Monsieur Brown," he heard Boucher wheeze, and the fat man waddled into view. He had evidently brought his "helper" along with him, a big, beefy-looking type whom Shannon assessed as being good at lifting things but slow-moving. Marc, he knew, could move like a ballet dancer when he wished. He saw no problem if it came to trouble.

"You have the money?" asked Boucher as he came close.

Shannon gestured to the driving seat of the truck. "In there. You have the Schmeissers?"

Boucher waved a pudgy hand at his own truck. "In the back."

"I suggest we get both our consignments out onto the ground between the trucks," said Shannon. Boucher turned and said something to his helper in Flemish, which Shannon could not follow. The man moved to the back of his own truck and opened it. Shannon tensed. If there were to be any surprises, they would come when the doors opened. There were none. The dull glimmer from his own truck's lights showed ten flat, square crates and an open-topped carton.

"Your friend is not here?" asked Boucher.

Shannon whistled. Tiny Marc joined them from behind a nearby barn.

There was silence. Shannon cleared his throat. "Let's get the handover done," he said. He reached into the driving compartment and pulled out the fat brown envelope. "Cash, as you asked for. Twenty-dollar bills. Bundles of fifty. Ten bundles."

He stayed close to Boucher as the fat man flicked through each bundle, counting with surprising speed for such plump hands, and stuffing the bundles into his side pockets. When he had reached the last he pulled all the bundles back out and selected a note at random from each. By the light of a pencil flashlight he scanned them closely, the samples, checking for forgeries. There were none. At last he nodded.

"All in order," he said and called something to his helper. The man moved aside from the truck doors. Shannon nodded at Marc, who went to the truck and heaved the first crate onto the grass. From his pocket he produced a knife and prised up the lid. By the light of his own flashlight he checked the ten Schmeissers lying side by side in the crate. One of them he took out and checked for firing-mechanism pin and breech movement. He replaced the machine pistol and smacked the loose lid back down tight.

It took him twenty minutes to check all ten cases. While he did so the big helper brought by M. Boucher stood nearby. Shannon stood at Boucher's elbow, twelve feet away. Finally Marc looked into the open-topped crate. It contained five hundred magazines for the Schmeissers. He tested one sample magazine to ensure it fitted and that the magazines were not for a different model of pistol. Then he turned to Shannon and nodded.

"All in order," he said.

"Would you ask your friend to help mine load them up?" asked Shannon of Boucher. The fat man passed the instruction to his assistant. Before loading, the two beefy Flemings removed the potato sacks, and Shannon heard them discussing something in Flemish. Then Boucher's helper laughed. Within another five minute the ten flat crates and the carton of magazines were loaded in Marc's truck.

When the crates of arms were loaded, Marc placed the board in position as a tailgate which came halfway up the back of the truck. Taking a knife, he slit the first sack, hefted it onto his shoulder, and emptied the contents into the back of the van. The loose potatoes rolled about furiously, finding the cracks between the edges of the crates and the sides of the van and filling them up. With a laugh, the other Belgian started to help him. The quantity of potatoes they had brought more than covered every trace of the ten crates of guns and carton of magazines. Anyone looking in the back would be confronted with a sea of loose potatoes. The sacks were thrown into the hedge.

When they were finished, both men came around from the back of the truck together.

"Okay, let's go," said Marc.

"If you don't mind, we'll leave first," said Shannon to Boucher. "After all, we now have the incriminating evidence."

He waited till Marc had started the engine and turned the truck around so that it was facing the drive back to the road before he left Boucher's side and leaped aboard. Halfway down the track there was a particularly deep pothole, over which the truck had to move with great care and very slowly. At this point Shannon muttered something to Marc, borrowed his knife, and jumped from the truck to hide in the bushes by the side of the lane.

Two minutes later, Boucher's truck came along. It too slowed almost to a halt to negotiate the pothole. Shannon slipped from the bushes as the truck went past, caught up, stooped low, and jammed the knife point into the rear offside tire. He heard it hiss madly as it deflated; then he was back in the bushes. He rejoined Tiny Marc on the main road, where the Belgian had just ripped the stickers from the sides of their vehicle and the false number plates off front and back. Shannon had nothing against Boucher; he just wanted a clear half-hour's start.

By ten-thirty the pair was back in Ostend, the truck loaded with spring potatoes was garaged in the lock-up Vlaminck had hired on Shannon's instruction, and the two were in Marc's bar on Kleinstraat, toasting each other in foaming steins of ale while Anna prepared a meal. It was the first time Shannon had met the well-built woman who was his friend's mistress, and, as is the tradition with mercenaries when meeting each other's womenfolk, he treated her with elaborate courtesy.

Vlaminck had reserved a room for him at a hotel in the town center, but they drank until late, talking about old battles and skirmishes, recalling incidents and people, fights and narrow escapes, alternately laughing at the things that seemed hilarious in retrospect and nodding glumly at the memories that still rankled. The bar stayed open as long as Tiny Marc drank, and the lesser mortals sat around and listened.

It was almost dawn when they got to bed.

Tiny Marc called him at his hotel in the middle of the morning, and they had a late breakfast together. He explained to the Belgian that he wanted the Schmeissers packaged in such a way that they could be smuggled over the Belgian border into France for loading onto the ship in a southern French port.

"We could send them in crates of spring potatoes," suggested Marc.

Shannon shook his head. "Potatoes are in sacks, not crates," he said. "The last thing we need is for a crate to be tipped over in transit or loading, so that the whole lot falls out. I've got a better idea." For half an hour he told Vlaminck what he wanted done with the submachine pistols.

The Belgian nodded. "All right," he said when he understood exactly what was wanted. "I can work mornings in the garage before the bar opens. When do we run them south?"

"About May fifteenth," said Shannon. "We'll use the champagne route. I'll bring Jean-Baptiste up here to help, and we'll change to a French-registered truck at Paris. I want you to have everything packed and ready for shipment by May fifteenth."

Marc accompanied him down to the car ferry to Dover, for the truck would not be used again until it made its last run from Ostend to Paris with its cargo of illegal arms. Shannon was back in London by early evening.

He spent what remained of the day writing a full report for Endean, omitting to mention from whom he had bought the guns or where they were stored. He attached to the report a statement of expenditure and tally of what was left in the Brugge account.

The first morning mail of that Friday brought a large packet from Jean-Baptiste Langarotti. It contained a sheaf of brochures from three European firms that manufactured the rubberized inflatable semi-rigid boats of the kind he wanted. They were variously advertised as being capable of use as sea-rescue launches, power boats, speed craft for towing water-skiers, pleasure boats, launching vessels for sub-aqua diving, runabouts, and fast tenders for yachts and suchlike. No mention was made of the fact that they all had been developed from an original design produced to give marine commandos a fast and maneuverable type of assault craft.

Shannon read each brochure with interest. Of the three firms, one was Italian, one British, and one French. The Italian firm, with six stockists along the Côte d'Azur, seemed to be the best suited for Shannon's purpose and to have the best delivery capability. Of their largest model, an 18-foot launch, there were two available for immediate delivery. One was in Marseilles and the other in Cannes. The brochure from the French manufacturer showed a picture of their largest example, a 16-foot craft, speeding through a blue sea, tail down, nose up.

Langarotti said in his letter there was one of these available at a shop for marine equipment in Nice. He added that all the British-made models needed to be ordered specially and, last, that although there were several more of each type available in brilliant orange color, he was concerning himself only with those in black. He added that each could be powered by any outboard engine above 50 horsepower, and that there were seven different makes of engine available locally and immediately which would suit.

Shannon replied with a long letter instructing Langarotti to buy the two models made by the Italian firm that were available for immediate delivery, and the third of French manufacture. He stressed that on receipt of the letter the Corsican should ring the stockists at once and place a firm order, sending each shopkeeper a 10-per cent deposit by registered mail. He should also buy three engines of the best make, but at separate shops.

He noted the prices of each item and that the total came to just over £4000. This meant he would overrun on his estimated budget of £5000 for ancillary equipment, but he was not worried by that. He would be under budget on the arms and, he hoped, the ship. He told Langarotti he was transferring to the Corsican's account the equivalent of £4500, and with the balance he should buy a serviceable second-hand 20-hundredweight truck, making sure it was licensed and insured.

With this he should drive along the coast and buy his three crated inflatable assault craft and his three outboard engines, delivering them himself to his freight agent in Toulon to be bonded for export. The whole consignment had to be in the warehouse and ready for shipment by May 15. On the morning of that day Langarotti was to rendezvous with Shannon in Paris at the hotel Shannon usually used. He was to bring the truck with him.

The mercenary leader sent another letter that day. It was to the Krediet-bank in Brugge, requiring the transfer of £4500 in French francs to the account of M. Jean-Baptiste Langarotti at the head office of the Société Général bank in Marseilles.

When he got back to his flat, Cat Shannon lay on his bed and stared at the ceiling. He felt tired and drained; the strain of the past thirty days was taking its toll. On the credit side, things seemed to be going according to plan. Alan Baker should be setting up the purchase of the mortars and bazookas from Yugoslavia for pick-up during the early days of June; Schlinker should be in Madrid buying enough 9mm. ammunition to keep the Schmeissers firing for a year. The only reason he had ordered such an excessive amount of rounds was to make the purchase plausible to the Spanish authorities. Clearance for their export should be obtained for mid to late June, provided he could let the German have the name of the carrier by the middle of May and provided the ship and its company were acceptable to the officials in Madrid.

Vlaminck should already have the machine pistols stowed for transporting across Belgium and France to Marseilles, to be loaded by June 1. The assault craft and engines should be loaded at the same time in Toulon, along with the other ancillary gear he had ordered from Schlinker.

Apart from smuggling the Schmeissers, everything was legal and aboveboard. That did not mean things could not still go wrong. Perhaps one of the two governments would make problems by taking overlong or refusing to sell on the basis of the provided documentation.

Then there were the uniforms, which Dupree was presumably still buying in London. They too should be in a warehouse in Toulon by the end of May at the latest.

But the big problem still to be solved was the ship. Semmler had to find the right ship, and he had been searching in vain for almost a month.

Shannon rolled off his bed and telephoned a telegram to Dupree's flat in Bayswater, ordering him to check in. As he put the phone down, it rang again.

"Hi, it's me."

"Hello, Julie," he said.

"Where have you been, Cat?"

"Away. Abroad."

"Are you going to be in town this weekend?" she asked.

"Yes. Should be." In fact there was nothing more he could do and nowhere he could go until Semmler contacted him with news of a ship for sale. He did not even know where the German was by this time.

"Good," said the girl on the phone. "Let's spend the weekend doing things."

It must be the tiredness. He was getting slow on the uptake. "What things?" he asked.

She began to tell him in precise and clinical detail until he interrupted her and told her to come straight around and prove it.

Although she had been bubbling with it a week earlier, in the thrill of seeing her lover again Julie had forgotten the news she had for him. It was not until nearly midnight that she remembered. She bent her head low over the half-asleep mercenary and said, "Oh, by the way, I saw your name the other day."

Shannon grunted.

"On a piece of paper," she insisted. Still he showed no interest, his face buried in the pillow beneath crossed forearms.

"Shall I tell you where?"

His reaction was disappointing. He grunted again.

"In a folder on my daddy's desk."

If she had meant to surprise him, she succeeded. He came off the sheet in one movement and faced her, gripping both her upper arms hard. There was an intensity about his stare that frightened her.

"You're hurting me," she said irrelevantly.

"What folder on your father's desk?"

"A folder." She sniffed, on the verge of tears. "I only wanted to help you."

He relaxed visibly, and his expression softened. "Why did you go looking?" he asked.

"Well, you're always asking about him, and when I saw this folder, I just sort of looked. Then I saw your name."

"Tell me about it from the beginning," he said gently.

When she finished she reached forward and coiled her arms around his neck. "I love you, Mr. Cat," she whispered. "I only did it for that. Was it wrong?"

Shannon thought for a moment. She already knew far too much, and there were only two ways of ensuring her silence. "Do you really love me?" he asked.

"Yes. Really."

"Would you want anything bad to happen to me because of something you did or said?"

She pulled back from him, staring deep into his face. This was much more like the scenes in her schoolgirl dreams. "Never," she said soulfully. "I'd never talk. Whatever they did to me."

Shannon blinked several times in amazement. "Nobody's going to do anything to you," he said. "Just don't tell your father that you know me or went through his papers. You see, he employs me to gather information for him about the prospects of mining in Africa. If he learned we knew each other, he'd fire me. Then I'd have to find another job. There is one that's been offered to me, miles away in Africa. So you see, I'd have to go and leave you if he ever found out about us."

That struck home, hard. She did not want him to go. Privately he knew one day soon he would have to go, but there was no need to tell her yet.

"I won't say anything," she promised.

"A couple of points," said Shannon. "You said you saw the title on the sheets with mineral prices on them. What was the title?"

She furrowed her brow, trying to recall the words. "That stuff they put in fountain pens. They mention it in the ads for the expensive ones."

"Ink?" asked Shannon.

"Platium," she said.

"Platinum," he corrected, his eyes pensive. "Lastly, what was the title on the folder?"

"Oh, I remember that," she said happily. "Like something out of a fairy tale. The Crystal Mountain."

Shannon sighed deeply. "Go and make me some coffee, there's a love."

When he heard her clattering cups in the kitchen he leaned back against the bedhead and stared out over London. "You cunning bastard," he breathed. "But it won't be that cheap, Sir James, not that cheap at all."

Then he laughed into the darkness.

That same Saturday night Benny Lambert was ambling home toward his lodgings after an evening drinking with friends in one of his favorite cafés. He had been buying a lot of rounds for his cronies, using the money, now changed into francs, that Shannon had paid him. It made him feel good to be able to talk of the "big deal" he had just pulled off and buy the admiring bar girls champagne. He had had enough, more than enough, himself, and took no notice of the car that cruised slowly behind him, two hundred yards back. Nor did he think much of it when the car swept up to him as he came abreast of a vacant lot half a mile short of his home.

By the time he took notice and started to protest, the giant figure that had emerged from the car was hustling him across the lot and behind a hoarding that stood ten yards from the road.

His protests were silenced when the figure spun him around and, still holding him by the scruff, slammed a fist into his solar plexus. Benny Lambert sagged and, when the grip on his collar was removed, slumped to the ground. Standing above him, face shadowed in the obscurity behind the hoarding, the figure drew a two-foot iron bar from his belt. Stooping down, the big man grabbed the writhing Lambert by the left thigh and jerked it upward. The iron bar made a dull *whumph* as it crashed down with all the assailant's force onto the exposed kneecap, shattering it instantly. Lambert screamed once, shrilly, like a skewered rat, and fainted. He never felt the second kneecap being broken at all.

Twenty minutes later, Thomard was phoning his employer from the booth in a late-night café a mile away.

At the other end, Roux listened and nodded. "Good," he said. "Now I have some news for you. The hotel where Shannon usually stays. Henri Alain has just informed me they have received a letter from Mr. Keith Brown. It reserves a room for him on the night of the fifteenth. Got it?"

"The fifteenth," Thomard said. "Yes. He will be there then."

"And so will you," said the voice on the phone. "Henri will keep in touch with his contact inside the hotel, and you will remain on standby, not far from the hotel, from noon of that day onward."

"Until when?" asked Thomard.

"Until he comes out, alone," said Roux. "And then you will take him. For five thousand dollars."

Thomard was smiling slightly when he came out of the booth. As he stood at the bar sipping his beer, he could feel the pressure of the gun under his left armpit. It made him smile even more. In a few days it would earn him a tidy sum. He was quite sure of it. It would, he told himself, be simple and straightforward to take a man, even Cat Shannon, who had never even seen him and did not know he was there.

It was in the middle of a Sunday morning that Kurt Semmler phoned. Shannon was lying naked on his back on the bed while Julie puttered around the kitchen making breakfast.

"Mr. Keith Brown?" asked the operator.

"Yes. Speaking."

"I have a personal call for you from a Mr. Semolina in Genoa."

Shannon swung himself off the bed and crouched on the edge, the telephone up to his ear. "Put him on the line," he ordered.

The German's voice was faint, but reception was reasonably clear. "Carlo?"

"Yes. Kurt?"

"I'm in Genoa."

"I know. What news?"

"I have it. This time I am sure. She is just what you wanted. But there is someone else would like to buy her also. We may have to outbid them if we want the boat. But she is good. For us, very good. Can you come out and see her?"

"You're quite sure, Kurt?"

"Yes. Quite sure. Registered freighter, property of a Genoa-based shipping company. Made to order."

Shannon considered. "I'll come tomorrow. What hotel are you staying at?" Semmler told him.

"I'll be there on the first available plane. I don't know when that will be.

Stay at the hotel in the afternoon, and I'll contact you when I get there. Book me a room."

A few minutes later he was booked on the Alitalia flight to Milan at 0905 the following morning, to make a connection from Milan to Genoa and arrive at the port just after one in the afternoon.

He was grinning when Julie returned with the coffee. If the ship was the right one, he could conclude the deal over the next twelve days and be in Paris on the fifteenth for his rendezvous with Langarotti, secure in the knowledge that Semmler would have the ship ready for sea, with a good crew and fully fueled and supplied, by June 1.

"Who was that?" asked the girl.

"A friend."

"Which friend?"

"A business friend."

"What did he want?"

"I have to go and see him."

"When?"

"Tomorrow morning. In Italy."

"How long will you be gone?"

"I don't know. Two weeks. Maybe more."

She pouted over her coffee cup. "So what am I supposed to do all that time?" she asked.

Shannon grinned. "You'll find something. There's a lot of it about."

"You're a shit," she said conversationally. "But if you have to go, I suppose you must. It only leaves us till tomorrow morning, so I, my dear Tomcat, am going to make the best of it."

As his coffee spilled over the pillow, Shannon reflected that the fight for Kimba's palace was going to be a holiday compared with trying to satisfy Sir James Manson's sweet little daughter.

<u>SIXTEEN</u>

The port of Genoa was bathed in late-afternoon sunshine when Cat Shannon and Kurt Semmler paid off their taxi and the German led his employer along the quays to where the motor vessel *Toscana* was moored. The old coaster was dwarfed by the two 3000-ton freighters that lay on either side of her, but that was no problem. To Shannon's eye she was big enough for her purposes.

There was a tiny forepeak and a four-foot drop to the main deck, in the center of which was the large square hatch to the only cargo hold set amidships. Aft was the tiny bridge, and below it evidently were the crew quarters and captain's cabin. She had a short, stubby mast, to which a single loading derrick was attached, rigged almost vertical. Right aft, above the stern, the ship's single lifeboat was slung.

She was rusty, her paint blistered by the sun in many places, flayed off by salt spray in others. Small and old and dowdy, she had the quality Shannon looked for—she was anonymous. There are thousands of such small freighters plying the coastal inshore trade from Haifa to Gibraltar, Tangier to Dakar, Monrovia to Simonstown. They all look much the same, attract no attention, and are seldom suspected of being up to anything beyond carrying small cargoes from port to port.

Semmler took Shannon on board. They found their way aft to where a companionway led down into the darkness of the crew quarters, and Semmler called. Then they went on down. They were met at the bottom by a muscular, hard-faced man in his mid-forties who nodded at Semmler and stared at Shannon.

Semmler shook hands with him and introduced him to Shannon. "Carl Waldenberg, the first mate."

Waldenberg nodded abruptly and shook hands. "You have come to look her over, our old *Toscana?*" he asked.

Shannon was pleased to note he spoke good, if accented, English and looked as if he might be prepared to run a cargo that did not appear on the manifest, if the price was right. He could understand the German seaman's interest in him. Semmler had already briefed him on the background, and he had told the crew his employer would be coming to look the ship over, with a view to buying. For the first mate, the new owner was an interesting person. Apart from anything else, Waldenberg had to be concerned about his own future.

The Yugoslav engineer was ashore somewhere, but they met the deckhand, a teenage Italian boy reading a girlie magazine on his bunk. Without waiting for the Italian captain's return, the first mate showed them both over the *Toscana.*

Shannon was interested in three things: the ability of the boat to accommodate another twelve men somewhere, even if they had to sleep out on deck in the open; the main hold and the possibility of secreting a few crates below the flooring down in the bilges; and the trustworthiness of the engines to get them as far as, say, South Africa.

Waldenberg's eyes narrowed slightly as Shannon asked his questions, but he answered them civilly. He could work out for himself that no fare-paying passengers were coming on board the *Toscana* for the privilege of sleeping wrapped in blankets on the hold-cover under the summer stars; nor was the *Toscana* going to pick up much freight for a run to the other end of Africa. Cargo sent that distance will be shipped in a bigger vessel. The advantage of a small coaster is that she can often load a cargo at very short notice and deliver it two days later a couple of hundred miles away. Big ships spend longer in port while turning around. But on a long run like that from the Mediterranean to South Africa, a bigger ship makes up in extra speed what she spent in port before setting out. For the exporter, the *Toscanas* of the sea have little attraction for trips of more than 500 miles.

After seeing the boat they went topside, and Waldenberg offered them bottles of beer, which they drank in the shade of the canvas awning set up behind the bridge. That was when the negotiations really started. The two Germans rattled away in their own language, the seaman evidently putting the questions and Semmler answering.

At last Waldenberg looked keenly at Shannon, looked back at Semmler, and nodded slowly. "Possibly," he said in English.

Semmler turned to Shannon and explained. "Waldenberg is interested why a man like yourself who evidently does not know the charter cargo business, wants to buy a freighter for general cargo. I said you were a businessman and not a seaman. He feels the general cargo business is too risky for a rich man to want to hazard money on it, unless he has something specific in mind."

Shannon nodded. "Fair enough. Kurt, I want a word with you alone."

They went aft and leaned over the rail while Waldenberg drank his beer.

"How do you reckon this guy?" muttered Shannon.

"He's good," said Semmler without hesitation. "The captain is the owner also, and he is an old man and wants to retire. For this he has to sell the boat and retire on the money. That leaves a place vacant as captain. I think Waldenberg would like it, and I agree with that. He has his master's license, and he knows this boat inside out. He also knows the sea. That leaves the question of whether he would run a cargo with a risk attached. I think he would, if the price is right."

"He suspects something already?" asked Shannon.

"Sure. Actually he thinks you are in the business of running illegal immigrants into Britain. He would not want to get arrested, but if the price is right, I think he would take the risk."

"Surely the first thing is to buy the ship. He can decide whether to stay on later. If he wants to quit, we can find another captain."

Semmler shook his head. "No. For one thing, we would have to tell him enough beforehand for him to know roughly what the job was. If he quit then, it would be a breach of security."

"If he learns what the job is and then quits, he only goes out one way," said Shannon and pointed his forefinger down at the oil-slicked water beneath the stern.

"There's one other point, Cat. It would be an advantage to have him on our side. He knows the ship, and if he decides to stay on he will try to persuade the captain to let us have the *Toscana*, rather than the local shipping company that is sniffing around. His opinion counts with the captain, because the old boy wants the *Toscana* to be in good hands, and he trusts Waldenberg."

Shannon considered the logic. It appealed to him. Time was running short, and he wanted the *Toscana*. The first mate might help him get it and could certainly run it. He could also recruit his own first mate and make sure he was a kindred spirit. Apart from that, there is one useful precept about bribing people: Never try to bribe them all; just buy the man who controls his own subordinates, and let him keep the rest in line. Shannon decided to make an ally of Waldenberg if he could. They strolled back to the awning.

"I'll be straight with you, mister," he told the German. "It's true if I bought the *Toscana* she would not be used for carrying peanuts. It's also true that there would be a slight element of risk as the cargo went on board. There would be no risk as the cargo went ashore, because the ship would be outside territorial waters. I need a good skipper, and Kurt Semmler tells me you're good. So let's get down to basics. If I get the *Toscana* I'll offer you the post of captain. You get a six-month guaranteed salary double your present one, plus a five-thousand-dollar bonus for the first shipment, which is due ten weeks from now."

Waldenberg listened without saying a word. Then he grinned and uncoiled himself from where he sat. He held out his hand. "Mister, you just got yourself a captain."

"Fine," said Shannon. "Except the first thing is to buy the boat."

"No problem," said Waldenberg. "How much would you spend for her?"

"What's she worth?" countered Shannon.

"What the market will take," answered Waldenberg. "The opposition has fixed its own ceiling at twenty-five thousand pounds and not a penny more."

"I'll go to twenty-six," said Shannon. "Will the captain take that?"

"Sure. Do you speak Italian?"

"No."

"Spinetti speaks no English. So let me interpret for you. I'll fix it with the old man. With that price, and me as captain, he'll let you have her. When can you meet him?"

"Tomorrow morning?" asked Shannon.

"Right. Tomorrow at ten, here on board."

They shook hands again, and the two mercenaries left.

Tiny Marc Vlaminck was contentedly at work in the garage he had rented, while the locked truck stood outside the door in the alley. Marc had closed and locked the garage door also, so he would not be disturbed while he worked. It was his second afternoon alone in the garage, and he had almost finished the first part of the job.

Along the rear wall of the garage he had erected a workbench of solid timber balks and equipped it with what he needed, the tools bought with Shannon's £500, as the truck and the rest of the necessary items had also been. Along one wall stood five large drums. They were bright green and bore the trading mark of the Castrol oil company. They were empty, which was the way Marc had bought them, quite cheap, from one of the big shipping firms in the port, and they had once contained heavy lubricating oil, as was plainly marked on each barrel.

From the first in the line, Marc had cut a circular disk out of the bottom, and the barrel stood up-ended, with the gaping hole showing upward and the screw cap at the top of the barrel on the floor. Around the hole was a 1½-inch flange, all that was left of the original base of the drum.

From the truck Marc had taken two crates of Schmeissers, and the twenty machine pistols were almost ready to enter their new hiding place. Each gun had been carefully mummified from end to end in sticky masking tape, and each had five magazines taped to the weapon itself. Following the wrapping process, each machine pistol had been slipped into a stout polyethylene envelope, which Marc had then sucked empty of air and tied securely at the neck with twine. After that, each had gone into a second, outer envelope of polyethylene, which was again tied at the neck. Such wrapping, he reckoned, should keep each weapon dry until it was next brought out into the air.

He took the twenty stubby packages and with two stout webbing straps rolled them all into one large bundle. This he inserted into the hole at the top of the drum and lowered it to the bottom. The drums were the usual 44-gallon, or 200-liter type, and there was enough room in each for twenty Schmeissers and their accompanying magazines, with a little room to spare around the walls.

When the first bundle was secreted, Marc began the process of resealing the barrel. He had had fresh tinplate disks cut at a machine-shop in the port, and the first of these he fitted onto the top of the opened drum. It took half an hour of filing and rasping before the disk finally settled tight and neatly onto the drumhead, running right up to the rim in all places and nicely covering the 1½-inch overlap that remained of the previous end of the drum. Turning on his steam jet, powered by a gas bottle and burner, and taking a stick of soft solder, he began to "sweat" the tinplate to tinplate.

Metal can be welded to metal and, to get the hardest join, it usually is. But a barrel that has once contained oil or ignitable fuel always retains a residue of film on the inner surface of the metal. When heated, as it must be by welding, the film turns to fumes and can easily explode very dangerously. "Sweating" a piece of tinplate onto another piece does not give the same strength of join but can be done with steam heat at a lower temperature. Provided the drums were not laid on their sides and juggled about, which would produce a powerful surge inside, they would hold together against a fair amount of handling.

When he had finished, Marc packed any remaining crevices with solder and, when all was cool, spray-painted the whole area with a color the exact replica of the color of Castrol oil drums the whole world over. After leaving the paint to dry, he eased the drum gently onto its new base, removed the screw cap at the top, took one of several large jerrycans standing ready, and began to pour in the lubricating oil.

The emerald-green liquid, thick, sticky, viscous, flowed into the open aperture and gurgled its way to the bottom of the drum. Slowly it filled up the air spaces between the sides of the drum and the bundle of machine pistols inside, slid noiselessly into every nook and cranny between the individual weapons, and impregnated the webbing and twine. Despite Marc's sucking before twisting the ends of each polyethylene bag tight shut, there were still bubbles of air inside the bags, trapped in magazines, barrels, and breeches. These offset the weight of the metal so that, as the barrel filled, the cumbersome bundle of guns became almost weightless, bobbing in the heavy oil like a body on the tide, and finally sinking slowly below the surface.

The Belgian used two jerrycans, and when the drum was full to the brim he estimated seven-tenths of the interior was taken up by the bundle, three-tenths by oil. He had poured 60 liters into the 200-liter drum. Finally he took a pencil flashlight and scanned the surface of the liquid. It gleamed back at him in the light, slick and green, with hints of gold. Of what lay at the bottom of the drum there was not a sign. He waited another hour before he checked around the base. Nothing had leaked; the new base of the barrel was sealed tight.

There was a jauntiness to him as he rolled open the garage doors and ran the truck back inside. He still had the wood of two flat crates with German markings to destroy, and a disk of now useless tinplate to throw away. The latter would go into the harbor, the former onto a bonfire. He knew now that the system worked and that he could convert one barrel every two days. He would be ready for Shannon by May 15, as promised. It was good to be back at work.

Dr. Ivanov was incensed, not for the first time and doubtless not for the last.

"The bureaucracy," he snapped at his wife across the breakfast table, "the sheer, incompetent, stultifying bureaucracy in this country is bloody unbelievable."

"I'm sure you're right, Mikhail Mikhailovich," his wife said soothingly as she poured two more cups of tea, strong, dark, and bitter as she knew her husband liked it. A placid and contented woman, she wished her volatile scientist husband would be careful with his outbursts, or at least confine them to the house.

"If the capitalist world knew how long it takes to get a couple of nuts and bolts in this country, they'd die laughing."

"Shush, dear," she told him, stirring in the sugar for herself. "You must be patient."

It had been weeks since the director had summoned him to the pine-paneled office in the heart of the vast complex of laboratories and living quarters that made up the institute in the heart of the Siberian New Lands, to inform him that he would be in charge of a survey team being sent to West Africa and that he should take charge of the details himself.

It had meant forsaking a project that interested him deeply, and asking two of his junior colleagues to do the same. He had put in for the necessary equipment for an African climate, sending off his requirements to the half-dozen different supply directorates concerned, answering the petty queries as politely as he could, and waiting, always waiting, for the equipment to arrive and be crated. He knew from having been on a survey team in Ghana what working in the deep bush could entail.

"Give me the snow any time," he had told his team leader at the time. "I'm a cold-weather man."

But he had done it, on orders and on time. His team was ready, his equipment prepared and crated, down to the last water-purification tablet and camp bed. With luck, he had thought, he could be there, do the survey, and be back with his rock samples before the brief and glorious days of the Siberian summer had been eaten by the bitter autumn. The letter in his hand told him it was not to be.

It came from his director personally, and he bore the man no animosity, for he knew he was only passing on instructions from Moscow. Unfortunately the Transport Directorate there had ruled that the confidential nature of the survey forbade the use of public transport, but the Foreign Ministry did not feel able to instruct Aeroflot to put an airliner at the team's disposal. In view of continuing Middle East developments, neither would it be possible to use one of the military's Antonov freighters.

In consequence, ran the instructions from Moscow, it had been felt advisable, in view of the volume of equipment necessary for the survey, and the even greater volumes of samples that would have to be brought back from West Africa, to use maritime transport. It was decided that the team could be best transported by a Soviet freighter heading past the coast of West Africa toward the Far East. On its return, it would simply notify Ambassador Dobrovolsky that it had completed the survey, and, on instructions from him, a freighter heading back toward home would divert to take the three-man team and its crates of samples on board. Notification would be made in due course of the date and port of departure, and vouchers authorizing the use of state transport to the port of embarkation would be provided.

"The whole summer," shouted Ivanov as his wife helped him into his fur-collared coat and fur hat. "I'm going to miss the whole damned summer. And it'll be the rainy season down there."

Cat Shannon and Kurt Semmler were at the ship again the following morning and met Captain Alessandro Spinetti for the first time. He was a gnarled old man with a face like a walnut, a T-shirt over what was still a barrel of a chest, and a white-topped peaked cap aslant on his head.

The negotiating started then and there, before they adjourned to the office of the captain's lawyer, a certain Giulio Ponti, who ran his practice from one of the narrow side streets that lead backward and upward from the brawling, riotous Via Gramschi. To be fair to the signor, he was at least at the better end of the Via Gramschi, and the prostitutes in the bars they passed became progressively more presentable and expensive as they neared the lawyer's office.

Nothing to do with the business of the law moves faster than a snail's pace in Italy—and usually the pace of an arthritic snail.

The terms had been agreed on already. With Carl Waldenberg translating, Captain Spinetti had accepted the package deal Shannon offered: £26,000 cash for the ship, to be paid in any currency or country the captain cared to name; his own first mate to be offered a minimum six-month contract as the new skipper, at a salary double that he had received as first mate; the chance for the other two men, the engineer and the deckhand, to stay on for six months at existing salary, or part company with severance pay of £500 for the deckhand and £1000 for the engineer.

Privately Shannon had already decided to persuade the deckhand to leave but to do all he could to keep the engineer, a surly Serbian who Waldenberg said could coax those engines to hell and back, who said nothing and asked less, and, best of all, whose papers were probably not in order and who therefore needed the job.

For tax reasons, the captain had long ago invested £100 in forming a small private company, Spinetti Maritimo Shipping Company. It had one hundred ordinary shares, of which he held ninety-nine and his lawyer, Signor Ponti, held one plus the position of company secretary. The sale of the MV *Toscana*, the company's only asset, was therefore linked to the sale of the shipping company, Spinetti Maritimo, which suited Shannon perfectly.

What did not suit him so well was that it took five days of meetings with the lawyer before the details were in order. And that was only for the first stage.

It was a week in May, and Day Thirty-one on Shannon's private calendar of a hundred days, before Ponti could start drawing up the contracts. As the deal was going through in Italy, and the *Toscana* was an Italian-registered and -resident vessel, the contract had to comply with Italian law, which is complicated. There were three contracts, that for the sale of Spinetti Maritimo and all her assets to Tyrone Holdings of Luxembourg, that which contracted Tyrone Holdings to offer Carl Waldenberg the job of captain for six months at the agreed salary, and the third guaranteeing the two other crewmen their existing salaries or severance pay. This process took four days, and Ponti's attitude was evidently that he was breaking all speed records, although all participant parties were anxious to complete the sale as soon as possible.

Big Janni Dupree was content with life that bright May morning when he emerged from the camping-goods store, having placed the last of his orders. He had put down a deposit for the required number of haversacks and sleeping bags. Delivery had been promised for the next day, and that same afternoon he intended to pick up two large cardboard boxes full of military-style knapsacks and berets from a warehouse in East London.

Three bulky consignments of miscellaneous equipment were already on their way to Toulon. The first should have arrived, he estimated, and the other two should be in transit. The fourth would be crated and put in the hands of the shipping agent the following afternoon, which left him a week ahead of time. The day before, he had received a letter from Shannon, telling him to vacate his London flatlet and fly to Marseilles on May 15. He was to check into a given hotel in the French port and wait there to be contacted. He liked precise instructions; they left little room for errors, and if anything did go wrong, it could not be his fault. He had bought his ticket and was eager for the remaining week to pass so that he could be off. It was good to be going into action again.

When Signor Ponti had finally drawn up the necessary papers, Cat Shannon dispatched a series of letters from his Genoa hotel. The first was to Johann Schlinker to tell him that the ship that would be engaged to carry the ammunition from Spain would be the MV *Toscana,* owned by Spinetti Maritimo Shipping Company of Genoa. He himself would need from Schlinker details of where the arms shipment was supposed to be heading, so that the captain could draw up the appropriate manifest.

He included in his letter full details of the *Toscana* and had already checked with Lloyds Shipping List, to make sure the *Toscana* was listed there. He told Schlinker he would be contacting him within the next fifteen days.

Another letter went to Alan Baker, so that he could inform the Yugoslav authorities of the name and details of the carrying vessel, so the export license could be granted. Shannon already knew what the manifest would have to read. It would say the vessel was proceeding with her cargo from the Yugoslav port of embarkation to Lome, the capital of Togo.

He wrote a long letter to Mr. Stein as chairman of Tyrone Holdings, instructing him to prepare the papers for a board meeting of the company in his office four days hence, with two resolutions on the agenda. One would be for the company to buy Spinetti Maritimo and all its assets for £26,000 and the other would be to issue a further 26,000 bearer shares of £1 each to Mr. Keith Brown in exchange for a certified check for £26,000.

He dashed off a line to Marc Vlaminck, telling him the pick-up of the cargo in Ostend would have to be delayed until May 20, and another to Langarotti, putting back the Paris rendezvous to May 19.

Last, he sent Simon Endean a letter in London, asking him to meet

Shannon in Luxembourg four days hence and to have at his disposal funds amounting to £26,000 for the purchase of the ship to carry the whole operation to the target area.

The evening of May 13 was soft and cool, and several hundred miles along the same coastline Jean-Baptiste Langarotti was driving his truck westward from Hyères on the last stretch into Toulon. He had the window down and sniffed the smell of conifer and *maquis* coming off the hills to his right. Like Dupree in London, who was preparing that evening to fly to Marseilles, like Vlaminck in Ostend, who was putting the final touches to his fifth and last oil drum of guns, Langarotti was content with life.

He had in the back of the truck the last two outboard engines, bought for cash and equipped with underwater exhaust attachments for silent running. He was on his way back to Toulon to deliver them to the bonded warehouse. Already in the warehouse of Maritime Duphot were three inflatable black dinghies, each crated and unopened, and the third engine. Also there were four large crates of assorted clothing that had arrived over the past two weeks from London in his own name. He too would be ready on time.

It was a pity he had had to move from his hotel. A chance encounter with an old underworld friend as he left the doorway three days ago had forced him to make a quick excuse and move out the following morning. He was now in a new hotel and would have informed Shannon of this, except he did not know where Shannon was. It made no difference. In forty-eight hours, on May 15, he would keep his rendezvous with his chief at the Plaza-Surène hotel in Paris.

The meeting in Luxembourg on May 14 was surprisigly short. Shannon was not present. That morning he had taken delivery from Endean of the £26,000 purchase price for the ship. Just before the board meeting he had met Mr. Stein in his office and handed over to him the documents for the sale of the Spinetti Maritimo Shipping Company and its vessel, the *Toscana*, along with a certified check for £26,000, payable to Tyrone Holdings SA.

Thirty minutes later, Mr. Stein emerged from the board meeting and handed Shannon 26,000 ordinary bearer shares in Tyrone Holdings. He also showed him an envelope which contained the documents concerning the sale of the ship to Tyrone, and Tyrone Holdings' check in the name of Signor Alessandro Spinetti. He sealed the envelope, which was addressed to Signor Giulio Ponti at his Genoa office, and gave it to Shannon. The last document he handed over was a board decision to appoint Herr Kurt Semmler managing director of Spinetti Maritimo Shipping Company.

Two days later, in the Italian lawyer's office, the deal was finished. The check for the purchase of the *Toscana* had been cleared, and Tyrone Holdings legally owned 100 per cent of Spinetti Maritimo. In respect of this, Signor Ponti dispatched by registered mail the 100 ordinary shares in Spinetti Maritimo to the company office of Tyrone in Luxembourg. As a separate matter, Signor Ponti accepted a package from Shannon and locked it in his vault for safekeeping. He took two sample signatures from Shannon, in the name of Keith Brown, to be able later to certify the authenticity of any letter from Shannon regarding disposal of the package. Unknown to Ponti, the package contained the 26,994 controlling shares of Tyrone.

Carl Waldenberg received his captaincy and his six-month contract, and the Serbian engineer was kept on. One month's salary was paid to each man in cash, and the remaining five months' pay for each was placed in escrow in the hands of Signor Ponti.

The Italian deckhand was persuaded without difficulty to take his £500 severance pay, plus a bonus of £100, and left the crew. Semmler was installed as managing director.

Shannon had had a further £5000 transferred from Brugge to his credit in Genoa, and with this he had covered the two salaries of the crewmen who were remaining with the *Toscana*. Before he left Genoa on May 18, he handed the rest over to Semmler and gave him his briefing.

"How about the two replacements for the crew?"

"Waldenberg is seeing to it already," Semmler told him. "He reckons this port is crawling with men available for recruitment. He knows the place inside out. He also knows what we need. Good hard men, the kind who ask no questions and do what they are told, particularly if they know there is a bonus at the end of it. Don't worry, he'll have a good pair before the end of the week."

"Right. Fine. This is what I want. Get the *Toscana* ready for sea. A complete engine overhaul and servicing. Port dues paid up, papers in order with the new captain's name. Manifest prepared for Toulon to pick up general cargo for Morocco. Get her fueled and supplied. Take on enough stores for the crew plus a further dozen men. Extra fresh water, beer, wine, cigarettes. When she's ready, take her to Toulon. You have to be there by June first, at the latest. I'll be there with Marc, Jean-Baptiste, and Janni. Contact me through the shipping agent, Agence Maritime Duphot. They're in the port area. I'll see you then. Good luck."

SEVENTEEN

Jean-Baptiste Langarotti was alive, in part, at least, because of his ability to sense danger before it came looking for him. The first day he reported to the Paris hotel, he just sat quietly at the appointed hour in the residents' lounge and read a magazine. He gave Shannon two hours, but the mercenary leader did not show up.

On the off chance, the Corsican inquired at the reception desk, for although Shannon had said nothing about staying the night, it might be he had arrived early and taken a room. The reception clerk checked the register and informed Langarotti there was no Monsieur Brown from London in the hotel. Langarotti assumed Shannon had been delayed and would make the rendezvous at the same hour on the next day.

So the Corsican was there, sitting in the residents' lounge, at the same hour on May 16. There was still no Shannon, but there was something else. Twice the same staff member of the hotel peeked into the room and vanished as soon as Langarotti looked up. After another two hours, Shannon still not having come, he left the hotel again. As he passed down the street he had a glimpse of a man in the corner doorway showing a bizarre interest in the window into which he was staring with such fixed intensity. The shop window was full of women's corsets. Langarotti had the feeling the man was one component that did not fit into the pattern of that quiet back street on a spring morning.

Over the next twenty-four hours the Corsican began to sniff the wind in the bars of Paris where mercenaries forgather, using his old contacts of the Corsican Union in the Paris underworld. He continued to go to the hotel each morning, and on the fifth morning, that of May 19, Shannon was there.

He had arrived the previous evening by plane from Genoa and Milan, and had stayed the night at the hotel. He seemed in good spirits and told his colleague over coffee in the lounge that he had bought a ship for their operation.

"No problems?" asked Langarotti.

Shannon shook his head. "No problems."

"But here in Paris we have a problem."

Unable to strop his knife in such a public place, the small Corsican sat with his hands idle in his lap. Shannon put down his coffee cup. He knew if Langarotti referred to problems, that meant trouble.

"Such as?" he asked softly.

"There's a contract on you," said Langarotti.

The two men sat in silence for a while, as Shannon considered the news. His friend did not interrupt. He usually answered questions only when they were asked.

"Do you know who placed it?" asked Shannon.

"No. Nor who has taken it up. But it's high, about five thousand dollars."

"Recently?"

"The word is, the contract was placed some time in the last six weeks. It seems uncertain whether the contractor, who must be Paris-based, is the one who placed it, or whether he is acting for someone behind the scenes. The word is, only a good hit-man would take a contract on you, or a stupid one. But someone has taken it. Inquiries are being made about you."

Shannon cursed silently. He had little doubt the Corsican was right. He was too careful a man to go bandying unchecked information like that around. He tried to think back to any incident that might have given rise to the placing of a contract on his head. The trouble was, there were so many possible reasons, some of which he knew he could not even guess.

Methodically he began to go over the possibilities he could envisage. Either the contract stemmed from something to do with the present operation, or it came from a motive that lay further back. He considered the first option first.

Had there been a leak? Had some government agency received a whiff of intelligence that he was mounting a coup in Africa and decided to stop it permanently by snuffing out the operations commander? The thought even crossed his mind that Sir James Manson had learned of his ewe lamb's multiple ravishing—if that was the word for such an experienced Lolita. He rejected all three possibilities. It could be that he had offended someone in the murky world of the black-market arms dealers, who had decided to settle the score the hard way while remaining in the background. But such a move would have been preceded by an argument over a deal, a squabble over money, a stand-up row, or threats. There had been none.

He turned his memory further back, to the wars and the fights gone by. The trouble was, one never knew if one might at some time have angered a big organization without meaning to. Perhaps one of the men he had gunned down had secretly been an agent of the CIA or the KGB. Both organizations bore long grudges and, being peopled by the world's most savagely unprincipled men, insisted on settling scores even when there was no pragmatic motive, but simply for revenge. He was aware the CIA still had an open-ended hit contract out on Bruce Rossiter, who had shot an American in a bar in Léopoldville because the man was staring at him. The American, it had later turned out, was one of the horde of local CIA men, though Rossiter had not known this. His ignorance did not help him. The contract still went out, and Rossiter was still running.

The KGB was as bad. It sent assassins across the world to liquidate fugitives, foreign agents who had hurt the KGB and had been blown for all to see, and were thus unprotectable by their own former employers; and the Russians needed no practical motive, like the information in the man's head that he had not yet spilled. They did it just for revenge.

That left the French SDECE and the British SIS. The French could have taken him a hundred times over the past two years and made sure it happened in the jungles of Africa. Moreover, they would not place a deal with a Paris contractor and risk a leak. They had their own men, good ones, on the staff. The British were even less likely. Legalistic to the end, they would have to get permission from almost Cabinet level for a hit and used the method only in the direst emergency, to prevent a vital leak, to create a nasty example to encourage others to have confidence in the Service, or occasionally to even a score where one of their own men had been knowingly knocked over by an identifiable killer. Shannon was sure he had never hit a white-carded Britisher, and that left the motive of preventing an embarrassment. The Russians and French would kill for that reason, but not the British. They had left Stephen Ward alive to stand trial and nearly ruin the Macmillan government; they had left Philby alive after he was blown, and Blake too; in France or Russia both traitors would have entered the road-accident statistics.

That left a private firm. The Corsican Union? No, Langarotti could not have stuck by him if it had been the Union. So far as he knew, he had never upset the Mafia in Italy or the Syndicate in America. That took the matter back to a private individual with a private grudge. If it was not a government agency and not a big private firm, it had to be an individual. But who, for God's sake?

Langarotti was still watching him, waiting for his reaction. Shannon kept his face still, his air bored.

"Do they know I'm here in Paris?"

"I think so. I believe they knew about this hotel. You always stay here. It's a mistake. I was here four days ago, as you had said—"

"Didn't you get my letter, putting the meeting back to today?"

"No. I had to move from my Marseilles hotel a week ago."

"Oh. Go on."

"There was someone watching the hotel the second time I came. I had already asked for you by the name of Brown. So I think the leak came from inside this hotel. The man was watching yesterday and today."

"So I change hotels," said Shannon.

"You might shake him. You might not. Someone knows the name of Keith Brown. They could find you elsewhere. How much do you have to be in Paris over the next few weeks?"

"Quite a bit," admitted Shannon. "I have to go through several times, and we have to bring Marc's stuff down from Belgium to Toulon through Paris in two days."

Langarotti shrugged. "They might not find you. We don't know how good they are, or how many of them. Or who. But they might find you a second time. Then there would be problems, perhaps with the police."

"I can't afford that. Not now. Not with Marc's consignment sitting in the truck," said Shannon.

He was a reasonable man and would much prefer to have negotiated with the one who had placed the contract on him. But whoever it was had chosen to do it the other way.

Shannon would still have tried to talk to the man, but first he had to identify him. There was only one man who could do that for him: the man who had taken the contract to kill him. He put this to the Corsican, who nodded somberly.

"Yes, *mon ami*, I think you're right. We have to take the hit-man. But first he must be lured out."

"Will you help me, Jean-Baptiste?"

"Of course," said Langarotti. "Whoever it is, it is not the Union. It is not my people, so I am your man."

They spent close to an hour with a street map of Paris on the table in front of them. Then Langarotti left.

During the day he parked his Marseilles-registered truck at an agreed prearranged spot. In the late afternoon Shannon went to the reception desk and asked the way to a well-known restaurant a mile away. He was within earshot of the hotel clerk who had been described to him by Langarotti. The chief receptionist told him where the restaurant was.

"Within walking distance?" asked Shannon.

"But certainly, m'sieur. After fifteen minutes, maybe twenty."

Shannon thanked him and used the desk telephone to make a reservation in the name of Brown for ten o'clock that night. He did not leave the hotel all day.

At nine-forty exactly, carrying his overnight bag in one hand and a light raincoat over the other arm, he left the hotel and turned up the street in the direction for the restaurant. The route he took was not direct. It led down two streets even smaller than the one in which the hotel was situated. As he walked, he left the other pedestrians behind and entered streets in the first arrondissement which were dimly lit and where no passers-by came his way. He dawdled, passing the time staring into lighted shop windows, killing time until the hour of his restaurant reservation was long past. He never looked back. Sometimes, in the quiet, he thought he could hear the soft slap of a moccasin somewhere in the dim-lit streets behind him. Whoever was there, it was not Langarotti. The Corsican could move without disturbing the dust.

It was past eleven when he reached the dark, black alley he had been told was there. It led to his left and had no lights in it at all. The far end was blocked by a row of bollards, making it into a cul-de-sac. On each side the walls were blank and tall. Any light that might have entered the alley from the other end was muted by the bulk of the French truck that stood parked there, empty but with its rear doors open. Shannon walked toward the truck's gaping back and, when he reached it, turned.

Like most fighting men, he always preferred to face danger rather than knowing it was somewhere behind. He knew from past experience that, even when moving backward, it is safer always to face the danger source. At least, then, you can watch it. Moving up the alley with his back to the entrance, he had felt the hairs on his neck prickling. If the psychology was wrong, he could be very dead. But the psychology had been right. Keeping to empty streets, the man behind him had stayed well back, hoping for just such an opportunity as now presented itself.

Shannon tossed his bag and raincoat to the ground and stared at the hulking shadow that blocked the vertical streak of lamplight from the end of the alley. He waited patiently. He hoped there would be no sound, not in the center of Paris. The shadow paused, assessed the situation, and evidently checked Shannon for a gun. But the sight of the open truck reassured the hit-man. He assumed Shannon had simply parked it there for discretion's sake and had been all this time returning to it.

The shadow in the alley moved softly forward. Shannon could make out the right arm, out of the raincoat pocket now, held forward, holding something. The face was in shadow, the whole man was a silhouette, but he was big. His form stood dead center in the cobbled cul-de-sac, stopped now, raising his gun. He paused for several seconds as he aimed, then slowly lowered it again, straight-armed, down to his side. It was almost as if he had changed his mind.

Still staring at Shannon from the shadow-black face, the man slowly leaned forward and went onto his knees. Some shots do this to steady themselves. The gunman cleared his throat, leaned forward again, and placed both his hands, knuckles down, on the cobbles in front of him. The metal of the Colt .45 clattered on the stones. Slowly, like a Moslem facing Mecca at the hour of prayer, the gunman bowed his head, staring for the first time in twenty seconds not at Shannon but at the cobbles. There was a light splashing sound, as of a liquid running fast onto cobbles, and finally the man's arms and thighs gave out. He slumped forward into the puddle of his own aortic blood and went to sleep, quite gently, like a child.

Shannon was still standing against the doors of the truck. With the man down, a shaft of lamplight came from the lit end of the alley. It glistened on the polished black sheen of the four-inch bone knife-handle that protruded upward from the mackintoshed back of the man on the pavement, slightly left of center, between the fourth and fifth ribs.

The Cat looked up. There was another figure against the lamplight, small, spare, motionless, still standing fifteen yards from the body at the point where it had made its throw. Shannon hissed, and Langarotti padded noiselessly down the cobbles.

"I thought you'd left it too late," said Shannon.

"*Non.* Never too late. He could not have squeezed the trigger of that Colt at any time since you emerged from the hotel."

The rear of the truck was already laid with a large sheet of tough industrial plastic over a canvas tarpaulin. The tarpaulin had loopholes all around the edge for easy lashing into a bundle, and plenty of cord and bricks were stacked at the far end. Each taking an arm and a leg, the two men swung the body up and inward. Langarotti climbed in to retrieve his knife, while Shannon shut the doors. He heard them securely locked from the inside.

Langarotti climbed into the front seat and started up. Slowly he backed out, down the alley and into the street. As he swung the truck around before driving off, Shannon approached the driver's window.

"Have you had a good look at him?"

"Sure."

"You know him?"

"Yes. Name of Thomard, Raymond. In the Congo once for a short period, more of a city type. Professional hit-man. But not quality. Not the sort one of the big contractors would use. More likely to work for his own boss."

"Who's that?" asked Shannon.

"Roux," said Langarotti. "Charles Roux."

Shannon swore quietly and viciously. "That bastard, that stupid, ignorant, incompetent fool. He could have fouled up a whole operation just because he wasn't invited to come in on it."

He fell silent and thought for a while. Roux had to be discouraged, but in a way that would keep him out of the Zangaro affair once and for all.

"Hurry up," said the Corsican, the engine still running. "I want to get this customer put to bed before anyone comes along."

Shannon made up his mind and spoke urgently and rapidly for several seconds.

Langarotti nodded. "All right. Actually, I like it. It should fix that bugger for a long time. But it will cost extra. Five thousand francs."

"Done," said Shannon. "Get moving, and meet me outside the Porte de la Chapelle métro station in three hours."

They met Marc Vlaminck for lunch in the small South Belgian town of Dinant by agreement. Shannon had called him the previous day and given him the instructions and the rendezvous. Tiny Marc had kissed Anna good-by that morning, and she had given him his lovingly packed suitcase of clothes and his snack box with half a loaf, some butter, and a hunk of cheese for midmorning break. As usual, she had told him to take care of himself.

He had driven the truck, carrying in the back five 200-liter drums of engine oil by Castrol, across Belgium without being stopped. There was no reason why he should be. His license was in order, as were the permit for the truck and the insurance.

As the three men sat over lunch at a main-street café, Shannon asked the Belgian, "When do we go over?"

"Tomorrow morning, just before sun-up. It's the quietest time. Did you two sleep last night?"

"Nope."

"You'd better get some rest," said Marc. "I'll watch over both trucks. You can have till midnight."

Charles Roux was another one who was tired that day. All the previous evening, since he had received the telephone call from Henri Alain about Shannon walking to his restaurant meal, he had waited for news. There had been none by midnight, when there should have been a call from Thomard to say it was all over. There had been none by three in the morning and none by sunrise.

Roux was unshaven and puzzled. He knew Thomard was no match for Shannon on equal terms, but he was sure the Irishman would be taken in the back as he walked through one of the quieter streets on his way to the evening meal.

At midmorning, as Langarotti and Shannon in their empty truck were passing without trouble into Belgium north of Valenciennes, Roux finally slipped on a pair of trousers and a shirt and took the elevator five floors down to the lobby to check his mailbox.

There did not seem to be anything wrong with the lock of his mailbox, a container some twelve inches tall, nine wide, and nine deep, screwed to the wall of the lobby along with a score more for the other tenants. There was no indication that it had been opened, but of course a clever burglar would have picked the lock.

Roux used his personal key to unlock the door and swung it open.

He stood for about ten seconds without moving. Nothing changed about him except the normal ruddy color of his face, which slid into a chalky gray. Still staring, mesmerized, he began to mutter, "*Mon Dieu, O mon Dieu . . .*" over and over again like an incantation. His stomach turned over; he felt as he had at the moment in the Congo when he had heard the Congolese soldiers questioning his identity as he lay inside the bandages on a stretcher while John Peters smuggled him out from certain death. He felt he wanted to urinate, run, but could only sweat with fear. With an air of almost sleepy sadness, eyes half closed, lips gummed together, the head of Raymond Thomard gazed back at him from inside the mailbox.

Roux was not squeamish, but he was no lionheart either. He closed the box, went back to his flat, and started on the brandy bottle, for medicinal purposes only. He needed a lot of medicine.

Alan Baker emerged from the office of the Yugoslav state arms company into the bright sunshine of Belgrade, feeling well pleased with the way things were going. On receiving Shannon's down payment of $7200 and the End User Certificate, he had gone to a licensed arms dealer for whom he had occasionally done work in the past on a subcontractual level. As in the case of Schlinker, the man had felt the amount of weaponry and money involved in the proposed deal to be derisory, but he had yielded to Baker's argument that if the buyers were satisfied with the first consignment they might well return for more, a lot more.

So he had given Baker his flat to fly to Belgrade and make application for the purchase, using the certificate from Togo, duly filled out with the appropriate names, and with a letter of authority from the dealer appointing Baker his representative.

It meant Baker would lose a part of his cut, but it was the only way he could be received in Belgrade, and for such a small deal he had in any case allowed a mark-up of 100 per cent on the buying price of the arms.

His five days of talks with Mr. Pavlovič had been fruitful and had included a visit to the state warehouse, in which he had selected the two mortar tubes and two bazookas. The ammunition for both was standard and supplied in crates of twenty bazooka rockets and ten mortar bombs.

The Yugoslavs had accepted the Togolese End User Certificate without demur, and although Baker, the licensed dealer, and probably Mr. Pavlovič, must be aware the certificate was just a piece of paper, the air was maintained that the government of Togo was eagerly awaiting the chance to buy Yugoslavia's weaponry for testing. Mr. Pavlovič had also required full payment in advance, and Baker had had to pay over what remained of the $7200 Shannon had given him, after his travel costs, plus $1000 of his own. He was confident Shannon's balance of another $7200 would reimburse him and, even after the licensed dealer had taken his cut, leave $4000 for Baker's pocket.

His morning's talks had confirmed that the goods would be granted an export license and sent by army lorries to a bonded warehouse at the port of Ploce in the northwest, close to the holiday resorts of Dubrovnik and Split.

It was here that the *Toscana* should dock to take the shipment aboard, any time after June 10. With a light heart, Baker took the next flight for Munich and Hamburg.

Johann Schlinker was in Madrid that morning, May 20. He had Telexed the full details of the deal in 9mm. ammunition that he wanted to put through to his Madrid partner, a Spanish national, a full month earlier, and had later flown to the Spanish capital himself with his Iraqi End User Certificate, as soon as he had received Shannon's $26,000 in full payment.

The Spanish formalities were more complicated than those Alan Baker had discovered in Belgrade. Two applications were necessary, the first to buy the hardware, the second to export it. The application to buy had been made three weeks earlier and over the past twenty days had been vetted by the three departments of state in Madrid who concern themselves with such matters. First the Finance Ministry had been needed to confirm that the full purchase price of $18,000 had been received into the appropriate bank in hard currency. A few years earlier, only United States dollars had been acceptable, but more recently Madrid was more than happy to take German marks.

The second department was the Foreign Ministry. Its job had been to confirm that the buyer country was not a state to which Spain was opposed. There was no problem with Iraq, since the great bulk of Spanish arms exports habitually go to the Arabs, with whom Spain has always maintained close and friendly relations. The Foreign Ministry had no hesitation in confirming its approval of Iraq as a recipient of Spanish 9mm. ball ammunition.

Last, the Defense Ministry had been required to confirm that nothing in the proposed sale was on the secret list or among the categories of arms not for export. With simple small-arms ammunition, this too had been no problem.

Although there had been no sticky problems with such a consignment, it had taken eighteen days for the papers to pass through the three departments, accumulating more paperwork as they went, until the final dossier emerged with the stamp of approval. At this point the crates of ammunition were taken from the CETME factory and stored in a warehouse of the Spanish army on the outskirts of Madrid. From this point the Army Ministry took over, and notably the head of its arms-export section, Colonel Antonio Salazar.

Schlinker had come to Madrid to present personally the application for an export license. He had been in possession of the full details of the MV *Toscana* on his arrival, and the seven-page questionnaire had been filled out and presented. Back in his room in the Hotel Mindanao, the German expected no problems here either. The *Toscana* was a clean ship, small but belonging to a registered shipping company, Spinetti Maritimo, as Lloyds Shipping List confirmed. According to the application form, she would wish to berth in Valencia between June 16 and June 20, take the shipment on board, and proceed straight to Latakia on the coast of Syria, where the consignment would be handed over to the Iraqis for trucking to Baghdad. The export license should take no longer than another two weeks, and then application would be made for a movement order, permitting the crates to be taken from the army warehouse and detailing an army officer to mount escort with ten soldiers as far as Valencia quayside. The latter precaution, brought into force over the previous three years, was to prevent any risk of hijacking by the Basque terrorists. The last thing the government of El Caudillo wanted was to see Madrid's bullets being used against the Guardia Civil.

As Schlinker prepared to leave for Hamburg, he reflected that his Madrid partner was perfectly capable of ensuring that the liaison with the Army Ministry remained at a cordial level and that the crates would be waiting in Valencia for the arrival of the *Toscana* on time.

In London a third and seemingly unconnected meeting took place. Over the past three weeks Mr. Harold Roberts, the nominee director of Bormac Trading Company, controlling 30 per cent of the company stock, had been cultivating the chairman, Major Luton. He had several times taken him to lunch and once visited him at his Guildford home. They had become quite friendly.

Throughout their talks, Roberts had made it clear that if the company were to get off the ground and go back into business, whether in rubber or in some other area of trading, a large injection of fresh capital would be needed. Major Luton could well see that. When the time was ripe, Mr. Roberts proposed to the chairman that the company should make a new one-for-two issue of shares—a total, therefore, of half a million of new stock.

At first the major was aghast at the boldness of the move, but Mr. Roberts assured him that the bank whose nominee he was would find the necessary fresh finance. Mr. Roberts added that in the event that any of the new shares were not taken up by existing shareholders or new shareholders, the Zwingli

Bank would take up the rest at full value on behalf of its customers.

The clinching argument was that when news of the fresh share issue broke on the market, the price of Bormac ordinaries would be bound to rise, perhaps by as much again as their present value, which then stood at one shilling and threepence. Major Luton thought of his own hundred thousand shares and agreed. As is so often the case when a man has once weakened, he then went along with Mr. Robert's proposal without further demur.

The new director pointed out that the pair of them could form a quorum and hold a directors' meeting able to pass a resolution binding on the company. At the major's insistence, a letter was still sent to the other four directors, simply stating that it was intended to hold a board meeting to discuss company business, including the possibility of making a share issue.

In the event, only the company secretary, the City solicitor, turned up. The resolution was passed and the announcement of the new share issue posted. There was no need for a meeting of shareholders, as in the long-distant past an increase in capital had been authorized but never carried out.

Existing shareholders were given first choice to buy the stock and were sent allotment letters for the appropriate number of new shares. They were also given the right to apply for any shares not subscribed by those to whom they were originally offered.

Within a week, papers and checks signed by Messrs. Adams, Ball, Carter, and Davies, forwarded by the Zwingli Bank, were in the company secretary's hands. Each man opted to buy fifty thousand of the new shares, including those originally allotted to him because of his existent holdings.

The shares had to be issued at par, which was four shillings each, and, with the existing shares standing at less than a third of that price, it was an unattractive offer. Two City speculators noticed the press announcement and tried to offer to underwrite the issue, assuming there had to be something in the wind. They would have succeeded but for Mr. Roberts. His own bid on behalf of the Zwingli Bank was already in, wishing to buy any shares remaining at the closing of the offer that had not been bought by existing shareholders or Bormac.

Some idiot in Wales agreed to buy a thousand shares, even at the too high price, and another three thousand were bought by eighteen other shareholders scattered around the country, who apparently could not do basic arithmetic or were clairvoyant. Mr. Roberts, as a nominee director, was not in a position to buy for himself, since he owned no stock. But at three in the afternoon of May 20, the closing date of the offer, he subscribed for all the 296,000 remaining unsold shares in the name of the Zwingli Bank, which in turn was buying these on behalf of two of its customers. Their names happened to be Edwards and Frost. Again the bank used designated accounts of its nominee company.

In no case were the rules of the Companies Act regarding disclosure broken. Messrs. Adams, Ball, Carter, and Davies each owned 75,000 of the shares from their first purchase and 50,000 from their second. But as the number of shares now in circulaton had risen from 1 million to 1.5 million, each man held less than 10 per cent and was able to remain anonymous. Messrs. Edwards and Frost each owned 148,000 shares, just under the 10-per-cent limit.

What did not appear in public, or even to the directors, was that Sir James

Manson owned 796,000 shares in Bormac, an overwhelming majority. He controlled, through Martin Thorpe, the six nonexistent shareholders who had bought so heavily. They could, through Martin Thorpe, direct the Zwingli Bank in its dealings with the company, and the bank controlled his contracted servant. Mr. Roberts. Using their proxies, the six invisible men behind the Zwingli Bank, operating through Harold Roberts, could make the company do anything they wished.

It had cost Sir James Manson £60,000 to buy the original shares, and £100,000 to buy up the bulk of the new issue of half a million. But when the shares reached the predicted £100 each, which he was sure they would do after the chance "discovery" of the Crystal Mountain in the heart of Bormac's Zangaran franchise, he stood to make £80 million.

Mr. Roberts was a contented man when he left the Bormac offices after hearing how many shares his six Swiss-based stockholders had been allotted. He knew that when he placed the share certificates in the hands of Dr. Martin Steinhofer, there would be a handsome bonus for him. Although he was not a poor man, he was relieved to know his retirement in comfort was secured.

In Dinant, Shannon and Langarotti woke from their slumbers shortly after dark had fallen, to find Marc shaking them. Both were stretched out in the back of the empty French truck.

"Time to be going," said the Belgian.

Shannon looked at his watch. "I thought you said before sunrise," he grumbled.

"That's when we go over," said Marc. "We ought to get these trucks out of town before they become too noticeable. We can park by the roadside for the rest of the night."

They did park, but none of the men slept any more. Instead they smoked and played cards with the pack Vlaminck kept in the glove compartment of his truck. Sitting under the trees by the Belgian roadside in the darkness, waiting for the dawn, feeling the night air on their faces, each could almost think he was back in the African bush again about to go into action, except for the flashing lights through the trees where cars headed south on the road to France.

As they sat through the wee small hours, tired of playing cards, too tensed to sleep, each fell back into his old habits. Tiny Marc munched the remnants of the bread and cheese his girl, Anna, had made for him. Langarotti stropped his knife blade a little sharper. Shannon gazed at the stars and whistled softly.

EIGHTEEN

There is no great technical difficulty in running an illegal consignment across the Belgian-French border in either direction, and that includes a quantity of black-market arms.

Between the seat at La Panne and the junction with Luxembourg near

Longwy, this border sprawls for miles, and most of it in the southeast corner is through heavily wooded hunting country. Here the border is crossed by scores of side roads and tracks through the forest, and by no means all of them are manned.

Both governments seek to establish some kind of control, using what they call *douanes volantes,* or flying customs. These are units of customs men who pick a track or side road at random and set up a border post. At the existing customs points, one may reasonably assume that one vehicle in ten is likely to be stopped and examined. On the unmanned roads, if the flying customs on either side happen to be sitting there for the day, every vehicle going through gets a check. One can take one's choice.

The third alternative is to pick a road where there is definitely no customs post set up, and drive straight through. This method of running cargoes through the frontier is particularly favored by the smugglers of French champagne, who see no reason why this drink connected with mirth and gaiety should receive the attentions of the very unhumorous Belgian import duty. As a bar-owner, Marc Vlaminck knew about this route. It is called the champagne run.

Running south from Namur, the old fortress town of Belgium, following the line of the river Meuse, one comes first to Dinant, and from here the road runs almost due south over the border to the French town called Givet. Along this road there is a finger of French territory that juts upward into Belgium's underbelly, and this corridor of France is surrounded on three sides by Belgian tracks and paths. The main road from Dinant to Givet has a customs post on it—in fact, one Belgian post and one French, set four hundred yards apart but in sight of each other.

Shortly before dawn, Marc got out his maps and briefed Shannon and Jean-Baptiste on what he needed to be sure of getting across the border unspotted. When both men understood exactly what was required, they set off in convoy, the Belgian truck in front, driven by Marc, the other two in the French truck, two hundred yards behind.

South from Dinant the road is fairly well built up, with a series of villages whose outskirts almost connect with each other. In the predawn darkness these hamlets were quiet and obscure. At kilometer six, south of Dinant, there is a side road leading to the right, and this Marc took. It was the last they saw of the river Meuse. For four and a half kilometers they ran through undulating country of even-sized, rounded hills, thickly wooded and covered in the lush leafage of late May. The run was parallel to the border and into the heart of hunting country. Without warning, Vlaminck swung his truck off to the left, heading again toward the frontier, and after three to four hundred yards he pulled to the side. He climbed down and walked back to the French truck.

"Make it snappy," he said. "I don't want to wait here for long. It's too obvious where I'm heading for, with Ostend number plates." He pointed down the road.

"The border is down there at one and a half kilometers exactly. I'll give you twenty minutes while I pretend to change a tire. Then I get back to Dinant and we meet at the café."

The Corsican nodded and let in the clutch. The drill is, if either the Belgian or French customs men have set up a flying barricade, the first vehicle stops and allows itself to be searched. Being clean, it then proceeds south to rejoin the main road, heads into Givet, turns north, and returns via the fixed customs post to Dinant. If either customs post is in operation, it cannot return back up the road within twenty minutes.

At kilometer one and a half, Shannon and Langarotti saw the Belgian post. At each side of the road a vertical steel upright had been placed, embedded in concrete. Beside the right-hand one was a small glass-and-wood booth, where the customs men could shelter while drivers passed their papers through the window. If it was occupied, there would be a red-and-white striped pole, supported by both uprights, blocking the road. There was none.

Langarotti cruised slowly past, while Shannon scanned the booth. Not a sign. The French side was trickier. For half a kilometer the road wound between the flanks of the hills, lost to sight from the Belgian posts. Then came the French border. No posts, no booth. Just a parking area on the left, where the French customs car always parks. There was nothing there. They had been gone five minutes. Shannon gestured to the Corsican to go around two more corners, but there was nothing in sight. A glimmer of light showed in the east over the trees.

"Turn her round," snapped Shannon. "*Allez.*"

Langarotti pulled the truck into a tight turn, almost made it, backed up, and was off toward Belgium like a cork from a bottle of the very best champagne. From then on, time was precious. They shot past the French parking space, through the Belgian posts, and less than a mile later saw the bulk of Marc's waiting truck. Langarotti flashed his lights, two short, one long, and Marc gunned his engine into life. A second later he was past them, racing through to France.

Jean-Baptiste turned around more leisurely and followed. If Marc drove fast, he could be through the danger area within four minutes, even heavily laden with a ton of cargo. If any customs men hove in sight during the vital five minutes, it was bad luck. Marc would try to bluff it out, say he had got lost, hope the oil barrels stood up to a thorough checking.

There were no officials there, even on the second run. South of the French parking space is a five-kilometer stretch with no turnings. Even here the French *gendarmerie* sometimes patrols, but there was nothing that morning. Langarotti caught up with the Belgian truck and followed it at six hundred feet. After three miles Marc turned off to the right at another parking area, and for three more miles wended his way through more back roads until he finally emerged onto a sizable main road. There was a signpost by the roadside. Shannon saw Marc Vlaminck wave his arm out of the window and point to it. The sign said GIVET in the direction from which they had come, and pointed the way they were going with the word REIMS. A muted cheer came wafting back from the truck in front.

They did the change-over on a hard concrete parking lot next to a truckers' café just south of Soissons. The two trucks, open-doored, were backed up tight against each other, and Marc eased the five barrels from the Belgian truck to the French one. It would have taken Shannon and Langarotti together all their strength, the more so as the loaded truck was squashed on its springs, so the floors of the two vehicles were not at the same height. There was a 6-inch step-up to get into the empty truck. Marc managed it on his own, gripping each barrel at the top in huge hands and swinging it in arcs while balancing it on its lower rim.

Jean-Baptiste went to the café and returned with a breakfast of long, crisp baguette loaves, cheese, fruit, and coffee. Shannon had no knife, so they all used Marc's. Langarotti would never use his knife for eating. He had his finer feelings. It would dishonor the knife to use on orange peel.

Just after ten they set off agin. The drill was different. The Belgian truck, being old and slow, was soon driven into a gravel pit and abandoned, the license plates and windshield sticker being taken off and thrown into a stream. The truck had originally been of French make anyway. After that, the three proceeded together. Langarotti drove. It was legally his truck. He was licensed. If stopped, he would say he was driving five barrels of lubricating oil south to his friend who owned a farm and three tractors outside Toulon. The other two were hitchhikers he had picked up.

They left the A1 autoroute, took the peripheral road around Paris, and picked up the A6 south to Lyon, Avignon, Aix, and Toulon.

Just south of Paris they saw the sign to the right pointing to Orly Airport. Shannon climbed out, and they shook hands.

"You know what to do?" he asked.

They both nodded.

"Keep her under cover and safe till you get to Toulon."

"Don't worry, no one will find this little baby when I've hidden her," said Langarotti.

"The *Toscana* is due in by June first at the latest, maybe before. I'll be with you before then. You know the rendezvous? Then good luck."

He hefted his bag and walked away as the truck headed south. At the nearby garage he used the telephone, called a cab from the airport, and was driven there an hour later. Paying cash, he bought his single ticket to London and was home in St. John's Wood by sundown. Of his hundred days, he had used up forty-six.

Although he sent Endean a telegram on his arrival home, it was a Sunday, and twenty-four hours went by before Endean called him at the flat. They agreed to meet on Tuesday morning.

It took him an hour to explain to Endean all that had happened since they last met. He also explained that he had used up all the money both in the cash sum he had retained in London and in the Belgian account.

"What's the next stage?" asked Endean.

"I have to return to France within five days at the latest and supervise the loading of the first section of the cargo onto the *Toscana*," said Shannon. "Everything about the shipment is legal except what's in those oil barrels. The four separate crates of assorted uniforms and webbing should pass without any problem on board, even if examined by customs. The same goes for the nonmilitary stuff bought in Hamburg. Everything in that section is the sort of stuff a ship might normally take on as ship's stores: distress flares, night glasses, and so on.

"The inflatable dinghies and outboard engines are for shipping to Morocco—at least, that's what the manifest will say. Again, it's perfectly legal. The five oil drums have to go aboard as ship's stores. The quantity is rather excessive, but there shouldn't be any problem despite that."

"And if there is?" asked Endean. "If Toulon customs men examine those barrels too closely?"

"We're busted," said Shannon simply. "The ship impounded, unless the captain can show he hasn't a clue what was going on. The exporter arrested. The operation wrecked."

"Bloody expensively," observed Endean.

"What do you expect? The guns have got to go on board somehow. The oil barrels are about the best possible way. There was always that risk involved."

"You could have bought the submachine guns legally, through Spain," said Endean.

"I could," Shannon conceded, "but there would then have been a good chance the order would have been refused. The guns and the ammo together make a matching pair. That would have looked like a special order to outfit one company of men—in other words, a small operation. Madrid might have turned it down on those grounds, or examined the End User Certificate too thoroughly. I could have ordered the guns from Spain and bought the ammunition on the black. Then I would have had to smuggle the ammo on board, and it would have been a much bigger consignment. Either way, there has to be an element of smuggling, and hence of risk. So if it all goes wrong, it'll be me and my men who go down, not you. You're protected by a series of cut-outs."

"I still don't like it," snapped Endean.

"What's the matter?" Shannon mocked. "Losing your nerve?'

"No."

"So cool it. All you have to lose is a bit of money."

Endean was on the verge of telling Shannon just how much he and his employer stood to lose, but thought better of it. Logic dictated that if the mercenary was going to face prison, he would be as careful as possible.

They talked finance for another hour. Shannon explained that the payment to Johann Schlinker in full, and half to Alan Baker, along with the mercenaries' second months' salary, the £5000 he had transferred to Genoa to fit out the *Toscana,* and his own traveling, had emptied the Brugge account.

"Also," he added, "I want the second half of my salary."

"Why now?" asked Endean.

"Because the risks of arrest start next Monday, and I shall not be returning to London after that. If the ship is loaded without fuss, she sails for Brindisi while I arrange the pick-up of the Yugoslav arms. After that, Valencia and the Spanish ammunition. Then we head for the target. If I'm ahead of schedule, I'd prefer to kill the extra time on the high seas rather than wait in a port. From the moment that ship has hardware on board, I want her in port as little as possible."

Endean digested the argument. "I'll put it to my associates," he said.

"I want the stuff in my Swiss account before the weekend," countered Shannon, "and the rest of the agreed budget transferred to Brugge."

They worked out that, with Shannon's salary paid in full, there would be £20,000 of the original money left in Switzerland. Shannon explained why he needed it all.

"From now on I need a wad of big-denomination travelers' checks in United States dollars on me all the time. If anything goes wrong from now, it can only be of a nature where a fat bribe on the spot might sort out the problem. I want to tidy up all the remaining traces, so that, if we all get the chop, there are no clues left. Also, I may need to make cash bonuses on the spot to the ship's crewmen to persuade them to go ahead when they find out what the job really is, as they must when we are at sea. With the last half-payment for the Yugoslav arms still to come, I could need up to twenty thousand."

Endean agreed to report all this to "his associates" and let Shannon know.

The following day he rang back to say that both transfers of the money had been authorized and the letter instructing the Swiss bank had been sent.

Shannon reserved his ticket from London to Brussels for the following Friday, and a Saturday morning flight from Brussels to Paris to Marseilles.

He spent that night with Julie, and Thursday as well, and Thursday night. Then he packed his bags, mailed the flat keys with an explanatory letter to the agents, and left. Julie drove him to the airport in her red MGB.

"When are you coming back?" she asked him as they stood outside the "Departing Passengers Only" entrance to the customs area of Number Two Building.

"I won't be coming back," he said and gave her a kiss.

"Then let me come with you."

"No."

"You will come back. I haven't asked where you are going, but I know it has to be dangerous. It's not just business, not ordinary business. But you will come back. You must."

"I won't be coming back," he said quietly. "Go find someone else, Julie."

She began to sniffle. "I don't want anybody else. I love you. You don't love me. That's why you're saying you won't see me again. You've got another woman, that's what it is. You're going to see another woman—"

"There's no other woman," he said, stroking her hair. An airport policeman looked discreetly away. Tears in the departure lounge are not uncommon anywhere. There would be, Shannon knew, no other woman in his arms. Just a gun, the cool, comforting caress of the blued steel against his chest in the night. She was still crying when he kissed her on the forehead and walked through into Passport Control.

Thirty minutes later the Sabena jet made its last turn over South London and headed for its home in Brussels. Below the starboard wing, the country of Kent was spread out in the sunshine. Weatherwise, it had been a beautiful month of May. From the portholes one could see the acres of blossom where the apple, pear, and cherry orchards covered the land in pink and white.

Along the lanes that trickle through the heart of the Weald, the Maythorn would be out, the horse-chestnut trees glowing with green and white, the pigeons clattering among the oaks. He knew the country well from the time years ago when he had been stationed at Chatham and had bought an old motorcycle to explore the ancient country pubs between Lamberhurst and Smarden. Good country, good country to settle down in, if you were the settling type.

Ten minutes later, one of the passengers farther back summoned the stewardess to complain that someone up front was whistling a monotonous little tune.

It took Cat Shannon two hours on Friday afternoon to withdraw the money transferred from Switzerland and close his account. He took two certified bank checks, each for £5000, which could be converted into a bank account somewhere else, and from that into more travelers' checks; and the other £10,000 in fifty $500 checks that needed only countersignature to be used as cash.

He spent that night in Brussels and flew the next morning to Paris and Marseilles.

A taxi from the airport brought him to the small hotel in the outskirts where Langarotti had once lived under the name of Lavallon, and where Janni Dupree, still following orders, was in residence. He was out at the time, so Shannon waited until he returned that evening, and together they drove, in a hired car Shannon had engaged, to Toulon. It was the end of Day Fifty-two.

On Sunday the shipping agent's office was not open, but it did not matter. The rendezvous spot was the pavement in front of it, and here Shannon and Dupree met Marc Vlaminck and Langarotti on the dot of nine o'clock. It was the first time they had been together for weeks, and only Semmler was missing. He should be a hundred miles or so along the coast, steaming offshore in the *Toscana* toward Toulon.

At Shannon's suggestion, Langarotti telephoned the harbor-master's office from a nearby café and ascertained that the *Toscana's* agents in Genoa had cabled that she was due in on Monday morning and that her berth was reserved.

There was nothing more to do that day, so they went in Shannon's car along the coast road toward Marseilles and spent the day at the cobbled fishing port of Sanary. Despite the heat and the holiday atmosphere of the picturesque little town, Shannon could not relax. Only Dupree bought himself a pair of swimming trunks and dived off the end of the jetty of the yacht harbor. He said later the water was still damn cold. It would warm up later, through June and July, when the tourists began to pour south from Paris. By then they would all be preparing to strike at another harbor town, not much larger and many miles away.

Shannon sat for most of the day with the Belgian and Corsican on the terrace of Charley's bar, the Pot d'Etain, soaking up the sunshine and thinking of the next morning. The Yugoslav or the Spanish shipment might not turn up, or might be late, or might be blocked for some as yet unknown bureaucratic reason, but there would be no reason for them to be arrested in Yugoslavia or Spain. They might be held for a few days while the boat was searched, but that would be all. The following morning was different. If anyone insisted on peering deep into those oil barrels, there would be months, maybe years spent sweating in Les Baumettes, the great forbidding fortress prison he had passed on Saturday as he drove from Marseilles to Toulon.

The waiting was always the worst, he reflected as he settled the bill and called his three colleagues to the car.

It turned out to be smoother than they thought. Toulon is known as an enormous navy base, and the skyline at the harbor is dominated by the superstructures of the French navy warships lying at anchor. The center of attraction for the tourists and the strollers of Toulon that Monday was the battle cruiser *Jean Bart,* home from a voyage to the French Caribbean territories, full of sailors with back pay to spend and looking for girls.

Along the broad sweep of esplanade fronting the harbor, the cafés were full of people indulging in the favorite pastime of every Mediterranean country—watching life go by. They sat in brightly colored hordes, gazing from the shaded awnings across the half-mile of bobbing yachts—from little outboard-powered runabouts to the sleek sea greyhounds of the very rich.

Up against the eastward quay were the dozen fishing boats that had elected not to go to sea, and behind these were the long, low customs sheds, warehouses, and harbor offices.

It was beyond these, in the small and hardly observed commercial port, that the *Toscana* slipped into her berth just before noon.

Shannon waited till she was tied up, and from his seat on a bollard 150 feet away he could see Semmler and Waldenberg moving about the decks. There was no sign of the Serbian engineer, who was probably still in his beloved engine room, but two other figures were also on deck, making fast and coiling ropes. These had to be the two new crewmen recruited by Waldenberg.

A small Renault buzzed along the quay and came to a halt by the gangway. A rotund Frenchman in a dark suit emerged and went aboard the *Toscana.* The representative of Agence Maritime Duphot. Before long he came back down, followed by Waldenburg, and the two strolled over to the customs shed. It was nearly an hour before the two men emerged, the shipping agent to return to his car and drive away into town, the German captain to get back to his ship.

Shannon gave them another thirty minutes, then he too strolled up the gangway and onto the *Toscana.* Semmler beckoned him into the companionway that led down to the crew's saloon.

"So, what's been going on?" Shannon asked when he and Semmler were seated below.

Semmler grinned. "All smooth and easy," he said. "I got the papers changed to show the new captain, had a complete engine service done, bought an unnecessarily large amount of blankets and a dozen foam-rubber mattresses. No one asked any questions, and the captain still thinks we are going to run immigrants into Britain.

"I used the *Toscana*'s usual shipping agent in Genoa to book us in here, and the manifest says we are taking on a mixed cargo of sporting goods and leisure equipment for a holiday camp on the coast of Morocco."

"What about the engine-lubricating oil?"

Semmler grinned. "It was all ordered; then I called up and canceled it. When it didn't arrive, Waldenberg wanted to delay for a day and wait for it. I vetoed that and said we would get it here in Toulon."

"Fine," said Shannon. "Don't let Waldenberg order it. Tell him you've done it yourself. Then when it arrives, he'll be expecting it. That man who came on board . . ."

"The shipping agent. He has all the stuff still in bond, and the papers prepared. He's sending it down this afternoon in a couple of trucks. The crates are so small we can load them ourselves with the derrick."

"Good. Let him and Waldenberg sort out the paperwork. An hour after the stuff is all aboard, the fuel-company truck will arrive with the oil. Driven by Langarotti. You have enough money left to pay for it?"

"Yes."

"Then pay for it in full, cash, and get a signed receipt. Just make sure no one bangs it about too hard as it goes aboard. The last thing we need is for the bottom of one of the barrels to fall out. The quay will be waist-deep in Schmeissers."

"When do the men come aboard?"

"Tonight after dark. One by one. Just Marc and Janni. I'm leaving Jean-Baptiste here for a while. He has the truck, and there's one more job to be done at this end. When can you sail?"

"Any time. Tonight. I can fix it. Actually, it's rather nice being the managing director."

"Don't get too accustomed to it. It's only a front."

"Okay, Cat. Incidentally, where are we going when we leave?"

"Brindisi. Know it?"

"Sure I know it. I've run more cigarettes into Italy from Yugoslavia than you've had hot dinners. What do we pick up there?"

"Nothing. You wait for my telegram. I'll be in Germany. I'll cable you through the port office at Brindisi with the next destination and the day you have to arrive. Then you must get a local agent to cable the Yugoslav port in question and reserve a berth. Are you okay to go to Yugoslavia?"

"I think so. Anyway, I won't get off the ship. We pick up more arms?"

"Yes. At least, that's the plan. I just have to hope my arms dealer and the Yugoslav officials have not cocked it up. Do you have all the charts you need?"

"Yes, I bought them all in Genoa as you told me. You know, Waldenberg will have to realize what we are taking on board in Yugoslavia. Then he'll know we aren't running illegal immigrants. He accepts the speedboats and the engines, the walkie-talkies and the clothing as quite normal, but arms are something else again."

"I know," said Shannon. "It will cost a bit of money. But I think he'll get the message. There'll be you and me, Janni and Marc on board. Besides, by then we can tell him what's in the oil drums. He'll be so far in by then, he'll have to go along. What are the two new crewmen like?"

Semmler nodded and stubbed out his fifth cigarette. The air was a blue haze in the small saloon. "Good. Two Italians. Hard boys, but obedient. I think they're both wanted by the *carabinieri* for something. They were so pleased to get on board and under cover. They couldn't wait to get to sea."

"Fine. Then they won't want to be put ashore in a foreign country. That would mean they'd be picked up without papers and repatriated, straight into the hands of their own police."

Waldenberg had done well. Shannon met both men briefly, and short nods were exchanged. Semmler simply introduced him as a man from the head office, and Waldenberg translated. The men, Norbiatto, the first mate, and Cipriani, the deckhand, evinced no further interest. Shannon exchanged a few instructions with Waldenberg and left.

In midafternoon the two vans from Agence Maritime Duphot rolled to a stop by the *Toscana*, accompanied by the same man who had appeared that morning. A French customs officer, clipboard in hand, emerged from the customs house and stood by as the crates were swung inboard by the ship's derrick: four crates of assorted rough clothing, belts, boots, and caps, for the Moroccan workers at the holiday village; three crated large-size inflatable dinghies for sporting and leisure purposes; three outboard engines for same; two crates assorted flares, binoculars, ship's gas-powered foghorn, radio parts, and magnetic compasses. The last crates were listed under ship's stores.

The customs officer ticked them off as they went aboard, and confirmed with the shipping agent that they were either bonded for re-export, having arrived from Germany or Britain, or they were locally bought and carried no export duty. The customs man did not even look inside the crates. He knew the agency well, dealing with them every day.

When all was aboard, the customs man stamped the ship's cargo manifest. Waldenberg said something to Semmler in German, and the latter translated. He explained to the agency man that Waldenberg needed lubricating oil for his engines. It had been ordered in Genoa but had not been delivered in time.

The agency man noted in his book. "How much do you need?"

"Five drums," said Semmler. Waldenberg did not understand the French.

"That's a lot," said the agent.

Semmler laughed. "This old bucket uses as much oil as Diesel. Besides, we might as well get it here and have enough for a long time to come."

"When do you need it?" asked the agent.

"Five o'clock this afternoon be all right?" asked Semmler.

"Make it six," said the agency man, noting the type and quantity in his notebook, along with the hour of delivery. He looked up at the customs man. The official nodded. He was uninterested and strolled away. Shortly after, the agency man left in his car, followed by the two trucks.

At five o'clock Semmler left the *Toscana*, went to a phone in a café on the waterfront, rang the agency, and canceled the oil order. The skipper, he said, had discovered a full barrel at the rear of the stores locker and would not be needing any more for several weeks. The agency man was disgruntled but agreed.

At six a truck drove carefully along the quay and stopped opposite the *Toscana*. It was driven by Jean-Baptiste Langarotti in a bright green overall suit with the word Castrol on the back.

After opening the back of the truck, he carefully rolled five large oil drums down the plank he had fitted to the rear step. From the window of the customs house the duty officer peered out.

Waldenberg caught his eye and waved. He pointed to the barrels and back to his ship.

"Okay?" he called, adding with a thick accent, "*Ça va?*"

From the window the customs man nodded and withdrew to make a note on his clipboard. At Waldenberg's orders, the two Italian crewmen slipped cradles under the barrels and, one by one, winched them aboard. Semmler was uncommonly eager to help, steadying the drums as they swung over the ship's rail, shouting in German to Waldenberg on the winch to let them down easily. They slid out of sight into the dark, cool hold of the *Toscana*, and soon the hatch was back in place and clamped down.

Langarotti, having made his dispatch, had long since left in his truck. A

few minutes later the overall suit was at the bottom of a waste bin in the heart
of town. From his bollard at the other end of the quay, Shannon had
watched the loading with bated breath. He would have preferred to be
involved, like Semmler, for the waiting was almost physically painful, worse
than going into action.

When it was over, things quieted down on the *Toscana*. The captain and his
three men were below decks, the engineer having taken one turn of the ship
to sniff the salt air and then having gone back to his Diesel fumes. Semmler
gave them half an hour, then slipped down to the quay and came to join
Shannon. They met around three corners and out of sight of the harbor.

Semmler was grinning. "I told you. No problems."

Shannon nodded and grinned back with relief. He knew better than
Semmler what was at stake, and, unlike the German, he was not familiar with
port procedures.

"When can you take the men aboard?"

"The customs office closes at nine. They should come between twelve and
one in the morning. We sail at five. It's fixed."

"Good," said Shannon. "Let's go and find them and have a drink. I want
you back there quickly in case there are any inquiries still to come."

"There won't be."

"Never mind. We'll play safe. I want you to watch that cargo like a mother
hen. Don't let anyone near those barrels till I say so, and that will be in a
harbor in Yugoslavia. Then we tell Waldenberg what he's carrying."

They met the other three mercenaries at a prearranged café and had
several beers to cool down. The sun was setting, and the sea within the vast
bowl of land that forms the anchorage and roads of Toulon was ruffled by
only a slight breeze. A few sailboats pirouetted like ballerinas far out on the
stage as their crews brought them about to catch the next gust.

Semmler left them at eight and returned to the *Toscana*.

Janni Dupree and Marc Vlaminck slipped quietly aboard between midnight and one, and at five, watched from the quay by Shannon and Langarotti, the *Toscana* slipped back to the sea.

Langarotti ran Shannon to the airport in midmorning to catch his plane.
Over breakfast Shannon had given the Corsican his last set of instructions
and enough money to carry them out.

"I'd prefer to be going with you," Jean-Baptiste said, "or with the ship."

"I know," said Shannon. "But I need someone good to do this part of it. It's
vital. Without it we can't go through. I need someone reliable, and you have
the added advantage of being French. Besides, you know two of the men
well, and one speaks a smattering of French. Janni couldn't go in there with a
South African passport. Marc I need to intimidate the crew if they cut up
rough. I know you're better with a knife than he is with his hands, but I don't
want a fight, just enough to persuade the crew to do what they're told. And I
need Kurt to check the navigation, in case Waldenberg chickens out. In fact,
if the worst comes to the worst and Waldenberg goes over the side, Kurt has
to skipper the ship. So it has to be you."

Langarotti agreed to go on the mission. "They're good boys," he said with
a little more enthusiasm. "It will be good to see them again."

When they parted at the airport, Shannon reminded him, "It can all fall
through if we get there and we have no back-up force. So it depends on you

to do it right. It's all set up. Just do what I said and cope with the small problems as they arise. I'll see you in a month."

He left the Corsican, walked through customs, and boarded his plane for Paris and Hamburg.

NINETEEN

"My information is that you can pick up the mortars and bazookas any time after June tenth, and that was reconfirmed yesterday by Telex," Alan Baker told Shannon the day after his arrival in Hamburg.

"What port?" asked Shannon.

"Ploce."

"Where?"

"Ploce. Spelled P-L-O-C-E, pronounced Plochay. It's a small port almost exactly halfway between Split and Dubrovnik."

Shannon thought. He had ordered Semmler while in Genoa to pick up the necessary sea charts to cover the whole Yugoslav coast, but he had supposed the pick-up would be at one of the larger ports. He hoped the German had a chart covering the sea approaches to Ploce, or could get one at Brindisi.

"How small?"

"Quite small. Very discreet. Half a dozen wharves and two large warehouses. The Yugoslavs usually use it for their arms exports. The last shipment out of Yugoslavia I did by plane, but I was told at that time if it was to be by sea, it would be from Ploce. It's better if it's a small port. There's usually a berth, and loading facilities are quicker. Moreover, the customs there must be a very small unit, probably with one lowly man in charge, and if he gets his present, he'll see everything on board within a few hours."

"Okay, Ploce. On June eleventh," said Shannon.

Baker noted the date. "The *Toscana* is okay?" he asked. He decided to bear the *Toscana* in mind for later use. Shannon, he was sure, would have little use for her after whatever operation he was mounting was finished, and Baker was always on the lookout for a good boat for running his cargoes into deserted coves.

"She's fine," said Shannon. "She's running for an Italian port now, where I have to let her know by Telex or letter where to head for. Any problems at your end?"

Baker shifted slightly. "One," he said. "The price."

"What about it?"

"I know I quoted you fixed prices, totaling fourteen thousand, four hundred dollars. But the system inside Yugoslavia has changed over the past six months. To get the paperwork through on time, I had to engage a Yugoslav partner. At least, that's what he is called, though in fact he's another middleman."

"So?" asked Shannon.

"So he has to get a fee or salary for getting the paperwork through the Belgrade office. On balance, I supposed it was worth it to you to have the shipment ready on time and no bureaucratic hang-ups. So I agreed to engage him. He's the brother-in-law of the official in the Trade Ministry. It's another way of taking a kickback. But what can you expect these days? The Balkans are still the Balkans, and they've got wised up."

"How much extra will he cost?"

"A thousand pounds sterling."

"In dinars or dollars?"

"In dollars."

Shannon thought it over. It might be the truth, or it might be that Baker was trying to squeeze a bit more out of him. If it was the truth, refusing to pay would simply force Baker to pay the Yugoslav out of his own cut. That would reduce Baker's margin to such a small amount he might lose interest in the deal, not caring whether it went through or not. And he still needed Baker, and would need him until he saw the white wake of the *Toscana* heading out of Ploce harbor on her way to Spain.

"All right," he said. "Who is this partner?"

"Fellow called Ziljak. He's out there now, taking care of the shipment right up to Ploce and into the warehouse there. When the ship comes in, he'll get the stuff from the warehouse through customs and onto the boat."

"I thought that was your job."

"It is, but now I have to engage a Yugoslav as partner. Honestly, Cat, they left me no alternative."

"Then I'll pay him personally, in travelers' checks."

"I wouldn't," said Baker.

"Why not?"

"The buyers of this shipment are supposed to be the government of Togo, right? Black men. Another white turns up, obviously the paymaster, and they might begin to smell a rat. We can go to Ploce, if you like, or I can go alone. But if you want to come with me, you'll have to come ostensibly as my assistant. Besides, travelers' checks have to be cashed at a bank, and in Yugoslavia that means they take the man's name and identity-card number. If someone cashing them is a Yugoslav, there are questions asked. It would be better if Ziljak got cash, as he has asked."

"All right. I'll cash some checks here in Hamburg, and I'll pay him in dollar bills," said Shannon. "But you get yours in checks. I'm not carrying vast sums of dollars in cash around. Not to Yugoslavia. They get sensitive about that sort of thing. Security gets interested. They think you're funding a spy operation. So we go as tourists with travelers' checks."

"Fine by me," said Baker. "When do you want to go?"

Shannon glanced at his watch. The next day would be June 1.

"Day after tomorrow," he said. "We'll fly to Dubrovnik and have a week in the sun. I could do with a rest anyway. Or you can join me on the eighth or ninth, but not a day later. I'll hire a car, and we can drive up the coast to Ploce on the tenth. I'll have the *Toscana* come in that night or early on the morning of the eleventh."

"You go on alone," said Baker. "I have work to do in Hamburg. I'll join you on the eighth."

"Without fail," said Shannon. "If you don't turn up, I'll come looking. And I'll be hopping mad."

"I'll come," said Baker. "I still want the balance of my money, don't forget. So far, I'm out of pocket on this deal. I want it to go through just as much as you."

That was the way Shannon wanted him to feel.

"You do have the money, I suppose?" asked Baker, fingering a lump of sugar.

Shannon flicked through a booklet of large-denomination dollar checks under Baker's nose. The arms dealer smiled.

They left the table and on the way out used the restaurant telephone to call a Hamburg charter company specializing in package tours for the thousands of Germans who vacation along the Adriatic coast. From this company they learned the names of the three best hotels in the Yugoslav resort. Baker was told he would find Shannon in one of them under the name of Keith Brown.

Johann Schlinker was as confident as Baker that he could fulfill his arms deal, though he had no idea that Baker was also doing business with Shannon. No doubt the men knew of each other, might even be acquainted, but there would not be a question of discussing each other's business together.

"The port should be Valencia, though this has yet to be fixed and is in any case the choice of the Spanish authorities," he told Shannon. "Madrid tells me the dates have to be between the sixteenth and twentieth of June."

"I'd prefer the twentieth for loading," said Shannon. "The *Toscana* should be permitted to berth on or during the night of the nineteenth and load in the morning."

"Good," said Schlinker. "I'll inform my Madrid partner. He habitually handles the transporting and loading side of things, and employs a first-class freight agent in Valencia who knows all the customs personnel very well. There should be no problem."

"There must be no problem," growled Shannon. "The ship has been delayed already once, and by loading on the twentieth I have enough sailing time but no margin to fulfill my own contract."

It was not true, but he saw no reason why Schlinker should not believe it was true.

"I shall want to watch the loading also," he told the arms dealer.

Schlinker pursed his lips. "You may watch it from afar, of course," he said. "I cannot stop you. But as the customers are supposed to be an Arab government, you cannot propose yourself as the buyer of the merchandise."

"I also want to board the ship at Valencia," said Shannon.

"That will be even harder. The whole port is sealed off inside a chain-link fence. Entry is by authority only. To board the ship you would have to go through passport control. Also, as she will be carrying ammunition, there will be a Guardia Civil at the bottom of the gangplank."

"Supposing the captain needed another crewman. Could he engage a seaman locally?"

Schlinker thought it over. "I suppose so. Are you connected with the company owning the vessel?"

"Not on paper," said Shannon.

"If the captain informed the agent on arrival that he had permitted one of his crewmen to leave the vessel at its last port of call to fly home and attend his mother's funeral, and that the crewman would be rejoining the vessel at Valencia, I suppose there would be no objection. But you would need a merchant seaman's card to prove you were a seaman. And in the same name as yourself, Mr. Brown."

Shannon thought for a few minutes. "Okay. I'll fix it."

Schlinker consulted his diary. "As it happens, I shall be in Madrid on the nineteenth and twentieth," he said. "I have another business deal to attend to. I shall be at the Mindanao Hotel. If you want to contact me, you can find me there. If loading is for the twentieth, the chances are the convoy and escort from the Spanish army will run the shipment down to the coast during the night of the nineteenth to arrive at crack of dawn. If you are going to board the ship at all, I think you should do so before the military convoy arrives at the docks."

"I could be in Madrid on the nineteenth," said Shannon. "Then I could check with you that the convoy had indeed left on time. By driving fast to Valencia, I could be there ahead of it, and board the *Toscana* as the rejoining seaman before the convoy arrives."

"That is entirely up to you," said Schlinker. "For my part, I will have my agents arrange the freighting, transportation, and loading, according to all the normal procedures, for dawn of the twentieth. That is what I contracted to do. If there is any risk attached to your boarding the vessel in harbor, that must be your affair. I cannot take the responsibility for that. I can only point out that ships carrying arms out of Spain are subjected to scrutiny by the army and customs authorities. If anything goes wrong with the loading and clearance of the ship to sail, because of you, that is not my responsibility. One other thing. After loading arms a ship must leave a Spanish port within six hours, and may not re-enter Spanish waters until the cargo has been offloaded. Also, the manifest must be in perfect order."

"It will be," said Shannon. "I'll be with you in Madrid on the morning of the nineteenth."

Before leaving Toulon, Kurt Semmler had given Shannon a letter to mail. It was from Semmler to the *Toscana's* shipping agents in Genoa. It informed them there had been a slight change of plan, and that the *Toscana* would be proceeding from Toulon not directly to Morocco but first to Brindisi to pick up further cargo. The order, Semmler informed the agents, had been secured locally by him in Toulon and was lucrative, since it was a rush order, whereas the consignment of mixed cargo from Toulon to Morocco was in no hurry. As managing director of Spinetti Maritimo, Semmler's instructions were those of the boss. He required the Genoa agents to cable Brindisi reserving a berth for June 7 and 8, and to instruct the port office to hold any mail addressed to the *Toscana* for collection when she berthed.

Such a letter was what Shannon wrote and dispatched from Hamburg. It was to Signor Kurt Semmler, MV *Toscana,* c/o the Port Office, Brindisi, Italy.

In it he told Semmler that from Brindisi he should proceed to Ploce on the Adriatic coast of Yugoslavia, and that if he had no charts to negotiate the tricky straits north of Korcula Island, he should get them locally. He had to get the *Toscana* there on the evening of June 10, and his berth would be reserved. There was no need to inform the agents in Genoa of the extra leg from Brindisi to Ploce.

His last instruction to Semmler was important. He told the German ex-smuggler he wanted him to acquire a merchant seaman's card for a deckhand called Keith Brown, stamped and up to date, and issued by the Italian authorities. The second thing the ship would need was a cargo manifest showing the *Toscana* had proceeded straight from Brindisi to

Valencia without a halt, and would be heading from Valencia to Latakia, Syria, after taking cargo aboard in Valencia, Semmler would have to use his old Brindisi contacts to obtain these documents.

Before he left Hamburg for Yugoslavia, Shannon's last letter was to Simon Endean in London. It required Endean to meet Shannon at a rendezvous in Rome on June 16, and to bring certain maritime charts with him.

About the same time, the MV *Toscana* was chugging steadily through the Bight of Bonifacio, the narrow channel of limpid blue water that separates the southern tip of Corsica from the northern end of Sardinia. The sun was blistering, but mellowed by a light wind. Marc Vlaminck was stretched out, stripped to the waist, on the hatch cover of the main hold, a wet towel beneath him, his torso like a pink hippopotamus covered in suntan oil. Janni Dupree, who always turned brick red in the sun, was propped up against the wall of the after structure, under the awning, swigging from his tenth bottle of beer of the morning. Cipriani, the deckhand, was painting part of the rail around the forepeak white, and the first mate, Norbiatto, was snoozing on his bunk below after taking the night watch.

Also down below, in the stinking heat of the engine room, was the engineer, Grubič, oiling some piece of machinery that only he could understand but which no doubt was vital to keep the *Toscana* steady on her eight knots through the Mediterranean. In the wheelhouse Kurt Semmler and Carl Waldenberg were sipping cold beer and exchanging reminiscences of their respective careers.

Jean-Baptiste Langarotti would have liked to be there. From the port rail he could have watched the gray-white sunbleached coast of his homeland slipping past barely four miles across the water. But he was many miles away, in West Africa, where the rainy season had already begun and where, despite the fever heat, the clouds were leaden gray.

Alan Baker came into Shannon's hotel in Dubrovnik just as the mercenary was returning from the beach on the evening of June 8. He looked tired and dusty.

Cat Shannon, by contrast, was looking and feeling better. He had spent his week in the Yugoslav holiday resort behaving like any other tourist, sunbathing and swimming several miles each day. He looked thinner, but fit and tanned. He was also optimistic.

After settling into his hotel, he had sent Semmler a cable at Brindisi requesting confirmation of the arrival of the vessel and receipt of the waiting letter mailed from Hamburg. That morning he had got Semmler's telegraphed reply. The *Toscana* had arrived safely in Brindisi, the letter had been received and acted on, and they would depart on the morning of June 9 to make destination by midnight of the tenth.

Over drinks on the terrace of their hotel, where Shannon had reserved Baker a room for the night, he told the dealer from Hamburg the news.

Baker nodded and smiled. "Fine. I got a cable forty-eight hours ago from Ziljak in Belgrade. The crates have arrived in Ploce and are in the government warehouse near the quay, under guard."

They spent the night in Dubrovnik and the following morning hired a taxi to take them the hundred kilometers up the coast to Ploce. It was a boneshaker of a car that appeared to have square wheels and cast-iron suspension, but the drive along the coast road was agreeable, mile upon mile of unspoiled coastline, with the small town of Slano at the halfway mark, where they stopped for a cup of coffee and to stretch their limbs.

They were established in a Ploce hotel by lunchtime and waited in the shade of the terrace until the port office opened again at four in the afternoon.

The port was set on a broad sweep of deep blue water, shielded to its seaward side by a long peninsula of land called Peliesac, which curved out of the main coast to the south of Ploce and ran northward parallel to the coast. Up to the north the gap between the top of the peninsula and the coast was almost blocked by the rocky island of Hvar, and only a narrow gap gave access to the sea lagoon on which Ploce stood. This lagoon, nearly thirty miles long, surrounded on nine-tenths of its perimeter by land, was a paradise for swimming, fishing, and sailing.

As they approached the port office, a small and battered Volkswagen squealed to a halt a few yards away and hooted noisily. Shannon froze. His first instinct said trouble, something he had been fearing all along, some slip-up in the paperwork, a sudden block put on the whole deal by the authorities, and an extended stay under questioning in the local police station.

The man who climbed out of the small car and waved cheerily might have been a policeman, except that police in most totalitarian states of East or West seemed to be banned from smiling by standing orders. Shannon glanced at Baker and saw his shoulders sag in relief.

"Ziljak," Baker muttered through closed mouth and went to meet the Yugoslav. The latter was a big shaggy man, like an amiable black-haired bear, and he embraced Baker with both arms. When he was introduced, his first name turned out to be Kemal, and Shannon supposed there was more than a touch of Turk in the man. That suited Shannon fine; he liked the type, normally good fighters and comrades with a healthy dislike of bureaucracy.

"My assistant," said Baker, and Ziljak shook hands and muttered something in what Shannon assumed to be Serbo-Croat. Baker and Ziljak communicated in German, which many Yugoslavians speak a little. He spoke no English.

With Ziljak's assistance, they roused the head of the customs office and were taken off to inspect the warehouse. The customs man jabbered a few words at the guard on the door, and in the corner of the building they found the crates. There were thirteen of them; one apparently contained the two bazookas, and each of two others contained one mortar, including the base-plates and sighting mechanisms in each. The rest were of ammunition, four of them with ten bazooka rockets in each, and the other six containing the ordered three hundred mortar bombs. The crates were in new timber, unmarked with any description of contents, but stenciled with serial numbers and the word *Toscana*.

Ziljak and the customs chief babbled away in their own dialect—and it appeared they were using the same one, which was helpful, because there are dozens in Yugoslavia, including seven major languages, and difficulties have been known to occur.

Eventually Ziljak turned to Baker and said several sentences in his halting

German. Baker replied, and Ziljak translated for the customs man. He smiled, and they all shook hands and parted. Outside, the sunshine struck like a sledgehammer.

"What was all that about?" asked Shannon.

"Kemal was asked by the customs man if there was a little present in it for him," explained Baker. "Kemal told him there would be a nice one if the paperwork could be kept trouble-free and the ship was loaded on time tomorrow morning."

Shannon had already given Baker the first half of Ziljak's £1000 bonus for helping the deal go through, and Baker drew the Yugoslav to one side to slip it to him. The man's all-embracing bonhomie became even more embracing for both of them, and they adjourned to the hotel to celebrate with a little slivovitz. A little was the word Baker used. Ziljak may have used the same word. He did not mean it. Happy Yugoslavs never drink a little slivovitz. With £500 under his belt, Ziljak ordered a bottle of the fiery plum liquor and bowl after bowl of almonds and olives. As the sun went down and the Adriatic evening slipped through the streets, he relived again his years in the war, hunting and hiding in the Bosnian hills to the north with Tito's partisans.

Baker was hard put to it to translate as the exuberant Kemal related his forays behind Dubrovnik in Montenegro, in the mountains behind where they sat, on the coast of Herzegovina, and among the cooler, richer, wooded countryside north of Split in Bosnia. He relished the thought that he would once have been shot out of hand for venturing into any of the towns where he now drove on behalf of his brother-in-law who was in the government. Shannon asked if he was a committed Communist, having been a partisan, and Ziljak listened while Baker translated, using the word "good" for "committed."

Ziljak thumped his chest with his fist. "*Guter Kommunist,*" he exclaimed, eyes wide, pointing at himself. Then he ruined the effect by giving a broad wink, throwing back his head, and roaring with laughter as he tossed another glass of slivovitz down the hatch. The folded notes of his first £500 bonus made a bulge under his waistband, and Shannon laughed too and wished the giant was coming along to Zangaro with them. He was that kind of man.

They had no supper but at midnight wandered unsteadily back to the quay to watch the *Toscana* come in. She was rounding the harbor wall and an hour later was tied up alongside the single quay of hewn local stone. From the forepeak Semmler looked down in the half-light cast by the dock lamps. Each nodded slowly at the other, and Waldenberg stood at the top of the gangplank, consulting with his first mate. He had already been instructed, following Shannon's letter, that he should leave the talking to Semmler.

After Baker had headed back to the hotel with Ziljak, Shannon slipped up the gangplank and into the captain's tiny cabin. No one on the quay took any notice. Semmler brought Waldenberg in, and they locked the door.

Slowly and carefully Shannon told Waldenberg what he had really brought the *Toscana* to Ploce to take on board. The German captain took it well. He kept his face expressionless until Shannon had finished.

"I never carried arms before," he said. "You say this cargo is legal. How legal?"

"Perfectly legal," said Shannon. "It has been bought in Belgrade, trucked up here, and the authorities are of course aware what the crates contain. Otherwise there would be no export license. The license has not been forged, nor has anyone been bribed. It's a perfectly legal shipment under the laws of Yugoslavia."

"And the laws of the country it's going to?" asked Waldenberg.

"The *Toscana* never enters the waters of the country where these arms are due to be used," said Shannon. "After Ploce, there are two more ports of call. In each case only to take on board cargoes. You know ships are never searched for what they are carrying when they arrive in a port to take on more cargo only, unless the authorities have been tipped off."

"It has happened, all the same," said Waldenberg. "If I have these things on board and the manifest doesn't mention them, and there is a search and they are discovered, the ship gets impounded and I get imprisoned. I didn't bargain on arms. With the Black September and the IRA about these days, everyone's looking for arms shipments."

"Not at the port of embarkation of fresh cargo," said Shannon.

"I didn't bargain for arms," repeated Waldenberg.

"You bargained for illegal immigrants to Britain," Shannon pointed out.

"They're not illegal until their feet touch British soil," the captain said. "And the *Toscana* would be outside territorial waters. They could go inshore in fast boats. Arms are different. They are illegal on this ship if the manifest says there aren't any. Why not put it on the manifest? Just say these arms are being legally transported from Ploce to Togo. No one can prove we later deviate from course."

"Because if there are arms already on board, the Spanish authorities will not allow the ship to stay in Valencia or any other Spanish port. Even in transit. Certainly not to take on more arms. So they have to remain unmentioned on the manifest."

"So where did we come from to reach Spain?" asked Waldenberg.

"From Brindisi," replied Shannon. "We went there to take on cargo, but it was not ready in time. Then the owners ordered you to Valencia to pick up a new cargo for Latakia. Of course you obeyed."

"Supposing the Spanish police search the boat?"

"There's not the slightest reason why they should," said Shannon. "But if they do, the crates have to be below decks in the bilges."

"If they find them there, there's not a hope for us," Waldenberg pointed out. "They'd think we were bringing the stuff to the Basque territories. We'd be inside forever."

The talk went on till three in the morning. It cost Shannon a flat bonus of £5000, half before loading and half after sailing from Valencia. There was no extra charge for the stopover in the African port. That would present no problem.

"You'll take care of the crew?" Shannon asked.

"I'll take care of the crew," said Waldenberg with finality. Shannon knew he would, too.

Back in his hotel, Shannon paid Baker the third quarter of his bill for the arms, $3600, and tried to get some sleep. It was not easy. The sweat rolled off him in the heat of the night, and he had an image of the *Toscana* lying down there in the port, the arms in the customs shed, and prayed there would be no problems. He felt he was so close now, just three short ceremonies away from the point where no one could stop him, whatever was tried.

The loading started at seven, and the sun was already well up. With a customs man, armed with a rifle, walking beside the crates, they were wheeled on trolleys down to the dockside, and the *Toscana* hoisted them aboard with her own jumbo derrick. None of the crates was very large, and down in the hold Vlaminck and Cipriani swung them easily into position before they were roped down across the floor of the hold. By nine in the morning it was over, and the hatches went on.

Waldenberg had ordered the engineer to stand by for casting off, and the latter needed no second bidding. Shannon learned later he had suddenly become very voluble when he learned three hours out from Brindisi that they were heading for his native country. Apparently he was wanted there for something or other. He stayed well hidden in his engine room, and no one went looking for him.

As he watched the *Toscana* chugging out of the port, Shannon slipped Baker the remaining $3600 and the second £500 for Ziljak. Unbeknownst to either, he had had Vlaminck quietly prise up the lids on five of the crates, taken at random, as they came aboard. Vlaminck had verified the contents, waved up to Semmler on the deck above him, and Semmler had blown his nose, the signal Shannon wanted. Just in case the crates contained scrap iron. It has been known to happen, quite frequently, in the arms world.

Baker, having received his money, gave the £500 to Ziljak as if it came from himself, and the Yugoslav saw the customs chief did not go without supper. Then Alan Baker and his British "assistant" quietly left town.

On Shannon's calendar of a hundred days, given him by Sir James Manson to bring off his coup, it was Day Sixty-seven.

No sooner was the *Toscana* out to sea than Captain Waldenberg began to organize his ship. One by one, the three other crewmen were brought into his cabin for a quiet interview. Although none of them knew it, had they refused to continue to serve aboard the *Toscana*, there would have been some unfortunate accidents on board. Few places are quite as well suited for a complete disappearing act as a ship on a dark night at sea, and Vlaminck and Dupree between them could have pitched anyone else on board a long way from the ship's side before he touched the water. Perhaps their presence did the trick. In any case, no one objected.

Waldenberg dispensed £1000 of the £2500 he had received in travelers' checks from Shannon. The Yugoslav engineer, delighted to be back out of his own country, took his £250, stuffed it into his pocket, and went back to his engines. He made no comment one way or the other. The first mate, Norbiatto, became quite excited at the thought of a Spanish jail, but pocketed his £600 in dollars and thought of the difference that could make to his chances of owning his own ship one day. The crewman, Cipriani, seemed almost happy at the prospect of being on a vessel full of contraband, took his £150, said an ecstatic thank you, and left, muttering, "This is the life." He had little imagination and knew nothing about Spanish jails.

With this done, the crates were broken open, and all afternoon the contents were examined, wrapped in polyethylene, and stowed deep in the bilges, below the floor of the hold and inside the curvature of the ship's hull. The planks which had been removed to make this possible were replaced and covered with the innocent cargo of clothing, dinghies, and outboard engines.

Finally Semmler told Waldenberg he had better put the Castrol oil drums at the back of the stores locker, and when he told his fellow countryman why, Waldenberg finally did lose his composure. He lost his temper as well and used some expressions that could best be described as regrettable.

Semmler calmed him down, and they sat having beer as the *Toscana* plowed her way south for the Otranto Channel and the Ionian Sea.

Finally Waldenberg began to laugh. "Schmeissers," he said. "Bloody Schmeissers. *Mensch*, it's a long time since they've been heard in the world."

"Well, they're going to be heard again," said Semmler.

Waldenberg looked wistful. "You know," he said at length, "I wish I was going ashore with you."

TWENTY

When Shannon arrived, Simon Endean was reading a copy of *The Times* bought that morning in London before he left for Rome. The lounge of the Excelsior Hotel was almost empty, for most of those taking late-morning coffee were on the outside terrace watching the chaotic traffic of Rome inch past and trying to make themselves heard above the noise.

Shannon had picked the place only because it was in easy reach of Dubrovnik to the east and in line with Madrid to the west. It was the first time he had ever been to Rome, and he wondered what the ecstatic guide books were talking about. There were at least seven separate strikes in progress, one of them being among the garbage workers, and the city stank in the sun from the uncleared fruit and other rubbish on the pavements and down every back alley.

He eased himself into a seat beside the man from London and savored the cool of the inner room after the heat and frustration of the taxi in which he had been stuck for the past hour.

Endean eyed him. "You've been out of touch a long time," he said coldly. "My associates were beginning to think you had run out. That was unwise."

"There was no point in my making contact until I had something to say. That ship doesn't exactly fly across the water. It takes time to get her from Toulon to Yugoslavia, and during that time there was nothing to report," said Shannon. "By the way, did you bring the charts?"

"Of course." Endean pointed to the bulging attaché case beside his chair. On receiving Shannon's letter from Hamburg, he had spent several days visiting three of the top maritime-chart companies in Leadenhall Street, London, and in separate lots had acquired inshore charts for the entire African coast from Casablanca to Cape Town. "Why the hell do you need so many?" he asked in annoyance. "One or two would suffice."

"Security," said Shannon briefly. "If you or I were searched at customs, or if the ship were boarded and searched in port, one single chart showing the area of the ship's destination would be a giveaway. As it is, no one, including the captain and crew, can discover which section of the coast really interests me. Until the last moment, when I have to tell them. Then it's too late. Do you have the slides as well?"

"Yes, of course."

Another of Endean's jobs had been to make up slides of all the photographs Shannon had brought back from Zangaro, along with others of the maps and sketches of Clarence and the rest of Zangaro's coastline.

Shannon himself had already sent a slide projector, bought duty-free at London airport, onto the *Toscana* in Toulon.

He gave Endean a complete progress report from the moment he had left London, mentioning the stay in Brussels, the loading of the Schmeissers and other equipment onto the *Toscana* in Toulon, the talks with Schlinker and Baker in Hamburg, and the Yugoslav shipment a few days earlier in Ploce.

Endean listened in silence, making a few notes for the report he would later have to give to Sir James Manson. "Where's the *Toscana* now?" he asked at length.

"She should be south and slightly west of Sardinia, en route for Valencia."

Shannon went on to tell him what was planned in three days' time: the loading of the 400,000 rounds of 9mm. ammunition for the machine pistols in Valencia, and then departure for the target. He made no mention of the fact that one of his men was already in Africa.

"Now there's something I need to know from you," he told Endean. "What happens after the attack? What happens at dawn? We can't hold on for very long before some kind of new regime takes over, establishes itself in the palace, and broadcasts news of the coup and the new government."

"That's all been thought of," said Endean smoothly. "In fact, the new government is the whole point of the exercise."

From his briefcase he withdrew three sheets of paper covered with close typing. "These are your instructions, starting the moment you have possession of the palace and the army and guards have been destroyed or scattered. Read, memorize, and destroy these sheets before we part company, here in Rome. You have to carry it all in your head."

Shannon ran his eyes quickly over the first page. There were few surprises for him. He had already suspected the man Manson was boosting into the presidency had to be Colonel Bobi, and although the new president was referred to simply as X, he did not doubt Bobi was the man in question. The rest of the plan was simple from his point of view.

He glanced up at Endean. "Where will you be?" he asked.

"A hundred miles north of you," said Endean.

Shannon knew Endean meant he would be waiting in the capital of the republic next door to Zangaro on its northern side, the one with a road route straight along the coast to the border and thence to Clarence.

"Are you sure you'll pick up my message?" he asked.

"I shall have a portable radio set of considerable range and power. The Braun, the best they make. It will pick up anything within that range, provided it's broadcast on the right channel and frequency. A ship's radio should be powerful enough to send in clear over at least twice that distance."

Shannon nodded and read on. When he had finished, he put the sheets on the table. "Sounds all right," he said. "But let's get one thing clear. I'll broadcast on that frequency at those hours from the *Toscana*, and she'll be hove to somewhere off the coast, probably at five or six miles. But if you don't hear me, if there's too much static, I can't be responsible for that. It's up to you to hear me."

"It's up to you to broadcast," said Endean. "The frequency is one that has been tested before by practical use. From the *Toscana's* radio it must be picked up by my radio set at a hundred miles. Not first time, perhaps, but if you repeat for thirty minutes, I have to hear it."

"All right," said Shannon. "One last thing. The news of what has happened in Clarence should not have reached the Zangaran border post. That means it'll be manned by Vindu. It's your business to get past them. After the border, and particularly nearer Clarence, there may be scattered Vindu on the roads, running for the bush but still dangerous. Supposing you don't get through?"

"We'll get through," said Endean. "We'll have help."

Shannon supposed, rightly, that this would be provided by the small operation in mining that he knew Manson had going for him in that republic. For a senior company executive it could provide a truck or jeep and maybe a couple of repeater hunting rifles. For the first time he supposed Endean might have some guts to back up his nastiness.

Shannon memorized the code words and the radio frequency he needed and burned the sheets with Endean in the men's room. They parted an hour later. There was nothing else to say.

Five floors above the streets of Madrid, Colonel Antonio Almela, head of the exporting office of the Spanish Army Ministry (Foreign Arms Sales), sat at his desk and perused the file of papers in front of him. He was a gray-haired, grizzled man, a simple man whose loyalties were uncomplicated and uncompromising. His fidelity was to Spain, his beloved Spain, and for him all that was right and proper, all that was truly Spanish, was embodied in one man, the short and aged generalissimo who sat in El Pardo. Antonio Almela was a Falangist to his boot-heels.

Two years from retirement at the age of fifty-eight, he had been one of those who stepped ashore on the sand of Fuengirola with Francisco Franco many years ago when El Caudillo of modern Spain had been a rebel and outcast, returning against orders to launch war against the Republican government in Madrid. They had been few then, and condemned to death by Madrid, and they had nearly died.

Sergeant Almela was a good soldier. He carried out his orders, whatever they were, went to mass between the battles and the executions, and believed, deeply, in God, the Virgin, Spain, and Franco.

In another army, at another time, he would have retired as a sergeant-major. He emerged from the civil war a full captain, one of the ultras, the inner circle. His background was solid peasant, his education next to nil. But he had made full colonel, and he was grateful. He was also trusted with one of the jobs that in Spain is unmentionable and top secret. No Spaniard ever, under any circumstances, learns that Spain exports arms in large quantities to almost all comers. Publicly, Spain regrets the international arms trade as unethical and conducive to further warfare in a world already torn by war. Privately, she makes a lot of money out it. Antonio Almela could be trusted to check the paperwork, decide whether to grant or refuse permission for export licenses, and keep his mouth shut.

The dossier in front of him had been in his hands for four weeks. Individual papers from the dossier had been checked out by the Defense

Ministry, which had confirmed, without knowing why the question was being asked, that 9mm. bullets were not on the secret list; by the Foreign Ministry, which had confirmed simply that a sum of money in dollars, paid into a certain account in the Banco Popular, had been received and cleared.

The top paper on the file was an application for a movement order to shift a quantity of crates from Madrid to Valencia and export them on a vessel called the MV *Toscana*. Beneath this sheet was the export license, granted by his own signature.

He glanced up at the civil servant in front of him. "Why the change?" he asked.

"Colonel, it is simply that there is no berth available in Valencia port for two weeks. The place is crowded to capacity."

Colonel Almela grunted. The explanation was plausible. In the summer months Valencia was always crowded, with millions of oranges from the nearby Gancia area being exported. But he did not like changes. He liked to play things by the book. Nor did he like this order. It was small, too small, for an entire national police force. Target practice alone for a thousand policemen would use it up in an hour. Nor did he trust Schlinker, whom he knew well and who had slipped the order through his Ministry with a batch of other orders, including more than ten thousand artillery shells for Syria.

He glanced through the papers again. Outside, a church bell struck the hour of one, the hour of lunch. There was still nothing wrong with the papers, including the End User Certificate. Everything bore the right stamp. If only he could find one discrepancy, in the certificate, in the carrying ship of the company that owned it. But everything was clean. Making a final decision, he scrawled his signature across the bottom of the movement order and handed the file back to the civil servant.

"All right," he growled. "Castellón."

"We've had to change the port of embarkation from Valencia to Castellón," said Johann Schlinker two nights later. "There was no choice if the loading date of the twentieth was to be adhered to. Valencia was full for weeks."

Cat Shannon was sitting on the bed in the German arms dealer's room in the Mindanao Hotel. "Where's Castellón?" he asked.

"Forty miles up the coast. It's a smaller port, and quieter. Probably better than Valencia for you. The turn-around of your ship is likely to be quicker. The cargo agent in Valencia has been informed and will personally go north to Castellón to supervise the loading. As soon as the *Toscana* checks in with Valencia harbor authorities by radio, she will be advised of the change of port. She will only have a couple of hours' extra steaming if she diverts at once."

"What about my going aboard?"

"Well, that's your business," said Schlinker. "However, I have informed the agent that a seaman from the *Toscana* who was left behind ten days ago in Brindisi is due to rejoin, and given him the name of Keith Brown. How are your papers?"

"Fine," said Shannon. "They're in order, passport and merchant seaman's card."

"You'll find the agent at the customs office in Castellón as soon as it opens on the morning of the twentieth," Shlinker told him. "His name is Señor Moscar."

"What about the Madrid end of things?"

"The movement order provides for the truck to be loaded under army supervision between eight and midnight on the nineteenth, tomorrow. It will set off with escort at midnight, timing its arrival at Castellón harbor gates for six a.m., the hour they open. If the *Toscana* is on time, she should have docked during the night. The truck carrying the crates is a civilian one, from the same freight firm I always employ. They're very good and very experienced. I have given the transport manager instructions to see the convoy depart from the warehouse and to phone me here immediately."

Shannon nodded. There was nothing he could think of that might go wrong. "I'll be here," he said, and left.

That afternoon he hired a powerful Mercedes from one of the internationally known car agencies that have offices in Madrid.

At half past ten the following evening he was back in the Mindanao with Schlinker while they waited for the telephone call. Both men were nervous, as men must be when a carefully laid plan rests for its success or catastrophic failure in the hands of others. Schlinker was as concerned as Shannon but for different reasons. He knew that, if anything went badly wrong, a complete investigation into the End User Certificate he had supplied could be ordered, and that certificate would not stand up to a complete investigation, which must include a check with the Interior Ministry in Baghdad. If he were exposed on that one, other, and for him far more lucrative, deals with Madrid would be forfeit. Not for the first time he wished he had not taken the order in the first place, but, like most arms dealers, he was a man so greedy that no offer of money could be turned down. It would almost be physical pain to do it.

Midnight came, and still there was no call. Then half past midnight. Shannon paced the room, snarling his anger and frustration at the fat German, who sat drinking whisky. At twelve-forty the phone rang. Schlinker leaped at it. He spoke several words in Spanish and waited.

"What is it?" snapped Shannon.

"Moment," replied Schlinker and waved his hand for silence. Then someone else came on the phone and there was more Spanish, which Shannon could not understand. Finally Schlinker grinned and said, "*Gracias,*" into the phone several times.

"It's on its way," he said when he put the phone down. "The convoy left the depot fifteen minutes ago under escort for Castellón."

But Shannon was gone.

The Mercedes was more than a match for the convoy, even though on the long motorway from Madrid to Valencia the convoy could keep up a steady 60 miles per hour. It took Shannon forty minutes to find his way out of the sprawling suburbs of Madrid, and he supposed the convoy would know the way much better. But on the motorway he could take the Mercedes to 100 mph. He kept a careful eye open as he sped past hundreds of trucks roaring through the night toward the coast, and found what he was looking for just past the town of Requena, forty miles west of Valencia.

His lights picked up the army jeep keeping station to a covered 8-ton truck, and as he swept past he noted the name on the truck's side. It was the name of the trucking company Schlinker had given him. Driving ahead of the truck was another army vehicle, a four-door sedan, evidently with an officer sitting alone in the back. Shannon touched the accelerator, and the Mercedes sped past toward the coast.

At Valencia he took the ring road around the sleeping city, following the signs to the E26 highway to Barcelona. The motorway ran out just north of Valencia, and he was back to crawling behind orange trucks and early farm vehicles, past the miraculous Roman fortress of Sagunto, hacked by the legionaries out of the living rock and later converted by the Moors into a citadel of Islam. He drove into Castellón just after four and followed the signs labeled PUERTO.

The port of Castellón lies three miles from the main town, down a narrow, arrow-straight road that leads from the city to the sea. At the end of the road it is impossible to miss the port and harbor, for there is nothing else there.

As usual with Mediterranean ports, there are three separate harbors, one for freighters, one for yachts and pleasure craft, and one for fishing vessels. In Castellón the commercial port lies to the left as one faces the sea, and like all Spanish ports is ringed by a fence, and the gates are manned day and night by armed Guardia Civil. In the center lies the harbormaster's office, and beside it the splendid yacht club, with a dining room looking out over the commercial port on one side and the yacht basin and fishing harbor on the other. Landward of the harbor office is a row of warehouses.

Shannon turned to the left and parked the car by the roadside, climbed out, and started walking. Halfway around the perimeter fence of the port area he found the main gate, with a sentry dozing in a box beside it. The gate was locked. Farther on, he peered through the chain-links and with a surge of relief spotted the *Toscana* berthed against the far side of the basin. He settled to wait till six o'clock.

He was at the main gate at quarter to six, smiled and nodded at the Guardia Civil sentry, who stared coldly back. In the rising sunlight he could see the army staff car, truck, and jeep, with seven or eight soldiers milling around them, parked a hundred yards away. At 6:10 a civilian car arrived, parked next to the gate, and sounded its horn. A small, dapper Spaniard climbed out. Shannon approached him.

"Señor Moscar?"

"*Si.*"

"My name's Brown. I'm the seaman who's got to join his ship here."

The Spaniard puckered his brows. "*Por favor? Que?*"

"Brown," insisted Shannon. "*Toscana.*"

The Spaniard's face lightened. "*Ah, si. El marinero.* Come, please."

The gate had been opened, and Moscar showed his pass. He babbled for several seconds at the guard and the customs man who had opened the gate, and pointed at Shannon. Cat caught the word *marinero* several times, and his passport and merchant seaman's card were examaned. Then he followed Moscar to the customs office. An hour later he was on board the *Toscana.*

The search started at nine. There was no warning. The captain's manifest had been presented and checked out. It was perfectly in order. Down on the quay the truck from Madrid was parked, along with the car and the jeep. The army escort captain, a thin, sallow man with a face like a Moor's and a lipless mouth, consulted with two customs officers. Then the latter came aboard. Moscar followed. They checked the cargo to make sure it was what the manifest said and no more. They peered into nooks and crannies, but not under the floorboards of the main hold. They looked in the stores locker, gazed at the tangle of chains, oil drums, and paint cans, and closed the door. It took an hour. The main thing that interested them was why Captain Waldenberg needed seven men on such a small ship. It was explained that Dupree and Vlaminck were company employees who had missed their ship in Brindisi and were being dropped off at Malta on the way to Latakia. They had no seamen's cards with them because they had left their gear on board their own ship. Asked for a name, Waldenberg gave them the name of a ship he had seen in Brindisi harbor. There was silence from the Spaniards, who looked at their chief for advice. He glanced down at the army captain, shrugged, and left the ship. Twenty minutes later, loading began.

At half past noon the *Toscana* slipped out of Castellón harbor and turned her helm south to Cape San Antonio. Cat Shannon, feeling sick now that it was all over, knowing that from then on he was virtually unstoppable, was leaning against the after rail, watching the flat green orange groves south of Castellón slip away as they headed for the sea.

Carl Waldenberg came up behind him. "That's the last stop?" he asked.

"The last where we have to open our hatches," said Shannon. "We have to pick up some men on the coast of Africa, but we'll moor in the roads. The men will come out by launch. Deck cargo native workers. At least, that's what they'll be shipped as."

"I've only got charts as far as the Strait of Gibraltor," objected Waldenberg.

Shannon reached into his zip-up windbreaker and pulled out a sheaf of charts, half of the number Endean had handed him in Rome. "These," he said, handing them to the skipper, "will get you as far as Freetown, Sierra Leone. That's where we anchor and pick up the men. Please give me an arrival time at noon on July second. That is the rendezvous."

As the captain left to return to his cabin and start to plot his course and speed, Shannon was left alone at the rail. Seagulls wheeled around the stern, seeking morsels dropped from the galley, where Cipriani was preparing lunch, squealing and cawing as they dipped toward the foaming wake to snatch up a scrap of bread or vegetable.

Anyone listening would have heard another sound amid their screaming, the sound of a man whistling "Spanish Harlem."

Far away to the north, another ship slipped her moorings and under the guidance of a port pilot eased her way out of the harbor of Archangel. The motor vessel *Komarov* was only ten years old and something over five thousand tons.

Inside her bridge, the atmosphere was warm and cosy. The captain and the pilot stood side by side, staring forward as the quays and warehouses slipped past to her port side, and watching the channel ahead to the open sea. Each man held a cup of steaming coffee. The helmsman kept the vessel on the heading given him by the pilot, and to his left the radar screen gleamed and died endlessly, its iridescent sweep arm picking up on each turn the dotted ocean ahead and beyond it the fringe of the ice that would never melt, even in high summer.

In the stern two men leaned over the rail beneath the flag with the hammer-and-sickle emblem and watched the Russian Arctic port slip past. Dr. Ivanov clipped the crushed cardboard filter of his black cigarette between his teeth and sniffed the crisp, salt-caked air. Both men were wrapped against the cold, for even in June the wind off the White Sea is no invitation to shirtsleeves. By his side, one of his technicians, younger, eager for his first trip abroad, turned to him.

"Comrade Doctor," he began.

Ivanov took the stump of the Papiross from his teeth and flicked it into the foaming wake. "My friend," he said, "I think, as we are now aboard, you can call me Mikhail Mikhailovich."

"But at the institute—"

"We are not at the institute. We are on board a ship. And we will be in fairly close confinement either here or in the jungle for months to come."

"I see," said the younger man, but he was not to be repressed. "Have you ever been to Zangaro before?"

"No," said his superior.

"But to Africa," insisted the younger man.

"To Ghana, yes."

"What is it like?"

"Full of jungle, swamps, mosquitoes, snakes, and people who don't understand a damn thing you say."

"But they understand English," said the assistant. "We both speak English."

"Not in Zangaro, they don't."

"Oh." The junior technician had read all he could find, which was not much, in the encyclopedia borrowed from the vast library at the institute, about Zangaro.

"The captain told me if we make good time we should arrive at Clarence in twenty-two days. That will be their Independence Day."

"Bully for them," said Ivanov and walked away.

Past Cape Spartel, nosing her way from the Mediterranean into the Atlantic, the MV *Toscana* radioed a ship-to-shore telegram to Gibraltor for onpassing to London. It was to Mr. Walter Harris at a London addresss. It said simply: "Please announce your brother completely recovered." It was the sign meaning the *Toscana* was on her way and on schedule. Slight variations of the message about Mr. Harris's brother's health could have meant she was on course but late, or in some kind of trouble. No telegram of any kind meant she had not been cleared from Spanish territorial waters.

That afternoon there was a conference in Sir James Manson's office.

"Good," said the tycoon when Endean broke the news. "How much time has she got to reach target?"

"Twenty-two days, Sir James. It is now Day Seventy-eight of the hundred estimated for the project. Shannon had allowed Day Eighty for his departure from Europe, and that would have left him twenty days. He estimated the time at sea between sixteen and eighteen days, allowing for adverse weather or a two-day breakdown. He had four days in hand, even on his own estimate."

"Will he strike early?"

"No, sir. Strike Day is still Day One Hundred. He'll kill time hove-to at sea if he has to."

Sir James Manson paced up and down his office. "How about the rented villa?" he asked.

"It has been arranged, Sir James."

"Then I don't see any point in your waiting around London any longer. Get over to Paris again, get a visa for Cotonou, fly down there, and get our new employee, Colonel Bobi, to accompany you to this place next to Zangaro. If he seems shifty, offer him more money.

"Get settled in, get the truck and the hunting guns ready, and when you receive Shannon's signal that he is going in for the attack that evening, break the news to Bobi. Get him to sign that mining concession as President Bobi, date it one month later, and send all three copies by registered post in three different envelopes to me here.

"Keep Bobi virtually under lock and key until Shannon's second signal to say he has succeeded. Then in you go. By the way, that bodyguard you are taking with you—is he ready?"

"Yes, Sir James. For the kind of money he's getting, he's good and ready."

"What's he like?"

"As nasty as they come. Which is what I was looking for."

"You could still have problems, you know. Shannon will have all his men round him, at least those who survive the battle. He could prove troublesome."

Endean grinned. "Shannon's men will follow Shannon," he said. "And I can handle him. Like all mercenaries, he's got his price. I'll just offer it to him—but in Switzerland and out of Zangaro."

When he had gone, Sir James Manson stared down at the City below him and wondered if any man did not have his price. "They can all be bought, and if they can't, they can be broken," one of his mentors had once said to him. And after years as a tycoon, watching politicians, generals, journalists, editors, businessmen, ministers, entrepreneurs and aristocrats, workers and union leaders, blacks and whites, at work and play, he was still of that view.

Many years ago a Spanish seafarer, looking from the sea toward the land, had seen a mountain which, with the sun behind it in the east, appeared to him to have the shape of a lion's head. He called the land Lion Mountain and passed on. The name stuck, and the country became known as Sierra Leone. Later another man, seeing the same mountain in a different light, or through different eyes, called it Mount Aureole. That name also stuck. Even later, and in a more whimsical bout of fantasy, a white man named the town founded in its shadow Freetown, and it still bears the name today. It was just after noon on July 2, Day Eighty-eight in Shannon's private calendar, that the motor vessel *Toscana* dropped anchor a third of a mile out from the shore, off Freetown, Sierra Leone.

On the voyage from Spain, Shannon had insisted that the cargo remain just where it was, untouched and unopened. This was just in case there was a search at Freetown, although since they had nothing to discharge and no cargo to take on board, that would have been most unusual. The ammunition crates had been scrubbed clean of their Spanish markings and sanded down with a disk sander to the bright white wood. Stenciled markings showing that the crates contained drilling bits for the oil rigs off the Cameroon coast had been painted on.

Only one job had he allowed to be done on the way south. The bundles of mixed clothing had been sorted, and the one containing the haversacks and webbing had been opened. With canvas needle and palm, Cipiriani, Vlaminck, and Dupree had passed the days cutting the haversacks to pieces and transforming them into backpacks fitted with a score of long, narrow pouches, each capable of taking one bazooka rocket. These now shapeless and inexplicable bundles were stored in the paint locker among the cleaning rags.

The smaller knapsacks had also been altered. The packs had been cut away so that only the shoulder straps remained, with braces across the chest and around the waist. Dog-clips had been fastened atop each shoulder strap, and others at the belt, and later these frames would accommodate an entire crate of mortar bombs, enabling up to twenty to be carried at one time.

The *Toscana* had announced her presence while six miles offshore to the harbormaster's office of Freetown, and had been given permission to enter port and anchor out in the bay. As she had no cargo to load or unload, there was no need for her to take up room at the port's precious Queen Elizabeth II Quay. She had come only to take on deck crew.

Freetown is one of the favorite ports along the West African coast for taking aboard these brawny laborers who, trained in the use of tackle and winches, are used by the tramp steamers frequenting the smaller timber ports along the coast. They board at Freetown on the outward voyage and are discharged with their pay on the way back. In a hundred coves and creeks along the coast, where cranes and jetties are at a premium, ships have to use their own jumbo derricks to load cargo. It is grindingly hard work, as one sweats in the tropical fever heat, and white seamen are paid to be seamen, not stevedores. Locally recruited labor might not be available and probably would not know how to handle cargo, so Sierra Leonians are brought along. They sleep in the open on the ship's deck for the voyage, brewing up their own food and performing their ablutions over the stern. It caused no surprise in Freetown when the *Toscana* gave this as her reason for calling.

When the anchor cable rattled down, Shannon scanned the shoreline right around the bay, almost all of it taken up by the outer shantytown of the country's capital.

The sky was overcast, no rain fell, but beneath the clouds the heat was like a greenhouse, and he felt the sweat clamping his shirt to his torso. It would be like this from here on. His eyes riveted on the central area of the city's waterfront, where a large hotel stood looking out over the bay. If anywhere, this was where Langarotti would be waiting, staring out to sea. Perhaps he had not arrived yet. But they could not wait forever. If he was not there by sundown, they would have to invent a reason for staying on—like a broken refrigerator. It would be unthinkable to sail without the cold store working. He took his eyes away from the hotel and watched the tenders plying around the big Elder Dempster ship tied up at the quay.

On the shore, the Corsican had already seen the *Toscana* before she dropped anchor, and was heading back into the town. He had been there for a week and had all the men Shannon wanted. They were not the same tribal group as the Leonians, but no one minded. A mixture of tribes was available as stevedores and deck cargo.

Just after two, a small pinnace came out from the customs house with a uniformed man standing in the back. He was the assistant chief customs officer, white socks agleam, khaki shorts and tunic pressed, epaulettes sparkling, and stiff peaked cap set dead straight. Among the regalia a pair of ebony knees and a beaming face could be distinguished. When he came aboard, Shannon met him, introduced himself as the owner's representative, shook hands profusely, and led the customs man to the captain's cabin.

The three bottles of whisky and two cartons of cigarettes were waiting. The officer fanned himself, sighed gustily with pleasure at the cool of the air-conditioning, and sipped his beer. He cast an incurious eye over the new manifest, which said the *Toscana* had picked up machine parts at Bruindisi and was taking them to the AGIP oil company's offshore concession near the Cameroon coast. There was no mention of Yugoslavia or Spain. Other cargo was listed as power boats (inflatable), engines (outboard), and tropical clothing (assorted), also for the oil drillers. On the way back she would wish to load cocoa and some coffee at San Pedro, Ivory Coast, and return to Europe. He exhaled on his official stamp to moisten it, and placed his approval on the manifest. An hour later he was gone, his presents in his tucker bag.

Just after six, as the evening cooled, Shannon made out the longshore boat moving away from the beach. Amidships the two local men who ran passengers out to the waiting vessels in the bay heaved at their oars. Aft sat seven other Africans, clutching bundles on their knees. In the prow sat a lone European. As the craft swung expertly in to the side of the *Toscana*, Jean-Baptiste Langarotti came nimbly up the ladder that hung to the water.

One by one the bundles were heaved fom the bobbing rowboat up to the rail of the freighter; then the seven Africans followed. Although it was indiscreet to do so in sight of land, Vlaminck, Dupree, and Semmler started to clap them on the back and shake hands. The Africans, grinning from ear to ear, seemed as happy as the mercenaries. Waldenberg and his mate looked on in surprise. Shannon signed to the captain to take the *Toscana* back to sea.

After dark, sitting in groups on the main deck, taking with gratitude the cooling breeze off the sea as the *Toscana* rolled on to the south, Shannon introduced his recruits to Waldenberg. The mercenaries knew them all, as they did the mercenaries. Six of the Africans were young men, called Johnny, Patrick, Jinja (nicknamed Ginger), Sunday, Bartholomew, and Timothy.

Each of them had fought with the mercenaires before; each of them had been personally trained by one of the European soldiers; each of them had been tried and tested in battle many times and would stick it out however hard the firefight. And each of them was loyal to his leader. The seventh was an older man, who smiled less, bore himself with a confident dignity, and was addressed by Shannon as "Doctor." He too was loyal to his leader and his people.

"How are things at home?" Shannon asked him.

Dr. Okoye shook his head sadly. "Not well," he said.

"Tomorrow we start work," Shannon told him. "We start preparing tomorrow."

PART 3
The Big Killing

TWENTY-ONE

For the remainder of the sea voyage, Cat Shannon worked his men without pause. Only the middle-aged African whom he called "Doctor" was exempt. The rest were divided into parties, each with a separate job to do.

Marc Vlaminck and Kurt Semmler broke open the five green Castrol oil drums by hammering off the false bottoms, and from each plucked the bulky package of twenty Schmeissers and a hundred magazines that was inside. The superfluous lubricating oil was poured into smaller containers and saved for the ship's use.

Aided by the six African soldiers, the pair stripped the masking tape from each of the hundred submachine guns, which were then individually wiped clean of oil and grease. By the time they had finished, the six Africans had already learned the operating mechanisms of the Schmeisser in a way that was as good if not better than any weapons-familiarization course that they could have undergone.

After breaking open the first ten boxes of 9mm. ammunition, the eight of them sat around the decks slotting the shells into the magazines, thirty to each, until the first fifteen thousand rounds from their store had gone into the five hundred magazines at their disposal. Eighty of the Schmeissers were then set aside while Jean-Baptiste Langarotti prepared sets of uniforms from the bales stored in the hold. These sets consisted of two T-shirts, two pairs of shorts, two pairs of socks, one pair of boots, one set of trousers, one beret, one combat blouse, and one sleeping bag. When these were ready, the bundle was wrapped up, one Schmeisser and five full magazines were wrapped in an oily cloth and slipped into a polyethylene bag, and the whole lot was stuffed into the sleeping bag. Tied at the top and ready for handling like a sack, each sleeping bag contained the necessary clothing and weaponry for one future soldier.

Twenty sets of uniforms and twenty Schmeissers with five magazines per carbine were set aside. These were for the attack force itself, although the force numbered only eleven, with spares for the crew if necessary. Langarotti, who had learned while in the army and in prison to handle a needle and thread, altered and sewed eleven sets of uniforms for the members of the attack party until each man was fitted out.

Dupree and Cipriani, the deckhand, who turned out to be a useful carpenter, stripped down several of the packing crates that had once contained ammunition, and turned their attention to the outboard engines. All three were Johnson 60-horsepower units. The two men built a wooden box to fit neatly over the top of each engine, and lined the boxes with foam rubber from the mattresses that had been brought along. With the exhaust noise of the engines muffled by the underwater exhausts, the mechanical noise emanating from the engine casings could also be reduced to a low murmur by the muffling boxes.

When Vlaminck and Dupree had finished these tasks, each turned his attention to the weapon he would be using on the night of the strike. Dupree uncrated his two mortar tubes and familiarized himself with the aiming mechanisms. He had not used the Yugoslav model of mortar before, but was relieved to see it was simple. He prepared seventy mortar boards, checking and arming the primers in the nose-cone of each bomb.

Having repacked the prepared bombs into their boxes, he clipped two boxes, one above the other, to the webbing harness that had already been prepared from the army-style knapsacks he had bought in London two months earlier.

Vlaminck concentrated on his two bazookas, of which only one would be used on the night of the attack. Again, the main limitaton to what he could take with him was the weight factor. Everything had to be carried on a human back. Standing on the forepeak, using the tip of the flagpole sticking above the stern as a fixed point, his aiming disk slotted to the end of the bazooka, he carefully adjusted the sights to the weapon until he was certain he could take a barrel at two hundred yards with no more than two shots. He had already picked Patrick as his back-up man, for they had been together before and knew each other well enough to make a good team. With his backpack, the African would be carrying ten bazooka rockets as well as his own Schmeisser. Vlaminck added another two rockets as his personal load, and Cipriani sewed him two pouches to hang from his belt, which could contain the extra rockets.

Shannon concentrated on the ancillary gear, examining the magnesium-flare rockets and explaining to Dupree how they worked. He distributed one compass to each mercenary, tested the gas-powered foghorn, and checked the portable radio sets.

Having time, Shannon had the *Toscana* heave to for two days well out at sea in an area where the ship's radar told them there was no other shipping within twenty miles. As the ship lay almost stationary, heaving slightly on the swell, each man tested his personal Schmeisser. The whites had no problems; they had each in their time used half a dozen different submachine guns, and these weapons vary but slightly. The Africans took longer to get used to them, for most of their experience had been with bolt-action 7.92mm. Mausers or the standard 7.62 NATO self-loading rifle. One of the German carbines jammed repeatedly, so Shannon threw it overboard and gave the man another. Each African fired off nine hundred rounds, until he was accustomed to the feel of the Schmeisser in his hands, and each man had been cured of the annoying habit African soldiers tend to adopt, of closing their eyes while they fire. There was no point in testing the mortars, since they have no moving parts—the bombs do the work—and they cannot be fired with accuracy anyway from the deck of a ship at sea.

The five empty and open-topped oil barrels had been stored for later use, and these were now streamed astern of the *Toscana* for bazooka practice. At a hundred yards all of the men, black and white, could riddle a barrel before they had ceased their practice. Four barrels were destroyed and sunk in this manner, and the fifth was used by Marc Vlaminck. He let it stream to two hundred yards, then planted himself in the stern of the *Toscana*, feet apart and braced, the bazooka across his right shoulder, right eye applied to the sight. Judging the gentle heave of the deck, he waited until he was sure and fired off his first rocket. It screamed over the top of the barrel and exploded with a spout of spray into the ocean. His second rocket took the barrel in the center. There was a crash, and the boom of the explosion echoed back over the water to the watching mercenaries and crew. Fragments of tinplate spattered the water close to where the barrel had been, and a cheer came from the watchers. Grinning widely, Vlaminck turned to Shannon, ripped off the glasses he had used to protect his eyes, and wiped the specks of smut from his face.

"You said you wanted a door taken off, Cat?"

"That's right, a bloody great wooden gate, Tiny."

"I'll give it to you in matchsticks, and that's a promise," said the Belgian.

Because of the noise they had made, Shannon ordered the *Toscana* to move on the next day, and two days later he called his second halt. In the period under way, the men had hauled out the three assault craft and inflated them. They lay side by side along the main deck. Each, despite being a deep, dark gray in color, had a brilliant orange nose and the name of the manufacturer in the same luminous color down each side. These were painted out with black paint from the ship's store.

When they were hove-to for the second time, they tested all three. Without the muffling boxes placed over the top of each engine, the Johnsons made an audible mutter even when four hundred yards away from the *Toscana*. With the boxes in place and the engines throttled back to less than quarter-power, there was hardly a sound at thirty yards. They tended to overheat after twenty minutes at half-power, but this could be stretched to thirty minutes if power was reduced. Shannon took one of the craft out for two hours, checking throttle settings for speed against noise, to get the best combination. As the powerful outboards gave him a large reserve, he elected never to push them beyond one-third of full power, and advised his men to close down to less than quarter-power for the last two hundred yards as they approached the landing beaches of the target area.

The walkie-talkies were also tested at up to four miles, and despite the heavy atmospherics and the hint of thunder in the stifling air, messages could still be heard if read over clearly and slowly. To get them used to the notion, the Africans were also given trips in the power craft, at a varying range of speeds, in daylight and at night. The night exercises were the most important.

For one of them Shannon took the other four whites and the six Africans three miles out from the *Toscana*, which burned one small light at her masthead. On the journey away from the ship, the ten men had their eyes bandaged. When the masks were taken off, each was given ten minutes to accustom his vision to the blackness of the sky and the ocean, before the move back to the boat began. With the engine throttled down and dead silence maintained aboard, the assault craft moved quietly back toward the light that represented the *Toscana*. Sitting with the tiller bar in his hand, holding the power setting steady at one-third, then cutting back to less than a quarter for the final run-in, Shannon could feel the tension of the men in front of him. They knew this was what it would be like when they struck, and there would be no second chances.

Back on board, Carl Waldenberg came up to Shannon as the two men watched the crew winch the vessel inboard by torchlight. "I hardly heard a sound," he said. "Not until you were a couple of hundred meters away, and I was listening hard. Unless they have very alert guards posted, you should be able to make the beach, wherever you are going. Incidentally, where are you going? I need more charts if I have to proceed much farther."

"I think you'd all better know," said Shannon. "We'll spend the rest of the night going through the briefing."

Until dawn, the crew (with the exception of the engineer, who still slept with his engines), the seven Africans, and the four mercenaries listened to Shannon in the main saloon while he went through the entire plan of attack. He had prepared and set up his projector and slide transparencies, some of which were pictures he had obtained of Zangaro, others of which were the maps and charts he had bought or drawn for himself.

When he had finished, there was dead silence in the stifling cabin, the blue wreaths of cigarette smoke trickling out through the open portholes into the equally clammy night outside.

Finally Waldenberg said, "*Gott in Himmel.*" Then they all started. It took an hour before the questions were answered. Waldenberg wanted reassurance that if anything went wrong the survivors would be back on board and the *Toscana* well over the horizon before sunrise. Shannon gave it to him.

"We have only your word for it they have no navy, no gunboats," Waldenberg said.

"Then my word will have to do," said Shannon. "They have none."

"Just because you did not see any—"

"They have none," snapped Shannon. "I spent hours talking with people who have been there for years. There are no gunboats, no navy."

The six Africans had no questions. Each would stick close to the mercenary who would lead him and trust that he knew what he was doing. The seventh, the doctor, asked briefly where he would be, and accepted that he would remain on board the *Toscana*. The four mercenaries had a few purely technical questions, which Shannon answered in technical terms.

When they came back up on deck, the Africans stretched themselves out on their sleeping bags and went to sleep. Shannon had often envied their ability to sleep at any time, in any place, in almost any circumstances. The doctor retired to his cabin, as did Norbiatto, who would take the next watch. Waldenberg went into his wheelhouse, and the *Toscana* began to move again toward her destination, just three days away.

The five mercenaries grouped themselves on the afterdeck behind the crew quarters and talked until the sun was high. They all approved of the plan of attack and accepted that Shannon's reconnaissance had been accurate and precise. If anything had changed since then, if there had been an unforeseen addition to the town's defenses or improvements to the palace, they knew they could all die. They would be very few, dangerously few, for such a job, and there was no margin for things going wrong. But they accepted that either they had to win within twenty minutes or they would have to get back to their boats and leave in a hurry—those that could leave. They knew that no one was going to come looking for wounded, and that anyone finding one of his colleagues badly hurt and unmovable would be expected to give him one mercenary's last gift to another, the quick, clean way out, preferable to capture and the slow death. It was part of the rules, and they had all had to do it before.

Just before noon they parted company and turned in.

They all woke early on the morning of Day Ninety-nine. Shannon had been up half the night, watching beside Waldenberg as the coastline loomed out of the perimeter of the tiny radar screen at the rear of the wheelhouse.

"I want you to come within visual range of the coast to the south of the capital," he had told the captain, "and spend the morning steaming northwards, parallel to the shore, so that at noon we are off the coast here."

His finger jabbed the sea off the coast of Manandi. During the twenty days at sea he had come to trust the German captain. Waldenberg, having taken his money in Ploce port, had stuck by his side of the bargain, giving himself completely to making the operation as successful as he could. Shannon was confident the seaman would hold his ship at readiness four miles off the coast, a bit to the south of Clarence, while the firefight went on, and if the distress call came over the walkie-talkie, that he would wait until the men who had managed to escape rejoined the *Toscana* in their speedboats, before making at full power for the open sea. There was no spare man Shannon could leave behind to ensure this, so he had to trust Waldenberg.

He had already found the frequency on the ship's radio on which Endean wanted him to transmit his first message, and this was timed for noon.

The morning passed slowly. Through the ship's telescope Shannon watched the estuary of the Zangaro River move past, a long, low line of mangrove trees along the horizon. At midmorning he could make out the break in the green line where the town of Clarence lay, and passed the telescope to Vlaminck, Langarotti, Dupree, and Semmler. Each studied the off-white blur in silence and handed the glass to the next man. They smoked more than usual and mooched around the deck, tense and bored with the waiting, wishing, now they were so close, that they could go straight into action.

At noon Shannon began to transmit his message. He read it clear into the radio speaker. It was just one word, "Plantain." He gave it every ten seconds for five minutes, then broke for five minutes, then gave it again. Three times within thirty minutes, each time over a five-minute period, he broadcast the word and hoped that Endean would hear it somewhere on the mainland. It meant simply that Shannon and his men were on time and in position, and that they would strike Clarence and Kimba's palace in the small hours of the following morning.

Twenty-two miles away across the water, Simon Endean heard the word on his Braun transistor radio, folded the long wasp-antenna, left the hotel balcony, and withdrew into the bedroom. Then he began slowly and carefully to explain to the former colonel of the Zangaran army that within twenty-four hours he, Antoine Bobi, would be President of Zangaro. At four in the afternoon the colonel, grinning and chuckling at the thought of the reprisals he would take against those who had assisted in his ousting, struck his deal with Endean. He signed the document granting Bormac Trading Company a ten-year exclusive mining concession in the Crystal Mountains for a flat annual fee, a tiny profits-participation by the Zangaran government, and watched Endean place in an envelope and seal a check certified by a Swiss bank for half a million dollars in the name of Antoine Bobi.

In Clarence preparations went ahead through the afternoon for the following day's independence celebrations. Six prisoners, lying badly beaten in the cells beneath the former colonial police station, listened to the cries of the Kimba Patriotic Youth marching through the streets above them, and knew that they would be battered to death in the main square as part of the celebrations Kimba had prepared. Photographs of the President were prominently hung on every public building, and the diplomatic wives prepared their migraines so they would be excused attendance at the ceremonies.

In the shuttered palace, surrounded by his guards, President Jean Kimba sat alone at his desk, contemplating the advent of his sixth year of office.

During the afternoon the *Toscana* and her lethal cargo put about and began to cruise slowly back down the coast from the north.

In the wheelhouse Shannon sipped his coffee and explained to Waldenberg how he wanted the *Toscana* placed.

"Hold her just north of the border until sundown," he told his captain. "After nine p.m., start her up again and move diagonally toward the coast. Between sundown and nine, we will have streamed the three assault craft astern of the ship, each loaded with its complement. That will have to be done by flashlight, but well away from the land, at least ten miles out.

"When you start to move, around nine, keep her really slow, so you end up here, four miles out from the shore and one mile north of the peninsula at two a.m. You'll be out of sight of the city in that position. With all lights doused, no one should see you. So far as I know, there's no radar on the peninsula, unless a ship is in port."

"Even if there is, she should not have a radar on," growled Waldenberg. He was bent over his inshore chart of the coast, measuring his distances with compasses and set-square. "When does the first craft set free and move inshore?"

"At two. That will be Dupree and his mortar crew. The other two boats cast adrift and head for the beach one hour later. Okay?"

"Okay," said Waldenberg. "I'll have you there."

"It has to be accurate," insisted Shannon. "We'll see no lights in Clarence, even if there are any, until we round the headland. So we'll be on compass heading only, calculating by speed and heading, until we see the outline of the shore, which might be no more than a hundred meters. It depends on the sky; cloud, moon, and stars."

Waldenberg nodded. He knew the rest. After he heard the firefight begin, he was to ease the *Toscana* across the mouth of the harbor four miles out, and heave to again two miles to the south of Clarence, four miles out from the tip of the peninsula. From then on he would listen on his walkie-talkie. If all went well, he would stay where he was until sunup. If things went badly, he would turn on the lights at the masthead, the forepeak, and the stern, to guide the returning force back to the *Toscana*.

Darkness that evening came early, for the sky was overcast and the moon would not rise until the small hours of the morning. The rains had already started, and twice in the previous three days the men had weathered drenching downpours as the skies opened. The weather report from Monrovia, listened to avidly on the radio, indicated there would be scattered squalls along the coast that night, but no tornadoes, and they could only pray there would be no torrential rains while the men were in their open boats or while the battle for the palace was on.

Before sundown the tarpaulins were hauled off the equipment piled in rows along the main deck, and when darkness fell Shannon and Norbiatto began organizing the departure of the assault craft. The first over the side was the one Dupree would use. There was no point in using the derrick; the sea was only eight feet beneath the deck at the lowest point. The men lowered the fully inflated craft into the water manually, and Semmler and Dupree went down into it as it bobbed against the *Toscana's* side in the slow swell.

The two of them hoisted the heavy outboard engine into place over the stern and screwed it tight to the backboard. Before placing the muffler on top of it, Semmler started the Johnson up and ran her for two minutes. The Serbian engineer had already given all three engines a thorough check-over, and it ran like a sewing machine. With the muffling box on top, the noise died to a low hum.

Semmler climbed out, and the equipment was lowered to Dupree's waiting hands. There were the baseplates and sighting gear for both mortars, then the two mortar tubes. Dupree was taking forty mortar bombs for the palace and twelve for the barracks. To be on the safe side, he took sixty bombs, all primed and fused for detonation on impact.

He also took both flare-launching rockets and the ten flares, one of the gas-powered foghorns, one walkie-talkie, and his night glasses. Slung over his shoulder he had his personal Schmeisser, and tucked in his belt were five full magazines. The two Africans who were going with him, Timothy and Sunday, were the last into the assault craft.

When it was ready, Shannon stared down at the three faces that looked back up to him in the dim glow from the flashlight. "Good luck," he called softly.

For answer Dupree raised one thumb and nodded. Holding the painter of the assault craft, Semmler moved back along the rail while Dupree fended off from down below. When the craft was steamed astern of the *Toscana* in complete darkness, Semmler tied her painter to the after rail, leaving the three men to bob up and down on the swell.

The second boat took less time to get into the water, for the men had got the hang of it. Marc Vlaminck went down with Semmler to set the outboard engine in position, for this was their boat. Vlaminck was taking one bazooka and twelve rockets, two on his own body, the other ten carried by his back-up man, who was Patrick. Semmler had his Schmeisser and five magazines in easy-extraction pouches hung around his belt. He had a set of night glasses around his neck and the second walkie-talkie strapped to one thigh. As he was the only man who could speak German, French, and reasonable English, he would double as the main attack party's radio operator. When the two whites were ensconced in their craft, Patrick and Jinja, who would be Semmler's back-up man, slid down the Jacob's ladder from the *Toscana* and took their places.

The boat was streamed astern of the ship, and Dupree's painter was passed to Semmler, who made it fast to his own assault craft. The two inflatable vessels bobbed behind the *Toscana* in line astern, separated by the length of rope, but none of their occupants said a word.

Langarotti and Shannon took the third and last boat. They were accompanied by Bartholomew and Johnny, the latter a big, grinning fighter who had been promoted at Shannon's insistence when they last fought together, but who had refused to take his own company, as his new rank entitled him to, preferring to stick close to Shannon and look after him.

Just before Shannon, who was the last man into the boats, descended the ladder, Captain Waldenberg appeared from the direction of the bridge and tugged at his sleeve. The German pulled the mercenary to one side and muttered quietly, "We may have a problem."

Shannon was immobile, frozen by the thought that something had gone seriously wrong. "What is it?" he asked.

"There's a ship. Lying off Clarence, farther out than we are."

"How long since you saw it?"

"Some time," said Waldenberg, "but I thought it must be cruising south down the coast, like us, or moving northward. But it's not; it's riding to."

"You're sure? There's no doubt about it?"

"None at all. When we came down the coast we were moving so slowly that if the other had been steaming in the same direction, she'd be well away by now. If northward, she'd have passed us by now. She's immobile."

"Any indication of what she is, who she belongs to?"

The German shook his head. "The size of a freighter. No indication who she is, unless we contact her."

Shannon thought for several minutes. "If she were a freighter bringing cargo to Zangaro, would she anchor till morning before entering harbor?" he asked.

Waldenberg nodded. "Quite possible. Entry by night is frequently not allowed in some of the smaller ports along this coast. She's probably riding out until the morning before asking permission to enter port."

"If you've seen her, presumably she's seen you?" Shannon suggested.

"Bound to," said Waldenberg. "We're on her radar all right."

"Could her radar pick up the dinghies?"

"Unlikely," said the captain. "Too low in the water, most probably."

"We go ahead," said Shannon. "It's too late now. We have to assume she's just a freighter waiting out the night."

"She's bound to hear the firefight," said Waldenberg.

"What can she do about it?"

The German grinned. "Not much. If you fail, and we're not out of here before sunrise, she'll recognize the *Toscana* through binoculars."

"We mustn't fail, then. Carry on as ordered."

Waldenberg went back to his bridge. The middle-aged African doctor, who had watched the proceedings in silence, stepped forward.

"Good luck, Major," he said in perfectly modulated English. "God go with you."

Shannon felt like saying that he would have preferred a Wombat recoilless rifle, but held his tongue. He knew these people took religion very seriously. He nodded, said, "Sure," and went over the side.

Out in the darkness, as he looked up at the dim blob of the *Toscana's* stern above him, there was complete silence but for the slap of the water against the rubberized hulls of the boats. Occasionally it gurgled behind the ship's rudder. From the landward side there was not a sound, for they were well out of earshot of the shore, and by the time they came close enough to hear shouts and laughter it would be well past midnight and, with luck, everyone would be asleep. Not that there was much laughter in Clarence, but Shannon was aware how far a single, sharp sound can travel over water at night, and everyone in his party, in the boats and on the *Toscana*, was sworn to silence and no smoking.

He glanced at his watch. It was quarter to nine. He sat back to wait.

At nine the hull of the *Toscana* emitted a low rumble, and the water beneath her stern began to churn and bubble, the phosphorescent white wake running back to slap against the snub nose of Shannon's assault craft. Then they were under way, and by dipping his fingers over the side he could feel the caress of the passing water. Five hours to cover twenty-eight nautical miles.

The sky was still overcast, and the air was like that inside an old greenhouse, but a hole in the cloud cover let a little dim starlight through. Astern he could make out the craft of Vlaminck and Semmler at the end of twenty feet of rope, and somewhere behind them Janni Dupree was moving along in the wake of the *Toscana*.

The five hours went by like a nightmare. Nothing to do but watch and listen, nothing to see but the darkness and the glitter of the sea, nothing to hear but the low thump of the *Toscana's* old pistons moving inside her rusted hull. No one could sleep, despite the mesmeric rocking of the light craft, for the tensions were building up in every man in the operation.

But the hours did pass, somehow. Shannon's watch said five past two when the noise of the *Toscana's* engines died and she slowed to idle in the water. From above the after rail a low whistle came through the darkness—Waldenberg, letting him know they were in position for cast-off. Shannon turned his head to signal Semmler, but Dupree must have heard the whistle, for a few seconds later they heard his engine cough into life and begin to move away toward the shore. They never saw him go, just heard the low buzz of the engine under its muffler vanishing into the darkness.

At the helm of his assault craft big Janni checked his power setting on the twist-grip he held in his right hand, and held his left arm with the compass as steady as he could under his eyes. He knew he should have four and a half miles to cover, angling in toward the coast, trying to make landfall on the outer side of the northern arm that curved around the harbor of Clarence. At that power setting, on that course, he should make it in thirty minutes. At twenty-five minutes he would shut the engine almost off and try to make out his landfall by eyesight. If the others gave him one hour to set up his mortars and flare-rockets, they should move past the tip of the point toward their own beach landing just about the time he was ready. But for that hour he and his two Africans would be the only ones on the shore of Zangaro. That was all the more reason why they should be completely silent as they set up their battery.

Twenty-two minutes after he left the *Toscana*, Dupree heard a low *psst* from the bow of his dinghy. It was Timothy, whom he had posted as a lookout. Dupree glanced up from his compass, and what he saw caused him to throttle back quickly. They were already close to a shoreline, little more than three hundred yards away, and the dim starlight from the hole in the clouds above them showed a line of deeper darkness right ahead. Dupree squinted hard, easing the craft another two hundred yards inshore. It was mangrove; he could hear the water chuckling among the roots. Far out to his right he could discern the line of vegetation ending and the single line of the horizon between sea and night sky running away to the end of vision. He had made landfall three miles along the northern coast of the peninsula.

He brought his boat about, still keeping the throttle very low and virtually silent, and headed back out to sea. He set the tiller to keep the shoreline of the peninsula in vision at half a mile until he reached the limit of the strip of land at whose end the town of Clarence stood, then again headed slowly inshore. At two hundred yards he could make out the long, low spit of gravel that he was seeking, and in the thirty-eighth minute after leaving the *Toscana* he cut the engine and let the assault craft drift on its own momentum toward the spit. It grounded with a soft grating of fabric on gravel.

Dupree stepped lightly down the boat, avoiding the piles of equipment, swung a leg over the prow, and dropped onto the sand. He felt for the painter and kept it in his hand to prevent the boat from drifting away. For five minutes all three men remained immoble, listening for the slightest sound from the town they knew lay over the low hummock of gravel and scrub in front of them, and four hundred yards to the left. But there was no sound. They had arrived without causing any alarm.

When he was certain, Dupree slipped a marlin spike out of his belt, rammed it deep into the shingle of the shore, and tied the painter securely to it. Then he rose to a crouch and ran lightly up the hummock ahead of him. It was barely fifteen feet above sea level at its top, and covered in knee-high scrub that rustled against his boots. The rustling was no problem; it was drowned by the slap of the sea on the shingle and far too soft to be heard away in the town. Crouching at the spine of the strip of land that formed one arm of the harbor, Dupree looked over the top. To his left he could make out the spit running away into the darkness, and straight ahead lay more water, the flat mirror-calm of the protected harbor. The end of the spit of gravel was ten yards to his right.

Returning to the assault craft, he whispered to the two Africans to begin unloading the equipment in complete silence. As the bundles came onto the shore he picked them up and carried them one by one up to the top of the rise. Each metallic piece was covered in sacking to prevent noise if two should knock together.

When the whole of his weaponry was assembled, Dupree began to set it up. He worked fast and quietly. At the far end of the spit, where Shannon had told him there was a round, flat area, he set up his main mortar. He knew, if Shannon's measurements were accurate—and he trusted they would be— that the range from the tip of the land to the center of the palace courtyard was 781 yards. Using his compass, he pointed the mortar on the exact compass bearing Shannon had given him from the point he stood to the presidential palace, and carefully adjusted his mortar's elevation to drop his first range-finding bomb as near to the center of the palace courtyard as possible.

He knew that when the flares went up he would see not the whole palace but just the top story, so he could not watch the bomb hit the ground. But he would see the upward flash of the explosion over the brow of the ground behind the warehouse at the other end of the harbor, and that would be enough.

When he was finished with the first mortar, he set up the second. This was pointed at the barracks, and he put the baseplate ten yards away from the first, down the spine of the land on which he stood. He knew both range and bearing from this mortar to the barracks, and that the accuracy of the second mortar was not vital, since its purpose was to drop bombs at random into the acreage of the former police lines and scatter the Zangaran army men through panic. Timothy, who had been his sergeant on mortars the last time they fought, would handle the second mortar on his own.

He established a pile of a dozen mortar bombs next to the second tube, settled Timothy beside it, and whispered a few last instructions into his ear.

Between the two mortars he established the two flare-launching rockets and jammed one rocket down each launcher, leaving the other eight lying handy. Each flare was reputed to have a life of twenty seconds, so if he was to operate both his own mortar and the illuminations, he knew he would have to work fast and skillfully. He needed Sunday to pass him his mortar bombs from the stack he had built beside the emplacement.

When he was finished, he looked at his watch. Three twenty-two in the morning. Shannon and the other two boats must be off the shore somewhere, heading for the harbor. He took his walkie-talkie, extended the aerial to its full length, switched on, and waited the prescribed thirty seconds for it to warm up. From then on, it would not be switched off again. When he was ready, he pressed the blip button three times at one-second intervals.

A mile off the shore, Shannon was at the helm of the leading assault craft, eyes straining into the darkness ahead. To his left side, Semmler kept the second craft in formation order, and it was he who heard the three buzzes from the walkie-talkie on his knee. He steered his boat softly into the side of Shannon's, so the two rounded sides scuffed each other. Shannon looked toward the other boat. Semmler hissed and pulled his boat away again to maintain station at 2 yards. Shannon was relieved. He knew Semmler had heard Dupree's signal across the water, and that the rangy Africaner was set up and waiting for them. Two minutes later, 1000 yards off the shore, Shannon caught the quick flash from Dupree's flashlight, heavily masked and blinkered to a pinpoint of light. It was off to his right, so he knew that he was heading too far north. In unison, the two craft swung to starboard, Shannon trying to recall the exact point from which the light had come and to head for a point 100 yards to the right of it. That would be the harbor entrance. The light came again when Dupree caught the low buzz of the two outboard engines as they were 300 yards from the tip of the point. Shannon spotted the light and changed course a few degrees.

Two minutes later, shut down to less than quarter-power and making no noise louder than a bumblebee, the two assault craft went by the tip of the spit where Dupree was crouching, fifty yards out. The South African caught the glitter of the wake, the bubbles from the exhausts rising to the surface; then they were gone into the harbor entrance and across the still water toward the warehouse on the other side.

There was still no sound from the shore when Shannon's straining eyes made out the bulk of the warehouse against the marginally lighter skyline, steered to the right, and grounded on the shingle of the fishing beach among the natives' dugout canoes and hanging fishnets.

Semmler brought his own boat to the shore a few feet away, and both engines died together. Like Dupree, all the men remained motionless for several minutes, waiting for an alarm to be called. They tried to make out the difference between the humped backs of the fishing canoes and the shape of a waiting ambush party. There was no ambush. Shannon and Semmler stepped over the side; each jabbed a marlin spike into the sand and tethered the boats to it. The rest followed. With a low, muttered "Come on, let's go," Shannon led the way across the beach and up the sloping incline to the 200-yard-wide plateau between the harbor and the silent palace of President Jean Kimba.

TWENTY-TWO

The eight men ran in a low crouch, up through the scrubland of the hillside and out onto the plain at the top. It was after half past three, and no lights were burning in the palace. Shannon knew that half-way between the top of the rise and the palace 200 yards away they would meet the coast road, and standing at the junction would be at least two palace guards. He expected he would not be able to take them both silently, and that after the firing started the party would have to crawl the last hundred yards to the palace wall. He was right.

Out across the water, in his lonely vigil, Big Janni Dupree waited for the shot that would send him into action. He had been briefed that whoever fired the shot, or however many there were, the first one would be his signal. He crouched close to the flare-launching rockets, waiting to let the first one go. In his spare hand was his first mortar bomb.

Shannon and Langarotti were out ahead of the other six when they made the road junction in front of the palace, and already both were wet with sweat. Their faces, darkened with sepia dye, were streaked by the running perspiration. The rent in the clouds above them was larger, and more stars showed through, so that, although the moon was still hidden, there was a dim light across the open area in front of the palace. At 100 yards Shannon could make out the line of the roof against the sky, though he missed the guards until he stumbled over one. The man was seated on the ground, snoozing.

Shannon was too slow and clumsy with the commando knife in his right hand. After stumbling, he recovered, but the Vindu guard rose with equal speed and emitted a brief yell of surprise. The call attracted his partner, also hidden in the uncut grass a few feet away. The second man rose, gurgled once as the Corsican's knife opened his throat from carotid artery to jugular vein, and went back down again, choking out his last seconds. Shannon's man took the swipe with the Bowie knife in the shoulder, let out another scream, and ran.

A hundred yards in front, close to the palace gate, there was a second cry, and the sound of a bolt operating in the breech of a rifle. It was never quite certain who fired first. The wild shot from the palace gate and the snarling rip of Shannon's half-second burst that sliced the running man almost in two blended with each other. From far behind them came a whoosh and a scream in the sky; two seconds later the sky above them exploded in blistering white light. Shannon caught a brief impression of the palace in front of him, two figures in front of its gate, and the feeling that his other six men were fanning out to right and left of him. Then the eight of them were face down in the grass and crawling forward.

Janni Dupree stepped away from the rocket-launcher the instant he had torn the lanyard off the first rocket, and was slipping his mortar bomb down the tube as the rocket screamed upward. The *smack-thump* of the mortar bomb departing on its parabola toward the palace blended with the crash of the magnesium flare exploding away toward the land, over the spot he hoped his colleagues would have reached. He took his second bomb and, squinting into the light from the palace, waited to watch the first one fall. He had given himself four sighting shots, on an estimate of fifteen seconds for each bomb in flight. After that he knew he could keep up a fire rate of one every two seconds, with Sunday feeding him the ammunition singly but fast and in rhythm.

His first sighting bomb hit the front right-hand cornice of the palace roof, high enough for him to see the impact. It did not penetrate but blew tiles off the roof just above the gutter. Stopping, he twirled the traverse knob of the directional aiming mechanism a few mils to the left and slipped in his second bomb just as the flare fizzled out. He had stepped across the other rocket-launcher, ripped off the firing lanyard of the rocket, sent it on its way, and stuffed a fresh pair into the two launchers before he needed to look up again. The second flare burst into light above the palace, and four seconds later the second bomb landed. It was dead center, but short, for it fell onto the tiles directly above the main door.

Dupree was also pouring with sweat, and the grub-screw was slick between his fingers. He brought the angle of elevation slightly down, lowering the nose of the mortar a whisker toward the ground for extra range. Working the opposite way from artillery, mortars have to be lowered for extra range. Dupree's third mortar bomb was on its way before the flare fizzled out, and he had a full fifteen seconds to send up the third flare, trot down the spit a short way to actuate the foghorn, and be back in time to watch the mortar explode. It went clean over the palace roof and into the courtyard behind. He saw the red glow for a split second; then it was gone. Not that it mattered. He knew he had got his range and direction exactly right. There would be no shortfall to endanger his own men in front of the palace.

Shannon and his men were face down in the grass as the three flares lit up the scene around them and Janni's ranging shots went in. No one was prepared to raise his head until the Afrikaner was sending the hardware over the top of the palace and into the rear courtyard.

Between the second and third explosions Shannon risked putting his head up. He knew he had fifteen seconds until the third mortar went home. He saw the palace in the glare of the third magnesium flare, and two lights had gone on in the upper rooms. After the reverberations of the second mortar bomb died away, he heard a variety of screams and shouts from inside the fortress. These were the first and last sounds the defenders made before the roar of explosives blotted out all else.

Within five seconds the foghorn had gone on, the long, maniacal scream howling across the water from the harbor spit, filling the African night with a wail like a thousand released banshees. The crash of the mortar going into the palace courtyard was almost drowned out, and he heard no more screams. When he raised his head again he could see no further damage to the front of the palace and assumed Janni had dropped the bomb over the top. By agreement, Janni would use no more testing shots after his first on target, but go straight into the faster rhythm. From the sea behind him, Shannon heard the thud of mortars begin, steady, pulsing like a heartbeat in the ears, backed by the now monotonous wail of the foghorn, which had a life of seventy seconds on its gas canister.

To get rid of forty bombs, Janni would need eighty seconds, and it was agreed that, if there were a ten-second pause at any point after halfway, he would cease the bombardment so his colleagues would not run forward and be blown apart by a latecomer. Shannon had few worries that Janni would muff it.

When the main barrage began to hit the palace fifteen seconds after the thumps of their firing were heard, the eight men in the grass had a grand-stand view. There was no more need for flares; the roaring crash of the mortar bombs going into the flagstone-covered courtyard behind the palace threw up gobbets of red light every two seconds. Only Tiny Marc Vlaminck had anything to do.

He was out to the left of the line of men, almost exactly in front of the main gate. Standing foursquare to the palace, he took careful aim and sent off his first rocket. A twenty-foot-long tongue of flame whirled out of the rear of the bazooka, and the pineapple-sized warhead sped for the main gate. It exploded high on the right-hand edge of the double doors, ripping a hinge out of the masonry and leaving a yard-square hole in the woodwork.

Kneeling by his side, Patrick slipped the rockets out of his backpack spread on the ground, and passed them upward. The second shot began to topple in midair and exploded against the stonework of the arch above the door. The third hit the center lock. Both doors seemed to erupt upward under the impact; then they sagged on the twisted hinges, fell apart, and swung inward.

Janni Dupree was halfway through his barrage, and the red glare from behind the roof of the palace had become constant. Something was burning in the courtyard, and Shannon supposed it was the guardhouses. When the doors swung open, the men crouching in the grass could see the red glare through the archway, and two figures swayed in front of it and fell down before they could emerge.

Marc sent four more rockets straight through the open gate into the furnace beyond the archway, which apparently was a through passage to the courtyard behind. It was Shannon's first glimpse of what lay beyond the gate.

The mercenary leader screamed to Vlaminck to stop firing, for he had used seven of his dozen rockets, and for all Shannon knew there might be an armored vehicle somewhere in the town, despite what Gomez had said. But the Belgian was enjoying himself. He sent another four rockets through the front wall of the palace at ground level and on the second floor, finally standing exultantly waving both his bazooka and his last rocket at the palace in front, while Dupree's mortar bombs caromed overhead.

At that moment the foghorn whined away to a whisper and died. Ignoring Vlaminck, Shannon shouted to the others to move forward, and he, Semmler, and Langarotti began to run at a crouch through the grass, Schmeissers held forward, safety catches off, fingers tense on the triggers. They were followed by Johnny, Jinja, Bartholomew, and Patrick, who, having no more bazooka rockets to carry, unslung his submachine gun and joined the others.

At twenty yards, Shannon stopped and waited for Dupree's last bombs to fall. He had lost count of how many were still to come, but the sudden silence after the last bomb fell told him they were over. For a second or two the silence itself was deafening. After the foghorn and the mortars, the roar and crash of Tiny's bazooka rockets, the absence of sound was uncanny. So much so that it was almost impossible to realize the entire operation had lasted less than five minutes.

Shannon wondered for a second if Timothy had sent off his dozen mortar bombs to the army barracks, if the soldiers had scattered as he surmised they would, and what the other citizens of the town had thought of the inferno that must have nearly deafened them. He was jerked into wakefulness when the next two magnesium flares exploded over him, one after the other, and without waiting longer he leaped to his feet, screamed, "Come on," and ran the last twenty yards to the smoldering main gate.

He was firing as he went through, sensing more than seeing the figure of Jean-Baptiste Langarotti to his left and Kurt Semmler closing up on his right. Through the gate and inside the archway the scene was enough to stop anybody in his tracks. The arch went straight through the main building and into the courtyard. Above the courtyard the flares still burned with a stark brilliance that lit the scene behind the palace like something from the *Inferno.*

Kimba's guards had been caught asleep by the first sighting shots, which had brought them out of their lean-to barrack huts and into the center of the paved area. That was where the third shot and the succeeding forty quick-succession bombs had found them. Up one wall ran a ladder, and four mangled men hung from its rungs, caught in the back as they tried to run to the top of the enclosing wall. The rest had taken the full force of the mortars, which had exploded on stone flags and scattered lethal shards of steel in all directions.

There were piles of bodies, some still half alive, most very dead. Two army trucks and three civilian vehicles, one the presidential Mercedes, were standing shredded from end to end against the rear wall. Several palace servants about to flee the horror in the rear had apparently been grouped behind the main gate when Vlaminck's mortars came through. They were strewn all over the undercover area beneath the archway.

To right and left were further arches, each leading to what seemed to be a set of stairs to the upper floors. Without waiting to be asked, Semmler took the right-hand set, Langarotti the left. Soon there were bursts of submachine-carbine fire from each side as the two mercenaries laundered the upper floor.

Just beyond the stairs to the upper floors were doors at ground level, two on each side. Shouting to make himself heard above the screams of the maimed Vindu and the chattering of Semmler's Schmeisser upstairs, Shannon ordered the four Africans to take the ground floor. He did not have to tell them to shoot everything that moved. They were waiting to go, eyes rolling, chests heaving.

Slowly, cautiously, Shannon moved through the archway into the threshold to the courtyard at the rear. If there was any opposition left in the palace guards, it would come from there. As he stepped outside, a figure with a rifle ran screaming at him from his left. It could be that a panic-stricken Vindu was making a break for safety, but there was no time to find out. Shannon whirled and fired; the man jackknifed and blew a froth of blood from an already dead mouth onto Shannon's blouse front. The whole area and palace smelled of blood and fear, sweat and death, and over it all was the greatest intoxicant smell in the world for mercenaries, the reek of cordite.

He sensed rather than heard the scuff of footsteps in the archway behind him and swung around. From one of the side doors, into which Johnny had run to start mopping up the remaining Vindu alive inside the palace, a man had emerged. What happened when he reached the center of the flagstones under the arch, Shannon could recall later only as a kaleidoscope of images. The man saw Shannon the same time Shannon saw him, and snapped off a shot from the gun he clenched in his right hand at hip level.

Shannon felt the slug blow softly on his cheek as it passed. He fired half a second later, but the man was agile. After firing he went to the ground, rolled, and came up in the fire position a second time. Shannon's Schmeisser had let off five shots, but they went above the gunman's body as he went to the flagstones; then the magazine ran out. Before the man in the hallway could take another shot, Shannon stepped aside and out of sight behind a stone pillar, snapped out the old magazine, and slapped in a new one. Then he came around the corner, firing. The man was gone.

It was only then he became fully conscious that the gunman, stripped to the waist and barefoot, had not been an African. The skin of his torso, even in the dim light beneath the arch, had been white, and the hair dark and straight.

Shannon swore and ran back toward the embers of the gate on their hinges. He was too late.

As the gunman ran out of the shattered palace, Tiny Marc Vlaminck was walking toward the archway. He had his bazooka cradled in both hands across his chest, the last rocket fitted into the end. The gunman never even stopped. Still running flat out, he loosed off two fast shots that emptied his magazine. They found the gun later in the long grass. It was a Makarov 9mm., and it was empty.

The Belgian took both shots in the chest, one of them in the lungs. Then the gunman was past him, dashing across the grass for safety beyond the reach of the light cast by the flares Dupree was still sending up. Shannon watched as Vlaminck, moving in a kind of slow motion, turned to face the running man, raised his bazooka and slotted it carefully across his right shoulder, took steady aim, and fired.

Not often does one see a bazooka the size of the warhead on the Yugoslav RPG-7 hit a man in the small of the back. Afterward, they could not even find more than a few pieces of cloth from his trousers.

Shannon had to throw himself flat again to avoid being broiled in the backlash of flame from the Belgian's last shot. He was still on the ground, eight yards away, when Tiny Marc dropped his weapon and crashed forward, arms outspread, across the hard earth before the gateway. Then the last of the flares went out.

Big Janni Dupree straightened up after sending off the last of his ten magnesium flares and yelled, "Sunday."

He had to shout three times before the African standing ten yards away could hear him. All three men were partly deaf from the pounding their ears had taken from the mortar and the foghorn. He shouted to Sunday to stay behind and keep watch over the mortars and the boat, then, signaling to Timothy to follow him, he began to jog-trot through the scrub and bushes along the spit of land toward the mainland. Although he had loosed off more firepower than the other four mercenaries put together, he saw no reason why he should be denied all the action.

Besides, his job was still to silence the army barracks, and he knew, from his memory of the maps on board the *Toscana*, roughly where it was. It took the pair of them ten minutes to reach the road that ran across the end of the peninsula from side to side, and, instead of turning right toward the palace, Dupree led the way left, toward the barracks. Janni and Timothy had slowed to a walk, one on each side of the laterite road, their Schmeissers pointing forward, ready to fire the moment trouble showed itself.

The trouble was around the first bend in the road. Scattered twenty minutes earlier by the first of the mortar bombs dispatched by Timothy, which fell between the hutments that made up the barracks line, the two hundred encamped men of Kimba's army had fled into the night. But about a dozen of them had regrouped in the darkness and were standing at the edge of the road, muttering in low whispers among themselves. If they had not been so deaf, Dupree and Timothy would have heard them sooner. As it was, they were almost on the group before they saw them, shadows in the shadows of the palm trees. Ten of the men were naked, having been roused from sleep. The other two had been on guard duty and were clothed and armed.

The previous night's torrential rain had left the ground so soft that most of Timothy's dozen mortar bombs had embedded themselves too deeply in the earth to have their full intended impact. The Vindu soldiers Dupree and Timothy found waiting around that corner still had something of their wits about them. One of them also had a hand grenade.

It was the sudden movement of the soldiers when they saw the white gleam of Dupree's face, from which the dye had long since run away with his sweat, that alerted the South African. He screamed, "Fire," and opened up at the group. Four of them were cut apart by the steam of slugs from the Schmeisser. The other eight ran, two more falling as Dupree's fire pursued them into the trees. One of them, as he ran, turned and hurled the thing he carried in his hand. He had never used one before and never seen one used. But it was his pride and joy, and he had always hoped to use it one day.

The grenade went high in the air, out of sight, and when it fell, it hit Timothy full in the chest. In instinctive reaction, the African veteran clutched at the object as he went over backward and, sitting on the ground, recognized it for what it was. He also saw that the fool who had thrown it had forgotten to take the pin out. Timothy had seen a mercenary catch a grenade once. He had watched as the man hurled it straight back at the enemy. Rising

to his feet, Timothy whipped the pin out of the grenade and threw it as far as
he could after the retreating Vindu soldiers.

It went high into the air a second time, but this time it hit a tree. There was
a dull clunk, and the grenade fell short of where it was intended to go. At
that moment Janni Dupree started in pursuit, a fresh magazine in his
carbine. Timothy shouted a warning, but Dupree must have thought it was a
scream of elation. He ran eight paces forward into the trees, still firing from
the hip, and was two yards from the grenade when it exploded.

He did not remember much more. He remembered the flash and the
boom, the sensation of being picked up and tossed aside like a rag doll. Then
he must have passed out. He came to, lying out on the laterite road, and
there was someone kneeling in the road beside him, cradling his head. He
could feel that his throat was very warm, as it had been the time he had had a
fever as a boy—a comfortable, drowsy feeling of being half awake and half
asleep. He could hear a voice talking to him, saying something repeatedly
and urgently, but he could not make out the words. "Sorry, Janni, so sorry,
sorry . . . "

He could understand his own name, but that was all. This language was
different, not his own language, but something else. He swiveled his eyes
around to the person who was holding him and made out a dark face in the
half-light beneath the trees. He smiled and said quite clearly in Afrikaans,
"Hallo Pieter."

He was staring up at the gap between the palm fronds when finally the
clouds shifted to one side and the moon came out. It looked enormous, as it
always does in Africa, brilliant white and shining. He could smell the rain in
the vegetation beside the road and see the moon sitting up there glistening
like a giant pearl, like the Paarl Rock after the rain. It was good to be back
home again, he thought. Janni Dupree was quite content when he closed his
eyes again and died.

It was half past five when enough natural daylight filtered over the
horizon for the men at the palace to be able to switch off their flashlights. Not
that the daylight made the scene in the courtyard look any better. But the job
was done.

They had brought Vlaminck's body inside and laid it out straight in one of
the side rooms off the ground-floor hallway. Beside him lay Janni Dupree,
brought up from the seashore road by three of the Africans. Johnny was also
dead, evidently surprised and shot by the white bodyguard who had seconds
later stopped Vlaminck's last bazooka rocket. The three of them were side by
side.

Semmler had summoned Shannon to the main bedroom on the second
floor and showed him by flashlight the figure he had gunned down as it tried
to clamber out of the window.

"That's him," said Shannon.

There were six survivors from among the dead President's domestic staff.
They had been found cowering in one of the cellars, which they had found,
more by instinct than by logic, to be the best security from the rain of fire
from the skies. These were being used as forced labor to tidy up. Every room
in the main part of the palace was examined, and the bodies of all the other
friends of Kimba and palace servants that had been lying around the rooms
were carried down and dumped in the courtyard at the back. The remnants

of the door could not be replaced, so a large carpet taken from one of the state rooms was hung over the entrance to mask the view inside.

At five o'clock Semmler had gone back to the *Toscana* in one of the speedboats, towing the other two behind him. Before leaving, he had contacted the *Toscana* on his walkie-talkie to give the code word meaning all was in order.

He was back by six-thirty with the African doctor and the same three boats, this time loaded with stores, the remaining mortar bombs, the eighty bundles containing the remaining Schmeissers, and nearly a ton of 9mm. ammunition.

At six, according to a letter of instruction Shannon had sent to Captain Waldenberg, the *Toscana* had begun to broadcast three words on the frequency to which Endean was listening. The words, *paw-paw, cassava,* and *mango,* meant respectively: The operation went ahead as planned, it was completely successful, and Kimba is dead.

When the African doctor had viewed the scene of carnage at the palace, he sighed and said, "I suppose it was necessary."

"It was necessary," affirmed Shannon and asked the older man to set about the task he had been brought to do.

By nine, nothing had stirred in the town and the clearing-up process was almost complete. The burial of the Vindu would have to be done later, when there was more manpower available. Two of the speedboats were back at the *Toscana,* slung aboard and stowed below, while the third was hidden in a creek not far from the harbor. All traces of the mortars on the point had been removed, the tubes and baseplates brought inside, the rocket-launchers and packing crates dropped out at sea. Everything and everyone else had been brought inside the palace, which, although battered to hell from the inside, bore only two areas of shattered tiles, three broken windows in the front, and the destroyed door to indicate from the outside that it had taken a beating.

At ten, Semmler and Langarotti joined Shannon in the main dining room, where the mercenary leader was finishing off some jam and bread that he had found in the presidential kitchen. Both men reported on the results of their searches. Semmler told Shannon the radio room was intact, apart from several bullet holes in the wall, and the transmitter would still send. Kimba's private cellar in the basement had yielded at last to the persuasion of several magazines of ammunition. The national treasury was apparently in a safe at the rear of the cellar, and the national armory was stacked around the walls—enough guns and ammunition to keep an army of two or three hundred men going for several months in action.

"So what now?" asked Semmler when Shannon had heard him out.

"So now we wait," said Shannon.

"Wait for what?"

Shannon picked his teeth with a spent match. He thought of Janni Dupree and Tiny Marc lying below on the floor, and of Johnny, who would not liberate another farmer's goat for his evening supper. Langarotti was slowly stropping his knife on the leather band around his left fist.

"We wait for the new government," said Shannon.

The American-built 1-ton truck carrying Simon Endean arrived just after one in the afternoon. There was another European at the wheel, and

Endean sat beside him, clutching a large-bore hunting rifle. Shannon heard the growl of the engine as the truck left the shore road and came slowly up to the front entrance of the palace, where the carpet hung lifeless in the humid air, covering the gaping hole where the main gate had been.

He watched from an upper window as Endean climbed suspiciously down, looked at the carpet and the other pockmarks on the front of the building, and examined the eight black guards at attention before the gate.

Endean's trip had not been completely without incident. After the *Toscana's* radio call that morning, it had taken him two hours to persuade Colonel Bobi that he was actually going back into his own country within hours of the coup. The man had evidently not won his colonelcy by personal courage.

They had set off from the neighboring capital by road at nine-thirty on the hundred-mile drive to Clarence. In Europe that distance may take two hours; in Africa it takes more. They arrived at the border in midmorning and began the haggle to bribe their way past the Vindu guards, who had still not heard of the night's coup in the capital. Colonel Bobi, hiding behind a pair of large and very dark glasses and dressed in a white flowing robe like a nightshirt, posed as their car-boy, a personal servant who, in Africa, never requires papers to cross a border. Endean's papers were in order, like those of the man he brought with him, a hulking strong-arm from London's East End, who had been recommended to Endean as one of the most feared protectors in Whitechapel and a former enforcer for the Kray Gang. Ernie Locke was being paid a very handsome fee to keep Endean alive and well and was carrying a gun under his shirt, acquired locally through the offices of ManCon's mining enterprise in the republic. Tempted by the money offered, he had already made the mistake of thinking, like Endean, that a good hatchet man in the East End will automatically make a good hatchet man in Africa.

After crossing the frontier, the truck had made good time until it blew a tire ten miles short of Clarence. With Endean mounting guard with his rifle, Locke had changed the tire while Bobi cowered under the canvas in the back. That was when the trouble started. A handful of Vindu troops, fleeing from Clarence, had spotted them and loosed off half a dozen shots. They all went wide except one, which hit the tire Locke had just replaced. The journey was finished in first gear on a flat tire.

Shannon leaned out the window and called down to Endean.

The latter looked up. "Everything okay?" he called.

"Sure," said Shannon. "But get out of sight. No one seems to have moved yet, but someone is bound to start snooping soon."

Endean led Colonel Bobi and Locke through the curtain, and they mounted to the second floor, where Shannon was waiting. When they were seated in the presidential dining room, Endean asked for a full report on the previous night's battle. Shannon gave it to him.

"Kimba's palace guard?" asked Endean.

For answer Shannon led him to the rear window, whose shutters were closed, pushed one open, and pointed down into the courtyard, from which a ferocious buzzing of flies mounted.

Endean looked out and drew back. "The lot?" he asked.

"The lot," said Shannon. "Wiped out."

"And the army?"

"Twenty dead, the rest scattered. All left their arms behind except perhaps a couple of dozen bolt-action Mausers. No problem. The arms have been gathered up and brought inside."

"The presidential armory?"

"In the cellar, under our control."

"And the national radio transmitter?"

"Downstairs on the ground floor. Intact. We haven't tried the electricity circuits yet, but the radio seems to have a separate Diesel-powered generator."

Endean nodded, satisfied. "Then there's nothing for it but for the new President to announce the success of his coup last night, the formation of a new government, and to take over control," he said.

"What about security?" asked Shannon. "There's no army left intact until they filter back, and not all of the Vindu may want to serve under the new man."

Endean grinned. "They'll come back when the word spreads that the new man has taken over, and they'll serve under him just so long as they know who is in charge. And they will. In the meantime, this group you seem to have recruited will suffice. After all, they're black, and no European diplomats here are likely to recognize the difference between one black and another."

"Do you?" asked Shannon.

Endean shrugged. "No," he said, "but it doesn't matter. By the way, let me introduce the new President of Zangaro."

He gestured toward the Zangaran colonel, who had been surveying the room he already knew well, a broad grin on his face.

"Former commander of the Zangaran army, successful operator of a coup d'état as far as the world knows, and new president of Zangaro. Colonel Antoine Bobi."

Shannon rose, faced the colonel, and bowed. Bobi's grin grew even wider.

Shannon walked to the door at the end of the dining room. "Perhaps the President would like to examine the presidential office," he said. Endean translated.

Bobi nodded and lumbered across the tiled floor and through the door, followed by Shannon. It closed behind them. Five seconds later came the crash of a single shot.

After Shannon reappeared, Endean sat for a moment staring at him. "What was that?" he asked unnecessarily.

"A shot," said Shannon.

Endean was on his feet, across the room, and standing in the open doorway to the study. He turned around, ashen-faced, hardly able to speak.

"You shot him," he whispered. "All this bloody way, and you shot him. You're mad, Shannon, you're fucking crazy."

His voice rose with his rage and bafflement. "You don't know what you've done, you stupid, blundering maniac, you bloody mercenary idiot."

Shannon sat back in the armchair behind the dining table, gazing at Endean with scant interest. From the corner of his eye he saw the body-guard's hand move under his floppy shirt.

The second crash seemed louder to Endean, for it was nearer. Ernie Locke went back out of his chair in a complete somersault and sprawled across the tiles, varying the pattern of the old colonial marquetry with a thin filament of blood that came from his midriff. He was quite dead, for the soft bullet had gone through to shatter his spine.

Shannon brought his hand out from under the oak table and laid the Makarov 9mm. automatic on the table. A wisp of blue smoke wriggled out of the end of the barrel.

Endean seemed to sag at the shoulders, as if the knowledge of the certain loss of his personal fortune, promised by Sir James Manson when Bobi was installed, had suddenly been compounded by the realization that Shannon was the most completely dangerous man he had ever met. But it was a bit late for that.

Semmler appeared in the doorway of the study, behind Endean, and Langarotti slipped quietly through the dressing-room door from the corridor. Both held Schmeissers, catch off, very steady, pointing at Endean.

Shannon rose. "Come on," he said, "I'll drive you back to the border. From there you can walk."

The single unpunctured tire from the two Zangaran trucks in the courtyard had been fitted to the vehicle that had brought Endean into the country. The canvas behind the cab had been taken away, and three African soldiers crouched in the back with submachine carbines. Another twenty, fully uniformed and equipped, were being marshaled into a line outside the palace.

In the hallway, close to the shattered door, they met a middle-aged African in civilian clothes. Shannon nodded to him and exchanged a few words.

"Everything okay, Doctor?"

"Yes, so far. I have arranged with my people to send a hundred volunteer workers to clean up. Also another fifty will be here this afternoon for fitting out and equipping. Seven of the Zangaran men on the list of notables have been contacted at their homes and have agreed to serve. They will meet this evening."

"Good. Perhaps you had better take time off to draft the first bulletin from the new government. It should be broadcast as soon as possible. Ask Mr. Semmler to try to get the radio working. If it can't be done, we'll use the ship."

"I have just spoken to Mr. Semmler," said the African. "He has been in touch with the *Toscana* by walkie-talkie. Captain Waldenberg reports there is another ship out there trying to raise Clarence port authorities with a request for permission to enter port. No one is replying, but Captain Waldenberg can hear her on the radio."

"Any identification?" asked Shannon.

"Mr. Semmler says she identifies herself as the Russian ship *Komarov*, a freighter."

"Tell Mr. Semmler to man the port radio before going to work on the palace transmitter. Tell him to make to *Komarov*: 'Permission refused. Permanently.' Thank you, Doctor."

They parted, and Shannon took Endean back to his truck. He took the wheel himself and swung the truck back on the road to the hinterland and the border.

"Who was that?" asked Endean sourly as the truck sped along the peninsula, past the shantytown of the immigrant workers, where all seemed to be bustle and activity. With amazement Endean noticed that each crossroads had an armed soldier with a submachine carbine standing on point duty.

"The man in the hallway?" asked Shannon.

"Yes."

"That was Doctor Okoye."

"A witch doctor, I suppose."

"Actually he's an Oxford Ph.D."

"Friend of yours?"

"Yes."

There was no more conversation until they were on the highway toward the north.

"All right," said Endean at last, "I know what you've done. You've ruined one of the biggest and richest coups that has ever been attempted. You don't know that, of course. You're too bloody thick. What I'd like to know is, why? In God's name, why?"

Shannon thought for a moment, keeping the truck steady on the bumpy road, which had deteriorated to a dirt track.

"You made two mistakes, Endean," he said carefully. Endean started at the sound of his real name.

"You assumed that because I'm a mercenary, I'm automatically stupid. It never seemed to occur to you that we are both mercenaries, along with Sir James Manson and most of the people who have power in this world. The second mistake was that you assumed all black people were the same, because to you they look the same."

"I don't follow you."

"You did a lot of research on Zangaro; you even found out about the tens of thousands of immigrant workers who virtually keep this place running. It never occurred to you that those workers form a community of their own. They're a third tribe, the most intelligent and hard-working one in the country. Given half a chance, they can play a part in the political life of the country. What's more, you failed to recognize that the new army of Zangaro, and therefore the power in the country, might be recruited from among that third community. In fact, it just has been. Those soldiers you saw were neither Vindu nor Caja. There were fifty in uniform and armed when you were in the palace, and by tonight there'll be another fifty. In five days there will be over four hundred new soldiers in Clarence—untrained, of course, but looking efficient enough to keep law and order. They'll be the real power in this country from now on. There was a coup d'état last night, all right, but it wasn't conducted for or on behalf of Colonel Bobi."

"For whom, then?"

"For the general."

"Which general?"

Shannon told him the name.

Endean faced him, mouth open in horror. "Not him. He was defeated, exiled."

"For the moment, yes. Not necessarily forever. Those immigrant workers are his people. They call them the Jews of Africa. There are one and a half million of them scattered over this continent. In many areas they do most of the work and have most of the brains. Here in Zangaro they live in the shantytown behind Clarence."

"That stupid great idealistic bastard—"

"Careful," warned Shannon.

"Why?"

Shannon jerked his head over his shoulder. "They're the general's soldiers too."

Endean turned and looked at the three impassive faces above the three Schmeisser barrels.

"They don't speak English all that well, do they?"

"The one in the middle," said Shannon mildly, "was a chemist once. Then he became a soldier; then his wife and four children were wiped out by a Saladin armored car. They're made by Alvis in Coventry, you know. He doesn't like the people who were behind that."

Endean was silent for a few more miles. "What happens now?" he asked.

"The Committee of National Reconciliation takes over," said Shannon. "Four Vindu members, four Caja, and two from the immigrant community. But the army will be made up of the people behind you. And this country will be used as a base and a headquarters. From here the newly trained men will go back one day to avenge what was done to them. Maybe the general will come and set up resident here—in effect, to rule."

"You expect to get away with that?"

"You expected to impose that slobbering ape Bobi and get away with it. At least the new government will be moderately fair. That mineral deposit, or whatever it was, that you were after—I don't know where or what it is, but I can deduce that there has to be something here to interest Sir James Manson. No doubt the new government will find it, eventually. And no doubt it will be exploited. But if you want it, you will have to pay for it. A fair price, a market price. Tell Sir James that when you get back home."

Around the corner they came within view of the border post. News travels fast in Africa, even without telephone, and the Vindu soldiers on the border post were gone.

Shannon stopped the truck and pointed ahead. "You can walk the rest," he said.

Endean climbed down. He looked back at Shannon with undiluted hatred. "You still haven't explained why," he said. "You've explained what and how, but not why."

Shannon stared ahead up the road. "For nearly two years," he said musingly, "I watched between half a million and a million small kids starved to death because of people like you and Manson. It was done basically so that you and your kind could make bigger profits through a vicious and totally corrupt dictatorship, and it was done in the name of law and order, of legality and constitutional justification. I may be a fighter, I may be a killer, but I am not a bloody sadist. I worked out for myself how it was done and why it was done, and who were the men behind it. Visible up front were a bunch of politicians and Foreign Office men, but they are just a cage full of posturing apes, neither seeing nor caring past their interdepartmental squabbles and their re-election. Invisible behind them were profiteers like your precious James Manson. That's why I did it. Tell Manson when you get back home. I'd like him to know. Personally. From me. Now get walking."

Ten yards on, Endean turned around. "Don't ever come back to London,

Shannon," he called. "We can deal with people like you there."

"I won't," yelled Shannon. Under his breath he murmured, "I won't ever have to." Then he turned the truck around and headed for the peninsula and Clarence.

EPILOGUE

The new government was duly installed, and at the last count was ruling humanely and well. There was hardly a mention of the coup in the European newspapers, just a brief piece in *Le Monde* to say that dissident units of the Zangaran army had toppled the President on the eve of Independence Day and that a governing council had taken over the administration pending national elections. But there was nothing in the newspaper to report that one of the council's first acts was to inform Ambassador Dobrovolsky that the Soviet mining survey team would not be received, and new arrangements for surveying the area would be made in due course.

Big Janni Dupree and Tiny Marc Vlaminck were buried down on the point, beneath the palm trees, where the wind blows off the gulf. The graves were left unmarked at Shannon's request. The body of Johnny was taken by his own people, who keened over him and buried him according to their own ways.

Simon Endean and Sir James Manson kept quiet about their parts in the affair. There was really nothing they could say publicly.

Shannon gave Jean-Baptiste Langarotti the £5000 remaining in his money belt from the operations budget, and the Corsican went back to Europe. He was last heard of heading for Burundi, where he wanted to train the Hutu partisans who were trying to oppose the Tutsi-dominated dictatorship of Micombero. As he told Shannon when they parted on the shore, "It's not really the money. It was never for the money."

Shannon wrote out letters to Signor Ponti in Genoa in the name of Keith Brown, ordering him to hand over the bearer shares controlling the ownership of the *Toscana* in equal parts to Captain Waldenberg and Kurt Semmler. A year later Semmler sold out his share to Waldenberg, who raised a mortgage to pay for it. Then Semmler went off to another war. He died in South Sudan, when he, Ron Gregory, and Rip Kirby were laying a mine to knock out a Sudanese Saladin armored car. The mine went off, killing Kirby instantly and badly injuring Semmler and Gregory. Gregory got home via the British Embassy in Ethiopia, but Semmler died in the bush.

The last thing Shannon did was to send letters to his bank in Switzerland through Langarotti, ordering the bank to make a credit transfer of £5000 to the parents of Janni Dupree in Paarl, Cape Province, and another in the same sum to a woman called Anna who ran a bar in the Kleinstraat in Ostend's red-light district.

He died a month after the coup, the way he had told Julie he wanted to go, with a gun in his hand and blood in his mouth and a bullet in the chest. But it was his own gun and his own bullet. It was not the risks or the danger or the fighting that destroyed him, but the trivial black mole on the back of his neck. That was what he had learned from Dr. Dunois in the Paris surgery. Up to a year if he took things easy, less than six months if he pushed himself, and the last month would be bad. So he went out alone when he judged the time had come, and walked into the jungle with his gun and a fat envelope full of typescript, which was sent to a friend in London some weeks later.

The natives who saw him walking alone, and later brought him back to the town for burial, said he was whistling when he went. Being simple peasants, growers of yams and cassava, they did not know what the whistling was. It was a tune called "Spanish Harlem."